THE EMPIRE AT WAR

British Military Science Fiction

THE EMPIRE AT WAR

British Military Science Fiction

Andy Bigwood

P.P. Corcoran

Christopher G. Nuttall

Phillip Richards

Tim C. Taylor

The Empire at War
— British Military Science Fiction —

Cover artwork Copyright © 2016 by Andy Bigwood
"Mission Briefing: an introduction to The Empire at War" Copyright © 2016 by Tim C. Taylor
"Fallen Witness" Artwork Copyright © 2012-2016 by Andy Bigwood, Story Copyright © 2016 by Tim C. Taylor
"Discovery of the Saiph" Copyright © 2014 by P.P. Corcoran
"Haven One-Eight" Copyright © 2016 by P.P. Corcoran
"Their Darkest Hour" Copyright © 2014 by Christopher G. Nuttall
"C.R.O.W." Copyright © 2012 by Phillip Richards
"Escape from the Hive" Copyright © 2016 by Phillip Richards
"Marine Cadet" Copyright © 2014 by Tim C. Taylor
"The President's Son" Copyright © 2016 by Tim C. Taylor
"SitRep: The State of British Military SF" Copyright © 2016 by Tim C. Taylor
"Roll Call: British Military SF Authors" Copyright © 2016 by Tim C. Taylor

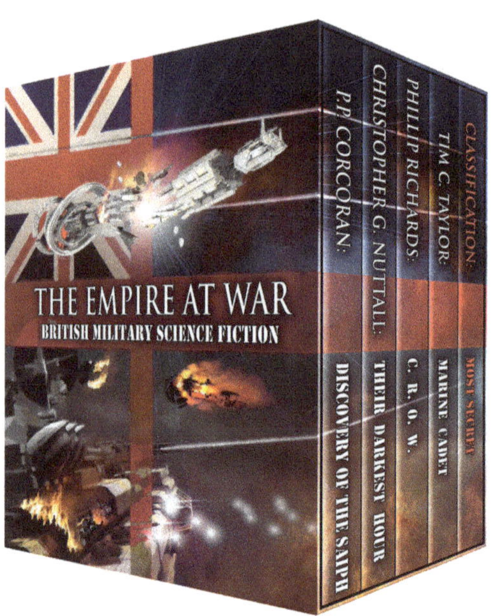

ISBN-13: 978-1-909636-13-2
Published by Greyhart Press
All Rights Reserved

Also available in eBook editions

www.EmpireAtWar.co.uk

CONTENTS

Mission Briefing: an introduction to The Empire at War — *Tim C. Taylor* 15

Fallen Witness I: — *Andy Bigwood (Art), Tim C. Taylor (words)* 9

Discovery of the Saiph — *P.P. Corcoran* 13

Haven One-Eight (exclusive short story) — *P.P. Corcoran* 99

Fallen Witness II: — *Andy Bigwood (Art), Tim C. Taylor (words)* 103

Their Darkest Hour — *Christopher G. Nuttall* 107

Fallen Witness III: — *Andy Bigwood (Art), Tim C. Taylor (words)* 227

C.R.O.W. — *Phillip Richards* 231

Escape from the Hive (exclusive opening chapter of his new series) — *Phillip Richards* 305

Fallen Witness IV: — *Andy Bigwood (Art), Tim C. Taylor (words)* 313

Marine Cadet — *Tim C. Taylor* 317

The President's Son (exclusive short story) — *Tim C. Taylor* 449

Fallen Witness V: — *Andy Bigwood (Art), Tim C. Taylor (words)* 457

SitRep: The State of British Military SF — *Tim C. Taylor* 461

Fallen Witness VI: — *Andy Bigwood (Art), Tim C. Taylor (words)* 469

Roll Call: British Military SF Authors — *Tim C. Taylor* 473

Fallen Witness VII: — *Andy Bigwood (Art), Tim C. Taylor (words)* 481

MISSION BRIEFING
—An Introduction to 'The Empire at War' —

Tim C. Taylor

From Downton Abbey to Doctor Who, Britain is going through one of its periodic phases of cultural success. Cool Britannia they called it last time around. Monty Python, 2000AD, Led Zeppelin, James Bond, Top Gear, scotch whisky and Sir Tom Jones… it's not that we Brits are better at 'doing' culture, but when we get it right, we do it a quirkily different way. Jason Bourne is as exciting to watch as James Bond, but one is American and the other British. To swap them around would utterly change the dynamic.

Or take comics. When I was growing up in England, America exported Spiderman, Batman, and the Fantastic Four, while the British answer was (and still is) 2000AD with its dark dystopias of Judge Dredd, the Volgan Wars, and Strontium Dog. I can't imagine Marvel Comics being British any more than 2000AD could ever have been American.

And that's a good thing. Readers get a more diverse range of material.

The British have supplied their fair share of science fiction authors too. Iain M. Banks, Tanith Lee, Arthur C. Clarke and many others have thrilled us for years, but British military science fiction?

That's an oxymoron.

Isn't it?

Conventional wisdom says that Brits don't do military SF, not unless you count the gaming tie-ins of Warhammer 40k. War is sometimes used as a backdrop, or a key event in a character's past, but portraying characters in a military organization who are fighting an ongoing war…? Well, that's the kind of thing we leave to the Americans. In fact, as we'll see in the essay *SitRep: The State of British Military SF*, the idea that Brits don't do military fiction was never quite as true as the standard narrative would have you believe, and yet even today the fallacy that British military SF is an oxymoron remains common, despite all the overwhelming evidence to the contrary.

And that evidence largely comes from Amazon through its bestseller charts, which for the first time in publishing history give a freely available and transparent guide to who is selling well and what kinds of books readers are buying. Not only is military SF selling in huge amounts, but British authors are playing a big part in this explosion of new talent.

In *The Empire at War* anthology, we showcase a sample of writing from top British military SF writers. We have all of us had multiple top-10 bestsellers in the Amazon.com military SF book charts in the past two years, and half of us have fought off the ferocious level of competition to claw our way to the #1 spot in that chart. British military SF first erupted into prominence almost 150 years ago, but this collection is not a dry retrospective of the history of science fiction; this is a sample of what is happening in science fiction *right now*.

The first novel in this anthology is *Discovery of the Saiph* by P.P. Corcoran. This is the opening book in an epic-scale adventure story of humanity's war for survival against an implacable enemy. Space battles, alliances and treaty negotiations, special ops and alien technology… it's all here in *Discovery of the Saiph*. Originally hailing from Scotland, but currently based in Northern Ireland, Paul Corcoran draws upon his experience of twenty-two years spent in the British Army, as an elite paratrooper in 5 Airborne Brigade, and subsequently in signals and intelligence.

Paul follows his novel with an exclusive short story: *Haven One-Eight*. A relentless foe seeks to murder the Faithful in their haven, but who are these unstoppable servants of Satan? The answer will shock you.

Alien invasion of the Earth is a popular theme in military SF, and an early British example is HG Wells with *War of the Worlds* (1897), which itself tapped into the invasion fantasies featuring German or French invaders that had been immensely popular for decades, ever since the stunning success of George Chesney's *The Battle of Dorking* (1871). It's astonishing to think that it is almost 150 years since British military SF's first period of huge commercial success. I hope we're doing that tradition proud.

I'm confident the next book in this collection does just that. Take *War of the Worlds* and *The Battle of Dorking*, add in the 1940 Blitz spirit of the Battle of Britain, and shift to the day after tomorrow. The result is *Their Darkest Hour* by Christopher G. Nuttall, a novel of alien invasion, occupation, collaboration and resistance. Though the descriptions of the (mostly) brutish German soldiers in *The Battle of Dorking* may seem coy to modern sensibilities, they outraged the Victorian audience at the time. Modern tastes are less easily perturbed, but the actions of British collaborators in *Their Darkest Hour* are powerful enough to appall contemporary readers, just as Chesney outraged his.

The *Their Darkest Hour* series is one of many published by Scottish author Christopher G. Nuttall in recent years, of which *The Empire's Corps* and *Ark Royal* are the most famous. Nuttall is not only one of the most prolific but one of the most successful new British science fiction writers of the decade, winning huge legions of fans, and along the way scoring many #1 bestselling titles on amazon.com, the #1 position in bestselling science fiction authors, as well as being a *USA Today* bestseller.

Phillip Richards is the only author in the collection who is not a full-time, professional writer. That's because he's otherwise engaged in his day job as a platoon sergeant in the British Army. *C.R.O.W.*, the first book in Richards' *Union* series, tells the story of Andy Moralee, a young Combat Replacement of War in the English Dropship Infantry, as he progresses through training and hazing through to his first experience of combat. Like P.P. Corcoran, Richards takes his service experience and applies it to his writing, but with completely different results. Corcoran's *Saiph* series features a large cast and many locations because, as he explains, that's how real wars are. As Andy Moralee progresses through Richards' *Union* series, and begins to take on promotions to NCO rank, his viewpoint remains limited. In what becomes a politically messy military campaign, the field commanders don't share every detail of their plans with a lowly enlisted soldier, and certainly don't ask for the advice of a junior NCO, as they often seem to do in the less convincing modern military SF. The results are sudden explosions of chaotic action that are unpredictable, sometimes injected with confusion, and always have you turning the page to find out what happens next.

The *Union* series is still ongoing, but Phillip is already planning another, less autobiographical, series. The opening chapters, entitled *Escape from the Hive*, are available for the first time in this collection. In this preview, Denrik awakes in a hold filled with unconscious soldiers hanging from the overhead like carcasses in a meat plant. Who is he, and why is he there? But all such questions are driven from his mind when a genetically engineered killing machine enters the hold, programed for slaughter.

The final novel is *Marine Cadet*. Unlike the other three novels here, the characters in *Marine Cadet* have never set foot on Earth, and have only recently been granted permission to learn of Earth's history. They are like the janissaries of the Ottoman Empire, cut off from their homes to fight in alien wars. The series starts in what appears to be a standard boot camp scenario, but this isn't the familiar tale of a gruff but decent drill sergeant teaching hard lessons to our young characters. That's present in the book, sure, but there are dark conspiracies maneuvering in the background, angling for advantage before this region of the galaxy explodes into a civil war, after which nothing will be the same again.

The characters in the *Human Legion* series have been isolated from the rest of humanity for centuries, but their distant ancestors were taken as children from Earth. In *The President's Son*, a short story exclusive to this collection, we hear the story of that first group of slave children.

There is one more story in the collection, and it's pretty special! The sumptuous cover artwork for *The Empire at War* was produced by Andy Bigwood, whose cover art has twice won the best artwork award from the British Science Fiction Association. Andy is a fully fledged contributor to this collection, and has supplied seven pieces of artwork that are interspersed with the other stories. I have written words to accompany each image, and together they tell a lavishly illustrated short story called *Fallen Witness*.

Next we have an essay, *SitRep: The State of British Military SF*. Non-Brits needn't be concerned because the essay is about more than *Doctor Who* and endless cups of tea. It has to be, since in order to grasp the current state of British military SF, we first have to understand how American science fiction publishing has transformed in the past five years.

To round off the book we have *Roll Call: British Military SF authors*, which tells you more about the authors in this anthology, and then goes on to provide information and links for notable British authors in the field, from established stars of the like of Karen Traviss and Neal Asher, to major new voices such as Michael G. Thomas and Tony Healey.

This, then, is *The Empire at War: British Military SF*. Now, go lose yourself in the stories within.

FALLEN WITNESS

—Vision I: Speedbird—

Art: Andy Bigwood
Words: Tim C. Taylor

When the lights dim in the auditorium, even the boys in the back row discussing last night's game calm enough to turn their attention to the stage. Heated debates about the relative merits of sporting heroes turn to furtive speculation. What is that movement they can hear on the darkened stage? Pupils from all over Second Landing are here to listen to a special history lecture, but the teachers have dodged every call to explain details. There have been whispered rumors all their lives, about holes in their history that grown-ups will never discuss. A few children are suggesting that today the truth would be revealed, but for most the big game is a far more enticing topic.

The children blink when a column of light stabs the left side of the stage. Caught inside the light is a tall figure, a woman holding a roll of something in one hand. It takes even young eyes a few moments to adjust to the bright light, but the way the figure's glossy skin gleams and sparkles is unmistakable. Whispers spread through the audience: *she's an android.*

"Good morning," she says, "and welcome to a special history lesson."

The pupils listen with rapt attention. The android's voice sounds like a human's. Are they allowed to do that?

"My name is Petty Officer Francine DeSouza, Royal Navy, and I'm a fallen witness."

Some of the children notice that DeSouza is wearing a military uniform. But it's a very old one.

"I'm also a liar. We only told your teachers this was a history lesson so they would bring you." She winks and the children start to love this strange android. "What we're really about to give you is a *future* lesson."

DeSouza unwraps a roll of what looks like smartscreen. She sets it to go rigid and then holds it high above her head. The screen illuminates, showing a spaceship with a nose like a raven's beak. The forward half looks beautifully streamlined, but the rear is dominated by a trio of huge engines. A curious ring is mounted amidships.

"Can anyone tell me the name of this ship?"

DeSouza scans the audience. A fair percentage think they know the ship's name, but aren't brave enough to volunteer an answer, or suspect their parents aren't supposed to have told them. There's a pair near the front, a boy and a girl, who are practically dislocating their shoulders in an attempt to raise their hands higher. She indicates the girl. "Yes, young lady."

"Is it *Speedbird*?" says the girl, suddenly uncertain. The shoulders slump on the boy beside her.

"Well done." DeSouza remembers to smile. "This is *Speedbird*, the last of the Clipper-class ships. They were built many centuries ago using a revolutionary new propulsion system that made them the fastest ships in existence. But they were ruinously expensive to run. Within twenty years, only *Speedbird* was still space-worthy, always on the edge of being scrapped, but kept alive for decades by generous donations of money and time from enthusiasts who couldn't bear to let the Clipper-class's dream of speed fade into history."

DeSouza points at the boy who clearly knew the ship's name. "You, why was *Speedbird* so important?" Her face no longer smiles.

"*Speedbird* carried news of the enemy," he replies. He speaks with confidence, and DeSouza lets her sight rest on him long enough to identify him from citizen records as Mahmoud Bhatti. She makes a note to contact Bhatti's family and recruit them for the special program reserved for those who pass on restricted knowledge to their children.

"She carried more than news," Bhatti continues. "She carried one of *them*… an energy wraith."

"Excellent. Thank you. In fact, it carried several wraiths. To many of you, the wraiths are monsters from stories, but it is my duty to inform you that they were real – creatures of pure energy who were snuffing out human colonies at will. As your teachers have no doubt told you, one of the biggest obstacles to appreciating history is that from the vantage point of the present, you children know how events turned out. The

people who lived through historical events didn't have that knowledge. Soldiers going into combat do not know whether their side will be defeated or emerge victorious. They do not know if they will fall in battle."

DeSouza has to take a breath. She has been doing this for a very long time now, but talking about some topics requires great resolve, no matter how well rehearsed you are.

"Imagine living on one of the core worlds five centuries ago. At that terrifying time, communication with the outer colonies was being cut off, one by one. People of that period often compared human civilization to a great tree of life, spreading its branches as more and more star systems were colonized at an ever-increasing rate. Now one of those branches was dying, and the withering disease was both spreading to neighboring branches and advancing toward the trunk. No one knew why. Was it natural disaster beyond anyone's understanding? Was one of the Federated Nations attempting to secretly carve out an empire? Was this a deadly new religious cult? Missions were sent to discover answers but none returned. Can you imagine how frightened everyone was?"

DeSouza senses the fear spreading through the auditorium and feels satisfaction. A part of her wonders how much of her satisfaction is genuine, and how much has been *programed*. She wrinkles her lip in disgust but she has a duty to perform, orders to obey, and so she notes the identity of the most frightened children. Her superiors wish to leverage that fear to influence their parents.

"Do you see the ring in the picture?" DeSouza asks the children. Most of them nod. "If you could see *Speedbird* in more dimensions, it would look more like a cylinder than a ring. It is the quantum foam turbine, a source of near-limitless energy and the secret to the ship's great speed. When a squad of energy wraiths boarded the ship, they were trapped within the turbine. The crew knew the importance of their strange and lethal cargo, and so they plotted a course to what they hoped would be a safe world. More energy wraiths were on the way to kill everyone on board. To escape, the brave crew set *Speedbird* to accelerate away at maximum speed, even though they knew doing so would crush the life from them.

"Their quick thinking and sacrifice allowed *Speedbird* to escape her pursuers. For the first time, news had escaped the slaughter of a world to explain the blight threatening to wipe out humanity. Finally, we knew our enemy.

"*Speedbird* saved the tree of human life but only because of her unique quantum foam turbine, and it was the only one in existence. If not for those civilian enthusiasts that kept the old ship flying, perhaps our entire species would have been wiped out. That's how close we got."

A fresh wave of fear sweeps through the children.

DeSouza smiles, satisfied that she has conducted her duty well. Now it is time for the next fallen witness.

Fallen Witness Vision II is on p103

DISCOVERY OF THE SAIPH

—Book 1 of the Saiph Series —

P.P. Corcoran

"the good must associate; else they will fall, one by one, an unpitied sacrifice in a contemptible struggle." —
Edmund Burke

CHAPTER ONE

Doorway to the Galaxy

Senate of the Terran Republic - Geneva - Earth

Senator Gillian Rae, representing the Boreland habitats on Titan, listened to the grey haired scientist who was concluding his testimony before the Senate's Science and Technology Committee.

"The ion drive is our most advanced light speed technology," the scientist said. "It is capable of speeds of up to one quarter the speed of light, which means it will reach the closest stars within twenty-five years, a vast improvement on previous attempts. The probe can gather images and data from the stars' planetary systems and send those images and data back to Earth by radio. My peers and I agree this is our best hope of identifying other worlds suitable for human habitation, thus ensuring our continued survival. Thank you."

As the scientist took his seat, Gillian glanced at her fellow senators. Many were nodding their heads in approval. She waited a beat, and then another, and then rose from her seat and got the attention of the president.

"Does Senator Rae wish to be recognized?" Bartholomew McMullen asked.

"I do, Mr. President."

"Very well. You have five minutes."

Gillian took a breath and began. "Mr. President and fellow Senators, I need not remind you of the consequences of fully autonomous machines with insufficient programming and little or no human override. Many of you know I was fortunate to have survived an incident involving one such machine."

Gillian paused to let her comment sink in. As most of her colleagues knew, she was one of the few survivors of the 'Boreland Blasts', a disaster triggered by a prototype of a fully autonomous mining machine undergoing trials on Titan. The machine mistook a fuel line for a mineral vein and used a laser cutter on it. The resulting chain of explosions and rapid decompression of living quarters killed 104 men, women and children.

Gillian heard murmurs of recognition and saw nods from many of her peers.

"Who knows what these probes will discover when they reach their destinations?" she continued. "Who knows how they will react to their findings in the face of unknown variables, which may be beyond their programming? Such autonomy may result in the loss of vital data, missed opportunities, or worse, the loss of life."

Gillian paused again. She saw more nods but also some puzzled faces. Behind her, she heard whispers.

"I propose we send out manned probes. I understand this increases development difficulty a hundredfold. It requires the expansion of our deep space environment technology program, and it will delay the probe deployments. Nevertheless, the benefits of having a human on the spot to make critical decisions will be worth the added time and expense. I hope my colleagues will agree the risks to our people are too great to ignore. Thank you."

Bartholomew McMullen, the twenty-third President of the Terran Republic, stood to address the Senate. "Thank you, Senator Rae. Senators, we are all aware of Senator Rae's personal and professional experience in this field. She is a devoted member of the Science and Technology Committee, where she has put her engineering degrees to good use, and I know she speaks with knowledge and expertise in this field."

The president paused and glanced around the chamber before continuing. "I call for a vote on Senator Rae's motion – the deployment of the unmanned probes suggested by our learned senior scientists should be delayed at least until the feasibility and practicalities of sending a human crew are investigated."

The holo cube in front of Bartholomew flashed as the senators' votes were recorded and counted. A few minutes later, a bell signaled the end of the voting. Bartholomew studied his screen before rising to announce the results. "Senator Rae's motion is carried."

Unbeknown to the president and the Senate, Gillian Rae, the former engineer from Titan, had just ensured the continued existence of the human race.

HASLETT RESEARCH STATION - ASTEROID BELT

Doctor Jeff Moore was having another bad day. He had decided his state of the art computer enjoyed driving him mad, and he was seconds away from reducing it to a heap of rubble when an incoming call tone sounded. Jeff turned away from the offending machine and answered the call, immediately regretting it when the smirking face of Valerie Hayes, Director of the Vega Star Probe team, appeared.

"The bad computer laughing at you again, Jeff?"

"What can I do for you, Valerie?"

"I was going to offer you breakfast in the staff canteen."

"The thought of breakfast in the staff canteen just made me lose my appetite."

"How about a cup of coffee instead?"

"What's the occasion?" Jeff asked.

"One of my engineers, Danny Dunlewey, pulled an all-nighter studying the data from the last Improved Ion Engine test, and he's come up with a few anomalies the computer disregarded."

The Improved Ion Engine was the reason Jeff was having a spate of bad days. He theorized a field of gravity waves projected in front of a steadily accelerating spacecraft would act like the bow wave of a prewar oceangoing ship and allow greater speed and less resistance. It was a great theory, but it seemed to work only at limited velocities. Whenever the test probes accelerated to two-thirds the speed of light, they exploded. At least he assumed they exploded. The last anyone saw of them was a flash of light, and they were gone, obliterated into particles too small to be picked up by optical or electrical equipment – or so he surmised.

Adding to his frustration, the cryogenics team at Caulfield Research Station in New South Wales had made rapid advances in techniques to ensure the safety of the Vega probes' human crew. Meanwhile, his efforts to reduce the probes' travel time to Vega had stalled.

"Is it real coffee?" Jeff asked.

"As real as the recycled air you're breathing," Valerie said. "See you in five."

Jeff left his office and took the lift two floors up to Valerie's office. He wondered what Danny Dunlewey had found—perhaps a way to track the larger pieces of his exploded drive.

Twenty minutes and a second cup of coffee later, Jeff felt as though his world had turned upside down. The data on the holo cube in front of him seemed to prove the impossible. Yet there it was, evidence of faster than light speed travel, a way to fulfil man's quest to travel to the stars.

Jeff moved his gaze from the screen to Valerie. "Where's Danny?"

"He's outside."

"Would you please get him?"

Valerie frowned. "Look, Jeff, I hope he hasn't led you on a wild goose chase. I know he hasn't been here long, but he does show a lot of …"

"Ask him to go to Conference Room One and set it up to present his data to the heads of departments, will you?"

"Oh. OK. Sure."

Jeff stood up. "I'm off to the Communications Room. I need to make a few calls to Earth."

OFFICE OF THE CHAIRMAN OF THE SCIENCE AND TECHNOLOGY COMMITTEE - CANBERRA - EARTH

Gillian Rae admired the sprawling city through the glass wall of her office, which towered 160 floors above Canberra.

Humanity had worked hard to reclaim the nearly destroyed Earth after the wars. Australia had escaped the worst of it and recovered more quickly than Europe or North America. As a result, it had served as the capital and base of the fledgling Terran Republic until Geneva became habitable again. The Science and Technology Bureau had sunk its roots deep in Canberra, and when the rest of the apparatus of government moved to Europe a decade earlier, Sci-Tech stayed behind.

Gillian had come to appreciate Canberra as a second home, so different from her original home on Titan, and now promoted to chair of the Science and Technology Committee, she felt even more at home. Australia provided another advantage, one Gillian had just begun to appreciate. With the president and the rest of the Senate tucked up in their beds half a world away, she had an extra few hours to get a grip on what the scientist and engineer perched on the couch in her office were trying to explain to her.

Gillian turned from the view of Canberra and faced Jeff Moore and Valerie Hayes. Jeff appeared even younger than his eighteen years as he sat alongside Valerie in one of the comfortable chairs. Valerie was chosen as the Director of the Vega Star Probe Team not only for her exceptional mind but for her political savvy, both proved to be invaluable assets when you push for, and get, authority from those in the corridors of power to employ young, fertile minds straight from university rather than choosing scientists and engineers with more… experience.

When Gillian received the urgent request for a face-to-face meeting, she immediately queried the necessity for the five-day inter-system shuttle trip by Valerie and Jeff, instead of the usual holo cube communications, but Valerie had refused any explanation and insisted on the in person meeting. Now Gillian knew why.

"Explain this to me again in simple terms, please. I'm only a humble politician." Not entirely true, but her double first in Spatial Engineering from Cambridge hadn't quite prepared her to understand completely what Danny Dunlewey had discovered.

Valerie took a deep breath and began. "As you know, Senator, we at Haslett Station are trying to develop an improved ion drive for the Vega Star Probe mission. Since Vega is more than twenty-five light years from Earth, our current best estimate is thirty-eight years travelling time, minimum. Accounting for the time required for surveying the system and radioing the data to Earth, it would be some sixty-six years before we heard back from the Vega mission."

Jeff continued. "The effort expended to get our probe there at near the speed of light would save at least thirteen years, well worth it we all thought. And so, for the past five years we," he indicated Valerie, "have been out in the asteroid belt building and testing the best engine ideas humankind can think up, but we reached some kind of wall, a hurdle we couldn't clear. We'd been unsuccessful getting beyond two thirds the speed of light before our probes exploded. Or so we thought." Jeff took a breath. "Our engineers put a failsafe on the engines. If, for whatever reason, the engine test beds lose continuous communication with Haslett base for two seconds or more, a cut-off switch is engaged, the engine is powered down and they begin transmitting a recovery beacon. We, as it turns out, wrongly assumed the previous four test engines were destroyed, thus, the computer ignored any transmission on their recovery beacon frequency. Dunlewey was analyzing the data from the fifth test engine before it too was destroyed when he noticed an anomaly. Remember the computer had been told to ignore, not delete, the recovery beacons from the destroyed test beds, and Danny found beacons from three of the five probes. They hadn't been destroyed at all."

"But why was their signal not detected before?"

"Because it's taken the first signal two and a half years to get back to us,"

"Hang on, are you saying our test engines are all in one piece somewhere out there?" Gillian gave Jeff an incredulous look.

"No, Senator. So far we've only identified the beacons from engines two and three," Valerie interjected. "If engines four and five survived, then we expect to hear from engine four in another year, and five seven months after four."

Gillian took her seat and peered across the low coffee table at Jeff as Valerie continued. "All telemetry received via the beacons indicates the engine shut down at the planned two seconds after the lost contact marker."

"But if the signal took two and a half years to reach us travelling at, err…" Gillian tried to drag the figure for the speed of light up from memory.

"290,792,458 metres per second," Jeff added helpfully.

"Thank you, Doctor Moore. So you're telling me your engines are sitting two and a half light years from here and covered the distance in two seconds?"

"Those're the facts as we read them, Senator," answered Jeff with a nervous laugh. "Our engines are half way to Proxima Centauri and if we figure out what we did right the Vega Star Probe will arrive at Vega in under seventeen seconds."

Gillian sat stunned for a few moments then faced Jeff and Valerie squarely. "But how? Short answer please, I may have to explain this to the public."

Jeff turned to Valerie. "Would you like to demonstrate?"

"OK," said Valerie moving into tutorial mode. "I need a piece of paper," her eyes searched the ultramodern office.

Senator Rae rummaged in a nearby drawer and pulled out a battered little diary, promptly ripping out a blank sheet and handing it to Valerie. "Sometimes it is useful to keep some old tech to hand." She smiled.

Valerie continued with her demo and scribbled on the page. "A good way to imagine this is by using this paper. See I've marked one end A and the other B?" Valerie showed the senator before placing the paper on the coffee table in front of her. Senator Rae nodded in acknowledgement.

"Now imagine an ant crawling across the paper from A to B. If you leave the paper flat on the table, it might take a little while. Now…" Valerie picked up the paper and folded it while she narrated. "If I pick up the paper and fold it so A and B are right next to each other, just so…" She demonstrated this to Gillian. "Now, imagine the ant moving from A to B."

"Of course, Doctor Hayes." Gillian nodded her head, slowly as realization dawned. "Fold space theory…"

"Exactly, Senator." Valerie continued. "Travel time is exponentially reduced. Essentially, this is what Doctor Moore's Gravity Drive has done. Completely by chance it has given us the means to explore the galaxy in our lifetime and at our leisure."

"This may change things slightly," said Gillian wryly. "Now my next question. How soon will a practicable vessel be ready?"

Jeff responded with the eagerness of a puppy, glancing from Valerie and back to Gillian. "Well with the ability to travel, for all intents and purposes, instantly, I would think the current research at Caulfield could be scaled back. Give us their environment researchers and engineers and we could probably produce a test bed within a year. We could be ready for a full scale launch within three."

"Make plans, Doctors. I think you will get everything you might ever need. And good luck." Gillian smiled and stood. She held out her hand. The two doctors, taking this as their cue, also stood before shaking the senator's hand. They made their way out of the senator's office.

As they left, Gillian placed a call to the president's private residence. The last Jeff and Valerie heard was Senator Rae's charming, playful, voice saying to a presidential aide "Well, wake him up gently then. But wake him up!"

CHAPTER TWO

First Flight

TDF *Marco Polo* - Deimos Dry Docks

TDF *Marco Polo* gracefully released the mooring clamps securing it to the dry docks orbiting Deimos. The Terran Republic's first interstellar manned ship lit off its reaction drive and slowly pulled away heading for the freedom of open space.

Its captain, David Catney contemplated the past five years. Doctor Jeff Moore had estimated three years to produce a ship ready to go to Vega but his estimation proved a little optimistic. Figuring how to build the automated recovery probes, which made it half way to Proxima Centauri to recover the original engine test beds, had taken eighteen months alone. Analyzing their data fully and beginning to design the *Marco Polo* had taken a further two years, all the while sending out more and more unmanned probes ensuring the jump to such phenomenal speed would not turn the crew into paste on the rear bulkhead.

However, as Valerie Hayes pointed out, "If my precious computer circuits can survive the jump into fold space and back to normal space, so can you."

Yeah, fills me full of confidence, thought David. All the same, here he was, along with his bijou crew. A carefully selected crew, as each displayed excellence in their respective fields. David took time out to consider his command team: Executive Officer commonly shortened to XO, Lieutenant Commander Roger Cromie, and Chief Engineer Susan Harper. They had become friends over the past six months of training on the *Marco Polo* and had come to trust each other's judgment implicitly. Also on the bridge were two civilian scientists: Doctor Walter Kernaghan and Doctor Amanda Allenby, physicist and xenobiologist respectively. Although they too trained alongside the Command Team, they had both remained a bit of mystery to David. There was no questioning their knowledge and expertise, but often science got in the way of real life and neither had really engaged with the rest of the crew as human beings, albeit there was mutual respect, friendship was out of the question.

Five years, David mused, *five years, the best minds humanity has to offer, a bucket load of cash and here we are, humankind, is about to take its first tentative steps into the unknown...* David said, "All ahead one third, Chief."

"All ahead one third, aye," responded Susan. The *Marco Polo*'s reaction drive pressed them back in their seats. The gravity sump, a spin-off of the Gravity Drive taking them into fold space, was not entirely effective at negating the acceleration forces.

Mixed emotions welled, excitement, trepidation even a touch of fear of the unknown. David pushed these aside, conscious he and his crew had an important mission to complete. He was also conscious if he felt this way, his crew likely was too.

"Everyone, it has been a pleasure training and working with you on the buildup to this mission. I regard you all as experts in your fields and as colleagues. Some of whom have become my friends, others I regard with the utmost respect." He glanced at the doctors as they sat by their control panels. "To each and every one, I thank you for your hard work and dedication in making this possible. Rest assured I will do everything in my power to ensure a successful mission and ensure we all return to friends and family having made history." David did not wait for a response, he took a breath and said in his best command voice, "OK. Let us make it look good for the press folks. Stand by on the sensors, Doctor Kernaghan, Doctor Allenby." Both of their

indicators went to green on the captain's repeater display, "Very well, Chief. Take us to all ahead two thirds."

"All ahead two thirds and three, two, one... fold!"

David felt a slight tremor run through the ship and then a second tremor as the computers automatically cut the Gravity Drive. "External view ahead." On command, the view ahead of the *Marco Polo* was projected into the main display holo cube to the front of the bridge. He let out the breath he did not realized he was holding. "OK, people. We're here." Under his breath, he said, "Wherever here is...

"Commander! Position fix – computer and manual if you please. Chief! Rotate ship and bring us to a dead stop. Doctor Kernaghan, Doctor Allenby, full sweep all sensors. Passive only, no need to let anyone know we're out here."

The doctors exchanged exasperated glances.

"But, Captain..." began Walter in protest, his thirst for knowledge outweighing his concern for his own and the ship's safety.

"No, Doctor Kernaghan. Passive only. Until I personally give orders to the contrary. Clear?" David addressed Amanda too.

"Yes, Captain," they announced in resigned unison.

David gave a nod and thought scientists could be such children. He operated the internal communications system and barked at his engineer, "Lieutenant! Are you still with us down there? And more importantly, how are my engines?"

"Give me a few minutes to do a complete system check, sir." Glendinning's reply was tinny and a little muffled.

"Very well. Report to the Chief on completion."

"Aye-aye, sir."

David observed his chief. He knew she would double check all Glendenning's results, not because she didn't trust him, but the old adage of 'two heads are better than one' sat well with David too, especially when you were two and a half light years from home.

"Commander, thoughts?" asked David of his XO.

Roger raised his gaze from his console and said deadpan, "Sir, so far we successfully carried out phase one of the mission. We're still alive."

David smirked. "And phase two?"

"Navigation computer puts us within the margin of error for the fold transit. Sensors report no contacts within passive range, and Engineering shows a green board." The news satisfied David as Roger continued, "All data has been downloaded to the courier drone, as per Standing Operating Procedure, and the drone is ready for launch."

Roger referred to the courier drone. Despite the huge scientific leap in technology borne out by the capabilities of the *Marco Polo*, still the most efficient means of communicating over these vast distances was by courier drone. It was fitted with an individual Gravity Drive and travelled from the ship's current location through fold space before docking back in the Sol System. Its aim was to bear news of the *Marco Polo*'s location and status of the crew and ship, and it allowed for the manual downloading of all data gathered during their mission. An effective system, a bit like a carrier pigeon really. As long as you had drones, you had communications. Thankfully, *Marco Polo* carried the standard twenty.

"Very well, Commander, launch the drone and plot our next Fold. I want to arrive at least ten AUs outside the Proxima Centauri System." David planned to exit fold space some 1,490,597,871 kilometers from the edge of the system, close enough for the passive systems of the *Marco Polo* to scan the whole system and far enough away to allow the *Marco Polo* sufficient warning of any danger.

"Understood, sir. Calculation running. Standby. Ready, sir."

David turned to Susan "Ready, Chief?"

"Ready, Captain."

"Very well, rotate ship to…" David glanced at the navigation repeater in front of him, "three one five decimal seven degrees by negative zero decimal seven degrees galactic and ahead two thirds."

"Three one five decimal seven degrees by negative zero decimal seven degrees galactic and ahead two thirds, aye-aye," repeated Susan "Rotation complete and three, two, one…… fold!"

This time the slight tremor went virtually unnoticed and the main display holo cube showed a dim red dwarf star, Proxima Centauri.

David reflected on the importance of this maneuver. They had done it! The first humans to visit another star. Damn, he felt good!

Back to business. "Same again people, confirm location, sensors on passive only. And bring us to a dead stop relative to the system primary."

A chorus of "Aye-aye, sirs" greeted David, and he began to relax as he watched his people go about their business. Suddenly he realised he was hungry, a small snack wouldn't go amiss. After all, he had travelled a long way he thought, with a wry smile. Out of the corner of his eye, he caught one of his scientists frowning at his sensor suite, punching new commands in as quickly as results were being displayed. "Problem, Doctor Kernaghan?"

"I'm not sure, Captain. I'm getting some strange readings here."

David sat bolt upright in his chair. "Explain strange." David felt an uneasiness creep over him. Unbidden, he saw his XO downloading the ship's logs into a courier drone and readying it for launch. Walter was still querying his computer.

David said "Now, Doctor!"

Walter shook his head slowly. "Well I'm seeing what looks like a… a…" He grappled for a word to describe the abnormal readings he could not believe he was seeing. "A power source," he finally settled on. Walter directed his next words straight to David. "It's from one of the inner planets, Captain. However, it is no natural source. It must be machine generated."

Without a second thought, David began to recite the ritual he had practiced so long and hard. A ritual he had hoped never to complete. "Computer, Alpha X-ray six four two initiate,"

A pause, then a flat emotionless female voice replied. "Voice print confirmed, Captain Catney. On your authority Alpha X-ray six four two is activated, courier drone launched. Bio readings indicate Lieutenant Commander Cromie is alive and unharmed. Does he concur?"

The two civilians regarded the captain in stunned silence. What was happening? Why was he communicating directly with the ship's computer? What was this gibberish?

"Computer," said the XO. "Bravo Yankee five three one, I concur."

Amanda had been virtually silent until this point, but now her face was flushing red with frustration and anger at the lack of understanding of events on the bridge.

"What the hell is this military double talk, Captain?"

David ignored her and instead addressed his explanation to the bridge. "On my command, all our logs were downloaded to a courier drone, this drone has now folded to a location held by the ship's computer. I have no idea of its destination. Only the computer knew. I say knew, past tense, because as soon as the courier was launched the destination was erased from the computer memory." There was silence on the bridge as they took in this information.

"When our return to the Sol System becomes overdue, a data chip will activate at Survey Command headquarters. This chip holds 200 possible locations of our courier drone. A recovery drone will be deployed to search and retrieve it." The civilians' faces paled. "If in the next sixty minutes the computer does not receive the correct coded halt cipher from two of this command team, Commander Cromie, Chief Harper or myself, then the computer will activate a fusion device hidden somewhere on board the ship."

"Are you serious?" Amanda's outburst was rhetorical.

David contemplated each of his bridge crew before resting his gaze on Amanda. "It's very simple, Doctor. Your colleague stated the energy source detected is mechanical. Meaning alien intelligence, potentially hostile alien intelligence. Humanity is vulnerable while our star travel is still in its infancy. We are all located in one star system. We…" He gestured to them all, "cannot afford to leave a breadcrumb trail back to Earth. The result could be the extinction of our very race. So, Doctors. You now have some fifty-five minutes to prove to my satisfaction this alien intelligence is no threat."

TDF *MARCO POLO* - PROXIMA CENTAURI - 4.22 LIGHT YEARS FROM SOL

"Well, Doctor Kernaghan?" asked David,

"In a minute. It takes time to narrow the location down at this distance," replied a harassed Walter. Beads of sweat visible on his forehead.

"A minute is about all we have," muttered his fellow scientist, Amanda.

"Twelve to be precise," said Roger tightly.

"Enough! Ladies and gents," said David from his command chair. "Doctor?"

"OK, I have it. Planet Three. There's a lot of background radiation but I have it isolated to within 200 square kilometers."

"Computer, display Planet Three region as specified by Doctor Kernaghan."

The holo cube lit up with what could have been a view from the orbit of the moon, if not for the red tinge of the system's red dwarf primary. Crater upon crater filled the holo cube.

"What am I looking for, Doctor?" asked David.

"Is this scene at all familiar, Captain?" asked Walter.

David stared harder. Yes, just like the cratering on the moon. Before he could answer, his Chief spoke.

"It's like the Midwest plains of North America, or the Urals of Russia after the nuclear strikes of World War Three."

Then David saw it, a strike pattern… There was nothing random here.

"Do you want the good news, Captain?" asked Walter.

"Yes, please." David thought the doctor was enjoying this now, but their personal countdown to destruction was still ticking,

"I would calculate using radiation decay rates this happened at least 700 years ago. It's old news."

"Are you positive? We can't afford to be wrong here."

Walter replied confidently, "Yes, give or take twenty years. The system is reasonably accurate even at this distance."

"What about the power source, Doctor?"

Walter ran through the data in front of him again. "There is no indication of any change in the level of output since the time we detected it."

"Very well." Turning to address his XO, David enquired, "Commander. Thoughts?"

"Given the doctor's calculations, I think it's safe to say whoever or whatever did this is long gone. As far as the power source goes, the fact our presence has caused no reaction leads me to believe it is not a weapon or detection system of any kind. I think we can assume we, and therefore, Earth, are in no immediate danger."

"I concur. Computer, Romeo Charlie Nine six three, execute."

A pause, then the computer replied, "Voice print confirmed, Captain Catney. On your authority Romeo Charlie nine six three previous auto destruct can now be countermanded. Bio readings indicate Lieutenant Commander Cromie is alive and unharmed. Does he concur?"

Roger spoke aloud, "Computer. Whiskey Zulu one eight seven, I concur."

"Auto destruct aborted, fusion weapon deactivated," the computer confirmed.

The relief on the bridge of the *Marco Polo* was palatable.

"OK, Commander. Plot us a course to Sol and take us home. You have the con. I'm going for a coffee while I think about what I tell our lords and masters."

CHAPTER THREE
Crossing the Rubicon

Innes Base - Planet III - Proxima Centauri

Robert Ignico considered the red dwarf that was Proxima Centauri, through the clear steel dome protecting them from the bitter cold, a touch above the average noon temperature on this scarred rock – minus 112 centigrade.

He searched for the reflection of TDF *Ferdinand Magellan* in geostationary orbit above the base, he knew it was futile, even though it was by far the largest interstellar craft humans had so far built. It was some 1300 metres long, 250 at the beam and weighed in at 110,000 metric tonnes. It carried the essential parts and personnel who initially constructed Innes Base on the surface of Planet III of the Proxima Centauri system. TDF *Ferdinand Magellan* had then shuttled back and forth to Earth, bringing more scientists and engineers and materials as Innes had expanded to become the current home to some 630 men and women, all of whom were searching for the elusive source of the power spike found by TDF *Marco Polo* six months before.

The engineer in charge of the drilling had promised Robert today was the day. He had been promising this for the past week. Although the source of the power spike had been located quickly enough, it was found to be some five kilometers underground. One of the first groups to arrive on the *Magellan* had been mining engineers. They had been digging ever since.

The crackling in his earpiece returned Robert to the present.

"Doctor Ignico?" called the disembodied voice of the duty controller.

"Go ahead."

"We're approximately ten minutes drilling time from the target"

"OK. I'm on my way thanks." *Time to go to work*, thought Robert as he headed off to his office in the control center.

————

Robert was seated at his desk facing the holo cube that filled the center of his office trying to figure out what his eyes and his chief structural engineer were telling him.

"Sorry, run that past me again?"

"Radar on the drill head is reporting a cavern some seventy-five metres across and at least four, possibly five buildings. We must wait until we learn more from the robot sled after it arrives at the bottom of the drill shaft in another thirty minutes or so." Sarah repeated herself while tracing the display on the holo cube.

"What's new?" said Robert. "Best tell them to start widening the shaft. I want to get down there as soon as possible."

"Yes, sir." Sarah began making the necessary calls to the drill team.

————

Five kilometers below the Surface - Planet III - Proxima Centauri

A long week of Robert's team trudging under the artificial lights illuminating the cavern and casting conflicting shadows around it. Mapping and measuring the squat, box like buildings arranged with one at each corner of a square and, what Robert and his engineers were assuming, was the power plant in the middle. None of the buildings showed any obvious doors or other access points — assuming, of course, whoever or whatever built this cavern had the same thought processes as humans. Now, with baited breath came the moment of truth.

"OK, Sarah. Let's do it."

Sarah Boone, Robert's chief structural engineer nodded and signaled to her cutting crew. Plasma torches flared and Robert began making his own door.

The walls had turned out to be two metres thick. This place had been built to last! All the evidence pointed to some form of nuclear bombardment on the surface. The five kilometers of rock had provided protection but whoever had built this place was obviously not taking any chances.

The plasma torches should have cut through the walls like a hot knife through butter but instead it took forty-five minutes to make a hole large enough for a human to fit through. *Well, the moment of truth*, thought Robert. "Rank has its privileges," he said. "Recorders on and let's go see what was worth all of this protection." Robert entered the building.

Robert circled where he stood. He stared at the walls covered from floor to ceiling in storage racks holding small crystals, no bigger than a finger, crystals of every colour. In the centre of the room was a small raised podium with something similar to a lectern upon it. The lectern had a small keypad on the right hand side and a slot on the left. Robert mused, "If I'm not mistaken the slot is about the size of one of those crystals."

Sarah's eyes widened incredulously, "You're not thinking what I think you're thinking, are you, sir?"

"We are here to find out everything we can about this place, and this seems to be the next logical step to me."

Sarah pronounced slowly, "You're the boss…" glancing apprehensively at Robert as he selected a crystal at random and carefully placed it in the slot in the lectern.

Nothing.

There was a collective sigh, as much of relief as disappointment. Then Sarah reached over with a wry smile, glancing at Robert who was watching her every action, she carefully removed the crystal and reinserted it the other way round.

A million sparkling pinpoints of light encircled the podium.

"Oh my God!" Sarah exclaimed.

"Whoa," said Robert.

"Now there's an understatement," commented Sarah. She was not sure where to look or what she was looking at.

Robert flung her a shriveling look before returning to stare at the lights. "Are these familiar, Sarah?"

Sarah paused to re-examine the lights, trying to focus on an image, writing, something familiar… "Eh, no I don't think so. Random light, a visible language maybe?"

"You diggers. Try looking up now and again. These, unless I am mistaken, are stars. This is a map of our galaxy. We, Sarah, have hit El Dorado."

———

Robert compiled a hasty report and forwarded it to the *Magellan* for onward carriage to Earth by courier drone. Finding himself overcome with exhaustion, he realised he had been on the go for thirty-six hours.

Stimulants could only keep you going so long, so with strict instructions to the scientists, who were virtually salivating at the mouth to take the other Block Houses apart, to touch nothing until he returned, he left for the surface and his quarters to grab a few hours' sleep. His head seemed to just touch the pillow when the incessant beeping of his Comm woke him. "Yes, what is it?" he barked.

The face of his chief xenobiologist stared at him from the Comm. "Sir, I think my team may have found something quite interesting. Would you come back down here please?"

Robert rolled himself into an upright position "With what I've seen in the past two days, this wants to be good, Ivan."

"You need to see this for yourself, Robert. Trust me."

Robert let out a grunt. "OK I'll be there within the hour Ignico out." Robert headed for the shower in the hope it would infuse some energy into his tired body.

Thirty minutes later Robert found himself inside Block House Five. "Alright Ivan what's up? I would have thought the astronomers and physicists would, if anyone, have been the first to come up with something."

Doctor Ivan Kulibin smirked. "We do what we can to play our small part, sir."

Robert smiled back. "Get on with it Ivan." Robert noted he had the 'cat who just got the cream' air about him.

"Didn't it strike you as strange how you were able to stand at the lectern?"

The penny dropped for Robert. The position, the size of the lectern – he had not paid much attention at the time. *Damn!* He thought, aloud he said, "Of course. Why would an alien race construct a lectern which fits the human form and posture so closely?"

"Well it was Sasha from ergonomics who first noticed it. She practically fell on her rear end, peering at the lectern's control panel, when she stood back up she naturally placed her hand onto the keypad and discovered the keypad is designed for five fingers. Five!"

Robert stood in stunned silence, trying to let his logical, scientific brain process the implications. Eventually he recovered the ability to speak. "Are you telling me whoever or whatever built this was approximately the size and shape of a human, even down to having five fingers?"

"It would certainly appear so, sir."

Robert closed his eyes in concentration for a moment then. "Alright Ivan. I want your team to work on that assumption. Split your team in half: the second half will play Devil's Advocate and try their best to find fault in your logic. There is no way we are telling Earth about this 'til we can firm it up, understood?"

"Yes, sir. I'll get on it right away. May I make a suggestion which could speed things up?"

"You know all suggestions are welcome,"

"Well we could open one of the other Block Houses in case this is just a one off."

Robert thought for a second. "OK, so authorized. Get Sarah back down here. Pick a Block House at random and proceed. I'm going back to bed. I can feel a long few days ahead for all of us." Patting Ivan on the back, Robert headed back to the drill shaft and bed.

INNES BASE - PLANET III - PROXIMA CENTAURI

"Ivan you look like crap. When did you last sleep?" Robert regarded the figure slumped in the chair in front of him.

Ivan smiled and replied, "In another life, sir."

Robert smiled back and cast an eye over Sarah Boone. She was perched on the arm of the other chair in his spartan office located beside the control room on the surface of Planet III, or Rubicon, as it was fast becoming known. Named after the Roman river which legend said if an army ever crossed it then nothing would ever be the same again. Nothing would be the same again if the snippets of information Robert was getting where anything to go by.

"Sir," Sarah began, indicating the holo cube in the corner of Robert's office where a diagram of the cavern located five kilometres below them appeared. "As per your instructions, we divided into two teams and began to assess the data from opposing views. With the opening of the second then, with your permission, the three remaining Block Houses, we found the raw data was forcing the two teams to reach the same inescapable conclusion. If I could briefly go over the relevant points?"

Robert nodded and the image in the holo cube changed to show the internal layout of Block House One.

"As you know, the basic layout of each Block House is the same." Sarah described the images displayed in the holo cube. "Four sides with floor to ceiling racks full of the data crystals and a lectern on a raised podium located in the center." The holo cube image changed to show the location of each of the Block Houses. "Working on the assumption of this layout being replicated in each of the buildings, we entered Block Houses Three, Four and Five from above, keeping any possible damage to the data crystals to a minimum." The Holo image rotated and settled on a 3D rendering of a single story Block House, with a smaller cube directly below the center of the structure.

"Each Block House is independently powered from a source located below its structure, here." Sarah pointed toward the smaller cube in the image, and then continued. "And each structure appears to contain specific information. The easiest Block House to decipher was the one containing the Sciences – some things are a given constant, such as the composition of the atom – so once we identified the key, things gathered pace."

The holo image expanded to show the other Block Houses, each numbered. As Sarah described each Block House, the holo cube highlighted each image in turn. "Block House One was the first entered. Two seems to contain what we are assuming is art and music by the images and sounds. Three appears to hold enormous amounts of written data. Four is of a similar nature though it seems to contain more graphics, it appears to be planetary mapping but not all showing the same layouts, a bit confusing at the moment but we're working on it. Using the data from Block House One as a common cipher, like our very own Rosetta Stone, the computers are slowly but surely beginning to identify key points. But the sheer volume of information is staggering." Sarah took a deep breath. "That leaves us with Block House Five." Sarah paused again, which caused Robert to search her face rather than the scrolling data in the holo cube.

"Go on Sarah," said Robert.

"Sir…" Sarah began hesitantly, "upon examining the lectern in Block House Five, one of the technicians noticed a subtle difference in its keypad make up. It's subtle but it's there. Therefore, we decided we had pushed our luck far enough for the moment. As you know, we have been randomly trying a crystal from one Block House in another Block House's lectern and they all seem interchangeable." Sarah paused. "All except those from Block House Five. No crystal from there will play in the other four lecterns, and we have been too afraid in case we damage them to try the modified lectern in Block House Five. In conclusion, sir, I would say we have found an entire civilization's reference library."

"Thank you, Sarah. Ivan?"

"I think Sarah's conclusion is correct, Robert. We have enough data here to keep every scientist and researcher from every field of study on Earth busy for the next decade."

"But not from Block House Five?" said Robert.

"Not yet, sir," replied Ivan.

Robert jumped to his feet startling the tired Ivan. "Well, let's see what we can do about that shall we?" He headed out of his office toward the shaft to the underground cavern, followed by Ivan and Sarah.

Robert stood in front of the podium in Block House Five, staring at the seemingly innocent keypad on the raised lectern, with Ivan and Sarah standing behind him.

"Are you sure you want to do this, sir?" asked Sarah.

Robert smiled. "Well if it all goes wrong, Sarah, you get an instant promotion." Without another moment's hesitation he stepped onto the podium and place his hand over the keypad while inserting a data crystal (chosen at random) from the surrounding wall racks.

He felt a faint tingling and a large, contorted shape appeared in front of him. No, not contorted. A spiral. With the groove on the left of the spiral being much larger than on the right, he heard Ivan gasp behind him but was too entranced to turn around. Then it came to him, Ivan was a medical doctor by training, Robert was not, though he still remembered the image from biology.

He was feasting on a DNA helix – his DNA helix – and, as he watched, whatever computing machine drove the lectern highlighted sections of the helix. One area… two… three… eventually some ninety percent of the helix was illuminated. How was this possible? How could this machine identify so much of the human DNA helix so quickly? The image disappeared and for a second there was nothing…

Then images began to appear. Soon they were all around him, replaced every few seconds by another.

"Schematics!" Sarah blurted, "Complicated schematics. Where's Taylor?" Activating her wrist Comm, she shouted, "Control. Sarah. Find Taylor, tell him to report to Block House Five immediately!" Without waiting for a reply, she signed off and returned to examining the schematics. She was a structural engineer but these were not building schematics. Taylor was a design engineer, he would be clued in to what these were. Where is he? She asked herself impatiently.

After a few minutes, an out of breath Taylor arrived. "Yes, ma'am?"

At last! "What are those? Best guess will do," Sarah indicated to the still changing images.

Taylor watched intently for a few moments then shook his head and watched for a few more moments, turned to Sarah and said, "Ships, ma'am. Not just any ships. I would say warships… Pretty big ones!"

OFFICE OF THE PRESIDENT OF THE TERRAN REPUBLIC - GENEVA - EARTH

Bartholomew McMullen, permitted by a special act of Senate to run for a consecutive third term as president, had won a landslide victory. In these rapidly changing times, it seemed the voters wanted someone familiar to trust their fate to and that someone was Bartholomew McMullen, twenty-third President of the Terran Republic.

Bartholomew sat at the base of a horseshoe shaped table, with his cabinet and trusted advisers arranged on either side of him. A holo cube easily ten metres across directly in front of him. He watched Robert Ignico's follow up report for the second time, having viewed it in private earlier in the day, describing the contents of Block House Five.

He took the opportunity to gauge the reactions of the group assembled around him as the report played out. Faces showed a multitude of reactions from enthusiasm at the prospects for the scientific advancement the new

information provided to apprehension as to why there was such detail on weaponry.

At the realization that the final lectern required human DNA to activate it, an air of thoughtful silence settled around the table. The report concluded and heads turned toward the president, waiting for him to speak. *I knew I should have retired*, Bartholomew thought.

"Well, ladies and gentlemen," he began. "Your faces look just as mine did when I first viewed Doctor Ignico's report a few hours ago. It's a lot to take in so let me hit the highlights as I see them." Bartholomew stood up and slowly walked around the back of table with his hands clasped behind his back. He summarized the salient points as he saw them. "Firstly, this seems to be an alien race's complete reference library. Everything they have ever done or been is stored here." Bartholomew paused his slow pace and brought his hands to his front, posing in a thoughtful manner. "Secondly, what is the significance of the massive and detailed military database? If I consider this with the obvious nuclear bombardment on the surface, I begin to wonder – is this library a last ditch attempt to preserve what was the accumulated knowledge of an entire civilization? If so, preserve it for whom?" Bartholomew walked back to his seat at the base of the table and sat as he contemplated aloud. "Was it a threat from factions within their own society or some external force? And thirdly, Block House Five." He regarded in turn each of the people sitting at the horseshoe table, catching the eyes of just a few who were brave enough to look directly at him, "How did the lectern in Block House Five recognize human DNA so quickly? And why did it trigger the release of the apparently encrypted information?" Bartholomew broke his gaze from those in the room and rested it downwards on the table. He shook his head slightly, before raising his eyes and addressing the room again. "This causes me the most concern and I am sure it will be the source of the most consternation and worry amongst our people."

Nods around the table assured Bartholomew he had hit the proverbial nail on the head.

"The only saving grace I can see, at this moment in time, is – according to the *Marco Polo*'s initial assessment and subsequent work by the *Magellan* — the nuclear bombardment on the planet's surface occurred some 700 years ago. This point must be emphasized to the general population, to allay fears of any immediate attack. Whatever disaster overtook this unfortunate civilization, we can rest assured it is not about to visit us tomorrow."

A gruff "We hope," sounded from Bartholomew's right.

Bartholomew eyeballed the source of the comment. Admiral Olaf Helset of the Terran Defense Force. Standing at a 180 centimeters tall, broad shoulders tapering to a narrow waste, blond, close cropped hair and chiseled jaw with grey eyes the colour of the North Sea (which his Viking ancestors traversed with impunity those centuries before). Helset was a man who spoke his mind and hated politicians of all ilk, in the way only a military man could.

"Do you have something to say, Admiral?" enquired Bartholomew with a smile, which failed to reach his eyes.

"I am a military man, Mr. President, charged with protecting the Terran Republic. However, for these past 150 years the only threat to the Republic has come from the odd pirate attacking merchantmen plying their trade within the Solar System. The Defense Force is more like a coast guard than any sort of standing navy. There has simply been no requirement for such a force. So I truly hope, and I mean this with all my heart, this civilization destroyed itself. If it didn't, and whoever did this comes calling on us, then it will be a very short, one sided fight."

There was a stunned silence for a moment before the room filled with a cacophony of noise as each cabinet member attempted to voice their concerns. Bartholomew banged his fist on the table and called, "Enough!" The room fell silent once more. Scanning slowly around the room, Bartholomew said, "Ladies and gentlemen, I think we all agree without more information any statement to the public at this time would be precipitous. I suggest our course of action is to wait until we have examined the data more thoroughly before we release any statements to the public. As I speak, our scientists at Stickney Base on Phobos are working on deciphering the Rubicon data, including Block House Five."

There was a general murmur from the room. "My decision is final: we wait."

CHAPTER FOUR

Our Rosetta Stone

Stickney Base - Phobos - Orbiting Mars

Stickney Base was located in Stickney Crater on the Martian moon of Phobos. Phobos was only seventeen by fourteen by eleven kilometers in diameter and Stickney Base was five kilometers across. The base filled the entire crater, making the base seem even larger than it actually was.

With an orbital period around Mars of only zero point three two Terran days it did have the effect of causing seasickness on many new arrivals to the base but not Patricia Bath. She had been on Phobos for what seemed most of her adult life.

Stickney was her first choice on graduating top of her language course at MIT and she had never looked back. As head of department, she was intimately involved in interpreting the data brought back from the Rubicon cavern so many light years away orbiting Proxima Centauri.

Patricia shook herself out of her melancholic mood as her Comm beeped for attention, "Bath."

"Patricia. I've been running the new interpretation cipher of yours…" It was Vince Kealey, a few years older than Patricia but content to let her be the boss. It allowed him to get on with the more serious work of decoding everything and anything he could get his hands on while avoiding the spectrum of paperwork Patricia dealt with on a daily basis.

"Yes, Vince?"

"Well, I made a few tweaks and I think we've cracked it! We've significant matches across the board and should be able to start producing good translated copy by early tomorrow."

Patricia smiled. "Not bad for an old man Vince. Even one whose brain clouds over with old age every now and then."

Vince laughed down the Comm. "You're not too old to be put across my knee young lady," replied Vince. "So get your behind down here and take over so an old man can get some well-deserved rest."

"Yes, Granddad. Be there shortly." Taking one last look at Mars whizzing past only 9000 kilometers away, Patricia turned and headed back toward her lab and the mass of data awaiting her.

Office of the President of the Terran Republic - Geneva - Earth

After a soft knock, the door to Bartholomew McMullen's office opened. An aide ushered Admiral Olaf Helset through the door. Olaf marched in, halted short of the president, who rose from his seat at the head of the small round conference table, and saluted him.

"Please join us, Admiral." Bartholomew indicated a seat at the table where two others were already seated. "You know Senator Gillian Rae and Senator Thomas Crothers, my Secretary of Finance."

Olaf nodded toward both politicians by way of greeting. When requested to meet with the president, he had assumed it was about the Rubicon Cavern (as the area of the discovered Block Houses was now known). It would explain why Senator Rae was here. But what was the Secretary of Finance doing here? Well, the only way to find out was to get on with the meeting Olaf supposed.

"Admiral," began Bartholomew. "I've invited both Gillian and Thomas to join our little discussion today. We're just waiting for two more guests before we begin."

Olaf remained standing and addressed the president. "Sir, with all due respect, perhaps you'd like to tell me why I'm here and what the meeting is all about?" Olaf's intonation conveyed he had better things to do than shoot the breeze with a bunch of politicians.

"Patience, Admiral, I beg you. Now, please take a seat."

With an audible sigh, Olaf sat down, somehow managing to sit as far from the three politicians as the table allowed. *Should be an interesting meeting!* Bartholomew thought.

Another knock on the door. The same aide ushered in a reasonably tall woman and a willow wisp, slightly greying and overweight man into the room before closing the door behind them. Bartholomew stood and approached the woman. "Ah, thank you for coming Doctor Bath, and you Professor Ballantine. Perhaps we could get started. Please be seated."

As his new guests found seats, Bartholomew composed his thoughts. *Damn, I should have retired when I had the chance!* "If you'd like to begin Doctor Bath, I don't know if you have met all my guests before so I'll do the honors - this is Senator Rae," he indicated Gillian then moved on to Thomas, "and Senator Crothers and, finally, Admiral Olaf Helset."

"Thank you, sir." Patricia directed her gaze around the table as she continued, "I am Doctor Patricia Bath, head of linguistics at Stickney Base on Phobos, and this," indicating Ballantine, "is Professor George Ballantine, head of xenobiology here at Geneva University." George nodded around the table at the introduction. "OK… eh… well I'll cut to the chase" Patricia paused "since successfully interpreting the language found in the Rubicon Cavern…"

Olaf interrupted her flow with a strangled "What! What did you just say?"

Patricia regarded him steadily and repeated herself "Since successfully interpreting the language…"

Olaf turned a brilliant shade of red "Just what I thought you said, Doctor!" Throwing Bartholomew a glare capable of stopping elephants in their tracks, he addressed Patricia. "And when did this happen?"

"Some five months ago, Admiral," replied Patricia.

If Olaf could have gotten any redder, he would have. He stood and approached Bartholomew. "Why wasn't the TDF informed? Who decided to withhold this vital information? It could mean the life or death for Earth –"

Without rising from his seat, Bartholomew cut the admiral off in mid flow. "I did, Admiral. Now, sit and let the doctor finish her brief."

Olaf hesitated, and for a moment, Bartholomew thought he was going to continue. Instead, Olaf retook his seat and sat there like a volcano on the brink of erupting.

Bartholomew took a breath before turning to Patricia. "Please continue, Doctor."

Patricia glanced from Bartholomew to the admiral and back to Bartholomew, took a deep breath and continued. "Thank you, Mr. President. Now, as I was saying, having successfully interpreted the alien language we began cycling through the accumulated data brought home by the *Magellan*. The sheer volume of information is staggering. The original estimate of a decade to translate everything may not be far off, there is just so much of it, but finding the index to each Block House has made our life much easier. So far, we have managed to translate five percent of the data, but we have been able to make some reasonably good assumptions."

"WAGs you mean, Doctor?" interrupted Olaf. Patricia looked confused. "Wild Ass Guesses" said Olaf helpfully.

"Ah, well yes, Admiral. But we think we have the data to support our guesses," she replied pointedly. "It seems pretty obvious this alien civilization was more advanced than ours. They had already explored parts of the galaxy. We have discovered at least seventeen different planetary maps from their astrological database, some of which we have been able to verify using our own known data. I think it is safe to assume they managed to colonize some of these worlds. Their medical databases also reveal insights into their physical make up."

This time Gillian Rae interrupted. "You mean we know what they looked like?"

Patricia's face broke into a large grin. "Yes, Senator." An image appeared in the holo cube in the center of the table. All eyes in the room fixated on the 3D image of an alien being

It was approximately one meter forty centimeters tall. Covered in light brown hair, not quite as thick as fur, two round eyes were set in a slightly pointed head with the ears mounted higher up the head than a human. The mouth and nose protruded slightly, a short thick neck leading to a barrel chest with two arms bending at an elbow and two legs with knee like joints. It could easily be mistaken for a relative of Earth's monkeys.

After a moment, Patricia continued, "That's right, ladies and gents. This image is very familiar to us and we may be forced to reassess our theory of evolution." Patricia could have heard a pin drop in the room.

"Doctor Ballantine and his team at Geneva are sure the DNA similarity between our alien friends and ourselves is not a coincidence. How could two species evolving in two different parts of the galaxy have so many points within the DNA helix that match? The odds are astronomical." Patricia paused for a second to allow the minds of the others in the room to grasp the implications of what she had just said, "It's our belief we have a common ancestor."

Olaf was going that shade of red again. "Whoa, stop right there, Doctor. Are you saying we are descended from aliens? Because I didn't realised today was April Fool's Day."

Patricia turned to the president. "Perhaps Professor Ballantine would be better at explaining this, it is his field after all."

With a nod from Bartholomew, Professor Ballantine stood up and cleared his throat. "Mr. President. Twenty-five or so million years ago, for some reason we still cannot explain, the rhesus monkey broke away from our particular chain of evolution. It has, also for an unknown reason, ten markers in its DNA helix, which really should not be there. We have been at a loss to explain them."

"Some 3,000,000 years ago the chimpanzee also broke away from our evolutionary chain. It is our closest DNA match with something like ninety-five percent duplication of human DNA. I have concluded both the rhesus monkey and the chimpanzee were failed attempts to produce an intelligent creature. I believe the aliens millions of years ago manipulated our DNA to produce as near a version of themselves as possible but tailored to the Earth's environment." His conclusion met with a deafening silence. It hung in the air.

Bartholomew's voice sliced through the silence "Thank you Professor Ballantine. Perhaps, Doctor Bath, you would continue?"

"Mr. President, the data is still sketchy but it would appear these aliens originated in the constellation of Orion, from a planet orbiting the star we call Saiph, some 2200 light years away."

"A hell of a long way to travel just to experiment with our DNA, don't you think?" asked Gillian. "Surely there's a more suitable planet closer to their home star?"

"Senator," replied Ballantine. "We are working on the premise the seventeen planetary maps so far discovered in the Saiph database are also locations where they experimented with the DNA of indigenous life forms."

"But why?" interjected Olaf. "If their goal was colonization, why not just send a ship full of – what did you call them – Saiph? It's certainly a lot quicker than waiting for a new species to evolve."

"Because they wanted to leave something behind, Admiral. A legacy if you will," said Patricia.

Olaf regarded her in puzzlement. "I'm sorry, Doctor. Leave something behind? A race so advanced doesn't just vanish overnight," he looked around the room at the others, "for all we know they are probably still out there somewhere."

Patricia stared directly at the admiral, knowing what she was about to say would change the future path of humanity. "I doubt that, Admiral, because they were at war… At war with a foe who was not out to conquer them but to annihilate them. To erase the Saiph's very existence from the galaxy. And the enemy was winning."

———

As the aide closed the door behind him, Bartholomew turned to his remaining guests. The two scientists had left, leaving the two senators and Helset. Thomas was staring intently at his coffee cup.

"Penny for them Thomas," asked the president. Thomas had been noticeably silent throughout the briefing. Glancing up, Thomas paused, then said,

"Mr. President, although the contents of the briefing have my head swimming, I keep returning to the same question."

"Go on Thomas," urged Bartholomew gently.

"It's not why the Saiph manipulated life on Earth and other planets or even how such an obviously advanced race could lose a war… Its why am *I* here? I understand the admiral represents Defense, Senator Rae – Science and Technology. But me? All I do is manage budgets."

Bartholomew began to chuckle, to the amazement of the others in the room, "Oh Thomas, you are probably the most important man in the room." Thomas seemed completely perplexed, Bartholomew continued. "Without you I can't carry out my plan."

"Which is… sir?" asked Gillian, Thomas' puzzlement reflecting in her own face now.

With his best vote winning smile, Bartholomew answered, "Why, simply to build a fleet of survey ships, in complete secrecy of course, to explore and find out what happened on the other seventeen planets." He beamed at the occupants of the room, before resting his gaze on the admiral. "Olaf here will provide the requirements and crew." His eyes moved to Senator Rae. "Gillian has the technical wherewithal to build them." Bartholomew brought his gaze back to Senator Crothers. "But you, my dear Thomas, will need to provide the millions of Feds to finance them. All without the senate or our citizens finding out. Simple? Wouldn't you agree?"

Thomas dropped his coffee cup onto the carpet. Staring open mouthed at the smiling President who had just declared himself as, potentially, the biggest embezzler of government money… ever…

CHAPTER FIVE
Operation Minerva

CHARON BASE - ORBIT OF PLUTO - SOL SYSTEM

John Radford stopped to get a look of his surroundings as he exited the shuttle door. "Now this is the quintessential middle of nowhere."

"Sorry did you say something, Captain?" asked the ensign assigned to meet this shuttle.

"Nothing, Ensign," John sighed, "Just remarking on the location my lords and masters at the Admiralty have decided on as my new assignment. I'm now wondering who I pissed off to be sent this far off the beaten track."

The young ensign impatiently expressed the 'I've heard it all before' look. "Your orders, sir?"

"Yes, sorry. Here." John handed over the data chip containing his orders and personal records. The ensign inserted them into his PAD. He confirmed John was indeed Captain John Radford and he was indeed posted to some unheard of Joint Service working group on the logistical requirements of establishing and maintaining manned bases outside the solar system.

A friend of John's had remarked the posting sounded like a barrel of laughs as he bought John a consolation drink on the last night of his shore leave, shortly before John caught the inter system shuttle which would deliver him to his home for the next three years.

Perhaps, his friend pointed out, John needed a few years to grow into his new rank after his recent accelerated promotion and the media circus which followed him. The press had sensationalized John's actions during the 'Alexandria Incident' and brought unwanted, and John felt unwarranted, attention to him and the Admiralty. John wholeheartedly agreed with him. Without a doubt this was the Admiralty's way of getting him 'outta sight, outta mind' for a while. John's face formed an unhappy scowl. With his experience, he should be out there exploring the galaxy and setting up those bases, not sorting out how many packets of toilet rolls it takes to support them.

As the ensign returned the data chip to John, he said, "If you follow me, sir. The admiral is expecting you. You're the last to arrive."

Oh great, thought John, *last to arrive. Hope the admiral is in a forgiving mood or this could be a long assignment.*

As the ensign escorted him to the briefing room, they passed down corridors bustling with navy, marine and civilian personnel. All seemed to be moving in a hurry and with a definite purpose. This struck John as odd, but when the ensign stopped at a doorway with armed marines guarding it he decided, something was definitely not right here.

The ensign turned to John and indicated a state of the art retinal scanner mounted on the doorframe. "Press your right eye to the retinal scanner, sir. You'll be met on the other side."

"You're not coming?"

"No, sir. I'm not cleared." The ensign turned on his heel and headed for his next task.

An ensign not cleared for a logistics meeting? Forgetting himself, he thought aloud, "What the hell?" He shook his head before placing his right eye in front of the retinal scanner. The door popped open and he stepped through. A greying female lieutenant commander wearing the insignia of Naval Intelligence confronted him.

She scanned him up and down and without a word of greeting said, "This way Captain. Admiral Vadis is expecting you."

John stopped dead in his tracks. "Admiral Aleksandr Vadis?"

The lieutenant commander had already taken several steps, she stopped and turned with a knowing smile. "The one and only."

John's mind raced. Aleksandr Vadis… the spook's spook. He had been immersed in the black side of intelligence work for some forty years until he was implicated in a corruption scandal, what – three years ago? He had been forcibly retired in disgrace. A sad end to a lifetime of service. What the hell was he doing way out here at the edge of the solar system? Better still – if he retired in disgrace – why was he in charge?

Full of questions John was led along a corridor. They reached another door, again guarded by marines. These ones seemed even nastier than the pair guarding the building's entrance. Another retinal scan, however, this time the lieutenant commander also presented her right eye.

As the door opened, the lieutenant commander led the way and they entered the room. It held an oval shaped table with four chairs on either side and two at the top. Already seated were three navy captains, two men and one woman, along with four marine majors, paired off – navy, marine, navy, marine. John's escort indicated the empty seat beside, what seemed like, an overly tall marine while she walked to the head of the table and took her seat beside, damn – it was he. Admiral Aleksandr Vadis.

"Welcome, Captain Radford," said Aleksandr with a smile suited to a fox about to thieve a few chickens. "I have no doubt you're wondering what the hell you're doing here, as I'm sure are the other men and women seated here."

Scrutinizing the faces around the table, John could see he was not the only one who had no clue of what was going on.

"This briefing," Aleksandr paused, "is so sensitive anyone who knows about it is either on this godforsaken rock, and will stay here for the rest of their natural lives, or in key positions within government. Not even all of the cabinet know about us."

John's stunned face reflected the others around the table. *What the hell?*

"As is general public knowledge the discovery of the Rubicon Cavern proved once and for all that we are not alone in the universe. It may be the library of a long dead civilization but the odds are, sooner rather than later, we will run into a living, technologically advanced civilization. Do we all agree?" There was a general nodding of assent around the table. "As I said, the Rubicon Cavern and the existence of its creators is now public knowledge. What is not is how this particular civilization came to its demise. The government has encouraged scientists to expound theories on the subject, but we have known almost from the start the Saiph were wiped out by a technically inferior but numerically superior race. They were outnumbered, not outgunned."

John thought he heard the jaws of the people gathered around the table hit the floor.

Aleksandr's smile resembled a fox. "Oh it gets better ladies and gents. We have since discovered the Saiph knew they were losing the war and so set out to tinker with the evolution of worlds to ensure part of them survived. One of those worlds was Earth. So we," he glanced around the table, "are the evolutionary result of their tinkering."

Silence filled the room as minds raced to comprehend Aleksandr's words.

"Now you understand why this has been kept a secret. From the Saiph's library, we have identified seventeen other worlds where they have… 'Tinkered', for want of a better word. It is your mission to find out what happened on these other worlds. In complete secrecy we have, over the past three years, designed and constructed four stealth survey ships. We have incorporated as much Saiph technology as we presently understand."

Aleksandr pointed toward each of the navy captains. "You will each command one of these Vanguard class ships. The marines will be inserted onto the surface of any planet deemed worthy of further reconnaissance. It is imperative you all understand the covert nature of our mission, both here at home and out there amongst the stars. At home, we cannot anticipate people's reaction if they find out an alien race manufactured them. Out there, we may make first contact with another intelligent species – peacefully we hope. But what if the race that destroyed the Saiph is still out there?" Aleksandr paused, making eye contact with each of the personnel gathered around the table. He continued in a tone he hoped relayed the gravity of his words. "We launch in six months, and you…" Aleksandr again slowly caught the eye of each of them, "have a lot to learn. I now turn you over to Lieutenant Commander Elizabeth Wilson, my chief of staff, to continue your introductory brief."

John appraised the Lieutenant Commander with fresh eyes. To be the chief of staff to Admiral Vadis you had to be something special. Before him stood a sixtyish, grey haired, slightly chubby woman who had the appearance of someone more at home playing with her grandchildren than helping to run a secret mission.

"Good morning, ladies and gentlemen, and welcome to Operation Minerva. Before we begin, I must emphasize the covert status of this mission. Few are aware of this operation and those participating are chosen carefully. You are amongst the chosen few, as am I. To give you a little of my background: I retired from active service seven years ago. I enjoyed civilian life, I was enjoying watching my grandkids grow up," With a quick glance and a smile at Aleksandr Elizabeth continued, "Until Admiral Vadis approached me and not so politely told me my commission had been reactivated. My mission was to go to the asshole of the universe and supervise the mining of some worthless rock. As you can imagine, I was full of the joys of spring at the prospect." Chuckles emanated from around the room. "I didn't actually know what my real mission was until I was on the transport out here and the admiral arrived at my door with a briefing pack and a strong brandy in hand. Sorry, I've no brandy for you!" Elizabeth smiled. "But I completely understand how you feel right now. So, to business." She touched a control on the panel in front of her.

An image of a ship appeared above the center of the table, slowly rotating to give everyone a 360-degree view. All the naval officers at the table lent forward for a better view, including John, who heard himself let out a low whistle. It was nothing like anything he had seen or heard of before. The marines tried not to show any interest in mere navy stuff – the navy was only there to provide them transport after all – but John could see out of the corner of his eye the marine beside him intently studying the small ship. Small but… elegant.

The ship was the black of darkest night, making it hard for John to make out details, as they seemed to merge. A blunted off wedge shaped bow morphed into a smooth rounded off superstructure. John only just discerned the stern where again it was wedge shaped. As the image rotated, John made out more details, sunken engine protrusions in the rear wedge. Spread along the length of the beam from bow to stern where small clusters. They appeared remarkably like small laser turrets. Mounted just after the wedge at the bow, top and bottom, there was mounted a shallow turret holding twin cannon with the same design of shallow turret mounted above and below at the stern. This ship may be small but it seemed she could handle herself.

"This," Elizabeth continued, "is the Vanguard class survey ship the admiral mentioned earlier, weighing in at 15980 tonnes and with a crew complement of 135 naval and eighteen marines. She is only 325 meters long and twenty-one at the beam…"

"Seriously?" John thought, then realised the word had actually come out of his mouth.

"Yes, Captain?" said Elizabeth. "You have a question?"

Foot in mouth again thought John as the whole table turned to him. *Oh well here goes. Deep breath.* "If I heard you correctly, Commander, you said the ship was only 325 metres long. With a crew of 135. Only four years ago, TDF *Marco Polo* was the best technology we had. The engines alone were something like 200 metres long and massed 600 tonnes each with a crew complement of 2100."

"If I may, Commander," interjected Aleksandr, "You are correct, Captain Radford. The difference between the *Marco Polo* and the Vanguard class is," he pronounced slowly and definitively, "RE-MARK-ABLE… I must point out something you said yourself. The best our technology had." He paused. "My staff have been moving heaven and earth to reverse engineer the Saiph's engineering library. It helps that it seems the Saiph knew whoever found and accessed their library had to be led by the hand. Therefore, our people have been racing ahead. We feel confident the Vanguard incorporates the best Saiph technology we currently understand. Does that answer your question, Captain?"

"Yes, sir. Thank you," replied John.

Aleksandr turned to Elizabeth, "Please continue, Commander."

"Sir, full technical specs are available in your briefing packs, but to summarize the high points, the Vanguards design is not for head-to-head combat. They are primarily stealth covert survey ships. Engineered to get you in and out of your objectives without alerting anyone to your presence. Each Vanguard incorporates the latest version of our chameleon stealth units, employing active optics to project whatever is behind the vessel onto the part of the vessel viewed by an enemy – effectively making the vessel invisible."

"Not everything is perfect, there is always the chance of failure. An enemy may not be deceived or may possess technology, which may defeat the chameleon system. To mitigate the risk, we have armed the Vanguard with four dual turrets of particle cannon. From the image you will see: two forward mounted above and below the hull, and two to the rear again above and below the hull. Spread across the hull, for close in defense, are Laser Area Denial weapons, which should kill anything that gets too close for comfort. Also embarked are two Tanto class covert insertion shuttles for use by the embedded marines."

"In relation to personnel. In your briefing pack, you will find the manning lists for your crew. They are the best the navy has to offer. There are some… um…" Elizabeth and Aleksandr exchanged a knowing look, "unorthodox individuals amongst them, but both the admiral and myself decided that for a mission of this importance we needed the best. Whatever their previous commanding officers may have said. I strongly urge you to read between the lines when you read their personnel jackets. Now, let me turn to the marine contingent."

At this the four marine officers sat up a little straighter, as if everything they had heard so far was just a preamble to the important bit, the marines.

"As you will have no doubt noticed, ladies and gentlemen, sitting to your right is a marine major."

John turned to his right and took his first proper look at the marine officer beside him. It was then he noticed he was not the atypical marine. The haircut was there, tight to the skull, but he did not have the expected massive body builder bulk. It was then he noticed his eyes: dark blue and unblinking, like an eagle. Lacking any emotion while displaying complete concentration. An unbidden shiver ran down John's spine, *the sort of man you do not want to meet in a dark alley.* The marine looked at him as if he were working out where to strike him, and then much to John's surprise, he stuck out his hand.

"Alec, Alec Murray," a thick Scottish accent softly rolled the 'r's and was accompanied by a small smile.

"John Radford," John shook the outstretched hand and held Alec's eyes briefly before flicking back to the main speaker in the room.

"Each of these marines command your marine detachments. You have quite a bit of leeway while on your missions and you may decide a ground reconnaissance is required. In consultation with the Marine Detachment Commanders on board, you have the resources to plan and execute any such ground reconnaissance." Elizabeth paused. "The key to mission success is information. This is not a guts and glory job. Earth badly needs to know what we are facing out there. The only way to do so is to explore, record the findings and get the information home. To this end, each Vanguard has a complement of courier drones embarked to allow each ship to get its information back to us for evaluation and dissemination. It is our intention to share all relevant information gathered by each Vanguard with the other Vanguards. As the mission is covert, the plan is for you to drop a stealthy communications relay buoy at your point of entry into each system. An incoming courier drone will hit it with a whisker laser to pass its messages. In turn, your ships can hit the buoy with a whisker laser and download any messages stacked there for you. If, however, we do not hear from a ship within a seven-day window, it will be classed as lost and no further attempts will be made to communicate with it." Elizabeth took the time to regard each of the men and women sat around the table. "Understood?"

There was consensus from the gathered officers. "At this point, I'd like, with the admiral's permission, to call a halt for today. Your senior officers will meet you tomorrow at zero nine hundred hours in the designated briefing rooms. An ensign is waiting for each of you at the outer doors to escort you to your accommodation. Admiral?"

Aleksandr stood. "Ladies and gentlemen, be under no illusions. You have the complete resources of the Terran Republic at your disposal. We must ascertain if there is any threat to humanity out there in the stars. Your mission is to locate, identify and return home without any one, or anything, knowing you have been there. Good day."

The officers stood to attention as the admiral left the room. John picked up his briefing chip, turning he was startled to find himself staring straight into the face of a smiling Alec Murray. "I don't know about you but I could do with a beer. What say we pull rank on the ensign and get him to take us to the Officers' Club?"

John gave a wary smile of his own unsure of Murray's motives "Sounds like an idea," John led the way to the door and punched the activator, he motioned Murray through "Lead on"

"Typical navy, Let the marines lead. Bet you don't have any money either."

John sniggered aloud and Murray smiled at his own joke. *A killer with a sense of humor? A novel thought!* John decided the marine might not be a bad lad after all "OK, first one's on me, Alec."

"Right answer! You're too easy, are you sure you're not English?" the smile reached Alec's eyes.

———

Watching the departing officers on his desk display Aleksandr looked up as Elizabeth entered the room, he gestured for her to take a seat as he stood and made his way to the small bar in the corner of his office. He poured two double bourbon on the rocks before placing a glass in front of Elizabeth and retaking his seat. Aleksandr took time to savor the bourbon's aroma. The Russian in him still rebelled at the thought of drinking bourbon rather than the traditional vodka. He inwardly reminisced, how he, as a shiny new ensign, had boarded his first ship all those years ago and was introduced to a dyed in the wool Kentucky CO who'd promised Aleksandr he would disavow vodka by the end of his tour and would have converted to bourbon. Surprisingly, his CO had been right. Aleksandr took a small sip of bourbon allowing himself a final moment of pleasure before returning to work.

"So what do you think of them Elizabeth?"

Elizabeth tilted her head slightly as she considered his question savoring a sip of her drink, it gave her more thinking time.

"As far as the marines go, the Corps has done us proud. You could not ask for a more professional and dedicated group. Of course, marines are not my area of expertise, it's the ships captains who are. As we've discussed before, Admiral, the final selection of the vanguard captains is entirely your choice and…"

A raised hand from Aleksandr stopped her mid-sentence.

"I asked for your opinion Elizabeth, don't beat about the bush."

She frowned, she hated being put on the spot and Aleksandr knew it. Sometimes she wondered if he did it just for his own amusement. Taking a deep breath she let it out as an audible sigh she.

"Captain Lewis is the most experienced. Having read his personal file it shows he has turned down promotion on more than one occasion until the time came when the Admiralty just stopped offering it. It explains why at fifty-six he is still only a captain. He is a born explorer, but take into account his Command Course results you will see he came top of the tactical phase. In my opinion, he should've been forced to take promotion… If this all goes wrong and we get into any kind of shooting war out there we'll need his experience in fleet command."

Aleksandr made a mental note to drop a line to his old friend and fellow admiral, Ai Jing about Lewis. Elizabeth was right some people should not be given the choice to avoid promotion.

"Captain Papadomas is a student of history and its societies, he's also a devoted family man. He joined as a seaman before making such a good impression on his commanding officers he ended up being offered a commission as a mustang. He is perfect for the role of exploration. A man with a keen thirst for knowledge but tempered by the need to return to his family, so… unwilling to take undue risks with his own or his crew's safety."

Elizabeth paused to take another sip of her bourbon.

"Captain Witsell, on the other hand, enlisted as a commissioned officer. Top of her class at the Academy she has not put a foot wrong in her career and is without doubt a rising star on the command track, thus her place on this mission. My only concern is she has not been tested in a combat situation. Not that we are expecting the Vanguards to go into combat but this is her first command of a major vessel. I'm afraid I must reserve judgment on her at the minute."

Aleksandr eyed Elizabeth over the rim of his glass. Noting they both needed a fresh drink he lifted Elizabeth's glass from her hands and went to the bar, still with his back to her he said, "I see you have left our young Captain Radford to last. Impolite of you considering he is senior to Witsell."

A harrumph emanated from Elizabeth and extracted an un admiral like grin from him, he quickly recovered before turning to Elizabeth and passed her the now refilled glass.

"Unlike you, Admiral, the exploits of Captain Radford do not impress me and you know fine well the only reason he is senior to Captain Witsell is because they appeared on the same promotion list and the letter R comes before the letter W."

Now it was the admiral's turn to buy himself some time by taking a sip of his drink. "Radford may be young for his position but the decisions he was forced to make during the 'Alexandria Incident' show when push comes to shove he puts the greater good and his duty first. Being responsible for deaths under your command so you can ride to the rescue of civilians could be seen as making a tough call or…"

Elizabeth locked eyes with her admiral. "Putting your crew in danger to satisfy your own need for glory hunting."

CHAPTER SIX

The Journey Begins

Charon Base - Orbit of Pluto - Sol System

John Radford sat back in his seat on the command deck of the new Vanguard class survey ship the *Henry Hudson*. It was so new his seat still squeaked. The last six months had flown past. From his first sight of what was to be his new ship still shrouded by the cradling arms of a construction dock to the myriad of briefings led by Lieutenant Commander Elizabeth Wilson and her underlings. Where did that woman get her energy? She seemed to be everywhere and had an answer for everything. If she did not know, she knew a man who did.

No wonder Admiral Vadis had dragged her out of retirement to be his right arm.

John glanced around the bridge, taking in the officers and ratings preparing the ship for launch. The admiral had not been joking when he said John and his fellow captains were getting the best the navy had to offer. His comment about reading between the lines of his crew's personnel jackets was so true. Taken at face value, the majority of his crew were the cream of the crop, but some appeared to receive strangely low ratings from their past commanding officers. Unless you read into it. You really could not blame their COs. The TDF was not a large force. Split into its composite parts of Ground, Marine, Navy and Survey it got even smaller. It would not be the first time, or the last, John was sure, a CO would write a neutral, if not slightly shaded, report on one of his subordinates in the hope of keeping them. Frustrating for the subordinate but good for a lazy CO.

John's own navigator, Lieutenant Carlo Danino, was a prime example. Before Vadis seconded him to Charon, he had been working out on the asteroid belt doing traffic control for the endless amount of freight traffic plying back and forth to the inner system. On his arrival at Charon John met him at the shuttle, as he had with each of his command crew, to get an initial feel for him. Danino arrived with the expression of a beaten man, resigning himself to another tour of another humdrum asteroid. John was not impressed. That evening while having dinner with Alec Murray, who had become not only a friend but also a good sounding board, he expressed his concern. "You should have seen him, Alec, he got off the shuttle and couldn't even look me in the eye."

"Well I don't know about you John but if I'd just finished a tour shuffling freighters around for three years and was told I was going somewhere even more remote for another three, I'd certainly wonder who I had pissed off."

"Yeah… I suppose your right. If he is such a shit hot navigator why don't we see what he's made of?" John tapped his communicator.

"Control?" a disembodied voice said.

"Control, can you tell me if any of the Vanguard simulators are free?"

"Wait one, Captain… Yes, sir. Simulator Two is free till zero eight hundred tomorrow morning."

"Thanks. Can you book it in my name for zero one thirty hours till zero four thirty hours and load a level four navigation scenario for me?"

There was a short pause on the other end of the link. "Sorry, sir. Did you say zero one thirty till zero four thirty and level four?"

"That's correct. I feel the need to push myself a little, brush off the rust so to speak."

"At level four, sir, I hope you're on the top of your game."

So do I John thought. "Radford out."

Alec sat back and raised his beer glass. "I salute a fellow humanitarian, a man who cares for his crew and thinks of their every need. So when do you give the good lieutenant the news of his make or break simulator test?"

"Oh," a large grin appeared on John's face, "about zero one ten hours," and sipped his own beer.

A very harassed and out of breath Danino came running round the corner at the end of the corridor holding the entrance to Simulator 2. John glanced at his watch. "Zero one twenty-five Lieutenant Danino. What took you so long?"

"Sir, I only arrived on the base this afternoon."

"Which has given you adequate time to check out the basic base schematic has it not Lieutenant? I don't expect excuses from any of my crew."

Surprise ascended Danino's face "Crew, sir? I thought I was here to do traffic control?"

John looked him square in the eye "That, Lieutenant Danino, is what we are here to decide. Follow me." Radford entered the simulator with Danino in tow. There was a sharp intake of breath behind him as Danino took in the view. A complete replica of the command deck of a Vanguard class survey ship. John smiled. "Close your mouth Lieutenant. You're not catching flies." Danino's mouth closed with an audible click. "Sit down over there Lieutenant." John indicated a seat surrounded by monitors against the left hand bulkhead and then took his own seat in the center of the command deck. "Until I am satisfied you're up to the job, we will run simulations. If, however, you do not come up to scratch, I think freighter controlling will be your calling. So do we understand each other Lieutenant?"

Danino did not even turn around as he busily tried to familiarize himself with the controls around him. "Yes, sir. Clearly, sir."

John sat back in his chair. "Then let us begin."

Three hours later and John's head was pounding. On the first two simulations, John had beaten Danino to the correct navigation solution but as the lieutenant became more familiar with the control system of the Vanguard, he was able to beat John by a greater and greater margin. If John did not know better, he would have sworn Danino was cheating. He was able to do complex math in his head and cut out the need to input the information into the nav computer. He did not have to wait for the results, and therefore missed steps out of the final computation… truly amazing.

After the final simulation, John saw a different side of Danino. As the lieutenant turned to face him, he was smiling from ear to ear. His whole body seemed to have come alive with raw energy, eager for the next challenge. John regarded him for a moment. "Well done Lieutenant. I stand corrected. Welcome to the *Henry Hudson*."

Giving John a quizzical look, Danino said, "Thank you, sir. But, eh… what is a *Henry Hudson*?"

John laughed aloud, nearly falling off his seat in the process. "Briefing room, zero eight thirty sharp and all will be revealed. Now go get some sleep. I know I plan to."

TDF *HENRY HUDSON* - CHARON BASE - ORBIT OF PLUTO - SOL SYSTEM

A call from the marine at the outer hatch informing him Admiral Vadis had just boarded and was on his way to the command deck broke John Radford's train of thought. A few moments later, the admiral strode through the hatch followed by Lieutenant Commander Wilson, his chief of staff.

"Admiral, a pleasure as always," John said in his best upbeat tone. Vadis saw right through him.

"You're such a poor liar, Captain. Nevertheless, ten out of ten for trying. You know and I know I only interfere when I have to. Most of the time I send my henchman – woman," he nodded toward Wilson, "to do my dirty work, but not this time. Could I ask you to assemble your senior staff in your briefing room in say… thirty minutes? Until then, why don't you show Lieutenant Commander Wilson and me the comfy chairs in your cabin?"

John glanced over at Commander Bill Talbot, his Executive Officer, seated at the other side of the bridge. Bill nodded and started making calls. "If you'd like to follow me, Admiral." John was not getting a good feeling about this.

The *Henry Hudson* was a small survey ship. The captain's quarters consisted of only one cabin and a small office attached to it. With John, Vadis and Wilson ensconced in it it was not exactly spacious. John stood behind his desk. The admiral took the other most comfortable seat and indicated for the others to sit.

"Well, John. As I said, we have had a slight hiccup. As you are well aware, I have been banging on about the covert nature of our mission and of Charon base. We have managed to keep the whole thing secret for nearly four years – a small miracle in itself. When President McMullen first authorized Operation Minerva, only the then Chair of the Science and Technology Committee, Gillian Rae, the Secretary of Finance, Thomas Crothers and Admiral Helset were even aware of its existence. When I was brought on board, I had direct contact with Admiral Helset only, the theory was simple. If I didn't know anyone and they didn't know me then leaks are kept to a minimum. In the spy business, we call it compartmentalization. When President Coston took over…" Vadis referred to Rebecca Coston, the new 24th President of the Terran Republic. She recently replaced the popular outgoing President McMullen. He had reached the end of his fifteen-year presidential term and, too much disappointment, was forbidden from standing again. After all, the permitted maximum term is fifteen years.

Vadis continued. "She was briefed by McMullen of our existence. Rebecca Coston agreed to keep not only the operation secret, but to keep key personnel such as Crothers and Rae in place." Vadis chuckled. "I would love to have been a fly on the wall when she told her party officials she was retaining two senators from the opposition party in their posts! Unfortunately, the president's party insisted on replacing Admiral Helset. He apparently made some of them feel uncomfortable. I can't imagine why…"

This time Wilson giggled like a schoolchild. "He always had a knack of annoying politicians," she said.

"True, Commander, but I digress. It is with his replacement that our problem lies."

John was confused "But surely his replacement is General Joyce? A marine through and through. You couldn't get a secret out of the man with an explosive charge."

"Quite right, Captain." Vadis exhaled sharply. "General Keyton Joyce will make an outstanding leader of the Defense Force. However, somehow, and I am personally investigating the reason, the eyes only briefing pack on Operation Minerva was delivered to the wrong office." Vadis was clenching and unclenching his fists as he spoke his words through gritted teeth.

This was not going to be pretty, thought John.

Vadis continued. "How do you deliver a sealed, eyes only, briefing pack inside a secure briefcase, attached to the wrist of an armed marine, to the wrong office? Then accept the wrong ID for it and walk away happy as Larry?"

Uh oh, thought John. Some poor marine officer was going to be in charge of chipping small flakes off an asteroid with an ice pick for the rest of his career.

"Anyway, to the point." Vadis physically calmed himself again. "The clerk who accepted the pack had no way of knowing its contents, just the code name — Operation Minerva. When the marine came running back into the

office to recover the pack, he apparently threatened the clerk with a fate worse than death if he ever mentioned the name 'Minerva' again."

Wilson turned to John, "And what do you think happened next?"

"Not funny, Commander," Vadis growled "Over a drink the same evening with some…" The admiral screwed up his face in disgust, "… reporter, he told the whole story. Said reporter did some snooping and spoke with a source in Finance who, being a good citizen, told him all about some project being run directly out of the Secretary's office… In addition, it appeared to be swallowing up significant portions of other projects' budgets. The reporter in question intends to run the story tomorrow with the bare minimum of facts and the maximum of conjecture."

"It would seem, Admiral," said John, "the cat is out of the bag. Where do we go from here, sir?"

Vadis looked at Wilson. "Commander, if you would."

"Yes, sir. The plan, Captain, is to bring the launch of all the Vanguards forward. Instead of launching two ships at a time to their respective destinations the ships will launch as and when they are ready."

John thought for a moment before answering. "Well, we could be ready to go in seventy-two hours, sir. We were scheduled to launch in six days anyway."

Wilson nodded. "About what I thought. Over the next fourteen days, we intend to launch all the Vanguards. The *Vasco De Gama* and Captain Witsell will take the longest to prep as they've been having some technical difficulties with their navigation systems but the yard dogs have assured me they will be able to rectify any problems before launch."

As Wilson finished, Vadis stood up. "We will not delay you any further, Captain. You have a tight enough schedule. You need to be meeting with your staff and sharing the good news."

It was John's turn to smile. "Yes, sir. I'm sure they'll be overjoyed."

The admiral and his Chief of Staff headed through the hatch, toward the outer air lock connecting the *Henry Hudson* to the dock, escorted by a marine. John headed for the briefing room a few doors up from his cabin, his brain doing flip flops as he considered how to squeeze six days of work into seventy-two hours. John paused at the briefing room hatch and smiled as he recalled that on any ship the XO handled the bulk of any task. Talbot was going to love him. He pressed the hatch release and entered the briefing room.

Commander William 'Bill' Talbot was attempting to cat nap while he waited for his computer to finish checking, what seemed like, an endless list of supplies and equipment: from rations to fuel to computer gel packs which the ship's supply officer, Lieutenant Kessler, had assured him were now safely on board the *Henry Hudson* and stored correctly. The last seventy-two hours had been ones of frantic activity. He was sure the captain had been smiling at him when he told the assembled staff of the quote, 'small change in plans', unquote. Ha! Talbot's well thought out detailed plans to be ready in five days were flung out the airlock. Instead, he created new plans off the top of his head. No wonder he was going bald!

The computer made an attention tone. Talbot opened one eye to see if the list was complete. It was still running. The noise was the hatch entry tone. Talbot reluctantly pressed for acceptance and wondered what problem was about to disturb his well-deserved snooze. Talbot stood up a bit too fast and swayed a little as he realised the captain was standing in the hatchway. "Steady now, Bill," John said with a grin.

"Sorry, sir. Just having a little cat nap while the computer finishes."

"Have a seat, XO." Talbot flopped back into his chair. "I bring a peace offering." From behind his back, John produced a bottle of cold – there was even frost on the bottle – Australian beer. "I believe you are partial to some of the amber nectar? Seeing you have managed to keep my promise to Admiral Vadis – I do appreciate it when my minions make me look good – I thought a small reward was in order. Not forgetting," as John produced a second bottle from behind his back, "a reward for myself for having the good sense to employ such a useful minion." Both men laughed as John passed over the beer and took the only other seat in the office.

Talbot took a good long pull of his beer and let out an appreciative sigh. "You know, sir, that was almost worth all the hard work… almost!"

"Enjoy it, XO. It's going to be our last for a while. Are you happy we're ready to go?"

Talbot paused for a moment before replying. "Yes, sir. The crew have worked their guts out to be ready. Every department head has got a green board and I have complete confidence in them."

"Well, XO, if that's your opinion, then it's good enough for me. I will inform Admiral Vadis the TDF *Henry Hudson* is ready in all respects for launch. After I finish my beer of course."

Talbot looked back at him "Of course, sir."

———

John Radford sat, once more, in the conference room in which he had first learned of the real reason for his posting to, what he thought at the time, a logistics assignment.

John was accompanied this time by his own command staff: Commander Bill Talbot, Lieutenant Commander George Taylor, his Chief Engineer, Lieutenant Commander Albert Remberts, Chief Medical Officer, Lieutenant Alexandra Falconer, Tactical Officer, Lieutenant Cai Tingkai, Communications Officer, Lieutenant Alfred Kessler, Supply Officer, and last but not least Lieutenant Carlo Danino, Navigation Officer. Also present was Major Alec Murray, CO of the Henry Hudson's marine contingent – a man whose judgment and common sense John had learned to trust over the previous six months.

A side door opened and all present stood at attention. Admiral Aleksandr Vadis entered, followed closely by his right hand man, Lieutenant Commander Elizabeth Wilson. "Please be seated, ladies and gentlemen," said Vadis as he himself sat at the head of the conference table. "I know you have accomplished a minor miracle in the last seventy-two hours, Captain, preparing for launch. No doubt your XO and supply officer are suitably harassed." Vadis smiled and nodded toward Talbot and a face reddening Kessler. "But now to business. The initial targets of the Vanguard ships will be those stars identified from the star charts recovered from the Rubicon data. We know the Saiph have visited at least seventeen star systems. It is prudent to believe these star systems were not chosen at random but were part of their greater plan to seed indigenous species, such as ourselves, with the physical and mental makeup to develop into advanced civilizations. We have no idea how well this seeding has taken root. It is your job to go out there and find out. But…" Vadis paused and allowed his eyes to rest on each person in turn, "your overriding priority is not the discovery of new life, it is the preservation of life on Earth. If, for whatever reason, something does not seem right to you, Captain, you turn tail and head for home. Do you understand?"

All present stood to attention once more as Vadis reached out and grasped John's hand in his.

"Good luck John. I wish it were I going. Do us proud."

"I'll do my best, sir," replied John.

The admiral left with Commander Wilson in tow. John turned to his staff and noted their expectant demeanor "Launch in three hours people so let's get those last minute checks done and be on our way."

Vadis watched John dismiss his staff from his office adjacent to the conference room before turning to Wilson,

"Well?" he said.

Wilson consulted her PAD. "*Henry Hudson* launches at fifteen hundred hours, Captain Papadomas and the *Jacques Cartier* is due to launch at zero nine hundred hours tomorrow with Captain Lewis and the *James Cook* at seventeen hundred hours tomorrow. Which only leaves Captain Witsell and the *Vasco De Gama*. The techs are still having problems with her navigation computers but assure me she should be ready for launch by twenty-three hundred hours."

Vadis was quiet for a moment as he thought. Four small ships representing man's first true attempt to explore the surrounding stars. All accomplished in utter secrecy… until that idiot went to the wrong office. He unconsciously scowled as dark clouds of anger entered his thoughts. *Enough!* He thought. *I have better things to worry about than things that have already passed.* The press and the general population would get the whole story in a matter of hours, when President Coston broadcast the details of Operation Minerva to the public.

Vadis preferred the survey ships were launched and returned safely before entering the public arena, but so be it. At least all the interest in Minerva had ensured the second prong of Operation Chimera had remained hidden from prying eyes. "When is Admiral Jing due to arrive Elizabeth?"

Wilson consulted her PAD. "He should be here by eighteen hundred hours today, sir."

"Good. I'm anxious to hear how he is progressing. I pray we never need Chrysaor, but we have no idea what's out there." Vadis paused as his thoughts wondered amongst the stars.

"With the admiral's permission?" Wilson interrupted, hinting at her wish to leave the office.

"Yes, of course Elizabeth." Wilson left Vadis alone with his thoughts.

CHAPTER SEVEN

First Encounter

TDF *HENRY HUDSON* - ORBIT PLANET II OF 70 OPHIUCHI

John Radford studied the unimposing planet suspended in the holo cube. By his survey's reckoning, it was one-third water and two-thirds land. Most of the landmass was desert wasteland, the planet orbiting just a little bit too close to its sun.

On arrival in the star system, John had held the *Henry Hudson* at maximum range while his crew searched for any possible signs of energy sources in the system and deployed the communications buoy and courier drone to inform Charon Base of their safe arrival. When no artificial energy sources were detected, John had instructed Danino to plot a spiral course, gradually bringing the *Henry Hudson* in system to the only planet within, what humans would consider to be, the life-bearing zone. If the Saiph had meddled with the DNA of an already indigenous species and, if they had gone for a similar type of planet to Earth, then John was betting this was the place. John frowned as he stared into the holo cube. Too many ifs for his liking.

"Penny for them John?" John glanced to his right and there stood Major Murray, his Marine Contingent Commander.

"Jesus, Alec! Are you sure you're not part ninja?"

Alec grinned. "No, just very sneaky."

Even with the tension, John could not help but grin back.

"So what do we have, Commander?" John asked his XO. Talbot was closely studying the information fed to him by the ship's computer and the dedicated biosciences section.

"Well, now we're in orbit and able to use our active sensors…" On arrival at the star system, John had stuck rigidly to Standard Operating Procedure and hung out system using only passive sensors until a threat assessment was completed. Better to be safe than sorry where the safety of the ship, the crew and Earth was involved.

"… Our initial ideas are firming up nicely. What life there is is mostly located around the dense tropical rain forests, around the equator of the planet. There are no obvious signs of civilization of any kind, no detectable power sources and no clusters of artificial structures. Nothing in the way of pollution in the atmosphere to indicate industrialization or contamination. The air is thinner than on Earth, by some eleven percent, but still capable of supporting life, which does appear to be thriving. I suggest our next step is to send a survey party to collect some plant and animal samples for analysis and to check for any evidence of Saiph influence."

John considered for a moment, "Agreed, XO. Prepare a survey team. Full biohazard gear. Alec, provide a protection detail. No need to take chances."

Both men chorused "Aye-aye, Captain," and left the bridge.

John took one more look around the bridge and stood to leave, "Lieutenant Danino, you have the bridge."

"Aye-aye, sir. I have the bridge."

John made his way toward his cabin, thinking he could do with a few hours' sleep before listening to Murray and Talbot's plans for their planetary landing.

Without warning, the Battle Stations alarm began its steady wail throughout the ship and the computers automated voice called "Battle Stations, all hands to Battle Stations."

John spun on his heal and ran back toward the bridge, scattering crew members with his shout of "Make a hole!" as they too ran for their stations.

Striding through the bridge hatch a scene of organized chaos greeted John. His crew swiftly and efficiently brought the ship to full readiness. "Report, Mr. Danino if you please." John said in his calmest voice.

Without turning, the young lieutenant replied, "Sir, a few moments ago active sensors detected a neutrino surge from a point just beyond the system's Kuiper Belt, approximately thirty-five AUs from our current location. As per your standing orders, I immediately sounded Battle Stations and have moved the ship into the shadow of the planet. There is now no direct line of sight between ourselves and the location of the neutrino surge."

John was assimilating this information when the XO and Alec Murray arrived on the bridge. Alec had his sidearm strapped to his leg – a pulsed energy projectile infrared laser pulse-emitting pistol, which creates a rapidly expanding plasma on contact with the target. The resulting sound, shock and electromagnetic waves stun the target and cause pain and temporary paralysis.

"Expecting boarders, Alec?"

Alec looked at him incredulously as he tapped the PEP in its holster, "better to be prepared."

"I bet you were a great Boy Scout," murmured Talbot moving off to his console.

"Sir," Lieutenant Falconer at Tactical called. "All departments report at Battle Stations. All plasma cannon and Laser Area Denial weapons are online. Marines report armed and standing by to repel boarders. Engine Room reports ready to fold on your order."

John turned to the XO. "Anything more on what caused the neutrino surge, Bill?"

Talbot was staring at his display and trying to make sense of the masses of information displayed there. "Sir, it appears Lieutenant Danino's initial reaction was correct. If I'm reading this data correctly, there is some sort of vessel at the spot where he detected the neutrino surge." All talk and movement on the bridge stopped as Talbot turned to his captain before continuing. "The Saiph database has made a tentative identification of the ship as one belonging to the enemy they were fighting."

My God! John thought. *They are still out there. Have they seen us?* "XO, download all data to two of the drones and get them off. Make sure their initial flight path takes them away in the shadow of the planet and they fold before they come out of the shadow. I want at least three folds per drone before returning to Earth."

Talbot nodded his head in understanding: John intended the drones to make multiple folds in case whoever was on the unknown vessel was able to track their initial flight path.

"OK people," John addressed the bridge crew. "If this vessel does belong to the enemy of the Saiph, I see it as our first priority to alert the Admiralty to their existence, hence the drones. Second priority is to gather as much information as possible on this potential threat. To that end," John turned to Danino, "Navigator, plot me a course away from the planet which will keep us in its shadow as long as possible, putting us above the ecliptic plane. When we clear the planet's shadow, I want the ship rigged for silent running. I want us to be a hole in space. Understood?" John scanned the bridge and a series of nods from his officers greeted him. "Good, then let's get to it people and let's find out who's out there!"

TDF *HENRY HUDSON*
TWENTY AUS ABOVE THE ECLIPTIC
PLANE OF 70 OPHIUCHI

Captain John Radford sat at the head of the table in the small briefing room on board the TDF *Henry Hudson*. For the past five days, the *Henry Hudson* had pretended to be a hole in space as it ever so slowly climbed above the ecliptic plane of 70 Ophiuchi in an attempt to get a good eyeball of the unknown vessel, which, in a burst of neutrinos, had appeared near the system's Kuiper Belt.

The past few days had been tense for the whole crew.

Had they been observed as they left the shadow of Planet II? Had the two message drones John launched on their multi fold flight to warn Earth been detected?

At least the passive sensors of the *Henry Hudson* had shown no obvious reaction by the unknown vessel to either the presence of his ship or the departing drones. *A good sign, right?* John contemplated as the heads of department gathered around the table. He cleared his throat to get their attention.

"OK, people. What do we know? XO, if you could bring us up to speed."

"Yes, sir," Commander Talbot began. "It appears Bogey One, as we're calling the unidentified ship, is making steady progress in system. Not moving swiftly and we are occasionally detecting strong electromagnetic activity. We suspect this is a sort of detector sweep which seems to be concentrated on the ecliptic plane rather than above it. We believe our chameleon system is so far obscuring our existence from Bogey One. It has made no move to intercept us after any of the sweeps. Either Bogey One doesn't know we're here or it's not interested in us." His comment elicited a smile from a few gathered at the table. "According to Lieutenant Danino, Bogey One's course should take it to Planet II. I agree it appears to be its most likely destination, as you can see by the display."

The holo cube in the center of the briefing table showed a schematic of the 70 Ophiuchi system with the tracks displayed of the course of both the *Henry Hudson* and Bogey One.

"We have been able to gather quite a lot of useful information by using only our passive sensors. We estimate the ship to be around 1700 meters long and some 400 meters at the beam, weighing in at around 220,000 tonnes."

"A big beast. Bigger than anything Earth has built to date," remarked Falconer.

"Correct Lieutenant," said John. "Please continue, XO."

"Sir, one of the most interesting things though is we believe we have discovered Bogey One's source of propulsion."

John sat up straighter. "Really, XO?"

"Yes, sir. If the Chief Engineer would explain." Talbot motioned toward Lieutenant Commander George Taylor and sat down as the Henry Hudson's chief engineer stood.

"Ladies and gentlemen, without turning your poor command brains to mush…" A ripple of laughter ran through the assembled bridge officers. The friendly, and sometimes not so friendly, rivalry between the command line officers, Engineering and Science officers was a well-known fact – had been since before man had entered space. Stretching back as far as the wet navies. From the view of the command line, they saw themselves as the decision makers while the engineers and scientists were there to make things work. On the other hand, the engineers and scientists saw the command line as, to be polite, stuffy, strutting marionettes who thought they ruled from Mount Olympus. Deep down, both lines knew they could not do their jobs without the other to rely upon, so the friendly rivalry persisted and the work was done.

Once the laughter died down, the chief engineer continued. "Sir, it appears Bogey One is employing a form of Alcubierre Drive. It contacts space in front of the ship while expanding space behind it. The net effect is faster than light travel. It explains the neutrino effect as they slow to below the speed of light. I know researchers at Haslett Research Station seriously considered it before the discovery of the Gravity Drive but I don't know how far they got. Whoever this Bogey One is, they seem to have perfected it. I reckon for travelling in system, as they are now, the drive can also use the Mach Effect doubling as an impulse engine to move them around at sub light speeds. What I find concerning is the velocity advantage at sub light speeds they have over us. On the other hand, our Gravity Drive permits almost instantaneous travel between the stars while they are restricted to multiple of the speed of light to get between the stars." John mulled it over for a minute before asking,

"So, Bogey One, in your opinion, has a tactical speed advantage while we have a strategic one?"

"Yes, sir. That's my take on it."

"OK thanks, Chief," replied John. "XO, anything else?"

Again Talbot stood. "Yes, sir. Having had some time to think over what the Chief thinks propels Bogey One, it brings us to another tactical point – which I think will have a bearing on our future options. Bogey One's power output and its threat envelope."

John was beginning to see where the XO was going with this, the sort of power required for an Alcubierre Drive could also power a formidable weapons package. The *Henry Hudson* was severely out gunned.

"If I could ask Lieutenant Falconer to carry on the briefing, sir?" John nodded his assent and Falconer took the floor.

"Sir. This new information, as the XO has pointed out, certainly gives me pause to think. When I consider the sort of reach and strength of any power generated weaponry Bogey One may employ against us I don't think it is much of a reach to say they could defeat our ablative hull armor without a second thought and, as they out mass us by some fourteen to one, I'm willing to bet they can take a lot more hits than we can."

John looked around the table at the fallen faces, solemn at the realization of what they truly faced if Bogey One became aggressive toward them. John turned his attention back to Falconer as she continued.

"On the brighter side, sir, as the XO said, it appears our chameleon system is worth its weight in gold. Though I advise, we get no closer than our current distance to Bogey One. If they get a sniff of us and come investigating, I can't guarantee we can avoid their sensors."

Now that is food for thought. "Thank you Lieutenant. Now, last, but by no means least, could you give us a quick supply run down Alfred?"

The diminutive German stood up. "As of zero eight hundred this morning we have sufficient perishable supplies for another fifteen days of operations. At our current level. This increases to twenty-two days if we employ rationing with immediate effect." There was a general groan from around the table at the thought of reducing the fresh food and replacing it with ration packs and worse still reducing showering time. Everyone loved a nice long hot shower.

Kessler continued as if he had not heard the complaints. "Our tactical ordnance is at full strength. No ordnance, to date, has been expended. Our spares for critical systems are still at ninety percent. This is no doubt due to the exceptional maintenance performed by the Chief's crew rather than my own department's foresight as to system requirements." John cast a quick glance at the Chief who was doing a very good impression of a kettle about to boil. People forgot Kessler had a very sarcastic side and for a mere Lieutenant to take the hand out of the ships third in command took some serious balls, but it still made John laugh. He could only imagine how the Chief would extract his revenge.

"Thank you Lieutenant." John looked around the table. "Thank you all for your hard work to date and please pass on my gratitude to your various departments. I shall not hold you back any longer. XO and Major Murray, join me in my quarters immediately after this. That is all." All around the table echoed "Aye-aye, sir," as John stood and left, heading for his quarters.

John sat behind his desk while Talbot and Murray sat in the only two remaining seats in the cramped quarters. This was John's inner circle. He had confidence in these two men and knew they would give him good council. "Well Bill. Options?"

Without a second thought Talbot said, "We break contact with Bogey One while we still remain undetected. Dogleg through a couple of Folds to ensure no one is tailing us and head for home with the information that whatever destroyed the Saiph is still out here. Albeit we've seen only one ship, we've no idea if he has any friends out there who could arrive right on top of us."

John had similar thoughts though he wanted to explore his options. "Alec?"

Alec looked from John to Talbot and back again. "To give you a good balance, I think I'll have to play Devil's Advocate here. If we continue to shadow Bogey One in system, we can confirm their final destination is in fact Planet II. It also gives us the opportunity to possibly observe their modus operandi when it comes to landing on planets and maybe give us a visual of them." Alec looked at Talbot and could tell he did not like the idea one bit, but Alec's job here was to give his captain options, and that was what he was doing. There was a long pause as John weighed up both options.

Head home and tell them the news, the enemy of the Saiph still lived.

Stay and take the chance the *Henry Hudson* would remain undetected and be able to give an invaluable insight into the operations of whomever Bogey One belonged to. Well, he supposed, this is why I get the center seat. John made his decision and stood up. As he did, so did Talbot and Alec. "I don't like it but for once I think I'll have to go with the Devil's alternative. The information we could glean is invaluable if we end up facing these people in a slugging match. Bill?"

"Sir?"

"I want fifty percent of the crew stood to at all times. We need to be ready to fight or flee at the drop of a hat. The remaining fifty percent go on enforced rest. Tell the Chief no routine maintenance is to be carried out and tell Alfred to institute rationing forthwith."

Talbot nodded his understanding. "Understood, Captain."

"Goes for you too, Bill. Either you or I are in the center seat every minute. Bogey One's tactical speed advantage means we cannot afford any critical delay in making a command decision. If you see something developing, use your own judgment — do not wait for my confirmation. You know I have complete faith in your judgment."

"Thank you, sir,"

"Alec."

"Sir?" replied the marine.

"Same goes for yourself. I want your marines armed and dangerous in every critical section, ready to fight or offer assistance as and when."

Alec gave that smartarse grin of his. "At your command my liege."

All three men smiled before John ushered them out. "Make it happen minions while I compose a message to Admiral Vadis detailing our daring and courageous plan."

All three men laughed before Talbot and Murray headed off and John returned to his desk.

CHARON BASE - ORBIT OF PLUTO - SOL SYSTEM

Lieutenant Commander Elizabeth Wilson entered the office of Admiral Aleksandr Vadis. He was leaning into his holo pickup with a finger pointed like the barrel of a plasma rifle and she could hear him shouting at some unlucky soul.

"No, I don't think you do understand! Look at my face and tell me you want me to visit you in your nice plush office in Geneva and kick you so hard up the ass that my boot comes out of your mouth! Do you understand me now?" Vadis waved Elizabeth to a seat, his hand out of view of the pickup.

Elizabeth sat, patiently waiting. She barely made out the mumbled apology from whoever was at the receiving end of the admiral's displeasure.

"Good! Now if I have to speak to you again about this matter it will be in person and my voice will be the last human voice you hear because for the rest of your living, breathing days all you will hear is the sound of penguins mating!" He cut the connection.

"Motivating the troops again, sir?"

Like night turning to day Vadis' face broke into a large smile. "Commander, I would never motivate someone under my command in such an overbearing fashion. A political weasel, on the other hand, is in need of much more of a… hands on approach. So to business Elizabeth. Has anyone in intelligence been able to make any headway with the information the *Henry Hudson* has provided us with?"

"Sir, it is their considered opinion, and I must agree with them, the ship Captain Radford encountered and subsequently identified as the alien race which the Saiph were at war with, is indeed what it appears to be."

This came as no surprise to Vadis. Having examined the data from the Henry Hudson's courier drone, the images had been unmistakable.

"The fact we now have indisputable proof this group of aliens are still out there, taken alongside the Alcubierre Drive, with its potentially massive energy output for weapons systems, the boys and girls down in intelligence are having kittens."

Again, this came as no surprise to Vadis. He may be an admiral working out of an office, but over the years, he had gained respect for a potential enemy's weaponry. "Has Doctor Moore's team at Haslett Research Station been able to give any insights into this Alcubierre Drive's performance?"

Elizabeth consulted her PAD. "As Chief Engineer Taylor stated in his initial brief to Captain Radford, Haslett had been working on a drive of the same principle but it was all shelved with the discovery of the Gravity Drive. Doctors Moore and Hayes are reviewing our research and using it to try and get a handle on the technology used by these aliens."

"What of Doctor Bath at Stickney? Has she not been able to at least give us a name for this group of aliens yet?" asked Vadis,

"It would appear, sir," replied Elizabeth, "the Saiph only seem to refer to them as the Others."

"What the hell does that mean, Elizabeth?" said Vadis. "How more cryptic can the Saiph get? No home star system? Not even a general location?" Vadis let out a deep sigh. "They were fighting these Others for hundreds, if not thousands, of years and the best they could come up with was the Others!"

Elizabeth waited as Vadis calmed down. "Seems so, sir. I remind you Doctor Bath has so much data to go through in the Saiph database – even when it is organized for ease of access –that she is simply swamped and her research is going to take time,"

"Time, Commander," Vadis said almost to himself, "is something which we may find ourselves in short supply of if the Others are able to pinpoint Earth." Vadis sighed again. "Please ensure courier drones are dispatched to the other Vanguards bringing them up to speed on what the *Henry Hudson* has found and our conclusions at this time."

"Yes, sir." Elizabeth stood up and left.

Once the door closed, Vadis sat still for a few minutes contemplating his next move. Coming to a decision, he pressed a control on his desk. The face of a young ensign appeared in his Holo cube.

"Communications, sir. Ensign Davies."

"Ensign, get me a secure priority link to Admiral Jing." Time to bring Chrysaor up to speed.

TDF *HENRY HUDSON* - 4 AUS ABOVE PLANET II OF 70 OPHIUCHI

Radford sat in his command chair as TDF *Henry Hudson* sat still in space, four astronomical units or 598,400,000 kilometers from Planet II of 70

Ophiuchi. It had taken another ten days of shadowing Bogey One before it settled into a geosynchronous orbit around the planet. The orbit obscured Bogey One from the *Henry Hudson* for half the planetary day but, as promised, the gathered intelligence was worth it.

From their position, the crew of the *Henry Hudson* had a great view of Bogey One sending its shuttle equivalent to the surface of Planet II. Sensors had identified four shuttles used almost continuously, moving between Bogey One and the same spot on the surface. Within hours of the first shuttle landing sensors detected independent power sources on the surface. Tactical surmised the crew of Bogey One were setting up a permanent base on the planet. *A fair assumption*, John thought. A call from Lieutenant Alexandra Falconer at Tactical interrupted John's musings.

"Neutrino surge, 275,000 kilometers to starboard,"

Too close, thought Radford. *They cannot fail to see us.* "Battle Stations Lieutenant."

As the wailing alarm sounded throughout the ship, Falconer continued, "Second vessel emerging. Designating Bogey Two. Initial sensor readings indicate a vessel of similar shape and size as Bogey One. Wait, wait, wait... Heading change. Bogey Two has changed heading. It is on course directly for us. I am getting strange power indications. The computer assesses Bogey Two is powering up weapons."

John displayed the characteristics that had gotten him selected for this mission. Thinking on his feet, he said. "Engineering, stand by to fold. Navigation, randomly select a destination from my prearranged list. XO, get the message drone away and a backup if you get time."

"Chief reports ready to fold. Coordinates locked, Navigation ready."

John spared a glance in the direction of Carlo Danino, all those hours in the simulator when he first arrived had been worth it for this situation alone.

"In your own time, Carlo." Danino did not acknowledge John, instead, he kept his eyes locked on the XO until he got the nod, message drone departed.

"Three. Two. One. Fold!" The *Henry Hudson* vanished from the 70 Ophiuchi system.

CHAPTER EIGHT

Fifty Thousand Light Years

TDF *VASCO DE GAMA* - CHARON BASE - ORBIT OF PLUTO - SOL SYSTEM

Ruth Witsell could not, by any stretch of the imagination, be said to be in a good mood. The captain of TDF *Vasco De Gama* was only five feet two inches tall and of slight build, however, at this precise moment, her bridge crew were avoiding her gaze as if she could strike them down in an instant.

"Lieutenant Winters, have we rectified our small navigational error yet?"

Her navigator, the aforementioned Lieutenant Winters, checked his board again before taking a deep breath and replying. "Yes, Captain. Our angle of departure is good. The engine room reports ready to fold."

Ruth knew it was not really her navigator's fault —on leaving the dock at Charon Base the ship decided the holding orbit of twenty kilometers should be twenty-five kilometers instead. The *Vasco De Gama* seemed plagued by a fault in her navigational computer. Neither the crew nor the yard dogs had been able to find the source. If time had been on her side, Ruth would have requested Admiral Vadis to delay her mission to Gama Leporn, some 29.25 light years distant, until the whole navigation system was replaced. However, Ruth was already three days behind schedule.

Ruth had watched President Coston's announcement, explaining to the citizens of the Terran Republic the mission parameters of Operation Minerva – to visit the seventeen known systems in the Saiph database. Ruth also observed the news media clamoring to get to Charon Base, to see for themselves how billions of Feds had been spent. It only reinforced her decision to lobby Admiral Vadis to release the *Vasco De Gama* and send it on its way.

Ruth glanced across at her XO, Commander Ronald Hopkins, who gave her a silent nod of agreement. Ruth addressed her navigator. "Very well, Mr. Winters, let's be on our way."

"Aye-aye, ma'am. Fold in three, two, one… fold." The Vasco De Gamma ceased to be in Sol space.

The transition into and out of fold space should have been seamless, but it certainly was not for Ruth. She suddenly felt groggy, the ship seemed to have bucked like a wild horse. The entire bridge crew appeared shaken in a similar fashion. The sound of an alarm blared into her consciousness, the proximity alarm. "Navigation. Report!"

Winters was, just now, beginning to react. "Ship is tumbling. Correcting now. Large object near, portside 52000 kilometers, moving away from us now."

Ruth's mind raced. They had been due to come out of fold space some twenty parsecs from the edge of the Gama Leporn system. So, what could be out this far? Some rogue comet perhaps? She noticed Winters was still working furiously away at his station.

"Problem Mr. Winters?" Winters appeared to ignore her. Ruth raised her voice and pointedly announced "Mr. Winters! Is there a problem?"

Winters turned toward her with a shocked face. Before he could say anything the urgent voice of Lieutenant Alice Balerno at Tactical rang out,

"Captain! Passives are picking up energy readings, lots of them!"

Ruth spun to face the holo cube "Bring it up, Guns." Ruth used the ancient nautical term for her tactical officer without thinking. Immediately, the holo cube filled with a primary, the system's sun and eleven planets orbiting. Two in the life zone on opposite sides of the primary, one close in, closer than Sol's own mercury. *Wouldn't that be a nice place to visit?* In addition, eight more extended out from the life zone to just beyond the orbit of where Pluto would be.

The two planets in the life zone were scattered with red blotches indicating artificially generated energy and, more interestingly, there were red dots orbiting both planets.

Artificial satellites perhaps? Hold on – was that one moving? By God, it was! Ruth realized. One of the energy signs was undoubtedly moving between the two planets. *This civilization is spacefaring!*

"Captain?" the XO called.

Ruth turned to face him, but Hopkins only pointed toward where Lieutenant Winters was, still staring at his captain with a pale face.

"Mr. Winters, report!"

Winters hesitated for just a moment. "Captain. This is not Gamma Leporn," he hurriedly added, "I have checked and double checked: this is definitely not where we should be." Winters noted Ruth's doubtful expression. "Captain, according to the Saiph database this system should only consist of seven planets."

Ruth studied the holo cube and the eleven planets it was undoubtedly displaying again. Damn, why hadn't she noticed the obvious? "Continue, Mr. Winters," she said.

"All I can put it down to is the error in the navigation computer which we couldn't track down, it must be exponential. When we left the dock, it took us twenty-five kilometers to a parking orbit instead of twenty kilometers… ma'am. If I work on that ratio it means instead of traveling the 29.25 light years to Gamma Leporn, the navigation computer has travelled an extra five kilometers for every twenty we've travelled. Twenty kilometers becomes twenty-five kilometers, sixty kilometers becomes 144 kilometers and so on," Winters paused, seeing his captain now worried.

"Go on, Mr. Winters," Ruth said with more conviction than she felt.

"Ma'am, if my math is correct, we are actually somewhere in the Messier 54 Cluster. Some 50000 light years from home."

The stunned silence was broken by a small gasp from Lieutenant Ben Leopold at communications. Years of training did not fail Ruth. She had not been chosen for Minerva for her lack of decisiveness.

"Navigation! I need an exact fix soonest."

Winters responded as though struck with a cattle prod. "Yes, ma'am."

"Tactical I need to know A, your best guess if we have been detected, and B get together with Bio and Mechanical Sciences – I want an estimate in comparison with Earth on the level of technology of this system."

"Aye-aye, Captain."

"Engineering, complete system wide check. 50000 light years is a long way to come and I want to know if we did any damage."

"Aye, Captain."

Finally, Ruth turned to Commander Hopkins. "Ronald, coordinate the department heads. I want answers and I want them quickly. Not at the expense of mistakes: more speed less haste. When navigation have a good fix on where we are exactly, I want you to plot a series of folds to get us home. Plot them manually, so you better dust off those navigation brain cells I know you used to have."

Hopkins's facial expression showed just how much work manually plotting folds takes. *The yard dogs would answer for this,* Ruth thought, *if Hopkins didn't get to them first.*

"XO, I'll be in my cabin." The bridge erupted into action. Ruth stood and headed through the bridge hatch. The marine on duty was standing smartly to attention, as if he could fail to notice the activity on the bridge.

"Thank you, Marine," said Ruth as she strode down the corridor to her cabin. A second marine came to attention as if on a parade ground. "Marine, give me ten minutes then I'd like to see Major Egnorov."

"Aye-aye, ma'am." Ruth entered her cabin and sat herself down on the chair behind her desk. 50000 light years. An unknown civilization. A crew demanding her leadership and direction. Ruth smiled. This is why she loves command. Now, if only she knew what to do next.

———

All told, the majority of the answers demanded by Ruth of her crew took the better part of three and a half hours. Now she was here, gathered with her department heads in the briefing room of the *Vasco De Gama* ready to hear those answers.

Ruth addressed Commander Hopkins "XO?"

Ronald Hopkins cleared his throat. "Captain, before I start I would like to point out the departments are working with the minimum of data. I decided on variables which were used in some decision making processes and some of those variables are only my best guess."

Ruth smiled at her haggard second in command, "Understood Ronald. I consider your best guess to be better than some people's facts so please continue."

Hopkins gave Ruth a tired smile of his own before continuing. "As you know, ma'am, due to an error in the navigational computer we are some considerable distance from where we should be." This brought a nervous chuckle from those around the table.

"Mr. Winters, using a hand comp and some math I was never taught at school…" Ruth could see young Lieutenant Winters reddening slightly around the cheeks. "… Was correct in his original estimation of 50000 light years. He has narrowed it down to 48975, but I wouldn't hold 1025 light years against him."

At this point, Winters' whole face went red and it appeared something on the deck at his feet had him completely engrossed. Ruth could not help let a small laugh escape from her. "I think we shall forego the keel hauling on this occasion, XO."

Hopkins said in deadpan seriousness. "The captain is too lenient." This time there were various snorts from around the table, and, if possible, Winters turned an even brighter red. "But I digress, Captain. We appear to be just outside a solar system consisting of some eleven planets. We know two are inhabited. Our current position puts us about sixty-one degrees above the ecliptic plane, we are in a very good vantage point to observe the system. As best as we can tell, there has been no reaction to our presence yet. In the three and a half hours since our arrival, we have noted some forty-six vessels moving between the two planets displaying energy sources. From the speed of the vessels, we estimate a traveling time in the region of eleven months between the two inhabited planets. Further, we have noted planet Messier A, as we have designated it, currently the planet furthest from us has substantially more energy sources than Messier B. Bio Mechanical Sciences theory states either planet B is less advanced than A or, and I will explain my thinking, planet B is a colony of A."

"Your thinking for this, Commander?" asked Ruth.

Hopkins paused for a moment, gathering his thoughts. "The emissions of planet A, although more numerous, are of varying strengths and types. Some are more efficient than others, whereas on planet B, all are virtually of the same strength, type and efficiency." Ruth nodded her understanding. "Those on planet B are similar in manufacture and being more efficient than the vast majority on A would indicate newer manufacture to a higher standard, i.e. you would send your best most efficient to a startup colony." Hopkins smiled. "That's how I see it, ma'am."

Ruth looked across at Major Egnorov who had the smile of a cat who had just caught the mouse with the cheese. Hopkins, slightly perplexed by the exchange between his captain and the marine, continued. "Considering the type and efficiency of the energy sources. The apparent transit timescale between planets A and B. The spectrographic analysis of the respective planets' atmospheres for pollution, radiation and so on, along with electronic eavesdropping of broadcasts in the electromagnetic band, I believe we could safely place this civilization as equivalent to pre-World War III Earth." As Hopkins studied his captain's reaction, he could not help but notice the small smile crossing her lips and, if possible, the smile on Egnorov's face got bigger.

"So you would rate any threat to ourselves from the planets as…?" asked Ruth.

"In our current location I would have to say negligible, Captain."

"Thank you, XO. Engineering?"

"A level one diagnostic shows no damage to either the ship or more importantly the Gravity Drive. The momentary dizziness we experienced was due to the time spent in fold space. No one has ever spent so long in transit before and the Chief Engineer…"

Ruth glanced down the table to Lieutenant Commander George Lee. He had studied under Doctor Jeff Moore, and to say Moore had been slightly upset when Lee was collared for Chimera would be an understatement. Moore saw Lee as a protégé the navy stole from him. "… Has assured me if we can keep the folds to under 5000 light years each in the future, then the engines shouldn't even notice it."

Now this was news. The rating for the engine was folds of only fifty to sixty light years. Ruth addressed Lee directly. "George, anything you want to tell me?"

"Captain, while running our drive checks I reviewed its performance in detail. I was able to identify the elements of a theory I had been working on with Doctor Moore before leaving Haslett Research Station. Our prolonged unplanned journey has given me empirical data to collaborate the theory and I believe with a few alterations, with your permission of course," Lee gave Ruth a lopsided grin, "I could extend the range of each fold to a comfortable and more importantly, repeatable 5000 light years."

Ruth thought for a second. "How long to make the alterations and what would be the downtime on the drive?"

Without hesitation Lee replied, "The software alterations can be completed offline then uploaded into the engineering mainframe with no disruption. The physical engineering alterations will take a maximum of thirty-six hours, with the drive offline for about seven of those hours."

Seven hours with no means of getting out of here in a hurry if needs be. *A big gamble*, thought Ruth. Hopkins lack of conviction was enough for Ruth.

"OK, prepare the software changes but do not install them. Same for the physical changes. Keep the XO up to speed on your progress. When you are ready to go, we will reassess."

The crestfallen Lee replied. "Aye-aye, ma'am."

Hopkins looked happier. The idea of being dead in the water for seven hours did not appeal to him either.

"Anything else, XO?"

"Yes, ma'am, just one more thing." At this, Alice Balerno, the Tactical Officer, and Lieutenant Ben Leopold, the Comms officer, both seemed to sit a bit straighter.

Hopkins continued. "During our evaluation of the inhabitants of the planets, we covered their electromagnetic emissions." Hopkins paused. "Lieutenant Leopold, if you please."

Leopold switched on the holo cube in the center of the table. A biped, possibly 168 centimeters tall, wearing a tan and brown uniform with some emblems at the waist, a small circular mouth with what appeared to be three slits either side of where a nose should be and two eyes set widely apart above the slits. There seemed to be no ears, or for that matter any hair apparent on the body.

"Captain," said Hopkins with a flourish. "May I introduce the sentient species of Messier 54?"

Ruth stared at the image for a few seconds before saying, "Ronald, your flair for the dramatic is never ending"

"But, Captain," said the XO, "I saved the best for last. May I draw your attention to the arms?"

Ruth examined the image once more. Two arms, but where the elbow should be there was a joint, which did not look quite right. Ah, double jointed! The elbow could bend in two different directions. A shorter forearm and a hand with, *I'll be damned*! Ruth turned to her XO and then to Egnorov.

Vladimir Egnorov matched her gaze and said simply, "When do I leave?"

UPPER ATMOSPHERE PLANET B MESSIER 54 CLUSTER – 50000 LIGHT YEARS FROM EARTH

Major Egnorov glanced around the Tanto covert insertion shuttle and then at the heads-up display projected into his left eye by the Wraith Combat Suit.

Issued to Force Recon Marines, the Wraith Combat Suit was composed of ultra-strong shock absorbing material. Constructed from inorganic nanostructures – five times stronger than steel – the Wraith Combat Suit, commonly simply called 'Wraith', remained highly elastic and provided a complete range of movement for the wearer. The assimilated exoskeleton provided immense strength through the servomotors utilizing high gauss permanent magnets and step down gearing to provide high torque, responsive movement in a small package. The combat suit was, therefore, unrestrictive to the wearer, allowing them to access even small surface areas. Power, provided by miniature solid oxide fuel cells, was easy to replace in the field and would sustain the suit at maximum power output for eight hours or with normal use, thirty-six. The suit was capable of use in a vacuum for short time periods – enough time for a planetary assault, for instance.

One of the key elements of the suit, for any Force Recon Marine, was its ability to communicate with not only other suits but also with ships in orbit. Comms were established by either suit to suit/ship radio or, more covertly, by use of whisker laser – a point-to-point communications system that could not be intercepted unless one happened to stray into the path of the laser — a highly unlikely scenario.

An equally vital element of the suit was the Chameleon unit, a stealth system integral to each suit. It was a compact version of the stealth systems used by Navy ships. Chameleon used optics throughout the Wraith Combat Suit, effectively projecting whatever was 180-degrees behind the suit to 180-degrees in front. If the enemy peered at the wearer, they effectively saw right through them. The wearer became indistinguishable to the naked eye and undetectable to any known electro optical systems. The Force Recon Marine became, essentially, invisible.

Egnorov's Wraith was counting down the altitude of both him and the shuttle as they descended through the atmosphere of Planet B. Egnorov and six other marines similarly suited in Wraiths were providing close protection for the ten Navy types commanded by the *Vasco De Gamma's* XO, Commander Hopkins. The mission was to collect as much material from soil, plant and animal samples as possible without discovery by the 'Baldies'. Egnorov chuckled. Some midshipman had christened the sentient species on Planet A and the colonizers of Planet B the irreverent nickname, but it had stuck.

Egnorov and Hopkins had been planning this mission for three weeks, as the *Vasco De Gamma* crept slowly in system, continually checking for the tiniest indication of detection as it closed on Planet B. It became quickly obvious that not only were the Baldies on the planet, but mining operations were also in progress within the asteroid belt. A steady flow of traffic had been observed between the belt and what appeared to be orbital facilities around Planet A. This same traffic provided a navigational headache to Lieutenant Winters, but the young navigator had proven his worth, spending endless

hours at the helm. Eventually, caught fast asleep in his chair on the bridge, Captain Witsell ordered him to his bed, along with strict instructions not to return for at least forty-eight hours.

The plan Egnorov and Hopkins devised was a variation of one the marine and Captain Witsell had deliberated long before leaving Charon Base.

Admiral Vadis spoke of the probable requisite for surface reconnaissance at his initial briefing on Operation Chimera, so, while Witsell prepared her ship and crew for their mission, Egnorov and his marines investigated potential scenarios warranting their own surface mission and identified their parameters.

When the captain had called him to her quarters and briefed him on their current predicament on arrival in Messier 54, Egnorov had been able to warn his small planning section to begin prepping for a mission. By the time Commander Hopkins briefed the captain, Egnorov knew he was going to command the first marines to visit a planet controlled by an alien species.

When he filled Hopkins in on this after the captain's brief, Hopkins understood the reason for the smile on Egnorov's face.

The jolting of the shuttle brought Egnorov back to the present. The pilot was bringing the shuttle in on an oblique angle, mimicking the trajectory of a meteorite. Although the shuttle was the stealthiest yet produced, Egnorov saw no reason to take unnecessary risks. He and Hopkins had chosen a landing site far from any detected population centers.

The planet sunrise dictated the night landing – land one hour after dark and leave one hour before sunrise. A quick in and out mission. His instructors at Marine Force Recon would have been proud.

Egnorov relished in happy memories of those long tiring days and nights at Recon School – maybe happy was not the right word. The highest praise Egnorov had heard out of the mouths of those marine gunnery sergeants was "Satisfactory Egnorov." By the end of the course of 160 initial candidates, only Egnorov and two others qualified as Marine Force Recon. As Egnorov graduated, his gunny instructor shook his hand and said "Satisfactory Egnorov." His instructor paused and, with a hint of a smile, tagged his comment with, "Sir."

Egnorov reminisced back to his arrival on Titan Base, shortly after his graduation, when he took up his post on Titan Base as Team Commander. A fresh faced lieutenant.

He recalled his arrival interview with the commanding officer as… brief. The CO was a long service naval admiral with a reputation of running a tight ship. He did not suffer fools gladly. Titan Base was the front line where they waged the fight against asteroid belt piracy. Marine Force Recon teams deployed from Titan to rocks thought likely to harbor pirates. They carried out surface reconnaissance in non-existent gravity and hard vacuum. Only the best were sent to Titan Base, which was why the 'satisfactory' Egnorov was slightly perturbed at his posting there. He recollected the conversation.

"Lieutenant Egnorov," the admiral had said.

"Yes, sir," a nervous Egnorov had replied.

"I see here your gunny instructor was Gunny Bates."

"Correct, sir."

"I've known Gunny Bates for more years than I or he would care to remember. As a young ensign, I carried out a boarding action with him on a pirate ship out past Ceres. Messy business. The pirates kidnapped the crew and passengers from a cruise ship and murdered most of those not worth ransoming. They knew it was the gallows for them if they were captured so they fought like animals." The admiral let out a short snort. "My pistol ran out of charge eventually. I was left facing two of them with the civilians behind me. Son, if anyone ever tells you your life flashes in front of you at times like that, it is a lie. I was too busy being scared. The only thing I had to hand was my survival knife… and survive I did. The pirates never reached the gallows. The navy in their wisdom decided to give me a medal."

Egnorov stood a bit straighter as he noticed for the first time a small blue and white ribbon on the admiral's chest. The Terran Medal of Honor. The highest award a military man could receive, awarded only by recommendation of the entire Joint Chiefs and the consent of the senate.

"Son, I managed to sneak a peek at the after action report years later written by Gunny Bates. Gunny rated my performance: 'Satisfactory. This officer has potential'. Beside it was a handwritten note from the then Chairman of the Joint Chiefs. It read: 'Recommended for the TMH on Gunny's say so'. Now if the Joint Chiefs think a satisfactory rating from a mere gunnery sergeant is something to stand up and listen to, then who am I to disagree? If Gunny said you were 'satisfactory', then I am damned glad to have you. So welcome aboard!"

The admiral stood up, shook Egnorov's hand and escorted him to the door. "Now get out. I've got work to do." So started Egnorov's career with Recon.

Whoa! Egnorov screamed back to the present, kept in his seat only by the restraining ties locked onto his suit as the shuttle made another wild maneuver.

"Thirty seconds," called the pilot. Egnorov did a brief team check via his suits on board computer. Bio readings of his marines were nominal, damn! He studied Gunny Alison Chew's readings again. If he did not know any better, he would swear she was asleep. *Are all gunnies the same?* He thought and shook his head making the helmet of his Wraith move slightly.

"Touchdown! Doors opening!" Egnorov and his marines were out in a heartbeat and moving off to a distance of 300 metres in every direction to form a secure perimeter around the Tanto. The navy personnel moved off next and formed a second perimeter close to the Tanto, ready to re embark at the first sign of trouble. Egnorov stood by the Tanto's boarding hatch. Using the Wraith's link to his marines, he quickly and efficiently completed a threat assessment. None of his marines detected any danger and it seemed they were down unnoticed.

Egnorov enabled his whisker link to the *Vasco De Gamma*. "Team down and undetected as far as I can tell, Captain."

In geosynchronous orbit, Ruth Witsell sat on the edge of her chair on the bridge and let out a breath she did not know she had been holding. "Very well, Major. If you are content the area is secure, please inform the XO to begin his survey."

"Understood. Egnorov out." Egnorov turned to Hopkins, who was kneeling in the center of the inner perimeter, "Captain says we have a green light, Ronald."

Hopkins nodded in understanding. "OK, people. Let's get started. Remember, no movement outside the marine perimeter without my express permission. And stay in your pairs." The Human's first exploration of an alien occupied world began.

"So," began Ruth, looking across the table of the *Vasco de Gama*'s Briefing Room at Major Egnorov and Commander Hopkins, "you are sure of your results?"

"I don't think there is any room for error, ma'am," Hopkins replied confidently. "The samples we recovered have been tested thoroughly. There is no doubt the Saiph visited this system. All the samples recovered leave me in no doubt the indigenous species are products of the Saiph DNA manipulation."

Ruth sat still for a moment, considering her options. "Well... now we have a decision. Do we make our way back to Earth with our findings? On the other hand, do we spend more time in this system gathering as much information on the Baldies as we can before returning home? Thoughts, gentlemen."

There was silence for a few seconds before Egnorov said, "I'm a Force Recon Marine and it's my job to gather as much intelligence on a target as possible..." Egnorov paused. "Despite this, our discovery here – another spacefaring species – Earth needs to know about this ASAP."

Ruth turned to Ronald. "Ronald?"

"Ma'am, the major is correct. We need to get this ship and the information home. Let the Admiralty get a proper first contact expedition set up and return here. We completed exactly what we set out to do – albeit," Hopkins grinned, "a bit beyond the intended target system."

Ruth and Egnorov both let out a short laugh.

"Ronald, your irony never ceases to amaze me. Very well Ronald. Get together with the chief engineer and let's get started on our way home."

CHAPTER NINE
Life No More

TDF JACQUES CARTIER DELTA PAVONIS - 19.92 LIGHT YEARS FROM EARTH

Captain Christos Papadomas sat alone in the briefing room of the TDF *Jacques Cartier*. He stared at the image of Planet III, spinning slowly in the holo cube. Dark clouds completely covered the planet, broken only by the occasional flash of lightning in the upper atmosphere. It seemed to promise so much, but the chance of life had been snuffed out by nature — wiping the slate clean ready to start again.

He touched a control panel and a small net of flashing lights began to surround the planet. A still functioning satellite network. Another touch of the panel and the image zoomed in, passing through the clouds, down even further until it reached the level of the ocean, and then carried on until it reached the ocean floor.

There, on the ocean bed was a massive crater some 600 kilometers across. A stream of data appeared on the right of the image: carbon dioxide (CO_2), soluble in seawater, was present in very large quantities. It mostly reported the bicarbonate radical ($-HCO_3$) stable at temperatures below fifty degrees Celsius – the normal sea surface temperature – but sea surface temperature could easily exceed this if or when an asteroid struck the ocean, inducing a large thermal shock. He understood in those circumstances very large quantities of CO_2 would erupt from the ocean as a heavy gas, and the CO_2 could quickly spread around the world in concentrations sufficient to suffocate air breathing fauna and animals. Asteroid impacts with the ocean might not leave obvious signs, but these impacts had the potential to be far more devastating to life on a planet than impacts with land.

He pulled the view back, and with a flick of his fingers sent it flying through the atmosphere over the nearest land – over the ruins of cities lying on the coastal region, struck by tidal waves up to a mile high, the damage subsiding the further inland he viewed. Even though the physical damage lessened, the result was the same, he noted. Everything requiring oxygen to breathe was dead.

His geologists put the impact at less than twenty years ago. Only twenty years ago and he would have seen a living, breathing planet with a world civilization who had put artificial satellites into orbit. But no more. The best he could do for them was to ensure that at least some memory of them lived on. He shook himself out of his melancholy, touching a control. The image of his XO appeared where the dead planet had been. "Robert, could you round up Major Draper and join me in the Briefing Room at your earliest convenience?" It was a rhetorical question.

Robert Ranking guessed at the purpose of the meeting with his captain. "Would you like me to bring Doctor Gunnerman?" Doctor Rudolf Gunnerman was TDF *Jacques Cartier*'s xenobiologist and a history buff.

"Good idea Robert. As soon as you can, please."

"Yes, sir." Ranking signed off.

Christos sat back in his chair and began to put together a plan to save as much of this dead civilization as his small ship could hold before returning to Earth with his solemn news. Life no longer existed in Delta Pavonis.

CHARON BASE - ORBIT OF PLUTO - SOL SYSTEM

Lieutenant Commander Elizabeth Wilson once again found herself in the office of Admiral Aleksandr Vadis, Commander of Operation Minerva on Charon Base, orbiting Pluto.

The solemn mood of the base reflected its commander. TDF *Vasco De Gama* had not made contact confirming its safe arrival at Gama Leporn. Vadis had authorized the dispatch of two courier drones to the system to make contact with the missing ship. Both had returned intact and reported there was no indication of either the ship or the communications buoy it should have released on its arrival in the system. Vadis was only delaying the inevitable by not declaring the ship lost but Elizabeth reflected, he was the admiral and it was his decision.

Vadis turned from the holo cube image of Gama Leporn to face Elizabeth. "So, Commander. Give me some good news."

"Sir, Captain Radford has safely arrived in the Sol system and is due to dock within the hour. We have received a courier drone from Captain Papadomas. He requests he be allowed a further seven days in Delta Pavonis to secure as many facts as possible on the indigenous civilization."

Vadis nodded. "Granted. Inform him as to the current situation with TDF *Vasco De Gama*. Make it clear he is to leave Delta Pavonis at the first indication of any trouble. We still do not know what happened to Captain Witsell and her crew. I don't want to lose another ship."

Elizabeth made the annotations on her PAD before continuing, "As for TDF *James Cook*, Captain Lewis reports safe arrival at 31 Aquilae. That is all at this time." Elizabeth keenly felt a sense of relief at this particular news. She and Robert Lewis had enjoyed each other's company while preparing for the survey missions and she missed being able to talk to him. Elizabeth shook herself internally. *Robert is old and bold enough to look after himself without you worrying like an old woman,* she thought, and promptly halted her pondering as she waited for Vadis to reply.

"Very well Elizabeth. Inform Captain Radford I expect a full briefing from him two hours after he docks, and please ensure the yard gets TDF *Henry Hudson* turned around as quickly as possible for redeployment."

"Yes, sir." Elizabeth stood to leave then paused. "Sir, if I may?"

Vadis broke his gaze away from the image of Gama Leporn in the holo cube. "Of course, Elizabeth."

"Sir, as you have pointed out, we have no idea what has happened to the *Vasco De Gama*, so maybe we should wait for a little while longer before we write them off?"

Vadis considered for a moment. "As always, Elizabeth, you know what to say and when to say it." Vadis gave her a small smile, the first she had seen since TDF *Vasco De Gama* had failed to make contact. "Maybe a few days more before I make any calls to the families." Vadis' eyes turned to reflect on the image of Gama Leporn. Elizabeth left the room.

CHAPTER TEN

Trip Wire

TDF *JAMES COOK* - 31 AQUILAE

TDF *James Cook* arrived at the pre-planned distance of 52 AUs from the primary star 31 Aquilae, some 49.41 light years from Earth. 31 Aquilae could be seen by the naked eye from Earth. The star was some 116 percent of the mass of Earth's own star and some 138 percent of its size. Spectrograph readings showed it as surprisingly rich in elements, with the exception of hydrogen and helium, for its age, some five billion years old – which put it about half a billion years older than our own sun. A blink of the eye on a cosmic scale.

Captain Robert Lewis viewed his bridge with paternal pride. His people were going about their jobs with the utmost professionalism and if truth were told, he felt outright redundant. Robert had been, perhaps, more surprised than the other captains on hearing of their selection to command Earth's first extra-solar survey ships. Robert was only a few years from retirement and had already been planning how he was going to spend his free time – commuting between his home on the south island of New Zealand and his daughter's home on the north island. He had gone as far as considering selling his place and moving lock stock and barrel to be closer to his daughter. However, his home on south island was where he and his late wife, Colleen, had lived, raised a family together and where, if it had not been for the cancer, they had planned on growing old together.

Robert shook himself out of his reverie. It was not to be. In any case, he had found a resurgent interest in his career. On receiving the briefing by Admiral Vadis and Lieutenant Commander Elizabeth Wilson on Operation Minerva at Charon Base, Robert had found himself spending many hours with Elizabeth going over details of the operation. Not only during work hours but also over the odd late dinner. Robert had been surprised to hear Elizabeth too was a widow, her husband had died in service early in her career. Lewis still thought he made a mistake in not inviting her to see New Zealand with him. Perhaps when this mission was over…

"Captain!" Commander Torrance, his XO, called and attracted his attention.

"Yes, XO?"

"Sir, if you would care to view the holo cube, astronomy have finished their plot of the system and have confirmed their findings." Robert spun his chair to get an unobstructed view of the central holo cube. As it sprang into life, Torrance continued. "As you can see, sir, the system consists of nine planets. Two are gas giants, three are effectively balls of ice, being too far from the system primary to receive anything in the way of heat, and another two are so close to the primary they make our own Venus seem a nice place to vacation. One is just outside the Goldilocks Zone and this one is just right," Torrance paused.

Robert interjected, "This sounds like the story of the three bears, Bruce."

Refusing to acknowledge the pun, Torrance carried on. "So far, sir, spectral analysis of the atmosphere has a high amount of carbon dioxide, methane, nitrous oxide and halocarbons."

Robert raised a finger to stop Torrance in mid brief. "XO, are you going where I think you are going with this?"

Torrance let a small smile reach his lips. "As usual, sir, you are a step ahead. I'm saying what you've already guessed —these are four of the principle greenhouse gases, which accumulate in the atmosphere, causing concentrations to increase with time. On our own planet, levels of this sort occurred in the industrial era."

"No sign of artificial power generation?" asked Robert.

"None, sir," confirmed the XO.

Robert sat back in his seat and involuntarily began to stroke his grey goatee. Torrance remained silent, allowing his captain to mull over the information.

"Very well," announced Robert, turning to face his navigator, Lieutenant Ash. "Mr. Ash, please plot us a spiral course for Planet IV. I want to survey the outer planets on the way in, no sense in taking any chances."

"Aye-aye, sir."

"Lieutenant Marcks. I want passive sensors only, but get as much information as you can."

Marcks, the Tactical Officer nodded, "Yes, sir."

"XO, I shall leave the bridge in your capable hands. Download all our information to a courier drone and get it away please. Ensure the deployment of the communications buoy."

"Understood, sir."

"I'll be in my quarters, taking my pensioner's half hour. We of the older generation require our midday snooze, you know."

Torrance allowed himself another smile. After watching how Captain Lewis had driven the crew in preparation for this mission, he had more stamina than half the crew put together and could give the marines a run for their money as well. Instead he replied, "I'll be sure to wake you for dinner, sir," before turning to carry out his orders.

————

Robert was fast asleep when his Comm buzzed urgently. Without even opening his eyes, he had hit the accept button. "Captain. Go ahead."

"Sir, Lieutenant Ash. Could you come to the bridge, sir? Passive sensors are detecting what Tactical are classifying as an artificial power source on or near Planet V. Approximately two point eight AU from our current location."

The request brought Robert to full wakefulness. *How could it be? There should not be an artificial power source out here.* "Signal all stop, Mr. Ash. Rouse the XO and get him to meet me on the bridge."

"Aye-aye, sir."

Robert swung his legs out of bed and dressed while ruminating the implications of an artificial power source in the system. Well, no need to over think until he received more information, he would just have to wait.

On reaching the bridge, Robert took his center seat just as Torrance came through the bridge hatch, slightly out of breath, and talking into his wrist communicator. Lewis smiled at him, "A little out of shape, XO?"

"Running and talking at the same time, sir. Need to get to the gym more I think."

As Torrance moved to his console, Robert noted more harried, out of breath officers were arriving. Torrance had been rousing the senior bridge staff to replace the night crew. *Better to have the A Team on duty, good idea Bruce*, thought Robert. For a few minutes, Lewis let his team get themselves up to speed before getting down to business, "OK, XO. What do we know?"

"Captain, approximately…" Torrance took a quick look at the bridge clock, "seven minutes ago, Tactical detected an artificial power source emanating from the general location of Planet Five, which has now been narrowed down to a point approximately point five AUs from the planet.

Although the power source is quite weak, Tactical are positive it is artificial, and having looked at the data so am I. Until now, we have not detected any attempt to sweep for us using active sensors."

"Can you be certain we remain undetected, XO?"

"I cannot guarantee it at this point, sir. Whatever is the source of the energy signature may have capabilities we cannot detect."

Food for thought, Robert mentally agreed, *well, we cannot just sit here.* "Recommendations, Bruce?"

Now it was Torrance's turn to take a breath. Robert waited patiently as his first officer ran through the various options in his mind, calculating what was best for the ship and the mission.

"Sir, I recommend holding station. We can observe the location of the power source with our on board passive optical equipment. Whatever it is, its twenty-two point four light minutes from us. There are no detected aggressive moves, we can get a good look at it before deciding on a course of action."

"Sounds good, XO, make it happen and let's see what we're really dealing with here. How long before we get results?"

"I'll meet with Lieutenant Curran from Supply and get the required equipment broken out of stores. Ensign Yamata has a first from MIT in Astrography and is my choice for setting it up."

Robert could see the cogs turning in his XO's head.

"Say three hours to locate, track, image and be ready to present the findings, sir."

"Make it happen Bruce. Tactical. I want a permanent passive weapons lock on the source, but do not power anything up without my express permission. And notify me the second we have any change in either its output or aspect."

"Aye-aye, sir," said Marcks at Tactical.

"XO, I also want everyone fed and watered. I fear we may have a long day ahead."

"Yes, sir. I'll see to it."

Robert left the bridge and headed for his cabin for what, he had no doubt, would not be his first mug of coffee this day.

––––––––––

Three hours later, Robert sat in his chair in the Briefing Room of the TDF *James Cook* with the rest of his command team and a seemingly aloof Major Karen Mills, the CO of the *James Cook*'s marine detachment. All were eagerly awaiting the XO's presentation.

Robert found it hard to relate to Major Mills. She was obviously competent or she would not be here, but she kept herself and her marines apart from the rest of *James Cook*'s crew. Robert did not like this aloofness, however, he understood his officers had their own command style. Until it became an issue, he did not feel the need to interfere. Robert looked across at Torrance, "XO?"

"Sir, the last three hours have been very productive. We can now confirm the source of the energy readings is in fact from an artificial object which is station keeping at that point." Torrance activated the holo cube. There was a small and, what appeared, quite battered object. It looked remarkably like an old style communications satellite without the solar panels – a large box, roughly the size of a ground car, with two long antennas protruding from it and a large dish mounted on it. As the image rotated, one side of the box appeared covered in glass lenses and, as the image rotated further, Robert could that see on the opposite side of the lenses there was an even larger dish, which covered one side of the box.

As the image rotated, Robert asked, "What is your assessment, XO?" A darker patch on the object had caught Robert's eye.

"Without stating the obvious, sir, we believe this object is not the product of any civilization in this system. Our analysis of the capabilities of Planet IV show no sign of space travel at their current level of development. It leads us to conclude it must have been placed by some other, unknown, nonindigenous civilization."

Silence descended on the table as people assimilated what Torrance had said: a civilization on Planet Four at a level of technology equivalent to Earth during the industrial revolution and, somewhere else, there was another civilization. This civilization not only had the technology for spaceflight, but also must have the technology for interstellar flight to travel to this system from which they did not originate. A sobering thought – man was not the only species currently traveling the stars.

"Going back to the object, XO. What are your thoughts?" asked Robert.

"If I were to equate it with our own technology, sir, I would say it was some form of surveillance platform. My best guess is the glass side of the box are the lens for some form of high definition space telescope. The protruding antennas gather any electromagnetic transmissions, the larger dish shape to the rear is a broadcast array. The platform is situated in a position where the lens is always pointed at Planet IV and, at this distance from the planet, even if the inhabitants were to develop the technology to put their own satellites in orbit, this platform would remain undetected, possibly for decades to come."

"Well thought out as usual, XO. It leaves only the questions of who is watching Planet Four and how do they collect data?"

"One other thing, sir"

"Yes, XO?"

Torrance fiddled with the controls for the holo cube and the image of one side of the platform enlarged. "If I could point out this particular image, sir…" It was the darker patch Robert had seen earlier. "This would appear to be a jagged hole in the structure of the platform. It is my belief something struck the platform causing the damage."

Robert regarded the image. "We have no way of knowing how long ago the damage was inflicted, XO?"

"We think we do, sir. Tactical noticed a slow, but steady, reduction in the power output of the platform. Now we have taken the time to observe it more closely, it appears to have a slight wobble."

Lewis thought he could see where this was going, "Do you have a proposal, XO?" Out of the corner of his eye, Robert was sure he saw the cool Major Mills turn her head microscopically toward Torrance.

"Sir, I would like to propose we close with the platform. Do an onsite inspection, and if deemed safe recover it, return it to Earth."

Robert regarded Torrance for a moment. It was obvious the XO had thought this through at length, "What you are proposing is very risky, XO. If whoever placed the platform here comes back looking for it to make repairs and it's simply vanished, it could prompt them to ask the same questions we are: Is there someone else out here?"

Torrance looked steadily at Robert. "Understood, sir. But I think the risk outweighs the gain on getting our hands on this technology."

Robert still was not convinced. At the end of the day, the decision lay with him. "Major Mills." If a marine could come to attention in a seat then Mills did so. "Get together with the XO and sketch out a plan to approach the platform, inspect it and, if possible, recover it. Cover all our bases here, Major. If you consider the plan unworkable, then we leave the platform where it is, understood?"

Mills looked from Captain Lewis to the frowning XO and back to Lewis, "Sir! Yes, sir!"

Robert stood up. "OK, people. We have a lot to think over. Communications. Get a courier drone away with images of the platform and a summary of my intentions. The rest of you are dismissed." Robert left the Briefing Room but not before noticing, astonishingly, what appeared to be a smile on the lips of Mills as she approached a still frowning Torrance.

––––––––––

The plan Bruce Torrance and Karen Mills developed was as straightforward and uncomplicated as they could make it. Karen was a firm believer in the KISS principle – Keep It Simple, Stupid. The more complicated the operation, the more chance there was Murphy's Law would come into play. This operation was too important to give Murphy any chance of screwing it up for them.

TDF *James Cook* hiding itself on the far side of Planet V was the basic plan. From there, a Tanto shuttle would launch with a joint Navy/Marine recovery team on board. They would approach the alien platform with the planet at their back so the natural electromagnetic radiation, generated by the planet, would help hide the miniscule amounts escaping from the covert insertion shuttle on the off chance the platform had the ability to detect objects approaching it. On arrival at the platform, the recovery team would perform an extra vehicular activity (EVA) – navy speak for going out in spacesuits – and get a closer look at the platform after the Marine Explosive Ordnance Disposal (EOD) had cleared the platform of any self-destruct mechanisms.

To Robert Lewis the plan was good one. The only problem was after the Tanto moved beyond the radio horizon of Planet V, he would have no contact with the recovery team until it broke the radio horizon on its return journey to TDF *James Cook*. Nevertheless, moving the *James Cook* behind the planet was the only way to get as close as possible to the platform without putting the ship within any possible detection zone of the platform. *No plan is perfect!* Thought Robert. From his seat on the bridge, Robert watched the Tanto move away from the *James Cook. Good luck and safe journey Bruce.*

Bruce sat in the troop/cargo area of the shuttle, completely enclosed in his armored spacesuit. Not as good as the marine issue Wraith suits, but good enough for him to survive and fight in a hard vacuum environment. Bruce looked for the hundredth time at the display in front of him as the Tanto made its stealthy approach to the alien platform. "Still no change in the power output, Gunny?"

Gunnery Sergeant Hazon was the Marine EOD and he had constantly monitored the platform's energy readings since the Tanto had started detecting them when it had broken the radio horizon of Planet V and begun its approach. Now only 100 meters from the platform, the Tanto sat stationary while Hazon confirmed there were no unexpected power spikes that might be a telltale signal of the Tanto's detection. Hazon took one more look to confirm his readings. "Still looking good, sir. I'm happy to say we have a go."

Bruce switched across to his private link. "Well Karen?"

"I'm with the Gunny, Bruce," replied Karen over the link. "If he's happy to deploy, it's his call. He's the one who has to approach the thing first after all."

Bruce had not been happy with this part of the plan, but Karen insisted. The platform had to be checked for self-destruct mechanisms. Bruce knew it was the gunny's job, but Karen had insisted the remainder of the team stayed within the added protection of the Tanto's hull until the gunny cleared the platform. It simply went against the grain with Bruce to send a man into potential danger while he sat in the relative safety of the Tanto. "OK, Gunny. You have a go."

Hazon released his seat restraining ties with practiced ease and moved to the troop hatch on the side of the Tanto. He operated the hatch mechanism, stepping into the air lock and closing the internal hatch without even a backward glance.

Over the team link, Karen called Hazon. "Gunny, no chances here. If anything looks even slightly wrong, back away and return to the shuttle. Communications by whisker laser only, let's do this thing by the book."

"Understood, Major. Just a walk in the park." Hazon activated his pusher pack and a small blast of high-pressure gas moved him in the direction of the platform. Hazon stopped at ten meters from the platform, and then using the pusher pack, he performed a complete 360-degree check of the platform. "Nothing obvious on an initial visual survey. I'm going to move closer"

"Understood, Gunny. Still looking good from here: no signs of any unusual activity on the platform," Bruce acknowledged.

Hazon moved in closer and found what he was looking for "OK, I have found what looks like an inspection panel. Are you getting a good visual?"

"I see it, Gunny." Bruce could see on his display a rectangular panel roughly a meter by half a meter with what looked like retaining lugs spaced equally around it, securing it to the main body of the platform.

Hazon reached to his tool belt and lifted off a small handheld laser cutter, "I don't have anything which will fit the lugs, so I'm just going to go for a straight cut to remove the lugs and then lift the panel free." Hazon started cutting away at the lugs, knowing any one of them could be attached to enough explosives to destroy the platform and spread him over this entire area of space.

Karen noted a rise in his respiration. "Everything OK over there, Gunny? Your respiration and heart rate are up."

Without pausing in his work, Hazon replied, "I think I have a cold coming on, Major."

Karen had to fight to control her laughter before activating the link again, "That explains it, Gunny. Make sure you visit sickbay when we get back, I don't need you spreading it to the rest of the detachment."

Listening in, Bruce could not believe what he was hearing. She was berating the man for having a cold and not going to sickbay all the while he was cutting away at a potential bomb. He would never understand marines. Torrance failed to notice the slight shoulder movements of the Wraith suits of the remaining marines as they laughed heartily, ensuring not to activate their own Comm links.

With the last of the retaining lugs removed, Hazon lifted the panel clear and secured it to the side of the platform. He was able to get his first clear look inside. A complex looking set of boards were joined by what looked like thick plastic strips to a central hexagonal shaped object about the size of a soccer ball.

"Hold there, Gunny. Zoom in on one of the connections to the object directly in front of you," Bruce ordered. As the Gunny zoomed in, Torrance looked at the connection more closely. "Gunny, run your PAD over one of those connections for me. I want to check something." Hazon did as instructed and fresh data appeared on Torrance's display. "OK, Gunny, confirmed. There is an electric current emanating from the central object. I think it's a safe bet this is the platform's power source. Unless there's a backup, we should be able to deactivate the platform by removing the source."

"Just give me a minute here, sir." Hazon removed his monomolecular blade from its scabbard at his shoulder. No marine went anywhere without a knife and the monomolecular blade was the ultimate knife. It could cut at the molecular level, carving through virtually any known material as easily as a hot knife through butter. Not something for the uninitiated to play with, but Hazon handled it with skill, giving not a second thought to the fact it could cut through his suit and expose him to vacuum. Hazon twisted his body to get into a better position and began slicing through the connections, careful not to touch the suspected power source itself, ever hopeful Commander Torrance was right about these connections and he was not about to be adjacent to a fatal, loud bang and expanding ball of gas. The last connection was severed. Hazon secured the blade in its scabbard and ran the PAD over the object again. No power readings. It looked like Torrance was right. "Are you getting this, Commander?"

"I see it, gunny. OK standby. I'll get the remaining team to you and we'll get this thing in the hold and secured." As Bruce turned to the rest of the team, he heard Karen over the link.

"And don't forget to report to sickbay when we get back, Gunny."

Keep me safe from marines! thought Bruce. *Does that woman never lighten up?*

———

Robert and the rest of the crew of TDF *James Cook* let out a collective sigh of relief when the Tanto carrying the recovery team finally made contact to report mission success. They had the alien surveillance platform on board and would shortly be docking with the *James Cook*. Onboard techs could not wait to get their hands on the platform and, if he was honest with himself, it had taken a conscious decision not to get his own hands dirty in the lab with them. Sometimes you just have to take a step back and let the experts get on with it.

The time had come to hear what they had discovered. Robert sat in the Briefing Room, with his command staff, all anxious to hear the results. "XO, if you please."

Bruce stood and regarded the waiting, expectant faces. "Captain, our initial premise for the purpose of the platform appears to have been correct. It transpires the optics we assumed to be a sort of telescope are in fact a high resolution thermal imaging system."

Robert was confused "A thermal imaging system, XO? To what purpose?"

"If I could pass to Ensign Yamata, sir, she has a theory on it."

The diminutive ensign, like the rest of the crew, had only joined TDF *James Cook* at Charon Base. Where everyone else on the crew had at least one tour of duty under his or her belts before selection for Operation Minerva, Shizuko Yamata was fresh from the Naval Academy. Glowing progress reports had singled her out, and Admiral Vadis, who had free rein with Personnel, directed her posting to Charon Base. Robert read the same reports and slotted the freshly commissioned ensign into a lieutenant's post, his faith in her had so far been fully justified. Bruce obviously felt the same way or he would not allow her to brief the command staff.

"Captain, ladies and gentlemen. Prior to the wars, which nearly destroyed Earth, some of our larger nations engaged in various ongoing programs, the aim of which was to detect planets orbiting stars. What was known as Direct Thermal Imaging had an advantage over Direct Observation. Detecting an exoplanet using visible light as the detection mechanisms in the near and mid infrared are of utmost importance for characterizing the physical and chemical properties of any exoplanets and their atmospheres. I believe this was the purpose of the alien surveillance platform. But with a twist."

"A twist Ensign?" asked Robert.

"Yes, sir." Shizuko paused, gathering herself to extol a theory, the reception for which she was unsure. "When employed by the larger nations, the system was used to detect exo-planets in orbit around distant stars. In this case, the system is within the same star system as the planet it is observing." Yamata took a breath. "Sir, I hypothesis the system was employed as a tripwire. If I could explain, sir?"

Robert nodded. "Please do, Ensign. Although I don't think I'm going to like it."

"Sir, as a civilization progresses, it expands its industrial base and population. As we observed on our arrival, Planet IV has detectable levels of the greenhouse gases in its atmosphere, all of which generate heat. If I could draw your attention to the holo cube…" Shizuko indicated two circular images, which appeared side by side in the holo cube. "As you can see, the image on the left is significantly dimmer than the one on the right. The one on the left is a thermal image of Planet IV, which we took on our arrival in the system and we used to make our initial analysis of its atmosphere, the one on the right is an image of Earth."

There was a moment of silence in the room, the significance of what the young ensign was showing them sank in. A gradual realization dawned.

"Sir," Shizuko continued, "if I was looking to identify an up and coming civilization, identify when it was becoming a potential threat, then place a surveillance platform in system with the ability to detect when it reached the equivalent of our industrial revolution – then this is how I would do it."

I knew I did not like where this was going, thought Robert. "Thank you Ensign and good work." Shizuko bowed slightly and retook her seat.

"Unfortunately, your hypothesis may be correct." Robert came to a decision. "XO, let's get us moving back to Charon Base. We need to make the Admiralty aware of our findings as soon as possible." He paused, then continued, "Dismissed people. Once again, good work."

Bruce stood, as did the rest of the staff, and left Robert alone in the Briefing Room. Robert contemplated the images of Planet IV and Earth side by side in the holo cube. Shizuko's hypothesis of the platform acting as a tripwire placed by an alien race to alert them of a key advancement in a civilization's industrial progress was indeed worrying. What would their reaction be when the wire was tripped? Would they just come and observe the planet's progress? Alternatively, would there be a more sinister purpose for their visit? The images of the nuclear-scarred surface of Rubicon, where the Saiph database was discovered, arrived unbidden into Robert's mind.

CHAPTER ELEVEN

Letters Unwritten

CHARON BASE - ORBIT OF PLUTO - SOL SYSTEM

Admiral Aleksandr Vadis sat in his office on Charon Base. He contemplated the old style paper in front of him. If he were aware of time passing, he would have realized he had been staring at the paper for ten minutes. Sitting perfectly still, the pen in his right hand having only touched the paper once in those ten minutes: 'Dear Mr. and Mrs. Yamata'.

TDF *Vasco De Gama* was now two weeks overdue, courier drones sent to the Gama Leporis had returned without any successful contact with the ship. Lieutenant Commander Elizabeth Wilson had urged him to delay informing the crew's family of the probable loss of their loved ones, but the time had come. It was not the first time Vadis had sent young men and women into danger, he knew it would not be the last. No matter how many times he had to write to the families of those who had died or simply disappeared, presumed killed in service, it still took a little more out of his soul. Get on with it Aleksandr! Vadis urged himself. The demanding tone of his Comm stayed his pen on the paper. Vadis pushed the accept symbol. The face of a smiling Elizabeth Wilson appeared above his desk.

"Admiral, I have the pleasure to report TDF *Vasco De Gama* has arrived in system, and Captain Witsell reports all hands safe. And apologizes for her tardiness."

Vadis felt his own face break into a smile. "Inform Captain Witsell her apology is accepted and be sure to inform her she is responsible for adding years to an already old man!" He cut the link and his eyes fell to the letter in front of him, he reached down and ripped it in half before depositing it in the waste.

———

Vadis, accompanied as always by Elizabeth Wilson, sat in the main Briefing Room of Charon Base surrounded by the captains of the four survey ships and their marine majors.

Only a scant seven months had passed since they had first arrived here at Charon Base and learned of their impending mission to take their Vanguard class ships to distant stars and look for evidence of the Saiph. What they had brought back! It caused the hairs on the back of Vadis' neck to stand up.

TDF *Henry Hudson* and Captain. Radford had found a life-bearing planet in 70 Ophiuchi. No sign of an intelligent species there yet, but analysis showed indications of Saiph meddling. Then there was the appearance of those Alcubierre driven ships identified by the Saiph database as having belonged to the Others. Not forgetting what appeared to be the establishment of some form of base on Planet II, the beginnings of a colony or perhaps a military base? The arrival of a second ship had caused Radford to make the prudent decision he had possibly pushed his luck too far and it was time to come home. Vadis would have done the same thing in his position.

TDF *Jacques Cartier* and Captain Papadomas discovered the remains of a freshly extinct civilization on Planet III in Delta Pavonis. The DNA extracts the *Jacques Cartier* returned with proved positive for Saiph intervention. From the crew's findings, it put the inhabitants of Planet II at the technology level of pre-World War 3 Earth, before their decimation by an asteroid, which snuffed out all life on the planet.

Captain Lewis and TDF *James Cook* returned with, not only the news of a living, breathing world around 31 Aquilae but news of the inhabitants of Planet IV reaching the level of pre-industrial revolution by Earth standards. The discovery of the surveillance platform brought all further observation of Planet IV to a grinding halt. It proved beyond any doubt, Man was not the only one exploring the stars and looking for new life.

Ensign Yamata's hypothesis, now backed up by Vadis' own experts on Charon Base, was worrying. The surveillance platform would only trigger a message to its makers when the atmosphere of 31 Aquilae showed signs of large-scale industrialization on the planet. The question now was what would be the reaction of the makers of the platform? His technicians had taken the platform apart and found symbols all over the inside. The linguists determined it was a language dissimilar to those found in the Saiph database. It led them to believe neither the Saiph nor the Others built it. So who had constructed it?

Finally, TDF *Vasco De Gama* and Captain Witsell. They may have missed their objective by a few thousand light years but what they had found was remarkable. A spacefaring civilization in Messier 54 had begun to colonize a neighboring planet within its own star system. Vadis was unsure the politicians back home would permit the nickname the crew of the *Vasco De Gama* had devised to describe the indigenous race, 'The Baldies', to stand. Vadis also gathered Doctor Jeff Moore was screaming for the return of George Lee, the Chief Engineer of TDF *Vasco De Gama*. Moore demanded his help to improve the current Gravity Drive, after Lee's modifications without a doubt had returned Captain Witsell and her crew home safely after a 50000 light year detour.

Overall, Vadis thought they had achieved the aim of the Vanguards mission. The Saiph had indeed interfered with the natural progression of life, within the star systems the Vanguards visited. Unfortunately, they had to weigh the fact the Vanguards had also encountered the Others against the successful mission. God only knew the implications.

"Ladies and gentlemen! If I could have your attention please!" The gathered captains and marines simultaneously ceased their small talk, turning their full attention to the admiral. "The information you have returned is remarkable and I thank you and your crew's for your efforts. However, it also brings troubling news. The Others are still out there. For the time being, I am halting all further survey missions. Until the threat is properly assessed by the Admiralty and the government back on Earth." Judging by the assembled faces, Vadis could see this news did not go down well. As each Vanguard returned to Charon Base there had been a mad scramble to turn the ships around, ready to head out to their next destination amongst the stars.

"On the plus side, I am authorizing shore leave on Earth for all crew members. I think two weeks should be sufficient, effective immediately." Everyone around the table smiled at this news. "Dismissed!" Vadis turned and made his way toward the hatch leading to his private office, only to stop as Wilson made to follow him. "Shore leave includes you, Elizabeth. You have been stuck on this rock with me for long enough. Go and visit the family or take a break somewhere warm."

"Why, thank you, Admiral. It has been some time since I was home."

Vadis noticed behind Elizabeth the Briefing Room was emptying, except for Robert Lewis waiting patiently. "I think Captain Lewis wants a word with you."

Elizabeth turned around and faced Lewis, who was rubbing his hands nervously.

"Commander Wilson, as the admiral has authorized shore leave for you as well, I was wondering if you had ever visited New Zealand?"

Elizabeth felt her cheeks reddening like a schoolchild. *Control yourself,* she thought. *You are a grown woman, for Pete's sake.* "I can't say I have, Robert. But it's a place I always meant to visit."

"Perhaps we could discuss it some, over coffee," said a smiling Robert as Elizabeth led them out of the door.

As the office door sealed behind them, Vadis regarded the seated figure of Admiral Jing. He moved across the room to join him, "So what do you think, Ai?"

Vadis and Jing had been friends for as long as either of them could remember, but where Vadis had moved in the shadowy circles of intelligence, Jing had always been in the command line. He had progressed up the chain of command in the relatively small Terran Navy, with turns at the Naval Academy teaching tactics, until he found himself as head of the Naval Strategy Board. And, if what Vadis was hearing on the grapevine was correct, Ai was to be the next Head of the Joint Chiefs on the retirement of General Joyce.

Jing leaned forward, placed his elbows on the table, and interlocked the fingers of both hands, a position Vadis remembered as Jing's thinking pose from the many occasions the two young officers sat late into the night discussing the strategic and tactical problems set by the instructors at the Naval Academy.

"All the data from the Vanguards is being collated and analyzed by the Strategy Board. I think I can safely say there will be a good many worried people back home. The existence of another spacefaring civilization in 'The Baldies' at their current level of development poses no immediate threat to Earth, but the fact remains we now have irreconcilable proof. The Others are out there and are capable of traveling between the stars. A worrying development," Jing stated.

Vadis nodded his head slowly in agreement. "So do we move forward with phase two of Chrysaor?"

"I think it would be only prudent, Aleksandr. The initial planning is in place. General Joyce has given his blessing for me to start scouting for a suitable base of operations in nearby star systems. If you could attach two of your Vanguards to Chrysaor then I'll get to work"

Vadis thought for a moment. "OK. When Captains Papadomas and Lewis return from shore leave, you can have TDF *Jacques Cartier* and TDF *James Cook*. Now, perhaps we can discuss how we are going to sell Chrysaor to the politicians back in the senate."

Jing looked at his friend with a wrinkled brow, "By telling them the truth."

CHAPTER TWELVE
Full Disclosure

OFFICE OF THE PRESIDENT OF THE TERRAN REPUBLIC - GENEVA - EARTH

Rebecca Coston sat at the head of the conference table in her private office with an air of apprehension. Arrayed around the table were Senator Gillian Rae, Chairman of the Science and Technology Committee, Senator Geoffrey Rawson, Secretary of Defense, Senator Thomas Crothers, Secretary of Finance. General Joyce, Chairman of the Joint Chiefs was accompanied by Admirals Vadis and Jing. Doctor Jeff Moore and finally Doctor Patricia Bath, Head of Linguistics at Stickney Base, made up the group.

This select gathering had been at the request of General Joyce. It was he, Rebecca turned to first. "General, I and my staff have had the opportunity to review the information brought back by Admiral Vadis' survey missions. I can tell you it has the top echelons of the government frightened. The discovery that the 'Others' are still out there, the possibility of another star traveling race, and another race are beginning to colonize planets within their own system, who may be on the verge of discovering star travel for themselves, and yet another race who are at the brink of their own industrial revolution."

Rebecca indicated Jeff Moore. "When Doctor Moore invented the Gravity Drive some seven years ago, we thought it promised us the means to explore the stars at our leisure. Who could have thought we would find the Rubicon Cave and all that followed from there?" Rebecca paused for a moment. "The discovery of the Saiph changed our understanding of not only the universe around us, but of ourselves and our own origins. It came as a huge mental blow to the general population. I now understand more than ever, why President McMullen urged me to keep Operation Minerva a secret for as long as I could. Once it was general knowledge, I was surprised at the reaction from the public. Yes, they were annoyed we kept the operation secret, but there was also a groundswell of support for the operation and its goals. The public wanted to know if any of the other planets the Saiph visited had survived and prospered as we have."

Rebecca now settled her gaze on Joyce. If he expected to railroad her into silence then he had another thing coming.

"So before you begin, General, you need to know I have no intention of keeping the results of Admiral Vadis' surveys secret. The people have the right to know, and it is my intention to go onto the floor of the senate tomorrow and inform them of the survey findings."

General Keyton Joyce had been a marine for nearly thirty-five years and in all that time, he could not remember anyone who had a more resolute look in their eyes than Rebecca Coston at this moment. "Madam President, this is exactly what I and the Joint Chiefs want you to do."

Rebecca opened her mouth, ready to argue with her top general, when she realized what he had just said. "Excuse me, General. You want me to tell all?"

Joyce smiled. "Yes, ma'am. It's important the citizens understand the full nature of the threat we face and the actions we must take to counteract that threat."

Rebecca was dumbstruck by this unexpected reaction, but, with the poise of an experienced politician, she recovered quickly. "What actions would they be, General?"

"The reason I asked for this meeting today, Madam President, was to go over an operation Admiral Vadis and Admiral Jing conceived and have been running in conjunction with Operation Minerva. We call it Operation Chrysaor."

Rebecca looked accusingly at Secretary Rawson. "Where you aware of this Geoffrey? And if you were, you better have a very good reason for not telling me!"

Geoffrey Rawson was a career politician and knew how to play the blame game. "I was aware of the operation, Madam President, but I was assured by General Joyce it was only a planning exercise. I had no idea it was anything more." He redirected the president's anger onto the military men.

"Well, General?" demanded Rebecca.

Joyce took a second to look at Geoffrey, as if he were something unpleasant he found stuck on the bottom of his shoe, before turning back to the president. "Ma'am, the aim of Operation Chrysaor is four fold: firstly, to analyze the information returned by the survey ships. Secondly, to identify any threats to Earth from the analysis. Thirdly, to devise a strategy to counter these threats and finally to implement that strategy." Joyce nodded to Jing. "Admiral Jing is, and this is difficult for the marine in me to acknowledge, the foremost tactician of the Terran Defense Force. He has been running Operation Chrysaor."

"Thank you for your confidence in my abilities, General," Jing said.

"I ask him to review his findings, Admiral?" Joyce sat down as Jing stood to address the group. Jing could feel the eyes of all present focus on him.

"Madam President, ladies and gentlemen. If I could take the first and second aims of Operation Chrysaor in conjunction. In analyzing the information returned by the survey ships and employing the work of Doctor Bath in decrypting the Rubicon Saiph database, we were able to compare the two and look for either similarities or discrepancies. As far as the threat posed by the civilizations in 31 Aquilae and Messier 54 are concerned, without further intelligence it cannot be fully assessed, however, the fact neither have star travel leads me to categorize any threat they may present to Earth at present as minimal."

"Reassuring at least," said Rebecca.

Jing nodded. "Agreed, Madam President. Unfortunately, the same cannot be said of whoever built the surveillance platform found in 31 Aquilae. It proves they are capable of star travel, and yet we have no idea as to their intentions. It would be prudent to take what precautions we can, although, on the other hand, we have yet no reason to believe they are hostile. As to the confirmed existence of the Others it, to use a sporting analogy, is a game changer."

"In what way, Admiral?" asked Rebecca.

"If I could ask Doctor Bath to explain, ma'am."

Rebecca looked down the table at the linguist. "Doctor?"

Doctor Patricia Bath cleared her throat before continuing. "Madam President, as you know the Saiph database provided us with a massive amount of information, so much so we were forced to prioritize. Our first priority was to discover the fate of the Saiph and find out why they lost their conflict with the Others."

"But I thought it was because they were simply vastly outnumbered?" interjected Senator Rawson.

"True," agreed Patricia. "But what we discovered during our research explains why they were so outnumbered."

"Go on, Doctor," urged Rebecca.

"Although the Saiph were able to travel between the stars, it seems they did not have any colony worlds. Yes, they visited other worlds and established research bases on some, but the vast bulk of the Saiph population remained on the home world. They had a stable population and saw no need to invest in colonies. The Saiph had been at peace with themselves for thousands of years. Add to the fact they had never come across another star traveling civilization since they began to explore the nearby stars and you can imagine how much of a shock it was when a fleet of warships, warships we now know belonged to the Others, arrived in the Saiph home system. The Saiph attempted to establish contact but the warships remained silent. They moved into orbit and began bombarding their home world. After so long at peace, the Saiph had no significant weaponry to fight back and the bombardment survivors headed for the research bases. The Others simply followed them and destroyed them as well. A few Saiph ships managed to escape. It was they who planned to tailor the DNA in the seventeen star systems listed in the database. They knew with their limited numbers, their race was doomed to extinction. They did what they could to make sure some part of them survived. Scattered around the star systems they visited, they left databases, like the one we found on Rubicon. Hoping, one day, one of their protégés would find it and use it to defend themselves from the Others."

As Patricia retook her seat, Jing stood.

"Madam President. This brings me onto the third aim of Operation Chrysaor: to devise a strategy to counter the perceived threats. If the Others were to appear in the Solar System tomorrow, we would find ourselves in the same position as the Saiph. We have no established colonies outside our own star system." He indicated the Chairman and Vadis. "Our main goal must be the survival of the human race. We see the easiest way to do this, in the short term, is the immediate establishment of self-sufficient colonies outside our own solar system. We already know there are planets out there, such as Planet II of 70 Ophiuchi, which will sustain human life and have no indigenous intelligent species of their own."

"But, Admiral, isn't Planet II where Captain Radford encountered the Others?" interjected Rebecca.

"Yes, ma'am, but they can't be everywhere. The Baldies of Messier 54 are such an example." Jing activated the holo cube and a star chart appeared hovering over the center of the table. "This is a diagram of what's known as the Local Bubble, a region within sixteen point three light years of Earth. Within this bubble, in addition to our own solar system, there are fifty-five stellar systems. Within these systems, there is a total of fifty-six hydrogen-fusing stars. Despite their relative closeness to us, only thirteen percent can be viewed with the naked eye. Besides the Sun, only three are first magnitude stars: Alpha Centauri, Sirius and Procyon. Admiral Vadis has already consented to two of the Vanguard survey ships being seconded to Operation Chrysaor. It is my intention, at the earliest opportunity, to send them as a pair, in case of mishap or an encounter with the Others, to scout these three systems for a suitable world on which to establish a human colony."

Rebecca caught the eye of Gillian Rae, who nodded her approval. "OK Admiral. I can see the sense in your approach. I thereby approve the sending of the two survey ships. But the logistics behind establishing a colony are massive, never mind the expense." In her peripheral vision, she saw Thomas Crothers' gaze fixed on the image in the holo cube. The president could also see the financial planning involved in the establishment of the colony running through his mind. A plan began to form in her own head as to whom she should entrust with the planning for the colony. *The party leaders are not going to like it,* she thought. She could see Jing was waiting for her permission to continue. "Please go on, Admiral."

"Yes, ma'am. Secondly, in conjunction with Science and Technology, we need to begin a crash program into weapons research."

Senator Rawson tried to hide a grin at the news as he considered the extra power and influence he was about to gain. Jing chose to ignore him.

"The designs held in the Saiph database are untried in real life. They only exist as technical drawings. With their main industrial base destroyed on the home world, the Saiph never got a chance to build them let alone try them. We need to incorporate their technology into ours – faster than we have been doing. Doctor Moore and his team have been working miracles but we need to expand his team, as rapidly as possible, to exploit the advantages of the Saiph technology."

Rebecca turned to Senator Rae. "Well Gillian? Can we do it?"

Geoffrey Rawson made a small coughing noise. "Madam President, surely the exploitation of the Saiph weapon technology would best be handled by Defense?"

Rebecca was beginning to regret allowing the party to force Rawson on her as Secretary for Defense.

"May I suggest a joint research and development team: Science and Technology to do the research and building while Defense review and prioritize the research and carry out testing," suggested Senator Rae.

"Sounds like a good plan," said Rebecca, smiling at Senator Rae and realizing the good senator had not lost her head for politics.

Senator Rawson looked rather crestfallen. "Yes… Madam President."

"Good that's that sorted. Anything else, Admiral?"

"Just three more things, ma'am. We need to halt forthwith the surveys being conducted by Admiral Vadis and Operation Minerva."

Rebecca's eyes widened with surprise. "But why Admiral? Surely it's more important than ever to find out what happened to the remaining worlds the Saiph visited?"

"True, Madam President, however, sending survey ships to known star systems the Saiph have visited increases the chance of an encounter with the Others. In turn, this increases the chance they discover Earth's location, and, as I discussed earlier, we cannot afford for that to happen until we are sure we can handle them."

Forced to agree, Rebecca reluctantly nodded and replied, "Understood and agreed, Admiral. Next?"

"If we are to assess the full threat the Others pose to us, we require good, sound intelligence. Currently, all we have is the contents of the Saiph database. Having discussed it with the Joint Chiefs, we are in agreement we should employ the two remaining Vanguards to insert a Marine Force Reconnaissance team onto Planet II of 70 Ophiuchi to observe and report back on the Others base there."

"A big step Admiral, are we sure the marines can get in and out undetected?"

General Joyce spoke up. "There are no guarantees with this sort of thing, ma'am. Nonetheless, those marines are the best at what they do. I have every confidence in their ability to complete the mission."

Rebecca was the first to admit the reputation of the Force Reconnaissance Marines was the best, but still… "I don't know if I'm comfortable with the suggestion."

Joyce answered for the military men. "We don't see any other way to get the intelligence we need, ma'am,"

Rebecca was still unsure. However, sometimes you have to take a leap of faith. After a thoughtful pause, she said, "OK, General, Admiral. I bow to your superior knowledge on military matters. And your final request, Admiral?"

"This is more to prepare you for what may be coming than for immediate implementation, Madam President."

Rebecca did not like the sound of this. "Stop beating about the bush Admiral, and get on with it please."

"Very well, ma'am. We must consider there will be a requirement for a massive increase in the size of the Terran Defense Force in the near future. At present, we are little more than a coastguard and if, and I do say *if,* we are to face a conflict, we simply do not have the strength to fight more than a skirmish before our enemy, if they are of any significant force, brush aside our forces. The numbers are against us, Madam President. Our standing forces need to be increased and these things take time. We have a solid core of experience to build on, but to build any sort of fighting force we need time and personnel and, to be blunt, the money to pay for it all."

Rebecca looked over at Senator Crothers. "Well Thomas? How to pay for things is your area. So what do you think?"

Thomas Crothers looked around the table uncomfortably. He did not like being in the spotlight, despite being a politician. "Madam President, our current standard of living is higher now than it's ever been in our recorded history. Our population is rising at an exponential rate and, to be honest with you, if we want to avoid overcrowding and keep the standard of living at its current level we would soon have no choice but to look for planets to colonize anyway. The threat from the Others is only making our decision to colonize come faster. Our excess industrial capacity could very quickly be converted to military use and with some time we would be quite capable of building dedicated production facilities for the military with minimal effect on civilian output." Thomas paused, regarded those around the table, and shrugged his shoulders. "The only thing I can't help you with is the personnel."

"Thank you Thomas. Well, gentlemen, it would seem Thomas has a point." Rebecca looked from Joyce to the other two Admirals. "Do you have an answer to the personnel issue?"

Joyce met his president's eyes steadily. "Madam President, ever since the human race almost caused its own demise, we've been ingrained with the importance of the continued existence of the race as a whole. Maybe it's time to tell the people what we face and see if we really are ready to put the greater good before the good of the individual."

OFFICE OF THE CHAIRMAN OF THE JOINT CHIEFS OF STAFF - GENEVA - EARTH

General Keyton Joyce let out a non-committal sound as he placed his coffee down on the table in his private office and turned off the sound on the holo cube on which he'd watched President Coston make her address to the senate. He, Admirals Vadis, and Jing had looked on in silence as President Coston outlined the survey ships' findings and then went on to explain the government's response. The Senate had sat in polite silence up until the point where the president had announced the immediate expansion of the Terran Defense Force, and then the Speaker of the House had no choice but to intervene and restore order. It had taken nearly ten minutes before the Speaker reinstated calm, allowing the president to continue. Now with her speech over, it seemed every senator in the House clamored to speak.

Keyton turned to his two guests. "Well, gentlemen, it looks like the proverbial cat is out of the bag. I think it's safe to say we are about to live out the ancient Chinese curse."

Aleksandr chuckled. "I hope you live in interesting times," he quoted.

"Exactly," answered Keyton with a short laugh of his own before becoming serious again. "The plans for the future structure of the Defense Force, with emphasis on the navy and marines, Ai has come up with will be implemented forthwith. We will deal with the work force shortfalls as and when they arise. I intend to create a post of Special Inspector with the rank of Rear Admiral working directly from this office. Their job will be to handle any problems arising from officers who become, how should I say? An obstacle to progress. We do not have the time to pussyfoot around, gentleman. Not with the fate of the human race at stake. You either get with the program or you will find yourself unemployed." Aleksandr and Ai both understood what was about to happen to the Defense Force was a necessary evil and found themselves agreeing it needed to happen as quickly as possible. The threat the Others presented was too great. Keyton could see the agreement in the faces of the two Admirals. "Unfortunately, Aleksandr, the first casualty comes from your command. With immediate effect Lieutenant Commander Wilson is promoted to Rear Admiral and transferred to this office." Joyce grinned. "She's my hatchet man now, Aleksandr."

Aleksandr grinned in return. "Only if I get to tell her she's just skipped three ranks and got her flag."

"Deal," said Keyton. "Now, back to business. Ai, what about fleet construction?"

Ai touched a control and the scene from the senate floor changed to a warship. "This is the design from the Deimos Yards I prefer. They named it the Talos class cruiser. 452 meters long, fifty-seven meters at the beam, weighing in at 24400 tonnes. It carries three Tanto shuttles and has a crew complement of 710."

Above the table, the image of the warship rotated giving Keyton and Aleksandr a good look at the first true warship Earth had built to fight amongst the stars. "As you can see, sir," continued Ai, "the designers at Deimos have combined as much Saiph technology R and D can reverse engineer with the latest version of the Gravity Drive from Doctor Moore's research, to produce the Talos class. Starting with the known capabilities of the Others' ships, we tasked the designers to develop a hull that could defeat an Others' ship in one to one combat and operate as part of a combat group.

They factored in speed, maneuverability, survivability and lethality. The Talos class mounts the same twin turret particle cannon as the Vanguard class but it has twenty-four such turrets spaced around the hull in five rings giving the Talos a 360 degree arc of fire with a minimum of ten turrets being able to engage at any one time."

Aleksandr let out a low whistle. "A lot of fire power in a small package, Ai."

Ai nodded. "True, and there's more! We noticed the Others use bombardment to reduce any ground-based target, so the Talos class will be fitted with a limited number of experimental High Velocity Missiles, or HVMs. They use a miniature Gravity Drive, similar to our courier drones, to deliver a small fusion device to a target. As it stands, the mathematics involved in using the Gravity Drive in such a tactical role is causing a few headaches, but Doctor Moore assures me his team are nearly there. To be honest, I'd rather have the HVMs as they are, than wait for a perfected version."

"OK, makes sense." Keyton gave Ai a knowing look. "But you still have something up your sleeve. So what is it?"

"I never could keep secrets," said Ai. "May I draw your attention to the bow of the Talos? See the two, large projections side by side?" Keyton and Vadis both nodded. These projections had prompted Keyton's query in the first place. "You are looking at the largest grazers ever mounted on a human warship."

Aleksandr let out an excited "Surely not! The power requirements alone when coupled with the rest of the weaponry must be staggering!"

Ai now smiled openly. "True, but those smart designers at Deimos have used Saiph technology to build in four separate and independent power sources. One for the Gravity Drive, one for general ships systems, one for all the other weapons systems and one for the sole use of the grazers – giving them a rate of fire of three shots per minute. The test firing resulted in a million watts per square centimeter, or put into perspective, one shot from the grazer will pass straight through the best armor on any ship we can produce, without even slowing down. And the ship will be left an expanding ball of plasma from the energy transfer."

"Very impressive, Ai," commented Keyton, "How quickly can we get a Talos from the drawing board through construction and into operation?"

Ai consulted his PAD for a moment. "For the first Talos, simply because it's a prototype, Deimos are currently estimating about ten months on construction. The Admiralty estimate three months for trials. So for the first ship to come on line, thirteen months in total. But…" as Ai's smile widened, "due to the modular construction employed in the Talos, Deimos are estimating their build time, when they start to benefit from the president's decision to expand our construction facilities, will eventually lead to a launch completed Talos every ninety days."

"My God!" exclaimed Aleksandr "Phenomenal!"

"The beauty of automated standardized construction," replied Ai, "The designers at Deimos have bigger and better things planned, and this particular design is only the first one to come off the production lines. The only problem I can envisage is one we have already identified – personnel."

Keyton changed the image on the holo cube back to a view of the senate floor and pointed a finger in its direction. "That, gentlemen, is a problem for the politicians. Our problem is this expansion, which must be handled well," gesturing at the holo cube and the still clamoring politicians. "We'll must head off anyone who thinks he can become a politician in uniform. There's going to be a lot of rapid promotions, and we need reliable people in command slots who can handle the pressure outside forces exert." Both the admirals understood what he was talking about – political interference in military decisions.

"If I may make a suggestion, sir?" interrupted Ai. Keyton nodded his assent and Ai continued. "We have a small pool of experienced flag officers, using Admiral Vadis as an example, some have been reactivated due to the exigencies of service. What I suggest is a board made up of a selection of these officers, none of whom has any current political affiliations, as they are retired and headed by an officer who we all know personally. And, if I may be so bold, scares the crap out of the Senate."

Keyton and Aleksandr looked at Ai before turning to look at each other and laughing aloud.

The three men held the mental image of the Senate faces when informed Admiral Helset was to be reactivated.

CHAPTER THIRTEEN

Enemy

TDF *HENRY HUDSON* - 70 OPHIUCHI

Admiral Jing's brief to John Radford and Ruth Witsell had initially excited John. Excited by the prospect of taking TDF *Henry Hudson* and TDF *Vasco De Gama* back to Planet II of 70 Ophiuchi and inserting the Force Recon Marines onto the surface for a closer look at the 'Others'. However, as he had gotten to the initial planning stages with Ruth and the two marine majors, Alec Murray from the *Henry Hudson* and Vladimir Egnorov from the *Vasco De Gama*, it did not take long for John's excitement to wear off, replaced by an impending sense of dread.

Six months ago, on his last visit to the system, TDF *Henry Hudson* had detected the first ship belonging to the Others. From an undetectable position, the *Henry Hudson* observed the Others approach Planet II, begin shuttling equipment to the planet surface and start construction of some kind of base. However, a second ship had arrived only 275,000 kilometers to starboard. It changed course toward TDF *Henry Hudson* and powered up its weapons. If it had not been for the alertness of his Tactical Officer, Lieutenant Falconer, and the quick thinking of the navigator, Lieutenant Danino, the *Henry Hudson* and her crew might not be here today.

John shook off his melancholic mood and returned his concentration to the present. On his tactical display, he could see the *Henry Hudson* approaching Planet II from the opposite side of the planet from where the Others had been establishing their base. TDF *Vasco De Gama* was in step, slightly behind and off to port. As John was senior to Ruth, the ultimate command of the mission had fallen on him. Communication between the two ships was strictly by whisker laser. Both ships were rigged for silent running with all electromagnetic emissions kept to a minimum. Both ships were employing the chameleon system to hide the ships from any prying eyes, both optical and electronic. John could only hope it worked as well as last time.

Lieutenant Cai at Communications interrupted his thinking. "Captain, Captain Witsell on whisker, sir."

"Go ahead, Ruth," said John as Ruth's face appeared alongside the tactical display in his holo cube.

Ruth looked as apprehensive as John did. "Major Egnorov informs me he and his marines are aboard the Tanto and ready to go."

John glanced at Tactical and got an affirmative nod from Lieutenant Falconer before addressing Ruth. "Major Murray also indicates ready. Best we get on with it then." John gave the order. "Tactical. Inform the marines to launch. I want a full passive lock kept on both Tantos until they cross the radio horizon."

"Aye-aye, sir," replied Falconer.

John's concentration returned to Ruth. "And so the waiting begins."

Ruth gave him a small smile. "Don't sweat it, John. They know what they're doing." She cut the connection.

"I hope so," John said to himself, "Stay safe, Alec."

Major Alec Murray, Marine Force Recon, Terran Defense Force, was forced to admit, as he surveyed the Others' base, he loved his job.

What other job in the world sends you to a distant star system, occupied by potential hostile forces, with God only knew what capabilities while six, (yeah, count them *six!*) 1700 meter long alien ships held geosynchronous orbit above your head? All while you lay dug into a hillside, covered in sheets of chameleon material with only one other marine for company. Murray laughed quietly so as not to wake the sleeping form of Corporal Semple beside him.

Alec and Vladimir's plan for what was termed a Close Target Reconnaissance of the Others' base was straightforward. The two Tanto shuttles had approached the base from opposite directions, until they detected emissions from the base, at which point the Tantos immediately grounded.

Group One, the marines of TDF *Henry Hudson*, split into a rear party of six marines under Gunny Young, to protect the Tanto and to act as an extraction force if Alec got into trouble. Alec took the remaining twelve marines of Group One forward, five kilometers from the base, at the Final Rendezvous Point (FRV). He split them into six by two man teams to form a loose semi-circle around the base and find suitable hide locations from which to observe.

Vladimir did the same with his marines, Group Two. Both groups were to stay in position for three planetary days before extracting to their respective FRVs, then head for the Tantos to return to the waiting Vanguards.

The only drawback to the plan was that apart from the marine beside him, Alec had no knowledge of what was happening to any of the other teams. All the Wraith suits the marines wore were in strict emissions control mode to avoid any chance of detection. The marines were under orders to break radio silence only if they came into contact and needed to fight their way out. In which case, all bets were off. Each team of two marines was to return to their FRV ASAP, wait for thirty minutes and, no matter how many marines made it, the senior man was to take command to get the marines back to the Tantos at best speed. It might seem callous, but on receipt of the initial contact report the Tantos would only remain on the planet for twelve hours, if you were late, your ride home would leave you.

Over the past two days, Alec and Corporal Semple obtained valuable intelligence on the composition of the Others' base. Observing construction techniques, identifying personnel accommodation, power plants, communication centers and what looked like weapon positions. Murray instinctively ducked as a shuttle passed virtually directly overhead at an altitude of about 300 meters. The Others appeared to be clock-watchers: every four hours another shuttle would approach the base from exactly the same direction and land at a large shuttle facility at the western edge of the base, and then offload its cargo before leaving along the exact same route it had approached on two hours later. Semple had suggested either the Others were anal about traffic management or the route the shuttles were using was a cleared lane through an air defense zone. Murray was inclined to agree with the latter. Murray settled back down for his remaining hour on watch before waking Semple.

Alec woke to an insistent nudging in his ribs, a brightly lit landscape revealed itself as he opened his eyes. Something must be wrong, his next shift was to start on the approach of nightfall. Alec turned his head toward Semple, his straight arm indicated to a small bluff maybe 250 meters from their dug in hide. Semple then made a fist, inverted it and stuck his thumb out, the hand signal for enemy. *Crap,* thought Alec, *Had the Others detected them somehow?*

Alec looked back in the direction of the bluff, as he watched two, what Alec could only describe as hovering sleds appear from around the bluff. Alec had observed the sleds moving around the perimeter of the base for the last couple of days but they had never ventured more than a kilometer from the perimeter. The sleds were rectangular, about three meters long and maybe a meter across with a bubble shape just short of a meter high toward the rear of each machine. Protruding from each side of the sled was the unmistakable shape of weapons pods. The sleds were flying maybe three meters apart and they were headed away at an angle from Alec's position. Neither appeared to have noticed the marines. There was no doubt in Alec's mind the two sleds were some sort of Others' clearance patrol sent out to sweep the area within line of sight of the base. Granted, this was the first patrol of this type they had seen since they had arrived, but it would probably not be the last. Alec came to a decision. As soon as the sleds were out of sight they would pack up their gear, make for the FRV and await the rest of the marines before heading back to the Tanto.

Ten minutes later, with all their gear stowed, Alec and Semple were on the move. Alec's worst nightmare played out as the shrill tone in his helmet informed him one of his teams was in contact. Semple immediately went to ground scanning the area for threats, knowing Murray would be preoccupied trying to sort out what was happening. Murray's heads-up display flashed the names of two marines in contact: Baker and Rodriguez. The display listed the distance and bearing to their location. Unbidden, Alec's head turned to the bearing, as if he could see the two marines.

What he did see was a large black cloud mushroom into the air, closely followed by a loud boom. The marines' names began to flash red in the heads-up display. The warning tone started up again. Alec cancelled the tone and cleared the display. He could do nothing for them now. Semple tapped his arm and indicated the Others' base. Alec used his helmet optics to zoom in. He could see more sleds moving from the base in the direction of the explosion, this time accompanied by larger hovering vehicles – troop transports if Alec was to make a guess. *From bad to worse,* thought Alec.

Alec gave the clenched fist jerking motion to Semple, indicating they were to double time it. Both men set off at a run, their Wraith suits building up to a steady and sustainable forty kilometers an hour. They covered the distance to the FRV in seven minutes and settled into firing positions to await the arrival of the remaining marines. They did not wait long. Alec was just catching his breath when his Wraith suit warned him a whisker laser, using the correct Identify Friend or Foe (IFF) challenge, had hit him. Murray ordered his suit to acknowledge and two marines appeared, as if out of nowhere, slotting themselves into firing positions expanding the perimeter of the FRV. Quickly, three more pairs of marines arrived. IFF issued its challenge to each pair before Alec acknowledged and granted permission to enter the FRV.

Alec moved to the center of the marines and tapped Semple's boot. The Corporal turned to face him and Alec pointed a straight arm in the direction of the waiting Tanto. Semple gave him the OK signal, then tapped the marine to his right and moved off in the direction indicated by Alec. The marine Semple had tapped allowed Semple to get a few metres ahead before they, in turn, tapped the next marine to his right, stood up and moved off. Each marine repeated the action until all the marines were on the move. Third in line was Alec. Not a spoken word or an electronic emission made during the whole process. No need to give the Others a sniff of their location.

The marines had been moving at a steady rate for over an hour when Alec's suit buzzed for attention. The heads-up display indicated a low threat warning. It detected an increase in electromagnetic radiation. The onboard computer classed the source as a ground search radar of unidentified class off to the right of his line of march. Alec kept an eye on it but the source did not grow in intensity. He kept the marines moving. After a few minutes, the suit buzzed for attention once more. On the display, Alec saw a second source

appear, this time off to his left. Alec did not like what he was seeing, he had an enemy contact on his right and now another on his left, time to step up the pace. Alec tapped the marine in front of him and indicated for him to double time it. Turning, Alec made sure the marine behind him got the same message.

Semple waited a few seconds to ensure the message reached the last man, and then set off at double time. Alec's suit buzzed for attention a third time. He saw a third source appear on the display, this one behind him. The Others were boxing him in. It was still over fifty kilometers to the Tanto. *Forget covert!* Murray thought. He activated his Comms, keeping the power low so it only broadcast to the marines with him. "The enemy have us on three sides, they either haven't got a blocking force into position in front of us yet or the blocking force is in position and we're going to run right into them. Unfortunately, they are between us and our ride home. Keep your eyes open and watch each other's backs — this could get messy very fast. None of the marines replied, they had all seen the same thing on their own display and were all experienced enough to read the signs.

Alec's suit buzzed and on the head-up-display, the blocking force appeared 300 meters ahead of them. The marines went to ground as Alec used his optics to scan the small ridgeline concealing the enemy. There! A slight movement in the vegetation. Alec switched to thermal imaging and the shapes of twenty or so Others were clearly outlined. The darker shape of long weapons they were aiming in his direction stood out in the display. Alec checked the groups to his left and right. They seemed to be holding position, as was the group to the rear, not wanting to walk into the crossfire from their own ambush, no doubt. Alec sent the information to his marines' suits so they could see what they faced, before opening his Comms link.

"OK, marines. Here is the plan. We move forward in a skirmish line, using the chameleon units in the suits to get as close as possible. On either effective enemy fire or on my command, we break into our pairs and fire and maneuver through the enemy line. Once you are through, you hightail it to the Tanto and tell Gunny Young he is to run for the *Henry Hudson* at the slightest sniff of the enemy or at his own discretion. The intelligence is more important than any of us, understood?" A line of green lights on his heads-up display acknowledged his orders. "On the count of three, cross deck all the information you have to every suit. Stand by. One, two, three." Again, a line of green lights illuminated in his display as his suit acknowledged receipt of the data from the other marines. "OK marines. Let's move out."

The marines shook down into a skirmish line, each marine advancing up the ridgeline a few meters apart, with Alec in the center. The marines slowly approached the enemy with their suits set to thermal vision. The Others' position was clearly visible to their front, still with no indication they had detected them. Only twenty meters from the enemy Alec's suit screamed at him as something his suit classified as a low intensity laser designator struck him. Somebody was pointing something nasty at him.

Alec swung his plasma rifle around and fired a short burst in the direction of the source of the laser. There was a satisfying scream, which was quickly cut off, a plasma rifle strike tended to kill quickly.

Alec's marines interpreted his action as their queue to break into fire and maneuver. One marine in each pair would provide covering fire while his partner moved a few meters forward, he would then fire while the first man advanced. It was an effective way to cover ground quickly while laying down constant fire. The marines advanced onto the ridgeline like the wrath of God, anything moving instantly received fire. The marines moved through the enemy position and broke for the waiting Tanto.

Alec looked into his heads-up display as it called for his urgent attention. His heart sank. The three remaining enemy forces were closing on his position. The suit projected all three would combine and intercept them while the marines were still fifteen kilometers short of the Tanto. Alec activated his comm link. "Corporal Semple. You plus Marine Chin, will continue to the Tanto. The rest of us will go firm here and attempt to delay the enemy."

Semple knew better than to argue. Instead, he grabbed Alec by the hand and shook it as he said, "Aye-aye, sir. Good luck."

Alec watched as Semple and Chin ran, at the suits' best speed, for the waiting Tanto, carrying the precious information bought by the lives of his men.

The marines set themselves up ready to receive the oncoming enemy force. Alec's suit was telling him it estimated nine sleds and three troop carriers. If the enemy forces he had faced on the ridge were of a similar makeup, then he should be facing upwards of sixty troops. Alec looked around at his seven marines. *Yeah!* He thought and a smile creased his face. He had them outnumbered!

The enemy forces came on at speed with the sleds in the lead. Alec let them close to within 100 meters before opening fire. The concentrated fire of marine plasma rifles cut through whatever armor the sleds had. Within seconds, there were seven smoking craters in front of the marines' position, the surviving two sleds searched for cover, to no avail. The marines switched fire and brought the two sleds crashing down. Thick black smoke from burning sleds now obscured the area in front of the marines, the heat from the fires interfered with the suits' thermal imagery. The marines resorted to the Mark One Eyeball. The second the marines opened fire on the sleds, the troop transports went to ground, there was no sign of the troops Alec was certain they were carrying.

A series of explosions, just short of the marines' position, warned Alec of advancing troops. They were firing what seemed to be some kind of kinetic energy weapon from a small roof mounted turret. Fortunately, the fire was not accurate, but it was enough to keep the marines' heads down, sufficiently distracting them for a few seconds —all they needed. A cry from a marine at the far left of their fire position enlightened Alec as to what had happened to the enemy who had been on the troop transports. They had left their transport behind and were attempting to outflank him. The telltale red in his display advised Alec, sadly, the marine's fight was over.

Alec quickly determined he had to swing his position or the enemy would roll him up. Just as he was on the verge of giving the order, his helmet filled with the voice of Gunny Young.

"Marines! Danger close! Get small!"

Alec curled into the smallest ball possible and hugged the ground. The entire world around him shook. Buffeted by explosions, flying fragments impacted his suit. The noise seemed to go on for an eternity but Alec knew it could only have been a few seconds, and then all was quiet.

The commanding voice of Gunny Young came through the comm link again. "Marines, count off."

Alec heard himself say "Murray here," and listened as his six surviving marines called in. Alec got to his feet and looked at the devastation around his position. The enemy troop transports were burning shells, the dismounted troops cut down where they had stood by the now grounded Tanto. The troop hatch opened, Gunny Young stepped down and walked toward Alec as the marines Alec had left with the Gunny fanned out eagerly seeking new targets.

Young stopped in front of Alec. "Heard you needed a lift, sir."

Despite himself, Alec smiled. "Appreciate it, Gunny. I take it you have Semple and Chin on board?"

"I do, sir. Although Corporal Semple is in restraints at the moment."

"Dare I ask why, Gunny?" asked Alec.

"He was very insistent on returning for you and the others, sir, after he ensured Chin's suit had all the data and it was good to be transferred to the Tanto. Went as far as using bad language to me, sir. You know I cannot abide bad language. I was forced to persuade him to remain on board. Medic says his teeth can be put back in when we get back to the *Henry Hudson* and the bruising should clear up nicely."

Alec could not help but let out a small laugh. "What can I say? He appreciates a good officer."

It was the Gunny's turn to smile. "Well, if I ever find one, I'll let you know, sir. Now, if you want to get yourself and the boys aboard, I'll give the area a quick once over and see if we can recover anything useful. Then I suggest we beat a hasty retreat for the *Henry Hudson* and get the hell out of this system – before the big boys up there make their presence felt."

Alec took a moment to look around. His gaze fell on a body of one of the Others and he moved closer to get his first good look at the enemy. The body looked to be about two meters tall and was covered head to toe in body armor, not dissimilar to the marines' own Wraith suits. Pale, almost translucent skin peaked out through a hole in the chest armor, penetrated by the impact of a Marine rifle. Alec used his boot knife to unseal the Others' helmet and opened it to reveal a broad face with two large eyes mounted further apart than a human. There was no appearance of a nose, and then Alec noticed what looked very like fish gills on either side of the neck. The mouth was more rounded than a human one and contained an impressive set of razor sharp teeth. Any further examination of the body would have to wait. The Others' ships in orbit had already demonstrated they could lay waste to vast areas of a planet's surface if they so wanted.

"Let's get to it, Gunny, and make sure we secure some of the enemy remains and equipment, and then we're out of here."

"Aye-aye, sir." Gunny Young started passing orders to the marines while Alec headed for a seat on the Tanto. They were not clear of this yet.

John Radford was asleep in his quarters when the urgent comm tone woke him, he was up and dressing as he pressed the accept button. "Captain."

The face of Lieutenant Falconer his Tactical Officer appeared in the holo cube. "Sir, passive sensors have picked up the returning Tantos. They're coming in at full speed, even a blind man could see their emissions."

Not good, thought John. *They must be in trouble.* "Contact the *Vasco De Gama* by whisker laser and tell them both ships are to make for a shortest time intercept with the Tantos. Sound battle stations. Full emissions protocol remains in place till we know what we're dealing with here." The wail of battle stations erupted throughout the *Henry Hudson*. The automated computer voice called the crew to their stations as John ran for the bridge.

John entered the bridge, immediately calling to Lieutenant Falconer. "Update please, Tactical." His holo cube sprang to life, displaying two Tantos moving at speed toward them. John wondered what spooked Alec and his marines so much they were throwing all caution to the wind, running at full speed. A fresh icon, circled in red, appeared in his display, promptly followed by another and then another.

"Computer is designating the new ships as Bogies One, Two and Three. They match the size and shape of the Others' ship we ran into last time we were here. Power output shows their weapons are hot," reported Falconer. Now John knew why the Tantos were running. The Others' ships were monsters compared to the lightly armed shuttles.

"Time till Bogey One can take the shuttles under fire?"

Falconer did some quick calculations. "Sir, our best guess at their armament would put the shuttles in weapons range of Bogey One in… eleven minutes with Bogies Two and Three entering weapons range in… sixteen minutes. Sir, if the computer's reading on the Others' weapons power output is even half right, a shuttle would not survive a direct hit."

John looked over at Lieutenant Danino, "Navigation. Time till we intercept the shuttles?"

Danino turned to look at his captain, "Fourteen minutes, sir."

Too late, thought John, *and there is nothing I can do about it.*

"Captain," Lieutenant Cai's voice at Comms cut into John's thoughts. "I have Major Murray for you."

The face of Alec Murray appeared in John's holo cube. What do I say to him? I cannot get to him in time…

Alec spoke before John could say anything. "Captain, we've run the numbers here. We know you won't get to us before we enter their firing range so I'm transmitting all the intelligence we gathered to you now."

John got a nod from Cai. "We've got it, Alec. Tell your pilots to go to evasive maneuvers, just buy us a few minutes. We can get to you."

Murray smiled at him. "Captain, you know the *Henry Hudson* has as little chance of taking on one of those monsters as we do in a shuttle. You have the intelligence. Get it home. Don't let our lives have been for nothing." The signal cut off. John stared at where the face of his friend had been. *There must be something he could do?*

Cai called for his attention, "Sir, *Vasco De Gama* for you."

A view of the bridge of TDF *Vasco De Gama* appeared in front of John. There was a bustle of activity around the navigator's position as Chief Engineer, Taylor, worked on a PAD and entered data into the navigation console before turning to Ruth Witsell. "Yes, I can do it, ma'am."

"Thank you Chief." Ruth turned to the pickup. "John, we think we can buy you some time."

"Tell me! I only need a few minutes and we can recover both shuttles," demanded John.

Ruth gave a small shrug. "By doing what needs to be done." She paused and looked down for just a moment before taking a deep breath and looking John square in the eye. "Get my people home John." She was gone.

"Captain, the *Vasco De Gama* has activated her Gravity Drive. She's gone," said a stunned Falconer. "No. Hold on… I have her again. She's dropped back into normal space. My God, sir! She's directly behind Bogey One, range 30000 meters," Falconer said in disbelief.

John spun to Cai at Comms. "Get me the *Vasco De Gama* now!"

Falconer began a running commentary. "*Vasco De Gama* is firing her particle cannon. Direct hit on Bogey One's drive. Bogey One is slowing."

"Get out of there Ruth," John heard himself shout.

"*Vasco De Gama* is ignoring our hails, sir," said Cai.

Falconer continued her commentary. "Bogey One is returning fire. Computer is designating the return fire as a Q Switching laser. *Vasco De Gama* is taking hits but the ablative armor appears to be holding. Attitude change from Bogey One: she's turning broadside on. Multiple separations from Bogey One. Computer is designating them missiles. *Vasco De Gama* Laser Area Denial Systems are going active and engaging."

John turned to Danino "Our time to shuttle intercept?"

Danino did not need to check. "Ten minutes, sir."

John calculated the math in his head. "Comms! Raise the *Vasco De Gama*. Tell them to get the hell out of there, now! They've bought us enough time." John saw a glimpse of light at the end of the tunnel. Maybe *Vasco De Gama*'s gamble would pay off.

A shout from Tactical. "Bogey Two is engaging the *Vasco De Gama*!"

John looked into the holo cube, just in time to see an energy beam cut the *Vasco De Gama* cleanly in half. Shortly after, the remains exploded as containment failed on the drives and weapon systems.

There was a deathly silence on the bridge of TDF *Henry Hudson*. The stunned crew stared, in shock, at where their sister ship had just perished along with 135 men and women. John broke the silence, trying hard to keep his anger in check. "Snap out of it people! We have two shuttle loads of marines who still need us and we're short on time. Let's not waste it."

The bridge crew moved to carry out his orders. There would be time to mourn their dead later. For now, the living took precedence.

CHAPTER FOURTEEN
Changes

ORBIT OF PLANET II
ALPHA CENTAURI B - 4.37 LIGHT YEARS FROM EARTH

"Well? What do you think, Captain?" asked Bruce Torrance from his seat on the bridge of the TDF *James Cook*.

Robert Lewis regarded the light blue and white planet centered in the holo cube as he contemplated the enormity of the decision resting on his shoulders. This was the third star system the *James Cook* had visited, accompanied by the TDF *Jacques Cartier*, in its search for an Earth like planet to be man's first colony outside his home system.

The first, Sirius, some eight point five eight light years from Earth, had proved to be a dead system. Any planet capable of bearing life became desolate when Sirius B had lost its outer layers when it had collapsed and became a white dwarf, the star's outer layers spreading through the star system like an unstoppable tidal wave of star plasma and radiation scrubbing clean all before it. The second, Procyon, some eleven point four six light years from Earth was deemed unsuitable as none of the system planets were found to have a stable orbit, almost certainly due to the main star's white dwarf companion, which was close enough to the orbit of the planets to influence them.

This led the search to Alpha Centauri. One of the brightest stars in the southern skies, it is the nearest stellar system to our own solar system, only four point three light years away. Alpha Centauri is actually a triple star. It consists of two stars, similar to the Sun, orbiting close to each other, designated Alpha Centauri A and B, and a more distant and fainter red component known as Proxima Centauri, where almost a decade ago, humans discovered the Rubicon Cave. Since the nineteenth century, astronomers have speculated about planets orbiting the stars, which make up Alpha Centauri. The invention of the Gravity Drive meant Man at last was capable of travel and could observe for himself. The recent clashes in the 70 Ophiuchi system, the loss of TDF *Vasco De Gama* and all on board and the threat posed by the Others to humanity all increased the impetus to settle beyond the home system. Alpha Centauri B is very similar to the Sun, but slightly smaller and less bright, with four planets orbiting it. One was so far from the star it was a frozen snowball, another was a gas giant, one orbited so close to the star its surface was molten, and then there was Planet II. The newly discovered Planet II the *James Cook* and *Jacques Cartier* were currently orbiting had a mass of a little more than Earth. The planet orbited about 106,000,000 kilometers away from the star, closer than Venus to the Sun in the Solar System. The orbit of the other bright component of the double star, Alpha Centauri A, keeps it hundreds of times further away, but it would still be a very brilliant object in the Planet II skies.

"The geologists say the planet has just come out of a period of glaciation?" asked Robert.

"Yes, sir. It's all in their report. Current surface temperatures are equivalent to just south of the Arctic Circle on Earth at this time, but they will slowly rise in time," answered Torrance while, he too, regarded the blue and white marble in the display. So reminiscent of Earth. "The scientists tell me, using the same techniques we used to successfully grow crops during the cleanup of Earth after the wars, the planet should be self-sufficient in food, dependent on population size, in no time. Native life appears to be limited, on land masses, to small mammals not much bigger than rodents, with the largest life forms detected in the oceans, some of them as large as our own whales."

Robert came to his decision. "Very well, Commander. Please inform Captain Papadomas to remain in this system and continue to survey the remaining three planets. We shall return directly to Earth. I need to speak to Admiral Jing so we can inform the Joint Chiefs I think we have found a suitable planet."

Torrance looked across at the lieutenant at Communications and could see she was already transmitting the instructions to TDF *Jacques Cartier*.

Torrance's attention returned to Robert as he asked, "One more thing, Commander."

"Yes, Captain," replied Torrance.

"Your watch discovered the planet so you get to name it. Have you given it any thought?"

Torrance had not… at least not till now. He looked again at the blue and white marble, hanging there looking so pure and untouched he smiled slightly, "Janus, sir, after the Roman god of beginnings. Hopefully, we can tend to this world better than we have Earth."

"Janus," Robert repeated and gave Torrance a smile of his own, "I like it. Very well. Let's be on our way."

Torrance gave an affirmative "Aye-aye, sir. Navigation! Plot us a fold for home and engage when you're ready."

TDF *James Cook* disappeared from the Alpha Centauri system leaving TDF *Jacques Cartier* to stand watch over the system.

STICKNEY BASE - PHOBOS - ORBITING MARS

A harried Patricia Bath was busy having a short lunch when a beep from her wrist Comm demanded her attention. With a wearied sigh, she wondered why she had ever let Senator Rae talk her into taking on the directorship of the newly founded Office of Research and Development. It may have given her control over all the ongoing research into the Saiph but she could not remember the last time she had taken a day off. Her wrist Comm beeped again, this time louder. *Oh well,* thought Patricia, *there goes lunch.* She activated the link. "Doctor Bath."

"Director, sorry to bother you over lunch. It's Doctor Fredericks. Could I have a moment of your time?"

Patricia thought Doctor Fredericks did not sound the least bit sorry for interrupting her lunch. "How about in my office in twenty minutes or so?"

"Would it be possible for you to come down to the lab as soon as you can? It is rather important," asked Fredericks.

Patricia looked at the salad, which was to be her lunch, and stood up. "I'm on my way, Bath clear." She cut the link and threw the remains of the salad in the recycling.

Ten minutes later, all thoughts of lunch had vanished as Patricia looked at the two DNA profiles displayed in the holo cube. She looked at Fredericks and said in a disbelieving, questioning tone. "Doctor, this can't be right?"

Fredericks stood shaking his head. "I know what you mean, Director. Nevertheless, I have double and triple checked the samples. The one on the left is from the Saiph database and is verified as the Saiph. The one on the right was taken from the remains of one of the Others returned by TDF *Henry Hudson*. I have taken samples from each of the remains and they all show the same results. The Others also show signs of Saiph DNA interference."

Patricia incredulously said, "There must be some mistake. Our searches of the Saiph database tell us the Saiph only began to meddle with the DNA on the seventeen planets after they were attacked by the Others millions of years ago."

Fredericks looked at Patricia, as a professor dispensing a lecture to a wayward student. "Director. Science does not lie. The Others incorporate the DNA of the Saiph. Now, I am the first to admit when it comes to weapons technology and engineering I am but a layman, but has it never occurred to anyone else, if the Others have been around for millions of years, why is their technology not so far advanced beyond ours as we are from the amoeba? It appears what you thought you knew for fact may not be true at all."

Patricia sat and stared at the comparative DNA profiles. How could this be? Her brain refused to digest this new information. The scientist in her eventually kicked in. They had to review everything they had extracted from the Saiph database with a fine toothcomb. This could set them back years. Shaking herself mentally Patricia brought herself back to the problem at hand.

"Is there anything else, Doctor Fredericks?"

With a few taps on his PAD, Fredericks changed the image in the holo cube, it displayed the neck of one of the Others. Patricia could just make out a dark image at the base of the skull.

"What… is… that?"

Another few taps of the PAD and the image enlarged. In front of Patricia was a rectangular box approximately two by four by four centimeters with a dark circle on the surface. Fredericks face settled into a puzzled frown.

"To be honest with you, Director, it has us all baffled here. We took samples of it and determined it was made of some type of metallic plastic composite."

It was Patricia's turn to look puzzled. "What do you mean it was made of? It's still there I can see it."

"That's the puzzling bit. According to the tests we ran, the object seems to have suffered a complete melt down and I mean literally. Whatever it was, was subjected to an intense heat source, which destroyed the inner workings of the object but left the flesh and muscle surrounding it completely untouched. Even more inexplicably we found microscopic tunneling along the spinal column and into the brain, all centered on the object."

Fredericks shrugged his shoulders and let out a sigh.

"Our best guess is the Other, this object was retrieved from, suffered from some form of spinal damage and the box was a kind of amplifier for the subject's own thoughts. Researchers have long tried to perfect a similar system to allow prosthetic limbs to be controlled directly by the user but so far they have only had limited success. Perhaps the Others had greater success. The tunneling extends as far as the limbs and vital organs on one side of the object and into what may be the movement control areas of the brain."

"Have you found any more of these objects in the other recovered remains?"

Fredericks shook his head. "Unfortunately all the other remains have been too badly damaged for us to substantiate our conclusions."

Patricia looked at the image for another few moments trying to puzzle out its purpose but nothing came to mind.

"OK, Doctor, type up your report and forward it to my office as soon as you can. I'll send it on to Canberra and we'll see what they can come up with."

Patricia turned on her heel and headed back to her office thoughts of her failure rebounding in her head.

————

Patricia sat at her desk with her head in her hands. How could she have been so wrong? It was more of a statement than a question. Following Fredericks' revelation she had tasked Vince Kealey, her colleague who had worked with her originally to decode the Saiph database, to take her work apart a piece at a time.

Vince had found the mistake quickly. A simple substitution in the decryption algorithm had completely changed the interpretation of a section of the Saiph language. Where the Saiph had indeed experimented with DNA on other worlds millions of years ago, they had, in fact, written the experiment off as a failure. It was not until the Others turned up in the sky, above their home world, they realized something productive had come from their meddling on other worlds. It was this final revelation that had Patricia sitting alone in her office. The Others had not destroyed the Saiph all those millions of years ago. The Others had rained destruction down on the Saiph less than 1000 years ago. A blink of an eye as far the cosmos was concerned.

Patricia thought of all those men and women who had relied on her interpretation of the Saiph database. Those sailors and marines who ventured out into the far reaches of space sure in the knowledge those who had destroyed the Saiph were more than likely dust in cosmic history by now and not actively traveling the space between the stars.

When Valerie Hayes had plucked Patricia out of obscurity and placed her in charge at Stickney Patricia had been young and arrogant. A real fire breather as some of the older researchers had referred to her. Others were not so kind, they wondered who this young upstart, Hayes forced on them, thought she was. Vince had every right to be one of those whose nose was out of joint by Patricia's arrival, instead he sat back and allowed her full rein, helping her when she struggled to cope with researchers who were more senior and encouraging her when she doubted herself.

She felt she had let them all down, Vince, Valerie Hayes, the president and most importantly the men and women who flew amongst the stars. All those who had held faith in her.

Patricia touched a control and her holo cube sparked to life with the face of the duty officer in communications. "Yes, Director?"

Patricia Bath took a deep breath, knowing this would be her last action as director. "Get me a secure link to the Office of the President."

OFFICE OF THE PRESIDENT OF THE TERRAN REPUBLIC - GENEVA - EARTH

The news from Stickney Base had been less of a surprise to some than others Rebecca Coston thought. The military had questioned amongst themselves why the Others technology had not given them an insurmountable edge, but they simply got on with their task and did not count their chickens. Many a politician attempted to lay the blame strictly at the door of the now ex-director of the Linguistics and Cryptology Division at Stickney Base, Doctor Patricia Bath as the media whipped the public into an unnatural fury at the desk jockey who had endangered the lives of those brave sailors and marines. The opportunists had jumped on the bandwagon and the broadcasts were filled with paid mouth pieces spouting their version of the truth and pointing out in retrospect Patricia Bath's mistakes. *Hindsight is a wonderful thing*, thought Rebecca.

Valerie Hayes had pleaded with her to refuse Doctor Bath's resignation but, unfortunately, the political heat was just too much and as much as her old friend liked the youthful Bath, Rebecca, with regret, would accept her resignation with immediate effect.

Not for the first time Rebecca reminded herself how much she hated politics. She genuinely liked Bath it was such a pity. Maybe when the media furore subsided she could quietly kick start her career again.

————

Rebecca turned to face the only other two people in her spacious presidential office, admiring the blue and white rotating ball that was the planet Janus. "So, General Joyce, how are we coming along with the refit of TDF *Ferdinand Magellan*?"

"Exceptionally well," replied Joyce. "The yards at Deimos are expanding as fast as they can and, with the added slips, the builders were able to basically redesign the *Magellan* and employ the modular construction we're beginning to see in all our ship construction. The basic dimensions of the ship have remained the same, 1300 meters long with a beam of 250 meters but we have managed to increase the gross tonnage to 250,000 tonnes. The reduction in size of the Gravity Drive engines is freeing up more space for cargo and a crew of only 130 with 6500 colony personnel. The Admiralty's plan is to have ten of this type of colony ship shuttling between Earth and Janus to enable the colony to be self-sufficient as quickly as possible. The ships would then be available for use, should we discover further suitable colony worlds."

Rebecca gave a small satisfied "Hmm… and when are we likely to deploy?"

Without the need to refer to the PAD in front of him Joyce answered, "The equipment is arriving steadily and being shipped directly into the cargo areas of the *Magellan*. The necessary foodstuffs, seeds and the minutia required to build a startup colony have been in planning and development since the decision to execute this phase of Operation Chrysaor. I estimate they should all be aboard in the next thirty days."

Rebecca gave a nod of approval, "Very impressive, General. That only leaves the trivial issue of personnel."

"If you remember, Madam President, the Joint Chiefs raised the problem of insufficient personnel prior to your decision, which we fully endorsed, to announce the findings of our initial Vanguard surveys. This led to a surge in volunteers for government service, from colonists to the military, and…" Joyce cast his eyes to the ground in a momentary gesture of respect, "with the loss of the *Vasco De Gama*, we expected this initial enthusiasm to dry up. However, the opposite has happened. The ranks of potential colonists and military personnel have continued to swell, to such an extent I have had to make more than a few calls to certain key members of industry to reassure them our automation program to replace skilled workers will bear fruit in the near future."

"Good to hear, General. How is said industry holding up Thomas?" Rebecca addressed the only other person in the room,

"Remarkably well, Madam President," replied the Secretary of Finance, Senator Crothers. "With the increase in construction and the shrinking base of available, experienced personnel, you would think it would leave industry in a bit of a jam. Nevertheless, the promised mass automation is coming online. The various industries have noticed how the machines, in comparison to human personnel, are cheaper to run, never tire, never argue about wages and don't get sick. All in all, the heads of industry are happier now than I have seen them in a long time."

"So, we are on the verge of establishing our first colony." Rebecca looked again at the planet Janus in the holo cube, soon to be the home to thousands, and one day millions, of humans. "Can you gentlemen think of anything else we may have missed which could assist the growth of the colony?"

Senator Crothers cleared his throat. "If I may make a suggestion, Madam President?"

"Go on," permitted Rebecca.

Crothers pointed at the image of Janus. "I have never pretended to be a military man," he said with a slight nod in the direction of Joyce, "but I am a man whose job it has been his whole working life to make things work while making a profit."

"Janus is not about making a profit, Senator. It's about the survival of the human race," interrupted Joyce angrily.

"I understand, General. Nevertheless, humans being humans always perform at their best when there is something in it for them. In the case of the men and women who head our industry – they want profit." Crothers

paused to collect his thoughts, "Our aim is for the colony we propose to establish to be self-sufficient in the shortest time period, but, as it stands at the moment, the government has to pay for everything the colony needs and eventually transports. Our finances are finite in any given year. I have been floating the idea, with certain trusted friends in industry, that the government would be willing to give massive concessions to any cargo line who would be inclined to build ships with Gravity Drives and haul goods to and from Janus. Further, the main contractor at Deimos has suggested, using the new automated construction techniques, he builds a second yard in the Alpha Centauri system, doubling our construction facilities at a stroke and providing redundancy in the event the Others locate our solar system and destroy our only means to mass produce warships." Crothers sat back and waited for the president and Joyce to reply.

"Well," said a very impressed Rebecca, "I see you have given this a lot of thought, Thomas. I have to admit we never thought of this before now. Why? I do not know. This lack of forethought, on my part, smacks of foolishness." Rebecca looked across at Joyce who seemed to be equally impressed.

"Don't take this the wrong way, Senator. But I never thought you had it in you," said Joyce.

Crothers smiled at him, as a teacher to a pupil who had just independently figured out a lesson he had been tutoring for months. "I'll take that as a compliment, General."

Joyce went on. "Admiral Jing raised concerns over us having only one production facility. He has looked at the raw economic data and figured the construction of a separate shipyard for Janus was at least five years away."

"On the contrary, General." Crothers was warming to his subject. "Taking into account industry financed participation, my projection shows we could have a viable, completely self-sufficient colony on Janus within two years."

Crothers' last sentence clinched it for Rebecca. "Well, Senator, it would seem the only thing left for you is to resign."

Crothers looked aghast, stumbling over his words "But… eh… why… Madam President…? Eh… I am only trying to improve the colony's chance of success."

Rebecca paused for a moment. "I understand completely, Senator. However unfortunate, I cannot have you double jobbing as Secretary of Finance *and* Governor of Janus. I accept your resignation forthwith."

Crothers' mouth hung open, like a fish. He wanted to say something but no words were forthcoming.

Joyce stood and stuck out his hand. "Congratulations, Governor!"

CHAPTER FIFTEEN
A New Beginning

JANUS COLONY
ALPHA CENTAURI B - 4.37 LIGHT YEARS FROM EARTH

Thomas Crothers, Governor of Earth's first extra solar system colony of Janus, looked out through the clear steel window of his office on the fourth floor of the Terran Republic building, in the center of the capital of the colony. A capital which by popular demand had been named Witsell after the captain of the TDF *Vasco De Gama* who had sacrificed herself and her crew to save the marines fleeing from the Others during the fighting in 70 Ophiuchi a year before.

Only a year? thought Thomas as he looked out at the bustling streets. The Magellan class colony ships had been shuttling people from Earth as fast as the expanding colony could take them. The current population was now over 1.5 million on just the surface of Janus. In orbit and in the asteroid belt, another 500,000 humans labored to supply the needs of the flourishing colony with its fledgling shipbuilding yards. If the projections were correct, given another year Janus would have a population of five million and be completely self-sufficient.

A descending shuttle caught Thomas' eye as it headed for the landing pads – that would be his visitors. With a sigh, he turned from the window and returned to the waiting, seemingly endless bureaucracy that came with the job, in a vain attempt to empty his inbox before their arrival.

Half an hour later, Thomas stood as the entry chime sounded on his office door. It swung open and allowed Fleet Admiral Jing, newly named Commander of First Fleet in the rapidly expanding Terran Navy, and a vice admiral he did not recognize into the office. The governor walked around his desk to greet the navy men. "Good to see you again, Admiral Jing, and…?"

The unnamed admiral smiled and shook the Thomas' proffered hand. "Vice Admiral Robert Lewis, Governor."

The name was familiar to Thomas and then his memory placed the name, "Of course, Captain of the *James Cook*. A well-deserved promotion if I may say so, Admiral."

"Please don't, Governor," interjected Jing with a chuckle. "Since being appointed my deputy at First Fleet, he has become insufferable. In fact, my trying to get rid of him is what has brought us to Janus."

Thomas indicated a group of comfortable chairs and the three men sat before Thomas asked, "And how do you intend to rid yourself of poor Admiral Lewis?" as he gave Lewis an apologetic look.

Jing pulled a PAD from his case and pressed his thumb against the DNA scanner to activate its secure contents. "It has been noted by many back in Geneva, Governor, Janus is well ahead of schedule and, without sounding like a sycophant, nobody back home is fooling themselves the success is down to anything other than your hard work."

"And many others who have put more blood and sweat into the building of the colony than I, Admiral," added Thomas.

A politician willing to put others before himself? Thought Jing. *How novel!* "Well your combined efforts enabled the TDF to bring forward its schedule by nearly ten months. The shipyards, here in Janus, have reached a level at which the Joint Chiefs believe a percentage of their production may now be dedicated to the production of military hardware."

"What sort of percentage are we talking, Admiral," asked Thomas apprehensively. "We still have a lot of work to do in the asteroid belt and the orbital habitats."

Jing consulted his PAD before answering. "Based on your own figures, we would be looking at switching over twenty-one percent at this stage, growing to thirty-five percent by the end of the year."

Thomas opened his mouth to protest, but Lewis got in first. "Governor, if I could explain?"

"Please do, Admiral Lewis," said Thomas unhappily.

"The speed with which the colony expanded beyond our planning has meant the Joint Chiefs feel the resources of the Sol system are being stretched to provide adequate defenses for both the home system and Janus. And, to be blunt, if you don't start to provide the material to defend yourself, then everything you are building here could be for nothing if the Others come calling."

Thomas paused for thought the admirals had a point. Everything the population of Janus had worked so hard to build could be taken from them if the Others stumbled on Janus. After all, the whole idea of Janus was if, God forbid, some disaster befell Earth, then humankind would be able to continue. Was it not his duty as governor to ensure the safety of the colony?

"My apologies Admirals. Of course, Janus must assume the burden of its own defense. Please continue."

Both admirals let out a small sigh of relief. They had expected a harder fight for the resources they needed.

"Governor," continued Admiral Jing, "it is the intention of the Joint Chiefs to expand the TDF's forces here at Janus. System defense needs to be brought up to par, and to do so the navy intends to build a fleet base here for what will eventually become Second Fleet, and Admiral Lewis has been chosen as its commander."

"Ah," said Thomas with a slight smile toward Admiral Lewis, "This would be Admiral Jing's cunning plan to get rid of you."

Lewis gave a small shrug of his shoulders. "So it would seem, Governor."

"So, down to brass tacks, gentlemen. What sort of forces can I be expected to provide?" stated Thomas, all business now the decision for Janus to build its own units had been taken.

Jing indicated for Lewis to continue. "In broad brush strokes, the first thing we need to establish is a sufficient defensive capability to ensure Janus can fend off any initial attack and buy enough time for forces from First Fleet in the Sol System to respond and come to our assistance. Once I believe our defense units are sufficient to secure Janus, we will switch production over to offensive units, which is where the main power of Second Fleet will be. It gives us the capability to respond to any calls from First Fleet for assistance as well as to go on the attack independently if needed. We plan to initially bring personnel from Earth to form a core of experienced crew for the ships but Janus will be expected to provide what it can."

"I don't see it being a problem, Admiral," said Thomas. "The people are proud of what they have achieved here and will want to protect it and their families who have settled here."

Lewis nodded his understanding. "People will always protect their families and what they have built themselves. We project the mainly automated orbital defenses should be fully operational in six months with the first fleet units operational between twelve and eighteen months from now."

Thomas held a hand up to stop Admiral Lewis "A suggestion, Admiral."

"Of course, Governor." Lewis looked across at Jing. Was the governor going to change his mind in supporting their plan?

"If I were to reduce your percentage of yard production from twenty-one percent to say, eighteen percent, how would this reduction impact on your production of the automated orbital defenses?"

Jing did some quick calculations on his PAD. "It would extend our orbital defense completion by a month or so."

Both admirals sat waiting patiently. The governor appeared deep in thought before his eyes refocused. "If I use the three percent to build additional yard units and build the navy its own dedicated construction facility, it could be incorporated into your fleet base. And means you roll out the first fleet units in eight months."

The admirals regarded Thomas in amazement.

Thomas went on, seemingly ignorant of the admirals' expressions, "Of course you would need to step up your personnel movements, but I'll have a word with the colony construction teams. I'm sure we can sort something out in the short term until your fleet base is up and running. Is there anything else I can do to help?"

Jing shook himself. "No, Governor, everything is covered."

"In that case, I shall organize a meeting with Admiral Lewis and the colony planning board for tomorrow and we can get things rolling." Governor Crothers stood.

The admirals stood and shook hands with a man who had just changed their perceptions of a politician's behavior.

OFFICE OF THE PRESIDENT OF THE TERRAN REPUBLIC - GENEVA - EARTH

Rebecca Coston walked through the entrance of her private conference room stopping the ongoing, quiet conversations as the gathered men and women turned, looking at her expectantly. Rebecca recognized most of those in the room but was surprised to see Edward Munro, Director of the Federal Investigation Bureau, Carol Manning, Secretary of Finance and Edvard Dietel, the Attorney General, present. "Please take your seats," said Rebecca.

Rebecca took her seat at the head of the table. "Ladies and gentlemen, I must assume this is an urgent matter or I would not have agreed to this meeting on such short notice. Would someone like to tell me what is going on?"

General Joyce cleared his throat nervously. "Madam President, as you are no doubt aware, we have been building warships and expanding our military forces as rapidly as possible in the face of the perceived threat from the Others."

"General, I am well aware of this," said Rebecca with some exasperation. "Has something changed that I am unacquainted with, for you to ask for this meeting so urgently?"

Joyce looked across the table at Vice Admiral Wilson, before continuing. "When the decision was made to begin the expansion, I put in place certain measures in the hope of containing any internal or external interference in it." Joyce nodded toward Wilson, "If I may introduce Vice Admiral Elizabeth Wilson, who works directly for me. Her job is to overcome any such obstacles."

Rebecca regarded Wilson. "You mean she's your hatchet man, General," she stated.

Joyce allowed a small smile to appear on his face. "Hatchet man is a fair description, Madam President, and due to Admiral Wilson I asked for this meeting."

Rebecca looked toward Wilson quizzically. "Surely you have not found some obstacle within the military the Chairman of the Joint Chiefs cannot deal with? Surely you do not require presidential intervention?"

"The issue, Madam President," replied Wilson "isn't within the military per se."

Rebecca was becoming a little irritated with all the pussyfooting around, "Please get to the point, Admiral."

"Very well, Madam President. Your Secretary of Defense, Senator Geoffrey Rawson, has been selling contracts for bribes and has been embezzling funds on a huge scale," Wilson said matter-of-factly.

Rebecca stared at the admiral for a few moments. *That weasel!* She thought. *Curse the day I ever agreed to him getting the post!* She took a deep breath and steadied herself before asking. "How much, Admiral, and for how long?"

It did not occur to Wilson the president had not questioned the validity of her claim for a second. "I first had an inkling something wasn't quite right when I compared the costing and output of the yards at Deimos with the yards at Janus. The discrepancy was nearly ten percent per unit, and even though they were using virtually identical equipment Deimos' construction time was fifteen percent longer than at Janus. Now we all know Governor Crothers has a knack for efficiency and cost cutting but the discrepancy was too much to be ignored so, with General Joyce's permission, I began an off the books investigation using outside agencies, investigators from the Federal Investigation Bureau and auditors from the Department of Finance…"

Rebecca was finding it difficult to remain calm. "I shall ask one more time, Admiral. How much and for how long?"

The room became very still. No one present had ever seen President Coston as aggravated as this before.

To her credit, Secretary Manning spoke up. "Madam President, my auditors discovered a trail which leads us to believe Secretary Rawson has been lining his own pockets since his appointment as Secretary of Defense. Our current estimate is approaching eight-three million credits between skimming the budget and bribes."

Rebecca let out a gasp. "Eighty-three million! How the hell did no one notice?"

"When Secretary Rawson took over at Defense, he brought a lot of his own people with him and it would appear many, if not all, are implicated. To be honest, we just have not had the time yet to go over all of their finances. Remember, Madam President, we have been flinging money at Defense hand over fist for the past three years and it would appear, according to Director Munro's people, anyone Rawson couldn't pay off was pushed out of Defense or an excuse was found to sack them."

Rebecca pointed at Director Munro. "I want rid of him! Not tomorrow, not at the end of the day. I mean right now. That man has not only stolen money from the Republic, but by slowing construction of our defenses he has put the lives of the people of the Republic at risk."

Director Munro hesitated. "Are you sure you want this done publicly, Madam President? I could have agents arrest him at his home this evening and give you time to prepare a press statement."

Rebecca fixed him a look to wilt a lesser man. Without taking her eyes from him, she addressed the Attorney General. "Is there enough evidence for a charge of Treason, Edvard?"

The Attorney General struggled to keep his voice calm and level. Treason was a crime which still carried the death penalty within the Republic. "Yes, Madam President. I believe the evidence I have seen is enough to justify the charge of treason."

Rebecca's eyes had not strayed from Director Munro. "Well, Director?"

Director Munro tapped his secure wrist link. "This is Director Munro. Inform the protection detail for Secretary Rawson, on the president's order, they are to secure the secretary immediately and await the arrival of agents from my office. The secretary is to have no contact with any person or access to any electronic system."

Rebecca stood abruptly. "I think that will be all for today, ladies and gentlemen. Thanks to you, I can pretty much guarantee the rest of my day is shot to hell."

As the people gathered in the room began to leave, Rebecca called, "General Joyce, a moment please."

The general halted and returned to stand by his seat at the table. Rebecca indicated for him to retake his seat as she sat herself.

"So, how long have you suspected Rawson?" asked Rebecca in a tired voice.

"Admiral Wilson came to me about a year ago with her concerns and I trusted her instincts enough to let her run with the investigation," replied Joyce.

"And you didn't trust me enough to let me know of your suspicions?"

"Madam President, with all due respect," replied Joyce, "when Admiral Wilson came to me to tell me she suspected the Secretary of Defense, a secretary you had appointed, what would you have done?"

For the first time in the day, Rebecca smiled wryly. "I would have trusted no one, General. You did the right thing. My problem now is when this scandal breaks, who will the people trust enough to be Secretary of Defense? And how quickly can we undo the damage done to our military buildup caused by Rawson?"

Joyce sat back in his chair and ran the numbers in his head for a few seconds, "The damage caused is mainly in production schedules at Deimos. The efficiency of the Janus yards goes part way to offsetting the delays, in fact, if we were to introduce the same procedures Janus employs at Deimos, we should be back on schedule within the year."

At least there is some good news, thought Rebecca.

"As far as a new Secretary of Defense goes, well, who takes up the post is a political issue, Madam President."

Rebecca knew the general was right. The people had to have confidence in its political leadership. Ever since the threat from the Others had become known, the citizens of the Republic had recognized their duty and had joined the military in their millions. They had complete faith in the generals and admirals to do their duty. The politicians will be distrusted, unless... An idea came to Rebecca.

"So, General, how goes the senior officer selection boards?" Rebecca asked conversationally.

Joyce, somewhat thrown by the president's sudden change of tone, could smell something brewing. "Ah, very well, Madam President. The board, run by Admiral Helset, has appointed the required number of senior officers, and the promotion requirements for further advancement of junior officers is in place and working well." With a small chuckle, Joyce carried on. "To be honest with you, it's working so well the admiral may find himself out of a job soon."

As soon as he said it, Joyce could have kicked himself. The crocodile smile spreading across the president's face told him he had just been played.

Rebecca knew Joyce now realized what was going on, but carried on with the charade regardless. It was not every day you got one over on the Chairman of the Joint Chiefs, "Oh well, I suppose it rests with you to let Admiral Helset know he is once again facing retirement."

Joyce was virtually squirming in his seat. Rebecca could have sworn he was mumbling a few choice words. "Yes, Madam President. I suppose that duty does fall on me. Perhaps you could suggest some gainful employment for him?"

With difficulty in keeping a straight face Rebecca replied, "I believe the position of Secretary of Defense has just become vacant."

OFFICE OF THE SECRETARY OF DEFENSE - GENEVA - EARTH

Secretary Olaf Helset sat behind his desk in the office, his for the past month, looking across at General Joyce and Admirals Jing and Vadis. Men he had served alongside for more than thirty years. "Well, tell me the bad news."

Joyce spoke for the military men present, "Well, Admiral... apologies, Mr. Secretary!"

Secretary Helset looked down his barrel like finger, now pointed at the Chairman of the Joint Chiefs. "You, Mr. Chairman, serve at the pleasure of the president, and in this room I act in her stead. If you continue in your disrespectful tone, I shall summon your own marines and have you escorted from here and keel hauled until you begin to show the degree of respect I require," before breaking into a large grin. "Now get on with it, Keyton."

Joyce bowed deeply at the waist. "Of course, your majesty. Although there is significant damage to production, it is repairable. And with the able assistance of men lent to us by Governor Crothers, we are nearly back on track."

Joyce regarded the display on his secure PAD for a moment then touched a control and a holo cube sprang into life, he began to explain what he saw. "As you can see, Mr. Secretary, our current strength is broken into three areas, the first of those being planetary defense." The display changed to show Earth and Janus side by side. "Over the past three years, our priority has been planetary defense of, firstly, Earth and secondly, Janus. As it has expanded, so have our defenses there. The Army has expanded and been shaped into a heavily armored reaction force to respond to any threat of actual planetary invasion. The Army also has responsibility for the ground based Planetary Defense Centers." Pin pricks, spread out over Earth and Janus, became animated on the display. "Installations scattered around the surface of both planets are armed with particle weapons and High Velocity Missiles. They can reach out to geosynchronous orbit."

The display changed. This time it showed two seemingly innocuous boxes. The box on the left, on closer inspection, consisted of an L shaped body on which was a pallet with nine square openings on one end. The main body had Laser Area Denial clusters on each of its four sides. The right hand box also displayed had the same L shaped body, but the pallet attached to it had only a single round protuberance set at its far end.

Joyce indicated to the first box. "Mr. Secretary, what you see here is a multi-functional disposable point defense platform. We call it Viper. The left hand Viper is armed with nine HVMs, each with a megaton nuclear warhead. The Viper on the right is armed with a single grazer with an integrated power supply. It's good for 100 shots. Each Viper, as you can see, has its own Laser Area Denial System for its own defense and can be controlled by a local Planetary Defense Center or it can be allowed independent action within a given engagement zone."

Helset let out a low whistle, "A lot of firepower, Keyton."

"Yes, sir," agreed Joyce. "Combined with the Planetary Defense Centers it gives us a layered defense capability with the ability to engage any ship, in theory, as far as it can be detected."

"In theory, Keyton?" asked Helset.

"Yes, sir. As you know, the HVMs have a limited amount of fuel. They can boost only so far and change direction only so many times until they exhaust their onboard fuel supply, then they either carry on in the direction they were traveling or self-destruct. The particle weapons have, in theory, an unlimited range. In reality, the range is restricted by the fact we have to be able to detect a target for our weapons systems to engage it."

Olaf could see the problem. "Am I to assume, then, you have a solution, Keyton?"

The holo cube image changed. Now, there was a third platform. The same L shaped body but this time the box on the pallet had an array of antennas protruding from it. "We call this Sherlock, outfitted with our best detection and target identification systems, it can update the Planetary Defense Centers or cross deck its information directly to the Viper units."

Olaf was suitably impressed. "So would it be safe to say Earth and Janus have enough of these units to defend against the Others tactic of bombardment?"

Joyce took a moment to look at the two admirals with him. "Mr. Secretary, nothing is a sure bet, but with what we have seen of the Others' tactics, we consider the Viper units to be our best defensive strategy."

Olaf held Keyton's eye for a moment. "Very well, Keyton. If it is the considered opinion of the Joint Chiefs. How long before you can begin deploying them to protect our habitats throughout the Solar and Janus systems?"

"Production of the required Viper units is in full swing." Keyton consulted his PAD briefly. "At current rates of production, another six months should be enough to provide sufficient cover for any strategically valuable asset in both systems, Mr. Secretary."

Satisfied Earth and Janus were adequately protected from any immediate danger, Olaf turned to Jing, "So, Ai. How goes things with First Fleet?"

Keyton turned his PAD over to the admiral who, with a few touches of the controls, changed the display in the holo cube.

"Mr. Secretary, on the display is the completed Order of Battle for First Fleet. The fleet will be broken into five parts, three battle forces, BatFor 1, 2 and 3. Each BatFor will consist of three battleships, four heavy cruisers, two light cruisers and ten destroyers. A Marine assault division of some 19000 marines consisting of four regiments, a tank battalion, a reconnaissance battalion, two light armored reconnaissance battalions, two combat engineer battalions and one orbital assault battalion. The entire division is lifted in ten assault ships and has a dedicated light cruiser and destroyer escort. And, as of zero eight hundred hours this morning, First Fleet is active."

"And what of Second Fleet, Ai?" asked Olaf.

"Admiral Lewis assures me Second Fleet, minus its marine contingent – who are still forming up on Earth and awaiting transport to Janus – will be up to strength within the next twenty-eight days."

Helset gave Ai a knowing look as he nodded slowly. "Very impressive work, gentlemen. Very impressive indeed. But there is something else, isn't there?" pointing a lazy finger at Vadis. "Otherwise, Aleksandr wouldn't be here, would he now?"

Vadis smiled slightly. "We never could get anything past you, sir."

Olaf regarded the three senior officers as a disproving schoolteacher. "No you couldn't could you? So let me guess. You got Keyton here to wax lyrical about the strength of the defenses and then poor Ai about how First Fleet has been activated and then how Second Fleet will be activated within the month, because you have some cunning plan up your sleeve and you want me to take it to the president for approval."

Vadis leaned forward in his seat and said flatly, "We want to go back to Messier 54 and 31 Aquilae."

Olaf did not even flinch. "I was beginning to wonder when you were going to ask."

CHAPTER SIXTEEN
In to the Fire

TDF *JACQUES CARTIER*- 31 AQUILAE

Commodore Papadomas sat in his chair on the bridge of TDF *Jacques Cartier* and regarded the holo cube to his front, it displayed three blue icons representing his survey flotilla.

A smile crossed his lips as he realized he considered the Vanguard survey ships as his. TDF *Jacques Cartier*, TDF *James Cook* and TDF *Henry Hudson* had been dispatched to 31 Aquilae under the newly promoted Commodore's command. His mission, as outlined by the Joint Chiefs was simple enough: enter the system and deploy surveillance platforms to observe not only the pre industrialized civilization inhabiting Planet III (or as some researcher had dubbed it, Garunda, apparently after the Hindu name for this constellation), but to deploy a shell of surveillance platforms around the system looking outwards. Research and Development assured him each of these new style surveillance platforms could detect the Others' Alcubierre drive out to a distance of a light year.

He turned to the duty communications officer. "Please signal the *James Cook* and the *Henry Hudson* I am beginning deployment of the planetary surveillance platform and they may begin their own deployments when ready and we shall meet them at the rendezvous point in three days."

The young lieutenant at communications replied, "Aye-aye, sir," without turning around.

"Commander Ranking, the bridge is yours. I'll be in biosciences if you need me." Without waiting for a reply, Papadomas got up from his chair and headed for biosciences to see for himself the initial take from the planetary surveillance platform, which they all hoped, would bring them a greater understanding of the life on Garunda.

TDF *HENRY HUDSON* - 31 AQUILAE

Captain Bill Talbot was enjoying a late lunch alone in his small cabin when the urgent chiming from the intercom demanded his attention. Bill reached over and activated the small holo cube, which sprang to life with the head and shoulders of his new XO, Commander Euan Campbell. "Problem, XO?"

The XO was concise and to the point. "Captain, approximately ten minutes ago platform twelve picked up indications of an Alcubierre drive. I ordered platforms nine and eleven re tasked to the same area. They confirm not one, but six drive sources headed for this system. Tactical identifies them as the Others. They have the same drive signature as those designated Buzzard class from 70 Ophiuchi."

"ETA, XO?" asked Bill.

The XO looked down at something out of the pickup's range, then back at Bill. "At current rate of advance Tactical estimates fourteen hours till they enter the system."

Bill's mind began to race. "OK, this is what I want to happen: download all our current data to four courier drones. Dispatch two to First Fleet and two to Second Fleet and launch when ready."

Bill could see his XO typing furiously and then felt a small lurch as the drone bays beneath the *Henry Hudson* came open and the four drones where launched.

The XO looked up. "Drones away, sir."

"Good. Is the *James Cook* still within whisker range?"

Without needing to check, the XO was able to answer, "Negative, sir. They completed the nearest portion of the surveillance shell a few hours ago and have moved to their next deployment area."

Bill thought through his options for a moment. "Very well, launch a drone to the *James Cook* and one to the *Jacques Cartier*. Inform them it is my intention to go to silent running and continue to monitor the surveillance platforms in real time for as long as I remain undetected by the Others, unless the Commodore orders otherwise. Then I want the crew placed on mandatory rest and get them all fed and watered XO. The next few hours could be tricky."

In the holo cube, Euan Campbell nodded his agreement. "Understood, sir. I'll get right on it."

"That order applies to you too, XO. I'll come up and relieve you in two hours," said Bill.

"Aye-aye, sir," acknowledged the XO.

As Bill cut the link, he wondered how the authorities back on Earth would react to the news of the Others heading for 31 Aquilae.

OFFICE OF THE PRESIDENT OF THE TERRAN REPUBLIC - GENEVA - EARTH

It was the early hours in Geneva when one of her aides wakened Rebecca Coston. The Secretary of Defense and the Chairman of the Joint Chiefs were on a secure link requesting to speak with her urgently.

In all her time as President, not once had she answered a call with such a feeling of dread as she activated the link, the faces of Secretary Helset and General Joyce appeared on the split screen in front of her. Rebecca did not like the look of worry etched on both men's faces. "Gentlemen, by the hour of the day I take it this is not a social call."

Olaf Helset shook his head slowly. "No, Madam President I'm afraid not. An hour ago First Fleet received a courier drone from the Vanguard survey ship, TDF *Henry Hudson* which, as you are aware, along with TDF *James Cook* and TDF *Jacques Cartier*, was tasked to the 31 Aquilae system to place surveillance platforms around the planet now known as Garunda and a detection shell around the system."

Rebecca's sense of dread deepened. "What have they found, Olaf?"

"Madam President, there are six Buzzard class Others' ships headed for the system. The captain of the *Henry Hudson* stated his intention was to remain on station and monitor their approach. Commodore Papadomas confirmed this decision in a second drone received by First Fleet fifteen minutes later. I estimate the Buzzard's arrival at just over twelve hours."

Both men waited patiently as Rebecca fought her drowsiness to understand the implications of this information. After a few seconds, the president asked, "Do we have any idea of their intentions, Olaf?"

Olaf shook his head and a frown appeared on his forehead. "Impossible to tell, Madam President. They could be coming to survey the system as we have done. On the other hand, I would remind you what happened to the Saiph home world. The Others arrived in orbit without a word and began to bombard the planet. The civilization on Garunda are pre industrial revolution." Olaf shrugged his shoulders. "They would have no defense against an orbital bombardment."

"What are our options, Olaf?" asked Rebecca.

The Secretary of Defense shifted in his seat and replied in a flat, neutral tone. "Option one, we sit back and allow the Others to enter the system and, if their plan is to carry out a survey, our ships sit in stealth and get as much intelligence about their tactics as possible." Olaf continued, his face contorting as if he had eaten something particularly distasteful. "Option two, they enter the system and begin to bombard Garunda and we watch the extinction of a civilization."

In her mind's eye, Rebecca could imagine the inhabitants of Garunda going about their business on just another day as, without warning, a fiery rain of destruction begins to fall on their homes and their lives are cut short. Rebecca cleared the images from her mind as she looked back at Olaf with steel in her eyes. "Not good enough, Olaf. I will not stand by and allow the extermination of an entire race. I want another option."

Olaf gave the only other answer he had. "We intervene, Madam President."

Rebecca regarded her two closest military advisers and felt the weight of an important decision bearing down on her. Taking a deep breath, she asked, "How?"

Joyce broke his silence. Until now, he had said nothing to allow his lord and masters to come to the decision he knew in his heart was the only viable one. "BatFor 1 is ready for immediate deployment, as is BatFor 3 from the Janus system if required. It is my recommendation that the deployment of one battleship force is required in this particular scenario."

Rebecca was well aware a deployment of human forces could well be a slippery slope. "And what would be their orders?"

"BatFor 1 would deploy to the edge of the system and observe the Others. They would only move to intervene if they believed the Others were about to attack the planet. If the Others simply carry out a survey mission and then leave, BatFor 1 would return to its base."

Rebecca had once spoken to her predecessor, President McMullen, about his decision to keep the existence of Operation Minerva secret. He remarked it was not the fact he kept Minerva a secret that was the hard part, it was the fact he realised when he made the decision it was his and his alone. President McMullen had told Coston about another leader from the time before the wars who had had a sign on their office desk, which read "The Buck Stops Here." Now President Coston knew what he had meant.

"Very well, General. Deploy your forces."

TDF *CARTAGENA* - 31 AQUILAE

From the Flag Bridge, Rear Admiral John Radford looked at the holo cube, which displayed the 31 Aquilae system before him. The blue icons of BatFor 1, First Fleet Terran Defense Force surrounded his Nemesis class battleship, TDF *Cartagena*, in a layered globe. Destroyers formed the outer shell, cruisers a mid-layer and the battleships at the heart.

Compared to John's last command, the Vanguard class survey ship TDF *Henry Hudson*, TDF *Cartagena* was nothing less than a monster. The Nemesis class battleship had been designed with only one thought in mind, to defeat anything the Others had so far fielded in a toe-to-toe stand up fight.

It was 980 meters long, 120 meters at the beam and weighed in at 52000 tonnes. Designed to close with, destroy and not hide from the enemy, the *Nemesis* utilized the most efficient particle weapons, grazers and missiles, which humans, using Saiph technology, could devise. The *Cartagena* was not alone. BatFor 1 comprised of a further two Nemesis battleships, *Lagos Bay* and the *Fort Royal*, four Vulcan class heavy cruisers, two Talos class light cruisers and ten Agis class destroyers. For this mission, BatFor 1's marine element was not required.

As John continued to watch his display, it split and the face of his flag captain, Joshua Ward, appeared.

"Admiral, I see we have customers," said Ward grimly.

In the display, the red icons of the Others' six ships moved past the outer surveillance shell in three groups of two ship formations and the lonely blue icon representing the *Henry Hudson*. "Well, Captain, there's the first good news of the day. The Others have either not detected or have chosen to ignore the *Henry Hudson*. The bad news is the Buzzards are still making a best time course for Garunda." Without taking his eyes from the display, John called, "Tactical, estimated time till the Buzzards reach Garunda?"

The lieutenant at Tactical checked her readouts before answering. "Current rate of advance would put Buzzard One's arrival in orbit around the planet in fifty minutes, Admiral."

The clock is ticking, thought John. "Project phase line Trafalgar onto the tactical display and give me an ETA for the Buzzards breaching the line."

A red globe superimposed itself around Garunda. Phase line Trafalgar – an imaginary sphere, which was the scientists' best guess using references from the Saiph database at the maximum of the Buzzards' planetary bombardment range. To John it marked his decision point.

"Forty-five minutes till phase line Trafalgar is breached by Buzzard One," called the lieutenant at Tactical.

John thought this could be the longest forty-five minutes of his life. With a voice calmer than he felt, John ordered, "Communications, signal to the fleet: All ships to battle stations."

John looked back to his display and the waiting face of Captain Ward, "Captain, I believe I may have some business for you shortly."

———

All conversation on the flag bridge of the *Cartagena* slowly tailed off as Buzzard One inexorably closed on phase line Trafalgar. John found himself staring intently at his tactical display. The Buzzards had retained their three two ship formations as they closed with Garunda. Then it happened: the leading Buzzard passed the red line.

"Phase line Trafalgar breached by Buzzard One, Admiral!" came the confirmation from Tactical.

Now we find out if all our hard work pays off, thought John as he gripped the sides of his chair that little bit harder. "Communications, signal to fleet: We will go with ops plan Nelson Two."

The communications officer transmitted the pre-arranged signal. Just as quickly, the ships of the fleet replied. "Fleet acknowledges Admiral. Nelson Two on your command."

John waited a heartbeat before ordering, "Execute!"

BatFor 1, Terran Defense Force disappeared from the outskirts of 31 Aquilae only to reappear a split second later barely 1000 kilometers from the leading two ship Buzzard formation.

John leaned forward and quickly studied his tactical display. BatFor 1 had reemerged from fold space, not in the globe it had entered in, but now arrayed in a conical formation with the three battleships at the point of the cone and the cruisers spreading out on the flanks. Of the destroyers, there was no sign. John shifted his eyes closer to the planet and was relieved to see the blue icons of the destroyers forming up as a shield between the Buzzards and the planet. They were John's last line of defense against any missiles fired at the planet, which leaked past his cruisers.

Well, phase one worked, thought John. The micro jump first performed by the *Vasco De Gama* in 70 Ophiuchi to get into a firing position behind another Buzzard had been repeatedly practiced as the tactical advantage it gave was now fully recognized.

Now for phase two. Without another word of command from John, all three Terran battleships fired their main grazer armament. The targeted Buzzards had no time to react: by the time their light speed sensors told them BatFor 1 was there, the light speed grazers were only seconds behind. As John watched, the grazers of *Cartagena* and *Lagos Bay* (four of the heaviest grazers ever mounted on a Terran ship) struck the flank of Buzzard One. They passed through the battle armor like it wasn't even there, taking off the rear third of Buzzard One and leaving the remaining two thirds to begin a steady tumbling motion in the same general direction the Buzzard had been originally headed on.

"Communications! Inform the nearest cruisers to engage what remains of Buzzard One with HVMs," ordered John without taking his eyes from his display. Damn! Buzzard Two had been lucky, only one of the grazers from *Fort Royal* impacted, but the bow of the Buzzard was now an expanding ball of plasma.

The gunners of Buzzard Two were quick off the mark and Q laser fire began hitting the armored hull of the *Fort Royal*. But this was what the Nemesis class of battleship had been designed for. *Fort Royal* shrugged off the hits as her forward particle cannon opened fire and she maneuvered to bring her grazers bear. As the particle cannon impacted on Buzzard Two, John saw in his display Buzzards Three and Four slowed to allow Buzzards Five and Six to catch up, and their formation was changing.

John's Tactical officer saw it too. "Admiral, aspect change of the remaining Buzzards. They're maneuvering broadside onto us, I would suggest to deploy missiles and to clear as many weapons as possible to engage us."

As the Tactical officer finished, a fresh set of red icons appeared on the display and began speeding in the direction of the Terran ships.

The Tactical officer reacted immediately. "Vampire, Vampire. Enemy missile release. The fleet now has weapons free for anti-missile assets. The cruisers are engaging."

Compared to the near light speed grazers and particle weapons, missiles might seem slow, but the anti-ship HVMs BatFor 1 carried moved at 60000 kilometers per hour and had a powered range of 300,000 kilometers. They carried either a nuclear or a conventional warhead controlled from the firing ship or by the missile's onboard computer. The anti-missile HVMs could accelerate up to 100,000 kilometers per hour but had a much shorter range, only 1000 kilometers. Again, they could carry either nuclear or conventional warheads controlled by the firing ship or onboard computers.

John watched the display as a shoal of anti-missile missiles flew from the cruisers of BatFor 1 as the battleships held their missiles in reserve. John knew this was the first major engagement between the Others and the Terran Defense Force and, although John would have loved to engage with everything at his disposal, this fight was a chance to learn how effective the Terran tactics and weaponry were, so, despite himself, John held back from committing his battleships fully.

"Second missile separation from the Buzzards," came the call from Tactical. "Fewer in number this time but with a larger energy reading."

As John continued to watch the battle develop, Q lasers continued to strike out at *Fort Royal*, but the Nemesis battleship seemed unaffected by the strikes. *The Fort Royal's* particle cannon were taking large bites out of Buzzard Two and as the *Fort Royal's* grazers came to bear, they fired in tandem, striking the Buzzard dead center. With a blinding flash, the Buzzard simply ceased to exist. Where a 220,000 tonnes starship had once been, there was now only an expanding cloud of debris.

Out of the corner of his eye, John saw the Tactical officer, whose fingers had been flying over his controls throughout the battle, as he coordinated the actions of the whole of BatFor 1, had paused and was looking intently at his repeater display. "Problem, Commander?"

In reply, the second volley of missiles from the Buzzards lit up in John's display. The commander at Tactical spun his chair to face John with a look of puzzlement on his face. "Sir, it appears this second volley of missiles, our count is twenty from each Buzzard, are on course to clear our engagement envelope. They won't come anywhere near our ships."

John looked again at the display, trying to discern the enemy's intention. Why fire sixty missiles in the middle of a firefight when all sixty head off at a tangent from the enemy? John started and sat bolt upright in his seat hoping to God he was wrong. "Tactical! Have the destroyer screen around Garunda shadow the trajectory of the second wave of missiles. I believe they're not aimed at us at all – they're going for the planet! They're just completing a dog leg course to avoid us intercepting them."

The battle continued to rage around John. His battleships had, so far, taken only minor damage, and John could feel a growing sense of confidence emanating from the flag bridge. The Others did not appear to have an answer to the heavy grazers mounted on the TDF ships, and the particle cannon, although not as effective, was still able to inflict significant damage. Anti-missile HVMs from the cruiser screen easily defeated the missiles fired at BatFor 1. John involuntarily relaxed a little in his seat. Maybe this was not going to turn out so badly after all. A call from Tactical changed his mind in an instant.

"Aspect change on the second flight of missiles we've been tracking." The commander paused checking his data. "Looks like you were right, Admiral. The missiles have changed course, and are now heading for the planet and are increasing speed. The enemy missiles are now traveling at 75000 kilometers per hour."

Damn! Thought John as his eyes moved across the display to focus on the missiles closing with Garunda. The missiles had formed into three distinct waves. The first wave consisted of thirty missiles, followed by two further waves of twenty missiles each.

John looked at the blue icons of his ten Agis class destroyers, which had interposed themselves between the oncoming missiles and the planet. The Agis class were designed as fleet protection ships. They mounted a complex Fire Control system, which allowed them to integrate their defensive fire with other ships. Their firepower was distinctly skewed toward the role of long-range anti-missile pickets specifically tasked to kill any missile threat to the fleet. Were John's ten Agis ships going to be enough against sixty incoming missiles?

John ran a quick scenario through his head, then turned to his tactical officer, "Tactical, re task the cruisers closest to the enemy missiles. I know it's a long shot and the chances of hits are minimal, but they are to engage the enemy missiles heading for Garunda with their particle cannon. I think the Agis can do with all the help they can get."

On John's display, he saw the re tasked cruisers shift position slightly to bring their weapons to bear on the new threat, and then all hell broke loose.

Three of the Buzzards slipped into a tight triangle formation and slowed noticeably. Before John or anyone else on the flag bridge could react, a bright blue beam shot out of the bow of each of the Buzzards and all three beams connected with the *Lagos Bay*. The sidebars on John's display had difficulty keeping up with the thermal blooming recorded from the battleship.

There was a stunned silence on the flag bridge. In the main holo cube, the blue icon representing the *Lagos Bay* changed to a blinking red, after only a moment, the red held solid. The *Lagos Bay* was gone… along with 2000 humans.

John shook himself. He was still in a firefight and the Buzzards were lining up for another shot, "Tactical, *Fort Royal* and the heavy cruisers are to concentrate fire on a single Buzzard. I want *Cartagena* and the light cruisers to swing around for a flanking shot. Let's give them two distinct targets and see if we can't split their firepower."

As BatFor 1 maneuvered to come at the Buzzards from two sides, the first wave of missiles headed for Garunda were engaged by the Terran destroyers in their desperate attempt to stop them reaching the planet. The command and control of the Agis ships was second to none: enemy missiles began to fall victim to coordinated anti-missile fire. The first wave was reduced to just eleven survivors. The Others sprang their next surprise.

At a range of only 50000 kilometers from the Agis destroyers, all the remaining eleven missiles detonated. A single bomb pumped x-ray laser shot from the nose of each missile and impacted on an Agis. Each x-ray laser beam was barely ten centimeters in diameter. It struck the hull of an Agis and blew chunks off the ablative armor where it hit a weak point. It penetrated deep into the core of the ship, destroying everything it touched until it reached the outer hull on the opposite side of the ship, where the armored hull halted its deadly path.

Chance is a fickle thing. Of the eleven surviving x-ray lasers targeting the Terran destroyer's, six shots were clean misses. TDF *Conquerant* and *Venomous* took one hit a piece, causing minor damage, but TDF *Oberon* was struck by three: one penetrated her forward missile magazine. The result was immediate and catastrophic. Megaton range nuclear weapons exploded before the crew of *Oberon* had an inkling something was wrong. *Oberon* died, along with 250 of her crew, in all-consuming nuclear fire.

Oberon's sister ships could not spare the time to mourn her passing as the dispassionate computers compensated for the hole left in the anti-missile net by *Oberon*'s passing. The second wave of missiles was upon the destroyers, the space around them filled with HVMs, particle beams, and laser defense cluster fire as computers on board the destroyers took over from their human operators – for only they were quick enough to prioritize and engage targets as the Others' missiles swept over the little destroyers.

The third wave arrived quickly on the heels of the second. Space filled with the defensive fire of the nine remaining Agis destroyers as they struggled to cope with the onslaught. TDF *Venomous* found itself rocked to the frame by the explosion of a fifty-megaton missile as it died under the fire of one of the *Venomous*' laser defense clusters. The shock caused the command and control system to go off line for a fraction of a second, and yet more time was lost as the system re booted itself. It was enough. Two of the Others' missiles made it cleanly past the destroyers and began their final plunge toward the surface of Garunda.

A shout from Tactical alerted John to the impending destruction on Garunda. "Leakers! We have leakers. At least two missiles moving beyond the engagement range of the destroyer screen and headed for the planet surface. Time to impact two minutes."

John knew in his heart that he could do nothing to stop the two remaining Others' missiles. He could only pray whatever their target, it was a thinly populated one and the attack resulted in minimal casualties.

John pulled himself back to his current predicament – the remaining Buzzards. *Fort Royal* and the heavy cruisers succeeded in destroying another of the Buzzards from the group of three that had killed the *Lagos Bay*. From the readings on his display, it appeared they had badly damaged another. That left only two to deal with. The remaining Buzzard from the three-ship formation and the single Buzzard that had, so far, hung back from the main battle.

As the *Cartagena* and her two Talos light cruiser escorts swung around, it brought the Buzzard broadside onto the *Cartagena*'s grazer. As John watched, the grazer fired, striking the Buzzard amid ship and cutting it cleanly in half. The smaller grazers mounted on the two Talos light cruisers fired, and the remains of the Buzzard were wiped from space.

John was staring intently at his tactical display, plotting his next move, when the icon for the Agis destroyer TDF *Dagger* vanished, only to reappear virtually touching the planet Garunda. It hung there for a few seconds before again disappearing and reappearing in almost the exact location within the tactical display from which it had vanished. John rubbed his eyes quickly, it must have been a brief fault. Dismissing it, John still had the last Buzzard to worry about.

"Aspect change on Buzzard Six, Admiral!" called the Tactical officer. "She's reversed course and is moving away."

John's reaction was immediate. "Communications! Signal all ships: Engage the remaining Buzzard immediately." The information the Buzzard contained was priceless. The Others had already witnessed the effectiveness of not only the Terran weapons but of their own weapons on the Terran ships. John had to stop this precious knowledge from getting back to them.

The commander at Tactical was fully engrossed in his display as he reported to John, "Direct hit on the rear quarter of Buzzard Six Admiral. Her speed is dropping, looks like complete engine failure."

The Others' ship was dead in space and John paused for a moment with his steepled fingers in front of him. He realized a golden opportunity presented itself. It would have to wait though for the time being – the Other's ship was not going anywhere any time soon.

John regarded the floating image of Garunda in the tactical display and felt the heavy burden of responsibility weigh on his shoulders. He wondered at the destruction caused by the two surviving missiles that had somehow avoided the destroyers' desperate attempts to protect the planet.

"Communications! Signal the destroyers to move into low orbit and compile a damage assessment of Garunda."

The commander at Tactical turned to John with a wide smile on his face. "The missiles didn't impact the planet, Admiral."

John looked at him incredulously as he felt the weight lift from his shoulders. "Explain, Commander,"

"Sir, on his own initiative Captain Engel carried out a micro fold and placed TDF *Dagger* just outside the upper atmosphere of Garunda where he proceeded to engage and destroy the two remaining missiles before returning to his place in the destroyer screen."

To say John was astonished by one of the gutsiest maneuvers he had ever heard of was an understatement. It would only have taken the slightest of miscalculations to place Engel and his ship in the atmosphere of the planet – no place for a ship designed to be operated in space. Yeah… gutsy was the word.

"Communications! Signal to *Dagger*: You and your crew have the personal thanks of the fleet commander for your actions this day."

John returned to his display. His fingers called up a more detailed image of the Buzzard and an idea began to take shape in his head. "Tactical. Have you enough data on the Buzzard to ensure you cleanly disable her engines permanently and identify all her exterior weaponry?"

The commander at Tactical turned slowly in his chair as he began to understand what his admiral was asking of him. "Sir, would I be right in assuming you wish to ensure Buzzard Six remains dead in space and you wish me to remove her ability to fire upon us but you don't want me to destroy her?"

John smiled and pointed a finger in his direction. "I believe, Commander, you may have read my mind."

The Tactical officer frowned as he thought over the complex task Radford had set him. "I can certainly use surgical strikes from our particle weapons to do as you want Admiral. But if I may ask, why?"

John's smile broadened as he turned back to the image of the Others ship. "Because, Commander, I intend assaulting that ship with marines and taking it intact."

As the battle raged around Garunda, a small surveillance platform sitting motionless high above the ecliptic plane and identical to that found around Planet V used its passive sensors to record the unfolding events and safely store them away. Its internal clock told it to expect the signal to download its take to the next visiting ship in just over three months.

CHAPTER SEVENTEEN

Boarding Action

TDF *CARTAGENA* - 31 AQUILAE

To John Radford's surprise, his request for marine support to carry out a boarding action of the remaining Buzzard was answered within the hour by the appearance of the marine assault ship TDF *Saint Nazarene.*

Based on the Vulcan class heavy cruiser TDF *Saint Nazarene* was an Excalibur class assault ship, carrying little in the way of offensive armament she relied on her extra armor to survive in battle. What she did carry was a marine assault battalion of 510 fighting men and women. Ten Buffalo assault shuttles to carry twenty wraith suited marines into a hot landing zone. Five heavy lift Gigant shuttles to carry the marines' heavy equipment and five Reapers to provide close air support on a planet's surface. The Reapers were a small, two man, highly maneuverable and lethal craft equipped with rapid-fire plasma cannon and HVMs. Overall, *Saint Nazarene* carried everything a marine battalion needed to carry out independent actions like those that the one John had in mind.

"*Saint Nazarene* is hailing us, Admiral."

"Put her through, Lieutenant," replied John as he spun his chair to face his personal holo cube. John felt his face break into a grin as the smiling face of Alec Murray appeared.

"Well, well, well. Look what the cat dragged in. Good to see you, Alec. I see you didn't waste any time getting here."

Alec shrugged his shoulders in his typically nonchalant manner.

"I hear the navy couldn't finish the job without us marines coming to the rescue… again."

John let out a short snort of laughter before getting straight to the point.

"That Buzzard out there could be a wealth of intelligence Alec. Just the chance to get our hands on one of their ships, a look at their technology. Maybe even the opportunity to secure their navigational data, find out where they come from and the extent of the area under their control. It could lend us insight into what we are facing in this war."

John's voice took on a somber tone. "And make no mistake, Alec, this is a war now. We may have won today but we have no idea of what we truly face."

In the holo cube Alec's life like image nodded its head in understanding.

"Time is of the essence here, Alec, the Others have a two-hour head start and if I were in command of their ship I would demolish anything and everything I thought useful to an enemy. We must get aboard that Buzzard and secure as much as we can before they destroy it."

John paused and Alec saw a frown appear on his friend's brow. "To be honest with you, Alec, I don't understand why they haven't abandoned ship and scuttled her already."

"It occurred to my planning team as well Admiral. We came up with only two options: one - for whatever reason they can't scuttle her or…" any trace of a smile left Alec's face, "two - they're waiting for us to board her, then scuttle her and take us with them."

Taking a breath John looked resolutely into the disembodied face of his friend, before he gave the order he knew could be condemning Alec and his marines to death.

"It's a risk we have to take, Alec. The prize is simply too big to pass up."

From the holo cube, Alec's eyes fastened on John. It was not the first time John had sent men and women under his command into danger and Alec knew his friend would not do it lightly.

"You of course have my full support for your plan, Alec…" the grin slowly returned to John's face. "You do have a plan don't you?"

This time it was Alec's turn to let out a short laugh. "It may not be pretty but I reckon it will do the job." Alec's gaze flicked out of the holo cube's field of view for a moment before returning to fix on John. "My marines are boarding the shuttles now. We launch in ten minutes."

"Good luck, Alec."

With a quick nod from Alec, the connection terminated. John sat back in his chair and quietly said a prayer for the marines.

———

Aboard his command shuttle, Alec Murray remained outwardly calm. To any observer everything was under control. The operation will run as smoothly as a Swiss watch… Alec reassured himself, so why was his stomach doing flip-flops and his brain running at a thousand miles per hour?

"Five minutes 'til contact, Colonel." The warm, honeyed southern accent of the female marine pilot called as if it was just another training flight.

Alec pulled up a real time flight plot on his Wraith suit's heads-up display. Nine Buffalo shuttles were formed up into three flights of three shuttles. Each flight of three performed an intricate weaving pattern designed to fool any enemy gunners as they approached the 1700 meters long, 220,000 tonnes enemy ship from the rear. The navy assured him by using pinpoint energy weapon strikes on the Buzzard's outer hull, they turned anything resembling detection equipment, anti-ship or anti-missile systems into worthless scrap metal. All the same, Alec saw no reason to take life-threatening risks. He was not complacent, although no enemy fire had been directed at his shuttles, it could mean the enemy were simply waiting until the shuttles reached point blank range before opening fire.

Alec's plan was simple, as he mulled on it a worried frown crossed his forehead. The plan was stripped back as he had no idea what he and his marines were going into. There was no intelligence to indicate the internal layout of the Buzzard. The crew estimate of 1400 was exactly that. Based on Intelligence's guesstimate on crew requirements for a human ship the size of a Buzzard. Alec had no idea whether his marines would face the Others version of themselves once they entered the Buzzard or whether it would just be armed ships' crew. Assuming of course they were able to enter the ship.

The Buffaloes were headed for what Intelligence had identified as airlocks spread along the hull of the Buzzard. Alec let out a sigh of resignation, they thought they were airlocks, they could be waste disposal hatches for all they knew. The thought of his marines blowing their way into the Buzzard only to be confronted by a mountain of rubbish was one which in any other circumstance, would bring tears of laughter to Alec's eyes, but not today. Intelligence rationalized the ports were spread evenly around the hull of the Buzzard and were roughly equidistant along its length.

Alec divided his initial assault force into three sub units: 'A' Company under Captain Brandon, the bow where all things being equal they would locate the bridge. 'C' Company under Captain Alonso, the stern where they should find the engineering spaces. 'B' Company under Captain Tanaka, with Alec's small headquarters element attached amidships where on human ships you would expect to find the computer core.

Of the three marine companies initially employed in the assault 'C' Company had, perhaps, the easiest yet most crucial task. Human warfare was governed by The Rules of War, it stated an enemy should be given the opportunity to surrender. In drawing up his assault plan Alec recognized he had no choice but to breach this rule, he could not afford to give anyone in the engineering spaces the opportunity to set off scuttling charges. 'C' Company were ordered to give no quarter, they were to secure the engineering spaces at all costs and hold until relieved. Captain Alonso's stoic look when he received said order indicated he understood tough calls had to be made at times and this was one of those times.

Following the initial insertion, the Buffaloes were to return to TDF *Saint Nazarene* and pick up the second wave of marines who would then insert through the breaches made by the assault force to reinforce, as Alec deemed necessary. This was guesswork on Alec's part but it was all they had to work with.

———

"One minute… doors opening. Gravity off." The command came in the same calm voice. The loadmaster pressed a control and Alec felt the bottom of his seat retract until his legs dangled below him. The marines were now secured only by the magnetic shoulder harness as the emptiness of space sped past below. Alec took a sharp intake of breath as, not ten meters below his feet, the scarred and gouged battle armor of the Buzzard suddenly appeared. Damn that hull was close! Alec hoped the pilot did not have to make any radical maneuvers. She had not left herself much wiggle room.

The shuttle came to a halt directly over a three by three meter hatch with some sort of locking mechanism off to one side. Alec assumed a rigid vertical position as the loadmaster touched the control activating the pusher system. The shoulder harness dropped explosively downward before disconnecting from the marines' suits, shooting the marines out of the shuttle bay akin to a cork exploding from a bottle. Twenty marines spat out of the shuttle bay doors at a speed only the integral Wraith suit computer could compensate for. The marines' shoulder harnesses were still retracting into the shuttle bay as the shuttle was piloted back to TDF *Saint Nazarene* for her next load. Alec felt his legs bend slightly at the knees as his suit automatically prepared to take the impact with the hull. With a jolt, Alec's feet contacted the hull and his suit activated its magnetic boots to secure him in place while he oriented himself.

With no word of command, the two marines carrying the breaching charges moved to the airlock doors and placed their cargo. The remaining marines stacked up a few meters clear, ready to enter once the charges went off. In Alec's helmet display a small clock appeared and a warning tone sounded in his ear. Five… four… three… two… one… flash! The helmet filters automatically dimmed what Alec knew was a blinding explosion, he felt a slight vibration through his body and knew the initial breach was successful. A marine moved forward and without exposing himself stuck his rifle barrel into the hole. Alec's heads-up display was filled by the image, courtesy of the marine's barrel camera of a room four by three by two meters with a second bulkhead at the far end. It was indeed an airlock.

"That's a beer I owe Intelligence," Alec muttered as his marines were occupied with the next stage of their assault. A marine maintained an over watch on the inside of the airlock while another, with a second breaching charge dropped in, his feet found the deck inside. "Internal gravity is on." Alec noted aloud.

The marine approached the inner airlock door and placed a second breaching charge before beating a hasty retreat to the outer hull. Five… four… three… Alec watched the countdown on his heads-up display as the warning tone sounded, two… one… Flash! Another successful breach. The airlock gushed atmosphere as the corridor beyond was subjected to explosive decompression. Atmosphere was not the only thing to rush out into the cold darkness of space. At least half a dozen unsuited crew were dragged through the airlock and ejected into space. They may be the enemy but Alec hoped the merciful embrace of death came quickly to them.

The marines surged through the airlock, into the now empty corridor beyond and took up covering positions.

"Williams! Scan!" Ordered Tanaka. Marine Williams produced a handheld device from a leg compartment of his suit and slowly turned in a circle.

The Buzzard's armor had previously defeated the TDF's scanning equipment. The layout of the Buzzard could not be determined without a navy ship closing with it and using a powerful penetrating radar, which would have damaged any computers and storage devices onboard and irradiated the crew. The decision to carry out a manual scan after the breach was not really a decision it was the only choice. Williams was doing a sterling job and within moments Alec's suit indicated it had begun receiving the data to build into a complete schematic of the Buzzard. Alec took the opportunity to check the progress of his other assault teams.

The other two 'B' Company teams amid ship had successfully gained entry and had as yet met no opposition. On the other hand, the three 'A' Company teams in the bow were meeting stiff resistance by space suited crew armed with laser rifles.

Alec's suit was having difficulty getting a solid link with 'C' Company. He was not unduly concerned as communication difficulties were to be expected. The engineering spaces on any ship were heavily shielded and would, no doubt, cause interference. Alec keyed his radio and called Captain Brandon as Williams finished his scan. A ship's schematic appeared in Alec's display containing the marines known positions.

"Sitrep, Captain Brandon."

"Team One is pinned down in the corridor adjacent to the airlock. I have three KIA and two walking wounded. Without using something heavier, I will be unable to make progress. Team Two met minimal resistance and are advancing to what they believe to be the main missile bays. I prioritized that task and have sent Team Three in support. I believe we have identified the bridge.

Our scan shows what appears to be a mass of command and control lines running to an area two decks above my current position, it's more heavily shielded than any other section in the bow. I intend to break through current enemy resistance and make our way to that section." A clear concise report, a sure sign Brandon was an experienced combat leader. Alec's own experience led him to read between the lines. Brandon's professionalism and dedication to his men prevented him from spelling out his worst fears, his marines would continue to die without the release of heavier weapons.

Alec unconsciously worried his bottom lip, a habit he developed in childhood, which reappeared whenever he had a tough decision to make. He was sympathetic to Brandon's position but using heavy weapons on board brought with it collateral damage and the possibility of destroying exactly what they had come to secure.

His marines though where taking casualties. Alec came to his decision. "Heavy weapons at your discretion, Captain, but don't get all John Wayne on me understood?"

"Aye-aye, sir."

"On 'D' Company's arrival in…" Alec quickly checked the progress of the second wave of marines. Damn! They were still sixteen minutes out. "Sixteen minutes I shall chop two teams to your command. Your mission is to secure the bridge ASAP."

"Roger that, sir. I'll use explosives to blow upward through the deck plates which should side step their defenses."

"Sounds good, Captain. Let's make it happen!" Alec cut the link and gave the sub vocal command "Suit, call Alonso." A pause followed by a double tone informed Alec his suit could not establish a link to Alonso, instead it automatically searched for the next active ranking marine.

"Go for Semple." The voice sounded strained and distracted. Alec's face paled as he did a quick mental calculation. Semple was something like tenth in the chain of command.

"Sitrep, Sergeant?"

"The situation is… let's call it fluid at the moment, sir… Wait. Jonas on your six! Two enemy on… Shit!"

On Alec's display, Marine Jonas' name flashed red then disappeared as Semple came back on the link.

"Sir, I have fifty-three KIA and virtually everyone else has an injury of some sort. The initial entry went as planned but enemy marines assaulted us in full up armor as soon as we cleared the airlocks. They were using some sort of plasma grenade. The suits can take a lot of damage but plasma in a confined space you can imagine…"

Alec heard the stress in Semple's voice and said, "Sergeant! Can you hold?"

"We've killed all the armored marines and secured all the entrances into engineering by bodging the breaching charges and using them to warp the bulkheads. If they want back in here, they'll have to either blow or cut their way in. I'm sweeping the area now for anything that looks like scuttling charges and enemy stragglers. They seem to be mostly suited crew armed with nothing more than improvised weapons but they'll attack a suited marine with whatever they can get their hands on. It's like they have some form of death wish or something."

Alec felt a surge of pride. 'C' Company had suffered fifty-three dead from a fighting force of eighty marines. According to Alec's readouts, the remaining twenty-seven had all sustained injuries to varying degrees. With all his officers and senior NCOs dead, Semple had assumed command continuing the mission until its successful conclusion.

Alec checked the arrival time of the second wave again. The clock was not going fast enough for Alec's liking and not for the first time that day, he wished he could control time.

"Sergeant. You'll have a team from 'D' Company with you in twelve minutes. Murray clear." A flashing icon in his display told Alec Captain Tanaka was waiting to speak with him.

"Go for Murray."

"Sir. If you'll check your schematic it looks like we've identified the computer core."

Alec scanned the schematics now showing in his display. An area highlighted in yellow was located at almost the center of the ship. It appeared heavily shielded, one small area at the heart, seemingly constructed of the same type of battle armor as the ship's hull.

Alec's brow furrowed in thought, it seemed to be overkill. If a deep penetrating weapon such as this struck, surely the ship would be lost. Why bother protecting a comparatively tiny area to this extent. Alec mentally shrugged, there was only one way to find out. Alec pulled up his marines' positions. His display showed Teams Five and Six, the other two amidships teams, were making their way horizontally along their respective decks, away from the computer core.

"OK, Captain that looks like our objective. Order Teams Five and Six to make their way there now." Tanaka cut the link to pass the necessary orders while Alec contemplated his next problem.

The Buzzard's battle armor was blocking all communication with anything beyond the hull, he couldn't talk to either the admiral or the shuttles carrying the second wave. At least this comms problem had an easy answer. Alec punched in the link for his two-man security/headquarter team. Gunny Wanderman and Corporal Fredricks.

"Gunny, you and Fredricks remain here. We'll use your suit's comms units to act as a relay for the marines inside the hull to the outside world. I'll stay with Captain Tanaka."

With a curt "Aye-aye, sir" the Gunny and Fredricks moved into the cover of the inner airlock and almost immediately the icon for the flagship began blinking.

"Go for Murray."

"Thought we'd lost you there for a minute," came the concerned voice of John Radford before turning business like, "Sitrep?"

"Admiral, we're taking casualties but we believe we have secured the engineering section. We are confident we have identified the missile bays, the bridge and the computer core and I have teams moving to secure them now. The Buzzard's crew are putting up stiff resistance in places but on the deployment of the second wave I am sure I can secure our objectives."

"Understood, Alec. Keep your head down."

"That's one thing you can be assured of. Murray clear."

Changing channels Alec stood up. "Let's go, Captain."

————

Gunny Wanderman followed the progress of the various teams and the imminent arrival of the reinforcement shuttles with one eye while keeping a wary lookout for the enemy with the other. He clocked Corporal Fredricks bracing herself in the upper corner of the airlock with her head poking out of the jagged remains of the outer airlock door, presumably to allow her suit's surveillance systems to get a clear image of the outer hull until its curved shape took it out of line of sight. Wanderman's thoughts were interrupted by a call from Fredricks.

"Gunny, I've got movement on the hull."

Wanderman brought the image up on his display. Sure enough, he made out at least four space suited figures cresting the curve of the hull about twenty meters from the airlock. None of the suits were transmitting an IFF code. Wanderman's heart rate rose several beats per minute, what were the enemy doing on the hull? He did not have to wait long for an answer. Two of the enemy figures raised a long tube onto their shoulders. Missiles!

Wanderman activated the emergency link on his suit, automatically overriding all other broadcasts on the marine net. "Vampire. Vampire. Enemy soldiers on the hull with missiles. Location twenty meters ship north of airlock four I am engaging with small arms. Wanderman clear."

Fredricks had already swung her whole body up through the outer airlock and was firing at the enemy soldiers. As Wanderman pushed himself upwards to join her he saw Fredricks' shake then, in gruesome slow motion he watched her lower half, neatly cauterized just above the pelvis, fall backwards into the airlock. Fredricks' remains hung, suspended by the suit's magnetic boots. Of her upper torso there was no sign.

Wanderman stuck his rifle up through the airlock and used his suit's targeting system to show him the enemy soldiers. Fredricks must have downed two before her demise there were only two left. One had taken cover behind a large section of damaged hull denying Wanderman a clean shot. The other, however, was advancing toward his position as fast as his magnetic boots would allow, he made no attempt to move from cover to cover. *More fool you*, thought Wanderman as he fired off an aimed shot that struck the advancing soldier squarely in the chest. The plasma round was traveling at a significant portion of the speed of light and went through the soldiers armored chest as if it wasn't there. Exiting through the back of the suit, it carried on into the infinity of space. Wanderman was contemplating moving onto the hull to get a clean shot at the remaining soldier when the shrill tone of a proximity warning sounded in his ear, interrupting his thought process. The starlight around him disappeared as a Buffalo shuttle came to a stop not two meters above him. The nose of the Buffalo was pointed at the section of damaged hull behind which the enemy soldier was hiding and, as Wanderman looked on, the nose-mounted rapid-fire plasma cannon discharged. The section of the hull and the soldier vanished in a brilliant flash. Twenty fully armed and Wraith suited marines dropped beside him and headed through the airlock to join the fight. The blinking icon of an incoming call caught Wanderman's attention.

He activated the link. That warm, honeyed voice said "Thank you kindly for the heads up, Gunny. The other Buffaloes are reporting missile teams were waiting for them at each of the airlocks. Could've been a nasty surprise if you hadn't got that warning out."

Despite recent events, Wanderman smiled. "My pleasure, ma'am."

"I think maybe we should hang around for a while in case you need any more flies scratched off your back."

"I'm obliged. Wanderman clear."

———

Deep in the hull, Alec Murray and Team Four were closing on their objective. The suspected computer core. During a natural pause between tactical bounds, Alec took a minute to check on the progress of the teams in the forty minutes since the initial breaching action.

Teams Two and Three had secured what appeared to be the main missile magazine with the minimum amount of casualties. The Lieutenants in charge of each team had gotten their heads together and came up with the idea, quickly adopted by all Team Leaders, of using a small charge on every bulkhead door they came across. The ones on either side of their route of advance got a charge large enough to buckle the frame making the doors inoperable. The ones on the actual route of advance were blown open and left that way. The net effect was that the entire line of advance was left in hard vacuum trapping the ship's crew in the areas that retained atmosphere. On reaching the missile bay, the marines had simply blown the bulkheads and allowed the atmosphere to escape before entering to minimal opposition. It may seem cruel to some but it kept marine casualties and collateral damage to a minimum. A good thing too as Team Two reported the crew had been in the process of rigging some of the nuclear missiles with dead man switches that would have allowed them to be detonated by hand rather than electronically. The detonation of a few nukes would have destroyed the ship, the crew and the marines.

Captain Brandon had managed to circumvent his immediate opposition by blasting his way through the deck plates but Brandon reported stiffening opposition from armored soldiers as he approached the bridge area but he was confident with the imminent arrival of reinforcements he could take the bridge in short order.

Sergeant Semple held the engineering spaces with the arrival of fresh marines he was in the process of evacuating his wounded, although he refused to leave himself. Memories of 70 Ophiuchi came to mind and Alec wondered if he was going to have no choice but to send Gunny Wanderman to Engineering to remind Semple of the consequences of refusing to obey orders.

"Moving."

The call on Team Four's net brought Alec back to his current position. According to the schematics, Team Four was less than twenty meters from the area that showed the heaviest shielding. The lead marine made his way to the corner of the corridor and went to one knee as he extended his rifle in front of him giving it, and by extension, his suit, which passed the image to the other suits of the team, a clear look along the marines' line of advance. Alec had the fleetest of moments to identify a barricaded position as the entire corner where the lead marine was kneeling exploded outward flinging the marine clear across the corridor where he bounced off the far wall and lay still. The red blinking name Morales appeared then disappeared in Alec's display.

The marines around him hugged the corridor walls for cover as two small, round, black objects rebounded off the corridors wall and fell by Morales' still form.

"Grenade!" screamed Alec, as he fell to the deck. The world around him rocked and his suit filters blackened as the first wave of superheated plasma passed over him. Alec sensed rather than felt being violently beaten onto the deck. The beating seemed to last forever. Alec prayed for his suit to maintain its integrity and spare his life.

The detached, rational part of Alec's mind knew only a few seconds had passed, not a lifetime, but a few seconds in combat was the difference between living and dying. He knew if he were in command of the enemy soldiers, he would order a follow up charge on the heels of the explosion.

Alec struggled to his knees as the first armor clad enemy soldier came around the corner. A lethal looking rifle in his hands was swinging in Alec's direction. Alec tried to raise his own weapon but his brain was finding it difficult to coordinate. Alec realized he was not going to make it and resigned himself to his fate… What the hell? Alec shook his head to clear the fog… he saw the hand of God pluck the soldier off the corridor floor, throw him high in the air before returning him as a million shredded pieces. Something tapped Alec's shoulder and he turned toward it. All external sound practically muted by the ringing in his ears, Alec concentrated on the moving lips he saw, and the muffled noises coming from them.

"Sir! Can you hear me? Sir! Are you all right?" Alec strained to hear the marine.

"Captain…" Alec struggled to get the word out as he re oriented himself. Muqimi repeated "Sir! Are you OK?"

Alec shook his head to clear it as his suit systems began injecting pain-numbing medication, enough to keep him mobile. He nodded in assent and Muqimi helped him to his feet, urgently grabbing at his arm and pulling with great strength while maintaining possession of his own weapon. Now on his unsteady feet, Alec looked around him and snorted at his own stupidity. It had not been the hand of God to the rescue it had been his reinforcements.

He sobered immediately on the realization that Team Four had ceased to exist. Twelve fellow marines gone in an instant. The survivors had sustained severe injuries.

"Muqimi, it must have been the plasma grenades," Alec gestured toward the destruction. "Semple came up against them in the engineering spaces," Muqimi nodded his understanding, "around the corner are the enemy who've just wiped out your fellow marines I want them to understand that killing a marine is a bad idea." Alec was almost running on a full tank of gas now, "Do you understand me?"

Muqimi, a marine for the guts of fifteen years, understood his commander perfectly. "Message received and understood, sir!" He switched to his team channel. "Marines covering fire on my command. Breaching charges forward. Standby. Standby. Fire!"

The wrath of God rained down fire, engulfing the enemy position as Team Fourteen poured plasma fire onto the killers of their fellow marines. Under this cover, two breaching charges were launched, their magnetic hooks held them fast against the enemy barricade. A heart beat later their shaped charge heads exploded, reverberating throughout the ship. The barricade and its defenders ceased to exist. The marines charged through the cloud of debris. A still shaky Alec with them. No quarter was given. The marines cleared the position leaving only death and destruction in their wake.

Before them lay the bulkhead leading to the computer core. As Alec approached the bulkhead, he felt, just for a moment, an unusual tingling. He checked his suit readouts. He had not imagined it and through the deck plates beneath his feet, he felt a deep rumble. "Suit, analysis!"

A male un intoned, synthesized voice replied, "Systems show a three hertz ultra-low frequency signal. Duration two seconds. Generated from indeterminate source located seven meters beyond the bulkhead. One second later, there was a thermal baric explosion. There is no electrical activity from that section, further I detect the only life signs aboard this vessel are those belonging to Terran Defense Force personnel."

CHAPTER EIGHTEEN

First Contact

OFFICE OF THE PRESIDENT OF THE TERRAN REPUBLIC - GENEVA - EARTH

Rebecca sat alone in her office as she contemplated the events of the past couple of weeks. Since the battle in 31 Aquilae, the press had been full of praise for the members of BatFor 1, especially one Captain Engel, who was swiftly becoming regarded as some form of hero for his actions in stopping the missiles, which would have wrought so much destruction on the defenseless planet Garunda. There was even a suggestion he should be awarded the Terran Medal of Honor, one which if put forward officially Rebecca would only be too happy to agree to.

A flash of lighting made Rebecca look out the windows of her office, a wry smile crossing her lips as she regarded the gathering storm clouds as they blew over the mountains. The first rain spoiled the mirror perfect surface of Lake Geneva.

A soft knock on the door drew her attention back into the room as the door opened and Secretary Helset and General Joyce entered the room. Rebecca came around her desk to greet them.

"Gentlemen. Glad you could make it." Rebecca shook both men's hands warmly as she indicated for them to take a seat around her private briefing table. "I'm eager to hear what progress the team from Research and Development are making on the captured enemy ship."

"Madam President, with your permission…" began Joyce. Rebecca nodded her ascent and Joyce inserted a secure chip into the holo cube concealed in the table. It sprang to life on command and displayed the interior of a ship, similar to a human ship but undoubtedly alien.

"Madam President, as you know, following the arrival of extra marine elements, Admiral Radford began a boarding operation of the last surviving Buzzard. During the operation, marine casualties were high. They were restricted in the weaponry they could employ on board without destroying the very thing they had come to capture and the crew of the ship fought tooth and nail for every meter of the ship." Joyce's voice faltered as he continued, "By the time the marines secured the ship, they had sustained eighty-four killed in action and 142 seriously wounded."

Rebecca shook her head slowly. "Any update on enemy casualties?"

Joyce paused and composed himself. "No living crew members have been located. It appears those who weren't killed fighting the marines committed suicide when it became obvious they were about to be captured."

Rebecca forced down a shiver. She had hoped, with the fight for the ship over, the search teams would find some of the crew alive. All of them dead? Some at their own hand? What sort of people are they? "Excuse me, General. Please continue."

"Colonel Murray's decision to seize the engine room and the missile magazines first undoubtedly saved lives. His marines found the crew in the missile magazines attempting to detonate the warheads and the engine room crew trying the same thing with the engines. If either group had succeeded, it would have destroyed the ship and killed our boarding party."

"Colonel Murray is to be commended, General," A furrow appeared on Rebecca's brow, "Murray. The name seems familiar."

Helset leaned forward. "Colonel Murray was promoted following the operation in 70 Ophiuchi where he commanded the marines who carried out the reconnaissance of the Others' base there, Madam President."

"A well-deserved promotion then, Olaf," commented the president. "Please go on, General."

Joyce manipulated the holo cube controls and a schematic of the Buzzard appeared in the air above the table, a forward section highlighted. "The team from R&D identified this as the source of the weapons fire which managed to destroy the TDF *Lagos Bay*. Initial analysis by the team leader states the weapon is a large x-ray laser similar to those the Others had deployed on their missiles used against the destroyer screen."

Rebecca held up a hand to stop the general. "Didn't the initial brief state those lasers were powered by a nuclear detonation? Surely, General, the Others don't detonate a nuclear device on board their own ships every time they fire that thing?"

In response, Joyce manipulated the controls once more and a line appeared on the schematic, weaving its way from one end of the ship to the other. "The R&D team believe the weapon is tied directly into the ship's engines, which might explain their sudden drop in speed just prior to the weapon being fired. It's slow firing and leaves them at a small tactical disadvantage as they lose speed but, as the destruction of the *Lagos Bay* shows, if it hits its intended target the effects are devastating."

The room stilled. The loss of the *Lagos Bay* and its crew of 2000 had been the largest single loss of life the Terran Defense Forces had ever suffered, but everyone in the room realized it would not be the last.

With a small sigh of resignation, Rebecca went on. "Have we learned anything more I should know about, General?"

"Yes, Madam President. The team have identified what they believe to be the main computer core. It's not intact but fortunately, the marines got to it before it could be wiped. We're hoping it holds vital intelligence. Rather than try and work on it in situ, the whole section containing it is being removed from the ship and will be taken back to Stickney Base for analysis there."

"That's the best news I've heard all day, General. Our lack of knowledge about the Others is our biggest handicap by far."

Joyce nodded his head in agreement. "I couldn't agree more, Madam President, although I must remind you to be realistic. Deciphering the computer core will undoubtedly take time."

Rebecca gave a small chuckle. "I understand, General. I'll try not to get my hopes up too high. Now, is there anything else?"

With a sound like a grunt, Helset cleared his throat.

Rebecca spared him a smile. "Olaf, you would never have made a good politician."

Helset returned her smile with one of his own. "Thank you for the compliment, Madam President."

Rebecca emitted a laugh. "You're welcome, Olaf. Now, how may I help?"

Helset sat a little further forward in his seat. "Madam President, the decision to intercept the Others and defend Garunda, while undoubtedly the right thing to do, has left us in a bit of a precarious position."

Rebecca could feel the involuntary frown on her brow forming. "How so, Olaf?"

Helset glanced at Joyce before continuing. "Our plans have always been centered on defending Earth and Janus, but with our action around Garunda I feel it has committed us to the defense of a third star system – a system containing a native civilization for which we are now responsible, for better or for worse."

Rebecca could feel the anger rising in her. "Are you suggesting we abandon Garunda to its fate, Olaf, after the sacrifices made in its protection?"

Helset raised both hands as if to ward off a physical attack from the president. "No, not at all, Madam President. Please don't misunderstand me. I am as committed to defending Garunda as you are. Please accept my apology if that is how my words were interpreted."

By the look of shock on the Secretary's face, Rebecca realized she might have over reacted a little. Getting control of her anger, she continued in a more even tone, "Apology accepted, Olaf. Please accept mine in return. I should know you would never leave those people defenseless."

Helset looked relieved. "Thank you, Madam President. My point is our current force deployment does not take into consideration the defense of a third star system." Helset touched the controls in front of him and the holo cube displayed three star systems, with a list of TDF assets displayed under each.

"Madam President, as you can see, the TDF have First Fleet in the Sol system securing Earth and Second Fleet to secure Janus. The assets in 31 Aquilae, protecting Garunda, are currently drawn from BatFor 3 of Second Fleet as BatFor 1 has been withdrawn to Deimos for repairs and refit. As things stand, it is the Joint Chiefs' intention to continue to rotate a BatFor into 31 Aquilae until such time as construction of new hulls and training of personnel allows for 31 Aquilae to have its own dedicated BatFor."

Helset gave Joyce a quick glance, one not missed by Rebecca. "Olaf, am I to take it you and the Joint Chiefs are in disagreement?"

When Helset did not offer an immediate reply, Rebecca became apprehensive. "Olaf, would you like to tell me what is going on?"

Unbidden, Helset stood, took a few steps away from the table and stopped with his back to the president, looking out of the wide windows being rain lashed by the approaching storm. Helset turned to face Rebecca and stood a little bit taller. "Madam President, when we discovered the Gravity Drive, it opened the stars to humanity and what we have found in the Others could destroy us all. But not only us. We have found three other civilizations out there, one populating Garunda, for which we have intervened and saved from destruction and another, Messier 54, which has, as far as we know, no idea either the Others or we exist. The third, the builders of the surveillance platform observing Garunda, we have no idea whether they are friendly or not."

Helset began to pace up and down as he spoke. "The problem as I see it cannot only be solved by military means. In the longer term, the Others will want to know what happened to the ships it sent to destroy Garunda. It makes more sense to build a fleet base in 31 Aquilae which will become the home to what I envisage will become Third Fleet. However, we can't just go building fleet bases in other people's star systems, even if they have no clue we exist. The problem needs a political solution."

"And what is this problem you're eluding to, Olaf?" asked Rebecca.

Helset stopped his pacing and looked directly at the president. "We need to make first contact with the indigenous populations of both planets, Madam President. Garunda first because we're already there, followed by Messier 54."

The silence in the room was palpable and seemed to stretch for minutes, even though Rebecca knew it was only a few seconds. "You always come to me with the hard ones, Olaf. I'll give you that."

Helset let a smile escape his lips. "If they were easy, Madam President, I would sort them myself."

Rebecca chuckled. "Indeed, Olaf."

It was Rebecca's turn to pause and think. The two men in the room waited patiently, knowing the importance of the decision the president faced.

Rebecca refocused her attention into the room. "I'll need to put this before the Senate, but I see the merit of your argument, Olaf. Leave it with me."

Both men stood to leave but Rebecca stopped them. "One more thing, Olaf. If we're to make contact with the people on Garunda and in Messier 54, it would appear prudent that more research into them is carried out prior to first contact. Could you get together with R&D and have a working group

set up before the Senate decides to do it themselves and lumbers us with a bunch of politicians looking to make a name for themselves?"

"Yes, Madam President. I'll get right on it." Helset turned to leave but Rebecca stopped him with a touch to the elbow.

"Oh and one other thing, Olaf. I would like Doctor Bath on the group." Both Helset and Joyce looked skeptical.

"Everybody deserves a second chance," said Rebecca, by way of reply to the unasked question. They left to carry out their president's orders.

———

Aaron Beckett, a career diplomat, had spent over fifty years traveling around the world and the various human habitats dotted throughout the solar system. He had acted as a troubleshooter for eight different presidents, negotiating everything from trade disputes to calls for more autonomy amongst the asteroid belt habitats.

Four years previously, as he turned seventy, Aaron had decided it was time to retire permanently. He moved from the hustle and bustle of Geneva to a small log cabin in the Rocky Mountains. Aaron's wife, Margaret, had died the year before in a freak transport accident, they never had children, as Aaron was always too busy. Now he faced a life alone, a life which modern medical science promised would keep him active well into his early hundreds.

Aaron was sitting on his porch, reading a book in the late afternoon sun, when he heard the unmistakable sound of a hover jet approaching from across the lake. He remained seated as the sleek transport had landed on the shoreline and a single passenger disembarked, their face hidden in shadow by the slowly sinking sun behind them. Aaron was unable to make out the face of the visitor until she was nearly at the cabin. Recognition brought him out of his chair in a hurry and his book fell to his feet.

"Good... eh, morn... I mean... afternoon... Madam President." The words tumbled out as best as Aaron could manage through his confusion.

A smiling Rebecca Coston reached forward, brushing away his outstretched hand, instead giving him a kiss on the cheek and a small hug. "It's been too long, Aaron. How have you been?"

Aaron gave a small shrug and a lopsided grin. "Good, Madam President. Thanks for asking. I've been catching up on my reading and just enjoying the quiet life."

"So what does a girl have to do to get a coffee around here?"

Aaron cleared some books from a bench seat, next to his own. "If you'd like to take a seat, I'm sure I could rustle up something."

While Aaron made the coffee, Rebecca took a moment to admire the view. A gentle downward slope to the shoreline, the lake water reflected the setting sun as it sank slowly behind snowcapped mountains. Beautiful, simply stunning.

Aaron returned with two mugs of piping hot coffee for them and set them on a small table. "I suppose this isn't really a social visit, Madam President."

Rebecca picked up her mug and blew on the hot coffee before taking a sip. "No, Aaron, it isn't. To be honest, I have a problem and there isn't anyone else I could think of could solve it for me."

With a deep sigh, Aaron took in the view for what he knew would be the last time for the foreseeable future. "How may I serve, Madam President?"

ORBIT OF PLANET GARUNDA - 31 AQUILAE

Two months on and Aaron found himself leading Earth's first diplomatic mission amongst the stars. The president's decision to include Patricia Bath, seen by many as controversial, was the key to unlocking the more commonly used languages on Garunda. The highflying stealth drones, employed to gather them from the different nations living on the planet, had unobtrusively recorded Garunda's languages.

Aaron looked again at the distinctly reptilian shaped form in the holo cube. The stump of what had been, in its genetic history, a tail was still obvious as was the elongated face covered in overlapping scales and the protruding pink eyes. Aaron's attention, as always, was drawn to the hands. Five fingers with opposable thumbs, the unmistakable sign of Saiph DNA intervention.

The decision on how best to approach first contact rested with Aaron. After all, he would be the one on the ground, so to speak. The sheer number of identified nation states ruled out the feasibility of visiting each in turn. After many hours' consultation with the leading lights in the field of sociocultural anthropology, Aaron concluded the easiest way to reach the majority of the population was to identify the state that appeared to control the greatest land mass in proportion to population. Surprisingly, it turned out to be a relatively small island nation in the southern hemisphere. It appeared to be in control of over one third of the planet. Many of the anthropologists drew on the similarities between that small nation and Britain in the late nineteenth and early twentieth centuries. Aaron inwardly laughed. He just hoped they were not as stuffy.

The beeping of his wrist comm interrupted his thoughts, Aaron touched a control on his desk. The face of Rear Admiral Analisa Chavez, Commanding Officer BatFor 3 Second Fleet replaced the native Garunda.

"Ambassador, your shuttle is prepped and ready for launch."

Aaron had come to know the admiral over the past couple of weeks spent aboard her flagship, he could see concern lurking behind her calm exterior. Aaron stood a little bit straighter. The decisive moment had arrived. "Thank you, Analisa. I'll be along shortly."

Chavez paused as she reached to disconnect the link, "Good luck, Aaron." Her face disappeared.

Good luck indeed, thought Aaron. *I'll need it.*

As the shuttle dropped from the Nemesis class battleship TDF *Mishima*, Aaron Beckett threw a furtive glance across the aisle at Patricia Bath sitting opposite him. Aaron saw the whites of her knuckles she gripped the side of the seat tightly.

Like many others, Aaron had his doubts when informed Doctor Bath was his official translator on this mission. He too had heard the media reports from the previous year, how her mistake in the translation of the Rubicon database led to an almost disastrous misjudgment by the military of the threat the Others posed to Earth.

Calculations corrected, after the discovery of Patricia's error, revealed the Saiph home world had been destroyed by the Others around the year 1187 AD and not millions of years previously as estimated. Patricia's detractors pointed to the Roman Empire, they existed on Earth for at least 1200 years before their eventual demise. There was, therefore, no reason to believe the Others were extinct, however, there was *every* reason to suppose they were still out there amongst the stars… waiting for a human ship.

Yes, this mistake could have held huge consequences, but aside from it, Patricia Bath had shown to be a remarkable interpreter. Aaron was no fool. He knew many of Patricia's critics begrudged her successes, after all, Valerie Hayes had selected her.

Valerie was notorious for finding exciting young talent to bring a fresh perspective to problems. She plucked Patricia from virtual obscurity at the ripe old age of twenty-two to heads-up the Linguistics and Cryptology Division at Stickney Base on Phobos. Unfortunately, Valerie also collected political enemies. Her promotion to Special Science Adviser to the president meant many disgruntled colleagues. These colleagues saw protégé Patricia's

mistake as an opportunity to damage Valerie's reputation… ending Patricia's career was simply collateral damage.

They took advantage, created a media storm, made Patricia the scapegoat and achieved their aim. President Coston reluctantly accepted Patricia Bath's resignation.

Aaron understood the president presented a hard political shell to the world, but having known her for most of her adult life he also knew that underneath was a warm beating human heart, so when the media storm died, Rebecca made a point of giving Patricia a second chance by ensuring a place for her on Aaron's staff.

So here they were, about to initiate man's first contact with another sentient species and the majority of the groundwork had been completed by this slim, auburn haired thirty-one year old. Patricia had spent the last two months either locked away in her office or sleeping in her accommodation aboard the *Mishima*. It had not escaped Aaron's notice that she had eaten all her meals solo in either her office or accommodation, politely refusing all staff invitations to share a meal, particularly avoiding any young males.

Aaron was concerned Patricia was distancing herself, until now he'd kept his worries to himself in the hope she would come out of her shell but now with no change in her distant behavior and the fact first contact was imminent he was left with no choice but to intervene… somehow.

He reached across and tapped Patricia lightly on the arm, "Doctor Bath." Patricia's head snapped around to face him, shocking Aaron with what he saw in her frightened childlike eyes, he quickly decided on a gentle approach and said softly, "Are you alright, Doctor? I'm sure the shuttle will be landing soon and we'll all be back on firm ground."

Patricia slowly shook her head. "Believe me, Ambassador, it's not the flight I find bothersome. I have been working on the language program for nearly eight weeks and you have based your decision on where to make first contact solely on my interpretation of the available data. I…" her eyes watered and her body began to shake almost imperceptibly, "I just don't want to let you down."

Aaron felt anger well in him as he realized her meaning. The media had not only almost destroyed this young woman's career but had quite clearly obliterated her self-confidence. Working day and night on board TDF *Mishima*, she had been in constant fear of failure and fear she would disappoint Aaron. He closed his eyes briefly, kicking himself with guilt he had failed to cotton on to the underlying issues behind Patricia's behavior. Well he could solve this problem.

"Doctor Bath… Patricia, the president herself came to me and personally recommended you for this mission. If she has such faith in your abilities then who am I to question them?" Aaron reassured her. "When we land I expect you to stand by my side as my personal aide de camp, not just an interpreter. You have carte blanche to intervene and make any suggestions you feel appropriate." Aaron smiled at the open-mouthed dumbfounded look on Patricia's face. "Close your mouth, Patricia, you'll catch flies." Patricia closed her mouth with an audible click.

Aaron reclined with a contented smile on his face, he considered what the media would say about his choice of aide de camp… Screw them!

Patricia's head was spinning. Chief Aide and Adviser to Aaron Beckett? Me? The repeater display in front of her sprang to life and halted her whirling thoughts. She got her first good look at the destination she had chosen as man's first meeting with an alien species… Oh God, let it all go as planned! Patricia offered her silent prayer as the shuttle cleared the upper atmosphere and the electro optical systems threw their destination into stark relief.

She had chosen a relatively small island nation in the southern hemisphere located just off the coast of one of the three major landmasses. At first glance, there was nothing special about this island. The reconnaissance probes had flown over it and other more populated areas of Garunda but flags only began popping up with the analysis of the compiled data.

While the neighboring continent appeared to be in the throes of what human history characterized as the first industrial revolution: chemical manufacturing, iron production processes, improved efficiency of water power, increasing use of steam power and the development of machine tools. This little island displayed signs it was already well into the period of a second industrial revolution. Technological and economic progress continued with the adoption of steam-powered boats, ships and railways, the large-scale manufacture of machine tools and the increasing use of machinery in steam-powered factories. Analysis showed a much more dense population than its neighbors and reconnaissance probes captured images of seagoing vessels flying the emblem of the island nation in various ports around the planet in a much higher proportion than any other. Taking all these factors into consideration Patricia concluded this small nation was a major planetary power, if not *the* major planetary power on Garunda.

Patricia wrinkled her forehead… Garunda. Humans had dubbed the planet 'Garunda' soon after their arrival in the system but through research it seemed the planet had been given many different names by its various nations and religious groups. She decided it was an issue best dealt with later, Aaron Becket had much bigger fish to fry than identifying the indigenous population's name for their world.

The shuttle levelled out and the display filled with views of well-defined fields of crops being worked by small groups of farmers. Their faces turned skyward at the unfamiliar noise of the shuttles screaming aero engines before Patricia saw them begin to run in all directions in what she could only assume was panic. Not one of the reconnaissance probes had shown evidence any Garundan nation had yet developed flight, not even rudimentary hot air balloons had been recorded so it was reasonably safe to assume the human shuttle was the first flying machine the Garundans had ever seen.

The rolling fields soon gave way to a more built up area of scattered houses, which within a few more kilometers thickened considerably. Large factories belching smoke into the sky were now mixed in amongst the dwellings. The pilot banked the shuttle into a large lazy turn and the extent of the city was fully revealed. A wide river ran through the middle of the city with numerous bridges spanning it and as far as the eye could see, there was factories and homes. Near the center of the city, lining the river was a large dock area with dozens of ships gathered along it.

Then, as the shuttle began to level out once more, Patricia caught sight of their final destination. A large group of overly ornate buildings set in what on Earth would be a large park. This was the only part of the city not covered by buildings and stood out like a sore thumb in the reconnaissance imagery. Patricia was convinced this cluster of buildings was the seat of power for this small nation and, as the shuttle came into to make a landing, she could make out dozens of figures scurrying away but more importantly she saw others dashing toward the site of their landing. All of them dressed in a similar fashion and taking up what even a novice of military tactics could see where defensive positions between the shuttle and the buildings.

The shuttle rocked slightly on its landing gear as it touched down a few hundred meters from the largest of the ornate buildings and Aaron released his restraints and stood. The two marines detailed as his close protection team were resplendent in their dress blues, which only served to draw the eye even more to the dull black pulse pistols secured at their waists. Pausing to straighten his jacket cuffs before taking a step toward the shuttle hatch he paused again and, without turning his head said "Are you coming, Doctor Bath?"

It had been agreed only Aaron and his two marine escorts would disembark the shuttle until the friendly status of the locals could be determined but obviously, Aaron had decided to fling that plan out of the airlock. Patricia fumbled with her restraints as she rushed to join him at the hatch and she swore she caught the sound of a subdued chuckle.

The shuttle hatch opened and the ramp extended until it touched the grass. The marines moved down the ramp and took up positions on either side of it at the position of parade rest. Bodies locked rigidly in place, hands clasped to the rear, heads up and eyes forward.

"Now for the moment of truth." Whispered Aaron as he stepped off down the ramp followed closely by Patricia. As he reached the marines at the bottom of the ramp, they snapped to attention in unison and gave a parade ground salute any drill sergeant would have been proud of. Aaron acknowledged the salute with a polite thank you as he moved past them a few paces and halted facing the buildings. The marines resumed the position of parade rest as Patricia passed them and took her place beside Aaron.

"You were right about the marines, Ambassador. They're very impressive."

"That they are, Doctor Bath, but their purpose is twofold. Firstly they saluted me and not you which identifies myself as a person of importance which, if you look at the number of Garundans in uniform currently arrayed in front of us and the fact we have no way of identifying their rank structure at the moment, gives them a polite advantage."

Patricia could not help but notice the numbers of uniformed Garundans, which had formed a loose circle around the shuttle. Their numbers seemed to swelling by the minute and the majority of them had a very ugly tri-barrel rifle aimed at her.

"Secondly. The marines are in an obvious uniform whereas you and I are not. I hope it indicates to whomever is in charge over there that we are civilians and not military. A distinction enforced by the marines saluting a civilian, I hope to show that although we do have a military capability it is subordinate to civilians."

A commotion interrupted any reply that Patricia was about to make, it came from the rear ranks of the Garundans located near the building. Patricia made out three Garundans making their way through the soldiers toward the shuttle. At last, the front row of soldiers parted and the three Garundans approached the waiting humans. Patricia noticed they seemed to have a slight side-to-side motion as they walked no doubt due to their tail stump. The group stopped only a few meters from Aaron and both sides regarded each other for a few moments before a particularly well dressed Garundan stepped forward and began to speak. The interpretation program took a few seconds to catch up before Patricia clearly heard his voice through her ear bug.

"I am Prime Minister Bezled of the Yeut Confederation. This is Governor Tzir of Makol and Chancellor Rol of Esper." On being introduced, each of the Garundans gave a curt nod to Aaron.

"I am Ambassador Aaron Beckett of the Terran Republic and I come to you in the spirit of friendship and cooperation."

The voice of an alien coming out in their own language made quite a few of the Garundan soldiers take a wary step back accompanied by a few gasps of surprise. Prime Minister Bezled and his companions hardly batted an eyelid. Aaron recognized the signs of skilled politicians when he saw them. Aaron indicated his wrist comm. "This device interprets my voice and yours so we may understand each other."

"A useful machine indeed Ambassador. May I suggest we continue our conversation inside I feel we have much to discuss."

OFFICE OF THE PRESIDENT OF THE TERRAN REPUBLIC - GENEVA - EARTH

Winter had descended on Geneva and snowflakes coated the ground as Aaron Beckett was ushered into the president's office.

"Welcome back, Aaron," said Rebecca with a warm and welcoming smile. After all, what he had achieved in less than a month was nothing short of miraculous.

He bowed his head slightly. "Madam President."

Rebecca ushered him into one of the comfortable informal chairs as a steward brought them both coffee.

"I've read the reports, but I'd like to hear a summary from your own lips to be sure there's no misunderstandings. It seems to me there is something missing from them."

Aaron put his elbows on the arm of the chair, steeple hands in front and a smile creased his face. "To put it plainly, Madam President, they were expecting us. They may not be as advanced as us, but they do have optical telescopes and more than one had witnessed the battle between the Others and us. In the time it took us to get my team together, get a handle on the main languages and make landing, they had already been in frantic communication with each of the other major nations and had decided to fight us as one if we invaded."

Rebecca was shaking her head in disbelief, which made Aaron chuckle. "You may find it hard to believe, Madam President, but imagine my surprise when instead of speaking to one national leader I was confronted by representatives from all the major powers."

This time it was Rebecca's turn to chuckle. "So how did you persuade them we weren't about to invade?"

Aaron looked at her a little sheepishly. "Ah, well, you see, Madam President, I may have slightly overstepped my authority there, which is why I thought it would be better if you heard this from me and didn't read it in a report."

Rebecca placed her coffee cup down on the table and sat back in her chair, looking at Aaron warily. "Go on."

Even after all his fifty years negotiating on behalf of presidents, Aaron knew this was the biggest gamble he had ever taken of his own accord. "Madam President, I knew going into this my actions would set the standard for every first contact we make from hereon in. I decided to be completely honest with the Garunda." Aaron took a deep breath. "I explained how we had found the Rubicon Cave and what we knew of the Saiph and their experiments in different star systems with indigenous life forms' DNA and how we came into conflict with the Others."

"Sounds reasonable so far, Aaron. But there's something else isn't there?"

"I offered them full access to the Saiph database and promised assistance in bringing their technology up to a level where they could defend themselves without our help."

Rebecca jolted out of her seat as if she had suffered an electric shock. She looked at Aaron disbelievingly. "You did what? My God! Aaron, do you realize what you have done? The information in the database is priceless. We've still got no idea what else remains to be discovered in it."

"Madam President," Aaron pleaded. "We needed the people of Garunda to trust us, and I think my openness did the trick."

Rebecca attempted to rein in her anger. "How so, Aaron?"

"For their entire recorded history, the people of Garunda have fought with each other, either as tribes or cities or as nation states like they are now. For God's sake, they couldn't even agree on a name for their own planet and they ended up adopting the name we dubbed it!"

"Our arrival has changed Garundan dynamics. The fact I met representatives from all the major nation states proves it. They also insisted on sending a small team of representatives back with me, to see how we came together as one planet. They realize as single nations they stand no chance against the Others."

The president stood perfectly still, "You mean – they are here now?"

Aaron nodded. "On board the same ship that brought me back."

"You could have given me a bit more warning we are about to hold an interstellar conference, Aaron."

Aaron simply shrugged his shoulders. "They insisted. And I thought it would be impolite to say no."

Rebecca gave him a withering look, but then a small smile appeared on her face. "Well, if I am to meet with them, I'm not going to do it on my own." The president pressed a control on her wrist Comm and the disembodied voice of her personal assistant came into her ear.

"Yes, Madam President?"

Rebecca looked at Aaron and her smile widened. "Jim, please inform the Vice President, the cabinet and the leaders of both houses we will be hosting a full state dinner tomorrow evening for a delegation from Garunda."

"Of course, Madam President."

"Thank you, Jim." As Rebecca signed off, she turned to Aaron, shaking her head. "You know, Jim has served three presidents and I have yet to hear of him ever being fazed by any presidential request. The man must have ice water running through his veins. Now you!" She pointed at Aaron like a schoolteacher berating a misbehaving pupil. "Get out of my sight! You have work to do. I want a detailed paper on Garunda etiquette with Jim before the end of the day so I do not make any major cock-ups tomorrow, or I will have your head on a block. Is that understood?"

Aaron stood and bowed his head in a newfound respect for his president. "Yes, Madam President. And thank you for trusting me."

Rebecca walked him to the door. "Aaron, if I hadn't trusted you to do the right thing, I would never have sent you."

———

Rebecca looked around the spacious reception room as she awaited the arrival of the delegates from Garunda. The balmy room was set to a temperature of twenty-six degrees centigrade, with a humidity of sixty-five percent, to better suit her guests. Rebecca could not help but scratch her left ear, where the ear bug protruded slightly. Doctor Bath assured Rebecca the translation program preset into her wrist comm would successfully translate the Garundan language and she would hear the Standard English output via the ear bug. The Garunda delegation had been similarly equipped. At least they should be able to talk to each other.

A low chime sounded throughout the room. All eyes turned to the entrance doors. They swung slowly open. The Master of Ceremonies announced the arrival of the Garunda delegation. *Well here goes nothing!* Thought Rebecca as she moved to the head of the reception line.

The first person through the door was Aaron. He was chatting amiably with a Garunda, resplendent in a light green uniform with a gold sash across the right shoulder. Apart from the sash, the only other decoration appeared to be a small diamond encrusted star on the left side of his chest.

The Ambassador came to halt in front of Rebecca. "Madam President, may I introduce Prime Minister Bezled of the Yeut Confederation who has, by agreement with the other major powers of Garunda, been chosen as their representative."

Rebecca regarded the Prime Minister for a moment before turning her back on him. She could hear the sudden intake of breath from the humans in the room as Rebecca carried out what any human could only describe as a calculated insult. To the human watchers' amazement, the Prime Minister waited a few seconds before saying, "Please turn, Madam President. Your faith in my honorable intentions is appreciated. And I offer you my back in return." As Rebecca turned to face him again, the Prime Minister turned and presented his back to Rebecca.

"Your honorable intentions were never in doubt, Prime Minister." Relieved she had performed the ritual correctly, Rebecca continued. "If I may introduce the other members of my government." Rebecca worked her way down the reception line, each person introduced gave a slight bow to the Prime Minister, as they completed the ritual of honorable intentions.

On reaching the end of the line, they came upon a very uncomfortable naval captain in his dress whites. He appeared to prefer to be anywhere else than in this room full of dignitaries at this moment in time. On the captain's chest was a small blue and white ribbon, the Terran Medal of Honor.

"Mr. Prime Minister, I believe you especially requested to meet the captain of the destroyer *Dagger*." Rebecca noticed the entire Garunda delegation tense slightly as they turned in the captain's direction. "May I introduce Captain Engel?"

"Captain Engel, when Ambassador Beckett came to us and told us of these… Batha!" the Prime Minister said in a tone which no human or Garunda in the room could mistake as anything but a term not to be used in polite company, "these Others had come to destroy our home, we were skeptical."

With a raised arm, he gestured around the room. "After all, how were we to know you were not just fighting the Others for control of Garunda, and after defeating them you would not invade us yourselves?"

Rebecca could feel this spiraling out of her control and began to protest. "Mr. Prime Minister, I can assure you that was never our intention. We –"

Prime Minister Bezled raised his hand and Rebecca fell silent as Bezled went on in an even and quiet tone. "Madam President. I am a politician as are you and words are just that. Words. But Captain Engel's actions in putting the lives of his crew and himself in jeopardy to stop those last two missiles, which I now know could have killed so many of our people, say more about your intentions toward us than any mere words could say. Your decision to send humans into battle knowing some could, and indeed, did die to protect Garunda speaks volumes for you and your people. If it was possible, I would thank each and every family who sacrificed a loved one that day so my people could live."

Bezled reached up and removed the small diamond encrusted star from his chest looking at it fondly. "Captain Engel, this is the Star of Yeut, it was presented to me many years ago by a grateful nation. I now ask *you* to accept it on behalf of your fallen comrades as a gift not only from my nation, but from all the people of Garunda."

Engel reached out and took the star from the Prime Minister. "I accept your gift on behalf of all those who cannot be here today, and I shall wear it proudly in their memory."

"I have no doubt, Captain. Now, Madam President…" The Prime Minister turned his attention back to the waiting president. "Shall we continue?"

Shaking herself, Rebecca said, "Of course, Mr. Prime Minister."

It did not escape the president's notice as each Garunda passed Captain Engel, they came to their version of attention and placed their hand flat on the center of their chest. *One to ask Aaron later,* she thought, wondering what further surprises were in store tonight.

Rebecca sat in a comfortable chair in her private living room, lit only by a solitary table lamp and the flickering flames from the wood fire burning in the hearth. Her shoes lay where she had kicked them off and she sat with tucked legs underneath her. She savored the smell of the brandy in the glass Aaron handed her.

"Aaron, did you know what Bezled was going to propose tonight?"

He sat in the chair opposite Rebecca and contemplated the flames for a moment before answering. "No, Madam President. It came as much of a surprise to me as to you."

Rebecca chuckled "Aaron, I've known you over twenty years, so when we're in here and alone, please call me Rebecca."

Aaron felt his cheeks redden slightly. "Of course, Madam… Rebecca."

Another chuckle escaped Rebecca's lips. "That's better. Now what about this proposal from Bezled?"

Aaron closed his eyes and rubbed the bridge of his nose as he thought through his answer. "To be honest with you, Rebecca, I still don't know what to think of it." Aaron shook his head slowly. "As it stands, Garunda is broken into a number of nation states, each with their own military forces. But the threat of the Others has made them realize for all their differences they are all Garundans."

"You mean in the same way our own near self-destruction made us realize we couldn't go on killing each other?"

"Exactly. Prime Minister Bezled is offering as many Garundan military and scientific personnel as we can train, each will give up their individual national identity and swear allegiance to a pan-national Garundan authority." Aaron felt a smile tug at the corners of his mouth. "I think we have just witnessed the birth of a planetary government."

Rebecca Coston raised her glass with a smile. "Then let's be the first to wet the baby's head. Cheers!"

CHAPTER NINETEEN
Friend or Foe?

31 AQUILAE

High above the ecliptic plane, the stealthy surveillance platform finished downloading its data to the ship keeping station alongside. On entering normal space, Sub Leader Verus was shocked to find the whole system, especially the area around Planet IV, teeming with energy signatures, which were unmistakably spacecraft.

It could not be right! The population of Planet IV could not possibly have developed space travel in the three years since the last ship had downloaded the surveillance platform's memories. The fact Sub Leader Verus could not establish contact with the other platform closer in system was also disconcerting.

To add to his confusion, the energy signatures did not match anything held in his ship's database, so unless the old enemy had developed a completely new form of space drive then it could not be them. Who were these people?

Scratching the short fur behind his right ear, in a motion his crew knew displayed his puzzlement, he called to the navigator, "Plot a course for home. We'll let the Council decide what to do about what we have found here." The navigator started the calculations as the captain sat back in his chair and wondered if he had discovered a new enemy or a new ally.

"Course plotted, Sub Leader."

Sub Leader Verus had one more look at the mass of energy signatures moving about the system while again stroking the fur behind his right ear. *We had best be on our way,* he thought. "Execute!" he said.

The navigator's index finger, in a hand comprising five fingers, pressed down on the control panel in front of him, and the ship entered fold space.

The lieutenant at Tactical on the Flag Bridge of TDF *Mishima*, in orbit around Garunda, stiffened as the console he was operating let out an urgent beep. "There it is again, Admiral!"

Rear Admiral Analisa Chavez, commanding officer BatFor 3, Second Fleet stood up from her command chair and crossed her flag bridge to stand behind the lieutenant at Tactical. Chavez's one meter thirty centimeters height, slight frame and long black hair had lulled many a recruit at the naval academy, who did not know her, into believing she was a little girl playing at being a naval officer. Until she beat them hands down at nearly everything on the syllabus, graduating top of her class. Behind those soft brown eyes, there was a mind as sharp as a razor and as cunning as a fox – the reason she was still on her flag bridge at half past three in the morning.

It followed a report from Tactical, just after midnight, they had a mere sniff from a Sherlock platform of an unknown energy signature well above the ecliptic plane. The signature, put through their database, was too weak for the computer to identify. If it had been the Others then surely the Sherlock platform would have detected it further out and not as a stationary point above the ecliptic.

Chavez chose to wait rather than send her force to battle stations and possibly scare off her quarry. It looked like her gamble had paid off.

"Well, Lieutenant. Has the computer got a better reading this time?" asked Analisa patiently.

The lieutenant did not answer immediately, Analisa allowed a little impatience to enter her tone. "Lieutenant?"

The lieutenant spun in his chair to face her and she could see the confusion evident on his face. "Ma'am, I've run the energy signature through the computer twice." The lieutenant swallowed. "We don't have an exact match in the database but the computer is giving an eighty percent probability match."

"Spit it out, Lieutenant."

"Ma'am, the closest match is a Saiph star drive."

PLANET PARS - PERSEUS ARM - 6400 LIGHT YEARS FROM EARTH

The room fell into silence as the Chairman of the Council of Twelve called for order. Chairman Tarrov was the longest serving chairperson in the 242 years of the council's existence. He was also the oldest serving member of the council at 163 years of age. His fur may have lost the moonlight black of his youth, replaced steadily by fine silver, but his mind was still as sharp as in his youth, even if it was now tempered with the experience his fellow younger council members still had to learn.

"My fellow councilors. By now, we have all had a chance to review the data Sub Leader Verus recovered from our surveillance platform. I think the time we all knew would come eventually is upon us."

Tarrov looked slowly around the table at the other council members. Some signaled their agreement, others stayed perfectly still, not committing themselves, but not one disagreed with him.

"When our forefathers left the original planet Pars, in the first wave of three colony ships, and headed out amongst the stars for a new home, they had no idea what they would find. Not all the probes deployed to the nearest stars had returned when the decision was taken to launch the first of the colony ships. How impatient we were."

Tarrov went on retelling the history every living Persai knew by heart. "Our forefathers made planet fall here. Ten years after leaving home. As planned, the colony ships were broken into pieces to form the basis of the new colony, knowing all the time the following ships would bring the parts and personnel required to expand the fledgling colony." Tarrov's tone became bitter. "But the ships never arrived. Two years after landing, we found out why."

The images of the ships appearing in orbit around the home planet, the frantic attempts to establish contact and finally the nuclear death that rained down, all transmitted to the stranded colonists with a final message. Save yourselves, for we are lost. You are all that remain!

"Between them, the three colony ships carried 12000 colonists along with everything needed to establish a viable colony. That is what we did. We named the colony Pars so we would never forget our home world." Tarrov looked around at the rough-cut stone walls of the council chambers. "But the threat from this unknown enemy still exists, so we decided to hide all signs of ourselves on this world, moved everything underground. That was when we discovered the true nature of our enemy."

Unbidden, all eyes in the room were drawn to the dais on which stood the raised lectern in the corner of the room.

"Our miners, looking for minerals stumbled on the cavern containing the Saiph library. Although it took us years, we decoded the information contained in them. We learned the truth. We are the descendants of some long lost Saiph experiment, which means nothing to us for we are our own people. Our only true link to the Saiph is our common enemy. The Enemy!

"As they have hunted down and exterminated the Saiph, so they might hunt us. The last of our people. We would simply cease to exist. A footnote in history." Tarrov's voice became hard edged "But we survived!" Around the table, the council members' heads rose proudly and they each had a glint of defiance in their eyes.

The entire room reverberated to the banging of fists on the council table, the feeling of intense hatred filled the room for those who had destroyed their home was a living breathing thing.

Tarrov allowed the cacophony to go on for a moment longer before raising his hand for quiet. "We learned from the library and, although we didn't have the resources to replicate exactly the ships from the library, we improvised and we overcame the technical challenges. The only thing we could never overcome was our need to husband our resources. For years now, we have kept our population artificially low, for any sign on the surface of organized farming could lead The Enemy to us. We looked beyond this star system. For the past twenty years, we have placed surveillance platforms in systems listed in the Saiph library, avoiding those which give off any form of electromagnetic signals, for fear they could be The Enemy. But now… now, my fellow councilors, we have seen The Enemy defeated."

Tarrov touched a control and an image of Radford's ship, TDF *Cartagena*, firing into the Others ship during the battle for Garunda appeared.

"Whoever these people are, the data clearly shows they have placed some sort of warning buoys around the system and detected the approach of The Enemy. But not until it became obvious The Enemy intended to close with the populated planet did they intervene and destroy The Enemy ships."

Tarrov rested his hands on top of the table. "The important thing is what happened next."

One of the junior councilors spoke up. "But, Chairman, nothing happened next. The unknown ships made no approach to the planet."

Tarrov's lips curled back, exposing a vicious set of canine fangs. "Exactly, my young friend. Exactly."

The same junior councilor looked confused. "I'm sorry, Chairman. I admit to not understanding your point."

Tarrov touched another control, and the data ran forward until it showed the formation of the ships of BatFor 1 following the battle. "If these people had planned to take the planet following their defeat of The Enemy, then why are they forming a defensive shell around the planet?"

Understanding slowly spread through the room and Tarrov gave it a moment to fully sink in. "Until Sub Leader Verus downloaded the data from the surveillance platform, it had recorded only the comings and goings of one small shuttle to and from the planet. Even after the original ships that had taken part in the battle departed and were immediately replaced by a force of similar makeup, no hostile move was made to either fire on the planet or invade."

Tarrov saw on the faces surrounding him the moment of comprehension. "Fellow councilors. For years, we slowly built a small but powerful fleet in the uncertain hope that one day we could have our vengeance on The Enemy. In our heart of hearts, we knew our fleet would be too small to take on the might of The Enemy." Tarrov pointed at the human ships "But these people stood up to The Enemy and defeated them."

Every Councilor in the room was looking at the image of the human ships. "I propose we return to the system in which the battle with The Enemy took place and offer an alliance with this unknown race."

There. Tarrov had committed himself.

The gathered leaders of the Persai spent a long moment looking from Tarrov and then back to the image of the human ships. One councilor began banging the table in a slow, methodical manner. One by one, the remaining councilors joined in until the entire room reverberated to a slow, methodical drumming.

OFFICE OF THE SECRETARY OF DEFENSE - GENEVA - EARTH

The weekly planning and coordination meeting with General Joyce was ending. With the rapid expansion the Terran Defense Force had overseen over the past few years, Secretary Helset had found that to stop himself being bogged down in all the minutia, it was easier for him to have Joyce brief him on a weekly basis. This allowed both men to raise any issues.

This week it was the planning of a timetable for the training and equipping of the Garundans. As Joyce had pointed out, although you could not fault their enthusiasm, it would simply take time to bring their basic understanding of the advanced human technology to a level where they could progress to and employ the same technology.

"So give me a ballpark figure then, Keyton."

Joyce leaned back in his chair. His face blanked for a moment as he ran numbers in his head. "Well, Mr. Secretary. If, for the sake of argument, we write off the current Garundan industrial base, start from scratch as we did for Janus, I would say we are looking at maybe two years before we have established sufficient in-system resources to begin constructing hulls. As far as training goes, the proposal is we introduce a tailored course at the Academy for Garundan officers, with an expanded syllabus to bring them up to the same level as our own officer corps. Other ranks will be treated in a similar fashion with extra classes added to basic training. We would look at moving them to the training fleet. It is felt and I must agree that hands on practical experience is more important than theory."

Haslet felt himself nodding in agreement. "It appears the Office of the Joint Chiefs has this pretty well in hand."

"Thank you, Mr. Secretary"

"Moving on. I read the proposal for the deployment of a permanent force to be based in the Garundan system."

"Yes, Mr. Secretary. Admiral Jing and the Strategy Board feel since we are now committed to the defense of Garunda for at least the next two years, rather than rotate a BatFor every three months, our first order of business is to establish a fleet base under a Vice Admiral. He or she would oversee the buildup of our forces and the integration of Garundan units as they come on line."

"Sounds like a wise move, do you have anyone in mind for the post?"

Before Joyce could answer, the urgent beeping of his wrist Comm demanded his attention. Both men knew only something of the utmost priority permitted interruption to this meeting. With a look to the Secretary for go ahead, the general accepted the call.

"General, Commodore Riesling, Duty Watch Officer. A courier drone just arrived in system with a priority message from Rear Admiral Chavez in the Garundan system."

The general and the secretary exchanged a worried look. Had the Others returned in force to finish what they had originally intended for Garunda?

"I'm in the Secretary of Defense's office, please patch the message through."

There was a brief pause before Helset's holo cube sprang to life and the face of Rear Admiral Chavez appeared. Helset touched the playback control and the message played,

"Central Command this is Admiral Chavez. At fourteen twelve hours, Terran Standard Time, an unidentified ship arrived in the Garundan system. The ship has not attempted to progress any further in system as of this time. It is my intention to dispatch a flotilla of destroyers to investigate and report to me before any further action is taken. It should be noted, however, the energy signature is a match for the one which we detected three weeks ago in the same general area as this ship. I must remind you at the time the ship was tentatively identified as Saiph. I will report to you when I know more. Chavez out."

TDF *Mishima* - 31 Aquilae

Analisa Chavez forced herself to relax as she contemplated the tactical plot displayed in the holo cube in her private briefing room. The plot showed the positions of all the ships constituting BatFor 3, but Chavez only had eyes for the three blue icons representing the destroyer flotilla she had dispatched to investigate the lone red icon which remained stationary some 39.4 AUs above the ecliptic plane.

Those three blue icons were now stationary and spread out in a line some 50000 kilometers from the unknown ship. Not for the first time, Chavez found herself cursing the huge distances involved in trying to retain command and control throughout an entire star system. For a radio message to reach her from the destroyers it took nearly five and a half hours, for them to receive her reply another five and a half — eleven hours in total. A lot could happen in eleven hours. To combat this, courier drones were employed to make micro folds. Nevertheless, there was still a time delay as a message was downloaded, a reply composed and uploaded to the drone and sent on its way back to Chavez. Yes, it dramatically reduced the communications lag but, and not for the first time, Chavez wished it was she who was out there. However, she knew her place was here, in overall command of BatFor 3, not gallivanting all over the star system.

Analisa's Comm beeped. She touched a control and the holo cube split to show Lieutenant Kyle at Communications. "Ma'am, a courier drone from *Rhin* has arrived and the message downloaded."

At last! Thought Analisa. TDF *Rhin* was the lead destroyer of the formation she had sent to investigate the unknown ship. Louis Chesneau, formerly her own Tactical officer before getting his own well-deserved command, captained *Rhin*. Analisa knew Chesneau to be cool and level headed under pressure, and Analisa had the utmost confidence in him. "Pipe it down to my briefing room, please."

The face of Chesneau replaced Kyle's and Analisa touched a control to allow the message to play. "Admiral, the flotilla is currently holding station 50,000 kilometers from the unknown vessel. As per your instructions, we are not using any active systems to scan the vessel in case they are misinterpreted as hostile. Our passive systems confirm your original analysis. The energy signature is an eighty percent match for a Saiph star drive. Now we are close enough for the passive systems to get a good look at the vessel, the computers are telling us, although not a perfect match for the Saiph designs in the database, many of the vessel's features are similar. In my opinion, they are too similar to be a coincidence."

Analisa paused the playback as she considered this new information. A ship emitting an energy signature virtually the same as that in the Saiph database? Now Chesneau was telling her he had identified design similarities as well. *The plot thickens,* Analisa thought, as she touched the control to allow the message to continue.

"It would appear the vessel has powered down all its systems except life support. Immediately upon our arrival, the vessel began to transmit a directional radio signal toward us, it repeated the same short message. We ran it through linguistics and surprise, surprise, we found a match in the Saiph database. As best as we can tell, the message being transmitted is one word: 'friend'."

Anyone else in the briefing room would have likened Analisa's face to a goldfish – her mouth dropped open and stayed that way for all of five seconds. She regained control and her mouth snapped shut. Analisa's mind raced. Had they made contact with some remnant of what they all thought were the long extinct Saiph? The authorities gave an admiral wide-ranging powers of discretion, but any decision making here was well above her pay grade. This needed direction from not just the Admiralty but from the top levels of the Republic. They were light years away. Analisa was the one on the spot, but she was no diplomat. Then a light bulb lit up in the admiral's head: Ambassador Beckett! He was back on Garunda as the Terran Republic's official ambassador to the new Pan Garundan Government.

Analisa touched a control and the face of Lieutenant Kyle appeared before her. "Lieutenant, download to *Rhin* they are to continue to hold position and take no action unless in defense of themselves. Then get hold of Ambassador Beckett at the Republic embassy and tell him I request his presence on board *Mishima* as a matter of urgency. And please attach the message from *Rhin*. Once the embassy confirms receipt of the signal, dispatch a shuttle to collect the Ambassador. Lastly, send a copy of *Rhin*'s message back to Central Command."

Without waiting for confirmation, Analisa cut the link and sat back in her seat with a wicked grin, imagining the faces of the Ambassador and those at Central Command as they watched the message from Chesneau.

CHAPTER TWENTY

Massacre

OFFICE OF THE PRESIDENT OF THE TERRAN REPUBLIC - GENEVA - EARTH

As she closed her eyes and used her fingers to massage her temples in a vain effort to ward off the oncoming headache, Rebecca understood why no president was permitted to run for more than three consecutive terms.

Rebecca put her burgeoning headache down to the latest message from Aaron. The Ambassador, accompanied by Doctor Bath, had been waiting for the shuttle sent for them by Admiral Chavez. They wasted no time, on their arrival on board the *Mishima*, to badger the admiral into relocating her flagship to join the destroyers sitting off the unknown vessel which had been hanging in space broadcasting the Saiph word for friend.

Bath was an expert in her field of linguistics and at Aaron's direction began a tentative dialogue in the language of the Saiph with the unknown vessel, all the while believing they had indeed encountered the Saiph themselves.

The crew of the unknown vessel agreed to a video conference. The image as it appeared in the holo cubes on board *Mishima* quashed the hope that man had at last found the Saiph. The central being was tall, well built, with short, almost silver fur and faintly familiar canine features. Tarrov, Chairman of the Council of Pars, stared back at Aaron, in the background, the leaders of a race calling themselves Persai could be seen. Aaron put a personal footnote on his message, Tarrov reminded him of an elderly werewolf. Rebecca smiled to herself as she thought the comment was certainly not politically correct, but the more she thought about it and recalled her first look at the images of the Persai she could see the resemblance.

Rebecca blamed her imminent headache on the rest of the message. Tarrov relayed to Ambassador Beckett the story of the destruction of their Persai home world, destroyed by 'The Enemy', or as it turns out, the Others. Tarrov continued with his tale, describing The Enemy's sudden appearance in orbit around the original Persai home world swiftly followed by its wanton destruction – despite the population's pleas for mercy. They had received no reply from the silent enemy. Tarrov told of the establishment of the colony, naming it Pars after the dead home world and of the colonists' decision to secrete themselves underground for fear of discovery by the Others. Then the all-important discovery of the Saiph library and the knowledge it brought. Armed with the knowledge the Persai had built starships and once more ventured out into the night sky in an attempt to discover the fate of the other worlds listed in the Saiph database. Caution tempered the Persai's curiosity. Deep down, they knew if the Others discovered the new Pars, then its fate would be as its dead namesake. The order went out, any system showing signs of artificial energy sources was to be avoided and would never be visited again.

Rebecca and her advisers thought the latter statement was possibly a little short sighted on the part of the Persai. However, when Tarrov explained the Persai had enforced an artificial ceiling on their population, a conscious decision made by them after taking into account their limited subterranean resources, Rebecca and her advisors began to understand their decision. The Persai made the conscious decision not to mine the asteroid belt of their system and take advantage of its abundant resources for fear of discovery by the Others. This led to the Persai's complete reliance on only what they could mine from the planet without leaving any telltale signs. Hence, the limited numbers of Persai ships.

The Secretary of Defense and the Joint Chiefs had initially been disappointed when they had heard the Persai had only a limited number of ships available. The thought of having to stretch the already overextended Terran Defense Force even more thinly was not an appealing one. Jealousy soon replaced this disappointment. The Persai had had over 150 years to examine the Saiph database. As their understanding of Saiph technology grew, so had the sophistication of their ships. Joyce and Doctor Moore, representing Research and Development, had been practically drooling at the thought of getting their hands on one of the Persai ships.

That was exactly what Tarrov offered. Access to Persai technology. In return, an alliance. Unlike Garunda, which was completely reliant on the TDF for defense from the Others until its own forces were up to sufficient strength, Persai had a limited number of ships available with which to defend itself. In return for access to Persai technology, Tarrov wanted a guarantee, if the Others were to threaten Pars, then the TDF would come to their aid.

Rebecca felt she was being inexorably dragged toward an unknown fate. From the very moment of the Gravity Drive's discovery, to the revelations of the Saiph database and humankind's first clash with the Others, which led to the rapid expansion of human forces, and then her decision to commit those same forces to the defense of Garunda. Now the Persai had arrived on the scene with their offer of advanced Saiph technology and an alliance that would again commit human forces to the defense of an alien world.

She closed her eyes and resumed massaging her temples. The urgent beeping of her comm forced her tired eyes open as she accepted the incoming message. "Yes?"

The face of her personal assistant appeared above her desk. "I'm sorry to disturb you, Madam President, but we've just received news from Central Command the research ship dispatched to Delta Pavonis has come under attack from the Others."

DELTA PAVONIS - 19.92 LIGHT YEARS FROM EARTH

The insertion from orbit progressed quietly. There was no sign the Others had detected their arrival in the system, never mind their stealthy approach to the planet. Vladimir Egnorov looked at his rescue team. They were the best of the best, men who had been Special Forces for most of their adult lives. Not one had backed down when he had asked for volunteers for the mission. Each marine knew the risks of dropping into potential enemy held territory. The scientists had made no contact with Earth since the first report via courier drone of a single ship, identified as one of the Others Buzzard class, appearing in orbit. Of that research ship and her crew, there was no sign. Hopefully, the scientists who had been on the surface at the research base had followed Standard Operating Procedure, powered everything down and moved away from the main research buildings to the pre prepared extraction point to await rescue.

The tinny sound of the pilot's voice over Comms interrupted his musings. "Two minutes from the drop point!"

The drop point was the lowest the shuttle could come to the planetary atmosphere without leaving a visible indication of its presence. The marines decided on a high altitude, high speed insertion by exo-atmospheric jump. Risky, to say the least. The marines in their Wraith combat suits would jump in a cocoon of armor, which they jokingly called 'eggs', designed to get them onto the ground as quickly as possible.

Vladimir acknowledged the pilot's message and gave the thumbs up to the loadmaster, who passed the message to the company of marines to get into their protective cocoons. Vladimir's heads-up display told him all his marines acknowledged the instruction and sealed their eggs before he too sealed himself inside his and awaited the drop.

With a gut wrenching pull, the egg dropped from the shuttle. He could see via his display the exterior of the egg heating up, its ablative armor burning away as it dropped into the atmosphere at supersonic speeds. Speed was life, the sooner he was on the ground the less time any enemy gunner had time to shoot him down.

The retro rockets firing forced him into his couch, and then the front of the pod blew off and he released his harnesses stepping out of the egg, bringing his rifle to the ready position as he checked 360-degrees around him for targets. None were visible.

Vladimir called up the location of his company's Eggs on the display and found all but two had landed safely. One had had a retro failure and had ploughed into the earth at a speed approaching Mach two, fatal for the marine inside. The other had not made it through the atmosphere and had broken up, spreading itself and its unlucky occupant over the upper atmosphere.

His heads-up display flashed a point on the map, the rally point, and he headed in its direction as fast as the Wraith suit would carry him. Better to clear the landing zone before the Others had a chance to bring fire down on it.

On reaching the rally point, Vladimir conferred quickly with his platoon commanders before they formed the troops up and began to move in the direction from where the scientists' beacon was located. Time was of the essence: the more time they gave the Others to gather their strength, the more chance the marines would be pinned down before they could link up with the scientists and the shuttles from the light cruiser TDF *Konigsberg* to lift them all to safety.

The landing zone was only a kilometer from the scientists' beacon and the marines made good time, covering the ground quickly but tactically, ready to react to any threat.

As the lead platoon reached the pickup point, they reported no sign of the scientists. Vladimir ordered the company on toward the main research base on the most likely route the scientists should have used to reach the pickup point.

The marines did not have far to go. Vladimir got a call from the lead platoon commander to come forward. When he reached their location, the sight of 264 dead scientists confronted him. Laid out in a line extending back toward the research station buildings, each scientist had a single, precise entry wound in their forehead, if he had to guess, from a handheld laser pistol. There was no sign of resistance on the scientists' part. No weapons in sight and each of the scientists had their hands bound behind their backs. The Others had executed them. Left their bodies laid out in a macabre message to whoever came to discover their fate. He struggled to keep his anger in check as he signaled the *Konigsberg* for pickup.

He understood the message. One day, he would make sure he replied in kind.

Office of the President of the Terran Republic - Geneva - Earth

The news of the massacre on Delta Pavonis spread like wildfire. Somehow, the press had gotten hold of the grisly video footage, which showed the neatly laid out bodies of the scientists with their hands bound behind their backs and the single hole in the center of each man and woman's forehead.

Maybe it was because the images evoked memories of humankind's own terrible past, that the reaction of the general population was so strong. The memories of the barbarism of the Nazis, the ethnic cleansing in the Balkans and throughout Africa. The religious wars of the mid twenty-first century had led to the near extinction of humans in World Wars Three and Four. This was something humanity thought consigned to history. But no, here, once again was an example of an evil man thought would never revisit him.

It was not that the people did not recognize the Others caused the extinction of the Saiph, or that they nearly caused the extinction of the Persai and the attempted extinction of the Garunda. It was not the losses BatFor 1 had taken in defending Garunda. This time, it was the coldblooded execution of unarmed men and women.

It must not happen again!

In the weeks following President Coston's office had been strangely quiet. Yes, immediately after the news broke, the president addressed the people and there had been the normal denunciations of the Others actions along with the government's promise to take whatever steps it deemed necessary to protect the Republic. Apart from that, the president refused all other requests for interviews. Unsurprisingly, her opponents in the Senate had pounced on her silence as a sign of weakness and were attempting to make what political capital they could from it.

Two months to the day after the massacre, President Coston's office contacted all the major broadcasting outlets and informed them the president requested airtime the same evening for an announcement. As news of the request spread, many a senator wondered if the president was about to announce her resignation, but try as they might to garner details of the address none of the president's staff were talking.

All around the world and on human habitats throughout the solar system, men, women and children watched as the face of President Rebecca Coston appeared in their holo cubes.

"My fellow humans. The events on Delta Pavonis have shaken us all to the core. It has wakened in us memories of days gone by, days we prayed we would never see again. Humankind saw so much pain and anguish at his own hands and in the end, you, the people, joined together to say *no more*! No more death and destruction at our own hands. No more senseless slaughter of the innocent. Out of that time of sadness, we forged a new beginning. We came together as one and the Terran Republic was born. We rebuilt our shattered world and brought peace and prosperity to all. As man has travelled amongst the stars, we have discovered many new wonders and, following the discovery of the Saiph database, have been forced to reassess our place in the universe. Our travels have also brought us new friends."

As the camera pulled back it showed on Rebecca's right, Prime Minister Bezled, now head of the Garundan Pan National Government and, on Rebecca's left, Chairman Tarrov of the Persai.

"But what we have also found is a race, the Others, whose only objective seems to be the destruction of everything they find to be alien. I am sure Prime Minister Bezled, Chairman Tarrov, you the people and I, agree the Others are a threat to us all. It is something we cannot and will not tolerate!"

"During the past two months, my office has been working frantically behind the scenes on a project I wish to reveal to you now. I believe neither the Republic, Garunda nor Pars have the resources individually to tackle the threat from the Others. Garunda, with our help, is still over a year away from the ability to resist any attack from the Others. The Persai are more technologically advanced than the Others but they find themselves in the same situation as the Saiph found themselves in. They are numerically inferior to the Others and would be simply swamped by greater numbers. Although we have defeated the Others in battle, we still have no idea of their total strength."

Rebecca took a deep breath and pushed on. "In consultation with my esteemed colleagues from Garunda and Pars, I propose we establish a Commonwealth Union of Planets incorporating our three civilizations. Together this Commonwealth would abide by a Commonwealth Charter, which would establish a common foreign and defense policy enshrine our belief in free trade and travel between worlds. A right to democracy, human rights and the rule of law. Each member planet would retain its own independence within the Commonwealth but every individual would have dual citizenship of their own planet and of the Commonwealth and would be afforded the same protection under law as any other citizen no matter where they are."

In millions of homes around the solar system, the silence was tangible.

"There is nothing really new in these proposals. When the Terran Republic was founded, the principles I have outlined to you were the same ones that allowed humankind to live in peace and harmony for hundreds of years, so why should they not allow the Garundan, the Persai and ourselves to do the same? We know from the Saiph database they visited at least seventeen worlds where they dabbled in the indigenous life form's DNA. Who are we to say that in the future we may not come across other civilizations on these worlds from whom we, and they, may benefit from being a part of this Commonwealth Union of Planets?

"What of the spacefaring civilization found by our survey ships in Messier 54? We know, for a fact, they are a result of Saiph intervention. But what of our own colony world of Janus? Is it not realistic to think, as its population grows and humans are born and raised on Janus that they grow up considering Janus not Earth to be their home? I foresee a day, in the not too distant future, when Janus will want to be its own world and not simply a colony. Rather than lose them, let us embrace them as an equal into the Commonwealth Union.

"As you can see, Prime Minister Bezled and Chairman Tarrov stand by my side. They have agreed in principle to the establishment of this Commonwealth. At the end of this broadcast they will return to Garunda and Pars to seek the approval of their people. I have ordered a plebiscite to be carried out on Earth and Janus thirty days from today. It will ask one question… Do we form this Commonwealth Union of Planets?

"In the meantime, I ask you to consider this question: Do we face the future together? Or do we struggle on by ourselves and hope we can overcome whatever else the universe decides to fling in our path?"

The camera zoomed in to show only the face of President Coston. "I have faith you will make the right decision. Thank you for your time, and goodnight."

KUIPER BELT - 31 AQUILAE

The Others' ship slipped into the Kuiper Belt of the 31 Aquilae system, home to the Garunda, and came to a halt. It used a small body approximately 100 kilometers across to mask its presence from the many energy signatures it identified as spacefaring vessels closer in system.

When the six vessels dispatched to erase the alien species detected on the fourth planet had not returned this single destroyer deployed from the nearest fleet base to find them. It had taken two months at maximum cruising speed for them to reach the system.

On its approach to the system the destroyer detected no signs of the ships it was sent to find, so the captain decided to drop back into normal space further than normal, just beyond the system's Kuiper Belt, about sixty AUs from the system's star. It allowed his ship to coast in unpowered. Covering the distance had taken his small ship nearly three weeks but it had been worth it.

The Kuiper Belt surrounding the 31 Aquilae system extended from around thirty-eight AUs from the star to around sixty AUs. Similar to the Sol System's asteroid belt, but far larger, it was composed of mainly small bodies left over from the formation of the 31 Aquilae system. Although circular in shape, the belt actually extended approximately ten-degrees below and above the ecliptic that made the belt more donut shaped than circular.

The destroyer captain used the ten-degree angle above the ecliptic plane to his advantage. He positioned his ship to look down into the solar system to get a clear look as to what lay in system. The presence of so many spacefaring vessels had surprised the crew. This system was supposed to be incapable of spaceflight, this incapability was the reason only six ships were dispatched to ensure its destruction, obviously a mistake.

It was obvious to the captain the race from the fourth planet had already been conquered by a technologically more advanced race, a race his people had not yet met. From his ship's readings of the inner system, there appeared to be heavy inter-system traffic indicative of mining operations in the asteroid belt and, if he was not mistaken, the beginnings of construction of ship yards in orbit around the fourth planet. He had seen enough. The fleet must know of this new threat.

With the same alacrity as he had used to get his small ship into the system, the captain edged his ship away again.

CHAPTER TWENTY-ONE
Pars

PLANET PARS
PERSEUS ARM – 6400 LIGHT YEARS
FROM EARTH

As TDF *Northern Lights* smoothly entered orbit around Pars its crew hastily prepared its single shuttle for departure. *Northern Lights* was one of the new fast courier ships, designated Clipper class, entering service and was specifically designed to get a small number of passengers from one planet to another as quickly as possible. The ship was designed around its Gravity Drive. Engineers fitted the biggest and most efficient drive into its small hull, and then squeezed the most accurate navigational computer into it. This allowed it to make longer jumps in fold space and to make micro jumps, thereby dispensing with the need for the normal reaction drives, which other larger vessels needed to use within a system.

With the successful formation of the Commonwealth Union of Planets the month before, the need for small courier ships of this type, to shuttle diplomatic missions around the new Commonwealth, had already risen exponentially and they would see a lot more of these little Clippers in the future.

On board today, the *Northern Lights* carried a very impatient Doctor Jeff Moore and a small, handpicked team from Research and Development eager to take up the Persai invitation to share their insights into Saiph technology. Accompanying them was Ambassador Aaron Beckett and his assistant, Doctor Patricia Bath, who had come to Pars to establish Earth's diplomatic presence along with a group of diplomats from Garunda with the same intention. Last, but not least, was Rear Admiral John Radford, tasked by the Joint Chiefs to assess the Persai military strength.

John was a last minute addition to the team after Admiral Wiggans from the Joint Chiefs' personal staff fractured his leg in a skiing accident. It was felt that John's input, as the only flag officer to have actually met and defeated the Others in a fleet engagement made him an ideal replacement.

Standing around the boat bay on the *Northern Lights* John found himself disagreeing strongly with the Joint Chiefs' assignment of him to the Pars mission. BatFor 1 was due to return to Garunda in a week's time following its stint in the hands of the shipyards that had been repairing the damage from the battle with the Others. As its commanding officer John felt his place was there, ensuring it was at its peak performance and ready to deploy – not light years away inspecting Persai ships which, from what he had gathered from the briefing pack, represented the equivalent of a small Terran battle force.

Sure, the additional ships would always be helpful, but could not some staffer from the Joint Chiefs' staff have been assigned instead of him? John thought irritably.

Since arriving on the *Northern Lights*, John had had his head stuck in the briefing pack and had only managed to catch glimpses of his fellow mission members as they had boarded. The Terran delegates he had only previously seen pictures of.

John sighed as he waited impatiently for the civilians to board the shuttle. The Garundan delegation was already aboard and had been chattering away like a bunch of excited schoolchildren. John felt a smile grow on his face. Who could blame the Garundans? Less than one year ago, they thought they were alone in the universe and were still using primitive steam engines. Now, they were an equal part of a multi star system Commonwealth which jumped their technology forward at least 300 years.

John's train of thought was broken as Beckett and Bath entered the boat bay, accompanied by a very animated Moore. John's smile returned as he watched Bath, whose pictures he had to admit did not do her justice, pretend she was interested in whatever Moore was talking about. Bath noticed John watching her and rolled her eyes at him. Caught unawares, John let out a small laugh, which he managed to cover with a not very convincing cough.

"Something caught in your throat, Admiral?" asked a smiling Patricia as she walked past him and entered the shuttle.

For the first time in a long time, John did not know what to say and he just shook his head and followed the small group into the shuttle. Maybe this mission was not going to be as bad as he thought.

––––––––

As the shuttle descended through the atmosphere, John got his first proper look at Pars, the home of humanity's latest ally in the struggle against the Others. The shuttle pilot had piped into the passenger area the feed from the nose camera. John had to admit he was not overly impressed so far. Speeding past below the shuttle John could only see kilometer after kilometer of rolling grassland and every now and then a herd of large herbivore that scattered in all directions as the shuttle shot past at almost tree top height. There were no signs of any buildings or even crops anywhere to spoil the completely natural look. Any passing survey ship would take the planet to be uninhabited. It reminded John of the veldts of southern Africa except the green of the grass was slightly off.

"The grass doesn't look right." Commented John more to himself than anyone else and immediately regretted opening his mouth.

Jeff Moore lent forward in his seat behind John so his head was protruding between the headrests.

"Oh, that's probably because of the slightly different shift in the yellow light emanating from the local star. We see because light bounces off things and then into our eyes, the colour that bounces off is what it looks like. Chlorophyll looks green because it stores the red and blue light and bounces off the green and yellow light which go to our eyes…"

John turned in his seat and gave Jeff Moore a look, which cut him off midsentence.

"Thank you, Doctor, for your succinct explanation."

As Jeff's mouth was left hanging open in midsentence, John could make out a muffled laugh from the seat across the aisle from him. Turning his head John regarded the source of the laughter. Patricia Bath was trying her best to fain interest in her PAD she was holding up at eye level. Noticing John's attention she tried to regain control of herself but continuing shaking of her slim frame gave her away.

John set his face in his best admiral's scowl and returned his attention to the passing terrain.

The shuttle was following a Persai ship, which met them as they had entered the upper atmosphere. John read the scrolling read outs along the bottom of the image when he noticed that both ships had slowed significantly. Perhaps they were at last approaching their destination.

With a small bump not completely cancelled out by the compensator, the shuttle crested a small rise and without warning dropped like a stone into a wide canyon. John heard a short gasp from Jeff Moore and for once John had to agree with him. Laid out before him was a canyon the like of which John could only equate to the Valles Mariners on Mars. The shuttle continued to drop as the canyon walls towered above the shuttle. John's repeater showed him the extent of the canyon as the shuttle levelled out after a descent of nearly eight kilometers. The canyon was only two kilometers across at its widest point, narrowing to under a kilometer in places and it ran for over 3000 kilometers. A massive, jagged scar ran across the equator of Pars.

John felt pressure on his headrest again as Jeff used it to pull himself forward.

"This canyon was probably formed by some massive tectonic event in the crust of the planet millions of years ago…"

John tuned him out as Jeff continued to wax lyrical about similar events scientists had discovered in the solar system. John's full attention focused on the scrolling read outs in his display and he brought up the virtual keyboard and began to tap away frantically. This got the attention of Patricia Bath and she unlocked her restraints and stood in the aisle so she could better see what had so interested the admiral that even the incessant lecturing of Jeff Moore had failed to distract him. As Patricia lent over to get a better view of John's display, he sat back with a satisfied grunt as a series of red blocks began appearing.

"What are those, Admiral?"

John let a small smile appear on his face. "Those, Doctor Bath…" As John extended a long finger and pointed at the red blocks. "Are weapons emplacements. Damn well shielded from electronic and optical sensors but definitely there and, from the sniff at the power readings I can get, I'd say that they'd give even the batteries on our most powerful warship a run for its money. These people are serious about protecting wherever we are headed."

Without warning, the shuttle rapidly decelerated and made a radical left turn. The compensators failed in their attempts to keep the turn smooth for the passengers. Patricia, standing in the aisle leaning over John's seat to view his display, tumbled head long into his lap in a flurry of arms and legs saved from any serious injury by the simple expedient of John wrapping his arms around her and holding her close to him as the shuttle once again regained level flight.

For the first time John became aware of the faint smell of her perfume as he looked into her wide emerald colored eyes and felt the warmth of her body next to his. In an instant, the moment was gone as Patricia's face flushed scarlet with embarrassment and she struggled to her feet and attempted to regain her demeanor flicking her hair from her face.

"Thank you, Admiral, and my apologies for my clumsiness."

John broke into a wide grin. "My pleasure, Doctor. And please call me John, after being so close I feel it's only right we call each other by our first names don't you?"

If Patricia's face could have gone even more scarlet, it did. "You may call me Patricia. Not Pat or Patty I am not a pet or a small child." She said in a stern voice as she sat back into her own seat and secured the harness while John looked on, a ludicrous childlike grin on his face.

"Patricia it is then."

As Patricia looked away, she caught the smiling face of Aaron Beckett regarding her from the seat diagonally across the small aisle. Fixing him a look a scolding parent gives their wayward child, she said "And you can take that smile off your face too."

Chuckling softly Aaron could only comment. "A good politician should retain their composure no matter the circumstances, Patricia."

In reply, Patricia stuck her tongue out briefly in a most unladylike manner before closing her eyes and wishing this flight would end before she could embarrass herself even further.

It seemed Patricia's prayers were to be answered as the shuttle came to a stop at the entrance to a large cave entrance. The Persai vessel led the way as the human shuttle followed closely behind, its external lights casting strange shadows across the walls of the cave. Jeff Moore let out a low whistle as the extent of the cave was revealed on his display.

"When nature wants to remind us we are only a small part of the cosmos it does it in style. According to the radar returns, the cave is 270 meters high, 160 meters wide and extends for approximately five kilometers. Some of the stalagmites are over seventy meters tall. This place even has its own river running through it."

The next five kilometers passed in near total silence as the each of the shuttle occupants marveled at the beauty of nature passing by above, below and on both sides of the slowly coasting shuttle. The shuttle came to a halt again as it reached the end of the cave, hovering in place in front of what appeared to be an implacable stone wall. As John looked on a sliver of light fractured the wall top to bottom, gradually the sliver widened to reveal what had to be the biggest airlock John had ever seen.

"Now that's impressive. Although I don't see any landing pads." John altered his display to show the pilots display and now it was his turn to let out a soft whistle.

Aaron turned to John. "Perhaps you would like to enlighten us, Admiral?"

Touching a few controls John sent the information he was reading to Aaron's display. "We're not seeing any landing pads as we still have something like two kilometers to travel."

The shuttle glided forward and the massive cave doors sealed behind it. An equally large set of what looked like battle-armored doors began to open in front of the shuttle revealing a sharply sloping shaft. This shaft had not been naturally formed. As the shuttle moved along the shaft, its smooth sides were indicative of very intense heat, probably from a powerful mining laser which had simply melted its way through the natural rock.

The Persai do not do things by half, do they? Thought John. Even with the best equipment available, it would have taken human engineers years to build something like this. The shuttle passed through another two of the massive armored doors before finally passing through into what was unmistakably a major shuttle bay which, although not as big as the natural cave at the start of their subterranean journey certainly gave it a run for its money. Shuttles easily the size of the one carrying the delegation were parked around the bay. The scurrying figures of their crew and maintenance personnel allowing John to use their known size to judge the true extent of the bay.

The shuttle made its way an oversize pad located near one corner of the bay where John could see a small crowd gathering. *Well*, thought John, *time to meet the locals. Let's just hope they're as friendly as I've been led to believe.*

The shuttle bounced lightly on its extended landing gear, the entire delegation released their restraints as the shuttle passenger door opened with a slight hiss, and John could feel his ears pop as the pressure equalized. This being a primarily a political mission Aaron Beckett led the way out of the shuttle and down the steps onto the bay floor and toward the welcoming party.

This was John's first meeting with the Persai. Of course he had seen images of them in the briefing packs but meeting one in the flesh, so to speak, was something else. Whoever had compared them to werewolves had it spot on. Even down to the slightly bent spines, which led to their heads, being carried less upright on their necks than humans.

John hung back as a Persai with more silver fur than the black of his younger entourage approached Aaron. This older Persai stopped in front of Aaron, raised his right arm and extended it out with the hand/paw facing the ground showing the exposed palm.

Through the translator bug in his ear, John heard the Persai address Aaron. "I am Tarrov, Chairman of the Council of Twelve and I welcome you as comrades in arms and hope that together we may vanquish our enemy."

Aaron extended his right arm and mimicked the pose of Tarrov. "I am Aaron Beckett, sent by the president of the Terran Republic as a sign of friendship and trust and in the hope we may become allies in our struggle against evil."

A Persai elicited, what John could only describe as, a low growl. The source of the growl stood slightly apart and exuded a sense of aloofness from the main welcoming group. Chairman Tarrov's mouth dropped open in what

John later learned was the Persai version of a laugh. "May I present Force Leader Taminth? The Force Leader will be your military liaison for the duration of your stay. Taminth has viewed your fleets' destruction of the enemy with relish and keenly awaits his opportunity to fight alongside you."

Aaron turned and beckoned John forward. "In that case the Force Leader may wish to speak to Admiral Radford. Admiral Radford was the commander of the human fleet which was victorious that day."

Taminth took a step forward and presented his hand in the same manner as Tarrov had. "An honor, Admiral."

Not missing a heartbeat John repeated the gesture. "The honor is mine, Force Leader."

Taminth stepped back and resumed his position as John did the same.

"May I suggest the remaining introductions be completed en route to your accommodation? I'm sure you could do with some time to relax and freshen up before we begin our various meetings." Tarrov indicated toward a bulkhead set into the wall of the shuttle bay.

"An excellent idea, Chairman," replied Aaron smoothly, "It has indeed been a long trip to get here and perhaps a few hours to recuperate would be more than welcome."

As the group made its way toward the bulkhead doors John found himself walking beside Taminth. The Persai said nothing but John had the feeling Taminth could not wait to hear all about the battle around Garunda. A distracted John nearly walked into the back of Jeff Moore as the scientist came to a dead stop a few steps through the bulkhead doors.

John was about to berate the scientist when the words died in his throat. The doors had opened to reveal what John could only describe as the most amazing thing he had ever set eyes on. Extending into the distance was a vast subterranean city, complete with parks, rivers and skyscrapers. As John took in the view, his eyes were drawn up the skyscrapers sides as they disappeared through… clouds! Clouds within a cave. Impossible!

Taminth came to a halt beside John and his mouth formed into the shape of a Persai laugh. "This is the place where my ancestors found the Saiph blockhouses. My people spent decades expanding this cave to hold our capital city. Everything we need to survive is here. Homes, power generators, hydroponic gardens, industrial plants. All concealed below the surface so our enemy will never find us."

"Amazing."

"And with your help, Admiral, perhaps it is time for us to come out of our caves and finally face the enemy who has haunted my people for so long."

John looked up into the face of Taminth. "You have my word, Force Leader."

A vaguely canine face smiled and exposed its short fanged incisors. "Well, what do you think, Admiral?"

"I'm suitably impressed, Force Leader Taminth," nodded John Radford from his seat at the rear of the bridge of the Persai battle cruiser *Vitaros*. In the nine weeks John spent with the Persai, Force Leader Taminth acted as his guide. Taminth was second in command of what John thought of as the Persai Navy. The battle cruiser *Vitaros* was its flagship. Although around the same size as the Terran light cruisers of Talos class, the *Vitaros* was a pure beam weapons platform carrying no missile armament at all. What it lacked in size it made up for in punch. Utilizing Saiph technology, the Persai equipped the *Vitaros* and her sister ships with a main armament of a single, high-energy plasma cannon, which Doctor Jeff Moore had assured John, was at least twice as powerful as the TDF's current heaviest grazer weapon. A similar, though less powerful, plasma cannon provided secondary armament, and finally close in defense was provided by a series of quick firing x-ray lasers – powered independently from the other weapons systems to ensure its survivability as a last line of defense. Well not quite a last line.

On discovering from the Persai the Saiph had been working on a form of energy shielding using exotic matter as a power source, John thought Moore's face was the picture of a schoolchild in a sweet shop. The Persai had been working to perfect it and actually had had success in generating an energy shield in the laboratory but their need to stay hidden from the Others had precluded their search for the right materials to make the energy shielding work on a practical basis. John had left Moore deep in discussion with Persai scientists about Bose–Einstein condensates and Quark—Gluon plasma. It all sounded very boring to John.

John's nine-week mission had culminated in the last two days of fleet maneuvers. The fifteen Persai ships had simulated an incursion into the Pars System by a force of forty Buzzard class Others ships, whose aim had been to close with Pars and launch on the planet. Having detected the Others approach using the Persai equivalent of the Terran Holmes platforms seeded throughout the system's asteroid belt, the Persai ships had ambushed them as they entered the system and using micro folds had out maneuvered the Others as they pressed on toward their objective of Pars. The Persai constant hit and run tactics had allowed them to attack and destroy the Others' fleet a few ships at a time and then micro fold away before suffering any significant damage themselves. The Persai had repeated the process without a break for two days until the Others' fleet had been reduced to manageable numbers before confronting them in a full fleet engagement, leading to the inevitable total destruction of the Others' fleet while the Persai suffered minimal losses.

John had to admit, the Persai ship handling and tactics impressed him. Although their lack of missiles limited the offensive range of their ships, the devastating main plasma cannon ensured any hit by it was a kill shot. If the TDF could re-equip its ships with the Persai plasma cannon, it would significantly increase its firepower.

Moore had assured John the Persai Gravity Drive, although differing from the one he had developed independently of the Saiph, was only slightly more efficient and not worth introducing to the TDF but the fusion generators the Persai used were smaller and more efficient and they were well worth adopting into TDF service.

The other part of the Persai Navy John had been impressed with was its small fleet of survey ships, like the one commanded by Sub Leader Verus who had first discovered the Terran intervention in Garunda. These ships had all the properties of the TDF's own Vanguard class survey ships but reflected the Persai fixation with remaining hidden from the Others. They were equipped with superior stealth technology. They also reflected the Persai issue of depth of trained personnel, due to their population limits. The Persai were forced to heavily automate ship's functions and relied on advanced computer systems, just one more thing Moore drooled over.

John stood and walked to where Taminth sat in the middle of the flag bridge. "A good day's work, Force Leader Taminth. And now perhaps we should return to Pars for a well-deserved rest and to allow me to compile my report for the Joint Chiefs." *And,* John thought, *a chance to see more of Patricia Bath.* He found Patricia increasingly in his thoughts, he hoped he was in hers too.

Taminth turned his head at John's approach. "With you and your kind by our side, Admiral, I think the time of our revenge on The Enemy is getting closer." Taminth's smile disconcertingly bared his incisors and John sensed Taminth's intense need for revenge. As he looked around the bridge, vengeance radiated from every Persai present. John hoped it would not consume the Persai if they ever came into conflict with the Others.

CHAPTER TWENTY-TWO
Return to Messier Fifty-Four

CHARON BASE - ORBIT OF PLUTO - SOL SYSTEM

Commodore Christos Papadomas had been expecting the call from Admiral Vadis ever since he was informed a Persai survey ship and two of their battle cruisers had arrived in orbit around Charon Base. Once the home to the secretive Operation Chimera, it was now the base for the Survey Command arm of the Terran Defense Force. The pace, of late, for Survey Command had slowed as the TDF recovered from the battle with the 'Others' around Garunda and the discovery of the Persai. To Papadomas and the leaders of the TDF, it became apparent that despite the fact the Vanguard class survey ships successfully avoided contact with the Others, if the Vanguards had been detected and come under fire, they would not have the necessary firepower to overcome the Others. The TDF could not rely on catching the Others out with a micro fold as Captain Witsell had done in 70 Ophiuchi.

Now he found himself waiting patiently in Vadis' briefing room accompanied by Captain Bruce Torrance of TDF *James Cook* and Captain Bill Talbot of TDF *Henry Hudson*.

Keeping his voice at a low conspirator's level, he said to Torrance and Talbot, "Well, gentlemen. Do you get the feeling they may at last have found a job for us poor relations in Survey Command?"

Talbot let out a little chuckle as he replied in a similar way. "Best keep your comments to yourself, Commodore. You know Vadis hears everything, he used to be a spy, you know."

The other two men laughed and quickly stifled it as none other than the said Vadis entered the briefing room, followed by a Persai who was deep in conversation with a human in smart civilian attire and a Garundan in what passed as their version of a suit. *Politicians…* Christos thought, as he and the other survey officers brought themselves to attention.

Vadis smiled his usual fox's smile as he walked to the head of the table and took his seat. The human suit and the Garundan sat without invitation while the Persai remained standing and gave the two politicians, what Christos could only assume was, a look of disdain highlighted by the visibility of his one bared incisor and a low one-word mumble. Christos attempted to hide a grin as he realized the military's dislike for all things politic appeared to cross all species boundaries.

Vadis indicated the vacant seats before his officers. "Please, gentleman. Take your seats and let's begin." Vadis touched a control and the image of the Messier 54 system appeared above the center of the table. "This, gentlemen, is why we are gathered here today."

Christos felt a nudge at his elbow as Talbot leaned his head toward him. "Told you."

Vadis ignored him as he went on with the briefing. "It has been decided the time has come for us to return to the Messier 54 system and attempt to make friendly contact with its inhabitants." Vadis smiled his smile again. "The Baldies."

The human suit coughed quietly. "Admiral, must you call them that?"

Vadis regarded the politician with a playful glint in his eye, "My apologies, Ambassador Schamu. I never was very good at political correctness."

Christos could see out of the corner of his eye the Persai giving the ambassador a look of distain again as he struggled to keep a grin from appearing on his own face.

Back to the briefing, Vadis continued, "The plan is relatively simple: three Vanguard class survey ships will accompany a Persai survey ship captained by Sub Leader Verus."

The Persai gave a small nod in the direction of the human officers.

"The Vanguards will carry out reconnaissance of the outer system and Sub Leader Verus will use his ship's more advanced stealth technology to get as much information on the two occupied planets as possible without being detected. The Ambassador and his party will then assess the information and formulate a plan to approach the Baldies."

At the use of the slang word, again, the Ambassador cringed. Christos was sure the admiral had done it on purpose.

Vadis went on as if he had not noticed the politician's reaction. "The Joint Chiefs have decided, although there is no indication of a presence of the Others in the system, from now on all Survey Command missions of this nature will be accompanied by warships to provide the mission with some teeth in case they run into any trouble. To that effect, two Talos class cruisers and two Persai cruisers have been attached to this mission."

Ambassador Schamu lent forward and interrupted Vadis. "May I point out this is the first mission to consist of representatives of all three Commonwealth Union members and I have been selected to lead our political representatives?" He sat back with a very smug look on his face.

Vadis continued as if he had not heard the Ambassador. "As such, the flotilla will come under command of the ranking Commonwealth Union officer, who will take into account the suggestions of the Ambassador. This officer will ultimately have command of the mission."

Schamu looked crestfallen at the announcement of the chain of command to everyone in the room.

Vadis smiled again as he turned to face Christos. "That would be you, Rear Admiral Papadomas."

It took a moment to register what Vadis said but a hearty slap on the back from Talbot brought him back to his senses. "Congratulations, Christos – sorry, Admiral Papadomas."

After a moment Vadis continued. "Indeed, Admiral Papadomas. Congratulations. Now I would suggest your first order of business is to let Commander Ranking, your XO, know he is now Captain Ranking, then get together with your other captains and Sub Leader Verus and familiarize yourself with the Persai ships' capabilities and formulate a plan. I expect your ships to depart for Messier 54 within the week."

––––––––––

Rear Admiral Papadomas looked around his rather spartan flag bridge on TDF *Cutlass*. Not designed to house admirals and the staff that inevitably came with them, the Talos class Cruisers had simply had the marine areas converted for the admiral and his hangers on use. A temporary measure until the shipyards built the new survey support cruisers.

Unashamed pride is what he felt. He found himself not caring one iota how his flag bridge looked because the important thing was, it was all his to command. This last week had been a busy time for the admiral and his new staff. Aside from getting to know how each other operated, he had the added burden of having to listen to the insufferable Schamu's incessant complaining – about everything: from his quarters to the quality of food… The sooner the Ambassador had something else to occupy him and his party the better.

Now the time had come. He and his newly named Survey Flotilla One were formed up and ready to depart. "Communications, has the flotilla signaled to the flag it is ready to depart?"

"Signal has been received and acknowledged, Admiral," replied the Communications officer.

"Thank you." He activated his link to Captain Mkhize whose face appeared in the admiral's holo cube.

Mkhize was from the Natal Province of Earth. With his striking ebony features, deep bass voice with its easily identifiable accent and seemingly irrepressible sense of humor, he and Mkhize found themselves drawn into a natural working partnership, where it appeared Mkhize occasionally had the uncanny ability to predict his Admiral's intentions without a word being said. Qualities an Admiral needed in his flag captain.

"Vusumuzi, I believe it is time we were on our way."

Mkhize smiled at his Admiral. "Your wish is my command, Admiral."

He could not help but smile as Mkhize's infectious good nature took hold. "Then the command is let's be on our way to Messier 54, Captain."

"Aye-aye, sir," replied Mkhize.

Papadomas cut the link and noted with satisfaction the flotilla moving as one, and quickly picking up speed as it cleared Charon Base.

His excitement grew as the commander at Communications called out to the bridge in general, "Fold in three, two, one." Survey Flotilla One disappeared from Terran space.

CHAPTER TWENTY-THREE
Stealth Attack

KUIPER BELT - 31 AQUILAE

TDF *Aurora* ran silently through the darkness of space, every active system on board shut down as she flew on a ballistic course through the outer reaches of the 31 Aquilae system. Her mission was simple: attempt to penetrate the system without detection by any of the watching Sherlock platforms or the patrolling warships of BatFor 4. The Joint Chiefs would periodically run these exercises to test unit readiness. The unit in question, the newly arrived BatFor 4, had no foreknowledge the destroyer *Aurora* was coming. If a unit commander was aware an exercise was scheduled, they may increase their operational tempo in response. It was their normal operations the Joint Chiefs wanted to test.

Aurora had been selected for this mission, as she was equipped with the latest chameleon stealth systems, which it had been promised, would raise the TDFs stealth ability to a level that should give it parity with the Persai. Right now, *Aurora* was fast approaching the Kuiper Belt circling approximately fifty AUs from the system primary, which Captain Francis McNamara intended to use to mask his approach.

McNamara had been busily planning his next move after clearing the Kuiper Belt when a call from Tactical interrupted him.

"Captain, I'm picking up something odd on the passive sensors."

"Throw it up on the main holo cube and let me have a look please, Guns." The holo cube sprang to life with a view of the approaching Kuiper Belt. The Kuiper Belt comprised the bits and pieces left over from the formation of the system, which normally were reasonably small. Some pieces could be as big as 100 kilometers across and some even large enough to qualify as dwarf planets with a diameter around 1600 kilometers. Centered in the image, McNamara was looking at, was exactly that – a dwarf planet. Scattered across it was a dusting of twinkling lights, like the stars on a cloudy night obscured and unobscured by the moving clouds.

McNamara's gut told him something was not right. "What am I looking at, Guns?"

"Captain, the light points you are seeing are computer generated renditions of fleeting energy signatures the passive sensors have detected but are having difficulty locking onto."

McNamara hated it when he was right. "Could they be ships running their power at minimum levels just like we are?"

The lieutenant at Tactical's forehead frowned as she considered the possibility. "If I were to take a guess… I'd say that is exactly what they are. It's hard to get a firm read on their numbers, but I guess at least thirty ships are out there. BatFor 4 only has twenty-two ships in its current order of battle including its resupply, fast replenishment ships. Could the Joint Chiefs be running some sort of major fleet exercise we're unaware of?"

McNamara felt his gut tightening. His mind raced as he tried to muster up an explanation as to why so many ships would be hiding out here in the Kuiper Belt. No matter how hard he tried, there was no alternative. There could only be one reason why those ships were here: the 'Others' had returned to 31 Aquilae, and this time they had come en masse.

McNamara hit the recessed control in his chair arm and the bone-penetrating wail of the battle stations alarm reverberated throughout the *Aurora*, urging the crew to their posts. McNamara gave rapid-fire orders in succession. "Guns! Bring the weapons on line and go active on all your sensors. Get as much on those ships as you can, then download all your data to the courier drones and append our current location and logs. I want the drones constantly updated and programmed to fold for Garunda on my command."

The young lieutenant spun in her chair as she went to her task. McNamara hardly noticed as he continued his orders. "Engineering! Standby the Gravity Drive. Communications! Hail those ships, identify us and request their identities and intentions."

"My God!"

McNamara looked across to Tactical where the unbidden remark originated "Guns! What are you seeing?"

A very pale faced lieutenant turned to face her captain, her fear evident in her voice. "Captain, those ships are powering up. I now make… forty-two ships. The computer identifies at least thirty as Buzzard class and," the lieutenant swallowed hard, preparing the delivery vehicle for bad news, "the remaining twelve… the computer puts at fifty percent larger than the Buzzards. Somewhere in the 330,000 tonnes range. Their power readings are at least twice the Buzzards."

Those on the bridge who overheard the conversation between the captain and his Tactical Officer stopped whatever they were doing, momentarily, in mid flow. All eyes turned to McNamara, pleading with him to order a fold jump, to let them escape from the nightmare the ships in front of them represented.

McNamara saw the anxious faces of his officers but knew if a force of this size caught BatFor 4 unprepared then it would be a slaughter. "Navigation, flight time for a Buzzard at maximum known speed to Garunda?"

Fingers flew over controls. "I make it seven hours from a standing start to insertion into Garundan orbit, sir."

Only seven hours, thought McNamara. Seven hours for Rear Admiral Thapa and BatFor 4 to prepare for the Others' onslaught. McNamara said decisively. "Communications! I want a flight of eight drones launched as quickly as you can get them away, two each for Garunda, Earth, Janus and Pars."

"Aye-aye, sir."

"Navigation! Plot us a fold back to Garunda. Let's get the hell out of here." McNamara felt the *Aurora* shudder as the courier drones began launching in rapid succession. He counted them off. One, two, three, four, five…

The near light speed energy weapons fired at them by the nearest Others ship guaranteed neither McNamara nor his crew saw home again. As the weapons connected with the small destroyer, the ablative armor held for a moment before the sheer volume of fire blew its way through it. TDF *Aurora* and all her crew had no chance of survival.

As the *Aurora* died, the Others' fleet formed itself up and moved toward Garunda.

As the Others advanced in system toward their ultimate goal of the planet Garunda, BatFor 4 raced to battle stations. On receipt of the devastating message alerting him to the massive enemy fleet heading toward him from the *Aurora*'s courier drone, Rear Admiral Thapa dispatched his own drones to Earth, Janus and Pars. He requested all available ships to make their way to Garunda.

Thapa was no fool. He knew his BatFor were in for the fight of their lives. The Others' fleet outnumbered him and this new type of Others ship, his

Tactical Officer had designated them Vulture class, outweighed his own TDF *Richelieu*, a Nemesis class flagship by four and half to one. Even if it had comparable weapons to the Buzzard class, he knew he could do little but slow the Others down and hope the cavalry arrived before the Others managed to range on Garunda and obliterate all life on that world.

The only way Thapa could see to buy time was with the lives of his own brave men and women. Thapa looked slowly around the flag bridge of the *Richelieu* and steeled himself for what was to come.

"Communications! General fleet signal: Ships are to form up on the battleships as per Case Yellow."

Without turning, the lieutenant at Communications acknowledged the order with a tense "Case Yellow. Aye-aye, sir."

As Thapa watched, a sidebar on his holo cube listing the names of the ships of BatFor 4 highlighted in turn as each ship acknowledged the order.

Case Yellow planned for this very scenario facing BatFor 4, an attack by overwhelming numbers on a shortest time course for Garunda. The plan was simple: BatFor 4 would place itself between the attacking Others and Garunda and fight a long range missile duel with BatFor 4 attempting to slow the Others progress to the planet and gain time for the reinforcements to arrive. Unfortunately, Case Yellow was conceived on the premise BatFor 4 would face Buzzard class ships only, not these new Vulture class ships. The readings gained by TDF *Aurora* had allowed Tactical to make a best guess at the range of the Vulture's weapons. It was exactly that – a guess. Thapa would not know for sure until his ships closed with the Others and engaged them.

As Thapa watched his display, he noted with satisfaction Commodore Nikulin and his three Ragusan class fleet replenishment freighters were already moving off with their escort of two Agis destroyers, while six of his remaining destroyers broke into pairs and moved to either flank of his three Nemesis battleships. Specifically designed to be anti-missile platforms, the Agis would augment each battleship's own anti-missile defenses. The four heavy cruisers positioned themselves two above and two below the line of battleships to protect against any attempted pincer movements by the Others. Many civilians did not know a space battle was fought in three dimensions, so protecting the space above and below you was just as important as your sides, front and rear. The two Talos light cruisers would fold to a position to the rear of the Others and use hit and run tactics in an attempt to cause as much damage to the enemy's drive systems as they could.

One lone destroyer left – TDF *Comanche*. Thapa watched it blink out of existence and only a moment later it reappeared high above the ecliptic plane, far from any danger. *Comanche* had the unenviable task of being the messenger to inform Earth of the seemingly certain death of BatFor 4 and the destruction of Garunda and her hundreds of millions of inhabitants. *Comanche* would hold her position and record the impending clash until BatFor 4 and Garunda's fate was decided.

Ensign Roawan looked around him in a state of mild confusion as the human crew of the Ragusan class fleet replenishment ship TDF *Wayfarer* seemed to move around him, as if he were a lonely outcrop of rock in a sea of people. Roawan was one of the first native Garundans to graduate from the Joint Naval Academy. He had specialized in communications and the *Wayfarer* was meant to be his maiden cruise where he would apply all the lessons he learned in the classroom in the real world. But right now, as he watched the humans around him move with a purpose, he felt like a spare cog in a very large machine. He knew he should, no, he knew he needed to be doing something. The Others were attacking his planet and he couldn't leave the humans to shoulder the burden of its defense. He was now a naval officer and it was his duty to do whatever he could to protect his people. With a new found purpose, Roawan headed for Comms and hoped he could be of some assistance.

He entered the Communication Center, a very grand name for a very small room holding two naval ratings and a chief petty officer who monitored the flow of traffic to and from the *Wayfarer*. Most of the traffic on the *Wayfarer* was generated from the bridge where the duty Communication's officer was stationed. Roawan had been working here since his arrival on board the *Wayfarer*. He found humans always treated him with the respect his status as an officer deserved, even if he was only an ensign and straight from the Academy.

The CPO heard the hatch open behind him. On the realization Roawan had entered the room, he quickly brought him up to speed. "Sir, we have established solid whisker locks on the escorting destroyers and *Splendid*. The *Maverick* has reported a fault with her forward whisker mount but we have a solid lock on her stern mount." TDF *Splendid* and TDF *Maverick* were the *Wayfarer*'s sister ships. "We have six courier drones prepped and ready for launch awaiting any downloads from the bridge and we are currently running health checks on our remaining ready couriers. I have also ordered a health check on all the courier drones we are carrying in the cargo holds." The CPO quickly checked his PAD. "Our current stock is forty-seven ready for immediate off-loading with eighteen down for essential maintenance."

Impressed by the CPO's comprehensive report, Roawan could not help but feel, again, he was excess baggage. "Thank you, CPO. What of the fleet's current status?"

The CPO touched another control and a small holo cube sprang to life in the corner of the room. The blue icons representing the fighting ships of BatFor 4 had folded away to a point approximately 200,000 kilometers from the oncoming enemy ships, and had begun to engage them at long range using anti-ship missiles in an obvious attempt to slow their progress toward Garunda. On a sidebar, Roawan saw the list of damaged and destroyed TDF ships growing slowly but surely.

These new Vulture ships of the Others might be slower than the Buzzards, but their weight of firepower was telling. Thapa was forced to continually maneuver to avoid the waves of anti-ship missiles being launched by the Others. These new Vultures carried a more powerful version of the Buzzard's x-ray laser which, if it struck a TDF ship, invariably caused massive damage or outright destruction. The admiral was forced to maneuver and keep the Others within his own weapons effective envelope. Roawan noted so far in the battle, BatFor 4 had been unable to cause any significant damage to these new Vulture ships. Tactical had identified another new type of Others' ship, designated Goshawk. The Goshawk was similar in size and construction to a standard Buzzard but it appeared to be an anti-missile ship designed to protect the larger Vultures. Similar to the role of the Agis destroyers within the TDF but on a much bigger scale.

So far, in battle, the Goshawks were very effective. TDF reports indicated only the standard Buzzards were taking casualties. No TDF missile had gotten close enough to the Vultures to cause any damage.

"How are communications with the fleet, CPO?"

"We are maintaining a steady stream of courier drones back and forth to the fleet. The bridge is having us launch drones back to Earth, Janus and Pars with status reports every thirty minutes."

Roawan's face contorted into the Garundan equivalent of a frown at the news. "We must be burning through our drones quite quickly then, CPO?"

Without consulting his PAD, the CPO answered. "With our current rate of expenditure, our stocks will be dry in nine hours." With a shrug, the CPO added in a quiet, resigned voice. "No matter, sir. It will all be decided by then anyway."

There was a moment of silence in the room. Even with the valiant efforts of BatFor 4, the Others were making steady progress through the system. At their current rate of advance, they should be within weapons range of Garunda in five hours.

Roawan could feel something nagging at the back of his mind, even as he contemplated the destruction of his home. Then it came to him. "CPO, you said at our current rate of expenditure we would be dry in nine hours."

Now it was the CPO's turn to be slightly confused. "Yes, sir. Nine hours is what the numbers are telling me."

"Are we not losing any drones to enemy fire as they arrive at the fleet?"

A large grin appeared on the CPO's face. "Well, sir. Before I moved over to communications, I used to be in navigation. I'm pretty good at calculating fold jumps." The CPO indicated the holo cube again. "As you can see, the Others and our fleet are moving at a relatively steady rate toward Garunda – almost a predictable rate. I have programmed each drone to emerge 30000 kilometers to the rear of our ships, redefine its location and identify the flagship and its current speed, then micro jump to within a kilometer of the ship. The drone is then shielded from enemy fire by the ship while it transmits its data, gets a reply and then micro folds away a safe distance and repeats the process in reverse to arrive back here."

Roawan was looking at the CPO in amazement. "How many drones have we actually lost to enemy fire?"

The CPO's chest puffed out with pride. "I lost two drones while I refined the computer programming. But since then? Not one has been lost." The grin on the CPO's face faded as he realized Roawan was no longer listening to him. An unusual blank expression fell over the ensign. "Sir, sir… are you alright?"

Roawan ignored the concerned CPO. He pushed past him to a computer terminal and began typing in commands as fast as he could.

The CPO watched over his shoulder as the load manifest of each of the replenishment ships was called up. Roawan became very still as he leaned on the terminal for support as if drunk. The CPO was forced to take a step back as the young ensign spun round to face him and grab him by the shoulders.

"CPO, do you know what you've done? You have given me the means to save my people!"

The CPO and the two ratings could only stare at the young ensign in bewilderment.

Roawan was making for the door, shouting orders excitely over his shoulder. "CPO! I want those drones downed for maintenance online as quickly as possible. Inform *Maverick* and *Splendid* to conduct health checks on all their available drones, ASAP."

Roawan stopped and turned at the entrance to the Comms Center to face its confused occupants. His joy replaced by determination. "Now we will see how well they die."

Radford looked across the table directly into the eyes of Patricia Bath and for just a moment held her gaze longer than he should, before Patricia broke contact. Her cheeks flushed slightly in embarrassment. When John first arrived on Pars, it had quickly become the norm for John, Aaron Beckett, Patricia Bath and Jeff Moore to meet for either dinner or a late supper and update each other on the events of the day. As the weeks passed and the humans became more and more pressed for time in their daily routine, it had left only John and Patricia to carry on the ritual.

John admitted to himself he was actually quite glad Aaron and Jeff could not make it anymore, for it gave him more time to spend talking to Patricia. Yes, the conversation always started about work, but recently work talk quickly tapered off. Each talked about their personal lives, their families and friends, personal likes and dislikes. John found himself wanting to know everything there was to know about Patricia.

The urgent tone of John's wrist Comm brought his attention back to the present. "Radford. Go ahead."

"Admiral." John immediately recognized the gruff tones of Force Leader Taminth in his ear bug. "We have received a courier drone from Garunda with some disturbing news."

John's body stiffened. Patricia must have sensed it too. Without thinking, she reached across the table and took John's hand in hers.

"The courier was from the TDF *Aurora* which has been trying to penetrate the 31 Aquilae system as part of a readiness exercise. It reports at least forty-two ships, identified as The Enemy, hiding in the Kuiper Belt of the system. From the *Aurora*'s sensor data it appears The Enemy have twelve ships of an unknown type at least fifty percent larger than their Buzzards. No more information is known at this time, but I feel certain The Enemy have come with the intention of destroying Garunda."

"Well we thought it would happen eventually. I just wish we had had more time; the fleet base isn't even fully operational yet. Thank God, the first phase of the Viper defense platforms are in place, it should at least give Garunda a decent chance of defeating any missile bombardment of the planet. John knew the Viper defense platforms with their two variants, one armed with nine high velocity missiles and the other with a powerful grazer good for 100 shots and the same ones Earth and Janus trusted with their defense. It was just a matter of how many had been deployed around Garunda.

"Admiral, Chairman Tarrov has activated our defense agreements under the Commonwealth Union Charter and the Persai will immediately dispatch units to the aid of Garunda. I would request you join me on my flagship as quickly as possible." As second in command of the Persai Navy, John knew Taminth's request was more of an order than a request.

"Of course, Force Leader. I shall be with you as quickly as possible." Taminth cut the link and John went to stand, only to find Patricia still held his hand. John looked down at her and thought he could see a small tear running down her cheek. He picked up a napkin and went to wipe it away but Patricia stopped him and gave his hand a small kiss.

"You come back to me John Radford. Do you hear me?"

John could hear the strain in her voice and realized he had fallen head over heels in love with this woman. "I promise," he said softly, hearing the strain in his own voice. He slowly pulled away from her, turned and headed for the shuttle pad.

Patricia sat alone at the table and stared after him, the tears she tried to hide from him now running freely down her face.

Admiral Jing regarded the faces of the three men and one Persai floating in the holo cube before him from his seat on the Flag Bridge of TDF *Reliant*. "Are you certain the automated drones are up to the task, Commodore?"

Without hesitation, Commodore Nikulin answered the ranking officer of the combined Commonwealth fleet, hastily cobbled together and now sat in hiding in the shadow of the only gas giant in the 31 Aquilae system. "I have complete faith in the system Ensign Roawan devised, sir."

Jing's fingers formed a steeple in front of him and he pursed his lips in his trademark pose. Jing knew time was of the essence. The Others were now only ninety minutes from being able to fire on Garunda. To commit his forces to a battle plan, which was ultimately reliant on an untested weapon, designed by an ensign, from a people who two years ago were still on the cusp of their own industrial revolution, was a big ask.

Around the *Reliant* floated the biggest fleet ever brought together by the Terran Defense Force. When the call for help arrived from Admiral Thapa and he stated he was initiating Case Yellow, Jing knew time was short. He organized his ships on the fly. Jing brought with him BatFor 2, which had been the alert BatFor, ready to respond to any incursion into Earth space, and the parts of BatFor 1 and 3 with enough men on board to fight. He stripped Earth's defenses to the bone. The politicians howled their disagreement as he ignored their calls and folded out for Garunda with seven Nemesis battleships, five Vulcan heavy cruisers, six Talos light cruisers and seventeen Agis destroyers.

Vice Admiral Lewis had not had to overcome the same whining politicians. Thapa and the men and women of BatFor 4 were based in Janus, and Governor Crothers had immediately given Lewis his blessing to take whatever he needed to come to their aid. Governor Crothers and the population of Janus felt a deep affiliation with the men and women of the TDF. In fact, a large percentage of the crew operating the ships of BatFor 4 had already applied to become citizens of the colony when they left the services. Lewis had arrived with two complete BatFors: six Nemesis battleships, eight Vulcan heavy cruisers, four Talos light cruisers and twenty Agis destroyers.

What was unexpected was the speed with which the Persai had reacted. When Jing arrived at the rendezvous point, behind the gas giant, he found ten Persai cruisers waiting for him. Force Leader Taminth had not hesitated in placing his ships under the command of Jing and Jing decided to leave Radford where he was on Taminth's flagship, *Vitaros*, as his liaison officer.

Jing caught the eye of Lewis in the holo cube and Lewis gave him a curt nod. Jing made his decision.

"Admiral Lewis, you will immediately fold with BatFor 5 and 6 and join with Admiral Thapa and bolster his defenses. Your aim is to slow the Others as much as possible. Try to keep them at arm's length, they are not permitted to enter weapons range of the planet at any cost. Commodore Nikulin, continue to deploy as many weapons as possible. You will launch only on my command but you can work on me giving that order…" Jing check the time displayed at the bottom of the holo cube. "Twenty-six minutes from now."

Jing turned his head to regard Radford and Force Leader Taminth, the last two members of this council of war. "Force Leader, for this to work I need those Goshawks providing anti-missile defense for the Vultures to be put out of action. Can you do it?"

Taminth's ears went back and his lips curled back to display his incisors, his voice in the admiral's ear was cold as ice. "Admiral Jing, my people have waited a long time for this moment. Again, The Enemy come to butcher the innocent, but this time they have met peoples who will not succumb without a fight. We of the Persai will do our duty or die trying."

"Very well, gentlemen. You have your orders. Admiral Thapa's people are dying out there, so let us get to it. Dismissed." The four faces vanished from the holo cube and as Jing watched, the tactical display changed as Lewis's ships folded away to join their comrades in BatFor 4, while the Persai ships left to begin their attack runs. Commodore Nikulin and the *Wayfarer* returned to Garunda to supervise the final deployment of the weapons the plan hinged on. Jing sat back in his chair and without thinking his fingers formed a steeple, fervently he hoped this was the right decision.

———

John gripped the arms of his seat on the flag bridge of *Vitaros* a little harder. For the first time, the *Vitaros'* sensors got a good look at the battle raging between the Others and the human ships defending Garunda. In the five hours since the Others began their attack, BatFor 4 had virtually ceased to exist. As John watched, a Vulture fired its main x-ray laser and the TDF destroyer *Black Skull*, which had strayed into the Vulture's weapons range, vanished in a blinding flash.

The arrival of Admiral Lewis and his reinforcements had been just in time. BatFor 4 was critically low on missiles – both anti-ship and anti-missile. If the Others had managed to coordinate their fire properly, they would have swamped BatFor 4's meagre defenses and ensured its destruction. For whatever reason, they had not yet managed to do so. Now the twenty Agis destroyers of BatFor 5 and 6 brought their own highly coordinated anti-missile systems into play, and the number of the Others' missiles getting through their orchestrated fire was slowing to a trickle as the battered remnants of BatFor 4 retired behind Lewis's fresh ships and full magazines.

Taminth gestured for John to join him. John left his seat to stand by the Force Leader's side as he regarded the main tactical plot. "Admiral, from the information supplied by BatFor 4 we have identified the twelve Vultures and their escort of two Goshawks apiece. My command will break into five pairs and we will attack as one wave with each pair assigned to engage the escorting Goshawks. I intend to attack the Goshawks protecting the Vultures closest to Admiral Lewis first, in an attempt to relieve some of the pressure on the admiral, and then sweep through the remainder of The Enemy fleet until all the Goshawks have been destroyed or until we have sustained sufficient critical damage which precludes any further offensive action."

Taminth's plan was simple in concept. John had seen the effect of the *Vitaros'* main high-energy plasma cannon in action. Unless the Others had another surprise up their sleeves, then the cannon should be sufficient to deal with the Goshawks. John's only worry was how the *Vitaros* and her sister ships' x-ray missile point defense lasers were going to hold up. *Vitaros* had to get within 10000 kilometers of the Goshawks to ensure a one shot, one kill ratio. If the Others got a lock onto the *Vitaros* while the Persai were getting a firing solution then their point defense x-ray lasers would be pushed to breaking point.

Well, John thought, *We'll just have to wait and see.* "Force Leader, I concur with your plan."

Taminth let out a short grunt as he put one hand on John's shoulder and turned to address the Persai on the flag bridge. "Let us send The Enemy to hell. Attack!"

The *Vitaros* winked out of existence only to reappear a moment later less than 9000 kilometers off the starboard side of a Goshawk.

The Persai at Tactical shouted, "We're being hit with rapid, high band radar, Force Leader! The computers are calling it targeting radar. Four seconds until main weapon is ready to fire. Targeting solution looks good. Firing now."

John stared at his readout as the invisible x-ray laser reached out, at nearly the speed of light, and touched the hull of the Goshawk dead center. John mouthed a silent prayer, hoping the Persai weapon proved effective on the Others' ships as all the simulations had said it would be… It was.

Before his very eyes, a large plume of escaping gases and debris exploded from the far side of the Goshawk, seconds later it exploded into a million pieces.

A jubilant cry went up from the bridge crew and Taminth had to shout to be heard. "Navigator! Get us out of here before they target us."

"Yes, Force Leader." The *Vitaros'* Gravity Drive took it away from the Others without suffering a single hit.

As the *Vitaros* reentered normal space, Taminth requested a status check on all the Persai ships.

The Persai officer at Tactical carrying out his order paused and became still. "Burrav disobeyed your orders, Force Leader."

Taminth struck the arm of his chair with his hand with such force John thought it would break. "What did that impetuous fool do?"

Taminth's Tactical Officer turned to face the Force Leader. His voice was hollow at the dishonor and needless sacrifice disobeying the Force Leader's orders had caused. "After engaging and successfully destroying his assigned Goshawk, Burrav attempted to engage the Vulture it had been escorting. By the time Burrav had a lock on the Vulture, he had come under fire from other Enemy ships. His ship simply couldn't stand up to the massed Enemy fire and it was destroyed."

Taminth bowed his head low for a moment. John thought he heard a mumbled prayer for the dead Persai before Taminth told the Tactical officer to continue with his report.

"We have confirmation all ten intended targets are destroyed, Force Leader."

Taminth nodded slowly and turned to John. "It would seem our plan is working. We will immediately re engage the remaining Goshawks."

"They'll be expecting us this time, Force Leader," said John cautiously.

Taminth nodded again. "Agreed, but time is running short and if Admiral Jing's plan is to succeed we must press our attack."

This time it was John's turn to agree. "True. By my calculations the admiral should be launching his attack in twelve minutes."

"Then we have no time to waste, Admiral Radford." Taminth spun in his chair. "Communications! Signal the ships to begin their second attack and continue until all Goshawks are destroyed."

Vitaros once again entered fold space and, as it emerged into normal space, John's repeater display filled with the bulk of a Goshawk. John's readout told him it was 4850 kilometers away. Damn! Spitting distance in a space battle. The *Vitaros'* navigator was good.

The Tactical officer was watching his display intently as the computers worked frantically to get a lock on the Goshawk. "Target locked. Firing in three, two –"

The Persai never got to say 'one' as the *Vitaros* was rocked by the impact of a Q Switching laser fired by the Vulture on the port quarter. The Tactical officer's station took the brunt of the impact as the laser penetrated the *Vitaros'* hull and entered the flag bridge. His voice cut off as his station exploded, his body shredded by deadly fragments.

John could only watch as the horror unfolded in slow motion. Taminth became the next victim. His chair was ripped from its mount and flew across the flag bridge to be stopped by an unyielding bulkhead. The sound of escaping atmosphere filled John's ears. He reached for the emergency helmet mounted in a rack at the side of his chair, secured it in place and said a silent prayer as all the telltales turned green. At least he did not have to worry about the lack of oxygen killing him. John punched up the weapons control on his repeater and was astonished to see the green ready light of the main armament still flashing its ready signal. John doubled checked to see the weapon was still locked onto the Goshawk and pressed down on the firing stud with all his might.

4850 kilometers away the Goshawk that killed Taminth expired itself.

The remaining Persai on the flag bridge were struggling to come to terms with the sudden violence and the death of their commanding officer. John had to act and act quickly before another of the Others' ships started using the *Vitaros* for target practice and they all died. John worked furiously at his terminal, fully expecting the next moment to be his last.

"Navigation! Fold us to the coordinates I've just sent you. Damage Control! Get the hull breach sealed. Communications! Slave fire control to your terminal and be prepared to fire on our next target." John barked his orders.

The *Vitaros* folded to the coordinates John had supplied and as it entered normal space, another Goshawk appeared in John's display. John bared his teeth behind the protective faceplate of his helmet. "Lock on and kill that son of a bitch."

The Persai at communications did not hesitate. "Yes, Force Leader." As the fire ready light turned green, the *Vitaros* fired and another Goshawk was guided into oblivion. John did not have the time to gloat, he punched another set of coordinates into his terminal and sent them to the navigator.

The *Vitaros* rocked as another laser hit her but she folded away only to reappear directly behind a Goshawk. John did not need any words of command. As the fire ready light turned green, the Goshawk joined its companions as rapidly expanding clouds of wreckage.

A red zero began flashing in John's display. *Time's up,* thought John, hoping they had done enough for Admiral Jing's plan to work. "Fold for the rendezvous point, Navigator."

"Yes, Force Leader." That was the second time a member of the bridge crew addressed him so. Maybe they had forgotten he was a human admiral and not a Persai.

Admiral Jing watched the clock inexorably counting down to zero. On his tactical display, the Others' fleet was approaching a line, which represented one hour's Buzzard flight time from Garunda. The time at which they would reach maximum launch range for any missiles targeted on Garunda. His display was constantly updated by the information arriving by courier drone from Admiral Lewis. Drones were arriving every five minutes now as the battle reached its most critical phase.

As the clock touched zero, Jing turned to his waiting Communications officer and uttered a single word. "Execute!"

Commodore Nikulin could cut the atmosphere on the bridge of the *Wayfarer* with a knife. Mad panicking over now. Either the plan would work or it would not. Nikulin could not help but smile as he watched Ensign Roawan nervously hopping from one foot to the other, as he lent over the shoulder of the *Wayfarer's* Tactical officer.

When Roawan had ran onto the bridge demanding to speak to him. Nikulin put it down to fear, fear he was about to witness his planet die before his eyes. Nikulin was wrong. Roawan explained his idea, flabbergasting Nikulin with its simplicity.

Take all the available courier drones on board the three replenishment ships. Remove the seeker heads and replace those with megaton range nuclear warheads from the anti-ship missiles Nikulin's ships were carrying, and finally load the software CPO Higgins had devised. And hey presto – immensely accurate, Gravity Drive-equipped, nuclear tipped, ship killers. Something R and D had been working on for what seemed like an age, a lowly Garundan ensign and a human chief petty officer had solved in a matter of a few hours.

"Commodore, courier drone from Admiral Jing. Download is one word: 'execute'."

Nikulin addressed the young Garundan. "Ensign Roawan, if you would do the honors."

The *Wayfarer's* Tactical officer pushed his chair back from his terminal and stood up, inviting Roawan to assume his post. Roawan sat, lent over the terminal and let his finger hover over the flashing red light, savoring the moment for just a brief second before pressing down with all his strength. "Weapons away, sir."

163 nuclear tipped courier drones picked up speed and vanished as their Gravity Drives engaged.

"Drones arriving 300 kilometers to our stern, Admiral!" Lewis rocked in his seat as another near miss shook the hull of the *Reliant*. His ships had only engaged with the Others for a little over half an hour but his list of casualties in ships and men filled the display.

Unlike BatFor 4, Lewis was forced to close with the Others as the distance between the enemy fleet and Garunda shrank. With the reduced gap, the Others brought their powerful main armament into play and increased the number of hits his ships took.

Now the decisive moment. "Tactical! Update your plot and prepare your strike package. I want ten drones assigned to each Vulture. It may be overkill but let's make sure of a kill. We only get one chance at this. The remainder at your discretion."

Reliant's tactical officer's hands flew over his keyboard as he prioritized his target list and entered the latest location data. "Targeting package ready, Admiral."

"Send it!" Lewis said with a sense of satisfaction.

The drones disappeared into fold space, only to reappear a second later, less than fifty kilometers from their intended targets. No living thing could react quickly enough. Computers on board the targeted ships tried. But on locking onto their targets, the drones accelerated as hard as their drives would go. Two seconds after lock on, multiple megaton-nuclear explosions racked twelve Vultures and five Buzzards. When the blast clouds dispersed not even wreckage remained to show where millions of tonnes of starships had once been.

The flag bridge of the *Reliant* broke into spontaneous applause and cries of delight, no doubt mingled with a sense of relief as they realized the untried weapons performed exactly as anticipated. All twelve Vulcans destroyed, along with five Buzzards. Add the twenty-four Goshawks the Persai killed prior to the launching of the weapons and the four Buzzards destroyed by BatFor 4 in their long retreat toward Garunda. Leaving only two Buzzards suddenly alone and facing the might of the combined Commonwealth fleet.

The Others beat a hasty retreat, their remaining ships reversed course, only to find Admiral Jing blocking the Buzzard's escape route after moving his ships from behind the gas giant.

The remaining two Buzzards did not even slow down or attempt to change course. They accelerated headlong toward Admiral Jing's waiting seven Nemesis battleships, five Vulcan heavy cruisers, six Talos light cruisers and seventeen Agis destroyers. The human ships ensured the Buzzards joined their recently departed friends in short order.

CHAPTER TWENTY-FOUR
Unexpected Guests

TDF *CUTLASS* - MESSIER 54 CLUSTER

Survey Flotilla One, in the Messier 54 Cluster for only twelve days, received the news of the second battle of Garunda. Rear Admiral Papadomas fleetingly considered halting his expedition to make contact with the inhabitants of Planet A and their colony on Planet B, and return to Charon Base, but could see no real purpose in doing so. Instead, he continued on his mission with his small survey flotilla of three Vanguard class survey ships, one Persai survey ship, two Talos light cruisers and two Persai battle cruisers.

Christos was in his private quarters, perusing the information his flotilla had thus far gathered on the Baldies and their civilization. A smile appeared on his face. He really should stop calling them 'Baldies', but every time he mentioned it in the presence of Ambassador Schamu it made the ambassador physically wince, it was so worth it!

Back to work, he chastised himself. Twelve days of frantic work had produced some solid results. He amended his initial plan slightly. He had two of the Vanguards, TDF *James Cook* and *Henry Hudson*, work over the asteroid belt and outer planets. The remaining Vanguard, TDF *Jacques Cartier* would provide over watch for the Persai survey ship, commanded by Sub Leader Verus, as it moved in close to first Planet B, then the Baldies' home world of Planet A. He held his own cruiser, TDF *Cutlass*, and the Persai battle cruiser, *Vitachi*, in geostationary orbit around the outermost planet of the system. He remained ready, at a moment's notice, to come to the aid of either pair of survey ships if they ran into something they could not handle.

The reports from the two Vanguards showed the Baldies had begun mining operations of the system's asteroid belt, but apart from what looked like smelters and other limited industrial habitats with limited populations there was no form of militarization present and no indication the Baldies were worried about visitors from other star systems skulking around.

On the other hand, the report from Sub Leader Verus in relation to his close approaches to Planets A and B made fascinating reading. When Captain Ruth Witsell and the TDF *Vasco De Gama* arrived in the Messier Cluster five years or so ago, following a fault in their navigation computer, they found Planet B in the initial stages of colonization by the inhabitants of Planet A. Eavesdropping on electromagnetic transmissions had produced an image of what are now known as the Baldies. Approximately 168 centimeters tall, wearing a tan and brown uniform with emblems at the waist. A small circular mouth with what appeared to be three slits on either side of where a nose should be. Two eyes set widely apart above the slits, with no apparent ears on the head. Two arms with double jointed elbows and shortened forearms, and no visible body hair – hence the term the crew of the *Vasco De Gama* came up with, Baldies. What sealed Saiph DNA tampering was the fact the Baldies had five fingers.

At the time of the *Vasco De Gama*'s visit, it was estimated the Baldies were at a level of technology roughly equivalent to Earth prior to World War Three. Their ships were powered by a low power ion drive which meant a one-way trip between Planet A and Planet B took around eleven months. Using similar propulsion methods meant a trip between the inner planets and the industrial habitats in the asteroid belt could take up to anywhere in the region of three years. Planet B's estimated population was at the time in the low thousands, which was why it was chosen by Captain Witsell as the site for a landing by her marines and a survey party, which had taken soil and plant samples, confirming Saiph interference in the natural progression of life. Captain Witsell never visited Planet A, preferring not to risk contact with the Baldies without the nod from the politicians.

Sub Leader Verus had been able to use his highly stealthy survey ship to slowly close with Planet A, until he reached a point where he could launch small reconnaissance drones to better observe the planet and its surrounding space. What his drones had discovered was a flourishing artificial orbiting network of space habitats, serviced not only by ships moving back and forth from the surface of the planet but two space elevators. Massive constructions, which were anchored to the surface of the planet by immensely strong nano fiber cables, which reached up into orbit and connected with a large cargo handling facility, located in one of the planet's Lagrange points, a point where the gravitational pull of the planet was cancelled out by its orbiting moon. These space elevators had been theorized on Earth, but with the disruption caused by the third and fourth world wars they had never been built, even with general agreement it was probably the cheapest and quickest way to get large payloads to and from orbit.

As far as population and governance went, current estimates put the planetary population at around the eight billion mark, which was probably why the Baldies were beginning to establish colonies on Planet B. From what was known of the political setup, it appeared there was a centralized planetary government but, and he found this next point rather unsettling, it would appear to be a very militaristic one. All news broadcasts were made by Baldies wearing the same brown and tan uniform and all the broadcasts ended in the same way. An image of an elderly Baldy, in uniform, accompanied by what he could only assume was some form of national anthem. Until the translation computers could provide accurate interpretations of communications, he could only guess and he was not willing to bet the success of this mission on guesswork.

All this information was passed to Ambassador Schamu and his staff. If the ship scuttlebutt was to be believed, then the Ambassador was as worried about the Baldies being a militaristic society as Christos was.

The urgent beeping of his terminal and a flashing red light interrupted him. He reached over to accept the emergency signal. The unsmiling face of Captain Mkhize appeared.

"Admiral, we've just received a courier drone from the *James Cook*. Captain Torrance states while conducting operations in the asteroid belt he has come across a vessel in distress. He states it appears to have suffered micro meteor damage to its engines and is venting atmosphere. The vessel is transmitting a repeating message in what has been identified as the language of the Baldies, but Captain Torrance believes the message is so weak it has little chance of reaching one of the Baldy installations before the vessel's atmosphere is completely vented into space."

He could tell by the look in Mkhize's eyes that Mkhize was thinking the same thing he was. A spacer's worst nightmare. A long, slow, cold death in space as the air in the suit ran low, the batteries supplying heat beginning to fail and the cold chills the body to its very core, before eventually the carbon monoxide scrubbers fail, darkness closes in and the body slips into unconsciousness. No life form, with a conscience, could allow that to happen to another.

"Send to the *James Cook*. You are to move to intercept the vessel in distress and render all assistance, which in your view is required. Any surviving crew of the vessel are to be treated with the utmost respect and brought aboard the *Cutlass* at the earliest opportunity."

The relief on Mkhize's face was obvious. "Thank you, Admiral."

"And oh, Vusumuzi, could you inform Ambassador Schamu we may be having extra guests for dinner this evening."

Mkhize let out a loud belly laugh, which took him a few seconds to control. "My pleasure, Admiral."

———

Christos and Ambassador Schamu stood together in the small, but well equipped, medical bay of TDF *Cutlass*. They watched Doctor Richards fuss over the three patients, each lying in beds surrounded by medical equipment. The beds were occupied by surviving crew of the Baldy ship, the same ship TDF *James Cook* had aided. The bodies of the other eight crew were currently in the *Cutlass'* makeshift morgue. Christos caught the Doctor's eye and she came to stand beside him while keeping her eyes on the patients.

"You asked to see us, Doctor?" said Schamu in a way which could only be interpreted as he had better things to do than stand in the medical bay.

Doctor Richards let out a small sigh. "The Baldy..." Christos noted a frown appear on Schamu's forehead at the Doctor's use of the slang term, he tried to hide his smile. "My apologies, Ambassador... The patient on the far left is recovering from his ordeal well. He is awake, our advanced translation program has told him he is in no danger and where he is. He should be fit enough to be discharged by the end of the day. Unfortunately, the other two are in a bad way. I'm keeping them sedated. They suffered severe lung and brain damage. I simply don't know enough about their physical make up to do much more than keep them alive."

Ambassador Schamu gave the doctor a stern look. "Not acceptable, Doctor."

"Acceptable or not, Ambassador, it is a fact. Unless those two patients get medical attention from their own people within the next twenty-four hours, their chances of making a full recovery are slim at best."

Christos looked from the doctor to her three patients and then back to the doctor. "Is it possible for us to speak with the patient who is awake without overtaxing him?"

Richards folded her arms and regarded the admiral and the Ambassador like a primary school teacher. "I don't see why not, Admiral. As long as you understand if he does show signs of stress, I may have to intervene."

"Thank you, Doctor. That will be all for now." With a nod, Richards left Christos and Schamu alone and returned to her patients.

"Well, Ambassador. I suggest you begin questioning our visitor as soon as you can for in twelve hours the *Cutlass* will be in orbit of Planet A and these patients will be off loaded to receive the medical attention they need."

To Christos' surprise, the Ambassador did not seem fazed at all. "I may seem a bit stuffy at times Admiral but even I would not let harm come to anyone for the sake of political expediency. If you'll excuse me, I have a lot of work to do and little time to do it."

Christos was left standing on his own as the Ambassador made his way over to the conscious Baldy. A large smile appeared on the Ambassador's face as he stretched out his hand in welcome to the confused Baldy. Christos shook his head in amazement at the change in the politician's demeanor as he turned to leave the medical bay and make his way back to his quarters. He had work to do as well if he was to be ready in twelve hours.

CHAPTER TWENTY-FIVE

They're Coming

OFFICE OF THE PRESIDENT OF THE TERRAN REPUBLIC - GENEVA - EARTH

Rebecca Coston entered her office to find her invited guests already waiting for her. "My apologies, ladies and gentlemen. But for some reason some senators believe the longer they go on, the more likely I am to give them what they want. They obviously don't know me very well." That got a smile and a few chuckles from Rebecca's guests. "Please sit. We have a lot to get through, so I suggest we just hit the high points."

As Rebecca took her seat at the head of the small conference table, she regarded each of the invited guests in turn.

Secretary Gillian Rae, Head of Research and Development. With the sharing of technology between humans, Garundans and Persai, her department was expanding every day and some of the technology being shared, such as the Persai shield initiative and nano technology, could change the way humans lived their lives.

Secretary Olaf Helset. The Terran Defense Force had expanded steadily for the past five years, but with the latest Others attempt to destroy Garunda it left the First and Second Fleets weakened, however, the main point to come out of the attack on Garunda was the determination of the new Commonwealth Union of Planets to act to protect its members. The size of the Vulture ships had been a shock – but as Rebecca understood, the hybrid courier drone/anti-ship missile had evened out the firepower imbalance and Research and Development were already rushing through a tailored design for mass production.

Ambassador Aaron Beckett, the man who helped her design the framework for the Commonwealth Union and was instrumental in its success, was convinced by Rebecca to retire from retirement and be her messenger to both the Garundans and the Persai.

Governor Thomas Crothers, Governor of Janus. Rebecca's one-time Secretary of Finance in whom Rebecca had entrusted the establishment of humankind's first colony world, Janus. In under five years, Crothers had taken it from zero to a colony with a population of over 20,000,000. A thriving, industrial world which now had its own shipyards, producing starships for trade and commerce and of course was home to Second Fleet under Vice Admiral Lewis.

Rebecca could see the day fast approaching when Janus would be independent and she would be addressing *President* Crothers.

"So to business, ladies and gentlemen. Aaron, I've managed to catch some of the reports coming back from Messier 54 so why don't you bring us up to speed on Ambassador Schamu's progress to date."

Aaron cleared his throat as at the touch of a control the Messier 54 system appeared in the holo cube in the center of the table. "Madam President, we now know Planet A is actually called Alona and Planet B is called Geta. Following a series of major wars on Alona, the military forces carried out a coup to stop further bloodshed. Military leaders in each country then came together for the greater good under the leadership of General Paxt, later declared Emperor of Alona. Every adult male and female must spend three years in a branch of the military performing tasks for the greater good of the people. If someone chooses not to join the military, then they are not considered a citizen of the empire and as such have no voting rights." The Ambassador took a breath then continued. "Although governed by an emperor, this position is not hereditary. On an emperor's death, the next emperor is elected by the governors of each 'District', who in turn are elected by the citizens of their respective Districts. Local law and statute is decided by the governor and his advisors. National law and policy is decided by the emperor. The system has been in place for 300 or so years and the people seem content. Alona began to explore Geta eighty-five years ago but serious colonization is only now beginning. Ambassador Schamu puts that down to population expansion."

A loud "hmm…" came from Gillian Rae. "So the military runs things in the name of an emperor. I don't know if I like the sound of it."

Aaron nodded his head in agreement. "If that was the way it actually was I would agree with you. However, over the years, society on Alona has developed to such an extent the military is not what we would regard as a military at all. It has diversified so it is responsible for everything from education to health to industry. If it's a dictatorship, it's a very benign one."

Rebecca interrupted him. "What progress has the Ambassador made in securing political links with the Alona?"

"So far, Ambassador Schamu has gotten agreement for a single embassy to be established to look after all the concerns of the Commonwealth Union. It is my understanding this has been agreed to by both Garunda and Pars."

Olaf Helset raised a finger and Rebecca nodded for him to go on. "For them being militaristic, according to the dispatches I have read from Admiral Papadomas, they appear to only have a small number of in-system gun boats which are used for anti-piracy operations. Papadomas reports there does not appear to be any form of sensor network in operation to alert them to the presence of any alien ships entering the system. Do I take it then the Alona are not aware of the 'Others' or of the Saiph?"

As Aaron started to reply, Rebecca raised a hand to stop him. "I'll answer that Aaron." Rebecca touched a control and the image in the holo cube changed to show the Earth at the center and two lines reaching out. One line ended with Garunda and the second line ended with the Pars.

"At this juncture I, in consultation with the other leaders of the Commonwealth have decided not to alert the Alona to the fact that sometime in their past their planet was visited by the Saiph. As far as any potential threat from the Others is concerned, Messier 54 is 50000 light years from Earth. The Others attacked Garunda which is 49.41 light years from Earth and the original Persai home world which was 34.36 light years from Earth."

Two more lines appeared in the holo cube. "We have encountered the Others in 70 Ophiuchi, 16.59 light years from Earth and at Delta Pavonis, 19.92 light years away. The Persai are 6400 light years away and have had no contact with the Others." Rebecca looked around at the others in the room, meeting each person's eye before going on. "This has led the leaders of the Commonwealth to the conclusion that the Others originate from one of the star systems listed in the Saiph database no more than 100 light years from Earth."

Olaf nodded slowly, "The Joint Chiefs have come to the same conclusion, Madam President. According to the Saiph database, not counting Earth, they visited eleven star systems. We can discount four of those systems as being the home of the Others because we have either run into them there or, in the case of the Garundans, it's a home planet of a Commonwealth member. That leaves us with seven systems. If I may, Madam President?"

Rebecca nodded her consent and Olaf added the seven systems to the display. "Gamma Leporis, 29.25 light years away, the original destination for the Vasco De Gamma, and which we have not gone back to. Tau Eridani, 45.58 light years. 16 Cygniz, 70.5 light years. 23 Librae, 83.7 light years. Algol 3, 92.8 light years. Regulus 4, 77.5 light years and last, but not least, 9 Ceti, 66.5 light years."

Olaf touched another control and a sphere ten light years in diameter appeared around Garunda. "This sphere indicates the distance a Buzzard at maximum speed can travel in six months – the maximum time we estimate the Others had to react to the destruction of its ships in the first battle of Garunda. As you can see, none of the seven systems are within that sphere. Our conclusion is the ships we engaged in the second battle of Garunda came from a naval base of some kind. Perhaps similar to the one we believe them to be constructing in 70 Ophiuchi."

Olaf could see he had the undivided attention of everyone in the room. "Using the information the Persai have gathered from their surveillance platforms, we have ruled out Tau Eridani and 9 Ceti." On the display, those two systems dimmed in response. "However the Persai platforms have shown artificial power generation in the remaining five systems."

"Are you saying the Others originate in one of those five systems, Olaf?" asked Crothers.

"It would certainly fit the facts as we know them Thomas. What also concerns me is the fact the Joint Chiefs believe the ships we faced in Garunda the second time were only what the Others had to hand at the naval base at the time. And it took the combined strength of First and Second Fleets aided by the Persai to defeat them. If they were to arrive in the Sol system with the forces we believe them capable of, then the TDF wouldn't have enough strength to even slow them down – never mind prevent them from decimating Earth."

The silence Olaf's last statement brought to the room was tangible. After a few awkward moments, Rebecca broke the silence. "I take it the Joint Chiefs have a recommendation, Olaf." It was not really a question.

Olaf's expression was one of resignation as he shook his lowered head before looking up into the eyes of his president. "Madam President. For most of my adult life, I was a military man. That doesn't mean I am a believer in a large military machine. But, to be honest with you, the only way I can see of securing our own survival, and in turn the Commonwealths, is to continue, and if at all possible, speed up our current military buildup and that of our allies."

Rebecca looked to Aaron Beckett. "Do we have a feeling for what the Garundans and the Persai would think if we went to a full war footing?"

Aaron thought for a moment before answering. "Well, the Persai have essentially been on a war footing ever since they arrived on Pars, and since we came on the scene they have gone into overdrive, their main problem is workforce. Years of enforced birth control has left them short of personnel. We can supply equipment to build their own shipyards and, as Gillian will no doubt back me up, they are freely supplying us with as much of their technology as we can deal with."

Gillian was nodding her head in agreement. "The Persai are sharing everything they have developed with us. My teams are like kids on Christmas morning. I actually think Jeff Moore is looking at emigrating to Pars if they would take him." That got a laugh from everyone in the room.

Aaron went on. "The Garundans, on the other hand, are virtually the opposite of the Persai. They have more personnel than they know what to do with. The Naval Academy is pushing them through as quickly as they can, but the naval base in Garunda is just nearing completion and the shipyards will not be able to supply completed hulls for at least another six months."

Crothers spoke up. "What if I freed up some space in my shipyards? I could probably complete one Nemesis class battleship every ninety days for them."

"Every little would help, thanks," said Aaron. "But by the look on Olaf's face, I think he would rather you concentrated on building hulls for use by the TDF."

Olaf's face reddened ever so slightly. "I hate to say Aaron is right. However, if the Joint Chiefs are right about the strength the Others may be able to field, I'm going to need every ship I can get my hands on. Besides, we'll need any spare yard space to carry out the retrofits of Persai weaponry on our existing ships."

"So where does that leave us, Olaf?" asked Rebecca from her seat at the head of the table.

Olaf touched another control and an order of battle in the holo cube replaced the image of the star systems. "This is the Joint Chiefs' preferred order of battle for the TDF. As you can see, the fleet has expanded to three times its current size. The Joint Chiefs envisage a force of eighteen BatFors equipped with the new Bismarck class battleships formed up in six fleets."

Thomas Crothers let out a low whistle. "That's a lot of ships and men."

Olaf turned to him. "We estimate a build and commissioning time of three years at the end of which we should be in a position to carry out the next phase of the Joint Chiefs' plan." Olaf glanced in Rebecca's direction. "With presidential approval of course."

Why did Rebecca get the feeling she was about to be railroaded into something? "And what sort of plan do the Joint Chiefs have up their sleeve this time, Olaf?"

"Madam President, our biggest problem is intelligence. We have been able, with Persai help, to establish where the home system of the Others may be, but we have no idea how big an area they control. It may be just a couple of star systems or they may have a massive empire we have just touched the edges of. We simply don't know."

Rebecca gave Olaf a look of frustration. "Get to the punch line, Olaf, if you please."

Olaf brought the image of the five star systems that could be the home of the Others up in the holo cube. Leaning his elbows on the table, he lent forward in his seat and pointed at the display. "The Joint Chiefs want to initially beef up Survey Command and then send these ships to these five systems to establish which is the home of the Others. We'll do it as stealthily as possible to avoid any chance of detection but I feel it's something we have to do. And in three years when the fleet is ready, we'll take the war to the Others."

Olaf sat back in his seat and awaited Rebecca's reply.

All Rebecca Coston could think of was hope. Hope the Others gave the Commonwealth the three years it needed so desperately to ready itself. Because three years or no… the Others were certainly coming.

Books by PP Corcoran

The Saiph Series:
Discovery of the Saiph, book 1
Search for the Saiph, book 2
Hunt for the Saiph, book 3

Ghost Soldiers (shorts):
The Province

Most books also available in audiobook (incl. Kindle Whispersync).

Visit www.ppcorcoran.com

HAVEN ONE-EIGHT

—An exclusive short story —

P.P. Corcoran

The single miniscule point burgeoned into a shimmering translucent portal, which encompassed the entire breadth and height of the reinforced concrete corridor.

First one, then a second, and finally, a third humanoid figure stepped from the temporary doorway. A thick neck attached the dull black metal-covered head to a wide-shouldered, metal encased body, which sprouted two similarly armored upper limbs carrying an oversized rifle.

The evil apparitions advanced stealthily on their two mechanical legs. A pencil-thin line of green, beamed from their heads, flicked back and forth, methodically searching the corridor for signs of life.

Wherever the green light moved, the barrel of their sinister mag rifles followed. As their scan revealed no life signatures, the black suits moved off down the corridor, their mechanically assisted legs whining and their metallic footsteps ringing out in unison.

"Movement in Level 8, Corridor 5!"

"Show me," ordered the Duty Watch Officer.

The large viewing panel in the Operations Room switched from the view of swaying, golden corn stalks under a clear blue sky to the gray, bland corridor. Nothing. The corridor was empty.

The Watch Officer eased his tension with a quiet prayer to the one and only true god. A few syllables passed his dry lips but the remaining words died in his throat, as three black figures moved into camera view and paused. The central figure's gaze locked onto the camera and the other two figures followed suit.

In the Ops Room an unearthly quiet descended. Every eye fixated in horror on the viewing panel, where they saw the Asatu Reapers descending upon them. The cold fingers of death unfurled and they knew death would not be satisfied until every man, woman and child in Haven One Eight was choked of their last breath.

The Watch Officer shook off the fear, which had almost paralyzed him. The Asatu's initial strike had been three years ago when they laid waste to every population center on planet Eden. Now, Haven One Eight held eighty-two thousand humans of the Faithful, the last remaining survivors of what had been a city of nearly six million.

The Asatu's first strike three years before had not been not unexpected.

Members of the Faithful had reported to the preachers on Eden that since the disconnection with Earth four centuries previously, Satan had infected every part of Earth's corrupt society. The preachers had ordered the Faithful to cleanse the Earth of the evil Satan, but their attempt failed. It had only been a matter of time before the evil ones' armies sought out the Faithful, to destroy the last vestige of god's light in the darkness, and the Asatu had arrived in Eden to do Satan's bidding.

The Faithful's lightly-armed militia had fought to its last. However, the Asatu Reapers and the larger, more heavily armed Specters, had simply been too powerful and numerous. It became an eventual slaughter.

However, the sacrifices of the militia had bought enough time for some of the Faithful to seek shelter in the deep mines scattered across the planet. Mines like Haven One Eight, named so, not because it was the eighteenth haven established by the government, but because it was eighteen kilometers underground.

The Asatu had taken three years to conquer the surface of their planet and in those precious years, the Faithful's engineers and technicians, forced underground, raced to complete the havens. They hoped many of the Faithful would survive undiscovered, long enough that, by the grace of the one true god, the Asatu and their cursed Reapers and Specters would return to their place beside Satan and allow the Faithful to emerge from their hiding places and rebuild.

Now, the Watch Officer saw three Reapers stalking the corridor, dashing all hope for the Faithful's survival. The image of his wife and son contentedly praying together this morning, before he left for his duty, flashed unbidden into his mind, and his eyes involuntarily flicked upwards. *God, why have you forsaken us?*

The Watch Officer barked out orders in rapid succession. "Seal the corridor! Get the QRF moving! Open the armories and let's get our people armed!"

The company-sized quick reaction force were ready to deploy at a moment's notice, but, the Watch Officer knew, their light weaponry was not adequate enough to stop a single heavily armored Reaper never mind three. Nevertheless he hoped to slow the Reapers long enough for the civilians to reach the armories and give themselves at least a fighting chance.

For fighting was the only option. When the Faithful retreated into Haven One Eight, demolition charges had sealed the entrance after them. There were no escape tunnels.

The Asatu had used their teleport technology to circumvent the millions of tons of rock which hid Haven. The Watch Officer gave a wry smile, as he thought of the numbers of Reapers which must have been lost as they probed the bowels of the planet in search of these last few survivors. No instrument could penetrate this deep into the rock to see what awaited it. The only option would be to open a teleport window and send a Reaper through. How many times had that ended in a Reaper being teleported into solid rock?

"QRF are holding at the entrance to Corridor 5."

Unbuttoning his collar, the Watch Officer reached under his shirt and extracted a thin plastic card hanging by a metal chain. Lifting it from around his neck, his trembling hand flipped a red cover on his control panel. Steading his nerves, he slipped the card into the slot. On the desk display, a phrase appeared.

'DEMOLITION CHARGES ACTIVATED
Please select a specific area or Haven-wide'

The Watch Officer selected Corridor 5 and tapped the accept key. The computer confirmed his selection.

'CORRIDOR 5 LEVEL 8 DEMOLITION CHARGES ACTIVATED
Time to activation 10 seconds'

The Watch Officer saw the figure 10 change to 9, change to 8. "Tell the QRF, fire in the hole."

The countdown reached zero and the camera on Corridor 5 blinked out. He removed his authorization card and returned it to its place, around his neck.

"Bring up Corridor 4."

The large vid display filled with the frantic efforts of the QRF as they erected makeshift barricades, blocking the way into Corridor 4. Meanwhile, the camera from Corridor 4 showed the once pristine Corridor 5 was now a pile of mismatched concrete rubble.

The steel reinforcing bars jutted from it like the spines of a porcupine. The dust had barely settled when a small, bright light sparked in the middle of the corridor, it rapidly expanded and from the emergent teleport field, stepped a dust-covered Reaper, its mag rifle already searching for targets.

The QRF fired first. Heavy ten and fifteen millimeter explosive-tipped rounds battered the Reaper which staggered under the impact, going to one bended knee. However, it did not fall and despite the constant impacts it raised its mag rifle and fired.

The Reaper let loose a withering burst of concentrated fire. The ball bearings ejected from the mag rifle accelerated to twice the speed of sound, courtesy of the magnets that lined the rifle's barrel. To the naked eye, each burst appeared as one continuous line of lightning.

The lightning disintegrated everything it touched, including flesh and bone.

A second Reaper exited the teleport field and joined the devastating fire fight. Before the third Reaper cleared the teleport field the fight was over. The Reapers stepped casually over the body parts littering the corridor and continued their steady advance into the heart of Haven.

"All armories report open, sir! Inner defenses are coming on line."

A grim, satisfied smile cracked the Watch Officer's features. The trickle of people reaching the armories would soon turn into a flood and, with the heavier weapons of the inner defense ring to back them up maybe, with god's blessing, they would be able to defeat the Reapers. A single call from the senior noncommissioned rank in the Ops Room dashed his meager hope.

"Reapers! Reapers emerging in Corridor 2 Level 4... Oh, almighty god. More emerging in Corridors 3... 4... 7... and 8 multiple levels."

The main vid screen changed from the shattered remains of the QRF into multiple picture in pictures videos, showing each of the new incursion points. The corridors were packed with the Faithful, trying desperately to reach their local armory. In their midst the Reapers stood like rocks in a stormy ocean, their mag rifles moving methodically from left to right as they fired continuously. The Faithful fell like stalks of corn to a farmer's scythe. When, eventually, the firing halted, it took the Watch Officer a moment to realize that, miraculously, there were survivors. His fleeting moment of hope left him, as he realised that only the children had survived.

His brain added the sounds of horror to the silent vid images he watched. He imagined the children's pitiful screams for their parents who lay piled around them. *Had the merciful God intervened to save the innocent?* Reapers moved forward and as they moved past each child, their metallic arm caressed each child who instantly fell, unmoving, to the floor of the blood-soaked corridor.

Somewhere in the distance a voice called to him, but, he could not take his eyes from the screen. The voice became louder, but, his body refused to move. The sight of Reapers culling the children ripped him to his very soul. *How could the almighty God allow the innocent to suffer such a fate?* A strong hand on his shoulder spun him around and he faced the craggy features of the senior noncom. The sound of his steady voice finally penetrated the Watch Officer's stasis.

"Sir, more Reapers are emerging. They are coming out directly behind the heavy weapons emplacements. The emplacements will quickly be overrun and the Reapers will be able to advance into the inner corridors at will. Only a handful of the Faithful have made it to the armories and without the support of the heavy weapons, any fight they can put up will be worthless...." The older man looked deep into his eyes as he held his shoulders. "Sir. You have a decision to make. And for all the Faithful's sake, you need to do it quickly." Releasing the young Watch Officer he turned and slowly walked back to his post.

The Watch Officer slumped as if physically exhausted into his seat. On the vid screen in front of him the story of death and sacrifice was laid bare for him and every person in the room to see. More Reapers were emerging into Haven. So many now that there was no point in reporting it. Everyone in the Ops Room were now mere spectators to events taking place in the building and corridors of Haven. The Watch Officer struggled with the decision he knew he must make. His fingers reached for the plastic authorization card. This time, it was cold to the touch. Minutes passed as he struggled to find an alternative action to what his faith and his conscience told him he must do.

One by one the cameras in the corridors surrounding the control room failed, and the sounds of fighting filtered more loudly through the heavily armored doors.

The Watch Officer knew time was running out. He knew his orders. He remembered the briefing from his commanding officer, the way she had paused, searching for the right words before she spoke. "In the event the Operations Room is breached, we must assume all hope of the Faithful's survival in Haven One Eight is lost. We must trust in the one true god and do our utmost to send the evil who hunt us back to the hell they came from. Your orders are to activate the nuclear demolition charge in the central core."

The gut-wrenching wail that came from his left caused the mounting feeling of dread to nearly overwhelm him. Turning to the direction of the sound he was confronted by a technician hunched over his monitors, his shoulders shuddering, his head slowly shaking. "What is it?"

The tech made no reply. Slamming his fist on his console the Watch Officer stood up so sharply his seat flew back on its wheels until it impacted with the wall, the loud bang drew furtive glances from the other technicians in the room.

The Watch Officer stalked over to the slowly whimpering man. *This is no time to go to pieces!* The Asatu were spreading throughout Haven and he needed everyone to stand to their duty. It only took one person to falter and the whole control room could fall apart. Reaching the tech he spun the hapless man's seat around, his arm raised, ready to slap him back into operation. His hand was already sweeping down when his eyes fell onto the station's monitor and his hand faltered in midair, his legs went weak and he was forced to grab the console's edge to keep himself upright.

In pin-sharp clarity he watched a line of Reapers pass a small bundle from one to another until the bundle was passed through the wavering pool that was the entrance to a teleport field. It took a moment for the Watch Officer to realize that each of these bundles were not quite perfectly wrapped, thin, short straps hung from each... No, not straps... limbs! The Reapers were passing the bodies of dead children through the teleport! As he watched, mesmerized by the sight of the small packages, a child's arm moved sluggishly and his knees almost buckled as he realized the children were alive.

The Reaper holding the child touched its metal hand to the child's head and the infant went limp again. Oh merciful God everything the preachers had taught was true! The Asatu were the handmaidens of the great Satan.

With new-found resolve he pushed himself upright and his eyes locked with those of the old noncom. This man had treated him with the gentle kindness of a loving father, gently guiding him through his first days of command whilst ensuring that the less respectful technicians knew that to question the young officer's decisions was to question his.

Under his guidance a young, green officer had become a confident, inspiring leader of the Faithful. Now, as he struggled with the biggest decision of his young life the older man's imploring eyes helped steel him for what he knew he must do. The Asatu and their evil master could not be allowed to corrupt the children. Better they should die than enter into a life that would deny them the chance of eventually bathing in the love of the one true god.

A loud explosion directly outside the control room doors caused a thin, haze of concrete dust to fill the air. Maybe it was this distraction or the dust hanging in the air which caused the Ops Room crew to fail to notice the tell-tale pinprick of light. Whatever the cause, the ringing of the Reapers' metal feet on the concrete floor as they emerged from the portal was the first warning they received and it was too late.

The evil snout of the mag rifle was already raised and without hesitation the Reaper opened fire. The rifle ripped through consoles and technicians with clinical precision.

Instinctively, the Watch Officer dropped to the floor as the concrete dust in the air was joined by the smoke from shredded consoles and mixed with flesh and blood as one after another the technicians he commanded fell to the withering fire.

Clinging to the floor, he raised his head only to see the Reaper moving in his direction, blocking his route to his console, and the children's only hope of salvation. The sound of metal on concrete resounded in his ears. Another couple of steps and it would see him.

From the opposite side of the room came a blur of movement. The Reaper's head and rifle spun in its direction as the older technician burst from behind a charred and smoking console, a fire ax raised high above his head as he charged directly at the metal monster.

With the Reaper momentarily distracted, the officer saw his chance, lunging for his command console. He reached it as the older man brought the heavy ax down on the Reaper's arm. By fortune or divine intervention, the ax landed exactly on the point where the Reaper's hand gripped the mag rifle. Sparks flew as the rifle's firing mechanism shattered. The Watch Officer reached his console and ripped the thin plastic card from under his tunic, thrusting it into the waiting slot. Behind him, the older man had begun to raise the ax to deliver a second blow. But, he never made it. With a speed that denied its bulk the Reaper released its grip on the now-useless rifle, its arm shot out and fixed around the old man's neck. With the whine of powered servos the fingers closed and a sickening snap rang out as fragile bone gave way to metal force. The fingers opened and the lifeless body dropped to the floor.

The fate of the old man made no difference to the Watch Officer's computer. With the card inserted the list of options appeared on its display. Aware that time was short the officer scrambled to select the correct listing for nuclear demolition. Yes there it was! His finger reached for the commit key, when he was violently thrown back against the wall, unbearable pain filled his chest, his vision blurred and he struggled for breath. Fighting back the waves of pain, he forced his eyes to focus, only to see the Reaper standing over him like some avenging angel. The Watch Officer commanded his arms to reach out in a final effort to push the commit button, but, as his arm reached out he realized it was futile.

The console was too far away. Above him the Reaper followed his movements and seemed to focus on the command card. The featureless face of the Reaper returned to stare at the dying officer. With a gentle hiss a crack appeared in the center of the metal chest. The crack expanded as the entire chest split in two, opening slowly like the petals of a flower to give him a view of the evil heart of the monsters.

His vision was failing and he blinked rapidly, refusing to show weakness as the heart of the beast was exposed. A heart that slowly unfurled and extracted itself from the metal shell. He knew his clouding eyes were lying to him as the evil heart coalesced into the lithe form of a woman, dressed in a figure-hugging, gray, one-piece uniform. The woman knelt by him, and brought her head close enough to his that he felt her warm breath through his excruciating pain. *No! Not human! Surely this is the last trick of the evil one?* With a shudder his eyes clouded over completely and he passed forever into darkness.

———

Corporal Mhairi-Anne Buchanan felt no remorse for the dead man lying on the cold floor of the Operations Room. Without a second thought she turned from the body, cursing under her breath, as her mag rifle, which she had used like an ancient spear to impale him before he could do god knows what at his console, was now a useless piece of expensive metal.

Reaching across the console, she removed the slim plastic card from its slot and watched as the lights on it changed from red to green. Slipping the card into a thigh pocket she allowed herself a cat-like stretch. Four hours in the battle suit was enough, even for the hardened veteran that she had become, over the past three years of fighting on this planet. Ironic, as Mhairi-Anne had never in her wildest dreams ever thought that she would be a soldier.

Her dreams had changed when the religious fanatics of Eden had re-ignited their relationship with their mother world after four centuries of isolation.

Earth had welcomed them with open arms, never once suspecting they were admitting vipers into the breast of humanity.

Then came the Day of Sorrow. It was the day that briefcase nukes exploded in over two hundred cities. Tens of millions died instantly. Hundreds of millions were scarred both mentally and physically. Men, women, children. The weapons ignited by the fanatics did not discriminate.

Mhairi-Anne had been out of town on business and her husband and two children perished. As they perished, a part of her also died.

The perpetrators made no secret of who they were. They called themselves the Faithful of Eden and had an unshakable belief that god was on their side. It was their destiny to cleanse the Earth of the unbelievers, they declared.

The various nations of Earth formed a military alliance and deployed the Allied Special Anti-Terror Unit, ASATU, to be the tool of their people's vengeance. Mhairi-Anne had joined the lines of willing volunteers. Vengeance burned in her heart.

From high orbit, the ASATU had demanded the surrender of those responsible for the murder of millions of its citizens. It was only then that the commanders of ASATU began to fully understand what they were facing. An entire world who shared the same slanted view of their divine destiny.

So entrenched was this belief that when the first ASATU units landed they faced not only soldiers but every man and woman on the planet. As the casualty figures rose a fateful decision was forced on ASATU. Every adult was to be treated as an enemy combatant, only the children were to be spared. The word went out and so the War of Annihilation began.

There could be no orbital bombardments. No heavy weapons. Not if the children were to be spared. ASATU soldiers fought street to street. Building to building. City after city fell. And when the enemy retreated underground the ASATU followed. After all the bloodletting this was the last bastion of the killers.

A wave of exhaustion swept over Mhairi-Anne and she rested a hand on her armored suit for a moment before shaking it off and climbing back into the pilot seat. Time to find a new rifle, to replace the one sticking out of the still form on the floor. The fight was not over yet, there were more children to free from the grip of this evil cult.

With the chest plate once more sealed, the metal suit turned in place and headed for the door, the ghosts of the dead riding high on its shoulders.

FALLEN WITNESS

—Vision II: Scapa Flow—

Art: Andy Bigwood
Words: Tim C. Taylor

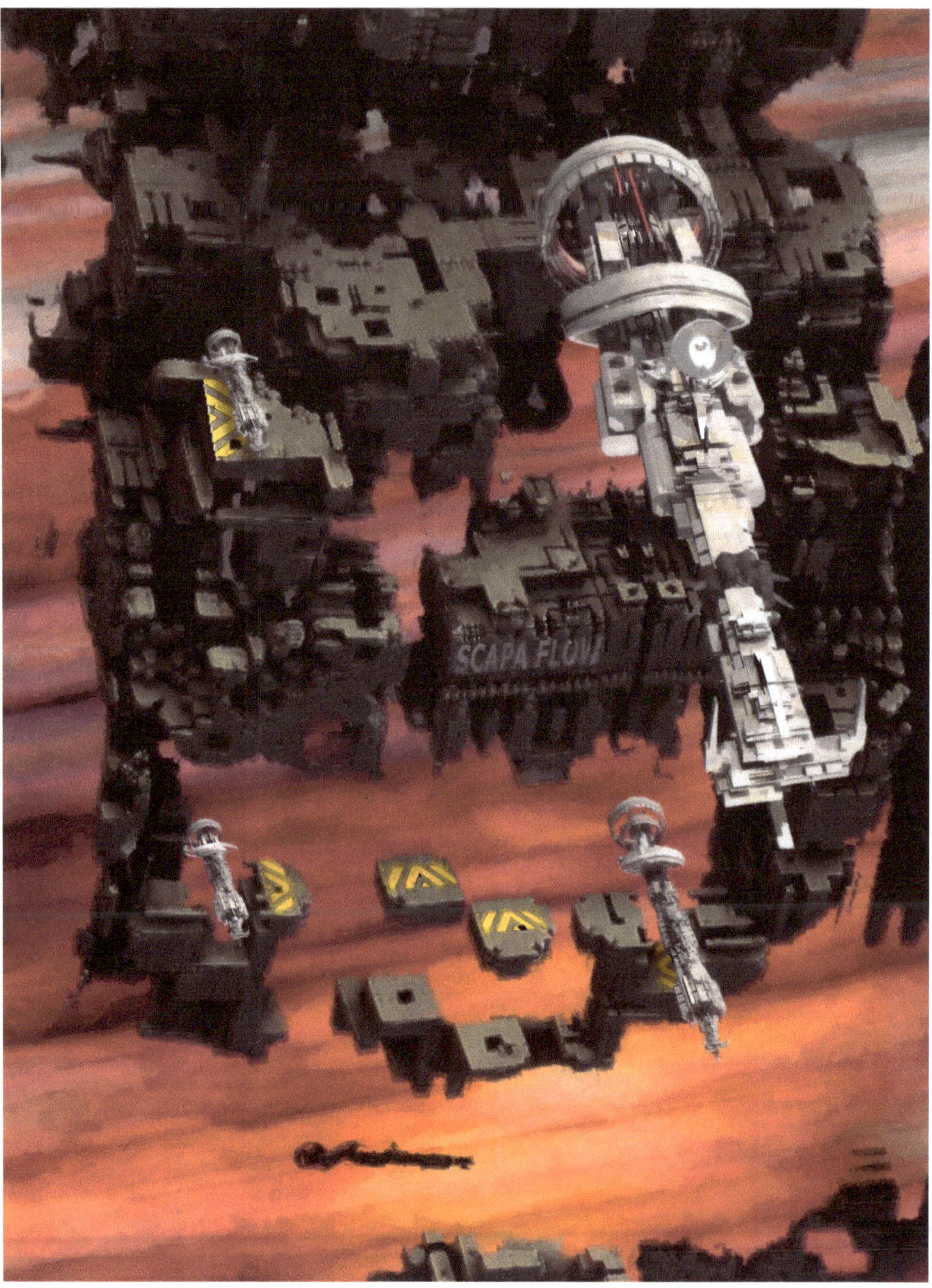
SCAPA FLOW

"My name is Flight-Lieutenant Karl Chalmers, and I am a fallen witness."

The second android is bathed in a similar cylinder of light to Petty Officer DeSouza. He is shorter than the first android and one side of his face is covered in burns. The children in the auditorium are confused. Why have they made an android with burns?

Chalmers holds aloft another rigid smartscreen. This shows a more complex image than the sleek *Speedbird*. Chalmers gives the children a few moments to make sense of the picture.

"This is Scapa Flow," he explains, "the Royal Navy dockyard orbiting Jupiter, a large planet in the Sol System. Many of the Federated Nations had naval facilities there, and Scapa Flow was the largest. There were private dockyards too, and industrial habitats bigger than any city on our planet. Jupiter and its moons were a rich source of fuel and raw materials, and its magnetosphere could easily be mined for energy."

A hand shoots up, the boy Petty Officer DeSouza has identified as Mahmoud Bhatti.

Chalmers frowns. *The battle for hearts and minds.* That's what they used to call this kind of mission. He sees its value but he doesn't have to like interruptions by civilian kids. He relents, nodding at the boy. "Yes?"

"Sir, that warship at the top-right. The one with the distinctive red flux tubes. Is that HMS *Warspite*?"

Chalmers nods again, this time with conviction. The boy knows his history. He probably knows why the fallen witnesses are here, but is playing along. That could make him a useful ally. His parents probably regard themselves as patriots, but will still need to be cautioned. Children are not supposed to learn this aspect of their history until they are told in the official way during their eleventh year. It holds more shock value that way.

"Very good," says Chalmers. "The military learned much from *Speedbird*'s data recordings and the energy wraiths imprisoned in her turbine. The leading Federated Nations vied with each other to construct the most powerful warships to combat the energy wraiths. There was great rivalry, but within a spirit of cooperation and the sharing of ideas. It was felt best that each leading nation should pursue their own vision of the perfect war machine, because this new enemy was so different. After all, even though they used matter to construct tools and the means to wage war, the enemy were beings of energy. They did not need to breathe air and they could move at will through the zero-gravity of the void, although without the protection of their ships, they would be seared by the stellar winds and planetary magnetospheres inside a star system. If you destroyed their warships, the ability of the energy wraiths to wage war upon us would be severely weakened, but they could simply beam themselves away and build another fleet. How could we defeat such an enemy? The answer of the British Nations was HMS *Warspite* and the class of ships she gave her name to. Take a look at the image and see if you can guess the main armament of the Warspite class."

Chalmers gives his audience a while to think. The more the children can feel the horror their ancestors knew, the better. Even after all these centuries, Chalmers can still taste the fear from the days when humanity stood on the brink of destruction.

A glance of understanding passes between Bhatti and Flight-Lieutenant Chalmers. The boy knows the answer but he understands why this is a future lesson more than a history one. Bhatti will keep quiet unless he is needed.

A few hesitant hands start to go up. Chalmers waits a few moments for the field of hands to grow before selecting a girl on the back row.

"Please, sir. The rings at the back… they look a bit like *Speedbird's*."

"Very good," said Chalmers, remembering to smile. "The Royal Navy's innovation was to turn *Speedbird's* accidental prison into a weapon of war, nicknamed Death Beat. In flight, the aft-most turbine provided thrust, just like *Speedbird*. But in combat, the Warspite-class ships had a second or even a third turbine ring mounted at an angle to the first. The angle was adjustable and would be set to generate a powerful interference pattern in the quantum foam, one directed at the enemy."

Chalmers lets that sink in before continuing with his standard explanation. "Have you ever traveled in a vehicle and opened a window or ceiling hatch by a small amount and heard a throbbing in the air? I expect if it was you who were to blame, your parents would shout at you to shut the damned window."

That wins a few laughs. A few recognize what he means. "That throbbing noise is called beating. Imagine the strength of the beating magnified a million times. Your whole body would explode. Now imagine that instead of setting up the beating in air, it was set up in the quantum foam that was to the energy wraiths what flesh is to you and me."

Chalmers gets a few puzzled looks for describing himself as flesh and blood. It's easy to forget he isn't. He presses on before his android nature becomes a distraction. "Royal Navy scientists and engineers had spent months testing their new weapon in virtual simulations but there was no way of being sure whether their simulations were accurate until they faced the enemy. But the Grand Fleet of humanity did know they needed one more thing before taking the fight to the enemy."

Fallen Witness Vision III is on p227

THEIR DARKEST HOUR

—Book 1 of Their Darkest Hour Series —

Christopher G. Nuttall

Prologue

The senior officers of the Conquest Force rose to their feet as the Command Triad entered the briefing room. *Ju'tro* Oheghizh bowed his head in submission as they took their three seats, each one representing and commanding an element of the fleet. Together, they would oversee the conquest – and pose no threat to the state, back home. They'd be too suspicious of one another to ever plot treachery together.

"We have been observing Earth for the past five of its rotations," *Va'tro* Nak'tak said. *Years*, Oheghizh reminded himself, careful to think in the language of the prey. "The humans are a curious race. They may well be more unlike us than the Uteck."

A rustle ran around the compartment as his words sank in. The Uteck, unlike most known races, didn't possess two arms, two legs and one head. They were utterly alien – which hadn't stopped them fighting the Eridiani to a standstill in fifty years of bloody warfare. The State still believed that they could defeat the Uteck and occupy their worlds, but it would be a long time before anyone saw fit to resume the war. It had simply been too costly.

"The humans have progressed remarkably unevenly," Nak'tak reported. "Their space presence is pathetic; they have yet to establish a base on their moon or start mining asteroids for war materials. They are literally unable to pose any threat to the Conquest Fleet, even once we are in orbit around their world. Furthermore, their ruling power seems curiously unwilling to crush its enemies – they appear to be willing to accept the hatred of their inferiors, instead of forcing their inferiors to submit. This is without a precedent in all of known space."

There was a pause. "However, in certain areas, they are actually more advanced than ourselves," he continued. "Their most advanced computer systems are more capable than the devices we use on these starships – and certain other advancements may pose a threat to the Landing Force once we start taking up positions on the planetary surface. In particular, they have an alarmingly high number of nuclear weapons and – we must assume – a willingness to use them if they face defeat."

Azhadib, the Director of Conquest, spoke into the silence. "Do you believe that this race will make acceptable clients for the State?"

"We believe that it may be harder than we expect to convince them to submit," Nak'tak said. "Unlike our previous encounters with low-tech races" – all of which had been brought into the service of the State, their development short-circuited by their natural masters – "they offer the promise of a workforce that will not require extensive training to grasp the basics of our technology, assuming that they are capable of grasping it at all. We have a secondary reason not to simply exterminate this race. They will be very useful to us."

He didn't mention the first reason, Oheghizh noted, in the privacy of his own mind. Known space had many mysteries – races blossomed to life, built their empires, dominated the galactic scene for a few million years and then faded away – but even the State had heard rumours of the Elders. They'd been warned that genocide would be harshly punished. Oheghizh wasn't sure if he believed the tales or not – the idea of someone being more powerful than the State was difficult to grasp – yet it seemed clear that *someone* believed them. There was no other explanation for the prohibition on genocide.

Earth spun in the centre of the compartment, a luminous orb glowing with blue-green light. It looked almost homelike, yet it was home to over seven *billion* humans. He glanced down at the reports the observers had filed in their long study of Earth, carefully monitoring the humans and devising plans for the invasion and conquest of their world. As one of the senior Land Force commanders, Oheghizh could expect high honours and rewards if he succeeded in bringing his portion of Earth under control – and endless infamy if he failed. The humans would pose a formidable problem, even to the State. But they would succeed. Failure would not be tolerated.

The assignments had been sorted out by the Command Triad and passed down as a unanimous decision. Oheghizh would be assigned to a medium-sized island nation, still one of the most advanced and developed states on Earth. Quite why they hadn't developed any form of unity was a surprise – technological advancement tended to unite previously separated nations – but it hardly mattered. Their political divisions would work against them when the Conquest Fleet revealed its presence. They would have no time to plan a unified defence before they were overwhelmed.

And slowly, but surely, Oheghizh and his companions drew up their plans against Earth. The Human Race would never know what had hit them until it was far too late.

Chapter One

RAF Coningsby/Salisbury Plain/London
United Kingdom, Day 1

"It looks like a busy day for us, boys and girls."

Flying Officer Alexandra Horton smiled as Squadron Leader Rupert Paddington opened the briefing. The men – and single woman – of No. 3 Squadron rarely had an uneventful day, even when they were patrolling the skies over Britain. After 9/11, every civilian aircraft that went off course sent ripples of alarm running through the United Kingdom Air Defence Region and it wasn't uncommon for Tornados or Eurofighter Typhoons to be scrambled in response to an aircraft that had simply lost its way. Not that anyone was allowed to become complacent, of course. The Eurofighters were scrambled with live weapons and everyone knew that one day a hapless pilot would be faced with the choice of shooting down a civilian aircraft or watching it plunge into the Houses of Parliament. Alex was mildly surprised that none of the thousands of terrorist plots monitored by MI5 had ever come close to taking off.

"We've been informed that the UKGDE boys have been tracking more ghosts," Paddington continued. "Someone higher up the food chain is getting just a little bit concerned with these reports and they'd like some hard data. You may be directed to perform an interception if a ghost shows up while you're in the air."

Alex frowned, thoughtfully. Over the last few weeks, radar sets in Britain – and America as well, she'd been given to understand – had been tracking a handful of transient contacts that seemed to be travelling right at the edge of Earth's atmosphere. The general feeling was that someone – perhaps in Britain, but more likely in the United States – was testing a new model of stealth drone by flying it through one of the most advanced air defence environments in the world. It wasn't an uncommon procedure, but surely *someone* would have said something by now, if only to prevent an interception that brought one of the craft down. Rumours she'd heard suggested that some of the top brass were more concerned than they admitted, at least to the pilots. There was a distant possibility that the Russians might have produced something new that they were using to probe NATO's defence environment.

She shook her head, reaching up to feel her short blonde hair. Her fellow pilots had nicknamed her Starbuck back when she'd started training to fly the Eurofighter and the name had stuck. Being assigned to No. 3 Squadron was hardly a blot on her record, even if defence cutbacks did make their position increasingly insecure. She'd heard that some of the top brass were worried about their ability to defend the UKADR if more squadrons were placed in reserve, or eliminated altogether. Buying the Eurofighter might have seemed like a good idea back before 9/11, but now the money was flowing to the army and aircraft that could provide support to British troops on the ground. The Eurofighter was an excellent piece of kit, yet it didn't have the close-support capability of an Apache helicopter. Their service in Afghanistan had always been far less decisive than the MOD had hoped.

"Horton and Davidson, you'll be on routine patrol, taking over from the lads out there now," Paddington said, finally. "Jackson and Stuart will be on QRA, ready to provide backup if there's a problem or you need to return to base. Don't forget to keep one eye on your radar sets at all times. You never know what you might run into up there."

There were some chuckles from the pilots, although they all knew that a mission could shift from routine boredom to sheer terror within seconds. Up in the air, *they* would be in the front line, not some paper-pusher in Whitehall who would happily question every little decision made by the men at the front. Alex knew pilots and soldiers who had been hounded out of the service by the MOD, or the government, merely for making poor decisions on the battlefield. It seemed to have escaped their notice that soldiers and

pilots had to make their decisions within seconds and there was no time to take a balanced view of anything…

She shook her head as Paddington dismissed them and headed for her plane. The flight plan said that she would be in the air within half an hour. There was nothing quite like flying over Britain as the dawn rose. And if she was lucky, it might even be a routine patrol.

———

Darkness shrouded Salisbury Plain, but the sound of humming engines could be heard – faintly – in the gloom. Dawn was approaching, the horizon starting to light up in the distance, leaving the French with little time to get across the river. Brigadier Gavin Lightbridge-Stewart allowed himself a tight smile as he lay on the ground, using his night-vision goggles to peer into the shadows. The French didn't know it, but the British Army had prepared a nasty surprise for when they tried to reach the mock town.

Full-scale exercises were rare – the days when the British Army could roam across Germany on exercises were in the past, and it was incredibly expensive to ship men and equipment to Canada or the USA – but the bean-counters had finally agreed to allow a joint exercise with the French. A section of French tankers had agreed to play the attacking force, simulating an attack from Russia into the European Union. Officially, the French were playing a fictional nation – it was typical of the politicians to be more worried about upsetting the Russians than helping out the soldiers who defended them – but everyone knew the truth. Russia had been rather more noisy than usual over the last few months and senior officers had been warning the politicians that important skills were being lost.

His lips twitched into a smile. The British Army was intimately familiar with the terrain and they'd used it to their advantage. A troop of Challenger tanks had been positioned to give the French a bloody nose, while ground-based air defence systems had been deployed to prevent the French from using a drone to spy out the British defences. Once the French tanks started to cross the river, they'd find themselves caught in a trap – unless they had a surprise of their own up their sleeves. The politicians on both sides of the Atlantic might deride the French, but the French military was tough and very professional. And it had picked up rather more experience in the years since Algeria than many outsiders realised.

He keyed his radio, speaking barely above a whisper. "Prepare to engage," he ordered, calmly. It wasn't common for a Brigadier to lead from the front, but he'd missed the advance into Iraq and knew himself to be less familiar with armoured warfare than he would have preferred. Besides, paper exercises were all very well, but it took real manoeuvring to gain a real understanding of what his force could – and could not – do. Murphy never failed to put in an appearance in the real world. "On my mark, launch flares and then engage at will."

———

"The bloody protesters are still there, I'm afraid."

Sergeant Robin Harrison, London Metropolitan Police, nodded as he strode up towards Buckingham Palace. A small army of men and women carrying signs protesting against the latest cause of the month were gathered outside the gates, shouting at passer-bys while sharing drinks and food amongst themselves. It seemed that there was no shortage of protesters in London; Robin knew from secret briefings that anarchist and other radical groups were streamlining their 'rent-a-mob' systems. The Police had responded by monitoring Facebook and other social networking sites, but the technical staff had warned that their ability to take down parts of the internet was very limited. Robin wouldn't have cared so much – people had the right to protest, as long as they behaved themselves – if criminal gangs hadn't started using protests as places to rob the protesters blind. It had only been three months ago when the Police had had to intervene when the dedicated protesters started turning on freeloaders within the camps.

"So I see," he said, tiredly. Overtime seemed to be a fact of life in the Police force these days, as was permanent tiredness and general unhappiness. The number of Bobbies on the street was going down and, despite the vast number of CCTV cameras all over London, crime was going up. Every few months, they'd even get new targets from politicians who didn't realise that they'd systematically crippled the Met over the last two decades. "Anything we ought to keep an eye on?"

"They seem a surprisingly nice bunch," Sergeant Singh said, seriously. He nodded towards the protesters, who were trying to convince a pair of pedestrians to join them. It didn't look as if they were having any success. "No real fights or anything, just shouting. A few of them keep looking daggers at us, I'm afraid."

"Nothing to worry about then," Robin agreed. The small police force would keep an eye on the protesters, some of whom might even be relieved that the police were there. They might claim to be an anarchist commune, but in his experience those broke down rapidly into chaos and the rule of the strong if there was no presence from the forces of law and order. It hadn't been that long since the London Riots of 2011. "Don't worry – we'll keep an eye on the Palace for you."

Singh gave him a one-fingered gesture and sauntered off in the general direction of the police station, where he'd catch something to eat and a few hours of sleep before he went back on duty. Robin watched him go and then turned to look back at the Palace. It was all lit up, allowing the protesters to see the very heart of the establishment they hated so much. The handful of policemen didn't waste time staring at the Royal Residence. They had to worry about keeping the peace.

A pair of protesters made eye contact with him, and then looked away as if they'd seen something dirty, or obscene. Robin wasn't too surprised. Some of the protesters saw the police as the enemy, the men who broke up protest marches and beat up protesters. His father had been a policeman, as had his grandfather, and neither of them had to endure the level of public distrust modern policemen faced. But back in their day, the police hadn't been cut back to the bone, to the point where ordinary citizens started to see them as the enemy.

He shook his head tiredly. Maybe he'd jack it all in early and find a place in a private security firm. They were hiring and the pay was generally better than the Met. And maybe then his family would get better care than they could from the NHS. His wife wouldn't even come into London. She preferred to live outside in the suburbs, away from the crowds and pressure. He couldn't really blame her at all. London just wasn't a safe place to bring up one's children any more.

———————

"Wake up," a voice snapped, in her ear. Doctor Fatima Hasid swallowed a word as her mother pulled away the blankets. "Get up, you lazy girl. You're supposed to be on your way to work."

Fatima scowled at her stepmother, but couldn't quite bring herself to snap at the older woman. At twenty-seven, she should be married and producing kids of her own – at least according to her stepmother. If only her father hadn't married again… but he had, leaving her to put up with an older woman who resented Fatima's presence in her life. Her stepmother had started putting forward the names of suitable boys, most of who lived in her grandmother's village back in Pakistan. Fatima had responded by taking more overtime with the NHS every time her stepmother arranged a meeting. None of the boys she had met had seemed keen to marry a woman who was far more qualified than they could ever hope to be.

She pulled herself out of bed and scowled at her face in the mirror. Dark eyes set in a dark face stared back at her, leaving her with an almost waif-like expression. The uniform she donned rapidly belonged to the nearest hospital, where she worked ever since graduating as a medical doctor. It would be years before she could pay off her debts and go into private practice and until then the NHS owned her, body and soul. She washed her face and headed downstairs, to where her stepmother was banging pots and pans

together. It wasn't as if she was doing anything useful either. Fatima had to get her own coffee and cereal before heading out of the house.

"They'll give you the sack and then where will you be?" Her stepmother demanded. Fatima ignored her as best as she could. Her father was already on his way to work, after visiting the mosque for morning prayers. "Who'll want you if you lose your job?"

"The boys you seem to think are suitable for me have no jobs," Fatima replied, as calmly as she could. It was true; her stepmother's family had been pressing her to convince Fatima to marry a boy from Pakistan, who could then be brought to Britain. The fact that Fatima herself didn't want to marry a stranger didn't mean anything to them. They'd all had arranged marriages and they'd turned out fine… well, publicly, at least. Fatima knew that at least one of her stepmother's relatives beat his wife. "And I still have an hour to get to the hospital before I start scrubbing up."

Her stepmother started to bleat again, but Fatima tuned her out with the ease of long practice. There were times when she cursed her decision to study medicine, even though it provided an independence many of her friends would envy. The screaming kids in the waiting room, the injuries inflicted by chance or deliberate malice, watching men and women dying slowly in front of her… there were days when she just wanted to walk away from it. But that wasn't an option, not when she still had to pay off her debts. The NHS was dreadful when it came to arranging life-saving medical treatments, yet somehow it was very good at tracking down students and demanding that they repay the loans they'd taken out to study…

She shook her head as she finished her coffee and headed for the door. She'd just have to endure until the day she could leave the NHS behind. And then perhaps she could set up in private practice, or maybe even leave the country. There were high-paying jobs for medical staff in America, she'd been told. Maybe she'd emigrate and leave her stepmother behind. The thought made her smile, even as she saw the dawn rising over the horizon. Another day was about to begin.

———————

He couldn't sleep.

Prime Minister Gabriel Burley stood in Ten Downing Street and peered through the bullet-proof glass at the protesters at the end of the streets. It seemed that there wasn't a day when the protesters weren't there, screaming and shouting as if they blamed Gabriel personally for the economic malaise that had gripped Britain over the last ten years. The country didn't seem to be able to hold together a government for more than a year either, not after the latest round of parliamentary scandals. Gabriel, two years ago, had been nothing more than an up-and-coming MP, a safe pair of hands for a Parliamentary seat that was solidly Conservative. He'd never dreamed of becoming Prime Minister, certainly not after his predecessor's career had been blown out of the water in the latest expenses scandal. His opponents had remarked that the only reason Gabriel had avoided being implicated in the scandal had been because he didn't have the imagination to fiddle his expenses, let alone do anything more interesting. There were times when Gabriel feared that they were right. Nothing he did seemed to please everyone, or even anyone.

He looked down at his desk and shook his head, bitterly. It was covered in folders, each one a wordy report from the Home Office, the Ministry of Defence or the Security Services. He was supposed to read them all, but reading them was a chore. Didn't anyone use plain English these days? He'd once spent an hour reading a briefing paper on recent developments in Iraq only to discover that it could have been condensed down into five or six sentences. At least he'd been able to make his feelings clear on *that* point. It was a shame that the Civil Service took so long to adapt. The next Prime Minister would probably not see any improvement.

One of the walls of his office held a large painting, commissioned by his immediate predecessor. It showed all of the Prime Ministers of the United Kingdom, from Pitt the Elder to Gabriel himself. He'd been surprised to receive it, only to be told that it had taken so long to produce that the Prime Minister who'd ordered it had left office by the time it had arrived. The Prime Ministers seemed to be gazing disapprovingly at him, as if they felt that he was letting the side down. They were probably right. When Gabriel compared himself to Pitt, or Churchill, or Thatcher, he always found himself lacking. But then, they'd never had to worry about an economic crash that was slowly bringing the country to its knees…

"Lucky bastards," he muttered, as he returned to his desk. The files sat in front of him, mocking him by their silent presence. His secure palmtop buzzed, reminding him that he had the daily security briefing in an hour, followed by several meetings with MPs before his speech in Parliament in the afternoon. The speechwriter had promised him a good speech, one he could read out before the assembled MPs, but it wouldn't go down very well. It never did, not when all he could deliver was bad news. There were times when he felt that the only reason the Opposition hadn't pushed for a no-confidence vote was because they didn't want to be saddled with commanding the sinking ship. They found it more congenial to snipe and shout abuse.

He opened the first file and looked down at it. It was just as he feared; a short summery, and then twenty pages he'd have to read, just in case some bastard with press credentials hurled a question at him. They'd have a field day with an ignorant Prime Minister. Cursing under his breath, he tapped the intercom and called for coffee. He'd read through one of the files, he promised himself, and then he'd have some time to relax. And then he'd attend the briefing.

And then all the alarms went off at once.

Chapter Two

Over Norwich/Salisbury Plain/London
United Kingdom, Day 1

"You know," Davidson remarked, "Becky has been quite jealous recently."

Alex rolled her eyes. The two Eurofighters were heading south-east, high over Norwich. It was definitely shaping up into a routine patrol, which was part of the reason they were bantering together as they flew onwards. It helped them remain alert and remind them that they weren't alone, even if they were flying single-seat aircraft. Fliers could forget about everything else while boring through the sky at just under supersonic speed.

"I thought you were dating Kate," she said, mockingly. Davidson's love life was the stuff of legends. Fast-jet pilots never seemed to have any difficulty finding female companionship while they were off-base. "What happened to the poor girl?"

"One of those Para bastards got his hands on her while I was looking the other way," Davidson admitted. His girls never stayed with him for long. "I think they were talking about getting hitched, last I heard."

Alex snorted. "And who does Becky have good reason to be jealous of?"

Davidson affected a hurt tone. "I'm shocked that you could think that I might cheat on her," he said. Alex snickered and made a one-fingered gesture towards his plane. "She's jealous of my Typhoon, Alex. I get into her and I take her to Heaven twice a day."

"I always knew that you were terrible in bed," Alex said, fighting down the urge to burst into giggles. "That joke is older than the CO's CO. And if you keep moving from woman to woman, you won't live long enough to get promoted into a desk job."

"You make it sound as if they'd kill me," Davidson protested. "I think…"

"Charlie One, Charlie Two, this is Sector Control," a new voice said. Alex straightened up at once, feeling ice shivering down the back of her neck. "We are picking up a single contact on intercept vector; I say again, we are picking up a single contact on intercept vector."

Alex glanced at her radar screen as… *something* blinked into existence. Dead ahead of the Typhoons, it was advancing towards them at Mach Four. For a moment, she thought it was a radar glitch, the kind of glitch that had caused panic during the height of the Cold War, or the years after 9/11. The contact remained alarmingly stable, refusing to vanish. She ran through the situation in her mind and realised that they'd be in visual range within two minutes. What the hell could travel at that speed? There were rumours of a hypersonic drone being test-flown in America, but what would it be doing over Britain?

"Acknowledged, Sector Control," she said. "Be advised that we will attempt to make visual contact; I say again, we will attempt to make visual contact."

"It could be a ghost," Davidson said. He sounded excited. Alex had flown a real-life interception mission before, back when the Russians had flown a pair of Blackjack bombers over the North Sea to remind NATO that they existed, but Davidson's military experience was limited to dropping bombs over Afghanistan. "You think we could be the first to see one with our own eyes?"

Alex glanced at her radar screen, and then peered ahead into the lightening sky. If she saw the craft… it was possible that someone higher-up would order them to avoid contact or to forget what they'd seen, if it *was* someone's secret test project. They should come into visual range in seconds…

Her threat receiver lit up like a Christmas tree. "What the hell…?"

A streak of light lanced out of nowhere and struck Davidson's Typhoon before he had a chance to evade. The weapon, whatever it was, hit its target so hard that Davidson's plane was blown into a fireball before he had a chance to realise that he was under attack. Alex yanked her plane into an evasive course just as a second streak of light – a very fast missile, according to her on-board displays – slashed through where she'd been. They were under attack! She almost froze in shock – only her training kept her moving. The radar was reporting *dozens* of new contacts now, appearing from nowhere over the North Sea and moving towards the British mainland. One finger uncovered her firing buttons as she tried desperately to call for reinforcements. The QRA aircraft should have been in the air the moment the radar controllers on the ground realised that something had gone badly wrong.

"Sector Control, this is Charlie One…"

Her radio screeched, loudly enough to force her to turn it down in a hurry. Someone was *jamming* her, preventing her from calling for help. The unknowns, whoever or whatever they were, were angling towards her, slowing as they came. Whatever they were flying seemed to outmatch her Typhoon effortlessly – who the hell were they? Alex gritted her teeth and activated her targeting systems. An enemy craft came into her sights and she launched a pair of missiles right towards it. The craft started to turn, but it was far too late. One of the missiles struck home and the enemy craft exploded in a shockingly powerful blast.

Another missile was screaming toward her. Acting on instinct, she corkscrewed her plane through the air, realising that she was utterly outmatched. But running could be as dangerous as trying to fight. A black shape appeared out of nowhere in front of her and she plunged the plane down, catching sight of an angular aircraft that reminded her of the F-117 Nighthawk, only several times as large. She took a shot at it anyway – it couldn't possibly be friendly – but she couldn't tell if she'd inflicted any damage. Whatever was screwing with her radio was screwing with her radar as well.

A brilliant flash of light caught her attention, from the west. Something had exploded on the ground, but what? The entire country couldn't be under attack, could it? The RAF hadn't had any reason to think that *someone* intended to attack Britain – or if they had, the senior officers had never bothered to tell the pilots. Her threat receiver screamed again, too late. The entire aircraft buckled around her…

Desperately, moving so quickly that she hadn't quite realised what she *was* doing, she pulled the ejection lever and exploded out of the aircraft, into the suddenly-hostile sky.

———

The first of the French tanks were coming into view, a trio of AMX-56 Leclerc Main Battle Tanks. There were a handful of soldiers flanking them, watching for antitank teams that could target the heavier vehicles with Javelin missiles, but Gavin could tell that a number of Frenchmen were missing. The French hadn't been engaged so far, which suggested that Lieutenant-Colonel Jean-Luc Baptiste had a plan of his own. Who knew what those missing French soldiers would be doing while the British attempted to take out the main force?

A streak of light slammed down from high above and struck the lead French tank. It exploded in a colossal fireball, the turret actually being blown into the air. Gavin stared in utter disbelief. What the *fuck*? Had someone in the Royal Artillery accidentally loaded live ammunition into the big guns? A second missile struck a tank, followed by a third that missed, almost toppling its target over through the colossal force of the explosion. Heedless of his personal safety, Gavin pulled himself back to his feet, his mind spinning with the sheer impossibility of the situation. They were under attack! They were in the heart of the British Army's Training Area and they were under attack!

He glanced back towards where the Challengers were positioned, hoping that their crews had enough sense to bail out before they were targeted too. Their unknown opponent – once might have been a dreadful accident, but two or more suggested deliberate malice – had to have gained control of the air. They could presumably detect any moving tanks… but who were they? There had been no report that Russia was planning anything drastic and the only other nation that might have had the capability to attack Salisbury Plain and the garrisons surrounding it was the United States. The thought that they might be at war with America was absurd.

Something caught his eye and he glanced to the east, towards Tidsworth Garrison. A streak of fire was falling from the sky towards the Garrison. It dropped below the horizon, seconds before there was a brilliant flash of light, followed by a massive fireball. The sound of thunder reached his ears seconds later. It looked almost like a baby nuke! Other fireballs were rising too. It didn't take his intimate knowledge of the training area to know that they were rising from the location of many of the other garrisons surrounding Salisbury Plain. He spared a brief thought for the men and equipment that had presumably been destroyed in the blasts, and then started to run for the command vehicle. The tactical command centre had been buried well behind the ambush point; it should – *should* – have escaped detection.

He waved a hand at Sergeant Gibbon as the Fijian soldier appeared from the concealed tanks. "Get a crew down to check out the French and get them under cover," he barked, trusting the Sergeant to deal with the situation. A number of young soldiers looked badly shocked, holding their personal weapons as if they were unsure what to do with them. He silently blessed his own insistence on issuing loaded weapons to the men, even on training exercises. It had been intended to ensure that the tankers were used to carrying them, but he had a feeling that they might be needing them to fight. "And then send a runner to each of the garrisons. I need to know what we have left in the fight."

The tactical command vehicle was half-buried under a small mountain of earth. Gavin pulled at the hatch and it opened, revealing a cramped compartment with the latest in communications and coordinating gear. He hadn't been too impressed with the entire concept when he'd first heard of it – the command vehicle wasn't even as well-protected as the wretched Snatch land rover – but it might have proved itself useful today. A pair of operators, both looking as if they were on the verge of panic, glanced up at him in relief.

"Report," he barked. "Who the hell hit us?"

"Sir, I don't know, sir," the lead operator said. He looked far too young and nerdy to serve with the army, but his skills at pulling information out of the ether were remarkable. "All of our communications links have gone down!"

Gavin swore. They had a laser link to the British-owned satellite communications network and various NATO systems. If they were all gone, it meant that their unknown opponent had somehow taken them all out seconds before launching the attack on Salisbury Plain. It was simply impossible to jam a laser signal, or even detect it. He keyed the radio and cursed when a wash of static blasted from the speakers. They were being jammed. His unit – and every survivor from the garrisons – had been cut off from higher authority. They were on their own, unable to coordinate with PJHQ or the MOD in fighting off the attack on British soil. But who were they fighting?

There was another screech of static, followed by a sudden shift into the BBC. "…Receiving reports of massive explosions in London," a voice said. "We have been unable to reach…"

The signal washed out of existence. For a moment, Gavin was sure that he could hear voices hidden in the static, but he couldn't make out what they were saying. The BBC had been unable to reach whom? The Government? He'd met the Prime Minister during a meeting at PJHQ and he hadn't been too impressed, but he *was* legal authority. And if they were at war… Dear God, just who the hell were they fighting?

He jumped out of the command vehicle and sighted a number of soldiers being alternatively bullied or cajoled into work by Sergeant Gibbon. A handful of men wearing French uniforms were with them, some badly wounded. The French hadn't been the only ones hit on the training area, he noted absently. It was easy to see which British units had been hit as well.

"Sir," a soldier yelled. It took Gavin a moment to place him as the commander of a Rapier missile launcher that had been deployed to provide some protection to the tankers. If they'd had armed weapons… but no one

had expected an attack from nowhere. "Sir, we got some data before they hit us!"

Gavin looked over at him. It was hardly the proper way to file a report, but under the circumstances he didn't care. The Rapier was supposed to be monitoring every aircraft flying over the range, including a handful that had been tasked to play enemy aircraft during the exercise. They should have picked up something…

"Sir, the attackers came out of nowhere," the soldier said. "But just before they started firing and we lost the network, the UKADR sounded an alert. So did the NATO network. Sir… some of those craft seemed to come from outer space."

"*Aliens?*" Gavin said, in frank disbelief. It was impossible. And yet it made a certain kind of sense. Who else would have the power to take out the satellites, drop bombs – kinetic strikes, perhaps - onto the garrisons and presumably hit London as well? It was impossible, but… he pushed his doubts aside. "Sergeant, pass the word. We'll regroup at Point Alpha – get the military police to sort out who we have left alive and what equipment we have that still works."

"Sir," Sergeant Gibbon said. There was a pause. "What about civilians, sir?"

Gavin winced. Salisbury Plain was a designated place of natural beauty, which meant that civilians could and did get underfoot most of the time. The military was supposed to have jurisdiction over the Live Firing Range, but the word from higher up was to be gentle, if possible. Gavin shook his head. The civilians would have seen the explosions – hell, perhaps the little green men or whoever would have targeted the towns around Salisbury Plain as well.

"Tell them to go back to their homes," Gavin ordered, finally. They'd never prepared for alien invasion. The possibility had never even been considered. "And see if the civilian telecommunications network is still working. We need to know what's left of our country."

———

The ground came up to meet Robin's face before he quite realised what was going on. He hit the ground hard enough to stun him, his body armour taking most of the shock below the neck. Everything seemed to have gone absolutely quiet. Dazed, unsure of what had happened, he started to push himself upright. His jaw felt as if it had been struck by a glass bottle and… what the hell had happened? There hadn't been any warning that someone was behind him, yet what else could have sent him falling to the ground?

He staggered to his feet and looked back at Buckingham Palace. It was gone. He was so dazed that it was several seconds before he realised that something was terribly wrong, and several more seconds before he realised what had happened. Buckingham Palace, the home of the British Monarchy, was a smouldering pile of rubble. Many of the protesters who'd been outside had been hit by flying debris and were badly injured – or dead. They seemed to be whispering, making shapes with their mouths that never became words, almost as if they were miming. He couldn't hear anything, apart from a faint ringing in his ears. It took him several moments to realise that he'd been deafened by a sound so loud that it hadn't really registered on him. He could only hope that it was temporary.

Pulling his radio off his belt, he keyed the emergency switch. Every copper within five miles should start converging on his position, as if they wouldn't be on their way already. This was Buckingham Palace; surely, someone at Scotland Yard would have noticed the destruction of the King's residence. They'd have the fire brigade, ambulances and entire regiments of policemen on their way right now. They might even get to the Palace before some fucking terrorist wannabe started singing their own praises on YouTube, claiming that it was another strike against the oppressive state. Who knew? Maybe the Government would be so angry that they'd take off the gloves and just hit back.

He stumbled towards the protesters, intent on doing what he could to help, when he realised that Buckingham Palace hadn't been the only target. Smoke and flames seemed to be rising into the air from all over London. He'd thought that it was a terrorist attack – even though he couldn't understand how they'd managed to get a bomb into the Palace – but this was on a different scale altogether. There were at least seven different plumes of smoke… he rubbed at his ear, cursing the growing ringing. It was impossible to call for help if he couldn't hear the reply. How could terrorists have pulled off such an attack?

The first protestor, a young girl barely old enough to drink, had been crippled by the blast. Robin did what he could for her, praying that the ambulances would be on their way. But if London had been hit several times… he'd been in enough crisis situations to know that it took time to get organised, time to throw off the shock and take control. How long would it be before someone took command and started funnelling help to the wounded? And what if the unknown attackers had taken out the Government? One of the plumes of smoke seemed to be coming from the direction of Whitehall.

And if they'd taken out the government… he shuddered, unable to face the implications. If they'd taken out the government, they'd committed an act of war.

But who *were* they?

Chapter Three

London
United Kingdom, Day 1

"What…?"

The emergency doors burst open as two men hurled themselves into the Prime Minister's office. Gabriel had no time to react before they grabbed him bodily and carried him over to one of the office walls. It opened, revealing a hidden shaft leading down into the bunker below Ten Downing Street. He yelped in shock as they dropped him, feet first, down the shaft and towards what felt like certain death. Instead, the tube seemed to twitch around him and he found himself slowing and sliding out into the bunker. A man wearing a black uniform caught him by the arm and pulled him away from the tube, just before the first of his own assailants popped out of the tube. Gabriel's mind finally caught up with the string of events and he realised that the Personal Protective Detail assigned to Ten Downing Street were doing their jobs. He'd been briefed on the emergency procedures – everything from terrorist gunmen to chemical or radioactive weapon being deployed against Whitehall – but he was ashamed to realise that he didn't know their names.

One of the men – the leader, Gabriel assumed – tapped a key into a concrete wall. A hatch appeared out of nowhere, revealing a set of metal stairs that led down into the bunker. It was illuminated by flickering lights that seemed to be having trouble remaining alight, suggesting that the power supply to Ten Downing Street had been cut off. There was an emergency generator in the basement, Gabriel remembered, as well as a handful of other precautions, but as far as he could recall they'd never been tested. They certainly hadn't held an emergency drill after he'd become Prime Minister. The oversight, he realised as he clambered down the stairs, might have cost lives.

Another doorway opened at the bottom of the shaft, revealing the Crisis Management Centre. Gabriel had been inside a handful of times, but he'd never grown to like the drab concrete walls and the effect of being cut off from the rest of the world. The only decoration was a painting of a cobra a previous Prime Minister's child had produced, a reference to the COBRA Committee that served as Britain's emergency council. No one had had the heart to take it down. The team leader pointed Gabriel to a seat and headed over to the bank of computers and communications equipment placed against one wall.

The ground shook, alarmingly. Gabriel glanced up as the light hanging over the conference table swang from side to side, proving that he hadn't imagined the explosion. Something on the surface… was there anything left of Ten Downing Street? He silently thanked God that his wife hadn't been in the building. She'd been on a visit to Edinburgh to meet with the First Minister of Scotland, carrying messages from Gabriel that he didn't dare entrust to anyone else. Dear God – had Edinburgh been hit too?

Gabriel took a moment to calm himself, and then tried to sound professional. "What happened?"

The team leader glanced over at him. "I'm not sure, Prime Minister," he admitted. He looked a tough young man, but Gabriel had enough skill at reading people to know that he was nervous. "We picked up a FLASH warning from PJHQ warning that an attack was underway – we immediately grabbed you and got you into the bunker. But most of our communications lines appear to be down and…"

Gabriel stared at him. "Has Downing Street been destroyed?"

"No, Prime Minister," the team leader said. He frowned, looking down at the console. "I can't get through to anyone else – not PJHQ, not Edinburgh, not anyone. The radio network appears to be being jammed. I'm not sure…ah."

He looked up as the main door to the conference room opened, revealing Major-General Sir Alan Robertson. Gabriel allowed himself a moment of relief. Robertson commanded the Household Division, the main body of troops in London. Among other duties – both operational and ceremonial – the Household Division was responsible for evacuating the Monarch, the Prime Minister and other government ministers from London in the event of an emergency. Robertson wore a combat uniform and carried a pistol on his belt. He was followed by three other soldiers, all carrying rifles and wearing combat uniforms.

"Prime Minister," Robertson said, relieved. "Thank God you're safe."

"You too," Gabriel said. A fourth soldier had arrived – but he looked more like a man dressing up rather than a real soldier. He had a pair of glasses and looked slightly overweight, carrying a small laptop under his arm than a weapon. "General… what the hell is going on?"

Robertson looked… worried. "Prime Minister," he said, slowly, "we're at war."

"At war?" Gabriel repeated. "Who with?"

The fourth soldier looked up. "Aliens," he said, flatly. "We're at war with aliens from outer space."

Gabriel stared at him, unsure if he should laugh or cry. "Aliens?" His Personal Protective Detail seemed to be having the same reaction. "*Aliens*? And I suppose that Doctor Who is going to come along any minute to tell them to piss off?"

"Please, Prime Minister," Robertson said quietly. "Hear him out."

The fourth soldier put his laptop on the conference table. "Fifteen minutes ago, the entire orbital communications network – ours, NATO's, the Russians – went down," he said. "Bare minutes later, we lost contact with the Deep Space Tracking Network – that's a joint operation largely run by the Yanks, but there are stations on British soil and we have access to the live feed. The last report we had from RAF Fylingdales reported a number of incoming missiles that appeared to have come from orbit. One of their projected endpoints – their targets – was the base itself. The entire Ballistic Missile Early Warning System has been taken down.

"At roughly the same time, ground-based radar stations picked up a number of unknown aircraft breaching the UKADR – that's the United Kingdom Air Defence Region," he continued. "RAF aircraft on alert were vectored towards the intruders – we lost contact shortly afterwards with both the aircraft and their bases. It appears that we have been hit badly all across the country. We have lost contact with almost all military bases within the United Kingdom."

"Which leaves us no choice," Robertson injected, "but to assume that they've been destroyed."

Gabriel felt… weak, unsure of himself. It seemed impossible, yet… if the unknowns, the aliens, had the capability to hit British military bases, there seemed no reason why they wouldn't – if they were hostile. His thoughts ran in circles. Why would aliens be hostile? What did Earth have that would make them worthwhile targets? He'd always been taught that a civilisation advanced enough to master space travel would have outgrown the desire to fight purely for the sake of fighting…

"It gets worse," the soldier said, softly. "We have confirmed that a number of strikes fell in London itself. The Permanent Joint Headquarters has been destroyed, along with a number of railway stations, road junctions, and – for reasons unclear – Buckingham Palace."

"The King," Gabriel said. "What happened to him?"

"He was in residence at the time, along with his wife, his eldest son and *his* wife," Robertson said. "We've had no word. I send a small detachment to the Palace to see what they could find, but first reports say that the devastation was almost total. There is a very good chance that Prince Harry may be the next in line to the throne."

Gabriel shook his head slowly, unable to quite believe his ears. Robertson was talking about the death of the Monarch – and the deaths of thousands of military and civilian personnel – as calmly as if he were ordering dinner. How could he be so dispassionate? Or was he trying to remain calm in the hope that Gabriel himself would remain calm? If they'd really been hit as badly as Robertson implied, the chances were that his position as Prime

Minister was no longer viable. God alone knew what he would be able to do for his country.

"Contact," one of the soldiers said, suddenly. "I got a link through to Salisbury Plain!"

"Excuse me," Robertson said.

Gabriel nodded as the General slipped away, heading towards the bank of computers. How could he deal with an alien invasion? Had it only been an hour ago that he'd been battling with the economic crisis? What would happen if – when – the British population realised what had happened to their country? He looked over at Robertson and found himself envying the man's calm. Maybe he should have gone into the military instead of politics. But then, he would have made a poor soldier.

"We managed to get in contact with Brigadier Gavin Lightbridge-Stewart," Robertson said. The name meant nothing to Gabriel. "He appears to be the senior officer left at Salisbury Plain; the preliminary reports say that the garrisons there have been hit badly. We managed to fill each other in on a few details, but we simply don't know much of anything."

He shook his head. "The Brigadier will be establishing defensive lines and preparing our counter-attack," he said. "We need to get you to the command bunker under the training area. It appears to be intact, thankfully. The aliens don't seem to know about its existence."

"Or they would have hit it," Gabriel said, slowly. "*Can* they hit it and… ah, destroy it?"

"They can drop rocks from orbit," Robertson said. "If they knew about the bunker, they could have taken it out – we assume." He seemed about to say more, when one of the consoles started to bleep an alarm. Robertson glanced at it and then swore aloud. "We've managed to set up a passive detection system outside, Prime Minister. It looks as if they're sending in shuttles."

Gabriel stared at him. "They're coming *here*?"

"They're coming to London," Robertson said, grimly. "I have two rifle companies in the city, armed for dealing with terrorists rather than alien invaders. We can bleed them – I assume – but we probably can't stop them from landing in the city. We have to get you out of here."

He looked down at the table for a long moment. "Normally, we'd get you and your ministers out through the tunnel network, but parts of it seem to have caved in under the bombardment. I'm not sure if the aliens intended to trap you or if it was merely a fluke, yet we cannot risk using the network. We need to get you upriver as quickly as possible." He raised his voice. "Butcher?"

One of the uniformed soldiers looked up. "Sir?"

"Check the boat and prepare it for immediate launch," Robertson ordered. He looked back at Gabriel. "Butcher served four years in the SAS before being asked to serve as a Close Protection specialist. Hughie and Mother" – a thin man and a taller man who looked as if he had muscles on his muscles – "both came to us through the SBS. They'll take care of you if anyone can, Prime Minister."

"Thank you," Gabriel said, quietly. "General… what are you going to do?"

"I have to get back to the surface and take control of my men," Robertson said. "We have to assume that they're carrying out a decapitation strike – an attempt to capture or kill you and the rest of Parliament. I intend to give them a bloody nose when they try."

Gabriel hesitated. "Don't get yourself killed, General," he warned. "The country will need you."

"We've barely been at war an hour," Robertson said, "and already we've been hurt worse than Hitler or Napoleon ever managed. God alone knows what's happening to the rest of the world. We never planned for alien invasion, Prime Minister. Hell, the last time we planned for a military invasion was back during the Cold War."

He shook his head. "The lads will take care of you," Prime Minister. "Linux" – he nodded at the soldier with the laptop – "will go with you. He'll be needed at the bunker. Good luck."

"And to you," Gabriel said, automatically. He was struck by the sense that he would never see Robertson again. "General…"

Robertson saluted, and then left the room.

"Come on, Prime Minister," Butcher said, two minutes later. "It's time to go."

Gabriel had never had the chance to explore the entire tunnel network. From what he recalled from briefing papers he'd never had a chance to read properly, the military had taken advantage of commercial tunnelling to add their own network for emergencies. Some tunnels linked government buildings together, allowing swift and silent evacuation; others led to hidden bunkers and archives that were never intended to see the light of day. Some information was in the public domain, he remembered, but the government had managed to keep a lid on most of the specifics. Or so they hoped. Gabriel had also been told that the Russians had gained access to far too much data on the tunnel network and emergency procedures.

Perhaps it was his imagination, but they seemed to be heading upwards – and the air seemed to be getting damper. A faint smell reached his nose, a stench that made him want to recoil, just before they turned into a chamber that held a large boat. Butcher held up a hand to halt Gabriel while he clambered up and into the boat, vanishing over the side. There was a moment's pause, and then the engine roared to life. The soldier reappeared and held out a hand to help Gabriel climb up. He was ashamed to realise that Butcher had simply lifted him at the end.

A thought struck him. "Why Butcher?"

"Dad was a butcher," Butcher said. "We don't stand much on ceremony, Prime Minister. Once someone passes Selection, they're one of us. The lucky ones get to choose their own handle. The unlucky ones get someone else picking it for them."

He waved Gabriel to sit at the bottom of the boat. The sound of the engine grew louder as the other two soldiers climbed onboard and concealed their weapons and uniforms below blankets. It struck Gabriel suddenly that anyone who saw him would know that he was the Prime Minister, but it was already too late to express his doubts. The boat seemed to leap forwards – there was a terrifying glimpse of a grating ahead of them, followed by a smell that made him want to throw up – and then they were suddenly out in the open. He caught sight of the Houses of Parliament and stared, realising that flames were rising up in the distance, from the direction of the Palace.

The boat started to tilt madly to one side as Butcher pointed them upriver, towards the west. Gabriel struggled to remain calm, even though part of him was convinced that they were going to be thrown into the water at any moment. A handful of other boats seemed to be making their way downstream, clearly intent on getting out of London before something worse happened. He wondered, suddenly, just how much the civilians knew about the crisis. It had never occurred to him to ask… in the distance, he could hear the sound of sirens. The police were responding to the attacks, but did they know what they were facing? And if there really were aliens heading towards London?

It seemed like a bad science-fiction movie, but it was happening…

Twenty minutes later, just as they were leaving London, Hughie tapped him on the shoulder and passed him a pair of binoculars. Gabriel glanced at them in puzzlement, and then looked up into the sky. A flight of aircraft were heading down towards London from the west… but they looked odd. Gabriel pressed the binoculars against his eyes and gasped as he finally made sense of what he was seeing. The alien shuttles were larger than the largest jumbo jet the human race had ever produced and they were heading towards London. They'd escaped the city in the nick of time. He tried to estimate how many aliens could be on those aircraft before realising that it was impossible to produce anything like a reliable estimate. For all he knew, the aliens could be microscopic in size – or they could look like stone statues of weeping angels. And perhaps they wouldn't even be humanoid.

"We're still being jammed," Hughie said, quietly. The SBS soldier had a faint Scottish accent that echoed through his voice. "We can't warn the General or the troops in London."

"But they know that they're coming," Gabriel pointed out, desperately. Suddenly, he felt ashamed for running. "They must know that they're on their way."

"Maybe," Hughie said. "Or maybe the aliens have ways to avoid passive detectors. Any radar station that lights up is likely to get clobbered. I don't know, sir. We just need to get you up to the command bunker, and perhaps then we can go back to the front lines."

"Or the front lines will come to us," Mother grunted. "Look."

Gabriel followed his gaze. There were more alien shuttles now, hundreds of them, glowing red as they decelerated through Earth's atmosphere. Just for a moment, he wondered how interstellar logistics could make an invasion possible, before dismissing the thought. There was no way to know how alien logistics worked. For all he knew, the aliens mass-cloned soldiers whenever they wanted to overrun another world.

He closed his eyes and said a silent prayer for the men and women who were about to be caught up in a nightmare. General Robertson had been determined to fight – it crossed Gabriel's mind that he should have ordered them out, but it was too late. All he could do now was pray for them – and pray that the aliens weren't savages. An alien race could wipe out all life on Earth.

The sound of more explosions caught them as they headed onwards, echoing back from London. There was no way to know what was going on behind them either. All they could do was pray. And hope that, one day, they would be able to avenge themselves on the aliens.

Gabriel shook his head. An hour. An hour after the alien attack had begun and he was on the run. And to think that yesterday he'd been cursing problems he would have given his soul for today.

Chapter Four

London
United Kingdom, Day 1

"Anything we should know, sir?"

The military officer sighed. Robin had been busy organising what medical help he could for the wounded, after a handful of ambulances and policemen had *finally* arrived. They'd reported that London's railway stations had been hit as well, causing massive casualties as well as jamming up the road network. The emergency services were overwhelmed trying to deal with the chaos. And they still had no idea what was going on. The radio seemed torn between increasingly hysterical bulletins and requests for the public to remain calm and in their homes. Judging from the level of traffic on the streets, Robin suspected that that particular request was going unheeded.

"Yes," the soldier said. A handful of other armed soldiers had appeared, causing many citizens to start edging away from them. Robin wasn't so impressed, if only because he'd spent his probationary period in Southampton, wrestling Royal Marines on Friday nights. "There's a good chance that whoever did this to us" – he waved a hand at the pile of smoking rubble that had once been Buckingham Palace – "is likely to start landing ground troops. You're looking at ground zero for their invasion."

Robin stared at him. A terrorist attack was understandable, even if there had been a hideous failure in intelligence that should have allowed them to detect the plot in time to derail it. Even a handful of bombs detonated around the city was understandable; Islamic Fundamentalism had been suspiciously quiet over the last few months and the radicals knew that they needed to keep staging spectacular attacks to boost their cause. But an invasion… Robin had taken part in drills where the Met had been seconded to the military for a military emergency, yet no one had believed that Britain might actually be invaded. The nightmare of an uprising from the poorer – and Islamic – parts of the country seemed more plausible.

"We're at war," he stumbled, finally. "Against who?"

"We're unsure as yet and we don't have time to speculate," the officer said, firmly. "I need you to get the civilians out of the area as quickly as possible – starting now. God alone knows how much time we have left."

Robin allowed his eyes to trail over the gardens and the surrounding area. A small number of policemen and medics had finally shown up, allowing them to start treating the wounded – although only one ambulance had arrived, which had been pressed into service to take the worst cases to the nearest hospital. From what little he'd heard from other police officers, London was gridlocked. Everyone who had a car seemed to be trying to get out of the city and to hell with how it impeded the emergency services. The BBC wasn't helping. It was either jammed up with static or raving about explosions in a dozen cities.

"I can't get everyone out…"

"You have to," the officer said, quietly. There was an earnest tone in his voice that somehow stripped Robin's final doubts away. He saw a pair of soldiers carrying handheld antiaircraft missiles setting up a position on one side of the gardens. If the enemy intended to send in paratroopers, the British Army would give them a hot reception. "I don't know how much time we have left."

He strode off in the direction of his men, leaving Robin staring at his back. Robin's training asserted itself and he began to bellow orders. God knew how he'd wound up as senior officer on scene – the mobile command centre had probably been stuck in traffic – but at least no one was arguing. The wreckage of Buckingham Palace had probably concentrated quite a few minds.

"Start moving the civilians out of here," he ordered, sharply. "Draft able-bodied men as stretcher-bearers if necessary; start moving them at least a mile from this location." He found himself grappling with a completely unexpected problem. If an invasion force – absurd as it seemed – was about to land in Central London, where was even remotely safe. "Take control of the traffic and get it moving away from here – commandeer any vehicles that can be used for moving casualties and put them to work. If anyone gives you trouble, arrest them and we'll worry about charges later."

Time seemed to slow down as an endless flow of civilians, government civil servants and worker drones were pushed out of the area. Most of them saw the pile of debris and didn't argue, but a handful seemed insistent that whatever was happening had nothing to do with them. Robin ignored their pleas, then their threats, and finally had a couple arrested and dragged away. The remainder finally got the message and headed away from Central London. A few who might have protested saw the soldiers and their obviously lethal weaponry and made themselves scarce. Robin nodded at two of the soldiers as he checked his radio again, but all he could hear was static. Whoever was jamming them had neatly shattered the Police in London. There were thousands of officers on the streets, cut off from their superiors and probably facing their own private nightmares. Dear God – if the country was really being invaded, what did the invaders intend to do with the Police?

He pushed the thought aside as he helped a pair of constables manhandle a wounded civilian down towards a waiting van. A team of doctors were at least trying to separate the minor wounded from those who needed a hospital immediately, but it was a terrifying nightmare. Hardly any of the civilians were used to violence and anarchy on such a scale and many of them seemed to be on the verge of coming apart. Robin might have joined them if he hadn't felt responsible for managing the crisis. It was certain that no one senior to him had made it to Buckingham Palace. He remembered the explosions all over London and shivered. The invaders, whoever they were, might have taken out Scotland Yard. And if they'd done that, they would have fragmented the entire network.

"Sergeant," a voice bellowed. He turned to see the officer he'd spoken to before, looking grim. "How quickly can you get the rest of the civilians out of here?"

Robin blanched, reading the bad news in the officer's face. "Too long," he said. They'd managed to get most of the people on the move, but the traffic wasn't taking the hint and heading away from Central London. Entire streams of people were being pointed away from the Houses of Parliament and being told to run. It was all a horrible ghastly mess. "How long do we have?"

"Maybe five minutes, maybe less," the officer said. "Radar has picked up enemy craft heading towards London. The chances are that they're coming here. You have to get the civilians out of the line of fire."

Robin nodded and blew hard on his whistle. "Everyone away, now," he bellowed. The other policemen took up the cry. "Move… *now!*"

He looked up at the officer, who had one hand on his pistol. "I'm qualified to fire in the line of duty," he said, quietly. "I could stay…"

"You're needed elsewhere," the officer said. The sound of thunder – no, it wasn't thunder – echoed in the air. "Go!"

———

Fatima had never felt so pressured in her life. She'd been on duty at the hospital when the police had sounded the alert and had been rounded up to go to the remains of Buckingham Palace. Seeing the rubble had shocked her, but there hadn't been any time to sit down and cry – not when there was work to be done. Hundreds of people had been wounded and there weren't anything like enough medical supplies to treat them all. From what she'd overheard, the emergency teams that should have been first responders to any crisis had been caught in traffic, as had most of the ambulances in London. Her mobile phone was useless and the pager she'd been given as they ran out the door had gone blank. She had been forced to improvise splints and bandages for half of her patients.

"Lie still," she said, sharply. The wounded man in front of her had been one of the guards in front of Buckingham Palace when the bomb – or whatever – had blown it into a pile of rubble. His leg was clearly broken in two places and it was quite possible, judging from the bruises, that he had internal injuries as well. She'd bandaged him up as best as she could, but he really needed an operation. It didn't look as if he was going to get one any time soon. "I said, lie still!"

"They need me," the man insisted. He sounded delirious, or perhaps he was going into shock. Fatima put her hand firmly on his chest and held him down gently. "I need to…"

"You need to get better," Fatima said. She'd heard stories of what happened in Pakistan and other less-developed countries when bombs exploded without warning, but she'd never expected to see it in Britain. Someone should have taken control at once and started coordinating all of the emergency response teams. Instead, everything was chaotic and the only people who were trying to establish order were a handful of policemen, who looked as frightened and helpless as the rest. "You can't go back to your unit with a broken leg."

She wanted to give him something for the pain, but there were no painkillers left. A pair of civilians pressed into service as stretcher-bearers appeared and gently lifted the wounded man onto a makeshift stretcher. Fatima checked his leg carefully, warned them to ensure that their charge didn't try to sit up, and then waved for them to go. There was no time to rest – she had to deal with the next wounded person. It seemed that there was no end to the wounded; men, women and children, half of them looking as if they didn't quite believe what had happened to them. This was Britain, not some Third World country where the natives killed each other at the drop of a hat. Disasters weren't supposed to strike the British mainland.

A hand fell on her shoulder and she jumped. "You need to get on your way," a policeman said. He looked about as worried as Fatima felt, but he seemed to have it under control. "You need to escort the patients back to the hospital. This place isn't going to be safe much longer."

Fatima looked up. All over the area, policemen and soldiers were shouting at civilians to move. The wounded were being carried off, followed by those who could walk on their own and the remaining medical staff. She started to follow them automatically, and then stopped dead. This was London. What the hell was going on that meant they had to risk moving so many wounded people at once?

"All I know is that this place is about to get very unsafe," the policeman warned. He was holding something back. Fatima had done a course in reading people back when she'd been studying to be a doctor. "I think you'd better start moving – now."

He sounded so earnest that Fatima picked up her bag before quite realising what she was doing. She could hear the sound of thunder in the distance and see plumes of smoke rising up into the sky. Something was clearly badly wrong… shaking her head, she started to follow the wounded. They'd need her when they reached their destination, wherever that might be. It seemed as if the police and soldiers were closing off all of Central London…

<hr>

"I think that's most everyone out," Constable McEwen reported, grimly. The sound of thunder was growing closer. Robin hadn't been able to stop himself from scanning the horizon, looking for incoming aircraft. God alone knew what was heading their way. "Sergeant…"

"Time for us to leave, then," Robin said. The armed policemen might be a help, but it was far more likely that they'd just get in the way. It wasn't as if they'd trained with the soldiers – hell, all the plans to hold major exercises had been curtailed by the shortage of cash. He remembered his wife, suddenly, and shivered. At least Helene was out of London, safely away from the chaos that had gripped the city. God alone knew how long it would be before the more rowdy element of the city's population decided that it was a great opportunity for looting, raping and burning. "Get everyone back to the cordon and keep moving the civilians further away…"

He covered his ears as something *screeched* by overhead. A tiny black dot, seemingly flying as low as it could over London, flashed by and headed into the distance. No missiles arose to challenge it, although Robin had no way of knowing if the soldiers had held their fire or if they didn't have enough antiaircraft missiles to spend them freely. Given how much it cost to produce equipment for the Met, he suspected the latter.

"Jesus Christ," he whispered, as he started to run. He'd hoped that it was nothing more than a terrorist bombing, even though the officer he'd spoken to had seemed certain. "It's really happening."

<hr>

Trooper Chris Drake perched on the roof of the Ministry of Defence's Old Admiralty Building and peered down towards Green Park. Smoke was rising up from all over London, suggesting that the enemy – and he still found it hard to believe that the brass took the stories of little green men seriously – hadn't concentrated their attentions on Buckingham Palace. From what he'd heard before the CO had dispatched him and a handful of others to vantage points where they could see for some distance without being seen, the enemy had bombarded the railway stations and several junctions. The result of one attack away from the Palace was easy to see. Westminster Bridge had been hit by… *something* that had knocked it effortlessly into the water. Chris didn't need to be a CO to know that that ensured that it would be harder for any reinforcements to reach Whitehall. Of course, if some of the other stories he'd heard were true, there was little left *to* reach Whitehall.

He'd seen action in Afghanistan, but he'd never expected to have to fight a war in England – no one had. Some of the lads had been worried about their wives, girlfriends and children and in truth Chris knew that he couldn't blame them. The CO had worked hard to keep them focused on the incoming threat, but without it Chris suspected that some of his comrades would probably have seen to their own families. They'd expected months – perhaps years – of warning before Britain itself came under threat. No one had expected an attack that had crushed them under its treads within a few hours.

The sound of engines pulled his attention back to the here and now. One of the tech guys down on the streets below had been able to rig up a passive detection system – or so he'd heard – but radar coverage was a thing of the past. It was possible that their enemy – little green men or whatever – would manage to get tactical surprise, even though the troops were dug in about as well as they could given the short notice. He started scanning the skies with binoculars, looking for trouble. Who knew what alien landing craft would look like? Flying saucers, or something humanity might have built itself, or maybe even tiny blue boxes that were bigger on the inside. There were just too many possibilities.

When he finally caught sight of the craft heading towards London, he was almost disappointed. They were big, all right; larger than any aircraft he'd seen in his career, massive shapes that seemed oddly unsteady in the atmosphere. The wings seemed too stubby to keep the craft in the air, although the roar of their engines suggested that whatever was powering them was more advanced than anything on Earth. In fact, they reminded him of something out of *Thunderbirds*. Despite himself, he felt a little relieved. They might not be as badly outmatched as he'd feared. The thought of facing the aliens from *Independence Day* had scared hell out of the soldiers.

The craft roared closer, moving with deceptive ungainliness. He formed a mental picture of a SAM blasting one of them out of the air, but realised quickly that the CO would want to hold off on that if possible. God alone knew how much damage a crashing alien transport would do to London, or to the civilians who happened to be caught in the blast. He reached for his radio, checked the channel quickly, and keyed the switch twice. They'd discovered that they could beat the jamming to some extent, if they used higher frequencies. Chris suspected that the aliens might be relaxing the jamming – whatever they used to coordinate might not be too different from what the humans used – but it hardly mattered. The entire city would have seen those craft making their final approach.

They flew over Hyde Park and started to shower tiny objects down towards the park below. Chris peered at them through his binoculars, trying to make out shape and form. They looked like paratroopers, but there were no parachutes. He wondered if they'd smash themselves into bloody ruin on the ground below, before realising that they had to have some way to slow their fall. Some of the SAS operatives had talked about opening their parachutes at terrifyingly low levels, barely slowing their fall before they touched down.

Other paratroopers were falling now, heading towards St. James Park. Chris leaned forward as the first of the black objects touched the ground and straightened up. The sight was so surreal that, just for a moment, he was convinced that he had to be dreaming. He hadn't wanted to believe it, but it was true. The aliens had landed.

Chapter Five

London
United Kingdom, Day 1

Tra'tro The'Stig braced himself in the cramped confines of the landing shuttle as the pilot started to count off the final seconds. Like most of the other assault formations, Assault Landing Unit #352 had been tasked with decapitating the prey – the *humans*, he reminded himself – before they could rally their troops and counterattack. The *Kyg'pa* - the Land Force – had had plenty of experience carrying out assault landings on hostile worlds and much of that experience suggested that the prey were easier to beat if their leaders were dead. In all of the endless briefings after they'd been pulled out of their stasis pods, they'd been warned that the humans – although primitive – were dangerous. Anything that weakened them before their world was occupied and their new position as Workers of the State was explained to them was all right by the Land Force. The concerns passed down to them about capturing the human infrastructure intact were irritating. It meant that the starship crews were unlikely to fire down at the planet's surface without authorisation from the Command Triad.

He kept his concerns to himself. Anyone who served the State knew that dissent was not considered welcome, at least from the lower ranks. The people at the top had the right to determine everything from troop dispositions to attack strategy and they didn't need his input. If he kept working away, and survived the coming war, he might just reach the higher levels where he could actually influence policy. And it was just as likely that the humans would roll over and surrender without a shot being fired.

The alarm echoed through the transport as it started to slow down over the human city. The'Stig had seen images taken by spy drones during the briefings and had to admit that the humans didn't seem to know when to stop building. Their city seemed completely disorganised, while their buildings would be alarmingly tight for his soldiers. They'd probably have to start establishing their own headquarters on the surface rather than using human buildings, if only because of the size difference. Humans seemed to be shorter and thinner than his people and their buildings had been built for their comfort. They hadn't thought to widen them for their new masters.

He flinched as the drop field caught him and propelled his unresisting form towards the hatch, followed by the remainder of the Assault Landing Unit. As always, there was a moment of sheer terror as he tumbled down towards the planetary surface, just before the counter-gravity field caught hold of his form and cancelled his motion, a mere second before he would have slammed face-first into the ground. Earth smelt funny – it was clear that the human disunion even affected their older cities – but he pushed that aside. The Assault Unit was spreading out, looking for trouble. Intelligence had stated that the humans had already lost their command and control networks, but the next thing Intelligence got right would be the first. They were really nothing more than well-connected officers who had the ability to avoid being assigned to front-line combat missions.

A dead human lay on the ground, not too far from his position. He glanced down at the body, recoiling in shock from its oddly-disjointed form. The humans looked as if they were permanently on the verge of falling over when they moved, with a suppleness that was alien to his people. A brief glance at the frontal area confirmed that they were looking at a male. There was no way to tell how the human had died.

The radio network hissed, suddenly. "Contact," it snapped. The sound of human weapons almost drowned the coordinator's voice out. "Engage and destroy!"

The'Stig cursed and dived for cover. Intelligence had made its usual flawed assessment – they'd landed right in the midst of a *Grisna* nest and the wretched little creatures were stinging like mad. Hefting his weapon, he led a small detachment forward, towards the buildings that served as the human centre of government. The human leaders were probably long gone, but

taking their buildings would show their impotence. Or so Intelligence promised…

———

Chris Drake couldn't believe his eyes. He was still half-convinced that he was dreaming, perhaps after a night of too many curries or kebabs. The aliens – and they *had* to be aliens, not men in funny-fitting suits – were landing in St. James Park, right in front of him. He keyed the switch on the camera that should have sent a live feed back to the CO, wondering what the straight-laced officer would make of it all. The aliens… were very alien.

His first thought had been humanoid dinosaurs, but they moved with an eerie grace that belied their hulking forms. They were larger than humans, carrying weapons that looked too ungainly for humans to use, wearing camouflage uniforms that seemed to automatically blend with their surroundings. What little skin he could see was gray and leathery, reminding him of elephants in the jungle, but their eyes were dark and very cold. Their faces seemed to be almost immobile, although he couldn't tell if they were naturally inscrutable or if he just couldn't recognise an alien expression when he saw it. One of them seemed to be the leader on the ground, using hand motions to advance his troops forward; the others seemed to be grunts. He reminded himself not to count them out too soon. The British Army used its best troops in the Air Assault Role and he had to assume that the same was true of the aliens.

He looked down at their weapons, trying to see what they were carrying. They didn't *look* that fancy, certainly not compared to weapons he'd seen in a hundred different alien invasion movies; indeed, he was sure that they weren't much more advanced than anything he'd seen on Earth. There was a crudeness about their design that reminded him of some of the makeshift weapons they'd pulled out of caves in Afghanistan, or weapons produced with a Russian eye towards functionality rather than appearance. Some of the weapons seemed to be almost portable machine guns; it struck him, suddenly, that they could probably carry more weight than the average human. Their transport aircraft were heading off in the distance…

The CO gave the order and the fighting began. A number of British soldiers had been positioned in nearby buildings, using them to pour fire down onto the hapless aliens, while a team of mortar gunners started to lob shells towards their landing zone. It was a shame that they hadn't had a few days to prepare, Chris thought, as he saw a couple of aliens hit the ground, dark blood staining the grass around their bodies. The Household Division had never expected to be fighting a major action in the heart of London. Some equipment that they'd used in Afghanistan was outside the city. It might as well be on the other side of the moon.

For a moment, he was sure that the aliens were doomed, before they started to return fire with surprising accuracy. Their handheld weapons had the same rate of fire as a GPMG and their aim was better than anyone would have expected. A pair of their leaders – he assumed, seeing they seemed to be in charge – were slipping forward, leading a direct assault against Whitehall. One of them was shot down by a sniper, while the other managed to take cover against a damaged car. It exploded a second later – the IED team had been putting their expertise to work – blowing the alien backwards. Chris watched dispassionately as it crashed back down to Earth and lay still, presumably stunned or dead. The remaining aliens had taken cover and were laying down fire towards the defenders. From what little Chris could pick up on his radio, they'd managed to pick off many of the soldiers through heavy fire. A handful of buildings were burning as alien grenades set fire to their interiors.

A dull roar echoed overhead as a second flight of alien transports roared down the Thames. This time, a team with a Stinger was cleared to engage the enemy craft, launching their missile at almost point-blank range. Whatever countermeasures the aliens had were ineffective at such a distance and the missile struck the alien craft on the side of its fuselage. For a moment, it seemed to have survived… and then it flipped over and came crashing down into the river. A colossal fireball blew up from where it had come down, throwing debris everywhere. If any aliens had survived, Chris couldn't see how they could get out of the water and into the fight. A second alien transport was hit just before it could start unloading its cargo. This one was damaged and managed to stagger away over London before coming down in the suburbs. Chris breathed a silent prayer for the civilians living where it had crashed before dragging his attention back to the main battlefield. The remaining alien transports had started to deploy alien tanks.

The British Army had considerable experience moving light armour around by air, but the aliens clearly had better technology than anything available to the Army Air Corps. Their tanks looked bigger and nastier than a Challenger II, although there was something funny about their design. It took him a moment to realise that they seemed to be lacking any treads, almost as if they were designed to be nothing more than moveable pillboxes. They hit the ground and bounced; Chris cursed as he realised that they were riding an air cushion, rather like small hovercraft. Each of the alien tanks started towards the defence line as soon as they landed, big guns rotating around with terrifying speed to challenge the puny humans ahead of them. They weren't completely dependent upon the big guns either, he saw. The alien tanks carried what looked like small machine guns, four to a tank. They probably could engage multiple targets simultaneously.

A streak of light announced that one of the antitank teams had engaged the nearest target. The alien tank stopped dead as the missile blasted through its upper armour and presumably killed the crew, but its comrades opened fire at once. Chris felt the building shake as they raked the windows with machine gun fire, while using their main guns to clear any large obstacles on the ground. The entire building seemed to be on the verge of collapse as a shell detonated inside; frantically, he scrambled backwards to the fire escape and started to slide down to safety. Judging by the noise, the aliens were responding to any attack with savage force. *They* didn't seem to have to worry about civilian casualties.

Cursing, he ran towards the rally point, just as the Old Admiralty Building started to collapse into a pile of rubble. Other soldiers joined the retreat, falling back to regroup and reform the defence line – but would it be enough? They'd been warned to be ready to slip out into London and try to escape the alien dragnet. Perhaps the time had come to leave…

A thunderous roar sent him falling to his knees. Behind him, the aliens were advancing, carefully. The rubble slowed their pace, but it also provided cover for their infantry. At least they hadn't yet realised just how small humans were, compared to their hulking forms. Humans could hide themselves in places no alien could follow. A handful of soldiers were taking advantage of the confusion to use grenades to set up makeshift IEDs. The aliens might take Westminster, but they'd take nothing more than a pile of rubble – and a very bloody nose.

The'Stig ducked as a human bullet cracked just past his ear. He couldn't count just how many times he'd come close to death; the humans might have been small and puny, but they knew how to fight. If it hadn't been for the tankers, the Assault Unit might have been wiped out in the first hour of the assault. Even with the tankers, the humans were bleeding them hard. At least their backs were to the river, he told himself firmly. They'd have nowhere to run when the tanks closed in on their positions. Any rational species would have realised that the position was hopeless and sought terms.

He wasn't sure who was in command right now, not after the humans had taken down the transport carrying two superior officers and their mobile command network. The threat of human-portable weapons had clearly been underestimated, part of his mind noted, cursing Intelligence under his breath. Several units had been shredded, leaving him as the senior officer within eyesight. He didn't even know half of the troopers who had been drawn into his orbit. All he could do was keep them moving forward and hope that the tankers sucked up most of the incoming fire.

A pile of rubble allowed him a chance to slip under cover, just as one of the troopers saw what looked like a pile of metal discs on the ground. The'Stig was just a second too late in ordering him to stop; he picked the discs up and an explosion blew him into bloody fragments. Even their body armour couldn't protect them against such an attack. The'Stig scowled and inched backwards, eyes scanning the piles of rubble and peering through the smoke in hopes of seeing the humans before they saw him. The entire area could be mined, but he doubted that he'd be able to get a team of experts to come down and remove the mines safely. Reporting their presence to his superiors – once they were appointed – would only mean that they'd be told to be careful. They needed to take the human leaders alive.

Something *moved*, right at the corner of his eye. Instinct sent him jumping backwards, just in time to avoid a knife thrown at him by a young male human. The human was wounded, he realised, and it had *still* attempted to take his life. Was the entire species insane? He fired a burst towards the human and watched bright red blood splash on the rubble. They looked so fragile and yet they could kill and kill and kill…

And they could hide. Hindsight, always clearer than foresight, showed him just what had happened. He'd ignored the human's hiding place because it was too small for one of his people. If he'd taken a longer look, he might not have been surprised so badly. And some of the other troopers who'd been ambushed might have remained alive, if they'd been more aware of what the humans could do to them. They'd have to learn quickly on this world.

He motioned for his troopers to hold their positions. The tankers were coming up behind them and more reinforcements were on the way. Let the tankers take a few bullets – which would only glance off their armour in any case. His troopers needed a rest before they pushed onwards – and besides, the humans were trapped against the river. They'd have to break through the assault lines to escape and *that* wasn't going to be easy.

"They're sending in their tanks, sir!"

Major-General Sir Alan Robertson nodded, sharply. After some thought, he'd established his command post in the Houses of Parliament, assuming that the aliens wanted to take Parliament relatively intact. They didn't seem to be *that* concerned about many of the other historic buildings in Central London, but it made sense. It would have been easy for them to take out the civilian government from orbit if they'd simply wanted them dead.

But his force was in an untenable position – which, he admitted to himself, he'd known about long before the aliens actually landed. The aliens seemed to be bringing in more reinforcements and their supplies of Stinger missiles were running low; it seemed that the aliens did have some form of effective countermeasure. Besides, he didn't want to shoot down another craft and see it crash in London. The team he'd positioned in the London Eye had reported that fires were spreading out of control from where one of the alien transports had crash-landed.

"Send in the Javelin teams and tell them one shot each," he ordered, sharply. The British Army had ordered thousands of Javelin missiles, but most of them had been stockpiled in the countryside or deployed to Afghanistan. No one had thought to equip the Household Division with more than a handful of antitank weapons. Who in their right mind would have considered that they'd be needed? "And then tell them to head for the tunnels. They're to get out of the city and link up with the rest of the army."

The ground shook violently as the aliens started bombarding Whitehall. Alan swore under his breath, realising that the aliens were clearly using orbital or drone surveillance assets to track his men. Their advance was almost unstoppable now, particularly not with what remained of his two companies. There was no point in getting more men killed for nothing.

"Sound the retreat," he ordered. He keyed his radio and issued the command. "Get the lads out of here…"

High overhead, an alien drone detected the signal, locked onto his position and fired a single missile. Major-General Sir Alan Robertson died before realising that he was even in danger.

————

"We're to get out of here," a sergeant was yelling. "Move, you stupid…"

Chris picked himself up, just as the alien advance broke through one of the makeshift defence lines. He fired a quick burst from his SA80 in the hopes of slowing the aliens, just as he realised that they'd blocked him from reaching the tunnel that should have led down into safety. Before he had a moment to think about it, he turned and ran towards the embankment, jumping down into the Thames. The river would carry him downstream and he'd be able to link up with what remained of his unit once he got out of the water.

Behind him, London burned.

Chapter Six

London
United Kingdom, Day 1

"My God."

From his vantage point, Robin had been able to see some of the fighting – too much of the fighting. What he'd seen had left him silently grateful that he wasn't close enough to see the rest of it. The aliens had landed in force – two of their transports had been shot down, including one that had crashed into the other side of the Thames – and taken Whitehall. God alone knew how many soldiers had been killed in an ultimately futile last stand.

He looked down towards the streets. They had been emptying with remarkable speed as people fled the battle, heading towards their homes in the hope that they might find safety with their families and friends. Robin suspected that there was going to be no such thing as safety in London for the next few weeks, if not ever. What the hell did the aliens want? Part of him refused to believe that there *were* aliens, but the evidence was undeniable. The flames and smoke rising up in the distance suggested that the world had indeed turned upside down.

"Sergeant," one of the other policemen said, "what the hell do we do?"

Robin silently cursed him for asking that question. In truth, he had no idea *what* they should do, because the Met had never seriously considered that London might be invaded. The last time the British police had considered the question had been back during World War Two, when – if he recalled correctly – they'd been ordered to maintain public order, but avoid giving any help to the Germans. But the Germans had never invaded and the plans had never been put to the test. What would the aliens do now they'd won themselves a city?

His radio buzzed, suddenly. The jamming seemed to have stopped, suggesting… what? Logically, the aliens would have wanted to keep the police and military forces fragmented, but perhaps their own communications were affected by their jamming. Or perhaps they were going to be hunting down any remaining soldiers and hoped that some of them would be foolish enough to use their radios. Or perhaps… he pushed the thoughts aside as a cold voice, utterly inhuman, echoed out over the airwaves. The aliens were finally making their demands known.

"Attention," the voice said. "This is *Ju'tro* Oheghizh, speaking for the Eridian State. All humans are to pay careful attention to this message on pain of punishment. Planet Earth has been conquered and is now part of the Eridian State. Your leaders have been captured or killed; your military forces have been scattered. Further resistance is futile. Accept your new position in the universe or you will be destroyed.

"All civilian humans are to remain within their homes until instructed to report to the occupation authorities," it continued. "Any attempt to impede the passage of my forces will result in severe punishment. Human military and police personnel are to turn themselves in to my forces. All weapons are to be surrendered to the occupation authorities. Failure to report will result in…"

"Severe punishment," Robin muttered. The aliens didn't seem to hide their intentions. There was no guff about coming to liberate humanity from human leaders; nothing, but naked force. And they'd already taken London. "And what happens if we report in?"

The message came to an end and then started to repeat itself. Robin listened a second time, but there were no differences – and no clue as to the fate of police and military personnel. If he recalled correctly, Iraq had collapsed into chaos partly because of the *absence* of a proper police force, yet the aliens might not care about chaos on the ground. Their attacks on London had shown a frightening lack of concern for civilian casualties. He glanced up as another alien transport roared overhead, dropping what looked like heavy crates towards the ground. They'd probably start pushing out from Westminster as soon as they felt strong enough to brave the surrounding city. God knew it wasn't as if there was much in the way to stop them.

"We go to the nearest police station," he said, finally. Scotland Yard might be gone, but it was far from the only police station in London. "We take the weapons and we conceal them somewhere before they think to secure the stations for themselves. And then we wait and see what happens next."

He watched as the policemen leapt to work, grateful that someone had finally told them what to do. Robin shook his head as they started to run through deserted streets, avoiding crashed and abandoned cars, hoping against hope that they would find someone more senior to issue further orders. He didn't have the slightest idea what to do next.

———

Ju'tro Oheghizh stepped off the shuttle and onto Earth, looking around him with ill-concealed interest. The humans seemed to have built habitations suitable for smaller creatures than themselves, although many of their buildings had been levelled by the first wave of assault troopers. A handful of humans, several wounded, sat in the middle of the grassy park, watched by armed guards. It was difficult to read human expressions, but some of them were clearly watching his troopers and considering how best to escape. Others seemed to be completely unaware of their surroundings. The discovery that there were other races out among the stars was always a shock to planet-bound races, even ones who had conceived the possibility long before they reached into space. He doubted that the humans would be any different from the other races brought into the State. It would take time to hammer their new status into their heads.

"The lead assault units were badly hurt," *J'tra* Rahol reported, as soon as they exchanged salutes. "The humans fought bravely and well. We're still finding traps left behind in the ruins – their small size gives them an advantage that cost many of our lives before we adapted."

Oheghizh narrowed his snout. "And the surrendered humans?"

"Many appear to be in shock," his subordinate reported, as they walked into the makeshift command centre. Oheghizh had hoped to set up in the human buildings, but if the humans had had time to leave surprises behind them, it would be unduly risky. "I do not believe that we have captured any truly important humans. Their leaders appear to have fled before we landed in their city."

"Unsurprising," Oheghizh said. There had always been an awareness that the human leaders might have been able to get out of their city – London, they called it – before the assault force landed. Some of the Land Force Commanders had called for targeting the human leadership with strikes from orbit, but the Command Triad had overruled them. They needed to bring the humans into the State as quickly as possible and having their leaders alive would make that easier. It would take too long to rebuild human society directly. "Do we have any idea of their current location?"

Rahol tapped the computer display. "The humans appear to be attempting to regroup their forces to the west," he said. "A number of human military units apparently escaped destruction during the opening minutes of the bombardment, including a number of air defence units. We have targeted active sensor emitters from orbit, but they appear to have learned from experience and are keeping any remaining active sensors turned off. Their effectiveness will decrease rapidly as we have destroyed their bases and supply dumps."

He pointed one long finger at the human road network. "Our own forces are landing around the cities, trapping the human civilians within our grasp," he continued. "There have been a handful of engagements between our forces and human military units, but most human units seem to be attempting to avoid contact. We have broadcast our demands for surrender on all human military and civilian channels. So far we have received no reply."

Oheghizh nodded, slowly. The humans were no doubt shocked by their sudden fall from power on their homeworld. Given time, they could probably regroup and launch a series of counterattacks that would cost the State dearly – and put a hold on his personal career ambitions. Logically, they needed to maintain the pressure as much as they could; practically, they needed to get set up on the ground before the naval forces surrounding Earth insisted on withdrawing most of the transports. The humans had managed to shoot down a number of shuttles, more than any of the planners had expected. Logistics were going to be weaker than anyone had expected when they'd drawn up the plans to invade Earth.

But it wouldn't last. The humans were just as dependent upon supplies to keep their forces moving as the State – and their supply dumps were flaming ruin. Their effectiveness would fall sharply over the next few days, leaving them without the ability to do more than harass his forces. And then they'd be in control and well on the way to turning Earth into a productive outpost. The humans were certainly more capable of labouring for the State than several other races he could mention!

"Keep grouping our forces for a push westwards," he ordered, finally. There was no way to know how the great mass of human civilians would react to their presence. The human government seemed to believe that keeping the civilian population disarmed was a good thing – although some of their measures had seemed so absurd he'd wondered if there was a translation problem – but it was clear that they'd never quite succeeded. Orbital observation indicated mass unrest in parts of the human city. It couldn't be tolerated. The Land Forces would have to open up the roads to allow supplies to be moved around the region. "And expand our patrol perimeter. I want the humans to feel our foot on their chest."

———

Garden House School had been a primary school yesterday, when the world had made sense and aliens were just figments of human imagination. Now, it had been turned into a makeshift medical centre, following emergency plans that had been drawn up sometime during the cold war. Classroom tables had been pushed together and covered with blankets, allowing the wounded somewhere to wait for treatment. Fatima wanted to close her eyes and rest, but there was no time. The small number of medical staff in attendance were doing what they could, yet there seemed to be no end to the wounded. And the civilian volunteers were doing more harm than good. She bandaged up a wound that really needed an operation in a proper hospital, knowing that she might have condemned the patient to a slow and unpleasant death. Any half-trained doctor knew the value of a sterile environment, but they didn't have a hope of maintaining one in the school.

She removed her scarf as she saw the next patient, a small girl barely old enough to go to school. Her parents seemed to be in shock, pointing at their daughter's arm as if they expected Fatima to be able to know what was wrong just by looking. She always hated treating children – young children couldn't tell doctors what was really wrong with them – but there was no choice. She wrapped the scarf around the child's arm, turning it into a makeshift sling. It crossed her mind that her stepmother would be horrified to see her in public with her hair uncovered and she almost broke down into helpless giggles. After everything else that had happened since the first explosions, it was almost a relief to worry about something so petty.

"She's in pain," the mother insisted. "Can't you give her something for the pain?"

Fatima shook her head, grimly. The school had had a well-stocked medical room, but they'd used almost all of the painkillers within the first hour. They'd sent runners to the nearest hospital in the hopes of getting more, yet none of the runners had returned. Fatima's superiors had been reduced to urging policemen to take painkillers from nearby shops, along with what other medical supplies they could find. And there still seemed to be no end to the wounded. Leaving a child in pain tore at her heart, but what else could they do?

She heard the sound of screaming from outside and closed her eyes. London had had riots before, but what would happen with an alien invasion force in the heart of the city? She breathed a silent prayer as the sound of gunshots echoed out in the distance, followed by a faint humming that seemed to echo in the back of her head. One of the doctors walked over to the classroom door and peered down the corridor. He jumped back, his face white as a sheet.

"They're coming," he said. His legs buckled and he collapsed on the floor. "They're coming!"

Fatima braced herself as the first of the aliens came into view. It was clear that the alien – she couldn't tell if it was male or female – seemed to be having trouble in corridors designed for humans. The weapon it carried in one hand looked too large to be carried by a human, although she had to admit that she knew almost nothing about weapons. Dark eyes, seemingly without any colours at all, peered around the room. Fatima met them for a second and was struck by just how *alien* the alien seemed to be. It turned and headed onwards, followed by a small number of other aliens. Fatima realised, as she felt her own legs give way, that they were expanding outwards. God alone knew what they'd do when they ran into resistance…

And, despite herself, she hoped that they would place the makeshift hospital under guard. If London really did dissolve into chaos, the hospitals and chemists would be among the first places targeted for drugs. Who knew *how* the aliens would react to rioters?

———

Building by building, the advancing assault unit swept through the human city. Outside their government centre, it seemed that there had been no time to rig traps or other surprises, although *Tra'tro* The'Stig knew better than to take anything for granted. His superiors had noted his achievement in the first battles by granting him a lead role in the expansion, along with reinforcements that had been dispatched from orbit. It was a honour he would happily have foregone. The oddly misshapen humans seemed either curious or terrified of his patrol; he watched in amusement as some ran away, while others just stared at them as if they'd never seen a non-human before. He shifted his weapon towards one of the humans who was paying too much attention to them in hopes of scaring the little creature away. The human emitted a high-pitched whine and fled.

The humans had abandoned many of their vehicles in positions that made it harder for the tankers to advance in support of the ground troops. Two of the tanks had already started pushing human vehicles to one side, but the remainder were holding back, nervous about the consequences of meddling with alien technology. Besides, the humans had shown a flair for creating traps and no tanker wished to lose his vehicle to a mere improvised bomb. The'Stig cursed them under his breath, even as he saw another group of humans ahead of him. They were staring at his patrol as if they couldn't believe their eyes…

A human voice yelled a command and the first projectiles crashed down around them. The'Stig's first thought was that they were under attack by human soldiers, but they were throwing glass bottles and stones rather than grenades and bullets. A moment later, one of the bottles crashed down on top of a trooper's head, sending him sprawling down onto the road. The humans might not be soldiers, but they could harm his troopers. Their defiance could not be tolerated.

He snarled as he pulled down on the firing trigger and sprayed bullets over the humans within eyesight. They fell to the ground in bloody heaps, their comrades suddenly running back as if they'd realised that it wasn't a good idea to challenge the occupation force. The'Stig refused to let them go easily; he lunged forward, firing burst after burst as he moved. The attack ended almost as quickly as it had begun, with a number of humans dead and two of his troopers mildly injured. He silently made a note to praise the body armour in his report. If they hadn't been so well-protected, they would have certainly had more injured, if not dead.

"Advance," he ordered, sharply.

The force continued on its way, coordinating with other groups as they pressed out along the human roads. It dawned on him suddenly that they weren't really controlling the city at all, merely the main roads they intended to use for transporting supplies. They simply didn't have the numbers to maintain control over the entire city. After a moment of thought, he kept that insight to himself. His superior officers no doubt knew all about it and intended to deal with the humans in another manner. Their city was dependent upon food supplies from outside, wasn't it? They could simply be starved to death if they refused to cooperate.

He smiled darkly as the first assault drone hummed overhead, watching for further human ambushes. The humans who had escaped the brief engagement – if he dignified the one-sided massacre by calling it an engagement – would spread the word. Any attempts to slow the occupation force would not be tolerated. Maybe the humans would learn quickly enough that the occupation force could relax.

The drone reported what looked like another ambush up ahead. He checked his weapon as the force moved carefully onwards, ready to deal with the ambush when it was triggered. The humans would learn – or they would die. In the end, he told himself firmly, Earth would belong to the State. The only real question was how many humans would have to die before the rest realised that they had no choice, but to submit.

Chapter Seven

Long Stratton
United Kingdom, Day 1

"I saw you come down," a voice called. Alex barely heard him. "Are you all right?"

Alex shook her head. Her entire body was shaking with post-combat stress. She'd left RAF Coningsby expecting nothing more challenging than a routine patrol and an attempt to intercept one of the mysterious 'ghosts.' Well, the ghosts weren't a mystery any more, were they? They belonged to the bastards who had blown Davidson out of the sky and shot her down, whoever they were. She'd practiced ejecting before, but she'd never had to eject from a Typhoon in the midst of a battle… she cursed her own weakness as she tried to stand up. Her legs refused to cooperate and she stumbled before grasping the proffered hand gratefully.

"I… thank you," she managed. Normally, a pilot bailing out of an aircraft would have been tracked by ground-based radar stations and a SAR helicopter dispatched from the nearest base. Now, she had the unpleasant feeling that the rest of the RAF had more important things to worry about than a single Typhoon pilot. The explosions she'd seen as she drifted down to the field suggested that the entire country was under attack. "Do you have a mobile phone?"

"I tried to call an ambulance when I saw your parachute," the farmer said. He looked older than her father, but there was a toughness around him that reminded her of the RAF Regiment soldiers who guarded the RAF's airbases. His face was tanned by the sun. "There's no signal at all."

Somehow, Alex wasn't surprised. The unknowns – whoever they were – had to have taken out the communications satellites, as well as jamming ordinary radio frequencies. There was no reason why they couldn't jam mobile phones as well. She cursed under her breath as she realised that she wasn't entirely sure where she was, or how to report in to whatever remained of her unit. The country was at war and she had enlisted to defend it. She needed to return to the base. And that might be impossible.

"I can take you down to the farm," the farmer offered. He held out a calloused hand. "My name's Giles, Giles Smith. I own the land about here."

"Alex," Alex offered, as they shook hands. "I didn't mean to land on your farm…"

"Don't worry about it," the farmer said. He frowned, for a long moment. "I don't suppose you know what those flashes I saw in the distance were?"

Alex filled him in on what little she knew as they walked down towards the farmhouse. It was a neat little building, surrounded by a field of sheep and cows, almost like something from a bygone era. She would have been charmed if she hadn't been so worried about the situation – and the smell from the fields. The people who suggested that humanity should abandon technology and go back to the land had never smelled the countryside. *She* was happy with air conditioning and filtering.

Inside, she allowed the farmer's wife to give her a cup of tea while she tried to call the base. The telephone line buzzed and clicked alarmingly, and then went dead, without even a dial tone. At Smith's suggestion, she tried the internet and was pleasantly surprised to discover that the farmhouse had broadband. Smith explained, when she asked, that the farmhouse often played host to young people and they all demanded internet access.

"And the wife likes watching streaming video from London," he added with a wink. "I know better than to get in her way."

Alex smiled as she tried to access MILNET through the internet connection. It should have accepted her password and allowed her access, but the link seemed to keep dropping out, as if some of the network nodes were malfunctioning. The unknown enemy had launched their attack without being detected, at least until it was far too late. There was no reason why they couldn't have launched a cyber-attack as well and taken out most of the military's secure network. The pilots had briefed that that was supposed to be impossible, but the unknowns had done far too much that should *also* have been impossible.

Finally, the system blinked up a warning; enemy troops in London and several other cities. Alex stared at the screen, not quite believing her eyes. How could *anyone* have simply landed in London? Where the hell was the rest of the RAF? The thought – the thought that she had been trying to avoid – floated back to the surface of her mind. She'd been blown out of the sky, along with her wingman. It was quite possible that the remainder of the RAF had met the same fate, or had been caught and destroyed on the ground. Who the hell were they fighting?

A set of general orders, directed to soldiers and TA reservists, flickered into existence. They were ordered to make their way out of the cities and rendezvous with officers at certain locations, each referred to with a different codename. Alex stared at them, before realising that whoever had taken command of the British military wouldn't have wanted to put their instructions on the military network, no matter how secure it was supposed to be. The unknowns were probably monitoring every move they made.

But *she* had no idea where to go. The RAF had never anticipated needing to establish covert rendezvous points, certainly not since the end of the Cold War. She could find a list of military bases online, yet the chances were good that they had been destroyed or attacked and occupied by the unknowns. The unknowns… their enemy didn't even have a face! Who the hell were they fighting?

She clicked on one of the options and an answer, of sorts, floated up in front of her eyes. Aliens. It seemed impossible, but so did the ghosts – the ghost aircraft that had blown her out of the sky and killed her wingman. She covered her eyes for a long moment, feeling the world spinning around her, and then looked back up at the screen. The damning words were still there.

"Aliens," she whispered. How long had it been since she'd watched the television show where the RAF had accidentally shot down a UFO, only to find themselves caught in the middle of a war between two alien races? Years… she'd been a child at the time. "It's not possible…"

But she could think of no other possible explanation.

Smith came back into the room and she filled him in, leaving out nothing. The farmer listened carefully, without interrupting, and then nodded. "I suspected as much," he admitted, after she'd finished. "The BBC has been raving about monsters in London. They must have seen the aliens…"

"But what do they *want*?" Alex asked, helplessly. "What does puny Earth have that they might want for themselves?"

"I have no idea," Smith said. He shrugged. "Listen; I have to go to the Parish Council and tell them what's going on. God alone knows what's going to happen if London's been occupied and we have to see to the crops. Lots of people might come running out of the cities and heading for the farms. I'd like you to come with me."

Alex hesitated, and then nodded just as her stomach rumbled loudly. "Have something to eat first," Mrs Smith said, firmly. "And you as well, Giles. You don't eat enough as it is."

———

Alex had never been to Long Stratton before, but Smith was happy to fill her in as they rumbled into the town and headed towards the Town Hall. Long Stratton was a civil parish with a population of roughly three thousand people, many of whom seemed to be thronging the streets as if they expected answers to be handed down from above. It struck her that many people around the country would have only seen explosions or heard thunderclaps, or perhaps listened to the ranting from the BBC – and wouldn't have the slightest idea of what was going on. How long would it be, she asked herself, before confusion turned into panic? And how long would it be before the aliens made their demands known to humanity?

Smith parked by the Town Hall and nodded towards the old-style stone church. "There'll be hundreds of people there, seeking guidance," he said, softly. "Everyone knows everyone else here, not like in the big cities. We have a real community here, despite everything London can do to ruin it. Little green men aren't going to take this place from us without a fight."

Alex kept her opinions to herself. Some of the farmers would have shotguns, or hunting rifles, but most of the population would be unarmed. It was quite possible that they could produce Molotov Cocktails and other makeshift weapons, yet how could they stand up to the alien onslaught? The defenders of Long Stratton and its sister towns might just be marking themselves for extermination. What was her duty to them if they decided to challenge the aliens directly?

Smith led her into the Town Hall after a brief chat with the policeman standing outside, looking rather worried. Alex saw his hand toying with his radio and realised that the police in Long Stratton had been cut off from London by alien jamming. She thought about telling him what she knew, and then realised that it would be pointless. He couldn't do anything about it, but panic. Shaking her head, she allowed Smith to lead her into a small room. Three men were gathered there, looking deeply worried. She smiled inwardly as they saw her uniform and frowned, uncertain what to make of her presence. God alone knew what she was going to tell them.

"This is the Parish Council, or as much of them as could be assembled," Smith said, without preamble. "Rupert Leigh; Tory MP for his sins, but a good man outside politics." A tall thin man nodded impatiently. "Timmy Simpson; used to farm quite a bit, but now pretty much retired." Simpson snorted, making a gesture with his fingers that suggested counting money. He was an older man, with a hunch that suggested that he was bowed under some great weight. "And the Reverend Macpherson, shepherd of our little flock."

"I should be in the Church," Reverend Macpherson said, shortly. "People need to come together and pray to God for guidance."

Smith nodded and started to outline what he'd heard from Alex, starting with the story of how he'd found her in his field. Halfway through, when he reached the bit about aliens, all three of the councillors stared at her. They looked as if they wanted to call in the policeman and have the pair of them arrested for public drunkenness. Smith finished by reminding them of some of the more hysterical statements on the BBC – "we live in strange times," he said.

"I wish I didn't believe you," Leigh said. His voice had an upper-class edge that reminded Alex of a certain breed of officer. They'd sounded as if they'd been absolutely certain about everything too. "But aliens… dear God, what are we going to do when we tell the people?"

"We shall inform them in the Church," the Reverend said. "They will have time to reflect on God's will instead of panicking."

Leigh snorted. "But what are we going to *do*?"

Alex had been giving the matter some thought. "They made us study recent military history back when I was a trainee pilot," she said. "The first few hours after an invasion are always the most dangerous for ordinary people, because the occupation force will be on edge and unsure of its ground. You may not see very many aliens this far from London, or they may decide to take stock of the entire country. I think you need to consider what you're going to do when they arrive – and what you're going to do about others."

She scowled. "Right now, London and a dozen other cities are war zones," she continued. "The population is going to start fleeing the cities and heading for the countryside. You're not that far from Norwich – and that's got upwards of three hundred thousand people who will find themselves starving very quickly. What happens when they start flooding the farms? You have food here – and animals that can be slaughtered for human consumption. What are you going to do when they arrive?"

"There's the police," Leigh said, slowly.

"I think you have to assume that the police and the military have been knocked on the head," Alex said. She didn't want to admit it, but it was quite possible. "Even if there is still a working government and military out there, they are going to have more on their hands than helping you. You need to start planning for the worst."

"Good God," Leigh said. He stared down at the table, helplessly. "I don't think that there *is* anything we can do if the situation is that bad. We can't hold back swarms of starving humans…"

"We may have no choice," Simpson said, flatly. "Do you want to wait and see your families starving because you gave all your food to refugees?"

"I would remind you," the Reverend said sharply, "that charity is your duty towards your fellow man. Remember the parable of the Good Samaritan."

"The Good Samaritan," Simpson replied, "was in no danger."

He shook his head, slowly. "We may be in serious trouble anyway," he warned. "It isn't as if we keep stockpiles of food and seeds out here – normally, we could just order the supplies when we needed them. How dependent are we on the rest of the world? International trade is probably shot to hell."

"No doubt," Alex agreed.

"Then we put it to the vote," Leigh said. "We can speak to the people in the Church – ask them to work together to safeguard our farms and the rest of our property. And then we can hope that this whole crisis is just going to blow over."

"Hark at him," Simpson crowed. He laughed, unpleasantly. "Stupid politicians *always* think that the world will go back to normal if they just keep their eyes closed long enough. The country has been *invaded*, you idiot! Even if the army does manage to give those thieving bastards a damn good thrashing, do you think that *anything* is going to be the same ever again? Really? I want some of whatever you've been smoking."

Leigh reddened, but he somehow managed to keep his voice calm. "If the worst does happen, we're probably doomed," he said. "I refuse to stop hoping for the best even as I try to prepare for the worst."

"Typical politician," Simpson said. He looked up at Alex, amused malice glinting in his brown eyes. "You want to bet that we're all dead a week from today?"

"That will do," the Reverend said. He stood up from the table. "I believe that it is time to sound the bells and summon the townspeople to the Church. We can tell them what we know and then we can decide what to do." He looked over at Alex. "I'd like you to remain at hand. You may be needed to answer questions."

"I don't know what else I can tell you," Alex admitted. "I've told you everything I know."

Simpson shrugged. "Some people will probably feel better knowing that someone in a uniform is telling them not to worry," he said. "Back in the War" – it took Alex a moment to realise that he meant the Second World War – "they used to tell us to keep calm and carry on. And we did too."

"You lived out here, safe on your farm," Smith pointed out, with some amusement. It was clear that he and Simpson were old friends. "I think the people in the Blitz probably felt a little different."

"I have no doubt of it," Simpson said. He looked up at Alex. "After the meeting in the Town Hall, let me know if you decide to stick around. I have some items you may be interested in using."

***

The announcement and discussion in the Church was just as bad as Alex had feared. Nearly two hundred people had crammed themselves into the building and they all wanted to talk. The children had picked up on their parents' emotions and looked fearful, apart from the ones too young to know that something was wrong. Alex found herself targeted by irate people who wanted to know what had happened to the RAF, or why the invasion had been allowed to take place. After trying to point out twice that she had been taken completely by surprise, she did her best to ignore the louder protesters. It wasn't as if there was anything else she could do.

"We can survive this if we all pull together," Leigh said, once the general panic had calmed down slightly. The sheer unreality of the situation helped, although the BBC had clearly managed to cause panic in some quarters. One report claimed that London and Manchester had been occupied by giant elephants. Alex couldn't help, but feel that little gray aliens would have been more traditional. "We don't know what's going to happen, but we *will* get through it all."

The crowd didn't ask for specifics, luckily. Alex allowed herself a moment of relief that it seemed to be quietening down, even though she wasn't sure what she wanted to do now. Where did she go to report in? RAF Coningsby was almost certainly destroyed – or occupied by alien forces. The RAF had been taken completely by surprise.

She stepped outside and looked up at the darkening sky. An entire day had gone by and she'd barely noticed. High overhead, the stars were coming out – and there were a handful of trails burning their way down towards Earth. The remains of humanity's pathetic space program, she assumed. Some of the other lights would be alien starships…

In the distance, she heard the sound of thunder and shuddered.

The night no longer felt safe.

Chapter Eight

Salisbury Plain
United Kingdom, Day 1

"Prime Minister?"

Gabriel shook himself awake, surprised that he'd managed to fall asleep. After they'd left London, they'd followed the Thames upstream, with only minor delays caused by bridges that the aliens had targeted from orbit. A couple of hours later, they'd left the boat and transferred themselves to a Land Rover Butcher had recovered from somewhere. Reading between the lines, Gabriel guessed that the vehicle had been stolen, but he had found it difficult to care. Exhaustion had overwhelmed him soon afterwards.

They had parked in the midst of woodland, with the vehicle half-hidden under the trees. A small group of armed soldiers wearing camouflage uniforms had surrounded the vehicle, glancing around nervously as they waited for the Prime Minister to disembark. Gabriel knew very little about the military, but he could tell that the soldiers were worried. No matter how he looked at the situation, there seemed little cause for optimism. A day ago, he'd been Prime Minister of the United Kingdom. Now… his position as Prime Minister seemed almost meaningless. No Prime Minister had ever had to flee London for fear that enemy troops would capture or kill him. Even Charles I had managed a reasonably dignified departure from his former capital.

Butcher led him into the woods, down towards a small concrete building marked PRIVATE, KEEP OUT. The soldier opened the door, revealing a ladder leading down into the depths of the Earth. Unwilling to show fear in front of the soldiers, Gabriel followed him down and realised to his relief that the lower levels of the bunker were properly lit. A uniformed soldier was waiting for him. The man looked deeply worried, but relieved when he saw the Prime Minister.

"Prime Minister," the soldier said. "I'm Brigadier Gavin Lightbridge-Stewart. Welcome to the bunker."

Gabriel followed the Brigadier as he led the way through a hatch into a large concrete room. It seemed primitive compared to some of the other emergency facilities he'd seen over the years, clearly not a facility that had been intended to return to active service. A number of maps had been scattered on the table, with red lines drawn on them by a handful of military personnel. Several more officers were working what looked like an older set of radios, trying to get back in touch with the rest of the world. Oddly, Gabriel felt a pang of relief as he took in the scene. The situation was bad – disastrous – but experienced personnel were trying to come to grips with it. They might not be so outmatched after all.

"Please, be seated," the Brigadier said. "I have a military brief for you, but you might prefer a shower and a change of clothes – and a hot meal. The situation is unlikely to change in the next few hours."

Gabriel hesitated. In truth, he wanted the shower, and some food, and a few more hours of sleep. But he needed to know what was going on before he could come to grips with the situation. Perhaps they could find out what the aliens actually wanted – assuming they wanted anything. If invasion and settlement was their goal, surely they'd have some kind of plan to deal with the human governments. He remembered the report that alien craft were heading towards London – the craft they'd seen as they headed upriver – and shuddered. The aliens had made at least one of their goals quite clear.

"I'd like the briefing first," he said, finally. The Brigadier nodded, as if he understood perfectly. Neither of them could do much to influence the situation, but they couldn't just rest while the entire country was in danger. "How much do we actually know about what's going on out there?"

The Brigadier tapped one finger on the maps. "Most of our military communications network has been badly hammered," he said. "We never anticipated the physical destruction of the network nodes or the satellite network orbiting the planet, although most of the hardwired connections – the land lines – are undamaged. Our intelligence is therefore very limited and changes frequently, but I've had several intelligence and signals units working on what we do have and trying to put together a comprehensive picture."

His expression darkened. "The aliens – whoever they are, whatever they want – have clearly not limited their attentions to us," he added. "We have intermittent contact with the Americans and they confirm that Washington has been invaded; we also picked up a brief report from a French military unit that implied that Paris had also been hit. I'm afraid that we have been unable to make contact with American or French government officials – the outlook, Prime Minister, isn't good."

Gabriel nodded, bitterly. He'd hoped that they would be able to call on NATO for support, but it was clear that NATO had fragmented, with the national military forces on the run – fighting their own hopeless battles. The American President was a friend and he'd managed to make some progress in talking to the French President… what had happened to them after the aliens landed? America was so powerful that he assumed that the aliens had devoted much of their attention to smashing them flat. It was quite possible that the President and everyone else in their line of succession was dead.

"We have been attempting to make contact with personnel in Europe – we have officers at NATO Headquarters and a British Army base in Germany – but so far attempts have proven fruitless," the Brigadier said. "I think we have to assume the worst; the units have been destroyed or scattered. Parts of the internet are still working and we may be able to establish contact, but…"

He shook his head. "Overall, Prime Minister, the news is about as bad as it can get," he continued. "From what reports we have received, the Royal Navy has been effectively destroyed from orbit. We've picked up witness reports of warships being hit by missiles or kinetic energy weapons, leaving them ablaze and sinking. There are reports that suggest that many large container ships have also been sunk. We assume that the other major naval forces have also been destroyed, but we've heard nothing apart from a brief internet message from Toulon reporting a sinking carrier."

"My God," Gabriel said. How many sailors had died before they'd even known that they were under attack? "What about the air force?"

"The RAF has lost most of its bases to orbital strikes," the Brigadier said. "The aliens have been dropping in on some of the bases and converting them – I suspect – to bridgeheads. I've issued orders for material to be removed from the remaining bases before the aliens arrive and take possession – the RAF Regiment has orders to briefly engage them and then withdraw before they can be destroyed by superior firepower. A handful of aircraft survived the first strikes and attempted to hit back at the aliens, but results were… not optimum. The aliens have also been landing on civilian airports and deploying their forces to take up positions on the ground. Our ability to impede them is very limited."

He waited, perhaps expecting Gabriel to say something, but there was nothing to say. "They also bombarded most – not all – of the army garrisons in the country," he concluded. "Damage was very significant, but enough soldiers survived to allow us to begin preparations for underground war – if necessary. I've had teams of soldiers return to the damaged bases and remove as much equipment and weaponry as we can from storage – as well as rounding up soldiers, reservists, and anyone with military experience who is willing to volunteer. I suspect that the aliens won't leave us alone here much longer – they have to know that we're attempting to regroup."

Gabriel shivered. "Brigadier… I need an honest answer," he said. The Brigadier looked oddly insulted by the question. "Can we stop them if they come here?"

"Unlikely," the Brigadier admitted, after a moment. He drew out a line on the map. "I have positioned our remaining armour – that's Challenger II tanks, the best tanks in the world – in positions where they can give the aliens a bloody nose when they come westwards. They're backed up by antiaircraft weapons, small antitank teams and a whole series of booby traps. We can and we will give them a bloody nose, Prime Minister, but we can't stop them. They have complete air supremacy and the ability to drop rocks on us from space. A straight fight will be disastrous for us."

"I never claimed to be a military man," Gabriel said, slowly, "but why are you talking about fighting them if you can't stop them?"

The Brigadier frowned. "Prime Minister… in recent years, we have had to operate on reduced logistics that have, quite frankly, cost lives. Normally, we would be able to draw ammunition, fuel and spare parts from our depots on the mainland, although we could never afford the stockpiles that we believed to be necessary for modern warfare. Military units burn through their supplies at terrifying speeds, even under the best of circumstances. Right now, our logistics train has effectively been destroyed. I imagine that we will become unable to operate the tanks within the next week. And, of course, they have eyes in the sky. They'd be able to detect us moving the tanks and blow them away from orbit.

"What that means is that our *best* chance for actually hurting them badly is now," he added. "From what we've seen of their armour in London – we managed to get pictures from the battle – we should be able to give them a rough reception. Our tankers have been given orders to hit the enemy hard, then fall back and abandon their vehicles. We should be able to make them more careful about advancing into unsecured territory while we prepare our fallback option."

Gabriel shook his head slowly. Yesterday, he'd been thinking about the economy. Now he was forced to think about war raging across England's green and pleasant land. It should have been unthinkable. He rubbed the side of his head, feeling a headache pounding inside his skull. How could anyone come to grips with what was tearing the country – the world – apart?

He looked up at the military officer. "And what do we do after they've smashed our tanks?"

"The only thing we can do," the Brigadier admitted. "We fight an underground war – an insurgency – until they decide that humans are too dangerous to keep as slaves."

"But…" Gabriel stopped, unsure if he should believe his ears. The thought of waging an insurgency against the invaders was romantic in the abstract, but in the real world he *knew* it would be horrific. God alone knew how the invaders would react to insurgents – human history showed a wide range of possible alternatives. Hell, for all he knew the invaders had technology that would allow them to read human thoughts or track human soldiers by their scent. "Can we hope to win?"

"I don't know," the Brigadier said. "All I can say is that it seems to be the only alternative – unless we want to raise the white flag and surrender."

Gabriel settled back into his chair, feeling the strength flowing out of his body. Surrender? Winston Churchill had rejected the very idea of surrender, insisting that Britain would fight on the beaches and fields and streets – but Churchill had known that invading Britain would be a monumental task for Adolf Hitler. Would his attitude have been different, Gabriel asked himself, if the Nazis had actually landed? Europe had seen bitter fighting in towns and cities, but Britain had been spared. But now… the aliens had succeeded where a long string of enemies had failed. They'd landed in England and the remains of the British military was on the run.

And yet… what did the aliens have in mind for humanity? He'd wracked his brains, but he hadn't been able to come up with one solid reason for an advanced alien race to invade the Earth. All they could take from Earth was humans – and surely if they were advanced enough to cross the gulf between stars, they were advanced enough to make machines that would replace slaves. Maybe they were just mindless monsters, intent on exterminating all other races, but then they could have just dropped rocks from orbit. Or maybe there was something he was missing. If only he wasn't so tired…

"I don't know what to do," he admitted. He cursed himself a moment later, for forgetting the one thing that should have been a priority. "What's happening with the civilian population?"

The Brigadier's expression hardened. "The aliens have come down in force around London, Manchester and a dozen other cities," he said. "From the reports we've had, they've been refusing to allow anyone to leave and they're backing up that refusal with live ammunition. Other parts of the country have seen riots and unrest – I think that they're only going to get worse as people realise that the government has been crippled. We're trying to get reservists out of the cities, but…"

He shook his head. "I'm afraid it's going to get worse, Prime Minister," he added. "It won't be long before we see starvation. God alone knows how many people are going to die."

Gabriel silently cursed his predecessors – and himself. Over the years, Britain had become increasingly dependent upon food imported from overseas – upwards of fifty percent of British food came from outside the country. And with the global trading network shot to hell by the aliens, there were likely to be shortages very quickly. The damage the aliens had inflicted on Britain's road and rail networks wouldn't make distributing what was left any easier. There had been calls to establish a national strategic food reserve that would allow the government to feed the people, if necessary, but successive governments had chosen to avoid the issue rather than pay for the necessary precautions.

"We never planned for this sort of global outrage," he admitted. Perhaps, he added to himself, because the prospects were so horrifying. "What do we do about it?"

"I don't think we *can* do much about it," the Brigadier said. "I think that we will have to hope that the aliens choose to feed our population – we sure as hell can't do it for ourselves."

Gabriel tried to find some of Churchill's determination within himself, but it seemed impossible to believe that there was any hope of victory – or even survival. His position as Prime Minister was meaningless…

"Have a rest," the Brigadier advised. "I have teams working on our long-term plans – it's possible that the aliens will give us enough time to lay the groundwork for a long-term insurgency."

"Or they won't," Gabriel said. He pulled himself to his feet. The room seemed to be spinning around him and he was suddenly aware of the people covertly watching him. He had to be strong for them, he told himself firmly. It didn't help. "If we can't beat them, Brigadier, what's the point of even fighting?"

———

Brigadier Gavin Lightbridge-Stewart watched, his face impassive, as the Prime Minister's bodyguards helped him down the narrow corridor. There was a small selection of rooms under the bunker, where he could have a shower and a long sleep – God knew he needed it. The man wasn't a soldier and hadn't even considered the possibility that he might find himself on the run; for all the bellyaching about British politicians and the seemingly endless scandals, Britain wasn't Afghanistan or one of the other countries where political leaders knew to keep a bag packed for flight at all times.

He looked down at the map on the table, trying to force himself to remain optimistic. The situation was grim, but the reports from London made it clear that the aliens weren't gods. They seemed to have a slight shortage of force fields, directed energy weapons and all the other miracle technology that any self-respecting fictional alien race should possess. In fact, some of their technology looked to be *inferior* to human tech – although there was no way to be sure. The analysts had taken a look at the images of the alien landing shuttles and concluded that they shouldn't fly, at least with any technology known to mankind. Their best guess was that the aliens had some form of negating gravity. The shuttles actually seemed to be more fragile than human craft. They'd been hit with Stingers and blown out of the air.

How long do we have? He asked himself. They'd been spoiled by modern technology. The fog of war, once banished by overhead reconnaissance and satellite imagery, was back with a vengeance. There was no way to know what the aliens were doing – at least until the scouts were in position to start reporting back. And the aliens could presumably track their radio transmissions and direct their aircraft to pick them off…

The Prime Minister had looked as if he was on the verge of collapse. Gavin couldn't blame him; no one, in their worst nightmares, had imagined an alien invasion. He didn't want to *think* about what the civilian population was feeling, looking out into the darkening sky and wondering what would happen to them now that their country had been invaded. Britain had been a good place to live for many; now… now it might become a nightmarish alien-ruled land. Or perhaps the aliens would choose to work through human proxies.

He shook his head. There was no way to know.

Passing command of the bunker to one of his subordinates – who had been commanding a troop of tanks until Gavin had pulled him out to serve in the bunker – he headed for the ladder up to the surface. He could inspect the defence lines and chat with the soldiers, just to see how they were coping with the situation. And he could start laying the groundwork for underground resistance. The PM might swing towards coming to an accommodation with the aliens, but Gavin had other ideas. His country had been invaded.

He wasn't going to let that pass without a fight.

Chapter Nine

London
United Kingdom, Day 2

Westminster looked like a war zone.

No, Alan Beresford, Member of Parliament for Haltemprice, corrected himself. It *was* a war zone. Alan prided himself on his cynical approach to life – it had certainly served him well in politics – but even he felt a pang as he saw the damage the aliens had inflicted on the heart of the British Government. The Houses of Parliament were scorched – by the aliens or their human defenders – and Big Ben had collapsed inward on itself. There had been hundreds of dead bodies scattered about, but from what he'd heard the aliens were collecting them up and disposing of them. He didn't want to think about *how*.

At thirty-five, Alan had been in politics for most of his life. His father had been a well-connected MP who had arranged for his son to receive employment within the office of another MP, who had in turn opened up a whole series of doors for his friend's son. Alan knew little about the world outside politics and cared less. All he cared about was the chance to make money, increase his personal power base and pass his legacy on to his son. He'd dreaded the prospect of an effective Prime Minister in Ten Downing Street for a long time – the thought of someone like Thatcher taking a look at his hidden secrets was terrifying – and he'd done a great deal to keep the position in the hands of a pathetic non-entity. Alan no longer believed in Britain, but then – why should he? The great British population, blessed with the gift of democracy, freely chose to elect men with few real qualifications for government – and then blamed those men for what they did to the country. No one had ever really held Parliament to account for a very long time.

But now… the world had changed overnight. Aliens had arrived, real aliens. Alan hadn't seen any of the battle at first hand, not when he'd been cowering in his upmarket flat fearing that every second might be his last. He'd believed that it was more likely to be terrorists and the BBC's increasingly absurd broadcasts just another sign of panic caused by the bastards. The news had only penetrated his skull when his political fixer had staggered in, bleeding from his shoulder, and raving about massive aliens. And then he'd heard their broadcast…

His position as an elected MP was useless now, Alan knew. The British Government was on the run – no one had seen hide or hair of Burley and his ineffectual Cabinet since the aliens had landed. Alan knew better than to assume that Burley could turn the situation around, which meant that it was every man for himself. The aliens, on the other hand, wielded real power. He could make an alliance with them and offer his services in exchange for protection, wealth and more power than he'd ever dreamed possible. Who knew what sort of rewards a race that could cross the gulfs between stars could offer their faithful servants?

He stopped dead as he saw the alien patrol turning towards him. Despite his belief that the aliens needed allies, it took all of his strength not to turn and flee. The massive brutes loomed over him, carrying weapons that seemed too large to be real. Alan had used shotguns and hunting rifles while staying at estates owned by his friends, but the alien weapons were very different. It struck him that the aliens had to be less socially developed than humanity – yet it hardly mattered. They'd crossed the gulf of space to reach Earth and impose their will upon humanity. It had taken them barely a day to crush most of humanity's defences.

Alan smiled and held up his hands, hoping that the aliens would understand the gesture. Their dark eyes showed no sign of human emotions; their faces seemed curiously immobile, almost as if they didn't have emotions at all. Or perhaps he was just looking in the wrong place. They might show their thoughts by how their hands moved when they spoke.

"I come in peace," he said. "Take me to your leader."

"Follow us," the lead alien grated. The voice didn't seem to come from its mouth, but from a small device hanging down below its oversized chin. Alan wasn't too surprised that they could speak English. They were clearly advanced enough to monitor human broadcasts and decipher human languages. "Do not attempt to escape."

The area surrounding Ten Downing Street and Buckingham Palace had been devastated. Alien machines were moving through the rubble, pushing it aside and exposing the hidden network of tunnels under Whitehall. A set of alien-designed buildings had already been erected in Hyde Park, allowing them to come and go freely, rather than trying to fit into human buildings. They'd have problems using human vehicles and aircraft, Alan told himself, and smiled. Even *he* appreciated that the aliens were on the end of a very long logistics chain. They'd be delighted if he could convince thousands of humans to serve their new overlords.

One of the aliens held up an oversized hand to stop him in his tracks, while a second waved what looked like a metal wand over his body. A security check, he realised, and allowed his mobile phone to be confiscated without demur. He hadn't been able to get a signal to call anyone – the landlines seemed to be badly damaged, or perhaps the staff just hadn't reported in after the aliens had landed – and he made a mental note to suggest to the aliens that they restore mobile phone communications as soon as possible. It would go a long way towards allowing them to win hearts and minds.

The interior of the alien building was oddly disappointing. It seemed more like a giant tent than anything else, with dozens of aliens working on small consoles and barking orders – or at least he assumed they were orders – at their subordinates. A massive image of Britain was displayed against one wall, covered with red and green markers that appeared to surround most of the larger cities. For the first time, Alan allowed himself to doubt the wisdom of his course of action. The aliens seemed to have won the war in the first day. Perhaps they wouldn't need him…

His escorts opened a door in the side of the building and pushed him into an oversized office. It was easy to believe that it was a power office, like the rooms favoured by CEOs he knew, but perhaps it was just normal for the aliens. They would need more living space than humans – a large human office might be uncomfortably cramped for them. A single alien was half-crouching in front of a desk, tapping away at what had to be a computer terminal. He – Alan decided to assume that it was a male, at least until it was proven otherwise – wore a simple black uniform, decorated with golden writing. Assuming the aliens prized gold as much as humanity, he was looking at a senior officer. He stepped forward and did his best to place an interested expression on his face. Who knew how the aliens would react to a man offering to help them?

"I am *Ju'tro* Oheghizh," the alien said. Alan assumed that *Ju'tro* was a title of some kind – General, perhaps, or Leader? It was unlikely that the supreme commander of a force invading the entire planet would be based in Britain. "You wished to talk with me?"

"Yes, sir," Alan said. Perhaps the alien wouldn't understand human respect, but there was no reason to take chances. "I am a high official in the government of this country. I wish to offer you my services."

There was a long moment as the alien's unreadable eyes bored into Alan's face. "We know who you are," the alien said, finally. Alan's mind raced; he hadn't seen them communicating, but who knew what they might be able to do? They might have communications implants in their skulls. "You will assist us in bringing humanity into the State."

"Of course," Alan said, quickly. He allowed himself another smile. "I would be happy to serve."

———

"You know," Sergeant Singh observed, "I was rather hoping that it would be a nightmare."

Robin nodded in agreement. They'd found their way to a police station, hidden most of the weapons in what he hoped was a secure hiding place, and then gone to sleep in the station's dormitory. A handful of policemen with families had gone to their homes to check on their loved ones. No one had attempted to dissuade them. Robin had considered trying to slip out of the city and make it to his house – and his wife – but the aliens had blocked all of the roads out of London. He had kept trying the telephone, only to hear nothing, not even a dial tone.

He pulled himself out of the bunk and checked the shower. The station's internal water supply was still working, thankfully, as was the internal generator. Most of London's power had been lost overnight, although there was no way to know if the aliens had done it deliberately or if humans had simply shut the power stations down before they fell into alien hands. London had seemed uneasily quiet after the events of the invasion, but Robin had no illusions. It wouldn't be long before the veneer of society fell away and what remained of social order collapsed into anarchy. And without the police on the streets, it was likely to spread rapidly. God alone knew what would happen then.

"I managed to get some news from the BBC," one of the constables reported after he entered the briefing room. Had it only been two days ago when he'd been on patrol, back when the world had made sense? "They were claiming that negotiations are in progress and it was all a terrible mistake."

Robin snorted. "That was no mistake," he said, flatly. He couldn't see how a race that could cross light years could launch an attack on London by *accident*. The BBC had never impressed him as a policeman, if only because it tended to side against the police force whenever its honour, capability or competence was called into question. "The planet has been invaded and we're at war. God help us."

He scowled over at the darkened terminal. Normally, it would have been glowing with updates from across the city, as well as items of interest, lists of suspects and all the other information that the modern policeman needed on a daily basis. Now, it was dark, suggesting that the police communications network was still down. Each of the police stations would have been cut off from the others… he shook his head, bitterly. What were they supposed to do now? Report in to the aliens and see what they had in mind for police officers?

"I've got something," one of the other constables said. "I heard a voice…"

He fiddled with the radio again and the static faded away to a background hiss. "…Speaking for the Conquest Force," a voice – unmistakably human – said. "I am the sole surviving member of the British Government. We have been defeated. The Eridian Conquest Fleet has destroyed our defences. We can no longer offer resistance to their invasion force. I am therefore ordering all remaining military units to surrender at once to the nearest Eridian force. Their leaders have assured me that they will be treated well, in accordance with *their* Rules of Law."

Robin swore. "Who the hell is *that*?"

"That's Beresford," Sergeant Singh said. "I think he's sold out to the aliens!"

"We must accept the fact that human independence is over," Beresford continued. "They have informed me that humans who are willing to serve will receive good treatment and a chance to climb within their ranks. Humans who refuse to serve them will be treated as criminals and rebels against the new lawful authority on Earth. I have been charged with making the process of human assimilation into their society as smooth as possible. There is no other hope for the survival of humanity. The aliens rule the skies. Long-term resistance will only result in the deaths of millions of humans.

"Accordingly, I am ordering all civil servants and policemen to report for service at once," he continued. "Those who do not report will be treated as deserters and will face the consequences when they are caught. Our priority must be the reestablishment of law and order within Britain. Those who do not submit to their rule will be punished."

There was a long pause. "We have grown used to human despots concealing their true motives behind fancy language," he concluded. "The Eridians do not seem to share our attitudes. They wanted Earth; they took it. Their attitudes will not be swayed by pleas or protests. They believe that

might makes right. Do not, for the sake of all humanity, seek to challenge them. They will respond with deadly force."

A moment passed, and then the message began to repeat itself. "Turn it off," Robin snarled, savagely. He couldn't believe his ears. There was no way to doubt that Beresford had sold out to Earth's new masters. They'd probably promised him wealth and power if he served them. "What the hell do we do now?"

One of the constables put their choice into words. "They seem to want us to work for them," he said. "If we do that…"

"Collaboration," someone else growled.

"If we work with them," the constable continued, "we would insulate the ordinary people – the people we swore to protect – from the aliens. If we refuse… we put our lives and those of our families in danger. We all know how the aliens react to challenges."

Robin nodded, bitterly. A group of louts – if he could be excused a moment of political incorrectness – had attacked an alien patrol with glass bottles and little else, apart from bad intentions. The aliens had opened fire and killed many of their attackers before the remainder fled for their lives. It hadn't been the only encounter between the aliens and humans who had tried to fight either. The aliens didn't seem to care that the humans were young, barely armed, and powerless… they'd seen a threat and dealt with it. They didn't have lawyers and politicians in uniform holding them back from handing out a good thrashing.

"There's another possibility," Sergeant Singh suggested. "We join up – and prepare ourselves to turn on the aliens if necessary. They might have *told* us that they've crushed all resistance, but we know that that might not be true."

"I won't push anyone into the decision," Robin said. He'd made up his mind. "If anyone wants to leave, they can do so now – without fear. I will go and see if I can shield humans from them…"

"Maybe," Sergeant Singh said. "Or perhaps they'll expect us to do as we're told. And we might be told to do something truly awful."

———

Fatima rubbed her eyes as she pulled herself from the depths of sleep. She'd just run out of energy – after seeing so many patients she'd lost count, she'd ended up finding a quiet corner and just collapsing into an uneasy sleep. Never in her worst nightmares had she imagined having to help so many people – and watch others die though lacking the supplies to save them. Maybe it had been a dream… she shook her head, cursing her own weakness. It had been no dream. They were still in the makeshift hospital and she could hear patients moaning in pain.

She pulled herself to her feet and headed towards the corridor. It was crammed with patients, lying on the floor; only the lucky ones had blankets to insulate themselves from the cold. The sight appalled her; the NHS hadn't been the best medical service in the world, but it wouldn't have allowed such conditions in a hospital. Now… now there was nothing they could do for their patients, but try to make them as comfortable as possible. They'd raided all the nearby chemists and supermarkets – and they were *still* short of supplies.

A hand fell on her shoulder and she jumped. "You all right, missy?"

It was a policeman, wearing what looked like riot-control gear. "I'm tired," she said, bitterly. "What are you doing here?"

"It seems that they want us to take care of the hospitals," the policeman said. He sounded as if he didn't quite believe his own words – or the changes in the world since… had it really been only a day ago? "There's fifty of us assigned here and over a hundred at the nearest hospital. Someone's been helping them assign us, that's for sure. Did you hear the broadcast?"

"I've been sleeping," Fatima admitted. Her body ached and she was uncomfortably aware that she stank. The white jacket she wore had been stained by blood. Her supervisor would have been furious at her if she'd turned up to work looking as if she'd walked out of a slaughterhouse. "What happened?"

"One of our beloved MPs has sold out to the aliens," the policeman explained. "I think we're expected to bow and scrape before them now – or they'll be offended. And it seems that their response to offense is to open fire."

Fatima shivered. "Is there nothing we can do?"

"It seems that we've been beaten," the policeman said. "Maybe there'll be a chance to do something about it later, but for the moment we just have to keep our heads down and see what happens. Maybe the remains of the military can beat them off, or… something. Perhaps the Americans will fly a captured UFO up to the mothership and blow them up…"

He shook his head. "All we can do is wait and see," he said. "The fighting seems to be at an end – and we lost. The country has been invaded. And God alone knows what is going to happen next."

Chapter Ten

Near Salisbury Plain
United Kingdom, Day 2

"You know," Chris Drake said, "I never thought I would be pleased to see a redcap."

The Military Policeman smiled, a little weakly. "It's been one of those days," he agreed. "Name, rank and unit?"

Chris smiled. He'd allowed the Thames to push him out of London before climbing out and finding a convenient place to dry himself. There had been a small charity shop nearby where he'd picked up enough clothes to keep himself warm as he walked the long way around London and up towards Salisbury Plain. He'd been lucky enough to find a civilian Range Rover, which he'd borrowed to complete the rest of the journey, but he'd been forced to stay off the main roads. The aliens, according to the radio transmissions he'd picked up, *liked* roads. They would, he assumed, have shot him or captured him the moment they saw him.

He'd relaxed a little as he headed westwards, until he'd run into the military police unit. He wasn't the only soldier who'd been separated from his unit and forced to travel alone to the rendezvous point, although as far as he knew he was the only soldier who'd escaped the Battle of London. The others had been supposed to link up in a disused warehouse and consider either making it out by foot or carrying on the fight against the invaders – God alone knew what had happened to them. He'd trained beside them, fought beside them – and now he was alone. Unless he was very lucky, he'd be pushed into a new unit to make up the manpower shortfall.

"You were in *London*?" The MP said asked, clearly impressed. "We've got orders to forward all survivors from London to the RV point. It seems that some of our superiors will want to talk to you."

Chris hesitated. There *was* a defence line being constructed that should slow the aliens down – he doubted that a force with air supremacy could be stopped – and part of him wanted to join it, to get stuck into the aliens who had killed so many of his friends and comrades. The rest of him knew that it was his duty to brief his superiors, to tell them what had happened at London and to ensure that the Household Division's last stand went down in the history books. But would the people writing the history books be human – or alien?

"They're going to be waiting to hear from you," the MP said, a moment later. "I suggest you brief them quickly. They're going to hit us soon."

Chris nodded and gunned the engine. He knew the area around Salisbury Plain fairly well – a legacy of the time spent boozing after exercises in the Live Firing Training Area – and it shook him to see so many deserted houses. The civilians would have been warned to leave the area as quickly as possible, whatever the aliens might have had to say about it. They probably wouldn't care if human civilians were caught in the crossfire. Everything they'd done suggested a certain lack of concern for human life. The sight of refugees heading north or south tore at his heart. Britain hadn't seen such deprivation since the Civil War – and that, by European standards of the time, had been remarkably civilised. He caught sight of a tank hidden under camouflage netting and waved to the man standing beside it, clearly planning an ambush. They should get in at least one good shot before the aliens started dropping killer crowbars from orbit.

Two miles further on, he ran into a second group of military policemen who ordered him to abandon the Range Rover and proceed on foot. The woodlands seemed crammed with human soldiers, including Royal Marines and RAF Regiment personnel, all forced together by circumstances. Chris had fought beside the Royal Marines in Afghanistan and while he thought – naturally – that the soldiers had the advantage, he had to admit that the Royal Marines were tough, professional fighters. The military policemen were sorting them out, sending some further away from Salisbury Plain while holding others to join the defence line. It *looked* as if someone was in command, thankfully. Perhaps everything he'd seen in London would be useful after all.

But the aliens controlled the high orbitals over Earth. They could bombard the planet into submission, or hammer any human military force foolish enough to show itself openly. How could an insurgency hope to win against such an enemy? God alone knew if they could do more than sting the enemy…

"Down here," a military policeman said. There was a hatch hidden in the woods, seemingly leading down to nowhere. Given how many other bunkers, bases and supply dumps were scattered around Salisbury Plain, it made sense to think that there was a government bunker hidden there too. "They'll meet you at the bottom."

Chris nodded and began to descend down the ladder.

———

"Are you decent, Prime Minister?"

Gabriel snorted at Butcher's mock-falsetto tone. He'd slept for several hours and awoke feeling as if he hadn't slept very long at all, but his watch told a different story. Butcher – who had apparently been assigned as his permanent bodyguard – had pointed him at the shower and told him to take his time. Someone had brought in a spare set of clothes, allowing him to lose the suit and tie he'd worn during the mad rush from London. The military seemed to have maintained its sense of efficiency, he told himself, and wondered how long that would last.

"I think so," he said, finally. He hadn't been able to shave and his cheeks felt rough with stubble. "Have we been discovered?"

"I don't think so," Butcher said. "But there have apparently been developments. I'll leave it to the Brigadier to brief you."

They walked down the concrete corridor and into the conference room. Most of the operators he remembered from last night were missing, their stations shut down and marked for destruction. In fact, the entire bunker complex seemed emptier than he recalled – even though he could hear the sound of people talking in low voices down the corridor. He assumed that they hadn't been detected – they would have fled the bunker if they had even *suspected* that the aliens knew where they were – but it was clear that something had changed. The Brigadier, when he made his appearance a moment later followed by a young soldier, looked deeply worried.

"Prime Minister," he said. "I'm afraid that there have been developments."

Gabriel listened carefully as the story of the Battle of London came pouring out of the young soldier. Two companies of British soldiers had fought and held the aliens for nearly an hour, before the aliens finally pushed through by brute force. London itself had been damaged in the crossfire, with at least one alien transport crash-landing in Central London. The thought was impossible to grasp – it just wasn't supposed to happen in Britain. Even the suicide bombers who'd killed far too many civilians on 7/7 hadn't even dreamed of causing so much pain.

"It gets worse," the Brigadier added. "I'm afraid that the aliens have found themselves a Petain."

He tapped a console and the recorded radio message played out, twice. Gabriel found himself listening with growing anger as Alan Beresford – an MP who had been implicated in a dozen scandals, yet nothing quite seemed to stick – recited the alien message to the British population. God alone knew what the public would make of it. They'd be frightened, isolated from the rest of the world, unsure of their place… far too many would simply grasp the straw Beresford was offering them. And the aliens themselves…

If Beresford was to be believed, their social development had not matched their technological development. But then, a case could be made that humanity's development hadn't matched its technology either. The aliens… they'd come, they'd seen and they'd conquered, with as little regard for the rights of mankind as Julius Caesar had shown to the barbarians he'd crushed beneath the heels of his legions. It was tempting to believe that Beresford was a liar – Gabriel wouldn't have believed that the sky was blue if Beresford had said it – but so far everything the aliens had done matched what he'd said. But then… if Nazi Germany had won World War Two, everyone would have been raised to believe that Nazism was right.

"My God," he said, finally. "What do we do about it?"

The Brigadier scowled. "The last reports have the aliens massing forces here, here and here," he said, tapping locations on the map. "I believe that they intend to advance westwards within the next few hours and scatter our forces before we can regroup and take the offensive. I'm afraid that we're going to have to put our emergency plan into operation before too long."

Gabriel nodded. "What do we have to do?"

"You're going to a secure location in the north – an old estate that belongs to a family that has been linked with the British Government for centuries," the Brigadier said. "It was always envisaged as the final resort – and so there haven't been any mentions of it on our computers or anywhere else. Butcher and his team will escort you there and then take care of you, once you've recorded a message for the civilians. You have to tell them that there's a government still out there fighting…"

"But won't that encourage them to fight themselves?" Gabriel asked. "Won't we just be prolonging the agony?"

"I wish I knew," the Brigadier admitted. "Back when I did a stint at Northwood, I saw some of the contingency plans and scenarios dreamed up by civil servants. They all tended to change depending upon the underlying assumptions, but I think we have to assume that the majority of the civilian population will not resist the invaders. But there's a fine line between not resisting and outright collaboration and… if they believe that there is a government left out there, fewer people will collaborate. I think that the aliens have to have limits on their manpower. Whatever their FTL drive, shipping millions of troops across interstellar distances cannot be cost-effective."

"And the fewer collaborators they have, the harder it will be for them to rule Earth," Gabriel said. The Brigadier nodded. "But what do they *want*?"

"If we take that traitorous bastard at his word, they think they have the right to rule everyone too weak to stand up to them," the Brigadier said. "Or maybe they have some other goal in being here that they're keeping to themselves – perhaps because they fear we could spite them in some way. Overall… we don't know what they want.

"The good news is that we managed to make contact with two of our missile boats," he added. "The aliens hit our submarine bases pretty hard, but we had three of the four boats at sea and two of them have been appraised of the situation. Using them may be tricky with the aliens controlling space, yet we do feel that there are possibilities. We've also managed to pull most of the tactical nukes from their storage bunkers and I've given orders to conceal them…"

"They are not to be used without my express permission," Gabriel said, sharply. The thought of nuclear war on British soil was horrifying. "I want you to make that clear to your officers."

"They know to keep them in reserve," the Brigadier said, flatly. "Overall, most of our deployed submarines – the attack submarines as well – seem to have survived. They may be usable in the future, but for the moment we have no firm plans."

He stood up. "We'll make a stand when they come west and give them a bloody nose, then fall back to prepared positions," he concluded. "And then most of the lads will go underground and carry on the fight. The aliens have ordered all military and police personnel to surrender themselves – they've clearly started putting the police to work, but no one thinks they intend to make use of the soldiers! It seems that they're already establishing detention camps near the cities. Most of the lads would sooner die than go into one of them."

"People of Britain," Gabriel said, twenty minutes later. It didn't sound good. Normally, back in Ten Downing Street, he would have had a speechwriter,

a make-up artist and a careful briefing on who was expected to be in the media crowd and what questions they might ask. He'd spent so much time preparing for speeches that it had often struck him that he'd done little else in his brief time as Prime Minister. And now… half the population would probably curse him as a man who'd fled, leaving them to face the aliens. "Our nation has been invaded."

He took a breath. "I won't lie to you," he continued. He'd wanted to be honest in his speeches, but the crowd of advisers had warned that too much blunt speaking could backfire. The public seemed to believe that politicians were always liars, yet they elected men who made them feel good about themselves – instead of telling them the truth. At least now he could go with his instincts. "The situation is dire. Many of our cities have been invaded directly; others have lost power and water supplies. Anarchy is threatening to grip our streets.

"Many of you will be frightened. Many of you will wonder if we can resist the aliens, or even if we *should* resist the aliens. Others will seek to take advantage of the chaos for their own benefit. I know that many of you will be looking to safeguard your families and friends, rather than thinking about the welfare of the country. I cannot blame you for worrying about your own lives, or those of your friends and families. The entire country has suffered a devastating blow. Our world has been turned upside down.

"But Britain has a long and proud history of resisting tyranny. It was us who stood alone against Nazi Germany, though we were bombed and half-starved and suffered defeat after defeat. We played a full part in the containment of Communist Russia, preventing general war from engulfing Europe for the third time. We stood firm against Napoleon when he threatened to invade our shores. The situation is dire, but it is not hopeless. We can fight back against the latest invaders.

"The British Government has survived and it will carry on the fight as long as possible," he concluded. "I will not order you to resist – I want you to decide for yourselves. If you wish to stand up and fight for Britain, for the freedom of our island nation, join us in resisting the enemy. Take care of yourselves, plan carefully – and hit them as hard as you can. There will be many dark days ahead, days where we can assume nothing, but blood, toil, tears and sweat, but there will come a day when we live freely in our own land once again."

He tapped the switch, ending the recording. "Very good, Prime Minister," Linux said. "I'll have it online tonight, once this bunker has been evacuated. The entire world will hear your speech…"

Gabriel frowned. "But the aliens will try to wipe it from the internet," he pointed out. Their jamming had certainly prevented any attempt to reclaim the airwaves. "How can we stop them purging it before it reaches its intended audience?"

"Leave that to me," Linux said. "There are thousands of people on the internet who devised all kinds of programs to share files – despite the best that governments and big corporations could do to stop it. We'll get your message to the world – after that, it's all up to them."

"Thank you," Gabriel said. He wanted to ask what would happen to the young soldier, but the words wouldn't form in his mouth. How could he ask anyone to fight for Britain when he was going to run away and hide?

Butcher cleared his throat. "Prime Minister?" He said. "It's time to go."

"Understood," Gabriel said. He hesitated for a moment, and then nodded. "Let's go."

The climb back up into the open air made him feel oddly claustrophobic. It was a relief when they finally reached the surface and emerged in the midst of a small group of armed soldiers. Butcher spoke to them briefly, and then led the way northwards through the woods. Gabriel could hear the sound of birds chirping in the distance, ignoring the presence of human soldiers in their habitats. Their lives would go on regardless of who ruled the planet. He looked up into the bright blue sky and shivered. There was something impossibly surreal about the whole scene.

"The scouts reported refugees gathering to the north," Butcher said, as they reached a civilian car that had obviously been commandeered by the military. "We'll try to give them a wide berth. The aliens don't seem to care about civilian vehicles, but I think that will change once they realise that we've been using them to ship men around under their noses."

Gabriel opened his mouth to ask why *they* were using a civilian car, before realising that there was no other choice. He couldn't have made it to the north on foot. The SAS men were used to walking for miles in a single day, but *he'd* just slow them down. They had to rely on the car and hope that the aliens didn't start blasting vehicles at random.

He glanced over towards the east. No plumes of smoke marred the sky, but he knew that the aliens were present – and planning their offensive. He wondered how many people still didn't realise what had happened, or what was going on – there had to be entire communities that hadn't had any contact with the aliens. No matter how advanced they were, he couldn't see how they intended to occupy every last town and village on the planet. If he was in their shoes, how would *he* do it? Target America, Europe, Russia and China… and let the rest of the world collapse into chaos?

And how long could Gabriel accept his people suffering while he hid from their new masters?

Chapter Eleven

Long Stratton
United Kingdom, Day 2

For a moment, Alex was half-convinced that she'd been having a nightmare. She lay in a comfortable bed, so comfortable that she wanted to return to slumber. Instead, she opened her eyes and beheld an unfamiliar room. It reminded her of the room she'd shared with her boyfriend back when they'd gone on vacation together, right down to the sunlight streaming in through the window. The presence of her pistol where she'd left it within easy reach brought her back to reality. Her country had been invaded and it was her duty to report in to superior authority – or carry on the fight alone, if possible.

The scent of frying bacon from downstairs made her stomach rumble and she pulled herself out of bed. Smith had brought her back to the farm and convinced her to remain for a day or two, just to see what happened. Who knew – perhaps someone would succeed in finding a way to drive the invaders away from Earth. Alex, who knew that such things only happened in bad movies, was much less optimistic. The farmland surrounding her seemed too mundane to be touched by the aliens, but the fireworks in the sky told her that the world had changed. God alone knew what was going to happen next.

Smith's wife – who'd turned out to be called Jean – had loaned her a dress and a shirt that was only a size or two too big for her. Alex pulled it on anyway; her uniform had been growing increasingly rank and it would only attract attention when – if – she set out to contact higher authority. There was no way to know what the roads would be like, or how many people would be fleeing the cities for the countryside now that the world had turned upside down. The modern RAF had never designed contingency plans for regrouping after an invasion of the British mainland. It had never even been a serious possibility.

She went to the toilet, splashed water on her face, and headed down the stairs towards the kitchen. Jean was already hard at work, frying what looked like bacon, eggs and potatoes in a massive frying pan. It looked wonderfully unhealthy, just the kind of food she'd eaten back home, when she hadn't been worrying about her weight. Whatever else could be said about life in the military, it ensured that soldiers, sailors and airmen got plenty of exercise. There weren't many fat personnel until one reached the higher levels of military leadership.

"Take one of the plates and pass it over to me," Jean ordered. "I've pulled you some fresh milk, straight from the cow. You'll have to learn to milk her for herself if you live longer – it's one of those experiences no one ever tells the city-folk until they come out here and stay with us."

Alex took the milk with some trepidation. "Is it safe to drink?"

"Of course it is," Jean said. "Of course, those bureaucrats think otherwise – and they do have a point, if the milkman isn't very careful. But no one here wants to go down in history as the farm that got a few hundred people killed. If those aliens" – she pronounced the word with a snort, as if she didn't quite believe it – "happen to kill all of those interfering meddlers who know nothing, plenty of people round here will raise a glass in their honour."

Alex frowned, sipping the milk. "But isn't that a bit disloyal…?"

Jean snorted, again. "You seem to think that the government is always a good thing," she said. "Do you know how much red tape we have to jump through, every year? Government seems determined to bury us in red tape and endless paperwork. Dear God – there have been years where I've seriously considered just urging the man to walk away from the farm. No one seems to *want* us to do anything, but fill in forms. You can't make a man a farmer by sending him to impractical courses run by people who aren't farmers…"

She shook her head. "I won't miss the government, young lady," she added. "And I think that many people here will feel the same way."

There was a hiss as she turned a pair of rashers over, and then piled them onto a plate with potatoes and eggs. "Eat up," she said, cheerfully. "As far as anyone knows, you're one of the city-folk who booked a holiday with us so you could experience life on a farm. You're going to have a busy day ahead of you."

Alex ate slowly, savouring the natural taste of the bacon and fresh eggs. She didn't mind working on the farm – for all she knew, money was worthless right now – but she knew that she couldn't stay for long. The farm would probably soon be visited by the aliens, who'd want food for themselves – if they could eat human crops. Alex was fairly sure that they'd like Earth as a new home; they wouldn't have bothered to invade if Earth was useless to them. Unless they were just nasty bastards, of course – and that was quite possible. They certainly hadn't bothered to demand surrender before they started shooting.

She tossed the thought around her head as she ate, trying to guess what the aliens would do next. There was no way to know. The last messages she'd seen on the internet reported that the aliens were securing London, Manchester, Birmingham and a number of other cities. There had been clashes between their forces and human mobs, clashes that had gone very badly for the humans. Somehow, Alex wasn't surprised. The aliens seemed to prefer brute force to anything more subtle and nothing stamped one's authority on a situation like brute force – provided that there was enough brute force, of course. But the aliens controlled space. They could lose control of large parts of Earth and still win the war. Hell, for all she knew, they were deliberately provoking humans to attack them so they could wipe out potential resistance fighters before they could get organised.

"Ann and Sue dropped in this morning," Jean said, as Alex was chasing the last of the egg around her plate with a slice of bread. "They left their home yesterday and camped out before making the rest of the drive here. Ann had to pay for petrol the old-fashioned way, damn it. Maybe the aliens can do something about the price of fuel while they're at it."

Alex frowned. The old-fashioned way? It took her a moment to realise that Ann had probably had to go down on the petrol station's owner to get fuel for her car. The thought was sickening, but it was probably only a taste of the future. If the aliens had blocked off supplies of fuel as well as food, the civilian population would lose its mobility very quickly – once the rest of the fuel ran out. The RAF had had stockpiles of aviation fuel for its aircraft, but the aliens might have destroyed it. And that would leave what remained of the RAF permanently grounded.

"Maybe they can," she agreed. "What did they say about the roads?"

"The aliens have been broadcasting orders for people to stay off the main roads," Jean said. "Speaking of which" – she clicked the radio and music started to echo out – "listen to this. Someone will start speaking in a moment…"

"People of Britain, my name is Alan Beresford and I am the sole remaining member of the British Government…"

Alex listened in disbelief as the message played out and then started to repeat. She knew of Alan Beresford by reputation – no military officer could afford to be a virgin where politics were concerned – and she knew that he wasn't well-regarded, but outright treachery? The message played again and again, before music started to fill the airwaves once again. Maybe Alan Beresford believed that there was no way to resist the aliens, or maybe he'd just seen a chance for advancement and taken it. There was no way to know for sure.

"That bastard," she said, finally. "He's sold us out to them!"

"So it would seem," Jean agreed. She picked up Alex's plate and stuck it in the sink. "Go wash your hands and then report to the man outside. He'll keep you busy until lunchtime."

Alex nodded and obeyed. The next three hours were an education. She'd never realised how much had to be done each day on a farm, from mucking out the pigs – who eyed her with disconcerting eyes – to rubbing down the horses. Smith explained that they also made money by renting out their horses to a nearby riding school, which had ties to a college for young ladies that specialised in turning their brains into mush. Alex had never thought much about horses, but it seemed that the young girls honestly had no idea how to treat them when they finally got to ride on their backs. Some of the horses were very docile, even with young and inexperienced riders; others seemed nasty, including a big black horse that eyed her balefully.

"Stalin there won't allow himself to be ridden," Smith commented. Somehow, Alex found it difficult to turn her back on the horse. Stalin – a play on words, she realised after a moment – seemed to be waiting for a moment to kick her or trample her into the ground. "Someone treated him very badly, poor thing, and he's been good for nothing apart from breeding ever since. A couple of people have tried to ride him and always come off worst."

"I'm surprised he wasn't put down," Alex said. Horses… but then, jet aircraft could be temperamental too. Too many missions had had to be aborted because multimillion pounds worth of equipment had failed at the wrong time. "Isn't he a danger to everyone?"

"No kids around here," Smith said, "and the wife and I know better than to relax around him."

He shrugged. "After lunch, do you want to go see old Nathan Archer? He was saying that there's something he wants you to see. The Parish Council meeting last night rather impressed him."

Alex looked at him, sideways. "*Should* I go?"

Smith snorted. "Nathan's a harmless old man," he said. "He used to run a large farm, but much of it got sold off in the seventies, leaving him with just a couple of fields. His wife died years ago and his kids never visit. I think he'd be glad of the company."

"I'll go then," Alex decided. "Are we going to have lunch now?"

"Hungry?" Smith asked. He laughed. "I hear the same from everyone who stays here – and no, it isn't lunchtime yet. We've barely begun to work."

He was still chuckling as they walked over to the field. "But you're not doing too badly, not like some of the visitors," he added. "We'll make a farmer out of you yet."

<hr>

Nathan Archer's farmhouse looked older than Smith's farmhouse, although Alex wasn't entirely sure why she had that impression. It was a long low building, with a large door and roses growing up the side of the house. Most of the windows looked too small for their positions, almost like portholes in the side of a ship. A pair of heavy axes had been nailed above the doors, reminding her of some of the decorations she'd seen in Afghanistan. They looked securely fastened, but she nipped under them as quickly as possible. She tapped on the door and waited. It was several minutes before Archer opened the door and peered out at her.

"Welcome to my home," he said. His accent was more rustic than Smith's accent, suggesting that he didn't spend much time watching the television. "Did you come alone?"

Alex tensed at the question, despite the pistol concealed within her jacket. "Yes," she said, finally. "I only told Farmer Smith where I was going…"

"Smith can keep a secret," Archer said. He picked up a stick, closed the door and hobbled out around the house. Alex heard the sound of dogs barking as they rounded the house and came up to a small fence marking out the rear garden. A small army of dogs were yapping away, some large enough to make her glad that she was carrying the pistol. She didn't recognise half of the breeds, but then she'd never been a dog fancier. Cats were far less trouble to keep. "Down boys, now!"

Alex watched in some amazement as the dogs sat down, their tongues lolling out of their mouths as if they were exhausted. "I used to be able to take them for walks every day," Archer explained, "but I can't do that now and I can't bear to give them away. I just have to let them have the run of the garden and hope that they don't make too much of a mess."

He led her over towards a barn, standing alone in the middle of a field. "I was a young farmer of nineteen when the war started," he said. Alex took a sharp look at him, realising that he was talking about the Second World War – just like the person she'd met at the Parish Council. That would make

him over ninety years old, surely. "I volunteered for service at once, only to be told that I was in an essential occupation. The young men of the parish called me coward as they marched away and I bloodied my fists on many of their faces."

His mouth opened in a crooked smile. "We were all so much more *vital* back then," he added. "None of this self-obsessed whining of the modern generation – we worked, we knew where we stood, we knew that we were responsible for ourselves. And there was no embarrassment over fighting to defend our country from the Hun. A quarter of the map was coloured pink and we loved it. All those whiners who say we shouldn't have had an empire never understood what it was like to have pride. Now, no one has any loyalty to their country.

"But I'd registered when I'd volunteered and they found a job for me," he said. "Everyone knew that it was just a matter of time before that little German Corporal led his dragoons over to England. They started preparing for war – for a war that would still continue even if the Germans occupied London and banished the King to Canada. And farmers like me were given a secret role to play when the Germans had defeated the army and believed themselves secure."

They reached the barn. Archer pulled an old set of keys out of his pocket and opened the padlock, pushing the doors open wide enough to allow light to stream into the confined spaces. It was empty, the floor covered with decaying straw and pieces of animal waste. Alex wrinkled her nose at the smell, before Archer pushed her to one side and started digging through the piles of straw. It struck her that something was concealed *under* the barn, something that might have lain in hiding for a very long time…

"They told us to keep it safe," Archer said. There was a click as he found a hidden board of wood in the floor and pulled it up. A few moments of struggling revealed a hatch neatly hidden, one that he had problems lifting alone. Alex walked over and helped him to pull the hatch all the way up, revealing a darkened space under the barn. Archer pulled out a small electric torch and shone it down into the darkness, revealing a number of bundles that looked as if they hadn't been touched for years. "First there was the Nazis, and then there were the Communists – oh yes, we were worried about them. I always believed that they would come and recover the dump's contents, but the government never bothered to come pick it up."

Alex stared at him, and then back down into the chamber. "How long has this been here?"

"Some of it has been here since 1940," Archer said, with some pride. "We had some changed during 1944 when we got new equipment from America – and some more got changed during the 1950s. And then the officials stopped visiting and we just kept on taking care of it. And it has never been touched."

"My God," Alex said. Now that he'd reminded her, she recalled a case where one such dump had been discovered fifty-odd years after the war. The farmer who had been charged with taking care of it, knowing that he was growing older, had contacted the police, who'd reported it to the army. Only in Britain could an entire repository of weapons and explosives meant for an underground resistance have been forgotten through bureaucratic oversight. But of course they wouldn't have wanted records. They would have led the Germans – who had disarmed their subject peoples as a matter of course – right to the cache. "What… what are you going to do with it?"

Archer let the hatch fall back down. "I'm really too old to feel that I have much to lose," he said. "The country has been invaded, young lady, and I took an oath to carry on the fight even if the government has been destroyed or forced to surrender. I intend to fight and I expect that you will fight with me against the bastards."

There was no give in his voice. Alex nodded, slowly. He was right; there was little hope of linking up with what remained of her unit, but she could carry on the fight. Maybe they were doomed, maybe the aliens could defeat them with ease… she shook her head. They had to fight.

It was the only hope of freedom.

"Very well," she said. "How many others know about this?"

"Not many," Archer said, "but enough to start a small army. And then we can teach them that humans don't come cheap!"

Chapter Twelve

Near Salisbury Plain
United Kingdom, Day 2

"Coming through clear as day, sir," the technician reported. "It seems that the Yanks were right and the bastards can't track microburst transmissions."

Brigadier Gavin Lightbridge-Stewart nodded. They hadn't been able to pull much information from the ongoing war in the United States, but the Americans had apparently had some success with stealth aircraft and UAVs. The SAS had been loaned a Shadow Hawk UAV by the CIA to support British troops operating in the Middle East and it had survived the bombardment of British bases across the mainland. It was currently orbiting high over Basingstoke, watching the alien land forces heading west, and relaying what it saw to the mobile command post.

A small alien detachment had apparently been ordered to lay siege to Reading, with alien troops taking up positions on the roads and discouraging civilians from escaping by firing over their heads. Despite that, a vast number of refugees had managed to leave the cities and towns and were currently scattered all over the area, often causing confusion and delays for the British military. The aliens seemed to have fewer problems, if only because their standard response to anyone trying to get in their way was to open fire. Their hover-tanks – or so the young soldiers on the front lines had dubbed them – seemed to combine the armour of a Challenger tank with the speed and agility of a far lighter vehicle. It hadn't escaped Gavin's sense of irony that they'd overrun Woking with terrifying speed. If their infantry hadn't been slower than their tankers, they might well have crushed the remaining British defences before they'd had time to regroup.

Part of his mind mulled over what the alien technology and observed capabilities seemed to suggest about their motives. They'd come as an army of occupation and they'd obviously come loaded for bear, but they seemed to lack the flexibility that every Western army tried to drill into its personnel. They seemed to have poor coordination between the armour and infantry, a problem that had caused many defeats in human history. In fact, given a level playing field – with no orbiting starships ready to drop rocks on their heads – he was sure that the 1st Armoured Division would have hammered the aliens. Their coordination between their aircraft, their ground forces and their spacecraft was surprisingly limited. It all suggested book-learning, rather than actual experience – and yet they were clearly experienced at taking control of their conquests. The speed with which they'd found collaborators and pressed them into service proved that beyond all doubt. It was all very odd.

But I bet the armies of Oliver Cromwell or King Charles would have had some problems understanding what we do as a matter of course, he thought, wryly. Maybe the logistics of an interstellar power worked differently to those on Earth. There were seven *billion* humans on the planet, but for all he knew the aliens had seven billion soldiers and the ability to deploy them to Earth. He rather hoped not, yet it remained a possibility.

"Contact the advance parties," he ordered. At least they'd been able to set up some limited signalling capabilities. The aliens struck the source of any transmission very quickly, but his men had set up a series of expendable transmitters. "Tell them that they are cleared to engage at will."

"I got the signal, boss," one of the soldiers outside the Challenger II tank said. "The enemy are on their way."

"Understood," the Commander said. He'd never anticipated fighting an all-out war in the heart of the English countryside, but he was damned if he and his tank were to be found wanting when the shit hit the fan. "You lot had better scarper. We'll be along presently."

His tank and a handful of others had been involved in the exercises when the aliens had announced their presence by bombarding the garrisons around Salisbury Plain. Shocked and horrified, he'd rallied his men and reported in to the remaining military command structure and had been ordered to take up a position watching the A342. They'd used their remaining fuel getting there – it had been a nightmarish journey – but they'd made it. He now scanned the horizon waiting for the first alien tanks to come into view. They seemed to like human roads.

Absently, he patted the side of his Challenger. Pound for pound, the Challenger had a fair claim to being one of the best Main Battle Tanks in the world – when tested, during the invasion of Iraq, they'd performed brilliantly. As they were unable to retreat, he'd had his position heavily camouflaged and the tank's engine switched off, leaving them – hopefully – undetectable. If they were wrong – if they'd been tracked during the night – they'd probably die before they knew what had hit them.

Suddenly, much faster than he'd expected, he saw the first alien tank heading up the motorway. He studied it with considerable interest, noting that it didn't seem to have been designed to face a modern environment. Their armour hadn't been much better than anything in the human arsenal, according to the reports from London, and it didn't look as if they'd designed it to deflect incoming fire. Maybe they only ever faced handguns, he considered, or perhaps they rarely had to go one-on-one with enemy tankers. Or maybe… he shook his head. There was no time for speculation.

"Take aim," he ordered, quietly. They'd get one shot, maybe two, and then they'd have to run for it. Their escorts had left a few surprises down below for the alien infantry when they finally came into view, but they wouldn't be able to survive rocks dropped from orbit. "On my command, fire and then switch to the next target."

"Understood, boss," the gunner said. The tank's heavy main gun rotated as it locked onto its target. "Ready when you are…"

"Fire," the Commander barked. The Challenger shook as it fired a single shell towards the enemy tank. "Reload and…"

The enemy tank went up in a colossal fireball. "Good shot," the Commander said, sharply. "Take aim… fire!"

A second enemy tank died, followed rapidly by a third. The fourth enemy tank returned fire, hurling a shell that went safely over their heads and came down somewhere in the distance. They ignored the chance to take out a fourth enemy target and climbed out of their vehicle, running for dear life. Another explosion shook the world around them as the enemy tank zeroed in on its target. The Commander felt a moment of contempt. He understood the rationale behind firing back as quickly as possible, but a *human* force wouldn't have missed so many times. The aliens were out of practice…

He heard a whistling and then the world seemed to explode behind him, the force of the blast picking him up and hurling him into the ground at terrifying speed. His last thought was the brief hope that some of his crew might have escaped…

"Get moving, you idiots," *Tra'tro* The'Stig shouted. The thrice-damned humans had shot up one of the infantry's personnel carriers and instead of disembarking and taking the fight to their foes, the infantry unit inside was cowering. They'd never been under fire before, even in the exercises, but that was no excuse. "Get out before they hit you again!"

He cursed the humans again as the infantry unit finally started to disembark, half of them forgetting their training and looking as if they wanted to retreat at once. The humans had shown a positive *gift* for preparing the ground, with nasty traps and snipers scattered everywhere. If one of those human snipers happened to see a few dozen infantry without enough protection, he could wreak havoc without fear of retaliation.

"Get moving," he yelled, again, pointing them towards the small cluster of large human buildings on the outskirts of a small town. The humans had hidden a small team there and if they moved quickly, they might manage to catch and kill the vermin before they escaped. Small human teams had hit the advancing force, inflicted some kills and then broken off, obviously trying to bleed the assault units without risking themselves unduly. "Kill the *Karna*-spawned devils before they kill you!"

A streak of lights fell to the ground some distance from their position, followed rapidly by a series of explosions that shook the world around him. The humans had made a stand – but in making a stand, they'd revealed their own location. At least they had no means to avoid bombardment from orbit, or the assault unit might have been chewed to ribbons before it finally broke through the human defences.

He led the charge at the human building, relying on speed to protect him from any human fire. Some of the infantry unit followed him, holding their own weapons at the ready, while others seemed stuck and unwilling to proceed further. The'Stig cursed their cowardice in the face of the humans, even as he tried to restrain some of the others from charging onwards. One of them ran through a doorway that seemed too large for mere humans, detonating a trap hidden within the building. His body was flung backwards and he landed on the ground, torn to bloody ribbons.

"You can't trust anything human," he snarled, angrily. A human vehicle seemed to be heading away from them, probably carrying the human soldiers who had stung his people so badly. He pointed his weapon at the vehicle and fired off a long stream of bullets, watching as they slashed through the human vehicle and killed its passengers. "Keep an eye on where you're walking – and don't relax, ever!"

The fighting seemed to be slacking off, but he knew that it was far from the end. They hadn't beaten the humans at all, not really – they'd fallen back to new positions they'd prepared for the next engagement. He wanted to know what was happening with the other assault units, but there was no way to know – it wasn't as if the Command Triad was going to bother to brief an ordinary infantry soldier. Rumour, however, suggested that there was fighting going on all over Earth. At least the humans would burn through their stockpiles of advanced weapons sooner rather than later. But of course they'd know that themselves…

He wanted to relax, but he didn't dare, not when so many units had been mangled together. It crossed his mind that he had probably shown that he deserved promotion – not that anyone would have noticed. The commanders who should have been watching their troops for potential officers were either at the rear or had gotten themselves killed heroically. He wondered, absently, if the humans had the same problem. Maybe they weren't so alien after all.

———

"Dirty murdering bastards," Corporal Tommy O'Neill muttered to himself. From his vantage point, he could watch helplessly as an alien patrol stumbled over a group of human refugees – and murdered them in cold blood. The humans hadn't even tried to fight, but it hadn't mattered. They'd been shot down and their bodies left abandoned on the side of the road. "Dirty fucking filthy murdering bastards."

He hadn't known that the refugees were there either, until two of them had started to run. No doubt they'd thought that they were well-hidden, unaware that the war was about to break right over their hiding place. He cursed his own oversight as he prepared himself for the coming engagement, promising to make the aliens pay for what they'd done. Civilians tended to shy away from soldiers, at least in his experience, but it was his duty to protect them. And if he couldn't protect them, he would at least avenge them.

It had taken several hours to lay the trap and it looked perfect, at least unless the aliens decided to start shooting human vehicles up at random. But even aliens from outer space had to have logistic needs; the briefing they'd received on the battle in London and other brief engagements between human and alien forces suggested that there was nothing magical about their weapons. They shot projectiles, just like human guns. Some of the troopers

had wondered why the aliens – who could clearly cross space with ease – would limit themselves, but Tommy suspected that he knew the answer. Their weapons would be far simpler than directed energy ray guns right out of science-fiction. He smiled, feeling a moment of kinship with the aliens before it faded away. No doubt they'd had 'wonder-weapons' devised by boffins and tested in laboratories that hadn't worked anything like so well in the field too.

He reached for the detonator as the aliens passed the single abandoned vehicle. Gambling that they wouldn't know how to inspect the human-designed car, he'd stuffed it with explosives and laid a cord to the detonator, which he'd placed near his vantage point. Uncapping the safety, he waited until one of the alien tanks was right next to the car and jammed down on the button. The results surprised even him. A colossal explosion flipped the enemy tank right over and literally vaporised most of the alien infantry. The remainder looked stunned and disorientated. Tommy allowed himself a tight smile and picked up his rifle. A new alien patrol was advancing towards their stricken comrades, watching carefully for any more traps. Tommy took aim and opened fire. The lead alien staggered backwards, inhuman blood flowing from its forehead, while the remainder opened fire in Tommy's general direction.

Poor shooting, he thought, as he moved to the next target. The aliens seemed to be learning quickly, although they seemed oddly reluctant to take cover. It took Tommy a moment to realise that they were scared of other booby traps, which was a crying shame – he hadn't had time to set up any more. He fired a final shot and started to crawl backwards. He had already marked out an escape route back to the RV point and he intended to be gone before the aliens gave chase. And if they didn't… well, that was good too.

———

"Go."

Captain Danny Jackson knew that he was lucky to be alive. He and his wingman had been on exercises with the British Army when their base at Middle Wallop had been destroyed by the aliens. As far as he knew, the two Apache helicopters they were flying were the last in Britain – perhaps the last in the world. There had been some Apache helicopters in Afghanistan – although never enough – but the aliens had probably clobbered them too. Danny couldn't do anything for his mates who were either dead or trying to fight their way out of a country that was probably swinging back under Taliban control, yet he *could* try to avenge them.

The two Apaches had been flown under cover of darkness to a location where they'd been hidden under camouflage netting, awaiting their chance to take the offensive. It seemed that they were about to get their chance; the aliens were shipping in more ground forces as they attempted to push their occupied zone further to the west. They were also shipping in armour – the direct feed from the orbiting UAV reported that there were at least fifty hover-tanks heading west – but the pilots had been given clear orders. Their principle targets were the alien troop carriers. If they were really lucky, they would kill a great many aliens who hadn't realised that the safety offered by their vehicles was really nothing more than an illusion.

He took control of his aircraft and pulled her into the sky. There were no illusions about their chances of surviving the battle, but they were going to be operating right on top of the enemy forces. Surely, the aliens wouldn't call in orbital strikes that would be dangerously close to their own forces. Or perhaps they would. Humans had done all kinds of horrible things to other humans in their long history and why shouldn't the aliens do the same? What cause did humanity have to complain?

Because they're not human, he thought, wryly. *And because we didn't pick a fight with them.*

They flew low and fast, only coming up above the treetops when the alien troops came into view. Danny didn't give them any time to recover from their surprise; he took the Apache in a firing run right over the alien position, allowing his gunner to unleash hell on the aliens. There was no time to aim properly, but it hardly mattered – the only targets on the ground were hostile. Hellfire missiles slammed into alien troop carriers, while the chain gun raked down entire columns of alien soldiers. He yanked the helicopter upwards as an alien-launched missile lanced by them with bare meters to spare. Part of his mind noted that the aliens hadn't keyed their missiles for proximity detonation, an odd oversight. Human missiles were capable of detonating close to their targets and taking them out with shrapnel.

An alien helicopter came into view, looking rather like a larger version of the Apache. It opened fire on the two British craft, launching a spread of missiles towards them. Danny retaliated by launching a Sidewinder – the only one they had – and deploying flares in the hope of decoying the alien missiles. The alien missiles were fooled long enough for him to take them low and fast away from the ambush sight, hopefully heading for a place where they could set down. They might not be able to rearm and resume the attack – if there were any more Hellfire missiles in Britain, they were probably misplaced – but they might escape with their lives…

He cursed as his threat receiver lit up. An alien missile crew had fired a missile from directly below them and it was climbing right up their tailpipe. There was no time to escape; the alien missile struck the Apache's armour and blasted through into the compartment beyond. And the world went away in a blast of red-hot fire.

Chapter Thirteen

London/Near Salisbury Plain
United Kingdom, Day 2

"What in the name of the seven hells is happening?"

Ju'tro Oheghizh stared down at his updating display. The damned humans simply didn't know when they were beaten. Any sensible race would have sought to come to terms with its new masters by now, but the humans kept fighting – even threatening to kill their fellows who didn't have a modicum of sense in their heads. The advancing Land Force spearheads, convinced that they were mopping up the remains of the human military force, were being ambushed and forced back with chilling regularity. And the humans didn't even stick around long enough for his starships to pound their positions into dust.

"They don't have many resources left to throw at us," *J'tra* Mak'kat pointed out. He'd served with Oheghizh in previous campaigns and didn't bother to mince his words. The State didn't approve of officers being too familiar with their subordinates, but Oheghizh found it hard to care. "They're burning up what they have left rather than abandon it. And many of our troopers haven't been in combat before. They're making mistakes through simple unfamiliarity with the alien landscape."

Oheghizh couldn't disagree. In hindsight, it was clear that the humans – who hadn't started uniting themselves, unlike almost every other race in their stage of development – had plenty of experience fighting each other. The sociologists were still trying to discover exactly *why* the humans hadn't advanced into space, but it was clear that space-based forces hadn't played a significant role in their internal struggling. They'd have had a much better appreciation of how badly they were outmatched if they had, he told himself, although it was a case of not being grateful enough for what they had. A space-faring race would have been a far tougher morsel to digest.

"Order our forces to take extra care," he said, slowly. "And pass me the figures on their advanced weapons. Let me see what they have left."

The planners were right about one thing, he thought, as he studied the figures and compared them to their projections. It was clear that the humans *were* running out of advanced weaponry. Their tanks were holding their ground rather than falling back – as their own tactical doctrine ordered – and the advancing spearheads were reporting fewer and fewer contacts with human armour. The aircraft backing up the ground forces, after a handful of embarrassing losses, reported that the humans had been reduced to deploying portable antiaircraft weapons rather than the sophisticated weapons they'd deployed in the opening hours of the invasion. And soon enough they'd run out of those too.

He watched through a set of advancing sensors as yet another human habitation was carefully explored. The humans had a whole series of unpleasant surprises for the troopers that first entered their dwellings – and a nasty sense of humour. He didn't want to think about the hundreds of injured or dead troopers that would have to be reported to the Command Triad. They would look down from high overhead, see the amount of casualties he'd suffered taking a relatively small area, and draw unpleasant comparisons with the Land Forces in the region the humans called the Middle East. It was hardly *his* fault that the terrain in the desert was far better suited for land warfare – and that the humans there seemed to have no idea of how to fight properly.

It could be worse, he told himself, dryly. The Chinese humans, after what looked like a successful opening strike to the invasion, had fired nuclear rockets at their own cities to destroy as many Land Force units as possible. Most of their primitive missiles had been knocked down by point defence units, but a handful had got through the network – and several more tactical nuclear weapons had been deployed by enemy ground forces. They didn't seem to care about the suffering they were inflicting on their own people, or the fact that they just couldn't win. At least the humans in Europe and America seemed smart enough to refrain from using nuclear weapons. The Conquest Fleet had gone to considerable trouble to decapitate the enemy command and control systems to prevent one or all of them authorising a nuclear strike.

Or they could be waiting for us to get into position, he thought, grimly. *Who knows what these humans will do?*

———

Yunt Ra'Sha watched in astonishment as humans fled their habitations, swallowing down the urge to hurry them on their way with a few rounds from his cannon. They'd been told to try to avoid engaging humans who weren't part of their military, but how was a lowly *Yunt* meant to tell the difference? Some of the smaller humans were clearly younglings, yet they seemed willing to throw rocks at the invasion force – and their seniors had all kinds of nasty surprises up their sleeves. His unit was still reeling after the death of their commander – killed by a human who'd driven a vehicle right into his position. They'd killed the human, but that hadn't brought their commander back.

"Ugly creatures," one of his fellows muttered. It was true. The humans seemed to half-run, half-walk wherever they went… and they were covered in fur! At least they had the decency to wear clothing rather than show off their strange bodies, moving in ways that no civilised race could ever duplicate. "We should just kill them all and leave their bodies piled up high."

"Better not let Ha'She hear you say that," Ra'Sha said. Orders were orders – and the lowly sluggers who did most of the work weren't allowed to question their orders. "He thinks he's officer material, the fool. Just because his father has a medium-ranked position in an industrial combine he thinks he walks on water. Maybe the humans will kill him and that will be an end to it."

He braced himself as they advanced on the first human dwelling, a two-story house surrounded by an oddly-shaped garden. The houses they built were too small for him to feel comfortable, even the rooms that were large enough to house a fully-grown trooper. They just made him feel claustrophobic, even restrained – while the damned humans had complete freedom of action. The beasts could nip down corridors that were too thin for him and set up their next ambushes by the time they finally reached their lair. And then they'd just keep falling back, and back…

They'll run out of country soon, he told himself firmly, trying not to think about some of the injuries he'd seen on the other wounded. The humans seemed to prefer to wound rather than kill, although some of the wounds he'd seen would probably have killed a grown human. But then, they didn't have any experience with other races. They were probably still thinking in terms of killing their fellows, rather than bigger tougher aliens with excellent medical technology. He snorted at his own thoughts as he slipped up to the human house and peered through the glass window. If he started thinking so deeply, he'd probably qualify for officer material himself. Not that there was any hope of promotion, of course. The officers looked after their own first and foremost, with newcomers only accepted if they were a cut above the rest. And all *he* wanted was to survive the war and return home in time for mating season.

The interior of the human habitation looked empty, but he threw an explosive pack inside, just in case. It exploded with a satisfying flash and he leapt inside, holding his weapon at the ready as he scanned for threats. There was nothing, apart from piles of smashed furniture and a handful of fires. He ignored the heat and checked the rest of the house, pushing his way up tiny staircases that creaked alarmingly under his weight, and allowed himself a moment of relief when he found nothing. The remainder of the patrol inched outside and waited for him. There was still the rest of the human village…

They checked two more houses before coming up on what looked like a human shop. Small piles of canned food lay everywhere, suggesting that the population had made a hasty departure. He caught sight of a half-opened packet of meat and had to resist the urge to taste it. The scientists swore blind that there was nothing on Earth that could kill them – at least they could eat everything the humans could eat – but it might have caused him to fall sick. And the penalties for rendering oneself unfit for combat were severe…

"Look," May'tha said, pointing to a large white container. It was smaller than the smallest member of the patrol, but it was clearly large enough to hold an adult human – maybe two, if they were very friendly. Adult Eridian didn't like being crammed so close together, yet the humans seemed to enjoy it – at least if the sociologists' interpretation of some of their videos was accurate. Or maybe they were nothing more than the human version of sexual movies. He'd enjoyed watching many of them when his childhood scales had started to fall off, revealing the adult skin below. "Do you think one of them could be hiding there?"

Ra'Sha reached for the handle, lifting his weapon into firing position. The reports from some of the other units had claimed that the humans were very good at concealing themselves – aided by the fact that they were smaller than the average Eridian. It was quite possible that one of their soldiers was hiding inside, waiting for the right moment to come out of hiding and attack them from the rear. He caught hold of the handle, pulled it open…

…And the world went away in a wash of fire.

———

"Well, damn me," Chris Drake muttered to himself, from where he'd been watching events. "I wasn't sure if that was going to work."

The aliens seemed to be learning – and they were moving faster as they realised that the British defenders were running out of tanks and antiaircraft weapons. They didn't seem to be learning as quickly as British and American forces had done in Afghanistan – indeed, there was still an oddly-robotic aspect to their performance – but they were definitely learning. He smiled at the fire in the distance before he started to crawl backwards. That alien patrol would never have a chance to report its findings to superior authority. The aliens seemed to be tougher than humans, but he doubted that any of them had survived the explosion. He'd gone to some trouble to ensure that the blast would be as nasty as possible.

There were no more aliens in the town, as far as he knew, but he kept to the shadows as he ran westwards. The RV point wasn't far away, yet there was no way to know how long it would be before they pulled out, leaving anyone who hadn't made it in time to get out on their own. If the aliens pushed forward faster than expected, they'd have to leave, just to preserve what was left of Britain's fighting men. Upwards of five thousand men had fought on the defensive line. God alone knew how many had survived the experience.

He saw the flash of light and hurled himself to the ground as the world seemed to come apart around him. The aliens weren't taking any more chances with the town, even though they'd chased out the sole human defender. When he pulled himself to his feet and peered back to the east, most of the town had been blasted into smoking ruin. Any remaining surprises – he didn't think that there were any, but they'd been operating on a strict need-to-know policy – would have been destroyed. The aliens would make one sweep through the wreckage and then continue heading west. Any humans caught up in their advance would be lucky to escape with their lives.

Shaking his head, he started to walk west. They'd be waiting for him, he told himself, and if not he could probably make his own way to one of the dumps. And then he would carry on his part of the war. He wondered, just for a second, how the PM and Prince Harry – no, *King* Harry – were coping, before he pushed the thought aside. They'd all have to learn to cope in the forthcoming days.

———

"They broke though the final defence line, sir," Major Foster reported. The tiny command post had been carefully hidden, but his deputy's command

post had been equally well-hidden – and the aliens had dropped a missile on their heads. "Colonel Bannerman is requesting permission to start Exodus."

Brigadier Gavin Lightbridge-Stewart hesitated. His instincts told him to keep fighting, to keep bleeding the aliens – and they *had* bled the aliens. It was difficult to be sure, but he was certain that they'd killed upwards of a thousand of the oversized bastards, perhaps more. They'd certainly adapted their tactics, he acknowledged. After several tries at engaging British troops in house-to-house combat, they'd pulled back and dropped rocks on the fighting positions. It was clear, no matter how much he wanted to hide it, that further open conflict was no longer an option.

The thought was a bitter pill to swallow. Ever since the development of modern communications, British commanders had been in control of their forces at all times – sometimes to excess. After all, performance in the field was rarely improved by having a distant superior with an imperfect grasp of the tactical scene issuing orders that were impossible to obey. But now the British Army – what was left of it – was going to fragment into a thousand tiny partisan groups, each one operating with minimal oversight from higher authority. God alone knew how it would work out. Outside of the Special Forces – the SAS, the SBS, the SRR and a handful of other units that were still highly classified – they'd never planned for insurgency warfare. The possibility of having to fight one in Britain itself had never been envisaged.

Clearly our imagination was somewhat limited, he thought, sourly. It would be very difficult to produce weapons, or bring in supplies from overseas. God knew that many civilians were already starving, unable to feed themselves or their families. Far too many of them would start collaborating with the aliens if it was the only way to keep their families alive. How could he blame them, let alone start issuing orders for the cold-blooded murder of collaborators…?

"Pass the order," he said. "All units are to execute Exodus immediately. And tell them I wished them good luck."

The field support team was already stripping down the mobile command post, removing all the sensitive equipment and preparing it for transfer to hiding places in the north. They'd have to abandon the vehicles themselves – there was no way to hide them from prowling alien aircraft – but at least they could leave a few surprises behind for the alien soldiers. A handful of grenades had already been set aside for improvised IEDs.

"Brigadier," Lieutenant-Colonel Jean-Luc Baptiste said. Gavin hadn't even noticed the Frenchman until he spoke, if only because he was lost in thought. There was no longer any point in giving orders. They'd have to rely on their own men in the field. "I think it's probably time for us to go."

Gavin frowned. He wanted to tell them to stay, but he understood their position. France had been invaded too, and they wanted to join the French Resistance – if there was a French resistance. They'd barely been able to make contact with isolated French units before the aliens had started their push west. Baptiste and his men would be risking their lives walking to Dover – being careful to give London a wide berth – and then trying to find a boat to take them across the Channel. And after that…? Baptiste had been honest enough to admit that he didn't know. France had been hammered just as hard – perhaps harder – than Britain. It was quite possible that *no* political authority had survived the Battle of Paris.

"If we can't convince you to stay," he said, and held out a hand. Baptiste took it and they shook hands firmly. "Travel with one of our detachments heading towards London, at least at first. They'll give you some cover if you need it."

"We'd be better on our own," Baptiste disagreed. Gavin didn't really blame him. He'd had to detach a number of Londoners to try to slip into the city in hopes of producing up-to-date information, but he knew that the odds were stacked against them. Every man was a volunteer, yet that didn't make it any easier. He'd never had to order men into a position where he *expected* they would die before now, before the world had turned upside down. "We'll meet again after all this is over."

"I hope you're right," Gavin said. The last French Resistance had been aided by Britain – and it had never come close to forcing the Germans to leave France alone. Now… Britain was invaded too, as was America and the rest of the world. How long could they keep an insurgency going when there were no outside sources of supply? "I wish you the very best of luck."

———

"Time to pull out, lads," the burly Royal Marine Sergeant said. No one argued with him. They'd expected nearly a hundred soldiers, but only thirty-seven had made it to the RV point. Some of the brief stories they'd exchanged in whispers had been horrifying. No one was really surprised that higher command had finally ordered them to leave. "Let's go."

Chris marched with the others, hearing the sound of thunder in the distance as the aliens continued their advance. If they were lucky, they'd escape the aliens and reach a place where they could build shelters and hide from the advance. And then they'd return to the fight.

Chapter Fourteen

London
United Kingdom, Day 6

"You have to give the bastard credit," Constable Richardson muttered to Robin. "How many people does he have here, do you think?"

Robin scanned the school's assembly hall and frowned. Someone had *definitely* been busy; a set of tables had been lined up, with chairs, laptop computers and a handful of coffee machines bubbling merrily away in one corner. The men behind the desks were civil servants, the epitome of evil to most British citizens – which probably explained why so many had agreed to serve the aliens. Their families would be starving if they refused, Robin knew, but the cynic in him wondered if the civil servants cared. They certainly spent most of their time creating red tape for the harassed coppers on the beat.

"Twenty here," he said. They'd opened dozens of makeshift registration halls, converting schools, gyms and warehouses into places for their collaborators to work. Robin had spent a few minutes puzzling over why they'd only used large buildings before realising that the aliens would have problems in smaller human dwellings. But then, they'd certainly shown no reluctance to remodel human buildings with high explosive. London had spent six days shivering on the edge of anarchy and only fear of the aliens had kept it in check. "There could be thousands in London alone."

The thought was a chilling one. Hundreds of thousands of people had worked for the British Government. Many would have been killed in the fighting or the chaos that had gripped parts of the city, but many more would have survived – and grown hungry. The aliens were offering them food and drink and Robin couldn't blame many of them for agreeing to serve the aliens in any way. Their families would have starved otherwise. The thought kept mocking him. His wife might starve if he refused to serve the aliens. And yet… where did collaboration end?

There were thirty policemen in the building with orders to keep order – and use whatever force was necessary to remove trouble-makers. The aliens had converted London's stadiums into makeshift detention camps and – according to rumour – they'd established much larger holding centres outside the cities. Anyone who caused trouble was to be removed to the detention camps and no one knew what would happen to them afterwards. The aliens had caused so much damage to London that Robin suspected that one of the jobs assigned to prisoners would be clearing up the debris and clearing blocked roadways of ruined cars.

The policemen were unarmed. Robin cursed the Home Office under his breath, even as he silently remembered the weapons they'd hidden in the city. The aliens had insisted that all weapons be surrendered – and they'd had the records to see how many weapons were unaccounted for. Robin was privately astonished that they'd accepted that several hundred pistols and rifles could go missing – or be reported destroyed – and it made him wonder if the aliens had already penetrated his little cell. Maybe they were only waiting for the policemen to be surplus to requirements before they dropped a hammer on their heads.

He felt dirty as the bell finally rang and they opened the doors. The aliens had been broadcasting the same message for days – using their so-called Prime Minister Beresford as the speaker – ordering all of London's residents to present themselves for registration. Anyone who failed to register within the week, they'd warned the public, would be arrested when they failed to produce a registration card and face indefinite detention. In truth, Robin had no idea just what the aliens intended to do with humanity in the long-term. Slavery seemed unlikely for a race that could cross the interstellar gulfs of space. But unless there was a hope of victory, he didn't dare start to fight back.

"Form lines," he ordered, silently praying that no one would start anything. Many of the people waiting outside looked desperate. They would be hungry; London's shops had been looted and there hadn't been much of anything brought in from outside the city. "Remain calm and form lines – you will all be dealt with in time."

Some of the citizens were staring at the policemen with sullen, angry faces. Others seemed too nervous to care, or were perhaps even relieved that they were dealing with human police, rather than aliens. Some probably didn't even *believe* in the aliens. The internet – what was left of it – had included a conspiracy theory that suggested that there had really been a military coup and the whole story of aliens was intended to keep the British public quiet while the Generals took over. Robin might have been tempted to believe the story if he hadn't seen the aliens. They were chillingly real.

The lines snaked towards the civil servants, who started processing the citizens with bland indifference. They'd been told to bring ID – driving licences or passports – which suggested to Robin that the aliens had managed to capture almost all of the government's records. There would be no chance for anyone to change their name and identity in the chaos, not if the aliens – and their collaborators – had anything to say about it. Robin silently prayed that everything would go perfectly, without him and his men having to intervene. God alone knew how the aliens would react if they had to run the city on their own. They could simply leave the civilian population to starve…

"Here," one oversized man bellowed, suddenly. "How am I supposed to eat this, you dozy cow?"

Robin started towards him, one hand dropping to the truncheon at his belt. The man was staring at a package of food from the piles behind the tables, food produced by the aliens. Robin had had a taste and wondered if anyone could actually be induced to *like* the stuff – it tasted faintly of leather, at best. The aliens insisted that the semi-bread was good to feed a family for four for several days, but Robin knew better. If nothing else, eating the same bland food for more than a few days would be severely demoralising.

"You cut it up and you put it in your mouth," the civil servant repeated in the same bored tone. She'd been working for the Department of Transportation before the aliens had arrived, just another pen-pusher in a department that had more pen-pushers than it had drivers or engineers. "It's perfectly simple…"

"It's muck," the man proclaimed, loudly. There was a murmur of agreement from several in the crowd. The lines were starting to jostle. "I can't feed my family on this shit!"

Robin caught his arm. "That's enough, sir," he said, trying to project a mixture of stern warning and the promise of excessive violence into his voice. They'd been told that appearing confident and unmoveable would prevent people from trying to pick fights with the police. Personally, Robin would have preferred a year of hard labour for each yob who thought he could get away with chucking a beer bottle at a hard-working policeman. "The lady's just doing her job…"

The man swung around and threw a punch at Robin, who jumped back automatically, whipping out his truncheon. A lady – a sad, beating-looking mother of two kids – tried to hold her husband back, but he shrugged off her arm and came after Robin. Robin didn't hesitate; he carefully lashed out with his truncheon, hitting the man in the chest. He folded over and hit the floor with a terrific crash. It would have been a media circus in the old days, with reports of police brutality hitting the airwaves faster than light, but now… he shivered as he realised that they could get away with almost anything, as long as they obeyed the aliens. The thought was terrifying. He knew dozens of coppers who would have liked to take the gloves off and just teach young hooligans some respect the hard way. What would they do without restraints?

He pushed the thought aside as he used a plastic tie to secure the man and then dragged him into a corner. "Don't worry about him," he said, to his wife. She was on the verge of either crying or lashing out at him herself. He couldn't really blame her for either. "I'll try to see to it that he gets back home ok."

The lines moved quicker now that the police had shown that they were ready to deal with any challenge. It didn't get any easier. Crying children constantly drowned out every other sound, despite the frantic attempts by their parents to calm them down. Older children looked around, bemused by what they were seeing, while their parents were clearly terrified. Robin understood just how they were feeling. The world – the world they'd grown up in – was no more. All of the old certainties were gone.

He caught sight of a dozen different ethnic groups and winced inwardly. Indians and Pakistanis, Arabs and Jamaicans… some from communities that had a long history of confrontation with the police. He had to wade in to stop a Pakistani man from attacking one of the civil servants, apparently outraged because he'd been told that his wife had to remove her veil. The mood in the building rapidly turned ugly, but he resisted the urge to call for backup. An alien patrol with live weapons would arrive and probably shoot a few dozen innocent citizens to restore order. That was the last thing he wanted.

Another scuffle caught his eye, one that seemed to spring out of nowhere – and then he saw the ID card. It was a military ID, one that identified its bearer as a serving member of the Royal Navy. He didn't want to act, but there was no choice. The policemen closed in rapidly and led the sailor away, leaving his wife behind. They'd been given no choice in the matter – all serving members of the military, whatever the service, were to be arrested and handed over to the aliens. He told himself that the sailor would have a chance to escape – they'd carefully not secured the holding area they'd made in one of the classrooms – but it was small comfort. The eyes of the sailor's wife and baby child would haunt his nightmares for the rest of time.

Dear God, he prayed, silently. *Please let this be over soon.*

He ran through the figures in his head. The population of Greater London was estimated at around eight million. Some would have died in the fighting, or in the chaos, or… maybe of simple starvation. The remainder were all expected to register within the week, or face arrest. How long would it take to register eight million people? It could take weeks, or even months.

Silently, he damned himself. But what else could he do?

Doctor Fatima Hasid had never liked crowded rooms, even as a child. She'd skipped classes at the mosque because there were too many girls crammed into the small room put aside for women – the boys had a far larger room, and a better teacher – and she'd stopped going to them shortly after she entered secondary school. The NHS had had its fair share of crowded rooms, but as a doctor she'd been able to avoid them and see patients one by one. Entering the registry office was a foretaste of hell.

The lines seemed never-ending and she was silently relieved that she'd managed to convince her superiors to give her the afternoon off. London still had thousands of wounded on its hands, but they'd finally managed to get the worst of the wounded into proper hospitals – even if they had had to distribute them over Britain. The remainder, the ones who hadn't been seriously injured, had had to be sent home. It had broken her heart to do it, but there'd been no choice. Their supplies had dropped to dangerously low levels.

Ahead of her, some boys were pushing and shoving. She hated to think what it was going to be like when her stepmother and her overweight sons and their relatives came to register themselves. Some of them were talking about refusing to register – after all, they'd had as little to do with the British Government as possible, except when it came to claiming benefits. Fatima suspected that if they tried to defy the aliens – the aliens they didn't really believe in – they'd find that the aliens hammered them into the ground. The stories she'd heard from some of her patients were horrific.

She pulled her arms around herself as the queue kept inching forward, finally allowing her to catch sight of a desk. It was no surprise to see a human – a set of humans – standing behind it, trying to handle the paperwork. The aliens wouldn't have wanted to waste their manpower on such a piddling task. Whatever the claims that they were all-powerful – the radio had certainly been assuring the British population that resistance was futile – there had to be limits on their manpower. Alien-power? She was still mulling

that over when she finally reached the desk and sat down in front of the civil servant.

"Name, address, proof of identity…"

The words rattled out and Fatima did her best to answer. It seemed that no one else from her family had registered yet, which was hardly a surprise. The amount of data the aliens were collecting puzzled her for a long moment, before she realised that they probably had sophisticated computers capable of mining through the vast datafiles and drawing conclusions in a way that no human could match. It struck her that they were experienced at invading and occupying planets – and if that was the case, who else had they fought? There had always been stories of UFOs flying around and kidnapping people, flown by little grey men with anal fixations. Maybe they were real after all…

"You're a doctor," the civil servant said. "You're in one of the protected categories."

Fatima frowned, leaning forward. "Protected categories?"

"They're looking for people with certain skills," the civil servant admitted. "Doctors and nurses… they're needed right where they are, so they probably won't send for you and put you to work somewhere else. Others… they're not so lucky. The men who register today who aren't in a protected category will probably find themselves ordered to do brute labour in a week's time."

"I see," Fatima said. "And you know this… how?"

"I don't," the civil servant said, "but I think it's a reasonable guess, don't you?"

Fatima couldn't disagree. A machine on the desk buzzed and whirred, and finally discharged an ID card. Fatima studied it, trying to keep her consternation off her face. She hadn't even *noticed* the camera, but there was a picture of her on the front of the card. It seemed that there were limits to alien technology after all, part of her mind noted. Every photograph she'd had taken for official purposes had managed to make her look bad, mad, dead or some combination of the three. The alien technology was no better.

"Carry it with you at all times," the civil servant warned. "There's a hefty fine if you lose it – and failing to produce it on demand could mean arrest, or worse. I don't think they have lawyers telling them what they can and cannot do to prisoners…"

Fatima thanked him and left. Outside, night was already starting to fall and so she hurried home. A curfew had been declared and there were already terrible rumours about what happened to those caught outside by the aliens. And her stepmother would bitch and moan if she was home late. They were supposed to be hosting guests soon and she was required to help. She would almost sooner have faced the aliens.

Alan Beresford stood in an office that had once belonged to a banking CEO and stared out over London. The city was finally coming back to life at nights, even though the curfew meant that many who would once have been outside partying would be tucked up safe at home, doubtless wondering when their world would shatter around them once again. It was *his* world now… well, his and a few aliens, but it seemed they didn't care about the perks he claimed for himself as long as he did a good job. And he *had* done a good job. It had been his idea to put the civil servants back to work, along with the men who ran the electricity and water companies. London was coming back to life – and so was the rest of the country.

The aliens were ruthlessly pragmatic, but they clearly didn't have the manpower to govern all of Britain, let alone the world. Alan was still unsure of what they actually wanted in the long run, but he was confident that he would be able to find a way to be useful to them. And he had his own long-term plans. He'd put friends and cronies in positions of power all over the country, laying a network that could be used in his own interests as well as those of his masters. It helped that the Prime Minister appeared to have vanished somewhere in the chaos of the first few days. Apart from a single message which was proving alarmingly persistent on the internet, no one had heard anything from him. It was quite possible that he was dead.

Losing Prince Harry was equally annoying. Harry was King now that his father and brother were both dead. Alan doubted that the population of Britain would rise in outrage at losing their King, but Harry could have made an excellent figurehead for a new Britain. Or perhaps not. He'd been a soldier and would probably have old-fashioned ideas about loyalty and honour and service to his country running through his veins.

Foolish, Alan told himself, and smiled. Loyalty and honour meant nothing these days – and they'd meant little before the aliens arrived. All that mattered was what one did for one's own self – and if it meant stamping on a few toes… well, you couldn't make an omelette without breaking a few eggs.

He lifted his glass – an expensive wine, but it had been easy to obtain in starving London – and drank a silent toast. To power, he told himself… and to those bold enough to seize it.

Chapter Fifteen

North England
United Kingdom, Day 8

Haddon Hall was one of the original stately England manors, built before the English Civil War by a loyalist who had lost his life fighting for Good King Charles. It was a regal building, although hopelessly impractical for military purposes, surrounded by gardens that regularly won awards in regional and national contests. Some people would have found it a paradise, a chance to play at being an English aristocrat. Gabriel Burley found it maddening. It was a prison by any other name, a place where he could do anything – except leave. The handful of security staff – really soldiers wearing civilian clothes – were polite and friendly, but they wouldn't let him leave. He was too important to risk falling into enemy hands.

The thought made him snort in disgust as he paced the massive library. Two years ago, he'd been a junior MP with ideals, ideals that were being worn down by contact with real-life politics. How could he hope to achieve anything without compromise – and by compromising, he was steadily turning into a true politician, a man who compromised everything for the sake of power and position. A man like Alan Beresford.

He snorted again as he picked up a book, glanced at it and put it down again. His host had given him the run of the house, and the use of an extensive collection of books, DVDs and even old-fashioned records, but it was still a prison. He couldn't concentrate on anything, apart from his feelings of hopelessness. His position as Prime Minister was meaningless, save in name only. The invasion that gripped the country proved that, whatever he told himself; he could hardly command the aliens to leave, could he? Their forces held the entire country now, surrounding cities and trapping the civilian population within their homes. God alone knew what they would do when the resistance went to work. They'd certainly shown no sign of any scruples when dealing with unarmed civilians.

The television remained bland, with old movies and soaps being played regularly, rather than the BBC's news programs. Gabriel knew some of what was going on all over the world, but it didn't help his mood. The aliens were tightening their grip – Dear God, had it only been eight days since they'd revealed themselves and descended upon a shocked and paralysed Earth? Gabriel almost wished that they would discover his hiding place and try to snatch him. At least running away would be doing something. Instead, all he could do was wait and hope that someone – somehow – found a way to hurt the aliens enough to make them leave. The military hadn't been too hopeful. As long as the aliens dominated space above Earth, they could call down strikes against rebel towns and cities – or, if worst came to worst, exterminate the human race. Gabriel remembered all the films he'd seen with asteroids crashing into the planet and shivered. The aliens would have no trouble pushing an asteroid towards Earth and the human race wouldn't be saved by a patriotic scriptwriter. It even made him long for *Independence Day*.

There was a cough behind him and he jumped, one hand falling to the pistol he'd been told to carry at all times – and save the final bullet for himself, if the aliens caught up with him. Brigadier Gavin Lightbridge-Stewart seemed rather amused – Gabriel hadn't even realised that he'd entered the room – but Gabriel was pleased to see him. He hadn't been allowed an internet connection, not when the aliens might use it to track him down. Outside news – accurate outside news – only came in fits and starts.

"Prime Minister," Lightbridge-Stewart said, gravely. "I trust that you are well?"

"I've told you to call me Gabriel," Gabriel said, impatiently. He didn't know where Lightbridge-Stewart had made his headquarters or even any operational details at all. What he didn't know he couldn't tell – and he had no illusions about his ability to hold out under torture. Or perhaps the aliens had perfect lie detectors and truth drugs. "What have you heard from the… outside?"

Lightbridge-Stewart smiled. "Elements of the Royal Scots are preparing fall-back positions in the Highlands," he said. "The aliens may control the cities, but they'll find extending their control into the Highlands a little harder than they'd prefer. They may even decide to abandon the Highlands altogether."

Gabriel nodded, half-wishing that he could go north and join the Scots. There were plenty of areas in England where humans could hide out from the aliens, but Scotland had a smaller civilian population at risk. But he knew that he could never take an active role in the fighting to come. They couldn't risk their Prime Minister, even if the position *was* meaningless.

"King Harry isn't adjusting well," Lightbridge-Stewart added. "He wants to fight back, not hide out somewhere in Scotland. But I'm afraid we don't have much choice."

"I can't disagree," Gabriel said. He hadn't even been in politics when there had been an almighty political struggle over deploying then-Prince Harry to Iraq and Afghanistan. In the end, he'd been allowed to go – as long as it wasn't made public. It was ironic, really; the British Monarchy had held mostly ceremonial roles, yet Harry hadn't been allowed to be a public sign that the Monarchy was willing to fight too. What made Harry any better than the hundreds of other soldiers who'd lost their lives in Iraq or Afghanistan? There had been no good answer, save that the enemy would have made capturing him a priority. His presence would have risked the lives of other soldiers.

Lightbridge-Stewart shrugged. "There's some good news," he said. "And some bad news as well, I'm afraid. We managed to recover a dead alien body in the retreat from Salisbury Plain and get it to a… well, a covert military medical research establishment. The doctors there took some time to dissect the body and draw a number of conclusions. I brought copies of their reports, but the interesting detail is that they're really not that different from us."

"They look like leathery dinosaurs," Gabriel observed. It still pained him that he hadn't seen any of the aliens at first-hand, but his minders had been clear. He couldn't risk being recognised. "And yet they're not that different from us?"

"Compared to what we were expecting, yes," Lightbridge-Stewart said. "Which isn't really good news in the long run. They can make use of our planet and presumably eat our crops – although I don't know if they'll actually *like* them. However, the doctors believe that they cannot catch our diseases – which rather puts the leash on any *War of the Worlds* scenarios we might have been hoping for."

Gabriel frowned. "And can we catch *their* diseases?"

"They don't think so," Lightbridge-Stewart said. "But they don't really have any samples of alien diseases to study."

"No," Gabriel agreed. "They wouldn't."

He'd studied history, back when he'd thought about becoming a historian. Back when Europe had discovered America, they'd brought their diseases with them – diseases that the Native Americans had had no resistance to. Smallpox alone had killed millions, leaving a void for the Europeans to expand into and eventually control. The empires built on native labour had collapsed; the empires based on settlers had survived and prospered. And if an alien disease got loose on Earth…

It might not even have to be natural, he realised. He'd certainly had enough briefings about the dangers of biological warfare, up to and including genetically-modified diseases that were resistant to every known vaccine. The aliens didn't have to reshape one of their own diseases to produce a monster that would exterminate humanity. They could simply rely on a simple human disease, with a little modification. Britain had no – official – stocks of Smallpox, but if the aliens had captured the stores in Russia, or America…

He pushed the thought aside. There was no point in worrying about it. They were at the mercy of the aliens and would be for years to come.

"The analysts think that the aliens will probably start growing their own crops on Earth sooner rather than later," Lightbridge-Stewart said. "Unless they've somehow managed to produce stable wormholes that reach from planet to planet, their logistics have to be rather touchy. Growing their own food will allow them to send more weapons and military supplies instead…"

"And there's nothing we can do about it," Gabriel said. "I don't suppose that anyone else has come up with a possible solution? Maybe hacking into their computers and shutting down their weapons…?"

"This is the real world, unfortunately," Lightbridge-Stewart said. He frowned, suddenly. "What I can tell you is that there is a certain… crude nature to most of their technology. We've captured samples of their weapons and taken them apart to study – in many ways, their weapons are actually less advanced than our own. That could be just them being practical – the more complex a piece of kit, the greater the chance it will break in the field – or their overall technology level could be less advanced than we've assumed. And for that matter…"

He hesitated. "It's hard to be sure, but their tactical doctrine sucks," he added. "If they didn't have those starships in orbit, we would have beaten them – and so would almost every other First World nation on the planet. Hell, even the Saudis would have given them a very hard time. I don't know who they're used to fighting, but they clearly haven't learned much from the experience. The analysts have studied the problem, yet they can't see any clear solution. It's possible that someone else gave them their technology…"

Gabriel stared at him. "Someone else *sold* them their technology…? Who?"

"There's no way to know," Lightbridge-Stewart admitted. "Another alien race, we presume – or maybe they captured technology from another alien race and somehow discovered how to duplicate it for themselves. We certainly didn't hesitate to sell tanks and guns to the Middle East, even though there was a strong chance that they would wind up being pointed back at us. For all we know, they stole the starships they have in orbit – and the weapons they're using against us on the ground may be their own designs."

"But there's no way to know," Gabriel said. He shook his head slowly. "Is there any good news?"

"Well, I've had a team of signals experts – very bright boffins, these lads – studying the alien communications system," Lightbridge-Stewart said. "It really isn't as advanced as our own – but then, we don't really understand their language yet so we may have problems unlocking some of their secrets." He smiled, briefly. "But we do have some idea of how their command-and-control network functions. It seems that their junior officers don't have much independence of action. They may not even have the ability to call in strikes from orbit without permission from higher authority."

He looked down at the floor, shaking his head. "God knows we had enough problems with calling in strikes while we were in Afghanistan," he said. "It may account for odd delays in their response times – we managed to get troops out of positions we knew would be bombarded before the hammer finally fell. Or we may be making a dreadful mistake because their system *looks* familiar to us. They're aliens and their idea of logic may not make sense to human minds."

"They've been taking prisoners and registering the entire population," Gabriel said. "Doesn't that make sense from a human point of view?"

"I'm very much afraid so," Lightbridge-Stewart agreed. "We have – had – political considerations in how we treated civilians caught up in occupied zones. It was never politically possible to impose our control with an iron hand – and that cost us badly. The aliens, on the other hand, seem to be registering our people with an eye to keeping them under firm control – and weeding out those who might be able to resist. Luckily we managed to get most of the TA and reservists called up and out of the cities before the aliens started arresting military personnel. God alone knows what they're doing with them."

Gabriel shivered. The reports had all been the same, even though they'd come from places as far apart as Southampton and Aberdeen. All civilians had to be registered – and military personnel were taken away, along with police and other emergency service workers who refused to collaborate. No one knew where the aliens had taken them, but Gabriel had no difficulty picturing them being executed by alien gunfire… or simply tossed from alien shuttles into the Pacific Ocean. The aliens had set up detention camps, but they all seemed to be for civilians. He could only hope that the military personnel were kept alive, elsewhere. The alternative was too depressing to contemplate.

"And we don't know what they have in mind in the long run," Lightbridge-Stewart added. "Perhaps they intend to isolate fatties and have them cooked for dinner – we believe they could probably eat human flesh."

Gabriel felt sick. "I don't think that any civilised race would want to eat human flesh," he said – but then, what *was* a civilised race? He'd thought that humanity, for all its faults, was making progress towards a better world for all, yet the aliens had knocked humanity down within two days of their arrival. The reports from Africa – where the aliens had almost no presence at all – suggested that mass chaos was spreading across the continent. Was the inner savage as far removed from the civilised man as he wanted to believe? "I'm sure they have something less… extreme in mind for us."

"I don't know," Lightbridge-Stewart said. "I just don't think we'll enjoy it when the penny finally drops."

"I haven't enjoyed anything since the aliens arrived," Gabriel said, ruefully. He hesitated. Even now, there were things he didn't feel comfortable discussing. "Is there… anything we can do about their damned puppet?"

"You mean assassinate him?" Lightbridge-Stewart said. "I admit that we've been looking at the possibility. But the aliens keep him under very tight guard – it's almost as if they think we might take a shot at him." He smiled. "We're working on the possibility, Prime Minister, but it may take some time."

He hesitated. "And we have to decide if we're going to wage war on collaborators as well as the aliens," he added. "Some are joining up because they need to feed their families; some are joining up because they believe that it's for the best… and some are joining up because they want power. And as long as the aliens have thousands of expendable humans to deploy against us, it will be a great deal harder to convince them to withdraw."

Gabriel shivered. Western Governments had been alarmingly sensitive to casualties and bad publicity, something their enemies hadn't hesitated to use against them. The terrorists had targeted soldiers, intent on causing as many fatalities as possible, and done their best to provoke incidents that could be spun against the Western troops. Any civilian deaths were always blamed on the West – and the fact that they'd been used as human shields by men who wore civilian clothes, or caught in bombs planted by their fellow countrymen, was never mentioned.

But they had no way of knowing what the aliens would consider acceptable losses – or bad publicity. Perhaps their homeworld had protest marches, with thousands of young and idealistic aliens marching to 'save the human,' or perhaps they were a fascist state, with all dissent ruthlessly suppressed. And if it was the latter, they might be prepared to endure terrifying losses to keep Earth firmly under their control – or blow up the planet if they felt that they had no choice, but to withdraw.

"So we go after the aliens first," Gabriel said, "and only go after the collaborators if they're nasty bastards who abuse their power?"

"Sounds like a plan," Lightbridge-Stewart agreed. "But there *will* be casualties, Prime Minister. We don't even know how many civilians died in the last few days."

Once, Gabriel would have been appalled – hell, he still was appalled. But there was nothing he could do about it. The aliens couldn't be ordered out of Britain by the Prime Minister.

"We have managed to set up a reasonably secure communications link with America," Lightbridge-Stewart said, after a moment. "Most of the American personnel in Britain want to go home and fight there, although that will be tricky. The aliens aren't allowing big ships to leave harbour – we can get them to Ireland, which hasn't been occupied, but I don't see how we can get many of them to the United States. It may be possible to use submarines…"

"But that would mean risking a boat," Gabriel said, slowly. Lightbridge-Stewart nodded. The remaining submarines in the Royal Navy – as well as ones belonging to America, France and the rest of Europe – had been ordered to run silent, run deep. The aliens didn't seem to be capable of tracking submerged boats from orbit, but they could see a surfaced submarine and drop a rock on it. "Are the Yanks going to take the risk?"

"I don't think so," Lightbridge-Stewart said. "They took higher absolute losses than we did and their country is much more heavily occupied. I suspect they can probably keep an insurgency going for longer than we can, but…"

He shrugged. "If we could just get them out of orbit, we could deal with their garrisons on the surface," he concluded. "But as long as they're in orbit, they can hold a gun to our heads."

Gabriel couldn't disagree. They could hurt the aliens, but they could never beat them. And if they couldn't beat them, was there any point in fighting at all? And yet, if they surrendered, there was no way of knowing what the aliens had in mind for the human race.

"Thank you for coming," he said, cursing his own weakness. "Will you stay for dinner?"

"I have to link up with a couple of others," Lightbridge-Stewart said, reluctantly. "We have plans to make. And then we can start reminding the aliens that we exist."

Chapter Sixteen

Long Stratton
United Kingdom, Day 10/11

The convoy looked like something out of Iraq, or Afghanistan. It comprised a handful of trucks, each one carrying a dozen policemen, and a pair of alien Armoured Personnel Carriers. It was escorted by a pair of helicopters, bristling with weapons, that flew elaborate patterns over the vehicles. From her vantage point, hidden near the town, Alex wondered if the alien pilots were showing off, or genuinely concerned about the threat of portable antiaircraft weapons. There was no way to know, but she suspected the former. The aliens, despite appearances, didn't look as if they were expecting trouble.

She gritted her teeth as the aliens started to dismount their vehicles, weapons at the ready, followed by their tame policemen. The internet had been ranting and raving about collaborators – and so many rumours that it was difficult to know what was fact and what was fiction – but actually seeing collaborators in the flesh was a different story. They looked as if they were confident, expecting no opposition – and they might be right. The BBC had been claiming that the remainder of the British military had been destroyed; looking down at the aliens, Alex started to wonder if they had been telling the truth. She might be the last surviving servicewoman in Britain.

No, she told herself firmly. That couldn't be true. She was isolated, but there would be others out there somewhere, waiting for the chance to hit back at their new enemies. And even if she *was* alone, she still had her duty. All she had to do was wait until the right moment. Until then, she just had to watch and allow the memories to become burned into her mind. The aliens and their collaborators had arrived in Long Stratton.

They'd developed their own procedure for securing towns and villages by now. The policemen used loudspeakers to summon all of the townsfolk out of their homes and ordered them to wait on the green while the aliens searched the village. Looking at their big hulking forms, Alex felt a chill running down her spine. She would have sooner believed in a rogue military officer launching a coup than in aliens, even though she'd seen their aircraft. The clattering of the helicopters grew louder as one skimmed over her position, so low that Alex was convinced, just for a few moments, that she'd been spotted. There was no way to know what the townspeople were telling the policemen down below.

She shuddered. The aliens had made their instructions quite clear; everyone in the country was to be registered, fingerprinted and given an ID card – no exceptions. And the internet had made it clear that the moment they discovered that she was a RAF pilot, they would take her away and no one would know what had happened to her. So she'd taken the risk of hiding, along with a handful of young men who were willing to resist the aliens. Alex hoped that it wasn't all just mindless bravado. There was no way to know what someone was made of until the shit hit the fan, by which time it might be too late. It was one of the reasons why military training was so intensive, in the hopes of weeding out the unsuitable before it was too late.

And if her little band was caught…? There was no way to know. The aliens might simply execute them on the spot, or take them to one of their detention camps or… she shook her head, concentrating on the scene before her. One by one, the townspeople were being processed and registered. Smith and his wife had remained on their farm. They probably wouldn't be processed until later – she hoped. And they'd been warned not to breathe a word about her…

One hand touched the pistol at her belt as the hours wore on. Watching made it seem almost surreal, with the aliens watching over their collaborators – their unarmed collaborators. Alex found that a warming sight; it was clear that the aliens didn't trust the policemen with live weapons. Perhaps the police hadn't been so badly subverted after all. But she couldn't count on anything…

Down below, a scuffle had broken out. She peered, wishing she'd dared bring a pair of binoculars, trying to make out what was going on. The policemen had pulled a man out of the crowd, a middle-aged gentleman she didn't know. Why… she realised why a moment later, just as she saw his crying wife and older children. He'd been in the army and returned to life as a civilian. It hadn't been enough to save him, or his son. The young man had lunged at a policeman, only to be knocked down and arrested by another. God alone knew what would happen to them.

She gritted her teeth again, forcing herself to watch. Whatever else happened, she would not forget. And those who had been killed would be avenged.

———

Night was falling as she approached the disused barn, one that had once belonged to a farmer who had sold out and left the country. It had fallen into a dilapidated state, but her small team had done wonders to ensure that no light could be seen coming from the barn in the darkness. The aliens didn't seem to patrol the country very effectively, yet there was no point in taking chances. They were taking quite enough with the elderly explosives as it was.

"They used to put this stuff in flour," Archer was saying to his small group of students. "The Chinese would use it to smuggle gunk past the Japanese – it could actually be baked and eaten without poisoning the poor bastard who actually ate it. We may have to use it the same way."

Alex frowned. The collection of weapons and explosives from World War Two had been looked after carefully, but an alarming number had decayed badly. Some of the detonator pens – designed for early IEDs – were unreliable. They'd been state of the art in 1940, Archer had assured her, but now… they would have to be careful. There were some nasty tricks that could be played with even disused explosives, yet… she had nightmares where one of the students accidentally blew up the barn or the weapons store. At least they'd managed to scatter smaller dumps around the area. Losing one wouldn't cost them everything.

"I think it's time for a break," Archer said, as he spied her. The young men stood up and scattered. They'd been warned to be very careful – and avoid the aliens at all costs. "Did you find out what you wanted to know?"

Alex nodded, but waited for the barn to empty before she spoke. "They're parked in a camping field, some miles away," she said, flatly. "I think they'll have to leave the way they came, unless they intend to go cross-country."

Archer nodded. "I have the surprise all ready for them," he said. "I'm coming with you…"

"No, you're not," Alex said, flatly. "You know much more about these weapons than I do. We can't afford to lose you – at least not yet."

Archer didn't look pleased, but he accepted her comment. "Make sure you place it properly," he said, firmly. "I spent too much trouble making it to have you fail to blow up the right people."

Twenty minutes later, Alex and two of the lads headed out over the countryside, heading for where the collaborators were parked. She was mildly surprised that the aliens had chosen to stay with them, but it worked in her favour. Assuming that the aliens were jumpy and had night-vision gear, she kept her small force from going any closer than the grit bin she'd noticed by the side of the road. It took longer than she'd feared to empty the grit into the road and pack the bomb into the bin, but they made it. Her first IED didn't look very professional, yet it should do the trick. Or so she told herself.

Sending the two boys back to their homes, she found a hiding place and settled down to wait. There was no way of knowing just when the collaborators would start to move, but the aliens – according to the internet – were hard taskmasters. They might well decide to start when dawn rose above the horizon, whatever their human subordinates thought. Besides, it was almost traditional to attack at dawn. Any human force would be awake and on guard at that point, at least if it was on deployment.

She was yawning when she heard two helicopters high overhead, followed by the sound of vehicle engines rumbling into life. It wasn't quite dawn yet – perhaps the aliens were harder taskmasters than she had assumed. Or perhaps they were just bastards. It hardly mattered. A moment later, she saw lights in the distance, suggesting that the aliens were on their way. She'd been worried about accidentally blowing up civilians, but most civilian vehicles had run out of petrol in the last few days. The remaining supplies were being carefully hoarded.

The lead alien vehicle came around the bend and accelerated down the road. Alex was mildly impressed by how it seemed to glide above the ground – it was almost silent compared to the trucks carrying policemen – but there was no time to stare. She reached for the detonator and held it in her hand, cradling it while running her finger over the button. There were no safety features, Archer had told her, with a thin leer. They'd been less careful in those days. Of course, the planned resistance cells in Britain had also had more training than Alex had ever received. If there was ever a day when the RAF returned to service, she made a mental note to insist that ground combat skills were included in what they taught their pilots.

Just before the alien vehicle reached the grit bin, she pushed down on the button. There was a heart-stopping pause – and then there was a thunderous explosion. The alien vehicle was picked up and flung right into the following truck, crushing a number of policemen under its weight. An engine caught fire and another truck went up in flames, just before two more trucks collided with the vehicles ahead of them. The second alien vehicle was untouched, but the alien infantry dismounted anyway. They moved with eerie grace as they surrounded the scene, clearly expecting another attack at any moment. Alex silently cursed her own oversight. She could have had several men with hunting rifles in position to pick off most of the aliens – but then, they would have had to risk remaining at the scene long enough for reinforcements to arrive.

She'd had time to plan her own exit and so she ran, keeping her head down and praying that she wouldn't be noticed. The alien helicopters had returned to the convoy to hover menacingly over the ruined vehicles, no doubt looking for enemy insurgents to target and kill. She almost fainted as she heard the sound of gunfire, before realising that the aliens were shooting at rabbits. The noise had flushed a number of the little beasts out of hiding and the aliens had thought that they were humans! She was still grinning at the thought when she headed further into the countryside, back to her hiding place. They'd never find her.

———

"You hit the bastards," Smith said, three hours later. The aliens had visited their farm yesterday and given the farmer and his wife their ID cards. Alex had examined them and concluded that the aliens had actually encoded information into the cards – hardly an unfamiliar form of technology, but one with ominous implications for population control. "What do you think they'll do in response?"

Alex shrugged. There was no way to know. She'd actually offered to leave, knowing that her presence would bring danger to their house, but they'd refused to hear of it. Besides, as Smith had assured her, they needed help on the farm. The aliens had stated that they would be expected to start expanding their yield and Alex suspected that failing to produce food for the aliens would result in losing the farm. Their children were still lost somewhere in Britain, unable to return to their home.

She looked down at Smith's ID card. The policemen had been very clear on what the farmer could and could not do. Leaving the county without permission would result in arrest. Failing to produce the card when requested would result in arrest. Their grown children and their families, if they ever arrived, would be expected to report to the aliens through the local police station – or they would be arrested. It seemed that putting even a single foot wrong would result in arrest. Alex could almost understand why they were issuing such edicts; it was as demoralising as hell and it certainly

kept humanity under foot. Given enough time, the aliens could start organising the country to suit themselves.

The sound of helicopters – they had to be alien – nearby sent another chill down her spine. How much could they mobilise to hunt her and her little band down? An entire army, a small force of soldiers… or would they bombard the nearest town purely for the hell of it? There was no way to know, but she would have to find out – somehow. She rubbed her face, fought down a yawn, and headed outside. There was work to be done on the farm.

———

"But the last time I fought was in Malaya!"

Major Terrence Smyth scowled at the aliens, who seemed unresponsive. For all he knew, they couldn't speak English. It wouldn't be the first time that some conquering bastard had thought that keeping his soldiers from speaking the native tongue would stop them from developing any attachments to the locals. Of course, humans had always been able to communicate, even if by gestures alone. And they'd always wanted the same things – women, money, a chance to go home without having certain vital parts separated from their bodies. The thought of the aliens paying attention to human women was sickening.

The policemen at least looked ashamed, when they bothered to meet his eyes. They'd taken his son away somewhere, purely for the crime of trying to defend his old man. Terrence had fought in Malaya before leaving the British Army, decades ago. It seemed that the aliens didn't give a damn about how long ago a person's military service was – if a person had military experience, he or she was to be arrested and taken away.

He stared around the small holding pen. It was a simple fence of wire, holding seventeen men and one woman, surrounded by the aliens. Escape seemed impossible; even if they'd been able to cut or climb the wires, the aliens would shoot them down before they managed to run away from their base. Hell, he didn't even know what they'd done to the area – they'd set up a handful of oversized buildings surrounding the holding pen. And he wasn't entirely sure of where he was.

Must be getting old, he thought, bitterly. And to think that he'd been planning a comfortable retirement. He was in his seventies, after all, but still as active as ever… well, maybe not as active as he'd been when he'd been a young soldier in the trenches. His wife wanted to travel the world and he'd been happy to oblige her. But now…

He looked up as a heavy lorry roared its way into the camp. The driver was a human, probably yet another of the damned civil servants who'd managed to find a soft landing in the arms of the aliens. Terrence glowered at him, before deciding that he was being unfair. The arsehole might have joined up to feed his family. Not everyone in Britain lived on a farm.

The policemen opened the gates and waved the prisoners forward. They didn't bother to shackle them, but what would be the point? Inside the lorry, they'd be prisoners just as much as they were prisoners inside the holding pen. He shuffled as slowly as he dared until it was his turn to climb into the vehicle, and then he pretended that his leg had failed, staggering down and collapsing on the ground. A moment later, a policeman helped him into the lorry.

He found a place to sit as the doors were closed and the big vehicle made its way out of the camp. There were no windows to allow him to see where they were going. A quick check revealed that they couldn't force open the rear doors to escape. The sound of engines grew louder, suggesting that they had joined a small convoy. Or maybe it was a very large convoy. He found himself praying that resistance fighters – or the remains of his old service – were still out there, ready to attack the convoy, but nothing happened. The hours wore onwards as the truck took them further and further away from the land he'd known.

It almost made him want to cry. His wife, his children… would he ever see them again? Or would the grandchildren grow up without knowing their granddad? He told himself that they wouldn't keep him prisoner forever, but there was no way to know. For all he knew, he might be going to his own execution. But they could have killed him easily without bothering to transport him halfway across the country. Maybe they wanted slave labour, or maybe they just had a holding camp for former military personnel somewhere isolated from the general population. They'd grow old and die there while the aliens took control of the rest of the country they'd sworn to defend. His grandchildren would grow up in a world where the aliens were a fact of life.

Shaking his head, he remembered the hills he'd once climbed as a younger man… and wondered, bitterly, if he would ever see them again.

Chapter Seventeen

London
United Kingdom, Day 15

"They're doing it on purpose," Aashif proclaimed, loudly. The small gathering of young men around him murmured in agreement. "They are showing no respect for our religion at all!"

Seated halfway across the room, with the women and young children, Fatima could still hear him voicing his anger. Aashif was twenty-one years old, born to a family and community that was largely excluded from the mainstream population. A stronger person might have broken down the barriers or carved out a career for themselves, but Aashif – like so many others – had chosen to fall back into his community and wrap himself in a tissue of imaginary grievances. She'd heard it all before; the world was against him, no one liked or trusted him because of his religion, and he had *rights*. It never seemed to have occurred to him that his failures were a result of his personality, or that he could have made something of himself if he tried. He found it so much easier to blame others for his failings.

She rolled her eyes. Men like Aashif were a persistent pain in the posterior. Deprived of the sort of wealth and power they thought the world owed them by rights, they turned upon the women in their lives. Aashif's sister was terrified to talk to strangers for fear that her brother would hear of it and beat her; his mother was a pale shadow of a woman, scared of the boy she'd brought into the world. Only his grandfather had ever been able to exercise any kind of restraint on the young man, and he'd passed away two years ago. She listened to his bragging and shuddered, inwardly. There was a new conviction in his voice that had been missing several months ago.

Not that she could really blame him. The aliens had taken over every building large enough to hold their oversized forms – and that included a number of London's mosques. Even the police had been reluctant to just barge into the mosques, fearing the effect such provocative acts would have on the Muslim community. But the aliens had just taken the buildings and evicted everyone who complained. They'd done the same to a number of churches, yet they seemed to have targeted mosques deliberately. Given the rumours coming from the Middle East – and spread over the internet, along with far too much outright nonsense – it seemed as though they were attacking Islam directly. From what she'd seen herself, Fatima suspected that the aliens simply didn't care. Humans were their property now – and property didn't get a vote, or the right to complain.

"We're going to do something about it," Aashif continued. Bragging about his connections to the underground *Jihad* movement wasn't new either, but she'd always known that he was just a poser, someone who would probably faint dead away at the thought of being asked to blow himself and a great many innocent civilians up. There were too many girls out there who were prepared to allow such claims to overpower their common sense. "I'm going to see to it personally."

Unseen, Fatima rolled her eyes. Of course he would – and while he was at it, he'd create the perfect Islamic State... never mind that such a state only existed in the deluded rants spouted by preachers with nothing better to do. There were times when she was tempted to believe that suicide bombers were God's way of weeding out the unworthy from the Muslim community. The young fools who died for a dream rarely got to spread their seed.

She shook her head, and then helped her stepmother and the rest of the girls clear away the dishes and wash up. They knew their place, all right – and the fact that she was a doctor cut no ice with the men. Men like Aashif wanted women to stay in their place. It was the only way they could convince themselves that they were in charge. She smiled, in a moment of dark humour. The world could hardly be worse if women were in charge.

————

Sergeant Abdul Al-Hasid was feeling dirty. Not the feeling he'd had when he'd first discovered pornographic magazines, despite knowing that his God-fearing father would thrash him to within an inch of his life if he'd been caught looking at naked sluts. And not the feeling he'd had when Salma – his first girlfriend – had allowed him to touch her bare breast. It was the feeling of knowing that he was doing something utterly wrong – and the fact that the people he was helping to do it wanted him to help them didn't make him feel any better. He couldn't shake the feeling that he would be called upon to answer to God and that no answer he could give, nothing he could offer in his own defence, would help his case.

He'd grown up in a strictly Islamic environment – so of course he'd rebelled. School hadn't given him much in the way of qualifications, so the Army had seemed a logical choice. And it had been the making of him. He'd knuckled down at it and worked hard for the first time in his life, deploying to Iraq and then Afghanistan with the Green Jackets. Along the way, he'd seen just what living under Islamic Law really meant – the only people who wanted Taliban-style rule were the people who had never had to live under it. He'd seen enough to convince him that the rulers, for all their dedication to making others follow the rules, enjoyed breaking them every chance they got. Walking through a Taliban-run whorehouse had been enough to convince him that they had to be stopped. They'd killed the girls rather than risk having them freed by the British Army.

After the aliens had invaded, he'd volunteered to return to London with several other Londoners. They'd known that it would be dangerous – no one could describe the military as a safe job in the best of times – but he'd known people who might be able to help them fight the aliens. Wearing civilian clothes, he'd wandered through the communities with his ears wide open, listening carefully. Finding the would-be suicide bombers had been depressingly easy. Like so many others, they had bad intentions – and no contacts with the underground world. Obtaining explosives on the black market wasn't exactly easy. He'd lost count of how many idiots seeking a quick death had tried to buy weapons and explosives off police informers.

He glanced around the garage, rolling his eyes. Like many other businesses in the area, as much of the business as possible was done off the books – just to keep the taxman from taking an undue interest in their profits. He found it hard to blame the struggling small businessmen for trying to keep their profits for themselves, but the garage had clearly been involved in preparing stolen cars to be released back onto the market. The tools to rig up a small van with enough explosive to really ruin someone's day had been easy to find. God alone knew what had happened to the owner and his family. They hadn't returned to work in the days since the invasion.

A tap at the door brought him to full alertness. He half-drew his pistol with one hand as he padded over to the door and peered through the one-way glass that the previous owner had installed. The young fool was standing there, waiting for him. Abdul rolled his eyes, silently grateful that he wouldn't have to rely on such fools forever, knowing that the man wouldn't have bothered to walk in a manner that might deter a shadow. His confidence that God would protect him was grossly misplaced. In Abdul's experience, God helped those who helped themselves – although He probably wouldn't want to help suicide bombers. Part of him wanted to tell the young fool to go home and enjoy the rest of his life, but there was no real alternative. They had to remind the aliens that they existed before the aliens broke their determination to resist.

He opened the door and waved the young man into the garage. The young fool had dressed for the job, all right. He'd washed, cut his beard and then dressed in his finest white robes. If he'd paid as much attention to his schoolwork as he had to his appearance, he might have made something of himself without slipping into bitterness and paranoid conspiracy theories. Abdul shook hands with him firmly, and then nodded towards the white van. It was ready to leave the building.

"I've been watching the alien guards," he said. Quite why the aliens had bothered to take over a technical college in London was beyond him, but it was clearly important to them. They weren't using their tame policemen to guard it. Instead, there were upwards of thirty aliens on guard duty and they weren't shy about urging human onlookers away from the scene. "You should be able to get into the parking lot if you leave in twenty minutes."

One thing that had been hammered into his head time and time again during the dreaded Combat Infantryman's Course at Catterick Garrison had been that they should never be predicable. Any routine was dangerous because a watching enemy could pick the best moment to launch an attack, catching the defenders by surprise. But the aliens didn't seem to have realised that. Their guards patrolled in regular, easily predicable patterns, changing every hour. He could almost set his watch by their movements. It had taken him two days of observation to be reasonably sure that it wasn't a trap of some kind, although they were definitely going to get more than they bargained for if he was wrong. The van carried enough explosive to be fairly sure of totalling the college when it exploded.

He walked over to the van and opened the door. "When you turn the corner onto the road, push down on the switch there," he said. "That arms the bomb. When you want it to detonate, take your hand off the switch and it'll explode. Don't try to brake once you're around the corner – just drive for the gate as fast as you can."

The young man nodded. He looked confident, at least. Abdul silently pitied him – and his family. It was rare to see a suicide bomber blessed by his family, at least in Britain. Their deaths tended to come as a shock to their friends and relatives, giving them the grief of losing someone while dealing with increasingly pointed questions from the security services. Part of his mind pointed out that such a young fool would find a way to harm himself sooner or later, perhaps lashing out at a member of his family. At least this way his death would count for something. He told himself that, time and time again, but the dirty feeling refused to fade from his mind.

He reached out and touched the young man's sleeve. "You don't have to go through with this," he said, flatly. "If you want to back out…"

"I know what I'm doing," the young man said. Abdul sighed inwardly at his tone. He'd heard it before from young recruits, the kind who needed to be broken down before they could be built up again. But that required dedication and determination – and the young would-be bomber had neither. "It needs to be done, for what they did to us. You have the video?"

Abdul nodded. He'd used a simple civilian camcorder to record a brief statement, a message to be uploaded onto the internet after the bomb exploded. The young fool would explain why he'd bombed the college, stating that it was in response to the occupied mosques. *He* seemed to believe that the aliens had meant to insult and degrade Islam. Abdul suspected that they simply didn't care. Given their size, they needed larger buildings – and mosque prayer halls were wide open, easy for them to use. A church would need to have the pews removed before it would suit the aliens.

"It's ready for uploading," he said. Actually, he'd moved the uploading laptop somewhere else. He had no way of knowing what surveillance capabilities the aliens had in place, which meant that they might be able to trace the van back to the garage. And if they caught him… he was sure that there were other soldiers operating within London, apart from his small cell, but he hadn't been given any details. He had to assume that their death meant the end of resistance within London. "Remember; push down on the switch once you turn the corner, and then *keep your hand on the switch*! You let go of it early…"

"Understood," the young man said. He turned the key and the engine rumbled to life. It was lucky that the garage owner had kept a small reservoir of petrol under the building, or they wouldn't have been able to fuel the van. Civilians had almost no petrol in London these days. The air was cleaner already. "And thank you."

Abdul watched him go, silently wondering if God would hear his prayers in the future.

He'd just sent a young man to hell.

Aashif knew how to drive, but he'd never taken the formal test and he had never tried to drive a van before. It felt heavy and unwieldy compared to his

father's car and if the roads hadn't been almost empty, he was sure that he would have crashed – or at least scraped off some of the paint – by now. His sweaty hands felt slippery against the wheel, forcing him to keep a tight grip. He could hear his heartbeat pounding inside his skull. A collaborator's car pulled out ahead of him and he had to push down on the brakes to avoid a collision. He'd been warned that if he did crash, for any reason, he had to abandon the van and run. The moment they saw the explosives, the police would know what he had in mind…

His breath was coming in patches, leaving him feeling unwell as he turned the corner carefully. There were no traffic lights in London these days either. He'd been told that he would feel calm, that the peace of God would overwhelm him, but instead he just felt frantic, almost terrified. It would be easy to park the van and just run… he could walk away from his own death. But there was nowhere to go. The people he knew were the ones he had bragged to about his role in the *Jihad*. It had seemed so easy at the start to use his inflated claims to gain power and influence – God knew that the younger Muslims had had enough of older clerics telling them what to do. Pakistan was on the other side of the world – gone, if some of the more alarming reports on the internet were true – and it wasn't *right* that they should be controlled by village elders who couldn't even protect them from racists or the police…

And then there were the temptations of the West. Women leaving the homes and working for a living, instead of doing their duty as mothers, daughters and wives. Music, drugs… everything that polluted the mind and wore away at faith. And homosexuality… how could anyone tolerate a world where men could love men? It was disgusting how the West prided itself on its own tolerance. Even though it provided a shield for the faithful, for those determined to turn back the clock… how could anyone *stand* to live like that?

And then there were those who suffered while he lived in luxury…

It had been easy to pretend, until his dream had become a nightmare. And yet he couldn't back out. He'd recorded the video, the one where he'd damned the aliens and their collaborators for what they'd done to Islam. If he left the van and ran, he knew what would happen. The video would be released and everyone would laugh at him. He'd know that they were laughing, even as they pretended to be sympathetic. How could he ever show his face in their company again?

His heart beat faster as he turned the corner. The college was just up ahead, a place for smarter kids who didn't want to spend the rest of their lives flipping burgers at McDonalds, or claiming benefits. He reached for the switch and hesitated. It wasn't too late. He could park and run away and maybe find a new home somewhere else. There were always possibilities for those with the determination… but he'd lacked it. In a rare moment of self-assessment, he realised that he'd never had the determination to make something of himself. Instead, someone else had made something out of him. He wanted to run and yet he didn't quite dare…

He pushed down on the switch, hearing an ominous click. His hand felt as if it were drenched in sweat as he gunned the engine, sending the van forward faster. The aliens hadn't bothered to put up a gate, merely a pair of guards. He saw their ugly forms and pointed the van right at them, wondering if they had the sense to jump out of the way. It wouldn't save them, though. There was enough explosives in the van to reduce the entire building to rubble… or so he'd been told. Maybe they'd lied to him…

There was a popping sound. It took him a moment to realise that they were shooting at him. A burst of pain spread over his chest, sending him flopping backwards against the seat. It was suddenly very hard to think. His chest was warm… blood was pouring from a hole… he slumped forward, his hand falling off the switch. He had a second to realise that he'd released the switch… and then the world went away in a flash of white-hot flame.

Chapter Eighteen

London
United Kingdom, Day 15

Robin and Constable Riley had been parked in a police car when they heard the explosion. It was thunderously loud in a city where most noise had dimmed away to almost nothing. The cars that had once produced a constant backdrop were silent; no massive jumbo jets flew in and out of the city. Indeed, it had been so quiet that Robin had wondered if the penny was ever going to drop. And the massive fireball rising up in the distance suggested that it had. Someone was striking back at the aliens…

"Start the car," he ordered, grabbing his radio. The aliens had allowed them to use them, although Robin suspect that they intended to use them to monitor their collaborators. "This is Zulu Bravo; we are heading to the incident site. I say again, this is…"

"Trouble," Constable Riley commented, as he flung the police car around a corner. "They were doing something at that college…"

Robin stared, not quite believing his eyes. There had once been a large building, home to a technical college producing graduates with degrees that should get them good jobs in the computer industry. It had been smashed by the explosion, along with several other buildings nearby. A number of cars were burning brightly – he keyed his radio to summon the fire brigade – and an alien armoured vehicle had been tipped upside down. It was a weakness in their design, he guessed; their hover-cushion gave an unexpected blast the leverage to throw the vehicle right over. He doubted that it would happen to a human-built tank.

"Dear God," he breathed. There seemed to be hundreds of people caught in the blast. Most schools hadn't reopened in the days following the invasion, but the aliens had been very interested in the technical college. No one had quite been able to figure out why. "How many people did they kill?"

"It really makes you wonder," Riley said, as they climbed out of the car. The whole scene was overwhelming, worse than Buckingham Palace. "Which side are we supposed to be on?"

Robin glared at him. If he'd been alone, if no one else had been in danger, he might have joined one of the resistance cells being talked about on the internet. But there was his wife… and there was the simple fact that innocent civilians were going to be caught in the midst of the fighting. The police existed to protect civilians… which didn't change the fact that they'd effectively started working for the aliens. But if they hadn't, who knew what the aliens would do in response? If they used live ammunition to respond to broken bottles, what the hell would they do in response to a bomb that had slaughtered upwards of twenty of them?

"Call ambulances," he ordered. He wasn't sure where to begin. With the wounded – or with two bodies that were very clearly not human? The aliens didn't seem to have survived the blast. Maybe they had some wonder-technology that could resurrect the dead, but he wouldn't count on it. "Call medics. Call everyone."

He shook his head. Where the hell did they even *start*?

———

Fatima had been trying to relax when her pager went off, alerting her to a medical emergency. It had come just in time. Her stepmother had been boring her again with more suggestions for suitable boys, even though they'd lost touch with the old country. The internet said that India and Pakistan had nuked each other in the wake of the invasion and, despite her best hopes, she suspected that it was true. Too many sources were repeating the same claim time and time again.

She picked up her overnight bag and ran out of the door, glancing down at her pager to see where she was going. A massive plume of smoke was rising up over London, reminding her of the hellish first days when the aliens had arrived. At least they'd managed to get most of the wounded to their own homes, she told herself as she started to run. Five minutes later, she saw an ambulance and flagged it down, hoping that the driver would have time to stop. He did, allowing Fatima to climb onboard before he gunned the engine again, heading towards the plume of smoke. She felt sick as she realised where they were going. Gilmore Technical College had played host to several of her friends, back when they'd dreamed of careers. And now it was just a pile of rubble.

A number of Incident Coordinators had arrived and taken charge, thankfully. They'd been missed during the desperate attempt to treat the wounded in Central London, during the invasion. Fatima didn't even bother to throw them accusing glances – they were collaborators, after all – as she scrambled down from the ambulance and ran towards their position. Police and firemen were helping the wounded away from the fires, trying to get them processed and into the queue for medical treatment. She closed her ears to their screams and pleas, knowing that there was little she could do to help. God alone knew if they had enough medical supplies on hand.

She rapidly found herself assigned to triage. It wasn't something they'd practiced before, outside of a pair of paranoid exercises they'd done before the invasion. She glanced at the first casualty, swiftly assessed his condition, and marked him down as category two. He had a broken leg and was probably in shock, but he'd survive without immediate medical treatment. It broke her heart to leave him without help, yet there was no choice. The next person, a young girl barely out of her teens, was too badly wounded to live without immediate hospital treatment. Fatima marked her down, knowing that she would probably never be taken to hospital and receive the treatment she needed. At least she was too badly injured to be aware of her surroundings. If God was kind, she would pass away without ever waking up.

The hours seemed like days as they tried to clear up the mess. Over two thousand humans had been in the building when the bomb exploded, along with a number of aliens. Most of them were dead, or so badly wounded that the only thing the doctors could do was inject them with painkillers and watch them slip away. One of the bodies, plonked down in front of her, was clearly inhuman. She forgot her fear and helpless anguish as she stared down at the alien body. The inner bone structure was very different from a human skeleton, as far as she could tell; despite their great size, they seemed almost *weaker* than the average human. But the internet insisted that the aliens had an advantage in hand-to-hand combat… their leathery skin, far tougher than human skin, might help hold them together. Perhaps they were less used to trauma than humans.

A leathery hand pulled her away from the body. She jumped… and found herself staring up into an alien face. The alien pushed her aside with casual ease, allowing two of his – she assumed that it was a male, although there was no way to tell – comrades to pick up the body and cart it away to one of their floating trucks. They weren't bothering to tend to any of the human wounded, or even help moving away the dead. As far as she could tell, they only cared about themselves.

"Don't get angry at them," a soft voice said. She looked up to see a policeman, staring down at her. There was something damned and suffering in his eyes. "Just be grateful they're letting us handle this."

Fatima opened her mouth to deliver an angry retort about collaborators – and then she swallowed it, knowing that it would do no good. What choice did they have? And what choice did *she* have? She had opened herself to charges of collaboration by coming to help the wounded, even though most of the wounded were humans. And to think she'd wondered why Iraqis had had so much trouble deciding which side to support during the war…

She pushed the thought aside and returned to work. There was an unending stream of casualties to tend to, and hopefully save. And then perhaps she might find something else to do with her time.

———

From his vantage point, Alan Beresford watched as the plume of smoke slowly faded away. It had been nearly four hours since the blast and the emergency services had worked like demons to cope with the damage. There was no threat to any other building, at least as far as they could tell, and they had a preliminary list of the dead. And as far as they were concerned, Alan knew, they'd done an excellent job. It was a pity that there was nothing left of the bomber, but the blast had been powerful enough to bring down a fairly large building. The bomber himself would have been reduced to atoms.

But that wasn't the important point, Alan knew. The aliens didn't share details about their security – or their long-term objectives – with him, but he did know that they had taken a handful of losses recently. Small, compared to the casualties they'd suffered during the invasion itself, but irritating. And all the more irritating because they'd trusted Alan to provide security for their people. They'd given him power and responsibility and all they'd asked was that he kept his word. What would happen to him, Alan asked himself, if they decided that they no longer wanted him to control the country for them? Somehow, he had no doubt that the aliens would simply kill him and put an end to it.

The thought was intolerable. He'd risen high in pursuit of power – he wasn't going to let it end without a fight. And if the aliens decided that he was expendable… no, it was unthinkable. He wasn't going to look as ineffective as the British Government had looked against the IRA, or the more recent threat from Muslim fundamentalists. He'd show them that Alan Beresford was still a good investment. And if a few innocents got mashed in the gears, well… one couldn't make an omelette without breaking a few eggs.

He turned and faced his small Cabinet. And small it was. Many of the ministers who'd served Prime Minister Gabriel Burley – wherever the hell he was – were dead, or in hiding. It seemed unlikely that they would be able to remain undiscovered forever, but that was small comfort. He'd had to promote a handful of his cronies, a number of men who owed him favours, and the senior surviving police officer in London. Some of them followed him because they believed in him, others followed because of the dirt he had on them… and at least two were there because they had nowhere else to go. But that could change, Alan reminded himself, savagely. How long would it be before one of them realised that they could make their own deals with the aliens? And then how long would Alan last?

"We have a problem," he said, addressing his Media Officer. Catherine Stewart knew where the bodies were buried, sometimes literally. Alan had once heard a joke about how many people would attend the funeral of a world-famous columnist, just to make sure that the old bat with the poison pen was finally dead. It applied just as much to Catherine, whose blonde good looks concealed a razor-sharp mind and a complete absence of scruples. "The scum who did this killed innocent Londoners. They have to be found. I want you to make sure that that party line gets out there right away, without any dissent. Try and prevent the internet from taking any other line."

Catherine nodded. It hadn't taken her more than a week to start building her own empire – but then, she was the only source of employment for countless spin doctors and muckrakers who no longer had anywhere else to go. They'd make damn sure that the media toed the line, or he'd have some of them shot to encourage the others. And he wasn't joking either. Given enough time, he was sure that they could shut down most of the internet in Britain, but it seemed difficult to do without taking down what remained of the government communications network. The aliens had refused to allow them to use the alien network.

"Of course, sir," she said. "How do you wish us to proceed?"

Alan's temper boiled over. "I expect your fucking subordinates to do their jobs," he snapped. "I want pictures of the dead and wounded – the younger and sexier the better. I want sob stories on who died and how much promise they had in front of them before they were assassinated by the wretched terrorists. I want total media coverage – interviews with the survivors and relatives, talking heads on how some people just cannot forget the past, and tearful interviews demanding that the legitimate government do something about them. Do you understand me?"

"Yes, sir," Catherine said. She lowered her eyes, but Alan wasn't fooled. There was nothing submissive in her nature. "I shall see to it personally."

"Now go do your damned job," Alan snapped, and waited for her to leave the room. She was too smart for her own good, at least in a world he controlled – as long as he pleased the aliens, of course. Given time, he was sure that she would be the one to challenge him. The woman was just too ambitious for her own good. "Chief Constable – give me some good news, *please.*"

Chief Constable Gerald Rivers hadn't been Chief Constable for very long. His predecessor and his deputy had been killed when the aliens took out Scotland Yard and Rivers' only real qualification for the job was that he'd been the senior police officer to agree to serve the aliens and keep the peace. He was a short man, inclining towards stoutness, but there was a hard edge underneath him that Alan had no difficulty recognising. It was a shame that he genuinely believed that the only way to protect the public was to work with the aliens, rather than allowing ambition to drive him forward… Alan shrugged. One couldn't have everything and Rivers wasn't likely to try to unseat him.

"We did manage to repair most of the CCTV network nodes over the last few days," Rivers said. London had had the greatest number of CCTV cameras per person in the world – until the aliens had arrived and wrecked a few hundred when they'd taken out Central London. "I've had crews working on the footage – we did manage to trace the van back to its base. And we got some good pictures of the bomber himself, but we think he had at least one accomplice. The explosives used in the blast were military-grade."

Alan scowled. The Household Division had put up a vicious little fight in Central London – and the aliens had been certain that they hadn't rounded up all of the surviving soldiers. Some of them had been killed trying to get out of London, but others had clearly stayed inside the city – and had been planning to carry on the war against the aliens. He cursed them under his breath, even as he tossed a few ideas around in his head. Perhaps there was a way to escape blame for the disaster… no, the aliens wouldn't be interested in excuses. From what he'd heard, they were only interested in results.

"I assume the bomber blew himself to fuck," he said, flatly. The swearword felt good on his lips, even though he had been careful not to swear in public before allying himself with the aliens. The Leathernecks, as some were calling them. "What about his accomplice?"

"I'm afraid his ally was too careful," Rivers admitted. "Our CCTV coverage near Regents Park has never been what it should be – and whoever was behind the blast knew to stay out of the camera's field of vision. The chances are good that we have some footage of the bomb-maker, but we don't know it. At least, not yet."

He shrugged. "The bomber himself, we believe, was Aashif Shahid," he continued. "He does have a file – he came to our attention after a number of outspoken comments in the mosque about the need to wage war on the Great Satan – but MI5 took a look at him and decided that he was nothing more than a loudmouth. No real contacts with the radicals who could provide explosives or weapons – and no sign that he was trying to build his own. And as for why he decided to attack the aliens…?"

Alan shrugged. "Get a team out to the garage and see if you can pick up any clues that might lead to the bomb-maker," he ordered. "And then draw up a list of his friends and family. I want them arrested and charged with harbouring a known terrorist…"

"With all due respect, sir," Rivers pointed out, "there is no evidence that anyone else knew about his plans…"

"Do it anyway," Alan ordered, sharply. He glanced over at the alien communicator on the table. God alone knew how it worked, but it was quite possible that the aliens were watching him at all times. Fear leaked into his voice as he spoke. "Do you want *them* to do it?"

Rivers met his eyes in shared understanding, if for different reasons. The aliens could do it, all right, or they might bring in the heavy weapons. It was easy to imagine them calling down strikes on London, blasting entire buildings to rubble, just to teach the imprudent humans a lesson. And then they'd be looking at thousands dead and God alone knew how many wounded. And it wouldn't give them a chance to track down the remainder of the resistance cell. And…

"See to it," Alan ordered, quietly. "We can't risk losing control now, or we might lose everything."

Chapter Nineteen

London
United Kingdom, Day 15

From a distance, the old garage looked harmless. Just another old business, struggling to stay afloat in the depression – and perhaps making questionable deals with criminals or terrorists to keep the money rolling in. But Sergeant Terry Graves knew better than to relax. CO19 – the Central Operations Specialist Firearms Command – had broken into terrorist bases before and, no matter how innocent they looked, they often had unpleasant surprises waiting for unwary armed police officers. The irony didn't amuse him as he beckoned the rest of the team forward, leaving two men behind to watch from a safe distance. They'd been sent into battle unarmed, at least without firearms. The alien ban on human firearms was still firmly in place.

Terry cursed silently under his breath as they crept closer. In an ideal world, he and his team would be fighting the aliens – and they'd had time to conceal a small number of firearms around London in places they could reach them if the shit hit the fan. But for the moment, they had no choice, apart from collaboration. And if they failed to catch the insurgents who had struck out at the aliens, the aliens would take steps of their own. Given their willingness to use indiscriminate weapons fire in the midst of the civilian population, he had no doubt just how bloody and violent their steps would be.

He held up a hand as he inspected the garage's door. It was quite possible, judging by the blast that had levelled an entire technical college, that they weren't dealing with would-be terrorists at all. The moron who'd driven the truck could have been told that he would have time to make his escape, or maybe he'd known that he was going to die. And the person behind him, far from being an international terrorist, might be someone trained and armed by the British Army. Terry had seen enough SAS troopers during their cross-training sessions to dread the possibility that one of them might have gone rogue.

The thought made him snort. From what they'd been able to pick up from the internet, the remains of the British military had been ordered to carry on the fight for as long as possible. They weren't chasing a rogue, but someone intent on carrying out his orders and hurting the aliens until he was finally hunted down and killed. There might be an entire team of Regiment soldiers waiting for them, or perhaps they had already vanished, leaving no traces behind. Terry envied them their freedom of action. His own family had been moved to a place where they were being held – for their own good, of course. And if he turned against the aliens, they would kill his entire family.

They seem to be getting an idea of what makes us tick, he thought, sourly. *God knows how long they were watching us from space. They don't seem to be particularly subtle at all – do as we want or we will kill you. And if you vanish, we will kill your family…*

The garage seemed deserted, but he clutched his baton tightly as he pushed at the door. There was a single click and then the door swung open, revealing a deserted interior. It looked as if someone had been busy – there were tools scattered everywhere – but they had clearly abandoned the building. Judging from the skill shown by the bomb-maker, he'd probably assumed that the suicide bomber would have been caught on camera and traced back to his base. Someone from the Regiment would have known just how the Met used the CCTV network to look backwards in time and try to localise a terrorist base. Or catch bad parkers, for that matter.

He beckoned two other officers inside and they spread out, checking for traps while carefully not touching anything that might carry fingerprints or DNA evidence. The pit below where the van had rested was deeper than he expected, suggesting that the original owner of the garage must have been a very tall man. Or perhaps he'd just been an expert at scrambling out of pits. There was no sign of a ladder or any other way back to the ground floor.

"In here," one of the officers muttered. "I found papers."

Terry followed his gaze. The back of the garage was a small office, stinking of half-eaten kebabs and burgers. Judging from the smell, the food had to have been decomposing for several days, perhaps a week. London's endless series of kebab houses had been shutting down as supplies from outside the city tapered off, leaving the population dependent upon the tasteless alien muck. It struck him as odd that an SAS soldier would leave contaminated food behind, but maybe it was intended to deter intruders. *He* certainly wouldn't have wanted to go into the office without a gas mask and perhaps a flamethrower. The forensic team were going to have to wear full NBC suits if they wanted to pull anything useful out of the room.

"Maybe they left something behind to tell us where they were going," the officer said. Terry doubted it. It was rather more likely that the garage's owner had left the papers behind, wherever he was now. Teams of researchers were already looking through the records to see what had happened to him – maybe he'd registered with the aliens – but Terry wasn't too hopeful that they would lead the Met to the bomb-maker. It was far more likely that it would be nothing more than a wild goose chase. "Or perhaps…"

He opened one of the drawers, a second before Terry could shout out a warning. There was a second click, followed by a wave of fire that blasted out and into the garage. Terry yelled in pain as his skin burned, even as he stumbled backwards trying to find the way out. The flames were spreading with terrifying speed, suggesting that the entire garage had been rigged to catch fire quickly and efficiently. He felt as if he'd caught fire himself… somehow, gasping for breath, he managed to find his way out without falling into the repair pit. Another officer wasn't so lucky; Terry watched in horror as he fell, just before the flames roared into the pit. They seemed to be almost crawling across the ground towards the policemen. He heard a scream that cut off seconds later.

Outside, he could hear the sounds of fire engines already on their way. It was far too late. The flames had consumed much of the evidence, if there had ever been any evidence at all – it was, he realised grimly, a trap intended to kill a number of policemen as well as wipe the slate clean. It was clear that the bomb-maker had a nasty sense of humour.

His skin still burning, he found a place to sit and waited for the fire brigade. Somehow, he was sure that they wouldn't find anything in the ruins of the garage. The bomber had gotten clean away.

———

Robin glanced up at his small force of policemen. They were all wearing riot-control gear, which should provide some protection if the situation turned violent. And it might well turn violent – Londoners weren't used to seeing hundreds of people torn from their homes and transferred to detention camps, even during the terrifying days after suicide bombers had struck the London Underground. People might resist – and if they did, it was likely to get bloody. And they'd still been denied firearms. The aliens had promised that they would have a force on standby to help out the police if necessary, but Robin was determined not to call on them. They'd kill civilians indiscriminately in the name of restoring order.

The vans pulled up outside the house and halted. Robin opened the doors and led the way out and up to the door, pressing down hard on the buzzer. A second team had been deployed to the back of the house, where it would snatch up anyone trying to climb out the rear window. There was a brief pause, and then a middle-aged Asian woman opened the door, her dark eyes clearly alarmed. The police weren't very popular in this part of London, despite attempts to recruit more officers from ethnic minorities. And they were about to become a great deal less popular…

Robin grabbed her, frisked her with casual efficiency, and then spun her around and slapped on the cuffs. She let out a yelp of shock that became a scream when he shoved her into the arms of another policeman, who would put her out in the garden until they'd rounded up everyone in the house. Her yelp brought two teenage boys out to see what was going on; Robin barked at them to keep their hands where he could see them, just before taking advantage of their shock to handcuff the lead youth. The second tried to swing a punch at Robin, only to be sent falling to his knees when Robin slammed his baton into his chest. He vomited, but Robin had no time to see to his health. As soon as the cuffs were on, he crashed onwards, into the next room. Two younger girls were cooking something that smelt hot and spicy; he gave them a moment to turn off the gas before cuffing both of them and pushing them outside.

Five other policemen had clumped up the stairs, finding three middle-aged gentlemen and an elderly lady who looked old enough to be Robin's great-grandmother. Her ID card claimed that she was sixty. The policemen cuffed her anyway, shouting at the men to keep them subdued as they were hauled downstairs. Robin kicked his way into the suicide bomber's room, but saw little of interest apart from some pamphlets produced by radical fundamentalists calling on the Muslim community to rise up and slaughter the infidel. He picked a new-looking booklet up and glanced at it, realising that the fundamentalist arseholes had demoted America from Great Satan to Middle Satan. The aliens seemed to be the new Great Satan, although he wasn't sure why. He'd heard that some fundamentalists were claiming that the aliens had bombed Mecca, but as far as he'd been able to tell they'd largely ignored the Middle East. The region was sinking into chaos after they'd smashed the military bases and left the rest of the region to sink or swim on its own.

Outside, a crowd was already gathering. The policemen ignored them as the next set of vans pulled up, ready to take the prisoners to the detention camp. Robin shuddered as the prisoners set off an awful racket, yelling and screaming for help from their fellow Muslims – and everyone else in the area. He felt sick at what he was doing – the Nazis had done the same to the Jews, as well as everyone else who'd incurred their hatred – but there was no choice. The looks some of the civilians were giving him suggested that they wouldn't accept his excuses, or his self-justifications. They saw him as a monster serving an inhuman enemy.

But we've no choice, he wanted to shout. *They can kill the entire human race.*

A rock was thrown by one of the crowd, followed rapidly by a small volley of stones, bricks and bottles. Robin ducked for cover as objects began to bounce off the side of the vans, or strike policemen. They were wearing armour, but no body armour was totally perfect. Two of the policemen fell to the ground, bleeding. One of them was caught up by the advancing mob and stomped to death.

Damn you, Robin thought. *Don't you know what the aliens will do to you?*

He barked an order and the water cannons activated, spraying water over the advancing crowd. They staggered backwards, some of them choking for breath as the hose was played right over their faces. Some of them seemed to have the sense to run, but others seemed far too aware that the police vans could only carry a small amount of water. A few minutes and they'd run out completely. And then they'd be forced to use the gas…

The engines roared to life and he barked orders. They'd have to leave the body of their fallen comrade behind, even though it tore at him to leave it. The only way to recover the body was to use gas – and he wasn't ready to use it unless they were in desperate straits. He watched as the remaining policemen scrambled for the vans, and then beat a hasty retreat. Absently, he wondered how the other teams were coping. The aliens had designated three hundred relatives of the suicide bomber and his friends for capture. Some of them would probably be arrested easily, but the others…? The Islamic community might hide them from the aliens.

He let out a breath he hadn't realised he'd been holding as the vans lurched down the empty streets. They'd made it out without having to kill any of the civilians. But next time…

Next time, he was sure, it would be a different story.

————

"I strongly suggest that you don't go any further," a man's voice said. "You're already in deep shit."

Fatima jumped. She'd been walking home from the bomb site, lost in her own thoughts – and yet surely someone should not have been able to surprise her. The streets of London weren't safe – hell, they hadn't been safe before the invasion. She had been asked to take up lodgings at one of the hospitals, but she'd declined. There was no way to explain it to her stepmother. Respectable girls lived in the family home until they married, whereupon they moved to their husband's home and found themselves slaving for their mother-in-law.

"Don't worry," the man said. "I'm on your side. Call me Abdul."

"Right," Fatima said. She'd met men who thought that they were God's gift to women before, brimming with unjustified confidence… but this man seemed to be more relaxed than confident. "What's going on?"

She glanced around the corner and stopped, dead. There looked to be a small army of policemen outside her house, and a growing crowd of friends, relatives and neighbours surrounding the policemen. As she watched, her stepmother was hauled out by two of the policemen and dumped in the garden, her hands cuffed behind her backs. The rest of her extended family followed moments later. Fatima realised, in growing shock, that she would have been arrested herself if she'd been in the house.

Abdul caught her arm. For once, she wasn't offended at a man touching her without an invitation. "Walk with me," he hissed. She could feel his breath against her ear even though the scarf. "Pretend we're a married couple and walk slowly. We don't want to attract attention."

Behind her, Fatima heard the sound of angry shouting in three different languages and the sound of hosepipes. She felt her heart clench inside her as they walked away, nearly fainting when a row of police vans shot past them and down the road at terrifying speed. The district was normally crammed with cars inching their way through the streets, but now it was empty, allowing the police to move fast. And they were taking her family away… she wanted to scream after them, but what good would it have done?

Abdul looked down at her. Oddly, she felt safe with him. "I'm afraid your… cousin managed to blow himself up earlier this morning," he said. "The police – and the Leathernecks – identified him and marked your family down for retaliation. You're a wanted woman now, I'm afraid. The moment you show that ID card of yours, they'll snatch you up and put you in one of the camps."

Fatima stared at him. "How do you know that?" She demanded. Something else crossed her mind. "And who are you?"

"My name is Abdul," Abdul repeated. "And I'm part of the resistance. And now so are you."

They reached a small apartment block, one that catered to students at London's universities. Some of the students, Fatima had heard, had managed to get permission from the aliens to return home, while others had found themselves trapped in London. It seemed an odd place to hide a resistance cell, but it did make a certain kind of sense. The landlords would be used to people coming and going at all hours of the day and they'd turn a blind eye to certain activities. They walked up two flights of stairs and entered a small suite of rooms, clearly ones that had been abandoned in a hurry. Somehow, she was sure that Abdul himself wasn't a student. He walked more like a mature and experienced man of the world. The kind of man her cousins had wanted to become.

"But I can't," she protested, finally. Her entire body was shaking. She had to be in shock, she realised. Her entire life had just fallen down around her. God alone knew what would happen to her family. "I can't just leave and… I've got patients to see!"

"The moment you show yourself," Abdul said, kindly, "they will arrest you. There'll probably be a reward on your head before too long. You can't do anything for your patients now – the only thing you can do is get yourself arrested."

He placed one hand on her shoulder. "We have this flat for the next fortnight, at least," he added. "Get a shower, have a long rest – and I'll see you tonight. You're a doctor – the resistance could make use of you. Certainly better use than the aliens could…"

Fatima found her voice. "But what will happen to my family?"

Abdul looked, just for a second, uncharacteristically guilty. "I don't know," he admitted, "but I don't think it will be anything good. It's rather more likely that they will execute them – to encourage the others, as they say. The only thing you can do now is help us to avenge them."

Fatima watched him go, her mind spinning. Her world had turned upside down… and she couldn't even cry. What could she do now?

Chapter Twenty

Near Gayhurst
United Kingdom, Day 20

"I just got the buzz," Private Cole muttered. "The Leathernecks are on their way."

"How unlucky for the Leathernecks," Chris Drake muttered back. The aliens were certainly predicable, all right. It seemed odd that they made mistakes that human armies had learned to avoid, but from what he could tell, they might have good reason to believe that this particular alien routine wasn't dangerous. There were reports suggesting that, two days ago, several men armed with hunting rifles and shotguns had tried to take on an alien convoy. They'd been killed without harming a single alien. "How long do we have?"

"Fifteen minutes, at most," Cole warned. "Maybe less. They do seem to speed up from time to time."

Chris shrugged. The alien hover-tanks moved at speeds that Challenger tanks would have found flatly impossible. Even the smaller armoured vehicles in the British Army – or the barely-armoured Snatch Land Rover – would have had trouble matching their speed. But human trucks and lorries were slower and the aliens, it seemed, were willing to press human drivers into service to help their logistics. It stood to reason that they'd prefer to use human labour where possible, but it didn't seem to have occurred to their commanders that this meant that their convoys were slower than they might have preferred. Or perhaps their commanders simply didn't care. Chris had encountered a couple of senior officers who issued orders that forced the soldiers on the ground to do more with less – and mistook the map for the terrain. And given that the aliens seemed alarmingly inflexible, they probably didn't give their troops on the ground any latitude at all.

Of course, we had to learn, didn't we? He thought to himself. *I wonder if we'll be the lucky ones who run into an alien junior officer with the guts – or family connections – to do his own thing…?*

The M1 motorway was one of the longest motorways in Britain, connecting London to Leeds. It had also been one of the busiest, at least until the aliens had arrived and managed to do what years of protest and campaigning by environmental freaks hadn't. Now, the motorways were almost deserted, used only by the aliens and their collaborators. Indeed, a handful of shot-up cars signified the dangers of using the motorways in a world where armed men were intent on waging war against the occupiers. Most families were conserving what little petrol they had left for emergencies.

From his vantage point in Gayhurst Wood, he could see the eerily deserted motorway stretching away into the distance. The aliens seemed to be running regular convoys up and down Britain's motorway network, supplying their bases around British cities. In fact, Chris knew that a number of other attacks had been planned over the coming few days, although he hadn't been given any specifics. It was strange to feel as if they were both isolated and connected to the resistance underground, but there was little choice. The aliens would presumably have no qualms about using torture to get information out of prisoners.

But we still don't know what they do to military prisoners, he thought, grimly. The resistance had attempted to trace the prisoners, using assets within the police forces that were serving the aliens, but they'd been unable to come up with any answers. All military personnel had been handed over to the aliens and taken away to an unknown destination. Given that the aliens ruled the entire world, it was quite possible that they'd been taken overseas, perhaps to the Middle East. Or maybe to Antarctica.

He pushed the thought aside as the sensor beside him started to bleep. They might not have any active radars any more, but they could tell when the aliens were using radar – and when one of their drones was heading towards their position. The aliens used drones to provide an outer layer of security for their convoys, a trick that probably explained why they'd picked off the civilian insurgents before they'd had a chance to spring their ambush. This time, however, things were going to be different.

"Get ready," he muttered. The moment they revealed themselves, the aliens would try to cut them down, perhaps by using something like a drone-mounted Hellfire missile. It was astonishing how advanced UAVs had become in the years since 9/11. Even the Taliban hadn't been up to evading their unblinking gaze. "Engage as soon as they come into range."

Nr'ta Silick studied the live feed from the constantly orbiting drone and relaxed, slightly. The humans were determined opponents, far tougher than anyone else they'd encountered at a comparable technological level, but they clearly didn't realise how easily their movements could be monitored by the Land Forces. A handful of convoys had been hit by concealed explosives and snipers, yet they'd never managed to take on a whole convoy – and never would. Their failure to develop space like any sane race left a gaping hole in their capabilities, one that a truly advanced race could use against them.

He snorted at the thought. The troopers who'd led the first landings on Earth had warned the reinforcement units that humans were sneaky, but he hadn't seen any evidence of human sneakiness in the four days since he'd landed on Earth. Sure, they'd managed to use treachery to kill many troopers, yet they'd also killed thousands of their own kind. No race, even one as strange as humanity, would carry one like that – their own kind would turn against them. And the humans who drove the trucks were properly loyal. They knew their place – and they also knew that any sign of disloyalty would result in their families being executed.

Earth itself was an odd world. Its climate was rarely perfect, often being too hot or too dry. The rainstorms they'd had just after landing had been refreshing, but they'd really been too cool for proper enjoyment. It wasn't too surprising that the local weather patterns had been screwed up – the Land Forces had bombarded human bases and centres of resistance with KEWs, while the Chinese humans had been insane enough to use nuclear warheads against their own cities – and the weather experts promised that it would get better soon. Indeed, they'd even pointed out that accelerating the greenhouse effect would make the planet warmer, melt the ice caps and generally make it more habitable. He couldn't understand why so many humans seemed concerned about global warming. Didn't they *want* a warmer world?

But the human opinion didn't matter, not now that their world had been absorbed into the State. They would learn to live on the reshaped world or die, while many of their fellows were shipped away to serve the State. And then…

He glanced down at the drone's feed as it shrilled a warning. It was in danger! Someone was using a seeker head to target it… he hesitated, convinced it had to be a malfunction, and then a flash of light in the sky marked the end of drone coverage. And then the world blew up in his face.

It had been surprisingly easy to gain access to the maintenance tunnels running under the motorway. Indeed, none of the soldiers could *think* why anyone would *want* the tunnels, but they'd come in handy. They'd loaded enough explosive into the tunnels to blow up half the motorway, while lurking in ambush and waiting for the aliens to respond. The destruction of their drone had been the only risky part of the ambush Chris had planned; if the aliens had realised that they were driving right into a trap, they might have deployed or simply turned back and called for reinforcements. But everything had worked perfectly…

He watched in delight as the lead alien vehicle – a tank, he suspected – literally vanished within the blast. Several human-built lorries were blown to atoms, their cargo picked up and scattered across the motorway. He heard the sound of brakes as the other vehicles struggled to come to a stop, but it was far too late. They crashed into the broken vehicles and caught fire themselves. Two alien vehicles crammed with their soldiers managed to skim to one side and up the embankment, a display of initiative he wouldn't have expected from the Leathernecks. Not that it was going to help them. He'd planned on the assumption that they wouldn't catch any of their escorts with the oversized IED.

"Go," he bellowed. Two Milan antitank missiles leapt towards their targets. One slammed into an alien vehicle before the aliens had a chance to dismount, blowing the vehicle and its passengers into bloody chunks. The other vehicle was luckier, or perhaps its commander had already issued the order to dismount before the aliens realised that they hadn't escaped the trap completely. Half of its passengers were already out when it was hit and sent careering into the motorway. "Hit the bastards!"

He smiled as the two GPMGs opened fire with savage intensity, sweeping the alien positions down below. An alien tank, bringing up the rear, skimmed around and opened fire, although it seemed that they were reluctant to risk coming any closer. Chris couldn't blame them. A Challenger II had been hit with a Milan and hundreds of RPGs in Iraq and survived, but few tankers would have been happy about driving straight up and charging into the teeth of antitank missiles. The alien tank's main gun fired twice, tossing high-explosive shells into the wood. Chris had to admit that it was an effective tactic, assuming that the aliens didn't have any way to localise their enemies. But why weren't they shooting back at the machine guns…

The alien infantry had responded with impressive speed. Most of the survivors had taken cover and were firing back, trying to force the insurgents to keep back from the remains of the convoy. A pair of human bodies on the ground suggested that they'd killed their collaborators, perhaps assuming that one of them had betrayed them to their enemies. Or perhaps they'd been shocked and hadn't realised that the collaborators were their allies. Chris waited long enough to be sure that all the aliens were out and fighting, and then he barked a second order. The three L16 81mm mortars fired as one, tossing high explosive shells down into the teeth of the enemy position. Their cover was effective against bullets, but the mortar shells landed *behind* their cover, tearing their positions apart. The aliens appeared to be tougher than humans – they certainly had tougher skin – yet they couldn't stand up to mortar shells landing far too close to them. Fire spread through the remaining vehicles as the second round of mortars was fired, just before the mortar teams started breaking down the weapons. They'd been reluctant to leave ahead of the rest when the plan had been drawn up, but Chris had been insistent. Moving a single mortar without a vehicle was difficult – artillerymen were *strong* – and they'd slow the rest of the unit down if they attempted to leave together.

He cursed as the alien tank reversed course and fled, denying him the satisfaction of a complete victory. Seeing it run puzzled him; whatever else one could say about the Leathernecks, they weren't cowards. Perhaps the tank commander had thought better of remaining close to antitank weapons, or perhaps his superiors had decided that it wasn't a good idea to risk losing another tank. It took far too long to produce a human-designed Main Battle Tank. God alone knew how long it took the aliens.

Another series of explosions ran through what remained of the convoy, followed by an uneasy silence, broken only by the sound of fire. Chris barked an order and his men held fire, staring down at the wreckage. Most of them had seen action in Afghanistan, but even the Taliban hadn't been able to wreak so much devastation on a British convoy. The training and equipment of Coalition forces had given them an advantage. He looked down for a long moment, and then nodded to the rest of his platoon. Carefully, weapons at the ready, they headed down towards the convoy.

Up close, there was something eerie about the alien vehicles, something that suggested that their designers worked from different ideas about how the universe worked. Their armour didn't seem to be quite up to human standards, although Chris was uneasily aware that once they ran out of antitank missiles, it was likely to be a great deal harder to inflict losses on the alien vehicles. He glanced inside one and saw a set of charred alien bodies,

blackened and burned by the heat. The stench was appalling. He had to fight to keep himself from throwing up his lunch into the alien vehicle.

"Look for prisoners," he bellowed, although he had no hope of finding any. The alien soldiers had been caught by the mortars and shredded. He moved from vehicle to vehicle, glancing inside and shaking his head at the carnage. Judging from the remains of some of the human trucks, they'd been transporting food rather than weapons. He couldn't blame the aliens for being reluctant to arm their collaborators. Who knew when a collaborator might change his mind?

The final vehicle – an alien troop transport – had been tipped on its side. Most of the aliens inside were clearly dead, but one was alive – if badly wounded. A human wounded so badly would need immediate hospital treatment – he flashed back to waiting on Afghanistan's plains for a medical chopper, knowing that the Taliban would shoot it down if they could – yet he had no idea if the alien could be saved. He met dark expressionless eyes and shivered, studying the alien's wounds as dispassionately as he could. Inky dark blood was leaking out of gashes in the leathery skin and spilling onto the ground. It didn't seem to be congealing like human blood.

"I'm sorry," he told the alien, as he pointed his Browning at the alien's face. It seemed to sigh and bow its head, an oddly-human motion that tore at his heart. He pulled the trigger once, putting a bullet right through the alien's brains. Oddly, the alien skull seemed to take the shot better than a human skull. He hesitated for a moment, and then scrambled out back onto the motorway. The sound of approaching helicopters could be heard in the distance.

He glanced back at where they'd hidden the IED. There was now a colossal hole in the motorway, leaving a major problem for the aliens to solve if they wanted to continue sending trucks to London. Their own hover-vehicles wouldn't have any problems navigating if they just shoved a small pile of earth into the hole, but any human-designed vehicle would have to be very careful. He scrambled up the embankment, hearing the sound of helicopters approaching from the west growing louder. The enemy tank that had withdrawn from combat – although the statements on the internet would say that it had fled – had clearly summoned reinforcements. He smiled as he saw the two helicopters finally come into view. They were moving slowly, dancing about as if they expected to run right into a trap of their own. Maybe they'd managed to spook an alien commander…

"Time to go," he said. Most of the unit had already bugged out, leaving only his platoon behind. He did have a pair of soldiers with Stingers to cover their retreat if the aliens decided to forget caution and come after them with everything they had. Hopefully it wouldn't be necessary. They had fewer Stingers than he would have liked. "We did good work today."

———

Tra'tro The'Stig dismounted from the transport and ran towards what remained of the convoy, hunting for survivors. At first glance, it seemed that there would be none, but orders from his superiors insisted that the effort be made. It didn't take a genius to realise that someone higher up was starting to wonder if there had been too many casualties on Earth, even though it had only been a handful of days since they'd landed. Given a few months or years, long before the first reports reached the State, they'd have pounded the humans into submission.

Or at least forced them to expend their advanced weapons, he thought, ruefully. This part of the world didn't seem to be as heavily armed as some others. The Russian humans seemed to have an inexhaustible supply of weapons, while the American humans seemed to have scattered weapons everywhere. Some parts of America had been crushed without the need for further fighting, but other parts were too far from the population centres to be brought under their control. At least Britain was small enough that the bases could support each other – although that meant less than it seemed. A planet was *big*.

His radio buzzed. "Report," an insistent voice demanded. The'Stig snorted, quietly enough not to be heard. No doubt it was someone senior enough not to be out on the front lines. "How many survivors have there been?"

"None," he reported, after a moment. There was a long pause, allowing him a chance to spy a couple of human bodies amid the wreckage. He tried to tell himself that they were human insurgents, but it seemed more likely that they were collaborators. The human insurgents seemed determined not to leave their bodies behind. "I cannot find any bodies."

"Understood," the voice said. "Please stand by…"

The'Stig snorted again and started to issue orders to the rest of his unit. They'd scout around and secure the area, maybe pick up on the human trail before they had a chance to go to ground. And then maybe they could extract a little revenge. Maybe…

Because if losing convoys became a habit, they were going to start running short of supplies. And if they had to start using shuttles again, they would risk losing them…

And then their ultimate victory would be in doubt.

And *that* would risk bringing in other powers.

Chapter Twenty-One

London
United Kingdom, Day 21

"How many people are down there?"

"At least five thousand," Gerald Rivers said. The Chief Constable looked uneasy. His policemen were out there, without any weapons more dangerous than water cannons and CS gas. The aliens had forbidden weapons even for those guarding their collaborators. "There will be more when people realise that the aliens aren't going to do anything to stop them."

Alan cursed. Down below, outside the security perimeter he'd had erected around his headquarters, thousands of protesters were gathering. The raids and arrests had galvanised large sections of London, bringing thousands of people out onto the streets. He couldn't help, but remember how crowds had toppled a number of regimes across the Middle East – or how they'd pressured the British Government during the run-up to Iraq. And the crowd below transcended racial or religious borders. The first series of arrests might have been targeted on Islamic families, but the next series had been equal-opportunity repression.

But there was no choice, he told himself, desperately. The poorer parts of London were becoming hotbeds of resistance activity. Young men, men who had had little hope of rising out of poverty before the invasion, were actively targeting the police – and even the aliens themselves. A dozen had died only yesterday in the wake of a failed petrol bomb attack on an alien patrol. And London wasn't even seeing the worst of the violence. Manchester had been consumed by a riot that had torn through Moss Side before the police had finally managed to restore order.

He shivered as the crowd's chant grew louder. As an MP, he'd seen the reports from the security services on radical trouble-makers who enjoyed infiltrating protest marches and causing havoc. A number with ties to London's criminal underworld were down there, arming the protesters with gas masks and even crude weapons. There might even be resistance fighters with the crowd, ready to take out a handful of collaborators. And what would the aliens do, he asked himself, if the crowd broke into his headquarters and lynched him? Perhaps they'd simply sit back and drop rocks on the crowd, thrashing the survivors into submission. Or… there were too many possibilities and none of them were pleasant.

"Give us back our children," the crowd demanded. "Give us back our wives!"

The roar grew louder as the words spread. It was simple enough to understand; dozens of wives and children, apparently innocent, had been swept up by the raids. No one knew what had happened to them, at least no one outside the alien garrison where Ten Downing Street had once been. Alan knew that they'd been taken outside the city, but then…? The aliens had refused to tell him anything, which suggested that they might simply have been killed.

But that didn't make sense either, he tried to tell himself. What was the point of punitive executions if they didn't inform the country that they'd been carried out? But the aliens were aliens and something that made sense to them might appear strange to the human mindset… he looked down at the crowd again and shuddered. He'd wanted power, hadn't he? And yet he was quailing at the thought of what he would have to do to *keep* hold of that power, to keep the population under control and the aliens happy…

He looked up at Rivers. "Disperse the crowd," he ordered, sharply. "Get rid of them. Now."

———

Robin felt sweat trickling down his back as the noise grew louder. The crowd had blurred into a single mass of humanity, screaming and shouting all along the barricades. Robin knew that if they decided to push forward, a lot of people were going to be hurt. Mobs lost all sense of proportion or civilisation; if they caught a policeman, he was likely to be trampled to death. And if individuals wanted to get away from the mob, they would find it very difficult, almost impossible. The mob mentality sucked in individuals and turned them into mindless automatons.

And yet, part of him wanted to throw away his uniform and join them. The mob was right – they *had* arrested hundreds of people without due cause. Sure, some of them had deserved arrest – one firebrand preacher deserved worse, but the pre-invasion government had been reluctant to take the political flak for arresting him – but others were innocent, their only crime being related to the suicide bomber and his friends. And some had been scooped up for no reason that he could see. They'd become worse than the Nazis in a far shorter space of time – and to think that the Met had once prided itself on its ethics. How far were they willing to go to collaborate.

He glanced behind him, seeing the same doubts written on the faces of his fellows. Some of them, at least, had been reluctant to follow orders and even join the police force blocking the way to the building housing the collaborating government. Others, on the other hand, seemed almost delighted at the prospect of violence, the ones who had learned to hate protest marches during the summers of rage, where it had been politically impossible to hand out the thrashing many of the protesters had deserved. They'd never done a day's work in their life, they'd argued, and yet they deserved to be fed and clothed at taxpayer's expense. Many policemen had little sympathy for protesters. If they put the energy they put into their protests into bettering themselves instead, they would actually find that there were other options than permanently living on the dole.

But they had their orders. The crowd had to be dispersed. Even now, other policemen would be setting up barriers, using them to push the crowd back and block off several lines of retreat. They'd be forced away from the building complex, pushed all the way back to where they'd come from – and any who tried to fight back would be arrested. Or at least that was the plan. Robin knew that many of the protesters would have come armed, intent on picking a fight – or merely intent on preventing a humiliating retreat. And the police had been denied firearms. The protest organisers might be better armed than themselves.

He braced himself as the loudspeaker crackled on. "ATTENTION," the speaker said, loudly enough to be heard over the crowd. "THIS IS AN ILLEGAL GATHERING. YOU ARE ORDERED TO DISPERSE. YOU ARE ORDERED TO DISPERSE."

The crowd started throwing objects towards the police lines. There had been no order, as far as Robin could see, merely a shared desire to hit back at the collaborators. Some of them were throwing rotten fruit and vegetables, others were throwing stones and empty bottles. Those made him wince, remembering the petrol bombs that had been thrown at the aliens and even some policemen. If they'd been filled with petrol and set alight… no flames enveloped the police lines and he allowed himself a moment of relief. A handful of policemen had been injured, but their comrades were already helping them back towards the emergency treatment centre they'd established in the corporate gym. Robin hadn't been able to believe just how many amities they'd managed to fit inside their buildings. It was a wonder that they ever went home for the night.

There was a hiss as water cannons came on, spraying furious gusts of water towards the protestors. The water was drawn from the mains, this time, providing a nearly infinite source of freezing cold liquid. Many protestors, drenched to the bone, would have thought better of being in the protest moments after they'd been hit, but the ones behind them wouldn't let them retreat. The water started to push them back, sending many protesters falling to the ground as they tried to seek shelter from the water. He allowed himself to hope that they'd succeeded in breaking the protest…

He saw the objects flying through the air before he quite realised what they were, too late. The grenades detonated beside the water cannons, blowing them and their operators apart in brilliant explosions. A great blast of water roared into the sky, leaving drops falling on police and protesters alike… the protesters howled and roared forward like a single living entity. He caught sight of young teenage girls caught up in the crush and felt a moment of pity, until they lunged forward at the police. The policemen fell back as their lines fell apart; it wasn't until he happened to glance towards where the Captain had been that he realised that someone had *shot* him. There was a sniper on one of the surrounding buildings, picking off the police commanders one by one. They hadn't even heard the shot over the sound of angry protesters scenting victory.

"Fall back," Robin yelled. The police lines were wavering. Few had been really enthusiastic about facing the protesters and it was clear that they were losing control. Several policemen with only a few months' experience had taken to their heels and fled. "Get back to the second lines, now…"

The mob surged forward and he found himself facing a young man with a shaven head and a pair of knuckledusters. He lashed out with his baton, sending the man crumpling to the ground, before the protesters trampled over his victim and kept coming. It was all he could do to back away slowly, rather than turning and joining the others in flight. He'd never faced such a situation in his entire life. Behind him, he heard the sound of gas being deployed and grasped his mask. He'd had one sniff of the gas during training and that had been quite enough. But somehow he doubted that it would be enough to stop the protesters…

His nerve broke and he turned, running for dear life. The next set of lines might be enough to stop them, or it might fall… and then the protesters would be able to pour into the buildings and rip the core of the collaborator government apart. And then the aliens would have to govern London on their own.

Somehow, he didn't think they would let it get so far.

———

"Get everyone up to the helipad," Rivers ordered. Alan barely heard him. The attempt to disperse the protesters had failed badly, not least because someone was clearing their way, picking off police commanders. He found himself looking at the other buildings, wondering which one held the sniper – or snipers. There might well be more than one. "Sir, we have to evacuate this building."

As a child, Alan had been frightened of heights and reluctant to enter tall buildings. That old fear came back to him as the building shook, suggesting that the protesters were breaking in through gates that were supposed to be sealed. Perhaps the police had fallen back deliberately, allowing the lynch mob a chance to gain entry and wipe out the collaborator government. He looked over at Rivers, wondering if the Chief Constable had ambitions to take over, before dismissing the thought. Rivers could have turned the police against him without needing to stage a riot.

"Come on, sir," Rivers said, catching him by the arm and half-dragging him towards the door. The CEO who'd owned the building had placed a helipad on top of the massive skyscraper, allowing him to fly in and out each morning without having to drive through London. Alan's government had planned to use it to keep certain movements out of the public eye. "We don't know how long it will be before they get up here."

Alan nodded, trying to remain dignified. It wasn't easy. "Where are we going?"

"The only place we can," Rivers said. "One of the alien garrisons outside the city. And pray to God that they're not feeling trigger-happy today."

Outside, on the roof, a gust of wind almost sent Alan to his knees. The entire building was shaking, as if it was on the verge of being blown over. Somehow, with help from Rivers and one of his men, he managed to climb into the helicopter and close his eyes. His entire body was shaking with fear. The sound of the engines grew louder and then he felt the helicopter lurch into life. It seemed to hop into the air, falling back for a heart-stopping moment before settling out and heading away from the building. Alan opened his eyes and stared down at the crowd below.

It struck him, suddenly, that the resistance might have hidden an antiaircraft team nearby, that they might have staged the entire protest to catch him when he was vulnerable. He opened his mouth to insist that they landed at once, before realising that the pilot wouldn't be able to hear him over the noise of the engines. Instead, he stared out at London, feeling the old fear crawling through his heart. If they were shot down, there would be no hope of survival…

London was burning. He could see plumes of smoke from where rioters were looting shops in the richer part of town, while the crowd of savage humanity seemed to have no end. It was easy to imagine what was going on down there, the frenzy of the lower classes as they worked out their class anger on defenceless targets. And then they would become savages, looting, raping and burning their way through London. He felt anger pushing away his fear as the helicopter banked away and headed westwards, up towards the alien positions around the city. How *dare* they lift a hand against him?

———

Tra'tro The'Stig had to fight down his fear as he dismounted, alarmingly close to the mob of humanity thronging through the area. There were *thousands* of the creatures, yelling and screaming as they raged against their leaders, against the few who had been smart enough to realise that they were beaten. The whole idea of a protest march was alien to those who served the State – surely, even the humans could not be so foolish as to allow protests from their juniors to shape policy. The'Stig, still in command of the mixed remains of several units, felt nothing, but contempt. Didn't these humans have the wit to know when they were beaten? Didn't they know that further resistance would only result in a great many deaths for absolutely nothing?

Behind him, more troop transports and tanks had arrived, bringing a large and powerful force right to the heart of the collaborator government. From what they'd heard through the grapevine – officially, they were only told what they needed to know, as determined by their superior officers – the rioting humans were tearing through the offices owned and operated by the collaborator government. The'Stig wasn't sure what they hoped to achieve. The computer records that detailed all of the registered humans weren't stored with the human government, but outside the cities at the Land Force Base. Even if they burned down the entire area, they would achieve nothing more than irritating the Command Triad. And they weren't even going to get that far.

He hefted his weapon and took aim into the mass of humanity. They seemed to become aware of him at the same moment, changing to lunge towards the troopers and their armoured vehicles. It was absurd. What possible harm could they do to armoured vehicles? Sure, some human antitank weapons could inflict harm on the tanks, but they had none. The only weapons they had were sticks and stones, which might harm the troopers on the ground, yet they wouldn't be enough to win. If they were smart, they would have realised that they were beaten and surrendered.

The machine guns mounted on the tanks opened fire, directly into the mob. Bright red blood seemed to splash everywhere as the bullets, designed to punch through thicker skin than humanity's, tore through the mass of humanity. He saw human bodies disintegrate under the assault, coming apart and falling in a sickening pile of flesh. It wasn't war, but a bloody slaughter. In seconds, hundreds of humans had been killed. The few survivors were screaming in pain, abandoned by the few who were able to run for their lives. The'Stig winced as the orders to advance came in through his headpiece, sending him forward. His feet seemed to slip on the blood-stained pavement, blood splashing everywhere. The handful of wounded humans were too badly injured to help, even if the Land Force had been inclined to assist humans too stupid to know not to charge tanks with sticks and stones.

Bit by bit, they cleared the human mob away. Panic was settling in, with thousands of humans running for their lives, abandoning others to the tender mercy of the advancing forces. He saw a handful of policemen, wearing the uniforms they'd been told to respect, staring at the troopers, their faces pale with horror. Hadn't they realised what was going to happen? The'Stig slipped on another patch of blood and stared down at the young human who had lost his upper body. A life had been wasted when he'd chosen to join a futile and pointless protest march.

He snorted in disdain. And it had all been so futile. Didn't the humans have the sense to know when they were beaten? He couldn't feel proud of what they'd done. They hadn't fired on the deadly humans, the ones who had been ambushing convoys and sniping at Land Force Bases. Instead, they'd killed thousands of humans who might have been useful, if they'd had some sense knocked into their heads instead of simply being slaughtered. The State would understand what they'd done, but would others? Even he didn't want to go through it again.

His radio buzzed. "Clear the plaza," the order came from above. "We're bringing in prisoners to clear away the bodies. Others will dig a pit outside the city where they can be dumped."

The'Stig snorted, again. Higher authority seemed stunned too. Who knew? Perhaps they would be so stunned that they'd change their tactics. Stranger things had happened.

Chapter Twenty-Two

North England
United Kingdom, Day 25

"We can't go on like this!"

Gabriel couldn't face the television set. For the last four days, the BBC had been broadcasting images from the riot in London – and its bloody end. Alien tanks firing directly into the crowd, alien soldiers crushing human skulls under their armoured feet, hundreds of orange-suited prisoners clearing away the bodies and piling them into trucks, the bodies being dumped into massive pits outside the city… the images were firmly burned into his mind. Nothing in Britain's history, at least that he could recall, matched the sheer horror the aliens had unleashed. God alone knew how many humans had been killed in the riot. The BBC claimed that *no* aliens had been killed, or even injured.

The news had shocked the country. From what few reports Gabriel believed from the BBC, there had been other riots in Newcastle, Glasgow, Edinburgh and Birmingham. The aliens, however, had managed to cow most of the rioters; their soldiers had quelled the other riots by their mere presence. Most of the insurgency had slipped back to IEDs and attacks on collaborators and alien patrols, although much of it seemed to be random violence. It helped that almost all human communities had a common enemy in the Leathernecks. Violent groups that ran the political spectrum from neo-Nazis to Islamic fundamentalists and ecological pressure groups were actually working together to bleed the aliens.

But the country was bleeding too. The BBC was heavily censored these days, controlled by the collaborator government, but enough was leaking through to worry Gabriel. People were starving, families had been shattered… each disaster might have been tiny, on a planetary scale, but they added up to untold misery. Britain wasn't supposed to be like that, he told himself, even during the Blitz they'd been spared the suffering inflicted on continental Europe by the Nazis. Britons saw disasters on television and donated money to help the dispossessed. They didn't suffer disasters themselves. He'd once read a book where an extinct volcano in Edinburgh had come back to life, forcing British emergency services to cope with the disaster. They hadn't done a very good job.

He sat back in his chair, trying to think. How could they convince the aliens to leave? But the aliens only seemed to respect force – and the entire human race hadn't been able to convince them to back off. Barely a month ago, the United States had been so far ahead of the rest of the world that it could do almost anything it liked. It was now invaded and occupied, the massive aircraft carriers that had given the Royal Navy fits of envy sunk by rocks dropped from orbit. Russia and China had been crushed, the Chinese suffering the effects of their own nuclear weapons as well as alien KEW strikes. And Europe…

The latest reports, such as they were, suggested that Europe was suffering from famine. France and Germany, the two powerhouses of the European Union, had been crippled, the continent-wide distribution network for food breaking down under the pressure of the alien offensive. Eastern Europe had attracted less attention from the aliens, with the result that millions of refugees were thronging through the countryside, desperately seeking a safety that no longer existed. The war in Bosnia had restarted, with a dozen different groups trying to exterminate their enemies before the aliens decided to intervene. But why *would* the aliens bother to intervene? Their human enemies were killing themselves off nicely.

And all he could do was sit and watch as his country was taken apart. He stared around the library, at the old books lovingly collected by the library's owner, and cursed himself for his weakness. His position as Prime Minister was meaningless in all, but name. Even if he were to issue orders, it was uncertain how many people would even hear them, let alone obey. The resistance seemed to be held together very loosely, if at all. He'd been assured that it was the only way to prevent the aliens from uncovering them all if they captured men from one particular cell, but it still felt flimsy to him. How long would it be before the resistance became nothing more than bandits?

A month. That was all it had been – and it felt as if he had been cooped up in his gilded cage forever. He thought, briefly, about the soldiers on the outside, providing security for his august person… did they feel resentment or relief that they were out of the fight? And how long would they *stay* out of the fight? The collaborators had offered a hefty reward for anyone who brought them Gabriel's head, preferably not attached to his body. He wasn't blind to the advantages the aliens would gain from having the legitimate Prime Minister as a collaborator, although he suspected that they wouldn't find him as useful as they would have expected. The slaughter in London would have destroyed whatever legitimacy the collaborator government had once enjoyed.

But what could they *do*? The aliens held control over the high orbitals – if worst came to worst, they could pull out of London – or any other city – and drop rocks on it from orbit. He thrilled to the stories of ambushes and IEDs planted in positions where the aliens would run over them, but they could never force the aliens to retreat and abandon Earth. And what would happen if the aliens decided to simply exterminate the human race altogether?

Alone in the library, Gabriel continued to worry. He wanted to do something, to take a stand, but what could he do? His only contribution to the resistance was a second video, one condemning the aliens for the slaughter in London and calling on all loyal British citizens to join the fight. And how many of them would hear him and die because they'd listened to a Prime Minister skulking in a hole?

But what else could he do?

———

"There's a great deal about this we don't understand," Linux said. Brigadier Gavin Lightbridge-Stewart – who was, as far as he knew, the senior surviving British military officer – nodded. Computers might have been extremely useful, but he didn't pretend to understand what went on inside them. "But the alien computer network is actually surprisingly primitive."

Gavin gave him what he hoped was an encouraging look. Linux – and his friends – hadn't joined the army in the traditional manner, let alone worked their way through the Combat Infantryman's Course at Catterick. They'd been computer hackers who'd gotten their kicks by breaking into secure databases, at least until they'd been caught and offered a blunt choice between working for the government or spending a number of years in jail. They did have some sense of social responsibility, yet they had no sense at all of military etiquette. It was sometimes refreshing to chat to them, but not now. The entire country was under enemy occupation.

"It seemed so odd that we were convinced they were screwing with our minds," Linux continued, cheerfully. "They can travel faster-than-light, their starships are several kilometres long and they clearly have at least some form of antigravity system – their shuttles couldn't fly without something along those lines. And yet they are oddly primitive in some areas. Their precision weapons aren't very precise and their computer networks are surprisingly crude."

Gavin nodded, although he had his own theories about alien precision weapons. From what they could see, the aliens seemed less inclined to worry about accidentally hitting their own troopers as well as enemy positions – and they showed a frightening lack of concern for civilian casualties. If they hadn't had the political impetus to design smarter and smarter weapons, maybe they simply hadn't bothered. Besides, the aliens didn't seem to bother with inventing justifications for their invasion of Earth. They'd come, they'd seen – and they'd invaded.

"They do have wireless networks comparable to our own, but their security technology is several generations behind ours," Linux continued. Two SAS men had slipped close to a major alien base to establish a passive listening post linked directly to the resistance's computer geek headquarters. They'd been monitoring alien traffic ever since. "One thing we can confirm is that the aliens are definitely top-down commanders. Orders flow down from the starships or the command base in London and the poor grunts on the ground do as they're told."

He grinned. "It took a week to find a way to slip *into* their networks, but we're finally starting to pull files out from their systems for examination elsewhere," he added. "We stumbled across another puzzle almost at once. Our translation software isn't very good, but theirs seems to be better than ours – even though their computers are less capable. But it isn't as good as it could be."

Gavin frowned, considering the puzzle. The aliens hadn't done much with the civilian population, but one thing they had done was take over a number of computer-related colleges and research labs. If the alien computers were primitive, maybe they were intent on absorbing human technology into their own society. But why were they primitive in the first place? Gavin could accept that they wouldn't be so concerned with producing precision weapons, yet why didn't they have superior computers? They certainly should have possessed computers equal to mankind's best designs.

"One of the programs we pulled out and studied was definitely designed for English," Linux informed him. "The others, however, aren't for any recognisable language. You'd think they could speak French or Russian or Chinese, but they don't seem to have programs for those translations. I assume that they might not bother to outfit a force landing in Britain with such systems, yet it's an odd oversight…"

"Very odd," Gavin agreed. It struck him a moment later. "There are other aliens out there!"

"So it would seem," Linux said. "At least six, unless the translation programs are for other Leatherneck languages. We have different languages on Earth – why shouldn't they have something comparable on their worlds. Unfortunately, we were unable to locate any files on the other alien races. But we're still looking. I'm afraid they didn't bother to design any search engines for their computer networks."

"Or maybe you haven't found those yet," Gavin said. "Tell me something. Can you alter their files? Twist the data they're gathering on our people? Slip records into the registries…?"

"I don't think so," Linux admitted. "I told you the system was crude – well, it's very crudeness provides some protection from people like me. We can read the files – hell, we've managed to download terabytes of data we can study without having to remain linked to their network – but altering them would certainly be noticed. Their core memory systems are ROM – ah, Read Only Memory. We can't change them without physical access to the system."

"Which we're not likely to get," Gavin agreed. He patted the young man on the back. "Good work."

"The intelligence staff are working their way through the dump," Linux added. "They're finding it slow going – if there is a listing or filing system, it isn't one that we recognise. It used to be possible to lose files inside computer networks unless one happened to know its precise location. I have a feeling that their superior officers probably have their own files concealed from everyone else. Who knows? Maybe they all gather dirt on their fellows for advancement."

"I was hoping you'd be able to tell me more about their society," Gavin admitted. "I don't suppose you pulled something like Wikipedia out of their database?"

"I don't think they'd want Wikipedia if they could support it," Linux said. "Or Google, for that matter. Or any of the other computer programs that put power in the hands of the users, rather than systems administrators and the big corporations…"

"I think they have more problems right now," Gavin said, dryly. He had a relative who had worked for Google Ireland. The Leathernecks had largely ignored Ireland, apart from bombarding its military bases and destroying the fragile truce between Ireland's various factions. After the remaining British soldiers had been pulled out, Ireland had degenerated into fighting between different factions, with thousands of refugees trying to make it to Britain. Perhaps the aliens would intervene if they thought there was something in Ireland worth taking. Or maybe they had too many other problems on their hands. "What can we do with the access we have? And can they block us out if they realise that we've hacked their systems?"

"I rather doubt they can block us unless they're willing to cripple their networks," Linux said. "But if they do have enemies out there, they may have security tricks we haven't seen ourselves. Maybe their enemies have a cunning plan to hijack their wireless computer networks and render their fleets helpless. And then sexy androids will rule the galaxy."

He saw Gavin's face and cleared his throat. "Sorry, anyway… we may be able to piggyback on their network to send messages to our own people," he added. "And seeing that they all radiate wireless signals, we could probably start tracking their movements. Or… we could rig up a sensor and link it to an IED. When the signals reach the right intensity, they trigger the IED and it explodes in their face. Or…"

Gavin held up a hand. "Good thinking," he said. "Let me know if there's anything else we can do…"

Linux hesitated. "It *might* be possible for us to interfere with the network," he said. "We might be capable of taking it down completely for short periods of time, cutting their small detachments off from higher authority. The result would be absolute chaos… but they'd know what we'd done. God alone knows how they'd react."

"I see," Gavin said. "I'll have to give that some thought."

He scowled. After the slaughter in London, they needed to find a way to hit back at the aliens, one that would convince them that slaughtering humans would draw a massive response. But how could they do that without revealing what few aces they had in their hand? And what if the aliens decided to destroy the entire human race in response?

––––––––––

"Panda Cola," the logistics officer said. He tossed a can at Chris, who caught it neatly and scowled down at the label. "All kept nice and cool for our gallant fighting men."

"Piss off," Chris said. Panda Cola was included in the British Army's Horror Bags – the packed lunches that were served to soldiers on duty. It was generally believed that it was produced by forcing a Panda to drink ordinary Coke, then bottling their urine and passing the cans to soldiers, who would then have to drink the foul liquid. Chris had heard during his training that the Ministry of Defence allocated 47p to procuring each can of Panda Cola, which raised the question of precisely what happened to the remaining 42p. "You'd think we could get better rations now we're living off the land."

He scowled around the resistance base. Calling it a base was really too much; they'd built shelters under the trees, trenches just in case the aliens stumbled over their position and a latrine some distance from the sleeping rolls. Some units, he'd heard, were living in civilian homes, but the aliens were getting better at running random patrols through seemingly-deserted hamlets. The base was safer, apart from the possibility of poisoning themselves by drinking army-issue Coke. He opened the can, braced himself and took a swallow. It tasted just as bad as he remembered.

"At least we're eating rabbits," one of the other soldiers pointed out. It was true; hunting skills they'd been taught were actually coming in handy. The woodland was full of small animals and vegetation that could be eaten, although they were being very careful with the mushrooms. If one of the soldiers managed to poison themselves, they wouldn't be able to get them proper treatment. "We could be eating that foul muck they served us in Edinburgh."

"I told you that you should have taken the pizza," his friend pointed out. Chris felt a pang for the comrades he'd lost in London. They'd all been jammed together from various units that hadn't made it out intact, but some of them had known each other beforehand. "When has the Army ever fed us well?"

Chris snorted. The Army Chefs – the Ration Assassins – had the hardest training course in the British Army. It had to be – no one had ever actually managed to pass, or so the soldiers joked amongst themselves. Now, he almost missed them, even though fresh rabbit stew was surprisingly tasty. Despite himself, he found himself wondering how they were going to cope when winter finally came along. It would be much harder to find food then – and the aliens, the crafty buggers, were being careful about what they doled out to the civilians. It would be easy to see if certain civilians were eating more than they should.

He pushed the thought aside, remembering the horror stories that had floated up from London. They'd have to make the aliens pay for that, but how? It had to be something spectacular... absently, he remembered the interior of the alien vehicles. Humans probably couldn't drive them without major effort. But they did have collaborators driving their vehicles...

Slowly, a plan started to come together in his mind. It would be risky as hell, but they were used to that by now. And they might just have a chance to inflict major damage on an alien base. Perhaps they could even shatter the ring of steel around London.

Absently, he reached for a notepad and started jotting down ideas. The pad would have to be destroyed, of course, but by then he should have a solid concept. They'd have to link up with other units. They couldn't do it alone. He smiled to himself. It would be good to know that they weren't alone.

And the aliens were in for a very unpleasant surprise.

Chapter Twenty-Three

Command Base
United Kingdom, Day 27

By long tradition, each separate Land Forces Commander was expected to remain within his Area of Responsibility until relieved of command. The Command Triad, on the other hand, was supposed to remain on their starships, a legacy of the time when a primitive race managed to kill the Command Triad in charge of subduing their world and wreck havoc while their subordinates were still bickering over who was in command. No one seriously expected other powers to send starships to Earth, while humanity had no ability to reach the command starships in orbit. The Command Triad were therefore isolated from the dangers on Earth.

Ju'tro Oheghizh watched as the teleconference slowly came into being. Each of the Land Force Commanders would link into the conference from their bases on the ground, while the Command Triad would attend from orbit. Given what they'd uncovered about human computer systems, it seemed likely that the whole process would be improved in the next few years, once the human technology was understood and integrated into the State. The humans seemed largely unaware of the potential of their own technology, but no one could deny their skill. They would make a very useful client race in the coming decades, serving as soldiers, technicians and inventors. The State would grow far more powerful.

"It has been one local month since we established ourselves on Earth," *Tul'ma* Jophuzu said. The Land Forces Commander had taken the lead, as was right and proper. His formations were the ones mainly engaged on Earth. "The humans have proved a more capable foe than we expected, but we have successfully taken and kept vast swaths of their territory."

The display lit up on his command. There were enclaves on both sides of the American continent, smaller enclaves across Europe, Russia and Australia – and enclaves scattered over Britain. Oheghizh allowed himself an interior sneer. His command might be smaller than the enclaves in America or Europe, but it was far more promising in the long run. Besides, the American humans seemed to keep fighting even when the situation was hopeless. They even seemed to have two guns per adult human. The only other place that had put up such a fight was Switzerland and the mountainous country had been bombarded into submission after the first landings had been repulsed with heavy losses. It would be a long time before they recovered. If only because no one was interested in helping them.

"The plans for the final disposition of their military personnel are already under way," the Land Forces Commander continued. "They will serve us on other worlds – and be kept separate from wild humans who could learn from their skills. However, our other plans to use Earth as a source of knowledge and technology have been crippled."

Oheghizh kept his face blank and his body still, refusing to show any emotion. He'd hoped to push forward the schedule for assimilating human technology into the State, but his dreams had vanished when the human suicide bomber – a tactic that made little sense to him – had destroyed the technical college. There were others, of course, but now he had to divert resources to protect the human computer experts and their families – which risked allowing the humans a chance to deduce one of the State's weaknesses. The humans had more experience in using their technology than the State. They had probably invented thousands of different ways to use computers as weapons.

Va'tro Nak'tak spoke from his position. "We may have misunderstood human social psychology," he said. "Humans are a contradictory bunch. Some humans will see us as terrifying and will submit to us without hesitation. Their fear, however, will make them less useful than we might have hoped. Some humans will refuse to allow us to cow them and will continue the fight, at least until they are killed in combat. We cannot expect any form of submission from them – and we couldn't trust it if we got it. Some humans will just try to live their lives as if we didn't exist, doing whatever it took to survive. We have been unable to put together any explanation for their psychology.

"Unfortunately, it seems that humans are often contemptuous of those who see sense and choose to submit to superior force. The humans who agree to work with us, of their own free will, are hated by their fellow humans and often targeted by them. We have seen collaborators attacked in many different countries, suggesting that the disdain for submission is a common human trait. They seem far more understanding of those we force into collaboration – by holding their families hostage – but there are fine lines that we do not understand. Rather than work towards securing themselves positions within the State, humans will continually lash out at the State.

"Worse, a number of the collaborators are considered… *deviant* by human standards. Some of them have sexual tastes for young humans who have not yet reached sexual maturity, tastes which we have allowed them to indulge. The vast majority of humans, however, regard the protection of children as a duty and recoil in horror at what we have permitted to occur. This horror has certainly fuelled many attacks on us."

Oheghizh snorted, along with many others. The idea of a race that seemed to be permanently in mating season wasn't new, but the humans took it to extremes. It wasn't too surprising that they'd drawn up sexual customs that looked strange to alien eyes, or that those who defied those customs were hated by their peers. But they made little sense. Among the Eridian, a female who entered mating season would be considered sexually mature – and outside mating season, there would be no sexual contact between males and females. The children of the mating, assuming that one took place, would be raised by the females. There were few permanent sexual bonds between male and female – but they certainly existed among the humans. Many of the humans who had launched suicidal attacks had claimed to be acting in the name of a dead mate.

"In the long term, we expect that the humans will eventually be ground under and reshaped into proper servants of the State," *Va'tro* Nak'tak said. "However, we may always have to make allowances for their alien natures. The State may have to devise new rules for them."

There was a pause. "The human sexual nature rears its head whenever male and female humans are put together. It even appears when some humans have a sexual attraction to their own sex, something unknown among us, but very common to the Paklet. Indeed, some human sects appear to consider females useless for anything other than breeding more humans, even though it is clearly inaccurate. The Paklet, however, do not have intelligent males. Their emotional connections are forged with other females.

"For humanity, we will need to create new rules. We have already started segregating humans in our detention camps by sex. It is quite likely that we will have to rein in our collaborators, if only to prevent us being tarred by the same brush – as the humans would put it…"

Tul'ma Jophuzu snorted. "We can make concessions to their nature once they have submitted," he said, flatly. "We have crushed their defences and raid where we will, yet they do not submit in large numbers. How do we force them to submit?"

"In the long term, they will submit," *Va'tro* Nak'tak said, flatly. "We must simply continue to hold our ground and refuse to abandon territory on Earth. They need to be constantly reminded that all of their attacks have not forced us to withdraw – and that we will never withdraw. They'll submit in the long run."

"The longer we wage war on this planet, the greater the chance that one of the other powers will intervene," *A'tar* Esuxam said. The Space Forces Commander lifted one clawed hand to stroke his leathery chin. "We may have claimed this system by right of conquest, but we don't have the firepower to keep a raiding force out if they wanted to hit us – or the coverage to prevent them slipping help to the humans on the surface. And if they realise what a treasure trove we've found here, they will be very tempted to intervene."

Oheghizh couldn't disagree. Humanity *was* a treasure trove, even if some of their decisions made little sense to a properly rational race. Their imaginations suggested all kinds of interesting weapons and tactics – and their computers would go a long way towards evening the balance between the State and several of its peer powers. Those powers wouldn't hesitate to intervene on Earth if they realised the danger – and the humans would certainly seek to make deals with them if they could. The enemy of my enemy, they said, is my friend.

"We need to tighten our grip on their planet," *Tul'ma* Jophuzu said. "I want all resistance crushed before they have a chance to find help from outside the system."

That, Oheghizh thought in the privacy of his own head, would be easier said than done. Humanity just didn't respond like a rational race, which raised the question of how they'd ever managed to develop atomic weapons without blowing themselves and their world into radioactive debris. Some of the observers had seen human claims of alien contact and wondered if someone might have been covertly assisting humanity's development, but the starships hadn't picked up any signs that anyone else might have visited the system. But how else could one explain a development that defied all of the understood rules?

They're alien, he reminded himself. *They might play by different rules.*

The Land Force Base near the human city of London was immense. It had been built on top of a human air force base, once the ground had been swept for hidden surprises, and simply expanded outwards. Three fences prevented human insurgents from getting into the base itself, while the outer edge was patrolled regularly by elite infantry units. A series of drones floated high overhead, backed up by attack helicopters and strike fighters. It should have been impregnable.

Tra'tro The'Stig walked across the human runway and up to the prefabricated building. Two guards checked his identity before allowing him to proceed, even though no human could have disguised himself to look like an Eridiani. The very thought was absurd, but the humans were full of nasty surprises. It was better to be paranoid than dead.

The interior of the building felt pleasantly warm and damp to his skin, a change from the cold breezes outside. There were parts of Britain where it never seemed to stop raining, but the rain was always cold and uncomfortable. Even the humans seemed to find it unpleasant, which didn't stop them from using the rain to cover their movements. The interior was also large enough for him to move freely, without needing to worry about holes torn in human walls or tiny humans lurking in holes too small for an adult Eridiani. It was definitely better than staying in one of the human buildings that had been adapted for their purposes. He saw a pair of females and concealed a wry smile. The seniors were making sure that they were in the right place when the females entered their mating seasons. If he'd smelt the scent that marked a female in heat, he would have fought any other male – superior or not – who tried to prevent him from mating with her. Outside mating season, it was a matter of amusement rather than irritation.

He stepped into the office and thumped his chest with one hand, claws sheathed. *Ju'tro* Oheghizh was far superior to his lowly position, which made the summons rather more than a bit worrying. He hadn't done anything wrong, as far as he knew, but it wasn't always necessary to screw up before being raked over the coals. And yet… he had found himself in command of a scratch Assault Unit made from the remains of several other Assault Units that had been ripped apart by the humans. Had he exceeded his authority badly enough to warrant punishment?

The State demanded nothing, but obedience from low-ranking officers and males. In the privacy of his own head, *Tra'tro* The'Stig wondered if that was the best way to handle fighting a war. It took time to call for orders from higher authority, time that the humans used to good advantage. How many human insurgents had escaped death because the KEW bombardments had to be ordered by superior officers, rather than the ones on the ground? But if he'd vocalised any of those thoughts… the best outcome would be remaining forever frozen at his current rank. At worst, he would be sent to a punishment unit or a re-education camp.

He waited for his superior to speak, as was proper. "You have served well during the course of the invasion," *Ju'tro* Oheghizh said. His superior officer didn't seem angry. "You fought well and survived the experience."

The'Stig wondered, just for a moment, if he was being mocked. Yes, he'd survived – and he'd learned never to take anything for granted. The humans had plenty of skill at concealing IEDs in apparently harmless positions, while they were learning how to hurt unwary Assault Units with simpler weapons and tactics. Officers fresh from suspension on the starships, assuming that the war was already over because the human cities had been occupied and their militaries hammered from orbit, had been caught by surprise. Many of them hadn't survived their first encounter with human insurgents.

"You are promoted to *U'tra*," *Ju'tro* Oheghizh said, almost casually. The'Stig forgot himself and stared at his commanding officer. He was being jumped up two grades…? It had to be a mistake. But then, hadn't he been serving as an *U'tra* even without the rank? "You will take command of the reformed Assault Units and commence sweeps for enemy insurgents. I expect you to find them and destroy them. Do you understand me?"

The'Stig saluted, hastily. Yes, he understood all right. The reformed units wouldn't be neat and orderly, certainly not as orderly as a more conventional commander would have expected. And if he failed in his mission, he could be demoted just as easily. He almost started to laugh at himself. Hadn't he been sure that he could do better, if he'd been in command? And now he *was* in command. Failure wasn't an option.

"I understand," he said. "I will not fail the State."

The alien helicopter touched down in the centre of their base and one of his guards half-pushed Alan Beresford towards the hatch. He scrambled out with as much dignity as he could muster, unable to prevent himself from staring at the massive shuttles and other aircraft scattered over the base. The alien buildings seemed dauntingly large, as if they'd been put together by designers without a sense of proportion. He winced at the sound of a jumbo jet coming into land, wondering if it was being piloted by humans or aliens. It seemed unlikely that aliens could fly a human craft, but they'd have to be insane to allow humans to land on their bases. 9/11 had proved just how much damage a crashing jumbo jet could do.

His escort marched him up to one of the alien buildings and into a network of corridors that looked large enough to hold hundreds of aliens at once. The smell was all around him, a scent that reminded him of mucking out a barn on his grandfather's estate. He'd never realised that the aliens smelled before, but then he'd never been in a building that had housed so many of them at one time. Human buildings probably smelled rank to them too.

He shuddered as they pulled him through a door and into an office. The aliens couldn't have been very happy with the recent riots in London, or the fact that part of the city had become a no-go area for the police. Their system for controlling the city – and the human population – was breaking down sharply. God alone knew how they planned to respond. He looked up at the oversized desk and saw one of the aliens crouching behind it. They didn't seem to need chairs, unlike humanity. Or perhaps it was a way to tell him that he wasn't important to them any longer.

"Your people have proved most disruptive," the alien said. Was it the one he normally dealt with, or was it another one? There was no way to easily tell them apart. "We are not pleased. We will be launching sweeps to catch human insurgents and we expect you and your people to cooperate fully with us. Failure to cooperate will have the most disastrous consequences."

Alan didn't need to be a politician to realise that that was a threat. "I will be honoured to cooperate," he said, quickly. "Perhaps if you could outline what you wish us to do…"

"We will carry out the sweeps without your assistance," the alien informed him. "We wish you to round up a number of humans and their families. We have a use for them."

"But of course," Alan said. There was no point in refusing now. The aliens would simply kill him and move on to another collaborator. "Might I enquire as to the purpose you have in mind for them…?"

"You will do as you are told," the alien said, flatly. "If you are incapable of carrying out your orders, we will find someone who is more capable."

Alan hesitated. If he started rounding people up without explanation, there would be resistance. People would start thinking that the aliens intended to *eat* them or something equally stupid, which would naturally provoke more resistance. And then his police force, already demoralised, would find itself unable to proceed further. But how could he explain that to the aliens?

"I will carry out your orders," he said, finally. "I await your command."

Chapter Twenty-Four

Near Dereham
United Kingdom, Day 32

Alex lay on her belly and considered the town below her. The aliens had arrived in force, coming up at Dereham from Norwich and surrounding the town before anyone quite realised that they were there. Dereham had been ignored by the aliens after the population had been registered, leaving the people to try to get on with their own lives in a world turned upside down, perhaps even to pretend that the world hadn't really changed. Their delusion, if they'd indulged themselves, had come to an end. The town was surrounded and the aliens were moving in.

"We can't just stay here and do nothing," Henry hissed. He was too young – but then, there had been younger soldiers fighting and dying in Afghanistan. "What are they going to do to the people down there?"

Alex shrugged. The aliens had been alarmingly active over the last few days, sweeping through parts of the countryside without anything that looked like a clear plan of action. Alex's best guess was that they were looking for insurgents – the internet noted hundreds of attacks carried out against the aliens – but she wasn't sure why they had returned to Dereham, or why they hadn't attempted to track her down. Perhaps they were following a doctrine formed on another world. Or perhaps they believed that there was a centre of resistance in the town and they intended to destroy it. There was no way to know.

"We can't do anything, but get ourselves killed if we go charging into the town," she hissed back. They'd carried out three strikes at the aliens so far, but she'd insisted on being very careful. If the aliens had decided to sweep through the area for insurgents, it was possible that they'd catch someone who wasn't registered or uncover an arms dump. Either one would be disastrous. "All we can really do is hope and pray that they don't find anything that justifies a massacre."

The images from London had been broadcast over the BBC. Alex had watched in horror as hundreds – perhaps thousands – of humans had been shredded by alien guns. The entire country had seen the bloody suppression of a riot, galvanising resistance to the alien occupation. If the internet was to be believed, there had been hundreds of strikes against the aliens over the last few days. It certainly explained why the aliens were being so determined to sweep for insurgents. Anything was better than waiting to be hit, hoping that superior firepower would allow them to slaughter anyone foolish enough to attack their positions.

There were upwards of 15,000 people in Dereham. It looked as if the aliens were systematically pulling them out of their homes and ordering them to gather in the roads, waiting for their fate to be decided. The aliens were ransacking the buildings, searching for weapons and anything else that might imply a link to the resistance. Alex could see a handful of policemen looking uncomfortable as the searches continued, unsure of just what they were feeling. Some policemen had been pushed into collaboration, no doubt about that, but others had been willing to serve the aliens without threats. It was hard to blame someone who served because his family was at risk, yet how could they tell the difference between that and a man who was serving the aliens for personal gain? Some of the rumours on the internet were shocking.

"Come on," she hissed. "We can't stay here."

It had taken nearly two hours to walk cross-country to Dereham and they'd arrived just in time to see the aliens establish themselves in the area. Alex had no illusions about what they would do once they'd secured the town; they'd sweep out, probably in the direction of Norwich. They had a major presence in that town and given enough time, they could probably safeguard the roads as well. A few of Alex's allies had been placing IEDs in the area, but that had its own dangers. The last thing they wanted to do was accidentally catch a farmer with an IED.

She scowled as they made their way across a field, which had recently been planted with an alien crop. One of the stranger points about British farming before the invasion had been that the government had paid a number of farmers to leave their fields lying fallow, rather than growing crops. It had been cheaper, apparently, to bring in food from overseas, which had worked perfectly until the country had been cut off from the rest of the world by the aliens. The aliens, on the other hand, had made a list of every farmer with fallow fields and ordered them to start growing seeds they'd provided. They hadn't gone into details, but they seemed to believe that the crop would be grown before winter, allowing it to be harvested and a second crop planted after the winter snows had faded away. Alex wasn't too surprised to see that they were planting crops from their world, but Smith had been furious. Adding something new to the ecology could cause chaos across the entire country.

"It was bad enough when they started planting those damn genetically-modified crops," he'd said, holding up one of the alien seeds. It hadn't looked very alien, but someone down in the town had looked at it through a microscope and confirmed that it bore no resemblance to something from Earth. "These things are likely to spread further and there won't be anything we can do about it."

The thought was chilling – and the internet speculation had been downright horrific. Introducing rabbits to Australia had been disastrous because the rabbits had had no natural predators and had bred like... well, rabbits. Alien plants might be resistant to Earth's formidable array of crop-destroying pests, while alien animals might be tougher than foxes or weasels or the other predators that hunted rabbits and field mice. Alex had tried to imagine an animal from the alien homeworld, but had drawn a blank. They could look like anything.

She could hear the sounds of alien helicopters in the distance as they walked onwards, watching carefully for any sign of an alien or collaborator patrol. They'd had some close calls in the days since they'd started trying to ambush the aliens, but the aliens seemed to have preferred to keep their distance. Maybe their current sweep was intended to change that – no matter what some of the young men thought, she had no illusions. They were barely pin-pricking the aliens. The aliens might not consider them significant enough to bother killing.

"You could come to the dance with me," Henry said, breaking into her thoughts. "It would be a fun time to let your hair down."

Alex rolled her eyes. Henry was seventeen; she was twenty-five. And she wanted to minimise the contact between her and the townspeople as much as possible. Officially, she was Smith's niece from across the country, but it wouldn't be long before someone guessed at the truth. There had been quite a few fugitives who had found new homes in the countryside, yet the aliens were alarmingly good at using human files to track down military personnel. And if they caught Alex... no one knew what would happen to her.

And Henry was clearly interested in her. Part of her was tempted, despite the age difference – Henry wasn't a bad person at all. But the rest of her knew better. She'd been between boyfriends when she'd been shot down during the opening days of the invasion and... if she opened herself up that far, it risked creating emotional ties. One day, she would have to leave Long Stratton if the aliens threatened to take over the area directly – and then she would have to avoid looking back.

"It wouldn't be a good idea for me to be seen," she said, finally. There were younger girls in the town, she told herself firmly. He'd find someone closer in age to himself. "I need to spend more time at the hole anyway."

The thought made her smile. Smuggling guns and explosives to hiding places well away from the town had been a challenge, but once they'd completed the program it had been easy to separate the different resistance cells. The aliens might catch one of them, only to discover that they had no leads to the next one. Or so she hoped. If someone had defied orders... she shook her head. The RAF had tried to control every aspect of her life as a pilot, but the resistance needed a much looser organisation. She would just have to trust that they knew what to do – and knew better than to contact her.

Henry said nothing for the rest of the walk back to the coppice that served as a rendezvous point. Alex's RAF training hadn't included building shelters, but Archer had uncovered a couple of ex-poachers who were remarkably talented at slipping unseen through the night, or building hidden dumps for the weapons. She knew she could live alone out in the countryside for quite some time, but that would mean giving up the fight and walking away, forgetting her oath to the country. They dumped most of their weapons in the stash and headed down towards Smith's farm. He'd been spending the last few days planting the alien seeds in the ground, cursing the aliens all the while. At least they'd gotten a petrol ration out of it.

"That's funny," Henry commented. "Where is he?"

Alex looked over at him, and then down at her watch. It was early afternoon, the time Smith normally worked in the fields. Henry was right. Where was he? More carefully now, Alex walked forward to the farmhouse and quietly peered around the corner. There was no sign of his Range Rover in the shed. He had to have gone out and... she touched the door and it opened, revealing that it was unlocked. Alarm bells ringing in her head, she inched into the farmhouse and looked around. There was no sign of Smith, or his wife.

"No sign of a struggle," Henry pointed out. Alex relaxed slightly. He was right. It looked as if Smith and Jean had had to go down to the town, leaving the door unlocked for her. And yet... something wasn't quite right. She slipped upstairs and checked the bedrooms, finding nothing that suggested trouble. "They might have just gone out for a drive..."

"Maybe," Alex said. "Or maybe..."

The sound of alien helicopters echoed out of nowhere. Alex started, and then ran for the door, suddenly certain what she'd see outside. Five helicopters were racing towards the farmhouse, aliens already rappelling down ropes to hit the ground just as the helicopters came to a halt. Alex reached for the gun she'd shoved into her belt, but it was far too late. A dozen aliens were advancing towards her, weapons pointed right at her chest. How the hell had they known...? It struck her, suddenly, that the aliens might have been watching as they walked back from Dereham. They could have orbited a drone so high overhead that the naked eye couldn't have made it out against the sun's glare...

"Put up your hands," the lead alien ordered. "Resistance is futile..."

Henry drew his pistol and opened fire, shooting madly towards the aliens. Alex could have told him not to waste his energy. The handguns they had weren't that accurate and alien body armour was more than enough to protect them, unless they were hit in the uncovered parts of their heads. They opened fire, their shells blowing Henry apart and scattering his bloody remains across the farmyard. Alex kept very still, thinking hard. Who had betrayed her? Smith and his wife, or someone down at the town? Probably the latter, she told herself, and she hoped that she was right. She didn't want to think that Smith might have betrayed her.

The aliens came closer, dark unblinking eyes fixed on her form. Their hands seemed to end in oversized fingernails – no, those were claws – and she had to fight not to cringe back as they tore at her clothes, removing her pistol and everything else she'd been carrying on her person. The claws seemed sharp enough to cut through her bare skin, convincing her that trying to fight hand-to-hand with the aliens was a bad idea. They kept two weapons pointed at her at all times, even after they'd finished searching her and wrapped a plastic tie around her hands, binding them behind her back. She wanted to laugh, or cry. They'd caught her – and if they knew how important she was to the resistance cells, they'd torture her until she talked. If they hadn't caught Archer, perhaps he'd know to order the cells to scatter before Alex broke. He'd assume the worst, wouldn't he?

They pushed her to the ground and left her there while they searched the house. It was hard to see what they were doing from her position, but it sounded as though they were tearing down most of the walls and smashing the windows. God alone knew what they were looking for, unless it was a weapons dump. She snorted at the thought. The only weapons kept in the house were her pistol and Smith's shotgun. They wouldn't find anything else. Finally, they pulled her to her feet and marched her towards one of their

hover-vehicles. The interior was surprisingly roomy compared to some of the vehicles she'd seen in Afghanistan, but it would have been designed for alien bodies. They clanged the hatch shut behind her, leaving her in darkness. There was no light at all inside the chamber.

A faint hum echoed through the vehicle and she realised, after a moment, that they were on their way. There weren't supposed to be any IEDs hidden around Smith's farm, but she found herself hoping that someone had disobeyed orders and planted one in a position where it might catch the alien convoy. If they interrogated her... she resolved to hold out as long as possible, or invent lies to keep the aliens happy. She knew that there had been hundreds of attacks on the aliens that had had nothing to do with her little band – if she claimed credit for them, it should confuse the aliens a little. It might even slow down their sweeps in the belief that they'd caught the resistance's leader...

Or maybe that was just wishful thinking.

She had almost lost track of time when the hum faded away and she heard the sound of scrabbling on the outside of the vehicle. The hatch clicked open, revealing a pair of aliens looking down at her. One of them reached for her leg with a clawed hand and pulled her towards the hatch, while the other held a gun pointed at her head. Alex almost burst out laughing, wondering just why the aliens thought she was so dangerous. She was alone, her hands were bound behind her back and she was unarmed. Did they think she was Wonder Woman or someone else with superhuman strength?

They pulled her out of the vehicle and held her upright long enough to regain her balance, before pushing her towards a gate in a massive fence. Inside, there were a large number of humans – all female, wearing rags. A second camp, some distance away, held men. They didn't look to be in any better shape. One of the aliens caught her hands, clipped the plastic tie free, and then shoved her through the gate. It closed behind her with an ominous click.

"Alex," a voice said. "Thank God you're alive!"

Alex turned to see Jean, Smith's wife, standing there. "Someone in the town betrayed us," she said, bitterly. It looked as if she'd been crying. "They came for us, arrested us and dumped us here. I hoped you'd get away."

"I walked right into them," Alex admitted. It gave her no pleasure to admit the truth, but there was no point in lying. She looked at her fellow captives and shivered. Most of them looked to have spent weeks in the detention camp, fed on very little. They looked thin and worn. There were some blankets to lie on, but no shelters. Alex realised that many of them were suffering from exposure. The aliens didn't seem to care. "And then they just brought me here."

Over the next few hours, she chatted to many of the women. They'd all been taken as prisoners by alien sweeps, apparently because they were linked to one or more of the insurgents. Several of the women thought that they'd been picked up at random, although they liked to think that their husbands or brothers were still fighting the aliens. A number had had military personnel in their families, although Alex was the only actual military person in the camp. The male camp didn't look to be any different. In fact, both camps appeared to be reaching capacity.

Jean caught her arm. "What are we going to do?"

Alex looked up, past the wire. They were inside an alien base, surrounded by aliens – and she didn't even know where they were. The alien vehicles moved with astonishing speed. They could be in Scotland, or Wales, or on the other side of London... there was no way to know for sure. It looked as if the aliens had built their base on top of a RAF base, but it wasn't one she recognised. That really only excluded a handful of bases from consideration.

And if they were removing military personnel, why hadn't they taken her? A moment later, it struck her – they *hadn't* identified her. They presumably thought she was just a civilian insurgent, rather than a military officer carrying on the war. And that gave her an edge, if she stayed alive long enough to figure out how to use it.

"I don't know," she admitted. No, that wasn't quite true. "We can't do anything at the moment, so we wait. Who knows? Maybe the horse will learn to sing."

Chapter Twenty-Five

London
United Kingdom, Day 35

"No, I don't know why they want you," Robin said, as patiently as he could. "All I know is that we have been ordered to pick you up and hand you over to them."

Silently, he cursed his orders under his breath. The aliens had ordered their puppet Prime Minister to round up several hundred people from London, people who seemed to have little in common. They certainly didn't have any links to the resistance as far as Robin could see. Once rounded up, they were to be handed over to the aliens and then… there was no clear answer. It didn't sound very good, but what choice did they have? The aliens wouldn't be anything like as patient with reluctant humans.

The young man they'd been sent to pick up didn't look very healthy. In fact, like most of the city's population, he'd clearly been losing weight now that he had nothing to eat, but the tasteless mush the aliens supplied. Real food was only available for collaborators and on the black market and their target lacked the contacts to obtain something that would have been readily available a month ago. Robin couldn't think of any reason why the aliens wanted him in particular, but they had clearly made up their minds. The young man's mother and father looked just as worried, even though they weren't coming with him. And the looks they were casting at Robin when they thought he wasn't watching…

He shivered. It was normal for people to be a little nervous around the police. Everyone had something weighing on their minds, even if it was comparatively minor compared to serial killing or paedophilia. The police represented law and order. But now…? Now the entire city – the entire country – was afraid of the police. The slaughter in Central London had broken their reputation once and for all. On their drive to the young man's house, they'd avoided several stones thrown at them by youths – and there were parts of the city that were no-go zones for them now. Robin hated conceding anything to the thugs who called themselves community leaders, but the alternative was to ask the aliens to help. And that would mean another slaughter.

Some policemen, including several he knew personally, had deserted, vanishing into London's overcrowded city blocks. Several others had killed themselves, swallowing vast quantities of painkillers or hanging themselves from the ceiling. Even those that had tried to remain on duty had been demoralised, after the slaughter. They knew that they were forever tainted by what the aliens had done, even though they'd never ordered it or wanted it to happen. How could they ever seek forgiveness from an angry population?

"It's going to be fine," Robin said, although he suspected otherwise. "You're allowed to take an overnight bag with you, so pack clean underwear and anything else you think you might need."

They waited while the young man and his mother packed a bag. Robin half-hoped that their target would take the opportunity to vanish out of the back door and into the side streets before they could catch him, but he didn't seem to have the nerve. He returned to the door with a large bag slung over his shoulder and an expression that suggested that he was going to his own funeral. Robin, who'd had a moment to study the awards pinned to the wall, suspected otherwise. The aliens had lost one of their projects when the suicide bomber had blown up Gilmore Technical College, but they were still interested in human computers. And the people on the list they'd been ordered to bring in had vast computer experience. It made little sense to him – the aliens could cross the stars, which suggested they should have better computers – but it was the only reason he could imagine. Or maybe they just wanted hostages to shoot.

He escorted the young man down and into the police car, scowling at the rotten egg someone had smashed across the windscreen while they'd been in the house. A quick check around the vehicle revealed no signs that anyone had tried to place an IED under the car, like the bomb that had killed two policemen three days ago. The resistance seemed to be conserving its weapons, which hadn't stopped it and various criminal gangs improvising weapons and using them to attack the police. Who would have thought that something would unite London's disparate political and religious factions against a single target? Robin would have been mildly impressed if he hadn't been the target.

The drive through London's empty streets took longer than he had expected. Several cars had been moved out of place and used to block or divert police traffic, while several groups of young men looking for trouble had made threatening motions towards the car. At least the gangs weren't trying to attack the alien base in Central London, not after they'd realised that the alien guards had authority to return fire with live ammunition. It hadn't stopped the resistance from setting up a mortar every few days and lobbing shells into the alien positions.

He winced as he caught sight of the prostitutes on one street corner. So many women had been rendered homeless or broke by the invasion that there were currently thousands of prostitutes in London. Many of them would have preferred to be doing something – anything – else, but the aliens weren't interested in relief programs. They doled out their tasteless food and otherwise left the population to live or die on its own. Robin knew that some policemen had suggested finding roles for the women within the civil service, but the suggestion hadn't found favour with the collaborator government. Perhaps the civil servants had managed to cobble together a union and get a ban on scab labour. The thought made him smile. If there was anything capable of working through an alien invasion, it was the British civil service.

"So," the young man said, "where are you taking me?"

"We're taking you to the aliens," Robin said. He wanted to tell a comforting lie. "I don't know what they want to do with you."

"And you work for them," the young man asked. "How do you sleep at night?"

Robin bit down the response that came to mind. The truth was that he didn't sleep very well at night, something shared by almost all of the policemen he knew. When he closed his eyes, he saw the slaughter the aliens had unleashed, or the helpless looks on their prisoners as they marched them off to an unknown fate. He thought about his wife, safe yet isolated outside the city, and shivered. If she knew what he'd done in the name of the aliens, she would never want to sleep beside him again. Some policemen had started popping sleeping pills and antidepressants, just to keep themselves going. He wondered how long it would be before he found himself doing the same thing, or perhaps taking one of the concealed weapons and putting a bullet through his own brain.

"Badly," he said, finally. He took firm hold of his temper before the urge to lash out grew too overpowering. The young man wasn't to blame. Several policemen had given into the stress and started beating their suspects, but he didn't want to fall that far. "If I'd known what they would be like back then…"

But they hadn't had a choice, had they? How easily they'd clambered onto the slippery slope! And how hard it would be to wash the blood from their hands. They'd told themselves that they were protecting the people, but they'd become the tools of the aliens – the same aliens who had slaughtered thousands in London just to keep the peace. They weren't protecting the people any longer, were they? They'd become another alien tool.

And yet… what choice did they have?

He remembered the weapons and shivered again. They could take them and fight back… and be destroyed when the aliens started using heavy weapons on London. There were reports that the aliens had already destroyed a number of small towns for daring to fight when the aliens arrived, or that they'd wrecked havoc in other parts of the world. Against such firepower, what could they do? The only thing they could do was die bravely. And every day, the thought of death seemed more and more attractive. He looked down at his hands and wondered if he would ever be able to wash the bloodstains off his soul.

They came to a halt by the alien fence and waited for the alien guards to confirm their identity. Once they were satisfied that they had the right person, the aliens took the young man away, leaving Robin and Constable Jasper to their own devices. Robin watched the gate swing closed behind them and then ordered Jasper to take them back to the station. He had a bottle of brandy he'd picked up from one of the abandoned houses in his locker. If he drank it all, perhaps he would get drunk and forget about the rest of the world. Or perhaps he'd just wake up with a hangover and have to go back on duty anyway.

And tell me, he thought, rather sourly. Bitter self-hatred welled up within him. How many had died because he had chosen to collaborate with the aliens? Each of his justifications felt less and less logical every time he thought about them. *What exactly do you deserve?*

———

"I can't do much for the wound," Fatima admitted. "The best I can do is separate it properly and bandage it up."

"You mean amputate my arm," the man in front of her said. He'd taken an alien bullet that had punched right through his upper arm, shattering his bone to dust. His arm now hung limply from what remained of his flesh, bound up with cloth to prevent it from tearing loose and falling to the floor. "There's nothing else you can do?"

Fatima shook her head. The resistance had gathered what medical supplies they could, but London had been short on medical supplies and equipment ever since the invasion. There were wounded that would have made a full recovery – if they had the right equipment – who would almost certainly be cripples for the rest of their lives. The man who'd lost an arm was hardly the worst of them. She honestly didn't know how some of them had held on to their lives. Determination to hurt the aliens before they died, perhaps.

"I'm afraid not," she said, as she started to wash her hands. The NHS had a poor reputation for keeping hospitals clean, but none of the ones she'd worked in had been anything like as bad as the abandoned house they'd turned into a medical centre. It had taken her hours to clean the place to a minimum standard and even then she had a feeling that it was still alarmingly unhealthy. "We don't have prosthetics we could use to give you a new arm, or replace the shattered bone. Even if we did have, I'm not sure you could recover after that level of trauma."

The man nodded, scowling down at the floor. He'd been given a large dose of painkillers, but they clearly hadn't been enough to keep the pain from making it harder for him to think. Fatima wasn't too surprised. Taking too many of the painkillers would have been bad for his health too.

"And if I chose to stay like this?" he asked, finally. "I could…"

"You wouldn't recover any function in your lower arm or your hand," Fatima said, flatly. She didn't really blame him for refusing to realise the truth. Humans hated losing parts of their bodies. Trauma victims never fully recovered. "You would be left with a useless dangling piece of flesh - one that would have to be bound to your body at all times. My best advice is to have it taken off, which would at least prevent the wound from becoming infected."

"Take it off, then," he said, finally. He smiled, although Fatima could see the pain written over his face. "I guess there's no hope of a proper rest afterwards?"

"Probably not," she said, as she prepared the local anaesthetic. He should have been put out completely, but she preferred to avoid doing that if possible. They had had to abandon two other makeshift hospitals and unconscious patients were difficult to move. "Just lie back and let me get on with it."

An hour later, she headed downstairs and washed her hands under the shower. The small apartment had been abandoned, according to Abdul and his men, which made it an ideal place for a resistance cell. Fatima hoped that they were right, if only because she didn't want to have to abandon her patients. Most of the wounded resistance fighters were scattered over

London, but the seriously wounded fighters were kept near her. She was their doctor, after all.

She sat down on the sofa and closed her eyes, fighting back tears. As a medical student, and then as a doctor, she'd taken pride in her work. She'd saved lives. Men and women who would have died a century ago had lived because of her – and the medical knowledge of hundreds of years. Now… she hated doing a bad job, but the truth was that there were limits to what she could do without proper equipment and supplies. Many of her patients needed a real hospital, not a makeshift set of beds which they might need to flee at any time. She'd asked if they could find a way to slip a patient into a real hospital, but Abdul had vetoed the idea. The aliens had insisted that the NHS doctors check their patients details and if they stumbled across a resistance fighter…

Fatima shook her head, wondering – again – what had happened to her family. There'd been no announcement of their fate on the BBC, just a terrible silence that was somehow far more terrifying than anything else. Anything could have happened to them – the aliens could have killed them, or enslaved them, or simply dumped them in a detention camp outside the city. After the bloody slaughter the aliens had unleashed, few dared to ask them – or to demand that the prisoners be returned to their families. For all she knew, they could have been shipped to Africa and dumped there.

The only thing keeping her from crying was the knowledge that her patients needed her – for all the good she could do for them. She had to watch many of them die because she didn't have the equipment to save them – and as they died, a little of herself died as well. If they hadn't needed her, she would have volunteered to drive the next truck loaded with explosives into the alien base. And that would be the end of her.

"Hey," a soft voice said, "are you all right?"

Fatima glanced up to see Lucas, a young man who'd been serving the resistance as a runner, ever since his family had been caught up in the invasion and killed. He'd wanted to join the fighters, but his knowledge of the area made him far more useful as a runner. Or so he'd been told. Privately, Fatima suspected that Lucas wouldn't have made a good fighter. He only wanted to hurt the aliens and didn't care if he got hurt himself.

And he was attracted to her. She found him attractive too, and attentive, but how could she afford more emotional ties with anyone? Her family was gone, perhaps dead… anyone else she invited into her heart might go the same way. She didn't dare take the chance.

"Just tired," she said, pulling herself to her feet. She should have a rest, but there was no way she could sleep long enough for it to do her any good. "And yourself?"

"I got told to bring you a warning," Lucas said. "The aliens did a sweep through a few blocks a mile or so away. They may have caught someone who knows about this place."

Fatima swallowed a curse. Her stepmother would have slapped her if she'd realised that Fatima even *knew* such a word. The aliens had the services of the police – and the police knew how to get suspects to talk and implicate more people. If they knew who they'd bagged, they might uncover the makeshift medical centre. Abdul had made it clear that no one – even himself – was to know everything, but the aliens might uncover more than one cell if they managed to capture the medical centre.

And three of her patients really shouldn't be moved.

"Go tell the patients upstairs that we might have to move," Fatima ordered. Given time, she was sure that she could get all of the patients out, but could they do it without alerting the aliens and their collaborators? "Is anyone else coming to help?"

"The Big Man says he's sending some of his men," Lucas said. He grinned. When he wasn't passing on messages, he spent most of his time with the soldiers. They were teaching him tricks he might need when he finally joined the fight. "Anyone who can't move under his own power will be helped."

Fatima nodded. And after that, she knew, they'd leave an IED behind, just in the hopes of bagging an alien or a few collaborators. They'd done it before. Abdul had pointed out that creating an impression of a network of IEDs slowed down enemy deployment, even if there were only a handful of real IEDs in the area. It had worked in Afghanistan and now it was working in London. Absently, she wondered how men who'd fought in Afghanistan liked using their enemy's tactics against the enemy of the entire planet?

"Come on then," she said. "Let's start moving the patients."

Chapter Twenty-Six

Alien Detention Camp
United Kingdom, Day 36

The first few days in the detention camp were unpleasant. Alex wasn't sure why the aliens hadn't bothered to provide shelters for their prisoners, which meant that when it rained – as it did every night – the bedding became soaked and refused to dry until the morning. A number of the prisoners were already suffering from exposure and were at death's door, but the aliens didn't seem concerned. When she was feeling charitable, which wasn't very often, Alex guessed that the aliens *liked* the rain and believed that the humans would like it too. The other explanation was that the aliens were deliberately torturing their captives and breaking their will to resist. It seemed as likely as any other possibility.

She had spent the first day studying the alien base, what little she could see of it from behind the wire. It seemed to be a small military base, although it was definitely not as active as Bastion or any of the other major bases she'd deployed to before the aliens had invaded and turned the entire planet upside down. Judging from the way they'd extended the wire several times since the invasion – several of the prisoners admitted to have been behind the wire since day one – they might just have intended it as a prison for rebellious types.

The next few days had been worse. She'd wondered endlessly who'd betrayed them – and why? Had the traitor been terrified for his life, or the lives of his family – or had he merely wanted thirty pieces of silver? The conditions outside the cities were better than inside the cities – at least if the internet was to be believed – but no one had been very safe. Perhaps the traitor, hearing stories about entire towns being blasted from orbit for daring to harbour resistance fighters, had decided that Long Stratton would be left unmolested if the resistance was handed over to the aliens. Absently, she wondered if Archer or any of the others had made it out safety, or if they'd been caught by the aliens. She tried to form mental pictures of them blasting their way through entire alien formations, but she had to admit that they weren't particularly likely. Archer had suggested heading into the national parks or other undeveloped parts of Britain and setting up long-term bases there. She hoped – prayed – that they managed to get out and carry on the fight. They would have to do it without her.

Every time she heard a noise in the sky, she looked up, wondering what she would see. Sometimes she saw the massive shuttles the aliens used to land troops from orbit, too large to fly without some kind of antigravity device; sometimes their attack helicopters, larger than the outdated Russian helicopters that had been flown around Afghanistan. She allowed herself to hope that one day she'd see a streak of light shooting down one of the helicopters, but the resistance seemed to be very thin on the ground around the detention camp. The aliens, according to some of the older prisoners, had simply uprooted thousands of humans and ordered them away from their bases. Remembering some of the havoc caused by dickers – civilians who reported British military movements to the enemy – in Afghanistan, Alex couldn't blame them, even though the mobile phone network had never been restored.

She shook her head. The Taliban had never scored a major victory, but they'd kept up the pressure and they might have won in the long term – if the aliens hadn't invaded. But the Coalition had been bound by rules of engagement dreamed up by decent – if ignorant – politicians. The aliens didn't seem to care about civilian casualties and they were perfectly willing to obliterate entire towns to punish resistance. Weaker forces had defeated stronger forces before – or had at least convinced them to withdraw – but Alex couldn't remember if they'd ever done it when the stronger forces had also been the barbarians.

When the call came, it took her by surprise. A pair of aliens were standing by the gate, bellowing for her in their toneless voices. She hesitated, considering hiding within the crowd, before realising that it was pointless.

Bracing herself, she strode out with as much dignity as she could muster and stopped in front of the aliens. One of them pointed his cannon-like weapon at her chest, as if he imagined that she was a threat. Alex couldn't keep the giggles from forming deep inside her chest. She was half-naked, half-starved and completely unarmed… and he thought she was a threat?

"Turn around and place your hands behind your back," the alien ordered. Alex obeyed, unsurprised to feel a metal tie contracting around her wrists. They weren't taking any chances, all right. Their voices were almost robotic. "Walk with us. Do not attempt to escape."

The alien swung her around and marched her towards the gate, which clanged shut behind them. Despite her growing nervousness, Alex was privately glad of the chance to inspect the rest of the base. A number of human-designed buildings were still intact, but others had clearly been knocked down and were being replaced by prefabricated alien buildings. She caught sight of what looked like a futuristic car at the end of one building, before her escort marched her onwards, half-pulling her whenever she tried to slow them down. The sound of alien voices speaking what had to be their own language – it sounded like grunting to her ears – caught her attention and she looked up. A small group of aliens was staring at her, their dark eyes wide. Surely she wasn't the first human they'd seen…

And these aliens were smaller. For a moment, she wondered if they were children, before realising that they were differently proportioned than her escort. Alien females? She'd assumed that the aliens had their own version of keeping women barefoot, pregnant and in the kitchen, but maybe they made better use of female labour than some human societies. Their clothing was different too… she wondered, absently, how the aliens mated, before pushing the thought aside. It was clear that she was about to have far more serious problems.

A human designed building loomed up in front of her and the aliens pushed her right into the darkness. For a moment, Alex was completely disorientated before her eyes adjusted to the gloom. There was a chair in the centre of the room, bolted to the floor, and the aliens pushed her down onto the cold metal. She yelped as they stubbed her bound wrists, before, fixing a bar around her chest and walking away. The door closed behind them with an audible clunk.

"Well, well, well," a voice said, from the darkness. "What have we here?"

Alex started, peering ahead of her. In the gloom, she could make out two figures, both clearly human. They didn't *seem* to be restrained. The light came on suddenly, almost blinding her. The two men definitely weren't restrained. Alien collaborators… or something else? But what else could they be?

"Who…?" Her throat was dry. She could barely speak. "Who are you?"

"Our names aren't important," one of the men said. They were both wearing masks to cover their identities, but the speaker was clearly taller than the other. "All that really matters is satisfying our masters."

He stood up and advanced towards Alex, rubbing his hands together. "You've been a very naughty girl," he said, mockingly. "The government surrendered – and you kept the war going all on your own." His mouth, what little she could see of it, leered. "But now the war is over and you're a prisoner. No one even knows where you are."

Alex braced herself, remembering the dreaded Conduct After Capture course they'd been put through during training. The Geneva Conventions had become a joke after the end of the Cold War and the MOD had – reluctantly – admitted that British personnel *would* be tortured and forced to talk by their captors. They'd been given guidelines, but the decision on how much to say and cooperate had been left with the captured personnel. Alex remembered seeing captured personnel broadcasting from Iran and shuddered. At least a personal broadcast from her wouldn't have any effect on the rest of the resistance. She barely knew *anything* that could be used against anyone else.

"Cooperate with us now and you will be well-treated," the interrogator said. She could feel his breath on her ear. "We have good food and you can rest. You did your duty – now it's over. You can relax."

His finger reached out and traced her chin, gently pulling her head up so she was staring into his eyes. "It's over," he said, gently. "Who else was involved with your resistance cell?"

Alex looked down and shook her head. "Come on," he said, gently. "There's really nothing to be gained by further resistance. We *are* going to get it out of you, one way or the other. Why not make it easier upon yourself?"

He stepped back and reached for a small tray lying on his desk. When he stepped back into view, he was holding a small bar of chocolate in his hand. "You know, you used to be able to get as much chocolate as you wanted for a few pounds," he said. "Now… now you can't get chocolate at all, unless you have *connections*." He spoke the last word with another leer as he opened the packet. "Wouldn't you like some chocolate?"

Alex recoiled as he held a piece out under her nose. After a few days in the detention camp, part of her wanted the chocolate – and part of her refused to take anything from her interrogator. He held it closer, just above her mouth, waiting to see what she would say. Her mouth was watering, but she shook her head. Perhaps he was right, perhaps it was hopeless, yet she wasn't going to break so easily. She swore to herself that she wouldn't break at all.

"You seem to believe that you can remain silent," the interrogator said. He popped a piece of chocolate into his mouth and ate it with evident enjoyment. "But believe me, you will talk."

Without warning, he slapped her across the cheek. Alex gasped in pain, feeling blood trickling down the side of her face. Her entire face hurt. He leaned closer and pushed his face against hers, almost as if he intended to kiss her. When he spoke, his voice was a dull whisper.

"You will talk," he said. "We have all the time in the world to break your resistance. You will be broken apart and then you will tell us everything we want to know. Do you understand me? Resistance is futile."

He slapped her again. Alex felt an unholy ringing in her head, which faded slowly. She hadn't had anything like enough to eat over the past few days. Chances were they'd held her long enough for hunger to set in and weaken her resistance. Her lips felt bloody and broken after the two slaps. The strap around her chest seemed to be contracting, squeezing the breath out of her. It was all she could do to remain aware and alert.

A glint of light caught her eye and she froze as the interrogator advanced towards her with a knife. He was going to cut her throat… for a moment, she was gripped with absolute terror, just before realising that they would hardly let her go that easily. She felt a tug as he pulled at what remained of her shirt, slicing it away from her bare skin. Her bra followed, leaving her breasts exposed to their gaze. She cringed back as he pinched her nipple, before turning his attention to her trousers. When he had finished, she was naked and exposed – and helpless. No amount of struggling would break the tie they'd put around her chest.

"Do you understand me?" The interrogator whispered. "You will talk, one way or the other. Talk now and we won't have to hurt you any longer…"

Alex tried to lose herself in thought. Where had the interrogator come from? She knew that some policemen were collaborating, but surely they would draw the line at such an interrogation… But the aliens had presumably taken the prisons as well. They'd have plenty of volunteers for an interrogation crew if they broke open the cells containing violent offenders. Some of the stories she'd read in the newspapers over the years had been horrific, like the brother who had casually tortured his own sister to death. He'd been jailed for a very long time – but had the aliens freed him and put him to work?

They didn't seem to enjoy making people suffer themselves. The aliens stamped hard on resistance, and they were indiscriminate when it came to applying heavy weapons, but they didn't have the sadistic urges that many human despots had indulged. But if they'd found humans who did enjoy making people suffer… the thought was sickening. If someone had suggested it to the aliens…

A hand grabbed her breast and squeezed, hard. Another reached down and clawed between her legs. Alex screamed for the first time, trying to bring her leg up to kick out at her tormentor. He slapped it down and then yanked at her breast. Alex felt her mind start to blur as he slapped her time and time again, the pain threatening to drag her down into the darkness. She'd lost track of time. How long had she been tortured… she heard a hiss and opened her eyes, in time to see a single jet of blue fire right in front of her eyes.

"You won't be such a pretty face when I'm through with you," her interrogator whispered. There was no doubt at all that he was enjoying himself. Alex cringed back as the heat came closer and closer to her face, only to be pulled away just before it started to burn her skin. "Do you know how many women I've beaten and broken here? How many are nothing more than my slaves, dependent upon me for everything?"

Alex tried to speak, but it was so hard to concentrate. She wanted to give in, and yet some stubborn part of her nature refused to surrender. The pain was growing; she was suddenly aware that he'd freed her from the chair, only to roll her over so she was bent over the chair, her buttocks lifted up for his inspection. Something sent a wave of pain over her rear and she screamed again, feeling a desperate desire to be sick that sent a tidal wave of vomit out of her mouth. Everything she'd eaten in the camp, as mushy and tasteless as it had been, seemed to be spilling out of her.

She felt his hands on her rear, spreading her thighs. And then she felt him pressing his hardness into her… the pain and humiliation overwhelmed her, sending her crashing down into darkness. Her last thought, shining out against the blackness, was that she'd told them nothing…

———

"Are you all right?"

Alex opened her eyes slowly, unsure of what had happened to her. She found herself in a small cell, staring up at a naked girl. The bruises on her skin told their own story. Every single piece of Alex's body *hurt* in ways she would have thought unimaginable. It hurt to try to open her mouth and speak. The pain around her breasts was horrific.

"Remain still," the girl urged. "He's cut you, the bastard. I don't know if you'll recover…"

Somehow, despite the pain, Alex managed to pull herself up into a sitting position – and instantly regretted it. Her buttocks felt as if they were on fire. Carefully, she inspected herself and saw red marks and cuts covering her skin. Some of them looked to have broken the skin, only to be allowed to heal on their own, without interference. She glanced around the dirty cell and realised that there was a good chance that one or more of the scars would become infected. And then… she doubted that they'd give her any medical treatment. Maybe the infection would finish her off quickly.

"What…?" She managed to say. Her mouth still hurt, even when she touched it. They'd slapped her, she recalled. Maybe they'd knocked out a tooth or two. Or maybe… hadn't she read a book, once, where the hero had had his teeth removed to make him talk? She didn't seem to be missing any teeth, but her mouth hurt too much for her to be sure. "What happened to me?"

"They dumped you in here," the girl said. "I don't think you told him anything. He was proper raging when he left you here and told me to take care of you. I think he's probably afraid that the Leathernecks will be angry with him for failing to get anything out of you."

"Good," Alex managed, finally. Maybe they'd send him to be interrogated instead. A taste of his own medicine would teach him a lesson. "Where… where did they get you?"

The girl hesitated, and then shrugged. "My brother was killed by the bastards and I was taken away," she said. "When I woke up, I was here – at his mercy. You… you don't know what they've done to me…"

"I think I can guess," Alex said. The bastard had raped her, just as he'd raped Alex. Part of her wanted to crawl into a corner and die, but the rest of her wanted revenge. There would be a chance to kill the bastard and she intended to take it. It was the only thing left to her. "Do you have more water? Something to wash?"

"There's a shower over there, but the water's always cold," the girl said. Alex pulled herself to her feet, despite the pain, and staggered towards the little chamber. "They do it on purpose, the bastards."

"Probably," Alex agreed. Her body was stained with blood – and his seed. She wanted to be clean again, even though she felt as if she would never be clean. "But we will get them, one day."

Chapter Twenty-Seven

Near Alien Detention Camp
United Kingdom, Day 40

"Jimmy!"

Jimmy Coates scowled as he heard his wife calling his name. What did the dumb bitch want now? It was bad enough that she picked a fight with him about each and every little thing, but she wouldn't allow him to respond to her stupid arguments. So what if he drank too much and came rolling home drunk? She'd come rolling home drunk if she saw half the shit he had to see, as well as the looks people gave a collaborator when they thought one of the aliens wasn't watching. And who cared if the fucking cooking club bitches had voted to throw Ginny out on her arse? Just because they didn't want a collaborator's wife…

"What?" He demanded, furiously. There were times when he thought that going to the whorehouses would be a good way to punish a shrewish spouse. It wasn't as if there was a shortage of whores these days. Pussy was cheap when so many were starving, kept alive by the mush the aliens doled out every week to those who bent the knee to them. "What's so fucking important that you have to drag me out of the bathroom?"

"They're saying there's going to be a national announcement in twenty minutes," his wife shouted back. God – what had he been thinking when he married her? She'd trapped him, all right; she'd told him that she was on the pill. But she'd gotten pregnant and her father had insisted that he marry her, or else. Jimmy still remembered the moment when he'd realised that he'd been trapped, forced into a marriage to a girl he didn't love. And even though they'd had three brats together, he still didn't love her. "You have to watch it too."

Jimmy snorted, but didn't argue any further. The BBC was wholly controlled by the aliens these days and they used it to make sure that their subjects heard announcements that might otherwise be missed. When they weren't issuing orders, they were showing old soap operas and movies, rather than anything else. The once-famed BBC news service had terminated two days after the aliens landed, never to be replaced. It seemed that the aliens believed that humans were only to know what they needed to know, rather than have news from all over the world pumped into their living rooms. Jimmy was almost relieved. His wife and her cooking group had held sales for every lost cause across the world, apart from Britain itself. No one was allowed to mention how Britain had problems…

He stumbled down the stairs, cursing the five pints of beer he'd downed after leaving work earlier, and crashed into the living room. She'd decorated it, of course, with all of her frilly decorations, rather than the beer table and fridge he would have preferred. Surely a man could design at least one room in his house. But no, it was all her own work – and it had cost him a pretty penny too! He sat down in the armchair and pretended not to see his wife's lips thinning with disapproval. So what if he was half-drunk? It wasn't as if he wasn't providing for her, was it? She still got half of his salary – real alien money – and there were goods in the shops for those who had alien money. They ate better than all of their neighbours.

The television was showing the end of one of the soap operas he so detested, but he told himself to be patient. It wasn't easy, not when his wife was either looking at the television or scowling at him, giving him the look that suggested that she regretted marrying him almost as much as he regretted marrying her. But it wasn't as if he'd had any choice… and then there were the kids. He loved his kids, or at least he told himself he did, and he wouldn't want any harm to come to them. They'd be shattered if mum and dad broke up… maybe he would go to the whorehouse after all. It wasn't as if his wife was giving him access to her body any longer.

He looked up as the music announcing an alien broadcast caught his attention. The aliens always announced their broadcasts in advance, warning everyone to watch – or else. Jimmy had no idea what had got into their minds this time, but he knew better than to avoid watching, not when his very career depended upon them. The aliens seemed interested in recruiting thousands of humans and they paid well, although they were really the only paying employers these days. No doubt the wretched banking CEOs and others who made it impossible for a man to overcome his debt and stand tall had sold out to them. No one had any principles any longer.

"Case in point," he grunted, as the collaborator-in-chief appeared on the screen. Alan Beresford was just another MP who proved that there was no point in being loyal to the country. Why should he be loyal to a government that pardoned outright criminality among its own members and at the same time lectured him to improve his lifestyle? What fucking business of theirs was it if he smoked twenty fags in a day, or drank himself senseless every weekend? It wasn't as if there were any dreams any longer. How could they claim his loyalty when they so manifestly didn't deserve it? The last Prime Minister was probably hiding in an aristocratic mansion somewhere, while his successor was an outright collaborator.

His wife looked over at him. "Yes, Jimmy?"

"Oh, shut up," Jimmy grunted. He wanted a beer, any beer. But he'd stashed all of his cans upstairs and there was none within reach. "I thought you admired this guy anyway."

"These have been tragic times for our country," Beresford said. Jimmy snorted. Somehow, he didn't think that Beresford had found them very tragic. It was clear that he was well-fed and content, even if he was the focus for a great deal of anger. The aliens would protect him if the lynch mob ever reached his door. "We have been forced to adapt to a new world order – and yet there are those who are resolved to fight to the bitter end. But their fight is hopeless – we are part of a greater universe now and it is time to earn our place in it."

"By whoring for the aliens, no doubt," Jimmy sneered. "Bet you're not worried about thugs slashing your tires when you park and go for a beer."

He smiled at the memory. It hadn't been that long ago that he and his fellow lorry drivers had caught a pair of young kids slashing their tires. They hadn't bothered to call the police, knowing that the little brats would only be let off with a warning. Instead, they'd thrashed hell out of them and abandoned them some miles from town. Jimmy had half-expected them to inform the police, but there had never been any comeback. Perhaps the police had figured that the brats deserved their treatment.

"We have broken many cells of bitter-enders, people who believe that they must still fight on," Beresford continued. "It is with great regret that I am forced to confirm that those fighters – who have killed far more innocent humans than aliens – will be executed in two days. Their deaths will serve as a warning – being a bitter-ender will bring you nothing, but grief. The entire population will see their executions on television. And then let us pray that that will be an end to the fighting. Our poor country has suffered enough.

"But you haven't suffered at all," Jimmy bellowed, and threw the remote at the television set. People like Beresford never suffered. They simply attached themselves to the centre of power and made themselves indispensable, at least until a new centre of power arrived. Bottom-feeders, the lot of them. "Do you really think that we will be impressed?"

"It gives me great pleasure to announce that the daily ration will be increased in response to the increasing number of people who have seen the inevitable and started to work with the aliens to build a new world," Beresford concluded. "Together, we will build a new Britain."

His face vanished from the display. Moments later, the next soap came on, while a small line of text underneath the pictures warned that the alien broadcast would be repeated every hour on the hour. Everyone in Britain would see it. And then they would watch in horror as the aliens executed their captives. Jimmy shrugged as he stood up. What had Britain ever done for him that he should fight for it? He'd been nagged by the nanny-state since he was a little kid. Don't smoke, don't drink, don't question… we know what's best for you, never mind that you don't like it…we have the right to reshape you as we see fit…

He rolled his eyes, just as the doorbell rang. Jimmy blinked in surprise; ever since he'd gone to work for the aliens, their circle of friends had dwindled away to almost nothing. His wife had taken it harder than he had – he was happy as long as he had beer and a place to sleep. Perhaps it was one of the religious freaks who went around offering salvation – in exchange for a cash donation, of course – or someone collecting for charity. It seemed that the only endangered species unworthy of assistance was the white male.

Carefully – there *were* bitter-enders out there – he peered through the tiny spy hole and frowned. Two brisk young men stood in front of the door, wearing civilian clothes. They didn't *look* like religious freaks. Maybe they wanted to sign up with the aliens – it wouldn't be the first time he'd been approached by someone looking for a job. He opened the door and scowled down at them. They didn't seem intimidated by his face.

"We need to talk to you," one of them said. He stepped forward, put his foot neatly in place to prevent Jimmy from shutting the door, and pointed a gun right at his face. Jimmy jumped back in shock, feeling the pleasant haze of near-drunkenness fading away. "You're going to help us rescue our friends."

Jimmy found himself on the floor, looking up at them. "And if you don't help," the man added, "you're really not going to enjoy what happens next."

———

Alex rolled over as she heard the sound of the cell opening. They seemed to take her to a different cell after each interrogation session, sometimes with someone in the cell, sometimes empty so she had a chance to brood on what would happen to her next. Her body just ached constantly, the pain blurring together into a single mass tearing away at her mind. She was half-convinced that they were torturing her for the fun of it, or perhaps they were waiting for her to break. They certainly hadn't bothered to ask her any questions.

The light came on, revealing a man with a blood-stained face hobbling into the cell. Like her, he was naked, with dark blue-black bruises covering his entire body. She found herself wondering if she would recognise him, but as her eyes adapted to the light she realised that he was a stranger. The blood on his face suggested that he'd been tortured worse than she had, at least physically. Being at the mercy of a pair of sadists who could do anything they wanted to her was taking its toll. The only thing keeping her from breaking was a bitter determination not to give them the pleasure.

"Hi," Alex said. So far, all of the other prisoners she'd met had been women. She hadn't even known that there were any male prisoners in the complex, although she wasn't really sure how large the complex actually was. It felt as if they were underground, but there was no way to know for sure. God alone knew if they were even still in Britain. "What did they do to you?"

The man stumbled to his knees, grunting in pain as he hit the stone floor. "They caught me two days ago," he said, quietly. Alex blinked in surprise. It looked as if he had been worked over more than once, but maybe she was mistaken. "They were lying in wait – wiped us out, apart from me. I was the lucky one they took alive."

There was a bitterness in his voice that was alarmingly convincing. "I was in Chester's group," he added. "Good old Chester – Shiny Two's Colonel. He's dead too, now."

Alex winced. Shiny Two was the nickname for 2 Para, one of the toughest units of fighting men in the British Army. She'd flown missions supporting their operations in Afghanistan, before returning to Britain and flying in defence of the UKADR. If they'd been wiped out, what hope was there for anyone else?

"We lost contact with everyone else," he admitted. "Who were you with?"

"No one," Alex admitted. The memory was a bitter one, although if he was telling the truth it would seem that the professional soldiers hadn't done much better. "I don't want to talk about it."

"It's over," the man insisted. "None of us are ever going to see the outside world ever again. What possible harm could it do now?"

Alex considered the point for a long moment. She didn't know who had betrayed her and she probably would never know. It was nice to think that Archer and the others would carry on the war without her, but the traitor might have betrayed them as well. And if that had happened, their resistance cell would have been blown open and destroyed. The supplies that Archer had guarded ever since 1940 would have been confiscated by the aliens.

"I don't want to talk about it," she repeated. She wasn't going to break, not after everything else she'd been through. "I need to rest."

"But they'll kill you," the man protested. "You can't help your friends now…"

Something clicked in Alex's mind. She'd been slapped and beaten and raped and, afterwards, she'd found it incredibly difficult to walk. The man looked to have been tortured worse and yet he was still walking, if badly. They should have shackled him, yet they'd left him free to walk. And he didn't sound as though he was in pain…

"Go fuck yourself, collaborator," Alex said, wondering if it would be the last thing she'd ever say. He might lash out at her and she was in no state for a fight. "You're nothing more than a goddamned Walt!"

There was a pause, and then the man stood up and banged on the cell door. His limp seemed to have vanished, she noted, as the door opened and he was hauled outside. She could hear the sound of someone screaming from further down the corridor before the door was slammed closed and the light went off, leaving her alone in the darkness. Alex chuckled, despite the pain it caused her to laugh. They'd tried to trick her into talking and failed.

She lay back on the hard bed and closed her eyes, trying to relax. It wasn't easy; the pain kept her awake. She wasn't sure how much more she could take before she broke, even though she was determined to hold out as long as possible. But what was going to happen to her afterwards? She had a feeling that she wouldn't enjoy the answer.

The cell door banged open without warning. A dark silhouette appeared, standing against the faint light from outside. "Well, you're certainly posing an interesting challenge," the tall man said. He sounded more amused than annoyed. "I thought that you would have been fooled for sure."

It was a mistake to talk to one's captors, but Alex couldn't resist. "Fuck you," she said. "I won't tell you anything."

"I've already fucked you," the tall man said, nastily. There was a faint chuckle, an inhuman sound for all that it came from a human throat. "I come with good news. Your suffering will soon be over, my dear. Our masters have decided to execute a number of people caught in the act of waging war against the new world order. They announced it on the BBC and everything. And unless you talk, you're going to be one of the ones executed by firing squad."

He leaned closer. "You could talk right now," he said. "I'll have your wounds treated and you'd even be able to rest properly, without any more suffering. There are places where you could live out the rest of your life, far from the maddening crowd. All you have to do is tell us what we want to know…"

Alex braced herself, and then threw a slap at his face. But she was wounded and drained and she moved far too slowly. He stepped back, effortlessly avoiding her desperate blow.

"I suggest you make your peace with yourself, bitch," he said, in the same casual tone. "Tomorrow, you will die. And don't even think that they will care, all the people you're protecting. They will just forget you, or forever wonder if you betrayed them…"

"Go fuck yourself," Alex said, as harshly as she could.

"I'll fuck someone else tonight," the tall man said. "Enjoy your last day on Earth."

The door banged closed behind him, leaving Alex alone once again. She'd known that there was a prospect of violent death from the day she'd first joined the RAF. And she'd known that she might be shot down over enemy territory and interrogated. It had been one of her few nightmares, back when the world had made sense. If only it had stayed in her nightmares… quietly, alone in her cell, she prayed to a God she hadn't spoken to for years. At least her death would have some meaning…

And perhaps it would be quick.

Chapter Twenty-Eight

Alien Detention Camp
United Kingdom, Day 41

"I strongly suggest that you don't fuck up," Chris said, looking over at the lorry driver. It hadn't taken much to pigeon-hole their unwilling assistant as someone who could be threatened, although never fully trusted. "One mistake and they'll have us – and they will never believe that you weren't part of it."

Jimmy Coates nodded, clearly nervous around the soldiers and their weapons. The aliens had summoned three of their tame lorry drivers – and their vehicles – to the detention camp, a stroke of luck that Chris intended to use against them. Each of the lorries could hold upwards of twenty soldiers, along with some heavy weapons. The remainder of the assault force had positioned itself nearer the camp, watching and waiting for the balloon to go up. Chris had devised the plan, but right now – on the verge of implementing his plan – it struck him that there were too many things that could go wrong. If they fucked up…

"I'm going to be in the cab with you," he added. "If you betray us, it will be the last thing you ever do."

He bellowed for the soldiers to clamber into the lorries, and then nodded to Coates to climb into his cab and start the engine. Chris had ridden in army lorries before, but it had taken some careful work to prepare the civilian vehicles for their use. They weren't designed to carry passengers in the rear, let alone heavy weapons. Chris hadn't mentioned it to the lorry drivers, but if necessary they wouldn't hesitate to abandon the lorries and leave them behind. The aliens would know who had assisted the resistance, which would mark the drivers for death when they were caught. Their families were already safe and the drivers, assuming that they survived the mission, would be allowed to join them.

"Come on," Coates bellowed. "We need to get moving!"

Chris nodded and scrambled up into the cab. It was warmer than he had expected, smelling of something he didn't quite want to identify. Jimmy turned the key and the engine roared to life as Chris pulled on his seat belt and checked his Browning. He'd stashed a small bag of grenades and other surprises below the seat, out of sight of any alien patrols. If nothing else, the mission should convince the aliens that they couldn't rely on their tame collaborators – at least not completely. And Coates, a drunkard with a shrew of a wife, would go down in the history books as a hero.

The vehicle lurched into life and headed off down the road, followed by the other two lorries at a safe distance. Chris wasn't too surprised to see how empty the roads had become, even though the aliens had started doling out petrol to their collaborators. Most vehicles were driven by collaborators and they'd been targeted by resistance fighters – or just local youths – for destruction. Not many people picked on the aliens these days. The Leathernecks were clearly learning; not only had they improved their reaction times, but they didn't hesitate to blast nearby towns and villages in retaliation for attacks on their vehicles.

Chris gritted his teeth as the roar of the engine grew louder, thinking hard. How long could they continue to fight if the aliens retaliated massively for every little attack? They had plenty of weapons, but the aliens would simply keep wearing them down – and force the local population into more active collaboration. If they started warning the inhabitants of towns near their bases that any attack would result in the destruction of their town, the inhabitants might betray the resistance fighters to the aliens. Chris couldn't really blame them, even though it would make carrying on the war difficult. How could they keep fighting if they didn't have a real hope of victory?

The internet – passing messages from cell to cell – was clearly trying to keep their hopes up, but he could tell that the resistance was fraying at the edges. None of the lads had ever expected to have to fight a war in their own backyards and many had seen to their families, only to be rounded up by the aliens and shipped… where? It bothered him that they still had no idea what happened to human military personnel. There were hundreds of rumours, but none of them had ever seemed more than marginally likely. Perhaps they'd just been taken somewhere isolated and murdered. It was as likely as any other suggestion.

Once, the motorways had been jam-packed with traffic, making it impossible to move along at anything above a crawl. Now, from what he'd heard, those collaborators who drove out found driving almost pleasurable – at least while they weren't dodging rocks. He couldn't really blame them for that, even though he hated them for collaborating. The longer the country remained under alien control, the more and more people who would find themselves pushed into collaboration, or at least accommodation, with the aliens. And then…

There were parts of the country that had been used for military training and exercises for years, places where few civilians lived. The Scottish Highlands could hide a resistance force for years; indeed, the aliens seemed less interested in human activities above Dundee. They did have a small alien force in Aberdeen, but they hadn't bothered to expand outwards or even start supervising the locals as closely as they did in London. It was reassuring to know that there were limits to their manpower, even though it was likely that they didn't consider the Highlands very important. He could go there and join the Scots Guards who were preparing their own fallback positions, or… maybe he would just carry on the fight until his luck ran out and the aliens killed him.

He glanced down at his watch. It was 1024. The executions had been scheduled for 1100 precisely. Apparently, the aliens were sending a number of bigwigs from London and the other occupied cities down to watch as they pumped bullets into captured resistance fighters, perhaps as a warning to anyone who would consider playing both sides of the fence. It was possible that Beresford himself would be there. Now *there* was a pleasant thought. If they had a shot at him, Chris intended to take it. Maybe it would teach the other collaborators not to sell themselves, body and soul, to the enemy of the entire world.

The light came on, shockingly bright.

"On your feet," a man ordered. Alex gasped in pain as strong hand grasped her legs and pulled them off the bed. A moment later, she was yanked to her feet and pushed against the cold wall while her hands were tied behind her back. Her two captors, both wearing the black masks that obscured their features, shoved her towards the door. Despite nearly falling onto her face, Alex found the masks rather heartening. They were clearly concerned about retribution from the resistance.

Outside, a number of other naked prisoners – male and female – were being pushed towards a flight of stairs leading upwards. Many of them were silent; others were crying out, begging for mercy from their masked captors. None of the captors seemed particularly impressed, although a few were taking advantage of the situation to grope the women in the group. Alex snarled at a man who grasped at her breast and he jumped back, clearly not having expected any resistance at all. The thought made her smile as she was pushed up the steps and out into the cold morning air. They seemed to be on the far edge of the alien detention camp.

She heard someone calling to her and glanced over towards the fences. Both the male and female camp populations were staring at the small parade, despite angry shouts and threats from their masked escorts. Alex wondered, absently, what had happened to the aliens. Surely they would be watching while their human pawns abused their captives… or perhaps they were ashamed. Hadn't there been a fictional race of aliens who had discovered the Nazi concentration camps and destroyed them in horror? If only Earth had been invaded by those aliens. The war wouldn't have lasted longer than a few weeks and Earth would have won with ease. Unless the aliens managed to drop asteroids onto the planet instead of landing in force…

"Move, bitch," one of the guards snapped, pushing at her. Alex was tempted to fall to the ground and force them to carry her, but it was clear that there would be little point. The handful of prisoners who had been tortured so hard they couldn't walk were being dragged along the ground by their hair or feet. A pair of alien helicopters flew overhead, the sound of their engines a mocking reminder of everything she'd lost since the day her Eurofighter had been blown out of the sky.

They rounded what looked like a gym and came to a halt in front of the wall. A set of aliens were waiting for them, with a smaller group of humans standing nearby. They looked like collaborators to her, although some of them clearly looked as if they wanted to be somewhere – anywhere – else. She wondered if she'd recognise any of them from the parish council – maybe one of those politicians had betrayed her – but none of them looked familiar. There was no sign of Beresford or any of his inner circle. Perhaps the aliens felt that they'd seen the slaughter in London and didn't need another lesson in alien ruthlessness.

"Get them against the wall," one of the humans ordered. The guards obeyed, pushing and shoving at the prisoners to make them move. Two of the badly-beaten prisoners sagged to their knees as soon as they were pushed against the wall, unable to remain standing upright on their own two feet. Alex leaned backwards and relaxed against the wall, feeling oddly calm. The aliens would kill her and that would be the end. No more torture, no more suffering, no more desperate attempts to prevent her treacherous tongue from speaking aloud… it would be the end.

A cold wind blew across the field as the collaborators prepared themselves. Alex was suddenly very aware that the entire country was going to see her naked – somehow, she found herself chuckling at the very thought. She'd once broken up with a boyfriend because he'd wanted a naked picture of her on his mobile phone; absently, she wondered if that ex-boyfriend would be watching as the aliens blew her apart with their handheld cannons. Perhaps her death would inspire him to go out and kill a few aliens… or perhaps it would just terrify him into submission. She did her best to stand upright, despite the increasing pain from her legs and feet. One way or the other, it wouldn't be long now.

———

"Here we are," Coates said. "They don't normally bother to look inside the lorry…"

Chris braced himself as they reached the alien checkpoint. After the suicide bomber in London, and a handful of copycats from all over Britain, the aliens had installed blast walls and double-fences to prevent any more suicide bombers from getting into their bases before they detonated their bombs. They'd done the papers properly, using MI6's forgery experts, but if the aliens decided to check the lorries anyway… they would have to fight their way into the base. The plan had been to rescue the prisoners and, ideally, give the aliens a colossal black eye. It would be much harder if they were caught outside the fence.

One of the aliens came stamping up to the cab and Coates passed him the papers. The driver was clearly nervous, although Chris suspected that it wouldn't be so obvious to an alien. Some suicide bombers in Iraq had given themselves away by being nervous as they neared their target… he glanced at his watch, noting that they only had ten minutes before the executions were scheduled to take place. A delay could ruin the entire plan. Carefully, he allowed his hand to drop down into his rucksack, where he'd concealed the grenades. If they had to fight their way into the camp…

The alien stepped back and waved one clawed hand. Coates wasted no time in gunning the engine and sending them around the blast walls, while the other lorries were checked and then waved into the base. Chris was almost disappointed at how easy it had been, although there was some evidence that this base wasn't really important to the aliens. They'd only flown a handful of their shuttles down to the base, while they kept flying them to the garrisons outside London and the base they'd built on the remains of Ten Downing Street and Buckingham Palace. He remembered,

briefly, the friends he'd lost in the brief, but violent last stand of the Household Division. They'd be watching from the next world as he led a mixed group of soldiers and marines against the alien base.

According to a handful of collaborators who had maintained ties to the resistance, the aliens had two main detention camps and a number of buildings that served as their local headquarters. Several prisoners had been taken into those buildings and never seen again, although there was no clear explanation as to what had happened to them. The aliens, it seemed, maintained a human interrogation team who interrogated prisoners of particular interest to the aliens. At least one of the interrogators had been identified as a particularly unpleasant sadist and murderer who had been serving thirty years in jail when the aliens had arrived. Chris gritted his teeth at the thought of anyone he knew falling into their hands.

History hadn't been a particular interest of his before the invasion, but he'd been reading about the French Resistance to Hitler. The French Resistance had been rather more low-key than it had claimed particularly after VE Day when the membership of the resistance skyrocketed, but it had had some successes. But it had also had problems with Frenchmen who threw themselves completely into serving the Nazis, as had the Russians and several other occupied countries. The locals had sometimes been worse than their foreign masters, having little or no regard for their own country. Some of the stories had been sickening. People had betrayed their fellows for food, drink, or merely some shelter in a world gone insane, but others had used it as a chance to play out their fantasies.

"Here we are," Coates said, nervously. The three lorries had parked near one of the human buildings. "How long do you want me to wait here?"

"I suggest you get out to the gate once the shooting starts," Chris said. Coates hadn't realised it, but the moment the aliens realised that they were under attack, they'd blast every human vehicle moving near the base. The only thing preventing them from dropping KEWs on their heads would be the presence of hundreds of their own people. "You know where to go to link up with our people."

He scrambled down from the cab and rapped on the back of the lorry. The first bunch of soldiers, wearing the brown uniforms that the aliens issued to their collaborators, opened the doors and jumped down, weapons in hand. If they were lucky, the aliens would start gunning down their collaborators, convinced that they had turned on them. And even if they didn't, they'd be confused.

"Come on," he said. The aliens didn't allow their collaborators firearms. They'd know something was wrong the moment they saw the SA80s and antitank weapons. "Let's go."

———

The problem with trying to make a defiant impression as one was waiting to be shot, Alex decided with a flash of humour, was that it took time for the enemy to get around to actually shooting. Their collaborators were busy making speeches, cursing the bitter-enders who felt that they had to carry on the fight even though it was hopeless. After the first speech, a second had begun, followed rapidly by a third. The viewing public would be getting very bored by now, Alex told herself, wondering if there was something she could do to speed up the affair. It was growing colder and she was hardly dressed for the weather.

She caught sight of a group of aliens marching towards them, carrying their weapons at the ready. There was already one group of armed aliens with the collaborators, but perhaps the aliens had decided they needed two groups – or maybe three. What sort of threat did they think they were facing? They seemed almost laughably paranoid about their prisoners, even though they were tied and suffering the effects of torture.

"And so, it is with the deepest regret that we must execute those who feel that they must resist the new world order," one of the collaborators finally droned. Alex straightened upright as the aliens levelled their weapons, pointing directly at her head. Their bullets were larger than human-designed bullets, she'd noted, perhaps a testament to the tough leathery skin that protected the aliens from outside threats. "Their deaths will serve as a warning to those who feel that they can resist with impunity…"

Alex closed her eyes, expecting the shot to come at any second. Instead, she heard alien grunts of alarm. She opened her eyes, just in time to see a small band of armed collaborators advancing on the aliens. *Armed* collaborators…? The aliens, caught in the open, swung around, too late. Alex threw herself to the ground as the newcomers opened fire, mowing down the aliens before they could take cover or return fire. A handful of collaborators were shot in the legs, knocking them to the ground. Alex glanced up as a figure bent down and sawed the plastic tie away from her wrists.

"What…?" She managed. It was suddenly very hard to speak. "What's going on?"

"Isn't it obvious?" The man demanded. "You're being rescued!"

Chapter Twenty-Nine

Alien Detention Camp
United Kingdom, Day 41

Tra'tro Yak'shat had been studying his records when the attack began. The Detention Camp wasn't officially part of the Land Forces, although they provided the troopers who guarded it from insurgent attack. Instead, it fell under the purview of the Sha'ra, the intelligence service that safeguarded the State from enemies both inside and outside its territory. There hadn't been an intelligence network on Earth prior to the invasion – too great a chance of being discovered ahead of time, or so they'd said – and the intelligence officers were working overtime to build up networks they could use to hunt down human insurgents. It wasn't going too well.

The Sha'ra had wide latitude when it came to intelligence gathering, and he'd been told that he had no need to know any of the gory details, but he'd heard enough to gather that they were using human rogues to torture their prisoners and extract confessions. Anything was permitted in the service of the State – and if the humans were unwilling to dispose of their own rogues, they had only themselves to blame – yet he found it hard to accept that such torture was permissible. The humans seemed to be their own worst enemies. Even the Sha'ra had been shocked at some of the rogues they'd allowed to live. Using them in the service of the State was…

He jumped up as he heard the first explosion. The Sha'ra had ordered the execution of some of the prisoners – even to the point of bringing in their own executioners – and he'd been told to keep him and his troopers away from the execution ground, but explosions suggested that the base was under attack. The alarms sounded a second later, summoning the troopers to grab their weapons and repel the human insurgents. He picked up his own sidearm and ran towards the hatch. If the humans intended to attack his base, they'd get a few unpleasant surprises. He'd been careful to keep half his garrison under cover at all times, in the hopes that any human watchers would believe that he only had half as many troopers as he had. They'd be deploying now…

Outside, the sound of gunfire was alarmingly close. The humans were already inside the fence… how was that even possible? And he could hear the sound of human mortars lobbing shells into the base. Explosions flared up from where they'd parked their helicopters and the shuttle that had brought the Sha'ra execution crew down from orbit. The entire base shook, seconds later, as the fuel dump exploded, blasting a colossal fireball into the air. Much of the base had been built to be fire resistant, but if the shuttle fuel had caught fire the prefabricated buildings would start to melt very quickly. Fire was already starting to spread over the grass the humans had used to mark out their runways. It wouldn't be long before the entire base went up in smoke.

He lifted his weapon, too late, as he saw a pair of humans running towards him. The weapons in their hands flashed fire… and he felt a brief moment of pain, before he fell down into darkness.

———

Chris saw antitank rockets smash into the guardpost, destroying the firing position before the aliens could bring their machine guns to bear on either side of the fence. The assault force outside had already taken out the other posts, allowing them to get close and start taking down the fence and push the blast walls aside. It would have been simpler to knock down the fence in a dozen places, but combat reports from America suggested that the aliens scattered mines between the two fences and they didn't have time to clear a path. Besides, it might be easier to get people out over the road.

"Get the prisoners moving," he bellowed. Sergeant Haywood heard him and started pushing the prisoners towards the gates. A second team headed towards the cages holding the remainder of the prisoners. Some of them prisoners looked as if they'd been beaten half to death, but they were all moving, if poorly. He'd have to assign people to help them get out of the base if they ran out of other options. "Get a team over and concentrated on the alien barracks!"

The aliens seemed to have had a number of troopers hiding in a large building that had clearly been designed to serve as a fortress. Chris watched as they fired from portholes, forcing his men to stay back. Whoever had designed the building knew what he was doing, he admitted to himself; the aliens could cover all of the possible angles of approach, except directly above their building. He detailed two platoons of Royal Marines to keep the aliens pinned down, while rounding up a platoon to follow him towards the human-designed buildings. If their intelligence was correct, the humans the aliens had been using as interrogators would be based there.

A small group of aliens had gone to ground behind a blast wall and were firing down towards the detention camp. Chris nodded to two of his men, who threw grenades over the blast wall and ducked for cover. Two shattering explosions tore through the aliens, sending bloody chunks of flesh flying everywhere. The alien body armour was *good*, he noted, with a flicker of envy. Several of the alien bodies were intact, even though they'd been stunned or killed by the grenades. They put a bullet in each of the alien heads, just to be sure, as they reached the hanger. Inside, there was a small alien helicopter and a pair of aliens who had to be techs. They reached for weapons hanging by their sides, only to be shot down before they could draw them and open fire. Chris watched them fall and then glanced at the alien helicopter, wondering if they could fly it out of the base. A quick check revealed that it had been designed for beings with very different proportions than humans and it would be very difficult for a human to fly. Maybe two humans, with proper training… he pushed the thought aside as they ran towards the stairs. There was an entire underground complex underneath the hanger, one built back when the base had been preparing for war against the Russians. The aliens would probably have found it uncomfortable claustrophobic…

"Incoming," one of the sergeants yelled. Chris glanced up to see an alien helicopter swooping over the base, firing down towards the humans on the ground. A Stinger leapt up and slammed right into the alien craft, sending it heeling out of the sky and down to the ground, where it exploded in a massive fireball. "Sir…"

Chris unhooked a grenade from his belt and motioned for the soldiers to get ready. A second later, he hurled it down the stairs, where it exploded. He followed it down, weapon ready to deal with anyone lying in ambush, only to see nothing more than scorched walls, illuminated by flickering light bulbs. They moved down and started to check each of the small rooms one by one. Most were empty, but a couple held wounded prisoners and one held a man who'd somehow managed to bite though his own wrists and commit suicide. Judging from the condition of his body, he'd been tortured so badly that he'd thought that he was on the verge of breaking and decided to silence himself permanently. Chris would have liked to take his body out of the alien base and bury it somewhere properly, but there wasn't time. The aliens would be responding, even now, to the attack on their territory. How long would it take them to get reinforcements to be base, or decide to cut their losses and drop KEWs on their heads? The only thing keeping them from doing that was the aliens holding their building on the surface.

The final set of doors were locked, but Chris slapped an explosive pack against the doors and jumped back, allowing the explosive pack to blow the door off its hinges. Inside, there were five men, cowering under the table. Chris recognised two of them as people the aliens had recruited to serve as interrogators, which probably meant that they were *all* interrogators. He nodded to his men, who seized the interrogators, searched them roughly, and then bundled them back towards the stairwell. They'd be taken back to the resistance base, interrogated themselves, and then executed. After seeing what they'd done to the prisoners, he had no room left in him for mercy.

A shuffling sound further down the corridor caught his attention and he unhooked his torch from his belt, pointing the beam of light into the darkness. Dark eyes stared back at him and he almost fired reflexively, before realising that the alien was unarmed. How could it even *be* in the underground complex? Chris wasn't claustrophobic, but he'd had to crawl through all kinds of tunnels at Catterick and the alien had to find the human tunnels proportionally worse than he'd found the drains he'd had to explore. It struck him a moment later that the alien had to be one of their intelligence officers. Who else would want to be so close to the interrogation rooms?

He pointed his gun at the alien's head and glared at him. "Can you understand me?"

The alien seemed to quiver, and then nodded. "You're coming with us," Chris said. "We won't hurt you as long as you behave yourself, understand?"

There was a pause, and then the alien nodded again. A student of humanity, perhaps? Human body language had to be alien to the Leathernecks, just as their own body language was almost unreadable to humanity. He looked at the alien's clawed hands and winced, inwardly. The last thing he wanted was the alien behind him with those natural weapons. He'd heard stories that suggested that the alien claws could cut through flesh and bone.

He jerked the gun upwards and the alien shuffled to his feet. Chris stepped to one side and motioned for him to move towards the stairs and he obeyed, slowly. He couldn't tell if the alien was moving slowly because he was claustrophobic or because he was hoping that its fellows would come to the rescue. Chris poked the alien impatiently in the rear end and the alien jerked, before moving a little faster. His massive bulk blocked half the corridor.

"Get him to the surface and out of the base," Chris ordered, before peering through the remaining tunnels. The lighting was failing, suggesting that the base's emergency generator had been damaged in the fighting. Or maybe it was just designed to add to the effect. "We'll finish searching down here and then get up to join you."

The remaining rooms were empty, apart from one which had a pair of laptops and several large hard drives piled on one table. They were definitely human manufacture, which seemed rather odd – even though the aliens had been noted as having an interest in human computers and rounding up human experts they could put to work somewhere outside Britain. He picked them up anyway, remembering their intelligence sweeps through Taliban hideouts back before the invasion, where they'd found all kinds of interesting information – and porn – on their software. The intelligence staff would study the laptops and determine if the interrogators had stored anything useful on their systems. Who knew? There might be videos of their interrogation sessions that could be played at their trial.

He glanced into the final room and blinked in surprise. The interrogators had turned what had once been a small kitchen into a chamber of horrors. A small pile of tools lay beside a hospital table, which was stained with blood and shit and piss. He recoiled, despite himself, wondering how anyone could get their kicks by torturing helpless victims. A cigarette lighter, a welding torch, a dental knife, a rattan cane, a pair of wire cutters… he could see how they'd used each and every one of them to break their victims. He felt sick, fighting down the urge to go find the interrogators and put a bullet through their brains. Even the Taliban hadn't been so unpleasant to their captives.

A glance in a cupboard revealed a small fortune's worth of cannabis and heroin, as well as some luxury foodstuffs that had been unavailable since the invasion. He couldn't tell if the interrogators had used them for themselves or tormented their captives with them, although he could see how they might addict someone to a drug and then leave the withdrawal symptoms as yet another form of torture. One compartment held booze, mainly the muck that various farmers were trying to brew in the absence of government officials to tell them not to make their own. Some of the bottles, however, were old enough to impress even the hardened officers in the mess. Chris couldn't imagine what the torturers had done with the booze.

"Splash the fuel around here and let's go," he ordered, harshly. He didn't quite recognise his own voice. Outside the room, back in the darkened tunnels, he could see just how easily the torturers could break their victims. They'd be able to convince them that the tunnels went on forever, that there

was no hope of escape… the bastards must have been laughing as they enjoyed making people suffer. Perhaps they hadn't even produced results.

He unhooked a small bottle from his belt and splashed the contents around as they headed back to the stairs. The compound had been devised by chemists – it was a distant relative of napalm – but they'd never been allowed to use it in action. They'd followed the ROEs carefully when the world had made sense, yet they no longer mattered now. He pulled a small detonator from his belt as they reached the top of the stairs and tossed it down the shaft. It produced a spark which ignited the liquid, sending flames roaring through the underground complex. The torture chamber, the supplies the torturers had hoarded and the evidence of their grizzly task went up in flames. By the time it burned itself out, it would have incinerated everything, leaving the aliens nothing, but ashes.

"Get the prisoners out to the RV point," he ordered, as he headed back out into the open. The sound of shooting grew louder from the direction of the alien strongpoint. They were merely keeping the aliens pinned down, rather than trying to kill them – and invite the aliens to bombard the base from orbit. "Have we emptied the wire?"

The aliens had established two detention cages, one male, one female. They'd cut through the wire once they'd driven the aliens back from the execution grounds, but several of the prisoners were too terrified to move. Others had started streaming out as soon as the wire had been cut, heading out to the countryside and hopefully away from the aliens. Chris had detailed men to round up the prisoners and take them to resistance hideouts, but if any of the prisoners wanted to go their own way, that was fine with him. The further they were spread over the countryside, the harder it would be for the aliens to round them all up again. He did hope that they were smart enough not to go home. The aliens and their collaborators would presumably have lists of who had escaped and where their families lived, assuming they had families.

He glanced back at the alien base and allowed himself a quick smile. They'd devastated the place. Many of the buildings were tough enough to take the flames without being completely wrecked, but they'd killed dozens of aliens and destroyed their interrogation program. And they'd even destroyed a handful of alien vehicles. No one was quite sure how long it would take for the aliens to get resupplied from their homeworld, yet it would throw a crimp into their invasion and occupation plans. And even *that* didn't take account of how badly their reputation would suffer. Once the news of the raid got out on the internet, resistance fighters all over the world would take heart and try their own attacks on alien bases.

"Sir," Sergeant Gravesend snapped. "I just picked up a flash message from the watchers. The aliens are on their way!"

Chris nodded. "Good," he said. "Let's see just how badly we can maul them this time."

———

Alex's entire body hurt, worse than anything she'd ever experienced, but she would have endured worse for the chance of freedom. One of the rescue party had passed her a coat which she'd used to cover her nakedness, yet she wouldn't have minded even that. Her feet hurt from the broken tarmac and grass they had to cross – they didn't have any shoes – and she felt as if she was half-stumbling from the pain, but she kept moving. She wasn't going to allow this chance to escape because of the pain.

A burly man ahead of her was breaking the escapees down into small groups. "You're going with Group Five," he said, pointing to Alex, who nodded. Her heart was pounding like a drum, the rhythm seemingly echoing inside her head. Could she hear the sound of alien helicopters, or was it just her imagination? "Follow Wilson there and don't slow down. The Leathernecks are on their way."

She caught sight of a pair of bound men being pushed along by some of the soldiers and realised, with a burst of unholy delight, that one of them was the tall man who'd tortured her. The thought kept her moving, even as the sound of alien helicopters grew louder; there would be a chance for revenge. Maybe she could torture him herself, if he proved unwilling to talk… she pushed the thought aside, disgusted at herself. And yet it had a seductive appeal…

"Keep running," Wilson snapped. "You're not safe yet!"

Alex bowed her head and kept moving.

Chapter Thirty

Alien Detention Camp
United Kingdom, Day 41

The line of alien tanks moved with astonishing speed, racing cross-country towards the detention centre. Chris watched them come through a pair of binoculars, noting that the tanks had outraced their troop-carriers they'd presumably been supposed to be escorting. But the aliens trapped in the detention camp had presumably been screaming for help ever since they'd realised that the only thing keeping them alive was their value as hostages. The aliens would want to save their lives, if possible.

His original plan had been a quick smash and grab; get into the base, free the prisoners and then start running. The resistance commander, insofar as the resistance had a commander, had modified it into a better mousetrap, reminding him of stunts the Taliban had pulled during the early years of the war in Afghanistan. They'd been fond of attacking one place to lure a relief force into a trap, but they'd always paid highly for it. Chris had wondered if the resistance was likely to make the same mistakes, yet he'd been overruled. Besides, planting IEDs was all very well, but it wasn't spectacular enough to be inspiring.

"Sir," Maxwell called, "I have their overhead drone in my sights."

Chris nodded. No one was entirely sure just how capable the alien drones were, but the Americans had designed and produced fantastically capable platforms before the invasion, ones capable of tracking individual fighters and dropping Hellfire missiles on their heads. He had to assume that the aliens were just as capable, even though they didn't seem to be designed to operate in a threatening environment. But then, few Taliban fighters had ever had working Stingers. The briefers had commented that possessing such a weapon would make someone a Big Man – and if they fired the missile, they wouldn't have the weapon any more, would they? It had struck Chris as absurd, but they had clearly had a point. The aliens, facing people less concerned with their tribal status, had lost a number of drones to handheld missile launchers since the invasion had begun. But why hadn't they started to take better precautions?

He looked back towards the alien tanks. They'd be within engagement range in a matter of seconds and they all had to be taken out quickly, or they'd be lethal once they realised that they were under attack. Their main guns would be useless against insurgents, but they all carried heavy machine guns and their armour could stand off bullets and even grenades. The gangs in London, according to the internet, had thrown petrol bombs at the aliens, but the alien tanks had simply shrugged the blows off and kept on coming. Their soft-shelled vehicles were easier to disable or destroy.

"Fire," he barked.

Maxwell launched his Stinger upwards towards the alien drone, while the antitank teams fired on the alien tanks. Chris saw a flash in the sky from where the drone had been hit, moments before four of the alien tanks exploded. The fifth ground to a halt and sank to the ground – the rocket had struck the underside of its carriage – but returned fire with its machine guns. Chris cursed as two of the antitank teams were wiped out before they could fall back, while the remaining alien vehicles slowed down and started deploying their troopers. He watched the alien shapes emerging from cover and swore again. They were going to be on him faster than he had planned.

"Fall back," he ordered, raising his voice to be heard over the sound of the tank's guns. The aliens seemed to be shooting at random, raking the ground near their position. He wasn't sure if they were having targeting problems or if they were just trying to keep the humans pinned down. "Fall back to the next line."

Crawling through mud wasn't fun, but it beat being shot in the back by alien machine guns. The second set of surprises had been positioned along the route they assumed the aliens would come, yet the aliens had managed to get there before it was quite ready for action. He slipped down into the half-dug trench – any protection was welcome on a battlefield – and grasped

his rifle, looking for targets. The alien infantry were still advancing, more carefully now that their tank was no longer providing cover. Chris wondered what was going through their minds, before realising that it probably wouldn't be that different to what went through his mind when he advanced on an enemy position.

He glanced upwards and cursed as he saw a trio of alien aircraft roaring overhead. The aliens didn't deploy aircraft with the same enthusiasm as NATO had – they could drop rocks from orbit – and seeing them now was a surprise. They swept low over the ruined base, firing rockets at anything that looked remotely dangerous. Chris saw an explosion billow up from where two of the Royal Marines had been positioned and knew that they were both dead. A Stinger chased one of the alien aircraft as it headed into the distance before coming around for another run, but the aliens dropped flares and the missile, decoyed away, exploded harmlessly.

"Grenades, then run," he yelled, unhooking the last of his grenades from his belt and pulling the pin, before throwing it right into the alien position. The others followed suit, and then started to crawl away, using the explosions to cover their departure. Unless the aliens got very lucky and guessed that they were starting to retreat, they should hesitate long enough to allow the fighters to lose them. He reached for his radio and keyed it once, sending a simple message to the other two positions, and then abandoned it. The aliens would zero in on its position and drop a bomb on him.

The grenades shook the ground as they scrambled away, keeping their heads down. Outside the detention camp, they'd had a chance to scope out possible ways to retreat, including two that led through villages the aliens had ordered abandoned by their human residents. There was plenty of cover for resistance traps and they'd set up several IEDs, enough to keep the aliens carefully sweeping for more while the fighters made their escape. Several men had volunteered to make a last stand in the houses, but Chris had vetoed the idea. They needed every man they could get and futile stands would only cost them lives for nothing. The aliens could simply fall back and hammer the houses from orbit.

He heard the sound of alien aircraft overhead and instinctively sought cover. The ground shook a moment later, a colossal explosion that sent a fireball roaring into the air. God alone knew who or what the aliens had seen, but they'd certainly killed it. He kept moving, knowing that there was no longer any point in trying to fight. They'd split up into smaller groups and meet up again at the RV point.

There was a brief burst of firing, not too far away, followed by silence. Chris wondered briefly what had happened, but it hardly mattered. Assuming that the aliens believed that their men were still in danger, they would have gone to liberate the camp first and then give chase to the resistance fighters. Or perhaps they would simply drop rocks from orbit on the deserted villages, hoping to trap some of the resistance fighters in the blasts. It struck Chris as excessive, but the aliens probably regarded it as efficient. But then, they'd never know for sure how many they'd killed.

Shaking his head, he kept moving. There was a long way to go before he could relax and start heading towards the base. He'd have to be careful that he wasn't followed, either. The aliens might be holding back deliberately, hoping that he would lead them to a base. That was the last thing the resistance needed.

———

U'tra The'Stig knew that he wasn't supposed to lead relief missions in person, but many of his subordinates were either inexperienced in fighting humans or too low-ranking to be given overall command responsibilities. With the new access his promotion had granted him, it was alarmingly easy to see just how badly the humans had mauled the Land Forces – and caused them to bring in reinforcements earlier than the planners had expected. The humans might not be the most advanced race the State had ever encountered, but they were certainly the most stubborn. A sensible race would have started seeing what niche it could carve out for itself in the State by now.

The detention camp had been devastated. They'd blown through the gate, despite the blast walls that were supposed to prevent anyone from getting in without permission, and somehow secured much of the base long enough to cut through the cages and release the prisoners. Most of them would have been in no state for running, but they wouldn't have been given much of a choice. Even so, he could see a number of dead humans who clearly weren't insurgents, unless the insurgents had decided to fight while naked. The prisoners had been shot down in the crossfire, probably by their guards.

He watched as the remains of the base's garrison stumbled out of their barracks. At least they'd managed to hold out – although he had a feeling that they'd been left alive deliberately, if only to prevent higher authority from cutting their losses and dropping rocks on what remained of the base. The superior officer, an intelligence officer, came over and glared at The'Stig, before snarling orders for him to track down and kill the human insurgents. The'Stig tapped his badge, a droll reminder that he actually outranked the intelligence officer, and waited for him to calm down.

"They've destroyed all our work," the intelligence officer said, finally. "We were using humans to track down other humans and they've destroyed our work!"

"They do that," The'Stig agreed. The intelligence officers had a reputation for arrogance, but they did produce results. "I'm deploying my unit to hunt for the humans. I expect you and your unit to stay out of my way."

Ignoring the intelligence officer's splutters, he ordered his mobile command post set up in one corner of the ruined base. They were already deploying drones and attack aircraft to support the Assault Units on the ground. If the humans had managed to go to ground, they might be able to smoke them out before the operation was called off. Given the recent events in America that had forced the redeployment of several Assault Units and Security Units, it was quite possible that the humans would manage to hide. But they'd certainly do their best to rattle the humans as they fled.

———

"What the hell do we do with this guy?"

Chris looked over at their single alien prisoner. The alien didn't seem to be doing anything deliberately to slow them down, but there was no denying that his bulk made it harder for them to hide from the advancing alien patrols. Chris had climbed a tree and seen several aliens advancing in their general direction, hunting for human fighters. There was an IED nearby, hidden in their path, but the aliens had become much better at spotting and neutralising them over the past few weeks.

"Cut off his clothes and leave them here," he ordered, finally. It was possible that the aliens had hidden tracers in their clothing. Chris would have, if he'd been in their shoes. "And then we get him to the safe house and hope that they haven't tracked us."

It was the first time he'd seen one of the aliens naked and he had to admit that he was curious. Their captive's leathery grey skin seemed to shift unpleasantly over his bones, almost as if the alien had lost a great deal of weight recently. There was no sign of any sexual organs, between the alien's stumpy legs, but judging from what looked like coiled muscle under the skin the sexual organs had actually retracted into the body. Human penises did tend to shrink if the human was nervous, yet it looked as if the aliens didn't deploy their penises unless they were aroused. He found himself trying to envisage how they would mate before deciding that it hardly mattered. They could answer that question once they were safely away from the aliens chasing them.

"Come on," he ordered. "Let's go."

Fifteen minutes later, they seemed to have broken contact with the main body of the aliens, but Chris still felt uneasy. The skies seemed to be crowded with alien aircraft, some clearly hunting for the escaping insurgents, others flying down towards the base. One of them was blown out of the sky by a missile, but its comrades launched rockets towards the missile's point of origin. Chris hoped that whoever had fired the missile had abandoned the launcher and run the moment the missile had been launched, yet he suspected otherwise. The aliens had reacted with alarming speed.

The sound of alien aircraft slowly tailed away, leaving only the occasional sound of helicopters chopping their way through the skies. Chris kept glancing upwards anyway, wondering if they were being watched by a drone. No one knew for sure how good alien sensors were, but the Americans had performed miracles. The aliens might be just as good, or they might have stolen American technology – or perhaps they'd pressed Americans into service as collaborators. Many of the reports they had from across the Atlantic were confusing, or contradictory. People had welcomed the aliens, some said, while others claimed that the entire country was at war. But America had far more land surface to hide resistance fighters. Maintaining a resistance in Britain was growing harder by the day.

He looked over at the alien, stumbling his way through the undergrowth, and wondered just how he felt about being a prisoner. How many humans had the aliens taken as prisoners – and just what were they doing to military prisoners? Perhaps their captive knew the answer to those questions. They'd have to ask him, once they found a secure place to keep him – did he even know how to speak English well enough to answer complex questions?

Shaking his head, he kept walking – and silently prayed that they weren't being tracked from far overhead.

———

"Maz'Bak is missing," the intelligence officer said. "We have been unable to locate his body."

The'Stig looked down at the remains of the underground interrogation chamber. The humans had burned it, incinerating everything they hadn't taken with them. They'd left nothing, but ashes behind. It was quite possible that a body had been burned so completely that it would need a full DNA sweep to prove that it had been there, but he could see the intelligence officer's point. A missing trooper would be bad enough – the humans could do anything they wanted to him – yet an intelligence officer was far worse. He would know details that needed to be kept from human ears.

"The humans have largely made their escape," he said. It wasn't a pleasant thing to concede, but given how quickly they'd had to respond to the disaster, it was almost unavoidable. Small parties of troopers were still out in the gathering darkness, hunting for the humans, yet he'd had to pull most of his force back to the base. The drones might just pick up humans trying to move under cover of darkness. "If they had your officer with them…"

It wasn't a pleasant thought. An adult Eridian had a brighter heat signature than a human, but if the humans were careful there wouldn't be anything for the drones to detect. They'd already figured out weaknesses in some of the sensor networks surrounding Land Force Bases – did they know, perhaps, that the Assault Units had inferior night vision equipment to the devices the humans had invented? And if they had an intelligence officer to interrogate…

"I insist that you start searching for him at once," the intelligence officer said, angrily. "The loss of one of my people is a catastrophe of the highest order!"

Particularly for his career, The'Stig thought, with a certain amount of private amusement. He'd have to keep that to himself – intelligence officers made nasty enemies, even if they were outranked by Land Force officers – but it was funny. The intelligence officer would have to explain why they hadn't taken more precautions, or vetted the human collaborators more thoroughly or… they'd be blamed for the entire disaster. Losing an entire detention camp, to say nothing of the propaganda victory that had just been scored by the human insurgents. Someone would have to take the blame.

"I will detail units to continue the search," he said. It would be straightforward to push blocking forces forward, although he had the feeling that the humans would successfully evade contact. They'd had plenty of time to plan their retreat. "I suggest that you start thinking about what your officer could tell the humans. Who knows what they will do to him to make them talk?"

He'd heard rumours about how the intelligence service was conducting its interrogations, ugly rumours. The humans certainly wouldn't hesitate to retaliate in kind, once they learned the truth. And it would only stiffen their resistance. If they had enough Assault Units to tie down most of the country… but they didn't. They'd have to call in reinforcements from the rest of the world and that wasn't going to happen. Earth had already absorbed far more Assault Units and troopers than the planners had believed necessary.

The Command Triad would have to make some decisions, sooner rather than later. Perhaps if they pulled out of some parts of the world and left them to rot, they'd be able to return later, once the humans had finished killing each other off. The Middle Eastern humans had unleashed nuclear weapons on each other. Who knew what the British humans would do?

Chapter Thirty-One

Resistance Hideout, Near Coventry
United Kingdom, Day 42

"Well, you've been through the wars," the doctor observed, cheerfully. "Let's have a careful look at you, all right?"

"Let's not and say we did," Alex said. Her body still hurt, even though she'd had a good meal and a proper sleep once they'd evaded the alien pursuit and found their way to a resistance base near Coventry. "I don't want anyone to look at me ever again."

"I need to examine you if I am to prescribe treatment," the doctor said, patiently. "I'm sorry that I'm the only doctor here, but…"

"Never mind," Alex said. The original owner of the house had left a dressing gown behind when they'd abandoned their property for the illusionary safety of the countryside. She shucked it off and climbed onto the examination table, wincing as she saw the bruises covering her body. The interrogation team had seemed more interested in hurting her than actually dragging information from her unwilling lips. "Get on with it."

"Lie flat," the doctor said. He started by examining the bruises covering her chest, including a nasty one right across her left breast. "They hit you with a cane, I presume?"

Alex nodded. "Canes can break the skin, which is why some people use them for S&M frolics," the doctor observed. "There's an extra layer of danger as the cuts can become infected and cause greater hardship down the road." He studied the cuts in view and relaxed a little. "There's no sign of any infection, but I'm going to give you some cream to rub on them every night before you go to bed. It should encourage faster healing."

"They lashed my feet as well," Alex said. She couldn't keep the bitterness out of her voice. "Do people do that for fun as well?"

The doctor snorted. "There are people who choke themselves nearly to death for the thrill it gives them," he said. He studied her feet carefully. "Luckily, your feet weren't too badly damaged – I expect they wanted you to be able to walk under your own power. A couple of the wounded we plucked from the alien base were hamstrung – the bastards cut the nerves in their ankles, making it impossible for them to walk properly. It's hard to tell if they were being paranoid or sadistic. Roll over for a moment."

Alex obeyed, tensing as she felt his fingers working their way over her back and buttocks. "I can't see any infection," the doctor said, after a moment. "I think you've been very lucky. The disgraceful conditions in that camp would have meant that you would have picked up something, sooner or later. A number of the prisoners from the main detention cages have been suffering vitamin deficiencies, of all things. We don't have the resources to treat all of them here, so we've had to spread them out a bit and hope that the aliens or their collaborators don't realise what we've done."

His hands grasped her buttocks, pulling them apart for a moment. "There's far too much scarring down here," he said, grimly. "How many times did they rape you?"

"I can't remember," Alex admitted. It was shameful, but no amount of thinking could unlock the puzzle. She should have remembered. "Why don't I remember?"

"They gave you a mild drug in your food," the doctor said. "I took a blood sample last night and found traces of a particularly obnoxious date rape drug. My guess is that they were working to break down your resistance by disorientating you – it probably would have worked, given enough time." He winced. "Turn over and let me have a look at you from the other side."

Alex had always been embarrassed when her sexual organs had been examined, even by a female doctor, but she submitted without complaint. "I assume that you weren't a virgin when you fell into their hands?" The doctor asked. Alex flushed, but nodded. Her first time had been nothing to write home about, although it had gotten better over the weeks that had followed. "There's quite a bit of scarring down here – I don't see any signs of any STDs, but I don't have the equipment to do proper tests. I'm going to give you a course of antibiotics and I expect you to take them for at least a month."

He shrugged. "Normally, we would have sent you for counselling as well, but we don't have any of the trained specialists here," he added. "I spent half my time as a civilian GP referring people for counselling who didn't need it and now there are more trauma cases on my hands than I ever saw in my worst nightmares."

"It's tough all over," Alex said, as she sat upright. It still hurt to move, but it was getting better – or maybe she was just getting used to the pain. Her hands shook as she reached for the dressing gown and she found herself having problems picking it up. The doctor gave her a sympathetic look and helped her stand upright. "I… why don't I feel balanced?"

"Delayed shock," the doctor said. "I've seen it quite a bit in military and police personnel. You keep plugging onwards while the crisis is going on and then you start coming to pieces. My advice, my very strong advice, would be to rest for the next few weeks. You don't need to spend any time on the front lines…"

"The entire world is on the front lines," Alex pointed out, dryly. "What happens if the aliens come crashing in here and demand our immediate surrender?"

"Try and relax," the doctor said, with a faint smile. He hesitated, briefly. "One other thing. I'd strongly recommend that you refrain from sexual intercourse for the next month or two, at least while you're taking the antibiotics. You really need to let your body heal before you do anything else."

"I don't think that that's going to be a problem," Alex said. She caught sight of herself in the mirror and scowled. Her blonde hair had been hacked off by a maniac, her face was bruised and covered in tiny cuts and what little of her legs could be seen had been marked by the cane. "No one's going to be interested in me for a few weeks anyway."

The doctor shrugged. "I'd suggest refraining anyway," he said. "I should warn you – some people putting out propaganda on the internet want to use your story to embarrass the collaborators. They will certainly want to talk to you about it, maybe have you filmed talking about it or take pictures of your wounds. If that bothers you, tell them to go to hell. They captured enough footage from the interrogation chamber to thoroughly embarrass the collaborators without needing your input."

Alex looked up at him. "Footage?"

"The bastards recorded all of their interrogations," the doctor said. He looked sick, even at the mere thought of it. "I saw a handful of them when they wanted a medical opinion. My considered opinion is that they were torturers first and interrogators second. At least one of them was supposed to be locked up in jail for the rest of his life. One of their sessions was the slow murder of a young girl with no real connection to the resistance. God alone knows what they did with the body."

Alex remembered some of the reports from London. "The aliens had their prisoners dig pits and they simply dumped the bodies there," she said. "Maybe there's another pit near the detention camp. The girls in the cage told me that quite a few of them had died while they were in alien custody."

The doctor shrugged. "I'd suggest telling that to the review team," he said. "They may want to go back and look."

He looked her up and down, and then nodded. "I'll have the antibiotics and cream sent up to you," he added. "We don't keep them all here, for obvious reasons. And then I strongly suggest that you get plenty of rest."

Outside, she met a young man who was wearing civilian clothes, but carried himself with a military bearing. "I'm Gus," he said, with a faint smile. "I was wondering if you would be willing to discuss your time with the enemy with me?"

Alex blinked in surprise, even with the doctor's warning. Part of her wanted to forget the entire experience, but the rest of her knew that telling the entire world could serve as a warning to other resistance fighters not to get caught. Or perhaps they'd be too scared to resist the aliens when the time came. But that would be their choice – and besides, perhaps talking about it would help her get over it. The headshrinker who'd visited the squadron after they'd lost a pilot to equipment failure had certainly believed that that was the case.

"If you wish," she said, finally. "I'm afraid I intend to ask as many questions as you."

Gus led the way into a large room that had once been a living room, with a sofa, a plasma television and a computer placed against the wall. "We have been going through the recordings taken by the collaborators," he said. He nodded towards the television, which was showing a frozen scene from one of the recordings. Someone – Alex was relieved to see that it wasn't her – was being whipped. Blood was dripping off his back and down to the ground. "Some of it is for propaganda, but the rest of it is for building a case against them. We have them as prisoners, you see."

"Shoot them," Alex said, sharply. She remembered the girl who had tried to help her, after her first session with the torturers. And the others, only half-remembered in the haze her memory had become, who'd been there. "Is there any fucking doubt that they deserve to die?"

"None at all," Gus said, seriously. "But we intend to put together a series of videos for the internet that will prove them guilty, before we execute them. There's been quite a bit of debate over the issue, I'm afraid."

Alex snorted. "They chose to serve the aliens," she said. "What excuse is there for their actions? They weren't pushed into collaboration and they didn't have any noble motives – they wanted to indulge their fantasies. And they did."

She shuddered as she remembered the feelings of helplessness that had almost broken her, the awareness that she had lost all control over her body. Alone in the dark, she had come far too close to breaking, to begging them to listen to her as she spilled everything she knew. Who knew what might have happened if they'd been allowed to keep working on her for longer?

"We have to prove that," Gus said, quietly. "And we need your help to do it."

The next hour passed slowly. Alex watched one of the videos the torturers had recorded, fighting down the urge to be sick. She hadn't even been the worst-treated person in the underground complex. Two men had been sawn apart by their tormentors, while a girl had been practically raped to death. She told herself that she was right, that the torturers had been more interested in hurting people than learning anything the aliens could use, but it was no mercy. How could anyone indulge themselves by torturing helpless victims?

Alex had known how Third World countries treated their prisoners. She'd always known that being shot down and landing in enemy territory was a possibility. Saddam's regime had had entire corps of torturers, many of whom were nastier than the people the aliens had found and put to work. Iran and Saudi Arabia tortured dissidents and democrats with equal abandon, but they were both barbaric states. The thought of anyone in Britain willingly torturing someone was horrifying. And it was so pointless!

She recorded a brief interview with Gus, where she explained what had happened to her and how she'd been rescued from the firing squad. Gus proved to be a surprisingly good interviewer, although as an army intelligence officer he'd probably been trained to talk someone into revealing more than they intended. He replayed it for her and she was struck by the sense of hopelessness she saw in her eyes. The video would be put out on the internet and the entire world would see her. She'd never wanted to be a film star, but it was worth it if it turned hearts and minds against the aliens.

"So," she said, finally. "What happens to me now?"

"You recover," Gus said. He paused, just for a moment. "Did you hear about the Area Commanders the aliens have been creating?"

Alex shook her head. After she'd been arrested and sent to the detention camp, she hadn't heard anything new from the outside world. The last she'd heard was that the aliens were handing out seeds and expecting the farmers to plant them and raise crops before the onset of winter. Maybe they could, but Smith hadn't been too confident of it.

The thought reminded her of her friends. "What happened to the others from the camp?"

"The ones we got out are scattered over the country," Gus said. "Most of them will go into action units once they've recovered from their ordeal. I'm afraid we don't keep records here…"

"For fear the aliens will capture them," Alex said. Al Qaida had been notoriously good at keeping records, too good. Documents uncovered by raids on their hideouts had often led to more hideouts. "Who are the Area Commanders?"

"Senior collaborators," Gus said. He picked up a folder and placed it in front of her. "From what one of our sources says, they're going to be responsible for integrating Britain's economy with the alien empire. We believe that the aliens are doing something similar in America and France, but we don't have any confirmation. I was wondering if you recognised any of them."

Alex opened the folder and skimmed through the photographs. None were familiar, apart from one she vaguely remembered as having been an MP during the Expenses Scandal. A note beside the photograph claimed that he'd volunteered for alien service, rather than being press-ganged into unwilling collaboration by the aliens. She put the photo to one side and glanced down at the next – and swore.

"That's Rupert Leigh," she said, in shock. He'd been one of the few who'd known who she was, and what she had been before the invasion. And he'd known about the resistance movement she'd led even though he hadn't been an active member. "He…"

It clicked in her mind. "He betrayed me!"

"Almost certainly," Gus agreed. "From what we have been given to understand, Leigh was offered a chance to rule the entire county – in exchange for his service to the aliens. He probably was the one who betrayed you, along with several others. He's marked down for death if we ever get a clear shot at him."

"I want to go after him," Alex said, sharply. "You cannot deny that I have the right to kill him…"

"Maybe, but that doesn't mean that you should," Gus said. He held up a hand before she could say anything. "The doctor said that you should rest – so rest. There will be time to kill the traitor afterwards."

———

The underground chamber was cold, illuminated only by a single overhead light. Chris strode into the chamber and stopped in front of the five chairs positioned in the centre of the room. The men sitting on the chairs had been cuffed to render them immobile and hooded to make sure that they saw nothing, just in case they managed to escape and run back to the aliens. Besides, being blind was disorientating and demoralising. Chris hadn't enjoyed it during his training and he doubted that any of the collaborators would have enjoyed it either.

He reached for the first hood and pulled it off, revealing one of the alien torturers. The man stared up at him desperately, but the ball someone had stuffed in his mouth prevented him from speaking. Chris removed each of the hoods in turn, revealing the remaining torturers and collaborators. They had all featured in the videos they'd recovered from the alien detention camp. There was no doubt whatsoever about their guilt. Chris had watched the videos himself, just to prepare himself for the task ahead.

Quickly, he pulled his own facemask on and looked up at the cameras. "Start filming," he ordered. The set of cameras within the chamber came to life, recording the five faces – and Chris, standing behind them. They wouldn't see his face behind the mask. "Each of you has been found guilty of collaborating with the alien occupiers and of torturing your fellow humans for your masters. The evidence has been placed on the internet, there for all to see. For your crimes, there can only be one penalty. The sentence is death."

He lifted his Browning and put it to the head of the first torturer. The stench of shit arose as the man fouled himself, suddenly realising that the game was truly up. Chris felt nothing as he pulled the trigger, putting a bullet through the man's brains. The torturer had deserved far worse than a quick death. He moved to the second torturer, remembering the videos he'd seen that were now firmly burned into his mind. The man had gloried in watching helpless people screaming in pain. He pulled the trigger a second time and watched as the man died, bound and as helpless as his victims.

The remaining three were less guilty, but they'd definitely been involved. Chris shot all three of them and then stepped back to allow the cameras to film their dead bodies. The video would be uploaded to the internet tonight and then the entire world would see what had been done for the aliens – and what had happened to those who had done it. Maybe the next set of collaborators would be less willing to torture their captives…

Shaking his head, he walked away from the chamber, leaving the bodies behind. They'd be buried when night came, left to rot in an unmarked grave. And that, he hoped, would be the end of it. He didn't want to have to do it again.

Chapter Thirty-Two

North England
United Kingdom, Day 44

The alien had been placed in a large holding cell, with foodstuffs that had been liberated from one of the alien bases by a collaborator who had ties to the resistance. It – no, Gavin reminded himself, *he* – had been well-treated, with the intelligence crew's best guess at the kind of environment the aliens would find comfortable. Given the temperature of their buildings, they seemed to prefer a sauna rather than the open air. The alien certainly didn't look uncomfortable, although there was no way to know for sure. He didn't seem to speak English properly without his voder, but there was no way they could risk bringing it to their hiding place. The aliens might have been able to track it down.

"I doubt that we will ever be able to talk their language properly," Linux reported. They were standing together in front of the monitor, watching the alien and two of the intelligence team experimenting with a prototype translator. "Their mouths and ours are just too different. We'd have better luck trying to speak fluent pig."

"I've known a few intelligence operatives who claimed that they spoke fluent donkey," Gavin said, wryly. "Can we ask him questions?"

"Once the techs have finished, I think so," Linux said. "We copied their translation programs onto a pair of laptops and started working away at it. I think there will probably be quite a few glitches, but on the whole we have something that should work fairly well."

Gavin nodded, looking down at the reports from the pair of doctors who had examined the living alien. Most of what they said tied in with the reports from the handful of aliens who had been dissected around the world, but there were some interesting additions. The alien seemed to have undergone some form of surgery at some time, yet it seemed cruder than anything humanity had devised for itself. Their best guess was that the aliens actually seemed to be able to take more punishment than humanity, but any serious injuries healed slower than comparable damage to a human. It didn't make much sense to Gavin, yet the doctors seemed convinced that it fitted in with what they'd observed about alien behaviour.

Added to the files they'd pulled from the alien computer network, they'd also been able to identify different ranks, at least for alien soldiers. Their military appeared to be strictly top-down, without any of the special arrangements human forces made for their Special Forces, although their intelligence service – which appeared to be completely separate from the military – had no formal rank structure. Gavin suspected that they were missing something, if only because that little datum didn't seem to fit in with the rest of the alien structure. But their intelligence service might not keep its files on the general system, if only because they would fear hackers from Earth.

The two technicians finished working with the alien and left the chamber, leaving the alien alone in the heat. He seemed to prefer bright light, even at night; the technicians had shown him knobs that he could twist to adjust the light and heat to whatever he considered natural. Some of the researchers had wondered if the alien homeworld was permanently illuminated – they'd come up with all kinds of models to demonstrate how a habitable world could float at the gravitational point between two stars – but Gavin suspected that the alien simply didn't want to be in darkness. He was alone, miles from any of his own kind – and light years from home. If humans could get uneasy being only a short distance from their own kind, how would an alien feel when the distance to his homeworld was something unimaginable?

He stepped into the chamber, one hand half-covering his eyes against the glare. He'd had to leave his Browning outside the chamber, leaving him feeling oddly naked. The alien's heaving mass was stronger than him, although he could move quicker if he had to dodge the alien's grasp. One of the laptops had been left on the bench, proofed against damage caused by the humidity. He picked it up and sat down facing the alien. Dark eyes looked back at him. The alien seemed to be taking his captivity well, all things considered. Humans would probably have been bouncing off the wall by now, demanding release.

There was a note on the screen waiting for him. *The alien's name is Maz'Bak.* Gavin read it quickly and then looked up at the alien, Maz'Bak. No one really understood how the alien names went together – if there was a forename and a surname, or if there was some other way they constructed their names – but it was an issue that would hopefully be addressed once the war came to an end. Who knew? Perhaps they could force the aliens to accept something less than total conquest of Earth. And the key to unlocking many mysteries was right in front of him, breathing heavily. Up close, there was a faintly musty smell around the alien. It wasn't entirely pleasant to the nose.

He tapped the laptop, bringing up the translation program. "My name is Gavin," he said. The translation program produced a number of grunts, followed by his name. It was clearly smart enough to recognise that there was no direct translation of Gavin. "I am here to ask you some questions."

The alien made an odd motion with one hand. It seemed almost a shrug.

"Start with the easy question," Gavin said, dryly. "Why are you here?"

There was a pause, and then the alien grunted back. "I was captured by some of your men and transported away from my people," the laptop said. Gavin had to smile. "They brought me here and put me into the care of your doctors."

"That isn't what I meant," Gavin admitted. There was something almost simplistic about the alien's reply. He had to remind himself sharply that the translation program would be simplifying things as much as possible, perhaps editing out some or all of the meaning in the process. A *Star Trek*-style universal translator would have been very useful. "Why have your people invaded Earth?"

The alien grunted, several times. Gavin listened carefully, but as far as he could tell it was just grunts. The subtle points were impossible for humans to hear. "This world is in an important location for us," the laptop said. "We chose to claim it to forestall others from claiming it."

"Interesting," Gavin observed. "So you have enemies? Races on the same level as yourselves?"

The alien said nothing.

Gavin looked up at the dark eyes. "We have videos of what your human allies were doing to your prisoners," he said. "We could attempt to force the information from you."

"And then the State will extract its revenge," the alien said, through the laptop. Gavin had to admit that the alien had a point. The aliens were in a position to extract revenge, simply by bombing human population centres. "Your world is ours because we were strong enough to take it from you. We do not understand why you did not climb into space and secure yourself from races like us. And yet there is much about you that can be added to the State. Your race is a wealth of knowledge for our superiors."

Gavin glanced at the laptop, suspiciously. He'd tried primitive translation programs before in Afghanistan and they'd never really impressed him. If the alien was speaking truthfully – and the translator was working perfectly – the aliens had taken Earth because they could, rather than any desperate need for real estate… unless their mysterious enemies had wanted to take Earth and the Leathernecks had wanted to get there first. It struck him as oddly primitive, but it tied in with other statements the aliens had made since the invasion had begun. They didn't bother coming up with elaborate justifications for their actions. They just did what they thought needed to be done.

"You've been rounding up military personnel and computer specialists," he said. "What happens to them?"

The alien seemed to rock forward, slightly. "We intend to use your knowledge to enrich ourselves," he said, finally. "Your computer specialists will assist us in creating the next generation of warship computers, giving us an edge over the…"

Gavin frowned. The laptop had declined to translate the final grunt. If that was the name of their enemy… it did make a certain kind of sense. They had an enemy out among the stars, maybe more than one. And human computers were generally better than alien designs… of course they would want to add human technology to their warships. It would be an unpleasant surprise for their enemies when they restarted the war.

In fact, he could think of several other things the aliens might want. Ever since HG Wells had written a story about invaders from Mars, humans had been writing vast science-fiction epics that explored all kinds of fictional technology. But the aliens didn't find it fictional – they already had some kind of FTL drive, even if their computers weren't up to human standards. What if they started to implement ideas humans had devised into their warships, or their tactics, or…? There were thousands of possibilities. Maybe tactics from *Star Wars* could be used, or *Babylon 5*, or even *Doctor Who*.

"So you're taking the specialists away from Earth," he said, slowly. There were thousands of reports of people just taken away by the collaborators, leaving friends and families behind. They would never know what had happened to their missing relatives, not unless the aliens deigned to tell them – and it seemed unlikely that they would even understand the human need for closure. "What are you doing with the military personnel?"

The alien said nothing.

"Oh, don't give me that," Gavin snapped, angrily. "We know that you have captured thousands of British and American military personnel – and we assume you've done the same everywhere you've landed. What are you doing with them?"

He stared up at the alien's dark eyes. "We need to know," he said, quietly. "Where are our soldiers?"

"They have been taken off-world," the alien said, finally. His bulk seemed to quiver, just for a second. "They will serve the State on the disputed worlds. As subjects of the State, it is their duty to serve as the State decrees. They will fight for the State or die."

Gavin blinked in surprise. "You're expecting them to fight for you?"

"Of course," the alien said. "Their world is in our claws. We own your planet now and your people exist to serve the State. Your military personnel will be expected to take the disputed world or lose the right to return to their homeworld."

"I see," Gavin said. "And most of them will die in service to the State?"

"To die in the service of the State is a great thing," the alien said. Gavin stared down at the translator, convinced that there had to be an error. How could the aliens have developed such a society – and at the same time, developed FTL drives that had allowed them to spread out into interstellar space? For all he knew, someone had *given* the aliens FTL technology – or someone had landed on their homeworld and they'd captured their starship.

But then, what would have happened if Hitler had won World War Two? There would have been a fascist state, with children indoctrinated into believing Hitler's warped racial theories from birth – theories that would have been 'proven' by the Nazi victory. How long would it be before someone decided to question the fascist state's nature? And if they'd all been brought up to believe that genocide was acceptable in the name of the state, who among them would even question?

A few years ago, he'd read a book about the American South – and how slavery had been an integral part of society. They'd *known* that blacks were inferior to whites, which had played a large part in keeping society ordered, rather than have the poorer whites realise just how badly they were being screwed by their social superiors. And generations of children had been raised to believe that blacks were inferior… it had taken generations and a civil war to start the long task of changing their minds, and the scars were still present when the Leathernecks had invaded Earth. How long would it be before some Leatherneck version of William Wilberforce raised his voice to challenge the ruling party?

"One final question," he said, finally. "How can we get you off our world?"

The alien seemed almost amused by the question. "You can't," he said. "Earth belongs to the State."

———

"We have been bouncing questions off him for some hours," the intelligence officer reported. She was a slight woman, barely strong enough to get through the army's basic training before being streamlined into intelligence. "I'm afraid that most of what he told you, General, seems to fit in with what else we know about them. They came, they saw and they conquered Earth."

She tapped her laptop and the display changed. "We now know more about how they're organised," she continued. "At the time, there's a Command Triad; three officers, one from the Land Forces, one from the Space Forces and one from their intelligence service. Below them, there are Land Force Commanders who serve as the principle officers on the ground – we have one assigned to Britain, there are several assigned to the United States and at least three assigned to Europe. Below *them* – she tapped the laptop again – "there are a number of units assigned to the various Land Force Commanders. Apparently, we've been bleeding them pretty hard and they've had to shift units around fairly regularly on fireman drills."

Gavin smiled, despite his tiredness. Earth might be tiny by interstellar standards, but she was still a pretty big planet and most of the regional theatres were separated by large bodies of water. The aliens might have upwards of two million soldiers in their conquest force, yet it was nowhere enough to hold down the entire planet. But they didn't really *need* to hold down the entire world. The fighting in the Middle East, the chaos sweeping through Africa, the mass slaughters in the Balkans and Central Asia – the humans were still fighting each other, even when there was a more dangerous threat in orbit. It might not have been that important – the aliens were perfectly capable of bombarding parts of the planet they didn't need into submission – but it would have been nice to think that humanity could unite against a common foe.

Linux looked up from where he'd been sitting. "We're fairly sure that we could take their command network down for some time," he said. Gavin nodded, remembering when it had been first proposed. "But it would only work once. After that, they would start isolating their systems and making it impossible to take them down again."

Gavin snorted. "I still don't understand why they even offered us the chance to do it once."

Linux smirked. "How many people really know what happens inside a computer?" He asked, clearly remembering his pre-military days. "Every time a person's identity is stolen by a hacker, it happens because someone was careless or ignorant and left the front door to their computer wide open. People use the same passwords for different computers, even though they should know better. Do you know how I broke into the Pentagon's computers?"

His smile grew wider. "One of their officers used the same password for accessing their computers as he did for buying stuff on Amazon," he explained. "I cracked one password and then I had access to all of his Pentagon files. And that was someone who really should have known better. I'd be surprised if the alien troopers know anything about what happens inside a computer. They certainly don't seem to be interested in telling them anything more than they need to know."

"Maybe we should hold off for a few years and let them absorb our computer systems," Gavin mused. "And then we could take down their entire system at one fell swoop."

"Unless they're complete idiots, they will take precautions," Linux pointed out. "I would – if I had human specialists working for me."

Gavin shrugged. "And so we go back to the old problem," he said. "The aliens are in a position to bombard us into submission. Even if we take out their forces on the ground, we would still be knocked back down and forced to surrender."

"Maybe we could find a way to contact their enemies," Linux said. "The enemy of my enemy is my friend."

Gavin had been giving that some thought. "I don't see how," he admitted, finally. "Unless we can build an FTL communicator…"

"They don't have one," Linux said.

The door burst open as one of the operators ran into the room. "Sir," he said, "there's an important broadcast on the BBC. You have to see it!"

Gavin followed him back upstairs, leaving a pair of soldiers behind to keep an eye on the alien. The broadcast was already repeating when he reached the dining room, where two of the staff had been monitoring the

BBC. He was mildly surprised that the aliens hadn't bothered to put out their own version of the attack on the detention camp, but their propaganda efforts seemed feeble, almost uninspired. Their collaborators weren't quite working as hard as they should.

Alan Beresford's face appeared on the screen as the message started again. "I have been informed that the bitter-enders have taken one of our alien friends captive," he said. The collaborator-in-chief sounded as if he sincerely believed every word he said, although that was a necessary skill for a politician. "They have informed me that they no longer intend to allow the bitter-enders to frustrate Earth's admission to the galactic state. Therefore, if this captive is not released, a large number of humans will die."

He leaned forward. "I understand that change always worries those who do not want to see any change in how the world is run, but I appeal to those who are still fighting the aliens," he added. "They are not bluffing. Unless the captive is released within two days, they will take punitive measures against a city on the British mainland. Please, for the love of God, release the captive before millions die."

Chapter Thirty-Three

London
United Kingdom, Day 45

The entire city had gone crazy.

"Damn it," Robin yelled, as he ducked to avoid a hail of rubbish being thrown at them from the flats. "Where the hell is our backup?"

"Caught up in their own riot," Sergeant Wiggin shouted back. They'd entered the East London housing estate looking for a suspected resistance organiser. And then the entire estate seemed to have exploded around them. The alien threats against a human city had triggered off a whole series of riots. "They're stuck for the moment!"

Robin gritted his teeth. The housing estates had been slowly decaying into criminality for years, despite programs designed to give the inhabitants pride in their community. They were notoriously unfriendly to the police, even before the invasion. Their police car had been tipped on its side and they'd had to flee into an alley in the hopes of escaping the crowd. It was apparently worse along the outside of London, with humans desperate to escape the city clashing with police and alien guards equally intent on keeping people in. The internet had named a hundred different cities that might be targeted and they'd all gone crazy.

Outside, there were over five hundred youths, probably all members of the same gang. The gangs had been defending their territory ever since the invasion, even though they were drawing food and drink from the aliens. If they were waiting before giving chase to the policemen, it suggested that they were expecting others to arrive and fall into the same trap. Or maybe they were just biding their time. Robin wished, once again, that the aliens had allowed them to carry firearms. The crowd outside was better armed than the police.

He looked around and saw a drainpipe leading up to a window. Quickly, before he could think better of it, he ran over to the pipe and scrambled up it. It was a harder climb that he'd expected, but the crowd outside the alley was a powerful motivator. He managed to push the window open and fall face-first into the flat, gasping for breath as the stench of death reached his nostrils. Someone had been using the flat to smoke drugs, but had overdosed – or perhaps it had been a murder. Judging from the condition of the body, it had been at least a fortnight since death had taken place. He leaned back out of the window and waved frantically to Wiggin. Wiggin was older and fatter than Robin, but with a little help he made it into the flat.

"Jesus," he muttered, as he tried to avoid breathing. "What the fuck happened here?"

"No idea," Robin said, shortly. He glanced around the flat as they came out of the bedroom and up to a bolted door. Someone had attached no less than five bolts to the door, making it much harder for anyone to enter without breaking down the door. Drug dealers tended to be paranoid, not without reason. Their list of enemies didn't stop at the police. "I bet you that the back door outside is blocked off too."

"That's a fire hazard," Wiggin said. They shared a droll look as they opened the door. It didn't smell much better outside. An overpowering stench of urine almost sent them staggering backwards. Robin had never been able to understand how anyone could willingly live in such a dump, although he had to admit that most of them never stood a chance. The gangs were simply too powerful for ordinary people to overcome. Who would bother cleaning the stairwell if they knew it would simply be vandalised again within the week?

Robin glanced outside through a broken window and saw that the mob was getting stronger. There was little hope of anyone coming to help on the ground, unless they were armed and willing to cut down enough of the gang members to convince the others to flee. It wouldn't be long before they decided to go after the two trapped policemen – and it wouldn't take their leaders long to guess where Robin and Wiggin had fled. He glanced down

at the crowd again before heading up the stairs. There should be a way to get onto the roof from the stairwell.

The stench seemed to grow stronger as they raced up the stairs. Robin had made arrests in places like the estate before and knew that the closed doors hid all sorts of crimes – and people living their lives of quiet desperation. A drug dealer, a prostitute and her pimp, terrorists, racists... all hidden behind closed doors. The BBC might prattle on about the benefits that alien rule would bring to the country, but he doubted that any benefit could help those trapped on poor estates. Very few people born and bred on such an estate ever managed to climb out and build a proper life for themselves. The pressure just to sink into criminality was overpowering. There were some girls who were grandmothers at thirty, assuming they lived so long.

At the top of the stairs, he glanced up and saw the hatch leading to the roof – and a small set of metal climbing handles. Quickly, he climbed up and pushed at the hatch, before making the mistake of looking down. Dizziness almost overcame him, but he closed his eyes and pushed at the hatch again. It opened and fell to one side with a loud bang, almost as loud as a gunshot. He scrambled out onto the roof and peered out over London. A dozen fires were burning brightly in the distance, towards the centre of the city. He could hear the sound of alien weapons being fired, suggesting that the rioters were trying to take out the alien patrols. Maybe they'd even succeed...

"Call for a helicopter," he ordered, as Wiggin scrambled up beside him. Peering over the side of the building brought on another fit of vertigo, but he managed to overcome it long enough to realise that the crowd had realised that its hostages were missing. They were thronging around the block, looking for trouble. "Tell them we need an emergency pick-up right now."

He closed the hatch and dragged a number of fallen bricks over to make it difficult for anyone to reopen it from inside the building. The rioters had probably used the rooftop as a place to defend their territory in the past, throwing bricks down towards their enemies. Wiggin joined him and between them they stacked up nearly fifty bricks. It would be almost impossible for someone to open the hatch, Robin told himself, and hoped that he was right. After their escape, the crowd wouldn't be feeling merciful to the policemen if they caught up with them.

The sound of helicopter blades grew louder and he allowed himself a moment of relief as a police helicopter came into view. A rope ladder was already falling down towards them as it slowed and came to a hover directly over the estate. The sound of the crowd grew louder as Wiggin took hold of the ladder and started to scramble up into the helicopter. Robin heard a series of bangs and thuds from under the hatch that suggested that someone was trying to push the hatch open and come climbing out onto the roof. He took tight hold of the rope ladder and climbed up himself, following Wiggin. The helicopter seemed to bank in the sky the moment he reached the top and was helped into the cabin, tilting away from the estate and heading back towards Central London. From overhead, entire streets seemed to be jammed with rioters, or protesters. He could see riot teams unleashing CS gas on some mobs, while leaving others to shout themselves hoarse. It looked as if London was dissolving into chaos.

"They want every available officer out manning the barricades," the pilot called, as they flew lower. "The Leathernecks are moving up forces from outside the city. If we don't put the rioters back in their box, they're going to start mowing them down!"

Robin wasn't alone in believing that more vigorous policing and less politically correct bullshit would do more for the city than any amount of urban improvement schemes, but there were limits. And the aliens wouldn't hesitate to gun down thousands of humans to convince the remainder to do as they were told. He sat back and covered his eyes as the helicopter slowly came in to land at the makeshift New Scotland Yard. They'd be expected to go back out on the streets at once and he didn't know if he had the energy. All he wanted to do was crawl into a bottle and die.

"Well, mighty master of all you survey," Catherine said, dryly. "I think that some people are a mite upset."

Alan Beresford ignored her. The new seat of government for the collaborators was a small fortress, protected by the aliens. It said something about how effective they were at dealing with urban mobs that no one had risked attacking them, even though the deadline for the return of the alien captive was counting down towards zero. But the remainder of London didn't have that immunity to the chaos gripping the city. The entire city seemed to be out of the streets, trying to get out or to take down an alien or two before it was too late.

"You might have done better not to tell the world about the threat," she added. Just think about how long it is going to take to clear up the mess..."

"Shut up," Alan snapped. He didn't want to let her get under his skin, but there were limits to what he was prepared to endure. Catherine was preparing herself to challenge him and perhaps become the next Prime Minister – and tool of the aliens. "You know as well as I did that there was no choice."

The aliens had made their feelings quite clear. They wanted their kidnapped officer back – and they were prepared to threaten mass murder to be sure that they got their way. Alan knew them well enough by now to know that they weren't bluffing. In fact, he wasn't sure that they had the ability *to* bluff. They seemed to prefer the simplest and most direct way of doing things possible – and if that meant a great many humans got hurt, they didn't seem to care. Alan might have admired their ruthlessness if he hadn't been all too aware that they would turn on him if he stopped being useful. And his usefulness might just have run out.

Alan had managed to get most of the city's workers back to work, particularly ones who could help the aliens administer their new territory. The registration process had identified a vast number of people who could join the alien government and work overseas, perhaps in France or America. Alan had calculated that the aliens wouldn't want to bring in locals if he could produce servants, even if they would be at risk from the local resistance fighters. But now most of his civil servants seemed to have gone on strike, or were being hunted down by mobs in London. The rest of the country wasn't much better. Every city or large town that didn't have an alien ring of steel keeping the population trapped was emptying out into the countryside, spreading panic and disorder over the entire country. It wasn't as if they could all be fed outside the cities.

He glanced down at his watch. Two days, the aliens had said; two days for their kidnapped officer to be returned or else. And one of those days was nearly over. If he'd had a link to the resistance, he would have begged them to return their captive, if only because his usefulness would expire if the aliens decided that he'd lost control of his people. But there was nothing he could do, apart from waiting and hoping. It had been a long time since he'd prayed.

Catherine walked up behind him, looking out over the darkening city. "Do you remember when we thought that we were in control?"

"We will get back into control," Alan said, flatly. He was not going to let her rattle him. They were on the verge of losing everything – if the aliens bombed a city, it would be the end of his provisional government – and the damned woman was making a power play! "The resistance will release their prisoner."

"But how do you know?" Catherine said. "They might just believe that chaos is better for their goals than a country under your foot."

Alan prided himself on his self-control, but the woman was driving him insane. "And what happens if the aliens decide to administer the country themselves?" She asked. "What use will they have for us then?"

A hot flash of anger boiled through Alan's mind. He slapped her, right across the face. She staggered backwards, one hand raised to the ugly red mark where he'd struck her. Alan stepped forward and slapped her again, knocking her to the floor. He bent over her and put his hand on her throat, ignoring her feeble attempts to push him back. A sense of dark power roared through him as he stared down at her. He could do anything to her; rape

her, choke the life out of her... and who could stop him? The old order had died the day the aliens had landed in Britain and the rest of the world.

"You will do your fucking job or I will kill you," he hissed, finally. Part of his mind pointed out that it would be unwise to let her live, but the feeling of triumph overruled it. "Now get out and find a way of convincing the sheep down there to go back to work nice and peacefully."

He took his hand off her throat and stepped back, half-expecting her to lunge at him. Instead, she pulled herself to her feet and walked towards the door. Alan watched her go and then turned back to the window, shaking his head. He'd mounted a tiger when he'd made his bargain with the Leathernecks. They didn't care how he ruled the country, provided that he ruled it for their benefit. But the moment he stopped being useful, they'd kill him.

Outside, the fires were growing brighter. Alan watched, feeling cold despair replacing the exultation he'd felt when he'd humbled the bitch. If he stopped being useful...

"Damn you," he muttered, knowing that no one would hear him. "Why did you have to go and spoil it?"

"They shot up a crowd as they headed to Whitehall," one of the resistance fighters said. "At least thirty wounded, fifty dead – should I have them forwarded to here?"

"Only if you get me more supplies," Fatima said, tiredly. She'd been working like a demon, almost non-stop since the riots started to tear London apart. Hundreds of wounded had been brought in, passed across her table and then sent somewhere to recuperate. Many of them wouldn't survive, no matter what she did. They needed a proper hospital and one wasn't available. "Didn't Joe get some from the nearest hospital?"

"Only a few," the fighter said. "They're inundated with wounded too. We're trying to slip some of our own into their system, but if they're not registered..."

Fatima nodded, and then yawned. Tiredness caused people to make mistakes – and yet she hadn't been able to get any rest since the day had begun. She wasn't the only medical doctor in the resistance, but the others were scattered out over the city; like her, they were fighting to keep people alive who really needed proper treatment and a hospital...

She yawned again, feeling the room spinning around her. Had it only been last year when she'd taken the last two weeks of Ramadan off because she had worried about what would happen if she grew too hungry? What a joke! She'd worked herself half to death over the last few days and now she could barely keep herself together.

"Bring them in," she ordered, tiredly. Her last patient, someone who had been shot through the shoulder by one of the alien bullets, would probably never recover the use of his arm. One of the soldiers had commented that the aliens seemed to use elephant guns, something that made sense given how tough they were. Ordinary ammunition wasn't quite good enough against Leatherneck skin. "I'll have a look at them as soon as I can."

"You'd be better off getting a nap," a new voice said. She looked up to see Abdul. "You look too tired to work properly."

"I feel dead." Fatima admitted. She hadn't seen Abdul in days, ever since he'd brought her to the first of the makeshift hospitals. From what she'd heard, he'd been too busy organising attacks on collaborators and the alien patrols. "Can you have someone else take care of the patients?"

"I'll do my best," Abdul promised. He hesitated. "I think you need at least five hours of sleep, so get to bed and stay there. We'll wake you up if we have to vacate this place in a hurry."

Fatima looked up at him, nodded, and then stumbled into the next room. God alone knew what it had been originally intended for, but they'd set up a cot for her beside the window. Outside, she could see fires in the distance. London was burning – absently, she wondered if someone on the other side would realise that the resistance hadn't set any fires near its hideouts. But judging from the chaos, the collaborators had too much else to worry about before they started hunting the resistance again. They'd have to put out the fires, calm the rioters and – if the aliens carried out their threat – provide help to a destroyed city and its stricken population.

She closed her eyes and felt sleep overcome her.

Chapter Thirty-Four

North England
United Kingdom, Day 46

"There isn't any question about it," Gabriel said, flatly. "We're going to return the alien prisoner."

He held up a hand before Brigadier Gavin Lightbridge-Stewart could say anything. He'd come to the Prime Minister's hiding place despite the security risks, because it was one conference that they couldn't trust to the internet. The Leathernecks had a great many human computer experts in their hands now, people who could presumably track messages through the internet and locate their destination. Gabriel found their dependence upon messengers and carrier pigeons oddly ironic, given the circumstances. The longer the war continued, the more primitive the resistance would become.

"I know that the alien represents a treasure trove of valuable information and biological data," he continued, "but keeping him isn't worth a few million human lives. We can shove him out somewhere and one of their patrols can pick him up."

Lightbridge-Stewart frowned. "There are complications, Prime Minister," he said. "The first one is simple; if we give in to their threats, we create a precedent. If they feel that they can threaten us into submission, they will use it again and again, blackmailing us into surrendering our only hope of carrying on the fight. What would you say, a week from today, if the aliens threaten to bombard London or Edinburgh or Newcastle if you don't surrender yourself to them?"

Gabriel hesitated. "I'm aware of the risks," he said, flatly. "Doesn't the fact that they haven't threatened mass bombardments suggest that they don't intend to push it that far?"

"They may not have believed that it would work," Lightbridge-Stewart countered. "From what we have been able to draw from our alien friend, we know that humans are often more barbaric than the Leathernecks – we're certainly a lot better at justifying inhuman treatment to ourselves. If we give them proof that it will work, they may try it again. Where do we draw the line and say where we will no longer allow them to threaten us into submission?"

"But this is one point where we have to make a decision," Gabriel snapped. "We have an alien prisoner – and they want him back. Now, do you think that keeping that alien a prisoner is worth the loss of God knows how many of our own civilians?"

He pressed on before Lightbridge-Stewart could say anything. "And what happens to our reputation if we refuse?" He asked. "How many of our own people will turn against us after we lose an entire city?"

"The entire planet is at stake," Lightbridge-Stewart said. "What decision we make here and now will have an effect on the entire world. What if our captive can tell us how to contact the other intelligent races out there? What if we could get help from someone who could take out the alien starships hovering over our heads, poised to bombard us into submission if we rebel?"

"But we don't know that we could," Gabriel said. "We have the insight into their computers – maybe we can get the information some other way. I won't put so many lives at risk because we have one captive. The dangers are just too great."

He looked the military officer in the eye. "Correct me if I'm wrong," he added, "but am I not the ultimate civilian authority?"

Lightbridge-Stewart didn't hesitate. "You are, and if you want to order him released, I will carry out the order," he said. "However, there are other complications. Moving something the size of the alien cross-country will not be easy. Wherever they find him, they will certainly suspect that he was concealed somewhere nearby and start searching for his hiding place. There is a distant possibility that they might come here."

"It's a risk we have to accept," Gabriel said. He glanced at the television. The volume was down, but the BBC had helpfully displayed a ticking clock counting down the seconds to when the alien ultimatum ran out. He'd watched images of desperate rioters battling the police and the aliens, or fleeing out across the countryside like locusts. Others had boarded small boats and set sail for Ireland or the Scottish Islands, where the aliens hadn't bothered to establish a presence. They might find safety there. "We can abandon this building if necessary."

"Yes," Lightbridge-Stewart said. There was a long moment when they both contemplated possible futures. "I can see to his release, if that is your command."

"It is," Gabriel said, "Please see to it."

———

"Did I do the right thing?"

Sergeant Butcher shrugged. The three SAS men stayed close to Gabriel, while a small unit of soldiers were outside, maintaining a secure perimeter. Gabriel was rather surprised that the aliens or their collaborators hadn't bothered to investigate the old manor and register the people staying there, but Haddon Hall had been off the official radar for many years. The owners having ties with the security services had advantages for them. Gabriel would have been surprised if they even got taxed.

"I don't think that there was any right answer," Butcher said, after a moment. He looked down at the board for a long moment. All of the three SAS men played Chess and Gabriel had found it a good way to relax. "You have to make the decision and then stick to it."

He moved a piece forward and smiled, thinly. "I used to serve in Africa on missions that officially didn't exist," he added. "The locals really didn't trust their own governments – not without reason. If there was a foreign interest willing to spend big bucks on bribes, the governments would roll over and use troops to clear away the locals if they got in the way. I don't think you could afford developing a reputation as someone willing to throw British lives away for one alien."

Gabriel frowned, considering the board. "And what happened to most of those unlucky people?"

"The radicals would arrive and start convincing the people that the only hope was to fight," Butcher said. "And most of them wound up being slaughtered while the government disguised effective genocide by claiming that it was waging war against radical Islam. There are some truly shitty places out there, boss. Even worse now that the aliens have smashed anyone who might have been able to impose order by force."

He shook his head as Gabriel moved another piece forward. "Checkmate," he said, moving his queen into position. "You're getting better, sir."

"Thank you," Gabriel said, dryly. "You're masters at unarmed combat, sneaking about… and Chess?"

"There was a trooper up at Hereford who was a five-star chef," Butcher said. Gabriel couldn't tell if he was being serious or joking. "And there was a little old woman who knew absolutely everything about plants and kept massive greenhouses. Every six months, a dozen lads from Hereford would gather around this tiny old lady and learn what they could safely eat in the wild. She never had any problems with vandals either. I wonder why."

Gabriel opened his mouth, and then looked up as the butler entered the room. "Pardon me, sir," he said, "but the Brigadier has returned from his trip. He is waiting for you in the library."

"Good," Gabriel said, standing up. Butcher moved ahead of him, watching for assassins lurking in the corridor. Gabriel had tried to talk his close-protection detail out of being so paranoid, but Butcher had pointed out that the aliens had human collaborators who might be more adroit at tracking him down. Haddon Hall's small staff had just had to get used to the three men watching their every move. They were all security-cleared, positively vetted, yet none of them had expected to be suddenly living in an occupied country. Gabriel hadn't expected it either.

Lightbridge-Stewart stood up when Gabriel entered the library. "We got the consignment underway," he said. The alien was on his way back to his people, then. "I wanted to discuss a possible operation with you, while I was here. My staff have been putting together a plan we've entitled Operation Hammer."

Gabriel frowned as he took his seat. The Americans loved bold and purposeful operational names – Operation Enduring Freedom, Operation Iraqi Freedom – but the Ministry of Defence preferred to assign names at random, on the grounds that anyone who heard the name wouldn't automatically know what it meant. Using a purposeful name was unusual and it suggested that someone intended for it to become public sooner rather than later.

"The core problem, Prime Minister, is that we cannot prevent them from moving wherever they please – and, if necessary, bombarding us into submission," Lightbridge-Stewart said. Gabriel nodded, concealing his impatience. "They have the ability to hit us wherever they want, put bluntly, and it cripples our ability to mount a sustained insurgency. We need to show them that we are not going to roll over for them and surrender."

"Particularly after we returned their captive," Gabriel agreed. "How do you intend to hammer the message into their heads."

"We can cripple their command and control network," Lightbridge-Stewart said. "Maybe not for very long, but we can bring it down long enough to mount a series of attacks on their bases – and the collaborator government in London. At the very least, we would force them to fall back and rebuild their collaborator force from scratch. We might even give them enough of a bloody nose that they pull out of Britain altogether."

"I doubt they will feel inclined to surrender," Gabriel said, dryly. "It's much more likely that they'll take a step back and hammer us from space."

"It's possible," Lightbridge-Stewart agreed. "The problem, however, is simple; do we take advantage of the one chance we are likely to get to hurt them, and smash their collaborator government, or do we surrender the initiative to them? We know they've been working on building networks for controlling our civilians and putting them to work on alien projects. How long is it going to be before the last resistance fighters are pushed to the Highlands, or the North Yorkshire Moors, or…"

Gabriel nodded. "We're stuck," he said. "We can keep irritating them, but if we piss them off too much they might just decide that they're better off without us."

"Maybe not," Lightbridge-Stewart said. "We were talking to the alien captive about them committing genocide – about them wiping out the entire human race. From what we were told, they can't – there are interstellar laws that prohibit genocide."

"There are *human* laws that prohibit genocide," Gabriel pointed out. "I don't recall anyone actually stepping up to the plate and stopping the slaughter in Sudan. The laws aren't enforced, so…"

He shrugged, remembering how frustrated he'd felt before the aliens had landed and shown him just how helpless many people in undeveloped countries must have felt over the years. It was easy to get governments to condemn genocide, but much harder to actually convince them to *do* anything about it, no matter how clear-cut the case for intervention. He had no doubt that they could have stopped the slaughter in Sudan or any of the other stricken countries in Africa, yet the cost would have been horrific and there was no hope that anyone else would pick up the tab.

"Apparently, the interstellar races do enforce the laws," Lightbridge-Stewart said, slowly. "There's no law against invading a planet that can't defend itself, it seems, but there is one against deliberately causing a genocide. That's something we can use against them."

"They can kill a hell of a lot of us without committing genocide," Gabriel pointed out, sourly. Dear God – had he ever wanted to be Prime Minister? One less scandal and he might have died in London when the aliens landed, or perhaps found himself drafted into the collaborator government. The entire weight of the world rested on his shoulders. "How sure are we that the aliens wouldn't exterminate us?"

"I think we are reasonably sure," Lightbridge-Stewart said. "But they will certainly push back hard when we start pushing them."

"True," Gabriel said. They needed a victory. They needed something they could use to inspire resistance all over the country. And after the aliens had forced them to surrender their captive, they needed one desperately. "I authorise the operation."

He hesitated. "And I hope to God that we're not making a terrible mistake," he added. "The aliens won't hesitate to hammer us if we push them right out of the country."

———

Tra'ti Gra'sha kept one eye on the countryside around him as his small patrol skimmed down the human road, looking for trouble. It all looked peaceful, apart from the handful of birds flying through the air, but the undergrowth had been known to hide all kinds of surprises over the past few weeks. The humans were past masters at burying an IED and using it to hit a patrol, and then bringing in armed bands to catch the survivors before they had a chance to escape. Some of the Land Forces patrolling the ground around their bases had taken the opportunity to burn as much as they could of the local foliage, making it impossible for the humans to use it as a hiding place.

The armoured vehicle slowed as the driver caught sight of a group of animals blocking the road. Gra'sha hefted his weapon, alert for trouble; it wouldn't be the first time that some enterprising human had used animals to block a patrol's route while preparing an ambush. The driver had similar thoughts and turned the vehicle onto the embankment, relying on the hover-cushion to keep it upright and moving. A fence splintered as the vehicle brushed against it, but they ignored it and kept moving. The humans knew better than to complain about their damaged property. If they wanted to keep their property and their lives intact, they could stop harbouring the rogues who ambushed patrols.

He heard the sound of the animals protesting as the vehicle skimmed past them and back down onto the road. A pair of young humans – females, judging from their increased frontal development – jumped back in shock, clearly not having heard their approach until it was far too late. Gra'sha resisted the temptation to wave in their direction, knowing that they would probably be planting bombs or taking shots at him in the next few years. At least this bunch of humans seemed reluctant to send their young to war. There were tales of human children carrying bombs right up to patrols in some other parts of the world, although they could be just rumours. Rumour-spreading was officially forbidden, which didn't stop troopers from exchanging rumours and survival tips at every opportunity. Even the newcomers from the homeworld had finally learned to listen to those who had landed on Earth with the first invasion force. They'd survived the worst that the humans could throw at them.

Two aircraft flew overhead, matching course with the armoured vehicle for a few moments. It always made Gra'sha feel better to know that there were aircraft overhead, watching and waiting to provide support if they ran into trouble. They were supposed to run a random patrol, but there were only a handful of possible routes from the base they could run and the humans knew them all. Even if they didn't run into an ambush this time, they were likely to run into one the next time… and some human ambushes had been *nasty*.

He was still watching the environment when he saw a single naked Eridiani standing by the side of the road. For a moment, Gra'sha refused to believe what he was seeing – and then he connected it with the missing intelligence officer the Command Triad had warned them to look out for. It was just typical of intelligence to insist that the troopers on the ground poured out all the stops for a missing intelligence officer – not that he would ever dare say that out loud, of course. Intelligence officers tended to spend more time watching their subordinates for disloyalty rather than monitoring their human enemies. Absently, he wondered if that were true of the human intelligence organisations too. Probably. Certain things were universal, even among the non-humanoid race that had been the State's first major foe.

The vehicle pulled to a halt near the missing officer and Gra'sha dismounted, quickly. It was quite possible that the humans were using their captive as the bait in a trap, although quite what they hoped to gain from it was beyond him. The intelligence officer seemed rather disorientated as Gra'sha reached him, but looked very relieved to see a friendly face. How had the humans treated him while he was their captive? They did all kinds

of horrible things to their fellows, according to the briefings they'd received
– what would they do to a captive trooper, let alone someone who could
actually tell them what they needed to know.

"It's all right," he said, as the intelligence officer staggered towards the
vehicle. It looked as though the humans had just dumped him, presumably
some distance from their base. They'd take a look at the orbital coverage and
see if they could trace the humans back to where they'd kept their captive.
"You're safe now."

He helped the captive into the vehicle and remounted, hefting his
weapon as he surveyed the horizon for human threats. Somehow, he was
sure that none would materialise. The humans had wanted to give them the
captive – they wouldn't blow them up now. He smiled as the vehicle
hummed back into life and started heading straight back to the base.
Whatever the humans had had in mind, there was a good chance of
promotion or a bonus from their superiors. And that would give the small
crew a chance with the females when mating season rolled around.

And if they managed to trace the humans back to their lair, they might
just be able to decapitate the resistance in a single blow.

Chapter Thirty-Five

London
United Kingdom, Day 47

"Maz'Bak's debriefing has been completed," the intelligence officer informed Oheghizh. "The humans treated him fairly well by their standards. They did, however, interrogate him quite extensively."

"And as an intelligence officer he had a great deal to tell them," Oheghizh said. Curiosity was not encouraged by the State, but intelligence officers were an exception to that rule. Indeed, rather than stamping on excessively curious youths, the intelligence service preferred to recruit them. Their curiosity could be put to work on behalf of the State. "What did he tell them, precisely."

"It's all in the report," the intelligence officer said. "They know a great deal more about us than they knew before they raided the detention centre."

Oheghizh skimmed through the report, barely keeping himself from swearing out loud. The humans weren't supposed to know anything about any of the other races out among the stars – but now they did, along with far too much information on the galactic geopolitics that had led the State to Earth. And they knew how the command network on Earth was organised, the location and identities of the Command Triad… anywhere else, the information would have had a disastrous impact. If the humans had climbed into space, like any halfway sane race, it would have given them a decisive advantage. Instead, they were still trapped on the bottom of Earth's gravity well.

The Command Triad was not going to be pleased. Nor was the State, when superior authority heard about it. Earth had already soaked up more resources and combat power than anyone had anticipated, which meant that reinforcements had to be diverted from other planets. The human military personnel they'd taken off-planet and sent to disputed worlds might redress the balance, but how could they be trusted completely? They weren't even mercenaries; they'd been pressed into service. And they'd know it.

"On the other hand, we did manage to trace the humans back to their lair," the intelligence officer added. "They must have a fairly major command post of their own hidden in the general area. If we wait a couple of days, and then attack… we might be able to cripple the human resistance."

Oheghizh nodded, sourly. In truth, he wasn't sure that it would do more than hamper the human resistance organisation. The American command and control structure had been shattered by the opening blows of the invasion, but they were somehow still managing to mount a creditable challenge to the State. Intelligence was fairly sure that there was no overall commanding authority, which raised worrying questions about how far the Americans took the concept of leaderless resistance. It was an idea alien to the State.

"Prepare an assault force," he ordered, finally. "And have the former captive shipped to orbit for a more extensive debriefing. I want to know everything he told his captors – and I'm sure that the Command Triad will too."

He watched the intelligence officer scuttle out of his office, and then he turned to look out over London. The riots that had threatened their grip on the city had died away after the BBC had reported that the alien captive was safe and well, back with his own people, but they'd come alarmingly close to overwhelming their ability to govern the city. Part of him was tempted to just pull out and leave the humans to slaughter each other, yet he knew they needed as much of the local economy functioning as possible. The registry was already being used to earmark humans for clean-up efforts – and if they refused to work, they would starve.

And if they did manage to cripple the human resistance, perhaps they could bring the whole campaign to a successful conclusion.

Robin lay on his bed, staring up at nothing. It wasn't his bed, not really. The flat had been abandoned in the opening days of the invasion and the police, needing living space for policemen who had been forced out of their homes, had commandeered it. Robin had no idea who had owned the flat before he'd moved in, but they had had excellent taste in wine. He'd downed no less than six bottles over the last two days and was seriously considering finishing off the rest. It could hardly have made his life any worse.

Back before the invasion, he'd been a loyal policeman, upholding the law even when he'd wanted to forgot proper procedure and just kick some young thug's head in, or turn water cannons on protestors who had no idea how lucky they were. And then the aliens had invaded and he'd told himself that he had to go to work for them, just to keep the public safe. His own justifications rang hollow in his ears, mocking him; how safe was the public in a world at war? Outside, parts of the city had been torn apart by rioting, dead bodies lay everywhere and what remained of the police force was working for the aliens. And they weren't the only ones. Some of the special constables the aliens had recruited weren't policemen, or even soldiers. They just wanted to get their kicks by pushing around helpless civilians.

He reached for the bottle and cursed when his trembling hand knocked it down onto the floor. Somehow, he managed to roll over, just in time to see the red wine draining out of the bottle and soaking the carpet. It would probably drip down to the flat underneath, giving the inhabitant a scare. He pulled himself upright and rubbed at his head. Maybe a few more drinks would make him drunk and then he could forget the world for a while. If he could go home, if he could see his wife… but she didn't want anything to do with him now, not after the chaos in London. The entire world hated the policemen, those who had joined up to serve the aliens. If he'd known…

…Perhaps he would have gone underground too.

The thought was a bitter one. There were policemen, unmarried policemen, who had deserted their comrades and gone off to join the resistance. But they were the ones who had no hostages to fortune – or to the aliens. The married men knew that their wives and children were known to the aliens, and that they would be killed if their husbands or fathers showed any signs of disloyalty. Perhaps his wife could have evaded them if he'd vanished in the early hours of the invasion, when so many had gone missing, presumed dead, but it was now far too late. He reached for another bottle, struggled with the cork, and then took a long swig. Who cared about going on duty now? Maybe they'd just kill him and that would be an end to it.

How long had it been, he asked himself, since he'd walked his first beat? Not long at all, really; he'd known that he didn't want to go anywhere else. The endless red tape that strangled real policing, the politically-correct rules invented and enforced by politicians that made it impossible to nick real villains or monitor terrorists… despite all the trials and tribulations of modern policing, he'd loved his job. And now he was nothing more than a filthy quisling. They didn't need to drag up examples from France or Norway any longer, not when there were thousands of collaborators in the United Kingdom. They'd be calling them Robins in the future, no doubt.

His hands started to shake and he put the bottle down, quickly. He should get up and shower before donning his uniform, but he really didn't care any longer. The weapons they'd stashed away… maybe he should go to the stash, pull out one of the pistols, and put a bullet through his own brains. What else could he do? Resistance was futile. He was halfway to his feet before realising that suicide would probably mean doom for his wife, if the aliens decided to view his suicide as a kind of desertion. Did they even *have* suicide as a concept? There was no way to know, although given their tough bodies, killing themselves probably required poison. Or maybe they just jumped out of their starships and burned up in the atmosphere below. The thought made him giggle, a sure sign that he was drunker than he realised.

"You know," a voice remarked, "there's little sillier than a drunken policeman."

Robin's eyes snapped open. He'd been alone. Unlike some of the other policemen, he had no intention of bringing a whore back to his flat. He still loved his wife, despite everything – and besides, at least some of the whores had murdered their policemen and vanished into the underground. No one loved the police these days. Through his rather hazy vision, he saw a young Asian man standing by the door, wearing a policeman's uniform. Robin didn't recognise him – and there was something about the way he wore his uniform that suggested that he wasn't a policeman at all. But someone wearing a policeman's uniform could walk around the complex without being questioned...

"Don't worry," the man said. "I'm not here to kill you."

"Right," Robin growled. His head felt as if someone had smashed it with a brick, repeatedly. Mixing the different kinds of alcohol had probably been a mistake. It was hard to form words in his mind, let alone say them out loud. "What do you want then?"

"My name is… well, they've been calling me Abdul," the man said. Despite his light, almost flippant tone, his brown eyes never left Robin's face. "You may have heard of me. I believe the reward on my head is currently enough luxury food to keep someone eating for the next few months."

The name seemed to shock Robin out of his drunken haze. Of course he'd heard of Abdul – he was supposed to be one of the ringleaders behind the resistance, linking together groups as disparate as National Front racists and Islamic Fundamentalists. The name had been mentioned by captured insurgents during their interrogation, but none of them had known where Abdul based himself. Some policemen had thought that the name was a joke, yet the aliens had taken it seriously. The reward on Abdul's head was massive.

"Don't worry, they don't know I'm here," Abdul assured him. One hand rubbed the uniform, mockingly. "It's amazing how many people spy the uniform and don't look past it to the face."

"We don't know what you look like," Robin managed. Up close, Abdul was almost unmemorable. He had no beard, but otherwise he could simply have faded into the crowd and vanished. Bearded Asian men had often been targeted by the aliens, purely on suspicion. One of Robin's fellow policemen had joked that the aliens found beards intimidating because they couldn't grow them themselves. "And now… why are you here?"

"I was told that you might know where some weapons are stashed," Abdul said, lightly. "I think that it is time we talked, don't you?"

Robin staggered to his feet and stumbled over to the shower. The water in London was often turned off and then on again by the aliens, purely to remind Londoners who was in charge, but there was never any problem with the water in police complexes. He turned the knob and blasted cold water over his head, shocking himself awake. Part of him wanted to sound the alert and call for help, but the rest of him… if Abdul knew that Robin had been involved in hiding weapons, what else did he know? It wouldn't take much to alert the aliens to his betrayal – and they'd definitely see it as a betrayal. All weapons were supposed to have been surrendered to them.

"Fuck," he said, as his mind finally caught up with him. "Who told you?"

"Does it matter?" Abdul asked. "All that really matters is that we need to talk."

Drying up the water dripping from his hair gave Robin a moment to think. He hadn't been the only copper involved in hiding weapons, and two of the ones who had had deserted after the first riots. One or both of them could have found Abdul and shared confidences with him, naming Robin as someone who had hoped that he would be in the position to do something about the aliens one day. But that day had never come…

"Very well," he said. "What do we have to talk about?"

"You know that the aliens won't ever leave on their own," Abdul said. "Do you really believe that that collaborator asshole they have speaking for them can influence them in any way?"

"No," Robin said. He'd never trusted Alan Beresford, even when he'd been MP for Haltemprice rather than a collaborator claiming to be Prime Minister. The man smiled too much, among his many other failings. There had been rumours of shady dealings, but nothing had ever been proven. And now it was too late. "Do you believe that fighting them will make them give up and go away?"

"It's all we have left," Abdul commented. "You do know that the Vietnamese drove the Americans away after years of inconclusive warfare?"

"Years," Robin grated. It felt almost as if the aliens had *always* been on Earth. Had it really been less than two months? "Do you think that we can keep fighting them until they give up and leave us in peace? Or simply drop a massive rock on our heads and slaughter the remaining humans on Earth?"

"There's little other choice," Abdul said. He leaned forwards, warningly. "We need your help to hit them, policeman. Think about your people and join us."

Robin hesitated. "My wife..."

"We can get her out of their reach," Abdul assured him. "We'll fake her death and hide her in one of our bases. All it needs is for you to decide which side you're on. Do you support your fellow humans, or ugly aliens intent on turning us all into slaves?"

Robin looked down at his hands. How much blood was on them? How many had died, at least in part, because of him and his fellow collaborators? The aliens had slaughtered humans when protest marches had gotten out of hand, to say nothing of threatening mass slaughter to get one of their captives back. And they'd succeeded. The resistance had surrendered their captive, despite endless complaints on the internet that one city was a worthwhile trade for an alien who might finally provide real answers.

"My fellow humans," he said, finally. He reached for his uniform, feeling a flicker of the old pride he'd felt when he'd first donned it as a fully-fledged policeman. "What exactly do you want me to do?"

Abdul smiled and told him.

"Write a letter to your wife," he said, afterwards. "We'll make sure it gets delivered."

———

I should be part of the attack force, Alex thought sourly, as she parked the car outside the house. It was situated in one of London's surrounding towns, a nice place to live if you could afford the rent. *I want to hit back at the bastards, not play secret agent…*

Most of her wounds were healing, thankfully, but the medics had been insistent that she should avoid actual fighting for at least another month or two. Alex had pointed out that they could hardly send someone back home to recuperate when the aliens had occupied the entire country, yet they'd been insistent. She'd been tortured, raped and abused and she really needed time to recover. They seemed to expect her to break down at any moment, rather than being determined to get back out there and keep fighting the Leathernecks. The doctor had strongly urged her to go to the Highlands of Scotland or one of the other long-term resistance bases and had been surprised when she'd refused.

She climbed out of the car, ignoring the handful of sharp glances from pedestrians as she locked the door behind her. Only collaborators had fuel for cars these days; the aliens hadn't touched this part of Britain as much as they'd touched London, but their presence was keenly felt. They had a base only a few miles away, part of the ring of steel surrounding London proper. She touched the Browning she'd stuffed into her coat pocket – just in case, even though she had papers that should have fooled the aliens – and walked up to the house. There was the faint sound of music coming from inside.

Calmly, she pushed the button. There was no sign that the neighbours had realised that the house's lone occupant was married to a collaborator, but if they ever found out… some wives and children of collaborators had been bullied, or isolated, or even murdered by their former friends and neighbours. The door opened a crack and a lady with Italian features peered out.

"I have a letter for you," Alex said. "I suggest you read it now and then come with me."

Helene Harrison skimmed through the letter, her eyes going wide. "I am to come with you?"

"Yes," Alex said. There was no time to argue. "Don't worry – you've nothing to worry about. Just come with me for your own safety."

There was a pause as Helene picked up a bag she'd positioned at the doorway and then came outside. Alex felt an odd flicker of jealousy as she realised just how beautiful Helene was, before seeing the fear in her eyes. She hadn't seen her husband for over a month and yet her neighbours would condemn her, if they ever realised that he was a collaborator. But he could have died when the aliens hit Scotland Yard… Alex glanced at Helene and realised that she pitied the girl. The Helene Harrison's of the country were whom the RAF had existed to defend.

She climbed into the car, checked that Helene was buckled in, and started the engine. They had a long journey before they reached the safe house – and they'd have to abandon the car along the route. Who knew how closely the aliens monitored human vehicles?

Chapter Thirty-Six

Near London/London
United Kingdom, Day 50/51

They approached from the west, crawling low to be sure that they weren't seen as they neared the isolated station. A simple chain-link fence provided security, barely a moment's delay for SF soldiers who'd been taught lock-picking as part of their intensive training before they were unleashed on Britain's enemies. No one should have been anywhere near the station, but they checked twice before relaxing slightly and locating the keys they'd taken from the bunker. The door clicked open, revealing nothing, but darkness inside.

Chris Drake pulled a torch from his belt and clicked it on, aiming it into the darkness. They'd been briefed that the isolated station – part of a contingency plan that had been drawn up during the Cold War – had been left untouched for years, but it wouldn't be the first time some vagrant had set up home in an isolated building. The building looked untouched, however; a thick layer of dust bore silent tribute to the years since it had been built and then abandoned. He found the hatch on the ground, inserted a different key, and breathed a sigh of relief as the hatch opened without trouble. It led down a long rusty ladder to an isolated part of London's sewer network, one that had been sealed off from the main network years ago. Chris hooked the torch onto his belt and started to climb down the ladder, bracing himself for the smell. None of these tunnels had been cleaned for decades.

"Clear," he called back up, once he'd reached the bottom. The sewer network extended all the way from London out into the countryside. London was honeycombed with tunnels, some known to the public; others known only to the government, or simply forgotten in the years since they'd been built and abandoned. It was a way to get in and out of the city without being detected or stopped by the aliens. "Come on down. The smell is terrible."

The others chuckled as they clambered down and found themselves in an abandoned sewer, standing on a walkway that led into the darkness. "Better not fall into that," one of the Marines commented. "Worse than that shitty pond at Kandahar."

Chris snorted as he started leading the way down the walkway. "You want to bet that some mutant turtles have been breeding down here," he said, flashing the beam of light over the still water. "People used to put crocodiles down here with the rest of the shit they threw out."

"Thank you, sir," the Marine said. "I won't ever be able to wipe that image from my mind."

The walk seemed to stretch out into hours. It was strange to think that the aliens were just above them, watching for any signs of trouble. Chris knew that smaller parties of insurgents were meant to be launching a series of attacks to keep the aliens busy, but there was no way to know just how they were faring down in the tunnels. The torch flickered once as they reached a crossroads, reminding him of all the horror stories he'd read of monsters lurking deep underground. Aliens from *Alien*, sewer monsters from *The X-Files*… as a kid, he'd loved watching horror movies. And even as an adult, the memory still sent a chill running down his spine.

They reached the end of the tunnel and stopped dead. There was supposed to be a way around the blockage, into the parts of the sewers that were still working. Chris puzzled over the chart, before realising that they had walked past a smaller tunnel that connected to the main stream. The roof seemed to be closing in on them as they passed through a hidden door and out into the main body of the sewers. From what he recalled, most of the sewage was pumped out of the city, cleansed and then… actually, he couldn't remember what happened then. They weren't allowed to simply pump it into the Thames any longer, if he recalled correctly.

"Jesus," one of the men commented. "What a fucking pong."

Chris nodded, trying hard to breathe through his nose. In the distance, he could hear the sound of pumps pushing the sewerage through the tunnels. The environment was a breeding ground for rats, according to the briefing – he saw one running along a pipe before vanishing into the darkness. They seemed to have almost no fear of humanity, running up and almost touching their boots before jumping back to avoid kicks from the soldiers. Chris remembered that rats had carried diseases in pre-modern times and shuddered. The aliens had broken down a great many health and safety systems. There were probably places in Britain where scurvy and other long-forgotten diseases had returned to torment the human race.

He saw a light in the distance and reached for his pistol, before realising that it was the welcoming committee. Two of the soldiers who had been in London ever since the invasion were waiting for them, including someone he hadn't seen since the Battle of London, when he'd been swept out of the city by the river. He called his name and ran forward, heedless of the danger of slipping and falling into the shit. It had been far too long since they'd seen one another.

"Bongo," he said, as they hugged. "I thought you were dead!"

"I thought *you* were dead, you old pirate," Bongo said. He'd come from Jamaica to join the British Army and had been streamlined into the Household Division. "What the fuck blew you out of London?"

"The aliens," Chris said, as Bongo pointed to the ladder leading upwards to the safe house. He couldn't imagine which civil servant had been so paranoid as to designate a handful of houses as emergency evacuation points, but he had to admit that the paranoia had made it a great deal easier to slip into London. "What have you been doing with yourself, then?"

Bongo filled him in once they reached the top and clambered out into the safe house. Chris had seen a couple like it while he'd been on close-protection details, places where MI5 could debrief defectors or notable public figures could hide from the media. It looked perfectly normal from the outside, but most of the building would be wired for sound and the tapes stored at a different location. He hoped they'd taken out the bugs once they'd started to use it as a base.

"Oh, we're not based here," Bongo said, when he asked. "There's too much chance that someone will come across a reference to the place in the files – too many damn bureaucrats went over to the aliens. We just use it because it has access to the sewers."

He made a show of glancing at his watch. "We'll have to wait here until the sun goes down," he added, "so we may as well have a brew. I hope you bought some teabags from outside…?"

"And a few army-issue packed lunches," Chris said, with a grin.

"Bastard," Bongo said, without heat. "Anyway… what have you been doing with yourself since Westminster?"

———

It was an hour before Bongo decided that the night had fallen far enough to allow them to slip out onto the streets. The aliens and their collaborators had put a stop to London's once-celebrated nightlife by enforcing a curfew, but they didn't really have the manpower to keep it firmly in place outside Central London. Bongo and the rest of the resistance could still move about with impunity as long as they didn't go too close to the aliens, who had night-vision gear and a willingness to open fire without confirming that the contact was actually hostile. Most humans knew to give them a wide berth.

Chris had grown up in London and had loved the city, even though he'd left school with few qualifications and little hope of a worthwhile job outside the army. Looking at the city now tore at his heart. Buildings had been destroyed, or reduced to blackened shells of what they'd once been; the once-endless traffic had been driven off the road, leaving London's population forced to walk from place to place on foot. Burned-out cars were everywhere, a reminder that the aliens sometimes used them for target practice; others had bullet holes through their windscreens or superstructure. He saw a handful of dead bodies as they slipped onwards and wondered just how many had died in the weeks since the aliens had landed. London had had a huge population once, but now… now there was no way to know how many were left. He only saw a couple of living humans as they walked through the gloom.

Bongo had said that many of the gangs had wiped each other out. They'd been dependent upon selling drugs to customers, drugs that were no longer available because the aliens had sealed off London and destroyed world shipping. The gangs had been reduced to fighting over the last few bags of cocaine or heroin, while their customers had been forced to go cold turkey, weaning themselves off the drugs the hard way. Chris had nothing, but contempt for those who became enslaved to the needle or snorting powder, yet many of the addicts would have suffered greatly for lack of their crutch. One more crime to blame on the Leathernecks, he told himself, as they reached what had once been a large housing estate. The locals probably knew that the resistance had a base there, but hadn't breathed a word to the police. They'd probably felt that having the resistance there was good for them. The resistance certainly didn't waste time taking protection money or all the other tricks the gangs used to pull.

"Come on," Bongo hissed. Inside, the massive block of flats smelled faintly of urine. "I'm sorry about the stench, but we can't risk standing out from the crowd."

Chris nodded as the doors closed behind them. "Welcome to one of our staging bases," Bongo said. He nodded towards a team of four people who had been waiting for them. "Abdul – SAS dude, very brave or thoroughly crazy. Jake – local volunteer, smart-ass. Janet – our… ah, contact with some of the police. And Fatima – our doctor."

"Welcome to London," Abdul said, dryly. He might not have been wearing a proper uniform – none of them were – but he managed to *look* as if he was dressed for parade. "I think you'll hate what we've done to the place."

He shrugged and stood up. "There are places to sleep here, so get some rest," he added. "In the morning, we will start checking out our targets and planning the final stages of the operation. And then we're going to send a lot of people out through the tunnels before the shit hits the fan."

Chris nodded. "Let the CO know that we got here," he said. "How do you plan to check out the targets?"

Abdul smiled. "Let's just say that we had a little help and leave it at that," he said. "You don't need to know the precise details."

———

The following morning, after a breakfast that mainly consisted of the ration packs they'd carried through the tunnels, Abdul led Chris and a couple of others out into the city. They'd all been issued ID cards that noted their occupation as workers, people who moved from place to place to do manual labour for the alien overlords. London had simply too much damage to clear up and almost everyone who wasn't in a priority occupation had been tasked to help with the work – or starve. It was an attitude that Chris found rather understandable – it would certainly have helped clear up many of Britain's inner cities and housing estates – but the aliens didn't care about the niceties. From what many of the resistance fighters who'd stayed in London had reported, the aliens pushed the workers as hard as they could.

Dozens of work gangs roamed the city, clearing up smashed or burned-out cars, carting away debris from fallen buildings and even picking up dead bodies from where they'd been abandoned. Chris wouldn't have been surprised to discover that Londoners had an epidemic on their hands as well as everything else, just from the number of dead bodies that had been left to rot for a few days. The teams that cleaned up the dead wore NBC suits and were apparently granted special privileges by the aliens. Chris doubted that anyone could be given enough privileges to make the work worthwhile.

And there were policemen everywhere in Central London. Chris watched them checking ID cards as they patrolled, remembering the stories he'd heard about the French Resistance and those who had collaborated with the Germans. The police might have started to collaborate out of a desire to keep

the public safe, but now they were nothing more than a millstone around London's neck. Some of the men wearing police uniforms reminded Chris of the torturers he'd pulled out of the Detention Camp and executed, men who wanted to indulge their dark tastes and were willing to serve the aliens in exchange for having their way with their victims. Others looked ashamed and tried to do as little as possible.

The aliens themselves were very much in evidence. Chris watched as they ran armed patrols through London, waiting for one of the resistance fighters to take a shot at them. When they were engaged, they threw back a hail of bullets, with an alarming lack of concern for civilians who might be caught up in the crossfire. They didn't seem to recognise that some people just wanted to get on with their lives and ignore politics; anyone they caught close to the resistance fighter was often dragged away and dumped in the back of an alien vehicle.

"They go outside the city to one of the camps," Abdul muttered, as they busied themselves carting away rubble. "The Leathernecks sometimes press them into service, but mostly they just seem to leave them in the camps. We don't know why…"

"We don't know a great deal about them," Chris muttered back. They'd been studying the alien base they'd built on the remains of Buckingham Palace, a base that was heavily guarded, without any humans allowed to pass through the fence. The intelligence briefing had stated that the alien commander charged with invading and occupying Britain was based there, which explained the precautions. They had to feel more isolated than the Americans in the Green Zone in Baghdad had felt during the war in Iraq. "It's not going to be easy to get in there, not if they don't let humans into the building."

"There are some humans allowed in," Abdul said. "Their collaborator-in-chief, for one. I don't think he'd help us unless we pointed a gun at his head and I think the aliens would probably notice if we did."

Chris chuckled. The aliens did seem to be curiously uninterested in some human activities, although there seemed to be no rhyme or reason to their disinterest. They didn't seem to be interested in what humans were wearing, or in sex, even though both of them were clues to another human that something might not be right. He picked up another piece of rubble and dropped it in the cart, shaking his head. The aliens had their weaknesses, just like humans. All they had to figure out how to do was use their weaknesses against them.

His lips twitched with sly amusement. If it was that easy, he knew, everyone would be doing it.

They'd definitely realised that having their troops keep a fixed routine was a dangerous mistake. The patrols through London seemed to be random, while the guards patrolling the fence surrounding their base were varying their routine. Chris suspected, from the way they were moving, that there were probably reinforcements inside the base, just as there had been at the Detention Camp. But apart from that…? The closest major alien base was outside the city. If they could pin down the forces defending the base itself, they could run riot before the aliens could respond…

———

"I think you're going to be going out of the city tonight," Bongo said. Fatima nodded, tiredly. Her skills had helped save lives, but she'd watched too many people die because she didn't have the supplies or equipment to save them. "Once you get through the tunnels, you'll probably be taken up north with some of the others."

Fatima sighed. She'd never really been out of London, apart from a brief trip to Edinburgh. Her stepmother had wanted her to go to Pakistan, but Fatima had refused – she'd suspected that her stepmother had intended to marry her off. And now… where was her stepmother? The aliens had taken her away and… what? Had they killed her, or imprisoned her, or… she wasn't anyone important, not really. Hardly the kind of person they'd want to interrogate thoroughly.

But she'd been related to the first suicide bomber. That alone made her a person of interest.

"I see," she said, finally. "When do you want me to be ready?"

"Get your stuff ready when you have a moment," Bongo said. "We'll have to wait until dark anyway. They might spot us moving through the streets in daytime."

Fatima grinned, realising that she was being teased. As far as she knew, the aliens still wanted her for the crime of being related to a young man foolish enough to blow himself up – along with hundreds of humans and a dozen aliens. The collaborator government kept making that point on the BBC, reminding everyone of the evils of suicide bombing. Fatima couldn't really disagree, even though she'd disliked the young asshole. He'd thought that all women should be neither seen nor heard.

"Right," she said. "Will you be coming with me?"

"Probably not," Bongo said. "I have work to do here."

Fatima nodded. "Good luck," she said. "May God go with you."

Chapter Thirty-Seven

North England
United Kingdom, Day 51

"I think we have a problem."

Gavin looked over at the operator. He was manning one of the computer stations monitoring alien activity in the region, using their own computer networks against them. It gave them a view of what the aliens were doing, although he had to keep reminding himself not to take it for granted. The aliens, if they ever worked out what the humans were doing, could get around it by simply disconnecting from the network.

"The aliens have dispatched a flight of aircraft coming right towards our position," the operator said. "Their ETA is roughly ten minutes - perhaps less. I think we've been rumbled."

The damned captive, Gavin thought, angrily. The decision to release the alien might have made sense, but there had been no time to conceal their tracks properly. All the aliens had had to do was look at their orbital observations and they might well be able to track the small team back to the holding cell. And the PM and several other officials were based nearby as well.

"Send the alert to the PM's bodyguards and tell them to get his ass out of there," he ordered, flatly. Seven minutes… not very long at all. There wouldn't be any hope of completely disassembling the base and vanishing before the aliens arrived. "And then start the destruct sequence on our computers. I want nothing left that could lead the aliens to any other bases."

"Aye, sir," the operator said. There was a bleep from his console. "Sir, they've also started detailing land forces in our general direction. Should I send an update to the picketers?"

"Yes," Gavin said. He'd scattered small teams in positions along the roads leading to the base, teams armed with antitank weapons. They could slow the aliens down, but there was no easy way to slow down the aircraft. Their stock of antiaircraft missiles had largely been earmarked for Operation Hammer. "Tell them to land one good punch and then bug out. I don't want a stand-up battle if we can avoid it."

He glanced down at the map. The aliens had used helicopter assaults before, often with just as much bravery and skill as their human counterparts. They presumably wanted to take the alien captive's interrogation team prisoner, if possible – did they know that they were close to the PM, as well as Gavin himself? There was no way to know. No one outside the base knew what it hid, a security precaution that had seemed rather paranoid at the time.

"And then start making your way to the exit," he added. "You know where to go if we get split up?"

"Yes, sir," the operator said. He watched as Gavin checked the SA80 he carried slung over his shoulder. There'd used to be regulations against arming soldiers who weren't on duty. Those regulations no longer existed, along with the MOD that had sometimes seemed more paranoid about its soldiers being armed than about security. "Good luck."

Gabriel had been sleeping lightly when the door burst open. He jumped awake, one hand reaching for the pistol on the table. He'd never fired a weapon before the invasion began, but Butcher and his team had insisted that he learn and spent several days in the forest showing him how to load, fire and clean a Browning automatic. It felt oddly reassuring in his hand, even though he knew that he would never be a crack shot. The SAS men regularly shot birds out of the sky and made it look easy.

"Prime Minister," Butcher said. "We just had a warning from the OP. The aliens are on their way, coming here. You need to get up, now."

He pulled Gabriel out of bed and tossed him his dressing gown. "There isn't any time to dress," he said, as he scooped up the overnight bag they'd insisted that Gabriel pack when they'd first arrived. "They'll be on our heads in five minutes."

The thought made Gabriel shake off his drowsiness and follow Butcher down the stairs. A handful of staff were at the bottom, talking urgently among themselves in grim voices. Butcher ignored them and pulled Gabriel towards the rear of the building when he started to slow down, nodding to Hughie and Mother as they appeared in front of them. The two men were armed to the teeth, carrying what looked like enough rifles and grenades to fight a small war. Judging from the military's statistics Gabriel had read back before the invasion, they barely had enough for a brief skirmish with the enemy.

Outside, the morning dew hung heavily in the air. He could hear the sound of birds awakening from their slumber, but nothing else, not even a hint that someone was heading towards them with bad intentions. Gabriel almost opened his mouth to ask if it was a drill, before hearing the first sounds of helicopters in the distance. These days, there were only a handful of human aircraft in the air, all operated by collaborators. The aliens were definitely on their way.

Haddon Hall's rear gardens blurred into the forest surrounding the estate. In his first week at the hall, Gabriel had enjoyed walking through the woodlands and watching the animals scuttling around, untouched by the war marring Britain's soil. Now, there was no time to sightsee. He relaxed slightly as the trees and branches closed in around them, providing a limited amount of cover. The aliens might lose them within the gloom. He found himself praying as they stopped, briefly, near a cache of supplies Butcher had hidden in the forest, including a small change of clothes. They could pass for poachers trying to supplement their rations if the aliens caught up with them, although they had no ID cards. If the aliens demanded that they produce the cards… what could they do, but fight?

The sound of helicopters grew louder. Gabriel glanced up and saw dark shapes moving over the forest, heading towards the hall. He cringed back, only to be pulled back into a run by Butcher. The aliens might come down right on top of them if they lingered. Behind him, he could hear the sound of gunfire. Someone in the hall was giving the aliens a hot reception.

"We'll head to the coast and grab a boat," Butcher said, as they headed further away from the hall. The SAS man didn't even have the decency to pretend he was winded. Gabriel knew that he was the one who would slow them down, if they encountered the enemy. He'd once asked Butcher if they would put a bullet in his head if capture was certain. Butcher had ducked the question. "And then we can head north to somewhere a little safer."

Gabriel nodded, breathing hard. He'd had more exercise at the hall than he'd had in his entire life – with three SAS men as instructors – but he still felt winded. But there was no choice. They had to keep moving or the aliens might catch up with them. And then… Gabriel had no illusions about what they'd do to him. They'd force him to betray his country on television and then take him outside and put a bullet through his brains. They didn't need the old Prime Minister when they had a collaborator willing and able to do everything they asked.

Behind them, the sound of gunfire grew louder.

The aliens appeared with terrifying speed, their attack helicopters swooping low over the forest, followed by a pair of heavy-lift helicopters loosely comparable to Chinooks. Gavin watched them come closer, knowing that the bigger helicopters were the dangerous ones. The aliens, if they wanted prisoners, couldn't simply hose down the hall with bullets and rockets; they'd have to put boots on the ground. And the only way to do that quickly was through landing them from the air. They had their own version of the

HALO parachute tactic, according to the internet. They'd used it while assaulting a French position in the south of France.

He keyed his radio. The aliens would be monitoring their traffic, but they shouldn't be able to get real-time decryptions – at least if the intelligence on their computer software was accurate. British forces in Afghanistan had been able to monitor their enemies transmissions and use it against their foes, sometimes as targeting information. It was a risk, but one Gavin felt was worth taking. The same considerations about wanting prisoners ensured that the aliens couldn't simply drop a rock on the transmitter from orbit.

"Fire," he ordered.

The forest seemed to erupt as the concealed GPMGs opened fire on the larger helicopters, while a single Stinger – the only one at the hall – roared upwards towards one of the attack helicopters. It struck the helicopter on its armour-plated underside, sending the helicopter staggering off in search of a good place to put down, smoke billowing out from its lower regions. The aliens had clearly been armouring up their helicopters, Gavin noted, as the other attack helicopters turned and started to fire back towards the soldiers in the forest. They stopped firing and started to run, but some weren't quick enough to escape. Gavin saw them die, just before one of the larger helicopters heeled over and fell towards the ground. It came down with a terrifying crash, but didn't explode. A moment later, he saw alien troopers emerging from the wreck, shooting to force the humans to keep their heads down. It would have been admirable if it hadn't been aimed at his troops.

He cursed as the attack helicopters made a second run over the hall, firing down with heavy machine guns towards the British positions. His men had had plenty of time to prepare defences, but building something to stand off a helicopter without being noticed by alien orbital satellites would have been difficult. The aliens knocked two of the positions out – he forced himself not to think about the men inside – before their second transport helicopter started dropping aliens down towards the ground. From his point of view, it looked as if they were dropping out on bungee cords. The moment they touched the ground, the cords broke, releasing them before they could be yanked back up into the air. Gavin's soldiers, positioned at the windows around the hall, opened fire on them; the alien attack helicopters, sighting the firing positions, hurled a deadly storm of lead towards the windows. Their heavy fire smashed chips off the stone walls and blasted through the windows. Below, two alien assault teams ran forwards carrying what looked like an antitank weapon. They launched it into the main doors and shattered them backwards, smashing through the interior walls like paper.

Gavin clicked his radio twice – the signal to the outside teams to break contact and retreat to the RV points – and then abandoned the radio on the ground, kicking it under a bush. It would be too dangerous to use it now that the aliens controlled most of the ground. He could see a fireball rising up in the distance from where one of the larger IEDs had detonated, but he had no illusions about their ability to prevent the aliens from taking the hall. His close-protection detail spread out around him as he started to walk away from the hall. The remaining soldiers inside the building should be running for the exits, where they would link up with their fellows and start walking east. Gavin was the only one who knew that the PM and his team had headed west; the eastbound soldiers should provide some cover for his escape.

Another flight of alien helicopters swooped overhead, lowering a pair of light armoured vehicles to the ground. Gavin had seen the reports on their use against civilian rioters, but there hadn't been any report of them being used against resistance fighters before. They weren't as heavily armoured as Viking or Jackal vehicles, which should make them easy prey for antitank missiles or IEDs. On the other hand, they carried heavy machine guns and what intelligence claimed was a portable mortar launcher. It gave the aliens a surprisingly heavy punch for such light vehicles.

The ground shook as the first explosive charge inside the hall detonated. It had taken some specialist work by the defenders to position a fuel-air explosive in the basement, intended to send the entire hall up in flames. The aliens, picking their way into the building, were caught by a sheet of flame that seemed to roar up and out of nowhere. Gavin had been told that the main structure of the hall *might* survive – they'd known how to build tough buildings in those days – but anything the aliens might have been able to use to track the resistance to their next base would be destroyed. They'd never

know for sure how close they'd come to decapitating the resistance, or bagging the PM. The Prime Minister's ability to broadcast to the country, using the internet, had helped keep the resistance going. Gavin said a silent prayer for his safety as they continued to head into the countryside. The aliens would be putting up roadblocks and cordoning off the area, intending to trap them before they could escape. They had to move quickly before time ran out.

Behind him, he heard another series of explosions, followed by rapid gunfire. It was impossible to guess at what was happening, although most of the gunfire seemed to be coming from alien weapons. They kept running through the forest, despite hearing alien helicopters overhead, searching for fugitives. If they'd managed to improve their tracking technology, part of Gavin's mind insisted on reminding him, their helicopters or drones could keep track of them and steer a blocking force right into their path. Or maybe they'd just hose down the forest with bullets and leave their targets to bleed out and die.

The forest came to an end suddenly, broken by a road leading northwards towards the motorway. They crossed it rapidly, just as they heard the faint humming of alien vehicles racing towards them. Gavin heard the sound of gunfire and threw himself to the ground, trying to bury himself in the mud. Bullets were snapping right over his head, smashing through trees and branches with equal abandon. He heard one of his men yelp as a bullet slashed across his back – an inch or two lower and it would have shattered his spine – before the sound of alien helicopters came closer. The aliens, if they were still tracking the small party, would be sending in ground troops...

"Come on," one of his escort detail hissed. "We need to get out of this trap..."

The aliens were firing to force them to keep their heads down, but they could still crawl. Gavin squelched through the mud, just as he heard what sounded like incoming fire. An explosion, far too close to him, sent mud and branches flying towards his position. The second explosion picked him up and threw him through the trees. He crashed down and felt his arm snap under his weight. The pain almost overwhelmed him, even as he tried to stagger to his feet and run. Everything seemed to be shifting around him. It was almost impossible to move.

A dark shape appeared in front of him, pointing a gun towards his head. The alien's dark eyes seemed to meet his, and then pull back a little. Gavin remembered that they wanted prisoners and tried to reach for his pistol, but his hand refused to obey orders. He had to be more seriously injured than he'd thought...

The alien lifted a clawed hand and snapped it down across Gavin's face. There was a brief moment of shattering pain, and then he plunged down into darkness.

———

Gabriel was completely exhausted by the time they reached the coast, heading down towards a small village along the shore. It had probably once been a fishing village, but with the decline of the fishing industry it had turned into a tourist attraction, with boat trips to the Isle of Man, Ireland and the Scottish Islands. Gabriel found a place to sit and catch his breath while Butcher walked down to the small harbour, looking for a boat that could take them north. He'd admitted that he'd steal a boat if necessary, but he'd prefer to avoid it if possible. The last thing they needed was an outraged village calling the aliens and reporting their escape.

He closed his eyes. The next thing he knew was Mother shaking him gently. "We have a boat and an ex-Royal Marine to sail it," he said. "Come on. We'd better get moving before the aliens catch up with us."

The sound of helicopters in the distance underscored his words. Gabriel followed him down to the harbour and blinked in surprise when he saw the boat. It was an elderly sailing boat rather than a more modern design, but it did have an outboard motor at the stern. The owner, a man who looked old enough to be a granddad, nodded when he saw Gabriel and then started the motor.

"You'll be heading north, right?" He said, as they motored out and into open water. Gabriel wondered if the shape he could see in the distance was

Ireland, or if they were too far north to see the Emerald Isle. "I hope you've got somewhere safe to stay."

"Yes," Butcher said, shortly.

"I'll get you there, safe and sound," the sailor said. "Don't worry about a thing."

Gabriel half-turned, looking back at the receding shoreline. The green hills of England seemed to be illuminated as the sun beat down from high overhead, creating a marvellous picture. Despite himself, he wondered if he'd ever see them again. If they had to flee to Scotland, where would they go when the aliens came after them again?

"I'm not worried," Butcher said, stiffly. "I just want to be away from here before our friends catch up with us."

Chapter Thirty-Eight

London
United Kingdom, Day 55

"We're still on, then?"

"It looks that way," Abdul said, from where he was studying the laptop. London's internet connections were starting to collapse, although no one was quite sure if the aliens were doing it deliberately or if the wear and tear on the system was finally taking a toll. Probably both, Chris considered. The aliens had to know that the internet was being used to coordinate the resistance and they were recruiting computer experts. "We're too far advanced with the planning to back out now. If some groups don't get the message in time…"

Chris nodded. The alien attack on Haddon Hall – which had apparently been serving as a crucial resistance node – had scattered some of the resistance's fighting men, but it hadn't shattered the command network. Some people had suggested abandoning – or at least postponing – Operation Hammer, but too many people were already briefed and making preparations. Delaying the operation only increased the danger of the alien intelligence service figuring out what was coming before the operation was launched.

"Then" – he made a show of checking his watch – "we move from here in three hours and hit the aliens right where they live," he said. Offhand, he couldn't recall a bigger operation in recent history – let alone one mounted on such a shoestring. The cost of failure would be alarmingly high. "I take it that everyone is ready?"

There were nods from the small team. London was large enough to hide a couple of hundred fighting men – as well as the volunteers, gangsters and trouble-causers who were giving the collaborator government fits – in places close to their intended target. Thanks to Abdul's careful preparation – he'd recruited louts to smash CCTV cameras all over the city – the aliens and their collaborators would have difficulty realising that the assault force was being prepared, although they had to know that they were going blind. Chris privately suspected that one of the reasons the aliens had started insisting that people worked for their food was to keep control over the population, rather than leave people to their own devices. They might start getting ideas about lashing out at the aliens.

"Good," Chris said. He grinned to relieve the tension. "I feel like saying something terribly dramatic."

Abdul chuckled. "Once more into the breach, dear friends, once more," he said. "Consign their parts most private to a Rutland fence."

Chris laughed. He'd missed laughing and joking with his comrades before an operation, or telling great lies about female conquests… anything, but taking about the coming battle. They'd prepared carefully and rehearsed as much as they could, yet the tension would continue to rise until they were actually moving out and heading towards contact. The only thing that would make it settle was actual engagement.

London wasn't what he remembered any longer. Even Basra or Kabul at their worst didn't match what the aliens had done to London. Chris would cheerfully have killed every last one of the aliens for what they'd done, both for the damage they'd inflicted upon London's monuments and for the fear that pervaded the lives of ordinary citizens. There was no longer any faith in the law, or the police; the police served the aliens and the law was a joke, unable even to protect those who had spent their entire lives following it. Many people had been arrested by the aliens after being denounced by their neighbours out of spite, or because the neighbours wanted to pay back old grudges… no one trusted anyone any longer. Chris imagined that Moscow under Stalin or Berlin under Hitler would have had the same aura of fear, of mistrust and suspicion, that seemed to have settled over London like a shroud.

No amount of joking could convince him that things were normal, or that they would ever be normal again. One of the guys he'd met during the briefings had commented that the discovery of alien life alone had changed the world, and it would have done so even if the aliens had been friendly, or indifferent to poor struggling humanity. And if the latest intelligence on the internet was to be believed, there were at least six other alien star-faring races out there. Humanity was a very small fish in a very large pond.

He looked down at his SA80 and shook his head. He'd already checked, cleaned and rechecked it twice in the last two hours. They should be resting and preparing themselves, but he'd never been able to rest before an operation. Some of the others didn't share that particular problem. They were sitting against the wall, snoring loudly. Their comrades would make sarcastic remarks later.

"Don't worry," Bongo said. "It'll be alright on the night."

One of the other soldiers managed to twist his voice into a shrill falsetto. "It's all right, dear," he said. "We'll try again in a few minutes. Just take a look at some of these naughty pictures…"

Chris glanced at his watch, again. Would zero hour never come?

———

Robin had had some difficulties in altering his duty schedule to fit the operation's requirements, but by calling in several favours he'd been able to have himself and four others assigned to the force guarding the collaborator government's headquarters. It helped that Beresford was something of a micromanager, intent on keeping as much as possible of his government's operations under his thumb. The old Civil Contingencies Centre had been destroyed during the alien invasion of London, but a new command centre had been set up under Beresford's headquarters and outfitted with the latest in communications and surveillance equipment. Many of the officers who worked there had become more tainted by collaboration than anyone else.

There was no difficulty in getting through the security checkpoints outside the building, not with police uniforms and ID cards. Robin was almost disappointed. Part of him thought that he was being treacherous to men he'd known and worked beside for years, even though they were serving the aliens – and he'd been serving the aliens until recently. But there was a fine line between doing what they could to keep the public safe and actively helping the aliens achieve their goals and many of the operators had crossed that line. And if there was an element of hypocrisy, even self-hatred, in that thought, Robin no longer cared. It was time to put an end to it.

They walked down the stairs and into the canteen, where they would wait until ten minutes to zero hour. The police had been getting more and better food lately, a bribe to keep them on the streets in the face of public hatred and near-constant attacks from gangs of resistance fighters. He poured himself a cup of tea and waited, glancing from time to time at his watch. They weren't meant to go on duty for another hour, but the collaborator government didn't approve of lateness. Even a few minutes late was grounds for a reprimand.

He tried to push his thoughts out of his mind as the seconds ticked down. In truth, he didn't expect to survive the next few hours. The aliens had their own guard force on duty by the gates and if they weren't taken out in the opening moments of Operation Hammer, they would certainly respond to rogue policemen. Operation Hammer, even the small section he'd been told about, had simply too many working components for everything to come off perfectly. Years of experience in the police force had taught him that the more moving parts in a particular operation, the greater the chance of something coming apart at the wrong moment. The day they'd had to arrest nearly fifty suspected terrorists across Britain had come alarmingly close to being unglued.

His watch vibrated a warning and he nodded to his allies, standing up and heading down to the lockers. He'd stuffed the briefcase in the locker he used as a matter of course, just to keep someone from trying to open it too early. Between them, they were carrying assault rifles, grenades – and one large briefcase that had been converted into a makeshift IED. Picking up the final briefcase, Robin headed to the lift and down towards the bunker. It had started life as a corporate gym, but the collaborator government had lost no time in installing the latest computers and assigning operators to watch over the city. Robin had done a few shifts at Scotland Yard before the aliens had destroyed it and he had to admit that the collaborators had been very efficient. If they hadn't lost so many CCTV cameras over the past few weeks, they might realise what was going on before the operation began.

He strode through the chamber and up to a set of lockers assigned to senior personnel. One of them belonged to a detective-inspector with a habit of using the same combination for everything, a combination that he shared with some of his assistants who needed to use the locker. Robin opened the locker, cautioning himself to act normally and not make any moves that might attract attention, and placed the briefcase inside the locker. He had a cover story planned, but it wasn't necessary. People had a habit of assuming that anyone inside a secure perimeter had been cleared to be there. Closing the locker, he walked back out of the compartment and up the stairs to where his allies were waiting. The timer was ticking down the final minutes to zero hour. He took his rifle, pistol and a handful of grenades and led the way to the stairs. They were at the third floor when the building shook, violently. The IED inside the briefcase had detonated and taken out the command centre.

"Come on," he snapped, as they broke into a run. The emergency procedures insisted that everyone had to abandon the lifts and take the stairs, which meant that they would find it harder to get up while everyone else was heading down. He winced as the security alarm started to sound, even though it would add to the confusion. The procedure for security alerts was to remain where you were and wait. Panic would start sweeping the building.

The hardcore of dedicated collaborators were on the twentieth floor; men and women who had completely dedicated themselves to the alien cause. Some of them were intent on their own people, others had tastes they wanted to indulge – tastes that made Robin and his allies sick at the mere thought of such people being allowed out of jail and left free to prey on an innocent population. He kicked open the door and led the way into the first conference room. The collaborators looked up at him in shock, saw the weapons, and started to babble helplessly. Robin pointed his rifle at the closest man, shot him through the head, and then moved onto the next. They would decapitate the entire collaborator government before they were done.

A woman – blonde, with long legs revealed by a very short skirt – ran for the other door. Robin hesitated, but one of the others didn't, putting a bullet in her back. She collapsed, blood leaking onto the carpet, as Robin turned his attention to the remaining collaborators. They were trying to run, or begging for mercy, but it was far too late. They were gunned down and abandoned, left to die like so many of their victims. Robin remembered the guilt and shame he'd felt when he'd served the aliens and refused to feel sorry for them. They'd chosen to serve the aliens and deserved to pay the price.

He kicked open the next door and ran into the office. A personal assistant – one he knew had been hired for her looks rather than her brains – took one look at him and started to scream. Robin ignored her and checked the next room, almost running straight into the Director of Human Resources. He'd always hated Human Resources departments – personnel departments had been much more friendly – but this one had served the aliens, turning humans into their servants. Cleaning the debris one day, burying the dead the next… they'd been shamelessly intent on selling out the entire human race. Robin hit him in the chest, knocked him down and then put a bullet through his head. Behind him, the assistant continued to scream.

All the alarms were going off now, deafening him. The people downstairs would be probably running now, despite security procedures. He headed back to the stairwell and ran up to the top floor, leaving the others behind to finish off the rest of the collaborators. It had once belonged to a rich businessman, but the collaborator-in-chief had taken it over to serve as his living space. God alone knew what had happened to the original owner. Far too many people had gone missing in the chaos since the aliens had landed. He kicked open the door and stormed into the penthouse. It was time for the bastard to pay for his crimes.

<hr>

"What's that noise?"

Alan snorted, rolling over in bed. "I'm not paying you to talk," he sneered, through his yawns. He'd planned a late morning after a night spent enjoying himself with one of the whores his assistants had found for his pleasure. Prostitution was a buyer's market these days, particularly when one had access to real food and drink. The girl was young, barely legal age. Indulging himself with her was a sign that he had truly arrived.

A moment later, the alarms shocked him awake. The emergency panel beside his bed was buzzing, reporting… an explosion? Every alarm seemed to be going off at once, demanding his attention. And had the entire building shook just now? If something had exploded down below, would it bring the entire building down…?

The girl looked over at him. "What's happening?"

She sounded frightened. Alan couldn't really blame her. "This building appears to be under attack," he said, as evenly as he could. Crisis… it was a crisis, but he knew how to deal with a crisis. The secret was to remain calm and alive. Everything else came second. "Get down on the floor and stay there…"

He heard the sound of someone breaking down the door in the next room and swore. If someone was intruding on his privacy, it almost certainly wasn't someone friendly. He'd made the point to his allies time and time again – he wanted his privacy while he slept. Desperately, he tore open the drawer and removed the pistol he'd hidden there, despite the alien edict against human firearms. The door burst open and he swung around, lifting the gun and pulling the trigger. It kicked in his hand, just as the intruder fired at him. There was a brief moment of pain, and then he fell into darkness.

<hr>

Robin hadn't expected Beresford to have a gun. The collaborator's bullet passed through his chest, just above his heart. It felt as if someone had stabbed him with a red hot poker. The pain was so great that he almost fainted, before dropping to his knees and pressing one hand to the wound. Blood was spilling down, warm against his hand – and he knew that he was dead. It hurt to move, but there was no choice. He had to know that Beresford was dead.

Somehow, drawing on his every last ounce of determination, he managed to stagger towards where the collaborator had fallen. Beresford's dead face, twisted with agony, looked back at him. He was barely aware that there was someone else in the room until he saw the naked girl jump up from where she'd been lying and run towards the door. Robin wanted to call out to her, to warn her that she was running right into danger, but his mouth refused to cooperate. The pain was growing stronger and stronger, threatening to drag him down into the same blackness that had swallowed Beresford.

Should have had someone come with you, he thought he heard, at the back of his mind. It seemed to take hours before he managed to sit upright, keeping one hand pressed to his wound. It felt as if the bullet had lodged itself in his body rather than coming out of his back. He could hear the sound of alien weapons in the distance, demanding his attention, yet he was so tired. His other hand reached for his pistol and tried to pull it from his belt, but it refused to come free from where he'd stashed it. It was all he could do to pull one of the grenades free as he heard the sound of heavy footsteps clumping up the stairs.

His vision was starting to blur, but somehow he managed to keep his eyes open until the first alien form lumbered into the room. They'd killed his fellows, then, or forced them to retreat… it hardly mattered. All that mattered was that he was dying – and that he wouldn't die alone. He pulled the pin from the grenade and looked up at the aliens as they advanced on him. They hadn't realised the danger. Perhaps they hadn't even realised that he had turned on them. They'd probably thought of him as a very loyal servant.

He thought, briefly, of his wife. They'd said that she was safe, somewhere to the north. He hoped that she would understand one day, and find happiness with someone else. There was no reason anyone had to know that her husband had been a collaborator, if only for a short period. And besides, he'd turned on the aliens. That had to count for something, didn't it? But that would depend on who wrote the history books. Humans – or Leathernecks? The winners always wrote the history books to please themselves.

"Fuck you," he managed to say, and jerked the grenade free. "Fuck you, you…"

The aliens jumped back, but it was far too late.

Chapter Thirty-Nine

London
United Kingdom, Day 55

"If this fails…"

"It won't," Abdul said. "Have a little faith in your fellow man."

Chris nodded, watching from his vantage point as the alien patrols headed towards their checkpoint. They were very careful with their routines these days, even though he was sure that there was a pattern in their movements. He couldn't blame them for that, or their decision to exclude human vehicles from their bases. The resistance had attempted to capture and drive a handful of alien vehicles, but the experiments hadn't been successful. They'd found the alien vehicles difficult to operate with human drivers.

The alien base loomed over London, a brooding metal shape that mocked humanity's pretensions to historical monuments. They'd built it on the remains of Buckingham Palace, just to illustrate the fact that the Earth belonged to them by right of conquest. Chris had heard that they'd done the same with the White House and the Kremlin, knocking them down to make room for their buildings. Perhaps it made sense from their point of view, rather than waving a red flag in front of the human bull. They'd certainly shown no particular willingness to give a damn about what humans thought. There was a certain blunt honesty in their actions that contrasted oddly with human political thinking. All the politicians who'd talked about not giving offense to people who harboured terrorists intent on killing British troops…

Abdul tapped his shoulder. "The policeman should be moving by now," he said. "Two minutes left. You ready?"

"Yes," Chris said. He glanced back at his team. They looked ready, even though they knew that challenging the aliens on their own base was incredibly dangerous. The aliens might just cut their losses and start dropping rocks from orbit. "Get the Javelin teams into position."

The laptop buzzed once. They'd spliced it into one of the underground telecommunications links that had made up the backbone of the British communications network before the aliens had arrived, using it to link into the internet. The final countdown had begun. All over the world, countless computers were being linked into the alien communications system, attempting to hack into it and bring it down. Chris wasn't sure if he believed any of the more extreme promises, but they should certainly disrupt the alien response. It was all they'd need to get in, hit the bastards and get out again. The final seconds ticked down to zero.

He clicked his radio. "Go," he ordered. The snipers positioned on nearby rooftops opened fire, picking off the aliens within view. Their patrollers fell to the ground or dived for cover, trying to bring their own weapons up to return fire. They'd have some problems spotting the snipers, Chris hoped. "Javelin teams – go!"

The Javelin teams ran forward, taking up position to launch their antitank missiles directly at the alien gates. Chris had seen them used before to take out bunkers and other fortified positions, but as far as he could recall no one had ever used them to take out a gate. The missiles were fired before the aliens had a chance to react, blasting down towards the alien positions and slamming into their heavy gates. Chris watched as the gate he could see personally toppled inwards, squashing a couple of aliens who had been behind it when the attack began. The alien defences had been crippled.

He keyed his radio again. "Mortar teams, go," he ordered. "Fire at will."

The sound of mortars started to echo out over London as the teams opened fire, lobbing shells into the alien base to force the defenders to keep their heads down. Other teams all over London would be assaulting alien patrols, hoping to prevent them from turning and charging to the rescue of their leadership. In the early hours of the invasion, human military and police forces had been badly scattered, their command and control networks broken down and fragmented, leaving them facing their individual nightmares. Now the boot was on the other foot. The aliens were going to have to deal with an unfolding crisis as individuals.

He glanced over at Abdul, who was monitoring the results of the mortar strikes. "Not too bad," he commented. "Shame we couldn't get into the tunnels – we could have popped up right in the midst of them."

Chris shrugged. "Alpha team," he said, picking up his rifle, "go!"

As one, they started to run towards the alien gates, covered by the snipers. Up close, the sound of the mortars was louder. A single shell falling short might take out friendly soldiers, yet there was no time to call off the strikes. No one was entirely sure what the aliens used to build their base, but they did know that it was strong; alien bases across the world had stood off everything from RPGs to guided missiles. They had to keep the aliens penned up while they deployed into position to assault the base itself.

He smiled as he saw a pair of wounded aliens staggering back inside the base, only to be shot down before they could escape. They took cover behind what remained of the gate and glanced around, taking out any remaining aliens outside before they advanced into the base proper. Maybe they'd die without ever knowing what had hit them, but the aliens' faith in their own invincibility was about to suffer one hell of a knock.

"Go," he ordered.

———

Ju'tro Oheghizh had been reading the report from the latest round of interrogations when the attack began. There had been rumours that *something* was being planned, but an attack in the centre of London hadn't been expected. Everyone had known that the aliens and their collaborators controlled the city and attacking their base was merely a way to get encircled, trapped, and then exterminated. But it was clear that the humans hadn't gotten the message. The hooting of the aliens was growing louder, just as the first shells started impacting on the metal shielding.

He lunged towards the command room, expecting to see his officers already reacting to the crisis and summoning assistance from the other garrisons scattered over the city. Instead, the big board had lit up with glowing icons – and then frozen. His officers were trying desperately to reactivate the command network, but it had clearly crashed. Or hacked – the humans were marvels with computer technology. They'd developed entire libraries of tactics for attacking and defending their own computer systems – why wouldn't they be able to come up with something targeted against *his* computer systems?

And if they'd taken down the systems assigned to him, had they taken down everything?

The sound of the human bombardment grew louder. They didn't have a properly-trained computer tech at the base and they couldn't assume that someone who was only familiar with their own systems would be able to fix the damage the humans had inflicted, even if they had had a tech. And that meant that they'd been thrown back on their own resources. The higher commanders had loved the communications systems – it allowed them to supervise operations from on high – but the humans had turned it into a colossal weakness.

"Leave the computers," he ordered. There *were* emergency procedures for computer failure, although he had no idea how many would have the time to implement them if the humans were attacking everywhere. "Get the radios passed out" – unless the humans had managed to set up a jamming system – "and then arm yourselves. This base is under attack."

He picked up a weapon himself to illustrate the point. The command techs were unused to being in danger – they certainly hadn't been on the first drop into London, or on any of the more dangerous landings after the pre-invasion bombardment – but there was no choice. They'd be able to summon help from the bases surrounding London, if they could hold out long enough for help to arrive.

Another explosion shook the base. The command techs, almost on the verge of panic, cried out in shock. "If they had anything that could break through the shield, they'd have used it by now," Oheghizh snarled at them. A nuclear weapon could have broken through – they hadn't been able to account for some of the human tactical weapons, let alone the devices they'd installed on their missile submarines – but the humans had been oddly reluctant to use nuclear weapons against the invaders. Apart from the Chinese… and China was now a wasteland of competing warlords, trying desperately to survive. "Get out of here and down to the inner defence lines. We don't know how long we have until they start breaking in."

———

The first warning of attack had come when the shells started landing inside the base. *U'tra* The'Stig, who had been preparing for the latest sweep against human insurgents, had taken immediate action, ordering the base's own counter-battery weapons to return fire. He didn't realise that the entire command network had been taken down until he'd deployed two Assault Units to sweep the area around the base and capture, kill or drive away the human insurgents. It was only when higher command had failed to take command that he'd discovered the truth.

"Get the radios out," he ordered. He was supposed to direct his units from the mobile command vehicle, but half of its communications functions had been disabled. There was no way of knowing what the humans had done and they didn't have time to try to fix it. The handful of reports they had had before the system failed had warned that the entire network of bases around London had come under attack. "And then prepare for immediate deployment."

For a moment, he found himself lost in indecision. There was clearly a major attack underway, yet he didn't know what was being targeted – which meant he didn't know where he should send his troops. The base itself had only been lightly shelled, but the humans were tricky. It could have been an attempt to force them to stay in the base, a diversion… or merely the prelude to a more intensive bombardment. He'd have to keep shifting his troopers out and hope that the humans hadn't anticipated his actions and taken precautions. There were horror stories from many other bases about deploying their forces in pursuit of human raiders, only to walk right into an ambush that bled them heavily before they fell back.

"I managed to get a radio link to the London Base," one of the techs reported. They'd been working on the radios, the only system they could fall back on if the command network had gone down. "They're under heavy attack. The humans are threatening the base itself."

The'Stig cursed. It was bad enough having the humans gloating over how they'd pulled their people – the ones who were due to be executed – out of the detention camp, but if they managed to take out the central base in London it would give them a major propaganda victory. And if they'd learned better than to try to take prisoners, they'd wipe out the administrative staff – human and alien – who were trying to assimilate the humans into the State. The entire program would be set back weeks, if not months.

"I want us moving in five minutes," he ordered, finally. There was no choice – they had to assume that they were the only ones available to relieve the London Base before it fell. The radio operators still hadn't established contact with half of the nearby bases. The'Stig hoped that the bases had merely had problems establishing their own radio links, but he had to assume the worst. The humans might have taken the bases – and the troopers guarding them – out. It was a horrifying thought. "We need to head into London."

There was a pause. "And get the helicopters up too," he added. "We're going to need air cover."

———

Chris ran to the next piece of cover, heading towards the main entrance to the alien base. A number of aliens had taken up positions just inside, firing towards the humans as they came closer. Their shooting didn't seem to be particularly accurate, but they were definitely forcing Chris and his men to move carefully. He fired twice and then ducked down as a burst of alien bullets nearly took his head off.

Two men ran closer, holding grenades. They pitched them into the alien building and then ducked for cover themselves as the grenades detonated. A number of aliens were caught and wounded by the blasts, but the others kept firing, determined to keep the humans from getting inside. Chris waved to the Javelin team as they reached a position where they could fire directly into the doors, ordering them to take their shot. The missile blasted into the base and exploded, smashing through their defences. A handful of grenades polished off the remaining aliens.

"They're trying to snipe from the windows," his radio buzzed. "Our snipers are sniping back."

Chris nodded as he ran forward, into the wreckage of the alien front door. They'd been paranoid enough to set up firing positions inside, but the grenades had wrecked them. A single alien seemed to still be alive, yet he was so badly wounded that there was nothing anyone could do for them. Chris shot him and led the way forward, into the alien base. He'd crawled through Taliban hideouts before, seeing some of the horrors they unleashed upon their own people, but there was something oddly inhuman about the interior of the alien base. He laughed at himself a moment later. Of course there was something inhuman – it had been built by aliens who needed more space than their human counterparts. Their rooms and doors were far larger than anything a human would build.

There had been no way to get an accurate picture of the base's interior layout, but he headed towards the centre on the assumption that the alien command staff would be in the safest place on the base. The aliens seemed to have vanished, leaving the soldiers glancing nervously from side to side, looking for the next threat. It came in a burst of alien gunfire as the Leathernecks sprang an ambush, taking down two soldiers before they were forced to retreat by Chris and his men. Chris unhooked a grenade from his belt, tossed it into the side room, and headed inside as soon as the grenade had exploded. One alien was dead; the other, somehow, was completely unharmed. His shot missed Chris by bare millimetres. Abdul put three bullets into the alien head, shattering his skull.

One by one, the remaining rooms on the lower level were swept. Some of the rooms were completely bare, with nothing to show what the aliens had done in them. Others were packed with alien equipment, sleeping cots and other gear that was vaguely recognisable. A handful of aliens tried to surrender, but there was no time to take prisoners. All they could do was gun them down. Chris knew that it would bother him later, yet there was no time to worry about it now. They had to keep moving.

"I think this is the way up," one of the soldiers called. He'd kicked down a plastic door, revealing what looked like a bumpy ramp leading upwards. Chris had visions of disabled aliens trying to make their way up the stairs in wheelchairs before realising that the aliens probably found human stairs uncomfortable. There had certainly been some reports of aliens either becoming trapped or simply ignoring the upper floors, although no one had been quite sure why. "There's a blockage at the far end."

Chris smiled. It would have been an effective defence against the aliens, but humans were smaller and nimbler. Grenades cleared the way, allowing them to get up to the second floor and start pushing the aliens back. They didn't seem to be particularly well coordinated, reminding him of the times that headquarters staff had found themselves in contact with the enemy in Afghanistan. They'd found themselves roughly handled by the Taliban. It stood to reason that the aliens had similar people in the rear. He wondered, absently, if they had their own word for REMFs.

He glanced down at his watch as alien bullets snarled overhead. There had been no way to calculate how long it would take before the aliens started sending in reinforcements from the bases outside London. One theory had claimed that the aliens would wait for orders before doing anything – orders which were never going to come. Chris suspected otherwise; some alien commanders were clearly more capable of acting on their own initiative than others. Assuming that they left their base as soon as the attack began… there were too many variables to calculate any likely ETA. They'd just have to assume the worst and push on as fast as they could.

They punched through a plastic wall and came into what looked like a control room, almost comparable to the stations Chris had guarded while on active duty. The aliens fought back savagely, but it was too late. Grenades shattered the room, leaving most of the aliens dead or wounded. The remainder seemed stunned, unable to resist effectively. And one of them was clearly in charge.

———

Oheghizh stared at the human, wondering what the humans would do to him. Did they even know his rank? Probably, he told himself. They'd certainly be able to read the gold buttons and know that he was important. But they'd never be permitted to take him prisoner. The Command Triad would simply repeat the threat of bombarding a human city if he wasn't returned, alive.

Two human soldiers marched him back down the ramp and out towards the open air. There was a brief pause, then one of them produced a black bag and pushed it down over Oheghizh's head. The command network was down, but the satellites would still be watching… and all they would see, he realised in horror, would be a black mass. They wouldn't know he was a prisoner…

He wanted to fight, but it was far too late.

Chapter Forty

London
United Kingdom, Day 55

David Lamb watched the alien convoy making its way through London, led by its tanks. They were clearly out for blood, judging by their response to a handful of pot-shots as they'd entered the city. They'd responded with heavy machine gun fire and even HE shells from their armoured vehicles. But there were only a handful of ways to get into London and head to Buckingham Palace, at least if they wanted to get there directly. They pretty much *had* to come this way.

He smiled as he reached for the detonator. The aliens had killed millions of humans, without remorse; they probably didn't know that they'd killed Carol Lamb, wife of David, or their son Thomas. But David knew. He'd been wanting to fight ever since he'd discovered that his family had been caught up in the invasion and cut down in the crossfire. The resistance had trained him and given him a vital role in the counterattack. He had no intention of fucking up and failing to kill as many aliens as he could before they finally killed him. The alien tanks slowed as they spotted the plates they'd left on the road – they looked like mines, if someone was feeling paranoid – and started to move around them. David pushed down on the detonator and braced himself.

The entire world seemed to explode. They'd placed explosive under the road, in two parked cars and in buildings facing the alien position. The blast was terrifyingly loud and the building he was using as a lookout point rocked alarmingly. To the aliens, caught up in the blast, it had to look like a foretaste of the hell awaiting them when they died. He couldn't hear anything through the ringing in his ears as he pulled himself up and staggered towards the fire escape, knowing that the aliens were likely to be ready to murder any human they encountered – assuming that some of the aliens had survived the blast. Someone had definitely survived. He saw a flash of tracer pouring up into the air, but there was no way of telling if humans or aliens had fired the shot.

He saw something moving out of the corner of his eye and turned to see a pair of alien helicopters, moving rapidly towards the billowing cloud of smoke. They were shooting down towards the ground, aiming at resistance fighters – or maybe civilians who had been caught up in the battle. A missile rose up from the ground and slammed into one of the helicopters, sending it spinning over and down into the ground, where it vanished in a colossal explosion. The second helicopter climbed higher, all the while firing rockets down towards where the missile had come from. David took one final look, knowing that the aliens would never feel safe again in a human city, and then hurried down the stairs to safety. He'd been warned not to linger.

———

The shock of the explosion was so powerful that it nearly destroyed the command vehicle, despite the heavy armour that should have protected it from harm. The'Stig cursed as the vehicle spun around on its hover-cushion, almost crashing into one of the other vehicles in the convoy. Judging from what little he'd seen, the blast had almost certainly taken out four tanks, the vehicles he'd placed at the front to deter any humans from ambushing his force. He'd put them out there to be slaughtered.

There was no time to curse his own mistake. The humans were firing down at the convoy from all directions. Bullets were pinging off the command vehicle's armour, while the troopers in the troop transports had to dismount to seek cover before their vehicles were ripped apart by the human assault. Hundreds of mortar shells seemed to be crashing around them, trapping them in a killing zone. The air cover he'd ordered should be able to deal with the mortars, if the humans hadn't brought antiaircraft

missiles along to the ambush. They'd probably anticipated that he'd bring his helicopters with him.

"Order the tanks to return fire indiscriminately," he ordered. He'd set out to relieve London Base before it fell, but it looked as if he was going to have to cut his way out of the ambush first. The rear of the convoy was in chaos. One of the tanks had ploughed into a troop transport and ground to a halt. The surviving troopers had managed to dismount and start providing cover for the tanker as he tried to get his vehicle back into operation. "Tell them to clear the streets."

The tanks swung their main guns around and started firing shells into the surrounding buildings. Mighty explosions sent human buildings toppling to the ground, hopefully trapping and killing human ambushers before they could escape. The'Stig had only a moment to register the fact that one of his helicopters had gone down before the second one came under heavy fire from a hidden machine gun and had to break off, trailing smoke as it limped back out of the city. The radio kept buzzing with scraps of isolated chatter, but all his attempts to raise the fighter jet bases outside the city failed. It didn't take much imagination to realise that the humans might have taken out the bases, or at least forced them to keep their jets under cover.

"Start moving back," he ordered the rear units, as the human fire started to slack off. There was no point in trying to push ahead, even though the hover-cushions could probably allow the tanks to get over the rubble. The humans might have anticipated that and set up a second ambush, firing straight into the tanks vulnerable undersides. "Move the troopers to cover the tanks as they head back."

He glanced down at the map. Without the command network, it was far harder to coordinate his operations, which gave the humans an advantage. There were other routes to London Base, but if they were also mined… they might walk right into a second trap. The humans had clearly set out to delay them and they'd succeeded admirably.

But if he failed to get to London Base in time, the humans would inflict disastrous damage on the occupation force…

———

"Ned, Eccles," Chris's radio snapped. "The pig is in the poke."

Chris nodded. The first alien attempt to relieve their base had been ambushed, but the aliens could presumably shoot their way out of the trap. They had enough firepower to break through, or fall back and try to get to London via a different route.

"Start spraying," he ordered. There hadn't really been time to pull any papers or documents out of the command base, but they'd certainly ensure that nothing was left for the aliens to recover. Each of the soldiers carried a flask containing an extremely flammable liquid. Sprayed over the aliens, it would ensure that very little was left – and conceal the fact that the resistance had taken a second high-ranking prisoner. "Everyone else, start falling back to the city."

He finished emptying his own flask, tossed a detonator into the centre of the alien command room, and then waved for Abdul to precede him back down the alien ramp and into the lower levels. The sound of firing in the distance was growing louder, although there was no sign of any alien aircraft. They'd based antiaircraft teams throughout the city on the assumption that anything flying would be hostile and they'd clearly forced the alien aircraft to keep their distance.

"Not a bad day's work," Abdul said, as they made it outside. There were small fires burning throughout the remains of the alien base, with hundreds of dead alien bodies scattered around, waiting for the aliens to recover them. The human bodies had already been dragged away to where they would be buried. There would be time for a proper ceremony later. "I think we taught them a lesson."

Chris smiled, counting the men out as they left the remains of the alien building. Once everyone was confirmed as having left, he pushed down on the remote control, triggering the detonator he'd left behind in the alien control room. The flames would rapidly destroy the equipment and records as well as most of the DNA traces, making it almost impossible for the aliens to be certain of who'd been in the chamber when the fire started. They'd never know that they'd lost a high-ranking prisoner, not this time. And who knew what he could tell the human race?

The main body of the base would survive – he doubted fire would melt the material they'd used to build it – but it would be a blackened shell. Humans all over the world would take new hope from the story, as they would from all the other stories. The global counteroffensive would have hurt the aliens badly. Maybe, just maybe, they'd hurt the aliens badly enough to convince them to retreat and leave Earth alone.

He keyed his radio one final time, sending the signal to retreat, and then turned it off. It was time to make themselves scarce.

"Impressive," Abdul muttered.

Chris followed his gaze. Great plumes of smoke were rising up over London, revealing where resistance fighters had mounted attacks on the police and the other collaborators, as well as a handful coming from alien bases outside the city. He'd only known snippets of the overall plan, but it was clear that they'd hammered the aliens hard. God alone knew how many Leathernecks had died in the last few hours.

"Yeah," he said. "That's something they can take for granted. Humans don't ever give up."

———

Battered bloody, the remains of The'Stig's force finally broke through the human resistance and reached London Base. It was already too late. The base was a broken ruin, flames licking out through portholes that had been intended to allow the defenders to fire out at human opponents. There seemed to be no living thing left alive, not even the small collection of animals some of the command staff had kept as pets, despite edicts against it. Some humans – the Russians, in particular – were very good at using pets and other trained animals to take out tanks and other armoured vehicles.

He dismounted from the command vehicle and stared at the devastation. The entire base would need to be torn down and rebuilt from scratch. He cursed the humans as he realised that they'd wiped out vast quantities of equipment, all of which would need to be replaced from the homeworld. With all the other demands on the homeworld's resources, it was possible that they'd decide to slow Earth's progress into becoming part of the State. The humans would have a chance to prepare themselves for the next round of fighting, and the next.

The human collaborator government had been totally destroyed. Somehow, the humans had sneaked explosives and insurgents into the building – perhaps through using some collaborators who hadn't really decided to collaborate. They searched the remains of the human building as best as they could, but found that almost all of the senior collaborators were dead. It was clear that they'd been shot down by the insurgents in cold blood. The destruction of most of the records would make it much harder to be sure of who was still alive, or of who could be trusted. Personally, he wouldn't have trusted *any* human. They were a shifty treacherous race. Even their collaborators had been treacherous.

There was no sign of any living human. They'd done the smart thing and made themselves scarce. The'Stig couldn't blame them, not really. His troopers were in a murderous mood, intent on taking it out on the first group of humans that they encountered. Their city almost felt deserted, even though he knew that it was an illusion. The gunfire he could hear in the distance proved that some humans had been left alive.

"I managed to get a link to the Command Triad," his aide called. "The command network has been crippled, but they've managed to clear some functions."

The'Stig nodded and made his slow way back to the command vehicle. The Command Triad would not be pleased. Someone was likely to take the fall for everything that had happened to the Conquest Force. He wondered,

mordantly, if they'd try to blame him. It was possible, although almost unthinkable, that he was the senior surviving officer in Britain.

But that couldn't be true, could it?

———

"I think they've probably got their network back up now," Abdul said, as they gathered in the estate after the battle. "They've certainly been coordinating the forces they've been moving around the city more effectively."

Chris nodded. The Leathernecks hadn't been shy about re-establishing order, even though their collaborators had been killed or forced to flee. It would take them weeks to calm London down, weeks before they started rebuilding the collaborator government. Assuming, of course, that they could find anyone willing to become collaborator-in-chief. The last one had been gunned down by a policeman who was supposed to be loyal to the new government.

The reports on the internet kept changing, but it certainly looked as if Operation Hammer had been a success. They'd hit the Leathernecks all over the world, despite problems with international communications; the Leathernecks had to be badly shocked by the experience. The PM and several other world leaders, hiding out, had already uploaded messages of congratulations to the fighting men. Some of the soldiers had been contemptuous of the PM remaining in hiding, but Chris had reminded them that the aliens wanted him dead – or alive, serving as a collaborator. They needed to keep the PM alive and free. Defeating the aliens was all that mattered. The Leathernecks wouldn't give up easily, but they had been hurt. They knew they'd been hit hard…

And if they didn't know that they'd lost a senior officer…Chris smiled at the thought, before realising that getting the prisoner out of London would be difficult. The Leathernecks were searching lorries, they'd never be able to get him down the tunnels… maybe they could float him out on a boat. He had a brief mental vision of a submarine slipping up the Thames before realising that it was absurd. After the Americans had lost a submarine when it came too close to the surface what remained of the Royal Navy wouldn't take the risk. They'd need to find a boat to get the prisoner out.

Standing up, he headed outside and walked down the stairs to the basement. The estate, like many others in East London, had once had a gang in effective control, before the resistance had moved in and taught the gangs what *real* organised violence was all about. Now, it was guarded by soldiers in plain clothes, watching against collaborators and alien spies. They had no hope of stopping the aliens destroying the base if they discovered its existence, but there would be time to destroy the computers and escape.

The alien prisoner was held in the basement, guarded by three soldiers. Like the previous alien prisoner, he had been stripped of everything that might have carried a transponder, but his living quarters weren't so good. They didn't have the equipment to make it as hot or humid as the alien would probably have preferred. Chris looked through the window set into the door and scowled. The alien looked thoroughly miserable. It was dangerous to ascribe human thoughts and feelings to the Leathernecks – they weren't even sure what an alien smile or frown *looked* like – but he was fairly sure of his ground. The alien looked very unhappy.

Chris opened the door and stepped inside. The alien looked up at him, his dark eyes seemingly expressionless. Maybe the alien was hungry. All the experts claimed that the aliens could eat human foods – they wouldn't want Earth if they couldn't – but he hadn't touched the food he'd been given. Perhaps he was trying to starve himself to death.

"You do realise that they will come for me?" The alien said. He had to repeat himself twice before Chris understood. His English, spoken through an inhuman mouth, was mushy. "You won't be allowed to keep me."

"They don't know we have you," Chris said. The aliens had certainly not demanded his return. But then, they'd said almost nothing to humanity since Operation Hammer. "And even if they did, there's one thing about humanity that you folks need to understand."

The alien looked over at the wall. "What?"

"We don't give up," Chris said. "We will keep fighting until we're free."

The alien said nothing.

Chapter Forty-One

Deep Space
Day 70

"Don't try to move," a feminine voice said. "You've had a nasty shock."

Gavin opened his eyes. He saw a young woman, wearing a shapeless tunic, bending over him. It was so unexpected that he was almost convinced that he was in heaven. And then he remembered… the aliens had attacked, they'd run… and something had knocked him over and out. He was a prisoner. There was no other explanation.

"Lie still," the woman said. "It takes a moment for your body to adapt to the change in the environment. You'll be on your feet in no time."

She pushed something to his neck before he could object. He felt a brief stab of pain, almost as if he'd been pricked with a needle, and guessed that he'd been injected with something. A truth drug? Something to make him pliable? If the Leathernecks knew who he was, they'd want to interrogate him – and he knew what they did to make people talk. He just hoped he could hold out long enough for his men to scatter, assuming they knew that he'd been captured. The chaos as they'd retreated from Haddon Hall meant that they might not realise that the aliens had taken him alive. Not even the Leathernecks could get answers out of a dead man.

He tried to sit up, only to feel his head spinning. There was something subtly *wrong* about the environment. The young woman put a hand around his shoulder and helped him to stand upright. He had it a moment later, even though he'd never experienced anything like it in his entire life. The gravity in the compartment was barely two-thirds of Earth's gravity. Some of the scientists had speculated that the Leathernecks came from a world that had a significantly lower gravitational field than Earth, he recalled, but he had dismissed it at the time. The Leathernecks were so much stronger than the average human that he suspected it was the other way around.

"Who…" His throat hurt. He had to swallow hard before he could finish the sentence. "Who are you?"

"Sharon Cordova, US Navy Corpsman," she said, briskly. "I was a medic before the invasion, which is why they put me in here." She shrugged. "You seem to have come through the suspension process unharmed. Some guys swear blind that they remained aware even though they were floating in a stasis field."

Gavin stared at her, confused. She smiled at him. "If you're feeling better, I have someone you need to meet."

"One moment," Gavin said. The gravity wasn't the only odd thing about their environment. He could feel a faint queasiness in the back of his mind, hear a constant thrumming just loud enough to be on the edge of perception. "Are we prisoners?"

Sharon grinned. "Not exactly," she said, as she helped him towards the door. It opened as they approached, revealing a compartment large enough for a small party of Leathernecks. "Like I said, I have someone you need to meet."

Gavin walked through the door and stopped dead, unable to believe his eyes. The Leathernecks were humanoid, if not human. Some of the scientists had speculated that humanoid was evolution's default form, suggesting that all the old TV shows with humanoid aliens might have had a point after all. But… the alien in front of him was anything, but humanoid. A great mass of orange-gold tentacles, constantly spinning around the central egg-shaped mass… his mind almost refused to grasp its existence. The body – he assumed it was the alien's body – seemed featureless. There were no eyes, no mouth… no way of deducing how the alien collected data about its environment. Merely looking at it made him dizzy. It seemed to be incapable of remaining motionless.

"This is Protector Hank," Sharon said. She had the grace to look embarrassed. "They don't have names, not like us – we had to call him something."

"I am very pleased to meet you," Hank said. Its voice seemed to come from a small device hanging below the central body. The alien certainly sounded a great deal more natural than anything the Leathernecks had ever produced. "We have a great deal to talk about."

"I think I need to sit down," Gavin said. "And perhaps something to eat."

"Certainly," Hank said. The alien didn't need to turn; it just started wobbling its way down the corridor. Gavin wondered if the alien had had its back to him, before realising that 'front' and 'back' probably meant little to the aliens. They could head in any direction they liked without turning, leaving him wondering how they saw. Some form of mental vision? A sense of perception? Or maybe they saw through their tentacles. "We have become accustomed to feeding humans over the last few weeks."

———

"They captured me in Missouri," Sharon explained, twenty minutes later. They were seated around a table that had clearly been designed for humans, rather than Leathernecks… or Hank's race. "We had a base camp for wounded there – somehow, they discovered our location and raided us, rather than dropping a hammer on our heads. They took us off-world, loaded us into suspension pods… and the next thing we knew, the Leatherneck ship had been captured by our new friends. I think they'd been lurking around Earth for the past few months, waiting for a chance to stick a spanner in the works."

"That is correct," Hank said. "We took advantage of the remoteness of your planet to cause one of their ships to go missing. They will not understand what has happened until it is far too late."

Gavin stared at the alien. "You mean to say you did nothing while they invaded our world?"

"You misunderstand the nature of interstellar travel and communications," Hank informed him. "It can take months to travel between stars. By the time we discovered that the Leathernecks had found you, it was already too late to intervene – they had already dispatched the Conquest Force. There was nothing we could do, but watch and wait for an opportunity to act."

There was a long pause. "We first encountered them roughly two hundred of your years ago," Hank added. "It was hate at first sight. We spent fifty years fighting them before coming to a reluctant agreement that neither of us were likely to win outright. The victor in the conflict would be badly weakened, while the loser would be pushed to the brink of extermination. And that would have… consequences. We made a truce with them. Since then, both of us have been pushing out as far as we can, attempting to gain a decisive advantage before the war resumes. Your world was invaded and occupied as part of that process."

"They want to add our technology to their own," Gavin said, softly. "And start using us as expendable fighters too…"

"They tend to think in terms of brute force," Hank observed. "Their socio-political development led not to the victory of capitalism, as on your world, but a fascist state that managed to overcome many of the flaws that threatened to bring it crashing down. They were quite successful at absorbing the rebels, the thinkers, into their system. Those who might point out that the Emperor has no clothes, to use one of your world's sayings, end up supporting the State."

"You seem to know us very well," Gavin observed.

"We have… sources within the Leatherneck State," Hank said. "They collected a great mass of data on your world's society, even if much of it made little sense to their researchers."

Gavin smiled. "People who realise that the Emperor has no clothes?"

The alien didn't bother to deny it. "Unfortunately, their traditional way of coping with the universe – brute force – has given them an advantage over you," it said. "You barely started to exploit space – they had massive space stations in orbit within twenty years of developing rocket technology. From there, they eventually cracked the secrets behind warp drive – and they did it with computers inferior to yours.

"There is some speculation that someone else gave them a hand," Hank added, "but there has never been any proof of outside interference. Your world's history should inform you that predicting technological development is a difficult task. The Leathernecks approach problems from a different angle to your own race, but that doesn't make them stupid. They have already crushed your world."

"Yes," Gavin said, flatly. "Are you going to destroy their ships in orbit?"

"An open act of war would restart the conflict," Hank said. "We would prefer to avoid outright conflict before we were ready to win."

"You captured one of their ships," Gavin pointed out. "Isn't that an act of war?"

A human would have smirked. "Not if the Leathernecks never find out what happened to their ship," Hank countered. "And they won't. Ships go missing all the time."

"Maybe the Leathernecks are capturing your ships," Gavin said, dryly.

"It's possible," Hank agreed. He didn't sound particularly concerned. "Both sides have been pushing the truce to the limits."

"Right," Gavin said. "So… what are you going to do to help?"

"Provide you with support," Hank said. "Provide you with weapons. Provide you with tools you can use against your alien overlords. Help you to recover your world."

"And you'd get an ally for the coming war," Gavin said. He couldn't say no. Whatever had happened back on Earth, they needed help if they were to kick the Leathernecks off the planet. "When do we start?"

Hank's tentacles seemed to slow, just for a second. "How about now?"

End of Part One

The Story Will Continue In:

The Devil and the Deep Blue Sea

FALLEN WITNESS

— Vision III: The Huygens Gap Incident —

Art: Andy Bigwood
Words: Tim C. Taylor

"We had learned whom we faced and their approximate location," says the third fallen witness, after identifying herself as Spacer Ramilly Cutts, "but that wasn't nearly enough."

She grimaces, as she always does at this point. The preparations for war back in Sol System were humanity's greatest endeavor, but she was about to skip past nearly all of that in favor of the drama to come. Only the Huygens Gap Incident is deemed exciting enough by her superiors to mention in any detail.

"Two principle problems faced the combined fleet," she says, wishing she could expand her list. "One. How to locate the main enemy force and draw them into battle. Two. How to solve the problem of the limited weapons traverse of the human fleet. It was the genius of Admiral Nwosu of the Pan-African Squadron who devised the solution."

A hand shoots up from one of the children.

Cutts acknowledges the query with a nod.

"Why didn't our ships use turrets? Then they could aim wherever they needed."

There is a titter of amusement from the other children, which Cutts crushes when she answers: "A very good question. Thank you for showing more intelligence than anyone else here. Why no turrets? In fact, there *were* turrets on the Warspite-class ships, and they played a vital role. But the turrets carried conventional weapons, and while they could damage enemy ships, they couldn't kill the energy wraiths themselves. Each federated nation designed their own weapons that do that job, and each of them came up with weapons the size of the warships that carried them. Or larger. The North Americans had their energy whip. The Pan-Africans had spine-mounted railguns that shot a wide spray of tactical nukes. As for the Russians, they had the largest weapon of all. Four Russian warships would lock together into a square formation that formed an interior skein of disrupted space-time. A fifth ship positioned behind this square would fire dark energy torpedoes that picked up the exotic material of the skein and delivered it to the target."

Her answer seems to satisfy the questioner.

"The Royal Navy's Warspite-class ships had the same problem. In order to aim the Death Beat, the ships – each massing over a thousand tons – had to maneuver until their prows pointed at the target. And do you think the enemy would politely keep still while we aimed our main weapons at them?"

The children laugh, and Cutts feels relief that she isn't losing her audience's attention.

"Admiral Nwosu's solution to both problems was to use bait. At first she wanted to use *Speedbird* with her cargo of trapped energy wraiths as the lure, with the unwieldy weapons of the Grand Fleet lined up on the old ship. But *Speedbird* had been so damaged by her encounter with the energy wraiths that she was in no state to ever leave Sol System again. In *Speedbird's* place one of the Warspite-class ships, HMS *Brilliant*, was modified to power a huge energy dish, which would serve as a new prison for the energy wraiths. The prisoner transfer was going to be incredibly risky, and so the Admiralty set a trap. You can see it in this image if you look close enough."

Cutts waits for the children to see the trap. Of course, none of them do.

"Here you can see HMS *Brilliant* inside the spectacularly beautiful ring system around the planet Saturn. The rings are mostly made from water ice, and you can see the ice piling up on the edge of one ring like snow piles on the side of a road in winter. Rather than snow plows clearing a road, it is the gravitational disruption caused by Saturn's many moons and moonlets that piles up the ice and carves gaps in the rings, such as the Huygens Gap where HMS *Brilliant* is pictured. Saturn's rings are fascinating to see with your own eyes. They look fixed in the image, but they are resonating like the plucked string of a musical instrument, and the piles of ice are often miles high. Plenty big enough to conceal a trap. Several of them, in fact. The traps were called Q-Platforms, artificial ice mountains, each of which concealed an energy ring similar to *Speedbird's* but producing a more directional field."

A shiver runs down Cutts' back. They only had one chance to transfer the wraiths, and that meant every Q-Platform had a human weapons team on hand to operate the energy ring failsafes in case the automatic firing systems did not operate correctly. They were deployed inside the ice, and died there.

"The trap was set. As she passed the Q-Platforms, *Speedbird* would turn off her energy ring. The energy wraiths would emerge, but would immediately be caught in *Brilliant's* energy dish. As the wraiths fought to free themselves, the Q-Platforms would emerge behind them and pulse their energy beams in a way that would drive the wraiths into the dish, which would then close around them, trapping the bait inside forever. That was the hope, in any case. As a last line of defense, the entire Grand Fleet was at hand with their prototype weapons to blast the energy wraiths should they escape. What could possibly go wrong?" Cutts let out a mournful sigh. "Everything."

Fallen Witness Vision IV is on p313

C.R.O.W.

—Book 1 of the Union Series —

Phillip Richards

Language: UK English Edition

COMBAT REPLACEMENT OF WAR

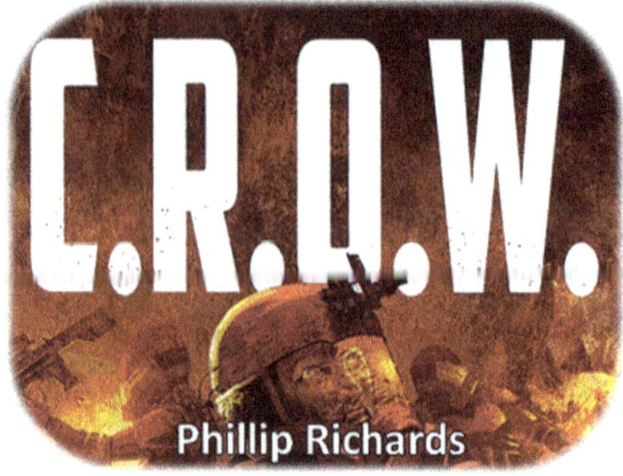

The Author

Phillip Richards was born and raised in Chichester, south England. He joined the Infantry at the age of seventeen, where he has remained ever since. During his service he has taken part in two operational tours in Kosovo, four in Iraq and a further two in Afghanistan. He is now a Sergeant, and this is his first science fiction novel, which has been significantly influenced by his experience within the Army. This story and all of the characters within it are entirely fictional, however, so if you know him and think that you recognise yourself for good or bad reasons, you are mistaken!

Acknowledgements

Thank you to Panagiotis Vlamis, 'Weaselpa', for producing the exceptional artwork for my cover. It has been a joy to work with you.

Thank you, mum, for reading and finding all the silly errors in my work that I hadn't noticed!

Thank you especially to my wife, for her support over the last few years. You stood beside me during my darkest hour time and time again. When I walked through the valley of the shadow of death, it was you who walked with me.

Lastly, and so very importantly, thank you to all of those who I have had the honour of serving with, who made me laugh when I should have cried, who kept me alive when I should have died. It is because of you that I am here to write this book.

'War is delightful to those who have no experience of it.'
– Desiderius Erasmus

1: The Drop

You can't ever be fully prepared for your first drop. You can train in simulators, practice drills for hours on end and sit in a million classroom lessons, but nothing ever comes close to the real thing.

I still remember my first drop, clear as day, from high above the atmosphere of Uralis, home of the Infantry. I remember wondering if it really was necessary that I had to be strapped in so tightly, I remember the nausea I felt when the troopship disengaged her artificial gravity ready for release, and I remember the intense anticipation of what lay ahead. But most of all I remember the fear, a fear so powerful it felt as though a storm raged within my bowels. I feared the unknown - for there were no windows in a dropship - its designers had decided that it was better for us that we couldn't see out, and so all I could do was imagine what was going on outside the tiny eight-man crew compartment. A million questions raced through my mind; what would it feel like to fall from space? Would the landing be hard? Would I be sick and look like a coward in front of my mates? Would I even survive the drop at all? Even in training, the odd mishap was inevitable. And mishaps at speeds I could barely imagine all came to the same obvious conclusion.

Of course I survived that drop, and the many that would follow it during an intensive final exercise that lasted several weeks.

But this time was different.

A bead of sweat ran down my forehead and slowly made its way down my nose. You would think, with all the millions of Euros it had cost to make a single dropship, and with all the technological wizardry that my section commander in training could only describe with a shrug, that it would be capable of keeping its human cargo cool.

'Just be glad you're not melting, the engine works at over five hundred degrees, and its right above you.' A loadee flicked his head upward as he checked our straps were secure. Nobody answered, but I knew we were all thinking the same thing … *Cheers for that bit of useless information, mate!*

The loadee walked between our two rows of seats, double checking that we were fastened tightly enough by tugging roughly at the straps across our chests. His white naval uniform contrasted starkly against our blood red combats, designed to camouflage us once we landed on the surface of New Earth. He wouldn't be dropping with us; he would stay on board Challenger and face the enemy in orbit. I listened intently as he went to speak to my section commander, who was sat beside me at the rear of the compartment, closest to the ramp exit.

'Remember, listen to the intercom and …'

My section commander waved the loadee silent. 'I know the score, mate, cheers.' One word from Corporal Evans was enough to stop a man in his tracks. His voice boomed with authority, and his words carried a confidence that could lead young men into the gaping jaws of hell itself. Corporal Evans was a giant of a man, at least half a foot taller than me, with broad shoulders and a chiselled jaw. The platoon worshipped him as a god, he was one of the few veterans left of the war on Eden, and had completed several combat drops during his ten-year service, including one on New Earth two years ago during the infamous Betrayal. I wondered what he thought about returning to the war torn Alpha Centauri system once again, but as ever, his hard eyes betrayed nothing.

The loadee nodded and left the compartment, and as he did so the rear ramp raised. We peered through the closing gap as our home - or what we had almost come to call home - disappeared for the last time. Challenger was one of the countless troopships sent through the stars to wage war on the Union's mortal enemy. It had been a hell for me, but it couldn't be anything worse than what was in store for us all kilometres below. The door closed with a loud dull thud, like the door to a tomb. We might die inside our tiny compartment, we all knew it. Everyone knew the statistics. Only two in three made it down. An electrical hum sounded somewhere above us, which I assumed meant the engines were warming up or something.

'Check your kit, lads, you won't get another chance,' Corporal Evans ordered.

All eight of us checked over ourselves. We had already done so a hundred times already, but there was a simple saying in drops: *'Check, check and check again, because you can't check when you're dead.'*

I went over my kit like a drill. I always checked my respirator first, because there wasn't much use in me having a rifle that was loaded and comms that worked if I was choking to death. New Earth's atmosphere was a toxic mixture of chemicals that could kill a man breathing unaided in a couple of minutes.

I placed the respirator over my face and looked through the visor. An amazing piece of equipment, the respirator visor was an advanced targeting system, and could give me a near perfect image by night. A microphone was built into the mouthpiece, as well as a headset that could receive transmissions from my section and protect me from noises that might otherwise deafen me.

The next most important thing to check was my personal weapon, which in my case was the MSG-20. The staple weapon of the armies of the Union, the MSG-20 had been in service long before I joined up. It was a super high velocity weapon system which used a series of magnets to drive steel darts sharpened at a molecular level to supersonic speeds. They could punch through armour and flesh at ranges of up to two kilometres, depending how good a shot you were, of course. The weapon could communicate with my visor display via a wire that ran up my sleeve, which allowed me to fire without the need to look along the length of the barrel to aim, although the weapon was said to be far more accurate fired from the shoulder. In addition rounds could be angled as they left the barrel by the magnets to effectively 'steer' them towards targets identified by my visor, thereby correcting my aim.

I checked my rifle was fastened into its rack beside me securely, so that it didn't bounce around the cabin as we dropped, breaking every bone in our bodies. I then checked its battery still read 'full'. It would last for days of constant battle before it would lose its charge.

I checked my magazine pouches. I carried ten magazines around my waist, with two on my weapon. Each held a total of sixty-five darts, which gave me a grand total of seven hundred and eighty; enough for me to fight a small war by myself, I liked to think. I also carried a belt of six grenades which were strapped to my body, as well as an assortment of smoke grenades, flares and anti-personnel mines that I carried in the daysack strapped to my back.

I finished off by checking myself, making sure everything was secured correctly, pouches were clipped shut, my water pack was full and my helmet was ready to put on when ordered. Satisfied, I sat back and waited for the others to finish.

It was waiting that made it worse. If I had something to focus my mind on I found that I could almost forget what was going on around me, and I wouldn't be afraid. But as soon as I stopped, my mind raced and my heart pounded against my rib cage: I was so scared I wanted to be sick.

Corporal Evans appeared to know that we needed to be kept busy. 'Let's do a quick comms check again then, lads.'

We made sure our respirator earpieces were seated properly over our ears.

'One at a time, then,' Corporal Evans called each of our names over our section intercom.

'Moralee.' That was me: Private Andrew Moralee, a new recruit fresh out the factory by a few months.

I stiffened by instinct. 'Corporal!'

'Berezynsky.'

'Corporal!' Tony Berezynsky was sat across from me. He'd joined not long before I did, plucked out of the slums of southern England as the colonial wars intensified. Like me he was a young nineteen-year-old trooper of average build and height, with boyish features. I didn't know much about him except that he was a quiet lad who kept himself to himself, still trying to find his place within the section.

'Climpson.'

'Corporal!'

Climo was senior to me and Berezynsky by a year. He was still barely twenty, but his small build hid a ferocious temper that had earned him respect as one of the most dangerous men in the platoon. I wouldn't pick a fight with him, that was for sure, but fortunately for me he was a friend who had stood by me - at great cost to himself. Although he hadn't experienced combat, his reputation had landed him with the MAM-G, or 'Mammoth' as we called it, for its brutish size. It was essentially a much larger version of the MSG-20, capable of far greater rates of fire at similar ranges. The funny thing about heavy weapons is that everyone wanted to fire them, but nobody wanted to carry them. Even though it was seen as a privilege and a mark of respect in a trooper's ability to carry such a weapon, Climo and many others would still grumble about it. In his case it had been given to him as a punishment for violence, which had already seen him do time in Challenger's claustrophobic brig.

'Brown.'

'Corporal!' Brown, heavily tattooed and muscular in build had landed himself the MAM-G like Climo due to his growing seniority in the platoon and his reputation of being one of the tougher - though by far not the toughest - members of the platoon. Unusually, I think he actually really liked carrying it. It was a symbol of status amongst the blokes, you didn't give the support weapons to any common idiot, and Brown was one of those troopers who desperately wanted to climb the platoon ladder to become a 'senior private', the first step to becoming a Non-Commissioned Officer; NCO. I didn't like Brown, and he had made it blatantly obvious that he didn't like me either, and he especially hated Climo for humiliating him days before and almost leaving him in hospital.

'Rawson.'

'Yeah.' Michael Rawson had served for several years, and had completed a couple of drops during the Eden campaign. In his mid-twenties, he was ready for promotion, but had been taken away from his promotion course on Uralis to join us in the fight for New Earth. He was essentially a lance corporal in waiting, and because of this he carried an automatic grenade launcher attached to the underside of his rifle. A trooper had to really know what he was doing in order to use such a weapon effectively, and *not* kill all his mates with a badly launched grenade. Mike was the section joker, always good for a laugh, and although he had never been friendly with me - no senior trooper was ever friendly to a new bloke or 'crow' as they were known - he had never given me any trouble.

The last of the privates to be called was Chase, another lance corporal in waiting, affectionately known as 'Chase the Face' for his extraordinary good looks. Supposedly he could leave Uralian women weak at the knees without even removing his respirator! He also carried a grenade launcher, and had been attached to the section after another senior trooper, a bully named Woody (who had tormented me since arriving to the platoon), had been beaten half to death in the last few days of our voyage.

'Joe, you got me?'

Lance Corporal Joe Mac was a massively muscular man in his mid-twenties with a big nose and so many tattoos I'm surprised he hadn't died from ink poisoning. He gave Corporal Evans a thumbs-up from where he sat furthest from the rear door. He was the section second in command. My section, like every other was divided into two fire teams, Charlie fire team commanded by Corporal Evans and Delta fire team commanded by Joe Mac. Overall control still went to Corporal Evans though. Joe Mac also dealt with ammunition resupply, casualty evacuation and the general administration of the section both in and out of combat. When Corporal Evans came up with a plan, it was Joe who enforced it and made it happen. Being section second in command was no easy task, plus if Corporal Evans took a dart, he would step up to take command. I hoped that would not be necessary.

We all removed our respirators after the comms check; we always kept them off until the last safe moment. They weren't particularly uncomfortable, but I'd still rather not wear mine if I had the chance. I wiped more sweat from my brow with a gloved hand.

'Right then, lads.' Corporal Evans spoke in his powerful voice, instantly seizing our attention. He was listening to the intercom through his respirator earpiece, something that only the section commander could do. It was so that he could tell us only what we needed to hear and leave out irrelevant information about the bigger battle that might confuse us - apparently. I suspected the real reason was probably so that he could keep us from hearing bad news like a fellow being shot down on entry. 'We've got a few minutes

until we drop. Challenger is already preparing for entry into New Earth orbit. The fleet vanguard has encountered heavy resistance in the northern hemisphere, but is already reporting success, so with any luck, we should be pretty safe until we enter the atmosphere.'

At that moment I imagined our troopship Challenger and the rest of the fleet, painted black as space itself, soaring toward the planet New Earth at incredible speeds. I imagined the epic battle being fought between the two great navies of the Union and the Chinese somewhere ahead of us. I imagined stricken ships belching gases in their last throes of death as they hurtled down into the atmosphere of New Earth, and then I imagined others, powerless, drifting out into space all alone in the dark. I shook off the thought.

'Lads, this is it.' Corporal Evans met our gaze one at a time as he looked around the crew compartment. 'I'm not a big man for speeches. All I'm gonna say is do what you've been taught, do as you're told, by me or the senior toms.' He was looking to me and Tony when he said that, we were the newest members of the section. 'Do that and you will get out of this alive. When we hit the deck, as soon as your seatbelt undoes itself you debus. You run into cover and then you fire. You keep firing until I give you a fire control order. Understand?'

'Yes, Corporal!'

A voice uttered something unintelligible from Corporal Evans's respirators, and I knew it would be the pilot on the intercom. He held it close to his ear, his face an expressionless mask. I wondered what he was being told. Something clicked from within the dropship and the electrical hum was then accompanied by a high pitched whirr that increased in noise and pitch, growing louder and louder until it became too much for me to bear, and so I slipped on my respirators and clipped it around the back of my head. The in-built headphones cut out the noise automatically, only allowing in sounds that they deemed worth my hearing. The rest of the section followed suit moments later. I knew that Corporal Evans was being told that it was nearly time and a fresh wave of fear passed through my body, it jangled every nerve from my very core out to my fingertips.

I looked up at Berezynsky at the same time as he did at me and for a moment we both gazed into each other's eyes from across the tiny compartment. We were so close to each other that our knees touched. Tony barely ever said a word to anyone, and I realised that even though we had been in the same platoon for weeks I barely knew a thing about him. I wondered if Tony was feeling the same fear as I was, then I wondered if he was wondering the same about me. Tony looked away.

'We're coming into orbit, lads,' Corporal Evans briefed us. 'Chinese warships have been driven away, but we're receiving heavy anti orbital fire from the surface. It's going to be a rough ride down, in other words.'

We knew that anyway. The Chinese had spent the past two years since defeating the Union and its Russian allies preparing for the inevitable counter attack. New Earth was worth too much to both sides to be given up without a fight, but the Union had never anticipated a Chinese invasion. Our enemy would not repeat the same mistake with us.

I had spent weeks during our voyage being lectured on the scale of the Chinese forces garrisoned on New Earth, and it was sobering: hundreds of battalions of infantry and artillery, hundreds of warships ranging from tiny gun boats and orbital weapons platforms, to mighty battleships and carriers stocked with robotic aircraft. Again I imagined the battle that raged around us outside our tiny little compartment, and it made me feel very, very small and defenceless.

Suddenly the lights switched from bright white to a dim blood red. We all knew what that meant - it was time.

'Helmets on, lads! Let's do this!'

As one, we put our helmets on over our respirators, clipping them under our chins. With the last part of my body covered except for a few square inches of my neck I began to sweat profusely. The respirator automatically made its best attempt to keep my face cool, its tiny fans whirring madly, but it was never quite enough and this time was no exception.

'One minute, lads!' Corporal Evans warned over the intercom, just as the artificial gravity generated by Challenger disengaged. The sudden feeling of weightlessness turned my insides and I resisted the urge to puke. The dropship was moving, I could feel it. The launch bay had depressurized and we were being moved by a robotic arm into position, ready to fall from Challenger for the last time. The bay doors above us would be gaping open, and I knew that we were hanging upside down over the red surface of New Earth kilometres below.

'Thirty seconds!'

Joe Mac pumped his fist. 'Come on, boys.' His bared teeth were visible through his visor as he leant forward to see us all. 'Let's get angry! We're gonna have these bastards!'

The intercom filled with our personal battle cries. I couldn't think of anything good, so I just screamed out, 'Wooooo!' Better than doing nothing at all I guess, and surprisingly it made me feel a lot better.

'Ten seconds!'

We were in frenzy; blokes were shaking fists and screaming obscenities I couldn't possibly repeat.

I did think of something to say then, something that at the time I felt would be inspiring to myself and the lads sat around me, but then I couldn't remember what it was I was - good job - because I never got the chance to say it.

We suddenly dropped.

We fell from Challenger toward the surface of New Earth and G-forces tore at my body as the dropship began its violent manoeuvres to achieve an optimum entry, and it was then that I was glad there were no windows to see out of. Again I fought back the urge to be sick. Everything happened so fast and violently, I'm not sure I was even able to breathe!

All I could do was hold Berezynsky's gaze. I don't know why I did it, but I always ended up locked into eye contact with one of the lads sat across from me. I guess without anything else to look at, it was the only thing to keep me from losing it. Tony's eyes were wild and terrified and I'm pretty sure that mine were too.

Dropships were at their most vulnerable during the entry stages of their drop, particularly from missiles and ground fire. Speed was one of their primary means of defence during that stage, and therefore instead of slowing to a more acceptable shuttle entry speed, they just kept going. Underneath a dropship was a patchwork of tiles designed to absorb the extreme heat created by the friction between the ship and the atmosphere on entry, initially at speeds as high as thirty thousand kilometres per hour.

Everything shook as the dropship entered the New Earth atmosphere, tilting backward to allow the tiles to do their job. High above us, Challenger and the other troopships would be firing us in, using an assortment of missiles and orbital artillery to cut through the enemy's air defence and soften the objective for our landing, as well as making it difficult for enemy anti-air batteries to distinguish between dropships and ordinance.

There was one single fact that terrified me, a point made again and again during my training to prepare me for the reality of a 'Hard' drop: *not everybody would make it*. On previous operations against the Indians, the Japanese and the many other enemies of the Union, statistically one in three dropships were destroyed by enemy fire during their perilous landings. And there I was, sat in one of those very dropships, strapped in so that I could hardly move, one missile away from becoming a statistic. The maddest thing about it all was that we were all troopers voluntarily; in fact we were one of the few arms in the Union military that *were* voluntary. In a world where freedom was only for the wealthy, we had made the only choice we were ever allowed to make; we had chosen the infantry.

I pictured phalanxes of missiles speeding toward us from every direction, blasting our mates out of the sky and sending molten metal streaking across the upper atmosphere, and then my fears intensified even more. The initial shock of the drop and the atmospheric entry were gone and my conscious mind began to contemplate what was happening. Despite what I was taught, every muscle in my body tensed and my heart felt like it was about to hurtle through the top of my skull, never mind it pumping! Some people had been known to soil themselves during a drop, and I think during training one of my mates actually did, although he always denied it.

We fell from the heavens at impossible speeds, slowing rapidly as the atmosphere thickened. The dropship would have to sacrifice its speed in order to enter the lower atmosphere without burning up, or splatting us onto the surface of New Earth like a bug on a windshield. In order to counteract the loss of speed it would then substitute with daredevil manoeuvres and

more importantly use its twin Vulcan cannon, capable of firing thousands of rounds a minute. Since our straps prevented our bodies being thrown about the crew compartment, our vital organs just threw themselves about inside our rib cages instead.

I felt the dropship dip its nosecone - enabling the Vulcan to fire. No sooner had it done so then the crew compartment shook. It didn't take the brains of a scientist to know that the vibrations were caused by the Vulcan firing, and that meant enemy missiles. Anti-air missiles of all types and sizes, which could not hope to hit us before, would now be in their element as we slowed in the lower atmosphere.

'Screw the nut!' Climo shouted in protest at yet another sudden drop that left our stomachs where our mouths should be. I'm still amazed he even got the words out.

'Keep it together, lads,' Corporal Evans boomed. 'We'll be flat to the deck soon. Anti-air ain't even getting close!'

I chose to believe him, although as it turned out he was actually lying. The Chinese air defences had successfully taken down dozens of dropships and gravtanks from our battle group, which had been one of the first to drop. They had also caused significant damage to our fleet in orbit, despite being completely outgunned. However, Dropship Infantry were organised to operate with the grim acceptance that ships would be lost. In a modern war against a well-matched foe like the Chinese, it was inevitable. To lose ten or so ships wasn't actually that bad going, believe it or not.

I could feel us begin to level out. Dropships had a symbiosis between pilot and machine that enabled them to fly at breakneck speeds only a few metres from the ground, making them harder to detect and engage. Rather than just dropping straight onto an objective, which made us an easier target, we would drop to a location a few kilometres away and then fly in flat to the deck with the gravtanks in support. The final stage of the drop was known as the 'run in', and it was just as dangerous.

I could imagine outside our tiny compartment the armada of ships forming up as it came closer and closer to the ground, blasting missiles away with sprays of Vulcan.

We levelled out suddenly with a jolt, and I knew then that we were on the surface of New Earth. The objective would be in the distance, obscured by clouds created by smoke bombs dropped by the fleet to mask our approach. Not much defence against the advanced targeting systems used by robotic enemy fighters and missiles, but a smoke screen was better than absolutely nothing!

We jerked to the left and right as the dropship weaved around unseen obstacles, through valleys, around hills and whatever else my imagination could cook up. We were really going for it, even though we were only travelling at a fraction of our entry speed, the G-forces of the final run in were easily enough to turn my stomach a few times. We 'leapt' over something, and I honestly thought all my intestines had dropped out of me.

It was then that Brown puked into his respirator. *Oh God!* I thought. I couldn't see his face, just what he'd had for breakfast smeared all over his visor. In other circumstances, I would have considered what I saw as hilarious. I despised Brown, but I didn't want to see him choke before he even made the landing.

'Brown, sort your life out! Now!' Joe Mac snarled as Brown struggled to remove the respirators.

I can't really say that I blame Brown for puking, lots of people do from time to time, and it's a wonder I didn't puke too, because I was absolutely terrified. Imagine the maddest rollercoaster on Earth and then get thousands of people to shoot at it, and that still wouldn't even come halfway to a drop!

Outside we were beginning to get into an assault formation. The company was assaulting with two platoons up front, with one to the rear in reserve, I remembered from my briefings. In each of those platoons were four dropships, in a box formation with two up front and two to the rear. In front of each platoon were the gravtanks, at a ratio of one to every two dropships. They were essentially a dropship, but with a lower profile, more armour and a turret mounted rail gun. Each ship would be a few hundred metres apart in order to minimise the damage the company could take from explosive area weapons used by the enemy. From above the formation would look like a large triangle, concealed in smoke and the dust and sand thrown up in its wake, hurtling toward its target.

Brown removed his respirator and tipped the puke onto the floor at his feet. He looked like he was about to cry. He shook it and tried to wipe the inside on his knee.

'No time for that now, you lizard!' Mac scorned. 'Put it back on!'

Brown obeyed. The respirators might well stink, but it would work, and that was the main thing.

'Thirty seconds boys!'

Funnily enough I felt almost elated. I had survived the drop with all of my section. Whatever happened when we touched down and the back door opened, at least I would have a chance to do something about it rather than sitting there, strapped in and ready to die.

I doubt that Tony Berezynsky felt the same; he looked like he was losing it.

'Tony you'll be alright, mate,' I offered him encouragement. It was a pretty empty gesture, but something is always better than nothing I liked to think.

Tony shook his head. 'This is crazy!'

'You're right there, mate, this is mental!' Climo shouted. The Vulcan was going berserk and we were slowing down rapidly. Party time.

It wasn't just mental, it was unreal. Here I was, sat in a marvel of science and engineering turned into a weapon of war - on an alien planet light-years from Earth, about to go into battle. How do you explain that to your kids? If you make it that far that is?

My elation was all but gone, and for the first time in my life I made a prayer to God.

'Twenty seconds!'

Dear Lord, please don't let me die.

'Okay, okay!' Corporal Evans hurriedly answered to the pilot on the intercom, then turned to us, 'Lads, when you exit, you go left! There's a ditch you can get in. Left, Berezynsky you got me?'

Tony would be the first man out, 'Yeah I got you!'

If you let me live I promise I'll change.

'Ten seconds!'

I'll believe in you. I'll go to church. I'll never pick up a weapon again.

'Five! This is it, lads!'

My stomach lurched for the last time as the dropship came to an abrupt standstill. My straps disengaged automatically and I reached for my rifle by instinct. Light poured in as the rear ramp began to fall.

It was raining on the surface of New Earth.

The noise outside was deafening even with my earphones on. The dropship was unleashing everything it had to cover our exit.

'GO, GO, GO!' Corporal Evans screamed, but Tony hesitated.

'GO, you knob!' Climo shoved him out the door, and I followed.

2: One month Ago: New Arrivals

I probably wouldn't have felt the gradual return of gravity and the gentle thud of the shuttle mating with Challenger's airlock had I been asleep like the others. I had been comfortable enough, the shuttle was far less cramped than a dropship compartment and the zero-G was quite relaxing once you got used to it. But I hadn't found myself able to fall asleep during our ten-hour voyage into deep space, instead I had passed the time staring at a tiny green computer screen at the far end of the compartment, our only illumination since the pilot had turned off the internal lighting. For the best part of the journey it had flashed on and off, with a single message, 'NO INTERFACE.' At times during the journey I had pondered over its meaning, but coming up with no answers I had long since given up and simply watched it blinking on and off. Like a clock ticking, it counted the seconds to our arrival.

I never could sleep during shuttle journeys, not necessarily through fear or excitement, but rather through anticipation of whatever I might encounter at my destination. My mind raced through scenarios of what might happen when we stepped aboard Challenger for the first time, wondering if the reception would be frosty or friendly and if the ship would be vast and awesome like the troopship that had taken me to Uralis for my training, or cramped and uncomfortable like the warrens of Fort Abu Naji, deep beneath the Uralian surface.

It would be my second time aboard a ship of the Union Navy. Well, it would be my third, but the second time didn't really count - we had flown up from the surface of Uralis by dropship, docked with an old decommissioned warship and then dropped only fifteen minutes later - we never even left the crew compartment. The thing that made Challenger different was not to do with the ship itself, it was who was on it. Challenger was a troopship with a formidable cargo, it was home to A Company of the 3rd Battalion English Dropship Infantry, a company of fully-trained and combat-hardened drop troopers and it was preparing for war. Onboard the comparatively tiny transport shuttle there were only fifteen of us, the rest of the platoon I had trained with had been split up into the flotilla of troopships that orbited silently, high above the brown and white surface of Uralis. Soon we - the fresh meat - would be the minority, instead of the majority as we had been in training. Challenger carried two hundred and fifty men, a hundred of whom were drop troopers.

I remembered the final words of wisdom from my section commander, the man who had trained me, before we nervously boarded the shuttle to leave Uralis for the last time, 'Be the grey man. Do what you're told and never answer back. Keep your head down and eventually you will be accepted.' I told myself I would follow his words to the letter.

Suddenly the compartment lights switched on, blinding me with their intensity. I covered my face with my hands as the shuttle AI spoke over the intercom with an almost mockingly cheerful voice and a strong German accent.

'Ladies and gentlemen, welcome aboard challenger! The time onboard is 0400 hours. Please wait while the docking procedure completes, this may take a few minutes.'

The compartment filled then with the groans of troopers unimpressed by their rude awakening, straining against their straps in an attempt to stretch their limbs.

As if anticipating what the lads in the compartment would surely attempt next, the AI added, 'Please may I remind all personnel that it is not permitted to remove your safety harness until the docking procedure is complete.'

'Yeah, thanks for that one,' somebody moaned sarcastically, followed by the sound of buckles being unfastened.

'Somebody tell that robot to ram it, I need a few more hours!'

'Yeah, let's do a lap round the planet or something.'

I smiled at the absurdity of the last comment. Of course we had no choice in the matter, not anymore anyway. Sign up to the dropship infantry and you choose not to have a choice.

A chime and a light at the far end of the crew compartment announced that we were allowed to remove our straps and I quickly unbuckled myself, flexing unused muscles and massaging aching joints. Uralis had added years onto my body, and sometimes I felt more like a middle-aged man than an eighteen-year-old boy. We stood and it felt good to feel gravity working against my bones again, even if I did know that it wasn't the real thing - like on Earth. Although I had learnt to handle zero-G without puking all over the place, it always reminded me how far from home I really was.

'Ladies and gentlemen, we are successfully docked with Challenger, please ensure you collect your equipment when you disembark, or you will not see it again.'

'No ladies on here!'

'No gents, either!'

I ignored the moans and rants of the other recruits, disconnecting my sausage bag from the straps that held it in place beneath my seat, straps that prevented it from bouncing around the compartment in the event of decompression. I had always thought it quite ridiculous, none of us were given suits, so decompression - however unlikely - meant certain death anyway. Who gave a stuff about things bouncing around or shooting out of the crew compartment?

I slung the bag over my shoulder. It could be no heavier than 10 kilos, the maximum permissible weight a passenger could bring aboard a military shuttle. It had been weighed to the milligram, and searched thoroughly for bacteria somehow smuggled accidentally from Earth - or worse – contraband goods. Heaven forbid I be in possession of beer or pornography before I go to my death, and how I would have gotten it to Uralis anyway was beyond me!

I carried very little in my sausage bag, most of the kit and equipment I had used in training had been taken off of me on Uralis before I left. A new set of equipment would be issued to me aboard Challenger, equipment more specific to where we were going. I travelled light, as was the norm in the Union military. To be exact, I carried 8.4529 kilograms. That was the weight of everything I owned, minus the clothes I wore on my back.

'Nervous?' Peters, a London lad who had been in my section in training, picked up his own sausage bag from where it had sat next to mine.

'Nah,' I lied. 'Can't be any worse than Uralis!'

Peters raised an eyebrow and chuckled, 'I sure hope you're right, man,' he patted my arm. 'Hopefully we end up in the same platoon.'

I nodded, and I hoped beyond hope he was right. Peters was the only lad from my training section who had been sent to Challenger, the others had all been sent elsewhere. There was nobody else on the shuttle I knew or got on with quite like Peters. Even though we were from different cities, him from London and me from Pompey, we had similar personalities, likes and dislikes, and so were mates since the very beginning. Having a good friend nearby to talk to, I knew, would really make a difference on board Challenger.

'You think anyone's up?'

I shook my head. 'I doubt it, reveille's probably at six I would have thought.'

'Yeah, fair one. I wouldn't wanna get up early to check out a bunch of new guys anyway. Hopefully we get an hour's extra head down.'

Without warning the crew compartment's airlock door slid open silently, revealing the airlock that led into Challenger. Within the two stood a figure dressed in a suit, its helmet tucked under its arm. For a second I blinked at the figure, who was bathed in blinding white light.

After couple of seconds it spoke irritably, 'Come on then, you lizards, let's go!'

That was the first greeting I had on board Challenger. *Was I ever in for a treat*, I thought as one by one we filed through the airlock, past the rather grumpy looking airlock technician. I couldn't quite figure out what her problem was - it was her job to maintain, check and cycle the airlock after all - but then I wasn't in a position to say anything.

Challenger's lock room wasn't the enormous cathedral sized room I had entered on board the Fantasque, the enormous troopship that had taken me and hundreds of other recruits from Earth to Uralis, and neither was it tiny or cramped, in fact it wasn't really much at all. Apart from a few suits hanging from hooks along the walls, the room was completely bare and not very interesting to look at. If I could describe my first impression aboard Challenger with a single expression, it would have to be 'anti-climax'. Or as most troopers would say – 'pump'. We formed up into three ranks with hands clasped behind our backs, sausage bags at our feet, which were shoulder width apart in the correct position of 'at ease'. Rarely had we practiced any form of drill on Uralis, most of that was done on Earth during basic training, but old habits never die, and we were eager to please our new unit.

The technician emerged from the lock, having checked that nobody had been left behind. Seemingly unimpressed by our smart parade ground formation, she counted us with an outstretched finger. The Navy loved to count things, I had learnt. I presumed she was counting us in case somebody had been left behind, which I would have thought would have been highly unlikely. Either that or she just wanted to appear more important than she really was - which I thought was probably more likely.

'Just waiting for your lot to come get you,' she finally said, jabbing a thumb over her shoulder, 'I just work the lock.'

We said nothing, unsure of the rank of the woman addressing us. We didn't fight in vacuum, that was what the marines were for, and so we didn't work closely with navy personnel, they were simply our means of getting to where we were going.

I listened to the new sounds of the ship, the rush of air being circulated through her network of ventilation ducts and the faint hum of powerful and exotic machinery deep within her bowels, echoing through the metal superstructure that surrounded us. Even though I had never seen how awesome a ship like Challenger was from the outside with my own eyes, I could imagine from images I had seen that she was an incredible thing to behold, a glorious machine half a kilometre long, her harsh angular lines and bristling weaponry revealing her true purpose as a machine of war with the ability to project the Union's power across the cosmos.

We waited for five minutes, fidgeting awkwardly while the technician busied herself resealing the lock, until finally somebody came to collect us.

The grey haired lance corporal held up a tablet and read our names aloud, 'Jones!'

'Here, Corporal.'

'Rai!'

'Here, Corporal.' He continued down the list of fifteen names. Satisfied, the lance corporal lowered the tablet and returned it to his pocket. I assumed he must be a store man or something; he was too old to be fighting within the sections. The aging process could be slowed or almost stopped in our day and age, but we certainly weren't rich enough or worth enough in the eyes of the Union to receive treatments worth more than our own equipment. If troopers didn't promote fast enough in the dropship infantry, they were either honourably discharged (which is basically the same as being dishonourably discharged!) or found themselves in a simple job that nobody else wanted - if they even lived that long of course.

I read the lance corporal's name badge sewn onto his fatigues shirt. It read 'Stokes'.

Lance Corporal Stokes sighed deeply and rubbed one eye, 'Right then, fellas. It's four in the morning, I'm tired and you're tired, so we'll get this done quick. You will be split equally into the three platoons. When I take you to your rooms get your heads down, reveille is at 0600 hours. Happy?'

We nodded, and chorused, 'Corporal.'

'Good, coz I want to get back to bed. Follow me.'

We followed Stokes through a bulkhead door and into the ship. It slid open and closed behind us with a deceptively quiet hiss. We were told that in the event of catastrophic decompression the doors were designed to close so fast and with so much power that they could crush a man's body beneath them and still achieve a perfect seal. I wouldn't want to find out if that was true.

We walked along a wide corridor, lined with even more closed bulkhead doors. Every ten or so metres another door would slide open, and behind us another would close automatically. Decompression could cause the entire ship to 'blow out' in less than a few seconds, I had been told. To prevent this from happening, the ship was divided by hundreds of bulkhead doors. The philosophy was - better to lose a section of the ship and a few good men - than have the entire ship blow out.

'This is the main access corridor,' Stokes explained as we walked, his voice echoing against the metal. 'It runs the full length of the ship from the bridge to the lock room, where we just came from. You can pretty much find whatever you need along here, and it keeps you away from headquarters, they tend to use their own access corridor. Stay clear of headquarters unless you're specifically told otherwise.'

Somewhere below us a line of gravity generators created an Earth-like gravitational field along the length of the ship, and we lived in a cylindrical world that surrounded them. There were several access corridors like the one we walked along, each running from aft to stern. What I found really weird were the circumference corridors. There were ten in total, each equally spaced along the ship like the ribcage of a gigantic monster. Each one was a good three hundred metres long, and curved around the ship to end where it began. The first time I walked around one I almost wanted to vomit, the sense of vertigo it gave me was overwhelming what with the horizon only a few tens of metres away. I found the best way to overcome it was to imagine as I walked or ran that I was rotating the massive cylindrical world with my feet, rather than going around it upside down or whatever. It was much easier to imagine that you were always up, and everything else was below you, rather than the other way round.

The back end of the ship contained stores, engine rooms, life support and everything that kept us alive and our ship functioning. To the bow was the bridge, headquarters, gunnery rooms and, of course, the dropship hangars. She carried a total of four gravtanks and sixteen dropships, four for each platoon and then a remaining four for headquarters.

The accommodation section was located amidships around two circumference corridors. Stokes explained that the stern section contained the three platoons and that we needn't ever stray into the forward sections.

'The fore accommodation section is for the ship's crew, jacks and officers,' he warned, 'Stay well clear or you'll end up in a world of pain. Each platoon bulkhead is clearly marked, so you have no excuses for getting lost.'

We stopped outside one such platoon bulkhead half way around the circumference corridor. Its sign read 'One Platoon' in large black stencilling.

Stokes harrumphed, the corner of his mouth turning up into a smirk. 'Good luck, if you're in one platoon. The platoon sergeant is, shall we say … excitable?'

The huddle of troopers said nothing, staring back with blank expressions.

'Right.' Stokes drew out his tablet and examined it. 'Berezynsky. Gilbert. Greggerson. Moralee. Kane. You're one platoon.'

My heart sank. I was to be separated from Peters.

'Walk into the accommodation, you will find a long corridor with rooms either side. Your names are marked on the doors and you will clearly see which bunk is yours, because nobody will be sleeping in it. Comprende? Any questions that can't wait for the morning?'

'Um, Corporal?' Greggerson asked meekly. He was a timid lad from Kent, but with a slight build and a voice as quiet as a mouse. I never fully understood how he managed to get through training, but then sometimes I wonder how I made it.

Stokes was clearly tired, and he shot Greggerson an angry look. 'What?'

'Where's the ablutions?'

Stokes frowned at Greggerson for a second, before shaking his head. 'Right, we're off. Reveille zero-six.'

The huddle of recruits disappeared over the horizon, leaving us stood outside the door to our new accommodation, and our new platoon. Like it or lump it, we would serve - and possibly die - with the men through that door.

'Well I'm not standing out here like a mug,' Gilbert, a country lad and the largest of all of us stepped toward the bulkhead and it opened. We followed cautiously.

Initially the platoon lines were pitch-black before a movement sensor spotted us and the neon lights that lined the ceiling flickered on, revealing our new home. Dark red camouflage netting hung from the walls and ceiling in huge sheets, as a form of decoration to break up the boring grey of the metallic walls. We were in a corridor that stretched for twenty metres until it came to a T-junction, lined with bulkhead doors.

I studied images that adorned the walls as I walked up the corridor, at the same time looking for my own room. Some were just of young lads out drinking in bars and nightclubs on Earth, but others were taken of alien worlds visited by Challenger. I recognised a few shots of Uralis, presumably taken during some form of exercise in preparation for New Earth. Since Uralis was a dead planet, and similar to New Earth, it was ideal for use in preparing the Union forces for the invasion that nobody spoke of too loudly, but everybody knew was coming.

I also recognised images of a green world: Eden. Its jagged, rocky surface was covered in the dark green lichen that typified the planet, a world more like Earth, rather oddly, than New Earth, in that it was able to support basic plant life without artificial assistance. It was believed that, after several hundred years of terraforming, unlike all of the other dead rocks, Eden was fully capable of supporting an Earth-like ecosystem. It was to be a Utopia. Our instructors in Fort Abu Naji had all been there but not one would talk about what it had been like for them. In a war between three separate Colonial powers, Eden belonged now solely to the Union, but at what cost I couldn't say.

I realised that whilst I had been staring at the walls the other lads had all disappeared into their rooms. I rounded the corner of the T-junction, eventually finding my room at the far end of the left hand corridor. The names of the occupants were stencilled onto the bulkhead with black spray paint: Woody, Climpson, Brown and me. The paint for my name was still wet.

I entered the room and thankfully the lights didn't come on automatically. Waking up my new roommates at four in the morning by turning all the lights on wasn't the best way to introduce myself. I stepped into the room, allowing the bulkhead to close automatically behind me and shut out the light from the corridor. From within the room somebody snorted and stirred, but then settled and appeared to drift back into a deep sleep. I used the backlight of my wristpad to find my bunk and was relieved to see the free bed was at the bottom - less chance of disturbing the bloke on top. I slipped quietly out of my fatigues and into the ready-made bed.

I must have laid there for a good couple of minutes; taking in the sounds of heavy breathing from the room's three other occupants. We were tightly packed into a room probably better suited for two men rather than four. I listened to the sound of an air vent gently blowing fresh air into the room and felt the cool breeze against my face. If I closed my eyes I could imagine it was the wind through an open window, and that I wasn't on a warship in another solar system potentially going to war, but lying in bed at home without a care in the world. I slept.

3: Reveille

I woke with a start to a screaming alarm, wrenched from sweet dreams of life back in Portsmouth with my family and dropped back into reality with a crash. It was the alarm calling the ship to reveille. I checked my wristpad - six on the dot. I was exhausted as I had barely slept in twenty-four hours.

Above me my bunkmate groaned loudly and swore, the bedsprings protesting under his weight as he rolled himself over in response to the noise.

I fought against my body's urge to do the same, I couldn't allow myself to appear lazy to my new roommates. I twisted out of the bed and rubbed my eyes with the backs of my hands, my bare feet cold against the metal floor. I felt around in the dark for my sausage bag, slid it over and began digging out my wash kit.

As I slipped on my sandals the bulkhead door slid open, revealing a muscular figure wrapped in a towel and covered in tattoos. He slapped a button on the wall beside the door, switching on the room lights. I half closed my eyes against the blinding neon light.

'Get up, lads, let's go!' he ordered with authority.

'Yeah, we're moving,' whoever slept above me answered unconvincingly. There was movement beneath the covers of the other two bunks.

The tattooed man caught my eye briefly but said nothing. He disappeared from the open bulkhead and it promptly closed behind him.

I wrapped my towel around my waist and made my way toward the door.

'Ah, hello,' a voice called from behind, causing me to pause. I looked back to the top of my bunk, where a round face was peering from beneath the covers.

'It's rude not to say hello when you meet people for the first time,' he said when I didn't respond.

'Sorry, I didn't want to disturb you.'

The face smiled, 'That's okay then. I'm John Wood. People here call me Woody. What's your name?'

'Andy Moralee.'

'Pleased to meet you, Andy Moralee.' Woody extended an open hand from beneath his bed covers and gestured for me to shake it. I noticed his arms were even more muscular than those of the man who had come to the door to wake us, 'I won't bite, mate!'

There was something I didn't like in Woody's over-friendly nature, it sounded fake, even patronizing perhaps. I couldn't not shake his hand, though, for all I knew it was a genuine welcome. I stepped over gingerly and took his hand, and he squeezed mine so tight I thought my fingers might break.

'There you go. We're mates now.'

The lads in the opposite bunk were climbing out of their beds. One was young, about my build, with light blonde hair. The other appeared a bit older, with a lean athletic build and colourful tattoos up his arms. I knew from the sign on the door that one must be Climpson and one was Brown. They paid me little interest as I shook hands with Woody, instead busying themselves with their own towels and wash kits.

I withdrew my hand. 'I'm gonna go grab a wash.'

'Okay, Andy,' his voice was deliberately patronizing, I was sure of it. 'You go grab a wash.'

I left to find the ablutions myself without asking for directions. I didn't want to talk to Woody for longer than I had to, his friendliness was purposefully exaggerated to the point of being unpleasant, and I doubted I had found a new best friend. It was easy enough to find the ablutions anyway - I just had to follow the line of men wrapped in towels making their way in through a nearby bulkhead.

There were about ten sinks in the ablutions, but there were thirty men in a dropship platoon and so I ended up in a queue. I was tiny compared to many of the troopers in the platoon, most of whom clearly spent a lot of their time in the gym training. I was ignored, people spoke around me but nobody chose to acknowledge my presence. I had expected as much, I supposed. It was my introduction to that Woody character that played on my mind - there was something about it that had made me feel uneasy.

As I stood and waited in line, a finger prodded me in the back. An older looking trooper in his mid-twenties was stood behind me in the queue with his arms folded. His ears stuck out like the handles of a jug, which made his attempt at looking intimidating slightly amusing. I chose not to point that out.

'Just got here?'

I nodded, 'Yeah.'

'You know where we're going?' He asked, as if he presumed that I didn't know and would be surprised if he told me.

'Yeah,' I replied. Everybody knew, our training staff had dropped enough hints, and our training had been geared toward it. It was inevitable that the Union would return to New Earth to seek revenge. New Earth, a symbol of mankind's future in the stars, and the first settled world outside of the solar system was once again to be ripped apart by war.

Interested now, he leaned closer and others in the queue turned to listen to what I had to say. 'What have you heard?'

I blushed under the sudden attention. 'Nothing, really,' I answered. 'Just rumours.'

'About what?'

I shrugged. 'We're here for a few days to pick up fresh recruits and supplies. We're then forming up just outside the system before heading for New Earth.'

'That's it?' He sounded disappointed.

'That's it.'

The trooper sighed, deciding that I had nothing else useful to tell him and then everybody went back to ignoring me again. A sink had freed up anyway, and it was my turn.

I shaved the tiny bits of stubble away from my boyish face, rinsing the razor blade in the puddle at the bottom of the sink. I wasn't capable of growing a beard yet, I reckoned I could probably get away with not shaving for a day or so before anybody noticed. I never tried of course - it was drummed into me that shaving was an essential part of my daily routine wherever I was. Facial hair could affect the seal between a trooper's face and his respirator, a mistake that on most Earth-like worlds would result in death.

'Do you know what you're doing this morning?' a gruff voice asked from next to me. I looked at the man shaving beside me; it was the heavily tattooed man who had switched the lights on in my room.

'No,' I said.

'We've got morning PT at zero-eight. Breakfast is at zero-six thirty. After that you have a ship's brief while we work with the stores.'

'What PT is it?' I hoped my PT kit hadn't creased up in my bag. We didn't press our kit on ship, but we were still expected to look presentable.

'Just shuttles, I think. Shorts and trainers.'

'Okay, thanks, mate.'

The man bristled, 'I'm not your mate.'

'S-sorry,' I blurted awkwardly, but he was finished and walking away. Another trooper took his place at the sink.

'Work out who people are before you start calling them 'mate',' the trooper said coldly. 'He's an NCO, and you're a crow.'

'Oh,' I said, my face reddening.

'Get a move on, crow!' somebody shouted from behind. I realised that it was me being shouted at and I was taking too long at the sink. I drained the sink and dried my face quickly before making my way out of the ablutions. As I passed the queue I saw Greggerson waiting, towel wrapped around his tiny child-like frame. He looked especially sheepish as he caught my eye, but said nothing. None of us wanted to attract attention to ourselves.

I knew what 'crow' meant - it was a word our instructors had often used to address us on Uralis. It was used as an offensive word that stood for Combat Replacement Of War: the new guys, replacing much better troopers who had promoted, left having served their time, or worse, died.

Thankfully nobody was in the room when I returned, so I quickly changed into my PT kit and made my way out onto the circumference corridor. I decided to find my way to the galley by following the crowds of troopers spilling out of the accommodation.

The galley was around the opposite side of the wheel that was the circumference corridor, and as I had suspected it was almost identical to the galley on board the Fantasque. It was a square hall a good fifty metres across with long neat rows of plastic tables and chairs. The interesting thing about the galley was that unlike the smaller rooms on the ship it had quite an obvious curve, much like the circumference corridor, and could appear quite odd when it was full of troopers, some apparently standing at unnatural angles against my own perspective.

On one side of the galley food was being issued to a growing queue from a window in the wall. Nothing on board the ship was cooked like you might expect, instead it was heated by a kind of microwave inside a white ration box, not entirely unlike the sort that we would be issued to eat on the ground. The box was often referred to as a 'horror box', which simply came from the expression upon the faces of people when they first looked inside one, or took their first bite. Nobody could ever claim that space nutrition was pleasant.

I slowly inched forward with the queue as the galley slowly filled with drop troopers, the room resonated with the sound of their chatter, angry exchanges and laughter. I kept myself to myself, being careful not to make eye contact with anybody lest I attract unwanted attention.

It didn't work.

'Oi mate, does your mum know you're here?'

I cursed in silence, turning to confront the voice from behind. A tall trooper looked down at me, his friends behind him grinning maliciously.

'Yes,' I replied flatly.

He chuckled. 'Well aren't you all grown up now, then, eh? You ready for New Earth, are you?'

'Yes.'

'Fair enough,' he smiled, though more out of amusement than friendship. 'What platoon are you?'

'One platoon,' I answered.

'One platoon?' He shook his head in mock dismay. 'Enjoy that, mate.'

'Why do you say that?'

'You'll find out.'

A 'horror box' was thrust into my hands. Startled, I realised I had reached the window. A trooper stared back at me through the opening, the next ration pack in his hands ready to be handed out. He looked fed up, and probably was since you only got microwave duty if you were being punished for something. His scabbed knuckles suggested his crime was probably fighting.

The trooper frowned at me. 'Well go on, then!'

'Sorry,' I made my escape whilst the queue behind me laughed.

I ate by myself on a table out of the way from everyone else, occasionally scanning for my mate, Peters. I saw a couple of lads I had known from training, but none chose to acknowledge me. I presumed jealously that they were probably getting on with their platoons far better than I was, and in the end I gave up and concentrated on my food.

I was quite used to eating space food after over a year spent outside of the solar system. Each horror box was divided into six sections, each containing a different colour slush that could be eaten using the spoon attached to the lid. The green one was the worst and I always ate it first, it tasted like peas and perhaps it once was - but I hated peas anyway - which didn't help. The brown and the red sections were probably my favourite, but I couldn't tell you exactly what they were, only that they tasted like some kind of meat. We were taught to eat all of the sections, supposedly they made up a perfectly balanced diet and not eating a section resulted in poor nutrition. I would never know the truth of that, but the horror boxes were surrounded in rumours and conspiracy theories. Some people said they contained drugs to make us more obedient, or chemicals that could be combined with a gas released by the ship's life support system to render us unconscious in the event of mutiny. In reality, they were probably just really cheap food mass-produced to be fed to the millions of men that made up the Union military.

'Mind if I sit down?' a tiny voice asked, causing me to look up. It was Greggerson.

'Yeah, have a seat, mate.' I gestured to a chair, trying to sound nonchalant. Secretly I was grateful to have some friendly company, no matter who it was.

'What are the lads in your room like?' Greggerson asked, sitting awkwardly with his hands on his lap.

I shrugged. 'Alright I suppose.'

'My room's alright, I think.'

Greggerson watched while I ate, then finally began to eat his own food. 'Kind of weird isn't it, being here.'

'I guess so,' I replied between mouthfuls. 'But then what have we done for the past year that you haven't found weird?'

Greggerson nodded with a childish grin. 'Yeah, you're right. We've done some pretty mental stuff.'

I could feel him thinking about what to say next as I ate. But I didn't mind the poor conversation, it was still company.

'You think they'll tell us about New Earth soon?'

'I dunno, mate. To be honest I don't think anybody knows anything, it's all just rumours. A bloke was asking me for gossip from Uralis earlier on.'

'In the ablutions?'

'Yeah that's right, the bloke with the ears.'

'His name's Stevo, he's in my room. Apparently he should have been dropped off on Earth a few months ago when Challenger stopped to re-supply. It's the end of his five years, but they refused to let him sign off, though.'

I raised an eyebrow. 'Really? What, for New Earth?'

'That's what he thinks. Sounds like it, coz apparently there were loads of blokes who couldn't go. But he was saying it puts all the platoons above normal manning.'

'Extra blokes?'

'Yeah, now we're here one platoon is three men over strength.'

I knew where Greggerson was going with this. 'Spares.' I said.

'Yeah.'

There was something chilling in the revelation. In the military you were a number. Oh, of course you were encouraged to use your initiative and develop your own character as a trooper, but in the end you were still just a number. Challenger carried more drop troopers than it needed to carry because the Union knew that men would die, and so the more the merrier.

I saw that Woody was walking toward us, the trace of a grin on his face. He was a big lad, far larger than me or Greggerson and probably in his mid-twenties, with a rounded face and a thick mop of brown hair.

'Hurry up, you two. The toilets don't clean themselves.'

My heart sank, should have seen that one coming. Even in space you had to clean the ablutions, and conveniently the platoon now had extra pairs of hands to help out.

'We're just finishing off,' I said, trying to sound like it didn't bother me.

'Well hurry up, coz I'm not doing it.'

So there we ended up, on our first day aboard a warship orbiting a planet in a star system light-years from Earth, cleaning out toilets and sinks like we'd done everywhere else. All five of us new lads had been rounded up for the task and had been left alone to do the job without help.

'This is *pump*,' Gilbert summed up what everyone was thinking.

That was when the doors to the ablutions slid open. I only had a couple of seconds to see as a gang of troopers charged into the room wearing respirators to hide their faces, each with a pillowslip filled with boots slung over his shoulder like a crude weapon.

None of us had time to defend ourselves, we were quickly overwhelmed by a flurry of blows that forced me to fall to the ground and curl into a ball. I didn't say a word, I just took it. What else could I do?

'Welcome to Challenger, crow bags!' somebody jeered.

They were gone as suddenly as they came - whooping and laughing as they made their exit from the ablutions, leaving us battered and bruised on the half-mopped floor.

Welcome to Challenger, I thought, *Home sweet home.*

4: PT

The other new lads, including me, followed the platoon to a circumference corridor at the stern end of the ship, our battered sides still smarting. I pretended it didn't hurt, not wanting to give anybody the satisfaction of seeing me in pain. Occasionally somebody in the crowd would look over at us whilst we walked and smile. They whispered amongst each other, no doubt talking about what they could do to us next. I tried to ignore them and focused my mind on what was coming up instead; my first fitness session with my new platoon.

Physical Training for troopers on board a troopship was a serious business for obvious reasons. Without constant training a company could rapidly become unfit, and so their ability to fight would suffer as a consequence. The age old saying went '*a drop of sweat in training is worth a pint of blood on the battlefield,*' and it was true. Not only did poor fitness affect our ability to run and to fight, it also increased the risk of medical complications during the high G-forces of a drop or caused problems for us breathing with the respirator.

There were two types of fitness training carried out on ship. The first was gym sessions using the comprehensive equipment kept in the ship's gymnasium. The problem with the array of machines, however, was that no matter how good they were they couldn't replicate the true motions of running - which was something we would do a lot of by the very nature of our job as dropship infantry - and they also became awfully boring.

The solution to this was the second option - running. Because the ship had so many circumference corridors it was easy for the Physical Training Instructors to close one of them off and get us to run around them. Still sounds boring, right? Well, it was the job of the PTIs to make PT the opposite of boring - as absolutely horrible a thrashing as they could make it.

It was enough to make me forget my bruised body seeing our PTI for the first time though. Even in battalion they fulfilled their stereotype, with slick gelled hair - how did they get it up to the ship anyway, and more importantly - why? And their unnecessarily tight t-shirts that barely contained their bulging muscles.

'We'll be doing shuttle runs today gents, relatively simple,' the PTI rubbed his palms together gleefully in anticipation of the session he had planned for us, 'Nobody is to *jog* around the corridor. Sprint the whole way. I'll be watching you, so don't cheat! Cheating equals pain!'

We listened intently, jogging on the spot to warm our muscles up.

Not intently enough, apparently, 'Am I *boring* you…?' A mischievous smirk grew on the PTIs face.

We shook our heads, all thirty or so of us. Somebody chuckled from within the huddle, knowing full well that we were to be thrashed whether we looked interested or not.

'Oh, so now you think it's funny - *two laps sound funny?*'

'Yes, Staff,' somebody replied.

The PTI smiled. It was all part of the session - he was going to send us anyway. I never fully understood how a PTIs mind worked, and I probably never would.

'Two laps, then. Last fifteen go again ... GO!'

We sprinted around the corridor and my battered body protested painfully as I went. I focused on rotating the giant wheel that was Challenger with my feet as I desperately tried to get to the front of the pack. Although they had spent four months on ship from Earth, and then a whole week of shore leave on Uralis, the platoon was surprisingly fit. Instead of being right at the front as I had expected to be I found myself fighting to stay in with the middle of the pack.

The PTI appeared again over the horizon, calling out to us as we ran, 'Come on, let's go, don't be the last fifteen and go again! It pays to be a winner, gents! Get up there, you!' The PTI shouted at me as I passed him for my second lap as fast as my legs would take me, trying to overtake the man in front.

I pushed myself harder, as it was the first time I had taken part in fitness with my platoon I was eager to show off how fit I was, but in the end I only managed to just scrape in with the first fifteen. The remainder were sent around again as I fought to regain my breath.

'You're crow, aren't you?' The PTI was talking to me, I realised, and I straightened to attention automatically, as had been drummed into me by months at the mercy of the training staff on Uralis.

'Yes, Staff!'

'You should be at the front, then, shouldn't you,' he scolded.

'Yes, Staff,' I panted.

Out of all of the new arrivals only me and Greggerson had managed to avoid going round the corridor again, but I doubted it would be wise to mention that to the PTI. Why was I the one being gripped?

Once the unlucky fifteen had finished their second lap and stood gasping for breath, the PTI began the explanation of his PT session. We were lined along the wall in two ranks and paired off. The man stood at the front of the pair was the number one and the man behind was the number two. The number one did a lap of the corridor, whilst the number two performed an exercise dictated by the PTI, press-ups for instance.

'Nice and simple, today, gents,' the PTI summarised. 'Let's burn some of that shore leave off them bellies!'

I was the number one, so it was me who would run first while my partner exercised.

'You better be fast, man,' my partner threatened from behind. 'Or you and me will fall out big time.'

'Number two's will be doing wide arm press-ups! In position - ready!'

The number two's dropped to the ground and adopted the wide arm press up position, 'One lap! Stand by ...' We braced ourselves to run. '...GO!'

Half of the platoon, including me, sprinted around the corridor as our partners did press-ups. The idea was that the fear of letting down your team mate drove you to push even harder than you might normally, because the faster you were the less exercises he had to do. It was a simple yet effective method of getting troopers to annihilate themselves whilst the PTI barely had to do a thing.

'Every single day we do this,' the young blonde lad from my room moaned to me as we ran.

'You must be sick of it,' I replied between gasps.

'Shut up!' a young skinny man hissed from beside me. I shook my head in disappointment at myself, I should know better than to talk during PT. If I had the breath to talk it meant I wasn't working hard enough.

The PTI emerged over the horizon again along with the line of troopers in the press up position.

'All the way in!' he called. 'Don't jack on your mate!'

One by one we relieved our partners, releasing them from their exercise. We stood, jogging on the spot to keep our muscles moving and prevent them from seizing up, it kept the PTI happy too. I was chuffed with myself - I had been one of the first to get back - so my partner couldn't say I'd jacked on him. In the military, 'jack' is a very dirty word. If you're jack it means you're not a team player, you let people down and only look out for yourself. People who were jack got other people killed and were hated more than anything. You could call somebody all sorts of words and he might not bat an eyelid, but call a man jack, and he would never take it well, especially if it was true.

'You got a problem, boy?' A harsh voice asked, and I jumped. The man who moved to stand in front of me was dressed in PT kit identical to mine, but it was easy to see he had some kind of rank, though what it was I was unsure. He was a broad-shouldered man in his late twenties with piercing blue eyes and severe acne scarring to his face. He had an additional scar that formed a near perfectly round, albeit broken, circle on his cheek, obviously the result of being stabbed by a broken bottle in one of England's notoriously classy drinking establishments. His eyes stabbed at mine as he leaned close to my face, his unpleasantly odorous breath burning against my cheeks.

I chose to go with the safe option, mid way in the rank structure.

No ... um ... Corporal.'

'I'm not a *Corporal*,' he spat the word as though he found it distasteful. 'Try again.'

'No, Sergeant.' I cursed inwardly, and my cheeks flushed with blood as I felt the eyes of the entire platoon upon me. Even the PTI had stopped to look. During PT the PTI was in charge, but ultimately the platoon sergeant was God; the terrifying disciplinarian who ruled the platoon with an iron fist and I had somehow already managed to annoy him.

'That's right, I'm your platoon sergeant. So if you haven't got a problem, why are you shaking your head at one of my lance corporals?'

'I didn't, I ...'

'I watched you do it.' The sergeant jabbed a massive finger at my chest. 'Are you calling me a liar, boy?' He was from Southampton, I recognised the accent. Being from Portsmouth I was never going to be in his good books, as the two cities despised each other since time began.

I gulped - I couldn't argue - not with the platoon sergeant of all people. Within a dropship platoon the only man higher than the platoon sergeant was the platoon commander, but even that was up for debate!

'No, Sergeant.' I focused my eyes on the wall behind him, not daring to look him in the eye.

'So now you're the liar, then?'

There was no response I could give that wouldn't be wrong. I chose not to say a word and instead tried to look as scared and stupid as I could for the sympathy card. In retrospect, I probably didn't need to try; I was probably scared and stupid enough.

The platoon sergeant drew closer, his teeth bared. 'Mess with me, boy, and you won't even make it to New Earth, understand?'

'Yes, Sergeant.'

He looked across to the PTI. 'Carry on, mate.'

'Roger! Number one's in position!'

I dropped to the press-up position, my hands cold against the metal. Bruised abdominal muscles screamed as I fought to keep my back straight.

'Number two's, one lap, stand by ... GO!'

As I pushed the world away a familiar voice taunted me from my right, 'You ain't gonna last five minutes here, crow bag.'

I looked over and saw Woody performing press-ups two down the line from me, grinning from ear-to-ear. It was probably his idea to get us in the ablutions and attack us, I thought. The sick bastard was enjoying seeing me suffer. I decided there and then that I had never hated anybody as much as Woody.

I realised my eyes were wet and looked to the ground and blinked it off.

What had I done to deserve this? I hadn't done anything wrong! As I exercised in my own little world of pain I finally realised that I had made a terrible mistake joining the dropship infantry - and I was going to pay for it.

The PT session went on for another fifty minutes, going up to two laps and even three at times as the PTI pushed us to our limits. I kept my mouth shut throughout - well, not to talk anyway - not even daring to look at anyone.

After PT the platoon was sent back to the accommodation to shower and change, while me and the other new lads were kept behind by the platoon commander. We lined the wall of the circumference corridor, which had become silent in the absence of the platoon's heavy breathing. I listened to the strange and ghostly sounds of the ship echoing through the superstructure whilst the lieutenant shared a whispered conversation with the platoon sergeant.

'Well,' the platoon commander began, walking out in front of the five of us. He was a slight man who appeared a little younger than the platoon sergeant. It was normal for a platoon commander to be younger than his platoon sergeant, the latter of whom had climbed up through the ranks from being a private like me. Platoon commanders came into command directly from their training, but that was because their training lasted several years and was far more selective than ours was. 'I don't know if I'm the first to say 'welcome on board' but … welcome on board.'

He wasn't the first to welcome us, I thought, and I had the bruises to prove it. I remained still, my hands clasped firmly behind my back.

'My name is Lieutenant Barkley and I am your new platoon commander. I apologize for not greeting you immediately upon arrival, but it *was* early in the morning, plus it gives you a chance to settle in and get your heads around it. This platoon and this ship are your new home.'

Like all officers I had met during my short time in the army, the platoon commander was extremely well-spoken, with an accent that I had never encountered until being conscripted into the Union army. He wasn't necessarily from a particularly affluent background, the dropship infantry was one of the few places in the Union where money and background didn't count for anything. Officers did, however, have to be of a certain intellectual calibre, most notably in language, since they were expected to be able to communicate with unit commanders from any one of the Union states who might not speak English. He had undoubtedly been to college, and perhaps even university, a privilege reserved for the gifted - or the rich.

'I take it you all have an inkling of what might be coming?'

We nodded as one. 'Yes, Sir.'

The platoon commander returned the nod, everyone knew that the Union would return to New Earth and that the time for battle would be very soon indeed, 'We're waiting for an announcement within the next couple of days, and potentially we might leave the Hope system very soon. Therefore I appreciate that this is a difficult time for any trooper to arrive from training. You have a great deal more to learn - and very quickly. No doubt you're feeling very homesick, lonely and scared right now, especially with this daunting task laid out before you.

Despite what you may have heard, at least two thirds of the platoon has never seen combat operations, neither have they seen New Earth or Eden. That includes me and several NCOs. Everybody is a little scared, if they say they aren't then they're probably lying. The platoon has been on voyage for four months and although I know you have spent just over a year away from Earth training, they too are homesick.

What I'm getting at is that we are all in the same boat together, metaphorically as well as literally. Talk to the lads in your sections, from the junior privates to the senior troopers. Share your burden with them and you will find you become part of the family very quickly, and you will forge a bond that will give you the courage and the strength to see the job through to the end.

You're going to be busy settling in, I urge you to use the next few days to do so before, potentially, we go to war. I will try to find the time to chat to you each in turn very soon. Until then, though, I will leave you in the very capable hands of Sergeant James.'

The boss glanced to Sergeant James, who stood off to a flank like a ferocious monster held back on a leash, waiting impatiently to be released, 'Sergeant.'

Sergeant James made an attempt to smile sweetly at the platoon commander, but instead it looked more like a grimace. He wasn't accustomed to smiling, as I would learn over the time I knew him. 'Permission to carry on, Boss.'

The boss nodded, almost surprised by Sergeant James's politeness, 'Of course, Sergeant.'

The stocky platoon sergeant stared expectantly at the boss, but it took a couple of awkward seconds for the message to sink in. 'Oh. Of course, well I'll be seeing you all around then.'

We waited as the platoon commander's footsteps slowly receded around the corridor and our new platoon sergeant paced in front of us, looking down to the floor as if he were examining his shoes.

I had been the ward of three separate platoon sergeants, one on Earth, one on the Fantasque, and then one on Uralis, and they had all been quite something in their own way. Sergeant Cooper on Earth had been a bully who could barely keep up with us on runs, a fat man who it was safe to say we all despised. Sergeant Talon on Fantasque was quiet as platoon sergeants go, but had a temper that could suddenly and without warning explode in our faces. Sergeant Jacob on Uralis was an amazing man, fit as any of us, and appeared to genuinely care for us, at least so long as we didn't wind him up too much. Sergeant James was by far the meanest looking platoon sergeant that I had ever come across, and that really was saying something.

The platoon sergeant was many things. He was first and foremost the platoon second in command, ready to step up to assume the role of the platoon commander if he was injured or killed. He managed the sections not being used by the platoon commander during the battle, using them to protect the platoon's flanks and assist in the movement of spare ammunition and casualties. He co-ordinated the smart launchers - rocket launchers that fired robotic missiles at threats in the air and on the ground with pinpoint accuracy. He managed the triage and extraction of casualties and managed the platoon's supply of ammunition, water and food, calling for more if required. He also dealt with discipline within the platoon, enforcing it either by sheer force of character, or sheer force, whatever came best to him. The platoon sergeant was more than just a high-ranking NCO, he was the heart and soul of the platoon, the platoon commander was its brain. You never, *absolutely never*, got on the wrong side of him, because if you did - you mark my words - you would regret it.

The sound of a bulkhead sliding open somewhere around the circumference corridor told us the platoon commander was gone. Sergeant James finished his pacing and eyeballed each of us in turn, as if sizing us up for a fight. I doubted any of us could take him, for he was a monster of a man. His eyes lingered on me and I felt my cheeks burning under his hateful glare.

'I ain't scared, and if any of you lot are, I seriously suggest you snap out of it,' he resumed his pacing, slower now as he continued to watch us. I didn't move a millimetre.

'I am Sergeant James,' he said. 'And whoever you thought was the big man in your world, you can forget him. I am your daddy now, and your mummy. I am the ruler of your little world.'

That wasn't the first platoon sergeant 'Don't mess with me' brief that I had ever had, but in our vacuum surrounded prison his words still carried great menace.

'You will respect your junior NCOs in my platoon. Lance Corporals are still Corporals here, and you will address them as such,' his eyes returned to me, 'You will obey their orders as if they came from me. They are my enforcers, and don't think for a second they won't resort to a swift back hand if you mess about. Complain if you want, but remember this, what goes on ship, stays on ship. Your complaints won't go far. Screw the nut, do what you're told, that's all I'm after. Go against me and I'll ruin you, and if you wanna go home tell me, so I can drag your disgusting body to the airlock and chuck you in the right direction. Understand?'

'Yes, Sergeant.'

'Welcome to Challenger, enjoy it while it lasts. Now get your awful bodies out of my sight.'

We ran back to the accommodation to whatever was in store for us next.

When I arrived back, half of the platoon was already queuing for their only shower for the day, chatting amongst themselves and thankfully uninterested in me and the other new lads. Steam escaped from the open ablutions bulkhead and was sucked up into the many air vents.

I paused as I entered my room and my jaw dropped. My sausage bag had been opened and tipped to the floor at the foot of my bed, the contents scattered across the floor like rubbish. For a moment I stood there, shocked by the complete lack of respect for my personal possessions.

Calm down, I told myself, *they just want to get a rise out of you*. Don't give that bastard Woody the satisfaction - it had to be his doing.

I bit my lip, and then began to gently pick up my things and place them neatly onto my bed. A picture of my mother smiled at me from my personal tablet, a happy smile from years gone by. I missed her so much, never before had I felt as far from home as I did that moment, even after all that I had been through up until then.

'*Eventually you will be accepted.*' Corporal Thomson's words echoed through my mind. How long was eventually? And after that I only had New Earth to look forward to.

I hadn't noticed the blonde-haired lad who had got me in trouble during PT enter the room, a towel about his waist.

'You need to get all the new blokes and go to the galley for a brief at zero-nine-thirty,' he said, then made as if to begin getting dressed and hesitated. I was more interested in scrolling through all of my family pictures, making sure none of them had been deleted or messed with. I swore to myself I would start swinging if one was missing and to hell with the consequences, but they were all there.

'He didn't do anything to it,' the blonde lad said finally.

I didn't look up.

'This crow thing, it doesn't last forever. Everyone gets it, believe me.' He started getting dressed into ship's fatigues whilst I finished gathering my things. 'I'm Climo, by the way.'

'Moralee.'

'Nice to meet you, Moralee.'

That was probably the only proper welcome I would ever receive aboard Challenger.

I went for my shower.

5: The Tour

Our introductory brief took the best part of the day, where all of us fresh recruits were taught everything we needed to know to get by on board Challenger. It was delivered by several different officers, each covering a different subject and using the galley as a makeshift lecture hall. It was long and at times extremely boring, but I wasn't bothered. It was a welcome relief from the platoon and I was reunited with my comrades from Uralis, including my friend Peters. We couldn't talk much, but I found his presence comforting.

You couldn't possibly expect to explain to us mere privates exactly how something as incredible as Challenger actually worked. Supposedly there was once a time when it was believed that soldiers of our time would have to be the most intelligent of individuals, hand-picked from the very top of the higher classes. The truth was that although we were required to be much smarter than regular conscripted troops, we were pretty below average as far as intelligence went. The average drop trooper was from a poor background, most likely living within the city slums which sprawled across much of England, and he probably had a very poor education - any of the smarter lads were kept for more specialized roles within the Union war machine, or became officers. We drop troopers didn't need to understand why things worked, or how things actually happened, what we needed to know was what they did and how they affected us. A trooper trying to comprehend how the magnets in his rifle worked wouldn't be putting all of his concentration into the task at hand - using it to kill the enemy. Or as one of the lads in training had said; *if we were smart we wouldn't be stupid enough to ask to join the dropship infantry instead of the regulars in the first place!*

Challenger was a troopship, or a 'stellar assault ship' to use her proper designation. She was designed to transport a company of troopers between star systems with a complete complement of sixteen dropships and eight gravtanks and then provide orbital 'top cover' whilst they made their landing. She was completely incapable of entering a planet's atmosphere. That would simply tear her apart.

Challenger was capable of travelling faster than the speed of light on a technicality, a loophole that she exploited in the laws of physics, and that was about all I was really expected to understand. I knew that when she accelerated or slowed she didn't experience G-forces as we might expect, which was just as well or we would all become a red, congealed mush at the back of the ship!

Challenger was armed with an array of weapons to aid her in her task, including banks of lasers for engaging enemy ships in vacuum, four Vulcan cannons as a last defence against missiles, and then an array of missile tubes and orbital artillery pieces designed to pound the ground beneath her with molten metal. But despite her impressive arsenal she was not designed to operate independently. A dropship battalion required a total of five identical troop carriers, three carrying the fighting companies and the remaining two carrying a fire support company armed with the more sophisticated, specialised weaponry - and a further headquarter company charged with the management and co-ordination of the others on the ground - as well as tasked to fight the unseen electronic battle. Typically a planetary assault force might consist of as many as fifty ships, and then at least half that number again would be the frigates and destroyers that escorted them.

'Challenger has been in operation since 2349 when she was commissioned in a New Earth shipyard,' a young naval lieutenant with a nasal voice told us all, 'Since then she joined the 1st Fleet and has been the home of A Company of the 3rd Battalion ever since. During those fifteen years most notably she has been involved in the Eden campaign, as well as the New Earth Betrayal three years ago.'

We stiffened, suddenly interested. We all knew that the company had seen action during the vicious Eden campaign fought against the Indo-Japanese alliance, but we had never been told anything about involvement in the Betrayal, when our Chinese allies had turned upon us without warning and forced us and the Russians off of the planet and then out of the Centauri system.

Perhaps sensing our intrigue, the lieutenant went on, 'Unfortunately the fleet was unable to enter safe orbit around New Earth, and instead gave cover as the surviving Union forces withdrew from the planet and left those unable to escape to their fate at the hands of the Chinese.'

What a terrible day that must have been for them, I thought. For every European at home, the shame of seeing the heart of our growing interstellar empire shattered so brutally by our historical allies tore at the very soul. My stomach churned with bile and my heart pounded at the very thought of the injustice that had been done to us those two long years ago. I could barely imagine how awful it must have felt to watch powerless as the Union forces trapped on the ground fought a helpless battle, enveloped and outgunned by Chinese warships, and then to leave the Centauri system, a system once hailed as the dawn of European influence in space.

'It was a sorry time,' the lieutenant said with feeling. 'Since then Challenger has undergone extensive refitting in Earth orbit,' he continued with renewed cheer, 'And has been involved in extensive exercises on both Uralis and Eden, showing the world that it was business as usual.'

Gilbert raised his hand. 'Sir, couldn't you attack their ships or something, over the last two years?'

'No,' the lieutenant answered, slightly irritated at the interruption.

'Can't we just go bomb China or something?'

'Of course not,' the lieutenant snapped. 'I'm afraid that the world is not that simple, Private. If we were to attack China on the home planet the consequences would be too dire to even think about.'

'Sorry, Sir.'

Mutually assured destruction, or MAD as they called it, was the result of any kind of conflict that spilled over onto Earth soil. It was an Armageddon the likes of which were written about in books centuries ago, and that which would rock the human race to its foundations and threaten the extinction of the species itself. Even the Chinese weren't that crazy, and so Earth had been largely locked into stalemate for generations. Only the poorer, non-space faring nations continued to war with each other on Earth, to minimal global interest. Technically the Union and China had been at war since the Betrayal, but barely a shot had been fired. Both sides were building their strength to make the next move, but it looked as though it would be the Union who would strike to regain absolute control of New Earth. And if the Union defeated the Chinese, then she would become a true colonial power in the eyes of the world.

Gilbert settled and the lecture of Challenger's history continued, but I sensed he didn't fully understand the lieutenant's explanation, and probably never would. It was difficult for anybody to fully understand how our world appeared to work these days, it had become more complicated perhaps than the human mind was meant to grasp. I remember something my dad had once said when I was younger, after watching the Betrayal pan out on the news channels: *'We're all running into space to escape this lousy planet. But what we don't realise is that we take everything lousy about it with us.'*

We were then taken around the ship and shown everything we needed to know and understand; the gymnasium, the classrooms, the combat simulation rooms, armouries and kit stores. The bridge was pointed out to us, as well as a secondary command deck midway along the ship that could assume command in the event of the bridge being destroyed. We weren't allowed in either, and they were protected by coded doors. We decided on board the Fantasque that it must be in the event of a mutiny, but we never asked.

As we walked around between each place I chatted to Peters, enjoying his company.

'How are you getting on so far?' I asked as we walked along one of the warship's many corridors with an officer at the lead.

Peters shrugged. 'It's alright, I guess. What about you?'

Peters was an outgoing lad, even for a Londoner, and everybody always got on with him. I imagined he had already made a load of mates and would be settled within the week, which was more than could be said for me.

'Yeah, it's not too bad,' I lied. My sides still hurt from my beating.

'You do PT this morning?'

'Yeah, it was good to blow off some cobwebs.' I didn't want Peters to know I had a rough time, I guess I just didn't want him to think less of me.

'We went up the gym, got smashed on the old CV machines. Proper smashed, mate. PTIs a raging nutter.'

'Yeah?'

'Yeah, man. Shame you didn't get to come along, you'd have loved it, mate.' He was clearly being sarcastic.

'Sounds great,' I replied with equal sarcasm. 'But rather you than me, mate.'

What am I on about? I asked myself. I would have killed at that precise moment to come across to Peter's platoon, just to be near to my mate. Once the tour was over, I knew I would have to return to my platoon who were currently working in the ship's stores and endure whatever they had lined up for me next.

We were taken to the dropship hangars then. Vast, packed with girders, wires and equipment, they were one of the few places onboard the ship where her true purpose was on brilliant display. There were four such hangars, each home to four dropships which hung from the girders and wires, just low enough so that their rear ramp doors could be lowered to the ground. Four great hangar doors along the ceiling were closed against the vacuum outside.

'You won't come in here very often,' our officer guide pointed out as we took in the spectacle with awe.

I had never seen a dropship hangar before, I had been in one, but I had never been outside of the dropship. It was like some kind of massive metal temple of war, and the dropships with their deep red camouflage were suspended and then cradled by wires and equipment like they were sat in a shrine.

Noticing our gaping mouths and craning necks, the officer smirked. 'Pretty smart, right?'

There's something about a dropship that always sends a tingle through my body. They were much bigger than you would think they were - when you're stuffed into their tiny crew compartments like sardines - with fat, stubby wings that hid their arsenals inside them during entry to the atmosphere. There were no windows to speak of, only cameras that you had to get right up close to see. They were smooth yet squat in their appearance, their underbellies black and tiled with heat absorbent panels that prevented them from burning up in the atmosphere as they dropped from the sky.

I think the thing that made dropships so stunning to see was the fact that every part of them was designed for a purpose, and not a single panel, line or drop of paint had occurred through chance or want of beauty. They were the evolution of hundreds, no, thousands of years of war, like the wolf who had evolved from millions of years on the hunt, and in their own terrible way they had become beautiful.

Nobody spoke as we looked at the craft that would take us to war, potentially, in a few months' time.

Becoming aware of the time, the officer harrumphed, 'Right, then. Again, you shouldn't be entering this room without permission - normally the access bulkheads will be locked and coded. Obviously I'm sure you all appreciate the consequences of somebody playing around with one of these things. Whenever you do come in here, however, I simply cannot stress enough that you are not to touch *anything*.'

He didn't have to tell me twice, somewhere in that room was probably the button that sucked the air out, I guessed.

The final part of our brief was back in the galley, which covered the 'Actions On' whilst on board the ship. The action on hearing the ship's call to quarters alarm was to return to the accommodation to await further instructions. Or if it was twenty-two-hundred hours, go to bed for the artificial 'night'. Similarly in the event of hearing the 'Action Stations' alarm we were to return to our accommodation again and don suits in case of decompression. We then did bugger all else and let the ship's crew deal with whatever the alarm was called for, be it a fire, structural damage, or worse, an attack. We would be strapped into place so we couldn't be sucked out of a hole if our compartment decompressed, but failing that we were told to adopt the 'decompression brace position', which was literally curling into as much of a ball as our suits allowed. I found the idea laughable, as even if such a position did protect me from bouncing around in the blast of escaping air, it would probably be the least of my worries!

It was nothing I hadn't already heard before, really, but never-the-less I enjoyed the final few minutes of freedom before I had to return to my platoon.

After the brief me and Peters promised to meet for evening meal – it would give us the chance for a chat and to catch up. We then made our way back to the accommodation. Woody's sickly smile haunted my mind, his words repeating in my head. *You won't last five minutes here.* I hoped he was wrong.

6: True Colours

You couldn't be any more isolated than when you were in the void, there was no more law and order there than that which we brought with us in our tiny ships. The captain of Challenger had the authority of the President of the Union himself - the power of life or death over her crew and her infantry cargo. Beneath her and in charge of our company was the officer commanding, who with the company sergeant major oversaw everything from discipline to the planning of future operations on the ground. They were all busy, with far more important things to deal with than issues within the platoons themselves.

'What goes on ship stays on ship', was a saying I had first heard aboard Fantasque and one I would never forget. To me it meant you kept your mouth shut, and you never grassed on your mate. It meant if you had a problem, deal with it, because nobody was going to be able to help you in your tiny prison surrounded by infinite vacuum.

'What goes on ship stays on ship.' The golden rule of the trooper - it was a lesson I was to learn hard.

The first punch connected with my cheek bone, taking me by surprise and knocking me off balance, but it was the second punch that took me down, striking me so hard on the eye socket it created a flash of white on my retina. My body collapsed like a sack of potatoes, my limbs limp and useless.

Woody wasn't finished with me, though. He never wanted me to forget what a beating from him felt like, and with sharp hisses of exhaled air he drove home a flurry of punches into my unprotected abdomen. I was so dazed I was barely even able to choke, much less breathe.

'Think you can mess with me, eh? Think you can gob off?' Woody spat through curled lips.

We were in our room but we weren't alone. Climo and Brown merely stood by and watched without a word as my helpless body was savagely beaten in front of them. I could swear Brown was smiling.

My confused mind tried to understand why Woody had turned on me so suddenly and viciously. *How had I gobbed off to him?*

When me and the other new lads had returned to the platoon from our tour, they were moving ammunition boxes from the lock room where they had recently been unloaded by shuttle to the ship's ammunition store. They were under the direction of the screws and lancejacks, and they were almost finished.

Woody had asked me, 'Where the fuck have you been?'

And my only answer had been, 'I've been getting my arrival brief, haven't I?' Was that gobbing off? Perhaps I had used the wrong tone of voice and had been misunderstood, but did that warrant me being set upon in my room, just before I was about to go to eat my lunch?

I tried to slap at Woody with feeble, weakened arms, but he straddled me and held me to the ground. God he was heavy! He grasped my neck in his hand and pressed down against my Adam's apple.

'I'm the senior bod in this platoon. Do you know what that means?'

I tried to gulp for air but couldn't, and only managed a gasp. 'No.'

'It means you don't mug me off, you don't gob off and you do what I tell you to do, you little weasel!'

I couldn't speak, my cheeks were burning and my eyes were watering as my lungs struggled for air.

'What do you say?'

I didn't understand.

'You say *sorry*.'

'S-sorry,' I managed.

'Sorry, Staff. From now on you call me *staff*, get me? Like a PTI.'

'Sorry … Staff.'

Woody smiled, with that sickening smile of his that I had come to loathe in less than six hours. 'Good. Mess with me again and I swear on my mum's life I'll have you out the nearest lock!'

With that, he released me and my lungs sucked precious air back into them, my heart pumping hard as it tried to return oxygen back into my organs. I clutched my throat and my eye which was already beginning to swell.

'I'm off to scoff,' Woody said to Climo and Brown. as they watched me with blank expressions. 'You coming?'

'Yeah,' Brown replied instantly, but Climo hesitated.

'You coming?' Woody repeated harshly.

Climo looked at Woody, then at me. 'Yeah.'

'Don't worry about that little prick,' Woody said as the bulkhead slid open for them. 'He needs to learn. That's how it works.'

The door was shut and I was left alone on the floor in my room, my body slowly recovering and my breathing coming back under control. As soon as I was able to, I dragged my bruised body to my bed where I cried for what seemed like forever.

After a while and without warning the door slid open. Startled, I quickly wiped the tears from my eyes.

A corporal frowned as he looked down at me. He was so tall that he appeared to fill the entire doorway, with sharp chiselled features that made him appear almost god-like. 'What are you doing down there?'

My eye was half-closed already and I could feel it swelling. There was no way he didn't know what had happened. My skull throbbed in pain.

'I just … um … fell over, Corporal.'

The corporal screwed his face up into a quizzical expression, 'Right. Who did you fall over onto?'

'Nobody, Corporal,' I insisted.

He nodded slowly. 'Right. Tell the lads in the room Corporal Evans says thirteen-thirty hours back up at the stores.'

'I will, Corporal.'

Corporal Evans continued to stare at me. 'Do you know what you should do when you fall over, lad?'

I shook my head.

'You get back up.'

I realised that I was still hunched up against the frame of my bunk bed. I quickly picked myself up off the floor, tucking my shirt back in and brushing down my trousers. 'Sorry, Corporal.'

'Don't be sorry.'

'Corporal.'

'It's Private Moralee, right?'

I nodded, uncomfortable in Corporal Evans' steady gaze. 'Yes, Corporal.'

The NCO nodded thoughtfully. 'Okay. Watch your step next time, Moralee, this ship is littered with trip hazards.'

He knew I had been beaten up, I thought as Corporal Evans disappeared behind the closing bulkhead, but he chose to say nothing. Senior troopers were part of military life, I had been warned, and were responsible for much of the discipline behind closed doors. Unfortunately it was just my luck that I had managed to find the worst of the bunch.

I didn't go to eat, instead I washed my face in the sink and nursed my half-closed eye. It was already beginning to change colour, but it was still working and I assessed that no bones appeared to be broken. Under my shirt my body was black and blue with the bruises from two separate beatings received in a single day. I longed for somebody to reach out and help me but there was nobody, not even Peters could help me. I resisted the urge to cry again, clenching my fists until my nails bit at the skin of my palms. *Damn you for being so weak, Andy*, I said to myself, *what if Corporal Evans catches you like that again?*

\#

'What the hell happened to you, boy?' Sergeant James scowled at me as the platoon arrived at the stores, a warehouse almost as large as a dropship hangar stacked with crates of ammunition of all sizes and natures.

I said simply, 'I fell, over, Sergeant.'

He spluttered and then frowned. 'Onto a fist?'

'The floor, Sergeant.'

The burley platoon sergeant rubbed his forehead stressfully, as the platoon set about their work amongst the ammunition. Woody eyed me threateningly as he walked past and disappeared into the maze of crates.

'You silly prat,' he said after a pause.

'Yes, Sergeant,' I agreed, with little other option. I had enough bruises for one day.

He drew in a deep breath and sighed resignedly. Behind those blazing blue eyes I think he could sense the predicament I was in. I wasn't going to tell him that I had just been filled in by a senior bod and earn myself another hiding for grassing him up.

'If you fall over, Moralee, you put your hands out, know what I mean?' He looked away. 'Get out of my sight. Go on.'

I followed the platoon to where we were unpacking crates containing smart missiles. They needed to be checked by an armourer before reloading them onto pallets to be lifted by forklift onto huge shelving systems a good ten metres high. Most of the lads noticed my black eye but chose to say nothing about it, I was sure they would be talking about it when my back was turned.

Greggerson and the other new lads all noticed and were keen to find out what had happened. 'I don't want to say,' I said to them all in turn. 'Let's just leave it, yeah?'

It was hard to lift things when I could hardly see out of one eye and my body had been used as a punch bag. I pretended I was fine and that I wasn't struggling with my injuries, I didn't want anybody to think I was a soft target or I suspected things would only get worse for me, plus I think a little part of me wanted to pretend it hadn't happened and wanted everyone else to pretend it hadn't happened as well.

A couple of times I passed Climo as we worked and he looked away from me awkwardly.

In the end I found myself carrying out the solitary task of cutting open the seals to the crate lids with a knife, before the others emptied the half-metre long missiles for the armourer to inspect them. They were well sealed and it took a good five minutes to open each crate - and there was a seemingly endless supply of crates being delivered by the forklift - but I was happy to be doing something that gave me a good excuse not to talk to anybody. Instead I listened to the other lads in the platoon who were working nearby chatter about their exploits on shore leave in the Uralian capital, Forsta Byn, glad to keep myself to myself. *Be the grey man, Andy*, I told myself once more, *watch the platoon and learn your place.*

The day had been such a whirlwind of emotions and information that I had barely even had a chance to work out anything about my platoon, who its NCOs were, the names of anyone outside of my room or even which of the three sections I was to be placed in.

Every platoon in the dropship infantry was divided into four distinct groups, much like the company was divided but on a smaller scale. First of all there were the three rifle sections which were the fighting units within the platoon, each one being eight men strong with a further six man headquarter group. This group included the platoon commander and his signaller, the platoon sergeant with his runner, and two smart gunners. Each section also included a section commander who had the rank of full corporal, or 'full screw' as he was known, a word carried through the centuries which supposedly originated from prison inmates - no surprise there, then.

The full screw was in charge of the section and made all of its decisions, managing the men beneath him both in and out of contact with the enemy. I suspected that I was in One section, because I could overhear the lads in my room sometimes referring to themselves as One section whilst they talked. It was often normal practice to put all of the section men in rooms together so that they developed the distinctive bond that only existed between troopers, or in my case so that they beat any new blokes senseless.

Corporal Evans was likely to be our section commander, I presumed. He wasn't working with us in the stores, but then I didn't expect him to, being a full corporal with far better things to do than lug crates. There was something about full corporals that filled me with awe and wonder and Corporal Evans was no exception. They were god-like men; fit, tough, tireless troopers with years of experience serving the Union, and they were only ever over-shadowed by the overpowering presence of the platoon sergeant. They would likely be away with the platoon commander, probably planning our training and discussing whatever the future might have in store for us all. Or perhaps relaxing in Challenger's modest recreation room probably, I figured.

Each section was divided further into two smaller teams of four or 'fire teams' as they were known, one of which was called 'Charlie' and commanded by the section commander, the other was called 'Delta' and was commanded by a lance corporal or 'lancejack' as they were known. Overall control of both fire teams still came under the section commander, however. Every platoon in every regiment in the Union used the same basic breakdown, although they might use different words to describe the same thing.

The lancejacks were second in command to the section commanders, and they took control of the sections in their absence. They were often in charge of administration within the sections, ensuring ammo states were correct, that the men were fed and hydrated and overseer of any other minor trivia that might otherwise distract the section commander's attention from the bigger picture - the battle itself. They worked under the platoon sergeant, who was to them as the platoon commander was to the section commanders. In the stores it was they that were in charge, as the commanders never got involved in the platoon sergeant's administration.

I had never worked with lance corporals before, having never had any within my training platoon on Uralis. Instead we had been expected to practice the role of section second in command ourselves under the watchful eyes of our instructors, as every rank in the Union army was always trained to be able to carry out the job of the man at least one rank above him. We were, after all, only one dart away from having to step into their boots, or further.

The lancejacks appeared to be much friendlier with the regular troopers than most screws I had met. They worked alongside everybody and chatted with them freely, only stopping to check that everybody was doing what needed to be done. I supposed that they had probably not long ago been promoted from troopers, and so the line between NCO and private was still slightly blurred.

The younger looking skinny lancejack who had got me in trouble during PT was Lance Corporal Reece, who the lads referred to as 'Reecy'. He appeared to be fresh out of the Junior Leaders course, a ten-week thrashing conducted on the surface of either Earth or Uralis by instructors pooled from across drops. He was loud and boisterous with an angry face that was trapped in an almost permanent scowl. Even when he smiled he still managed to look angry. He caught me looking his way that afternoon and stopped his work to return the stare.

'Oi, don't stare like you fancy me! Fancy me do ya? Get on with your work or you'll end up with another one of those black eyes, mate.' I blanched, and the platoon laughed mercilessly.

I didn't look his way again, and thankfully that was the last I heard of it.

Lance Corporal Cham or 'Chammy' as he was known was as young and skinny as Reece. He was a total comedian, and spent much of his time telling jokes and funny stories of his past antics that had the lads roaring with laughter.

The third of the three lance corporals was Lance Corporal Joe Mac. He was the tattooed man who had checked on my room that morning and had told me off for calling him 'mate' in the ablutions. He was large for a drop trooper, with a beak like nose and dark, thick black eyebrows and he looked like he could handle himself in a fight. He appeared friendly with Woody and Brown, and I suspected that he was my section second in command.

Our work kept us busy until close to seventeen-hundred hours, our evening meal being an hour later in the ship's artificial Earth-like day. By the time we finished my stomach had begun to rumble, and depressed or not, I understood the need to eat.

Thankfully Peters was there in the queue for food and spotted me straight away, and it didn't take long for him to notice my eye.

His friendly smile turned into a concerned frown. 'You okay, mate? What happened, man?'

I could feel the eyes of troopers eating at the tables upon me, amused at the sight of a new trooper already learning the hard way about how his new world worked.

'I'd rather not talk about it, mate,' I said quietly.

Peters looked left and right at the other lads in the queue, understanding that we weren't in a safe place to talk about it.

As soon as we were sat down I spilt the beans. 'There's this lad in my room, Woody,' I said softly, not wanting anyone to hear from the other tables.

'What? And *he* did that?' Peters blurted loudly, and I flinched.

'Alright, keep it down, mate,' I hissed.

Nobody appeared to have heard anything from any of the other tables around us, and in retrospect they probably weren't interested anyway.

'Yeah, a couple of hours ago,' I continued as Greggerson took a seat with us, followed by Gilbert. They had probably been waiting to find out what had happened to me all day.

'Why'd he do it?'

I shook my head. 'I think it was just the way I spoke to him before, I don't know. One minute I'm in my room waiting for lunch, then he just attacks me out of the blue.'

'Was it Woody?' Greggerson asked as he opened his horror box.

'Yeah, who told you that?'

'He's a bully,' Greggerson said, 'Everybody says it in my room. He likes to pick on new blokes and he's the platoon senior bod so he gets away with it.'

'Proper bastard,' Gilbert agreed in his thick country accent. 'One of the lads told me earlier, he abuses any new bloke until more recruits come in. Gives him a kick. Proper nasty piece of work, he is.'

'You don't say,' I pointed at my swollen eye. 'I reckon this morning was all his idea too. That's great, so when do we pick up the next intake, a couple of years?'

'Mate, it won't be that bad,' Peters said, attempting to reassure me and failing miserably.

'My sides are still killing me from this morning,' Gilbert said, and Greggerson nodded furiously. 'Took a right kicking, us lot, and Kane and Berezynsky too.'

'Really? What happened?'

We told Peters about how we were savagely beaten that morning by a gang of troopers masked in respirators, and the look of shock on his face told me all I needed to know - I was in the wrong platoon.

'Some sort of initiation the lads in the room were telling me,' Gilbert said in between mouthfuls of brown mush, "New bloke' here is a dirty word.'

'That's two words, Gilly,' Peters corrected.

'Whatever.'

And then our conversation descended into the usual idle chatter and banter that perhaps without our knowing had got us through our lives in space, and the army, with our humanity intact. I sat back in my chair having eaten my meal, and for a few minutes at least forgot where I was and enjoyed the sweet moment of company with friends.

———

I returned to my room with caution, not sure what to do if I was to be attacked again by Woody for some other random infringement, but he wasn't there to greet me with his sick smile. Glad for the time alone, I changed quickly into my track suit, as was the dress for after the evening meal on ship or in barracks, unless told otherwise. I couldn't shower as I had not been to the gym, as were ships rules, and besides I wanted to get the rest of my bag unpacked and locked away into my locker where it would be safe from ransacking.

I placed my tablet inside my locker and selected a picture of my family for it to display, gently brushing the image with my finger. I took no comfort from the touch. Instead the loving faces of my family, trapped by Earth's poverty, wrenched at my heart and caused a sting in my eyes. For a second I wished that I could have had no love for my family, like many of my mates from broken homes, to be free of the terrible longing to be home. I desperately missed them, but I knew as we all did that I had no choice anymore, I had chosen to be here and that was that.

The dropship infantry was voluntary, even though military service wasn't. Conscripts often sat in garrisons across the Union and her far flung colonies with little else to do other than hold ground that was probably never going to be taken, and those that would come with us to war would follow only in our wake, only landing when we had secured a landing zone the size of a nation. We in the dropship infantry often referred to them as 'sandbag fillers' for their defensive role, and we resented them for their easy ride.

The day my conscription papers had come through had been not a week after my sixteenth birthday. Theoretically I had the qualifications to go to college and become something more, but my family would never have been able to afford it and I certainly wasn't smart enough to get an education grant from the Union, so like the rest of the impoverished masses of Europe I had been 'selected' to serve. My mum had cried that day, but my dad had taken it well.

'Don't worry, son,' he had said, 'You'll probably end up on a nice garrison somewhere warm on the Med or something.'

Why had I then chosen to enlist with the dropship infantry, whilst my unknowing family waited anxiously outside the recruitment office one cold day in Portsmouth city centre?

'To kill people,' was Peters' answer to that question. And to many of those who served within the Union's voluntary ranks that was the only answer that made sense, but I think there was more to it than that.

I think I wanted to do something, see something, and be part of the new world that man had made for himself up in the stars - even if it wasn't all that pleasant. I wanted to be more than another disadvantaged child who saw out his four years of national service on some lonely garrison, only to return to the slums with nothing to say for himself. I wanted to see more even than the galaxy; I wanted to fear, I wanted to see the whites of my enemies' eyes and I wanted to share in the glory of the Union's eternal war across the heavens. Unfortunately I was beginning to realize that life wasn't always quite so poetic, and that service in the dropship infantry brought with it pain, loneliness and sometimes, misery.

My mum was devastated when she found out what I had done and that I had been selected for training for the dropship infantry, she cried well into the night. Even my dad shed a tear, but he chose not to scold me.

'You've made your decision, son,' he had said woodenly.

I *had* made my decision, and there was no going back. My dad's smiling face, wrinkled around his squinting eyes stared through me from the tablet. I wished he was there for me, but he wasn't.

'You alright?'

Startled, I spun around from my open locker; it was Climo. I would have to be mindful of those bulkhead doors in future, I told myself, because I hadn't even noticed him enter the room.

'Yeah,' I answered curtly. I busied myself again with my locker while Climo changed into his tracksuit.

'How's your eye?'

'It'll heal, nothing broken.'

'Maybe you should see the doc, get it checked out?'

Climo appeared to be genuinely concerned for me, but I couldn't forget how he had watched as Woody pounded me while I lay helpless on the ground.

Climo must have read my mind, because he threw up his arms defensively. 'Look, mate, I'm sorry about what happened. What could I do? Woody's a senior bod, I've only been on ship just over a year.'

Climo's explanation only made me angrier, but I knew not to kick off with him, he was senior to me, and I had quickly learnt that on Challenger seniority was everything. 'It's fine, don't worry about it.'

I felt him staring at me as I turned my back, probably thinking of something else to say, but eventually he set about sorting out his kit in his own locker.

'Laundry drop off's at half-six in the morning,' Climo said, presumably trying to change the subject. Annoyed as I was, I took note of the time, my PT kit was soaked in sweat and I only had three sets of it.

'Where is it?' I asked.

'I'll show you in the morning, if you like.'

'Thanks,' I finished what I was doing and locked my locker. I stuffed my dirty kit into a laundry bag and slid it under my bed ready for the morning, then began undressing for bed.

'You going to sleep now?' Climo asked, surprised.

'Yeah.' Damn right, I had barely had a few hours of sleep in over a day, and the time lag between leaving Fort Abu Naji, and having almost had my head knocked off my shoulders hadn't helped.

Climo shrugged. 'Fair enough.'

As soon as my head hit the pillow I fell asleep.

7: The Call to Arms

The soft kiss from the lips of a girl I had once fancied at school was interrupted by a familiar screaming alarm. Startled, her lithe arms withdrew from around my body and her breasts no longer pressed seductively against my chest. Instead it was only my blanket that I felt against my skin, and her sweet voice was replaced by the groaning of troopers and the constant whine of the air ducts in our tiny four-man room.

It was zero-six-hundred aboard Challenger, and the beginning of a whole new day. But my soul plummeted into despair, and I had to force myself to sit up and put my feet down once more onto the cold metal floor of reality.

'Why do they have to make that alarm so loud?' Brown complained, thrashing in his bed.

My face felt wet, so I instinctively went to wipe it and my hand came away covered in shaving foam. How original, I thought. I quickly wiped it away with my towel before I stood up, so Woody and the others might think it had come off whilst I slept and their prank had been in vain.

'Morning, Moralee,' Woody's voice caused my heart to skip a beat as I stood.

'Morning,' I answered flatly.

'How's the eye?' he slid out from under the covers so that his legs dangled over my bunk. I knew he was big, but I hadn't realised quite how big he really was until then. Woody clearly worked out in the ship's gym a lot, his biceps were enormous and his stomach rippled with muscle. He had an awful tattoo of a man's face on his thigh, I couldn't work out what it was meant to be, and I never chose to ask.

'Not too bad,' I lied. It was agony. 'Hurts a bit.'

'Well, that's what you get for gobbing off isn't it? Got to learn your place, haven't you, Moralee?'

I nodded feebly. 'Yeah.'

'Yes, *what?*'

I hesitated. 'Yes, Staff.'

Woody giggled to himself, like a disturbed child might laugh whilst tormenting a small animal.

'Much better.'

What a freak, I thought as I wrapped my towel around my waist and made my exit for the shower. My locker was locked, so I knew there wasn't much he could do with it. If he broke the lock or damaged my bedding he would be charged, and I doubted even the most senior of troopers would escape the platoon sergeant's wrath if he messed around with his accommodation.

I joined the queue for the ablutions, ignoring the stares and the hushed chatter about my eye from other members of the platoon.

'You happy with what's going on today?' Joe, who I now knew was my section second in command, was on his way out of the ablutions. He seemed unhappy that he had to talk to me, and his tone was meant to convey that it was not a friendly conversation.

'No, Corporal,' I replied. Lancejacks were still corporals, and were meant to be addressed the same even though they were not on an equal standing with the 'full' corporals.

'Right, you need to make sure you check to find out what's going on every evening. Surely you know that?'

'Yes, Corporal,' I agreed.

He looked me up and down as if sizing me up, and then sighed in the same way my dad would sigh if I did something stupid, 'Gym circuit training this morning, then more work up the stores. More ammo came in last night.'

'Yes, Corporal.' How much ammo could this ship hold? The ammo store was already stacked almost to the ceiling!

Joe flicked his hand for me to go away. 'Go on, then.'

Later that morning Climo took me to the laundry drop off point, not far from the galley. Woody and Brown had looked across disapprovingly at Climo when we left, but said nothing, and Climo didn't appear to notice.

'There's a board up outside Corporal Evans' bulkhead where everything you need to know about the next day is written up, so just check that in the mornings,' Climo explained as we walked with our bags slung over our shoulders around the circumference corridor. There was an awkward silence between us, and I sensed that Climo was torn between guilt for not helping me the day before and fear of reprisals from a trooper senior to him. Apart from the time he had spent on ship, and presumably an exercise or two, Climo wasn't much more experienced as a trooper than I was, and not much more senior either. Perhaps he knew what I was going through, I thought, it couldn't have been long since it had been him who had been at the bottom of the food chain, and possibly at the end of somebody's fist.

'What's Corporal Evans like?' I asked. He was the only one of the three section commanders I had noticed so far, and he was clearly revered and loved in equal measure by the platoon. Without him needing to say a word, people stepped out of his way in queues, and stiffened when he entered a room almost as if he were the OC himself.

'He's a living legend,' Climo said simply. 'Probably the best section commander in the company. He's been in ten years or so, and he's served on New Earth, Eden, Rendezvous …'

'New Earth?' I interrupted.

Climo smiled. 'Yeah, that's right. He was with one of the last companies to manage to escape from the southern continent before the Chinese drove our ships out of orbit.'

I drew in my breath. Wow, now that was, *'hard-core'* - I said the word aloud.

Climo laughed. 'He never talks about it, so don't even think of asking him about it. He's qualified to promote to sergeant, but apparently there's no place for him.'

We slung our bags into the open laundry hatch and signed them in on a tablet attached to the wall beside it.

'He and Jamo don't get on, but they try to pretend they do,' Climo continued.

'Jamo' was Sergeant James' nickname, but you daren't call him that to his face if you value your life.

'Why not?'

Climo shrugged. 'Jamo's a bully, and completely mental. They're just two *very* different troopers and their personalities clash.'

People like Woody probably thrived in platoons run by people like Jamo, I thought.

'What's the boss like?'

'Seems okay, we don't see him all that much really. He pretty much lets Jamo run the platoon on ship, too new to have any sway over him.'

I nodded my understanding. In theory a platoon commander outranked his platoon sergeant and made all of the big decisions, but in practice a strong platoon sergeant would often run the platoon behind the scenes, pointing the young officer in the right direction until he was experienced enough to be trusted. Even then the platoon sergeant would watch him closely and sometimes, rarely of course, the two could come to blows.

As we made our way back toward the galley the ship's announcement system crackled into life, echoing around the circumference corridor, 'Attention, attention, all personnel are to report to the galley immediately, end of message.'

Climo smiled grimly. 'Guess you'll get to find out what the boss is like on the ground soon enough.'

He would be right.

'Come on, you lot, let's get a move on, eh?' A corporal waved the building crowds into the galley and me and Climo followed.

The galley was rapidly filling with troopers, sailors and dropship crew alike, easily over a hundred people. The air ducts blasted cool air into the hall in an effort to keep the room from overheating and its air turning stale. Like a herd of animals, we jostled with each other as we attempted to find our platoons and the right place to form-up. It was a rare occasion to see so many people in the same place at once on a Union warship, which meant something was afoot and people murmured and chattered to each other about the meaning of this sudden change to normal ship's routine, and almost every conversation I heard contained a familiar name that sent a cold chill down my spine; New Earth.

'One platoon! Close in over here!' A hand waved above the crowd to identify where we should form-up and me and Climo pushed our way through the throng.

The three rifle platoons of the company formed-up into ranks along one side of the galley, whilst company headquarters, the ship's crew and the dropship crews were forming-up opposite. I didn't often see the naval personnel on ship; we lived separately, ate at different times and worked in entirely different sections of the ship. Their white uniforms clearly identified them against our grey drop trooper fatigues. The dropship crews, dressed in a similar fashion to the naval lads could be told apart by their shaven heads, a throwback to days when they had to be connected to their dropships by an implant at the back of their skulls known as a 'jack', which earned them their nickname. Biotech had become taboo of recent years and the jacks had settled for small implants beneath the skull that connected wirelessly to the ship instead, but they still shaved their heads, perhaps as a fashion.

I fell in at the end of my platoon, finding myself on the front rank. I cursed silently, as being on the front rank meant I was fully on show to whoever took the parade and anything wrong with me - from the way I tucked in my shirt to how well I sewed my name badge and insignia - could be picked up and would earn me yet another telling off.

Sergeant James was rounding up the platoon like the other three platoon sergeants, ushering stragglers into the growing formation with barked orders and scathing insults.

'Hurry up you idle arse wipes! Get there - no - there! Reesy, get a grip on yourself and fall in properly like everyone else!'

Woody jogged across the centre of the galley as the last remnants of the company found their positions.

'Hurry up, Wood.' Jamo changed the tone of his voice to a lesser degree of disrespect, though I swear I saw his lips curl.

'Sorry, Sergeant,' Woody chirped indifferently.

The last man to arrive was Corporal Evans, who walked casually over toward the platoon sergeant. The two NCOs regarded each other like two Union class boxers might size each other up for a fight, one a brutish tank of a man, the other a stooping giant almost too tall for dropship service. Corporal Evans tipped his hat slightly. 'Alright, mate? What's happening?'

Jamo returned the respectful nod and led the section commander into the centre of the galley and out of earshot. I watched their whispered conversation but they gave nothing away in their body language and Corporal Evans merely nodded his head slowly. They were both trained platoon sergeants, I had discovered, but unfortunately one of them hadn't a platoon to go to and so had to remain a section commander, I imagined Corporal Evans must have hated being in such a position, and he must have resented Jamo.

The platoon murmured softly as we waited to find out what was going on, exchanging everything from complaints of the lack of breakfast to elaborate conspiracy theories.

'I heard a rumour we might be returning to Eden for another exercise, like a show of force and that for the Indians.'

'I'm telling you, mate, it's the captain, she's gone mental, apparently the other day she got some of the navy boys to ...'

'FALL IN!' I jumped at the almighty bellow. Corporal Evans and Jamo quickly scuttled behind us to where they were meant to fall in behind the platoon, and the room suddenly silenced as the company sergeant major walked in amongst the parade like a lion might stalk into a frozen flock of sheep, sizing up each and every one of us in turn with hard unforgiving eyes. He gripped his pacing stick in both hands in such a manner that it looked as though he was about to break it in half on his knee and use the broken ends as weapons. Gold insignia decorated his fatigues and his boots were so highly polished that they reflected the room like blackened glass.

'Stand still, you!' He jabbed his pacing stick toward some unlucky man on the front rank of one of the other platoons. I gulped as he paced along in front of us all, his eyes scanning. We weren't expected to be dressed as impeccably as he was - we were, after all, on board a ship of war - but if we weren't up to the standard he expected there was no telling what he might do. The company sergeant major was to the company what the platoon sergeant was to the platoon, he was its beating heart, its very soul and it was he who upheld its discipline.

The sergeant major stopped at me and looked me up and down with a scowl. 'And who might you be, lad?'

He was a Yorkshire man, the accent was unmistakably thick. Cold eyes stared deep into mine and I might as well have been looking at the Devil himself because I was terrified.

I stammered, 'I ... P-Private Moralee, Sir.'

'Moralee,' he repeated the word with a grimace as if he found it distasteful. 'Haven't seen you before? New lad is he, Sergeant James?'

'He is, Sir,' Jamo answered from behind. 'Arrived yesterday, Sir.'

He turned back to me. 'How are you finding it, Moralee?'

'V-very good, Sir.'

The sergeant major appeared unsatisfied with the answer. *'Good?'*

Everyone was listening in silence but thankfully they were all facing rigidly to their fronts and could not see me blush red. 'Yes, Sir.'

'You're on one of the great ships of the Union navy, lad, poised to go forth and see the world, and all you can say is its *'good?'* He rested the end of his stick on the ground and leant on it with the palms of his hands. He was bored, I realised, and was probably playing with me while he waited for something to happen.

Something did happen - somebody moved a few places to my left and the monstrous man's face contorted into rage so suddenly it made me jump. *'Who was that?* Who in God's creation was that?! Why are you moving, you little weasel? *Who are you?'* His stick pointed directly into the ranks - but I couldn't see his victim.

'Greggerson, Sir,' a tiny voice replied. I felt instantly relieved to no longer be the focus of the sergeant major's attention, but that relief quickly turned to guilt as I realised poor Greggerson was now on the firing line. I

hadn't known him well on Uralis, but he seemed a nice, if slightly timid young lad, who had been a friend to me during the past twenty-four hours.

'If you don't have the discipline to stay still during a parade then how will you have the discipline to assault the enemy at close quarters upon orders?'

'I-I don't know, Sir.'

'You don't know,' he spat, stalking toward his prey. 'Well God help the Union if you're all that England has left to offer. Sergeant James!' he snapped. 'This man needs to be educated!'

'Sir!'

We waited in silence while the sergeant major paced impatiently around the middle of the galley, tapping a tune only he knew with the golden tip of his pacing stick. Suddenly he noticed somebody emerge from a nearby bulkhead and snapped smartly to attention.

'Parade!' He screamed, and the formation of men appeared to grow several centimetres as we thrust out our chests and lifted our heads proudly upwards as one, 'Parade ... SHUN!'

Two hundred boots stamped against the deck with an almighty crump that echoed about the ship's metal walls as we came to attention, feet together and arms tucked firmly against our sides.

The ship's captain, unmistakable in her smart white uniform and peaked cap and glistening with medals and golden embroidery, strode into the centre of the formation where the sergeant major waited.

The sergeant major saluted her as she approached. 'Ma'am, A Company is formed up and ready for your address.'

The Captain returned the salute with a smile. 'Thank you, Sergeant Major, please have the men stand at ease.'

'As you wish, Ma'am.' Then, to us, 'Stand at ... EASE!'

Our boots crashed against the floor again so that we now stood with our feet shoulder width apart, hands clasped behind our backs.

The captain's smile faded as she looked around her at those under her command. She had absolute power over all of us, the power of life and death entrusted to her by the Union and not even the company commander who was a major by army ranks escaped her authority. She was a distinctly uninteresting looking woman were it not for her uniform, as white as a brand new set of bed sheets and glistening with polished campaign medals and golden buttons.

The captain frowned as she recalled a terrible memory. 'Two years ...' she began.

She allowed those two words to sink in, and instantly I knew exactly what she was talking about. We all did.

'*Two years* ago this fine vessel fled in defeat from New Earth with the few survivors of the third fleet. She fled without having even fired a shot, and her drop troopers never left their hangars.'

Somehow Corporal Evans had. He had been down on the surface of New Earth as the terrible and unstoppable onslaught of the Chinese invasion engulfed the colony. I imagined him and others like him fighting a futile defence and then making their desperate withdrawal to the dropships and then into space, and I shuddered.

'*Two years* on and still now the Union aches with the shame of its defeat. But nobody on Earth can possibly understand the shame brought upon Challenger and her crew. No politician sat in Brussels or Berlin can ever possibly feel the same hunger for revenge as we have done, patrolling the remaining colonies like starved dogs left to settle for scraps while the cowardly victors wallow in their ill found glory.'

The captain paused for dramatic effect. '*Two years* we have yearned for revenge against our traitorous old allies the Chinese. *Two years* we have bottled our rage and bitten our tongues and some people said we were trying to forget. But we never forget. We have planned. We have re-trained, rebuilt and recruited. Our new enemy thought that they had succeeded in cutting us off at the knees, ending the fight in us once and for all, but all they have done is fill us with a ferocious anger that cannot be subdued. We have been waiting, but now my friends, we are ready, and the waiting is over.'

The captain paced the room, sweeping her gaze across all of us as she spoke, her movements becoming more and more animated as she spoke with increasing vehemence.

'They say that the soil of New Earth is stained red with the blood of Union soldiers. But now it shall be *Chinese* blood that will flow freely across those unforgiving lands like rivers!'

'Guess we're going in, then,' somebody murmured behind me, clearly unimpressed by the speech.

A tingling wave shot across my nerve endings as I realised that the impact of the captain's announcement. We all knew what the captain was going to say next. In my mind's eye I pictured the dead surface of New Earth, and it was indeed as red as though it were stained by the blood of the thousands who had died there since it had been colonized centuries ago.

'I have received orders today for a move to a rendezvous outside of the Hope system with the third and first fleet,' the captain continued, reading now from a tablet she had retrieved and unfolded from her pocket. 'It contains the preliminary orders for a voyage into the Centauri system. Our mission is outlined within those orders and it reads as follows: "The third fleet is to capture New Earth in orbit and on the surface in concert with elements of the first fleet, in order to bring about the enemy's defeat in the Centauri system."'

The Captain returned her tablet and looked around us once more. 'More details with regards to those orders will be passed down to you through your relevant chains of command, and much more detailed orders will be received and disseminated in due course. What you need to know for now is that we will shortly be departing from Hope for our rendezvous which will take approximately two days. From there we will depart for the Centauri system.'

My nerves tingled again. *This is really it*, I thought, the reason why I had joined the dropship infantry: we were going to war. A strange mixture of emotions passed through my body; excitement at the thought of doing my duty and being part of something historians might speak of for hundreds of years but also a terrible sense of foreboding. Everybody knew the statistics of making a 'hard drop' onto a hostile surface. *One in three dropships didn't make it.*

'The Chinese have had two years to prepare for us. They have dug deep into the rock, so deep that only infantry will prize them out. They are highly trained, equipped and motivated. We must break their will. We will strike hard and we will strike fast to shatter their resolve, and we *will* win. People will die, I won't lie,' she shook her head gravely, 'Some of you won't return with us to Earth, some of you will lose friends, most of you will kill, and all of you will lose what is left of the innocence of your youth,' she was looking over to us, the drop troopers who would land on the surface and do the dirty work with dropships, gravtanks, rifles and, if necessary, bayonets.

'Get on with it,' another voice hissed in frustration. The vast majority of Challenger's troopers had never carried out a combat drop for real, but we were all volunteers and we had known what we were in for when we enlisted.

'Too long has the Union felt the shame of its defeat. Now it is time for us to show the world that we are not a fleeting nation on the brink of losing its grip on the cosmos, but a superpower who bows to no man. We *will* defeat the Chinese, and the Union will go on to rule the known galaxy for a millennium. Gentlemen, I wish you good luck. All of you. Sergeant Major, carry on, please.'

The sergeant major snapped again to attention. 'Parade … SHUN!'

We stood silently at attention as the captain strode away. Satisfied that she was gone and out of earshot the sergeant major relaxed and strode back into the centre of the parade.

'Ship's crew, continue under your own arrangements.' He ushered the crew away, leaving only the troopers and the jacks behind.

'Stand the men at ease, please, Sergeant Major.' A dropship major walked into view, as elegantly dressed as the sergeant major, but with a glistening ceremonial sword sheaved at his side. He was the OC, the highest ranking drop trooper on board challenger. It was he who would lead the company on its drop to the surface and hopefully would lead us back again. He was stocky in appearance, with an almost apish gait that I wouldn't normally expect of an officer. When he spoke he was clearly well educated, which sounded strange coming from a man who wouldn't look out of place on the streets of Portsmouth. His name was Major McColl, and he was known for being a no-nonsense commander and a shrewd tactician.

'You've heard enough from the captain,' the OC said, smiling knowingly at us all. 'I will speak with all of you in due course. I should like to speak with all three platoon commanders after this parade. The remainder are to prepare for jump. Let's get this done,' I wasn't sure if the last sentence was referring to us preparing to jump to the rendezvous or the invasion of New Earth itself.

We were brought to attention one last time whilst the officers left the hall, and then finally the company sergeant major ordered us back to our accommodation. Breakfast would have to wait, I guessed.

———

I could never hope to fully understand how Challenger worked. Strange ghostly noises echoed about the ship as we sat in our rooms, with the bulkheads sealed against decompression, locking us into our tiny room like a tomb. She was preparing to 'jump', her previously dormant space drive, powering up with immense surges of power generated by the fusion reactor deep within her core. Incomprehensible calculations were being created by the ship's array of navigational computers before being checked laboriously by a dedicated team of navigators. System checks would be methodically carried out by the crew and all unoccupied sections would have their atmosphere pumped out to reduce the risk of a 'blow out' - a sudden and catastrophic decompression which could cause a chain reaction that would destroy the entire ship.

I sat nervously on the end of my bed, ignoring Woody's legs which swung obtrusively over the edge of the top bunk, most likely with the intent to wind me up. Brown and Climo looked equally on edge, and sat waiting anxiously for something to happen.

'I hate this bit,' Brown said to break the silence. It was rare for him to speak, I had noticed, he barely ever said much more than a single sentence, especially not to me.

'Why?' Woody asked from above me. 'Nothing happens.'

'I just don't like it.'

Nobody likes making a jump, but Woody was right, nothing ever did happen. Challenger's space drive didn't work within the confines of the rules that governed us and not even the slightest of G-forces would be felt, mainly because she wasn't accelerating or decelerating as you or I might imagine. The only way I ever knew about a jump having been made was the announcement system telling me that it had. But it wasn't what *did* happen that freaked us out, it was what *could* happen. Power overloads, incorrect calculations or faults within the space drive itself could all lead to the terror of decompression or God only knew what else.

Alone in our thoughts and our fears, we waited in silence for the ship to jump. A Company was going to war.

8: The Jump

It was gone ten ship's time when we finally made the jump to the rendezvous. We would arrive in deep space after a relatively 'short' two-day jump, we were told by the platoon commander, after our bulkheads were unsealed, and there we would marry up with the remainder of the fleet.

'I know no more than you do at this stage,' the boss said, as the platoon crowded anxiously outside their rooms to listen, 'Anything I could say right now would be pure speculation and nothing more.'

'Well, what are your speculations, Boss?' Corporal Weston, one of the section commanders - who was a young, stocky looking Welshman - appeared irritated at the lack of information. The three corporals were huddled together in their own little group at the far end of the corridor with Corporal Evans in the middle. The 'screw club' as it was known amongst the lower ranks, was completely exclusive, and even the most senior lancejack was an outsider, however well he might be regarded.

The platoon commander sighed resignedly, 'At a guess, the OC believes that we will enter Alpha Centauri in a month's time. For those of you who don't know, the system is composed of three stars, two of which harbour nothing more than a few small rocky planetoids and a single gas giant. The first fleet is likely to be used to secure those outlying worlds with support from the marines, leaving the third fleet - us - to deal with Alpha Centauri Alpha and the capital planet. We are the senior unit in the fleet and likely to be one of the first to drop.'

'You mean the least upgraded, and so the most expendable,' the third corporal, Corporal David, retorted sourly. Jamo shot him an angry glance but said nothing.

The platoon commander pursed his lips. 'Right. Any other questions?'

One of the more senior privates raised a hand. 'Is it true, Sir, that the Chinese have a laser battery built on the surface that can shoot a ship out of the sky?' A few troopers murmured their agreement to the story.

'Shut up, Rawson, you moron!' Jamo finally snapped, silencing the platoon.

The boss, who appeared amused at the question, raised a hand calmly. 'I can assure you that if lasers made an effective alternative to guided shells and missiles from atmosphere to orbit or vice versa, then Challenger would be equipped with them by now. Any other questions?'

'That aren't stupid,' Jamo added angrily.

'No? Good. I will pass on any further information as it comes. In the meantime we will begin training in preparation. We have the range booked after lunch. Sergeant James, carry on, please.'

'Sir.' The platoon sergeant stared blankly at the boss.

'Right. I'll be going, then.' The boss took the hint and exited the accommodation toward his own quarters.

'Here we go,' Climo whispered under his breath.

'Listen in, you bunch of cretins.' The platoon sergeant's face contorted with rage as he stalked amongst us. 'First the Chinese will have giant lasers; next they'll have nanites that eat you from the inside out and genetically enhanced bodies that heal gunshot wounds in seconds - rumours - just stupid rumours. If I catch you making up stupid rumours I will punch a hole through you, do you understand?'

'Yes, Sergeant,' we answered.

He glanced across at Corporal David. 'That goes for all of you,' he said, and the corporal looked down. Corporal Evans said nothing, but looked back to the platoon sergeant as if he weren't bothered by his withering glare. 'Where is Greggerson?'

Woody pointed toward the small trooper with a grin. 'There, Sergeant.'

Jamo walked toward Greggerson, his fists clenched. 'Face or gut?' he demanded.

Greggerson blanched. 'Sorry, Sergeant?'

'Face or fucking gut?'

Fear spread across Greggerson's face as he realised what was meant, and he mustered courage to speak. 'Gut, Serg … oof!' Jamo's punch threw Greggerson to the wall with a thump. The hapless trooper crumpled as the platoon sergeant walked away.

'Discipline! Discipline is what will keep us alive on New Earth! It's gonna be ugly down there, and people are gonna die. Some of you lot,' he pointed around at us each in turn, '… will die! It's a fact of life. You need to have the discipline to respect rank and orders, to carry out drills correctly as you're taught and not be idle! You need to stand in the face of the enemy and not run, because it's the only way that we as a platoon stand a chance to survive. Stand still on parade, don't spread rumours, respect your superiors or I swear I will make this journey even more miserable than it has to be. Do you understand me?'

'Yes, Sergeant.'

'DO YOU UNDERSTAND ME???!!' We all jumped.

'YES, SERGEANT!'

'Do one to your breakfast before I lose my temper. Ev - ensure they make it to the simulators straight after.'

Corporal Evans nodded without a word and the platoon bundled out into the circumference corridor to grab their missed meal.

I hesitated and went back to crouch beside Greggerson who still lay gasping on the floor whilst the accommodation emptied. 'You okay, mate?'

He wiped tears from his eyes. 'Yeah.'

'Not the luckiest two, you and me, eh?' I chuckled sombrely.

'No,' Greggerson replied, finally sitting up with my help.

'You alright?' a familiar voice asked with concern; it was Climo.

Greggerson stood up. 'I'll survive,' he replied gravely.

'Making some new friends, Climo?' Woody sneered as he passed us. He laughed, and behind him Brown laughed too.

'Get on after your boyfriend, Browner,' Climo replied, loud enough only for Brown to hear.

'I'll be alright, Climo,' Greggerson insisted, but Climo was already gone, the bulkhead to the circumference corridor closing behind him. I wondered if he was afraid to hang around us for too long.

'This crow shit is really starting to wind me up,' I said, and Greggerson nodded.

'Do you ever feel like you've made a terrible mistake?' he asked as he regained his composure. 'I've wished you stayed with the conscripts!'

'Yeah,' I said with feeling. 'All the time.'

———

The usually loud and boisterous queue for scoff was subdued into concerned murmuring that morning as the hundred or so members of the company began to openly discuss the impending operation, and New Earth was the hot topic around the tables, spiced up by the inevitable and sometimes downright outrageous rumours.

'I heard it's true about that laser battery,' Climo said as he stabbed at his food with a plastic spoon. He had offered me and Greggerson a chair at his table, to the barely concealed surprise of the troopers already sat with him. What had prompted his decision to include us I didn't know, perhaps it was guilt or empathy from seeing how we were being treated or perhaps he was simply making an effort to befriend a new addition to his section. Although battle loomed on the not too distant horizon, at least for that moment it felt good to be a little closer to being accepted.

One of the troopers sat with us was a Southampton lad called Sam Wakefield, who rarely chose to acknowledge our presence, instead speaking only with Climo and the others. Now he blew a raspberry and rolled his eyes in mock disbelief. 'And who did you hear that one from, mate? Stevo?'

Climo's hesitation to answer gave Sam the confirmation he needed.

'Mate, don't listen to that stroker, he's the platoon gossip monger. Plus the bloke has less spine than a jellyfish.' The comparison brokered a laugh about the table and I joined in, even though I didn't really know Stevo.

'Stuff like that ain't gonna come from nowhere, is it?' Climo said defensively.

'Mate, that's exactly where it's come from: *nowhere*.'

Rumours were rife in the dropship infantry, as I'm sure they were in any other front line unit. Rumours, religion and superstition were an everyday aspect to many troopers' lives, perhaps because we lived so close to death, and whatever waited beyond.

'Who's Stevo?' I asked.

Climo jabbed a thumb towards the senior bods table, where the top boys talked loudly and laughed with the lancejacks. 'See the bloke with the air brake ears?' Stevo, I saw, was the lad who had asked me what I knew about our deployment when I had first visited the ablutions on Challenger, which kind of fitted his description as a gossiper. He did have rather large ears, with a chubby rounded face like Woody's but he lacked the build of the larger senior trooper. Stevo was sat beside Woody, with Brown sat across from him.

'Near enough all of the rumours on this ship come from Stevo,' Climo said. 'But nobody says a word, because he's the platoon senior bod and Woody's lapdog.'

'He loves a bit of gossip, Stevo does,' Sam agreed. 'That's why his ears are so big!'

'He's a tube,' Climo said.

'Go and tell him then,' Sam challenged and Climo shrugged.

I looked back to the senior table, where Chammy was working everyone into a frenzy of laughter with his jokes.

I wondered aloud, 'How long until you become senior?'

Climo thought about it. 'Dunno, just depends I guess.'

Sam frowned, and for the first time he spoke directly to me and Greggerson. 'You don't want nothing at all to do with them clowns anyway,' he said bitterly. 'Bullies, kiss-arses and idiots who are just waiting for the Union to let them go. That's all they are. Being a senior trooper should be all about ability but instead it's just time served. It's ridiculous that some of them have some sort of God-given right to tell us what to do. Trust me, that'll all change in a month's time …' He sounded ominous.

Climo laughed. 'Chill out, mate!'

Sam shook his head, his rant was in full flow. 'True though isn't it? See them two there,' he pointed discreetly at two uninteresting looking lads at the end of the senior table, 'Mitch and Harmes - the platoon smart launcher crew. They make out they're the masters at firing smart missiles. You just point and fire, point and fire - it's not hard - the missiles themselves are smarter than those two.'

'To be fair the missile is probably smarter than all of us,' Climo pointed out. 'You've got to be pretty stupid to do all this of your own free will.'

'Speak for yourself,' a tall Kentish lad, whose name was Davo, snapped irritably. 'I'm not here coz I'm stupid, I'm here coz I wanna serve my country.'

Woody and the senior table had finished their meal and passed us as they made their way to the waste chute.

'Don't forget to do the block jobs,' Woody said, scowling at me as he went. He appeared to hate any sign of me settling in, as if it was too fast for his liking.

'Yes, Sir,' Davo hissed under his breath.

'I hate that bloke.' Climo said what everybody was thinking. It was the first time he had openly admitted his disliking of the senior private and I felt some warmth in knowing that it wasn't just me.

Since we were back on the subject of seniority, I decided to find out more about Woody. 'Is he the most senior?'

'Nah, that's Stevo,' Sam said. 'But nobody takes Stevo seriously. If he wasn't sucking up to Woody all the time he'd be nobody. They're both on their last year, so they'll be off next time we swing by Earth.'

'*If* we do,' Climo said, stressing the '*If*'.

'Woody's a meathead and a bully,' Sam went on. 'That's about it. Nobody likes him. He likes to abuse the new blokes because they can't defend themselves.'

Without thinking my hand went to touch my bruised eye. It had been a day since Woody had assaulted me and still it hurt to touch the bone around the socket.

Sam saw me and smiled. 'Nasty piece of work, he is, with a wicked punch.'

'I heard he got bullied when he first got to battalion, used to hide in the ablutions and cry,' Climo said. 'That's why he's like he is.'

'I heard he bottled it on the Eden campaign.'

'What happened?' Greggerson asked. We had heard so little about Eden, it was a subject that nobody who had been there liked to discuss, but the less we heard of it the more we wanted to know. Eden, meant to be a great terraforming project that brought nations together in harmony, was a hell.

'He tried to get himself out of dropping, didn't he?' Climo asked, closing up his horror box.

Davo shrugged. 'Something like that, I heard.'

'He's not as great as he makes out, is he,' Sam said.

'Is that why Sergeant James is a bit funny with him?' I asked, recalling the way his lips had curled at the sight of Woody arriving late to our parade in the galley.

Sam laughed. 'Jamo? Jamo hates everyone.'

'At least he's consistent,' Davo pointed out with a smile.

'He definitely hates me,' Greggerson made a show of touching his belly where Jamo had punched him.

'Yeah he does hate you,' Sam said, scrapping the legs of his chair as he stood. 'Get used to it!'

————

Not more than half an hour after breakfast we were paraded back in the galley, which had been converted into a lecture hall with chairs laid out in neat rows to seat the entire company, plus the jacks, and with a hologram screen set up against the wall where the food was normally issued.

We then received an endless series of lectures on New Earth from the ship's intelligence officer - who was a lanky naval lieutenant with pasty white skin - the perfect stereotype of what we in the infantry knew as 'spooks'.

Some of the information he gave us was new to us, and some of it was old, but nevertheless we all sat and listened and watched images on the hologram intently, not wanting to miss a thing lest it cost us our lives.

New Earth was the oldest colony ever to be established by mankind outside of the solar system, first stood upon some three hundred years ago. Like every other world that humanity would discover in its corporation driven spread into the stars, New Earth was dead, as it had always been for the several billions of years it had existed. To look at New Earth you might identify a close similarity with parts of Mars: jagged mountain ranges, gaping canyons and vast empty deserts scattered with rocks from ancient asteroid impacts. New Earth had a similar mass, temperature and composition to Earth itself, hence its name. It sported a large surface of water – eighty-percent we were told - and a weather system that included rain and even snow. Like Uralis, though, and many of the other major colonies, New Earth's atmosphere was impossible to breathe unassisted, the deadly difference given away by her turquoise sky. Inhabitants wore respirators and lived underground, or in domes of glass or airtight buildings. We were used to such an environment anyway, so that made no difference to the way that we would operate.

The population of New Earth had increased since its colonization to somewhere in excess of fifty million, a number dwarfed by the billions living on crowded Earth - but for any colony that was quite a number. That fifty million was divided into three significant parts, the two larger and equal portions at twenty million a piece was made up of European and Chinese nationality, with the smaller part being Russian. There had been a tradition of acceptance between the ethnic groups, who lived as neighbours on sections of the planet's continents that had been neatly divided up by the colonial powers and the corporations. It was only in the recent few decades - as relations between the old allies began to cool - that tensions on the colony rose.

'The Chinese corporations wanted more land and demanded the Union give up her own territory,' the lieutenant explained to his audience, showing us a rotating New Earth atlas on the hologram, divided into sections that were coloured in the flags of the three colonial powers that controlled the surface. 'In particular the southern continent, where most of the Union mines were located.'

The lieutenant went on to describe more of the geography of New Earth and the patchwork of colonial territories that appeared to follow no obvious pattern across the four main continents and smaller islands. We learned about the planet's Union capital; the Emerald City, a beautiful arrangement of glass domes, spheres and tunnels lit with all the colours of the rainbow. With a population of two million, it could be seen from space.

New Earth had nothing in the way of materials that couldn't be found closer to the home planet. What made it so desirable was its booming manufacturing industry. Unlike asteroids and some of the moons found orbiting many gas giants, the planet had an abundance of raw materials from right across the periodic table. It had no need for imports and could support a large human population without assistance from Earth. Also, unlike Earth, the planet wasn't divided by a thousand borders, and so the movement of raw materials was simpler still. The planet was a leader in nanotech, and was a leading mass producer in everything from computers to warships.

Due to the large Russian and Chinese presence and the open trading society that had existed before the Betrayal, English was widely spoken, although within the Union sectors - German, French and Spanish were the primary languages. It wouldn't be a problem for us, since our respirator headsets and mouthpieces were programmed to translate for us.

It was hard to imagine what the population of that holographic planet had been through in recent years, no news had escaped New Earth since its capture, except for Chinese propaganda on the net back home that we were told to ignore, 'What do you think they've done to them?' I wondered aloud.

Climo shrugged. 'Slave labour probably. Who knows?'

Joe Mac turned from where he sat in front of me and Climo. 'Oi, shut up you pair of skid marks,' he hissed.

'Sorry,' we murmured. Out of the corner of my eye I noticed Woody leaning forward to look at us from a few seats down. His eyes bored into my burning cheeks, but I pretended not to notice him and eventually he returned his attention to the speaker. *Great*, I thought, no doubt he would come up with some way to make me pay for that later.

He did. As soon as the lecture finished and we were on our way back to our accommodation to wait for more timings, Woody rounded on me and Climo, with Stevo and Brown stood just behind him. The rest of the company crowded past us around the circumference corridor, either unaware or simply uninterested in the confrontation.

Woody scowled. 'What were you doing talking in that lecture? Not interesting enough for you?' Woody didn't care about the lecture, I knew, he simply wanted some reason to continue his campaign of intimidation against me, but this time his contempt was directed at both me and Climo.

I tried to cool things down. 'I'm sorry, we weren't thinking,' I admitted. 'It was really stupid.'

'Was I talking to you, crow bag?' Woody spat, then turned to Climo who had blushed crimson.

'Crow don't speak,' Stevo said to me from where he stood behind Woody's hulking frame. 'They get *spoken to*.'

'Are you missing your crow days, Climo?' Woody asked.

'No,' Climo said, defiance in his voice.

'You wanna hang out with crow now do you?'

Climo looked at me, then back at Woody and shrugged. 'He's alright,' he protested, and Stevo laughed as if such an idea was preposterous.

'You did your time as a crow,' Woody went on. 'Like we all have. I took you under my wing and sorted you out. I could have smashed you far worse than you got, but I thought you were a good lad. Now you're mixing with this weasel,' he jerked a thumb at me where I stood awkwardly to one side. 'Throwing all my hard work back in my face. What's that about, then?' He threw his arms up in the air in a gesture of futility.

Climo looked to me again. 'He's alright,' he repeated. I felt a lift to my spirits seeing him stand up for me. Even though half of the platoon seemed to hate me, at least there was one more person who I could call a friend.

'He's a crow,' Brown said, as if that were answer enough, but Climo, his defiance growing, shook his head.

'We'll be going to war soon,' Climo said. 'What's the point in …' he was cut short when Woody grasped him by the throat and pushed him against the corridor wall so hard that the metal panels echoed loudly about the confines of the ship. I jumped back instinctively.

'*Don't talk to me about war!*' Woody shouted, his face pressed up against Climo's nose. Climo struggled for air and grasped at Woody's arm in a vain attempt to release the grip, but like me he was not nearly strong enough. When he wasn't working Woody lived in the gym, and his huge muscles bulged against his fatigues.

'What do *you* know about war? Nothing, that's what. You think you got a pair now coz you did a few drops with us on Uralis? Crow do drops on Uralis. But that's what you are, really isn't it, Climo? A crowbag.'

'You know what crowbags get don't you?' Stevo prompted Woody with a grin.

Woody nodded, and then he punched Climo full force in the gut. He let go and Climo, winded, fell helplessly to the ground. For good measure, he then kicked him again in the stomach as he retched on the floor.

It was at that point that Joe Mac appeared over the corridor horizon and saw what had happened. I was relieved, there was no way that Woody could explain this away, they had been caught red-handed assaulting a fellow trooper in the corridor. He lifted his cap, stooped over Climo and frowned. 'Lads, screw the nut! Officers walk down this corridor.'

I gaped as Woody massaged his knuckles casually. 'Sorry, mate, won't happen again.' Climo still clutched at his stomach where he lay at our feet.

'Get him out of here.' Joe shook his head. 'Screw the nut, Woody.' The lancejack was only concerned that somebody outside the platoon might see what was going on. He was happy to let the blokes serve their own justice if

it kept them in line and it saved him work so long as no one was around to see it. He walked away without looking back.

Once Joe Mac was gone Woody looked to me. I was rooted to the spot, staring at my mate as he fought the urge to vomit on the metal floor. All the while Stevo and Brown stood ready, clearly wanting me to try something so they could have a go. It wouldn't be much contest - there were three of them - and even if I went for one, I doubted the other two would allow me a fair fight. Stevo was as old as Woody, in his mid to late twenties I guessed, but he was little larger than me and I could see weakness in the way he hid slightly behind Woody for protection. Brown was less afraid, and he eyed me like a predator might eye its prey, but he knew not to do anything without Woody saying so.

'Fancy a go, do you?' Woody asked threateningly. My silence gave him his answer and he smiled. 'Didn't think so. Save your new mate a bit.'

Once the three of them left I helped Climo up so that he sat with his back against the wall. There were tears on his cheeks and at first I thought that was because he was winded, but then he sobbed.

'Are you alright, mate?' I asked, crouching on my haunches beside him. A couple of troopers walked by chatting loudly, only briefly stopping their conversation out of curiosity as they passed. 'You alright?' I asked again, placing my hand upon Climo's shoulder but he shrugged it off angrily.

'Just give me a minute, alright?' Climo's voice was breaking as he tried to take control of himself once more.

I paused, thinking of something to say that might lift Climo from his misery. Normally it seemed like it was just me feeling miserable. 'I'm sorry, I should have done something.'

'Like what, Moralee?' Climo said harshly. 'Do you do any martial arts?' He shook his head and his voice softened. 'I didn't do much good the other day anyway, did I?'

I realised he was talking about the day that Woody attacked me and he had done nothing. 'No, not really,' I agreed and Climo shot me an angered look - but saw that I was smiling. After all we were only as bad as each other. Climo laughed and wiped his eyes. He put out his hand and I lifted him to his feet like we would when we were exhausted on Uralis and carrying too much kit to stand by ourselves.

'This place gets too much for you sometimes,' Climo admitted. He sniffed and regained his composure.

'You don't have to tell me that, mate,' I agreed. My eye was still bloodshot in one corner and probably would be for some time.

Climo frowned, 'I hate Woody,' he said angrily, as upset turned to rage. 'And his cowardly little minions. This senior private show won't count for nothing down on New Earth. You'll see.'

I nodded, not necessarily because I agreed, but because Climo had begun to seethe with anger and I wanted to humour him as we began to walk back to the accommodation.

'It's Andy,' I blurted, surprising both of us. 'My mates call me Andy.'

'Well then,' Climo exclaimed with a smile and renewed cheer, 'nice to meet you, Andy!'

We shook hands, and I made myself a new friend aboard challenger.

9: Training

As Challenger slipped through the cosmos at speeds I could scarcely imagine, the platoon began training under Sergeant James. Hand-to-hand combat practice was followed by first aid and respirator drills. We practiced weapon drills as well, but the limited space on board meant ranges and exercises were impossible. The fact is, skills fade when you're cooped up for a long time aboard a ship.

The simulators were the Union's answer to that problem. They could recreate anything - from ranges on Earth, to exercises on Uralis, to combat scenarios on Eden fighting the Indo-Japanese Alliance - and make you feel like you were really there by tapping into the neural structures of your brain. Troopers being troopers, the programmers were asked to recreate bars, nightclubs and even brothels, but they were always told the same thing:

someone would have to actually 'play' the female. We always joked about someone taking one for the team.

The most important weapon in our arsenal that we all had to practice with was the MSG-20, or magnetic assault rifle, far superior to the silly carbines we'd had in basic training. Its powerful magnets could propel a small steel dart, no larger than the end of your little finger, at supersonic speeds up to five hundred times a minute. It didn't rust, it had a trigger, a catch to remove the magazines, a firing selector to switch from single shot to burst to automatic, and three equally simple buttons to control the sight: change view mode, zoom, and focus. The MSG-20 was designed by a genius to be used by fools, in any environment, from Earth to vacuum, and made the sniper rifle - though not the sniper himself - almost obsolete.

Using the simulators, me and the other new lads slowly began to settle in and see how our new platoon worked. There seemed to be three distinctive tiers within the platoon that were almost as rigid as the rank system itself, even if it wasn't official. The senior bods ensured we turned up with the correct kit. Woody in particular appeared to take sadistic pleasure in dealing with anybody stepping out of line; he thought up no end of humiliating punishments, including one time when he made me and Gilbert clean the toilets with our toothbrushes as punishment for not cleaning them properly that morning.

'Don't forget to brush your teeth tonight,' Woody had said with that same sickly grin that I had come to loathe.

'God, what a sadistic freak,' Gilbert had cursed under his breath, careful not to be heard as we frantically scrubbed at green stains that had formed under the rim of the urinals. I agreed with him but chose to say nothing, lest I earned another black eye.

There were about ten senior bods in the platoon, three of whom made up parts of the headquarter element, including the platoon signaller - who was a slightly strange looking skinny man with eyes that were perhaps a little too close together - which earned him his nickname 'Cyclops'. He never spoke much, but supposedly he was a genius. By trooper standards that didn't necessarily mean a lot. Then there were of course Sergeant James' smart launchers, Harmes and Mitch, who were - as Sam had said - '… quick to point out the importance of their role and how hard it was'.

'The platoon won't get anywhere without the launchers,' Mitch would say, while Harmes would nod his head furiously in agreement. During breaks in between shoots we would be taken outside into the corridor so that we could practice handling the smart launchers, loading them and unloading them with drill rounds and practicing using the sighting system. It was ridiculously simple, most of the clever stuff existed within the small missile which was indeed probably smarter than all of us. All you had to do was verbally tell the missile what you wanted it to do, point and fire, the missile worked out all the rest. You could even fire it blind into the sky without saying a word and it would search for a target you hadn't seen and kill it.

'There's more to it than just fire and forget,' Harmes defended when one of the senior bods made a sarcastic comment. 'You gotta load it quick, fire from a good position and know how it thinks!'

'Yeah, you gotta know how it thinks, man!' Mitch agreed with far too much enthusiasm. They were like a comedy act.

'Be one with the missile! They're heavy, too, man, so you gotta be fit!'

'Gotta be fit!'

I lifted the launcher in both arms. It was over a metre long, but built using lightweight composites in the most advanced factories on Titan. It probably weighed less than ten kilos with the drill round loaded into it. I decided that Sam had been right about the two of them; they were idiots.

Jamo appeared to have a soft spot for the two smart launchers, who were clearly in their position because they were senior but none too bright. He would often refer to them as his *'boys with the toys'* whilst the platoon referred to them - in secret of course - as his *'boys who are toys'*.

The rest of the senior bods were split amongst our sections with an aim to spread their knowledge equally amongst the newer troopers. Woody and Rawson both presided over One section, one of whom was in each of the section's two fire teams. Woody liked to think of himself as the top dog in the section, being the biggest in bulk as well as the biggest bully, but we all knew that in fact the top dog was Rawson, who would have been a Lance Corporal had his Junior Leader's course not been cut short in anticipation

of the Invasion. Despite being a cocky joker, he was calm and capable. Rawson appeared to let Woody have his way, but both Corporal Evans and Joe Mac often turned to him when things needed to be done - much to Woody's apparent frustration.

Then there were the new lads - us - who sat at the very opposite end of the food chain. Even though some members of the platoon had warmed to us, including Climo who had become a friend, we were still widely seen as outsiders and not considered worthy of conversation. Some troopers, such as Sam and Davo, would extend us the courtesy of one word phrases but generally wouldn't go out of their way to speak to us. We were used for menial tasks that the other lads didn't want to do, such as running errands and cleaning the accommodation in the mornings, and we were always watched closely by troopers keen to spot our mistakes.

Those in the middle weren't referred to as anything specific, they were 'the blokes', 'the bods', 'the lads',' the toms'… whatever took your fancy. They ranged from having served a year - to four years - and formed the main workforce of the platoon. Some were clearly more capable than others, some even more so than the senior bods, but they were seen as not having had enough experience to be considered for additional responsibilities. Some, like Sam, outwardly resented this, but made no effort to change a system that had worked for centuries. Others, like Brown, followed the senior bods doggedly in an attempt to climb the platoon pile, and I despised them for their shamelessness.

The platoon itself had a hundred divisions, depending on where individuals came from, ancestry, social class and religious beliefs. Most of our battalion were recruited from the southern cities, but we did have some within our ranks who came from the north, and even the odd Welshman - such as Westy. The platoon accepted their differences, as only troopers could, united by a bond created by shared hardship.

The rumours amongst the platoon intensified as we neared the rendezvous, the platoon was nervous and rightly so, and nothing made troopers more edgy than being left in the dark.

'I don't think it's gonna happen,' Woody said one time as we practiced using the under-slung grenade launcher outside the simulators and away from the NCOs.

'So what, we're gonna just turn up and the Admiral says "Shorry ladsh, falsh alarm?"' Rawson mimicked the Dutch accent of the commander of the 3rd fleet and the invasion of New Earth.

'We'll get there, and they'll think about it, and somebody will say it's a stupid idea.'

'What's stupid about it?' Sam asked from where the rest of us watched the two senior soldiers practicing with the grenade launchers. We were supposed to be taking turns, but Woody had not handed his over for ten minutes, because he kept making mistakes. He blamed it on being tired from a rough session in the gym the night before, but we all knew better, senior troopers weren't all perfect and he was proving it, and getting angrier and angrier in the process.

'Was I talking to you, Sam?' Woody snapped.

Sam's eyes burned with rage but he said nothing, and Woody carried on.

'Think about it,' Rawson went on. 'We get the order to take New Earth from Brussels, and they would have thought about this whole idea a lot, not just drawn it up on a fag packet. The big corporations have so much money held up in that place, they're probably putting a load of pressure on the Union to do something.'

'Well, I think they'll bin it, we'll get slaughtered down there. Why don't the corporations just duke?'

Rawson shook his head, 'Isn't it obvious? The corporations have loads of men and women who could fight - if they were properly trained to - but we have *millions,* an unending supply. It's the only thing most nations have that the corporations don't.'

Woody bristled, 'Well why don't they just build some robots or something?'

Rawson laughed, 'Even in this day and age it's all about money. Why build a load of robots for billions when you can train a hundred troopers for millions? Besides that, humans are more flexible in combat, can't get hacked into by electronic warfare teams and can win hearts and minds. As long as there's war there'll be infantry, mate.'

'The Chinese'll be dug in deep.'

'Then we'll have to dig them out, wont we?'

During our voyage we began to practice fighting as a section within the simulator. Most of the simulator environments we used were set on the surface of Uralis and I recognised them from my voyage to the home of the dropship infantry on board the Fantasque. They had been reddened in colour, as the surface of New Earth was bloody red instead of the dirty browns and greys of Uralis, but essentially they were the same thing; rocky valleys, and expanses of desert, rolling hills and towering mountains.

We fought pitched battles against computer generated men, sometimes fighting across open ground or amongst jagged rocks. It was the first time I'd had a chance to work with my entire section and see who was in it. As I already knew, Corporal Evans was our section commander, and Lance Corporal McAllister was the section second in command. In addition to Woody and Rawson - Brown and Climo were also part of my section. Then there was also Berezynsky, a lad who had arrived with me as a raw recruit. He had kept himself to himself since arriving, rarely speaking even to acknowledge his old platoon team mates, but then I had remembered him as always being the grey man and Gilbert confirmed this with typically few words, 'He's boring,' he had simply said. Fair one.

We arrived at our rendezvous some time while I had been sleeping. Our only way of knowing that the jump was complete was a gentle chime on the ship's announcement system - which was only intended for the crew on duty to hear. Whilst the majority of their crew slumbered, the vast fleet assembled silently in the darkness. It was a fleet bigger than any that the Union had ever assembled, but none of us would ever see it, for Challenger had no portholes for us to see out of, even if there was anything to see in the dark anyway. Before lights out and the bulkheads were locked shut again me, and Climo had contemplated it under Woody's increasingly hostile gaze.

'Every Union ship is painted black as space,' Climo pointed out, although I already knew. 'Camouflage ain't it.'

'Even with all the sensors ships carry?' I wondered. 'Surely painting them black wouldn't make any difference?'

Climo shrugged. 'Every little helps, mate.'

I would later learn that a ship could reflect the rays off nearby stars, however little it might be. And although on an interstellar scale that light could take years to be noticed - if at all - it could easily give a ship in orbit away and that, after all, was where Challenger was designed to operate in combat.

And so without a soul to see it, the Union fleet amassed, ready to take war back to New Earth.

—————

While Challenger and the two fleets hung silent as ghosts in the night, and Generals and Admirals thrashed out their plans, we were taken to practice survival skills in the lock room at the back of the ship. We were all dressed in our freshly issued combat equipment, instead of our drab grey ships fatigues and peaked caps.

Most of the combat equipment we had been issued on the ship was new, specially designed for the unforgiving environment we were destined to fight in. It felt surreal looking at us all in the tightly packed lock room, our new gel armour and respirators coloured a deep blood red and streaked with sections of brown; the camouflage pattern developed specifically for the surface of New Earth. The last people to wear that uniform had retreated from a victorious Chinese horde two years ago and now here we stood wearing it, contrasted against the grey walls of the ship.

'It's red so you can't see the blood so much,' Stevo said ominously.

But Corporal Evans snapped at him. 'Don't be so stupid.' The public reproof given by the giant section commander embarrassed the big-eared bully into silence, and although I made no sign of it, inwardly I smiled.

The respirator filtration canisters which were connected either side of the mouthpiece were slightly larger than those we used on Uralis, supposedly due to an additional element in New Earth's atmosphere that needed to be removed before it entered our lungs. It wasn't what was absent from the atmosphere that made it deadly, but rather what was present; noxious gases that could make you giddy after a single breath, knock you out in under a minute and kill you not long after. The respirator's filters cleaned the air and forced it into the miniature atmosphere it held against the wearer's face. It could even direct the air flow and change its temperature to keep him comfortable, and more importantly, stop the visor from fogging up. It was equipped with an in built intercom system that allowed troopers to talk to each other over blasting dust storms or over the noise of battle, and sounds were heard through earpieces that hugged the user's head. They were designed to cut out any noise above eighty decibels - explosions for instance - but magnified quieter sounds such as whispering. As if that wasn't enough, the respirator visor used what was known as Full Spectrum Imagining, taking all forms of energy from heat to infra-red to create an image that was almost as perfect by night as it was by day. It featured a targeting system that identified friends and foe and could mark key points on the battlefield. All of this was controlled by a wristpad that every trooper wore on his forearm.

I tried the new respirator on and Corporal Evans checked that I had it fitted correctly by tugging roughly on the straps and shaking my head by the mouthpiece.

'Feel okay?' he asked. He wasn't interested in how I was feeling mentally, or I would have said 'pretty pump'. Corporal Evans wanted to know if the respirator had formed a correct seal and only I would know that. A simple green icon on my visor told me that the seal was fine.

It often felt weird when I first put a respirator on, they were designed to be as comfortable and unobtrusive as possible, and over time I could forget it was there, but initially I could feel nothing but the seal squeezing my face.

'Feels fine, Corporal,' I finally said when I realised that Corporal Evans was waiting for an answer.

'You've got to put it on, first, Moralee,' Rawson said, and several lads laughed - including me. Rawson was the sort who could somehow get away with bad jokes and still get a good laugh.

Clearly unimpressed by Rawson's joke about my looks, Corporal Evans checked quickly beneath my chin and then walked to the next man and repeated the process.

I removed my respirator, which caused a warning tone to sound in the headset until it finally realised that it was being purposefully removed, and had not accidentally lost its seal. I checked the drinking straw, which could be connected to a water pack we carried inside our daysacks, as well as the feeding straw, which could be connected to ration packs issued on the ground. Mix up the two straws at your peril, the resulting curdled mush was quite sickening!

The section commanders inspected each and every man in turn, including the Lance Corporals and then they inspected each other. One man had an incorrect fit and was ordered to run to the ship's stores to exchange it after a brief telling off for not realizing sooner.

We checked our wristpads and made sure that they were picking up our vital signs, information that would be freely available to the platoon sergeant on the ground and would tell him automatically if we were injured. We then checked our gel armour, making sure our tourniquets were attached into the legs and arms. We also checked that there was no visible damage to the auto-clotting system that was designed to detect trauma. This was a vital bit of kit that would automatically constrict the padded armour around a wound to compress it, before administering a quick clotting agent into the wound itself. Rather than absorbing blood, it was meant to stop its escape altogether. Originally the armour was meant to administer morphine and other life-saving drugs automatically, but what was found was that sometimes the auto-injectors became damaged or confused and activated for no reason at all!

Seemingly satisfied that our clothing would do the job, Corporal Evans addressed us all. It was the first time I had heard him speak to the entire platoon, and his booming voice and air of confident capability made every man listen intently. 'New Earth is a vicious place,' he began, as if remembering his last few days there. 'And its atmosphere is as unforgiving as Eden. But if you respect it and look after your kit correctly then it's as safe as any street in London, Earth.'

We laughed nervously. The streets of London were murderous.

'It's important we practice your drills with the kit so that if anything should happen to you or your mates then you can deal with the problem *instinctively*,' he stressed the final word, and then held his own respirator high in the air. 'The less time you spend worrying about this, the more time you have to worry about the enemy.'

We practiced a series of drills from the simple to the more complex. Changing damaged canisters and patching up cracked visor screens were simple drills which could be carried out rapidly by the individual concerned, as long as he didn't breathe in or lose his cool. If upon removing the respirator or losing the seal, we were required to hold our breath against the toxic atmosphere, and upon fixing the problem and achieving a seal again we were required to breathe out hard, helping the respirator canister motors to force out the bad air from the mini atmosphere held against our faces.

This was all stuff I had been taught before. Coming fresh from Uralis I was more used to working in the respirator than anyone else. We spent almost three quarters of the year-long course above ground in the harsh environment. Our instructors taught us to overcome the claustrophobic fear of wearing nothing more than a piece of rubber filled with motors, wires and sensors to protect us from the poisonous air by making us perform tasks with the respirators off, like stacking bricks and negotiating obstacles. There was nothing more amazing and liberating than feeling that alien wind, bitterly cold as it was, brushing against my face.

'Just hold your breath and don't panic', our training instructor had always told us.

We were practiced on dealing with unconscious casualties with damaged respirators, and then drilled on everything - with the lights off and the lock room plunged into darkness - with and without the aid of our night vision. We felt for cracks on visors with our bare fingers before placing the clear plastic sealing patches over the hole.

Very rarely was a mistake made, but when they were the section commanders were quick to point it out, often angrily. 'These drills need to be *instinctive*!' Corporal Evans would repeat. 'You shouldn't need to think about it. Every second you fumble is a second closer to death!'

Thankfully that evening Woody spent most of his time in the gym or in the recreation lounge, leaving me and Climo some peace and quiet in our room. He appeared to be ignoring me and Climo, having said nothing since our encounter after the lecture and if he had told anybody else they didn't show it. Brown stayed in the room with us, but he spoke little if at all and only to Climo. He wasn't much more senior than Climo. I heard he had served two years, which meant that he had been on exercise on Eden and Uralis and that was it, but he had clearly decided as Stevo had said, 'Crow should not speak, only be spoken to'.

We busied ourselves chatting about our lives at home, and Climo excitedly told me of how his home town of Crawley was the roughest town of all of southern England.

Later that night Greggerson entered the room, with the look of someone with something big to get off his chest.

'Alright, mate?' I said, half as a greeting and half as a question.

Climo nodded his own less obvious greeting, and then Brown, clearly deciding that the addition of Greggerson into the conversation was too much for him rolled his eyes and walked out. Greggerson jumped out of the way.

Uninterested in Brown's silent protest, Climo asked, 'What's up?'

The skinny trooper tried to appear nonchalant when he told his news, but he fooled no one. 'We're leaving tomorrow morning.'

Climo frowned. 'Who told you that, Stevo?'

Stevo was in Greggerson's section, with Westy, and so they were always rife with rumours that spread across the ship like wildfire, stuff about the Chinese having laser banks and giant robot armies - 'That's why you can't see their faces behind their visors!' - and random changes to our mission. Stevo, a bully who hid behind Woody for protection was also a gossip-monger, filled with pessimistic thoughts that further contradicted his role as a senior bloke, an example setter.

Greggerson waved off the suggestion. 'Sam told me.'

Climo raised his eyebrows. 'Oh.'

There were false rumours and there were true ones. Sam always told the true ones, and so wherever he had got the news from it was likely to be reliable. The walls on Challenger had ears, it was said.

We didn't say anything for a while, or at least what felt like a while. If we began our voyage tomorrow then there would be no way for the ships of the two fleets to communicate, and so an abortion of the operation would not be possible until we arrived at the Centauri system itself, right on top of the Chinese. As soon as we jumped we would be committed. The final inevitability knotted my stomach, and I instantly thought of home, my mum and dad, and my sister.

Climo sighed remorsefully. 'Why didn't I just stay with the conscripts?'

'What else did he say?' I asked finally.

'We're taking a place called Jersey Island,' Greggerson answered. 'Us, the Scots and the Danes. It's supposed to be as big as England. We're the first down.'

Nobody said anything for a while as the information sunk in.

'Jesus,' Climo said under his breath.

The ship locked down without warning just before we ate breakfast the following day, and we were rudely rushed by the NCOs back into our accommodation without explanation, although none was needed. Everybody on Challenger had probably heard the rumour, spilt out by either the Captain or Major's parties as they returned by shuttle from their several day-long orders with the Admiral. Surely somebody would end up locked in the brig for such a terrible slip of the tongue, though I often wondered the point in all the secrecy. Spies could not operate in the void of space in an undisclosed location outside of the Hope system. The main reason for secrecy was believed by the vast majority of us to be to avoid a mutiny. Others believed it was the officers enjoying keeping their men in the dark for some kind of sick power trip. Perhaps both of the two theories were true, but ultimately the root cause was most likely due to the chain of command forgetting a critical principle of war; the morale of their own men.

'Thirty-two days it will take,' Woody said from above me on his bunk, directed to nobody in particular. Brown grunted his agreement, even though he had arrived on Challenger after she had returned from her shame in Alpha Centauri, and so had no idea how long it might take. 'Thirty-one days until we hit Alpha Centauri Bravo, then another day until we hit New Earth and we drop.'

Me and Climo said nothing, for Woody was merely taunting us.

'Of course we might not make it to New Earth,' Woody warned. 'We've got the whole Chinese navy between us and orbit, *thousands* of Chinese warships,' he exaggerated, 'loaded with guns and lasers. Then there are the gun boats, and the surface missile batteries. Not to mention Stevo's laser battery,' he laughed at the absurdity of the final claim.

'There's no laser battery,' Climo said curtly. He was sat on the edge of his bunk, watching the seconds tick past on his wristpad.

'One in three don't make it down.' Woody repeated the statistic that filled every trooper's soul with fear. 'We could be shot out of the sky.'

'Well then we all die,' Climo replied irritably, implying that Woody would be in the same dropship as us. I thought Woody might use Climo's defiant tone as an excuse to attack him again, but he didn't.

'I don't care if I die,' Woody said after a pause. 'I ain't afraid. Are you?'

Climo looked up at where Woody lay on the top of my bunk. 'No.'

The bedsprings squealed under Woody's weight and his fat head peered down at me, 'Are you afraid, Moralee?'

'No.'

Woody smiled. 'You're lying. You're dumping in your little crow pants coz mummy and daddy aren't around to help you on New Earth.' I swallowed, awkward under the bully's gaze. 'You miss your mummy and daddy, don't you?'

'Stop it,' I said, my cheeks burning red.

Woody made a mockingly high-pitched voice, 'I miss my mummy!'

'Shut up!' I shouted, and Woody laughed, disappearing back onto his bunk. He began to hum some random melody loudly, whilst I closed my eyes and imagined that none of this was happening.

———

When the ship's lockdown was finally lifted, we were once again called into the corridor outside our rooms to be briefed by the platoon commander on what we already knew was going on. We looked on sullenly while the young officer explained to us the information he had received from the OC: that we were indeed on our way to the Centauri system and that our objective would indeed be Jersey Island, securing landing zones so that other battalions could echelon through and continue the attack. Nobody raised an objection as he revealed the overall plan, and we looked like men who had been charged to be put to death; perhaps we were.

As the boss had predicted, the first fleet would secure two of the system's three stars, Centauri Bravo and Proxima Centauri, whilst leaving the much larger 3rd fleet, which included us, to secure Centauri Alpha and New Earth itself. A total of thirty squadrons would battle to seize orbital power from the Chinese as we - the dropship battalions - would make the drop to seize the surface. We would be one of the very first battalions to drop.

'There are a total of three DZs on the Island allocated to the English dropship battalions,' the boss explained, 'Each Drop Zone one is a hundred kilometres across. Ours is located ten kilometres to the north of Jersey City, and we have been tasked with securing it and thus allowing other dropship battalions to echelon through. The intent is to create a ring of steel around the garrison there, and provide an interlocking air defence matrix that will deny enemy artillery from engaging the second echelon as it drops.' The platoon commander's military terminology made the whole thing sound like something clean and clinical, but I doubted that it would be. We would deny enemy artillery the ability to fire missiles up against the second wave of dropships sent to move through us, but nobody would do that for us if we were first to drop. 'The forlorn hope', I had once heard first drops being called - a name taken from days of old used to describe first assaults - where the risk of casualties was outrageously high. If you survived the drop you had a chance, but entire platoons could be wiped out by a single volley of missiles if the crews weren't on their game. The jacks had trained long through the days and into the nights since I had arrived on Challenger, no doubt for that very reason.

'We will have thirty-one days to prepare ourselves for the operation to come,' the platoon commander said, 'And we will use that time to train. We will train hard, because if we train hard then we fight easy and I can assure you thirty-two days from now we will all be fighting. The other platoon commanders and I will spend much of the following few days piecing together our plan for this operation and you can expect a detailed set of preliminary orders to be delivered after that. A final set of orders will then be given at D-minus-one so that the plan is fresh in your minds. Are there any questions?'

The platoon commander looked across the platoon, but nobody said anything. We knew what we needed to know for now; we were going. We would be the first down, bearing the brunt of all that the Chinese could throw at us. It was a brutal task however you explained it and there was no doubt that many within the battalion would die before they even reached the ground. 'One in three dropships didn't make it …'

'Mission specific training will begin almost straight away,' the boss continued after pausing to allow the new information to sink in, 'starting with a detailed planetary briefing at eighteen-hundred-hours. Gents,' the boss relaxed his gait with a sigh as he levelled with us, 'I know this has been a turbulent few days, and I know that it isn't going to get any better for a long time. Some of you may be afraid, and that's fine. But remember that there are European citizens trapped on that planet. *Europeans*,' - he repeated the word to stress the point - 'we owe it to them. We will free them from the *Chinese*,' Jamo spat at the floor as if the word caused him great displeasure.

'We have the simulators booked for the rest of the morning, Sergeant?' Jamo nodded. 'Sir.'

'Then let's not waste any more time.'

The platoon sergeant nodded again and then looked to us. 'Get to the simulators.'

So much for breakfast.

10: Happy Birthday

We hurtled towards New Earth, and we trained hard, my God we trained hard. Since receiving confirmation of the invasion Jamo was like a dog unleashed, terrorizing us day in and day out, from six in the morning until twelve at night. We ran around the ship until we were giddy, did strength exercises until we puked and used the simulators until we struggled to work out which was a dream and which was reality. Sometimes I would wake up in my bed and think I was still in the simulator room.

Sometimes we drew weapons and bayonets from the ships armoury and practiced on stuffed bags dressed in pink painted ships fatigues. Pink was the colour of the Chinese uniforms, supposedly, and Jamo had given them the nickname 'Pinkies'.

'What's the bayonet made of?!' Jamo would scream at us as we stamped our feet on the spot in the galley, clutching our rifles close to our chests and panting hard.

'COLD, HARD STEEL!' we would scream back, enraged after the typical thrashing that always preceded bayonet training. The ship echoed with our chants - once the ship's captain complained about the noise from the bridge!

'What's the bayonet made for?!' Jamo would walk amongst us spraying spittle at our faces as he screamed, his face contorted into a hatred of all things living.

'KILL, KILL, KILL!' was the reply. Bayonet training hadn't changed for hundreds of years, and neither had the bayonet. It was hard to think that with the modern weapons deployed by the colonial powers that such a barbaric weapon was still employed.

'On guard!'

We would advance forward onto our left feet, lowering our rifles until they were level with the ground, the vicious, sharpened blades of our bayonets reflecting the galley lights, 'ON GUARD!'

The dummies would be suspended to the ceiling, or placed on the floor to simulate the different types of enemy we might face, wounded soldiers on the ground or soldiers stunned by grenades or shell shock. Others might be armed with fake 'weapons' for us to parry away before we made our final thrust for the chest cavity.

'One thrust at the lying enemy, front rank, advance!'

We would scream, and we would charge at our dummies with a rage we were taught to summon from deep within our souls, stabbing at our foes like wild animals possessed by hate. But to me that dummy wasn't a Chinaman, it was Woody, smiling at me with that awful smile, mocking my family and my youth! The galley floor would be scarred by a hundred blades a hundred times before we would arrive at New Earth to use them for real.

'When your rifle stops,' Jamo roared once, 'stab with your bayonet! When the bayonet breaks, strike with the stock! When the stock breaks punch with your fists! When your fists hurt bite with your teeth!'

'YES, SERGEANT!' we cried, and our bayonet training would continue.

Tensions rose among the lads in the company as the days passed and our fate drew ever nearer. Tempers were lost easily and there were even fights in the galley over minor arguments.

Each of the troopers in the platoon dealt with the situation differently, some grew quiet and attempted to isolate themselves, others became loud and boisterous as if they were trying to hide that they were afraid - from themselves as well as the rest of us.

The NCOs watched us closely, seeking signs that people were cracking, and Corporal Evans even approached me on one occasion to ask how I was.

'Fine, Corporal,' I told him, but I was lying of course. I was as terrified as any other trooper, and what made it worse was that Woody was using me as some kind of emotional punch bag to abuse whenever he felt low, ridiculing me in my room and in front of others.

'I'm gonna make New Earth a hell for you,' he had threatened me randomly one evening when he had caught me alone. I doubted that would be difficult.

Corporal Evans nodded slowly, disbelieving. 'Right. Any issues with your training, any dramas in the section I need to know about?'

Yes, one of your senior blokes is bullying me, I thought. 'No, Corporal.'

Another slow nod. 'Okay, Moralee.' He made to leave and I fidgeted. 'What?'

I stammered, the man was like a god, exactly what the Union wanted you to believe a drop trooper looked like, and now he looked down at me with inquisitive eyes, 'W-w-what was it like on New Earth? And Eden?'

His face hardened. 'You'll find out soon enough.' And he was gone.

We received our orders two days into our final voyage toward New Earth. We drew close around the hologram of Jersey Island as the platoon commander tapped through pages on his tablet. Jamo stood off to his rear, eyeballing each of us, willing us to do something stupid that might allow him to issue swift justice.

The hologram displayed an image of the Drop Zone we had been tasked with securing in order to play our part within the invasion. We had already received numerous familiarization briefings on the ground we would be covering using the simulators; the very next best thing to being there. I knew that Jersey Island sat in a deep valley than ran from south to north away from the Southern Ocean. It was dominated by two large hills to its west and east known for the operation as Hill Alpha and Hill Bravo respectively, both of which stood a good five hundred metres above sea level. Most of the land was farmland, producing huge yields of crops that would feed the island inhabitants and be shipped across the planet from the city's small space port. The farmland was contained within endless rows of greenhouses that sustained atmospheres for the plants to thrive, irrigated by a network of ditches and pipelines.

Both of the two hills were originally used as defensive positions by the Union two years ago, and were each garrisoned by an entire battalion, dug deep into the rock for protection from orbital barrages. Warrens, as they were called, were a common feature on the modern battlefield. Weapons dropped from orbit could punch deep into the ground, taking only minutes from drop to impact, so armies had to move faster, or dig deeper. There was only one way to prise infantry out of a warren, and that was with more infantry.

'Situation enemy,' the boss began, pointing his laser pen toward the two hills which lanced light across the hologram. 'The enemy positions are not fully known, although what little information we have suggests that the enemy have occupied the two warrens, Alpha and Bravo, and repaired damages caused during their own invasion, which was minimal.'

The Chinese barely had to fire a shot to take Jersey Island, it had been overlooked during their invasion, and most of the Union garrison had withdrawn long before they arrived.

'The warren systems run deep into the hills and connect together beneath Jersey Island, which enables the enemy to move troops and vehicles across the battlefield rapidly without fear of orbital bombardment. The warren systems have probably been extended significantly by the enemy, and will most likely form part of a complex air defence matrix.'

The hologram moved as though we were flying across the landscape, with the suspected tunnel locations highlighted blue, deep below the surface.

'Obviously,' the boss went on, 'the warren network is a delaying feature designed to harass us on landing and then as we try to consolidate on the ground. It will be connected to trench systems and burrows in order to confuse us or even attack us from behind. It is believed that the enemy's intent will be to delay us from securing the DZ, to give him enough time to counter attack. He will hold onto the warrens in the hills at all costs in order to achieve this. His morale will be high, having held the planet for so long, and it is doubtful that he will surrender, but will instead only withdraw

deeper into the warrens with the intent to draw out the battle until the cavalry come or we lose orbital cover.'

Orbital 'top cover' as we called it was the name of the game in modern interstellar warfare. If one side held command of orbit then the other side had better start digging or running. Even relatively small ships like Challenger carried enough payload to pulverise entire battalions from orbit. As battles raged in space and top cover was gained and lost, so the battlefield below would be almost directly affected.

The boss went on to describe the friendly forces involved in the operation. Two battalions would drop first onto the Island to secure the Drop Zone by capturing the two hills, the 3rd Battalion English Dropship Infantry - us - and the 1st Battalion Scottish Dropship Infantry. We would be supported by two whole regiments of Danish gravtanks in addition to our own, who would form a ring of steel around the hills whilst unmanned aircraft would dominate the skies throughout. Our squadron of ships would remain in top cover, whilst the others would seek to dominate orbit above the rest of the Southern Continent. A further two battalions of dropship infantry would be waiting to drop once the DZ was secure, and even more conscripts would be waiting on troopships to mop up the mess once we were done.

'It's unknown what the Chinese may have done with the civilian population, and how they might handle them upon our entry into the Centauri system. It's likely that they will take refuge on the outskirts of the city, or possibly be hidden underground. The Chinese won't want refugees around their positions getting in the way. Be sure to identify your targets before you engage them, however. The civvies are believed to be on-side, but if you start shooting them all up, they'll soon switch sides and remember, you will have to live with them for a while afterwards.

'One platoon's mission,' the boss recited, and he repeated it twice for good measure, 'Destroy. Destroy all enemy encountered on Hill Bravo in order to secure the Drop Zone.'

The plan itself was a simple one. The battalion would drop at a location that would be decided only a few minutes before we entered orbit, which the boss thought was likely to be over the sea. We would then carry out what was known as the 'run in', a charge along the planet surface toward the enemy. Staying low on the approach made us less of a target for the enemy's anti-aircraft defences, which would have already caused us great damage.

The tanks would push forward of us, bypassing smaller enemy positions and cutting the city off from reinforcement. They were vulnerable to massed infantry, using warrens and trenches for cover, and so would initially avoid the hills whilst we cleared them. A Company was the lead company of the battalion, and of that company we were to be the front left platoon with two platoon to our right. We would be the knife edge, charging across the battlefield toward Hill Bravo until either we reached the summit or we made contact with the enemy. If we did make contact, and we surely would, we would attack the enemy and destroy him whilst the company would continue its advance, attacking position after position until it became bogged down by the enemy and would need to be replaced by another company from the battalion. We would roll over position after position in a massed orgy of death until we reached the summit of Hill Bravo, and then once our fight was seemingly over, we would send the next battalion into the warrens to prize the Chinese out with Union steel.

'Will we go into the warrens with them, Sir?' A trooper asked what we had all been thinking. We were all trained in tunnel warfare; I had spent months in the purpose built Uralian tunnel systems fighting imaginary enemies in the darkness. The real thing could only be bloody, and terrifying.

The boss shrugged. 'Hard to say since we know so little about the ground and how it might affect us on the run in. We might sit pretty on top of the hill and rain hell on the valley, or we might all be going underground. You need to prepare yourselves for the worst, and then you can only be pleasantly surprised.'

We laughed nervously.

'It's important that you all remember the platoon mission, and you play back and study these orders in great depth until you can recite them back to me.'

Halfway into the voyage we were offered a chance to write our 'last letters' which would go with us to our families if we returned to Earth in a box. I had never hand-written a letter before, and the grim purpose for doing so was unnerving. We handed them into the ship's captain during a special morning service to commemorate those who had fallen in the vain attempt to save New Earth from the Chinese invasion. Sergeant James had demanded that all of us write one, even if it we didn't have anybody to write to.

'Address it to 'The President',' he had said bitterly, 'then the bastard can read it at bedtime.'

The letters were taken during the service whilst we stood on parade with our heads bowed, and the captain prayed for our safety and victory for the Union. I wasn't a religious man, but I listened and prayed with the captain anyway, just in case.

But the captain wasn't finished after the service. 'I have one last thing to announce,' she said with a smile, and then looked down at her tablet. 'Lieutenant Reed, Seaman Tamba, Corporal Jones …' she read out a long list of names and ranks from across the entire ship's crew, from the naval personnel to the jacks and drop troopers, '… Private Moralee, Private Ri ….'

Why had she called out my name? Fixed to the spot in the position of at ease, my mind raced for an answer to her needing to mention me in front of the entire crew.

'You have been very busy, and I wouldn't want you to forget … happy birthday to you all.'

I felt relief mixed with surprise when I realised that according to ship's time, my birthday had indeed been two days ago. I had been so busy, so detached from my old life on Earth that I had forgotten my own birthday! I was nineteen years old … and on my way to war.

'Don't forget to clean the toilets, birthday boy,' Woody said upon our return to the accommodation after the service. We didn't have much time, fitness would be at half-seven, which only really left me with enough time to get changed. I knew that I would be crucified by Jamo if I was late for PT, but if I argued with Woody he would take pleasure in making an example of me.

'I'm going now,' I said, and joined the rest of the new lads cleaning the accommodation. Climo and a few others came to help us, but a lot of the platoon was still reluctant to help, enjoying having us to do it all for them. I didn't care anymore, I was used to it. Cleaning the ablutions and mopping floors in the morning had become part of my routine.

Once we were satisfied we had done as much as time allowed, I hurried back to the room. I was anxious to get ready for PT in time so as not to infuriate the platoon sergeant, but when the door to my room slid away I stopped. My PT kit was no longer laid out ready on my bed as it had been, but instead it was laid out on the floor. It had been written on with shaving foam, 'Happy birthday'.

Brown and Woody were in the room and laughed as I crouched down beside my ruined PT kit in horror. Jamo would kill me! What would I do? The simple answer was nothing; we had so many PT sessions every day that most of my PT kit was constantly being laundered. All I could do was wipe away the excess foam and take Jamo's wrath.

'Happy birthday, crowbag,' Woody sneered. I looked up at my tormentor. He knew what he had done; he knew that the consequences for me turning up in dirty PT kit would result in a punch to the gut or worse.

My bottom lip trembled. What had I done to deserve such unprovoked cruelty? And then something changed in me.

I felt the anger boiling up inside of me, surging like a storm of energy that raged across my body and caused my limbs to shake. I was angrier than I had ever been, angrier than I had been for the most brutal of bayonet training sessions. There stood before me was the man at the heart of all of my misery, he had almost single-handedly made my prison on board Challenger unbearable. He was a bully, a coward who used vulnerable people like me to feel powerful.

'You gonna cry for mummy?' Woody asked, and Brown laughed again.

Every trooper was trained to have a safety catch in his mind, his rage needed to be controlled, directed, or else he was little more than a mindless thug. That day I released my safety catch.

I screamed as I launched to my feet, throwing a punch straight toward Woody's jaw. He was unprepared but his reactions were quick and he jerked his head back away from the punch enough to deny me a clean strike. My fist still clipped his chin and I threw a second punch into his stomach, knocking the air out of him.

Woody staggered backwards in shock and made no attempt to block my third punch which struck him on the top of the head. I was no prize fighter; my unarmed combat training was only a few weeks long, but the furious speed of the blows I threw at him kept him stumbling backward. I hit him again on the head, and twice to the neck and shoulders. Woody withdrew himself into a blocking stance, his arms tight together in front of his head.

My attack was stopped when Brown gripped me by the shoulders and threw me backward and I slid on my arse across the room. He strode confidently toward me with his fists raised, he was nowhere near as big as Woody but he was strong.

'Come on, then, you little weasel,' he beckoned as I stood.

'Little bastard,' Woody groaned, clutching at his head in the corner of the room.

Woody would be fighting any second, I wasn't much of a fighter but I knew my only hope was to take out Brown before he recovered and the two of them finished me off. I was committed.

With a cry of anger, I charged back into Brown, my head lowered toward his waist. He punched out uselessly at my back as I connected with him, driving him into his bunk. This wasn't a matter of honour; there were two of them and one of me. I punched him once in the balls and once in the gut and then stood, giving him a final punch into his nose. Blood exploded from his nostrils but he didn't fall. Instead he hit me across the temple so hard that I saw stars and with a powerful swipe of his leg he kicked my left foot out from under me and I fell to the ground.

'You'll pay for that,' Brown clutched at his groin as he stooped over me but Woody checked him.

'He's mine,' Woody's face was screwed up with rage, and he stalked toward me where I lay dazed. Brown stepped away.

I stood, but too late. A mighty punch drove me back to the ground. Warm blood flowed from my nose and into my mouth and I spat it onto the deck.

'Fuck you!'

'Fuck me?' Woody gripped me by the throat. 'Fuck you, Moralee!' His fingers closed around my windpipe, squeezing it closed. He leaned forward and whispered rasping threats into my ear as I fought for air, 'Remember what I said, crow bag. Accidents happen all the time out here. People kill themselves. Jettison themselves out of airlocks. Then there's New Earth. People get shot - in the back. Happens all the time.'

I tried to speak but failed. I choked on my own blood and my eyes rolled back into my skull.

'I'm gonna kill you, Moralee, you're gonna die out here, do you …' he didn't finish.

A metal chair crashed down upon Woody's head and he collapsed onto me under its weight. His hand remained around my throat but the fingers lost their grip and I gasped desperately for air.

Brown watched frozen in horror as Climo struck Woody again with the chair, swinging it around with so much force that it knocked Woody clean away from me.

'How do you like that?' Climo taunted as Woody tried to lift his body up from the ground but the chair came down again and again. Woody lay still. Blood from his head ran onto the metal floor.

'Christ…' Brown gasped as Climo stood with the chair poised over Woody, waiting for him to move again.

Climo threw down the chair. 'Want a go?'

Brown went for Climo with a clumsy punch, but Climo blocked it with ease and struck him with a punch that connected with the base of his chin. Stepping forward in between Brown's flailing arms he clutched his collar to pull him close, swung an elbow into his nose, and then grasping the back of his head he thrust his face downwards onto his knee. Barely conscious, Brown fell to the ground at Climo's feet.

'Fuck you, Brown,' he spat at the unconscious trooper, and then at Woody. 'And you too.'

Slowly I sat myself up, there was blood everywhere. 'Jesus Christ,' I exclaimed.

Climo kicked the chair across the room and then sat down on his bunk. 'God that felt good.'

I staggered toward the door and leant out into the corridor.

'Man down!'

Surprised troopers peered out from their rooms, but the message passed rapidly, as it would on New Earth.

My anger forgotten, I ran back to Woody. He wasn't moving. He had a deep gash across his skull, but it didn't look bad.

'He's stopped breathing,' I told Climo. 'Help me get him over!'

Climo remained motionless. 'Leave him, he's better off dead,' he said darkly.

'Not if you get done for murder! Give me a hand!'

Climo came over just before Joe Mac arrived at the door.

'What the hell is going on?' he shouted, and then his eyes widened at the sight of Woody and Brown on the floor. 'Jesus!'

'He's been hit on the back of the head,' I told him. 'He's stopped breathing.' We rolled him over and I reached into his mouth with my fingers. There were a few pieces of broken teeth in his mouth which I tossed aside and then felt deeper. 'He's swallowed his tongue.'

Troopers massed at the door and more NCOs were shouting to find out what was going on. Mac pointed at the nearest troopers to the door. 'You two! Get on Brown over there. You, get the medics down here now! Moralee what the hell happened?'

I looked at Climo as I pulled Woody's tongue back from his throat with my fingers. 'I hit him.'

There was a gasp from behind Joe Mac. 'You *what*?'

'I hit him with the chair,' I repeated.

'Don't be stupid, I did,' Climo argued.

'Right, you two,' Mac beckoned more troopers. 'Take over from these two idiots.'

I felt for a pulse as two troopers came to replace me and Climo beside the casualty, but there was nothing, 'His heart has stopped!'

'Get out of the way,' Sam snapped, pushing me aside. He knelt beside Woody and began compressions onto his chest, trying to work his heart to force any air left in Woody's lungs around his body. Me and Climo were roughly led out of the room and into the corridor where the whole platoon, its routine disturbed, crowded curiously.

I stood outside the company sergeant major's office, deep within the headquarter section of the ship. I had never been there before, nor did I want to be. The CSM was also known as the 'Company Scary Monster', the disciplinarian, the man you never wanted to meet. He was meant to be scary, and he fulfilled his role to the letter. He was like Sergeant James multiplied a thousand times.

You never stood outside the sergeant major's office unless you had messed up severely, and my God I had. Woody was in the ship's infirmary under intensive care with several stitches to his scalp. Rumour would have it he died twice and had to be resuscitated, and that his scar was larger than it should have been because they had to operate on his brain. He was alive, as was Brown of course, but my God had he taken a beating off Climo.

The bulkhead to the CSMs office barely muffled the sound of shouting, Climo was getting an earful. He would surely be locked in the brig and taken back to Earth to be court marshalled, with a hefty sentence. I wasn't sure what was worse, being in that room or on New Earth.

'Face your front,' a naval NCO ordered. There were two of them, standing watch over me and Climo in case we did something stupid; ready to take us both to the brig once the CSM had his way with us.

I waited for what seemed like hours, until the door to the CSMs office finally slid open and Climo emerged red faced and into the arms of the two naval NCOs.

'Get that areole down to the brig!' the CSM bellowed from inside and Climo was marched away leaving only me behind.

I wondered if I should enter, hesitated, and then thought better of it.

'Get in here, Moralee!'

I marched into the CSMs office as smartly as I could. I had barely practiced any kind of drill since leaving Earth and the CSM winced as I halted awkwardly at his desk. He sat forward in his chair, tapping his fingers impatiently as if he were waiting for me to speak. I said nothing, facing my front with my chin held up high, not daring to look down and meet his gaze. I swallowed hard.

'What do you have to say for yourself, Moralee?' he asked finally. He seemed oddly subdued after having screamed the walls down at Climo; I braced myself for the worst.

'I started it, Sir,' I blurted, and the CSM raised an eyebrow. 'I attacked Woody first.'

That was the second time I had seen the CSM since arriving on Challenger, but it was the closest I had been to him, and alone in that room his presence was overwhelming. He was no bigger in size than the average trooper, but his face was hard as Jamo's, and his gaze twice as penetrating. He had seen it all, like many of the older NCOs, from Eden to the Betrayal, and he had survived to make it all the way to the top of the food chain. Now he looked at me like he was about to explode.

'Go on.'

I told him about how I had found my PT kit ruined, about how I had constantly been at Woody's mercy and how I had finally attacked him and Brown in a terrible outburst.

'I just lost it, Sir. I'm sorry.'

'Sorry?' The CSM picked up a tablet from his desk and frowned as he studied it. 'I have two troopers in the infirmary, one of whom is critically injured and I've got another trooper in the brig. That's half a section wiped out in five minutes. Do you understand the importance of our manpower right now?'

'Yes, Sir.'

'We have one hundred and nine troopers in this company, and every one of them is a rifle on the ground. Effectively we could have lost three rifles today, if you include that idiot Climpson, that's half a section's fire power wasted before we even hit the ground.'

'Yes, Sir.'

'Are you on the Chinese side?'

'No, Sir.'

The CSM slapped the table so hard I jumped. 'Then act like it, then! Every five minutes I've got troopers beating each other senseless, but this takes it to a whole new level!'

I said nothing, and then the CSM sighed. He tapped away at his tablet. 'I'm putting you on galley duty for the remainder of the jump.'

Surprised, I glanced down at him. 'You mean I'm not going to the brig, Sir?'

'No, you're not,' the CSM tossed the tablet onto his desk. 'You're not the one who wrapped a chair around someone's head, are you? If I put blokes in the brig for fighting it'd be overflowing in a few days. I'm sure the blokes in your platoon will punish you enough, anyway. It's not looked upon well to attack your senior privates, believe me.'

'No, Sir.'

The side of the CSMs mouth twitched. 'Even if they are arseholes.'

'Yes, Sir.'

'Don't think that this is the end of it,' the CSM warned, jabbing a finger at me. 'If I ever have you in my office again, for even as much as wasting a drop of water, I'll have you in that brig without a seconds thought, is that clear?'

'Yes, Sir.'

He waved a hand. 'Go on, then. Get out.'

I hesitated. 'Sir? Will Climpson be in the brig until …?'

The CSM looked up at me irritably. 'I'm sorry, have we just become friends? What's it got to do with you? Get out.'

I could only wish that Jamo could have been as lenient with me as the CSM had been, but then I guess the CSM knew that he would deal with me and so hadn't bothered. There was only one thing you could do when a man like Jamo gave you a debriefing, stand there and take it. He sprayed me with saliva in an angry rant that told me all I needed to know of how little he thought of me, the rant ended with me on the deck of the platoon corridor clutching my gut. And that wasn't the end of it. Jamo knew that the platoon was waiting in their rooms for him to leave.

Half the platoon hated Woody, but for every man that hated him there was one who either liked him or at least knew that he was a senior private, not to be attacked by some jumped-up new lad. They came from their rooms, cautiously at first in case there were NCOs to see or hear, and then I got my punishment.

'No head shots,' Stevo ordered the ten or so troopers who had come to take their revenge upon me. Rawson was amongst them, I saw.

It didn't matter if I broke a bone; it was nothing the infirmary couldn't fix rapidly for the invasion. I took the beating like I was in a dream, my mind shut off the pain and I allowed myself to be thrown around the corridor like a rag doll. I thought the NCOs might notice what was going on in their lines, but they weren't there, or at least if they were then they were turning a blind eye to it. After all what goes on ship stays on ship.

Happy birthday, Moralee. Not long now.

11: Alpha Centauri

Final preparations began several days prior to Challenger entering the Alpha Centauri system. We worked tirelessly; kit was packed, inspected and re-inspected. Ammunition was loaded onto the dropships along with our kit, so that all we had to do on the day was jump on board with the kit we were wearing. Then once everything was packed into the dropships we would have our kit checked all over again. Nothing could be left behind; once the dropships left the ship there was no going back, not because they weren't physically capable of returning themselves to orbit, but because the Chinese anti-air defences would make it hard enough to land, let alone take off again. For at least the first few hours and most likely several days afterwards anything that dropped to the surface wasn't going back up again.

Climo was released from the brig after only a week of solitary confinement, we would need every man to fight and so his crime was overlooked. Brown stayed in the section, much to my dismay, though he was moved out of my room to prevent further bloodshed. He glared at me whenever we saw each other, but never went near me for fear of being punished. Woody was still in intensive care, though he was rumoured to be rapidly on the mend. Climo assured me that there was no chance he would be returned to one platoon, and I hoped to God he was right.

Nobody touched Climo, though the NCOs made sure he spent most of his time on fatigues as punishment. It seemed none of the blokes wanted to take their chances with the man who managed to put Woody in the infirmary, and Climo seemed to enjoy the notoriety. Unfortunately it was that very notoriety that earned him the MAM-G, which had been Woody's weapon. The 'mammoth gun' as it was known was simply a larger version of the MSG-20 rifle, which was fed by a drum of three hundred rounds and was designed to be fired on fully automatic. We all knew how to use it but it was a heavy weapon, despite modern materials, and a pain to carry around.

'There you go, tough boy,' Joe Mac had sneered when he handed Climo the weapon at the armoury for the first time. He had never appeared to be best friends with Woody, but he clearly resented me and Climo remaining within the section while one of the senior bods was in the infirmary.

Climo hefted the cumbersome weapon, 'Bastard,' he uttered, though whether the utter was directed at Joe or the weapon I didn't know.

Corporal Evans remained aloof over the whole situation which had unfolded within his section, and allowed Joe Mac to discipline us as he saw fit, and to be fair, between Jamo, Mac and the CSM's galley duties, I don't think I could have taken much more punishment anyway!

'Ev saves his anger for when he needs it,' Climo said. 'And to be fair I don't think he likes Woody, but when he does get mad, dash and get down!'

Corporal Evans took one of the platoon's three spare troopers from within headquarters. Jamo wasn't happy, as he had planned to use the spare troopers as a work party to help him move casualties and ammunition, and he was quick to point it out to me and Climo.

'If we run out of stretchers, blame these two,' he said to the platoon.

The new addition was pretty senior, but thankfully not of the Woody variety. Chase was a lean trooper with a chiselled jaw, who was often referred to as 'Chase the face' for his good looks that supposedly left Uralian women weak at the knees.

Although Rawson had been involved in my violent punishment for attacking Woody, he had taken mine and Climo's presence in the section remarkably well, in fact he appeared more than happy with the trade-off for Chase, who he clearly got on well with. I didn't think he would ever admit it, but Rawson found Woody's personality tiresome.

Berezynsky remained as quiet as ever within the section, barely saying a word to anyone unless spoken to, which had begun to cause other troopers to ask if he had mental issues. As for the other new lads within the platoon, we had all found our own places within our sections, and even though we were at the bottom of the pile, we began to be treated like human beings at last. Woody's stooge Stevo had withdrawn himself since losing his protection, and the platoon began to feel balanced, even if it still wasn't always pleasant. Perhaps we were all beginning to finally realize that when the time came and we dropped into the New Earth atmosphere, it wouldn't matter who we were or where we came from or how long we had served. In the end we would all fight and die side by side up against the full force of our enemy.

The might of the Chinese was sobering - endless holographic briefings with the boss in the galley detailed the known weapons in their arsenal - and their estimated numbers.

The Chinese possessed a conscripted ground force in excess of two hundred thousand men, much like the sand bag fillers who trailed behind our invasion fleet. They, like our conscripts, were more about quantity rather than quality, but sometimes in war quantity had its own kind of quality, and two hundred thousand was a lot of men. They would all be dug deep into warrens, with a mind to turn the surface of the planet into chaos as soon as we hit the deck.

They had an estimated thirty dropship battalion based mostly on the surface, which roughly translated into an additional twenty-five thousand fully trained volunteers who would move rapidly by dropship and act as shock troops, striking at units bogged down by the conscripts.

Chinese soldiers were supposedly similar to us, but uniformed in a light pink camouflage with a visor that was black and hid their faces.

'Despite popular belief that the enemy soldiers are all robots,' the platoon commander smirked at the absurdity. 'The Chinese visors are black for reasons simply within the design.'

'That's what they want us to think, Sir,' Rawson pointed out with a hint of humour in his voice. One of Stevo's latest rumours was that the Chinese soldiers were 'Cyborgs', the very word sent shivers down trooper's spines. Cybernetics was taboo, reserved for the rich and the depraved, and what it could render men capable of was unknown to us. And all troopers feared the unknown.

'Well, why don't you prove it to me when we get down there,' the boss said challengingly, and we laughed.

Chinese dropships were larger and squatter in appearance than ours, as were their gunships, which were their answer to our gravtanks. They were designed much more like aircraft than our low profile ground hugging craft but their basic capabilities were much the same.

Chinese soldiers on the ground outnumbered us significantly; we had only twenty-six dropship battalions to their thirty and only one hundred thousand conscripts to take over the ground we captured. We were relying upon our navy to provide us with orbital supremacy and for our unmanned fighters to outmatch theirs and keep control of the atmosphere.

If the numbers we had were anything to go by - and where they came from I would never know - then the Chinese were outnumbered by our fleet as we brought with us an impressive sixty warships to their forty, but for unmanned aircraft we were only at best the Chinese equal. Chinese robotic fighters were the scourge of the Union army and we feared them, but none as much as the 'saucer'.

Amusingly the saucer was once seen by our ancestors as a spacecraft flown by creatures from elsewhere in the universe, and it invoked terror that transcended generations. The real thing made its debut on the battlefield years ago, piloted by a computer like many modern aircraft and manufactured by factories on human colonies. It too created terror, but a terror far worse, for this saucer was real, and it carried guns. The saucer was an unmanned aircraft that used a far more advanced propulsion system than our dropships did, and because it was unmanned it was barely limited to the speeds it could go up to or how rapidly it could change direction. If a man were inside it he could be turned into mush. It was so shaped in order to make it aerodynamic in all directions, which helped make it far harder to hit because one second it would be going one way and then the next. They were mostly used by modern armies as atmospheric fighters, but they also made devastating ground attack aircraft and the Chinese knew this all too well. A Chinese ground attack saucer was equipped with banks of smart missile pods, and a twin twenty millimetre cannon that could turn a platoon into mincemeat before they even saw the thing. We were scared of the saucers, and all desperately hoped that our lives wouldn't be brought to an abrupt end by one.

The day before we would arrive in Alpha Centauri I heard word from Greggerson that Woody had been released from the infirmary and would indeed make the drop.

'How can they be releasing him so soon?' I asked as my heart plummeted down into my stomach. 'The bastard died several times didn't he?'

Greggerson shrugged. 'He had ops on his brain too, apparently. He's gone to two platoon.'

Damn trooper's rumour, I cursed silently, knowing that there was no way Woody could recover to combat fitness that quickly if his brain had indeed been operated on and he had been in a critical condition for days. Modern medicine could do it, but drop troopers weren't worth enough to warrant such expensive medical equipment. After all, there was one advantage to infantry that ensured that we never became obsolete. We were cheap.

'Who told you?' I asked.

'Stevo,' Greggerson answered. 'I wasn't talking to him, I overheard him saying it,' he quickly added as if I would be disgusted at him talking to the senior tom. People in the platoon liked Stevo less than Woody, who he often hid behind. He was also full of shit, but this time I somehow knew that Stevo wasn't making up another one of his random false rumours. Woody was out, and surely he would be wanting his revenge.

———

Entering the Alpha Centauri system was an anti-climax, there were no sirens, no sudden shudders through the superstructure, just a chime on the ship's announcement system at four in the morning whilst me, Climo and our new room-mate, Chase, slept in our bunks. The sound woke me and I knew what it meant, we were there, and I waited for the captain to speak. The announcement system remained silent and after several minutes I realised that it would remain so. There was no need to wake us early, because we would not arrive at New Earth for another twenty-four hours at least, and we had already been briefed what we needed to be briefed. Besides, it would take the Chinese hours before they even realised we were even inside the Alpha Centauri system, and far longer before any contact would be made between the two mighty navies.

We were to be given a lie in that morning, until zero-nine-hundred. Bliss, given that our average sleep was only seven hours long, and a chance for us to recharge depleted batteries for what lay ahead for us.

I tried to get myself back to sleep, tossing my body to and fro across the bed to get comfortable again. Eventually I resigned to staring at the shadow of the bunk above me where Chase slept, unaware of our arrival and snoring loudly. Nothing had changed on the ship, the room remained the same, and the air vent continued to blow its light breeze against my face as it always had done. But something had changed, because somewhere out there in the unseen void was the enemy, and we were no longer alone.

There was also something else very different that morning though, as we washed and dressed for breakfast, instead of our dull grey ship's fatigues we wore our dark red gel armour that we would soon be fighting in. We were quiet, subdued even, and the NCOs barked orders and hurried us along and tried their best to keep us motivated.

'This time tomorrow you'll have a pinkie on the end of your bayonet!' Westy, the Welsh corporal in command of Greggerson's section grinned from ear to ear as though he relished the thought of the killing that came his way, and his section cheered enthusiastically on their way to breakfast.

Passing Corporal Evans in the corridor to the galley I thought maybe me and Climo might receive our own encouragement from our section commander, but he simply nodded.

'Carry on, lads,' he said, and we scurried away.

'Do you think he doesn't like us?' I asked Climo.

'Nah, he's like that with everyone. Trust me, mate, if there's a section to be in, it's his.'

I hoped to God that he was right.

Through the day we were fed tiny bits of information about what was going on outside Challenger's metal shell. The Union fleet had completed its jump successfully, and was moving toward New Earth and Centauri Alpha's four other worlds, which were either scorched wastelands or cold gas giants. The vast majority of the fleet moved toward New Earth, the primary objective of the operation, and just after mid-day we detected the first of the Chinese ships. It wouldn't be long until the first laser banks began to fire, and combat would commence.

We sat in the galley together as a company, and listened while the ship's captain and the OC made their speeches, and the captain told us that whoever our God was we should take him with us and that he would protect us, or something like that. I looked for Woody amongst the crowd that huddled close around the two officers, fearing for reprisals, but I couldn't see him and besides I had far worse things to worry about. Two hundred and twenty-five thousand Chinese soldiers, to be precise. Nobody spoke a word, we listened as though those words would be the last we would ever hear, and maybe they were. We tried to appear calm, but you could feel the tension amongst the company, the air was thick with it. We were scared. Sure we had volunteered to do our duty, but none of us wanted to die. We wanted adventure, we wanted purpose, we wanted money, we wanted guts and glory - there were so many things that made us chose to serve at the tip of the blade of the Union spear - but none of us wanted to die, and now on the verge of all-out war, we were scared.

The captain returned to her bridge to command the upcoming battle in space, and a naval officer finished collecting hurriedly written last letters to families and loved ones and then he too disappeared, leaving only the dropship infantry behind.

'Gentlemen,' the OC addressed us all, 'in the next few hours we will enter New Earth orbit. We will drop not long afterwards. I won't keep you any longer. It has been a pleasure to command this company, and it will be an honour to command you in battle. You are all the very best that the Union has to offer. Or at least I hope so …' A smile crept across his face, and we all laughed and cheered. The OC held up a hairy arm and the company fell back to silence. 'Gentlemen, I wish you all the very best of luck.'

The CSM received the nod from the OC. 'Platoon Sergeants! Get your platoons to your dropships, confirm when you're complete.'

I shook hands with Peters for one last time before I left for my dropship. I had barely seen him during our voyage, and I knew that there was a chance I wouldn't see him again.

'Take care, mate,' I told him.

'You, too, man, good luck.'

And he was gone.

———

We walked in eerie silence through the corridors of Challenger toward the dropship hangars, a crowd of red uniforms heading in only one direction. We wouldn't return to see our accommodation for weeks or even months, and that was if we made it back at all. Naval personnel stood back and watched blankly as the procession passed, they were neither glad nor sorry to see us go. We were going somewhere terrible where there was a good chance we might die, but they too faced their own perils over the coming days.

I had hated my prison on board Challenger, but now I longed to stay inside its protective superstructure, guarded by banks of lasers, missiles and Vulcan cannon. I had become used to it, for all the suffering it had caused me, but now I was faced with a whole new horror; an enemy whose numbers I could scarcely imagine who sat waiting for us, waiting for his prey to come to him.

There were no more speeches, we had heard enough. Instead we were lined up beside our dropships and counted in by our section commanders. They gave the nod to the platoon sergeant, and then he in turn told the CSM that the platoon was complete and fully prepared to drop.

'Double check all equipment,' I overheard the CSM speaking to Jamo, looking over all of us as he made his rounds through each of the platoon hangars, 'Ensure you check all comms, batteries, etcetera. You know the score, mate.' Jamo nodded.

Before the CSM left the hangar he looked over to Corporal Evans and gave a very slight but respectful nod. Our section commander's hard face gave nothing away as he returned the nod, but Jamo appeared to bristle visibly.

'The CSM was Ev's platoon sergeant,' Climo explained quietly, '… on Eden,' he added.

'Wow,' I exclaimed, 'they must have seen some shit together.'

'Yeah, the CSM absolutely loves Ev, and Jamo hates it. He thinks Ev should have had the platoon.'

'Shut up, you two,' Joe Mac rounded on us. 'This is still a parade, not a cheers-easy get together!'

'Sorry, Joe,' I said, as Climo glowered.

'Have you got a problem with me, Climpson?' Joe took a step toward Climo, who said nothing. 'You might think you're the new wide boy because you can hit people with chairs, but if you kick off with me I will spread you up the wall.' Brown was looking over. He said nothing, but he glared at me and I looked away.

'Joe,' Corporal Evans called for calm. 'Let's save it for New Earth, alright?'

'Sorry, Ev.' Joe stepped away from Climo, who still stared at him defiantly. 'He'll learn soon enough.'

We double-checked all of our equipment, trying to keep busy to keep our minds off what was coming our way. Whilst I checked the contents of my daysack were packed correctly, Brown crouched beside me. His breath burned the back of my neck and I shuddered.

'Woody's dropping with us, today, you know that don't you?' he said darkly.

'Yes,' I answered bluntly.

'He wants you to know that he'll find you.' His words were filled with hatred. 'And have an accident. With you and your new mate. That's if I don't get you first.'

I said nothing, what could I say? I tried to appear nonchalant and continued to pack my daysack.

'Go talk to one of your friends, Brown,' Climo said, seeing what was going on. 'Oh wait, that's right, you don't have any.'

It was Brown's turn to say nothing, he walked away.

'I hate that bloke.'

We loaded onto the dropship and began to put on our armour and daysacks ready to go. This is it, I thought, this was the end of my journey, the final climax of almost two years of training and preparation. My heart began to pump hard against my ribcage and my palms began to sweat. I was so scared, but I tried to hide it. Besides the enemy I had Woody after my blood, and a man in my own section would love to see me dead.

Climo patted my shoulder gently, 'It'll be alright, mate,' he said as we took our places in the tiny dropship crew compartment. 'Trust me.' He slipped something into the inside of his helmet.

'What's that?' I asked.

'Picture of my family.'

'Oh.'

He showed me the inside of his helmet, which he had lined with simple printed pictures of friends and family. 'If I die, I want to be surrounded by the people I love.'

'Wow. That's heavy, mate.' I secretly regretted not doing the same - all of my family pictures were kept on my tablet still locked away in my room. I suppose I didn't want my family with me when I did what I was about to do. I longed for them so badly and the pictures only made it worse.

'Stuff like that won't help where we're going,' Chaz said, strapping himself into his seat.

'Let's get a move on, lads,' Corporal Evans ordered from outside the dropship. 'We're approaching New Earth now.'

The waiting was over.

12: The Ditches

Rain pelted my visor, and my boots crunched on the gravelled surface of New Earth as I ran. I was driven not by rage or purpose, but through sheer terror. I ran after Berezynsky, who was barely visible in the thick hot smoke belching from the dischargers mounted on the dropship's stubby wings. It fired salvos of missiles into multiple targets, its twin Vulcan cannons roaring as they spat death toward the enemy. The dischargers too billowed hot smoke from its sides to help mask us from the enemies' sight and infra-red, and scores of flares shot into the sky to deter missiles. The dropship had become a deadly firework show so loud my earphones could barely filter it. It was necessary to protect us, as well as the dropship itself, from the enemy because they were close, very close indeed.

I ran in a crouch through the smoke, the fear of death in me as I followed Berezynsky toward the ditch that the dropship pilot had told us to use as cover.

We were the first ones out. There was an order to debussing that we were taught on Uralis and had practiced again and again using Challenger's simulators during our voyage. The section commander never went first, and neither would the second in command. This wasn't a cowardly thing by any means, the section commander was so busy commanding the section, listening to the company radio network and planning his next action he often wasn't paying much attention to his own safety. Corporal Evans was right behind me, though.

'Move!' he yelled, with an urgency I had rarely heard from him.

The air cracked and hissed around my head as steel darts punched through the air. We were being fired upon, and we were only being missed because of the sheer firepower being unleashed by the dropship. It wouldn't last forever, though. Adrenaline spurred my body ever faster.

'Get down!'

I threw myself into the ditch, rolling down the steep bank and into a pool of cold water. I felt it soak under my armour and seep into my boots.

It was a drainage ditch, designed to keep the crops from being drowned in the heavy New Earth rainfall. It ran for several hundred metres in both directions, and through the smoke my visor identified another section debussing from their dropship into the ditch a hundred metres or so off to my right.

Black smoke from the orbital bombardment drifted overhead from Jersey City a few kilometres away, mixing in with the white smoke created by the dropships and smoke bombs fired by our battalion's own artillery.

Rounds ricocheted off the lip of the ditch, chucking great chunks of dirt down at me where I cowered in the blood-red mud.

Yeah, you heard right, I cowered. Overwhelmed by the sights and noise around me I had curled almost into a ball in the bottom of the ditch like a frightened child. In my defence, I hadn't done it consciously, rather my body's natural instinct had kicked in and told me to stay low and hide. It hadn't even reached my comprehension that what I was doing was against everything I had been taught to do since becoming a drop trooper.

Berezynsky was five metres to the right of me, lying up against the lip of the ditch and firing in the direction of the enemy. He stole a quick glance down to me, his eyes a mixture of terror and anger.

'Moralee, what the hell are you doing?' he asked over the intercom. I think it's the most I ever heard him say.

To be honest I didn't have a clue what I was doing. The whole section had formed a line along the ditch and everyone was firing apart from me, but still I remained frozen to the spot.

The dropship began to close its doors and shot backwards, its guns still roaring. Along with its battle brothers, it would give fire support and air defence from the rear whilst it waited to be used again. I wished that I could have gone with it, for then it was just us, and the Chinese.

'Moralee, get up and fire you little weasel!' somebody shouted, I think it was Chase.

'Get some rounds down!'

I was paralysed with fear. The voluntary nature of Dropship Infantry and the intensity of its training often led people to believe that we were superhuman, incapable of fear. People can talk themselves up as much as they like, but until they're in a contact with the enemy for real they can never really know how they might react. My first reaction was a bad one, I was almost unable to even move, I was so scared.

Boots slapped against the water at the bottom of the ditch behind me, and Joe Mac grasped me by the throat and threw me against the bank, his teeth bared, rifle held up as if he meant to smack me round the head with it.

'What are you doing? *What the FUCK are you doing?*' he screamed, his face so close to mine our respirators almost touched. Spittle sprayed over his visor. He was beside himself, he must have run halfway along the ditch under fire just to get to me.

'I don't know!' I cried out, wild with terror.

'Get up there and put some darts down the range now!'

I guess that was what I needed, a good kick up the arse. Whatever the pinkies could do to me, Joe could probably do far worse. Training kicking back in, I crawled up the bank of the ditch and took aim.

The crimson red New Earth surface was as dazzling as it was terrifying. Angry dark pink clouds broiled high above, flickering with lightning, or perhaps the flashes of a battle between atmospheric fighters. Balls of flame would regularly break through the clouds and strike the ground far away, causing shockwaves so powerful that I could feel them through my respirator. It was as though some great deity had decided to wreak terrible revenge on the land, but it was in fact our ships, high above, dropping kinetic weapons onto the enemy. New Earth was already a war zone, and it looked like hell.

We were in a corn field halfway up the slope of a large hill kilometres across that towered above a deep valley. I guessed that it was Hill Bravo, as we had been briefed prior to our drop and that another large hill on the opposite side of the valley must have been Alpha. The corn was enclosed in greenhouses in every direction as far as the eye could see, turning the land into a patchwork of different shades of green and gold mixed with the red of the New Earth soil. Most of their glass roofs had been either riddled with holes or shattered leaving nothing but the supports, like the exposed rib cages of decaying animals. Others burned fiercely. Without the artificial atmosphere the greenhouses maintained, the plants would all die. In the far distance Jersey City burned, from where I lay up on the bank of the ditch I thought that nobody could be alive down there.

My respirator target display flashed red as it indicated targets it had picked up to my front. Sure enough, through the smouldering greenhouse crops, I caught fleeting glances of Chinese soldiers running a few hundred metres away. I could recognise their distinctive off-pink camouflage.

My finger pulled the trigger. The series of powerful magnets that lined the barrel of my MSG-20 screamed as they propelled a dart toward my target at sonic speeds, rocking my body with the recoil. I don't know if I hit anything, but I was now in the battle.

'Section, prepare to give rapid fire!' Corporal Evans was back on the intercom, 'Rapid … FIRE!'

We gave them hell. The mammoth gunners let rip and a few grenades left their launchers, disintegrating the remaining greenhouses to our front and churning plant life.

Suppressive fire is a concept as old as the first guns, and it was unlikely that for long as infantry soldiers existed on the battlefield it would ever become obsolete. Suppressive fire forces a soldier to take cover, and as long as it remains accurate, it will keep the enemy hiding, unable to lift his head to fire for fear of death.

Sure enough, the enemy fire had subdued significantly under the withering rate of fire we had returned. It was hard to see where the Chinese were, but I assumed they were a hundred metres away, or thereabouts, in some form of cover, probably another ditch. I guessed there weren't many of them, since they had been relatively easy to suppress, or perhaps they were simply withdrawing to counter-attack us somewhere else using the complex system of tunnels and trenches supposedly dug into the hill. I fired round after round into likely enemy positions amongst the crops. My MSG-20 would occasionally alter the trajectory of the rounds passing through the barrel, angling them toward fleeting targets moving close to my crosshairs. Whether I hit anybody, I couldn't be sure.

Several feet splattered in the pool at the bottom of the ditch in which I had cowered. I didn't look around at the new arrivals in our little part of the ditch - I was too busy trying to shoot accurately without exposing myself too much.

'Section!' Corporal Evans called out. 'Slow down your rate of fire! What's happening Boss? Shit …' He cut off his intercom.

We slowed our rate of fire as ordered. There was no sense in us firing at a rapid rate for too long against an enemy who had momentarily lost the fight. Corporal Evans had given the 'rapid fire' to cover the boss as he ran up to us from wherever his dropship had left him. If the boss got himself shot then the platoon sergeant or the most senior section commander would be able to step up, but better he didn't die at all! We were still suppressing, but using far less ammunition and it wasn't long until the Chinese gained the courage to get up and fire again.

Rounds cracked overhead, forcing me to duck. I found myself staring straight into the eyes of the platoon commander's radio operator, Cyclops, who was crouched close to the platoon commander, monitoring the various communication nets for important information. His eyes were darting nervously across the battlefield and he looked like he was absolutely shitting himself, though I supposed I must have looked the same to him.

The boss was crouched up against the wall of the ditch explaining to Corporal Evans what he wanted him to do. Occasionally he lifted his head over the top to see the ground to our front. He was caked in mud, presumably he had fallen over. A gash on his arm suggested a glancing blow from his dash to get to us. He was lucky, a good strike with a dart could take your arm clean off, and at short range could punch straight through helmets and gel armour, advanced though they were.

BOOM!

The ground around me shook with a wave of overpressure as a gravtank somewhere to our rear fired a rail gun round into an unseen target in Jersey City.

'Get some, pinkies! Woohooo!' Climo screamed triumphantly, punching a fist into the air.

I looked behind me at the gravtank twenty or so metres back. It was an imposing beast of a machine. A giant Union flag flew from its turret, erected by the crew sometime within the last couple of minutes. The flag flapped in the strong breeze, its blue background and yellow stars striking in contrast against the reds and pinks of New Earth. Its Vulcan cannon opened fire, strafing across the ground to our front.

You don't mess with gravtanks. They have the same manoeuvrability and speed of a dropship but as much - if not more - firepower than any ground-based vehicle. It was the Dropship Infantry's prize asset, a real battle winner.

'Right, listen in lads,' Corporal Evans was back on the intercom. We stopped and listened as he gave us the plan, there was no need for us to continue to fire, the gravtank was keeping the Chinese quite busy! 'One section didn't make the drop, so it's just us and Westy's boys!'

I gulped. '*Didn't make the drop*'. A whole section of our platoon had perished on their way down, along with their dropship and crew. Gilbert and Kane had been with them.

'Two section has got eyes on an enemy section one hundred metres to our front,' Corporal Evans continued with a confidence in his voice that lifted my spirits, 'They're in a good position to keep them suppressed.'

He was talking of the enemy soldiers I had been firing at. There were many more of them all over the valley, but in our little part of the battlefield the ones directly to our front were our main threat. The Chinese were heavily dug into the hill, an entire battalion of them, and it was our job to clear them out, or die trying. To our left and right flanks, as well as to our rear tens of platoons would be engaged in their own battles. We were surrounded, but we were troopers - we were meant to be surrounded.

'Two section will continue to suppress,' Corporal Evans continued, 'We will attempt to use the ditches to attack them from the right flank, but we need to be quick!'

'Have it!' Climo shouted, randomly.

The platoon was normally composed of three sections in order, to allow it to manoeuvre over the battle field with one giving covering for the others, although this could theoretically work with two. The concept of one covering, one moving, was known as tactical balance, or 'one foot on the ground'. The problem we faced was that we no longer possessed a third 'reserve' section, which would normally give us the flexibility to deal with changes on the battlefield. Assaulting with only two sections was a risky business, but we had no choice.

'Prepare to move!'

I carried out the drill for preparing to move as I had done on Uralis and the simulators on Challenger - check safety catch, check ammo pouches, crawl down into cover. I slid down into the bottom of the ditch once more. Corporal Evans was already running past me along the base of the ditch.

'Move! Follow me!' His voice was urgent again, and I understood why. The Chinese were on the back foot, they had no idea where exactly we might have dropped, that was the problem with defending against dropships, but now we were on the ground they might regain the initiative if we didn't keep up the momentum.

We ran along the ditch behind our section commander. Cold water splashed up between my legs, but I ignored it, scanning to my left and right for enemy. Missiles and aircraft streaked across the grey sky above as the two vast colonial air forces fought for supremacy in the New Earth atmosphere. Missiles and ordinance of all descriptions passed over our heads, seemingly with much more important targets elsewhere. We were infantry, cheap and plentiful, hardly worth wasting expensive missiles on, or at least that was what I hoped. Rain lashed sideways against us, hammering against our visors.

The drainage system for Jersey's vast farmlands was formed into endless square grids, with each square being around one hundred metres across and each containing at least ten greenhouses. We had planned to advance forward by use of the ditches, which were deep enough to conceal a man keeping his head low.

Ahead of us was the section I had seen debus, locked into a fierce fire fight with our foe over the top of the ditch. It was two section, I could hear their section commander, Corporal Weston screaming orders into his intercom as we approached. At the bottom of the ditch a trooper screamed and clutched at his bloodied arm whilst another lay lifeless in the water, their red camouflage identifying them to me as friendly.

We passed behind two section, and as we did Corporal Weston called out to Corporal Evans, 'They're to my eleven o'clock mate, in a trench or something. Got 'em pinned!'

'Roger!' Corporal Evans led us round the back of two section. The ditch ran into the distance, unnaturally straight. A few hundred metres away more Union troops crossed it as a nearby dropship burned. The battle was everywhere, and we were only a tiny part of it.

The wounded trooper was Greggerson. My eyes widened at the sight of him crying with pain, his arm swollen almost comically where his gel armour had turned itself into a bandage. I didn't stop for him, and I ran around the body of the dead trooper. He lay face down, his respirator sunk into the mud. A chunk of his helmet was missing, and through the hole blood glistened. For the sake of morale our visor targeting screens wouldn't identify

friendly troopers who had died, but out of the corner of my eye I caught a glimpse of his name printed across the back of his helmet. It was Davo. He must have died debussing from his dropship.

We turned left at a junction in the ditch just past the end man of two section. The remains of the greenhouses towered above us, some ablaze, some remarkably intact. Rounds cracked overhead as two section continued its fire fight above us. I guessed the enemy were somewhere close by.

We hadn't got far, maybe fifty metres in front of two section when Corporal Evans signalled with his free hand for us to get down and as one we took a knee at the bottom of the ditch. I clutched my rifle tight, waiting for the Chinese to appear out from the burning greenhouses. Occasionally I thought I could hear their voices, picked out and amplified by my headset, but I couldn't be certain.

Nobody dared to speak as Corporal Evans scanned the crops off to our left. I didn't know if he had a sixth sense for danger that he had developed on Eden, but he definitely wasn't happy with something. The only sound was that of the tiny filters in my respirator and the thumping of my heart. Rain hammered against us as we strained to hear our unseen enemy.

Corporal Evan's hand closed into a fist, with his thumb outstretched and pointing downwards; enemy. Slowly and deliberately he then opened his hand, pointing into the greenhouses to our left. That way.

Weapons quietly moved to aim at their new found target. The enemy were moving in the farmland to our left, directly in front of two section.

I heard them this time, there was no mistaking their strange language and accent I had been taught to recognise against European languages. I couldn't see anything in amongst the greenhouses, and neither could my respirator target display.

Corporal Evans carefully raised his rifle over his head and used it to 'look' over the top of the ditch with its camera.

'Chinese section, ten metres away,' he whispered. 'We need to be quick, Delta fire team you will give covering fire, Joe ensure you maintain protection on the right flank, I'll leave you Climo.'

Joe Mac nodded, he would have five men in his fire team now, leaving Corporal Evans with only three men; him, Berezynsky, and me.

Berezynsky checked his bayonet was fitted securely. I gulped.

We crawled up the bank of the ditch as high as we dared without exposing ourselves. Rainwater ran through the blood channels cut into the blade of my bayonet and dripped onto the red earth. Around us the battle raged on, the gravtank had moved away from us and out of sight, presumably with bigger and more important targets to engage than a few Chinese soldiers - soldiers who could easily destroy it with a smart missile if it hung around for too long.

Corporal Evans looked left and right at his section of eight. Then, with a single tap on Climo's shoulder his plan was initiated. Climo sprang up and sprayed automatic over the bank with his MAM-G, closely followed by the rest of Delta fire team. At that instant Corporal Evans was up and over the top of the ditch, with me and Berezynsky just behind.

I remember my first bayonet charge so vividly even now, like it is permanently etched into my memory. I remember trampling my way through the crops, screaming in a mixture of hatred and fear as I bore down on my enemy like a modern day barbarian. Although their strange black reflective visors revealed none of their faces, the Chinese were clearly surprised. They were barely even ten metres away and lying on their bellies from where they had been trying to crawl closer to two section without being noticed. Instead they had been caught at point blank range and they were dead and they knew it.

Those who tried to kneel up in order to bring their weapons to bear were the first to die, cut to ribbons by Climo and the rest of Delta fire team. The hail of supersonic darts punctured through armour and flesh like hot butter, hurling bodies to the ground like dolls.

I fired round after round into my enemy as I closed with them, my bayonet gleaming cold hard and cruel as I did.

One Chinaman fell onto his back as I shot him in the stomach. Despite his wound, he attempted to bring his rifle into the aim, but too late.

I stabbed the man several times. Blood sprayed up my legs and he lay still, without making a sound. Training had taken over my body completely, and without even thinking of what I had just done I withdrew my bayonet and checked that it was still fitted correctly to my rifle, as was the drill, ready for my next foe. There were none. The rest were dead on the ground, killed either by Delta fire team or by us with our rifles and bayonets.

There had been an entire section of Chinese, presumably attempting to sneak through the crops in order to attack two section from close range. Unfortunately they hadn't covered their flanks and we had beaten them at their own game quickly and violently.

'Withdraw!' Corporal Evans bellowed.

We darted back toward the ditch. More Chinese were firing at us instead of two section from within the crops, having been alerted to our attack.

'Get down, you stupid crow!' Corporal Evans struck my daysack hard from behind, driving my body down to the ground as the crops danced with enemy fire.

Without a clear line of sight the Chinese couldn't target us accurately, but with similar weapons to us they put down some serious firepower, and made an effective demonstration of how suppressing fire could really force troopers to keep their heads down. I'd never crawled so fast in my life, dragging my body through the mud and into the ditch, where the gloved hands of the lads in Delta fire team grasped me and dragged me down into cover.

'You alright, Moralee?' Rawson asked.

'Yeah,' I nodded, panting. My respirator filters whirred as they worked to clear mist from my visor.

'Jesus, there's blood all up him,' Climo exclaimed. Rounds still cracked overhead as Corporal Evans and Berezynsky were dragged into the ditch.

'There are two trenches,' Corporal Evans told Joe, pointing towards where the rounds had come from, 'Must be a platoon in that direction.'

'Well we can't stay here mate, we'll be shot to shit,' Mac advised, glancing apprehensively up the ditch.

Corporal Evans nodded his agreement, 'We need to get out of this ditch.' Then to Rawson, 'Give me smoke.' He indicated up the ditch with an outstretched arm.

Rawson's respirator barely concealed his grin. 'Roger that!' He brought his rifle up into a high aim, activating his under-slung grenade launcher at the same time. It was a simple weapon with a revolving drum that lobbed guided grenades, and it was devastatingly effective in the hands of an experienced trooper like Rawson. He fired a string of three grenades, all of which exploded into clouds of smoke and phosphor. Lethal as the phosphor was, the grenades were designed with one purpose, to create an instant cloud of hot smoke and tiny metallic fragments that could shield us from view from the enemy's sophisticated targeting systems, including thermal.

'Let's move,' Corporal Evans ordered, and we scrabbled up the wall of the ditch and concealed ourselves amongst a field of what I could only guess to be corn, its greenhouse roof shattered and collapsed. Glass cracked beneath my boots as I crouched as low as I could amongst the plants and took aim toward the dispersing cloud of smoke. My eyes suddenly focused on my bayonet; it was dripping with blood.

'Two section's gonna push through us along the ditch,' Corporal Evans announced, and I shook off my daze, 'we'll give cover from here.'

Suddenly rounds peppered the earth around us, flicking bits of soil into the air. Chase and Berezynsky were snatched backwards and I blinked, stunned.

'Contact front!'

The section weapons erupted in the direction of the enemy fire, but for some reason my visor hadn't identified any targets and I paused, as if in a trance. Someone was screaming.

'Man down, man down!' a ragged voice called over the intercom. It was Joe Mac, running toward the casualties.

'Well fire, then!' I realised that Corporal Evans was looking right at me from not even five metres away.

I needed no further instruction. My visor could not see the enemy themselves but it could pick up the direction their rounds were coming from so I took up aim and fired.

To the left of the ditch two section were advancing forward parallel to us, their weapons spitting death as they went. They were moving forward as fire teams, one team moving while the other covered, dashing forward through the crops. The enemy was somewhere ahead of them, but I still couldn't see where.

'Rawson!' Corporal Evans hollered, 'Westy wants frag on the position!' Two section's section commander wanted grenades fired toward the enemy in order to force him into cover.

'Roger!' Rawson wasn't smiling any more, the section had taken casualties. He fired another burst of three grenades and my visor warned me that they were high explosive. Instinctively, I ducked low to the ground.

The grenades exploded amongst the crops, and I finally saw what we had been shooting at. A hundred or so metres away and concealed within one of the greenhouses on the other side of the ditch was some kind of trench, surrounded by sandbags, but any enemy that had been there had disappeared, presumably blown to pieces.

'Have that, you bastards.' Climo shook his fist.

Two section were up and moving again, and they were upon the trench within seconds. A couple of rounds were fired and somebody shouted something unintelligible. Seconds later there was a loud thump and a pillar of red earth and dust leapt into the air.

'Position is clear, it's got a tunnel!'

My heart skipped a beat. Of course they had a tunnel, many of the Chinese positions would do. The hill was networked with kilometres of tunnels designed to protect defenders from orbital bombardment, a legacy left by the Union and then no doubt built upon by the Chinese themselves. The explosion had been a grenade tossed into the tunnel by two section in an attempt to drive back any enemy that might be planning to counter attack back onto the surface.

We were all nervous of fighting in tunnels, it was chaotic, claustrophobic, and units fighting underground could expect high casualty rates. I swallowed nervously.

Corporal Evans lifted his head and looked across the battlefield. The greenhouses and their crops made it hard to see anything past a hundred metres, but even if we couldn't see all the battle, we could hear it. My visor indicated that another platoon was in contact somewhere off to our right.

Corporal Evans turned to Joe, who was tending to Chase and Berezynsky. 'What's the score with the casualties, mate?'

'Berezynsky's dead, mate,' Joe answered gravely and I saw that he was right. Behind me Berezynsky lay with his head missing. The super high velocity of a magnetic dart had the potential to do devastating damage to the unlucky. Chase, on the other hand, had been struck on the leg, and his gel armour had solidified on impact and managed to deflect the dart enough to leave him with no more than a broken bone. Funny how things work out.

Chase moaned, but somehow managed to give a thumbs-up as the section 2ic checked his medical status on his wristpad. 'Chase will live,' Joe said.

The air cracked, and my visor display flashed red at more Chinese firing from fifty metres away, this time on our side of the ditch. 'Contact!' I screamed. God knows where they had come from, but they were there, bounding toward us in the same way that two section had done toward the trench.

As we hit the deck, Climo fired a burst in response, his mammoth's high powered magnets shrieking in terrible fury.

The section returned fire as more pink camouflaged soldiers appeared. They were close; soon we would share the fate of the section we had killed only minutes ago.

'Boss, this is Ev,' Corporal Evans was straight on the platoon intercom, we were in trouble. 'Contact, wait out!'

'They're gonna flank us!' Joe Mac had abandoned Chase, and was now shouting to Corporal Evans. Rawson fired a string of grenades blindly over the greenhouses. The grenades soared almost lazily into the air, and then darted toward the ground and detonated as they identified targets that my visor couldn't.

'Come on, then, you bastards!' Climo was stood now, strafing the crops with his MAM-G. Chinese scattered from the spray of supersonic darts that ricocheted from greenhouse frames and hacked the ground and tossed clods of earth away into the air.

A Chinaman shot Climo straight in the face. He was dead before he even hit the ground.

The remaining five of us crouched low in amongst the crops in our desperate last stand, our weapons spitting death.

It occurred to me that I was about to die. The Chinese had fixed us in position, and were moving around the greenhouses to our right flank for the kill. The gravtanks and dropships were either destroyed or otherwise engaged, because no help came. Two section were nowhere near and no doubt had their own problems, and three section, who would have been our reserve, had never even seen the surface. In a world where travel between the stars was the norm, we were on our own, no further than fifty metres from friendly forces. The feeling of helplessness was overwhelming.

'Keep firing!' Corporal Evans's voice boomed over the intercom. 'Keep firing or we all die!'

Rawson yelped and dropped to the ground in a spray of blood. 'Man down!' The section echoed the alert that struck at my heart like a knife.

'My call sign is overwhelmed,' Corporal Evans called to the boss over the platoon net. 'Four times casualties, enemy in section plus strength. I am withdrawing!' He was still in control. Despite suffering two deaths and two casualties his voice never gave the slightest hint of fear or defeat. He threw a phosphorus grenade toward the enemy and at the same time Joe Mac threw another. They exploded in great puffs of smoke and phosphor, momentarily concealing us.

'Joe, Brown, move!'

'Moving!' Joe and Brown grabbed Chase and Rawson. Rawson was screaming, creating a sound that I had never heard before, and hoped never to hear again. I couldn't describe it to you, only to say that it curdled the blood and sent shivers up my spine. His agony was absolute; his arm had been severed clean off at the elbow. His gel armour had automatically tightened an inbuilt tourniquet above the stump, stemming the flow of blood. They ran toward the ditch and two section beyond, while me and Corporal Evans fired through the smoke to give cover for them as they moved. The hot smoke interrupted my visor's thermal display, making it almost impossible for me to pick up targets, but that meant the same for the Chinese which was what we needed in order for us to escape. It was impossible to guess how many of them there were out there, but I imagined that they were close, moving through the crops and battered greenhouses. The air was thick with their fire, but thankfully it was inaccurate.

Joe Mac and Brown dragged their casualties into the ditch and then took up positions on the bank to give us covering fire.

'Moralee, prepare to move!' Corporal Evans called.

Safety catch, pouch ... the drills that had been forced into my head on Uralis took over. I looked at the bodies of Climo and Berezynsky. Climo's face was in pieces. Exposed cartilage and bone glistened in the New Earth rain. Climo had been a true friend, one of the few troopers in the platoon who had accepted me into its ranks. Now he was gone.

'Move!'

Rounds whizzed past my head as I ran back with Corporal Evans toward the relative safety of the ditch and two section beyond. Corporal Weston's section appeared to be stuck in their own battle with an enemy to their front, but I saw that one of them was firing grenades over our heads to cover our retreat. Detonations thumped behind me but I didn't turn to look.

I struck something hard with my upper arm, enough to send me stumbling. I glanced around me, but nothing was there. I zigzagged toward the ditch, adrenalin spurring my body forward.

'Down!'

We dropped into the ditch beside the others. I fired a volley of shots into a pink soldier emerging from the smoke fifty metres away. He disappeared behind a greenhouse and I never saw him again.

'Joe, keep eyes on up that ditch!' Corporal Evans pointed in the direction we had been originally travelling. I saw that the ditch was empty, but we were horribly exposed in that direction with all four of us focusing toward the enemy advancing through the greenhouses to our right flank.

'I've got it, Ev!' It was Chase. He had managed to prop himself up against the bank and was pointing his rifle up the ditch. Beside him Rawson wailed, but it looked like his tourniquet had stopped most of the bleeding. He would have to wait. Chase's armour had swollen around his injured leg to immobilize the break.

Corporal Evans was back on the platoon net. 'Boss, this is Ev, we can't hold this flank! I need re-enforcing!'

I heard the hiss of rounds passing close to my head, and my visor told me it had come to my left. My eyes widened, the enemy were in the ditch with us.

'Contact left!' Chase screamed, just before he died.

We fired up the ditch with everything we had, filling it with smoke, sparks and lumps of earth.

'Boss,' Corporal Evans screamed into the platoon net, enraged, 'I cannot hold! Where the FUCK are you?!' He swore a string of curses as we fired in all directions. We were finished. Despite the initial surprise the Chinese had gained the upper hand, we were under attack from along the ditch and from the greenhouses and the situation was desperate.

There was only one option left to save the section. 'Joe, prepare to withdraw!'

'Joe's down!' Brown replied over the din. There were only three of us left.

'Shit!'

My arm was aching from where I had struck it, so I reached to rub it and my hand came away wet with blood. I had been shot.

'I've been shot!' I cried.

'We're gonna die, we're gonna die!' Brown cowered behind the bodies of Chase and Rawson, both of whom were no longer moving. Chase's eyes stared lifelessly toward the heavens, unaware that his body was being used for cover.

I took cover with Brown, throwing my body into the bottom of the ditch behind the dead. It sounds wrong to hide behind a comrade, even now as I say it, but by then I think my survival instinct had properly kicked in, I was little more than an animal, desperately trying to survive. The super high velocity ammunition of the modern battlefield wouldn't be stopped by flesh and bone, but behind two sets of gel armour I had a chance.

'Get up, you stupid little shits!' Corporal Evans had not given up. He cursed and picked up Chase's rifle and grenade launcher, holding it in his left hand with his own rifle in his right. He fired both simultaneously. Empty cases from the grenade launcher scattered to the floor at his feet.

It was at that moment then that I stared in awe at my section commander's last stand from where I lay at the bottom of the ditch. Coated in a mixture of blood and mud, he stood tall, proud and undefeated, his teeth bared like an enraged animal. He was the living embodiment of everything that made the Union army the fearsome foe that it was. I realised at that moment that although wars were fought with weapons, they were won by men like him.

Then it came, the inevitable assault from the Chinese. The battlefield exploded into noise as tens of rifles fired simultaneously and I closed my eyes.

But it wasn't the sound of rifles, I realised, and I opened my eyes. Corporal Evans had taken a knee beside me, but he wasn't dead.

Above us the mighty gravtank hovered, its Vulcan cannon roaring as it cut a swathe across the greenhouses. Any Chinaman above the ditches would have been cut to ribbons by the onslaught.

A section of troopers whose helmets identified them as three platoon came charging past us, splashing us with red water as they jumped over the bodies of my dead comrades. The platoon was back on the attack with its new found support.

The boss and his radio op were the next ones to pass, and he stopped to look at Corporal Evans who now knelt amongst the sorry remains of his section.

'Ev ... you okay ...?' the boss began. The radio op was tugging at his arm, with some important message to pass on. His eyes were wild, because he held the burden of knowing everything about the battle around him.

Corporal Evans said nothing. His eyes burned with hatred, and I knew that he blamed the boss for not re-enforcing him soon enough.

'I couldn't ... sorry.' He backed away two steps from us and our dead, and then he was gone, up the ditch and into the battle. Something exploded a few hundred metres up the ditch, and gunshots sounded from amongst the greenhouses. Another section passed us, and as if satisfied that things were back in our favour, the gravtank shot away from the hill.

Corporal Evans looked down and regarded me and Brown like a lion would a pair of mice. I became self-conscious that I was still curled into a foetal position next to Rawson's body and quickly picked myself up. The ditch was littered with bodies. Chase had been shot again fatally, and Mac lay in a crumpled heap, his head and arm missing. Only his rank insignia could identify him.

'Ev,' Sergeant James greeted our section commander as he slid into the ditch, with his work party and the smart launchers in tow. The platoon sergeant stooped over our dead and checked their vital signs on their wristpads to ensure that they read the same as his own. They were all dead. Finally satisfied he looked up at Corporal Evans and for the first time his face softened. 'It's not your fault, mate.'

Corporal Evans said nothing.

'Strip their ammo and follow on up. Moralee, patch that gash up on your arm when you get a chance, and stop feeling sorry for yourself. Welcome to the real world.'

I remembered the wound on my arm. My armour had swollen tightly around it and administered a clotting agent that had already stopped the bleeding. My wristpad told me that the wound was superficial and didn't require medical treatment, and soon my armour would return to normal to allow me to dress the wound properly. I felt ashamed. 'Yes, Sergeant.'

Chase's cold, empty eyes stared up at me.

With nothing else to say, Sergeant James was gone, following up the boss and the rest of the platoon to the top end of the ditch, where a new battle was being fought.

Corporal Evans looked at me and Brown again.

'It's not over, get their ammo.'

Our section had taken advantage of a chance encounter and succeeded in destroying a Chinese section, but in doing so we had then been counter-attacked by a numerically superior force. Despite our aggressive defence, there was no reserve section to come to our aid and we had quickly succumbed. We had lost five of our brothers in arms, Chase, Berezynsky, Climo, Rawson, and our section second in command, Joe Mac. I had received a glancing blow from a stray round and was lucky to still have my arm.

We rummaged through the kit of our dead mates for ammunition, while balls of fire fell from the flickering red clouds to the surface of New Earth as the Union navy began a fresh bombardment.

13: The Counter Attack

Nothing wakes you up to the realities of life in space better than dragging the sorry remains of a fellow trooper unceremoniously through the red mud, a pool of blood sloshing about inside his respirator. Me and Brown slid Climo's body over the bank of the ditch and into the growing stream of water that flowed along it. We sifted through his kit for his magazines and grenades and I tried not to look at my friend's face, or what little was left of it. The dart that killed him had passed straight through his nose, and had taken flesh and bone with it. It was so gruesome I began to gag and I lifted my respirator just in time to vomit down my armour.

Brown stopped what he was doing. 'Don't breathe in. Get your respirator back on.'

I hated Brown. He was the absolute opposite of Climo, a bully and an arse-kisser. He had helped Woody to make my life on Challenger a complete misery. But he was right, and begrudging doing what he told me to I swallowed what bile was left in my mouth and replaced my respirator. I waited for the filters to do their job before finally breathing again.

'Poor bastard,' I finally said.

Brown packed Climo's mammoth ammunition into his daysack, slung it onto his back and offered the rest of what he found to me. 'Yeah,' he agreed grimly.

My eyes were wet, partly because the stench of my own vomit still clung to my nostrils, but mostly because I realised one of my best friends in the platoon had died. Climo was gone, and my friend Greggerson was severely

wounded, possibly dead too. Gilbert and Kane had never even made it to the ground, and Berezynsky had shared a similar fate with Climo. I felt as though every one of the few people that mattered to me had been taken, and all I had left was Brown, a man I despised. Why had he not died instead?

I took the ammo without a word and we moved up after Sergeant James who was a hundred metres along the ditch. Corporal Evans was gone, he had moved forward to make himself useful elsewhere. One section, one platoon was no more. We would now be used by Sergeant James as part of his work party, tasked with collecting casualties and prisoners as and when required, moving ammunition or re-enforcing sections if they lost too many men.

The platoon was static, having pushed forward a few hundred metres since our section had met its demise. Another couple of platoons had moved through us, taking the battle further up the hill and toward its summit. We were organised into a defensive position whilst we waited to be re-tasked elsewhere on the battlefield.

The Chinese had withdrawn back into the warren and trench system dug deep into the hill. Bombardment from high above and the ferocity of our offensive had driven them back into cover, but it was unlikely to be for long. The battlefield was strangely hushed, but distant explosions reminded us that the war was far from over. The Chinese would not give up their warrens without a fight, and we would have no choice but to dig them out. We all dreaded the thought of fighting underground.

Fighting in Warrens and Caves, or FIWAC as it was abbreviated, was known for being chaotic and violent to the extreme. Depending on the nature of the warren's construction, it was possible for engagements to be so close they often turned to hand-to-hand fighting. Warrens were a common feature of the modern battlefield, particularly when the enemy had the time to dig himself in and fortify. With the devastating effect an orbiting warship could have on ground forces the only option available to a defender was to dig himself underground, often to great depth. Even with today's technology no ship could detect anything underground, and the most sophisticated of weapons could only penetrate so deep. As for nukes, no side dared risk starting a nuclear war that could spill over back on Earth.

The Chinese were believed to have occupied and extended the existing Union warrens, stretching for kilometres in all directions. Tunnels were capable of moving vehicles and troops rapidly, with some even equipped with maglev trains. The thought of fighting in the pitch black, claustrophobic tunnels made me shudder.

'Think we'll go in?' Brown asked when we took a knee behind Sergeant James's two smart launchers, as if he had read my mind. Mitch spared us a worried glance and then went back to concentrating on his smart launcher's optics.

'Dunno,' I replied curtly. We waited in silence for something to happen, while the two smart launchers scanned the skies for enemy aircraft.

Ahead of us two section and the section sent to re-enforce the platoon concealed themselves amongst tangled greenhouse frames and burnt crops. I later learnt that the new section were the sole survivors of their platoon, the rest of them had never made the drop like our own ill-fated three section.

I shivered, my legs were soaked. The people who designed my gel armour had clearly decided against making it waterproof. At least my feet were almost dry, and the rain had stopped at last. The clouds still obscured the sky, though, and wind blew bitter and cold against my soaking wet body. The orbital barrage had stopped - presumably our ships had momentarily turned their attention onto something else. Above the blackened greenhouses smoke still rose from Jersey.

'I'm freezing,' I said.

'Me too,' Brown replied, and I think he might have been glad that I spoke, the silence was deafening. 'Where do you think Ev is?'

I gestured into the crops above the ditch. 'He's up with the boss, I think.'

We lapsed back into silence. What could we possibly talk about? Hiding behind a fallen comrade while a man stands alone to fight the enemy? Or perhaps about dragging our comrades' remains through the mud like pieces of garbage, one of whom Brown hated and I had come to call my best friend?

Guilt haunted the back of my mind - a guilt I fought to ignore. My mates had died, and I hadn't, quite likely due to my own cowardice. Brown's survival was very little, if any consolation, and if I'm honest I think I almost resented it.

The silence didn't last for much longer.

The two smart launchers bleeped furiously.

'Contact! Fast air!' Mitch cried in alarm.

I froze for a second, before realising what he was telling us. 'Fast air' was trooper speak for fast moving aircraft. Something not particularly friendly had broken through into our airspace and had been picked up by the launchers.

Me and Brown dove for cover, there was fat lot we could do against a fast moving aircraft.

The smart launchers were set up to launch in seconds. Sergeant James crouched low beside them, shouting orders.

'Quick boys, get em up! Get em up!'

'Firing!' The first smart missile launched.

'Firing!' The second followed close behind.

Smart missiles were an old weapon that had evolved over centuries. Each missile was equipped with a state of the art computer that allowed it to track its target, anticipating its moves and disregarding decoys. But an individual smart missile was ineffective against modern aircraft equipped with gravity drives; they didn't have the speed or manoeuvrability to keep up with them, especially if you consider that fighter aircraft were unmanned and had virtually no limit on the Gs they could achieve. Smart missiles were normally employed against ground targets, but they made an effective deterrent to aircraft, in fact they were the only air defence that dismounted infantry had.

More missiles fired from across the hill, leaving white vapour trails in their wake as they veered across the sky toward their target.

'Reload then, you lizards!' Sergeant James spat with clenched fists and the smart gunners frantically reloaded new missiles into their launchers. The weapon was deceptively light, but it was still cumbersome and took precious seconds for even the most experienced operator to reload.

It was then that a series of explosions a few hundred metres to our left announced the arrival of the enemy aircraft. In a blur of silver metal it moved impossibly fast, almost like a flying insect would dart forward and backward but much faster. It was indeed an unmanned aircraft, dubbed the 'saucer' for its shape. Saucers were built like upside down dishes to allow them to be aerodynamic in all directions, and were common in virtually all modern armies. They made lethal ground attack aircraft.

'Down!'

I hugged the ground as the saucer shot overhead, strafing the earth with its twin cannon.

'Shit the bed!' Brown cursed.

'Firing!' Another missile was up to join the wolf pack. The sky was becoming filled with missiles on the chase, leaving vapour trails that tangled through the sky like spaghetti. The air became thick with Vulcan cannon fire from the dropships and gravtanks across the valley.

'Two more saucers inbound!'

'Two section is in contact!' A shrill voice spoke across the platoon net, it was the platoon commander and he sounded worried. 'Contact enemy dropships!'

Enemy dropships were inbound, and with them would come crack Chinese dropship infantry.

'They're attacking!' Brown shouted from where we lay. No shit.

What we didn't at that time know was that high above us the Union fleet was being engaged by the Chinese. In a co-ordinated counter offensive, they were hitting us in orbit, then using the distraction to launch an offensive in the atmosphere and on land that couldn't be hindered by our ships. It was this level of co-ordination that made the Chinese an opponent that couldn't be underestimated.

From our position of cover in the ditch, I could see troopers amongst the greenhouses ahead of me firing at the enemy. Pink painted dropships were disgorging their cargo into the fray a few hundred metres beyond.

The battle that followed would be far more intense than that of our initial drop. The Chinese had been on the back foot, not knowing where to expect us to land. Now they would attempt to regain the initiative.

In our favour though were our experience and our cunning. Although nobody could doubt the Chinese technology or fighting spirit, they had many flaws that the Union knew to exploit.

Gravtanks, evolved from lessons learnt in combat against the Indo-Japanese Alliance on Eden, darted about the battlefield in and out of cover. Their low profile hulls enabled them to hide almost as low as the troops they supported, unlike the larger bulky designs of Chinese anti-gravity vehicles which were designed to fight like aircraft. Their Vulcan cannon sprayed the skies with a million tiny darts and their rail guns took on the enemy dropships.

Somewhere within our secured perimeter, newly established electronic warfare teams began to hack into the Chinese communications and robotic vehicles. The unseen electronic battlefield was a crucial aspect of modern warfare, robotic craft could be turned against their masters, communications could be blocked or changed and even computerized maps turned upside down. The technologically superior Indians and Japanese had not anticipated the strength in Union electronic warfare capability, a weakness that was to be their undoing on Eden, with the help of some old fashioned Union steel.

You could hack into comms and robot aircraft, though, but you still couldn't hack into soldiers, and there were a lot of Chinese soldiers out there. The hill became alive with gunfire.

'We're fighting for our lives now, boys!' Sergeant James bellowed to us over the noise. 'Brown, Moralee, join two section up front, you're no more use to me here, get going!'

We scrambled over the banks of the ditch as the platoon sergeant continued to control his two smart launchers. He would manage the platoon's air defence whilst we got on with the fight on the ground.

We zigzagged between the greenhouses, leaping over battered frames and crashing through smouldering crops. I hoped the smoke and flames would help make us unlikely targets to the enemy.

Behind us, there was a huge explosion that almost sent me off my feet, but I didn't turn to look. Clods of earth rained down at my feet and bounced off my helmet.

Two section were just in front of us in cover in another ditch. To their left and right other platoons had moved to help repel the attack. The Chinese were only fifty metres away, I reckoned there must have been more than a company's worth of them. Several Chinese dropships lay stricken on the ground, their ugly bodies scorched from impacts from rail gun shells.

Rounds whizzed overhead as we ran as deep into a crouch as our thigh muscles allowed. I took little comfort knowing I probably wasn't the target; there were so many enemy that the air was thick with their fire. An intense animal fear finally overrode my muscles and I dove for the ground.

'Brown, get down!'

We had covered a good thirty metres in our mad dash, but in retrospect we were right to have taken to ground. There were so many Chinese in front of us, and the fact that we hadn't been shot deliberately or by a stray round was nothing short of a miracle.

But not entirely a miracle, as we would later realise. The electronic battlefield was a weird and wonderful thing, and as it turned out we had another little trick up our sleeves. After our shameful defeat two years earlier, the Union had identified a fatal flaw in the Chinese integrated soldier technology. Their weapons communicated with their visor targeting system via a wireless link, unlike ours which instead incorporated a wire which connected our visors to our rifles. Our electronic warfare teams had found a way to jam the signal, and even feed it fake ones. In effect they were now either firing rounds wildly off target, or they would have to fire using the sights like a normal rifle. Rumour had it the Chinese were terrible shots without their visor targeting system.

We crawled toward two section with every ounce of strength our bodies could muster. You would be surprised how fast two men can crawl if their lives depend on it! I slid my body into the safety of the ditch. Several sections lined the far bank, firing rapidly into the enemy, the magnets of so many weapons screaming in a noise so loud I swear I could feel it vibrating through my body, even if my headset didn't allow me to hear it through my ears.

We clambered up onto the bank to join in the fight. As I did so I switched my intercom to two section's channel.

'My God!' I gasped as I stole my first proper glance at the enemy on the attack. There were loads of them, and they were advancing.

'We've gotta hold em, boys!' Corporal Weston shouted from off to my right. '4th Battalion are about to drop in, and they know it! We've gotta hold on to this rock!'

'Who are you?' a trooper to the left of me and Brown asked between shots.

'One section!' I answered.

'Well lads, welcome to the party …'

'Ray, shut up,' Corporal Weston cut in. 'Rapid fire, rapid fire! Chammy, get me more ammo up here!'

'I can't, mate!' Corporal Weston's section second in command replied on the intercom. 'Jamo's comms went dead, and everybody is pinned. What you got is what you got!'

'Shit!'

The enemy were closing fast, using smoke to cover those moving whilst others covered, in much the same way we would. Their weight of fire was heavy, but it was not enough to keep us from returning fire. Both sides were receiving massive casualties.

The Chinese knew that our battalion had secured a foothold on New Earth soil, but we were weakened by losses sustained in the drop and the battle that followed. If they broke us here, the 4th battalion would land with no support. If they didn't defeat us here, they were in trouble.

I fired into the advancing enemy, catching one Chinaman in the leg and sending him crumpling to the ground. Lumps of mud flicked at me as darts struck the soil to my front, and an unknown trooper next to Ray was flung from the bank without a sound. I didn't need to look, he was probably dead. Even if he wasn't, I had to leave him to the medics to deal with. Right at that moment every man was needed up and firing to repel the onslaught.

Rail gun rounds sent shockwaves through the air as they struck the enemy dropships. There were tens of them, all over the hill, unleashing their cargo and then speeding away as fast as they could, chased by missiles and tracer into the air. The Chinese were undeterred; they were coming for us now. The nearest enemy section was not more than twenty metres away. They were moving and they were exposed, but there were more of them than us.

I looked left and right at the other troopers firing on the bank. Some were shot but still fighting, the only people not fighting were either dead or severely and traumatically disabled. Medics dragged the injured down into cover to be treated, prioritising those they thought they could save, and leaving those they couldn't to die.

Nobody was going to hide now, because we all knew what would happen if we did. The only chance at living was up there on the bank of the ditch. I remembered a saying as I continued to fire into my foe: '*Look up and down in desperation, look left and right for inspiration*'. Nothing inspired a man to fight more than his own comrades. Corporal Evans, wherever he was now, had stood against everything that was thrown at him, almost surely to die, not for the Union, maybe not even for us, but because he was a trooper and that's what he did. It was my turn to do the same.

Voices screamed across the net.

'Incoming!'

'Take cover!'

Then the saucers strafed down our ditch.

Explosive rounds detonated on the ground, ripping apart bodies and tossing limbs and organs into the air like confetti. Nobody had a chance to move or take cover, it happened in an instant. Then the next saucer passed over. I clutched at the ground crying out in terror, my fingers clawing at the earth. If I could have burrowed into the ground with my own fingernails I would have done. Once again my whole body was gripped with an animal fear that paralysed me, and this time rightly so.

As suddenly as it had begun, the attack from above stopped. I looked up at the smoking devastation, still in shock. I was relatively unscathed, but what I saw filled me with horror. Bodies lay strewn, some together, others scattered in pieces. Organs littered the cratered earth, some mixed together so that you could tell which part belonged to which corpse. Injured troopers cried for help, clutching at severed limbs and bleeding wounds. One trooper was frantically removing his dead comrade's respirator to replace his own,

blood gushing from his head where shrapnel had hit him. Other shell shocked but unharmed troopers staggered, like me, through the smoke. It was like a terrible nightmare that I couldn't wake myself from. I fought my body's reflex to gag.

As I stared in dismay, my headphones registered the sound of darts passing over above the ditch, but otherwise there was a stunned silence. Then a single voice called across the intercom.

'Get up! The pinkies are coming!'

I looked around me for Brown, but smoke had reduced my visibility to ten or so metres.

'Brown,' I called quietly. I hated him, but for that moment I desperately wanted to find him, he was all I had left of my section and for some reason that made him terribly important to me. I staggered to where he should have been, but he was gone.

'Brown!' I called on the intercom. I wondered if he thought to change channel to that of our new section, and so I shouted his name again so that he might hear me without the intercom.

'Here they come!' the voice warned again. My battle shocked mind struggled to identify the voice, it sounded familiar to me but I couldn't put a finger on who it was.

Something dragged me back into reality. I looked up over the ditch into the smoke and my visor flicked to infra-red. They really were coming.

The Chinese were upon us, a brilliantly timed airstrike by several saucers had devastated our position, right in time for them to close for the kill. The company line was broken and soon the battalion would be in disarray. Its brief hold on New Earth soil would not be enough to secure a safe landing for 4th Battalion and the Union would potentially be unable to take Jersey.

'Death before dishonour, boys! Death before dishonour!' I recognised the voice. It was the company commander. The OC was speaking on the platoon nets, to all of us.

I had survived my section's last stand, but this time it was the entire company that stood at the brink of annihilation. A few tens of survivors with their rifles and bayonets were all that stood in the attacking enemy's way.

'For the Union!' somebody called.

I raised my MSG-20 and crouched low in the ditch, checking that my bayonet was still correctly fitted. It was stained red with blood.

My headphones amplified the sound of feet trampling close by in front of me as the enemy bore down upon us. Wherever Brown was now, he would have to wait. I set my rifle to automatic.

I crouched with the survivors of B Company as the shadow of the Chinaman came over the top of the ditch. He emerged from the swirling smoke, breathing heavily as his boots pounded in the mud.

He was ready to fight, his rifle raised to fire, but he was not ready for me to be crouched at his feet. He didn't even see me as I struck, thrusting my rifle up at his torso. The bayonet penetrated his gel armour and into his flesh with almost no resistance, blood squirting through the blood channels.

The Chinaman yelped in pain, but his inertia took him into me, sending us tumbling down into the wet mud at the bottom of the ditch as more of the enemy met the Union line.

My bayonet was still inside him, and with an animal strength I threw him over me. He was squealing, almost like a pig.

I was possessed with a rage that sent my body berserk. As the ditch erupted into battle, I stabbed at the man repeatedly until he was dead.

Those of us who hadn't died in the airstrike fought like demons as the Chinese charged through the smoke at the top of the ditch. We stabbed and we shot and we threw grenades over the bank in our desperate fight for survival.

I was knocked to the ground by the hulking frame of a charging Chinaman as I picked myself up from my victim.

He screamed a blood curdling battle cry as he raised his rifle to butt stroke me in the face. The giant Chinaman's visor concealed his face, and only reflected back my own look of terror. But he was never able to bring his rifle close to me, because Brown emerged as if from nowhere and smashed his mammoth butt onto the Chinaman's head with so much force his visor cracked.

The Chinaman fell on me without a sound, knocking the air out from my lungs. I struggled from beneath him but his weight had me trapped to the ground. God, he was heavy, I could hardly breathe!

'Get this stroker off me!' I gasped.

Brown fired a burst of darts into the melee, and then rolled the Chinaman away. If he wasn't dead, he certainly wasn't going to be getting up for a while, but I slung his weapon over the ditch just in case.

'I know they said some Chinese soldiers could be big - but he takes the piss!' I joked grimly, getting back to my feet.

Two gravtanks passed over our ditch. The air hummed as they soared past us, their mighty rail guns firing into the parting smoke.

The ditch was still ours, although at a terrible cost; the bodies of the dead and horrifically injured were plain for all to see.

'What's going on now, then?'

Brown regarded me for a moment, as if deciding whether or not I was worth a response, then he stole a glance over the top of the ditch. 'Looks like another company is attacking from the right, the pinkies are being smashed,' he said flatly.

Sure enough, with dropships and gravtanks in close support a company of troopers were sweeping through the remaining Chinese. The assault on their right flank must have halted their advance, and now with no sign of their saucers they were completely outgunned. As if to confirm the return of Union air superiority, two of our own robotic fighters streaked overhead.

A cheer passed up and down our ditch as we watched the Chinese attempting to withdraw. Brown glanced skywards, grinned and pointed. 'Here they come!'

I turned my head to the heavens to see a shower of flaming objects breaking through the clouds and plummeting toward the ground several kilometres up the valley behind us. Flecks of light sparked around the objects. Surrounded by sprays of Vulcan and escorted by an armada of robot fighters the 4th battalion was fighting its way through the sky toward the safety of the planet surface, the tiny sparks were the only indication of the distant battle. It would be less than five minutes before the fresh battalion would arrive to push through us and take the battle further up the hill and into the tunnels beneath it. We watched in awe at the spectacle.

'Oi, you two!' A welsh voice called from further up the ditch, bringing me back to the reality of the carnage around me. Corporal Weston tapped his helmet, the hand signal for 'Come here', and shouted 'Hurry up!'

We ran over to the section commander.

'Brown and Moralee, yes?' the stocky Welshman asked harshly. His visor display would have told him as much; but I didn't think it the right time to point that out. 'You're two section, now. Understand?'

'Yes, Corporal,' I answered automatically.

'Brown, get yourself and that gun back up on the bank and observe. Be aware there are friendlies moving to our front, now, so don't shoot unless you're one hundred percent happy what you're shooting at. Go.' Brown was gone and Westy turned his attention to me. 'Moralee, go find the 2ic and help him with the casualties.'

I gulped. In amongst the smoking, cratered ditch there were many casualties and they weren't pretty. The responsibility of having to deal with one and having his life potentially in my hands was almost as terrifying as facing the enemy himself. I became ever more aware of the screams and moans of the wounded.

'You want me to find Chammy?' I asked stupidly. I had been in the platoon long enough to know who the different 2ics were.

'Yeah, Chammy. He can't be far,' Corporal Weston replied distantly. He was busy scanning the ditch, trying to take stock of what manpower he had at his disposal and what to do with it. I could only count thirty able bodied men along the full length of the bank and fewer moving about amongst the dead and wounded at the bottom of the ditch. There had been at least two platoons of us there originally, sixty men in total.

'Where will I find him?' I asked.

'I don't know, do I?!' the section commander snapped. 'Look around you. It's a fucking ...' He trailed off, lost for words. *A fucking gruesome mess*, that's what it was.

'I'll find him, Corporal,' I promised, and I went.

I had searched for Chammy, but I never found him. His locator wasn't working, so I couldn't find him using my visor. Instead I made my way back toward where I hoped Brown and Westy would be.

A battle still thumped and rattled just over the brow of the hill whilst I walked as if in a dream amongst the dead and the wounded. A pair of medics worked frantically on a man who fought with them in the mud. He was trying to remove his respirator, making terrible rasping sounds with every laboured breath.

'Calm down, mate, you'll be alright,' one of the medics hushed, while the other tried to restrain the casualty. He had a sucking chest wound, a round had passed through his chest armour and through one of his lungs, causing air to enter the cavity and preventing what was left of his lungs from being able to inflate. The medics would have to treat the wound with a chest seal, and they would have to be fast.

'Come on, stay with us, you'll be fine,' the medic repeated. 'Come on, Peters!'

It was Peters, my friend from training. Horrified, I stooped over my friend to help him. 'Not you too, Peters!'

'Get away, mate,' one of the medics warned. 'We've got this, get back to your section. He'll be fine. Go. Go now.'

Backing away, I tripped over a dead man's leg and crashed into the mud. I looked up and realised to my dismay who it was that I had tripped over - it was Sergeant James. His clouded visor hid his face from view, but the markings on his helmet confirmed it.

'Christ!' I exclaimed, staring in disbelief at the body of such an important platoon figure.

A hand suddenly grasped me by the daysack and tugged me backwards and I yelped.

'Where have you been, you idiot?' I recognised the voice speaking to me. It was Sam.

'Looking for Chammy,' I replied quickly. 'Westy told me to.'

Sam released his grip on me and gestured toward a dropship that hovered nearby. 'Hurry up and get over there, we're out of here.'

I made to go, then hesitated. The cries of the wounded and the shouting of panicked medics cutting through me. A man wailed as a medic yanked on a tourniquet to stem the flow of blood out of his amputated leg. 'You found Chammy?'

Sam's face darkened. 'Yeah. We found him.'

The clouds were beginning to part as we prepared to load back into the dropships, revealing a brilliant turquoise sky. I stared bleakly at its beauty as we waited for our dropship to touch down. The sun beamed through the breaks in the cloud, casting long shafts of golden light through the clearing smoke. It was almost a biblical moment, as if God himself was reaching down to show us the beauty of the land upon which we were fighting. But beneath that near perfect sky, wrecked craft still burned across the blackened hill in amongst wilted crops and smashed greenhouses, and muddy troopers carried the dead and wounded away and searched the ruined bodies of their comrades for ammunition and salvageable supplies. Hill Bravo would one day be recognised as a battle honour for the battalion, where a battered company of drop troopers were beaten but did not know it, and instead fought on against a Chinese onslaught. But I remember that battle for what it really was - butchery.

Westy closed us together and counted us in - there were only six of us. I expected him to become irritated wondering where everyone was, but when he didn't I realised that we were all that was left.

'Is Greggerson okay?' I asked Sam, suddenly remembering my friend. He was the only friend I had left.

Sam nodded. 'He's one of the lucky ones,' he said sadly. Greggerson would be somewhere in the medical chain by then, probably in a hastily constructed field hospital somewhere within our landing zone. I took small comfort knowing that one of my friends was okay, and then grew jealous when I realised that for him the war was probably over.

'Somebody shoot me in the arm so I can get out of this hole,' Stevo said, thinking the same as me, but out loud.

'Shut up, Stevo,' Westy snapped, and Stevo looked to the ground.

'Westy,' a voice called. It was Corporal Evans who emerged from the ditch, his arms soaked with blood. 'Get your blokes loaded, mate, me and the boss will ride together.'

Westy nodded. 'Roger,' he said and waved our dropship down. It lowered itself until its ramp gently touched the ground, and we loaded ourselves into its tiny crew compartment, strapping ourselves back into our seats. I looked about me, at Brown and the other troopers in the section. Wide-eyed fear had been replaced by the troubled gaze of men who had seen and experienced the horrors of war. We were no longer the same inexperienced young drop troops who had loaded up on-board Challenger and her sister ships high up in New Earth orbit a few hours ago. We were already the survivors of one of the bloodiest battles fought during the New Earth landings, and we knew there would be more.

The dropship lifted and threw our bodies against the straps as it accelerated toward our next objective.

The remains of the battalion were moving to the recently seized peak of Hill Bravo, where we could look onto Jersey City as over watch, as well as providing protection while the 4th battalion began to clear deep into the Chinese warrens beneath us. We would be called upon again, there was no doubt of that, but the battle group needed time to re-group and re-organise itself whilst others took over the fight. The 4th battalion was fresh, and had suffered far fewer casualties on their drop than we had but the warrens were deep and everybody knew that fighting underground was brutal.

I wondered if the rest of the Union invaders had succeeded in their landings, after all Jersey Island was only a small land mass not much bigger than England itself. Across the planet the many armies of the Union would be fighting their own battles. We could only hope that they had been more successful than us, or the fight for New Earth would last for much longer than the couple of days we had originally expected.

'How many mags have you two got?' Sam asked me and Brown. 'I need an ammo state.'

I paused to think how many magazines I had used. I knew that I must have changed magazines during the battle, several times, but it had been such a blur that I could not remember. A magazine change is a drill, it's instinctive, plus I must have picked up tens of magazines off the dead. I checked my pouches and counted.

'Twelve mags,' I reported.

'Five hundred for the mammoth,' Brown added.

'What else you got?'

Sam nodded as we told him how many grenades we still carried, smoke, claymores and so on, making a note on his wristpad. It was smeared with blood, and Sam was clearly struggling to get to grips with using it, gingerly padding the screen with a gloved finger as the dropship threw us about. It would have been the wristpad of two section's 2ic, Chammy, with additional functions for commanders. Chammy had lost both his legs. The section senior trooper would then have to step up into his shoes, but in this case it happened to be Sam, and not Stevo. In theory a private was one dart away from becoming the section second in command, and only two away from becoming section commander. It wasn't uncommon on the battlefield for that to happen.

Sam looked to Westy. 'We've got seventy-one total, plus a grand for the mammoth. Seventeen forty mil grenades, twenty-one grenades and twenty-two smoke.'

'Okay,' Westy nodded. 'What about Jimmy's ammo? Did you grab that?'

'No,' Sam answered.

'Well, why not?'

Sam bristled, and his response was curt, 'Couldn't find any on him.'

'What do you mean "I couldn't find any on him"?'

Sam snapped, 'I said I couldn't find any, alright?'

Westy stopped his enquiry, and his voice softened. 'Alright, Sam. Alright.'

Jimmy was two section's second MAM-G gunner; he had been with them all the way up to the Chinese counter-attack. Sam later admitted to me that they had found Jimmy before we loaded onto the dropship, but that they didn't want to take his ammo. Nobody wanted to dig through the gory pulp that was once their good friend.

In our tiny crew compartment we sat in silence. Somebody in the far corner had begun to cry. The trooper's sorrow made me think of Climo, Peters and the friends that I had lost. It caused my eyes to become wet, so I shook the thought away.

Nobody ever did tell me the total of troopers we lost that day, and I never asked. I didn't want to know the grisly truth in figures, even though the sight of dead friends and comrades would haunt me forever after. The company had barely enough survivors to man two downsized platoons, which would mean cannibalizing its third platoon in the process. Jamo had died along with half of his platoon sergeant's party, killed by the Chinese saucer as me and Brown made our dash into battle. He didn't die straight away, apparently his last words to the medics trying to save his life were 'Go to hell,' though that may have just been a myth because I never met that medic to confirm it. Our platoon sergeant's death had left our platoon with so few men that we had ceased to be a platoon at all, and how its only section would be used I didn't know.

14: The Burrow

Gravel crunched beneath our boots as we debussed from the dropship back onto the surface of New Earth and the rocky peak of Hill Bravo, far above the farmland and the carnage. This time, out of contact, we ran outward of the craft, forming into a circle around it in order to give ourselves all around protection from any possible attacks.

As I took my position I was awed at the view from the top of the hill. Alpha Centauri Alpha was setting, casting long shadows across the farmland landscape below us, which was scorched black and littered with craters and wrecked vehicles. The valley, gouged deep into the rocky landscape by an ancient glacier, widened as it ran down toward the Emerald Sea where Jersey City smouldered. You could see why the Emerald Sea was so-called, in the clearing turquoise sky and setting sun it shimmered like it was made entirely of jewels. If I ignored the devastation wrought by man in the foreground, it was the most beautiful thing I had ever seen. Away from the valley to the north the surface of New Earth rolled away in hills and jagged mountains, brilliantly red in striking contrast to the turquoise sky. Distant wind turbines turned lazily in the fresh breeze that blew across the mercilessly rugged landscape, occupied by occasional buildings and farmland. On the horizon, explosions marked the on-going orbital bombardment, which I could only assume - and hope - was from Union ships.

I laid down on the red soil as we waited for the dropship to lift off. Despite the alien sun rapidly falling toward the horizon, it felt warm against the back of my legs, rapidly drying my wet body. My visor display read a temperature of seventeen centigrade, a high summer temperature for that part of the planet. As my body began to relax I became conscious of the water in my boots and the dried mud that caked my gloved hands. My arm was sore but hardly worth seeing a medic over, they had far more important things to deal with, I figured. My armour had returned to normal. The sleeve sagged around where the dart had penetrated despite the gel, exposing a deep gouge in my skin that had been sealed by a white substance, which was the clotting agent released from within the fabric of the armour. The rest of my combats were scratched and torn and speckled with blood, some my own, but mostly other people's. Friends and foe alike, mixed together in one colour of red almost identical to that of the soil of New Earth.

The dropship rose a metre above the ground, and then it was gone, throwing clouds of dust in the air as it shot over the edge of the hill and beyond. Like the rest of the company that perched on the high ground overlooking Jersey City, we were left to fend for ourselves once more. Even the gravtanks were elsewhere.

Smart launchers were again trained to the sky, silently searching for more of the dreaded Chinese saucers. After the devastation they had brought down upon us, I would never underestimate the Chinese unmanned craft. The thought of them strafing along that ditch, sending limbs and gore into the air like confetti still sent a chill down my spine. That anybody could have survived it, let alone me, was nothing short of a miracle.

'We're just waiting here while engineers dig in a position for us to occupy,' Westy announced on the intercom from where he knelt in the centre of our circular formation. 'Sam, get forward to the sergeant major with a few blokes to sort out ammo.'

'Yeah, roger, mate. I'll take just one, mate.'

There was a pause on the intercom. There were so few of us that if Sam took more than one trooper away there would only be half a section left. 'Yeah, take one.'

'Roger.'

I heard footsteps behind me, and a boot tapped my ankle. I turned to look at Sam who had crouched over me.

'Come with me, Moralee.'

We ran across the high ground between several other sections before locating the company sergeant major and his work party huddled around a pile of ammo crates left behind by his dropship. Corporal Evans was there in front of the CSM, both of them were kneeling, holding a quiet discussion. I couldn't tell what was being said as we approached, even with my headphones magnifying any non-background noises, but Corporal Evans was nodding a lot as he was being briefed. The sergeant major patted Corporal Evans on the shoulder gently, and then passed something to him. Corporal Evans cradled the object in his hand as the CSM stood, as if unsure of what to do with it.

As we arrived by the pile of ammo I caught the CSMs last grim words to Corporal Evans before he turned and walked away, 'Congratulations, Sergeant.'

I realised that the object in his hand was a set of Velcro sergeant stripes, that of a platoon sergeant who had met his end, no doubt. They were dirty, but with the colour of the New Earth mud it could easily have been blood. He must have felt our stare, because he turned and looked directly at us, at me. I averted my gaze, unable to hold eye contact with the man I felt I had disappointed beyond words. I knew he was wondering why me and Brown had survived and not Joe Mac, or Rawson or any other one of his better troopers. Me, a snivelling excuse for a crow and Brown, an arse-licking bully. *He must hate us both for it,* I told myself.

A nearby explosion broke the pause, causing us all to crouch and look. It was the engineers a few hundred metres away mounted on lightweight buggies, driving around 'explosive digging' a defensive position for us all to move into overlooking Jersey City and the valley on one side of the high ground and the vast expanse of rolling terrain out to the north.

Corporal Evans looked down at the stripes in his glove and then back to us. 'Close in, Sam.'

We moved over to our new platoon sergeant as he changed his Velcro rank badge on his upper arm.

'What's your ammo state?' he asked, tapping his wristpad. If he realised I was there he gave no sign of it.

'Seventy-one mags, half a grand of mammoth.'

Sergeant Evans tapped the screen as he entered the figures. 'Forty mil?'

'Erm …' Sam stared at his own wristpad and frowned as he deciphered the numbers. 'Seventeen.'

'You got both grenade launchers?'

'Yeah,' Sam patted the grenade launcher mounted beneath his rifle. Like Rawson and Chase, he had carried it as a mark of his growing seniority, although Sam was nowhere near as senior as they had been. 'Westy has taken the other.'

Sergeant Evans nodded. 'Good. Mammoth?'

'Only got the one. Got half a grand for it. The others in bits.' The owner of it was too.

'Grenades?'

'Twenty-one.'

'Smoke?'

'Twenty-two.'

Sergeant Evans looked down at the figures and seemed happy. 'Good. See the piles of ammo over there, ours is on the right,' he pointed and sure enough the ammunition had been divided by the CSM into platoon piles to be taken away.

'Roger, how much have I got?'

'Take two crates of darts, another grand for the mammoth and …' he paused as he checked his numbers. 'Thirteen more forty-mil. Puts you on thirty. Happy?'

'No dramas, Sergeant. Come on, Moralee.'

I was sure Sergeant Evans was watching me as I followed Sam over to the ammo pile, where two other work parties from the two new sections were already busy collecting their share. I wished that he would speak to me, just even to acknowledge me. I wanted to tell him I was sorry for the men we lost and tell him of the guilt I felt for still being alive.

'That's gotta be pump, mate,' one of the blokes commented to another, nodding his head in the direction of our new platoon sergeant. 'He gets his whole section smashed, then he gets to fill a dead man's boots.'

I said nothing. We collected our ammo and left.

———

We ended up sat an underground bunker or 'burrow' the Chinese had probably used as a shelter from overhead bombardment. It wasn't really a bunker, more a hole. A single long tunnel had been cut out of the rock, maybe twenty metres deep and angled so that we could crawl in and out and then a spherical cavern had then been made in which a section or two could take refuge. A second tunnel had lead from the cavern deeper into the hill, probably connecting with the Chinese warren. Engineers had 'plugged' it with explosives and placed vibration sensors to detect if the Chinese tried to tunnel back out. It was hard to imagine but there was a battle still raging beneath us that might spill to the surface at any moment. Sat in the middle of the cavern and angled up through the entrance was the smart launcher, assembled on its tripod ready to launch in the event of an attack from the air. Across the entrance we had placed thermal sheeting to conceal our thermal signature from above. If we fired the smart missile, it would take the sheet with it.

The sky had become dark, and barely any light entered the chamber. Our respirator visors automatically set themselves to a mixture of thermal imaging and light intensifier so that we could see inside the man-made cave as clearly as we could by day, not that there was an awful lot to look at anyway.

I huddled against the wall of the artificial cavern, close to Brown and the boys of my new section. Westy was away receiving orders, leaving the remaining five of us alone in the dark. We pressed our bodies against each other to share body heat, rather than freeze in the sub-zero night time temperatures. We couldn't heat our food, or produce any unnatural heat of any kind, lest we give off a heat signature that would identify us to Chinese warships, despite our thermal sheeting.

The Union navy were engaged in another great battle far above us, word had got round that several of our warships had been destroyed. The threat of the Chinese securing control of orbit over Jersey Island and turning their guns down upon us was very real, and terrifying.

Somewhere beneath us the 2nd and 4th dropship battalions were clearing through more of the Chinese warrens, while we waited in a ring of steel around the smouldering city. We weren't ready to take Jersey City yet, not without clearing out the warrens.

Filaments within my armour worked hard to keep me warm without letting heat escape. They were failing miserably. I had wrapped a bandage around the gouge in my arm, and a further one over the top of the armour to try to keep the cold air out for what little help that did.

'I'm freezing,' Brown whispered. We were all shivering.

'Yeah,' I replied woodenly.

'Must be what, minus ten?'

I glanced at my visor display. 'Three degrees above.'

Brown tutted irritably. 'How do you know that?'

'Says it on your visor display, you've just got to …'

'Yeah, yeah, I remember,' he interrupted sourly. 'Nobody likes a smart-arse.' I ignored the rebuke, knowing that Brown would be embarrassed for not knowing such a simple visor function.

'How long have you been in Drops?' Sam leant forward to look at Brown.

Brown sighed. 'Long enough.'

'Shouldn't you know how to use your respirator by now?' he mocked.

I realised that Sam hated Brown almost as much as I did for his connections with Woody, and relished the opportunity to attack Brown. 'That's not all of it,' I piped up without thinking, 'ask him if it smells good in his respirator!'

I couldn't make out Brown's face, but his voice conveyed menace. 'Be careful, Moralee.'

Ray sniggered. 'You puked in your respirator, didn't you?' He laughed at Brown's reluctant nod.

'Ray, you can't say nothing, you shat yourself!' Sam added.

'Nice one telling everyone, mate!' Ray said sarcastically.

I listened to Sam and Ray laugh and joke and share stories of each other's exploits in the bottom of the cave as the smart launcher sat in wait. Sometimes we would stop and reflect on things that had happened. It was how we coped, I guess.

I told the boys of two section about our near annihilation at the hands of the Chinese. I left out hiding and various other acts of cowardice. Not the best way to introduce yourself to a new section, I thought, and I think Brown probably agreed because he said nothing.

'Mate, that gravtank saved you, man!' Ray exclaimed. 'We couldn't get to you. Should have seen how many pinkies there was, they almost had all of us. They was all moving toward us through the greenhouses, had us pinned. Westy wanted to come get you, but the boss said no.'

'Did he?' I was shocked; the boss had stopped two section from attempting to rescue us.

'Mate, I'm telling you, they were coming for *us,* man! They were gonna kill all of us, if we left that position, we'd be over run in a minute.'

Sam mused, 'I don't know if he made the right choice, but I know I wouldn't want to have to make that decision.'

I remembered the boss's face as he looked at the bodies strewn across the ditch, and then at Corporal Evans - *'I couldn't … sorry'*.

'This is one messed up war,' Brown said.

We sat in silence for a few minutes, the only sound coming from the tiny motors in the launcher's optics and distant gunfire from another battle far away, echoing across the valley.

I thought about the battle being fought deep in the Chinese warrens and took small comfort in being far away from it, even though I knew that it wouldn't be long before we would be called forward again.

I then felt a pang of guilt return like a blade in my heart when I thought of Climo, dead in the mud of that ditch. If I had fought harder, fought better, then maybe he would have survived. How could I take more comfort in knowing that other troopers would again be dying instead of me?

'Do you think we're winning?' Ray was the first to finally break the silence.

'Westy said we're winning,' Sam said, as if that were enough, but a loud tut came from the other side of our huddle.

'Well he's probably not gonna tell you if we're losing is he,' Stevo said scornfully. I wasn't surprised at his defeatist attitude, Stevo had practically decided the Chinese had won before we even left Uralis. I hated Stevo as much as I hated Brown, he too was a bully who sided with Woody. But at least Brown wasn't afraid to do the dirty work himself. Stevo was a senior bod who liked to hide behind Woody for protection, but without him he wasn't nearly as intimidating.

'So, what you think we're losing?' Ray asked.

'If them pinkies get those ships above us, we're done. They smashed us off this crappy little rock once, what's to stop them doing it again?'

'Yeah, alright, Stevo, we get it,' Sam snapped.

'*If them pinkies get those ships above us, we're done!*' Ray mockingly exaggerated Stevo's words into a high pitch.

Everyone laughed as Ray got up and made an impression of a child having a tantrum, stamping his feet, 'I didn't sign up for this, I want to go home!' I was surprised that Ray had the nerve to mock a senior trooper, he had been pretty quiet on Challenger and I barely knew him. Now it was as if all of the fighting had caused him to come out of his shell.

'I never said that, Ray made it up!'

The joking wasn't harmless; it was an attack on Stevo. Everybody had hated him on Challenger, but Woody was gone and half the platoon was dead or injured and so his position as senior trooper in the platoon didn't count for anything. Just as Sam had said, I realised.

'I'll tell you what lads, we're battering these bastards,' Sam jumped in, ending Ray's display. 'They wanted a go at us, and now they're gonna be sent home, crying like Stevo here.'

'Screw you, Sam.'

'Likewise. We proved it today in the farmlands, lads. It don't matter how much funky kit you've got, in the end it all comes down to cold hard steel.' Sam patted the blade of his bayonet. 'They haven't got the fight in them like we have.'

I wasn't so sure of that, the Chinese looked like they had a lot of fight in them to me when they were closing in to kill the remainder of my section.

We sat in silence for another few minutes, listening to our respirators click and whir as they worked to scrub the air for us to breathe. They would also extract heat from our exhaled breath, in order to minimise heat loss, which not only lead to us getting colder, but made us easier to spot from above. A warship looking in the right place at the right time could spot even the slightest source of heat.

Westy slid down into the cave.

'Alright boys?' he asked his section, rubbing his hands together in mock enthusiasm.

'Alright Westy, we're fine,' Sam replied. 'Bit cold.'

Corporal Weston crouched close to us in the dark, looking to check his section were all okay, 'There's nothing I can do about that, boys,' he said softly in his thick Welsh accent. 'We're all cold, me as well. Soon as they get the all clear from orbit we can get some heat going and get some hot food down our faces.' We never would get the all clear.

'What's going on, then?' Sam asked what we all needed to know.

'The pinkies are putting up a good fight. There are at least a couple of battalions of them dug in across this area, hoping to go back onto the offensive if they regain top cover. Jersey Island is garrisoned with another two battalions, which we believe are also connected to the warren network. Combat in the warrens is going to continue through the night, and then into the best part of the day. There's a possibility that a company may get grabbed to form battlefield replacements, but it's just speculation right now.'

'Battlefield replacements?' Stevo snorted. 'Everybody's gonna be a battlefield replacement …'

Sam punched Stevo full in the gut, and I gasped in surprise. 'Shut up, you lizard!'

Stevo rolled onto the floor gasping for breath.

'Get that waste of oxygen sat back down,' Westy growled. Sam hauled Stevo roughly back up against the wall, holding him by the arm. He wheezed, trying to speak. Sam had knocked the air out of his lungs despite his body armour.

'I tell you what, Stevo,' Westy stooped up close to Stevo, as Sam tilted the trooper's head back by his helmet. Their visors touched. 'You need to get a grip of yourself. I am sick of your constant whining. Frankly, I'm sick of you and your weak attitude. You're not a senior trooper. I barely even class you as a human being. You gob off one more time, you cower in the face of the enemy, you do one more thing …' His silence said everything.

'I'm sorry Westy, I'm sorry,' Stevo squirmed in Sam's grip. Tension amongst us all was high, but I hadn't realised it had been that high.

'You're a waste of a respirator, Stevo and this is a war zone. It would be very unfortunate for you to lose it. But things happen out here, don't they Stevo.' Westy's words filled with menace. I wondered what Stevo had done to make Westy hate him so much, clearly the original lads from two section were hiding something. I remembered cowering at the bottom of the ditch when we first landed, then hiding behind my fallen comrades and the thought filled me with shame. Perhaps what Stevo had done was worse, but I doubted I would ever be told. I hoped Brown would never tell anyone about what we had done - or Sergeant Evans. Although my night vision couldn't show it, I could imagine Westy's face contorted into hateful rage.

'Please, Westy, please!' Stevo begged.

Westy stood up, and Sam released his grip. Stevo rocked where he sat and began to sob like a child.

'I just don't wanna die here, man! For God's sake!'

'Shut up and sit up!' Westy crouched back down amongst us to continue his brief. He paused for what felt like almost a minute while he collected himself. 'For the minute our orders remain the same. We are to stay put in this defensive position until ordered to move or until we're relieved. C company is tasked to maintain arcs to the north and east, B to the south and west, and we have the good deal with having to provide air defence. That's good news for us, gets us some chance to rest and just maintain a watch on the air. The companies will rotate their tasks every six hours, so make the most of it.

'Platoon sausage, if you didn't know, is now Ev, which I'm sure he's chuffed with.'

Westy was clearly being sarcastic, I somehow doubted that any section commander would want to jump up to platoon sergeant, dealing with casualties, ammunition resupply and the company hierarchy itself. Sergeant Evans' battlefield promotion wasn't particularly unexpected, he was the platoon senior corporal and so next in line to step up whether he wanted to or not.

'The company is a bit of a mix up at the moment,' Westy continued. 'At the minute we have most of three platoon attached to us, so we're back to three sections. Each section in the platoon will maintain an air watch with the smart launchers and stick to hard routine. That means no heating your horror bags, no external heat sources of any kind. Movement outside the burrows is to be kept to a minimum. The company are trying to get us some additional thermal blankets, but with little or no supply chain I don't see how we're gonna get them. Basically, all we need to do is keep the stag going, and just wait to see what happens next. I suggest you all get your thermal bags out and rest. Anybody got any burning questions?'

'What's going on up there, mate?' Sam thumbed up toward the sky.

Westy shrugged, 'I don't know much to be honest. Challenger has apparently been destroyed during the day, along with several other ships.'

'*Shit, man!*' Ray gasped in dismay, and my jaw dropped. Challenger had been my home for several months, and now it too was gone! It seemed like everything I had known was systematically being taken away from me, one bit at a time.

'Our ships managed to maintain control of orbit most of the day, as you probably saw. During the Chinese counter offensive we lost more ships. That's why the saucers and the pinkies managed to get all over us so easily. They're still trying to re-take orbit above us to regain the initiative. Apparently it's like this over most of the planet, the Chinese are in disarray and either extracted from the surface or dug into their warren network. If I were to guess, I would say they will skirmish with our ships in orbit, and where they can seize even temporary top cover they'll then attack using hit and run tactics on the ground.'

'When are we gonna take Jersey City?' Sam asked.

Westy shrugged, 'Dunno mate. We won't do anything until the warrens are clear, I reckon. We're probably hoping for the city to surrender, but I don't think the Chinese will let us have Jersey City that easy.'

'Cheese heads,' Ray cursed toward the tunnel entrance, as if the enemy could hear him.

Westy chuckled. 'Yeah, right, but there you go. That's about all I know, boys. All we need do now is just sit tight here, get a stag going and get some rest.'

'No worries,' Sam said. 'I've got a stag list ready.' He looked to Ray. 'You and Stevo are on first, mate. Wake me up in thirty minutes.'

Ray sighed morosely. He clearly didn't want to go on stag with Stevo. 'No worries, mate. Come on Stevo.'

The two troopers went and sat by the smart launcher while we took our thermal bags out from our daysacks. They were small, thin sleeping bags that would fit almost into your pocket, but they could be surprisingly warm. I slid myself into the bag, my boots left on just in case I was woken in a hurry. I propped my daysack behind my head as a pillow, its contents were not particularly soft and comfortable, but the padding that normally sat against my back was.

I closed my eyes and tried to sleep.

It wasn't easy sleeping with a respirator on. They weren't particularly restrictive, built of the lightest materials with motorised filters that enabled the wearer to breathe clean fresh air as if they were in a park somewhere on Earth. But it was still there on my face, and it felt un-natural.

I stared at the ceiling of the burrow, listening to the sound of rain pattering on the surface up above and rain water slowly trickling down the entrance.

Somebody to the right of me snored, who I couldn't tell. I toned down the amplification on my headphones to near zero, transforming them into a set of ear muffs. The silence was peaceful, but it didn't help me sleep. I always eventually slept with my respirator on, and I was used to people snoring, but something else kept me awake, and it wasn't the throbbing in my arm.

Like a movie on fast forward, my mind flicked through all the things that had happened since our landing.

I thought of Climo, and dragging his lifeless body into the bottom of the ditch like unwanted rubbish. I remembered the Chinaman I charged in our surprise attack and driving my bayonet into his body. I remembered Chase's cold empty eyes staring up into the heavens, and the carnage during our last stand against the seemingly unstoppable Chinese advance. I also remembered Peters battling for air while the two medics fought to save his life. I wondered if he was still alive.

I had already seen things that would haunt my mind until the day I died, however long that would be. Images were captured in my mind so clearly, that if I closed my eyes I could see them as if I was there.

I tossed and turned in my bag, desperately trying to sleep, until I eventually gave up and just continued to stare up at the ceiling of our miserable home.

A hand patted me hard on the helmet.

'Moralee, you're on stag.' It was Brown.

'Okay, mate,' I answered instinctively, forgetting my hatred for him. Brown seemed not to notice and was already sliding back into his thermal bag.

I dragged myself out of my own bag and quickly packed it back into my daysack. Normally in training on Uralis I would have struggled to wake myself for stag duty, much to the annoyance of my comrades, but I hadn't slept a wink anyway, so what was the difference?

'Could you sleep?' Brown asked as I closed my daysack and, surprised that he had chosen to speak to me, I stopped.

'Not really,' I replied.

'Me neither,' Brown rolled over, signalling that the conversation was over. I silently cursed his rudeness, and then switched my visor back to night vision and moved into the centre of the burrow where Sam squatted with the launcher.

'Alright, Moralee?' he whispered. The chamber was tiny, and he would have heard me and Brown talking about not sleeping.

'Yeah, mate,' I lied, and Sam nodded knowingly.

I placed my daysack down beside Sam and sat on it cross legged. We were both sat behind the launcher facing up the dark angled tunnel that lead out of our burrow. Its entrance was obscured by the thermal sheet.

The launcher sat idle, set to air defence mode, with arrays of sensors laid outside our burrow that gave it the ability to scan the skies above. If anything approached that it couldn't identify as friendly, the launcher would make its own decision and fire without us having to do anything but reload it. A single red light blinked to reassure us that it was switched on and actively scanning.

There was very little to look at, I quickly realised. Air sentries were only really present to make sure the launcher didn't do anything mental, and protect the burrow in case somehow the enemy managed to infiltrate and sneak in.

'How's your arm?' Sam said finally.

It was sore as hell. 'Not too bad,' I said, and Sam nodded.

'Cold, ain't it?'

I hadn't really been thinking about it. The temperature had dropped significantly whilst I was in my bag and my visor now read minus two degrees.

'Yeah, gibbering.'

Sam rubbed his gloves together vigorously. 'I could do with a few more hours in my bag, I tell you.'

'Did you sleep alright?' I asked.

Sam laughed. 'Like a log, mate, I was chinned!'

'I didn't sleep at all, I don't think,' I said grimly.

'Yeah? Don't think Brown slept all that well either. Must just be the cold.'

I nodded as we both stared up the dark tunnel. 'Yeah, must be.'

Sam looked over at me, his head cocked inquisitively. 'Are you scared?'

I looked back. 'Aren't you?'

Sam shrugged, 'Yeah. Not as scared as I was when we dropped, though.'

I thought about it. 'I think I'm about the same, really.'

'Hmm.' Sam seemed to mull it over.

We said nothing for a few minutes. I watched the seconds ticking away on my visor display agonisingly slowly, as if time had slowed down just for my stag. Scientists had been trying to mess about with dimensions and stuff to fiddle with time for centuries without success, but we troopers had discovered the secret eons ago. Stare at your clock on stag to slow time down, get in your thermal bag to speed it up. I tried to ignore my visor clock thinking that it might help.

'What did Stevo do to annoy you all so much?' I blurted, instantly regretting asking the question. What was I thinking? It was obviously a touchy subject in the section, and Stevo was far too senior for a crow like me to speak ill of him.

Sam grunted. 'I don't really want to talk about it mate, to be honest.'

'Oh,' I said. 'Fair one.'

'Everyone's afraid here, mate,' Sam was looking at me. I wasn't sure if he was following on from my question, or from when he asked me if I was scared. 'There's nothing wrong with being afraid. It's what you do when you're afraid that counts, know what I mean?'

For a second I thought that maybe Sam had been told by Sergeant Evans about me and Brown. I felt his eyes boring into my skull through our visors.

I nodded. 'Yeah, I know what you mean, mate.'

'You've got to realise that we are all in this shit together, and we ...' he went on, pointing at me, himself, and then the others where they slept. 'All of us are in this together. Who do you think we're fighting for?'

'Er ... The Union? The people of New Earth?'

Sam laughed bitterly. 'New Earth? These people don't care about Europe, mate, or the Chinese, or any of us. And does the Union give a damn about you? Of course they don't. The Union is ruled by a bunch of rich corporate bastards who couldn't care less if you lived or died. Want to know who I'm fighting for?'

I said nothing.

His arm swept widely. 'I'm fighting for these guys. My mates. You. Because out here in this shit hole we are just about all we have. I would die for these lot, because they're family.'

'Did Stevo hide?'

'Yeah, but it's worse than that.' The tone in Sam's voice suggested that was all I would get from him.

I couldn't think of anything worse than me and Brown taking cover behind two comrades in battle, I was disgusted by myself. We could only hope that nobody in our new section would find out, lest we both wound up at the other end of their hatred like Stevo. I wished that there was some way that I could redeem myself, fighting during the Chinese counter-offensive just wasn't enough. Maybe nothing would be.

'Were you on Eden?' I asked, trying to change the subject slightly.

Sam snorted and placed his hand over his heart with mock hurt. 'God, how old do I look, mate?'

I decided not to say that he did look easily old enough to deploy to Eden. He looked about thirty. 'So you weren't then?'

'No, you stroker. Half the senior blokes hadn't been, let alone me. I'm twenty-two, but I must have had a hard paper round then, eh?'

'Sorry,' I smiled.

'Yeah, well ... No I wasn't. Westy was. So was Jimmy ...' he trailed off, the memory of his mate's death was still raw.

I thought of my mate Climo lying dead in the mud, and my other friends being cut to ribbons in withering Chinese fire.

'He was a good mate of yours?' I asked.

Sam didn't say anything for a few seconds, then nodded slowly. 'Yeah. Davo was too.'

'Climo was a good friend of mine.'

'Really?' Sam said sarcastically and laughed. 'You two were thick as thieves. The bloke should have been banged up for what he did, even if it was Woody he did it to. You too.'

I didn't know what to say, but Sam simply patted my back. 'I'm sorry about Climo.'

'That's okay. I'm sorry about Jimmy.'

We sat in silence again for a minute. I realised that I hadn't thought about Woody since we had dropped, and found myself wondering whether he had survived, and whether he was still out for my blood. My visor would have identified him to me had I come across him, but then the battle and its aftermath had been so hectic that I probably wouldn't have noticed if I walked right past him.

'A lot of people died today,' Sam sighed, and then paused thoughtfully. 'But there will be more.'

I knew he was right, but I felt no wave of fear like I did when we dropped down from Challenger. Instead the fear had become constant and over time I could feel my body numbing to it, and my mind accepting it as the norm.

'Yeah,' I replied.

Sam stood up, slinging his daysack over his shoulder. 'I'm gonna wake Ray, mate.'

I checked my clock; a whole half hour had passed. 'Okay.'

―――――

The remainder of my stag was uneventful, spent listening to Ray's endless jokes. He was a nice bloke from what I could make of him, but if I hadn't been wearing all the protective equipment around my head I reckon he would have actually chewed my ear off. That bloke could talk forever.

I woke Stevo before getting back into my thermal bag. He was sound asleep, and awoke with a start when I nudged him with my boot. His eyes were wide open, and his hand moved toward his rifle instinctively.

'Alright, mate, it's only me.' I gently placed my foot on top of the weapon where it lay beside him so that he couldn't do anything stupid. I had heard stories of half-asleep troopers stabbing and shooting each other in the dark, which wasn't a way I wanted to go.

Stevo tugged lamely at his weapon, until realisation dawned upon his face and his muscles relaxed.

'You scared the crap out of me,' he whispered angrily.

I stood upright, returning my daysack to where it had sat against the wall of the burrow as my pillow. 'Sorry. You're on stag.'

'Again?' Stevo groaned, sitting upright in his bag. 'I've just come off ten minutes ago.'

Quite clearly Stevo's display clock would tell him otherwise, but I wasn't interested. He might be a senior trooper, but it was his turn on stag.

'Ray's already over there, mate. You up, yeah?'

For a long five seconds Stevo sat still, as if his mind had not fully awoken yet and was struggling to compute what was going on around him. Some people could be a pain to wake up because they were deep sleepers, but he was just plain being difficult, I could tell.

'Are you up?' I repeated irritably.

'Yeah. I'm up.'

I began to unpack my thermal bag again as Stevo re-packed his own. You kept everything you weren't using packed away in your daysack, lest you came under attack and had to leave it behind. I couldn't imagine losing my thermal bag. It was as important to me as my helmet or respirator, as it should be to any half decent trooper.

As I slid my body back into the warmth of my bag I watched Stevo take his seat beside Ray once more. The two sat by the launcher for at least ten minutes in absolute silence. Watching them, thankfully, I fell asleep.

―――――

Only bad things happen when you fall asleep in a remote burrow in a war zone billions of miles from home. Any dream, good or bad might as well be a nightmare. Bad dreams mixed alien monsters and demons with experiences I had endured during the landings, with horrific scenes of mutilation and a never ending sense of horror and foreboding. Several times over a two-hour period I woke with a start, convinced something terrible had happened before realising that it already had.

Or you can have no dreams at all - now that is shit. Troopers will sometimes refer to the thermal bag as the 'red time machine'. You're tired enough and jump into your thermal bag, you close your eyes just for a second and *bam*! You wake up to the joyous words of 'You're on stag, mate', or 'Prepare to move', or something equally morale sapping as if you never even got in the bag in the first place.

But the worst dream of all for me was a nice dream. Dreams of pretty girls I had met during my life, dreams of passionate reunions and romantic encounters that came with a sense of sadness that hung like a cloud over the horizon. I could try to ignore that cloud, but it would always be there, slowly closing in around me.

Then I would get woken up, and the reality of where I was and the fact that I was just having a nice dream would dawn on me with an impact more devastating than a shell dropped from orbit.

After two hours I was awoken from one of those dreams. Whilst chatting up a naval lieutenant I had always fancied on Challenger, I could swear that Brown actually entered my dream and shook my shoulder, 'Moralee, we need to get up.'

'Give it a rest!' I complained, but the girl faded and I opened my eyes. With my visor de-activated I could just make out his outline in the darkness.

'Get up, you wand, we're moving in an hour. Westy's gone to get a brief off the OC.'

My mind began to wake up and I was back in the burrow. Instead of the girl's sweet sounding voice there was only the ruffling sound of all the blokes packing away their thermal bags, and her sweet perfumed smell was replaced by the clean, bland air produced by my respirator filters. I groaned.

'Come on, mate, get up,' Sam said, and his voice carried with it a sense of urgency. I activated my night vision, slid out of my bag and began to pack it away ready to go.

'What's going on, Brown?'

'We're going into the warrens. Just our platoon. Casualty replacements.'

Now that was a wake-up call if ever I had one.

15: Descent into the Warrens

The sun rose slowly over the horizon as we patrolled down the northern slope of hill Bravo toward the grid we had been given for the entrance to the warrens. Small strips of cloud broke up the sky, glowing deep red and orange as the low angled sunlight struck them and began to turn the dark blue sky back into a brilliant turquoise. The air was a cool five degrees and slowly rising, feeling crisp against the exposed parts of my neck. On Earth it would have been a beautiful spring morning, with birds singing and people rising for another day at work. But on Hill Bravo the silence was only broken by the crunching of the gravel and sand beneath our boots.

We stuck to the ditches as much as possible in order to keep out of line of sight from any unfriendly observers. As long as the enemy held on to the tunnel systems beneath the hill it was still possible for him to find a way back to the surface without us knowing. Behind us the summit upon which the battalion maintained over watch dominated the horizon. I felt myself wishing I was back with them. Perhaps Woody was there somewhere, waiting for his moment to strike, but I felt safer on that hill with Woody than down in the depths of the warrens.

Occasional aircraft passing overhead and the wind turbines that towered in the distance were the only sign of life on the barren, rocky world other than us. The three platoon sections were widely spread, we daren't take the risk of bunching together, lest a saucer break through into our airspace, or worse the Chinese attack from orbit.

Sometime overnight, Westy had told us on our brief, enemy warships had made another raid on the Union blockade over the northern hemisphere, succeeding in taking control of top cover over much of the northern continent for almost half an hour. Half an hour may not sound much, but it was enough to lay waste to entire battalions and see divisions run in retreat. We had been lucky; much of Jersey Island was just outside of their optimum bombardment trajectory. It could have just as easily been us had the Chinese warships entered orbit elsewhere. Fortunately the Union had regained orbital top cover, and its ships guarded us like unseen angels that watched us from the sky.

I could have taken some small comfort knowing that there were ships high above us watching us and our surrounding area for the enemy, but the reality was that New Earth was a big place, and a ship would probably not notice an enemy platoon dug in and well hidden amongst the hills.

Our section patrolled slowly and deliberately, scanning around ourselves for any approaching menace, in a single line of men spaced at least ten metres apart from each other. If one bloke set off a mine or took a burst of enemy fire, at least we all wouldn't get some. Such thinking might shock somebody who had never served within the infantry, but to us it was simply good patrol discipline. A dead man is useless, and if half the section was to die in a single burst of fire because they were bunched together, that would be the section rendered combat ineffective in the blink of an eye. When I was in training I maintained patrol discipline because I was told to, but on New Earth I finally understood it. There if I got the simplest thing wrong, it could cost me my life.

My visor marked the locations of the other two sections and platoon headquarters through the wilted crops and scorched greenhouses, and occasionally I would catch a glimpse of them. The platoon was very different to what it had been when it dropped to the surface, two of its sections were formed of troopers from elsewhere in the company, none of whom I really knew. The boss was patrolling just behind our newly formed One section who were somewhere ahead of us, along with his signaller. Our new platoon sergeant, Sergeant Evans, was off to our rear with his work party, which consisted of Mitch and one other, since Harmes had died along with Jamo. Sergeant Evans hadn't spoken much since his promotion, except to hurry us out of our burrows that morning and assemble us ready to move. Once we were good to go the boss had asked him if he was happy for us to move off, but he had to repeat himself when the platoon sergeant didn't respond. 'Let's go, then', he had said icily.

Westy navigated the section using a map on his wristpad, weaving us in and out of the maze of ditches and greenhouses as if he knew the area like the back of his hand. Occasionally we would stop whilst he checked what he was doing against a paper map he kept in his pocket, just in case the wristpad let him down or became compromised by an electronic attack by the Chinese. We would sit and wait, straining our ears for the sound of a stalking section of pinkies that never came.

The ditches still flowed with small streams of muddy water, making its way down from the high ground where rain had collected the day before. I looked into the deep red flowing water, and I remember thinking that it was like a river of blood.

During our patrol we passed a battlefield where one of our companies must have fought as we had done the day before. The ground was scarred with blackened craters, some small, others almost a hundred metres across. Gravtanks with ruptured hulls still smouldered amongst chunks of earth, and great boulders that had been thrown into the air by artillery and orbital bombardment.

As we approached the base of the hill we walked along a re-entrant with sheer rocky slopes that towered high above us. At its base a tiny river flowed, having cut its way down through the rock over millions of years. We weren't the first humans ever to walk down that narrow re-entrant, though. Several Chinese soldiers, corpses now, lay around a crater a few metres across. They all lay facing away from the crater, most likely killed by the blast of a smart missile or something similar.

Westy stooped over one of the soldiers, and we all forgot ourselves and gathered around him. The soldier's black visor made him appear as menacing as the man who had tried to kill me, even though he was clearly dead.

'Scary looking ain't they,' Sam said, 'considering they're wearing pink.'

'Might as well see what the bastards look like,' Westy said and he pulled the soldier's respirator away from his face. We gasped.

'I told you, they're Cyborgs,' Stevo stepped back from the monstrosity before us. It was clearly a human, but with black devices covering its mouth, nose, eyes and ears.

'Shit, man,' Ray exclaimed. 'Look at him!'

Undeterred, Westy grabbed the device that covered the soldier's mouth and pulled it away. It detached from the soldier's skin as if it had been stuck on with glue. Westy pulled more of the devices away and we looked down at what was finally revealed.

'He's just a boy,' I said. He wasn't a Cyborg at all, and he couldn't have been any older than nineteen, like most of us.

'I didn't think they'd look like that,' Ray said.

'Well what did you expect them to look like?' Sam asked.

Ray shrugged. 'I just didn't think they'd look like us.'

'They're not aliens, mate.'

'So what are all these things that were stuck to him?' Brown picked up the device that had covered the Chinese soldier's eyes and turned it over in his hands.

'Who knows,' Westy said, and he patrolled off again. One by one we followed on, and Brown threw the device over his shoulder.

I spared a final glance at the face of our enemy.

'Not so tough looking now, is he?' Sam said.

'He looks peaceful,' I replied, not looking away from the boy's face. 'It's almost like he's asleep.'

Sam nodded. 'Come on then, you'd better get going.'

I followed on after Brown.

'We're approaching friendly forces,' Westy announced over the section intercom after a few minutes. 'Don't shoot anyone unless he wears pink.'

Sure enough, above us I noticed a Union helmet pop up along the skyline. The trooper gave a thumbs up, which was returned in kind by Westy and then the helmet was gone again.

Our patrol took us along the re-entrant until Westy turned a right and we climbed up a steep slope. As I crested the top of the slope I could see the extent of 4th battalion's defensive position around the warren entrance. Amongst the farmland at the base of hill Bravo I caught glimpses of communication antennae, vehicles and troops arranged into a formation kilometres across with a flying Union flag at its centre. The dark blue flag and its golden stars were instantly recognisable against the red New Earth landscape as it flapped in the wind.

I spotted the entrance to the warren a few hundred metres away. It was a large hole cut into the side of the hill surrounded by rubble from where the Chinese had blown it up to slow us down. Excavation equipment sat idle close by while engineers scurried about performing unknown tasks.

I gulped as we approached the warren entrance. Down inside that dark gaping tunnel the battle for Jersey Island still raged beneath tonnes of earth and rock. A little voice at the back of my head screamed for me to do something to prevent my descent, shoot my foot, bluff a leg injury or try running away … but still my legs moved, ignoring that little voice with every step.

The opening to the warren was as foreboding as the entrance to the lair of some alien beast. A perfectly round tunnel some ten metres in diameter had been bored into the ground with great precision, running at an angle downward for a few hundred metres before turning off to the right. I peered into the tunnel whilst the rest of the platoon patrolled in and crowded round to receive our brief by guides sent up by 4th Battalion to lead the platoon below ground. It was bare, with ribbed walls created by the machine that had cut it out of the rock. A series of red fluorescent bulbs ran along its ceiling, bathing the tunnel in a red glow similar to that of a dropship crew compartment which served only to enhance its menace.

The guides were coated in red dust from head to toe, and their visors were smeared and scratched from where they had been constantly wiping it away in order to see. There were three of them, with a lance corporal in charge. Their eyes were sunken and weary from hours of fighting in the dark below and occasionally when they met the gaze of me and the other lads they would glare back with hatred. Regardless of what we had been through, we

hadn't experienced what they had, and they hated us for it. We were just replacements to them, filling dead men's shoes.

'The main tunnels are like this one,' the lead guide explained to the boss in a thick northern accent, 'They're just large enough for vehicles, but there's smaller tunnels down there big enough for two blokes to walk side by side. Most of the lighting is out too. Night vision all the way.'

'What's it like down there?' the boss asked, meaning what was the fighting like. We listened anxiously - most of us had never experienced combat underground. Sergeant Evans flicked mud from his boots with his bayonet.

The guide regarded the boss for several seconds, as if deciding whether or not he was worth sharing his experiences with, 'Boss, I ain't gonna lie to you, it's pretty bad, like. Everything is booby trapped, the pinkies hear a peep and they blow out the tunnels. You's'll get more info off the OC.'

Sergeant Evans didn't seem bothered by the guide's warning, or at least if he was he hid it well. Instead he thumbed nonchalantly toward the entrance. 'Shall we get on with it, then?'

'Yeah.' The guide signalled toward his comrades to prepare to move. He then looked at each of us in turn as he gave us the score. 'Fellas, when you's follow me, make sure you keep a ten to fifteen metre space between you's all. Don't bunch up, coz if we get bumped and we're bunched up like sardines everybody gets a bit. Keep checking behind for your mate coz if one of you's takes a wrong turn it's easy to get lost. We've marked the route down anyway, so you shouldn't get lost. If you do, just stop and wait where you are, we'll come back for you's. Lastly fellas, keep the noise down and de-activate all electronic equipment you ain't using, the pinkies pick you up through the walls and then we're mince. Good to go?'

The boss nodded. 'Let's do it.'

One by one, with two guides at the front of the platoon and one at the rear we patrolled down into the gaping mouth of the warren, and as I walked down into the abyss I remember wondering if I would ever see daylight again.

A few metres into the tunnel sat two metal signs, left by one of our engineers.

The first read: 'Welcome to the Hill Bravo Warrens, courtesy of 4th Battalion the English Dropship Regiment'.

I read the second, and shivered as I read: 'As I walk into the valley of the shadow of death, I will fear no evil. For God is with me'.

'This is mental,' I whispered to myself.

We deactivated virtually all of our equipment. Rifles were powered down, so that the magnetic fields they generated could not be detected. The section intercom would be kept on standby, and would not be used except in emergencies. Chinese engineers, like ours, would be constantly scanning for their enemy in neighbouring tunnels. Even though I could be sure that the entrance tunnel had been secured, it felt as though the very walls around me were now the enemy, and in some ways they were.

As I patrolled down a good ten metres behind the man in front, who was Brown, I turned one last time to look at the light of the surface. Behind me Sam walked, his face hidden behind his visor. He nodded at me in the dim light, and gave me a thumbs-up. I turned the bend in the descending tunnel, and that was the last time I saw daylight.

A walkway began a few metres beyond the bend, it felt slightly padded beneath my feet as I walked on it, almost like a gym matt. I knew from FIWAC lessons in training that it was a specially designed material laid by either our engineers or the Chinese before us to dampen the vibrations created by troops running or walking in the tunnels. The slightest vibration could easily be detected from hundreds of metres away by a keen listener with a few gadgets to hand, and the information could be used by the enemy to decipher troop movements.

My respirator visor automatically switched to night vision as the light became too poor to distinguish my surroundings. Instead of the dim red glow of the tunnel lights, everything became a light green instead. Lights danced about the tunnel from the section's rifle mounted infra-red torches, invisible to the naked eye. I activated the torch on my rifle, scanning my surroundings as I walked. The lights cast shadows across the tunnel, creating dark figures against the walls which would jump from one side to another and circle around us, like ghouls mocking us as we walked down toward hell itself. The ribbing on the tunnel walls was further exaggerated so that it took the appearance of the throat of some horrible creature.

Ahead, the platoon halted. I took a knee on the walkway, and with my left hand signalled back to Sam with a downward gesture to do likewise. We sat in silence in the tunnel, alone to our thoughts.

Brown looked back at me and tapped his helmet, which was a patrol signal that meant 'Close in.'

I looked back at Sam, repeating the hand signal, and then closed up toward Westy and the rest of the platoon.

We bunched together as a platoon in a long line, our weapons in the aim and scanning the dark in all directions. Nothing was inconceivable in underground warfare; it was entirely possible for the Chinese to somehow find a way to attack from behind. We had to assume the enemy was capable of anything, and then just hope that he wasn't.

The rear guide was the last man to join our formation. The message was quietly passed up the line to announce his safe arrival, then Sergeant Evans quickly counted that the platoon was complete and nobody was missing. It wasn't unheard of for troopers to end up walking kilometres into tunnels on their own before realising they had lost their platoon, particularly if they weren't paying attention.

'That's everyone in,' the platoon sergeant whispered to the boss at the front of the line.

The boss acknowledged, 'Roger.'

'The tunnel zigzags for another five hundred metres,' the guide briefed the boss, pointing with an outstretched arm into the darkness. 'Then there's a separate tunnel leading off into a defence complex. Battalion headquarters is located there.'

The boss nodded. 'Okay.'

The guide continued, 'I'll take you's in as far as battalion, then you should get taken on from there to the relevant company.'

'Roger.'

The boss and all of the NCOs consulted their maps on their wristpads as we sat observing the dark tunnel, making sure that they understood the layout of the warren. I listened intently for sounds of the enemy, my headphones would amplify any sounds so that I would have heard a whisper hundreds of metres away, but I heard nothing. The tunnel was as silent as a tomb. Despite the relative inactivity, my heart was pumping like crazy, pounding against my rib cage.

That wasn't my first time underground. On Uralis the FIWAC training phase had been almost a month long, preparing us for a tactic that had become increasingly common in modern interstellar warfare. The warren complex we used to train on Uralis was almost identical, if perhaps a little smaller. Entire divisions could be hidden in the complex networks of tunnels that ran for kilometres in all directions. Normally the tunnel we were in would have been a major access tunnel, probably used very recently when the Chinese retreated underground and blew the entrance.

'Just like Uralis, but twenty times as spooky.' Sam sounded foreboding as he whispered close to my ear.

'I don't like it down here one bit,' Brown said.

One of the guides snorted, 'You ain't seen nothing yet.'

My blood boiled. I thought to mention our battle on the surface and all of the friends and comrades we had lost, but bit my tongue. Arguing wasn't going to achieve anything, except maybe earn me a punch from either Sam or Westy. Besides, how was I to rate what it was like down there? We hadn't done anything yet, and I was already scared.

'Prepare to move,' the boss whispered.

We carried out the drill without thinking; safety catch, pouch.

The boss patted the guide to tell him we were ready and then one by one we moved off again into the darkness.

We continued down the tunnel for a few hundred metres, which snaked to the left and right several times at sharp angles. This was in order to confuse any munitions sent into the tunnel, which was large enough to fit aircraft, let alone smart missiles and smaller drones. Occasionally I noticed damaged machinery and small craters that identified where the tunnel's defences and booby traps would have been destroyed by our engineers.

A smaller tunnel opened up to our right, marked by red light sticks which had been crudely hung around it on nails. One by one the men in front of me disappeared into the tunnel, briefly turning to check that they were visible to the man behind so that he didn't keep walking into the dark.

Brown turned to face me before he disappeared into the smaller tunnel, giving me an 'okay' sign with his forefinger and thumb. In trooper speak this didn't actually mean 'okay', it meant 'this is pump'. I chuckled quietly to myself, which didn't make any sense to me because I disliked Brown and I was in one of the most terrifying places in the universe. Perhaps it was the simple way we drop troopers would describe such a complex and terrible situation that made me chuckle. After all, it was pretty 'pump'.

The smaller tunnel was no more than two metres across, again perfectly cylindrical and with a similar ribbed surface. The walkway was somehow raised so that the ground was flat and there was no lighting except that from our rifle torches. Without using our visors, we would be walking in absolute pitch black.

My pulse raced as my mind cooked up visions of nightmarish aliens and monsters that lurked in the tiny man-sized tunnel. Brown and Sam seemed so far away from me and I felt isolated and vulnerable. I gripped my rifle tightly, my finger hovering over the power up button; the weight of the weapon feeling reassuring in my hands.

There are far worse things lurking in these tunnels than aliens and monsters, I told myself. If a monster grabbed me at least I could fight it. If the Chinese in some tunnel nearby picked up our vibrations they could detonate bombs that would pulverize us into the rock, just by pressing a button. Even though the walls of the tunnel were no more than a metre from me in any direction, I felt more exposed than if I patrolled across an open desert.

We came to junctions and turns, all of which were marked by light sticks artfully arranged into arrows that pointed us in the right direction. The tunnels had become a maze; we were in some form of defensive complex, a collection of tunnels designed to be near impossible to clear without severe casualties, many of which would be connected with trenches and bunker positions on the hill surface. Often tunnels would open into large caves strewn with boulders and debris where bombs had been blown, either by the Chinese or the Union. The trail of light sticks led us through the caves so that we didn't trip and fall on the rubble.

We began to pass troopers of the 4th Battalion, many of whom rested in the caves, some in thermal bags, others huddled in groups around torchlight like the homeless might huddle around a fire on Earth. Engineers worked along the walls installing listening devices, laying walking mats or working with other fancy bits of equipment I couldn't recognise.

We were regarded with indifference by many of the troopers we passed; they were far more interested in whatever it was they were doing, which generally appeared to be recovering from their battle to secure the complex.

Eventually we arrived inside a chamber lit by light sticks, large enough to house a gravtank. It was lined with computer monitors, with cables and pipes hanging from the ceiling like the roots of a plant growing above us. Virtually all of the wires had been cut, the console screens were smashed and pipes burst. The Chinese had made a good job of destroying everything they left for us, no sense letting us have their equipment intact. I assumed the room had been some form of control room, from which the enemy would have monitored the array of sensors, cameras and defence equipment that helped them to slow us down. *A lot of our comrades would have been killed by men in that room,* I thought.

'Wait here, fellas, I'll let them know you's're here.' The lead guide disappeared into another tunnel, followed by the others.

Happy we were in a relatively secure location; our sections huddled together while we waited for the guides to return. I felt safe knowing that all the tunnels around us would be occupied by friendly forces, and welcomed the sight of troopers occasionally passing through the chamber going about their business.

'I don't know about you but that was one of the spookiest patrols I've ever done,' Sam said to Westy.

Westy nodded. 'I've never been in an enemy warren before, not even on Eden.'

'They must have had it bad down here,' Stevo said gloomily, sliding down to the ground against a wall.

Westy didn't acknowledge Stevo. 'We keep it together down here, boys, we stay alive. I don't want to lose any more blokes in this hole, alright?'

We nodded assent.

'What do you think they'll have us doing?' Brown asked.

'I don't know, do I?' Westy snapped, surprising all of us. 'Don't worry about that just yet.'

We stood in silence. I noticed that both the boss and Sergeant Evans had found two separate corners of the chamber to sit alone, and I wondered if the latter would ever forgive the boss - or me.

'You alright, mate?' Ray nudged me, and I realised I had been staring into space. My head was awash with fear and misery.

I shook it off and lied, 'Yeah, mate, you?'

'I wouldn't worry about me, man,' he laughed, 'I'm not the one staring into space like a shuttle crash victim!'

Ray was a friendly lad, and he had not meant to offend me, so I laughed with him. 'Alright, mate! This is just a lot to take in, that's all.'

'What is?' Ray mocked. 'You're a trooper, in a cave. That's some pretty simple stuff.'

I threw up my arms defensively. 'Look at this place. This is mental! It's like a vision of hell!'

'Could be worse, mate …' Sam answered.

'How, exactly?' I demanded. 'How could this be worse?'

'Well … we could be in Pompey, couldn't we?'

'Oh that's right, bring Pompey into it, why don't you,' Ray retorted. 'Where are you from again?'

'Chichester,' Sam replied.

'Well, that answers a few questions, then, doesn't it?'

'Where is Chichester, Ray?'

'How the hell should I know, you wand?'

Sam snorted, 'Brilliant, I'm stuck in a section of morons.'

It's amazing how a bit of banter with your mates can take your mind off things, Ray and Sam seemed to thrive off it. Brown on the other hand, stayed quiet, not wanting to join in with any conversation I was involved in, I figured. He hadn't really said much at all since the landing. I didn't care, he hated me and I hated him in equal measure. The less he spoke the better.

A man walked into the chamber with his rifle held low at his side. Despite his visor hiding the details of his face in the low light I could clearly make out his insignia on his chest; a major.

Westy almost snapped to attention, but thought better of it. 'Alright, Sir,' he said instead.

'Almost, Corporal, almost,' the major warned light heartedly, as he exchanged handshakes with the boss. You didn't salute or brace up to an officer in the field, lest you made him a target, apart from to call him 'Sir' and show him the respect that his rank earned him.

A smile was just about visible on the major's face as he pointed through the solid wall that Stevo had slouched against, and where he now stood bolt upright. 'Chill out, fellas, the enemy is out there, not in this room.'

The major looked at each of us and nodded approvingly. 'Good to see you boys, very good indeed. We need every bit of manpower we can get, and I make no apologies for having you pulled down here. I'm the battalion second-in-command, as you can imagine the Commanding Officer himself is pretty busy.' He shook the boss's hand. 'How many more platoons do I have coming down from your battalion, Lieutenant, do you know?'

I had never met anybody from my own battalion's headquarters, since they had come to New Earth on a completely different ship to ours. The major looked tired, and maybe even a little edgy, but he still maintained a level of haughtiness that was often expected of the officers in the higher ranks.

'We're it, Sir,' the boss told him. 'The battalion has no more to spare.'

'Oh.' The major shook his head sadly when he realised what that meant. 'I'm sorry to hear that. But at least you're here, because mark my words we need you. So, one platoon …' The major was clearly doing some form of calculations in his head. Battlefield replacements would be steadily moving in to bolster his battalion for its next move. The main effort for the brigade was to secure the warrens before Jersey City could be taken, therefore all the battalions that made up the brigade would be sending down troops to support that effort. More platoons from elsewhere on the surface would be following our route down the same tunnels, one by one, as they would be in

many other tunnels leading into the warrens. I wondered if somewhere else in a separate tunnel casualties were coming out at the same rate.

'This defence complex is the location of our headquarter element, as well as the Regimental Aid Post,' the major explained as if he read my mind. The Regimental Aid Post was where casualties would be treated after the medics in the companies had done as best they could with them. At this early stage of the invasion that was as close to a hospital as you were going to get, since there was little chance of you being lifted off the surface. I couldn't even imagine being a casualty underground in this hellish place, but better treated in here than out on the surface where Chinese ships and saucers could get you.

'It's presently defended by our C Company,' the major continued, 'who are resting after combat further down underground. A and B Company are located in two other defence complexes where they are preparing to assault deeper. We believe the enemy are completely trapped within this particular warren and their morale is shaken by the loss of orbital top cover. They're desperately hoping that we will lose top cover so that they can go back onto the offensive. As it stands there is estimated to be several companies of these traitorous bastards down here, including aircraft, artillery and God knows what else, just waiting for that moment. Half of it is useless down here, but if they were to break back to the surface with orbital cover we would be in a lot of trouble indeed.'

Corporal Jones, one section's new section commander nodded. 'Which company are we going to then, Sir?'

None of us even raised an eyebrow when we were told where we were going. *Let's face it,* I thought, *it wasn't going to be C Company on rest, was it?*

'A company will be taking you.'

A company, just like my own company who were still perched up on the hills overlooking Jersey City. I could only hope that it would not be quite as ill-fated as we had been.

———

'A' company gave us a frosty reception when we entered their part of the warren, another collection of caves almost a kilometre beneath the surface of New Earth. In amongst the masses of red glowing light sticks they regarded us with almost hateful eyes, as if we were the enemy himself.

'Don't worry about them,' our new guide said when we came to a halt in a small empty cave, 'they've been through a lot.'

'No shit,' Sam replied testily. 'Haven't we all?'

The guide ignored Sam's response and turned to the boss. 'Just hang tight here, Sir.'

'No worries. Sit down lads, chill.'

As the guide disappeared into a connecting tunnel we sat down either side of the cave. It was long and narrow, only a little wider than a dropship crew compartment, so our outstretched feet interlocked together along its length.

'You all alright?' Westy asked us.

We chorused a very unenthusiastic, 'Yeah.'

'Pump, ain't it,' he smiled.

Another 'Yeah' resounded.

'I tell you what,' Sam said, 'if we get one more cocky northern 4th Battalion guide with a chip on his shoulder, I'm gonna have to hurt him.'

'Roger that,' Ray concurred.

'I get it. They've had a crappy time, but what about us? We're the remains of two sections!'

'There's no point getting yourselves wound up, boys,' Westy said. 'Let's just get this done and get out of this hole.'

With my visor set to normal vision, I scanned the hellish cave in which we sat, the red light sticks casting dark shadows along its jagged walls.

'This place is like something out of a horror movie,' I said.

'It wasn't made to look nice, mate,' Sam answered.

Ray sighed. 'Is there anything on this planet that doesn't look awful?'

'The sea looked nice,' Brown said.

'Yeah, it was weren't it? Do you know what?' Ray leant forward enthusiastically, 'If we get out of here in one piece I'm gonna swim in that sea. Who's up for it?'

'That's a big 'if', Ray,' Stevo said.

We ignored Stevo. 'Can you even swim with one of these respirators on?' I asked.

Sam shook his head. 'Nah, you got to wear a special one, I think.'

'A special one?'

'Yeah, one that doesn't get clogged up by water.'

'Well, what if you kept your head out?'

Westy sighed tiredly. 'Are we really going to have a conversation about respirators and swimming right now?'

Ray laughed. 'Looks that way.'

It's funny when I look back at it, some of the ridiculous stuff that we troopers would talk about in the most inappropriate places. Down hundreds of metres beneath the surface of New Earth, waiting for the unknown to happen, we had a full-blown conversation about whether somebody had designed a respirator that worked both above and below the water. Ray pointed out that the Chinese probably had them already. Well sod it - they had everything else … supposedly.

After several minutes the guide emerged from the tunnels again and looked to the boss. 'This way, Sir.'

We were spared the formality of being greeted by the company commander. I doubted that being as close to the enemy as he was that he was really interested in meeting new arrivals. The OC of a company of drop troops operating underground was often subordinate to the engineer masterminds that worked around him. He might know how to lead his men into battle on the surface, but he had no idea of what layers of rock made up the crust of New Earth, or what methods the enemy might use to slow our advance. But that didn't mean his job wasn't difficult for him, quite the opposite in fact. Organising a company of three platoons to fit the engineers plan in the mazes of tunnels and caverns that made up the warrens was no simple feat.

Instead the platoon was escorted deeper into the underground network. As we patrolled downwards I noticed the guide begin to move more and more cautiously, until eventually he was creeping forward with delicate steps on the mats.

I made sure I kept my spacing to ten metres, hoping that if the Chinese blew us up it wouldn't be me who got it.

An IR torch flashed ahead of us in the gloom. We had found our new company, and the front line.

16: Battle in the Dark

We huddled silently in the small tunnel. It was far smaller than the tunnels we had been used to, so small that two men would struggle to pass each other without having to remove their kit. The tunnel had been cut out of the rock by a robotic laser drill an hour or so ago, before it had been destroyed by a detonation, most likely caused by Chinese engineers.

The sound created by the powerful explosion, even a few hundred metres away from the drill with our headphones on was simply ear splitting, shaking the very ground beneath our feet and engulfing us in clouds of dust that took minutes to settle. The resulting collapse of the tunnel had rendered it impassable to us.

The Chinese had rigged much of the tunnel systems that led to their underground lair with explosives, so much so that it was impossible for anybody to use them to move around. Instead we had been forced to resort to digging our own tunnels, using automated diggers like the laser drill which were fast and not much noisier than a team of men with pick axes and spades. Robots, although no replacement for infantry even in this day and age, always had their uses and this was definitely one of those times. I was glad that it hadn't been me digging down in that tunnel!

Brown was crouched so close in front of me I could hear his respirator sucking in air. 'What happens now, then?

My reply was so quiet it would barely stir a mouse. 'I don't know. I think the engineers are trying to think of what to do next.'

'Get the hell out of this hole, that's what we should do.'

We looked on up the tunnel, listening. I doubted my respirator could hear as efficiently as the listening tools that the engineers would attach to the walls, but I still strained to hear the sound of the Chinese tunnelling. Sometimes I would hold my breath, sure I had heard something.

Minutes passed as our section sat and waited for something to happen. We were at the front of the whole company, much to our dismay. Having had no experience of combat with the enemy underground, nobody amongst us was amused at being made to lead the company into the caves. Not that we had a choice, the boss wasn't in a position to argue.

A message was passed verbally up the tunnel. Sam tapped my shoulder from behind, whispering, 'Engineers have picked up an enemy tunnel.'

I repeated the message to Brown, who carried it on down the line.

An enemy tunnel was somewhere within the rock a few hundred metres from where I was crouched. I wondered if they were listening in to us too. A stupid thought, of course they were.

'Are we gonna pull back?' I asked Sam, hopefully.

'No,' he whispered, 'I don't think so.' My heart dropped.

We crept forward toward where the drill had been working its way through the rock, taking care not to trip on the lines of pipes and tubes that ran along the tunnel floor to feed it power and extract its spoil. We finally came to a halt fifty metres from the end of the tunnel, tucked around the last of the corners purposefully left by the drill to keep us out of direct line of sight, in case the Chinese detonated a device or broke in somehow. Sweat dripped from my forehead despite my respirator attempting to cool my face. My breath was ragged with fear. They knew we were there, how could they not?

A man crept past us, his lower legs brushing against our shoulders. With my visor's night vision I could clearly see that he wasn't wearing anything apart from his armour and his respirator. He crept slowly, placing his feet like he was stepping on broken glass.

I knew that the man had to be an engineer, for nobody in his right mind would do what this man was doing. In his hands he was cradling a plasma charge, taking it forward to the end of the tunnel where it would be used to best effect. You could use a robot drone to do this, but they were often easily detected, far better to use a human being to deliver the payload. I could only imagine what it must feel like creeping all the way up that dark tunnel, all alone, knowing that if the enemy heard a peep from you they would blast you into the rock like beef patty.

'That …' Brown whispered, 'is tapped.'

I said nothing. To do something like that a man must have had either nerves of steel - or a few screws loose.

I watched the figure round a slight bend in the tunnel and out of sight.

The engineer was gone for at least ten tense minutes. If I could have done I would have bitten my fingernails, but instead settled for chewing on my drinking straw inside my respirator to calm my nerves.

When the engineer returned he was clearly no longer carrying his charge. He exaggerated his creeping almost comically, and I could have sworn he was smiling. Crazy.

A minute later a message was being passed up the line again, making its way past several sections before it got to us.

Sam patted my shoulder. 'Fire in the hole. We will enter the enemy tunnel and assault left.'

'Fire in the hole, we will assault left,' I repeated to Brown.

When the message got all the way up to Ray, the section point man and the furthest forward of the platoon, he then sent the message back again.

Whispering as quietly as our lips allowed, we passed the same message back up the line to its source, confirming that it had reached the whole platoon correctly. We lacked the ability to communicate by intercom without alerting our foe, but we made do with the mark one mouth and mark one ear.

From behind us a rifle IR torch flashed slowly and deliberately up the tunnel. I knew from my training on Uralis that it was one of the engineers counting down to detonation of the plasma charge, a powerful device designed to punch a man-sized hole through soft or weakened earth and rock. After the third flash the device would be detonated by remote.

Boom!

My body was tossed from the ground where I crouched and I landed flat on my face. The impact lifted my respirator seal away from my chin, allowing hot toxic air inside and then a cloud of dust as thick as emulsion enveloped me.

'Down!' somebody hollered over the noise of the explosion that echoed up and down the tunnel.

'Get fucking down!' another voice screamed, more urgently this time. I recognised it as Sergeant Evans, and I obeyed, keeping as low as I could.

'Firing!'

I couldn't see, but a smart missile was launched. Over my head it flew, its booster rocket driving it up the tunnel and away from us before the main rocket ignited. It negotiated the corner in the tunnel with surprising ease, knowing exactly where it was going without needing to be told.

'Firing!'

Another missile was fired, then another.

The racket down the tunnel was unbelievable, sending shockwaves through the earth beneath me where I lay stunned. Blinding flashes of light burst through the clouds of dust as the missiles successfully navigated the hole created by the charge and detonated their payload within the Chinese tunnel.

I picked myself up as quickly as I could, my respirator display alerting me to the loss of a correct seal to my face. I pulled it back down over my chin and blew out hard.

'My God,' I exclaimed.

'Let's go!' Westy screamed.

'Go! Go! Go!' Sam pushed at me from behind.

Brown was stumbling in front of me. I grabbed him roughly by the arm and charged.

We sprinted around the corner of the tunnel and then into the glowing, smoking hole that had been blasted out by the plasma charge. As I ran, tripping and stumbling on pieces of rock and debris in the cloud of dust and smoke, I powered up my rifle to be used. I had no idea of what I was running into. The outlines of my comrades faded in and out of the cloud as we went, the heat making thermal imaging as impossible as Infra-red, and thus rendering my visor virtually useless.

'This one's for you, Jimmy!' Westy screamed from somewhere in front of me, unleashing a burst of automatic.

Before I realised it I was in the Chinese tunnel. If there were any of them alive where the charge had punched through and the missiles had followed, it was doubtful that any would have managed to stay in less than a hundred pieces, much less survived.

Upon entering the enemy tunnel we turned left instantly, the section behind would turn right so that we would be assaulting along it in either direction. Westy and Ray advanced side by side, firing rapidly into the smoke so that sparks showered as darts struck at the tunnel walls and ricocheted. Unable to fire without shooting a mate in front of me, I followed behind with the others, ready to be used.

We had to be rapid, the minute the Chinese worked out what had happened they were likely to withdraw and blow the tunnel.

If any Chinese had died in there I didn't see any. Nobody could have survived the combined effects of a plasma charge, a series of missiles fired in enclosed quarters and then to top it off a good hosing down with steel darts. Westy halted us ten or so metres up the enemy tunnel.

'Withdraw!'

We didn't need telling twice. Even if the Chinese in this tunnel - if there had been any - had died, no doubt there would be more further back or in neighbouring tunnels, quickly readying their own response. We ran back toward our entry point as fast as our bodies allowed.

'Two times charges detonating, friendly charge, friendly charge!' The company commander had broken the intercom silence, his message relaying from one trooper's headphones to another in the confined space.

Whump! The earth shook as the first charge somewhere nearby detonated.

Whump! Another, further away this time.

'Fuck this shit!' Stevo screamed as we bounded around the corner and back into the hole we had created for our attack.

Corporal Jones' one section was withdrawing back into the hole with us, and the boss stood at its opening pushing us toward safety in near panic.

'Go, go! Move! Move!'

Back inside our own tunnel a figure was stood, pointing for us to go back to where we had originally waited for the engineers to place their charge.

'Get your arses moving,' Sergeant Evans shouted as we passed him, 'Stay low! Stay low, move fast!'

We ran in single file through the darkness, the smoke clearing and our visibility returning.

'Go silent, Westy, go silent!' The platoon commander ordered over our section intercom.

'Go silent!' Westy hissed back at us and we slowed to a walk, and then a cautious creep. I resisted the urge to bolt away, knowing full well that I would be heard by the Chinese. Besides, where was I going to go?

Two almighty explosions rocked the tunnel, throwing us against the walls and sending Brown crashing to the ground at my feet. Another wave of dust engulfed us, so thick it pressed against my body, almost like I was underwater.

I steadied myself with one hand against the tunnel wall and with the other picked up Brown from the floor. 'You okay, mate?'

'I'm not your mate,' he replied angrily, shrugging my hands away violently. 'And do I look okay?'

'Shut up, you belters,' Sam hissed urgently behind us. 'Get moving!'

'Close up,' Westy called above the din of another explosion. 'Stay with me.'

We closed right together so that we could keep eyes on the man in front of us, continuing to slowly make our way back up the tunnel.

When he was satisfied we had moved a good hundred metres away from the hole into the Chinese tunnel, Westy held up a hand to bring us to a halt. We crouched together in a tight huddle, like a small herd of terrified animals. Stevo was rocking.

'Snap out of it, Stevo,' Westy hissed. 'Get a grip of your body.'

I looked left and right. In the settling dust I could see another section ten metres behind us in a similar huddle. I assumed it was one of ours. Despite the risk of losing an entire section or more in one go, we couldn't communicate effectively if we spread out without using the intercom and so it was necessary for platoons to huddle close together. I was glad to be as close as I was to the others, even Brown, their proximity was comforting.

As suddenly as it had erupted into noise and violence, the warren became deathly silent as again we sat and waited for the next move to be made. Our respirator motors battled to draw air from the smoke. I hoped that the engineers were ventilating the tunnels, because otherwise we would run out of air for our respirators to filter, they weren't designed to breathe pure carbon dioxide.

The silence was broken when Stevo sobbed loudly.

'Stevo, shut up!' Sam whispered angrily.

It was then that I heard the distinctive click of a bayonet being disengaged from an MSG-20 and then a second, muffled sob escaped Stevo's mouth as Westy pressed the blade against his throat.

'Make a noise like that again,' Westy whispered darkly, 'and I will cut you open from ear-to-ear. Do you understand me?'

'I don't want to die,' Stevo's pathetic words were barely audible, even with my headphones.

'You're very close to dying,' Westy threatened, 'so I suggest you shut up.'

Sam leant close to me, so that our visors touched. 'That bloke is a total arsehole.'

I nodded, although it felt hypocritical; I was hardly a hero myself.

We waited for five minutes in the dark, without a sound. I wondered what had happened and what had caused the other explosions. It seemed likely that the closer blasts had been caused by the Chinese blowing out their tunnel in an effort to stop us advancing into it. The more distant explosions I couldn't explain. Warren fighting was a terrifying underground game of chess, and we were the pieces. Engineers of both sides were deciding how best to make their next move and we were just along for the ride.

Eventually, a solitary trooper made his way toward us from the way we had come. A runner, no doubt, tasked to pass messages in absence of the intercom. Nobody dared use the company communication network unless the warren got noisy, it would only allow the enemy to work out where we were and what we were doing.

The runner crouched close to Westy and whispered his message.

'Pinkies blew out their tunnel,' he said quietly, confirming what I had suspected. 'Engineers are checking it out. Five platoon assaulted into the same tunnel further back, that got blown out too. We're possibly gonna dig down into a transit tunnel beneath us, but we won't be moving for at least the next ten minutes.'

'Okay,' Westy acknowledged, 'That it?'

'That's it. Anyone else further up there?' He flicked his head toward the Chinese tunnel.

'Yeah, mate. One section I think.'

'Cool, I'm off, then.'

The runner continued on up the tunnel to pass on his message and we waited.

I brushed a layer of dust away from my gloves gently, sending puffs of it into the air. I watched the mini dust cloud slowly disperse and settle on the ground. We were coated in it from head to toe, just like all of our guides had been when they had escorted us down into the warrens.

Too afraid to even make the slightest sound, we waited, listening out for the sound of Chinese tunnelling. We waited for what felt like an age, staring blankly at the walls across from us, alone to our thoughts, and our own inner demons. Inside my head the memory of my actions with my original ill-fated section assaulted my mind and soul, and I found myself longing for home, for daylight, for peace from all of the misery. There could be nowhere worse to be than there in the bowels of New Earth, man's self-made hell.

Beating off the urge to cry or vomit, I was unsure which; I closed my eyes and imagined I was back on Earth in the warmth and comfort of my home.

———

My body jerked when a hand violently shook at my shoulder. I looked up in alarm at the figure standing over me.

'Moralee, wake up you lizard.' It was Sam. He shook me again to emphasise the point.

'I'm –I-I wasn't sleeping,' I blurted reflexively. Out of the corner of my eye, Brown shook his head in disgust.

'Shhhhh,' Sam placed an upward pointing finger across his visor where his mouth would be. 'Course you weren't, sweetheart,' he said sarcastically.

My visor read it to be ten-twenty-two, just past the New Earth mid-day. It had been at least an hour since we had gone firm and waited for the next move, and I could only remember five minutes of that time. Quite clearly I had indeed been asleep - my exhausted body must have just switched itself off.

'Sorry, Sam,' I whispered.

'Don't apologise, it's weak. We're moving back.'

'Why? Are we retreating?' I was almost hopeful.

'And miss all the fun?' I sensed that Sam was smiling as Ray passed us back the way we had come and away from the Chinese tunnel. 'Where did you learn that word anyway? 'Retreating' is a dirty word.' He waved a disapproving finger at me.

I sighed. 'Fair one.'

Westy was next to pass us, then Stevo.

'So what's going on?' I whispered.

Sam shrugged. 'Don't know yet, we just got the order to move. Probably gonna try somewhere else.'

'Oh.'

Brown patted my shoulder, announcing he was about to move off.

'Had a nice snooze, cheese head?'

I said nothing, embarrassed. Sam shook me again reassuringly.

'Don't worry about him, mate. He's just got sour grapes because no one likes him. But don't let it happen again.'

'Him and Woody have got it in for me,' I said, but Sam just laughed.

'I think those two are the least of your worries, mate. And you're the least of theirs. Come on, let's go.'

I moved off.

———

For several hours we followed a laser drill as it burrowed a twisting and winding tunnel through the rock, trailing hundreds of metres of piping that brought the excavated rock back past us and to the engineers somewhere behind.

Twice in a single hour the Chinese blew out the tunnel being dug ahead of us as we tried to connect it with theirs for a fight, once right on top of a laser drill as it worked, then a second time further up the tunnel toward us in an attempt to hit troops instead of just a robot. They didn't want a force-on-force fight, instead they merely wanted to buy time, hoping their ships might return to save them from their prison underground. The explosions came with such force they took our feet from under us, each time leaving us dazed and confused on the ground.

Each time we picked ourselves up and waited whilst the engineers reassessed their route, and then carried forward a new drill complete with its snaking pipes, before continuing the process again down a brand new tunnel.

The way I imagined tunnel warfare was kind of like worms fighting some kind of duel in the mud, probing forward, moving, and probing again. Eventually though, the stalemate was going to end. We couldn't go on like this forever, either we would run out of drills or the Chinese would run out of explosives. That or the whole of New Earth would cave in on top of us.

As we slowly followed the drills down their tunnels we laid out our vibration-proof mats as they were passed down from behind, along with water for our packs which were almost depleted. It was hot work down at this depth, what with the heat created by the drill. Somewhere to our rear engineers would be working hard to maintain a supply of cool air into the tunnels, shame it wasn't air that we could breathe without the damned respirators.

I sat with my section in the pitch-black, whilst ahead our drill burrowed away somewhere out of sight ahead of us. I could hear the distinctive hissing-popping sound it created as its powerful lasers melted their way through solid rock, its spindly little metal legs pulling it forward toward the enemy like some ugly insect.

'Why can't they just give one of them things a rifle?' I asked.

'God knows,' Brown replied curtly.

I took a thoughtful sip on my drinking straw as I listened to the sound of the drill. If I listened to it for long enough my mind began to play tricks, sometimes I could swear I could hear people talking up there, and other sounds I knew to be in my imagination.

Sam patted my shoulder, 'We're ten metres short of a pinkie tunnel. It opens into their defensive complex.'

I leaned close to Brown and passed the message. Despite the proximity of potential enemy we knew now to remain sat down, any explosion would merely have us flat on our faces again anyway. I resisted the urge to power up my rifle, but my finger hovered close over the button.

A familiar figure stepped over our legs in the gloom, cradling another payload of explosives in his arms. His infra-red torch flicked over us as he moved, temporarily dazzling my visor until it quickly adjusted. He was smiling, alright. Last time I wasn't sure but he was definitely smiling.

'That nutter's actually enjoying himself,' I told Sam in disbelief.

'Yeah?'

'Mate, he's *smiling!*'

Brown shook his head. 'Then he needs to get a grip of himself.'

I watched the IR torch move up the tunnel, becoming a single ring of light around the lone figure. He was about a hundred metres up our tunnel, with the drill fifty metres on from him and the Chinese ten metres through the rock past that.

He didn't get any further.

Whump!

The explosion this time was so powerful it still managed to toss us from where we sat into a crumpled heap on the ground. The overpressure created by the enemy device, whatever it was, would surely have ruptured my ear drums and caused my eye balls to bleed had I not been wearing all of my protective equipment. I rolled onto my back, in shock from the impact. Dust settled on my visor so thick I couldn't see.

'On your feet! On your feet! Rapid fire, now!' I recognised our platoon commander's voice. Where before he had sounded urgent but in control, now his voice was shrill. With a terrible chill that shot up my spine, I realised it was the Chinese who had detonated a device, but this time the overpressure had been far greater than before. The Chinese had used one of their own plasma charges to explosively dig into our tunnel. Much the same as we had done to them hours earlier.

'Shit!' I yelled as I realised what was about to happen.

I struggled to pick myself up off my back, wiping the dust from my visor. As I did so there was a sudden flash of light that blinded my visor, accompanied by a rush of hot air that seared the exposed skin around my neck and blew me back down to the ground.

There was a massive explosion from behind as the Chinese missile struck home somewhere in the centre of the company. Somebody screamed.

I knew what was coming next. I leapt to my knees and powered up my rifle, thumbing the selector switch to automatic.

Through the cloud of dust I could see Brown picking himself up off the ground in painstakingly slow motion. For a nanosecond my mind flicked to a picture of him being cut down by enemy fire as they stormed the tunnel, with me unable to fire for fear of killing Ray, Westy and Stevo who were all obscured by the smoke. There was only one thing I could do, and in the space of the tiniest fraction of a second I made a decision that only a day ago I would never have dreamed of.

Whereas before I had been driven by fear of reprisal from my mates, or the fear of death or just blind obedience, I was now acting on something entirely different; a fear for my comrade's lives.

Not again, my mind screamed, *not my section again!*

'Brown, get down!' I pushed Brown back to the floor as I barged past him, bounding to the front of my section. It took me less than two seconds to get next to Ray where he lay dazed at the front of the section. I took up aim into the dark and powered up my rifle. Any second the enemy would emerge and hose us down with darts while we still reeled in shock from their smart missile.

'Fuck you!' I screamed into the gloom and pulled the trigger.

Flashes of orange light danced up the tunnel as my darts ricocheted off the walls toward my unseen foe. Chips of rock smacked off my visor, but I was oblivious to the return fire from the Chinese that had mixed in with mine, bouncing past and creating carnage in the company behind me. Ray's body jumped and rocked as it was struck several times by supersonic steel darts.

I don't know why the pinkies didn't get me. Of course it was just blind luck, pure and simple. The Chinese, like us, couldn't see much through all the hot dust and smoke and would be firing almost blind in our general direction. Besides if anybody had deserved a miracle, it wouldn't be me.

Another trooper joined me in my defiance; it was Sam.

'We're about to get spanked, Moralee!' he shouted over the din, and at that moment I knew as Sam did what needed to be done. 'Charge 'em!'

We ran toward the enemy, our weapons roaring and our bayonets lusting for blood.

Now there is meant to be a method of clearing forward through the tight tunnels of a warren, advancing forward in pairs with one in a half crouch and one stood high just to the side and rear so that both troopers could fire. I'm pretty sure that me and Sam didn't do that.

We ran almost side by side toward the enemy, firing our rifles wildly into the smoke. We had lost all sense and reason and were driven forward by pure rage, with not a shred of thought for the drills we had been taught on Uralis. All I knew at the back of my mind was that the company was

battered, and that those who had lived through the blast of the missile and the enemy gunfire were probably still lying comatose on the floor. We had to take the fight to the Chinese, if anything to stall them and give the lads a fighting chance.

They were bunched up in the tunnel when we reached them, a mass of men desperately trying to drag casualties out of the way and bring their weapons to bear again. Our rounds hacked at them as we charged, spattering them with each other's blood. They were a thronging mass of chaos and confusion, like a herd of animals that had hurtled straight into the path of some terrible predator. They had not expected us to respond with such ferocity.

One of the pinkies managed to force his way around an injured comrade, bringing his rifle up to aim at the screaming Europeans bearing down upon him. He let off a burst at the same time as he died by my own rifle.

That was the last time I saw Sam.

I ran over the bodies of the dead and into the enemy, with the rest of the company following.

That was the beginning of what was to be one of the most violent and bloody underground battles fought beneath the surface of New Earth. I can't tell you that I remember all of what happened. I stabbed and slashed and hacked at my foe as if possessed. Where the enemy fell, I finished him with a thrust to his upper torso, or simply stepped over him so that somebody behind me could do it. When I was out of stabbing range I fired my rifle instead, and charged again, scarcely aware of comrades trying to keep up with me.

Sometimes a trooper fell, I think, but I didn't stop to see who it was. I was lost in my own world of horror and pain and misery, and before me were the very people I blamed for it all. If I killed enough of them, maybe it would all go away. Or maybe they would just kill me.

Suddenly a hand clasped my shoulder and threw me to the ground in a crumpled heap and then a knee landed on my back with the full weight of a man upon it. Pinned, I struggled to release myself, desperate to get back into the fight. But I had already been relieved - another pair of troopers were now ahead of me followed by a long line of troopers waiting to take their turn, all crouching as low as their bodies allowed. The noise of battle gradually receded up the tunnel.

A hand patted my shoulder gently, and a familiar voice said reassuringly. 'It's alright, Moralee.'

My eyes were wet. I bit my lip to keep it from trembling.

'I'm good, Brown,' I protested. 'Let me up!'

'Advance forward in your pairs!' the platoon commander ordered over the intercom. 'Everyone else should be keeping as low as possible! Smart missile prepare to engage incendiaries … fire in the hole, get down!'

I struggled again, but Brown was too strong and heavy for me to escape from under him. 'Let me up, Brown, I'm fine!'

Mitch and his smart missile launcher were only metres from us when he fired over the heads of our platoon, sending a missile screaming away at the enemy.

Brown got off of me, and as soon as he did so I spun around in fury, raising my fist toward him.

'You fucking bastard! Who do you think you are?!' I raged, and I threw a wild punch that Brown ducked with ease. Brown was a fighter, one far more dangerous than me, but he made no effort to retaliate.

'What are you gonna do?' Brown asked. 'Try and fight me again?' Gunfire rattled from up the tunnel.

'I hate you!' I screamed, my rifle raised ready to stab at Brown. He saw the gesture and took a step back, one hand raised defensively. 'Climo should have lived! You should have fucking died, you prick!'

Brown's voice became angry. 'Do you think I wanted Climo to die? What kind of sick bastard do you take me for?'

The anger in Brown's voice only enraged me further. 'You made my life a misery, that's how sick you are! Why did you stop me, I'd have died and you could have rid of me…'

'Because you're all I've got left!' Brown shouted, stunning me into silence. 'And I'm all you've got!'

We both just stood there stunned. 'Get out of the way.' A trooper shoved his way past me and Brown, followed by the first section of the next platoon making its way into the battle. We had broken the Chinese, so it was critical that the pressure was kept on and they remained off balance. If we paused for even a minute they would re-group, blow out their tunnels and counter-attack.

Brown slumped himself down against the wall of the tunnel, breathing heavily. I paused for a second, unsure of what to do, and then sat down beside him.

The intercom was filled with chatter from the platoon as it advanced into the Chinese defensive complex. The platoon commander was calling for the OC to task the next platoon to echelon through him and continue the assault before he became over extended. The company second in command announced that the OC was a casualty himself, and that he would send up what the company had right away.

'Where are the others?' My visor had identified every man and not one was from our section.

'Dunno,' Brown answered. We both knew that most of the section would be dead or wounded. I knew for certain that Ray hadn't made it, and I was pretty sure Sam had died or been injured during our charge up the tunnels.

'Well what do we do now?'

Brown shrugged. 'I dunno.'

The battle for control of Hill Bravo's warrens continued for two more bloody hours. The Chinese were unable to match the ferocious momentum of our assault and they began to fall back, allowing us to punch deep into the bowels of their warren. Instead of mazes of empty tunnels designed to be fought in, we encountered store rooms, warehouses and accommodation. Unable to find survivors of our own section in the noise and confusion, me and Brown attached ourselves to any section we could in the platoon, or what was left of them. We fought through the tight two-man-wide tunnels we had become used to, one section assaulting at a time with grenades, rifles and bayonets whilst the others followed behind, dragging back casualties and the dead, and sending forward ammo and replacement troopers. We fought along corridors and through rooms that looked not entirely unlike the warrens on Uralis but without the lights working and the doors not operating, and through large cathedral-like hangars filled with Chinese vehicles and weapons.

Me and Brown were leading the platoon through a maze of vehicles packed into one such hangar, the sounds of our footsteps and heavy breathing seeming to echo between the vast metal walls, when several Chinamen opened fire from only a few tens of metres away. They missed us, their aim was poor and they were too close for their rifles to compensate for the inaccuracy. The Chinese were known for being worse shots at close quarters. We dove for cover behind the nearest vehicle, some kind of artillery piece mounted on caterpillar tracks.

'Contact front!' I yelled and fired, catching one Chinaman on the arm and sending him tumbling to the ground. He tried to crawl away but somebody finished him off with a shot to the head.

'What's going on?' I realised that a section commander had managed to get right up behind me, it was Corporal Jones.

'We've got enemy literally on the other side of this vehicle,' Brown said, firing a burst with his mammoth.

'Grenade!' someone shouted, and we ducked, but the grenade exploded uselessly on the wrong side of our cover, sending pieces of shrapnel zinging off of the vehicles.

'Right, I'll go round the left,' the section commander said, but I had an idea and stopped him. I flicked my head upwards, and he took less than a second to understand.

Corporal Jones nodded and looked back to his men. 'Rapid fire, boys, we're going over the top!'

Several rifles opened fire as the three of us clambered up onto the artillery piece. Its armour was smooth, but covered with hand holds, presumably for people to climb up and maintain it. As I reached the top and perched beside the barrel of the massive weapon I could see at least five pinkies huddled on the other side of the vehicle. It looked like they were preparing to assault, their commander was pointing around the left side where Corporal Jones had wanted to go on a flank attack. No doubt there were more, but I couldn't see them and there wasn't time for us to ponder, we had to take advantage of the surprise.

I charged down the other side of the vehicle, somehow miraculously not losing my balance on the smooth, steep armour, and I fired repeatedly into the mass of men. We were on top of them so fast they had no time to react before the three of us stabbed and beat at those who hadn't died outright.

'Position clear!' Corporal Jones shouted, and more troopers poured past us. He patted me on the arm. 'Well done, mate,' and he was off. Brown said nothing, he simply nodded.

Casualties came thick and fast, the platoons at the front of the company often bearing the brunt. Though we sensed the Chinese were broken they still put up a good fight. Lone pinkies would spray wild bursts of automatic and charge with bayonets as if they were possessed and without fear, and they often got the better of us. Every pair of troopers behind the assaulting sections formed part of a human chain, dragging casualties back five or ten metres to the pair behind them until they reached the medics. I lost count of how many I helped move. Gunshot wounds and concussion from explosions were common. Sometimes we helped move casualties back who appeared almost uninjured, apart from a small trickle of blood from the nose or twitching like a crushed insect. Others had horrific traumatic injuries, missing limbs and gaping holes that exposed organs and burnt meat. I remember dragging one man back with Brown and noticing that he was choking and wheezing from within his respirator. A quick flash of a torch on IR identified the problem: a round had struck the visor of his respirator, passing through it at an angle and out the other side close to his face. Nobody had noticed it, for whatever reason, perhaps haste, and nobody had checked his vitals. We tried to patch the hole with our respirator repair kits but too late. He died before we even patched the first hole.

'Shit,' Brown simply said, flicking off his torch.

He was just another dead trooper now. We stripped his ammo and passed him rearward.

We were losing blokes fast, and as we did the structure of the company was beginning to break down. Blokes were being grabbed by section commanders of all three platoons regardless of whether they belonged to them or not. Platoon sergeants stalked the tunnels organising the ammunition and casualty chain of the entire company, since they would never be able to identify all of their own platoon in the maze, much less work out how much ammo they all needed. They spat orders and threw troopers about by the collar, enforcing rigid discipline in every individual they passed.

I was taken forward by several section commanders on numerous occasions, but I always managed to keep Brown with me. We no longer moved forward in a frenzy, but in calculated moves often initiated by the smart missiles or by tossing grenades around corners. I would crouch low whilst Brown would stand above and to the side of me covering my back. We would often move forward without firing unless we knew that there would be enemy, as we were getting through magazines fast and firing blindly often only served to tell the enemy where we were.

I stepped over bodies like any other man on Earth would step over a curb. Someone behind could search the body. One time we were clearing forward as the lead pair again and we came across a Chinaman who lay on his back with his feet toward us. His weapon was too far from him to reach, but he was still reaching for it anyway. My visor was relying upon thermal imaging and I couldn't really distinguish what injuries he had sustained, but I guessed he had been hit by shrapnel from a grenade we had thrown from around a corner.

He lifted his head to look up at us. 'Ma … ma …' I didn't have a clue what he was trying to say, even if he was trying to say anything at all. His voice sounded weak.

We stepped over the injured Chinaman as if he weren't even there, only taking the time to take his weapon away from him so that he couldn't shoot us in the back. Behind us the next pair quickly stripped him of his equipment so that he couldn't find any more weapons, or worse, a grenade.

I knew that the Union preferred to treat the enemy injured when the situation permitted, so long as the resources were available. If the enemy knew he would die anyway, he would fight to the death, which in the end turned him into a tougher opponent.

But I felt no pity for the Chinaman, only the same hatred I now had for all of them. The last shreds of humanity had left me down there in those caves. Nobody in the company said anything as one by one we left the man behind to die.

On several occasions I came to within centimetres of death. One such time I rounded a doorway into a room fitted with bunk beds just like the ones in training, failing to notice a pinkie in hiding to my right. Brown snatched me out of the way milliseconds before the Chinaman opened fire, before we both managed to get our own weapons round and fill him with more holes than a Swiss cheese. Upon checking me over we found no wounds, only several holes through my combats, including one that ran through the edge of my helmet just missing my respirator. To be fair, those holes could have been from as long ago as the landings, but we still had a good laugh about it.

Our biggest fear by far, though, was explosives. The Chinese had rigged them up everywhere, from high-tech devices to slabs of plastic explosives dug into a wall with a pick and spade. We relied upon our visor to hopefully detect anything before we got too close. Anything recently made could be picked up as a lighter patch on thermal, and anything that didn't match the shape of the tunnel would be flagged up by our visor display with a flashing red warning triangle. But eighty-percent of making sure you didn't get blown to bits was instinct. If we didn't feel good about something we pushed back and threw a grenade, just to be sure.

The Chinese defence was becoming less and less like that of a determined foe and more like the final desperate stand of a broken enemy. Reports from the surface told of total orbital top cover, denying the enemy an escape route to the surface, and one by one the hangars that held precious vehicles and equipment were being cut off and captured.

Toward the end of the battle we heard from the platoon commander that Westy had been concussed and evacuated out of the area to the regimental aid post closer to the surface. He didn't know anything about the others. So once again me and Brown were the survivors of a section that had been near enough destroyed, but this time we didn't even have a commander, or have a clue what to do with ourselves but make ourselves useful to anyone who needed us.

Combat below ground ended when the Chinese battalion we had been fighting surrendered. It would have been lunacy for them to have carried on, since we had captured or destroyed much of their critical supplies and life support equipment. Besides that, the vast majority of the vehicles and equipment that the warrens were meant to protect were already in our hands, giving them little purpose but to die for the sake of it, if not by us then by thirst or lack of air fit for their respirators. There was no cheer when the surrender was announced to the platoon, though, just a deathly silence from a sea of weary faces. There was so little to cheer about.

17: Return to the Surface

Me and Brown sat with the survivors of the company in an underground warehouse stacked several storeys high with ammunition crates. We had placed out as many light sticks as we could so that we could see without help from our visors. Figures squatted in small groups, talking quietly and resting for whatever would come next.

In total I could only count fourteen of us in my platoon, of which only three appeared to be NCOs. Corporal Jones, or Jonesy as his men called him, was the only full corporal to have survived along with two lancejacks from the sections that had been attached to us after the landings. Such a heavy loss of manpower had caused the organisation of the sections to dissolve so that it was hard to work out who belonged to which. Of the original platoon there were barely a handful of us left, including the platoon signaller and Mitch in headquarters. Our spirits were lifted by news that most of our casualties had not died, and even Sam had somehow been saved by the medics. Apparently he had been riddled with holes and had got through litres of blood in the Regimental Aid Post, but he had survived. Unfortunately Ray had not been so lucky, and Stevo's body was nowhere to be found.

Sergeant Evans ordered us all to eat at least one horror bag through our feeding straws after it became apparent that many of us were still carrying almost all of our rations from the drop. Fighting the Chinese had caused us to forget to look after ourselves, but it was Sergeant Evans' job to make sure that we did.

I always had to suck so hard to get anything out of a horror bag that eventually the muscles in my cheeks became sore from the effort. The effort became annoying, and I wasn't hungry anyway, but nevertheless I forced myself to eat. I didn't know when I would next get a chance.

'Apparently the pinkies have a tube that sticks food right in them, so they never have to eat,' Brown said. He had barely got halfway through his bag.

I tossed my rubbish over my shoulder. 'Yeah?'

'Yeah.'

'Should have checked to see,' I said, remembering the dead Chinaman whose respirator we removed. His childlike face still haunted me, along with the faces of my dead friends.

Brown said nothing for a few minutes, then muttered, 'We shouldn't have left that bloke.'

I looked across at him. He had stopped eating, and was staring at the half empty packet.

'Which one?' I asked finally.

'The one we fragged with the grenade. The one on the floor.'

I cast my mind back, vaguely remembering the company leaving a man who had survived the blast of a grenade.

'He was trying to call for his mum,' Brown said. 'I heard him. We all just left him, though.'

I hesitated, and then awkwardly patted the back of my enemy. 'He's Chinese. How do you know what mum sounds like in Chinese? He was reaching for a weapon, end of story. Somebody at the back would have dealt with him.'

Brown shook his head, and took a slow drag on the straw that connected to his horror bag, 'It sounded like he was calling for his mum. We just left that bloke to die calling for his mum, like it was the most normal thing in the world,' he sighed. 'I dunno. All I know is that this place is really hurting me.'

My respirator hid my surprise. I think that was probably the first time Brown had ever mentioned anything of his own feelings.

'I'm sorry about Climo,' Brown said, and I saw that he was sincere.

I paused, and finally nodded. 'That's okay.'

'How's your arm?'

I patted the fresh bandage I had applied to my wound - the other had been soaked with blood and pus. 'It's sore, and a bit nasty-looking, but it's okay.'

Brown nodded.

'I can't stop seeing Chase's eyes,' I said suddenly.

Another pause. 'Me neither. But now it's not just him I see when I close my eyes. It's everyone else, too.'

We sat in silence.

———

I couldn't believe it when we were re-united with Westy. Both me and Brown jumped to our feet as the burley Welshman appeared.

'God am I glad to see someone I recognise,' he said, grinning from ear to ear in the dim light of the hangar,

I thought about going in for a hug but thought it too much, instead shaking his hand furiously.

'So what happened?' I asked, gesturing toward Westy's sleeveless, bandaged arm. 'I thought you were at the Aid Post?'

Westy shrugged. 'I don't remember much after the engineer walked up the tunnel with his charge. The medic reckoned I was knocked out by the blast, and then I must have been hit by a ricochet when I was lying on the deck. I was just lucky.'

'You heard about the other lads, right?' Jonesy asked, and our smiles faded.

Westy nodded sombrely. 'Yeah. The company second-in-command told me when I managed to get back.'

I thought to change the subject. 'So, what, did you wake up at the Regimental Aid Post?'

'Yeah, I came to with this medic wrapping my arm up. It's just a flesh wound, nothing serious. It looks worse than it is coz my automatic tourniquet activated and the medic had to cut the sleeve off my armour to save my arm from dropping off! He tried to get me to stay at the RAP but I refused and done a runner after you lot. Still got pins and needles even now.' He shook his arm.

'You went running off into the tunnels?' Jonesy smiled.

'Yeah, I thought it was just me left, so I just followed the noise and attached myself to a random section.'

'Mate, you are mental,' Jonesy said, and we laughed. We shared stories of our exploits, the good parts and the bad. Westy told of his madness, volunteering himself to go in the lead pair for everything until one of the platoon commanders realised he was a corporal from another platoon and ordered him to stop.

I had noticed instantly from the second he had entered the hangar that something had changed in the way that Westy spoke to us. He had warmed to me and Brown, as if the barrier that separated the section commander from his junior privates had dissolved. At first I thought that he had finally decided that we had earned his respect in the battle for the tunnels, but then I remembered what Brown had said to me when we had argued and realised the truth. *We were all he had left.*

Brown took a deep breath and asked, 'So, what now, then?'

'The warrens are clear, most of the remaining Chinese have surrendered. Apparently B Company have found enough kit to start a whole new war down here, fortunately for us the enemy never had the chance to get it above ground. The pinkies must have worked out they weren't going to manage to get it all back to the surface anyway though, most of it was trashed, controls ripped out and all sorts. No point giving us their own weapons.'

'So no more fighting down here, then?' I asked. So many troopers had died down in the tunnels, it had been like fighting in the bowels of hell itself. I felt my heartbeat slow and muscles relax at the very thought of an end to it all. *Could I really have survived this brutal stage of my war on New Earth,* I wondered, *and would I really live to see the end to the whole thing?*

Westy shook his head. 'Doesn't look like it. But I wouldn't get too excited, it's still busy up on the surface. Apparently 2nd Battalion took a number of key positions around Jersey City, but the pinkies gave them a hard time. It looks like the Chinese won't surrender the city, so we're going to have to go in.'

Ears had pricked up from amongst the platoon and everybody, whether they knew Westy or not stopped to listen. Our war was far from over. It was generally believed that the Chinese would surrender or retreat from the city if they lost the warrens, but we had been overly optimistic. After all, retreat was a dirty word.

It wasn't long before the CSM closed the company into the centre of the warehouse for the OC, with a freshly bandaged leg, to announce our move back up to the surface. He told us that reports of success on every continent had circumnavigated the globe, and that the Chinese navy had all but given up hope of ever regaining top cover in orbit. We were winning, and I felt a sudden surge of hope wash across the company, like a static charge that almost stood my hair on end. But the elation we felt was short-lived, as he told us that we were moving in order to be reassembled into a fighting force to take Jersey City. Whispered curses hissed across the weary body of men as the OC described in simple and brutally honest terms how he saw the next few hours panning out.

'In the next fifteen minutes we will move back up to the surface as a company using a northern transit tunnel,' the OC told us. 'The warrens will be concurrently taken over by the conscripts.'

'Cheers, easy,' somebody uttered.

The company commander and sergeant major heard the trooper, I think, but chose to ignore him. I doubted they or anybody else disagreed with the sentiment. We had fought hard to gain control of Hill Bravo and the warrens beneath it, and now above us shuttles were disgorging hundreds of conscripts who would reap the rewards of our struggle. When we were out of the warren its breathable atmosphere would be restored, as would power and defence grids. The conscripted soldiers would settle down and wait until the invasion was over without even firing a shot. Bastards.

'On the surface the company will be re-organized and bolstered with battlefield replacements provided by the other battalions. I will then issue orders for an attack onto Jersey City. They will more than likely be a very quick set of orders, as we are pressed for time. The rest of the division is pushing north to clear remaining enemy off of Jersey Island in a few hours, and we are a crucial element of that move. We could be on our way back into battle in a matter of hours, and you need to be prepared for that now because it's not over yet. Any questions?'

'What about us, Sir, are we staying with you now?' the boss asked.

My heart skipped a beat. It had not crossed my mind that we might in fact be sent back to our own battalion and not used in the attack on Jersey City at all. The last thing I heard of my battalion was that they were holding the peak of Hill Bravo, having been rendered almost combat ineffective by the high casualties sustained on the landing. We were only within the 4th Battalion's ranks to give them a quick booster of manpower for the tunnels, and what with battlefield replacements coming in were we not better off in our own unit? I would much rather take my chances with Woody on the summit of Hill Bravo than with the Chinese in Jersey City. I felt shame in my cowardly thoughts, and shook them off.

It didn't matter anyway.

'Almost certainly, yes, Larry,' the OC answered, using Mr Barkley's first name. 'From what I gather now your battalion are firm on Hill Bravo and will probably remain so. To be frank, I need you and your platoon here. You're battle-hardened and experienced and I'm not letting you go if I can help it. I'm sorry.' His apology was genuine.

'Not at all, Sir.' The platoon commander waved the apology away. 'We're good to crack on.' I wasn't sure everybody else would agree.

The OC nodded respectfully toward our platoon commander. He had served the OC well, and so had the platoon. We had to respect the boss for the battle in the tunnels; he had led the platoon throughout the assault into the warrens and had never faltered, unlike some of his peers. I had heard tales of officers being relieved by their platoon sergeants and even section commanders as the fighting turned fierce. Perhaps he had made a mistake on the fateful day of our landing, but who was I to judge? Even Sergeant Evans seemed happy enough to stand next to the boss, and I earlier spotted them sat together in the warehouse deep in conversation. Maybe, I wondered, if he had it in him to forgive the boss, he could forgive me and Brown too. But then how could he if I couldn't even forgive myself?

'Any other questions?' the OC asked, and the warehouse fell silent. 'You'll get a much more detailed brief on the surface. Sergeant Major?'

The company sergeant major stepped forward, dwarfing the OC. He made Westy look like a midget. He was massive, and with his kit all on he looked bigger still, his shoulders were so wide and he stood so tall I wondered how he managed to fit down the smaller warren tunnels. I remembered seeing him stalking the platoons as we advanced, barking orders at the work parties as they carried out the injured and passed up the ammo, and working the waiting assault pairs into a frenzy in his deep northern accent.

'You kill them!' I had heard him scream. 'You kill 'em all! No mercy, lads!'

That was probably the most intelligent sentence ever to come out of CSM Robson's mouth, known as 'the bull' by the company because he was big, not too bright, but horrifically violent and foul tempered. Some people would say that those were the principle requirements of a sergeant major, as long as nobody was about to hear it.

'Right then, lads,' the huge man began, 'every man here had some food, yeah?'

Some from the other platoons didn't nod in response, and he shot an angry glance to the platoon sergeants who stood off to a flank. They would get a severe de-briefing for not administrating their men, I suspected, apart from Sergeant Evans who had thought to make us eat.

'If you haven't, I suggest you do, because you may not get a chance for a while. Okay, fellas, on the way up there will be a rolling replenishment of water, rations and respirator canisters. Make sure you all replenish your water! If your pack is full - and I doubt it is - then drink half of it and then fill it back up. Every man jack will take a further twenty-four hours-worth of space food. I don't care if it tastes like shit and you've been eating the flesh off a Chinaman's arse, you take the rations. That means if you've got rations in your daysacks left over from today I suggest you eat them or you'll end up carrying double. Platoon sergeants ensure this happens.'

The enormous sergeant major took a break from his rant to lift his respirator and spit. 'Also, respirator canisters will all be exchanged, including your spare. They have all been exposed to a shit load of dust, which can clog the filters. If you don't exchange your canister and you go man-down, I'll kick the sense out of you before you die. Happy on that?'

We nodded.

'Lads, remember these tunnels aren't completely safe, and we will be moving fast. Stick close together as we patrol to the surface and don't lose eyes on the man in front. If you find yourself separated go firm and activate your distress beacon. Any questions? No? Good. Ev?'

'Sir,' our platoon sergeant responded.

'Mate, let's have a chat. We have found something that belongs to you.'

The three platoon sergeants exchanged puzzled glances and then Sergeant Evans followed the CSM away into the gloom beyond the light sticks scattered about the warehouse.

The OC summarized his orders and asked for the platoon commanders to close in to him for a brief. The boss turned to the remainder of our NCOs. 'Commanders, let's get the blokes squared away, I'll be back with you in five. Be ready to move five minutes after that.'

The platoon busied itself packing away kit and preparing for the replenishment, blokes chugged at their water packs and force fed themselves their horror bags under the watchful eye of the remaining NCOs.

When Sergeant Evans returned to us, his face gave no indication of what he had been told.

'What's the score, Ev?' Westy asked.

'Stevo,' the platoon sergeant said flatly. 'They've found him on the surface.'

'Christ,' I exclaimed, forgetting myself, 'how did he get up there?'

Sergeant Evans looked irritated at the interruption and I blushed beneath my respirator. 'I don't know. But I want to find out.'

The company marched out of the tunnels at a rapid pace. There was no longer the need to keep quiet or minimise chatter, and no need not to bunch up as we moved. We kept close together so not to lose each other in the maze of smaller tunnels and made our way back to the surface.

We were replenished along a main access tunnel that had been used to evacuate casualties. I could tell it had been used for the injured because it was scattered with medical waste, blood soaked bandages and packaging. Clearly a lot of casualties had been through there, I assumed an aid post was probably close to the surface.

Our daysacks were opened for us by a line of conscripts and water poured straight into our water reservoirs using stacks of plastic bottles. Ration packs were unceremoniously chucked into our hands and our respirator canisters ripped out and replaced with new ones. Cool air breezing down from the surface kissed at our necks as we marched onward, up the tunnel toward the surface and away from the wretched warrens that had cost so many of our comrade's lives.

Me and Brown didn't see it coming, let alone Stevo, but Westy saw him where he stood, waiting at the entrance to the warren with the company sergeant major beside him. It was dark outside and I wouldn't have known it was him if it wasn't for my visor display identifying him for me.

'You!' Westy jabbed a finger at him.

Stevo started. 'Westy I …'

The Welshman launched at him, throwing a powerful punch that connected with his respirator mouth piece and sent him sprawling to the ground. Everyone, even the sergeant major stepped back in surprise as Stevo desperately tried to correct the broken seal to his respirator.

'You fucking coward!' Westy gripped Stevo by the collar and lifted him, his biceps bulging through the remaining material of his sleeves as he brought the stunned trooper close to his face. 'You fucking ran, don't you dare fucking lie to me! You fucking ran and you left us to die!'

'That's enough, Corporal,' the sergeant major warned, but Westy ignored him, shaking Stevo furiously like a child would shake a toy.

'Jimmy died because of you! You left him to die, you bastard!' His voice was breaking.

Gingerly I stepped closer and placed a hand on my section commander's shoulder, 'Westy, come on mate, it's not worth it.'

As if suddenly broken from a spell, Westy seemed to become conscious of us all watching him, as well as the disapproving gaze of the sergeant major. He let go of Stevo like his hands had been burnt, allowing the trooper to collapse to the ground in a crumpled heap clutching at his throat.

'They're all dead. All of them.' Westy dropped to his knees and sobbed.

The platoon began to move off again into the night, as we stared at our section commander in disbelief.

I had never had a chance to get to know Westy properly before I was thrust into his section by the sudden and brutal destruction of my own. The men he had commanded and worked with loved him because he loved them back in equal measure. That was his greatest strength, and it seemed, his greatest weakness. I always saw our section commanders to be invincible, gods amongst men. But finally I saw Westy for what he really was, a scared young man who had lost all of his friends.

'Westy, what's going on, mate?' Sergeant Evans emerged from the dark. He was following up the rear of the platoon, in case anybody became separated.

Westy caught his sobs and sniffed. 'Nothing.'

Sergeant Evans knew that Westy was lying. 'Well get up, then, mate. We haven't got the time.'

Westy picked himself up. 'Prepare to move, boys.'

We were still in shock, and murmured the command back to nobody in particular as a natural reflex. Brown helped Stevo up from the ground as we prepared to patrol off again, picking up the rear of the platoon.

'I'll speak to you later, Stevo,' Sergeant Evans said darkly, then to the sergeant major, 'Last man, one platoon.'

'Good, thank you, Sergeant,' the sergeant major replied, then turned to Westy. He spoke three words that carried with them the experience of a man who had seen it all before: 'Carry on, Corporal.'

Westy straightened. 'Yes, Sir. Sorry, Sir.'

'You don't need to be sorry, son, get your men moving.'

'You've got two new blokes,' Sergeant Evans said, pointing toward two troopers who waited amongst the company rendezvous. My visor identified them as Brooks and Daniels, two troopers whose sections hadn't taken casualties and so had men to spare. The company was forming into lines so that it could be re-organised for battle. Troopers chatted quietly in the dark while they waited, and others stared blankly into space, perhaps reliving some moment within the depths of the warrens. Somewhere on the horizon something big was burning and the glow flickered against the clouds.

Westy tapped the details of the two new attachments into his wristpad. 'That puts me up to six,' he said flatly.

Sergeant Evans nodded. 'I also need you to nominate a new 2ic, mate, the ammo's here and I'll need help to sort it.'

Brown was the only obvious choice for Westy to take. He certainly couldn't choose Stevo to be his 2ic, who had run from the Chinese in the tunnels, not stopping until he was collared trying to escape through one of the warrens many openings to the surface. He couldn't choose Brooks or Daniels, who he didn't even know and who I suspected weren't senior to Brown anyway.

'Moralee.' Westy pointed to me, and my jaw dropped. Instantly I looked across to Brown, expecting him to explode, but the darkness hid his expression beneath his visor, and he said nothing.

I made to protest, but was abruptly cut short by Sergeant Evans. 'Come on, then, Moralee. Let's get your ammo.'

I followed him gloomily into the centre of the rendezvous, where the CSM and his work party were unloading ammunition from a buggy and placing it into three distinctive piles, one for each platoon. Troopers scurried about the piles taking ammo away and returning the empty crates under the supervision of their platoon sergeants.

'Westy will keep a close eye on you,' Sergeant Evans said, counting out the crates and separating the different ammunition types. 'Any dramas or questions, you ask him, or me.'

'Yes, Sergeant,' I said, withering under his gaze. He hated me, and probably wondered why on earth Westy had chosen me to be his 2ic. I was wondering the same thing.

The tall platoon sergeant held up two fingers. 'Two things I want you to be all over: *ammunition* and *casualties*,' he stressed each word. 'Make sure you're constantly checking and updating your ammo state so I have a constant feed. Ensure that casualties are reported up the chain instantly, the more information you get up the better. Don't rely on the casualty information passed up automatically by their wristpads, physically check.'

'Yes, Sergeant,' I said grimly.

He dropped several crates at my feet. 'That's your lot. There's a salvaged mammoth on the buggy too, so you'll have two guns again.' He paused, remembering something, and took a commander's wristpad out from his daysack. 'I almost forgot, you'll need this.'

I took the wristpad and carefully turned it over in my hands as if I had never seen one before. It was the same as the one that I wore, but had many other functions tailored specifically to commanders. It was Sam's, and Chammy's before that.

'Upload me your ammo state when you know it,' he said, and he was gone, in search of the other two section 2ics.

I realised that Brown was behind me, watching me blankly. I wasn't sure if I should expect to fight, and when Brown made no move I threw up my arms. 'Why me?'

Brown shrugged. 'Why not you?'

'I'm a *crow*!' I hissed. 'Nobody's been in as short a time as me!' I pointed a finger at Stevo, who was sat on his daysack staring at the ground. 'Stevo's senior to me by four years!'

'He's also a coward,' Brown retorted. 'God only knows what he did to get Jimmy killed.'

'You're senior to me.'

Brown sighed. 'By what, a few months?'

'But you're still senior,' I insisted. 'Who's gonna do what I tell them? I'm no good.'

'What about what happened in the tunnels?'

'What?'

'When we got hit and you charged the pinkies? Then when you lead that attack in the hanger? Have you not seen how the lads look at you now?'

I shook my head, not sure where Brown was going with it.

'They're in awe of you. They're saying that the darts parted around you like you were being protected by God or something. They say you charged the pinkies with so much rage that they broke and run.'

I sneered, 'That's a load of shit and you know it. What about what happened on Challenger, doesn't that bother you? What about Woody?'

Brown laughed harshly. 'Who cares about Woody, anymore? What happened on Challenger is history. We're in a war zone, Moralee.'

'I thought you wanted to climb up the ranks. Wasn't that what being mates with Woody was all about?' I almost flinched, expecting for Brown to lash out.

Brown simply sighed. 'Maybe. Look, I'm a follower, not a leader,' Brown said. 'And God knows my moral compass leads me off course. Maybe you aren't the best choice for 2ic, but if it's out of the five of us it has to be you.'

Defeated, I sighed. 'Fuck.'

Brown grinned, his teeth just visible in the dark. 'Yeah.'

'Well,' I paused, thinking, 'give me a hand with the ammo?' I half expected him to walk off.

'No problem,' he said, and he began to strip open the crates that lay at our feet. 'You know I heard the boss was talking about writing you and Sam up? You may get medals for that charge you did.'

This time it was me who laughed harshly. 'Who cares about medals? We'll be lucky if we get off this rock, and I certainly don't deserve any medals.'

'Does anybody deserve a medal for this war? Better you than someone else.'

We worked for at least an hour, re-distributing ammunition and equipment. The replacement mammoth gun was given to Brooks, with Brown still carrying the other, but there was no grenade launcher other than the one carried by Westy. Sam had the other, but through the chaos he had been evacuated with it and there was little chance or time for us to get it back.

I had a chance to see a medic for my arm, which was just as well as he told me I was risking blood poisoning from not cleaning it properly.

'You've got to clean the clotting agent out or it won't heal,' the medic told me sternly. I winced as he cleaned out the wound with a white gloved hand. 'We've got enough to deal with without you lot not looking after yourselves.'

'I was kind of busy,' I replied curtly, but the medic only laughed.

'Haven't we all, mate, haven't we all.'

I was about to tell him where to go, until I noticed the blood that coated his combats.

'What's it like in the aid post?' I asked, wondering what conditions my wounded comrades had to endure. I hoped that Peters had survived, along with Greggerson and Sam. Supposedly the aid post, once fully established, was as good as any medical facility on our ships, since it remained too dangerous to attempt to leave the atmosphere with casualties. If troopers knew they would be cared for if they were injured, they would fight better, and so medical treatment was a high priority.

The medic shook his head as he finished packing the gouge in my arm and began to wrap it with a bandage. 'I don't know, mate. I'm a combat medic, I hand the casualties over before I get anywhere near that far back.'

'Oh.'

The medic smiled. 'You're new, right?'

'Yeah.' *Was it that obvious?*

'And carrying a commander's wristpad already?' He nodded at my forearm. 'Either you're awesome, or things aren't going so well.'

I bristled, who was he to talk like it was all some big cosmic joke? Friends of mine had died.

The medic noticed my annoyance and patted my good arm. 'I meant no harm, mate,' he smiled.

I let the medic finish wrapping my arm without a word. When he was finished he patted my shoulder gently.

'There you are, mate, good as new.'

'Thanks.'

'You're welcome. Hopefully I won't see you again.'

It took me a second to understand what he meant. 'Yeah, hopefully,' I hesitated … 'What's it like, being a medic?'

'Like dying a little bit every hour,' he said sadly, and then he was gone to his next patient. I watched as the blood-soaked medic changed his gloves and got back to his work.

18: The Trenches

When you have a digital clock in the corner of your visio it can be hard not to find yourself just staring at it slowly ticking the seconds away into minutes and then hours. We were sat in our dropship for a long time, having loaded not long after my arm was bandaged. We were thrown about as it rapidly and unpredictably manoeuvred itself across the surface of New Earth.

Westy kept us briefed on what the dropship crew were doing, moving to the rear of the 2nd Danish Gravtank Battalion as they swept across the rolling hills of Jersey Island's coast, probing forward, waiting, probing again. Although we could have probably covered the length of the island in only a couple of minutes we were taking hours to cover only a couple of kilometres. Occasionally the company would stop and dismount into the dark on some lonely hillside only to scan with our smart launchers and visors for what seemed like hours on end, watching grey clouds slowly drift across the ink black sky.

'How long do you think this will go on for?' I asked Westy as we loaded back into the dropship for the umpteenth time.

'I dunno,' Westy replied flatly, 'it's only a few kilometres between Hill Bravo and the city, but we're sort of hooking around to the western flank in a big circle.'

'It's doing my head in,' I complained to nobody in particular. 'Let's just get on with it.'

'No point in rushing death, mate,' Westy said ominously, and Brooks gulped. Apparently Brooks and Daniels had been very lucky up until then, their sections had - through nobody's fault - avoided most of the combat in the tunnels and they appeared nervous.

Every now and then the dropship vibrated as it fired a burst of Vulcan at something. Westy would warn us of incoming missiles, but there's little you can do about it except pray to your God and hope for the best.

Westy had been quiet since his outburst, barely speaking unless to tell us what was going on. He wouldn't even make eye contact with us if he could help it, and we respected his need for space. Stevo did his best to pretend not to exist, so as not to further enrage the Welshman. I wondered what he had done to cause the death of the section's old MAM-G gunner Jimmy, and decided that when the time was right I would ask Westy.

'Are you Moralee?' Brooks asked after a prolonged period - during which we sat in the crew compartment in silence. I nodded, slightly irritated by the question. Surely he knew my name from his visor display.

'*The* Moralee?' Daniels' eyes widened.

'Yes,' I replied curtly, beginning to become annoyed. Brown grinned.

'We've heard about you,' Brooks said. 'You saved the company.'

'I wouldn't go that far, there were others with me.'

'Who were they?' They were eager for a story. Troopers were obsessed with rumours and tall tales. They thrived upon it.

'Sam Wakefield,' I said, remembering my old section 2ic. I wished he was in the dropship with us, so that the responsibility no longer rested on my shoulders. He could have done the job with his eyes closed, but instead he was somewhere in the medical chain, along with Greggerson, Peters and many, many others.

'What happened to him, then?'

Westy bristled. 'Shut up, Brooks.'

Brooks looked down to the ground like a scolded child and the crew compartment fell back into silence. I went back to watching the clock on my visor display ticking the seconds away until battle would resume.

Finally, after what seemed like an age, the dropship came to a halt and its door lowered for the last time.

'That's us at the drop-off point,' Westy told us all as we dismounted into the dark, our visors instantly flicking to night vision as we did so. We weren't to dismount straight into the battle this time. Jersey City was just shy of five kilometres away to our East and we would make the rest of the journey on foot. In the darkness I could see the three platoons that formed the company all exiting their dropships and preparing to move off.

'Happy, Moralee?' I realised Westy had taken a knee beside me in the gloom.

'Yeah,' I lied. *Why couldn't Brown be 2ic?*

'I need you to bring up the rear of the section, just to make sure nobody wanders off,' he said. It was often standard procedure at night for 2ics to be at or near the rear of their sections just in case the unthinkable happened and somebody somehow disappeared, but I was pretty sure he was talking about Stevo.

'No worries,' I replied.

Westy nodded toward the first platoon of the company to move off into the night. 'That's us off, then.'

'Yeah.'

'What's your first name, Moralee?'

Nobody had wanted to know my first name since Climo, and I was honoured that a section commander would want to know it. 'Andy,' I said.

'You've had a shit time here, Andy,' Westy said, and waited for my reply, but I said nothing. 'You did well in the tunnels. It was noticed.'

So many had died or been wounded, it felt criminal to accept any form of praise. I said nothing and finally Westy nodded, accepting that silence was my reply. He clapped a hand on my shoulder.

'Let's get this done, then, Andy.'

We patrolled into the night, toward Jersey City.

We patrolled for over an hour in pitch darkness until we reached a forward slope that covered us from the last kilometre of open ground to Jersey City. In the green image created by my visor's night vision I could see the other platoons forming up on the slope.

I could hear the sound of our fire support from somewhere off to our northern flank, and a quick glance over to my left allowed my visor to mark the fire support location with a hollow blue square and a number to indicate the range, two kilometres. The fire support was too far away for me to make it out, or for my target computer to bother marking the passage of any ammunition, but I knew which weapons were being used by their sound. Vulcan from a distance could be mistaken for the sound of a power drill cutting through a wall, as it fired so rapidly. Rail guns would make a thumping sound from far away, caused by overpressure created by the magnetised round as it exited the barrel, and would then be followed not long after by a *whump* noise that announced its impact upon its intended target.

We were part of a great deception plan cooked up by the brigade commander, we had been told. Several battalions of dropships and squadrons of gravtanks had encircled the city and had begun pounding it with everything they had, softening the enemy ready for the dropships to charge in with their troopers to finish the job. The Chinese, who would have monitored our movements, would be ready for us. But the dropship charge was never going to come, because the 4th battalion - us - were coming in on foot. We had been dropped off by the dropships as they moved to surround the city. The enemy had no reason to suspect that the dropships would unload their troops several kilometres away, instead they would have seen a unit taking a tactical pause to consider its next move for no more than a few minutes.

Westy took a knee twenty metres from the top of the slope and we formed up behind him in a straight line. Brown and Stevo were with the section commander in Charlie, and I took my place with my Delta fire team behind them. I motioned with my palm for Daniels and Brooks to spread out, they seemed to be drawn close to me and each other like they were magnetised. Bunching together just made you a tasty target for smart missiles and risked the destruction of an entire section, instead of one or two individuals, but those two just didn't seem to get it. To be honest I didn't care much for their love affair with each other, they were just two more

troopers I expected to die very soon, but I had to try to keep them alive for as long as I could. The burden of responsibility for their safety hung heavily upon my shoulders.

I adjusted my knee position away from a rock that was digging into the bone through my armour, having to put my hand down to the hard, stony ground to stop me from toppling over. My kit was light as it ever was, but my tired, aching muscles protested with every movement I made, even something as simple as balancing in the kneeling position had become an effort. My arm, slowly healing under a fresh dressing, throbbed more than ever. I was tired, as we all were, perhaps because we sensed that it was almost all over, one way or another.

A cold, fresh wind breezed against my neck; it was minus one that night, an improvement on the previous night but still enough to cut into my skin through my damaged armour. I shivered.

Twenty metres to our front the slope crested and the ground disappeared beyond it. Above us the clouded sky occasionally flickered with light as unmanned aircraft duelled out of sight and well out of range. I knew from our orders that the ground beyond to the east dropped gently away down toward the city, with a few small hills and streams that offered very little, if any cover at all. To our north was a large high feature which had been appropriately named Table-top Hill for its rectangular plateau. Fire support had been located upon the hill and was largely composed of gravtanks and a few infantry-based artillery platforms. To our west rolling hills and deep valleys had allowed us to approach out of sight in the dead ground, but once we moved over the slope that cover would be no more and we would be at the mercy of the Chinese.

'Westy, in position,' Westy announced over the platoon net. As the section 2ic now, I could listen in to platoon net chatter at the same time as the section intercom.

The other two section commanders reported that they too were ready. They crouched in lines parallel to ours that ran back down the slope.

'Roger that,' the boss answered rather un-enthusiastically. 'H-Hour-plus-five in thirty seconds.'

I glanced briefly at the digital clock on my visor display. 'H' hour had been when the fire support had moved into position to engage and we had begun to form up on the slope. At H-plus-five minutes, the hulking battleship Hamburg would begin its barrage from high in orbit down onto the battlefield. It had two tasks, one of which played its part within the brigadier's deception plan. Its primary target would be the Chinese anti-air defences and other key positions within and around the city, but it would also drop a few bombs short into the open ground between them and us. The resulting craters would create a route for us to use to push across to the city without being cut to ribbons. The pinkies, whose attention would be diverted to the dropships forming up around the city, would never notice the dismounted troops creeping forward through the smouldering craters until it was too late - in theory.

We waited in silence. My heart pumped against my ribcage and tendons tensed across my body in anticipation. Explosions from within the city thumped like the beating of drums.

'Five seconds,' the boss said.

I looked back at Daniels and Brooks; they were both staring toward the sky. The silly bastards should have been observing outwards for enemy infiltration, and I thought to give them a shout to pay attention to the task at hand, but instead I turned my head up to the sky to watch the initiation of our assault onto Jersey City.

'Rounds in the air, rounds in the air!' the boss warned. We watched on.

The clouds flashed brightly as the first round broke through into the atmosphere, burning at temperatures as hot as a sun as it streaked toward the ground like a meteor. It disappeared behind the top of the slope just as another dropped from the sky.

The flash from the impact was not as spectacular as that of the round's entry to the atmosphere, but it was the sound of the explosion that followed seconds later that told of its power.

The blast knocked several troopers over, and caused me to have to put my hand down again to steady myself from falling too. A layer of New Earth dust leapt a few centimetres off the ground and then carried away with the wind.

Whump! Another round. *Whump! Whump!*

I placed both hands down and knelt on both of my knees as the barrage continued.

Daniels cursed behind me. I guessed he had fallen over, but didn't look. Clouds of smoke and ash billowed into the sky.

You have to see and feel an orbital bombardment at close range to believe how truly awesome it is. I had seen it before, but never so close. I stared in fascination at the spectacle, forgetting myself.

The bombardment went on for several minutes until the order to prepare to move was given by the platoon commander.

'Prepare to move,' Westy copied onto the section intercom. I pulled myself together; taking a grip of my rifle again with both hands and looking to check my fire team were okay. We checked our safety catches and pouches instinctively.

'We will move off behind two platoon,' the boss ordered. 'Jonesy, acknowledge.'

One section's section commander answered, 'Roger.'

'Two platoon is moving off now.'

Sure enough a line of troopers was running up between the dropships and over the slope a hundred metres to my right.

For a few seconds I felt a wave of fear as I realised I was going back into harm's way again. I fought it away, reminding myself that I had lost so many of my nine lives already; I was probably a dead man anyway. After what I had been through it was probably better that way. How could I go home to Earth, to Portsmouth and my family having seen and done what I had done? I was a million miles from home, both physically and in my mind. That horrible world of pain and misery was where I belonged, and it was where I believed I would die.

'That's one section moving off now, two section follow on!'

We picked ourselves up and ran after our lead section in single file, passing more waiting troopers and cresting the top of the slope.

On that dark night Jersey City appeared menacing. As it came into view I saw great black pillars of smoke that drifted slowly off into the wind. From amongst black silhouetted buildings small fires burned and sparks showered from the impact of rail gun shells.

The dark shadows of troopers dropped away from me in a straight line into the low ground that separated us from the city. In my image intensified view I could identify the craters created by Hamburg. There were loads of them, and we were dropping down into them for cover.

The warship's bombardment had finished, I noticed. She had completed her task over the city, but there were many other tasks for her elsewhere, as the remaining brigades of the division pushed north to force the enemy off of Jersey Island completely. We just weren't high enough a priority for her to stay. The thought left a bitter taste, so I pushed it to the back of my mind as I ran.

'Stay close, lads.' The platoon commander was panting from up front with the lead section. 'Make sure your boys don't drop back, I can't afford a split platoon!'

I wondered when to expect the first round of incoming; surely the pinkies had noticed the company coming over the slope? I sped up as I approached the first crater, eager to get myself out of line of sight from the city. It was a good twenty or so metres across and five deep, I estimated, smouldering and glowing in places. I leapt down into the crater, skidding on loose rocks when I landed. I was very conscious that if I was to fall on my arse it wouldn't kill me, but the glowing hot rocks would really hurt, and probably damage my armour.

'Close up!' Westy ordered from the far side of the crater. My visor indicated him for me and I headed straight for him, my boots crunching the churned earth.

I moved right up behind Brown and then counted Daniels and Brooks as they came in. 'All here, Westy.'

'Okay, cheers,' he replied. 'Boss, this is Westy, that's my lads in.'

'Roger.' The boss was right up on the edge of the crater, presumably watching two platoon bound forward into their next piece of cover as quickly as they could. The ground was flat as a pancake on the approach to the city and Hamburg didn't have enough shells to make us a trench out of craters that ran all the way into the city.

'Close right up, lads, stay low,' Westy ordered. 'Better down here than up there.'

I wasn't so sure I agreed, on the one side we were exposed and easy targets in the open ground, but on the other we were bunched together like sardines in the crater. One smart missile would have us all going home in boxes.

'I can't believe the pinkies haven't worked out what we're doing,' Brown said to nobody in particular.

'Fire support must have them distracted,' I said. The Chinese should easily have been able to spot us, but they had been hacked at by rail guns and Vulcan, and then battered by an orbital barrage. All of their attention was diverted away from us, or at least that was what we were hoping.

'We will bound forward through two platoon to the next bit of cover, one, two, three sections acknowledge.' The boss looked down into the crater and waited for the commanders to answer up over the intercom.

'One, roger.'

'Two.'

'Three.'

'Let's go.'

We scrabbled up the side of the crater using our rifles like walking sticks so as not to put our hands on the scorched earth. On Uralis some of our instructors would probably have had a fit over such a terrible misuse of our rifles, but if one of us had a negligent discharge and shot himself, he would probably have done himself a favour anyway.

'This is pump,' I heard somebody say as we ran across the open ground toward two platoon's crater a hundred metres ahead, and I smiled grimly. The universal phrase of the English speaking armies was never so much of an understatement as it was on New Earth!

As if to show us all that things could always get worse, it began to rain. Droplets of water bounced off my visor as I ran behind Brown and the rest of the platoon.

'You've got to be kidding me.' I cursed at the rain as we went firm in another crater. The boss put one section up on the forward edge to observe, as our sister platoon leap-frogged past us.

'*Wouldn't have it any other way,*' Brown replied sarcastically, quoting a phrase loved by drop trooper instructors. 'If it ain't raining it ain't training.'

'Well it ain't training is it?' I retorted, but Brown's sarcasm cheered me.

We continued to move across the open ground taking turns to move as platoons, with the third platoon that made up the company bringing up the rear a bound behind us. Sometimes we would find natural cover to occupy, like a small hill or river bank, sometimes we would use the craters, and other times we would be forced to spread ourselves out in the open and just hope for the best.

As we drew closer the buildings at the western edge of the city became distinguishable. It was still half a kilometre away, but nevertheless I thanked God for every ten metres we covered without drawing enemy fire, the closer we were, the less ground we would have to cover when it all went noisy.

We were a good three hundred metres away from the city when it went noisy - and God did it do just that.

Two platoon came under contact from only a hundred metres to their front. I heard the crack of gunfire, and my visor marked the passage of enemy darts with red lines that streaked between the advancing troopers and through the bodies of others, their shadowy figures crumpling to the ground. It was hard to tell though who had been hit and who was simply taking cover.

We were exposed and in the open, and two platoon - who were to our forward left - were directly between us and the contact point. Even with our modern targeting systems the risk of blue-on-blue was too great to risk. We hugged the ground as Westy cursed over the roar of the rain and gunfire. Little rocks dug into my ribs and belly where I lay, but I ignored them, my eyes fixed on the unfortunate platoon as they reacted to the contact.

However unfortunate they were, they had obviously anticipated and prepared for contact on the route in as we had, and they reacted fast. As soon as the troopers were down the wind carried the sound of a section commander giving his fire control order, his bellowing voice focusing his trooper's fire where he wanted it and taking control of the fire fight.

The battlefield erupted with gunfire as two platoon's lead section began to suppress their enemy, but we still could not assist them. Unable to give fire support we could only watch and listen whilst Westy swore. He shouted at nobody in particular, not in fear but dismay at the situation we had found ourselves in. 'Boss, it's Westy, I can't engage from here, we need to move!'

The Welshman's voice was urgent and almost an order, but the boss was having none of it. His response was abrupt and left no room for argument: 'No, wait.'

To the right of where me and the rest of the section lay in cover, the boss was watching the contact unfold intently. He would be listening to the contact report sent by two platoon's commander on the company net, a communication channel even higher than the one I was now able to listen to, and planning how best to assault if needed. I was beginning to trust our platoon commander, and I was beginning to realise that he was making decisions that many of us would be too afraid to make. I sometimes wonder what might have happened had he sent two section to Corporal Evans' aid before his section was wiped out, would the entire platoon have been destroyed before the gravtank reached us? I think Westy trusted the boss too, because he stopped cursing after that.

'There is a trench and burrow system a hundred metres to our front,' the boss announced across the section intercoms. 'Two platoon are going to affect the …' An almighty explosion cut him short. Sparks flew from the direction of the enemy trenches, and I could swear I heard the scream of a Chinese soldier. Vulcan raked the ground in front of us. 'Two platoon are going to affect the break in with fire support from the gravtanks,' he continued as we were showered in tiny stones blown into the air by the blast. 'We will then echelon through them and assault onto depth positions.'

I could already make out two platoon fire and manoeuvring forward toward the trenches, each trooper zigzagging as he ran before taking cover again and firing. Grenades and smart missiles were fired into the trenches as the platoon bounded forward, steeling whatever initiative the enemy had.

The pinkies had been caught off guard, upon being bombarded from orbit they had retreated into their burrows for safety and had only just returned to their positions by the time we were upon them. Instead of giving them a position to fight us from, they had instead given us some cover to occupy, so long as we could get into the trench system and clear it.

The break in was announced by a string of grenades detonating from within the trenches. I could tell they were hand thrown grenades by the sound they made, much louder than their rifle launched counterpart. They were shortly followed by rapid gunfire, as the troopers who had thrown the grenades stormed into the trench and laid waste to any stunned or wounded enemy they came across.

Unable to help our comrades in their assault we lay motionless, looking into the dark city skyline for enemy depth positions, or worse an attack from the flanks.

I looked across at Brown to the right of where I lay. He gave me a thumbs-up, which I returned. A glance back at Daniels and Brooks, who lay in fire positions to my left, confirmed that they weren't dead.

We were in a terrible position as a platoon, completely exposed in open ground with nowhere to go. I felt very vulnerable, keeping my body as low as I could get it, however little good it might do me.

'I don't like this,' Stevo warned. 'We should withdraw and come in a different way.'

'Shut up, Stevo,' me and Westy chorused almost comically. I understood and shared his fear, but his constant whining had become irritating.

It didn't take long before the boss was back on the intercom. 'Right lads, listen in. Two platoon has made their break in and are now clearing through the trench system. Fire support has eyes onto the trench system now.'

I was shocked that the fire support group, what with all their optical equipment and vantage point, hadn't had eyes on earlier. We already knew of trench systems and warrens off to the north and east of the city, but how we hadn't noticed a trench system on our route of approach, considering we had orbital top cover and aircraft operating overhead, was a mystery. *Somebody somewhere had clearly made a mistake,* I thought.

'There are more trenches to our front, so we are going to crawl toward them until we're either contacted or we are close enough to assault. One, two, three acknowledge.'

'One.'

'Two.'

'Three.'

'The enemy are either too distracted by two platoon or simply haven't seen us. Either way we will take advantage of the situation. Enforce battlefield discipline, not a peep from the blokes and they stay flat to the deck, Ev acknowledge.'

'Roger,' Sergeant Evans answered from somewhere at the back of the platoon. 'You take a casualty leave them to me and the reserve to pick up. Don't throw away momentum if a bloke goes man down, lads, or you'll get spanked in the open.'

The platoon commander gave the last of his instructions. 'One and two section will bring up the front. Three stay back with Ev in reserve. Let's go.'

We crawled forward on our bellies in a long extended line made up of two sections side by side, with ours on the left and Corporal Jones' section on the right, maintaining a five metre gap between each man. The move forward was painfully slow and rapidly became exhausting. My respirator motors whirred as they battled to keep my visor from fogging up due to my heavy breathing.

After what felt like an age of crawling, I noticed that directly in front of me the sea of green was dissected by a dark black line that ran off in either direction. I knew it was the trench and stopped.

'It's right in front of us,' I whispered to Westy.

'Yeah, roger that, I see it. Go firm lads.'

My heart was racing, and not just from the exertion of the crawl. The opening to the trench was as silent and menacing as the gaping tunnel that had led us into the warrens. A few hundred metres to my left the shouting and gunfire continued as two platoon continued their clearance, and I knew that soon that would be us. To my left, a kilometre or so away, the fire support continued their onslaught, while ahead of me the once beautiful Jersey City burned once more. A friendly saucer swooped over the city, dropping its payload in a string of explosions.

Like my old section had done in the farmland ditches, we waited in comparative calm, as if we sat within the eye of a storm, untouched but surrounded by its destruction. I clutched my rifle tightly, its weight and bulk was reassuring. I often seemed to clutch and squeeze my rifle when I was scared, I realised. Like a child does his teddy, I thought, and chuckled quietly to myself. It was a pretty odd time to start finding things funny, but then if you didn't laugh you could only cry I suppose.

I rolled to my side quietly and then gently unbuckled a grenade from its pouch around my waist. I brought it up in front of me, removing the safety pin and priming the dial to two seconds. I didn't want too much delay on detonation in case somebody down inside the trench saw it and threw it back. I glanced to my left and right, checking the others were in line with me.

'Andy, grenade, set the time short,' Westy whispered so quietly the intercom barely carried his message.

'Roger.' It was already in my hand. I knew what had to be done.

'Boss?' Westy was asking for permission to assault.

'Wait for one section,' was the reply.

'One section is ready.' Jonesy's message came only seconds after. We were set to assault.

A burst of gunfire sounded off to my right, causing me to jump. It had come from the trench. A foreign voice shouted something.

'Contact!' a voice screamed over the rain, and the right hand side of our line began to fire into the trench. The Chinese had heard us.

'Contact, contact!' Jonesy's voice was fast and barely intelligible over the intercom; he had been surprised and was flapping.

'Man down!'

'Two section, GO!' the boss ordered without hesitation.

'Do it, Andy!'

I tossed the grenade. As it left my hand the mechanical fly off lever sprung away from the main body, activating the timer. My headset beeped as a warning, as everyone else's would as the grenade bounced and rolled into the trench along with another grenade thrown by Westy.

The two grenades detonated almost simultaneously, and like an athlete waiting for the gun to set him free at the start line, I bolted forward.

I didn't shout or make a sound as I charged for the kill, I knew now that there was no need. Instead I ran forward in silence, not giving the enemy the chance to hear me as I closed in with him.

I crouched at the lip of the trench, my rifle up in the shoulder. There was a man curled into a ball at the bottom ten metres to my right. I couldn't make much out through my visor, but I was pretty certain he was dead. Brown put a couple of darts into him anyway.

We slid down into the trench on our arses, keen to get out of the open as the fire fight around us intensified. A deep puddle of water splashed beneath my boots as I landed.

The trench looked recently constructed; it had no drainage and hadn't been sandbagged to prevent the walls from crumbling. It was just under shoulder height and about as wide as a warren tunnel.

'Boss,' Westy panted, 'we're in, one enemy dead!'

'Roger, see if you can get your section round to attack the enemy in front of Jonesy from the left flank.' The boss was urgent, but hadn't lost his cool.

'Roger,' Westy looked to me. 'Andy, keep our rear covered and move up with me.'

'Okay, mate,' I nodded and turned to my fire team. 'Daniels, cover the rear. Brooks, watch out toward the city, in case the pinkies try to come in from the top. Got it?'

'Okay,' Daniels replied. They moved up toward me and took their respective positions, covering out over the top of the trench and to the rear.

The section moved quickly along the trench. The lead pair moved in a similar fashion to the lead pair in Warren clearance, with one at the front in a half crouch and one stood off to the side, both able to fire in the enclosed space. Westy had paired himself with Brown at the front; he didn't trust Stevo. I'm not sure if I did either.

Between me and the lead pair Stevo walked, scanning over the top of the trench like my fire team did behind me. A section can become too focused with trench clearance and forget the bigger battle; there is nothing to stop the enemy assaulting back into the trench from above. It was as important to keep eyes on outside the trench as it was within.

The trench turned to the right and then almost immediately back to the left. But as soon as we rounded the second corner Westy and Brown opened fire.

'Shit!' Westy cursed as the pair almost fell over each other in their effort to get back around the corner. A spray of darts peppered the rocky wall where they had stood only moments ago.

Westy held his rifle around the corner and launched a grenade. Even with the grenade being guided, and the rifle optics being connected to his visor I doubted his accuracy, but thankfully the grenade detonated within the trench and not on top of Jonesy and his section.

'There's loads of the bastards,' Westy shouted back to me.

'Pinkies in the open!' Brooks shouted suddenly. 'Running away!'

I raised my head and looked over the top of the trench. Sure enough, enemy were running away from where Westy had fired his grenade, probably three or four of them. One was limping.

'Well shoot them, then,' I ordered, angered at his stupidity. Did he really need me to tell him?

'Okay,' Brooks opened fire with his mammoth, cutting two of the soldiers down with a single sustained burst.

I looked to my left and saw that Stevo was just staring at me.

'Stevo, fucking shoot them!'

Stevo jolted, as if waking up from a dream. He took aim and fired. It was a turkey shoot, none survived.

'If you see enemy run away, they're not running off to get the next shuttle to Beijing,' I spat scornfully.

'Sorry, Andy,' Brooks sounded hurt, but he got the message, no mercy. Stevo said nothing.

'I'm going again, Andy,' Westy said and he rounded the corner along with Brown before I could reply and fired up the trench. 'Boss, this is Westy, I'm clearing along your front now, do not fire, do not fire!'

'Roger,' the boss answered. 'I can see you.' His own visor would mark our progress.

We followed Westy around the corner and further up the trench, stepping over bodies as we went. I stabbed each with my bayonet as I passed them, just to be sure, heartlessly and systematically. Stevo glanced back at one of the bodies and then at me, as if in surprise at my actions. I suspected behind his visor his face would be one of horror or disgust. Perhaps mine should have been too.

'Be aware I'm sending Jonesy forward to you,' the boss warned.

'Friendly forces coming in from the south,' I repeated to the lads.

As we pushed ever forward Jonesy emerged over the top of the trench ten or so metres behind us, crawling over the lip and slipping down to the ground with a splash. He hurried his men to come down. Sergeant Evans chattered on the intercom with the boss about bringing casualties forward and into the trench, but I was too busy to hear how many there were.

The trench turned to the left at a sharp angle and Westy paused at the bend whilst Brown prepped a grenade. He wasn't going to make the same mistake again.

Suddenly darts cracked over my head, and somebody punched me on the helmet. That's what it felt like, anyway. I span like a ballerina on one foot and then landed in a heap on the floor.

'Contact left!' Daniels screamed, and Brooks fired a burst over the lip of the trench.

The section stood up along the trench and fired at an unseen enemy. I lay face up at the bottom of the trench and watched as the boys fought, my body in shock. I felt cold water running down my back and soaking into my armour.

A respirator appeared in front of me, scaring me half to death until I realised it was attached to a comrade's head. My dazed mind could faintly recognise the features behind the visor screen.

'You okay, Andy? Andy!' It was Brown, his brow furrowed in concern.

'I'm okay…' I said cautiously. 'I think.'

Brown ran his hands over my respirator and then round the back of my head, searching for blood or holes as above us the fire fight continued. Boots slapped in the water as a section of troopers charged past us.

'I think I'm alright, mate,' I repeated.

Brown shook his head disbelievingly. 'It hit you, I saw you go down!' Eventually he checked my helmet, and stopped. 'Jesus Christ, mate!'

'What?' I was worried. I felt fine, what could possibly be wrong with me?

'There's a chunk missing from your helmet, mate! Some pinkie must have missed you by a centimetre!' Brown sounded amazed.

I felt the side of my helmet. Sure enough, a deep gouge ran along the side where a round had struck and deflected slightly away from my head. How the impact hadn't broken my neck I'll never know.

Brown laughed. 'Get up, you lizard.' He was genuinely relieved, and his relief raised my spirits so much that I laughed with him.

'Andy, get up here and suppress!' Westy hollered. 'Let's go!'

As I picked myself up I could see three section crawling into the trench where Jonesy's section had entered, dragging with them the platoon casualties. Sergeant Evans shouted orders at them.

I took aim over the top of the trench to see what we were firing at. My visor could only identify enemy a few hundred metres off to my left, and they appeared to be locked into a fire fight with two platoon. The whole section was engaging a much closer trench twenty metres to our front, but I couldn't make out any enemy along its length; they were probably keeping their heads down. Meanwhile Jonesy's section had been sent to attempt to clear the rest of our trench to the right, and potentially come around and attack the enemy in front of us from the flank.

Troopers were getting through their magazines quickly, every time one was expended, the firer took cover to change it, instinctively shouting 'magazine!' to warn his comrades that he was out of the fire fight.

We were firing rapid, which amounts to about one round every two seconds. It's the fastest accurate rate of fire that could still allow the firer to recover his aim after the weapon's recoil. The only drama with rapid fire was the speed you could get through ammunition. Maintenance of the section ammunition was the section 2ic's main role in combat, and that meant me.

I crouched low and tapped on my wristpad screen, which then glowed dimly from behind droplets of rain. The rain had washed off most of the blood.

'Daniels, how many mags have you fired?' I called over the intercom.

'One!'

'Brooks?'

'Two!'

With each response I tapped figures into the wristpad to get my final total of magazines and mammoth available to my section. The final total would then be sent up to the platoon sergeant who maintained a constant vigil on the platoon's ammunition totals. He could then request a resupply from the company sergeant major when needed, or redistribute the ammunition within the sections, giving more to where it was needed. Apparently the Chinese used a fully automated electronic system that managed their ammunition, making platoon sergeants and sergeant majors little more than glorified medics and anti-air sentries. Our electronic warfare teams had a field day with it.

I sent my total up to Sergeant Evans and then stood back up to join in with the battle.

'Westy, we've cleared the rest of our trench,' the boss was panting over the intercom. 'I'm taking one section around to assault the trench in front of you, be aware of friendlies to your front and prepare to switch fire. You should see my forward line now!' The boss was panting again. He would be up with Jonesy's section, the platoon commander always stuck close to the front of the battle, as all good leaders should.

Our visors clearly marked the friendly troopers as they moved along our front and into our arc of fire.

'Switch, fire left!' I shouted over the intercom. The section repeated the order and obeyed, switching their suppressive fire to further along the trench. Wherever the enemy were, they weren't coming up to play, which meant we were doing our job.

A grenade detonated in the enemy held trench, followed by bursts of gunfire. I heard Jonesy shouting for someone to move.

'Check fire, check fire!' the boss shouted and we obeyed, repeating the command onto our own section intercom.

'Observe your arcs, boys!' Westy ordered.

We watched over the top of the trench for one section's progress, and more importantly any further enemy positions within the trench system. I could see two helmets poking out, identified as friendly by my visor.

'That was mental,' Brown exclaimed, elation in his voice. I shared his sentiment, even though the battle was far from over I was in good cover and I was alive. However brief it might be we could take a breather.

'Mate, I thought that was me,' I said, feeling the gouge in my helmet.

'So did I, mate, you went down like a sack of shit! Ha-ha!'

'Why are you laughing, mate?' I asked, with mock hurt.

'Er … coz you're a sack of shit?'

Everyone laughed, including Westy, which was unusual; I hadn't really heard him laugh or joke since we left Challenger.

'Ev, it's the boss, keep Westy back in reserve and send up three section, please.'

'Roger, they're already on their way. Westy! Keep your section where they are, I need a work party to extract casualties!' Casualty extraction was part of the 2ic's job, and that meant me.

'No worries,' Westy looked to me. 'Take two, mate.'

I chose Brown and Daniels because I couldn't take both mammoths away from Westy and I didn't trust Stevo. We ran back to the entry point, where Sergeant Evans and his launchers remained with the casualties. Three section charged past us on their way into the battle. No doubt there would be depth positions within the trench system, plus there had to at least be a couple of burrows as well.

Sergeant Evans waited with the casualties while his two smart gunners scanned the skies. 'Moralee, you need to hand these casualties over to the sergeant major. Happy?'

I glanced down at the casualties; one had been shot through the stomach, and looked in a very bad way, barely conscious, probably through loss of blood. His stomach had been packed with a clotting foam and then wrapped in bandages. The other had received a dart to the thigh, and was lucky he still had it attached. His armour had been cut away and a bandage applied to his injury; obviously the automatic response had not worked properly. He had been administered morphine, you could tell because the used injector pen had been attached to his helmet as a simple marker for medics. Both had already been moved onto collapsible stretchers.

'What about the dead?' I asked. The body of one of our fallen comrades had been sat up against the wall of the trench, his head lolling back unnaturally.

Sergeant Evans was clearly in a rush. 'Don't worry about him, he's been stripped of his kit and he'll get picked up at the re-org anyway. Just get those casualties out or they won't make it. I need to make my way forward. Happy?'

'Yes, Sergeant.'

'Let's go then.' Sergeant Evans was off, running up the trench toward the battle with his smart gunners in tow.

The three of us lifted the two casualties on their stretchers out of the trench. The man with the morphine moaned drowsily, but otherwise they barely made a sound. The trooper with the abdominal injury cried with pain, his injury was such that morphine could not be administered or it might kill him.

'Don't worry, mate,' Brown said reassuringly as we heaved him onto the lip of the trench, 'you'll be fine.'

'I don't want to die,' the casualty said weakly, and sobbed.

'You're not going to die, mate,' Brown laughed, and patted the casualty's shoulder as he lifted himself up alongside him. 'You'll barely even get much of a scar from that! What's your name?'

'Jackson.'

'I promise you you're fine, Jacko.'

As I lifted myself out of the trench I marvelled at how Brown sought to set the trooper's mind at ease, something I could never have imagined him doing only two days ago.

I saw that the sergeant major had marked himself and his work party on my visor display with a bright blue crosshair. They were only about fifty metres away in a slight dip in the ground that barely concealed them from the enemy. Several troopers from the work party appeared to be arranged into a defensive formation around the sergeant major's buggy, a tiny little two-seater with a trailer and little more than a roll cage as protection. He beckoned to us furiously.

Both of the stretchers were designed so that the casualty could be strapped into them, and if necessary dragged by only one man. It wasn't a pleasant experience for the casualty, and it was exhausting for the bearer, but we could hardly have an entire section lost to casualty extraction. The casualty with the leg wound could be dragged, since the stretcher was designed to keep any muck out of his leg, but the other would need to be carried off the ground, and so would be better off with two of us.

'I'll take the leg wound,' I offered, but Brown had already snatched up the straps to the stretcher before I managed to get out of the trench myself.

'What, with those arms?' Brown asked sarcastically.

'Fine,' I said, knowing that there was no time for arguing, and knowing that Brown was far stronger than me. 'Let's go.'

We dragged and carried our casualties unceremoniously toward the waiting casualty party. I felt terribly exposed in the open ground again. It's hard to stay low when you're carrying a stretcher, and the trench system still roared with gunfire. Occasionally stray darts passed close by, I could only hope that they weren't meant for me, or my luck would surely run out.

'Hurry up, you lizards!' the sergeant major called over the noise. One of his work party ran out to help Brown, who was already panting heavily.

The rain was pouring now, hammering at the ground like a billion bullets. I wiped my visor with my sleeve.

Two troopers grabbed our casualties and hurriedly heaved them onto the back of the buggy, its suspension dipping with the extra weight.

Jackson moaned again, and Brown gave him one last gentle pat on the arm. 'You're fine, mate. Your war is over!'

Jackson laughed quietly. 'Thanks, mate.'

'No worries.' Brown stopped when he realised that I was watching him. 'What?'

I laughed. 'I think you're in serious danger of becoming a *nice* person, Brown.'

Our conversation was cut short. 'Get back to your mates, lads, and give that to Sergeant Evans,' the sergeant major said, passing Daniels a box of ammunition.

'Yes, Sir.'

'Go, then!'

We ran back toward the trenches, zigzagging across the open ground as we did so, and then sliding back down into relative safety. Westy had re-organized the remainder of the section so that they covered to the north of the point of entry. We hadn't cleared the trench off to the north, and although two platoon was out there, it was possible that enemy stragglers might be sandwiched in between us. Not an ideal situation to be in, ideally trench systems were only breached at a single point to avoid just such a scenario, but better that than staying out in the open.

The platoon had reached its 'limit of exploitation', Westy told me, if we continued to assault into the trenches we risked over extending ourselves and being attacked from behind. Instead three platoon was sent through to clear the gap in between us and two platoon, and the whole of C Company were sent after them to drive closer toward the city.

'I prefer Browner,' Brown said suddenly, as one after the other what seemed like hundreds of troopers slid into our tiny part of the trenches, and then moved off again into the maze.

'Sorry?'

He sighed. 'I don't like being called Brown.'

'Well, what's your first name?' I asked.

'Danny. But I don't like being called that either.'

'Why not?'

'It's what my mum called me,' he looked wistfully up toward the clouds, the rain collecting on his visor.

'Is she dead?' I wouldn't think to ask such a question if we weren't so close to death ourselves.

'No. I wish she was, though.'

After a while I realised that was all Brown was going to give me. 'Okay, mate, Browner it is.'

We waited again, listening to the sounds of the battle whilst the smart gunners crouched nearby maintaining their constant watch of the air. We had control over the skies, even if our orbital top cover was gone, but we all knew that could change in an instant.

Reports had come over the net that C Company had almost cleared to the eastern end of the trench system, where they had encountered numerous burrows in which the Chinese would have taken cover during the barrage from above. Scattered equipment suggested that many of the enemy had attempted to flee back toward the city, but they took no chances. Every burrow had a phosphorus grenade thrown into it, nobody would survive that.

The order came that our company would continue the advance for the final few hundred metres into the city outskirts, and affect the break in as soon as C Company had reached their limit, before the fire support depleted its ammunition beyond critical levels. The assorted anti-gravity vehicles and artillery pieces had already been firing for well over an hour and their ammunition supply was dwindling.

'What about B Company?' Browner moaned.

I shared his opinion - the third rifle company in the battalion would be poised behind us ready to echelon through C Company in order to continue the advance with fresh troops. Why couldn't they be used rather than us? I supposed we were just closer and faster to mobilise. That or we had already sustained casualties and the CO wanted to keep a fresh company for the city itself.

Westy shrugged, 'I dunno, boys, but at least we're in one piece and we'll only be doing a few hundred metres, hard fast and aggressive with a load of fire support.'

'It's ridiculous, that's what it is,' Browner replied grimly, 'Somebody hates us.'

Westy took no insult. He had warmed to me and Browner, especially since our jump to second in command and senior private respectively.

'Well, complain to the Union when you get home.'

'Screw the Union,' Browner spat. 'Half of them politicians in Brussels should be sent to New Earth, see how they get on.'

'They should be lined up and shot,' Brooks agreed. Like Daniels, he was a quiet man of few words, not that I had really spoken to either of them much anyway.

'You know you can get in a lot of shit for saying stuff like that,' I warned light heartedly.

'Yeah, well ...' Browner answered. 'I won't tell anyone if you guys don't. I doubt anyone disagrees here anyway.'

'Boys,' Westy turned serious again. 'Let's just get this shit done, yeah? I don't know if this war is right or wrong, and I don't care. Let's just get it done.'

We all nodded. There was a general feeling that this was the big push, the third day of the New Earth invasion. Tomorrow would be parades and medals, either that or a sorry voyage back to Earth packed into a fridge on a cargo freighter.

Suddenly Brooks adjusted his mammoth as if he were about to fire. 'What the hell is that?'

I heard them before I saw them, distant figures running through the darkness off to our southern flank, coming from the city. They were shouting something, but I couldn't make out what it was. I was about to tell Brooks to engage when Westy slapped him on the helmet.

'Don't shoot!'

I squinted at the figures. Even with my night vision on full magnification it was difficult to make them out in the rain, but the figures - there were several of them - weren't dressed in any kind of uniform and appeared to be waving white rags.

'Are the Chinese surrendering?'

'They're civvies,' Westy corrected.

We all watched curiously as the figures disappeared into the gloom. They were the first civilians that I had seen since landing on New Earth.

'Where are they running to?'

Westy shook his head. 'No idea. Anywhere's got to be better than in there, though.' he jerked a thumb back toward the city.

'They must be so pleased to see us,' Brooks said.

There were no more civilians, and after several minutes I decided to change the topic of conversation. 'What are you gonna do if you make it back?' I asked Westy.

Westy spluttered, 'Mate, do you *want* me to die?'

'You don't say shit like that, Andy,' Browner laughed. 'You'll jinx us!'

'When I get back I'm gonna get so messed up on drink and drugs I won't even remember my own name,' Stevo said.

'That's nice,' Westy answered frostily. 'Hopefully I'll forget your name too.'

Stevo shrugged dejectedly. 'Just saying. I don't want to remember any of this.'

'I try not to think about going home,' Browner said. 'It just gets me down.' I wondered what had happened with his mum, but knew not to ask. 'I just want to go for a paddle in that sea.'

'You want to go for a paddle?' I laughed.

'What's wrong with that? I reckon it would feel amazing after all this. Who needs home?'

'Feels like home is a different world,' Daniels added.

Browner patted Daniels' shoulder. 'Err ... I hate to break it to you mate ...'

'Daniels,' I asked, 'do you even know where you are?'

'You know what I meant ...'

Browner laughed loudly. 'He only went up the road to buy himself some sweets from his local, then he ends up on New Earth!'

'You mean we're on ... a different world?' I asked sarcastically.

'That's what Daniels here reckons.'

'I didn't ...'

'Shit, Daniels, why didn't you tell us before?'

'He kept it secret all this time ...'

The boss broke into our childish banter just as it began to raise our morale. 'Prepare to move.' We checked ourselves over, snapping back into trooper mode.

'Order of march will be three, then one, then two, acknowledge.'

The section commanders answered their call signs. It was time to go again, back into the fray. The dark outline of the Jersey City filled me with foreboding.

'Let's go.'

19: Jersey City

The company broke out of the trenches and began to manoeuvre across the last few hundred metres to the city outskirts under the cover of our fire support. The rate of covering fire had intensified and was focused along the city's edge in an attempt to deny the enemy any chance of engaging us on our final route in. It must have been successful, because during that final bound into the city there were only short sporadic engagements involving lone gunmen moving amongst the rubble.

One and three section bounded forward in extended lines side by side, one of the two bodies of men covering whilst the other moved forward, zigzagging across the open ground as they ran and diving to the ground after a dash of no more than ten metres. My section, now in reserve, followed close behind in a single file lead by Sergeant Evans, ready to be sent forward if needed.

The ground was scattered with the bodies of Chinese soldiers who had fled from the trenches, either falling fowl of the orbital bombardment or being shot by C Company as they ran. Fleeing enemy was still enemy to us, because he was only running away to fight again somewhere else. Some were only injured, and were quickly searched and left for the sergeant major to pick up. They would be treated by our medics as if they were our own, because if the enemy knew he would be treated well upon capture, he didn't fight to the death. Once or twice the sections encountered what appeared to be the entrances to burrows or maybe even warrens, and they would stop to throw in a grenade before continuing their advance. The process took no longer than a few minutes, even though it felt like an age. I prayed that the Chinese hadn't had enough time to re-organize themselves.

We stopped within a hundred metres of the city and I could see the buildings in much greater detail than before. They ranged from single to two level structures, heavily sandbagged and lined with concertina wire. A road appeared to run alongside the buildings, creating a border between the rocky New Earth surface and the city itself.

From my briefings on Challenger I knew that the buildings were built traditionally out of stone quarried locally by the inhabitants and painted white, with roofs made of red slate tiles. They were designed to take the appearance of traditional European homes, a style commonly seen across many of the planet's suburban dwellings.

Whatever they might have looked like before, the buildings were little more than ruins when I saw them. Walls had collapsed in the hour long onslaught from our fire support, as had rooftops, exposing the rooms inside. Some houses had collapsed entirely, leaving behind only their foundations amongst piles of scorched rubble. Not far from us a Chinese vehicle, some kind of rocket launcher on legs, burned fiercely.

'Pat, reference my mark …' As the boss spoke a blue crosshair appeared over one of the buildings on my targeting system. It was two floors high and looked relatively intact, apart from having more holes in it than a Swiss cheese - I guessed a result of a gravtank's Vulcan cannon. Whoever had been inside it must have had a really bad day, I thought.

I could see the shadow of Corporal Pattison - or 'Pat' as three section knew him - kneeling up to see the building. 'Seen.'

'You are first assaulting section. Go when you're ready.'

Pat didn't need to be told twice. 'Moving now!' Three section were already up and moving, closely followed by one section, they weren't going to sit in the open near to those buildings any longer than they had to. I

would rather take my chances clearing room-by-room than wait for a sniper to have my head off if I had the choice.

I watched three section run the last hundred metres up to the building, followed by Two section and mirrored to their north by two platoon who were going for a different building. We would attack both buildings simultaneously, obtaining a foothold within the city outskirts through which the other companies could echelon. Once the battalion had then pushed into the city, there were a further two battalions poised to echelon through us, driving into the heart of the Chinese position and shattering their defences. It often amazed me how much depended upon one or two sections in an operation as large as this one.

I could see our two sections move rapidly up to the wall of the building, weapons bristling from the mass of men like the spines of a porcupine. They took cover whilst two men placed something against the wall, which I recognised to be an entry charge.

Entry charges were low-tech bits of kit used for blowing holes into buildings, much simpler than anything we used in the warrens. They were a metal conical device the size of a dinner plate that could be placed against a wall by use of a thin metal frame, designed to direct a sufficient blast to create a man-sized hole in stone or brick walls without harming anyone a few metres away from them. They were ideal because you never entered a building by a doorway or window unless you had to because the enemy would almost certainly have them covered and booby-trapped.

The troopers ran away from the entry charge, and when they were a sufficient distance away it detonated in a cloud of dust, with a noise that was an anti-climax considering the sound that our grenades made. The two sections of men charged into the building, followed closely by a single trooper I identified as the boss. Normally a platoon commander would come with his own radio operator, a man who could take and send messages for him whilst he busied himself with the battle itself. Due to our small numbers, however, Cyclops was attached to one of the sections and the boss was having to make do without.

A couple of rounds were fired and voices echoed from within the gaping hole. A few seconds later a grenade detonated and then there were more shots. One section was next to enter the building to join the fight.

'Ev, this is the Boss, bring up the remainder, please.'

'Roger that, Boss.' Sergeant Evans looked to us and beckoned. 'Let's get it done, lads!' he called, and we went, weapons in the aim, covering the buildings in watch for opportunists and snipers. After the withering assault from the gravtanks, I doubted many pinkies had remained within the crumbling ruins of the city outskirts, but there were bound to be a couple.

A carpet of glass shards cracked and shattered beneath our feet as we crossed the road. Above our heads would have been one of thousands of beautiful airtight glass domes that had allowed the inhabitants of the city to walk without wearing respirators, through broad streets adorned with plants, statues and water features. At night they had been lit brilliantly by thousands of multi-coloured lights, turning the city into a glowing spectacle that could be seen from orbit. A single orbital shell would have shattered them all and showered the inhabitants in a lethal rain of glass.

As I closed on the gaping hole through which three section had entered I came face to face with a Chinaman. He was sat up against the far wall in a room not much bigger than a dropship crew compartment, coated with dust and littered with debris. His respirator was gone, so had half of his head and much of his torso. A member of three section met us by the opening, pointing Westy to take a door to our left and north.

We entered the building without hesitation, our rifles held up in the aim and our bodies crouched as low as we could manage without falling over. I could almost feel the adrenalin pumping through my veins, and my heart thumping hard against my ribs.

The boss and Pat met us in the next room, which had been stripped bare and walled head high with sandbags. A huge section was missing in the ceiling, covered by two troopers from one section. There was one doorway on the northern side of the room ahead of us which hung open, and a second to the eastern side which was closed. The room we were in had probably once been something quite normal, I imagined, like a living room or dining room. Now it was nothing more than a modified bunker that had probably housed Chinese troops.

'Jonesy only has five blokes now, including him,' the boss reminded Westy as we crouched beside him, 'He's launched into the next room but I don't want him to push any further.'

'Okay,' Westy nodded, looking intently toward the open door to our north. 'You want me to go echelon through him?'

The boss shook his head, 'No, I want you to move into the room to the east, and then we'll see where we go from there. Exploit no more than two rooms, and do not move further north without me saying so,' I nodded my head in agreement, understanding that the boss didn't want us to assault into a room alongside Jonesy's without him knowing, as there was a risk of us accidentally shooting each other.

Westy stood. 'Roger. Browner, let's go.'

Browner ran toward the door, drawing a sledgehammer he had taken out of the dropship hours before from his daysack like a man might draw a sword and at the same time Westy took a grenade from his pouch and turned the dial. They stacked up together by the door, weapons at the ready whilst the rest of us closed in behind them.

Internal doors in the majority of New Earth dwellings, we had been told, were air tight but simple in their construction, since they were not competing against a vacuum. They often swung on hinges and looked like a hybrid between a normal everyday Earth door and that of a fridge. Because of this it was relatively easy to take a locked one down with a sledgehammer - even in this day and age. It's amazing what you can do when you hit things!

As Browner raised the sledgehammer; Westy poised to throw his grenade. The section commander tapped him on the shoulder. 'Do it.'

Browner swung the sledge with all his might against the door with an almighty crash, but the door barely budged. He hesitated, surprised that the door had withstood the impact.

'Swing it again! Again!'

Browner struck the door a second time, and again. On the second swing the door seal broke fractionally and on the third a gap just large enough to fit a grenade was formed. Something was propped against the door on the other side. There were beams of light flashing around behind the door and I recognised them instantly- infra-red torches.

I think the Chinese opened fire slightly before Westy pushed the grenade through the gap, but I couldn't be sure because everything happened so fast. They sprayed automatic fire into the wall to the wrong side of the door in the mistaken belief that that was where we stood. Fifty-fifty chance - left of the door or right of the door - but they chose wrong. Darts punched holes through the wall as if it was made of paper, and we dove for the ground before they could hit any of us.

A Chinese voice screamed from through the door.

Westy had only dropped the grenade on the other side of the door. This wasn't ideal because it would be possible for the pinkies to throw it back, if it didn't frag us through the door anyway.

Realising the danger, Browner quickly grabbed the handle to the door and pulled it shut.

'Browner! No!' I shouted at my comrade as the rest of the section hugged the ground, but he wasn't listening, he was too busy fighting a tug of war with somebody on the opposite side.

The grenade detonated after three seconds, sending the door and Browner crashing to the ground in a cloud of smoke and dust.

'*Man down!*' The dreaded words were repeated by every man.

Immediately after the grenade detonated Westy charged into the room, kicking away the remains of a piece of furniture that must have been used to block the door, firing as he went. Stevo paused, so I shoved him forward after the section commander and then followed as well. I was desperately worried that Browner had been hurt, but my training took over and I knew we had to clear the room or lose the initiative over our enemy.

The room was as dark as a warren tunnel, forcing us to scan rapidly with our infra-red torches. It was a large lounge-type room that had clearly been used to sleep maybe ten to twenty Chinese soldiers. Thermal bags were strewn across the carpeted floor as well as random items of personal equipment.

I fired into an upturned table and couch in the centre of the room, possibly used to hide behind as protection from the blast. Splinters and bits of stuffing flew across the room like confetti.

A Chinaman emerged from a doorway to our left, strafing holes along the southern wall and barely missing me. If I hadn't been in a half crouch I reckon I would have got one straight in the head. Instinctively I span to face my foe and fired two shots back at him, only I didn't miss. The two rounds hit him square in the chest, punching straight through his body armour, and he dropped like a stone.

Brooks entered the room behind me, bringing his mammoth gun to bear on the doorway I had fired into.

The mammoth spat death, its magnets screaming like banshees as it ate into its ammunition drum. Thankfully my earphones filtered out the terrible noise as he sprayed along the wall with hundreds of supersonic darts. The high velocity nature of our weapons meant that they penetrated walls with ease, but the Chinese shared the ability. Nowhere in the house was safe.

I checked around the room as Brooks closed on the doorway. Two pinkies had died behind the couch, but by the state of them I figured it had probably been the grenade that had killed them, and not me. Another had died by the door where he had fought against Browner to return the grenade. Only a gory mess remained of him, barely distinguishable as a man. There were two windows on the eastern wall, but both were smashed out and sealed with sandbags.

'Room clear,' Westy hissed over the intercom; he didn't want the enemy to know where he was. 'One enemy dead. One doorway to the north. Two blocked windows to the east.' Westy described to the boss what he needed to know over the platoon intercom.

The boss was in a squat, leaning around the smashed doorframe we had entered by. If what had happened at the door fazed him, he didn't show it. Behind him I could see one of the lads in one section lifting the smoking door away from Browner. I spotted movement; he was alive, thank God. The relief was overwhelming.

The boss nodded. 'Westy, go again. No engagements to the west. Jonesy, get your boys in cover in case Westy throws a grenade in there. Ev, have three section ready to clear onto the top floor. There must be a stairwell here somewhere.'

'Roger that, Boss, they're at the entry point with me now.'

We were to assault again into the room to the north, but we had to be careful where we fired, because one section would be in the adjacent room as we entered, and if we weren't careful we could potentially shoot them through the walls.

'Andy, stay here with Brooks,' Westy ordered. He crept toward the open doorway with Daniels, ushering Stevo to follow him.

Westy looked over his shoulder at Brooks and pumped his fist up and down. Brooks recognised the message for rapid fire and instantly responded with another sustained burst, spraying the wall to the left of the doorway where the Chinaman had died by my rifle.

Using the distraction Westy bounded toward the doorway and lobbed a grenade into the room, throwing it as hard as he could so that it would bounce against the walls and would be impossible to pick up quick enough to throw it back.

'Grenade!' We collapsed to the ground.

Boom!

The grenade exploded, sending a shockwave through the building so powerful that plaster fell from the ceiling and clattered off our helmets. Westy and Brooks were through the door seconds later, followed by Stevo.

'Room clear,' Westy called over the platoon intercom. 'One room to the west, plus one stairwell and a window to the east!'

'Roger, the room to your west is occupied by Jonesy's section so do not engage. Cover the stairwell and the windows.'

'Okay,' Westy said quietly. The boss's voice seemed to calm him, as it did me. He was a smooth operator, he rarely seemed to flap.

'Three section move up. Westy keep your blokes spread out and low, remember those walls won't give you much protection.'

As three section filed past with the boss in tow, I took the opportunity to go back to check on Browner. It was one of my many jobs as 2ic to manage my section's casualties, after all.

'Is Browner okay?' I asked from the doorway, dreading the answer.

'Yeah,' one of the one section lads answered from where he continued to cover the hole in the roof, he daren't not look away even for a split second.

'Platoon sergeant is having a look at him at the entry point, mate, but he looks fine. The door saved his life.'

'Cheers, mate.'

I ran back to the entry point looking for Browner, to see him being shaken about like a rag doll on the ground by the platoon sergeant. Initially I feared the worst, but only for few seconds.

'I'm okay, Sergeant,' he insisted as Sergeant Evans ran his hands over Browner's limbs and then felt with his fingers under the edges of his armour and around his respirator.

'Not taking any chances,' he said, and slapped Browner's helmet a couple of times. 'Yep, heads still there. Alright, go on, then.'

I helped Browner to his feet. 'You lucky bastard!'

Browner shook himself off in a cloud of dust. 'That was one rough door!' he laughed.

Gunfire rattled overhead; three section were upstairs.

'Come on, you two,' Sergeant Evans pointed the way we came. 'Get back to your section, we're not finished!'

We ran back to the section to find the lads attacking the sandbagging that covered the windows with rifle butts and fists.

'Use your bayonets, lads, cut the bags open!' Westy hacked and slashed at one of the windows with his bayonet, and coarse sand spilt to the ground. Something exploded somewhere outside the building, far away enough for us to be safe, but close enough for us to be alarmed.

'Let's get some fire going out of this building!' Sergeant Evans bellowed, stalking the rooms of the lower floor like a caged animal with the taste of blood in its mouth.

A hole large enough to get a weapon through was created in one of the windows, and glowing orange light flooded into the room. Something outside was burning fiercely.

'Westy! Get a mammoth in that hole!'

'Brooks! Get in there!'

Brooks set up his MAM-G in the freshly made hole in the sandbags and no sooner had he taken up a fire position when he then opened fire.

'Enemy moving left to right!' he warned.

The whole building erupted into noise as more and more of us managed to get through the sandbags to fire into the city. The Chinese were attempting to set up a fire support base amongst the rubble, and brief glimpses of soldiers running across our frontage suggested that they were going to try to attack from the southern flank, which would mean our platoon would be hit from the side while we were still in the process of securing the building.

'They're coming round to the south!' I hollered.

Sergeant Evans peered through the hole I had made and instantly saw the danger. 'Jonesy! Jonesy!'

Jonesy answered on the intercom, 'Yeah?'

'Secure the southern flank!'

'There's no windows there, mate!'

'I don't care how you do it,' Sergeant Evans rebuked angrily. 'Just get it done!'

'Roger,' Jonesy knew not to argue, 'I'll see what I can do.'

Jonesy had acknowledged, but didn't sound sure of himself. Sensing this, Sergeant Evans swore and made his way round to him.

Daniels pointed frantically. 'Missile!'

There was no missile that I could see, the only thing that lit up the dark were the sparks from ricocheting darts and the fires that burnt from within the city.

It seemed such a stupid question, since any smart missile would have hit us before I could even open my mouth. 'Where?'

'Launcher,' Daniels corrected himself. 'There!' He pointed uselessly. How was I to see it?

He must have seen a Chinese smart launcher, I figured. Chances were that the brick buildings would withstand or at least reduce the effect of a smart missile, but they were so called for a reason - they were smart. If one managed to get through one of the holes we had made and detonated then we were done for. I resisted the urge to run into a room to the back of the house.

'For God's sake, mark it, then, you stroker!' Westy shouted, and seconds later a red crosshair flashed on my visor, a marker placed by Daniels. Just behind the marker and in the dark something moved.

'Grenade!' Westy fired his grenade launcher, and the round landed right on top of the crosshair. Nobody could have survived the explosion, and we whooped with delight.

Browner shook a fist jubilantly. 'Have it, you pink bastard!'

Enraged by the death of one or more of their smart launchers, the enemy seemed to open fire with everything they had, hacking at the house with supersonic darts and causing many of us to take cover. I ducked as a round struck a sandbag next to my head and ricocheted.

'Building clear.' The boss was on the platoon net; three section had finished the job upstairs. 'Keep a watch on the southern flank, Ev!'

'Already got Jonesy on it, Boss,' Sergeant Evans answered, sounding slightly out of breath after placing out one section somewhere just outside the house. Whatever had happened before in the ditches was forgotten, Mr Barkley and Sergeant Evans had become so slick working with each other that they were almost a joy to watch and listen to. I had no doubt that there was no one better for either job.

Sergeant Evans strode back into our room, where we continued to exchange fire with the Chinese. 'Do you want the launchers up there, Boss? They're useless down here.'

The two smart launcher crews, who had tucked themselves safely into the corner of the room, glanced up at him nervously in the dim light.

'Yeah, get them up.'

Sergeant Evans turned to them. 'Get up there, boys.'

As soon as the smart gunners left the room a trooper crashed through the western doorway, bouncing clumsily off an overturned piece of furniture. His helmet had tilted to one side and his kit looked like it was about to fall off him.

'Where's your lieutenant?' he demanded in the most well-spoken officer's accent - which might have commanded respect if he hadn't turned up looking like a trooper on day one, week one, on Uralis! I was shocked when my visor identified him as the OC of B Company.

Sergeant Evans flicked his head upwards. 'Up there, Sir.'

'Thank you, Sergeant,' the officer said, and disappeared into the next room, uttering, 'What a mess. A bloody mess.'

'What's he talking about,' Browner asked with a hint of humour. 'The battle or his kit?'

Sergeant Evans did a rare thing and laughed - only briefly - before turning serious again. 'Observe your arcs, Brown. And you, Moralee.'

'Firing!' somebody shouted from upstairs, and the first smart missile screamed into the city where it detonated in a flash and a shower of sparks. I marvelled that a smart missile by night was not entirely unlike a firework.

'Just like New Year's Day!' I shouted.

Several targets were indicated on my visor a few hundred metres away, it looked like the pinkies were withdrawing deeper into the city through the rubble and burning homes, and I took a couple of shots at them. My rifle corrected my aim if it was slightly off, and I was always a good shot even without the visor display. At least one of the Chinamen went down, and was dragged off by another. We let them go, even though any of us could easily have hit the slow moving target, we couldn't shoot a man helping a casualty, there was something just not right about it. Most of us knew what it felt like to drag a mate who had been injured, because we had done it ourselves.

'Contact!' My heart skipped a beat; it was Jonesy on the intercom. 'Contact to the south!'

'Hold your position!' Sergeant Evans ordered, then looked up toward the ceiling as if he could see through it. 'Boss!'

'Wait,' the boss snapped, and our platoon sergeant growled in annoyance.

He shook his head. 'What the hell is that stupid major up to?' I understood his frustration. Any time wasted was a loss of initiative, allowing the Chinese to re-group and counter attack. B Company should have launched through us without hesitation, because we were only the very tip of the blade, and if we lost our hold on the city fringe that blade would be blunted.

'There's loads of them!' Jonesy sounded desperate.

'Boss!' There was no reply. 'Fuck it,' Sergeant Evans scanned across us impatiently. 'Moralee, Brown, come with me!'

'Yes, Sergeant.' We obeyed instantly, moving away from the windows. 'Westy, hold here, mate.'

Westy was through one of the holes, firing a grenade at something. 'Roger, mate!'

We ran back through the building to the hole that had been blown out with the charge, and as soon as we emerged into the cold night air Sergeant Evans swore. The whole of B Company were waiting in the darkness, in the middle of the open doing nothing. I gaped. Our attack was stalling.

'Let's go.' Sergeant Evans ran around the southern side of the building and I saw that Jonesy and his four men were in cover behind a low wall, locked into a fierce fire fight with enemy in and around a building one hundred metres away to the south. Darts peppered the wall to our house, and we all dove for cover.

'Jonesy, what's going on, mate?' Sergeant Evans crawled up alongside the embattled section commander, while me and Browner crawled up to the wall and joined in with the fire fight. Multiple targets were identified by my visor, some within the windows of the two-level house and others amongst the rubble in front of it.

'There must be a whole platoon of them,' Jonesy said nervously. 'They just went for it - full frontal! We shot loads, but … that was mental!'

'What's your grenade state?'

Jonesy shook his head. 'Nothing for the grenade launchers, I used the last one just then.'

'Jonesy, your 2ic needs to tell me stuff like that,' Sergeant Evans scorned, and switched to a channel reserved for his launchers. 'Mitch, I need missiles to the south, I will mark the target.'

I couldn't hear the reply, I wasn't on that channel and I didn't have time to be curious. It didn't matter anyway because seconds after Sergeant Evans sent the message I suddenly had much more pressing matters on my mind, because the Chinese fired three smart missiles at once.

'Incoming!' We flattened ourselves behind the wall, clutching at the earth with our fingers, but it made little difference. The first two missiles struck the wall a few metres to my left, their detonations blasting a chunk from it and hurling troopers to the ground. The third struck the ground just in front of where Browner lay dazed, and his body was thrown like a toy to land in a heap against the house.

I lifted my head to look at the smoking remains of the wall. My body was still intact - the wall had somehow saved me from the third missile.

'Moralee!' It was Sergeant Evans who called me. Somehow he too remained unscathed amongst the rubble, with Jonesy's de-capitated body at his side. 'They're coming!'

My lips curled. Those fucking bastards. I looked over the wall at the charging line of Chinese soldiers, screaming their war cries, an unrelenting enemy that never knew when to give up. Whether the Union won or not, we were never going to survive New Earth, I realised, but instead of filling me with fear, that one thought filled me with a powerful resolve to do what had to be done.

'Prepare to move,' I growled, and Sergeant Evans smiled, his teeth visible through his visor. There was no time for Westy or Pat to get to us, we had to do something to stop the Chinese advance or B Company would be caught with its pants down.

'Boss, Ev.' Sergeant Evans spoke on the intercom and drew a grenade and adjusted the dial. 'Contact south, twenty enemy or more, one section has been destroyed, task a saucer now or you will be over-run. I am engaging.' He threw the grenade.

The Chinese must have been no more than twenty metres away when the grenade burst. Loose rubble and shards of glass enhanced its effect, slicing through flesh and severing limbs.

I moved first, then Sergeant Evans, bounding over collapsed walls and mangled metal. I fired into the enemy as rapidly as recoil would allow, two shots for each, aimed directly at the centre of body mass as I had been taught on Uralis. Blood sprayed when I shot one pinkie directly through the head.

'Bastards!' I yelled.

A pinkie emerged out of the rubble, his rifle broken, and he charged with his bayonet raised to stab me.

'Come on, then!' I beckoned him as he approached, my body fuelled with sheer rage. He tried to stab at me, but clearly he hadn't spent as much time as me practicing using his bayonet, because I parried his bayonet away with ease and lunged at him, my own blade glistening in the light from the burning city. It caught him by the cloth of his armour, but didn't penetrate, so the Chinaman let out some kind of piercing war cry as if he was going to bring his weapon back to lunge again. I brought up my foot and kicked him square in the stomach, sending him tumbling to the ground.

'Die, you bastard!' Why wouldn't he just die? I stabbed at him again while he sprawled on the floor, and again my bayonet was deflected by his armour. There was no hope for the Chinaman, though, and I think maybe then he knew it, because I had gone completely berserk. I kicked his rifle away from him and dropped on top of him, and he uselessly hit at my thighs and torso, before I beat at him with my stock. First he took it, his helmet saving him from the first blow, but his visor cracked, then it smashed, and I beat at his head until it was little more than a pulp. The Chinaman was dead, and only I remained. A foreign voice screamed in agony somewhere in the dark.

A series of massive explosions rocked the Chinese house, and I realised that Sergeant Evans had marked the enemy position and smart missiles were being fired by the platoon from the roof. The flashes cast long shadows across the rubble. I remember thinking that it looked like a graveyard in a thunderstorm.

I looked down at my mutilated enemy, the rage slowly leaving my body. What had I become?

And then I remembered Browner.

'Man down!' somebody called before I could get back to the house. Westy had brought out his section to re-enforce the wall where one section had been, now no more than a pile of bricks and dust and gore.

'Medic!' The message would rapidly relay to one of the company battlefield medics.

Browner wasn't dead, but in some ways I wished that he was.

Only my visor could identify Browner to me, because there was no way that I would have ever recognised him. My eyes widened as I ran up to him, just as Daniels ripped the first tourniquet out of his pocket.

'Oh, my God,' I exclaimed, and fell to my knees. Browner was a bloodied mess. The first two detonations had merely stunned him when it destroyed his cover, but the final smart missile had exploded directly below him, resulting in the traumatic amputation of both of his legs and half of his arm. None of his automatic tourniquets had activated.

'*Medic!*' Sergeant Evans shouted over the company net. 'I have casualties at my location! Don't just stare at him, Moralee!' He hit me about the helmet, snapping me back into life. I stuffed my hand into my pocket and pulled out my own tourniquet, quickly preparing to put it onto Browner's leg. Blood flowed from the stump onto the ground. Still conscious, Browner made a whimpering noise from inside his cracked respirator that pierced my soul and still haunts me even today.

'Get pressure on his groin, Moralee,' Sergeant Evans spat. I thrust my hand into Browner's groin area, trying to apply pressure onto the major artery that supplied blood to his leg, but now was only allowing blood to flow freely onto the ground. I ran my hands down his leg, searching for where the bone ended beneath the flaps of quivering loose flesh just above where his knee should have been, and then awkwardly slipped the tourniquet over his thigh and pulled it tight with my free hand.

Sergeant Evans pushed his hand into Browner's armpit to staunch the blood loss from his arm, rocking the tiny body with his weight. He began putting his own tourniquet over Browner's arm and pulled it tight with all his might, 'Listen to me, Brown, can you hear me?'

Browner whimpered again quietly.

'Brown, you'll be fine, mate, do you hear me? You'll be fine, we've got you.' He tugged the tourniquet one more time, and me and Daniels did the same. 'Mark the time of application on those tourniquets for the medics, Daniels. Moralee, get up here.'

I came up beside Sergeant Evans just as he removed Browner's respirator. He quickly inspected Browner's face and checked inside his mouth, promptly closing it again and replacing the respirator.

'Check his torso. I need to check the others.' I hadn't realised that there were other casualties. In fact Jonesy was the only man in his section who had died outright.

I ripped open Browner's bloodied armour, only to find that his stomach was riddled with holes, and I gasped, 'Shit!'

Daniels ripped out a packet of quick-clot foam, a substance designed to be packed into wounds to stop bleeding internally. Just as he began to stuff it into a hole in Browner's stomach, the first medic slid to the ground beside us, panting heavily.

'What's going on?' he asked, and I realised that it was the same medic who had treated my arm. I told the medic while he worked, frantically pulling out his specialist equipment.

A stretcher had been assembled behind me ready to receive Browner. One of the other casualties was already being carried away, while B Company finally began an assault onto the house occupied by the Chinese. A Union saucer pounded a nearby building with its cannon.

'Have you checked his back?' the medic asked me in alarm, looking up from Browner's wristpad. Daniels continued to stuff quick clot into a hole with a bloodied finger.

I shook my head. 'No.'

'Brilliant,' the medic said scornfully, and he unceremoniously lifted Browner onto his side. 'Pull his armour away,' he ordered, and I obeyed, unclipping the armour to expose his back. His combat shirt was soaked in blood.

'Oh my God,' I exclaimed again. A piece of shrapnel had punched through Browner's stomach and come out the other side of his torso, toward the top of his back. He had a sucking chest wound.

'He's not gonna die …' the medic promised, maybe to himself, as he ripped away Browner's armour. The wound was large and gruesome, pulsing with frothy blood. 'Not gonna die.' A grenade exploded within the enemy house and gunfire erupted, but I didn't turn to look.

The medic wiped away the excess blood and placed a chest seal over the wound, checking to make sure that it was fitted securely.

'Get him on the stretcher,' he ordered. 'With me on three.'

I braced myself to lift Browner's body onto the stretcher. 'You'll be alright, mate,' I told him, but he was now unconscious. It was almost a sob.

'Make sure he stays on his side or you'll cut the chest valve off. One, two, three.' We lifted Browner onto the stretcher, almost throwing him into the air, it was so easy. He was so small; I'll never forget how small he was.

'I'll go with him,' I said.

'Don't need you to, I have a stretcher party,' the medic said abruptly. 'Let's go, lads.' The stretcher party stooped around the stretcher.

'I'll go with him,' I repeated. Me and Browner had been through everything together. 'He's my friend.'

'I don't care if he's your dad, mate.' A trooper pushed me out of the way and took the grips to the stretcher. Another trooper took the other end, and together they lifted Browner from the ground.

'Let's go,' the medic said, and they carried Browner away in a trot toward the trenches, where the shadow of a buggy waited for its next batch of casualties.

I stood and watched helplessly as my friend was carried away, his blood still dripping from my gloves. Finally I leant against the wall of the house and slowly slid down until I sat on the floor. I stared blankly at the B Company assault onto the Chinese. Voices echoed from within the enemy house that it was clear, and then I saw troopers running deeper into the city, but I couldn't have cared less. This place meant nothing to me. I didn't care about Jersey Island, or New Earth. I just wanted my friends back, because without them my life was empty and pointless. I felt so numb that I couldn't even bring myself to cry and so I just sat there and stared.

I don't know how long I had sat there until Sergeant Evans found me.

'It's not over,' he said simply.

I said nothing.

Sergeant Evans sighed. 'The platoon may be re-tasked to clear out pockets of enemy. The city will fall by daybreak, but we will have to maintain momentum in order to keep the upper hand.'

I wouldn't even look at him. The image of Browner's quivering stumps was permanently etched into my mind.

'Andy.'

I looked up. Sergeant Evans crouched beside me.

'The platoon needs you. We have to finish this.'

I sat in silence, then after a few seconds I nodded. 'Okay, Ev.'

And so the platoon went back into battle.

20: The Emerald Sea

Browner died of his injuries in a field hospital somewhere underground. On top of three amputations and numerous wounds to the abdomen he suffered multiple organ failure and a collapsed lung. The medic later told me that by the time he died he had been given fifty litres of blood, more than his fair share out of a dwindling stock. He was a fighter, but he couldn't fight forever.

The Chinese began to withdraw from Jersey City just as the sun began to rise over the hills, riding on dropships concealed within the warrens beneath us on a futile flight across the emerald sea. Without any ships to return to, they would be harried by our saucers until they eventually surrendered to the Spanish on a continent several hundred miles away.

Our platoon never did see any further combat, if the further two battalions who echeloned through us weren't enough to finish the enemy themselves, the third battalion to pass through us - our old battalion - certainly was.

I was crouched alone at the side of one of the city's empty streets when I saw the first platoon of my old battalion pass me by. The rest of my platoon was within the buildings resting, but I found that I couldn't sleep.

I recognised some of the names of the platoon as they went by, but nobody I knew enough to want to chat to. If they recognised me they didn't show it, patrolling past me at a fast pace. Perhaps their boss was eager to get into battle, I mused, since the carnage of the ditches probably wasn't enough for him.

One of the troopers at the back of the platoon, however, slowed down as he passed me, and then stopped in the middle of the road. I knew who it was - I had seen his name on my visor display long before he had noticed me. Woody didn't move, he just stared at me as his platoon rounded a corner out of sight. His trigger finger slid slightly off the trigger guard of his rifle.

'Go on then,' I said.

Woody remained motionless.

My lips curled. 'Kill me then, be my guest. You'll probably be doing me a favour.'

Woody remained motionless for several seconds, and then his finger returned to his trigger guard.

'Didn't think so,' I sneered. 'Now, fuck off.'

Woody hurried on after his platoon. I would see him again, but he would never speak to me, and so at least some little good came of the war on New Earth.

A few hours after our success in Jersey City, it was announced that the Chinese had suffered similar defeats to the north of the island, and had withdrawn. Not long after that it was announced that all hostilities on New Earth had ended, and that the last Chinese ships were being chased out of the Centauri system.

It took a day to completely clear the remainder of the city and its surrounding areas. Most of the remaining Chinese knew that their commanders were gone and the city was lost, and so they surrendered in their tens and even hundreds, and the prisoners were led by us into a hastily constructed holding area close to their trench system. Occasionally we met some small resistance, including a lone sniper who had us pinned for almost an hour until a saucer finally spotted him and blew him into chunks with its cannon.

The civilian population had been living underground in parts of the warrens that the Chinese had left for them, and even a small town of atmospheric tents just outside the city, beside the beach of the emerald sea. We thought that they would have been jubilant to finally be freed from their Chinese oppressors, but not a single person cheered, clapped or thanked us when our platoon entered the multi-coloured tented town and told them that it was safe to go back into the city to rebuild their lives.

'What's their problem?' Brooks threw up his arms as the civilians slowly made their way across the barren red surface toward their city on the horizon. I swear one of them even lifted his respirator to spit in the direction of our dropships.

Ev smiled grimly. 'What were you expecting? A brass band? These people don't want us here.'

I watched the civilians pass us. It was the first time I had seen old people and children in a very long time, but their hostile glares were obvious through their clear, bubble-shaped respirators.

Stevo frowned. 'So they prefer the Chinese? Traitors.'

Westy looked like he was about to say something, but thought better of it.

'They don't want the Chinese either,' Ev laughed. 'Isn't it obvious? They just want to be free.'

'You mean we just did all that shit, and these bastards don't even want us here anyway?' Stevo kicked at the ground. 'Then what was the point?'

'I'm not sure that there is one, I'm afraid. Is there really a point to any war? Behind all of it it's just a bunch of businessmen cutting up a map, and people like us who fight and die.'

'Well then, why are we here?' Brooks asked.

'Because if you're not here some other poor lad comes here in your place.'

The platoon watched for a while as the procession of civilians slowly receded into the horizon. Brooks furrowed his brow. 'That doesn't seem like a very good reason.'

Ev sighed. 'Well, I'm afraid it's all you've got.'

Nobody noticed me when I wandered away from the platoon, they were too busy watching the civilians go, perhaps hoping that they might leave behind something worth stealing in their tents. I walked over toward a steep rocky bank where the land dropped away several metres onto a beach of blood-red sand. The emerald sea glittered and sparkled magnificently in the sunlight, and I took a second to marvel at its beauty before sliding down onto the coarse sand below.

My boots crunched in the sand as I walked toward the sea, my headphones magnifying the sound of the waves lazily lapping onto the sand. I bent over and took off my boots and socks, and placed my rifle and daysack down beside them. The wet sand felt rough between my toes as I walked slowly into the water. It was cold, but after several days in boots the sense of liberation was overwhelming. With every wave the water rushed around my ankles.

Well, Browner, I thought, *I did it. I'm taking a paddle in the sea for you.* But I wished that all of my friends were there to enjoy it with me.

I don't know how long I cried, my respirator motors whirring in their battle to keep my visor clear, before I heard feet crunch behind me.

'You okay, Andy?' It was Ev. I didn't turn lest he see I had been crying, though he had probably heard me anyway.

'Yeah.'

The platoon sergeant waded into the water beside me. 'He turned out to be a pretty good trooper. You all did.'

I said nothing for a while, just listened to the sounds of the sea. 'I thought you hated us.'

'Why?'

'The ditches.' I remembered my friend Climo, and Chase's cold, accusing eyes and I grimaced at the memory. 'We hid behind a man's body like cowards.'

'You were scared,' Ev corrected, and sighed. 'The death of those lads was my responsibility.'

I frowned, puzzled. 'Why?'

'I was the section commander. Whether they were right or wrong, my decisions led to their deaths. You had absolutely nothing to do with it, and neither did the boss. He did the right thing.'

'But we still hid.'

Ev laughed. 'Any sane man would. Can anyone blame a man for wanting to live?' Another sigh. 'For what it's worth, you did yourselves proud. I couldn't ask for better troopers.'

It doesn't bring my friends back though.

It was my turn to sigh. 'So, what now then?'

'We spend a few months here cleaning up - the planet's infrastructure is in ruins. The Chinese soldiers will need rounding up and shipping back to Earth to be exchanged for some trade deals, no doubt, and no doubt there'll be a few die-hards out there to keep us busy. Then we'll have a relief in place by fresh troops, and you'll be shipped back to Earth never to see this place ever again.'

'What about you?' I asked, noticing that he hadn't said 'we' when he'd mentioned us returning to Earth.

Ev smiled and looked out into the sea. 'Beautiful isn't it?'

'Yeah.'

He looked at me. 'On this planet, 'freedom' isn't just a word. It isn't called New Earth because of similarities with the home-world, it's because people believe that this is where we can start again, and do things right.'

I laughed bitterly. 'Well that hasn't worked out very well, has it?'

'And whose fault is that? The people who live here?' He shook his head. 'I've been all over this planet. There are no Chinese, or Europeans or Russians. They are *one people*, all yearning to be free to govern themselves in peace.'

'What are you saying?'

'It's not over, Andy.'

Boots slapped and crashed in the water as the platoon charged us, whooping and cheering. They splashed and swore at each other, and one or two fell into the water and had to lift their respirators to let the water out.

'I hope these canisters are waterproof!' somebody shouted, and we all laughed and joked until the boss ordered us back to the dropships.

Sergeant Evans's prediction was right, we did indeed spend the next three months rebuilding the mess that the war had left behind - alongside a hostile civilian population. Several battalions of Chinese fought on in vast warrens throughout the northern continent, but they eventually succumbed to starvation and surrendered.

Our ship had been destroyed, along with many others, and so the battalions were crammed into troopships to be transported victorious back to Earth - so that we might be paraded through Brussels. But our more severely injured comrades would be hidden away from the cameras.

Eventually I would meet Peters, Greggerson and Sam again, all of whom had survived their injuries, and I would keep in touch with them and the remainder of my platoon for the rest of my life. We had endured something that nobody on Earth could ever imagine, and it united us with a bond that could never be broken. We were more than just friends, we were brothers-in-arms; we were troopers.

As for Ev, he would disappear several days before the brigade were due to leave New Earth, and was never seen again. People outside the platoon would call him a deserter and a traitor for abandoning the Union at its time of triumph, running to hide in the warrens beneath Jersey City. But we who knew Sergeant Evans knew that he was no traitor. Perhaps maybe we would even see him again.

Because the battle for New Earth wasn't over …

Also by the Author

LANCEJACK

Lancejack is Book Two in The Union Series.

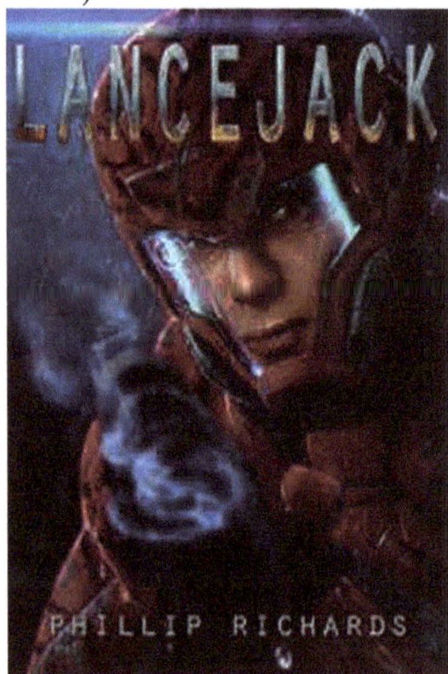

Andy Moralee is no longer the young and terrified recruit who had last set foot upon New Earth two years ago. Decorated for his bravery during the final hours of the invasion and promoted to lance corporal, he is still troubled by his memories and haunted by nightmares. He finds himself unable to cope with life back on Earth, and so he returns to the red planet, the only place where he feels he belongs.

But New Earth has changed as well. A growing insurgency threatens to turn the planet into a battleground once again, but this time the enemy has the ability to melt away into the population, and even turn the Union's weapons against them. Nobody can be trusted, even old friends.

Quickly swept up in the gathering storm Andy finds himself in the command of a section that resents his early promotion, and during the battle that follows his leadership, his loyalty, and even his faith in his comrades are put to the ultimate test in the face of an enemy that will stop at nothing.

(Kindle edition published March 2013)

Direct Amazon Links:
www.amazon.com/dp/B00BZODJZS - US/Worldwide
www.amazon.co.uk/dp/B00BZODJZS - UK

Amazon.com Reviews

5.0 out of 5 stars Outstanding, April 16, 2013
By Misico
This review is from: LANCEJACK (The Union Series) (Kindle Edition)

This second book is even better than the first if that is possible. The character development and fast action combine to make this a truly memorable series. I look forward to the next one.
***

5.0 out of 5 stars Great 2nd book and hope for a 3rd, April 14, 2013
By Theodore H Bertot

This review is from: LANCEJACK (The Union Series) (Kindle Edition)

This book was better than the first which I really enjoyed. I can't wait for the next book in the series. For a new author, Philip is outstanding.
***

5.0 out of 5 stars Very good, April 11, 2013
By Martin "ten98" (Canberra, Australia)
This review is from: LANCEJACK (The Union Series) (Kindle Edition)

As an ex grunt, I found the book excellent. I have worked in both jungle and urban warfare, and it brought back a lot of memories. Waiting for the next one.

ESCAPE FROM THE HIVE

—An exclusive preview of the new series —

Phillip Richards

A sudden tremor shook through Denrik's body. He stirred, an intense feeling of despair clouding his mind as if he had woken from a terrible nightmare. He was suspended in total darkness, his legs dangling freely below him. The still air suggested that he was indoors.

Denrik tried to recall where he was and how he had gotten there, but he remembered nothing. It was as though a black fog hung over his memories, black as the darkness surrounding him, leaving him with nothing other than an inexplicable yet almost overwhelming sense of loss and grief. He knew his own name, he knew that he was a soldier, but that was it.

Another tremor shook him, even more violently than the first. Metal groaned and machinery rattled noisily, as if he was within some kind of massive structure that was being pulled apart.

Denrik attempted to move, but something was restraining his body, trapping his arms at his side and holding his back rigidly straight. A sudden wave of fear passed over him, causing segments of his chitin armour to click as his muscles tensed. Something was terribly wrong.

What was holding him in place? He couldn't even move his head, as if something was clasping his skull firmly like a vice. His arms were trapped against his sides by what felt like manacles attached to his wrists, and numerous restraints were wrapped about his neck, torso and abdomen. Fear quickly mutated into dread, and Denrik became aware that his heart rate was rising steadily. Chemicals were being released into his bloodstream, as his body prepared itself for something terrible.

He struggled again, but could barely move. He was trapped, unable to fight, held aloft like a prisoner waiting to be executed. He suddenly became aware that there were others in the room – his comrades. They were all around him – he could somehow sense their presence despite not being able to see them. They were so close he could touch them if his arms were free, but their minds were dormant as though they were in a deep sleep. Then it occurred to Denrik, perhaps he wasn't *meant* to be awake either.

At that moment a long, ear-splitting groan reverberated around him, sounding like a mixture of protesting metal and the cries of an enormous injured beast. The noise caused whatever it was that held Denrik aloft to judder.

Wake up. Denrik urged his comrades, without saying a word. He knew that his mind could communicate with the other soldiers, and that normally they would respond in kind, but there was no answer. Their minds remained inactive.

Suddenly the whole room rocked violently, and something electrical sparked to his left, the light briefly flickering off rows of soldiers, hanging just above the ground like meat on a rack. The vision sent a fresh wave of terror across his body, and he struggled again.

Denrik shook his arms, trying to break free of the manacles so that he could attempt to wake his fellow soldiers. Perhaps his awakening had been a fluke, and the only way to alert his comrades was to remove them from the rack. Were they meant to be in the rack, or were they captive? He couldn't remember.

Metal screeched as the room shook again, but this time Denrik felt it tilt and fall downwards at alarming speed. He realised then that he was inside some form of massive aircraft, and sensed that it was about to crash.

He thrashed against his restraints with added urgency, desperately trying to release the manacles that held his wrists at his side. The manacle on his right was loosening, and he focused all of his efforts onto it, heart pounding as his powerful muscles battled to tear his hand free.

Another terrible groan, and more sparks showered, illuminating the racks properly for the first time. Denrik didn't have the time to count the number of soldiers before he was plunged back into darkness, but he guessed there was at least a hundred of them housed within a large chamber, all hanging in rows like dolls on a production line.

'Come on…' he growled at the manacle, his anger growing as he fought with increasing desperation. Finally, with one powerful tug of his arm, the manacle snapped away from the rack, the broken pieces clattering to the ground. Now all he had to do was use his free hand to remove the other manacle.

He was too late. With a mighty thump the aircraft struck the ground, and Denrik blacked out.

Another groan brought Denrik back to consciousness, this time a long, terrible groan as if the aircraft transporting him was crying out in pain. The room had tilted only slightly, suggesting that the aircraft had struck the ground on its belly.

Denrik used his free hand to work at the other manacle, ripping it away with relative ease before turning his attention to the restraints wrapped about his body. The restraints felt like an assortment of leathery cables and wires, all winding tightly about his armoured torso like the roots of a plant. He found a thick cable that ran around his chest and attempted to pull it away, but as soon as he did so a sharp pain pierced his stomach as if somebody had stabbed him with a knife. His muscles tensed as he resisted the urge to cry out in pain.

'What is this?' he asked aloud, tentatively tracing the cable with his hands until they stopped against the hard chitin armour segments that covered his abdomen. The cable went inside him.

Another shower of sparks illuminated the rack across from him, and he took the opportunity to study one of his comrades in greater detail. An identical cable ran out from the rack, coiling and twisting until it entered a hole in the soldier's stomach.

The aircraft groaned again, and Denrik's sensitive hearing could identify other sounds echoing from far away – gunfire. The aircraft was on the ground, and it was being attacked.

He gripped the cable again, his heart pumping faster as he prepared himself for the pain and whatever would follow. He had no idea what the cable did, what part of his body it was connected to, or what would happen when he pulled it out. All he knew was that he couldn't remain hanging in the racks, waiting for the unseen enemy to find and butcher him and his comrades.

'Come on,' he ordered his hands as they paused upon the cable, 'there's no choice…'

As soon as he pulled on the cable another stab of pain shot through his torso, but this time he continued the motion, slowly drawing it out of his body inch by agonising inch. The pain was so excruciating it caused him to baulk, and finally he gave in and screamed, his bloodcurdling cry echoing across the chamber as the cable, slick with blood, fell away.

He touched the hole left by the cable with shaking fingers, but although the wound was wet, there was no gush of bodily fluid flowing out of it.

He began to tear away the remaining cables and wires, but as he did so more pain seared across the back of his head, and he realised that another cable had been inserted into the base of his skull. The removal of his restraints was placing more weight onto the cable, and he realised that in order to drop to the ground he would need to pull it out as well.

This time the pain was even worse. The chamber reverberated with his screams.

Denrik hung silently from the rack for several minutes, clutching his head in his hands as he waited for the pain to subside. Slowly his heart rate and breathing returned to an acceptable level, and he began working at his restraints again.

The sounds of battle still echoed through the aircraft, though Denrik didn't know who was fighting who. His comrades still hung in their racks silently, oblivious to his struggle to free himself. They were still alive, he knew that much, but their minds were totally inactive. His only hope was to get to the ground and attempt to free them, in the hope that they would awaken before the enemy reached them.

A loud clang caused him to stop. Unlike the other sounds, its source was close, so close it was almost inside the chamber with him. He scanned around the chamber. The intermittent sparking of damaged electrical equipment provided little illumination, but he was almost certain that the chamber was empty except for him and his comrades.

Another clang, this time to his left. It was outside the chamber, he was sure of it, but it was very near, whatever it was.

Suddenly Denrik felt incredibly exposed in the middle of the chamber, totally unarmed. Where were their weapons kept? Perhaps the racks were keeping him and his comrades ready for their next deployment, so surely their weapons would have to be nearby?

The clangs continued, becoming louder and more frequent until they sounded as though somebody was battering at a door to the chamber, hammering it with furious blows.

He desperately wrenched at the last few restraints that ran across his belly, tough fleshy straps that were so tight he could barely get his fingers underneath them. Whatever it was that battered the door to the chamber, it sounded dangerous, and he knew that he needed to free himself fast.

He was too late, though. There was a sudden metallic screech, accompanied by an almighty clang as the door to the chamber gave way. Denrik froze.

There was a new sound in the chamber, something that Denrik hadn't heard before. Something was breathing heavily, something big.

With a high pitched squeal it launched itself into the chamber, the light from the sparks reflecting off bright, slick green skin as it struck the nearest soldier, thrashing at the unconscious victim with vicious claws. Blood splashed as it hacked chunks of flesh and armour from its helpless prey, before it leapt to another soldier, then another, squealing with rage.

Denrik watched from his rack, trying to maintain a posture similar to the others. The creature appeared to be attacking the soldiers mindlessly, so he guessed that it wouldn't notice that he was the only one that was awake. The ruse wouldn't keep him hidden forever, though, eventually it would be his turn.

More light flickered, and Denrik glanced down at the long cable he had pulled from his head, now lying on the floor. It was at least a meter long, and as thick as his thumb. Could he use it as a weapon?

The creature was close, leaving a trail of blood and gore as it slashed and battered its way along the racks. He watched as it made each attack, leaping with its arms out wide with claws extended and jaws wide open. Then, when close, it simply bit and slashed, using sheer aggression to overwhelm its opponent. Even if they weren't asleep, his comrades would struggle to fend off such a ghastly creature. What was it, and where had it come from?

Denrik knew that he couldn't wait on the rack to die. Maybe the creature would miss him and grow tired, but by then many more of his battle brothers would have perished. He couldn't allow that to happen.

He broke the last few restraints and dropped from the rack, landing in a crouch beside the discarded cable.

The creature stopped immediately, hanging from its latest victim as its ugly head swivelled to see what had disturbed its mindless slaughter. Its body was warm, so Denrik could see it easily with his thermal vision, but somehow it could see him too. He knew his armour gave off no heat, but perhaps the creature used sound and smell to track its prey, or something else entirely.

Denrik watched the beast warily, recognising it now that he could see it properly. It was strange that he knew what it was, even though he had no recollection of having seen one before. It was a "hunter", a monstrous animal that he and his comrades used as a weapon. He knew that they had very little intelligence, but they were vicious. This one was totally out of control, perhaps as a result of the crash.

His hands tightened around the cable. It was the only weapon available to him, and it would have to do. His chitin armour clicked, as he knew it did when he braced his muscles to fight.

The hunter let go of its victim and dropped to the ground, glaring at him with beady black eyes. Then with a shrill squeal it charged toward him, bounding with terrifying speed. Its jaws snapped as it approached, glistening wet with blood in the flickering light. It leapt into the air, spreading its clawed arms wide and opening its mouth to reveal rows of jagged teeth.

Denrik's powerful muscles snapped taut as they threw him out of the way, his head narrowly avoiding the hunter's talons as he whipped around it. It skidded as it landed, momentarily losing its balance, but that was all Denrik needed. He pivoted on one leg, kicking the beast in the back with so much power that it fell forward, landing flat on its face with a thud.

Claws skittered against metal as the monster shrieked with rage, thrashing its limbs as it stood and turned to face Denrik.

He studied the hunter as more sparks sprayed from a severed cable, trying to understand what it was thinking. Its eyes were black and tiny, barely visible above rows of blood-stained teeth, staring back at him with a mixture of anger and caution.

'Come on, then,' Denrik beckoned, adjusting the cable so that he held it as a noose in one hand.

The hunter charged.

Denrik dodged sideways, but this time he grabbed the hunter by one of its outstretched arms and swung it full force into one of the racks. It yelped in surprise as it struck the rack, but the sound was quickly cut short as Denrik threw the noose over its head with his free hand, jerking it back toward him.

The creature attempted to turn around, but Denrik moved too fast for it, shifting position so that he remained behind it as he took the cable in both hands and crossed them over. Then, in one fluid movement, he span around so that he and the hunter were back to back, and with all of his strength he bent forward, lifting it clear of the ground by its neck. It went wild, desperately trying to get its feet back onto the ground as the weight of its body began to choke it. Every time it moved Denrik pulled the cable tighter, crushing its windpipe so that its screams became wheezes as it fought for air.

The hunter thrashed for several minutes, trying its hardest to wriggle free, but it was no use. The harder it struggled, the tighter the cable became. Denrik kept its weight on his back, his muscles straining as they forced every last inch of life out of his victim. Once it finally stopped fighting he held it for another minute, making sure that it had definitely died. Then he threw it to the floor and tied its legs together for good measure.

Denrik didn't know why the hunter had attacked. He guessed that it had escaped from its cage, or from restraints similar to those that had held him in the rack. He knew that he needed to find a weapon before any more came.

He scanned the chamber, searching for clues to where he was and where the weapons were kept – if there even were any. He knew that he was aboard an aircraft, but that was it. Was this some kind of medical facility? Had he been injured?

He checked his body, searching for any signs of further injury. The large, smooth plates of armour that encased his body were all intact, except for the two holes where the cables had entered. He seemed to be fine – the only injuries he had sustained would have been caused by him pulling out the cables.

Denrik reached up to one of his comrades that hadn't been touched by the hunter, and tugged at the soldier's leg.

Wake up! He urged. **We're under attack!**

The soldier didn't move. His legs dangled lifelessly, like the limbs of a corpse.

This time Denrik grasped the cable that connected to the soldier's stomach and wrenched it out, but still there was no response.

'Wake up!' he ordered aloud, though he knew that shouting at his comrade would be futile. If the agony of having the cable pulled from his stomach wasn't enough to wake him, nothing else would. Not one of the soldiers had so much as stirred when the hunter attacked. It was as though they were all in a coma.

Another long squeal echoed through the aircraft, the terrifying sound sending a chill down Denrik's spine. He turned to where the hunter had battered its way into the chamber, expecting another one to appear at any moment. He could see the faint outline of an open doorway, and more darkness beyond. There were clearly more hunters outside somewhere and it was only a matter of time before one of them found its way into the chamber.

He broke into a trot, careful not to make too much noise as he hurriedly searched the chamber for a weapon or something that might help him to defend himself. He knew that he was a soldier. He knew that he ought to have a weapon. Surely there would be something nearby?

The chamber appeared to be circular, with ribbed walls that curved upward, networked by wires and cables that ran over every surface like blood vessels running over the surface of an organ. It was bare, but for the hundreds of racks that hung from the ceiling. Sparks poured down from severed cables, causing shadows to dance through the endless ranks of soldiers. It was an utterly terrifying spectacle.

There were no weapons in the chamber. As soon as Denrik realised this, he knew that he couldn't stay there. The only place to hide was amongst his comrades, but even that wouldn't save him if another hunter came – the beasts didn't seem to care if their quarry was conscious or not.

He cautiously approached the entrance through which the hunter had entered, treading carefully to avoid making a sound. He was heavy, and even though the ground beneath his feet appeared to be solid, it still thumped with every footstep.

The chamber entrance loomed menacingly over him as he drew near. It was almost twice his height, suggesting it had been designed for something far larger than him to pass through it. The door to the entrance hung open uselessly, twisted and warped where the hunter had beaten it open.

Denrik moved up to the edge of one of the doors, then slowly leant around it to stare into the darkness beyond. There was another chamber beyond the entrance, though this one was smaller and oval in shape. From its ceiling hung more racks, except there weren't any soldiers dangling lifelessly from them, instead there were weapons –– hundreds of weapons.

A wave of relief washed over Denrik. Though he couldn't recall using any of the array of weapons hanging before him like fruit from a plant, he knew what they all were and how they worked.

The nearest rack was only a few paces away, laden with dozens of rifles. He made a dash for it. Gripping the first gun, he tugged it downward, trying to release it from the rack, but it didn't budge.

Growling in frustration, he shook the weapon, trying to figure out how it detached from the rack. Leathery straps were wrapped about the weapon, similar to those that had held him and his comrades aloft. Presumably they were there to stop the weapons from falling down whilst the aircraft was in flight, but he had no idea how to release them.

He desperately tried to work his fingers under the straps, but they were almost fused to the weapon. He barely moved them.

Suddenly Denrik noticed a familiar sound of heavy breathing from the far end of the oval chamber. He glanced toward the source of the noise, but couldn't see anything. There was another hunter, somewhere just outside the chamber.

With renewed urgency, Denrik fought with the straps, shaking the weapon vigorously in his effort to free it from the rack.

'Come on!' he hissed at the straps, almost pleadingly. 'Come on, let go!'

Denrik realised that the hunter's heavy breathing had stopped, and the only person making any noise in the chamber was him. He froze, making a conscious effort to control his own breathing. His powerful heartbeat thumped like a drum in his ears.

The hunter's shrill squeal filled the chamber, causing him to jump. It knew he was there; the squeal was like a challenge.

There was no point in trying to keep quiet anymore. He tore at the straps, using his entire bodyweight to try to break the weapon from the rack.

The hunter burst into the chamber, charging toward him with an ear-splitting wail. It would take it less than a few seconds to reach Denrik, and he braced himself in anticipation of the attack.

The beastly creature was less than a few meters from Denrik when a mighty groan shook the chamber. The floor rocked beneath his feet, causing both him and the hunter to stumble. Metal shrieked in protest as the entire chamber flexed, as if a giant had gripped the aircraft in two hands and was attempting to bend it in half. Sections of floor cracked under the hunter, and orange flame belched through the crack, engulfing it.

Denrik lost his footing as a whoosh of hot air rushed over him, falling to the ground with a thump. The floor was beginning to tilt, and he felt himself beginning to slide away from the hunter – and the weapons.

Ignoring the wall of flame in front of him, he quickly scrambled to his feet and staggered back toward the racks.

The rack that held his weapon had partially detached from the ceiling. Seizing the opportunity, he yanked at the weapon with all his strength, finally breaking it away from the straps.

Only a few meters from him, the hunter scratched and clawed at the smooth, now slanting floor, desperately trying to gain purchase. It screamed painfully as flames from the crack continued to lick over its body, causing steam and smoke to rise from blistering green skin, but yet it continued unabated. It had no interest in survival, all it wanted to do was reach Denrik so that it could kill him.

Denrik quickly tested the rifle in his arms, as if he had done so a thousand times before. It was a large weapon, with an oversized trigger mechanism designed to fit his armour-plated fingers. He saw that it was loaded, and knew that it could fire fifty rounds before it needed a fresh magazine.

He pointed the rifle at the hunter as it attempted to crawl across the crack that had formed on the warped chamber floor, aiming between its eyes. It reached out toward him, clawed fingers flexing menacingly, before he finally pulled the trigger.

The rifle jolted against his shoulder as it fired. Flame spat from the barrel, propelling a round square into the hunter's head. It jolted with the blow, then let out another angry scream as if the round had merely angered it more.

'Die, you bastard!' Denrik roared, then fired a long burst of rounds into the hunter, not releasing the trigger until it had stopped moving.

There was no time to celebrate the death of the hunter. As soon as he stopped firing, three more hunters exploded into the chamber, their grotesque bodies illuminated in the orange glow cast by the flames.

Denrik fired a couple of rounds into the charging beasts, but still they came at him. He turned and ran back toward the first chamber, sped by the slope in the floor as well as the monstrous squealing behind him. He knew that his only hope was to return to his comrades and use the entrance as a choke point, channelling the hunters together so that his rifle could deliver maximum damage.

As soon as he was inside the first chamber, Denrik spun around and fired into the three beasts. They were much faster than he was, having cleared the crack in the floor and almost reaching the entrance. Seemingly unstoppable, they were barely slowed by the bullets that struck and tore through their sickly flesh.

They never reached Denrik, though, for just as the first hunter passed through the chamber entrance the ground rocked again, and this time he felt something give way beneath his feet.

Sensing the danger, he dropped the rifle, leapt upward to the nearest rack and clutched at the legs of one of his comrades, just before the ground beneath him fell away, taking the hunters with it. He watched in horror as the entire floor of the chamber disappeared, swallowed by a broiling cloud of inky black smoke.

Cold wind whipped at Denrik, who found himself hanging helplessly by the feet of his comrade, somewhere on the belly of the massive aircraft. The dark cloud of smoke closed in around him, so thick that it reduced his visibility to almost nothing. He had no idea how high up he was, but flickers of light within the smoke below him and the thumping of explosions suggested that the drop was significant.

The aircraft shook again, and several of the racks next to Denrik broke away, tumbling down into the smoke with their soldiers still attached to them. He watched his comrades as they fell into the void, wondering how long he could hold on until he fell as well.

Suddenly he heard a familiar sound over the wind, and turned his head up in horror. It was a hunter. The beastly creature had managed to escape the collapsing floor using the racks, just as he had, and had used the mass of cables and wires to climb above him.

The hunter reached down toward him, its wicked claws flexing within a hair's breadth of the fingers of his left hand.

Denrik strengthened the grip of his right hand on the soldier's leg and let go with his left, just before the hunter slashed through it. Blood sprayed into the wind as he swung away from the hunter, the sudden shift of weight almost causing him to fall. He clutched desperately with the one hand, but he knew that he couldn't hold on for long. He was far too heavy.

The hunter squealed as it lurched down toward him, thrashing with its free arm.

Denrik let go.

————

Pain. Denrik woke to terrible pain. His head and abdomen burned from where he had withdrawn the cables, and fresh waves of pain shot across his chest. The chitinous armour that encased him was strong enough to protect him from falls from a great height, but it was not invincible and neither was he.

Clutching at his abdomen, Denrik attempted to stand, but found to his dismay that a great sheet of metal had landed upon his legs, pinning him in place. He attempted to wriggle free, but the metal was too heavy for him to move.

He lifted his head to see where he had landed. The jagged, rocky landscape that surrounded him was scattered with flaming debris, causing shadows to dance across his vision.

He cast his head upward. The smoke had cleared enough for him to see the aircraft high above him, its dark, vast underbelly illuminated orange by the fires burning on the ground. It had landed upon a series of hills that held it aloft like great pillars of rock, leaving huge sections of its hull raised over the ground. The stress of so much weight was causing the hull to rupture, and he could see that the hole from which he had fallen was in fact part of a gaping tear far larger than the chamber itself. Sparks showered from severed power lines, and liquid poured from the torn hull like blood pouring out of a wound.

Denrik could hear the sound of gunfire distinctly now. A battle was being fought nearby, perhaps no more than a kilometre away. The unseen enemy had taken down the airship, and now they were going in for the kill. He had no doubt that they would slaughter all of his comrades, whether they were awake like him, or asleep in their racks. That was if the hunters didn't manage to kill them first.

Denrik turned his attention back to the metal across his legs. He needed to join in with the fight. Perhaps there were many more soldiers like him and his comrades, soldiers who had woken properly. They would need all the help they could get.

He pushed the metal upward with all his might, but it barely moved. He cursed as he dropped the weight back onto his legs.

Suddenly a familiar squeal sent a chill down his spine, and something emerged from amongst the debris like his worst nightmare made real. He froze.

The hunter had broken both of its legs, yet still it came at him, dragging itself forward with its jaws snapping viciously. Relentless in its hunt for blood, it wouldn't stop until it had killed him, even if that meant that it died in the process.

He cursed again at the metal, trying to lift it out of the way, but he knew that it would take too long. The hunter was nearly upon him, almost within striking distance. Denrik could make out pieces of flesh stuck in between its elongated fangs. It squealed at him, eyes burning with rage.

He looked around desperately, clawing for something to use as a weapon amongst the wreckage, but there was nothing small enough to wield.

Then he saw it. His rifle, the same rifle he had dropped when the floor gave way, had landed close to him. It was partially covered by another sheet of metal, though it didn't appear to be trapped like he was. He stretched out to reach it, his fingers brushing against the butt and threatening to push it away.

Just then the hunter slammed its claws against the ground next to him, missing his leg by centimetres. It dragged itself forward once more, then reared up as it prepared to deliver its fatal blow.

'No!' Denrik bellowed, straining his muscles as he made one final attempt to reach his rifle. His fingers closed around the butt, and he swung it with all his might toward the hunter's chattering teeth. It struck the creature's mouth with such force that it shattered several of its teeth instantly and sent it tumbling backward.

Denrik quickly adjusted his hold on the rifle and attempted to shoot at the hunter as it lay dazed on the ground, but the weapon didn't respond. The fall must have damaged its internal parts, rendering it useless. It took all of his mental strength to resist the urge to toss it aside in a fit of rage. It was his only weapon, functional or not.

The hunter let out a wheeze of air whilst Denrik used the rifle to lever the metal away from his legs, allowing him to slide free. He picked himself up and staggered toward the stricken monster. It looked up at him as he approached, blood pouring from its mouth, and he knew that despite its injuries it would soon attempt to attack him again. It knew nothing other than to hate and to kill.

'Die you bastard!' Denrik hollered as he brought the butt of his rifle down upon the hunter's head. He clubbed at the monster again and again, until its skull caved inward and gore splattered over him. Then, covered in blood, he dropped to his knees, swaying over the battered creature as he fought to remain conscious.

His vision dimmed for a moment, as his mind slowly began to shut down. His body was battered, and he was mentally exhausted from his ordeal at the hands of the hunters.

Suddenly he remembered a voice. He didn't know whose voice it was, but the memory was so vivid it was as though somebody was leaning over him to speak.

No! We can fight them!

Suddenly alert, Denrik's mind raced as he tried to recall the voice, and who it was that had spoken, but it was as though a black curtain had dropped once more over his memories. Whoever it was, their defiant words had brought him back to his senses, giving him the overwhelming desire not to give in and die amongst the wreckage of the aircraft. He had to fight.

'We can fight them,' he uttered, repeating the words of his memory.

He rose to his feet slowly, trying to ignore the pain. He was strong, and so was the armour that supported him. It would do its best to keep him alive for as long as possible, hopefully long enough to do his duty. The survival of his comrades, was all that mattered.

He picked up his rifle and inspected it. Whatever damage the fall had caused to its internal parts, there was nothing he knew to do that would fix it. He tested the weight of the weapon in his hands and grunted. It had become little more than a club, but it was better than nothing at all.

He limped through the smoke toward the sound of battle, negotiating the flaming wreckage as best as his battered body could manage. A couple of times he stumbled on the carpet of twisted metal and slick, molten organic tissue, trying not to cry out involuntarily as fresh waves of pain washed across his body.

Far off to his left a pack of hunters had fallen to the ground, squealing at each other as though they were discussing a plan of action. He crouched behind a large chunk of flesh-like material that had dropped away from the aircraft and watched the trio, expecting them to charge at him any moment. Then, thankfully, they charged off in the opposite direction, bounding into the smoke. Perhaps the acrid fumes and the stench of burnt flesh had affected their ability to sniff out their prey, or maybe they had found something better to hunt.

Denrik relaxed his muscles and turned back in the direction of the battle.

Suddenly, with a squeal that caused him to jump in surprize, a hunter leapt at him from where it had hidden beneath some metal panels. Denrik dodged away from its talons, smacking it around the head with his rifle as he did so. The creature skidded along the ground and then lay still, either dead or unconscious.

He had no idea how many hunters the aircraft above him contained, but it was clear that the enormous machine, as large as a city, carried entire armies in its belly. There would be hundreds, maybe even thousands of them, and for some reason they had decided to kill all of the soldiers they could find. Had the aircraft's controllers given a bad instruction to the hunters? Or were they simply out of control?

There was something wrong about the situation, but to Denrik the only option available was to find his way to the battle.

He was just about to head off again when something darted right up to his face, causing him to jump again and raise his rifle in alarm.

A tiny insect hovered in front of him, its wings beating furiously as it stared right at him with its single camera-like eye. It was a "follower", Denrik realised, a creature he and his comrades used to gain information on the enemy.

You scared the life out of me. Denrik told the follower, swatting at it in annoyance. **Go away.**

Dodging his hand with ease, the follower darted back up to his face, as if daring him to try again. It was harmless, of course, with no weapons to speak of. It was little more than a flying camera.

He attempted to swat the creature again, but it refused to leave, its camera eye staring at him intently.

'What do you want?' Denrik demanded aloud, throwing his arms up irritably.

The follower stared at him for a moment longer, and then darted away from him and the sound of battle. It flew until almost out of sight, and then returned, stopping in front of his face again, wings buzzing.

Denrik understood the message easily enough. It wanted him to follow it somewhere, but he was reluctant to do so. Followers were tiny creatures, and not particularly intelligent. They worked to orders passed down to them by other soldiers, but with the hunters seemingly intent to slaughter his comrades he doubted the allegiance of the follower. Was it trying to help him, or was it trying to lead him into the clutches of another pack of vicious hunters?

Another squeal echoed through the smoke, and Denrik made his decision.

Very well, he said. **I will follow you.** He walked in the direction indicated by the follower.

Satisfied that he was doing what it wanted, the follower took the lead, maintaining a distance several paces ahead pf him. It darted to and fro, as if checking that the route was safe, occasionally checking behind to make sure that Denrik was still there.

More squealing sounded behind him, presumably as more hunters fell to the ground and began their search for prey. The blood curdling sound drove him into a trot, which eventually became a run for safety. Denrik ignored the pain across his body as he ran from the hunters, weaving between chunks of flesh and metal that had fallen from the aircraft. Above him the mighty machine groaned almost painfully, and there was a huge crash as a large chunk of it struck the ground nearby, sending a great plume of dust and ash into the air.

Despite the fact that he was moving away from the sound of battle, Denrik felt no shame in his retreat. Curiosity drove him to follow his new-found guide, for he knew that somebody was controlling it. Who were they? Any where were they taking him?

The follower led Denrik away from the fallen aircraft, until he was no longer beneath it. He caught glimpses of stars through the veil of smoke above. Behind him the massive machine towered high into the sky, flickering as fires continued to burn across its hull.

Denrik stopped at the foot of a tall, rocky knoll surrounded by low vegetation. He was growing increasingly tired, every step getting harder as the energy sapped from his body. He knew that he needed to rest, and to think about what to do next. The knoll offered a good view, and perhaps from its vantage point he could get an idea of where the follower was taking him.

The follower watched impassively as he clambered toward the top of the knoll, grunting in pain every time he pulled his body upward. Finally, once he reached the top, he collapsed to the ground, his chest heaving. He resisted the urge to let out a moan, as he tentatively ran a finger along the edge of the open hole on his abdomen. It was still wet with some kind of liquid, though it didn't appear to be blood. The cable he had withdrawn from his body had clearly meant to be there, but what damage he had done by simply yanking it out he didn't know. Judging by the pain it caused, it wasn't good. How his body had survived so far was beyond him, but he doubted that the armour could keep him going forever.

His hands continued to search his body, following its contours and lines as if it was the first time he had felt them. His body felt alien to him. The large slabs of organic armour seemed overly brutish, and his thick, powerful jaw was almost frightening to touch. Who was he? *What* was he?

The follower landed on his knee, gently fluttering its wings as it came to rest. It studied him carefully with its little camera, as if concerned for his well-being.

I need to rest, his mind pleaded with the insect. **Just for a little while.**

It appeared to understand, and instead it slowly manoeuvred itself to look outward, back the way that they had come.

Once Denrik's breathing returned to normal, he studied the burning hull of the aircraft from which he had escaped. It was truly massive, as large as a city if not even larger. It was too large to call an aircraft – it was more like an air*ship*, a leviathan with a shell-like upper hull that gave it the appearance of an enormous beetle. It lit the evening sky like a torch, and as the pair watched something exploded beneath it with a flash of light. A few seconds later the air thumped with the sound of the explosion, and the vegetation around them shook with the force of it.

Quite a fight had been fought beneath the airship, but something told Denrik that it was lost. With many of the soldiers either dormant or butchered by the hunters before they could even draw their weapons, it was likely that the remaining creatures would succumb to the attack. Why had the hunters turned upon the soldiers, and why hadn't they been woken to defend themselves?

There were so many questions, but the biggest question of all spun around inside his head, until eventually he asked it aloud.

'Why me?'

What made him different to all the others? Why had he awoken in those racks, when all of his comrades had remained asleep, and why had one single follower flown through the smoke and the flames to find him, and led him away from the hunters?

The little insect turned and gazed up at him.

Why me? he repeated.

The follower stared back, unable to communicate even if it wanted to. It wasn't meant to communicate directly to all soldiers, only to those who controlled it. Eventually it turned back to gaze into the horizon, as if standing guard for him.

Denrik tried to think of what he should do next, but nothing came to him. Without the airship he knew that he wouldn't survive. He knew that he needed to sustain his body, but he didn't even know how to do that. He looked down at the hole in his abdomen. Was that how he fed? He shuddered involuntarily at the thought of it. Part of his subconscious mind knew that that was how he was meant to feed, but the thought was still repulsive.

It then occurred to him that he was probably going to die. Between the packs of hunters running wild, the enemy that had brought down the airship and nature itself, his chances of survival were virtually zero.

Where was he going? Could the follower be leading him somewhere where he could be healed? Where other soldiers were forming up to mount a counter-attack?

There were no answers. The follower couldn't tell him. All he could do was sit and watch as the airship burned before him, his eyelids growing heavy as he laid his head back to rest.

Denrik woke with a start, his pulse racing. A terrible feeling of loss and despair sat in the pit of his stomach, as if he had woken from a terrible nightmare that he could no longer remember.

His internal body clock told him that he had been asleep for the whole night, and that it was now early morning. Sure enough, the sun was slowly rising behind the towering silhouette of the airship, its light barely able to pierce through the ugly black cloud that now shrouded much of the sky.

A deep, distant humming sound caught Denrik's attention, and he cast his gaze off to the east. Another airship had arrived, its menacing, insect-like shape unmistakable as it slowly drifted across the horizon like a storm cloud. Before it was a large, sprawling city, presumably its target. He could make out the shapes of aircraft spilling from its belly like wasps swarming from a disturbed nest. The airship was headed straight for the city, presumably to finish what the other had started.

Perhaps the hunters had indeed been tasked to kill all of the crash survivors so that the enemy couldn't take advantage of them, Denrik considered, since there was clearly no plan to save them.

There was something quite unnerving about watching the distant airship attack. The airship he saw was filled with soldiers like him – his own kind – so why did he feel a chill when he saw it?

He realised then that the follower was still perched upon his knee, as though it too was watching the event.

'We should head that way,' he decided, nodding toward the new airship. 'It's our only hope for survival.'

The follower didn't respond, though. It remained motionless, facing toward the advancing airship. Denrik gently nudged the insect, and it fell from his knee. It was dead. They weren't meant to survive for prolonged periods away from the airship; their bodies needed sustenance and their batteries needed power.

Whoever had controlled the follower had saved his life by leading him from the hunters and a battle that was surely lost, but for what reason he simply didn't know. Was there a purpose to his survival that he didn't understand? Was there something that he was meant to do? Either way, his guide was no longer with him, leaving him to find his way on his own.

He looked down at the tiny insect that had been used to save him, and the feeling of loss became almost unbearable. It was as though somebody special had left him, and now he was on his own.

With an armoured hand he scooped up a clod of earth beside him and placed the follower into the hole.

'Thank you,' he whispered, before covering it over, patting the earth gently afterward.

He didn't know why, but burying the insect seemed like the right thing to do. Perhaps that was what soldiers did with their dead, he thought.

There was no more time for weighing up options, mainly because there weren't any. Only the distant airship offered Denrik the resources to survive, without it he would surely grow weaker by the day until he finally died, long before anybody found him. He had no idea how long it would take for the battle to end, but he knew that he wouldn't be alive by then if he simply waited out in the country.

He picked himself up and then half stumbled, half slid down the knoll, taking a mental note of the direction to the airship and the city itself. Unfortunately for him, his own stricken airship lay between him and the city, and it would be teeming with hunters, the unknown enemy, or both. The only solution was to skirt around the crash site, heading east for many hours before turning north. It was a long way to travel, but it was the only way he could hope to reach his own kind.

He stopped to take one last look at the attacking airship before it disappeared beneath the horizon. It loomed menacingly over the city, as if poised to swallow it whole.

There was something terrifying about the airship, though exactly what invoked such dread in him he couldn't tell. Was it simply its size, the way it dwarfed the city before it? Or was it the unseen masters of the massive craft who made him uneasy?

FALLEN WITNESS

—Vision IV: Beneath the Clouds of Saturn—

Art: Andy Bigwood
Words: Tim C. Taylor

"I'm Spacer Doyle, and I too am a fallen witness. Spacer Cutts has told you about the trap set at Huygens Gap for the captured energy wraiths. The plan was complicated, with many parts that all had to succeed. Military commanders hate plans like that because in combat your opponent rarely does what you expect, even when you belong to the same species. But desperation drove us to this approach. We needed HMS *Brilliant* as bait, and no one could think of a better way to achieve that.

"At first the plan seemed to work. With the *Brilliant* behind and the hidden Q-Platforms in front, *Speedbird* cut power to its energy ring. In less than a second, all five wraiths who had been trapped inside emerged into space around Saturn, thirsting for revenge against the fleet they found ranged against them. The naked wraiths could do little damage, but if they could capture one of the human ships, they could bend its systems to their will and turn its weapons on our vessels.

"Before they reached any of the ships, HMS *Brilliant* activated its energy dish, sucking the wraiths inside its invisible manifolds. The wraiths resisted with all the fury of a freed animal fighting against recapture. They were desperate, and that gave them strength. Soon, their descent into *Brilliant's* prison slowed and then stopped altogether. Then the wraiths began to wriggle free.

"At that moment the Q-Platforms threw off their outer skin of ice and focused their energy beams on the wraiths, tripping them up and bundling them back inside *Brilliant's* powerful grip. Only one wraith still resisted, clinging onto the edge of *Brilliant's* cone of effect, trying to squirm away. It clung on long enough to take in its surroundings and change tactic.

"The Warspite-class battleships were among the Grand Fleet warships guarding the Huygens Gap against an energy wraith breakout. They had the quantum turbine rings that powered their Death Beats powered up and ready to fire. The wraith that was still free grabbed at the nearest Warspite ring and pushed away from HMS *Brilliant* with all of its strength.

"The trick worked. Captain Beaufort was in command of the unfortunate HMS *Sirius*, and she must have watched in horror as the wraith was sucked into her ship and began to slaughter her crew. Beaufort had a clear idea of her duty, though. She ordered her helm to bring down her ship's prow and power into Saturn's heart.

"With *Sirius* still maneuvering, she shuddered to a halt as the energy field of her Death Beat snared in the beams of the Q-Platforms. A complex system of forces fought each other for dominance before *Sirius'* main drive won out and powered the vessel down into the planet below, dragging in her wake a dozen artificial ice mountains, and their gun crews, that she ripped from Saturn's rings.

"By the time *Sirius* reached the outer wisps of Saturn's' gaseous atmosphere, the energy wraith had already killed Beaufort and her crew, and was pulling the ship out of her death dive. You can see in this image the moment when the captured *Sirius* was re-emerging from Saturn's atmosphere, under the energy wraith's control. One of the Q-Platforms is in the foreground, on the way to disappearing beneath the clouds forever.

"The North Americans with their energy whip system saved the day. *Saratoga* and *Trois-Rivières* lashed out, the tips of their whips damaging the power conduits that fed the engines of the brave HMS *Sirius*. Saturn's gravity did the rest.

"As *Sirius* was dragged down into hell, Saturn's atmospheric pressure tightened its remorseless grip around her hull. Halfway to the planet's core, *Sirius* would have splashed down into a sea of liquid metallic hydrogen. Somewhere farther down, when the pressure was millions of times what we are experiencing today in this auditorium, the warship's hull integrity failed and the ship imploded."

The death of the *Sirius* blankets the audience in a somber mood.

One of the children is more afraid than saddened and asks a question. "If the wraiths are creatures of energy, did that mean it escaped from Saturn?"

"It's a good question. Most people at the time thought it perished with the *Sirius*. Even for an energy being, the center of a planet is not a safe environment. Nonetheless a permanent watch was placed around Saturn. It is still alert and ready today. But who can be sure? Maybe the wraith is still there, waiting."

When he sees the look on the child's face, Doyle suddenly remembers the time when he had children himself, and how elusive they sometimes find sleep. So he adds: "I'm sure it's no longer alive. But it's good the navy keeps watch just to be sure."

Fallen Witness Vision V is on p457

MARINE CADET

—Book 1 of The Human Legion —

Tim C. Taylor

—— PART I ——

Alien Lover

Extract from the *NEW ENGLISH DICTIONARY*, Patriot Publishing, Human Autonomous Region, 2671CE

human.

n. **1.** An individual of the species *Homo sapiens*, possibly also of derivative species. **See also:** *augmented-human.*

adj. **2.** Characterizing mankind, as opposed to aliens, animals, and machines (including AIs).

adj. **3.** [*meaning derived from common alien usage*] oppressed, the ultimate underclass, the hopeless ones, unwashed : **as in** *The Human Legion.*

—— Chapter 01 ——

Arun glanced into the darkness of the side tunnel as he thundered past with the rest of Delta Section. His eyes could see nothing in the branch, and his helmet visor didn't ping up any threats. No one said a thing. Arun was sure he wasn't the only one to feel the deep shadows of the side tunnel burning with threat, but what could they do other than ignore them?

Keep running. That was all they could do.

The rest of Blue Squad was pinned down by a Troggie redoubt. Delta Section had been tasked with pushing ahead and left to outflank the enemy position. Every time they passed a branch in the tunnel, Arun felt even more isolated, but there were only eight Marine cadets in the section. To peel off a pair to check out each fork in the tunnel network would be beyond madness. In this crazy twisting warren, there could be no such thing as a front line, not unless they had an entire regiment down here. The enemy could strike from behind at any moment.

He glanced across at Springer, her mottled gray battlesuit pumping her along at a steady 15mph, her SA-71 carbine just one safety away from spitting railgun death. The sight stirred his pride, and buttressed his courage. Together they were strong.

"Halt!" called Cadet Corporal Brandt.

Delta Section braked. What was Brandt thinking of now?

As Brandt pondered his move, Arun's resolve began to drain into the dirt floor.

A moment ago, he'd been buoyed by the momentum of his armored unit. Seeing them stationary had the opposite effect. There was an old Marine saying, drummed into them since the start of novice school: *stay still and die.*

Arun scanned the walls and ceiling for signs of ambush.

Scuttlebutt had it that Trogs could swim through the soil as easily as a human diver through water. He shivered, imagining alien eyes observing him through the dirt walls. If that rumor were true, they were utterly flekked.

No point worrying about what you can't change, he told himself, but only half believed it.

Whether or not the Trogs were watching, Arun was certain that his superiors were. None of the humans had ever met a White Knight. Never would, either, but through their vast network of nano-spies, the White Knights knew everything that happened within their empire, and they had no room for disloyalty or incompetence, even when the source was as irrelevant as a seventeen-year-old human dumbchuck. Like Brandt, for instance.

"I don't like it, because…" Brandt's words died away as he tried to organize the dust motes floating around his brain into a plan.

Brandt was indecisive rather than stupid, but hesitation could get you killed just as readily as dumb orders. Brandt had only been made cadet corporal less than an hour before, a temporary promotion that didn't entitle him to be addressed by the rank, only as 'sir'. Cadet Lance Corporal Majanita, Arun's fire team leader, would've made a much better section commander.

"We've penetrated too far without resistance," spoke Brandt in his best semblance of authority. "You heard the briefing. The Troggie guardians we're facing have regressed mentally to the borders of sentience, but we mustn't mistake that for stupidity."

"Do you think they're creeping up behind us?" asked Del-Marie.

"Err, yes," agreed Brandt. "That's exactly what I mean. Osman, go three hundred meters back the way we've come. Check our rear is still clear."

"Sir!" Osman raced off to obey. He wasn't going to give any cause for complaint now, but give him a cup of grok in a rec-chamber, and Osman would cheerfully tell you exactly what he thought of Brandt's order. For starters, sending a lone cadet to check a position was against their training. They should go in a pair. Buddied up Marines could cover each other. They were more than twice as strong as two Marines on their own.

Everyone knew that.

"McEwan!"

Arun only allowed himself to hesitate for an instant before answering: "Sir!"

"Recce that side tunnel we've just passed."

"Yes, sir."

And so Arun McEwan, a seventeen-year-old Marine cadet, chilled with foreboding, entered the shadows alone.

If the tunnels had been constructed by human engineers they would have been wider, well-lit, and level, but Trogs weren't human. As Arun cautiously penetrated the tunnel, he felt the wrap of alienness tighten around him with every step. He flicked his visor display to survey mode and confirmed one of his suspicions: the tunnel was rising and falling in its depth below the surface of the hill above. The change wasn't obvious as you walked, given the frequent twists and turns. Half-expecting an alien warrior to spring at him from out of the shadows, he quickly switched back to tactical mode, and breathed out when no threats were displayed, though it also told him that he was out of comms contact with his comrades.

Suddenly he was gasping, fighting to control his breath. Why hadn't Brandt sent Springer with him?

He calmed his breathing, but his instincts still told him he was in danger. With his visor tac-display showing no movement, no EM activity, and no inexplicable heat signatures, those instincts were indistinguishable from cowardice. To be afraid was inevitable, even for a Marine. To succumb to fear, though… that was punishable by death.

So Arun pressed on around a tight left bend and immediately came to a halt when he saw the tunnel narrow ahead. He would have to turn sideways to squeeze through the gap. Even if he were dressed in fatigues, it would be tight. The bulky battlesuit he wore meant he would have to force his way through.

Or try to. He could easily get stuck in there, deep inside enemy territory with no one to call for help.

He felt the crushing weight of earth envelop him, driving the breath from his lungs. He bent over, hands on knees, and fought to even out his short, rasping gasps. The walls ahead seemed to tremble, all the more eerie in the blue glow of his enhanced low-light display. That had to be his mind playing tricks.

Didn't it?

The tunnel was constructed from nothing more than trampled soil mixed with alien spit. The incalculable weight of soil overhead was not held up by some product of advanced materials technology, as with the human and Jotun Marine base. Just spit. Perhaps the shock waves from heavy weapons fire was bringing the hill down on top of him.

Arun wanted to go back. The fear was so intense he was on the brink of sobbing. If he triggered an ambush, then he'd die. If the ceiling collapsed he'd die. He'd been a cadet for just two weeks. What dungering use would dying be to anyone?

Flushing these tunnels of Trogs was supposed to be a training exercise, but the enemy didn't know that. The danger was very real. He took a deep breath. And another. To push his fears away was beyond him, but he rose above them enough to find sufficient air and calm for his brain to kick in and think!

Brandt wanted a recce. To advance five hundred meters down the tunnel sounded acceptable. Even though Arun had lost his Battle Net connection, he daren't lie about how far he'd gone down the tunnel. The chance that the Jotun officers were recording everything was too great. He would get to the five-hundred-meter mark, count out ten seconds, and then run back.

Now that he had a plan, a little confidence returned.

Pace by faltering pace, Arun squeezed sideways through the gap, using his power-assisted musculature like hydraulic rams to force his way through.

The earth was darker here. Damper too. Bubbles of foam oozed from the soil and stuck to his battlesuit; loosened soil tumbled to the floor, piling up almost to his knees.

It felt like climbing into the throat of an immense and hungry beast.

After a final series of twists, the constriction opened up again. He began to breathe more normally until the very walls began to tremble in a freakishly organic movement, as if the tunnel itself were breathing. Perhaps that was exactly what the tunnel was doing. He'd seen no obvious sign of ventilation and who knew what these aliens were capable of? His battlesuit AI, Barney, confirmed the motion: whatever was happening to the walls wasn't a figment of his imagination. This was for real.

Great, he thought. Just frakking great.

He checked himself. He was a Marine, and Marines *think*. He might not know much about the Trogs, but the Jotuns did and they had selected this exercise. The older cadets he knew, those in Class G and Class G-1, had all lived through similar exercises, though they were not allowed to discuss the experience. They'd survived. Logic said he should too. Probably.

Class G-1. Of all the cadets in the year ahead of him, Arun saw in his mind's eye the smooth oval face and dark midnight eyes of Xin Lee. She'd come through this alive. What would she think of him if she ever found out he'd gotten the scoojubbers in his first live fire exercise?

Emboldened by his logic — and thoughts of Xin — Arun switched his visor back to survey mode, and placed a target marker at the spot that Barney estimated to be five hundred meters into this tunnel. The target appeared as a glowing green cross slightly to his right, past a sharp bend, and an estimated distance to go of only sixty meters.

Once again the tunnel shimmered.

Switching his helmet to tactical didn't show up anything to fight.

"C'mon, Barney," Arun whispered to his suit AI. "Help me out."

Barney's response was to flash the green target marker at him again.

"Okay. Okay! I'm going."

The conviction that the walls were alive proved too much. Twenty meters short of his target, Arun lost his nerve. He turned and fled. The movement in the tunnel walls gave him something important to report. That was why he was withdrawing, he told himself, not because he was a coward.

From behind him came the sound of scuffling, the dull sprinkling of falling soil.

Something was digging through the walls!

He ran faster, a risky maneuver in a battlesuit over uneven ground. Nothing would be worse than losing balance and tumbling headfirst into the alien dirt.

The frantic scurrying sound grew in volume until it drowned out the digging.

When he reached the narrow gap, he realized he'd been trapped. He turned to face whatever was coming for him from behind.

He saw a blur of black insectoid bodies scuttling toward him along the floor, ceiling and walls. Each creature was half as big again as a human, with a halo of barbed horns surrounding the head, and vicious fighting claws adorning the front pair of legs.

Troggie guardians.

These barely sentient aliens had no concept of the words 'training exercise'. Only one thing drove the guardians: the burning desire to kill any intruder in their nest.

He didn't need to ask Barney to know that they were coming for him faster than he could push through the narrow passageway.

Reason said that his only chance was to stand and fight.

But reason had fled even faster than the rest of Arun.

Fear drove him to bully his way through the narrow constriction, gouging out more clumps of slimy earth from the walls as he went.

Then he was through to the far side. Still alive.

"This is only an exercise," he blurted to himself, but he knew death was only seconds away.

Fifteen meters ahead was a tight right turn and beyond that, the main corridor. He made it as far as the turning, but then his courage failed again and he had to turn and *see*.

Drawing on countless hours of combat drill, as he turned, he seamlessly readied his SA-71 carbine, bracing the stock tight in against his shoulder in readiness for the ferocious recoil kick he knew was coming.

Then he opened fire.

Every ten milliseconds the twisting railgun inside the barrel charged, launching a spinning kinetic dart out of the muzzle at Mach4. For the first two seconds of full auto fire, the darts whistled out the muzzle so gently it was as if Arun were blowing a stream of deadly butterflies. Then the recoil dampener tripped out. The carbine kicked and writhed with such fury that he couldn't aim with more accuracy than to point in the right general direction. But he didn't want sniper shots. He was after a withering barrage.

The SA-71 delivered.

Ichor and carapace fragments flew from the aliens. Horns shattered. Legs were chipped into fragments, making the insects trip and fall and stumble.

When the ammo carousel reported only 15% of the darts remained, Arun ceased firing. The alien advance was still pouring through the gap, drilling in and out of the solid walls as if swimming through a soil sea. *Would nothing stop them?* They powered around their fallen comrades. Every alien heart pumped hard to accomplish a single goal: to kill Arun.

Particulate matter from alien body fragments churned into a black fog that would have choked Arun if not for his helmet filters.

Oh, drent! His carbine wasn't going to be enough. He needed the tripod-mounted beam weapons and missiles of the Heavy Weapons Section.

Without really thinking about what he was doing, he'd turned away from the enemy guardians. Stumbling into a run, he unsnapped a grenade from his hip and rammed it into the launcher underneath his SA-71's barrel.

He swung around.

The lead Trog was about eight meters away.

He fired.

In that half-instant before the grenade blew, he saw more guardians emerging from the ceiling on his side of the defile, burrowing out from the earth. Their numbers were too great to count, but he saw enough to know that any aliens he slaughtered would be more than replenished.

Then the grenade's blast wave hit him, followed by a shower of alien ichor and gore.

Arun too sailed through the air and landed against a curve in the tunnel wall, his ears clearing enough to hear the hard body fragments clatter to the floor like frozen leaves in the fall.

Roof and walls began to drip with purple slurry in which black and brown rubbery chunks were mixed with clumps of falling soil. Then a half-dozen aliens fell through the top of the roof, bringing more showers of earth with them. Flailing all six limbs as they fell, they landed on the jumble of chitin below, skidding down to join the ungainly heap of living aliens scrabbling to right themselves.

The hordes behind kept coming, slipping and slithering into an ungainly mass that could not win purchase, only impede itself.

The grenade's shaped blast front had left Arun dazed but relatively unscathed. His visor had cracked, its display unavailable, including its low-light enhancers. Smart armor had reduced fatal shrapnel to punishing bruises, but his left knee was numb and unbending.

When his senses came back, Arun hurriedly switched on the lights at the side of his helmet. One of them worked, revealing that the wavefront of alien death had slowed more than he'd hoped. He estimated that his grenade had won him a fifteen second remission before he was sliced to a bloody pulp with those front-limb claws, or impaled on the wicked horns.

Last chance, then.

He activated *combat immunity*, the emergency combat-med that would numb all sensation within three seconds, and allowed him to keep focused on killing, even if he were critically wounded. He used his right leg to push up from the floor, feeling his left knee crunching as he did. By the time he'd gotten to his feet, the pain was gone and he charged at the onrushing insectoids. Grinding noises came from his left knee; he heard his leg tearing and splintering. He smelt the moldy stink on the aliens.

By the time he'd brought up the next grenade, and engaged it in the launch attachment, the pain had gone — *all* feelings had gone. He pressed his gun's trigger with his numb fingers and was lowering his head — too late — before the soil and chitinous armor blew over his face, almost burying him. Reaching round to the utility attachment patch on his back of his battlesuit, he snapped off another grenade, setting it to a new blast mode while he clicked it into place.

Barracks rumor — allegedly from older cadets — hinted that carrying extra grenades would be a good idea for this exercise, and that blast mode 37H might get you out of a tight spot in a Troggie nest. Whether his senseless fingers had actually punched the right code was another matter. Normally he'd tell Barney to set weapons modes, but his suit AI wasn't in a fit state to listen.

He had been trained since birth to be a Marine, bred for it, in fact. Between the years of drill and the combat meds, his mind was not much more than a spectator as he fired the grenade at the mass of aliens.

Another blast of soil and diced bodies flung itself over his disabled visor, but more subdued this time. The grenade had tunneled through the pile of aliens and buried itself deeply into the tunnel wall behind. This blast had wreaked much less destruction, but had won him time by giving the body pile such a kick that many Trogs lost their footing again.

The combat immunity drugs seemed to be trying to tell him something, to make him remember something from training. He didn't exactly have time to sit down and hum a memory-inducing meditative mantra, so he blanked his mind and followed his instincts… *to burrow!*

Instead of firing at the aliens, he turned his back on them, firing another grenade at the curve in the tunnel wall where he'd been flung by the first grenade.

The blast buried itself into the wall, hurling a cloud of spoil out into the tunnel and coating Arun who'd flung himself to the ground just in time. Even before he'd gotten to his feet and wiped his visor clean of soil and sticky gore, he'd set another grenade to code 37H — *emergency excavation blast mode*, an implanted memory informed him — and fired again into the small alcove carved out of the wall by the previous blast.

But it was all too little too late because he felt the impact of an armored claw slashing him from behind, just before the grenade blast blew him backward off his feet to fall onto hard unyielding carapace and slide down onto the sticky floor. His smart battlesuit armor soaked up enough of these blows to keep him alive for now.

Around him, the nearest aliens stirred feebly. Still half-stunned himself, Arun took a gamble. Instead of racing on into the hole his grenades had scooped out, he got himself up to a kneeling position and put one last 37H into the center of the cloud of alien body debris in front of him. This time he braced while the blast front rolled over him. Then he was staggering to his feet and stumbling on into the spray of soil and aerosol blood, and beyond into the hole the grenades had burrowed out of the soil. Clouds of spilling earth blinded him, but he judged he'd crawled in fifteen meters before the hole stopped and he could go no further. He abandoned his carbine, freeing both hands to burrow into the loosened soil, throwing it behind him like a gauntleted mole.

Euphoria gripped him. He'd abandoned his firearm, a capital offense, and the Trogs would dice him into a hundred bloody chunks any moment now, but he couldn't help but grin at the simple pleasure of using his hands like paddles. For this task, his combat immunity numbness actually seemed to help.

Then he reached soil that was still too compacted to shift. Actually he'd hit that barrier several moments or minutes ago. The sense of time's passage had numbed with most of his other senses. Even in the depths of confusion, one thing rang clear: Arun had nowhere left to run.

He screamed. High-pitched like a child. His scream cracked, turning into some hybrid of a sob and a gasp.

"McEwan, come in!"

Nowhere to run! Flekked!

"Report!"

Those aliens had done this. Those Trogs. He'd make them pay…

Arun twisted around and charged at the Troggie horde who'd gathered around the entrance to his hole.

He'd rip their legs off their stinking alien bodies.

"Report, cadet! Damn you! That is an order."

The irritation in Brandt's voice reached through the helmet speaker and sent a jolt of challenge into Arun's mind. He slowed as he wondered what the frakk he was doing charging along an alcove to head butt a pack of slavering aliens desperate to reach inside and kill him.

Damn those experimental combat drugs.

"I'm under heavy assault," he whispered into the helmet mike, more interested in putting his brain back into order than following reporting protocol. "I seem to be alive. I feel rather good, actually, thank you for asking."

"I didn't. I asked you to report."

"I did."

"I want a sit-rep. What's happening? We came back when Osman reported movement, but now he's dead and we're pinned down. What are you going to do?"

In front of him, Arun could see his carbine half-buried in the dirt where he'd dropped it. The gun looked so pretty there. Shiny. He wanted it. But the aliens were reaching into his hole, flicking their claws at him, and the gun was so close to the bad insects.

Big, *fat* insects. They were too big to follow the human into his hole, and whatever had let them swim through the walls earlier wasn't working here.

Arun shuffled around until his feet were pointing at the aliens and slid his left boot towards the waiting creatures, ever so gently.

Ever since they'd emerged from the walls and ceiling, the Trogs had been slavering, chittering beasts climbing over themselves in desperation to rend him limb from limb.

Now they froze. Arun froze too. His pulse was a dull drumming inside his helmet; there were no other sounds — until Brandt growled: "Well?"

"I think I'm going to kill them," Arun said. "Or maybe the other way around. I'm not sure yet. I'll report back when I know."

There was a way to turn off his comms unit, but he couldn't think what that was right now. He asked Barney to switch it off, but Barney wasn't listening for some reason. He tried out emergency eyeball gestures but they didn't work either. If he could, he would have taken the frakking helmet off and buried it.

Brandt was very annoying. If he couldn't turn him off, Arun decided he would drown out his voice. So Arun began to sing, a stirring ballad about the beauty of Old Earth, the precious homeworld left so very far behind. The chorus was rousing; just the thing to belt out with your pals at the end of a rec-evening.

His song got the attention of the Trogs. Each guardian shifted its head for the best reception of his singing voice. Perhaps his song was charming them to obedience, or sleep, or an even fiercer rage. Maybe they liked the words.

Inch by inch, he shuffled toward them, trying to slip his toe through the strap of his carbine. Ever so slowly… almost there…

"Are they coming in our direction? Report, McEwan!"

Oh, frakk! Brandt's voice had come out of his external suit speakers, spooking the Trogs so they were jumping around as if he'd rammed a red-hot poker up their butts.

Arun abandoned his attempt to be subtle and slid towards the gun as fast as he could.

At the same moment, the sea of alien motion flowed at his crude little tunnel and launched something at him, a dark blur of motion with hate in its alien head and coming right at him.

Double dung!

He'd wasted a precious heartbeat watching the thing come for him. The tip of his toe reached the gun strap. By yanking back his leg and contorting his torso so forcibly that this muscles spasmed, he whipped the gun his way and grabbed. Grabbed the *barrel* end.

He started shuffling back as this new thing came close.

Too late!

As he was spinning the gun round to point the killing end at the attacker, the beast finally reached him.

Arun looked up from his gun. At first he thought his opponent was a Troggie child but it was difficult to make out because it moved so very fast, all flashing limbs and flailing body and jaws. It was so close that the beam of helmet light didn't spread wide enough to pick out the limbs in detail.

When the creature flicked a claw across his leg, a realization hit him with pointless urgency: guardians are the last stage of the Trog lifecycle. There's no such thing as a guardian child.

What faced him was an adult guardian with four of its limbs ripped out. Only the front two remained, held out in front of its head as combined motive force and assault weapons. This was the hive creatures' answer to the narrowness of his crawlspace.

Spikes of pain flickered up his legs as the mutilated Trog cut into Arun, using the young cadet's flesh to pull itself closer until it could make a killing blow.

Arun wiggled his toes. And laughed.

Without most of its limbs, the Trog couldn't get power behind its attacks. Seeing as he could still move his toes, he probably wasn't going to die from its claw strike. Not just yet.

With a slightly firmer hold on his SA-71, he brought it to bear on this crazy alien. But the beast flicked the carbine out of his hands, which were still too numb from the combat immunity to grip properly.

Helplessly, he watched his gun sail overhead, out of reach, to land with a dull thud behind him, at the far end of the short tunnel gouged out by Arun's grenades.

Then the crippled guardian flopped its middle segment — its thorax, he supposed it was called — onto Arun's legs, pinning him with its weight. Arun flung his body left then right in a frantic attempt to wriggle free. His legs slid slowly towards freedom but not quickly enough.

The two-limbed Trog raised its legs up and sliced down, aiming in a coordinated attack that convinced Arun that these guardians knew a lot more about human anatomy than he'd given them credit for. It aimed that metal-sheathed claw directly at his heart.

At the moment the claws started to bite into his armor, Arun screamed.

He rampaged through his memories, trying to remember all of it while he still had a chance. He screamed all the way, only stopping when the realization hit him that he'd never properly been in love with a woman. It was so unfair to end it all now, when he was just getting his life started.

Then another unexpected thought struck him: he still wasn't dead.

Looking down at his chest, he saw the claw embedded inside his ACE-2/T training suit, and it hurt like frakk, but… his smart armor had caught and held the blow. The constraints of the narrow tunnel dimensions, the lack of limbs… whatever the reason, the claw was stuck!

The guardian thrashed madly, banging each side of the tunnel in turn, making Arun worry about a cave-in but allowing him to free his legs. All this time, the Trog made no sound at all except for the thudding of its carapace on the dirt walls.

Then it abandoned that tactic and reduced itself to flopping back onto Arun, trying to pin him to the ground.

"Only a matter of time before I get out, my friend," said Arun, beginning the work again of wriggling free.

The alien hissed at him. The sound was like a pressure valve release. Perhaps this meant challenge or hatred. It might be its death rattle or it might mean: "Well done, sir, for besting me." How could he know? It was a drenting, skangat alien for frakk's sake.

With his legs about halfway to freedom, Arun heard an answering hiss from the main tunnel, and a second mutilated alien launched itself at him.

One chance remained… Arun activated the emergency release on his battlesuit, gasping as the shock instantly hit his system. Emergency suit release felt like his body was turning inside out. Endocrine pumps retracted from insertion points. Myriad med-points detached from their hold through his skin. Waste pipes released his penis and slithered out of his anus. Clamps popped. Warm lubricants dripped.

Arun slithered free of his clothing in a short series of slurping wrenches.

The second Trog had reached its companion and tried to squeeze past. With three-quarters of its limbs missing, and the first Trog still stuck to the battlesuit's armored torso, the newcomer never stood a chance.

By the time the second Trog managed to push its head and thorax past its companion, Arun had finally reached his gun. He fired a controlled burst of darts.

The insect's front limbs exploded into chunks. Wet shrapnel of head and jaws and thorax peppered the area.

Arun released pressure on the trigger and inspected his handiwork. Both beasts were still twitching.

He switched the gun's ammo supply from kinetic darts to rocket rounds: *bangers*. The main purpose of bangers was to be fully recoilless, something very handy in zero-g combat out in deep space. But even here under a planet's surface, the rounds still made a decent bang.

Arun pumped ten seconds of fiery destruction into the two battered Trogs, imagining the blessed day when he would be issued with micro-nukes. Then the gun pinged that its ammunition was exhausted, and he remembered the downside of bangers: they were far larger than darts, so you couldn't fit many into an ammunition carousel.

After the black rain of chitin chunks had subsided, he tried cleaning his slick hands by wiping them on the walls, but the walls were soggy too. Maybe it was just as well they hadn't issued him with nukes.

The two mutilated Trogs that had attacked weren't moving, weren't even an obstacle any longer. Outside in the main tunnel it was a different story. An ocean of six-limbed aliens waited for him.

"Should have evolved the opposable thumb," he shouted at the enemy. As taunts went, it didn't have much effect. He reached for fresh ammo to reinforce his message.

Oh, drent!

That was when he remembered he had squirmed from his battle dress in order to escape from the aliens pinning his legs. He was naked, save for his helmet and gauntlets. His ammo was still attached to the battlesuit that he'd discarded underneath the two Trogs, the same Trogs he'd just liquidized with a volley of explosive bullets.

Frakk it!

As he crawled over the slurry he'd created, he struggled to spot his battlesuit under its covering of gore. Something of vaguely the right shape was there, pushed farther up his hole toward the waiting Trogs.

As he advanced, the Trogs outside stilled, and silenced. He preferred them manic; this was more menacing somehow. He ignored the guardians waiting just out of slashing range and wiped at the muck coating his half-buried suit. Arun flipped over the armor, which revealed shapes in the slurry underneath. Feeling with his hands, he found an intact fastening from an equipment pack, and two unused grenades. Underneath a shard from his drink bottle, he found an ammunition carousel. In a smooth and swift motion, he rammed the ammo into an unused socket in his carbine, took a kneeling posture, and fired.

Instead of the soft whine of darts, Arun heard an angry whir as his carbine rejected the ammo carousel, and then a faint plop as it fell to the wet ground.

When Arun crouched down to retrieve the bulb of ammunition, a wave of stench hit him: a Trog pheromone signal. It was an earthy smell; probably it carried layers of meaning to the aliens: taunts and an incitement to victory. To Arun it was remarkably similar to the pungent aroma of unwashed socks.

Zug might know what that scent meant, but his friend wasn't here. At this moment, his best friend was the AG-1 Ammunition Carousel, a dull-gray plastic bulb filled with bullets, darts and shells, a reservoir of sabot resin, and a power pack whose ability to recharge itself was as near as frakk to magical. Arun blew into the carousel's opened feed interface. Dark goop spewed out, gobbing into his eye. He blinked furiously.

Willing his tear-smeared eye to remain open, Arun snapped the slightly-cleaned ammo carousel into his carbine, which clicked and whirred hungrily… and carried on whirring. His gun was unhappy. A blue light lit up on its stock. He couldn't make it out. So he brought the stock to his head and thumbed for the carbine's AI to give an audio status.

"Ammo feed impaired. Risk of explosion. AG-1 contents only partially utilizable."

Partial, eh? Arun squinted out of his hole. He saw aliens as far as he could see. He shrugged. Once the dumb bugs worked out that all they needed to do was widen the opening to his bolt-hole, he was going to die anyway. *Partial* would do just fine.

Arun overrode the warning and fired into the waiting horde. He screamed incoherent sounds of battle fury as his weapon accelerated sporadic volleys of kinetic darts interleaved with frequent misfires. On and on he pumped death through the aperture of his hastily excavated hole, until he realized the ammo supply feed was clicking through an empty reservoir.

Drop by splatter, the aerosol of ichor and soil succumbed to gravity and cleared, engorging the dark pools already on the floor.

Recognizable fragments of carapaces, jaws, horns and legs poked out from the jumble of undifferentiated alien chitin… and… moved!

Icy fear cooled his battle fury. Dead aliens moving… he'd heard of undead aliens in the morbid rumors that frequently washed over the human community on Tranquility. Arun reckoned that ninety-five percent of this scuttlebutt was drent. That left five percent with at least an undercurrent of truth, such as the tales of alien warriors who could not be killed. Every time you snuffed out their life, they reconstituted, coming back stronger than before.

He shuddered. In front of him, as the spray of destruction cleared a little more, he could make out chitinous bodies jerking into movement, reassembling themselves. *Returning to life.*

Relief flooded his body when he realized what was really happening. He slapped a hand on his bare thigh and laughed so hard that he had to sit down. The dead Troggie guardians weren't coming back to life; it was their living nest-siblings removing their fallen comrades to clear the way for another attack.

As if to reinforce that common sense was returning to his world after that fright, he noticed the Trogs had lost their earlier attack mania, and were now using their combat claws to widen the entrance to his hole. They frequently stopped to examine the walls and roof, feeling them with their mid-limbs. These were guardians, he reminded himself: the last stage in the Trog lifecycle. He guessed these vecks weren't normally allowed to do any digging.

Arun backed away the short distance to the rear of his hole and counted down his last moments before evisceration. He'd heard you were supposed to cry for your mother when you faced certain death.

That didn't seem to be working for him, so he closed his eyes and tried to bring up memories of his mother.

She had been kind enough, but she had always known that one day she would be shipped out-system, leaving him behind. That she had kept her emotional distance was obvious to him now.

He couldn't even picture her face, just a name and rank: Sergeant Escandala McEwan.

Inefficient yet remorseless, the Trogs dug him out. Arun kept his eyes shut, but the unceasing scraping noise told him they were almost within range of a claw strike. As he waited to be sliced, his thoughts drifted to Stephen Horden. The older cadet had claimed to be descended from the President Horden of Earth who had signed the Vancouver Accord and condemned the ancestors of the Human Marine Corps to perpetual slavery.

Arun had never cared about lineage. What impressed him was how Horden had built quite a following with his secret teachings on Earth history, and compelling arguments about why Old Earth was something worth fighting for — worth *humans* fighting for — and, one day, returning to as free people.

Horden had graduated the year before, part of a replacement list sent off to some garrison fleet around the mining system of Akinschet. Arun's mother had been posted there. Perhaps the two would meet?

Fighting for humanity… as he waited to die a pointless death on behalf of uncaring alien masters, he wondered what it must be like to fight for a cause you could believe in, a new kind of Human Marine Corps that actually fought for humanity.

Without warning, every Trog simultaneously emitted a screech like poorly lubricated wheel brakes. A few seconds later came another pheromone-laden smell. Like rotten fruit this time.

Guess that meant contemplation time was over.

He opened his eyes. The guardians had withdrawn from his hole, standing motionless in the main tunnel corridor. Great! They must have found some digging-caste Trogs to get at him safely without bringing the roof down.

"Cease fire, humans!"

The voice seemed to be coming from within the tunnel walls, not from a single source but diffusely spread throughout this area of the hive. "This exercise is concluded. Cease fire!"

Within moments, the guardians calmed to a stop, listing woozily. If the notion wasn't so absurd, he'd say they had grown sleepy.

A ripple spread through the insectoid mob. The disturbance came from a new kind of Trog. Smaller and more lightly colored, this one lacked the halo of sharp horns. When the newcomer had pushed through the crowd and stood at the entrance to Arun's little cave, he could see its carapace was as black as the guardians but covered in fine red hairs that looked unexpectedly delicate, when picked out in the beam of his helmet lamp.

Instructor Rekka had explained in her briefing that this was a Trog in an earlier stage of the lifecycle: a *scribe*.

"The guardians will not harm you now," spoke the scribe via a box hanging around its neck, which whirred with gears as it generated a mechanical version of a human voice.

Arun wasn't convinced. But, what the hell? It beat cowering. He got down on hands and knees and slithered through the floes of spent sabots floating in a carnage sea. It was like crawling through a midden pit dug for an outdoor field exercise, except now he was so close to the chopped aliens, he smelled a tang of sweetened metal.

This had only been a training exercise.

But when he looked around at corpses of his supposed allies, killed by his own hand, he wondered whether the scribe would see things the same way.

—— Chapter 02 ——

The alien scribe stood motionless amidst the scene of combat carnage. Two pairs of glassy black bulbs — Arun assumed they were eyes — stared at Arun. If the creature was showing any kind of emotional reaction to the death of its fellows, it wasn't in a form a human could recognize.

Arun's combat drugs were beginning to wear off, enough for him to reason that the best thing for him to do was shut up, keep still, and await orders…

Thinking of orders… why wasn't Brandt shouting at him through the comms link in his helmet? Was Brandt dead?

"I have given them a pheromone order to render them dormant," said the scribe's box after a while. "You too should take on a dormant state, human Marine cadet."

He waited for the scribe's box to say more, but the creature had said all it intended to for now. The hairs on the insect thorax looked so soft, he wanted to reach out and stroke them. Although the alien made no menacing moves, Arun kept his hand to himself, worried that his sudden urge for intimacy might be connected to coming down from the combat drugs.

After the gnarled bulk of the guardians, the scribe seemed as cute as a cooing baby. It was only seven feet long rather than a guardian's nine plus, but still had the same three-segment body arrangement that looked like the head, thorax, and abdomen of Earth insects.

Arun was all too familiar with real insects. When his distant ancestors had been transported from Earth, the little buzzing, biting but pollinating pests had come too. The scribe only looked superficially like an Earth creature, though. It carried itself on three spindly pairs of limbs that ended in flexible suckers. Definitely not like an insect. The pre-mission briefing had mentioned these suckers, describing them as analogous to an Earthly elephant's trunk.

Although he wasn't one of the few who resisted the Earth-centric obsession, sometimes Arun thought it went too far. What kind of dumb veck thought it was a clever idea to compare Trogs to an animal on a far-off planet that none of the human Marines would ever encounter?

"I mean," he told the scribe, "really, it would make far more sense to describe an elephant's trunk as like a scribe's limbs, rather than the other way around."

On the scribe's motionless head, its two pairs of eyes blinked. Then it raised its antenna into a frenzy of wriggling.

Without warning, those feelers telescoped outward, directly at Arun's head.

He jumped back, settling into a loose crouch, ready for unarmed combat. But the feelers stopped their advance and Arun amused himself with the thought that he'd never been taught *unclothed* combat.

The antennae retracted slightly into a fixed pattern, a square shape that it maintained for a few seconds before saying: "I agree. I have read the same human texts. As if anyone on this planet would ever encounter an elephant!"

"That's exactly what I was thinking!"

Arun's squadmate, Zug, studied aliens with a passion. He'd be able to make sense of this conversation later.

"So…" Arun continued, wondering how you were supposed to change subject with an alien species you'd never met before, except to shoot at. (Arun glanced nervously at the carnage around him). "Er… did we win?"

"You failed to meet the success criteria of this exercise. We do not know the detailed assessment that will be forthcoming from the Jotuns and your senior humans. Our own assessment is that too many small-unit commanders proved inadequate, and your company commander lacked imagination. Most disastrous of all, you failed to keep reserves. The concept of a front line is tenuous when contesting a three-dimensional tunnel network. Counter-attacks can come from any direction. Have you not been taught the concept of a mobile reserve?"

"Oh." Arun's shoulders slumped. This was the scenario every human on the planet hated: being made to feel like children by older races that had seen it all before. He tried to put every iota of assertiveness into his voice and asked: "Were there any casualties?"

Speaking those words made him think of his fire team buddies: Osman, Madge and Springer. Were they dead? *Properly* dead?

"There were four minor injuries," the alien told him. Arun relaxed. "And one fatality. Name of Isabella de Grouchy."

Arun pictured bouncy brown hair, a hooked nose set into a serious, freckle-dashed face that was often frowning. De Grouchy had flashed him a momentary half-smile once; they'd never spoken but he'd seen her enough to paint a vivid picture of her in his mind's eye. And now she was gone.

Isabella hadn't exactly been the first to die. Not when Arun considered all those who hadn't survived to graduate from novice school as a cadet.

He glanced at the guardians still crowding the tunnel, apparently in deep sleep.

Arun idly flicked the larger chunks of mess off his body. He felt a throb of pain to his left leg and torso. He squeezed his right eye shut against the fierce pain that stabbed through it. Sensation was returning. And he was injured.

He froze, his wounds forgotten. He realized he'd just flicked a piece of Troggie body onto the scribe. Trogs lived in nests. Nest members, the briefing had said, were almost a gestalt entity, a hive whose members were far closer to each other than any human twin.

"Were…" Arun cleared his throat. "Were there many tropied on your side?" He winced, unable to stop himself glancing around at the combat slurry.

He could have phrased that better.

"A little over a thousand nest-siblings were… *tropied*. Is that the right word? You do mean *killed*, don't you?"

The alien had replayed a recording of Arun's voice when it said *tropied*. Seemed the translation software wasn't up to date with the vernacular used by the 412th Marines.

"Yeah, tropied. You know, *entropied*." Arun shrugged. "I'm sorry."

"Why?" The scribe twitched its feelers. "Because you humans killed so many?"

"Well…" Zug always told him that aliens don't do sarcasm, not that a human would ever understand, anyway. So Arun decided to take the alien's words literally. "Yes," he said, looking at the massed ranks of guardians. One word from the scribe and he'd be chopped meat himself within two seconds.

"I feel regret," Arun decided to add, "that so many nest-siblings were… slain."

Slain? He didn't think he'd ever used the archaic word before, but he couldn't quite bring himself to say *killed* with all those alien warriors standing there in the wreckage of their brothers and sisters — or whatever passed for gender within the nest.

The scribe twisted its antennae into spirals, and said: "You humans amuse us with your wild flights of emotion." It paused. "We also feel intense emotion at the appropriate stages in our life-journeys, but there is always a purpose to our emotion. But you, human, why do you grieve for fallen enemies?"

"Trogs aren't my enemies. We're all slaves of the White Knights on Tranquility."

"True. Just as those of my race are also slaves to our biological lifecycle, and to our nest's resource constraints."

The scribe relaxed its feelers and swayed slightly. "Today you killed my nest-siblings who were in the stage of our lifecycle you call guardians. An individual's body changes to the guardian state only because they failed in their previous life-phase. They are the oldest, on average, and so are expendable. In primitive nests, guardians are first to form the defensive wedge when rival nests attack. Without war between nests, our guardian population must be culled. For us, it is a kindness for humans to kill so many, because we remember these individuals from an earlier time in their lives when they were our friends, our children and our parents. Better you do it than we kill them ourselves. However they are culled, their role is not yet complete as we will shortly take their remains to be composted."

Arun pointed at one of the nearby corpses that was still relatively intact. "That one," he said. "Are you telling me you're going to chop him up and use him to help grow your vegetables?"

"Of course."

"Frakk!" Arun raised his hands, palms up. "*Aliens!*"

The Trog matched his gesture of bemusement, using its front limbs to approximate a shrug. "*Aliens!*" it exclaimed, playing the sound of Arun's voice through its box. "My thoughts exactly. See how you referred to that maimed Trog as *he* once you felt sympathy?"

"No. But… you're right. I did."

"You humans fascinate me." It paused. "May I ask you a question?"

"Go on…" said Arun, dearly wishing it wouldn't.

"You exhibit two incongruities that have led me to form a hypothesis. I should like to state my hypothesis for your review."

"O-kay."

"Firstly, I note that you are naked."

"No, I'm not."

"Forgive my imprecision. You are naked other than your helmet and your gloves."

"Right. Well, there's a simple explanation. I had to abandon my battlesuit because your nest-buddies had pinned me down."

"Secondly…" The alien extended both its feathery antennae to touch him in a place Arun really didn't expect an alien to ever make contact. Arun yelped in shock.

"Secondly, you have activated your mating prong."

Arun gasped, and slowly lowered his gaze. *Sweet final homecoming! Damn those frakking combat drugs and their drenting side effects.*

"My hypothesis," continued the alien, showing no sign of noticing Arun blush like a nuclear furnace, "is that you wish to engage with me in a sexual encounter."

Arun slapped one hand down to guard his genitals, and the other up to hide his face.

"It is my privilege to study alien behavior for the benefit of the nest. In the course of my research, I have observed many recordings of human copulation, and I surmise that you wish to penetrate first."

Collapsing to a ball on the tunnel floor, Arun willed the world to go away, or for him to die. Whichever came first; he didn't care, just so long as an end came quickly.

Through a crack in his fingers, Arun watched the alien turn side-on. Patches on its thorax had turned bright red, and a section of its carapace was… *puckering*.

"If my hypothesis is correct," said the alien, "you will find my reproductive opening on my flanks. I regret, though, that I cannot reciprocate."

Arun groaned loudly.

"Oh," said the alien, or rather its mechanical voice in a box, which managed to sound offended. "I hear your disappointment. My reluctance to penetrate you in return is not through lack of interest, rather that I would rip your opening and rupture your bowels."

"Cadet McEwan. Acknowledge ceasefire."

For several moments, the new voice confused Arun. It sounded deep and worn and it wasn't coming from the scribe. Then he remembered the comms link in his helmet.

"McEwan. Acknowledge! This is Sergeant Gupta. Acknowledge."

"Roger that. Sorry, sergeant."

"Relax, son. It's those frakking combat meds they keep tinkering with. There's always a few green cadets enter a combat fugue and never snap out. But you're coming round now. You'll be okay. And next time your body will find them a little easier to take. Hopefully."

"Sergeant… Brandt… why isn't Brandt…?" Arun found words that should come easily swirled and slithered away beyond reach. "Sergeant, is he—?"

"—dead? No, cadet. Well, Acting Cadet Corporal Edward Brandt is dead according to the rules of the exercise, but perfectly okay in real life. Mind you, I expect he will hope it was the other way around when I review his sorry performance with your instructors. Yes, I'm your new veteran squad commander."

Arun knew he should be paying attention to the NCO — a real one who had earned his rank. But he couldn't help but stare at the alien instead. Its antennae were bent at an angle. It looked like a person tilting their head when listening with interest. Maybe this gesture meant the same thing.

"Cadet."

"Yes, sergeant."

Gupta paused. "I did three tours of duty before they had me nurse-maiding you kids. I've been around for 180 objective years and that means I've seen a little of the galaxy. I want to share some of that with you now."

"Thank you, sergeant."

"Life has a habit of being unfair. Sometimes you just gotta suck it in. Cry on the inside if you have to, wail in private with your best pals if you must, but keep your head high and wait for your luck to change. Remember, a Marine never buckles under pressure. That's easy to say but now is your time to prove it."

"Yes, sergeant."

"Stay where you are, McEwan. Your injuries don't look too serious but I've marked you for medical evac just in case. So I don't want you walking out because that would make me look a damned fool."

"Yes, sergeant. Umm… Sergeant?"

"Hurry up!"

"Well, what you said. About life being unfair. I didn't quite follow. I survived. What's unfair about that?"

"Ah, frakk it, son. Everything in those tunnels was recorded. Video, audio, the works. What that bug-ugly just said to you is already flying around the base. *Why have you activated your muting prong?* Like it or not your comrades won't let you forget that, so I want you to roll with it. See the funny side. That's an order."

But Arun wasn't listening. He curled into as tight as ball as he could, and willed the lurking guardians to end his existence.

—— Chapter 03 ——

between nationalities reduced to misremembered fables, the Earth races had churned and averaged, to a norm of mid-brown skin and black hair. Except for the occasional individual, such as Zug.

"Say something," Osman insisted.

"Shut up!" Arun hissed. "I'm thinking."

Zug possessed by far the darkest skin color in his year, and that had made him stand out his entire life. He'd grown up being picked on and mocked for looking different, but he had never been cowed. He'd never been in with the popular crowd, but neither had Zug ever been isolated, never been singled out as a loser. Zug had even shaved his head bald to emphasize skin that was the color of the void.

If Zug could survive being different, Arun could too.

And so Arun put his trust in his friend and laughed. A brittle sound at first — obviously fake — he eased into the act and slowly the sound grew more natural. Soon, the crowd's interest waned. It was working!

Just when Arun began to imagine his ordeal was over, Xin Lee limbered her toned body out of her seat and sauntered his way.

Arun stood his ground, but his smile cracked.

Osman whispered: "Whatever she says, keep grinning."

Easy for you to say.

The girl who frequently turned his dreams feverish stopped in front of the little group of friends. She put her hands on her hips and gave Arun an appraising look.

"Well then, McEwan," she said. No, not said: *announced*. The class G-1 cadet — one year older than Arun — was addressing everyone there. Everyone listened. "I hear that you're an alien-faggot. Is that true?"

Arun felt his legs wobble. This was the first time that Xin had ever spoken to him in real life, and she had just invented a new term of derision. Just for his benefit. His heart sank. Speech was beyond him.

"Shame, really," she said. "After seeing your attempt at an erotic vid, it seems like a waste of good equipment."

Xin's gaze met his and taunted, those lovely dark eyes set into her smooth face, with the snubby little nose that he adored.

His heart accelerated up his spinal column and crashed into his brain, preventing him from saying anything beyond a plaintive grunt.

Xin decided his audience was ended, and marched out of the hall, flanked by a pair of girlfriends. Her every step was accompanied by catcalls and wolf whistles. She loved it.

In a way, she had saved him. By taking so much of the room's attention on herself, the excitement dissipated the moment she left the hall.

Arun fled to the nearest table, and hunkered down.

It was only as Arun approached the battalion chow hall, hobbling with the aid of the walking stick the medic had given him, that he knew for certain he hadn't gotten away with his embarrassing episode in the tunnel. At first, the complete shunters of the 412th Marine Regiment — his future comrades-in-arms, sworn to aid him in his hour of need — had acted as if nothing had happened, though he imagined he saw concealed smirks on their faces.

He began to hope he'd actually gotten away with it.

But now the cadets spilling out from the hall and into the approach corridor were no longer hiding their smirks. He ignored the little vecks as he pushed his way through and into the chow hall. As soon as he was inside, the door sphinctered shut.

Marine cadets of all years thronged the room, overwhelming the ventilation system to suffuse it with a sweaty pong, not unlike the stink of menacing Troggie guardians. Everyone in that room stopped whatever they were doing, and twisted around to stare at Arun McEwan.

Digi-sheets had been stuck onto every available surface. All of them looped the moment when the alien scribe grasped Arun's manhood with its feelers. Underneath the moving image, some wit had added the caption: 'Arun McEwan: so desperate he'll prong anything.'

The room erupted in a cacophony of cheers, catcalls, hoots and jeers. Some was good-natured. Most of it wasn't.

Osman slid over from somewhere and slapped Arun on the back, laughing along with everyone else in the room.

"Not you, too," groaned Arun.

Slapping his back all the while, Osman leaned closer and said: "Laugh, Arun. Laugh with them. It's your only chance."

"He's right," said Zug, who was standing a few paces behind Osman. "If they sense your humiliation, they will use this against you forever. Your status will be permanently degraded. What then for your sexual fantasy?"

Arun scowled at Serge Rhenolotte. *Zug* to his friends. He was about to remonstrate that Xin Lee was not a fantasy, but a real woman, when he realized that just then, Xin was a little *too* real for comfort. She was sitting only a few meters away.

"You can do it," said Zug. "Like I've done my whole life."

If the stories were true — and one thing you learned early on Tranquility was never to trust what you were told — then when the first humans had been brought to Tranquility, they had come in a variety of shades and shapes, reflecting the regions of Earth that had originally offered up their children to the White Knights. But that had been many generations ago. United in common service to their unseen masters, and with the distinctions

"Tough luck, pal," said Zug. "Your reaction to the combat drug was unfortunate, but hardly the most extreme on record. Some cadets die, you know, the first time they take combat-meds under life-threatening conditions. It's rotten luck, I know, but Xin was always a far from realistic proposition for you."

Arun frowned at him. "Eh? Didn't you just hear what she said?"

"Yes," said Zug. "Apparently, you're an alien-faggot."

Osman leaned over. "I think, Zug, that our friend was referring to Xin's second comment. Something about good equipment."

"Your friend is bang on correct," said Arun, feeling cheerful, "'I'm well in there."

Osman snorted.

Zug scratched his bald pate, trying to make sense. "It's hardly like she gave you her dorm code and invited you over to make jeem with her."

"Oh, I think that it was," said Arun, slapping Zug on the shoulder.

Osman face-palmed.

"Combat drugs are still addling his brain," Zug told Osman. "It's the only possible explanation."

"You're just jealous," said Arun, grinning.

Zug and Osman buried their heads in their hands and groaned.

Arun shrugged off his friends' disbelief. Newly entered into class G-1, Xin had nearly two years to go until she either graduated as a Marine, or was cast out of the Corps.

Today she had spoken to him, and with a dose of optimism, he could stretch those words into a compliment. It wasn't much to go on, but he had almost two years to win something more from her.

Arun relished a challenge.

He wasn't a natural leader like Majanita, as brave as Osman, nor as dependable as Springer.

Didn't need to be. Arun knew his strength: he never gave up.

One day, he'd win Xin Lee. Of that he was certain.

—— Chapter 04 ——

With evening inspection due in fifteen minutes, the atmosphere in Arun's dorm began to chill with fear.

The cadets in Arun's battalion had laughed at him mercilessly, but the story of the naked cadet had spread far beyond the 8th battalion… beyond even his regiment. The laughter had dried up in Arun's hab-disk and the battalion chow halls. Detroit was the home base for two other tactical Marine regiments and one Marine assault regiment, all of whom were now hooting with derision at the 412th.

Arun had brought shame on his regiment, shame on their regimental instructors.

And one of those instructors would be conducting the evening inspection very soon.

"I know what we need," said Arun, trying to raise the mood, "let's list our top five fantasy rack buddies."

The seven other cadets in the dorm groaned, even Cristina who gave an echo of disapproval from the head.

Arun was sitting at the dorm table with Springer and Majanita. He skidded his chair back to give him space to perform his best rendition of the Gallic shrug that Del-Marie had taught him. Del-Marie Sandure was no more French than Arun, but most people who'd survived this far into Marine training had adopted a personality weirdness or two. Everyone understood the need for a coping mechanism. If Del wanted to pretend he was French, his Delta Section mates were happy to indulge him.

"Oh, c'mon. Top fives are always fun," Arun insisted. His grin faded. "Or were until you all lost your sense of fun. Anyway, it'll give us something else to think about during inspection. I've got a feeling we might need distracting."

Lying on his bunk – or rack as they were learning to call them now they were cadets — Del-Marie sighed. "Arun, you're becoming tiresome."

"Oh, am I?" said Arun cheerfully. "You're only saying that because everyone already knows your list. Your favorite is Bernard. He's your number 2, 3, 4, and 5 too."

"His name is not Bur-nerd. It's Berr-narr." Del-Marie rolled his r's in a way Arun had never managed to imitate.

Madge reached over the dorm table and placed a well-manicured hand over Arun's. "Darling, Arun," she said in her breathy voice that some called flirtatious, and others called dumblitted, "I don't like to generalize but listing one's top vulley-buddies is such a boy thing. And an obsession strongest in the least mature of your gender."

Arun smiled, not minding the ribbing from Madge. Her vampish act had all but disappeared in the last few weeks, smothered under a heavy cloak of seriousness.

Springer snorted derisively, flashing her violet eyes at Arun — literally. Scattered through the Marine cadets were many unintended consequences of the genetic manipulations the Jotun scientists had engineered in their ancestors. The vibrant color of Springer's eyes, and the ability to illuminate them, was one of the more obvious. And attractive.

Madge steamed on. "A more useful topic for discussion is whether we're entering any teams in the Scendence competition this year."

"You're getting boring," Springer told Arun, ignoring Madge. He was shocked to see real anger in her eyes. "All you ever want to do is invent excuses to spout off about that skangat girl. For frakk's sake, why don't you ask Xin if she wants you to prong her? Then she'll shoot you down in a ball of plasma and–" Springer rolled her eyes "'– we won't have to listen to you prattle on about her ever again."

An impish grin came to Brandt's face. "Springer's only saying that because she wants you in her rack all to herself."

"Shut up, Brandt!" shouted everyone else in the room. He'd been assigned the section leader role in the tunnels, but his temporary rank vanished the moment the exercise ended.

Brandt seethed.

Cristina emerged from the head. "Did I miss something? What's going on?"

Several pairs of eyes glanced at Brandt and rolled in their sockets.

"The question remains," said Zug, ever the one to steer a conversation back on course, "how many Scendence teams are we entering?" He paused from cleaning the personal locker at the foot of his rack. "Alistair LaSalle will want to team up with Alice Belville. They'll take Gunnery and Deception and pick the best players in Charlie Company for the other positions. That'll probably include Hortez. Del-Marie we can trust to keep our secrets, but will be playing Gunnery in a team with Bernard. Am I correct, Del-Marie?"

Del nodded. "If I play this season, it won't be with any of you."

"Forget Alistair," said Madge. "As for Hortez, if our temporary squad leader thinks he's too good for the rest of us then let him play with Alistair. I don't care what they do, I intend to play Gunnery in a Blue Squad team." Madge's tone was serious again now. Cadets from other units often used to underestimate Majanita as either a shallow beauty doll or a salacious siren. They were both acts, to be dropped whenever the matter at hand was serious. And Estella Majanita – not many who knew her dared to call her Madge to her face – took the game of Scendence very seriously indeed.

Madge gave Springer an expectant look.

"Me too," said Springer reluctantly. "I'll take Obedience. I know what you're going to say, Zug, and you're probably right, but what the hell? I enjoy playing, and I enjoy winning. Perhaps we'll win some points for the battalion."

"Please understand," said Zug, "that I speak only for myself when I say that I shall not participate in Scendence this year. We've been in this hab-disk nearly three weeks. Three weeks since we ceased to be novices. Our every action now has the potential to win our battalion merit points–"

"Or demerits," interrupted Del-Marie.

Arun's gut churned. The fallout from the regimental humiliation in the tunnels had yet to settle, and if demerits were forthcoming he had scapegoat written all over him.

"Yes, my friend," said Zug. "Or de-merits. Everything we do has the potential to bring our battalion down closer to the Cull Zone if we fail. And if we do well, we put a larger margin of safety away from the Cull. All I'm saying is that if we don't think the time we put into Scendence training will pay off in merit points, then we should spend that time on something that will. The senior cadet companies seem eager to offer us G-2 noobs extra coaching. If they think that's a good investment of their time it's because we're all part of 8th battalion, and helping us gain merit points keeps them away from the Cull just as much as it does ourselves."

"And they're a year or two ahead of us," added Arun. "We should listen to what they're telling us."

"He's right," added Brandt who was hovering near the table. "I've already taken up every offer of coaching I can handle. I can't do that if I'm also doing serious Scendence training."

There was a moment's tense silence. Arun almost felt sorry for Brandt. He might be a dumb veck, and the way he'd led the section in the tunnels had landed them all in the drent, but Brandt hadn't volunteered to be a cadet corporal. Maybe, back in the days when there were human armies on Earth, he might have made a good officer one day. But there was no such thing as a human officer in the Corps, only NCOs. And Brandt just wasn't right to be an NCO.

"Brandt and Zug share an opinion," snapped Cristina, obviously an opinion she did not share. "That doesn't make them right. I'll be in the team too, if you'll have me."

If Brandt's words had been met with a moment of hostility, Cristina's brought out a silence that was altogether more tense.

Scendence was the hope, the passion, and the closest thing to freedom that would ever be experienced in the Corps. And not just the humans: other races played too on occasion.

While in crèche and then as novices, it had been possible – for some individuals, at least – to compete at Scendence purely for the thrill of doing so. Now that they were cadets, though, Scendence was a game played only to win. Not only were merit points a possibility, but the top 16 teams at the end of the season were granted immunity from the Cull. Cristina was not a good player. In any team she would be a liability. Winning immunity would be inconceivable.

"Of course we'll have you, darling," gushed Madge. "I'm playing Gunnery, of course, and Springer'll take Obedience. What role do you want?"

"Save it for later," said Brandt. "It's 20:58. Inspection in two minutes."

All eight cadets in the dorm scrambled to their positions at the foot of their bunks and stood to attention.

Although cadets had to be ready for inspection once in the morning, and again in the evening, on average each dorm was inspected about twice per week.

But after the company had been shot to pieces in the tunnels, and with images of Cadet Prong plastered all over Detroit, Arun's wrenching gut told him they would be certain to get a visit tonight. And he bet it would be the toughest of them all who would come: Instructor Rekka.

When, earlier that day, Brandt had dispatched him alone into that narrow tunnel, Arun had been terrified. Isolated.

He felt worse now.

Springer caught his eye. Her anger had vanished, replaced by a smile of support.

At least I've one buddy I can always rely upon.

Then the door hissed open and Arun snapped his eyes front.

The inspection had begun.

—— Chapter 05 ——

The dorm for Blue Squad's Delta Section was a narrow room with eight racks lined up against one wall. At the foot of each, a cadet stood at attention, awaiting the laser-sharp scrutiny of Instructor Rekka.

Arun had the sixth rack down. He kept his eyes front, but with four cadets already dealt with, he could sense Rekka advance to the fifth rack like an approaching storm front, her walking stick thumping aggressively on the deck like the sound of thunder.

Then came the worst part: the silence.

Like many of the instructors, Rekka was a former frontline Marine who had been too broken in combat to fight again, but too experienced to throw away.

The instructors who had trained them through novice school were in the process of handing over to the veterans who would command the cadets in battle after they had graduated as Marines. Although he would rather face an enemy division singlehanded than face an angry Rekka, Arun would miss the instructor's wardrobe of prosthetic legs, her habit of whistling in her rare carefree moments, and those precious few moments when she awarded hard-won praise.

Rekka was a hard person to like, but wasn't a sadistic bully, unlike some of the other instructors he'd endured. She was domineering because that was how instructors needed to be, but there was just one thing that made her boil with rage: when she decided the novices in her charge were abusing their precious gift of youth and health.

This evening, Rekka was beyond angry. The madder she got, the quieter and slower she talked. The instructor's words were barely a whisper.

Rekka had found fault with every cadet in the room. Del-Marie's bed covers had been creased. Madge's were folded at the wrong angle, and as for her long, blonde hair, that was a disgrace that needed to be shaved off. Zug had to do fifty one-armed press ups for not standing straight, and Springer a hundred for being caught glancing Arun's way.

Now it was Osman Koraltan's turn.

As Rekka built up to Osman's humiliation, Arun told himself endlessly not to rise to her bait when her attention turned to him. *Just suck it up, McEwan.*

"What is this… this *rag*?" Rekka didn't need to raise her voice. Everyone heard her disdain ringing loud and clear.

"It's a flag, ma'am," said Osman.

There was a faint swish, and Arun could picture Osman's flag picked up on the end of her walking stick and swirled around.

"A *flag*? Is this the regimental flag, cadet?"

"Ma'am. No, ma'am."

"Are you planning an insurrection, cadet?"

"Ma'am. No, ma'am. I would kill a traitor on sight, ma'am."

"Then what is the point of this article?"

"It's… the country I think I might have come from, ma'am."

"*You think?* The country you come from? On Earth. That is nova-frakking amazing. I'd always put you down as an uninspiring irrelevance, Koraltan. Someone I would forget the instant I'd handed you on to your veteran. Only a few days before I get to shake your hand and say good luck and good riddance, with a tear in my eye – you finally surprise me. I had no idea that you were born on Earth, Cadet Koraltan."

Osman kept silent, but Rekka wasn't going to let him off so easily. "Well, Koraltan? Did I get that wrong? Are you Earth-born?"

"Ma'am. No, ma'am. I meant the country I think my ancestors came from."

Rekka snorted. "You credulous imbecile. The very notion of nationality is a fantasy fit only for veck-heads. Do you really think there is any way you can trace your ancestry back to a region of Earth? Let me tell you what really happened. Your grandfather picked an exotic name and backstory out of a history book, and used it to impress your grandmother. You, Osman

Koraltan, are one of the disastrous unintended consequences of that unfortunate seduction. What country is this rag meant to represent anyway?"

"Turkey, ma'am."

"Turkey? Tur-key! It's the name of an avian species, you frakk-head, not a country."

Rekka limped over to the waste chute, the red and white flag held aloft on the tip of her walking stick. They all heard the grinding noise when the garbage input sensor recognized it had incoming, and began ripping apart the cloth at the start of its recycling journey.

Arun could feel the heat rise in his face. Osman had been given that flag two years ago. Two years during which Rekka had made no comment. But today, suddenly, it was a heresy to be rooted out and destroyed. Same as Madge's hair.

As Rekka returned to Osman, her stick once again thumping out her approach, she asked in a sneering tone that made Arun cringe: "Does anyone else know anything about Earth or that flag?"

"Ma'am, the flag was originally made…" Arun couldn't believe he'd spoken. He felt as if he'd stepped over a cliff and was staring in disbelief at the absence of ground beneath his feet.

All that was left to do now was fall.

"Yes, McEwan?" Rekka was in his face now. She was small and wiry, shorter than Arun. And yet she still managed somehow to loom over him, intimidating him with ease. "Did you forget to finish your sentence?"

"Ma'am. No, ma'am. Cadet Koraltan's flag was originally made by Sergeant Horden, ma'am." There, he'd said it! Projectile launched, brace for impact.

Instructor Rekka glowered at Arun for an eternity before spitting out that name. "Sergeant *Hor-den*. Are you referring to the man who *claimed* to be a descendant of President Horden?"

"Ma'am. Yes, ma'am."

Rekka curled her lip into a slow sneer. "According to the story of the Vancouver Accord, President Horden sold a million Earth children to the White Knights. My ancestors, Koraltan's and yours, all were amongst those children. Today we Marines swear by Horden senior and we swear *at* him just as often. *Horden's Bones! Horden's Children! Horden's Sweet Hairy Fanny.* Everyone on this base swears by Horden. Even *you*, McEwan. Have you sworn by Horden?"

"Ma'am. Yes, ma'am."

"Yes, ma'am. Of course you frakkin' have you stupid drent-for-brains. Horden's like all the devils and gods of every religion wrapped into one convenient package. The story also says that topping the list of slave children selected was his own first-born son. To claim descent from a specific person on Earth is the action of a deluded fantasist. But to claim that mega-veck, President Horden, as your ancestor is the deluded rambling of a truly sick individual, with megalomania only the start of the psychoses infecting their perverted mind."

Rekka leaned in even closer. "Feel free to disagree at any time, McEwan."

These past few weeks, Arun had been losing it. Acting wild in those Troggie tunnels, and speaking out of turn to Rekka: they were only today's disasters. He didn't know what had gotten into him, but he did know that right now he had to keep his mouth firmly shut.

"Now that we've established the nature of Sergeant Horden, this *so-called* authority, who produced a scrap of cloth purporting to be the flag of a hypothetical country, please explain to me, McEwan, why you saw fit to cite him."

"Ma'am, Sergeant Horden explained – I mean, *claimed* – that he had identified genetic markers, clues to our Earth ancestry." Arun stopped there. Horden had used Osman as an early test case. A successful one too. Either Horden was a fraud or Osman really was Turkish.

Rekka stepped back a few paces. "I know all about Horden's lies. Haven't you realized yet that we're all such a thoroughly jumbled-up mongrel mess that any genetic markers present in our distant ancestors have long since been lost in the homogeneous genetic paste that fills the bones of every Marine. And that's a good thing! I understand the human need for a tribe to belong to. You already have yours. Have you learned nothing, McEwan? Your nation is the Human Marine Corps. Your clan is the 412th Marines, or the 412th Tactical Marine Regiment for those who enjoy the long-winded

version. I don't hold with all this Earth drent that the Jotuns indulge you in these days. I've been out there in the wars, and I can tell you it's the belief in your unit, and in your comrade standing alongside you that holds Marines together. Not some dumb romantic guff about Earth."

She paused to stare at each cadet in turn, daring them to so much as breathe in a manner that she could construe as backchat. She stretched that moment of tension to her satisfaction before continuing. "Last I heard, Sergeant Horden was en route to the Akinschet system. I expect when he gets there that he'll change his tune pretty damned sharpish."

Rekka rocked back on the heels of her prosthetic legs. They were her everyday pair, encased in gleaming black plastic and silvered metal, except for the rubbery sole to the built-in feet. She lifted her stick and used it to poke Arun in the chest.

"I've warned you before about speaking out of turn, McEwan. Give me twenty squat jumps."

"Ma'am. Yes, ma'am."

Arun's anger returned in ever-increasing waves. Arun tried to suck it back in but today his self-control was shot to hell.

The instructors claimed that many of the rituals of training and command had been gleaned from practices used centuries before on Earth. The Jotuns reasoned that military training evolved over centuries to match the human psyche would be a better starting point than anything they could devise.

And so punishment for minor infractions often meant press ups, digging and filling in fighting holes, or similar pointless physical activity, even though in comparison with the original humans of Earth, the Marine cadets possessed immense physical strength and endurance. Wetware augmentation and genetic manipulation meant Marines were different mentally too. When not succumbing to a tendency toward ill-disciplined rage, they took an iron will for granted.

All of that meant punishment exercise was easy. Normally. But not today.

The anger in Arun's breast tempted him to glance meaningfully at his rack where he'd placed the walking stick the medics had given him.

He didn't. Rekka knew perfectly well that he'd suffered a leg wound. Drawing attention to his stick would be weak, and achieve nothing but win contempt from everyone in the room. Instead, he drew upon his mental strength and gingerly crouched down into a squat position. His wounded leg felt stiff, but only when he got into the deepest position of the crouch did his left knee grind, as if his joints were made from rusting steel that hadn't seen oil for decades. With a supreme effort, he managed to cap his scream of agony. He looked down at his limb, expecting to see the blood seeping out the wound opened up by the Troggie guardian's claw.

There was no blood, no bone shards poking through the skin over his knee.

"Begin!" Rekka ordered.

Arun jumped as high as he could, flinging his arms up as he leaped. He knew that if she decided he'd made a halfhearted jump, she would make him start again at the beginning.

At the top of his jump, Arun pointed his toes down and lifted his head high, as per the prescribed form. The jump was easy. The descent was not.

When he landed and his legs took his weight it felt as if hot blades were plunging into his injuries. Arun grunted but did not cry out. At the deepest point, when his legs changed from slowing his fall into beginning his ascent, those blades grew jagged edges and jerked around in his wound. Arun gasped before executing a perfect jump.

Determined not to give Rekka the satisfaction of hearing him scream, Arun willed his jaw to clamp firmly shut and stay closed.

I will not scream. I will NOT scream.

The second landing was even worse. The imaginary blades stabbing into his leg grew red hot.

I will not scream. I… I will not scream.

The blades exuded agonizing venom, which spread to his right leg.

I will not scream!

Arun's world became a foggy battlefield where pain fought against Arun's iron will for control of his body. He could even imagine the crump, crump, crump from a far-off artillery battery.

Then he realized that what he thought was incoming shellfire was actually the sound of Instructor Rekka's walking stick thumping the deck in front of him.

"I said stop!" She was shouting. "You've made 24 jumps. I only wanted 20. Can't you count?"

Arun decided he'd better not answer.

She narrowed her eyes. "I suppose there's something you want to ask me?"

"Yes, ma'am. This cadet requests permission to seek medical attention."

Rekka made a point of chewing over his request before replying. "Yes, I noticed your leg looks sore. You may get it patched after inspection."

Not bothering to inspect Zug or Cristina, Rekka turned and walked away. When she reached the door, she looked back at the cadets. "I'm disappointed in you. You were not fit for inspection and your performance in the tunnels today has made us the laughing stock of Detroit. The handover to your veteran NCOs began this week and already you have let us down. Badly. McEwan with his lewd display worst of all. Do not expect this to be the end of the matter. There will be repercussions. Mark my words."

After fixing them all with her baleful stare, Rekka dismissed them and stalked out.

Arun looked down at his leg. His fatigue pants were glued to his leg with sticky blood, but the blood flow had slowed or stopped.

"Hey, hero," said Osman. "Do you want me to help you get to the infirmary?"

Arun grabbed his stick and took a few test paces. "No, I'm good. Thanks, man."

He wasn't, but he didn't want to get his comrades into trouble. In theory they all had until First Sleep at 25:00 hours to do what they liked – training usually – but Arun knew he was toxic right now. He wanted his buddies to keep a safe distance.

As he limped out of the dorm, he was met by a variety of reactions from his squadmates. Pity he'd expected, and the concern he saw on Springer's face, but he also saw contempt and even anger from Brandt and Madge. He only half-cared, though. As he hobbled away to the med-center he kept thinking about what Rekka had said.

There will be repercussions.

—— Chapter 06 ——

"Rekka is purest evil," said Arun. "Just because she got her legs blown off, she's jealous of anyone still whole. What kind of instructor makes their cadets jump up and down on a wounded leg? Those squat jumps she made me do earlier – she could have saved us all the bother and just shot me in the leg. End result would've been the same."

"Too right, man," said Osman. "She was just worried about looking bad in front of Shlappo. And the senior instructor's no better. She made Brandt section leader and chose Alistair LaSalle to lead the company against the Trogs. What a pair of dwonks!"

Arun, Osman and Zug were sitting around the dorm room table. Zug was listening but saying nothing, as normal.

Cristina and Madge came over to join them. "Are you badmouthing Senior Instructor Nhlappo again?" asked Cristina.

"Osman's just speaking the truth," replied Arun, "because this is the only place we can say it. They're not supposed to listen in on us in the dorm room. I bet they are, though. In fact, I'm counting on it."

Madge shook her head in exaggerated disdain, flinging her long hair out behind her. "It's no use, Cris, he can't help it. It's because Instructor Rekka and Senior Instructor Nhlappo are both women." She leaned over the table, shoving her face against Arun's. "Admit it, you can't handle being given orders by a woman."

"Yes, I can."

"There's nothing to be ashamed of." She settled back in her chair and grinned at Cristina. "Boys of your age are emotionally immature. It's a proven scientific fact. You can't think too well because you've only one thing on your mind."

"Him more than most," added Springer, joining the group.

"Hey, that's not fair," Arun protested.

"Isn't it?" answered Madge. "How would you feel if I had led Delta Section instead of Brandt? Could you handle that?"

"Well, yes. Why wouldn't I?" It was true. Madge was a natural NCO, at least when she dropped the vampish act.

"You hesitated!"

"Leave him alone," said Osman. "I can't believe you're defending what Rekka did."

"We're not, turkey-man," said Cristina. "Rekka was cruel tonight, but we've all of us had that kind of drent in the past and we don't start crying every time an instructor says something to hurt our little-widdle feelings. At least, we women don't."

Springer joined in. "You know, if there's one thing useful I've learned from ancient Earth history, it's that they used to have all-male combat units. If our masters thought of the Human Marine Corps as a serious military force, rather than breeding stock, I reckon we'd have single-sex units. Anyway, lover boy here is always griping about Rekka or Nhlappo. Aren't you, Arun?"

Arun threw his hands in the air in frustration. "Oh, come on, guys. Rekka's given me a hard time, and Shlappo will tomorrow, or I'm a Hardit. And you," he pointed at Springer, "are supposed to be on my side."

Springer gave a curt laugh. "Rekka's giving you a hard time, eh? You seem to be having a lot of those recently. When you had your hard time with that alien scribe, were you thinking of our instructor? Did you imagine Rekka's sweet face on that Troggie body? Is that why you… oh, how did your alien friend describe it? … *activated your mating prong*?"

Cristina dug an elbow into Springer's side. "Lighten up on him will you? Arun's right. He's our squadmate. We should–"

"I know. Sorry." Springer looked serious. "I apologize for my inexcusable behavior… *Cadet Prong*." Laughter bubbled out of her. "Sorry, Arun. Frakk it, I couldn't resist."

Arun replayed Sergeant Gupta's words in his mind. He wouldn't crumble. He would get through this. "Guys," he pleaded, "get off my back. Please."

Springer studied him for a while before arriving at a conclusion. "Look, I tell you what, Arun. I won't call you Cadet Prong again if you promise not to call us 'guys'. I can't stand it when people talk to me as if I'm neuter, or a man. I'm a woman."

Cristina snorted. "Speak for yourself, grandma. I'm only in class G-2."

"Okay," admitted Springer, "girl or woman at your discretion, and then only until we're in graduation year. Deal?"

Springer extended her hand. Arun shook it.

"Thank goodness for that," said Madge. "Springer's been spouting drivel about you ever since we saw your mating prong performance. I think she's jealous." She winked at Arun and whispered to him loudly enough for all to hear: "You do realize she dreams about you?"

Arun laughed the same as everyone else.

But, no, he hadn't.

—— Chapter 07 ——

After all the excitement and pain of the day, Arun decided to turn in early, drifting toward sleep as soon as he closed his eyes. On the cusp of dreams, he imagined a familiar and comforting feminine scent.

"I'm sorry about before," said his dream girl.

He opened his eyes and discovered that, for once, reality was better than his dreams. Springer was crouching on the floor by his rack, with her hand on his shoulder. "I thought you could do with some company," she said. "Will you let me make it up to you?"

Arun grinned. "You're the best, Springer, but please don't put any weight on my left leg. Did I mention? I had a Troggie claw go through earlier today."

Cadet Phaedra Tremayne – named Springer by her friends due to her boundless optimism – grinned back and carefully clambered in beside him.

Springer was a squadmate, which meant they'd grown up together, shared the same school dorm for the past few years before making cadet, and then moving to the Charlie Company's underground hab-disk. That made his feelings toward her somehow both complicated and simple at the same time, but always strong. She was more than the comrade he was often buddied with in combat drills. She was a good friend, and several times recently she had *kept him company in his rack*, as she liked to call it. He tried hard not to think what that meant for their friendship.

Later, when they lay together in comfortable silence with Springer idly running her fingers through his hair, she suddenly blurted out: "I bet you're thinking of her right now."

"Her?"

"Yes, *her*. Xin Lee or is it Lee Xin? She can't seem to make up her mind."

Arun fumbled for a denial. He couldn't find one, though, because Springer was right. He'd been drifting into a heavenly dream existence filled with Xin's essence.

"Shhh, it's okay," she said. "More than okay. I think you having a crush on her is kinda cute." She kissed him tenderly on his forehead. "I was only thinking aloud. Xin is class G-1. At the end of next year, assuming she graduates as a Marine, they'll remove her contraceptive implant. She could have kids. *You* could have kids with her."

"Me? But I don't want to. I mean, I'm only 17. You and I are both only 17."

"Yes, but you *could*. I have to wait another two years and only then if I measure up to someone else's definition of what makes a good Marine."

"What's this all of a sudden about kids? Do you want to get pregnant?" Arun sat bolt upright. "Do you want *my* kids, Phaedra?"

Springer narrowed her eyes. There weren't many people she allowed to use her real name and get away without violence. "No and no. Not right now, and anyway, that's not the point. I don't get a choice. That's what gets me. I have to win someone else's approval to use my own body." She gave her head an angry shake. "You don't have the same implant. I guess you don't understand it. Not being a girl."

"We're all slaves, Springer. We're slave Marines. Bred to fight and die for the White Knights. Our bodies belong to them."

"True. But sometimes I think female cadets are slightly more slaves than you are."

He looked down at his friend who was staring wistfully up at the ceiling. She looked lost. Arun found himself echoing Sergeant Gupta's words. "Life isn't fair, Springer. Sometimes all you can do is suck it up and keep your head proud and high, the sign of a Marine. Wait for your luck to turn and then seize your chances with every fiber of your being."

Springer twisted round and stared at him, astonished. Then she rolled her eyes and shrugged.

The words didn't belong to him, and he felt an idiot to have spoken them. Arun didn't know what else to say – he never did – so he hugged her.

At first Springer relaxed into his embrace, but then she wriggled free and slipped away out of his rack. She was fleeing, unsteady on her feet.

"Don't go," begged Arun. "I'm sorry for talking such stupid drent."

"You didn't," she said. "I just want to be in my own bunk, is all." She paused trying to catch her breath. Arun swung his legs out of bed.

"No!" she shouted, her back to him still. "Get back in your rack and wipe that frown off your silly face. I worked hard to replace it with a smile. Don't you waste my efforts. There. That's better. Goodnight… *Cadet Prong*."

"I know you too well," he shouted, angry because she was hiding something from him.

The unspoken rule of the dorm – and the entire hab-disk – was that you pretended not to notice when its residents moved between racks during the night. Now he sensed hidden eyes alert, their owners poised to intervene.

Springer finally turned back and looked him square in the face. Tears streamed from those eyes, but those *eyes*! They were blazing beacons of violet. The skin of her eyelids was scorching, her tears vaporizing into emotional steam. He reached for the water canister he kept beside his bed and drenched her eyes with its contents. Her eyes were shut now, the lids still steaming.

"More water!" he barked.

Someone got the hint and threw another water canister to him. Arun tipped the contents over Springer's face, quenching the fire in her eyes.

"Thank you," she said, blinking away the drips.

She sounded abandoned, frightened. He would never forsake her, but she was half hidden behind a fringe of steam, and he could hardly blame her. He tried to hug her again, but again she pushed him away.

"Tell me, what's wrong."

"Nothing."

"Don't give me that. I know you too well. You had one of your visions, didn't you?"

"It's not a vision, Arun. I don't *see* things. I keep telling you that. I just get a feeling. Just now I felt that you…"

"What, that Rekka would hand me my ass on a plate?"

"No, not her. I don't know who. Really I don't, so just drop it. Get some sleep, instead. Please, for me. You'll need your strength."

"Strength for what?"

"Change. Yes, that's it. You're going through changes. Metamorphosis. You'll become something new. Or die trying. No – it's gone. Whatever I thought I'd sensed… it's gone. Arun, honestly, I probably just imagined it."

Unconvinced, Arun framed her face with his hands. "Be fair, Springer. You can't just dangle me by a thread and then cut the cord as if it doesn't matter. Think! What kind of changes?"

She shook his hands away. "Leave me alone, Arun."

Arun felt a confusing blend of emotions as he watched his friend pad away to her rack.

Then she stopped and turned around, bringing a flash of hope to his heart. "I'll tell you one thing, Arun." Her face creased into a frown. "At least you try to understand me. Have you noticed that since we made cadet everyone's turning into emotionless robots?"

Had they?

"There's not a single person in Detroit who could even attempt to understand me the way you did just now."

"Thank you."

She shook her head sadly. "I didn't mean that as praise. I love you, Arun, but I pity you even more."

Yeah well, I love you too, thought Arun. *But I wish you made sense sometimes.*

Solving the mystery of Springer's words would have to wait for another day. She'd retreated to her rack, wrapped in private thoughts.

Arun lay back down on his bed and closed his eyes, basking in the warm glow that came whenever he marveled in his good fortune at counting Springer as his buddy. Before long, though, his thoughts drifted along the passageway outside and down Helix 6 to hab-disk 7/14 where he pictured Xin asleep in her rack, the gentle ebb and flow of her breathing beckoning him.

Today Xin had acknowledged Arun's existence. Everyone laughed at him for falling in love with a girl so far out of his league, but today she had noticed him.

And Arun had a secret weapon to win her.

The meddling in the human Marine genome threw up a host of surprising side effects. Not all were as pretty as Springer's eyes. She had her visions of the future too, although they might be nothing more than vivid waking dreams.

Arun had his own special talent. Freakish genes might be what powered his ability. Or maybe he only thought he had a talent, and really it was a manifestation of psychosis. Whether true or imagined, if he set his mind a problem to be solved, on rare occasions he could feel his subconscious sifting through all the variables until an answer exploded in his mind, sometimes days later, leaving his brain feeling badly bruised.

He gave a brittle laugh.

So far he'd only used his ability to get into trouble.

He laughed again, softer this time. Getting into trouble was another talent of his. What else was youth for? No wonder Rekka was usually pissed at him.

Settling back into his pillow he immersed his mind in a new problem.

He held a woman's face in his hands, idly caressing the infinitesimally fine down on her cheeks. Just like he'd held Springer's face in real life scant minutes ago. The eyes regarding him from this face were not violet, though, they were as dark and dangerous as a Troggie tunnel. And this girl's skin was as perfectly smooth as ablative armor.

How do I get you to notice me? he asked Xin's face. *Could you ever love me?*

Xin gave the slightest of smiles, daring Arun to find out.

A sense of cogwheel teeth engaging filled his head, of noisy gears dripping with lubricant. It was a peculiarly mechanical sensation as if his mind were an apparatus constructed from brass, iron, hardwoods and oils. The gears turned faster; the smell of hot lubricant grew stronger. The floor of his mind rumbled with a low hum of power. This wasn't imagination. This was *real*. He, Arun McEwan, could do something no one else could.

He felt his problem being analyzed from scores of perspectives. Xin was chopped, sliced, and spun around to be measured from every direction. Whole universes sprang into being, filled with strategies and tactics, and their likely outcomes. Unpromising solutions died away, replaced with more promising lines of attack in a fecund blooming and culling of ideas.

Satisfied that he'd unleashed his talent, Arun left the hard work to his subconscious and drifted off to sleep. As his day finally floated away, he noticed the common thread that connected the galaxy-sized rooms containing the most promising solutions to his question.

For some reason he could not explain, the answers all involved him playing Scendence.

—— Chapter 08 ——

The following morning, Arun settled for a gentle walk in place of his regular pre-inspection workout. He kept away from the busy spineways and transit corridors, settling for the quiet passageway to the neighboring 6/10 hab-disk and back. *Gentle motion, nothing violent, and make use of your stick.* That's what the medic had said the previous night. She seemed to know what she was talking about. Given that less than a day earlier a claw had gouged a great chunk out of his thigh, and a shrapnel fragment had cracked his knee, he'd told the medic he was amazed he could walk at all.

"Why do you think the White Knights spent all that effort redesigning us?" she'd said. "Blast us and we get up again and carry on fighting. But your leg is now mostly filler and wishful thinking. It will still take weeks for your muscles to fully regrow, and knees are always troublesome healers. You'll have to recalibrate your battlesuit every other day to account for the changes in muscle strength."

As his stroll drew closer to his own hab-disk, his breath quickened. It wasn't the exercise; it was the sense of vulnerability. Rekka had left them with a threat and he felt sure it was aimed at him.

Before graduating to become a cadet, the worst punishment a novice could be given was to be discharged. Outside of the Marines there was a pale life of sorts in the Auxiliary, doing maintenance work and the dirtiest jobs in the mines here and on the moons. The luckiest Aux looked after the cadets and the Marines in the underground base as hab-disk servants. Now that he was 17 and a cadet, the penalty for insubordination or gross misconduct was public execution. And it wasn't an idle threat. Arun shuddered at the memories of what he'd been forced to witness.

Not wanting to be on his own, he slipped into the gym nearest to his dorm. There he found Osman pushing weights along resistance channels, and Springer climbing the endless wall.

Whether by coincidence or an empathetic sense of a squadmate needing support, Osman and Springer finished their exercise at the same time and left with Arun for the nearest shower room.

Usually, after stripping off, there would be a heap of banter between squadmates as they progressed through the various stages of the shower tunnel.

Shower time was normally a simple pleasure shared with friends. Not this morning, though. Today there was a new tension in Springer and Osman, something important but unspoken that poisoned the easy-going mood.

Eyes were averted.

Laughter stilted.

Was everyone else as frightened by Rekka as he was?

He thought that must be the explanation until they reached the spray booth at the end of the shower tunnel. Osman was pirouetting with both arms high while the booth sprayed a film of protective oils over his skin. That's when he blurted out the explanation for the discord.

"Arun, I'm joining the Scendence team."

Arun burst out laughing. "Is that it? All that edginess and it's just because you're joining the team? You bunch of dumbchucks. Have you worked out a team name yet? Here's one: three girls and an avian creature descendant. No, that was frakking awful. Give me a minute and I'll work out a better one."

To the sound of Arun's laughter, Osman walked out the tunnel looking mortified.

This was peak time in the showers. Arun, with his hands on his knees as he laughed himself silly, was holding up the flow of cadets in a hurry to get back in time for morning inspection. Springer pushed past and took her turn in the spray booth.

Tranquility's sun was anything but tranquil. Violent stellar flares flung vast quantities of high energy particles at their planet. The hab-disks were deep enough underground that the danger here was minimal, but at the surface, radiation peaks could be lethal. Detroit wasn't just a training depot, it was responsible for planetary defense too. It would not look good if an invasion force took Tranquility unopposed because the Marines delayed their deployment while they applied their sunblock.

"Moscow Express," said Springer indignantly. "That's our name. Majanita, Osman, Springer, Cristina. M-O-S-C-ow. Get it?" She lifted her arms and slowly turned around.

"Oh, I'm getting it," Arun said cheekily.

Springer narrowed her eyes, daring him to stare at her body.

He dared.

She narrowed her eyes even further, which made him laugh all over again. It was all a game, he thought. Springer loved the attention really.

Springer got her retaliation in by pointing at his crotch. "Your Xin said she admired some impressive equipment. As anyone can plainly see, she wasn't referring to you. She must have meant the Trog."

Arun laughed even harder at that, which won a giggle from Springer.

He caught Osman's attention. "You know," he said raising his voice so that Osman could hear above the chatter. "I don't mean to put a boot into a friend, but honestly? When it comes to Scendence, you're as useless as Rekka in a sexiest legs competition."

Osman winced. "I've no love for Rekka, but that's a combat injury you're mocking, man."

"Yeah, sorry." Arun colored with shame.

"You're right, though," Osman continued. "I stink. But they need a Deception player and it's better than letting them down, don't you think?"

"No, I can't say I do. But that's just me. Good luck to you, pal."

Springer stepped out of the tunnel joining Osman in the dressing area.

Arun took his turn under the spray. He could glimpse Osman. It wasn't easy to tell with his friend putting on his pants, but he looked genuinely unhappy,

"The only role I've any talent for is Deception," said Osman. "And even with Deception, I get a red mist. Can't resist going for the outrageous bluff. Promise me one thing. If the Corps is ever dumb enough to make me squad leader, I give you permission to shoot me first before my red mist gets us all killed."

"Acknowledged, future lance sergeant. I will implement your order without hesitation."

"Yeah, well. There *is* a way…"

"C'mon, man," Arun said as he emerged from the tunnel, washed, dried and coated in protective oils. "It's not like you to vulley around in circles. What's your plan?"

"For me to not be in the team."

Arun thought about that while he limped over to the clothing bins and selected underwear in his size. Just as he was about to step into his shorts, he paused. "No frakking way, man. You want me to take your place, don't you?"

Osman nodded, "The way I see it, if you don't then I will. If you think that's a waste of time, an opportunity cost because we won't be getting so many merit points elsewhere, then either way one of us will be wasting time on Scendence. So the way I figure it, there's nothing to lose if you take my place."

"That's butchered logic," said Arun, underwear on and selecting his pants.

"It's not like you have to," Springer told him. She was now fully clothed other than her shirt. "There are plenty of other good Deception players around."

"But will you?" asked Osman.

Arun frowned, thinking about those hints from his planner brain. "Is this what all that awkwardness was about? Is it really such a big deal to ask me?"

"No," replied Osman.

"Yes," said Springer simultaneously. "Well… yes it is a big deal, but…" Her shoulders slumped as if she'd melted slightly. "We're worried about you. I've never seen Rekka as angry as she was last night. She felt wounded, let down, and took that out on you. I'm not saying that's fair but it's the kind of drent that goes on all the time. Big deal. But what if someone more senior decides that they've been embarrassed? What if someone important goes looking for a scapegoat?"

"What? You mean a Jotun?" asked Arun. He hadn't considered the outcomes of petty training missions would be noticed so high up.

"Maybe," said Springer. "Who knows? It's a crazy world we live in. Let's face it, we're G-2 cadets. To us, this world still doesn't make sense."

"Springer!" Osman shouted. "We agreed not to mention being worried about him."

"Arun's not stupid, Osman. Except when he's vulley-dreaming about his skangat fantasy girl. I can't waste time on a bad lie to a good friend."

Osman didn't argue. He didn't agree with her either. He strode away back to the dorm, but at the shower room door he hesitated.

An instant later they saw why when Instructor Rekka burst into the room.

"Get your clothes on quickly and follow me." Her orders were directed at Arun.

Arun stood there, frozen.

"Hurry up, there's no time to waste," said Rekka, grabbing her walking stick.

He finished dressing as rapidly as he could.

Osman slunk back into the room waiting with Springer. Watching.

The instant Arun's boots were on, Rekka threw his stick at him. "You've been summoned."

He tailed her out of the shower room but took a last look back at Osman and Springer, and their expressions of horror.

Were there tears in Springer's eyes?

"Move it!" barked Rekka from the passageway.

Arun hurried after her as best he could. He wanted a chance to say a proper goodbye, maybe to say some things that had gone unsaid.

Too late. The next time he saw his squadmates, he expected to be on the wrong side of an execution squad.

—— Chapter 09 ——

In the end, Arun couldn't just stand there as silent and rigid as a statue, having his ass chewed out in silence. It was beyond unfair: he was being set up for a fall. He wasn't the sharpest blade in the set, but he knew nothing he did now would make any difference to his fate.

"Ma'am. Why me, ma'am?" he asked.

For a moment, it almost sounded like a reasonable question.

From the more comfortable side of her desk, Senior Instructor Tirunesh Nhlappo regarded him coolly. The braver cadets called her Shlappo behind her back, though they were always careful to do so very quietly. To look at her in a photo you would think she was nothing special: above average height, average build and with a shaven head that was probably the reason, Arun thought, why her ears looked ridiculously large. But when you meet Nhlappo in person you were struck by an intensity of personality that was so fierce you could practically see an aura crackling around her.

Nhlappo was one of the senior humans in the 412th, and one of her roles was as chief instructor for the 8th battalion. Until the handover to the veteran NCOs had completed, that meant the woman he'd just interrupted had power of life and death over him.

After a long pause – a very long and painful one for Arun – she spoke. "Excuse me?"

"Ma'am. Sorry, ma'am. I spoke out of turn."

All it took was an incremental shift in Nhlappo's expression and Arun knew without doubt that his answer was utterly unacceptable. He wasn't getting out of this so easily.

Dread spread through him like a virulent disease.

The other instructors quietly worshiped their senior, but Shlappo wasn't loved by the school novices or the cadets. In the five years in which she had been Arun's senior instructor he had never known her to say a single word of praise or encouragement. And training had been tough. Thirty percent of novices didn't make cadet grade. Horden only knew what happened to them all. The best thing Arun could say about Nhlappo was that she never took out her frustrations in the kind of petty humiliations some of her junior instructors had developed into an art form.

And yet she had spent the past ten minutes tearing strips off him. He'd never seen her do that before.

This was very bad.

Nhlappo's expression shifted once more, indicating Arun would have to answer now if he knew what was good for him.

"Ma'am. Our mission in the tunnels failed," he said. "But I wasn't even leading a fire team, and I did rack up the biggest kill count. Not saying I'm perfect – and I don't like what the combat drugs did to me – but do I really deserve to be the scapegoat, ma'am?"

After peering at him over steepled fingers, Nhlappo picked up her digi-pad and began writing notes. She handed the pad over to the man at her left, a senior sergeant according to his rank insignia. The sergeant read her notes, nodded, and then passed the pad back. His face was coated in the kind of perfect parade ground glaze that showed no reaction to anything.

"You know I admire your courage in standing up to me," said Nhlappo. "You've got backbone, son. I like that."

Relief gushed over Arun. He felt knots of muscles untie themselves. He'd thought he was in for a mega punishment, and here was Nhlappo offering praise for the first time in recorded history.

"To answer your question," she continued, "the reason I have selected you as – sacrificial victim – is because you're the laughing stock of the entire regiment. And beyond. If the Fates cherish you as their darling, it is just possible you might escape with your life." Her face went as hard as rock. "Don't count on it, though."

Arun held himself as tightly as he could, determined not to show any reaction to Nhlappo's honesty.

"I've served the Jotuns for 150 years," she continued in an infinitesimally softened tone. "All that time and yet I still don't understand them. They're lethally capricious, I can tell you that much. I have to guess what they want, and my guess is that they'll give us such a negative de-merit mark that our battalion is guaranteed to be Culled for years to come. If we humans deal with this first by having our squads disciplined and re-ordered, then that could mitigate any punishment. I have to at least attempt to make an example to prove we are taking this seriously. I have decided that it is your role, Cadet McEwan. You shall be that example. I believe the term your generation has rediscovered is *taking one for the team*."

Arun squared his shoulders another notch. "Ma'am. I understand, ma'am."

"Oh, no," said Nhlappo, suddenly angry. "No, cadet, that just won't do." Nhlappo shook her head in such a way that left Arun feeling the biggest idiot on the planet. "Don't misunderstand me, McEwan. I did not mean: '*You're my favorite really, yet I have no choice but to punish you. I'm sorry and I really hope you'll understand.'.*"

"No, ma'am. Of course not, ma'am."

"Good. Because you thoroughly deserved the punishment I was going to give you."

Relief flooded back. She'd said *was*. Had he gotten off somehow?

"Except you've made this worse," she said. "Standing up to me was brave but it was also exceptionally stupid, even for you, McEwan. You stood your ground because you felt your punishment was undeserved. You felt an injustice. Isn't that right, cadet?"

"Ma'am. No, ma'am."

Nhlappo gave an exaggerated cough. "Excuse me, cadet." She cleared her throat unconvincingly. "Nasty cough. Couldn't quite hear what you were mumbling. You know what, McEwan? An element of the novice training program has just come to mind. *Lying to a superior is punishable by death.* Did we remember to teach you that?"

"Ma'am. Yes, ma'am."

"Thank you. I feel reassured. I'll ask again, and speak clearly this time. Tell me, do you feel an injustice?"

"Ma'am. Yes, ma'am."

"Unacceptable!" Nhlappo slammed her fist against her desk. She rose, coming round the front of her desk to fix Arun with a close-up glare. Arun didn't dare to breathe.

"Marines are not permitted justice," she snapped. "Why not?"

Fumbling through her words for booby traps, Arun stumbled upon an answer that sounded plausible. "We are slaves, ma'am"

"Correct." Nhlappo's expression of disapproval lightened up half a notch, enough for Arun to breathe again. "If you live through today, perhaps you do have some chance of survival after all. Yes, of course, we're slaves. Only a fool would forget that for an instant. From the lowest of humans who fail to graduate school and so join the Aux for the rest of their short lives, to the senior Jotun system commander, and even the insectoids you slaughtered in your tunnel exercise: we are all of us slaves. To the White Knights we are nothing more than a rounding error in a troop strength list reported to the nearest million. As individuals we are less than nothing to them, but as battalions, regiments and Marine fleet contingents, our pain and servitude is just enough to earn a semblance of protection for our homeworld. Earth was free from alien occupation last I heard, though I never trust what I hear on that subject."

Arun took a sharp intake of breath. Nhlappo's words could be considered insurrection.

"My words appear to trouble you, cadet. Do you wish to contradict them?"

"Ma'am. No, ma'am."

"Good. You have a lesson to learn. Learn it well. You are a slave. Slaves must never imagine they deserve justice, because that is one short step away from rebellion. Any slaves who do not grasp this will be rooted out and destroyed. Understand?"

"Ma'am. Yes, ma'am."

"I believe you do. To be sure of that, I intend to extend your punishment. All members of your squad will suffer the same penalty I had intended for you. Furthermore I will make sure they know that you are the cause of their misery, and why."

Even if he were executed, they would curse his name. Springer too, he realized with a jolt.

"Most people would say I've just wasted the past ten minutes of my life by talking to you. By this time tomorrow, you will probably be dead. But the Jotuns possess an infinite capacity to surprise us, and so there remains a chance that you will live. That is why you and I are discussing this matter. *Attention to detail.* In warfare, administration, even romance, drama, literature – yes, I *am* familiar with those activities – attention to detail is frequently what separates success from failure. And, if you are to die, I want you to know why, and I want you to die well. Can you do that, McEwan? Can you die well?"

"Ma'am. Yes, ma'am."

Nhlappo judged him with a look. "Perhaps," she said grudgingly. She activated a control on the surface of her desk. "Let's find out, shall we?"

The door opened. Rekka entered, accompanied by two cadets: Hortez who had led Blue Squad in the tunnel exercise, and LaSalle who had been put in charge of Charlie Company in its entirety. The cadets looked deathly pale. Even Rekka looked troubled.

Nhlappo addressed Arun. "The reason I told you of punishments you *would have had* is because events are now out of my control. We've all been summoned by Colonel Little Scar to explain why everyone on the planet is laughing at his regiment."

She got out from her desk, leading her little group into the transit corridor outside.

Running was Arun's first instinct. Everything was stacked against him. Where could he run to? The one place he might find sanctuary was in the Troggie nest, but he would never make it that far. The forces of inevitability crushed any resistance from him and rooted his feet to the floor. All he could do was attempt some semblance of dignity.

He felt a shove in his back from the veteran sergeant – Arun still didn't know his name. It was enough to get Arun's legs working.

"Move!" he ordered. "The colonel will not expect to be kept waiting any longer."

Arun marched to his fate.

—— Chapter 10 ——

Senior Instructor Nhlappo led Arun and the doomed group through Gate Three and out into the eddying breeze on the planet's surface. Arun looked back at the heavily fortified entrance that bristled with gun emplacements manned by Marines.

"Eyes front, McEwan!" barked Instructor Rekka from the rear.

Arun reluctantly obeyed. Wrenching his gaze away from his home filled his gut with an aching sense of loss. The colonel hadn't invited them over for coffee and biscuits, that was for sure. Arun didn't expect to ever see his home again. Never see Springer's warm smile. And his plans for Xin were exposed as nothing more than a joke.

Look on the bright side, he thought, *you always enjoy any chance to come up to the surface.*

In Arun's experience there were four main reasons why cadets were allowed on the surface. A visit to the colonel was definitely not one of them.

A Marine was expected to fight in any environment: in the airless void of space, racing through endless hive tunnels deep underground, defending snowy mountain redoubts, or flushing insurgents from sweltering jungle thick with vegetation. Simulating these combat conditions was not an easy task, but the Human Marine Corps on Tranquility had access to an entire planet to provide as many training environments as required.

His use of the topside training grounds was the first reason why Arun was no stranger to the planet's surface.

Marines had to be in superb physical condition. Arun had climbed the endless Gjende Mountains that shadowed the Detroit base and had run, marched, and slept many times on the adjoining plateau, ignoring roads and crude paths to cut through fields of wheat, maize and more exotic crops, to the consternation of the Agri-Aux and the insistence of the instructors.

That was reason number two.

The third reason was to endure the mutual incomprehension of inter-species encounter sessions, where Jotuns and young humans would meet and attempt to get to know one another. In theory, the result would be human Marines who weren't so terrified of their officers that they were unable to function properly in combat. Arun saw no signs of that working, but the Jotuns had such an extreme phobia about being underground that the only way to move them beneath the surface was to render them unconscious first.

Arun's mind refused to think openly of the fourth reason why he might be summoned to the surface, pushing that cruel knowledge deep into his mind so that it only surfaced in his everyday thoughts as a persistent feeling of dread.

They pressed on in silence through service buildings, storage depots, and vehicle parks, and onward to Jotunville.

There was no official title for the complex of palaces topped with soaring spires and connected by glass walkways at obscene heights. Whatever it was called, to be summoned here was an ordeal few cadets ever experienced, and fewer returned to their underground holes to tell the tale.

As defense against orbital bombardment, Jotunville and the underground Marine complex nestled at the bottom of a narrow valley that meandered beneath towering mountain peaks. The transparent building material favored by the Jotuns would have generated a sense of space and warmth if their city had been situated out on the plateau, but most days inky shadow blanketed the valley floor, shrouding Jotunville with a chill aura of doom. Only once had Arun seen this phalanx of crystal spires at midday, when the illumination from the overhead sun caused it to gleam like a polished jewel.

There was little sun now, in the mid-morning. The lack of light made transparent walkways suddenly materialize overhead, making Arun fight hard against the instinct to duck. Distant palaces became ethereal phantoms that defied his attempts to grasp their shape. Jotunville was ghostly and threatening, as if its existence were only partially in the material plane. As they penetrated deeper into the city of glass spires, and the confrontation with the colonel grew closer, Arun's nerves began to shred.

How were the others coping? He hoped the two instructors were wetting themselves with fear, but they both had hearts of granite: they wouldn't be worried. The unknown sergeant following Nhlappo was no different. Maybe it was only Arun who was so scared that placing every foot forward took a supreme effort of courage. His fellow cadets were showing no signs of nerves. Hortez would be singing in his head to *clear his mind of darkness*, as he put it. As for Alistair LaSalle, he adapted to anything life threw at him, which was presumably why the instructors had tried him in the role of senior company sergeant for the tunnel exercise.

Mastering fear was about deflecting the anticipation of danger. The instructors had drilled that into him all his life. So he tried occupying himself by deploying an imaginary Marine company to defend Jotunville. Two squads up on either end of the overhead walkway would catch an enemy below in flanking fire, pinning them down while another squad, ready to launch flechette grenades, would sneak around and catch the invader from the rear. Then the command squad would fire a quick suppressing frag barrage before the remaining three squads charged the confused survivors.

But he was only replaying standard classroom tactics. The mental trick crumbled almost before he'd begun because they were in such deep shadow that he had to invent the layout of the surrounding buildings.

What made the fear so difficult to deflect was that this whole stupid business was so pointless. Arun didn't believe there was ever any glory in dying, no matter how you had to go, but there were deaths that at least counted for something.

To be executed for an embarrassing accident – that would mean his life had been utterly pointless.

He couldn't prevent his hands clenching into fists, his muscles readying to release explosive power. To fight injustice, to fall in a struggle for freedom. Now *that* would be worth dying for…

"Loosen those hands, McEwan," thundered Rekka. "You *will* march like a Marine, not an ill-disciplined brute."

Arun tried for his best parade ground form as they began to ascend a spiraling loop of transparent stairs, sheathed in a twisting tube. A quarter of the tube was open, exposing them to a blustering wind and a sheer drop that grew rapidly more lethal until he soon realized that he could end it all on his own terms by throwing himself off.

Suicidal thoughts haunted him, teasing fingers plucking at him through the opening in the tube. *A few seconds of falling and then it would all be over. The colonel's revenge would be cheated.*

Arun flung his arms out against the walls of the tube, bracing himself against the seductive thoughts in his head.

Jump…

No!

He wouldn't! Not while there was hope. And there *was* a slender hope. Nhlappo had said so.

Or had she planted false hope, in case of just such a moment as this?

"Keep moving, McEwan! Have you no dignity?"

Arun felt his jaw tighten. *No I haven't, you stupid veck!* For days, Arun had struggled to keep wild mood swings in check, and now Rekka's admonishment was like a flamethrower, coating Arun with incandescent fury.

He fantasized about grabbing the skangat of an instructor and throwing them both off the stairway tube. *But there was still hope.* He *had* to believe that. So instead Arun launched his final mental defense, the one marked: 'Do not use except in case of emergency'. He folded his conscious mind away and relinquished control to the unconscious parts of his brain. He had been engineered to do this during sentry duty, or when deployed for ambushes, waiting for hours or days with his finger on the trigger, waiting for an enemy to appear.

But this wasn't sentry duty. Would he wake up when he needed to?

That sense of unease stretched, infusing his mind for an eternity until–

Rekka slapped him… "That was a coward's escape," she sneered. "But at least it got you here."

Arun found he'd arrived on a transparent walkway, about to follow the rest of the group through a glass door that was sliding open. Of the journey here he had no memory.

He glanced down, but the ground was too far away to see.

Then he passed through the door and into the colonel's domain.

The humans were in the lower of two circular rooms built with the same transparent material as the walkway. They looked like two identical glass bowls stacked one atop the other but offset by a quarter of their diameter.

On the upper level, sitting at a double-banked work station, was the colonel of the 412th Tactical Marine Regiment. His name translated as Little Scar.

Only his head was showing over the back of his chair, but the nick in his left ear was enough for Arun to recognize the colonel from parade ground inspections.

From the tilt of his head, Little Scar was staring up at the clouds gamboling across the gleaming blue sky, his dangling bronze earrings in the shape of hammers brushing the back of his neck.

Sky?

The only view through these windows should have been shadowed mountainside. But that had been replaced by a sunny vista. Arun could even hear imaginary birds calling to each other as they flew through the spiraling walkway that led up through the roof.

Curved sofas covered in emerald green velour ran along the walls of the lower room, the huge size of these sofas making him feel like a small child sent to see the grown-ups, or a mortal approaching the gods. They could have been built for eight-foot tall humans if not for the additional armrests at shoulder level. Of course! Jotuns were hexapeds.

Zug would love this.

The thought of his alien-obsessed friend gave Arun a pang of loss. He tried smothering himself with numbness. Around him, he could sense fear begin to come off Hortez and Alistair, the mental defenses that had kept up their spirits on the journey had been stormed and breached by the presence of their officer. He couldn't blame them because they had everything to lose. Arun didn't.

However much he tried to believe in Nhlappo's slender thread of hope, Arun was certain he'd already lost.

Arun stared at Little Scar. *Whatever you're going to do, get on with it!*

As if the Jotun had heard his thoughts, Little Scar finally acknowledged the humans. Still with his back to them, he growled: "Study the softscreens."

Little Scar spoke with his own voice. Most Jotuns used the same voicebox translator technology as the Trogs, but those most skilled in human language could speak in a voice that sounded as if they had swallowed a box of razor blades.

To use his own voice emphasized that Little Scar had issued a critical command to be obeyed instantly.

But what did he mean? What softscreens?

Hortez saw them first, picking up a stack of transparent rectangles. Softscreen material was tough but years of use meant that the ones the cadets normally handled were scuffed enough to be seen even when inactive. These were pristine. Even when Hortez handed him one, Arun could barely see the device until his touch activated it and an image appeared of the Totalizer. He could see every cadet battalion in Detroit listed in merit point order. Arun's 8-412/TAC was two places and a little over seven thousand points clear of the Cull Zone. The image was real-time, with each score flicking up or down slightly, but the gap between each battalion was much too large for the positions to change while he watched.

After about ten seconds, the image changed. It still showed the Totalizer, but this time listing the live killscores for the past month. There he was, Arun McEwan, top of the leader board by a long margin, the result of blasting the insect horde in the tunnels.

The view switched to live plus simulated killscores. Arun was still ranked top, though by a lower margin.

The colonel must consider my killscore rankings to be important, thought Arun, *or else why is he showing them? If all Little Scar cares about are results, then I'm winning his heart.*

The more Arun considered this, the more it made sense. Zug was always saying it was a mistake to assign human emotions to aliens. It felt as if everyone on the planet had pointed out that Arun had made the regiment the laughing stock of Detroit, but now he thought of it, he'd only heard the jeers from other humans. Maybe Little Scar didn't care. Arun had won top killscore and a bundle of merit points for one of the Jotun's battalions. Perhaps Arun had been summoned to be personally commended by his commanding officer?

Suck on that, Shlappo!

The softscreen display shifted again and all his hope vaporized. Arun felt as if he were falling, plummeting farther even than if he had jumped off the Jotunville heights. If he'd suspected he was doomed before, he *knew* it now.

He peered at the screen. It showed a camera shot of Arun naked with the scribe, an image enhanced to simulate a spotlight focused on the source of his humiliation.

Someone had added the caption: *412th Marines. Always ready for ACTION!*

Arun willed the display to change again. It did, but he wished it hadn't. What it showed was so bad that the breath froze in his throat.

Cadets were lined up with their backs to the parade ground dais. This was the main parade ground, the one cut into the Gjende Mountains above Detroit. The camera took a close-up view of their faces. Most wore blank expressions, some were angry, a few trembled with fear.

Human text at the bottom identified the footage, as if it needed an explanation. This was the final reason for coming to the planet's surface that Arun had hidden from his mind. This was the fate that haunted every cadet.

This was the Cull.

The display looped around the moment of execution, but changed camera views from wide shots to close ups of individual twenty-year old cadet faces at the moment they were put to death.

The humans in his quarters had no choice but to watch. Little Scar had ordered that they should.

The Culled cadets died again and again, and Little Scar said nothing, sitting there up the steps in his upper room, not even deigning to glance in the humans' direction.

Minutes went past.

An hour.

While his subordinates watched endless variations on the same slaughter, Little Scar sat motionless in his chair, looking up into a sky that wasn't even real.

Then, at last, the time had come.

Little Scar turned and faced them.

<h1 style="text-align:center">—— Chapter 11 ——</h1>

Little Scar levered himself out of his deeply reclined seat and advanced a few paces toward the humans. His shaggy white fur, shot through with gray, jounced as he moved.

The size and power of the Jotuns was enough to scare the crap out of Arun at the best of times.

And this was not the best of times.

Arun's gaze was fixed on the digits of the alien's upper limbs. At present they were rubbery extrusions through the flat, horn-ridged pads that terminated his arms. But they could be retracted in an instant and replaced by claws like combat knives. With one blow, those claws could decapitate a human.

There was precedent.

The colonel halted at the top of the steps leading down from the upper part of the room, and delivered a roar that liquefied Arun's spine. Somehow Arun remained at attention, distracting himself with the way the colonel's earrings jangled as he folded his ear trumpets flat against his head.

Little Scar's mouth gaped wide. He did not speak, but the sounds of a male human came from his throat speaker. "You have seen footage from 32 years ago, from the last time my regiment suffered the dishonor of the Cull." He held up one upper limb. A single rubbery finger shot outward stretching as long as a human arm. And it was pointing straight at Arun. "I have had to explain to Supreme Commander Menglod why your image is posted throughout Detroit."

The colonel growled again. "Do I need to draw a connection between the two facts?"

Arun's sight glazed over. He couldn't breathe. He daren't.

The colonel retracted his finger. "The human cadets in the tunnel exercise are less than three years from graduation, from fighting in the war. Losing is a valuable lesson. It is best to lose at some point in your training. A warrior who has never been bested has never tasted the ash and tarnished mouth-feel of defeat. They remain untested and I do not wish for untested warriors in my regiment."

Arun breathed.

But then the Jotun extended his claws. They were serrated and so very sharp. "But to lose badly is unforgivable," he continued. "The stink of incompetence can linger forever. I must correct this now or execute the entire battalion. It wouldn't be the first time we had to discard a unit gone rotten. You humans have created this crisis and you are forever grumbling that you should run more of your own affairs. So you advise me. What should I do?"

Little Scar fixed his glare on Nhlappo. "You first."

She didn't hesitate. "Sir. Cadet McEwan is the source of the embarrassment. He should be executed immediately."

Nhlappo looked as if she had more to say but Little Scar pointed to Rekka. "You!"

"Sir. I agree with the senior instructor, sir."

The Jotun narrowed his eyes, glaring at Rekka. Arun allowed himself a little inward smile when he imagined how Rekka must feel under that attention.

Alistair and Hortez were next. Each took full responsibility upon himself, but evaded suggesting what punishment they should suffer.

Then it was Arun's turn. What could he say? He was trapped by his predatory superiors. So he spun the line that Nhlappo had ordered him to back in her office, dragging out the toxic words with as much dignity as he could manage. "Sir, you should remove the source of our shame by executing me."

He tensed his neck, expecting Little Scar to leap down the stairs and slash with those claws.

But the alien appeared satisfied and settled his attention on the sergeant whose name Arun still didn't know. "You are senior human sergeant for 'C' Company, 8th battalion. What would you do?"

If he was the senior veteran then he must be Staff Sergeant Bryant. He answered calmly. "Sir. It is the leader's responsibility to preserve the honor of his or her unit. To have lost a unit's honor is a catastrophic loss of authority after which no leader can function. So if a unit has dishonored itself, then its leader should be punished as an example. Even if the punishment isn't fatal, before the leader can return to the same position he or she must not only wait for a suitable period of atonement, but must also earn that position to the satisfaction of the unit."

"Quite so," said Little Scar. He nodded, a gesture of agreement, although with his pronounced brow ridge and bony skull crest the motion looked very much like an armored headbutt. "Of all of us, Staff Sergeant Bryant has most recently been tested in battle. It shows."

He pointed to Alistair and Hortez. "You are no longer Marine cadets."

A third finger extruded from his hand toward Nhlappo. "You! Ensure these failures are out of my regiment by the end of the day. Then hand over your remaining duties to your junior instructors. From midnight you are demoted to the rank of Marine private. Gold Squad has lost its veteran to resuscitation attrition. You will fill the gap. Pray that you are never presented to me again. I shall not be so lenient next time."

The merest hint of a protest sounded in Nhlappo's throat, but she cut it dead just in time.

"I have…" started Little Scar but stopped suddenly. He growled, flicking his ears wildly. "I have discussed your company's performance with Commander Menglod and we have agreed a unit-wide punishment for the 8th battalion. Examine your screens."

Arun looked down at the image of the Totalizer showing the leaderboard of battalions vying with each other to keep out of the Cull Zone. 8-412/TAC was 7,000 points ahead of the cut off. Arun steeled himself to see that safety margin diminish.

The screen refreshed.

8-412/TAC had disappeared. No it hadn't. It had shifted position. They were bottom!

"We have deducted 25,000 points from 8-412/TAC. This year's graduates *will* be Culled."

The colonel looked from one human face to another, daring them to protest. They were too stunned to speak.

"There is to be no further punishment of the cadets over this issue. Dismissed."

A mix of horror and relief flooded through Arun as he about-heeled to leave. He'd escaped but his friends had not. It should have been the other way around.

"No, not you, McEwan," said the Jotun. "You shall remain here."

Little Scar waited until the other humans had marched away before switching from his thought-to-voice system to speak in his own gravelly words.

"I want a chat with you."

—— Chapter 12 ——

With a wave of the rubbery tubes that passed for fingers, the colonel beckoned Arun to stand next to him at his workstation.

As he mounted the steps to approach the Jotun, Arun tried to guess what the alien was about to tell him. He had no idea.

Once Arun was standing next to the alien's chair, and had cast his gaze to the ground, Little Scar asked using his own awkward voice: "Would you like to see your brother?"

Not 'you will be executed at dawn' or 'you will be permanently assigned to the punishment battalion'.

Arun was so stunned that he let his pause drag on until Little Scar drew his ears back in annoyance.

"Sir. Yes, sir," Arun said quickly.

Little Scar smiled. There was little about the six–legged Jotuns that was human-like, but when they wanted to, Jotuns could smile just like the most endearing human child. And at that moment, the commander of the 412th Marines chose to smile.

"He is not here," said the Jotun, back to speaking through his artificial voice.

Inter-species familiarity sessions with the Jotuns often went this way. The exchanges mixed boredom on the part of the Jotuns with the terror of the young humans, blending them into an uncomfortable mutual incomprehension.

The worst part was that if you didn't understand, you were expected to ask.

And find a way to do so without having your face sliced off for insulting a superior.

Arun swallowed hard and then cleared his throat, trying to remember whether doing so meant a polite interruption or an insolent invitation to be decapitated. "Sir, this cadet begs permission to ask a question. Sir."

"Speak."

"Why did you ask whether I wanted to see my brother?"

The Jotun narrowed his eyes and stared at Arun, who flinched under this intense scrutiny. "Your incident in the tunnels. I was concerned it might affect your morale."

What? "Sir, that's… very touching, sir."

Arun cringed at his familiarity but the alien looked more puzzled than angry.

"Touching?" Little scar digested the word. "Ah. You mean you are overwhelmed by my emotional succor. Is that correct?"

"Sir. Yes, sir."

"Hah hah hah!" The voice simulator was stumped by human laughter. You couldn't tell whether the laughter was hearty, ironic, or uncertain. "You are right to think I care about your wellbeing, Cadet McEwan."

Arun couldn't quite believe what was happening. The commander of the regiment was talking to him like an indulgent uncle. Whenever he had spoken to Jotuns before, they had always assumed an attitude that humans were indistinguishable from each other. Little Scar was talking not only as if Arun were an individual sentient being, but an important one too. One that the regimental commander wanted to know better.

What the frakk was happening?

"I care about you…" said Little Scar, before pausing.

"Sir?"

"I care because the Night Hummers say you will be important."

Arun shivered. Floating in their tanks of churning yellow liquid, deep in the bowels of the base, the Night Hummers were bloated gas-sacs, prized for their pre–cognitive ability. Arun struggled to believe that anyone could actually see into the future – though he tried hard to keep an open mind about Springer's ability. Given the fuss the Jotuns made about them on behalf of their masters, the White Knights surely believed that Night Hummers could.

"I don't know why you are special," said the Jotun. "They won't say. Or can't." Little Scar flicked his ears back and bared his teeth, serrated little gray daggers that gleamed in the light from the artificial sky. "Perhaps you will betray us all."

Arun stood rigidly under the lashes of the Jotun's harsh stare.

"Only one other human has ever aroused the Night Hummers' interest. Strange how after several hundred years in which they never saw fit to even mention your species, here you are, both in my regiment at the same time."

Who was the other? Arun burned with the question but he didn't dare speak. It took all his courage to even breathe under the Jotun's withering gaze.

"And maybe a third human of interest is due to arrive in the system soon. Or… maybe not."

Little Scar moved his ears in circles, each rotating in a different direction. His training told Arun this indicated indecision, deep thought, or a sign of abdominal discomfort.

"Learn this, human. Night Hummers hint at their predictions. Forever they tell us: 'Act now to avert this disaster that will happen… or maybe it will not.' " He growled. "It is not a question of – what is your expression? – *hedging bets*. It is simply how the Hummers perceive the future – and sometimes the present. They allude, imply, and prattle. A collective of Hummers can be noisy, utterly tiresome. It is only by having a troop of Hummers, and keeping them under constant surveillance and analysis by AIs, that we ever realize when there is a temporary consistency to the Hummers' ramblings. Sometimes the pattern dissipates like mist and wind. Occasionally their minds march in lockstep and they all tell the same story, repeating their words over and over. We know then that they want us to listen."

Arun shivered as his pictured the Hummers in their yellow tanks, screaming Arun's name in unison.

"Human, your posture indicates inquiry. Did you want to ask questions?"

"Sir. Yes, sir. Thank you, sir."

"You may ask only one more."

"Sir. Who are the other humans the Night Hummers spoke of?"

Little Scar thought over the answer. "The one who maybe is to come and maybe is a misinterpretation has only the simplest description. No name, rank, scent, or title. All we know is that she is purple." He laughed, the artificial sound accompanied by a bass rumble from the alien. "Purple!"

Little Scar found the whole idea hilarious but Arun felt something else flooding him with sparkling warmth: hope.

Instructor Nhlappo had described the entire Marine Corps presence on Tranquility as nothing more than a rounding error on a White Knight fleet strength report. What if humans were important after all? And not in the mega long-term species survival plan some veterans talked of – but right here and now.

And, thought Arun, *Little Scar had referred to the purple human as a she…*

The laughter coming through Little Scar's speaker continued as he spoke. "I have seen pink and brown humans. Hrmph. Seen a few red ones too in battle – your species does bleed so energetically – but never a *purple* one."

Little Scar cut the laughter. "Now we discuss your brother." He brought out a mid-limb from where it had nestled in his deep chest hair, and pointed it up to the sky. "He's out there."

"Sir? You mean he's out there in the galaxy?"

"Yes. No." Little Scar thought it over. "He is in orbit. A lucky coincidence. I could let you meet if you would like."

"Sir. I would like that, sir."

Having written off the idea of family long ago, to meet a brother would be a curiosity. But it would also be fascinating to meet someone who had been out there, fighting between the stars.

"You would like," said Little Scar. "I would *not* like. But I may enable this in any case."

O-kay. That didn't exactly make sense. When Little Scar made no sign that he was going to elaborate, Arun asked: "Sir, is there something I must do first?"

"Yes. The insect scribe in your tunnel encounter showed sexual interest in you…"

"Not really, sir," Arun blurted out. When the officer didn't react to his interruption, he added: "Sir. The creature was academically interested in my unfortunate physiological reaction to the combat drugs. That's all, sir."

Little Scar showed his teeth again. He was not happy.

"Sir. Sorry, sir," Arun added quickly.

The Jotun allowed Arun's discomfort to continue for a few more seconds before slowly lowering his lips over his fangs. "Only speak when spoken to, human."

Was Arun supposed to acknowledge that? He decided to keep silent.

Little Scar sniffed at Arun, but then relaxed somewhat. "McEwan, you might dismiss your accomplishment, but such a display of sexual interest is unprecedented. These *Trogs*, as you call the hive creatures, run several mining operations here on Tranquility and on moons around the outer planets. They also service the cryogenic facilities, dig the network of defensive warrens, and form the bulk of the planetary defense force. The hive creatures are vital, yet we know very little about them. We need to aid each other to strengthen our defenses and add new contingency plans."

The first question that instantly struck Arun was why had they felt the need to strengthen their defenses. To ask, though, would be madness. He reckoned he had pushed his freakish familiarity with the colonel as far as it would go.

But Arun wasn't renowned for common sense.

"Sir. Permission to speak, sir?"

"There. Politeness was not so difficult, was it?"

A buried memory surfaced. The Jotun colonel sounded like his mom. He shook the thought away. "No, sir. Why are we needing to–?"

Little Scar hissed a warning. Arun had never heard that sound before. It sounded like human flatulence, but it came through the Jotun's teeth.

"I did not offer permission to speak, human. I merely commended politeness. Yes. We need to work more with the hive people. You have this connection with them. Therefore I want you to be our liaison."

Arun blinked repeatedly so that his emotions wouldn't show. His heart fluttered at the memory of the scribe's red flanks puckering…

"You may speak now," said Little Scar.

"*Liaison.* What does that mean, sir? What must I do?"

"Liaison means you will represent the interests of all humans and Jotuns in our dealings with the insect hives on the planet of Tranquility. Learn from them. Learn about them."

"Sir. But what are you expecting me to do?" *Surely he didn't mean…*

Little Scar hissed through his teeth – more a cross between heavy breathing and sighing than the flatulent growl of real anger. Arun interpreted this as irritation.

"Are you a child?" asked the Jotun.

"Sir. I'm 17," Arun replied. "No, sir, I'm not."

"Then you decide what liaison entails. I care nothing for means, only ends. Your first encounter is set for tomorrow." He paused. "Your honor is tarnished, Cadet McEwan. Combat drugs had taken control of your body. I understand. That is why I permit you to live. But the stink of failure hangs around you, makes me want to retch. How sweet it would be if you could take the cause of your dishonor, and transform it into a sweet-smelling triumph that will be celebrated for centuries."

"Sir. I understand, sir."

"Good. Understand this too. If you fail then I shall execute you personally. Dismissed."

— Urgent Info Message —

MESSAGE SUBJECT: Table of Organization & Equipment. Blue Squad, 'C' Company, 8th battalion, 412th Tactical Marine Regiment.

Additional instructions from Squad Leader, Sgt. Gupta:

Attention, Blue Squad.

Memorize the contents of this TOE. It sets out our initial structure, effective immediately. This includes semi-permanent NCO ranks

'Semi' means that if you screw up, or if you don't look at me in a way I care for, you get demoted.

'Permanent' means you lower-ranked cadets had better get used to addressing your seniors by their new rank.

To cadets newly assigned non-commissioned ranks: do not let your heads bloat! If any cadet NCO affords even the most junior full Marine with any less respect than that due a god, don't expect sympathy from me when I have to scrape up your pulped remains off the deck. Since graduating from novice school, you have risen in status within the Corps family. To a Marine, that now raises you to about the same level as pond scum.

We have yet to meet. Even the most dimwitted among you will therefore realize that I have set out this TOE mostly on the advice of your instructors. Those of you who impress me sufficiently to still hold NCO positions in six months' time will be sent to NCO training camp. There you will begin to understand that NCOs earn their privileges a hundred times over.

I understand that not all of you want to be a leader.

Tough shit.

Notwithstanding the ranks I am assigning today, you will all take turns to train in every role, including specialist, leadership, and those technical roles where your incompetence isn't likely to blow us all to hell. You are all of you only a few casualties away from being squad leader.

Sgt. S. GUPTA, 412th Marines.

Table of Organization & Equipment
==Blue Squad== [Sergeant Gupta]
Current strength: 1 Marine, 28 cadets

Command Section [Sgt. Gupta]
Sergeant Suresh Gupta
Cadet LSgt. - Edward Brandt [responsibility: ammo logistics]
Cadet LCpl. Puja Narciso [chief medic & casualty evac]
Cadet Christanne Cusato
Cadet Stok Laskosk [specialist: missile launcher]
Cadet Vilok Altstein [specialist: Fermi cannon]

Alpha Section [Cdt. Cpl. Hecht]
~~Fire Team Blue1~~
Cadet Cpl. Menes Hecht
Cadet Laban Caccamo
Cadet Giorgio Yakubov
Cadet Marcus Ballantyne

~~Fire Team Blue2~~
Cadet LCpl. Rozalia Naron
Cadet Kamaria Cimini
Cadet Rahul Bojin
Cadet Fadl Vallario

Beta Section [Cdt. Cpl. Khurana]
~~Fire Team Blue3~~
Cadet Cpl. Uma Khurana
Cadet Cheikh Okoro
Cadet Martin Sandhu
Cadet Johannes Binning

~~Fire Team Blue4~~
Cadet LCpl. Mbizi Sesay
Cadet Norah Lewark
Cadet Bernard Exelmans
Cadet Adeline Feria

Delta Section [Cdt. Cpl. Majanita]
~~Fire Team Blue5~~
Cadet Cpl. Estella Majanita
Cadet Osman Koraltan
Cadet Phaedra Tremayne
Cadet Arun McEwan

~~Fire Team Blue6~~
Cadet LCpl. Del-Marie Sandure
Cadet Cristina Blanco
Cadet Serge Rhenolotte
==1 Replacement Requested==

=MESSAGE ENDS=

—— Chapter 13 ——

Arun's leg still felt fragile, as if it were knitted together with spent carbine sabots. But as they jogged past the passageway that led from the hab-disk to Helix 62, that meant he'd now managed a full circuit of Ring 3 without his leg giving way.

"Let's pick up the pace, boys," he said, grinning. He felt indestructible.

"Take it easy, McEwan," said Del-Marie.

"I'm fine," Arun replied.

"Arun wouldn't have suggested it, if he didn't mean it," said Osman, who pulled away.

"I know," said Del-Marie as he accelerated to catch up. "But you're forgetting something crucial about McEwan."

"Go on," said Osman. "Tell me."

"The stupid skangat is afflicted with chronic idiocy."

"C'mon, fellas," protested Arun. "Quit joking around."

"I wasn't joking," said Del-Marie. "And I'm not your 'fella'. You saw the message from the sergeant. As of this morning, I'm a lance corporal. *Lance Corporal Sandure*. Still sounds kinda mutated, but you two had better get it right."

"Sorry, lance corporal," they chorused.

Arun refused to let Del get him down. His leg was healing – good enough to put in a few miles before breakfast. He'd even survived the fallout of Little Scar's displeasure. Nothing was going to spoil his good mood, so he changed the subject. "This rendezvous with the Trog I have to make at 14:00, you'll never guess what he's gone and done."

"He?" queried Osman.

"Yeah. 'He'. Referring to the insect as 'it' all the time is way too tedious. Anyway, he's suddenly changed the rendezvous point. We're to meet up in orbit."

"Why?" asked Osman.

"Search me. I tropied a lot of his friends. He might want to tip me out the airlock without a suit."

"You think too much, Arun," said Osman.

"Wouldn't you in my situation, pal? Allow me my thoughts because I might be dead this time tomorrow. I don't suppose Del would be too bothered if I didn't survive. Would you, lance corporal?"

"Stop your whining, McEwan. I don't like you. You're too soft, too distracted by childish emotions. Since the rest of us became cadets we've moved on and left you behind. I'm beginning to think someone else deserved your berth more."

"Finished yet?" Arun quipped.

"No. I also think you're an idiot, but I've got your back all the same because you're part of Blue Squad. So, no, I don't want you to be killed tomorrow."

Arun turned to Osman. "You see, Lance Corporal Sandure does love me! Bernard will get jealous if he carries on like that."

Osman frowned. "Look, I'm your friend, Arun. But Del's right. You're drifting away. Toughen up, man. Get serious."

Arun glared at his friend. *Get serious?* This from the same Osman Koraltan who two years ago converted his training rifle into a water gun and soaked the neighboring dorms in a water fight that spread throughout the company before the instructors shut it down.

"Oh, look at you!" Osman shook his head sadly. "It's all tantrums and emotions with you. You're supposed to be a Marine, for frakk's sake. You're meant to take your orders and then *act*. Marines don't sit down and debate an order, exploring how it affects their feelings. Sometimes I think the others are right about you."

"Right about what?"

"Frakk!" exclaimed Del. "You and your fat mouth, Osman." To Arun he said: "We're your squadmates. If you stay loyal to us, we'll cover your back, come what may. The rest of the battalion doesn't feel so generous."

Coldness suffused Arun. Del didn't have to spell it out. "I appreciate you two keeping down to my pace," he said, "but I'm slowing you down. Why don't you speed up and I'll meet up with you at inspection?"

A curt nod from Del-Marie and Arun's two jogging partners shot off like a starship engaging zero-point drive.

As he watched his comrades disappear around the curvature of Ring 3, Arun's good mood returned. Even at his slow speed, the rhythmic pumping motion of his run energized his body and cleansed his spirit.

Osman was right. Much of Arun's life felt abnormal. In unguarded moments, the others would agree that life as a cadet was cruel, even pointless. But none of that bothered the others – well, possibly Springer sometimes. Arun had always worried constantly, but he'd been able to keep that well hidden. Until these last few weeks. Now he couldn't even decide whether the Human Marine Corps was a proud family he was privileged to belong to, or a tyranny that should be smashed in the name of freedom.

But jogging… He loved jogging because it felt so natural. The books from ancient Earth said the human body had evolved adaptations specifically for long-distance running. He believed them.

The sound of pounding feet advanced on him from behind. He pulled over to let the faster runners overtake. To reduce congestion, joggers always pounded the rings in an anti-clockwise direction. He was surprised none had overtaken him earlier.

Two runners drew level with Arun, keeping pace with him. He glanced across and saw two cadets, heavy set, good looking, with cold eyes that hid a hot temper. They could almost be twins. Arun knew them: Chao and Burgamy, senior cadets from Checker Squad.

Whatever they had planned couldn't be good. He weighed his chances of sweeping their legs away and burying his fist in their faces before they realized he wasn't ready to be a victim. But with his bad leg, that was never going to work, and fighting was theoretically forbidden, although incidents were usually reclassified as over-exuberance. So instead he nodded a respectful acknowledgment and maintained his speed.

Chao gave a gesture of command to more runners arriving from behind who raced to take up positions in front. They were all from Checker Squad. Horden's Children! It looked as if the entire squad were here.

Some of the Checker cadets pushed between Arun and the wall, boxing him in entirely. Then they slowed, forcing Arun to slow with them until they halted altogether.

If they were trying to intimidate him, they were doing a grand job. Arun's muscles prickled with the need for action but all he could do was clench his fist and bite his lip.

Cameras would be recording everything, every word spoken, every action taken were constantly assessed by security AIs. It was vital that Arun didn't throw the first punch. He couldn't risk being blamed for starting a brawl.

Arun lowered his gaze, took a deep breath, and asked Chao: "Is there anything I can help you with, lance sergeant?"

The intensity of Chao's scrutiny heated the side of Arun's face, but Arun refused direct eye contact.

"I'm proud that my Checkers get first crack at you, McEwan. And in case you think we're some kind of rogue squad, let me assure you of one thing." Chao leaned in close enough for Arun to feel his breath warm his ear. "Every squad in every company throughout the 8th battalion… we're all lined up waiting for a piece of your ass. What do you think of that, loser?"

"Injuring other cadets is a serious offense, lance sergeant. You can be as much of a bullying veck as you like, but if you beat me up, you'll be executed. That's the one advantage of being a thing, owned by aliens. If you damage me, you damage someone else's property. That someone else is a White Knight. Are you big enough to take on the White Knights, Lance Sergeant Chao?"

"Ohh!" Chao sprang back in mock horror. "I'm a bully. Gosh, the shame." He laughed, the rest of the squad joining in on cue. "I'll spell it out for you, alien-faggot. It's not me. It's every last member of Checker Squad wanting to have a quiet word with you about why we're suddenly in the Cull Zone. Look around. Don't see everyone here? That's because the rest of the squad are up the corridor running interference so our little chat isn't interrupted. We're all equally involved. Who will the senior NCOs value most? An entire squad or one insect-loving loser? And if not Checker Squad then the next squad, and the next one. They'll have to choose who they want most – you or the rest of the battalion. They're odds I'm willing to stake my life on."

The world seemed to fall away from Arun. Chao was right. Actually, no… Not quite. "You forgot one thing, Chao. You aren't all equally to blame. You've acknowledged yourself to be the ringleader."

"Oh, yes." Chao gave a predatory grin. "Thanks for reminding me." The lance sergeant cried out in agony, clutching his ankle, scattering his squadmates in all directions – but not enough to leave an opening for Arun to escape.

Chao rolled around on the ground, pretending without much conviction to be in extreme pain. He sat up, still clutching his ankle. "I seem to have suffered a severe ligament strain. I will have to sit here for a short while to recover. Follow whatever course of action you see fit, Checker Squad. In my incapacitated state, I am unable to guide you."

A sinking feeling came over Arun as he waited for his beating to unfold with grim inevitability. He prepared to curl into a ball and bring up his arms to protect his skull.

It did no good. He felt two cadets behind him grab his arms. His legs were kicked away and Lance Corporal Burgamy lined himself up for the first kick.

"Vulley you, Chao." Arun spat in the direction of Checker Squad's leader.

"Really?" said Chao, still sitting on the floor. "Funny. I thought you only wanted to vulley aliens."

Then Burgamy landed the first kick and the breath was knocked from Arun's body.

He felt a burning need to curl over and reflate his lungs, but with his arms restrained he had to take the pain without the slightest respite.

Burgamy and the two cadets holding Arun's arms waited until the first wave of pain had subsided before running off down the passageway, resuming their jog as if nothing had happened.

Cowards!

Red hot anger exploded through Arun. He wanted to punch, kick, and bite. But being on his knees meant he couldn't throw his weight.

His arms were grabbed again and pinned against his back sharply enough to draw a yelp from Arun. As a tall girl, Schimschak, readied to throw a punch, Arun saw a line queue up behind her and sensed more cadets behind him, waiting to take their turn to restrain him.

Schimschak's punch smashed into his face. Arun twisted at the last moment. It was only a glancing blow to his left eye, but still enough to make him see blinding flashes until he shook them away – just in time to see Hardy land a roundhouse kick into his flank.

After that, the blows came in too fast for Arun to tell them apart. He was alone in a sea of pain that roiled with frustrated anger.

Then, suddenly, it dawned on him that the beating had paused. The sounds of a scuffle broke out around him.

Arun marshaled his strength and peered out through his right eye – his left wasn't cooperating. Around him, facing down the Checker Squad cadets, were Madge, Zug, and Springer. Others too, just out of sight.

Arun felt tears threatening to break to the surface. He hadn't cried for years – didn't want to now – but he'd felt so alone. So unwanted.

He collapsed to the floor and groaned. But the vibration of running feet came loud to his ears as he heard Checker Squad run off, hurling curses at Arun as they withdrew.

Arun didn't care. He gathered his strength as rapidly as he could and put everything he had into his dwindled power of speech. "Thank you." He propped himself up on one elbow and looked up at his rescuers.

He'd expected smiles and concerned expressions. Instead, many of the faces of his rescuers were as cold as Checker Squad's had been.

Madge seemed to be in charge. She stood over him, hands on hips, regarding Arun struggling on the ground as if he were something she'd

puked up. "Don't get all dewy-eyed on me, loser." She curled her lip. "If you weren't in my section I'd be the first in line to give you the kicking you deserve for putting us in this drent. Don't ever make the mistake of thinking I like you. And don't give me that crap about it not being your fault that you embarrassed the colonel. I don't give a damn whether it's fair or not, I'm still blaming you. Do you understand?"

Arun nodded.

"Frakk you, cadet. I asked you a question. I expect a respectful answer."

"Sorry, corporal. Yes, I understand, corporal."

Hands reached for Arun, helped him to his feet. But they weren't the corporal's. Cadet Corporal Estella Majanita, the friend he'd called Madge until yesterday, turned her back and walked away.

She did not look back.

—— Chapter 14 ——

The auto-shuttle docked with the unmanned orbital defense platform. Its two passengers alighted and made their way to the platform's observation room, the young human managing this with far more grace than his insect companion.

Arun tried to keep the hive creature in his peripheral vision. He didn't want to acknowledge the unwanted alien by looking directly at it – *him*, he reminded himself. Nor did he want to look completely away in case doing so was interpreted as a gesture of weakness.

Arun's alien masters had felt accurate timekeeping was important enough that they had augmented all human Marines with a range of time-keeping capabilities. So even though it felt like an age, he knew it took only 412 seconds before the alien broke the impasse by speaking through the voice box hanging around its neck.

"Look out the porthole," said the alien. "Tell me what you see."

Until that episode in the tunnel exercise, Trogs hadn't featured much in the lives of Arun and his comrades. The giant insects were grotesque fairytale monsters whose purpose, as far as the cadets were concerned, was to be an ingredient of the most indecent kind of insults. As to why they were really here, Arun had never heard any more than wild rumor until his interview with Little Scar. And who knew what truth lay behind the words of the Jotuns?

More to the point, Arun had been raised since crèche to know whom to salute and whom he could order around. The Trogs simply did not fit into that neat order. He resented this disruption.

And that made him feel dumber than ever. He couldn't help but feel he was a champion of humanity facing off against alien competition, and here he was second-guessing himself into knots.

It was very simple, he reminded himself. Little Scar had ordered Arun to cooperate with the Trog scribe, and the colonel was very definitely in the list of people to be obeyed.

So, after pausing enough to show he was treating the Trog's words as a request and not an order, Arun shrugged and pushed himself off from his perch. Thousands of hours logged in zero-g training meant the maneuver should have been as natural as walking. Not today, though. Arun's body had taken such a pounding these past few days that he gasped in pain as he pushed off.

"Do I need to apologize for the injuries inflicted by my species?" asked the scribe.

"No, you don't. Most of my injuries were handed out by my supposed comrades. I guess we're a pretty aggressive species."

"Of course," said the insect. "That is the species trait your masters recruited you for. What they have been breeding into you ever since."

"What do you know about what they've done to us?"

"Much. I request of you. Please answer my question: what do you see?"

Unsure how he'd been suckered into talking, Arun shut up and looked out the porthole.

"I can see the Serendine orbital elevator, the twin of the one that took us up from the surface. I can see flashes in a ring above the equator. I guess they're other defense platforms and satellites." He adjusted his sight to look farther out. "There's a disk of gleaming silver out at one of the Lagrange points, between us and… one of the moons, I'm not sure which one."

"Antilles."

"Right, Antilles. I've only got about 4x zoom with my eyes so I can't resolve the disk, but I reckon it's thousands of ore cans shot there from the asteroid belt and ready for processing on the moons."

"What about the planet? Tell me what you see below us."

"Okay… That's Tranquility. Nine light minutes from the sun. Two main continents: Baylshore where I live and the other one's called Serendine–"

"No. That's not what I mean. If you lived a hundred light years away, you could quote all those facts from a database. But you don't. This is your home. Do not tell me facts. Tell me what you see."

"Why?"

There was a pause before the alien replied: "Were you briefed?"

Insubordination from humans was not tolerated. The punishment would be fatal for him, and the demerits would push his battalion comrades further away from ever escaping the Cull Zone. A cadet called Mowad from the 420th had tried to dodge witnessing last year's Cull. The result was that Mowad found herself on the wrong side of the execution squad and her battalion went from fourth place from the top of the leaderboard down to fourth from the bottom.

"Yes, yes, I was briefed." Arun spoke hastily. "When I said *why*, I meant: what do you want me to describe?"

"Tell me what that view means to you."

Arun shrugged with one shoulder. "Like I said, it's a planet. Our planet. I suppose it's beautiful when you stop to look for a while and really *see* it. I like the way the atmosphere glows as it fades into the black of space. It's like your tongue, I guess. You don't think about your tongue 99.9% of the time, but when you do become conscious of it, it's actually really big, like…" He faded. Tongues were something he'd become aware of recently because he and Springer had kind of been exploring each other's, but anything to do with sex was definitely off topic. This was the insect creature who had humiliated him. Cadet Prong. Drenting stupid name. Drenting stupid alien who'd made him look so bad and now just perched there staring at him, saying nothing, only speaking out of his stupid voice box.

"I do have a tongue," said the alien. "If that is what bothers you. We do not consider it a taboo organ."

"Right."

"But I do not possess ears. I sense vibrations through my antennae."

"Okay."

"Nonetheless, I understand your reference. Antennae are with us from hatching through to death and our final recycling. We do not consider them 99.9% of time, as you say. But when we do they are large and awkward. At those times I do not know where to put them or how to angle them. I feel so self-conscious."

"Yeah. Well, the planet's like that. I've clocked so many hours in space doing boarding exercises, or waiting for atmos drops or TU attack exercises, that I take it all for granted."

"Very good, Cadet McEwan. Please continue."

Arun sniffed. It was a dumb exercise but not as difficult as keeping himself from punching this annoying insect. "Down below us," he continued, "is Beta City. It's the twin of Detroit, where I'm based, but on the other side of the world."

"What do you feel about Beta?"

What was with all this about feelings? "It's a dumb name. I feel contempt. No, that's too strong. They're still Marines down there. Mostly."

Arun looked at the alien, but the voice box was silent, and the insect's twin pairs of eyes seemed to be prodding him to say more.

"I guess I feel a little curious about them too," he said. "I mean, Beta is our twin. It's the depot base for three more Marine tac regiments and one regiment of Marine engineers. Do they train their Marines the same?

Probably, though some say the Jotuns forbid the Beta regiments to even mention Earth. The rumor mill also has it that Beta has a space-rat squadron based there."

"I apologize to interrupt, but I do not understand the term, *space-rat*."

"Human spacers. Starship crew. Born out in deep space, most of them. Raised there too, mostly. That's so frakkin' alien. Er, no offense."

"I still don't understand."

I still don't understand. Of course you don't. You never will because you're an alien.

That dry mechanical voice got under Arun's skin and shook him from mild irritation toward rage. It had been that voice that played over and over on those mocking vid recordings plastered all over the base. It was this voice and the alien behind him that had caused so much trouble.

When Arun got angry, all those combat enhancements that turned his body into a killing machine kicked in big time. Right now he needed to either blast something or run 20 miles. Sitting still wasn't an option. So he pushed away from the porthole set into the dull white plastic wall and shot through the open hatch into the next compartment.

When they'd docked, the alien had asked him to stay and talk in the observation deck. Well, they'd done that. He had never said Arun couldn't explore.

He emerged at speed into a cramped chamber with a central spine that fed cables into four transparent blisters set into the hull. He swung around the central spine and landed on a gunnery couch in one of the blisters. They looked like Fermi cannons, point defense weapons that could alter the laws of physics in a localized area, hopefully within the guidance system of munitions flung at the defense platform.

He stretched back and saw the Trog was still in the obs deck, struggling against the absence of gravity. *Good. It can stay there for a bit.*

Floating back to the cannon, he gripped the firing handles and hovered his thumbs over the firing studs, reveling in the power within his hands.

He pressed the studs.

Nothing happened.

The relief took the edge off his anger. He couldn't sense any power feeding through into the cannons. He hadn't really thought they were active, but he hadn't been sure until he tried them.

Arun perched on top of the gunnery couch and waited. The couch was designed for a hexaped – a Jotun, presumably. He'd done a theoretical course on ship weapons, enough to identify the three banks of controls: firing, targeting, and turret traverse. Humans didn't have enough limbs to operate them without doubling up. In a few weeks Blue Squad was scheduled to learn how to fire these beauties.

Strange, though, that there should be manual controls when the defense platforms were all automated.

The alien was still vulleying around in the other compartment. That was one up for the humans. Arun grinned.

Tired of waiting, he maneuvered over to the spine, surveying the controls there. The platform seemed to be on standby. He guessed that if active, he could control the main armament from here, the x-ray laser. It was a big one. Even the biggest enemy capital ship couldn't survive a direct hit from this beast on full charge, unless they launched an ocean of ablatives to soak up the power. Problem was, any enemy would probably know that too. There were 30 orbital defense platforms such as this around Tranquility. There were also several hundred dummy platforms, but Arun doubted you could hide for long amongst the fakes. The power build up on the real platforms was so intense, an enemy would have to be blind not to spot them.

Suddenly, the Troggie scribe came tumbling through the doorway at surprising velocity. It was flailing all six limbs, absolutely the worst thing you could do to stabilize yourself in zero-g.

Without thinking, Arun pushed off to help. Just before he grabbed the alien's limb he nearly panicked. This wasn't a comrade he was assisting; it was an alien with no reason to love humanity. And Arun was only dressed in fatigues. He didn't even have gloves.

Half expecting the alien limb to be bristling with spines, slime, or burning acid, Arun felt nothing unpleasant as he instinctively added his inertia to the alien's, steering him to a stable perch on one of the gunnery couches.

The alien's limb had felt no different from a human arm except the skin was cold, like a corpse.

"Thank you, my friend."

The artificial voice in the box around the creature's neck managed to sound breathless. Arun was impressed. Even the Jotuns couldn't do that.

"But why did you journey from the observation deck to this gunnery room?" added the voice.

"Why? Why not?"

"Ah, curiosity. At appropriate stages in our life-cycle, we too are consumed with curiosity beyond reason. I myself thirst for an understanding of other species, which is why you and I are here today. You see, we are alike more than you think, young human."

Arun laughed. He clutched at his middle and span forward as he floated, a never ending forward roll.

"Do you need assistance?" called the alien.

"No." Arun calmed down. "Why?"

"Your barking noise. And that spinning. Are you malfunctioning?"

"It's called laughter. It's a sign of amusement."

The alien froze in silence. He had hesitated like that before, and Arun began to wonder whether the big bug was consulting an implanted data store. "I understand. You have a violent way of showing amusement, which suits the violent nature of your species. When we laugh, we emit a pheromone and tilt our antennae like so."

The Trog angled his antennae about 15 degrees to its right. Arun realized the creature had already made this gesture several times, the cheeky little skangat.

Arun shook his head. This was frakking surreal. "Look at you, Trog," he said. "You say we're alike but you're an insect. You live underground in an immense social group and you can't talk with your own voice because you haven't got one. You make smells instead. And for frakk's sake, you've got those wiggly antennae things. How can you possibly say we're alike?"

The alien tilted its antennae about 15 degrees.

"Are you laughing at me?" Arun smacked his palm to his forehead, not quite believing what he was seeing.

"Yes, Cadet McEwan. We laugh together. It is true that we have gross physiological differences, but many of the problems faced by sentient social creatures are the same. Not only do we share similar challenges but many of their solutions too. This is vital because it leads to the possibility of cooperation between species."

"Isn't that what Tranquility is all about?" asked Arun. "Our Marine Corps officers are all Jotuns. You Trogs do whatever it is you do, and the Hardits do a lot of mining and maintenance work."

"Who says that humans must have Jotun officers? Who says that inter-species cooperation must take that particular form?"

Arun had the feeling he was stumbling into a trap. But he was too unimportant to bother with such elaborate deception, so he answered, though with caution. "The White Knights. They say Jotuns must be our officers and that we humans must obey without question."

Arun expected a response. The Trog said nothing, but it flung its antennae back to run flat along its head. Whatever that meant, it sure wasn't laughing now.

Was the Trog hinting that the slave species on Tranquility should – what? – get together to share expertise? Or was this something far more dangerous? Was the Trog proposing they should join forces and rise up against the White Knights? Arun was scared to even form such words in his mind. To speak them aloud was unthinkable.

The alien watched him and said nothing for a long time. Then asked: "*Why do you obey?*"

Arun's brain replayed a memory. Something the Trog had said just after the auto shuttle had left the orbital elevator. "There are no listening devices on the defense platform," it had said. "We may speak freely."

Arun had been bred, upgraded, and trained to fight in space. Being in a tiny bubble of atmosphere in the vacuum had never bothered him until that moment. He suddenly felt cold, vulnerable, and desperately isolated.

Either he was a melodramatic fool dreaming of conspiracies.

Or… he'd somehow been caught up in a rebellion. A fight to win freedom from the White Knights.

Arun kept his mouth rigidly shut, refusing to answer. Neither human nor Trog spoke again, embarking on their shuttle and descending the orbital elevator in silence.

Thoughts of freedom were not just treasonous.

They were insane.

—— Chapter 15 ——

I bet Sergeant Gupta mentions you," said Del-Marie from the seat to Arun's left.

"Unlikely," answered Zug to his right.

"Shut up the pair of you," snapped Madge from behind.

Arun let the banter wash over him, happy that his squadmates still acknowledged his existence. And after being hissed at by Colonel Little Scar, and threatened by Checker Squad, any disapproval by their new leader would be nothing.

The 27 cadets of Blue Squad were sitting behind their desks in one of hab-disk 6/14's briefing rooms, waiting for the first official encounter with their new veteran commander.

After the craziness of the past few days, Arun was looking forward to a simple classroom lesson.

Actually, he reminded himself, although the room layout was identical to the novice school classrooms, he'd finished with classes for good. He was a cadet now. This was a *briefing*.

A buzz of anticipation thrilled the cadets. When instructors had taken classes, in the back of your mind you always knew that you would leave them behind when you graduated. This was different: Sergeant Gupta would command their squad in battle. This was *serious*.

The door at the back of the room opened, launching a wave of standing and saluting.

Sergeant Gupta took his place behind the lectern emblazoned with the regimental flag: a black rectangle with the number 412 in silver set over a gold circle. The circle represented that spherical Tactical Unit warboats that put the *Tactical* into Tactical Marine Regiment.

Arun tried to get a measure of the man and found he felt disappointed at how unremarkable Gupta appeared. The sergeant was shortish, his shaven head not hiding that he was largely bald. His body looked more rugged than the cadets', sculpted by life on the frontier. Only Gupta's eyes revealed him as a force to be reckoned with. He was taking his time to study his squad. Unlike many of the instructors, he wasn't glaring, wasn't trying to domineer and scare. But there was a quiet intensity to the man's scrutiny. Gupta was not a person you would cross without consequences.

"Sit," Gupta ordered in a voice Arun remembered from the tunnels.

As the cadets took their seats, Arun decided he liked Gupta.

"That was me once," said the sergeant. "I was sitting there watching my first veteran commander give her first lecture. I wasn't listening. Not really. Was too busy wondering what kind of woman this was who would one day give me battlefield orders. It was a long while ago. I had yet to learn that your squad NCO is God as far as you lot are concerned. It's my job to keep you alive and pointing your SA-71 in the right direction long enough to do some damage to the enemy before you get hit. How I do that is my business. It is not my job to be your friend."

Gupta stared at every Blue Squad cadet in turn. His earlier scrutiny had been only a reconnaissance and now the cadets were exposed to the full effect. Many of them flinched under the sergeant's gaze. When he stared at Arun, he seemed to draw out every secret, expose every weakness, leaving Arun a shriveled weakling in awe of this terrifying man.

"Let me give you a flavor of just how long ago I was sitting in your place," said Gupta. "I was born on Tranquility and raised by my mother until I was nine. Then I was frozen for thirty years before they sent me to school. In the years before they froze me, a big change was spreading through what we still called Alpha Base. The Jotuns started allowing us to learn about Earth up till the moment of First Contact. When I was born we'd had to rely on race memories and a helluva lot of make believe.

"That's why so many of my age group were frozen. If the experiment had corrupted the older cadets and Marines – left them unwilling to fight – then the Jotuns would have exterminated them all and woken my cadre of sleeping kids from sleep to start over. I'll leave you to draw your own conclusions about why you are still forbidden to contact cadets from Beta Base."

Arun exchanged glances with Zug. This was news!

"These days squads are commanded by a sergeant, and fire teams are paired up into sections and led by a corporal," said Gupta. "Back then we still used the Jotun NCO ranks of 'old commander' and 'young commander'. I have to tell you I'm mighty glad I'm not called an old commander."

That brought out a smattering of laughter.

"We had *hands* instead of companies, *fingers* rather than squads and sections. As for fire teams of 4 to 6 Marines? Fire teams were the same in my day. But for the rest, they've given you a fresh coat of names and drills borrowed from a hotchpotch of ancient Earth armies. Strip all that away and one key detail is unchanged. Old commander or sergeant – that's as far as a human can ever be promoted. Sure, they invented new ranks: senior sergeant and staff sergeant, but all of them are firmly NCO ranks. Humans can never be officers, can never really be in command.

"That's the theory. That's what you've been taught. The truth is that the Jotuns can't provide officers in sufficient numbers for the Marine Corps. We breed more rapidly than the aliens ever accounted for. That's why so many Marines are kept in ice, and why the Cull gets even more of you than it did in my day.

"So they place us in operational command. If you were to read official regimental reports, a human senior staff sergeant is there in the battalion command squad to make the coffee for the Jotun officers, wipe their backsides, and amuse them with his or her performing monkey antics. Let me tell you, that human staff sergeant is actually the battalion executive officer."

Arun glanced nervously around the room. Was Sergeant Gupta allowed to say that?

A hand went up.

"Go on, Hecht. Spit it out."

"Sergeant. If the Jotun commander were killed in action–"

"Would a human take charge? What you really want to ask is this: can a human give orders to a Jotun? Is that it?"

A hush stifled the briefing room. Arun could taste the danger.

After a pained silence, Hecht replied: "Sergeant. Yes, sergeant."

"No. I don't want that sergeant sandwich crap. You aren't novices and I'm not an instructor. You reply 'yes, sergeant.' Got it?"

"Yes, sergeant," they all responded.

"Good," acknowledged Gupta. "That was well done, Hecht. All of you were thinking the same thing, but only this one cadet spoke that thought aloud. I'm going to have to work on this lack of initiative, but first your answer. The very idea of a human telling a Jotun what to do is preposterous. Worse than that, it is against the natural order of things, and we all know some very dangerous people who like to have everything and everyone in just the right place. Don't we?"

No one spoke.

"Don't we?" barked the sergeant.

Yes, sergeant. The White Knights," said Brandt of all people. Arun would have expected him to keep his head down.

"*The White knights*. Yes, indeed. I've never seen one. Don't expect to either and I can't say I understand them. But the Jotuns know them much better. Say they're obsessed with change, with evolution, and mutation, that sort of drent. They even pollute their world on purpose with a mutating cloud. Flek, people call it. The White Knights change themselves, celebrate their mutants and then – usually – cull them. I told you I don't understand them. The point you need to get inside your frail skulls is that our masters have a fascination with change, a fascination tainted with fear. They are alert to variation and if we upset the natural order then that is change, and they

will notice. I don't know about you, but I would much prefer to be so insignificant that we're ignored. Frankly, I think the Jotuns are working flat out to shield us from White Knight attention."

What the frakk was Gupta up? They were all so flekked.

Gupta paused for effect. "And so back to you, Hecht. No human can ever give an order to a Jotun. However…" He grinned. "There may be circumstances where a senior human NCO could make helpful *suggestions* to Jotun officers. After all, being attached to battalion or regimental HQ, even a dumb human would know what his Jotun superiors have been planning."

Gupta let the tension build. Arun began to wonder whether the sergeant was insane. Sometimes it happened when being thawed. Resuscitation attrition they called it.

"Yeah, I know," Gupta said. "Treason, eh? I'm going to get you all shot. Well, there's plenty that your instructors never told you. I'll teach you what, but all in good time. Here's your lesson for today. Any talk of dissent, to even raise the question of why you fight, of whether the White Knights are worth fighting for… that is treason. But that rule applies to you cadets. Not to we veterans. We're expected to question our role because – or so the Jotun theory goes – we have a psychological need to do so. Otherwise stress toxins build up and weaken us physically. The Jotuns reckon that when humans are in battle and it's either us or the enemy who are going to wind up dead, that's plenty enough motivation for us to obey orders. So long as you're talking with a vet, that treason immunity extends to you cadets too."

Gupta stopped talking and started sniffing the air. *What the hell was he up to now?*

"Anyone else smell hokum?" asked the sergeant.

When no one replied, he pointed to Osman. "You, Koraltan. Do you?"

Osman looked startled to be singled out by this mad veck. "Sorry, sergeant. I don't know what hokum is."

"Sheesh! It's sixty years since I was sitting in your place. I'll have to get used to your language, and you to mine. If you merge with another unit out there in space, you always get vocabulary issues. Frakking language won't sit still. *Frakking!*" He laughed. "That's a new one you kids have made up since I was last here, we used to say it a little differently. *Hokum*. It means bullshit, bollocks, balls, bullcrap – a lie that doesn't stand up to intensive scrutiny. Some of the petty rules and boundaries that you have lived with up all your lives are hokum."

Gupta suddenly pointed across the room at Uma Khurana without bothering to look in her direction.

"You've a face like you're afflicted with terminal constipation, Khurana. Do you want to ask a question?"

Arun glanced across. It was plain to see that Khurana would rather hide under her desk, but she judged that wasn't an option. "Yes, sergeant. Why? Why would we be told… *hokum*?"

"Good. Maybe there's some hope for you worms yet because that is the right question to ask. For an answer, let me share something I've learned about Jotuns. They are meticulous planners. They want to know every detail, to consider every possibly strategy and counter-strategy. We all notice they have six limbs, but if you shaved off all that shaggy fur, I reckon you would find six buttholes too, because Jotuns are so frakking anal. They don't do *petty*. When I said they set us petty rules and boundaries, *they only seem petty to us*. There will be a solid reason behind them. We just don't know what that is and the Jotuns ain't telling.

"So we fight. We fight for the sake of our buddies. We fight to protect our fleet and our Marine family here on Tranquility. Some of you see a big picture and imagine you fight in the long run for Earth. If that makes you run a little harder, prepare a little more thoroughly, and duck a little quicker, then that's fine by me.

"You're cadets now. The time for philosophy and theory is almost over. You've had 17 years of that useless crap. I'm here so some of my practical experience fighting as a Marine can rub off on you, and when you ship out-system I'll be with you, making sure you fight where, when, and how the officer expects. Well, here's a surprise. Just occasionally, sometimes philosophy can be practical too. I'll leave you with a Marine saying. I'm sure you've heard it before, but it's important and it might be a clue to answering Khurana's question of why you should fight. Here it is: Life as a Marine is awash with injustice, hardship and reverses. The mark of a good Marine is to suck that all up, keep your head held high, and wait for the advantage to swing your way so you can seize it! Seize that advantage and exploit it ruthlessly with every ounce of strength and without a second's hesitation. Shout out if you know who first said that?"

"You?" suggested Springer. Arun agreed, remembering that the sergeant had used almost the same words in the Troggie tunnel, but Gupta shook his head.

"Napoleon," said Brandt.

"I think you need to review your history," answered Gupta. "Napoleon wasn't in the Marines on account of he was too short. They wouldn't let him in. You…" He pointed at Hecht.

"Howlin' Mad Smith, sergeant."

Gupta nodded approvingly, "Better with the history, Hecht. General Smith was in the US Marine Corps, and maybe he did say something like that, but he isn't who I heard it from. I said that when the fight turns your way, a good Marine exploits it with *every ounce of strength*. But when I first heard this saying, the actual words were *exploit your moment with all six limbs*. Yes, cadets, it's originally a Jotun saying. Don't forget that Jotuns are Marines too. Perhaps as our fellow Marines, we should trust them to cover our backs."

Gupta appeared to be satisfied with the confusion he'd sown in his squad. "I want you to be very careful in what you say to each other," he said, "but I also want you to think deeply about what I've just said."

Given the nervous shuffling rippling through the room, Arun wasn't the only one thinking hard but understanding little.

"That is all," said Sergeant Gupta. "I'll see you later for EVA drill."

Arun saluted Gupta as he left but his mind was on the sergeant's words, not his back as he walked away.

What was the sergeant on about? Either he was just insane or… or what? The Jotuns always planned meticulously…there was a reason behind what they did even if they kept it hidden. Even if it was as weird as ordering a cadet to make friends with a Trog. Was Gupta trying to send Arun a message?

He'd only met the sergeant for five minutes, and already Arun had learned that after 17 years of such intensive training that a third of the novices hadn't made it to cadet, he still didn't know a damned thing.

—— Urgent Info Message ——

MESSAGE SUBJECT: Our Cull Zone punishment

To: 8th cadet battalion, 412th Tactical Marine Regiment
From: Staff Sergeant E. Bryant.

Our entire battalion has been punished. For some of you, the hard work of years has been undone in an instant.

This is disappointing.

GET OVER IT!

Life is filled with disappointments, but there are many chances for victory too. Good fortune smiles mostly on those who work the hardest at turning around their luck. Good Marines know this. When bad shit happens, they stick together, outlast the bad times, and go looking for their chance to turn things around.

Inadequate Marines turn in on themselves, pointing the finger of blame anywhere but at themselves.

We are in the Cull Zone.

Deal with it. As a unit.

The subject of how we were awarded the punishment is not to be discussed. Speculation regarding who might be to blame is forbidden.

And if I find any member of this battalion threatening a fellow cadet whom they blame for putting us in the Cull Zone, then I will burn out that canker of disunity with the utmost severity.

For those of you who think they can blackmail their superiors by acting as unified squads, I say this. Our Jotun officers and I are equally convinced that it is far better to have one company of good Marine cadets than eight companies of bad ones.

All of you can easily be replaced.

Don't forget that.

=MESSAGE ENDS=

—— Chapter 16 ——

384th Detroit Scendence Championships.
Day 1 – Practice Match

A cheer exploded through the crush of cadets near the exit to corridor 610. Arun swiveled his smart-plastic chair around to check out the fuss. It wasn't difficult to work out what was up. A group of cadets from Fox Company were jumping up and down in jubilation, pointing up at one of the sixteen large soft screens mounted on the wall.

Their player had just won a Scendence contest.

The fuss died down soon enough and the parade hall returned to the general low level excitement of a Scendence Day.

"Five minutes!" shouted Del-Marie.

Arun couldn't bring himself to cheer. Moscow Express had lost their first three contests of the day, which meant that however well Springer did in her individual match, the team result would be a loss. The Scendence season consisted of two practice matches before the knockout stage began. As the first practice, the result didn't matter anyway, but the mood from the chairs around Arun was still muted.

Another wave of excitement crashed over the parade hall. Arun looked up but couldn't see any cause. It was just your regular burst of Scendence Day excitement.

Just for a moment, his face fell. They were in one of the battalion's parade decks on Level 4. It was a dramatic space with a dais for NCOs to give speeches or lead large-scale training classes. Part of the wall behind the dais was built from the carcass of a Muryani attack cruiser, still scorched from the plasma fire that had disabled it before human Marines had boarded. The ship was a proud battle honor, but parade halls were used for many purposes, some not so positive. Arun had witnessed an execution in this room.

Executions made him think of the Cull. Across all cadet battalions in Detroit – currently there were sixty – the four with the lowest Totalizer score at the end of each year lost a tenth of their cadets to the Cull. If your battalion was one of the four in the Cull Zone then there were only two ways to escape the Cull. One was to die beforehand, the other was to reach the last sixteen in a Scendence championship and win immunity.

It didn't look like Moscow Express was going to be a means for anyone to escape the Cull.

Arun caught himself from slipping into one of his black moods of doom. Today was a Scendence Day. A day's vacation from such worries. An official day of fun.

He looked up at the screen the Fox cadets were watching, trying to borrow some of their jubilation. The screen replayed the moment of victory. This had been an Obedience-Stoicism contest. The players were each subjected to a random horror. If neither of them flinched, they would face a new horror, and another one until one of them gave way.

The match was running late because of an epic contest that morning between a human player and a Jotun opponent. That contest had gone an incredible twelve rounds before the Jotun had given way when they faced the horror of being buried deep underground in a tunnel collapse.

Not many Jotuns played Scendence and it was rarer too for them to lose to a human. Arun had taken a recording of the frenzied reaction in the room when the human had triumphed. A treasured moment to savor at moments of despair.

At any other time, a display of such disrespect toward the Jotuns would be unthinkable, but the officers expected rowdy behavior on a Scendence Day. It was just one more reason for Arun to think aliens would never make any sense.

The wall-screen now replayed a split view showing both competitors in the Obedience-Stoicism match. Each had their heads clamped and positioned in front of a perforated, black screen. A spike emerged from one of the holes turning slowly but relentlessly, aimed at the left eye of each player.

In real time the advance of the spike had been agonizingly slow. The replay sped up the action until the tip stopped a hand's-breadth from the eye. Then a needle emerged from the tip of the spike, pushing on toward the eye. Closer. Closer. Then it pierced the cornea. Neither player showed any reaction.

The spike had advanced in silence but now a motor purred as it pushed the needle deeper into the eye. Arun couldn't help but blink in sympathy.

A depressurization alert blasted out its twin tones. Depressurization drill was so ingrained in all of them that Arun nearly leaped from his seat. Just in time, he realized the sound was coming from the Scendence replay, a cruel trick to distract the players. They didn't react at all.

Then the clamps holding their heads in place fell away in a burst of compressed air.

Each player now had a needle inside their eyeball with only willpower keeping their head steady enough for it to do no damage.

Arun shook his head in wonder. He'd be blubbing like a baby long before this stage.

The loser lasted another four seconds before screaming and shutting his eyes. The scream turned to a wail of agony as the needle gouged a path of pain through his retina.

The Fox supporters jeered.

"Look at those foxies," said Arun. "I'd like to see them take a needle in the eye without blinking."

"I for one couldn't," said Osman who was standing just behind Arun, there not being enough seats for everyone.

"Cristina did," said Del-Marie.

Slumped in her chair across from Arun, Cristina gave a halfhearted smile.

"Yeah, we're proud of you," added Arun.

There was a grunt of agreement, which made Arun feel relief that his squadmates were beginning to act as if her were one of them again.

Cristina ignored them all.

In the morning session, she had taken the needle without flinching, but so too had her opponent. On the second round, she had screamed in pain when the poisonous scorpion in her mouth stung her. Her opponent had shown no reaction.

Osman's Deception-Planning had involved a card game, never a good scenario for Osman. His opponent hadn't even hesitated before he called Osman's bluff. Arun felt bad about that. Osman still wanted Arun to take his place in the team, but Springer had advised him to wait for now. Madge was still too mad at him after the battalion's Cull Zone punishment.

As for Madge, she was still on her way down from orbit after her Gunnery contest. She had done well but her opponent had done better still, which seemed to sum up Moscow Express's day.

Arun looked back at the wall-screen, which was now showing fluid being pumped back into the competitors' eyes.

The Scendence tortures had been virtual, but they had felt real to the competitors because they had been wearing total immersion suits. The irony was that in order to shoot images directly at the retina while bypassing the lensing effect of the eyes, the liquid inside each eyeball was drained when the suit was put on, and reinserted before removal.

Arun felt a kick against his chair leg.

"Springer's in position," said Del-Marie gruffly.

Flicking through the several hundred Scendence feeds offered on his softscreen, Arun quickly found several for Springer's contest. He picked one that showed his friend's viewpoint and offered audio commentary too.

Scendence players wore caps that strapped over the forehead rather like the training caps cadets wore during Second Sleep. You could tap into the player's mind, to see what they saw; hear what they heard. Some of the highest rated ACE-3 battlesuits, allowed you to do this too, tapping into the view from your squadmates. There weren't many of these advanced suits to go around and they were reserved for NCOs. They struck Arun as a very good idea.

"Here she goes," said Del-Marie, rather pointlessly as they were all watching Springer from various feeds as she walked out into a transparent box a dozen meters over the chilly water of Lake Tavistock.

The thin ice crust underneath had been melted for the contest. The commentary said the water temperature was only 4 degrees above freezing.

Each player was dressed in fatigues: boots, camo pants, and a thin shirt. Springer's viewpoint was shaking: she was shivering already.

Arun switched to a wider angle view. The two players were in a see-through box with a dividing wall between them. At the bottom of each compartment was sump filled with water. The objective was to fill the bucket they had been given, climb up a spiral staircase which ended in a hole at the top of the dividing wall. You had to throw the water through the hole to fill your opponent's compartment. The volume of water in each compartment started off the same. Once one player's compartment contained two thirds of the combined water volume, its floor would open up, dumping the loser into the lake below.

From his feed, Arun could see in the distance that a duplicate setup was positioned a short distance farther into the lake. A contest was already underway in the other setup.

Something about one of the figures in the other contest drew him in, making him zoom the view onto the other match as best he could.

It was Xin!

Springer's match wouldn't start for a minute or two, so he quickly found a feed that showed a closer view of Xin.

At the top of each compartment was an opaque box. Xin's match had progressed enough for it to open. It looked like it had deposited biting insects and a slimy goop over the competitors. Xin and her competitor looked like they had been half digested and then vomited up by some hideous monster, but Arun would kiss Xin in an instant.

Despite all the drent that had happened recently, he still felt exactly the same about that girl.

He wasn't watching Xin just to stare at her figure, he told himself. He selected another feed, one that showed a close-up of her face. Arun looked beyond her physical beauty at the determination that blazed from her eyes, the steadiness of her stride as she ascended the slippery steps. Her every movement was calculated, efficient, strong.

Xin put him in mind of a common saying about Scendence: *To take part is but a passing diversion. It is winning that matters.*

Her determination to win was almost machinelike. For all that he admired her, Xin scared Arun a little too.

The commentary feed was showing the score: 58% of the water was in Xin's compartment. She was losing!

"Come on," Arun whispered under his breath.

He delved through the commentary stats for the trends. Xin was losing but she was clawing back. She had been on 62% at one point, just 4% away from a long drop into the lake. Xin poured a bucketful into her opponent's compartment. Now she was on 57%. *Keep going!* Xin leaped down into the sump and began refilling.

Meanwhile her opponent slipped from the stairs, spilling out half the contents of her bucket. She took a moment to catch her breath before dipping her bucket in the sump again.

"Yes!"

With a grin, Arun realized that Xin wasn't losing, she was winning! She had paced herself. Her opponent had started off in a frantic burst of energy but had tired so much that she was visibly exhausted. Xin would carry on like a robot until she won.

Minute by minute, bucket by bucket, Xin came back from the brink to draw level with her opponent. And then claw her way into the lead.

"Thank Horden."

Arun looked up. That had been Zug's voice.

Following Zug's gaze to the wall-screens, Arun saw Springer splash up and down with glee in her compartment. She was grinning so wildly that her dimples were dark pits.

"Yes!" Arun punched the air in triumph.

Instantly, he realized something was wrong. A stony silence had replaced the jubilation around him. The guys were all staring at him.

Del-Marie was out of his seat advancing toward Arun.

It was like a bad dream. Arun couldn't quite believe this was happening.

"Give me that!" snapped Del-Marie.

He snatched the softscreen out from Arun's hands, the screen that showed Xin battling her opponent. Del paraded the screen around the squad, holding it aloft like a trophy.

Arun blushed with shame.

Del-Marie pointed up at the screen where Springer was bouncing up and down in delight. "There," he said. "There! That's Springer. You should be paying her attention. She is ours. You are hers. Frakking imbecile! You look at this cheap vulley-flit instead?"

"She's not a…" Arun stopped. Defending Xin wasn't going to help.

"Arun, it's not all right." Zug spoke calmly. Everyone listened. "This is not a small mistake of rudeness. You have let us down. No bulletin from Staff Sergeant Bryant is going to let you off this hook."

"I'm sorry."

"*Oh, I'm sorry*," echoed Del-Marie sarcastically. "Sorry isn't good enough."

"I swear, lance corporal," insisted Arun. "I promise I'll always put my squadmates first, in front of any… distractions outside of the section."

Del-Marie held Arun's gaze, but then he looked away, probably thinking of Bernard, his boyfriend from Beta Section. Where would Del's loyalties lie if pushed?

Osman joined in. "If you and Xin were an item," he said, "then it would be different. Slightly. But you aren't. She's just a vulley-dream. Come on, man, she's way out of your league. Time to grow up a little. Swear you'll put us before her."

"I already did."

"Then do it again."

"I will put my squad before Xin. I do so swear. On my honor and the honor of the Marine Corps."

The icy tension melted a little.

Zug got out of his chair and came over to Arun. He shook his hand, bent over and kissed him on both cheeks.

Zug sometimes claimed doing this was his cultural imperative because he was French. At other times, he admitted he did this to wind people up.

This time he kissed Arun to whisper a message in his ear. "I am still your friend. Make sure it stays that way."

—— Chapter 17 ——

At 13:00 hours, after a session at the firing range where he'd scored second best in the squad, Arun grabbed a bike from the Spineway B on Level 4 and cycled on his way to another meeting with the alien scribe.

At Helix 6 a thought struck him as he started coasting down to Detroit's lowest depths. This was their sixth talkie-talkie session and the Troggie scribe was showing no signs of growing bored. The opposite, if anything. And that meant they weren't going to end any time soon.

Referring to the creature as 'The Trog' was getting really old.

It was time Arun named his alien.

Arun laughed. He had no doubt that his Trog already had a name, but it was bound to come in the form of a smell or chemical signal. Asking for the scribe's name would have been met with one of those condescending speeches about how humans were stunted little creatures with no sense of smell, and such a limited concept of the world around them that it was a wonder they could get from one day to the next without accidentally killing themselves.

Arun was so lost in lists of candidate names that he'd picked up more speed than he realized. When the ramp curled round into the top of Level 8, he had to swerve suddenly to avoid hitting an assault tank on its side with the grav sleds off. The team of Hardits repairing the tank hurled abuse at Arun as he sped past, narrowly avoiding hitting one of the stupid monkey-creatures who was too engrossed in an engine diagnostic screen to look up.

Before he disappeared around the bend, Arun lifted up out of the saddle and mimed farting at the Hardits. Like the Trogs, the primary sense of this other alien species was smell, so he reckoned that was the best way to communicate his feelings to the Hardits in their own language.

It was only being polite really.

Judging by the roars of rage, Arun's message was received and understood.

Arun whistled cheerfully as he followed the tunnel round and round getting deeper with every turn. The helixes were the only route down for heavy equipment. If there was a major logistics operation going on in Helix 6, then Arun would be warned by the status map mounted on the walls at regular intervals. But today the helix was almost deserted. Being by himself for a short while was such a luxury that he decided it made up for missing the chow time that his comrades would be tucking into right now. By the time he got back, he'd only have the chance to grab a few scraps. And by then his squad would be going up the orbital elevator for an afternoon session of dropboat training. Another training session missed.

But Arun wasn't going to let that bother him today. This was the first time he'd ever cycled to these depths. Normally he met the Trog via one of the main surface entrances of the nest, in the forest to the southeast of Detroit. Today he was going to meet through the connection between the lowest level of Detroit and the nest.

Until last week he had no idea that the human base joined up with the nest. How many more secrets were waiting to be revealed?

Arun turned his mind back to his naming task. How about *Whistler*? Arun rolled the name around his mind, trying it out. He liked the idea: whistling was something only humans could do. It didn't sound right, though.

How about *Bike*? No. P*eddler*?

People said that bicycles were an entirely human invention, one that annoyed the Hardits in particular, given their specialism in technology and engineering. Mining human creativity was the reason Earth had been nurtured for millennia before begin fought over and eventually forced into the Trans-Species Union under the sponsorship of the White Knights. Technologically speaking, humanity was a million years or more behind the most advanced of their neighbors, but that also meant they didn't have a million years of precedent saying what works and what does not, stifling the ability to view old problems from an entirely new angle. Or so people said. But people said a lot of things that might be complete hokum, as Gupta might say. Still, it made for a good story.

But Peddler didn't sound right either. The name sounded like a guy he knew from Dog Company: Pedro.

Peddler. Pedro.

The connection was obscure and it was dumb. But it was dumb in a human way and that was what Arun was after. Pedro it would be.

————

"What did you call me?" The scribe spiraled both antennae, thrusting one forward and the other back. Arun recognized this as an expression of bemusement.

"I called you Pedro."

"Why?"

"Because that is your new name."

"But why? Why Pedro? What does it mean?"

Arun shrugged. "Why does it have to mean anything? It's just a name. Your name."

"You mean that Pedro is neither descriptive nor has a functional purpose, such as to denote rank or role? The name is a product of pure whimsy?"

Arun rolled his eyes. Pedro could over-complicate the simplest things. "Yeah, that's what I just said, Pedro. It's a frakking name. Don't any of you overgrown bugs have names?"

Pedro touched one antenna to Arun's shoulder. "No one in our nest has a name. We only have… *designations*, I guess you would call them. Just as you name and number the passageways and chambers of your tunnels. I cannot express how pleased this makes me. To be given a name is a great honor."

"Hold on. If none of you guys have names. How come it's a great honor to be given one?"

Pedro did that annoying gesture where he folded over his antennae in a loose approximation of human shoulders and then shrugged them. "Because I have decided that this is so. *My house. My frakking rules.*"

"You what? Are you quoting me?"

"I often repeat your phrases, though do not seem to recognize this."

"Figures."

Pedro rose on all six legs and skittered around in a circle making sudden little leaps in the air as he did. He'd explained once that this was his way of burning off dangerously high levels of excitement.

Even armed with that explanation, Arun couldn't help but be very conscious of the excitable creature's bulk even if it was bounding around playfully. Pedro must weigh upwards of 300 pounds. If he slipped and fell on top of Arun there would be badly broken bones, and broken Marine cadets were not worth the trouble of fixing.

Arun fiddled with the pheromone emitter dangling around his neck. Pedro had organized delivery of the emitter to Arun's hab-disk, with a note explaining that this made him smell like a nest sibling. Without the device, the Trogs defending their nest entrance would have killed him.

He needn't have worried. Despite the chaotic appearance of Pedro's little dance, the alien never once lost his footing. Arun suspected that the tiniest detail of his over-excitement dance was perfectly choreographed in advance, a pattern stored in its memory ready for use. They were obsessive about the details of life these Trogs.

Pedro halted abruptly and turned to stare at Arun. "With this name, you have assigned a gender to me. Do you believe that has significance?"

"I *know* it has no significance. It's you who are obsessed with sex."

"I see."

"*I see*? What in Horden's name is that supposed to mean?"

"You say more than you know, friend McEwan. Sometimes your subconscious tells me more than you consciously say. That's how I learn so much from you."

"Sure. Well I'm glad to be so transparent. Tell me, Pedro, what do you want me to reveal subconsciously today?"

"Today I want to hear about a day in the life of a human Marine cadet."

"*A day in the life*. You've been reading human books again, haven't you?"

Again with the shrugging antennae.

Arun sighed. "Get me some water, will you? I have long days. Better get my throat lubed up if you want to hear about them."

Pedro scuttled over to the water dispenser.

These sessions with Pedro had so inured Arun to the bizarre that he was only just starting to appreciate how weird this new room was. He recorded images through his eyes while Pedro was busy at the water dispenser – the same kind that was dotted around the human areas of the base. The Troggie tunnels were dark, but this room was brightly illuminated with red-tinged lamps. Arun was sitting in a swiveling sofa chair, deeply padded and covered in red faux leather. It looked brand new. Hung on the walls and ceiling were framed photographs of cadets. Arun was in most of the photos. All of Delta Section were there too. So was Xin. He wasn't going to ask why Xin was there. He'd never mentioned her, had he?

"Do you like this chamber?"

"It's… I don't know. I guess it's a good attempt to make me feel–" he glanced at Xin's photo– "I don't know what exactly but it makes me feel *something*."

"Ahh. I see you like the photograph of your beloved."

"My be-*what*?"

"Your beloved. The female you love."

"She is not my beloved."

"Correction. Ah, but your language is so messy. It is a minefield. This female is not one you are loving but one you wish fervently that you *shall* love in the future. You are in love but not…"

Pedro paused to regroup. Arun felt his face flush, caught precariously between anger and laughter.

"Let me rephrase," said Pedro. "That Xin is one hot chick." *That last sentence sounded suspiciously like it had been sampled from Arun's voice pattern.* "I guess you'd love a piece of her action." *So did that.*

The problem about Pedro, Arun decided, was that his face was an impassive mask. He couldn't help but feel Pedro was laughing at him from behind that mask. Whenever the conversation touched anything sensitive or awkward, Arun just wanted to punch the alien to wipe the hidden smirk off its face, even though that was a totally dumb thing to wish for, given that Pedro was physically incapable of smirking.

Arun stepped back from confrontation. It wouldn't help. That it wouldn't help just made Arun want to hit Pedro even more and that made him feel… feel that he'd rather Barney was there for a little advice and maybe a sedative too.

"You get those words out of movies and TV shows, didn't you?"

"Correct."

"Do me a favor," he told Pedro, "don't mention anything about girls again. You're just annoying when you do. Anyway, if you know all this stuff, why do you need me? I sometimes think you know more about humans that I do. What's the point of these chit-chats anyway?"

"Because…" Pedro twisted his body into something approximating an S-shape. It probably meant something profound. "Because I have read facts about humans. This is not the same as *understanding* your species. The distinction could become vital one day. Our future may present opportunities for cooperation."

Yup! There we have it, thought Arun. *Those stupid hints that I'm meant to be a messiah or freedom fighter or something.* He bit down on saying the words aloud, remembering that Pedro had gone to the trouble of meeting him in a mothballed orbital platform to escape the surveillance that permeated Detroit. After that first meeting, Pedro had never again hinted that there could be ways to live other than as slaves.

He laughed instead, noticing the manic edge to the sound, but why should he care if a dumb insect heard it? Depending on who you talked to, Arun was too soft, too much of a worrier, or just too much of a loser to be a proper Marine. Well, his emotions might have run wild recently, but he was no coward.

No one had ever accused him of being sensible either.

"Am I special?" Arun asked. *There, he'd said it*. And somewhere an AI would hear and record his words. "Is there something special I'm supposed to do? Is there something unique about me, Arun McEwan?"

Pedro pointed his antennae at Arun and then stood motionless and silent for a good minute. He might be a dumb insect, but he was perfectly capable of making Arun feel dumber.

"We are all unique individuals, Arun McEwan." The insect's artificial voice was so quiet it was barely audible.

"Unique? Horden's Organs, you dumbchuck, you're a *hive creature*. A drone. Uniqueness is an alien concept that you're trying to learn from me."

"I see I have upset you," said the scribe. "I apologize."

The alien wandered around for a while. The movement looked confused and aimless. It probably wasn't, but Arun had no idea what it meant.

When he was done, Pedro clambered onto a shelf carved into one dirt wall. Dim orange lamps were directed at the shelf. Basking in the resulting heat was probably a sensual pleasure. Arun had no way of knowing for sure without asking and he wasn't about to do that. The session had already edged too close to the borders of friendship.

"Tell me about a day in your life," said the scribe.

"You mean like an itinerary?"

"Sure. However you want to do it is fine. Then I'll tell you about my day. Shoot."

"Okay. Well, we wake at midnight. That's the end of First Sleep. We're woken gently. Basically, a switch in our heads is turned on by our internal clocks. We might take a leak, have a slurp of drink, but basically we put on our training cap, check it's attached properly and that we've inserted our suit AI chip. Then we go back to sleep."

"This sleep-training cap – what does it teach you?"

"Well, I don't actually know, seeing as I'm asleep at the time. I seem to know a lot of facts that I never learned in class or read in a book. I mean, we'll be training on a new weapon and I'll know burst radius, recoil strength, ammo variants and all that stuff, and yet I've never seen that kind of gun before. What else the caps do, we can only guess. Probably makes us superbrave and ultra-loyal to the White Knights."

"I expect that is correct."

Arun thought about that. He'd been joking, but he didn't think Pedro was. "So that's Second Sleep," he continued, "where they fill our brains with something. Then at 05:00, there's a buzzer sounds in our dorm. Doesn't give you any option but to be awake. I mean, if there were any corpses interred beneath the floor of our dorm then we'd know about it, because they would rise from the dead to complain about the noise."

"And who do you sleep with?"

"Hey! I thought I told you to keep off that topic."

"I have not gone *on* that topic. You have a dormitory, which I understand to be a separate room inside a habitation disk. Your hab-disk is designated 6/14 and houses Charlie Company and Dog Company from 8th battalion, 412th Marines. Is it always the same individuals who sleep in that dorm?"

"Oh, I see. Yeah. Now that we've graduated from the crèche to be full cadets, we get to live in a hab-disk and the dorm members are fixed, far as I know. Two fire teams make a section and it's one section per dorm. That's eight cadets. Me, Springer, Zug, Brandt, Majanita, Osman, Del-Marie and Cristina."

Pedro seemed satisfied, so Arun carried on: "It's quite relaxed first thing. The hab-disk has its own gym and firing range. So we stretch and work out – enough to get fit but not to tire us out before the day has started. Then we wash dress and clean ourselves ready for inspection between 07:00 and 07:30."

"You clean yourselves with water?"

"Sure we do. Why? What do you use to clean yourselves with?"

"Dirt. We sweat out toxins and scrub away by burying through dirt."

"Lovely. Don't you still smell?"

"We like to smell. We are our smell."

"O-kay. Anyway. Yeah, we have showers dotted around the disk. There's five of them. You can fit about ten people in each shower, twelve if you squeeze together. Sometimes you have to. It can get real busy at peak times."

"And these showers, males and females share the same facilities?"

"What is it with you? You're sex-obsessed."

"Possibly. Remember, my species has no genders. If smell defines my people, I think gender defines yours. This gender distinction is so fundamental to your species and yet completely absent from mine. How can we be so different? I do not understand this yet."

The insect made a good point. But how could Arun explain to someone who has no gender the horseplay that went on at the top and tail of a cadet's day? About how they were given license to let off a little steam? How dorm mates might vacate their dorm to give a couple ten minutes of privacy?

"It's different," Arun said. "In the showers, I mean. At other times, taking clothes off can be a big deal, but everyone has to get clean first thing and have their protective spray. It's mandatory. You get on with it. It's no big deal." That wasn't always strictly true, but it would do for an explanation. "Anyway, your idea of gender and sexual attraction is too simplistic. It isn't just a question of males liking girls and vice versa."

"What? You have more genders? Fascinating. Please elaborate… No, on second thoughts, leave that for another session. Please continue with your typical day."

Arun shrugged. "Like I said, inspection is 07:00 to 07:30. We stand by our racks – which I guess you could call single-occupancy sleep pods. Our kit cabins are open. Everything is stripped clean, assembled, washed. Absolutely perfect. Of course on most days an instructor doesn't come to inspect us. There aren't enough of them to go around. But we have to be ready just in case. Same goes for evening inspection between 21:00 and 21:30."

"Thank you," said Pedro. "I have two more questions. Firstly how much time do you have to yourselves in the evening?"

"Well, depends what we got to do. Inspection ends 21:30. We're supposed to in bed by 25:00 hours and sleep all the way through the remaining five hours until midnight at 30:00 hours. That's three and a half hours to ourselves. We don't just goof around, though. Some of us practice for Scendence. Sometimes we meet up with seniors from our battalion who

will help teach and train us. Our merit points help determine their Cull status, you see?"

"I do. Thank you. Final question. Who prepares food for you?"

"Well, the Aux of course. They do all the cooking and cleaning. Maintenance too. That sort of stuff."

"And these auxiliaries are lower caste humans, yes?"

Arun was about to deny that humans were so primitive as to have castes or a class system. The words caught in his throat when he thought of how he treated the Aux. He always tried to be polite, he supposed, but there was never any doubt in his attitude that he knew he was better than any Aux.

And from the vast majority of other cadets the best the Aux could hope for was indifference. Petty cruelty was more common because most cadets seemed to have had compassion bred out of them. They felt intense loyalty but struggled with the concept of kindness. And since the Aux were not part of their units, they might as well be aliens. Try as he might, Arun struggled to be so cold hearted. That made him a freak.

Before Arun could form an answer Pedro announced: "I must go now. I apologize for my abrupt departure. I am called away and cannot ignore the summons. I have a request, though. Please learn the name of one of your auxiliaries before our next meeting."

Pedro leaped from his shelf and raced away as if his life depended on it. Perhaps it did. There could have been a major cave in with thousands dead already, but not the smallest fragment of emotion could ever enter Pedro's artificial voice.

As he headed back up to the human levels, Arun silently cursed Pedro. How had the alien guessed that Arun didn't know the name of a single Aux?

—— Chapter 18 ——

384th Detroit Scendence Championships.
Day 2 – Practice Match

Arun was no xeno-linguist, which wasn't surprising, given there wasn't much call for that skill. If an alien was on your side then the Jotun officers could communicate with the xeno if necessary. For all other aliens, you didn't talk to them; all you had to do was aim your SA-71 and squeeze the trigger.

The only thing he knew about alien languages was that Jotuns used bifurcated nouns – a way of describing things from two perspectives. Zug said it came from the hexapeds having two pairs of hands.

Arun thought bifurcated nouns were an example of woolly thinking. Most humans agreed. But the Jotuns were in charge so they got to name the Scendence contests using their fussy nouns anyway. Equally naturally, the humans usually ignored this and simplified to a single noun.

So the contest of Deception-Planning was usually described as 'Deception' because most matches involved bluff and trickery. But sometimes – as with Arun's first match for Moscow Express – the planning side came to the fore.

After Madge had let him join, Arun was desperate to make a good showing – maybe that would raise his reputation off the deck in the eyes of his comrades?

He'd been taken to one of the tech labs in the Level 5 novice school where he'd faced a G-1 cadet from the 420th Marines whose shrapnel scars to her face gave her a grim appearance.

Their challenge was to plan blockade-running logistics to resupply a besieged planet until it grew strong enough to free itself from blockade. A range of ships was available to each player, each with varying characteristics such as troop-carrying capacity, build time, cruising speed, fuel consumption, nimbleness to evade the blockade, and firepower to blast a way through. The game AIs handled all the simulation mechanics – combat, random hazards, the success of crash landings other such factors – letting the Scendence players concentrate on planning the logistical operation.

Arun concentrated everything on massive troop carriers loaded with defensive fighter squadrons to protect the carriers and their main cargo: great clouds of single-use dropboats loaded with troops and supplies.

The carriers took such a long time to build that his opponent had already made two blockade-running missions to her beleaguered planet before Arun's carriers even reached his. Once there, his boats suffered a brutal 90% casualty rate as they passed through the blockade. And while his Scendence opponent's ships had degraded her enemy's defenses, Arun's had barely touched his, being all about evading rather than blasting a way through.

The 420th supporters watching the Scendence feeds were jubilant, the 412th's disappointed — except for Blue Squad, Charlie Company, 8th battalion. Some of Arun's squad had lost confidence in him as a Marine, but as a Scendence player they knew him too well to give up hope.

Blue Squad was right. Arun himself soon grew confident that victory would be his.

Although his troopship carriers took a long time to build, they didn't need rebuilding – they simply returned home to load the next cargo of cheap-to-build dropboats and the infinite supply of troops, who had no cost or build time. His opponent's fleets were single use, a replacement having to be built each time from scratch.

The key to victory was to exploit the abundance of his virtual Marines by spending their lives freely. Arun repeatedly flooded the blockade with such swarms of dropboats that enough survivors and their supplies got through to rapidly bolster the planet's defenders. It didn't take many waves before the game AI announced that his besieged forces had counter-attacked against the blockade, wiping it from orbit.

He'd won!

Arun allowed himself a smile when his overwhelming victory was announced.

Normally he would leap up and punch the air. But this time he felt dirty. There was a cruel parallel between the cheapness of his virtual soldiers' lives and those of the flesh and blood slaves bred to fight for the Human Marine Corps.

Still, a victory was a victory. And winning was all that counted.

The moment he entered the battalion mess hall after the game, a ragged cheer went up. Then he was surrounded by cadets wanting to slap him on the back, hug him, ruffle his hair or kiss him. After the mess in the tunnels, being mobbed as a hero felt so damned good.

It only took a few seconds for the mob to thin out and then disappear, revealing the cold truth: Arun had only ever had a handful of well-wishers. Most of 8th battalion was watching him with stony indifference or outright hatred. Gods! He hadn't seen many cadets outside of Blue and Gold Squads since he'd seen Little Scar – since his battalion had been demoted into the Cull Zone.

It didn't take a genius to work out whom most people blamed for that.

"Hey, well done on your game," called a female voice from behind. "I saw it all. An impressive performance."

Arun was grateful for any sign of support. "Thanks, pal. I do my best to…" *That voice!*

He stopped, turned around, and stared into Xin's face.

"Thing is…" Xin cast her eyes to the ground. She looked really uncomfortable. "Thing is, you're a whole lot better than the Deception player in my team."

Arun's reply was simply to gawp, too stunned to speak.

"Yeah, not too good on the vocabulary. I get that sometimes. But I studied your record. You've got good form."

"Well, yes, thank you. I wouldn't say I'm better than your teammate, but thanks. I saw you too. I think you're amazing."

"Oh, man. Don't go all twinkle-eyed on me. This is difficult enough as it is."

Arun chewed over her words, but he still couldn't make sense of them.

"Yeah. Lack of intelligence noted too, buddy. Still, you've got those plus points. And that's why I want you on my team."

"You… but… I can't. I'm already in the Moscow Express team."

"D'uh! I just saw you, remember?"

"Corporal Majanita has only just cooled down enough to let me on the team. I can't leave them."

"Yes you can. *Can't* is a word only used by losers. Now, *won't* is a word I'd accept, but can't is too pathetic for my ears to process."

Arun tried not to think too hard because he knew he'd hate himself for what he was about to say. "All right, Xin, I *won't*. I won't join you, much as I would dearly love to under any other circumstances, because… Well, you gotta see it my way. I can't let my squadmates down."

Xin gave a curt nod. "Fair enough. But will you at least do me a favor? Let me get you a drink and you give me five minutes of your time, because I've a couple of reasons to change your mind. If you still say no after that, then…" she shrugged sinuously. "No dramas. I won't ask again. Will you do that for me?"

Arun had the feeling he was getting conned here. Xin was dancing rings around him. Zug would know what to say. So would Springer, but Arun's usual way out of this sort of situation was to walk away or punch the person leading him a merry dance.

But with Xin, none of those were options.

"Hey, guys!" Xin was waving at some G-1 cadets sitting by the listening station, a zone of comfy chairs where ancient Earth music was beamed into stripped down battlesuit helmets modified for comfort.

A few minutes ago, Arun had felt like a hero in the making. Now, as he sat waiting for Xin, he felt like a child being bossed around by an adult. Or a bullying older child.

It wasn't long before Xin returned with a couple of drinks in cornboard cups.

Arun took his and drank half in one go. It was a grainer: rich, smooth and cool. He didn't recognize the flavor Xin had dialed up, but it was spicy enough to give a real kick but not enough to overcome the refreshing smoothness of the malt drink.

"It wasn't my idea to call ourselves Team Ultimate Victory. Frakking dumb name if you ask me, but do you think we'll live up to that name, McEwan?"

"Yes." He nodded. "You're superb, Xin. I don't think I've seen anyone play as well as you."

"It's not all about me, McEwan. Let me put it a simpler way. Do you think we'll reach the last sixteen and Cull immunity?"

"No," he said and immediately studied her face for a reaction. He'd given the right answer, he judged. "Too many weak points in the team," he added. "You'll come up against a team with no weak players and then you'll lose."

Xin grimaced. "You're right." Her leg started jerking up and down. Was she nervous?

Arun looked into her face. She looked unsure of herself. Other than that time after the tunnels, he'd only really seen her from a distance or through a camera feed. She'd always looked so perfectly beautiful, so fired up with determination that he thought of her more like an unstoppable force of nature than a flesh-and-blood girl. Seeing her up close like this… he wanted to stroke her straight black hair away from her face, look into those dark eyes, and tell her everything would be all right.

He didn't. Of course, he didn't. How could he when his hands were enormous clumsy lumps resting on his lap, barely capable of holding his drink cup? His tongue wasn't much more nimble, but his mind must have kept some of its sharpness because he found himself finishing off the implications of what he'd just said – *what Xin had led him to say.*

"And I would rate Moscow Express about the same," said Arun. "We won't win immunity either. So what you're proposing is to merge the strongest members of each team. That way we win more merit points for the battalion and start the climb out of the Cull Zone. We might just win immunity for ourselves too. That is what you're proposing, isn't it?"

"Congratulation, McEwan. You're not as dumb as you look. Don't you agree that playing in my team makes the most sense?"

"In terms of cold logic? Yes, I suppose it does. But there are other things beyond logic. Morale, loyalty. They count too."

"That's easy for you to say, McEwan. You're only G-2, this is only just becoming real to you. I'm a year further ahead. The Cull is much closer to reality for me. Much too close."

"Okay, I get that." Arun shuddered. He remembered the softscreen Little Scar had showing the last Cull of the 412th. The looks of resentment on everyone's faces. The dignified silence of the victims made even more poignant by the few who screamed for mercy. But there was no mercy in Arun's world.

"I can see you do," said Xin kindly. She laid her hand on his thigh. "I've witnessed a Cull too, don't forget. We see one at the end of every year." She shuddered, almost retching. "I don't want to be on the sharp end of one, but I don't think my class can escape the Cull Zone. The climb is too high."

"No one does," said Arun. "But I can't see my Moscow teammates going along with your idea. Do you think you can convince your team to bring me in?"

"Team? What team? Olmer quit. And without her, Pardi's thinking about walking too. I reckon I can persuade Lindet to stay, but I need reasons. You are reason number one."

Arun shook his head. The way Del-Marie had reacted after he'd been caught out watching Xin instead of Springer – he didn't even want to even think about how they would react if told them he was joining Xin's team.

"Hey! I'm still here," snapped Xin. "Stop thinking. It's not your strong point."

"Easy!"

Xin sighed. "I'm disappointed. That's all. I thought you'd like to spend more time with me."

"Well, yes of course."

"But you won't even consider my suggestion."

"Well, I–"

"All you need to do is play just one round with us. Then we'll see where we go from there. Just one. It's not much to ask and I'll make it worth your while… you *do* like me, don't you?"

"Like you? I do, I…"

"Oh, for frakk's sake, dunkchunk. When I say, *like*, I'm not talking about modest affection. Let me spell it out. You find me desirable. I find your Scendence talents to be desirable. Let's make a fair exchange."

"No. I can't."

"*Can't.* There's that loser word again. Won't is just as dumb in this case. Listen up, twinkle eyes, if I don't win immunity, I might wind up dead. And, oh, let's think for a moment… A year later, so might you. Bundle up all those soppy love tales you read as a kid, and fire a tac-nuke at them, 'cos this is the adult world you're living in now. I'm not some frakking fairytale princess. I'm not the villain either. I'm just a flesh and guts girl who wants to live long enough to get off this planet and I'll do whatever it takes to survive that long."

"Horden's Children! You're so romantic."

"Romantic? Listen up, McEwan, you'd better sort your drent out fast if you believe in frakking *romance*. Dumb veck. Romance is for… I don't know. People in stories, I suppose. Real people on Earth, even. We're not real people, McEwan. Don't you get that? We're slaves, you dongwit. Some of us are Culled every year. If we survive that, we'll die anyway, fighting out there in the void, warring on behalf of those skangat White Knights who probably don't exist anyway. But that doesn't matter anyway because I'll take my chances in any war. All I'm focused on right now is living long enough to earn my chance to die out there."

In the multitude of conversations with Xin that Arun had dreamed of, there had always been at least an undercurrent of steamy romance, often more like a flood to be honest. All he felt now was pity mixed in with disgust.

He felt mostly pity for Xin.

And mostly disgust at himself because he was actually thinking of joining her.

But then he pictured the disappointment on Springer's face.

"No," he said. He'd had to drag the word out but now he'd turned her down… he felt relief.

Xin cast him a withering look that made him feel two inches tall. She sniffed disdainfully. "There's a chance that if you do exceptionally well, your G-2 class might escape the Cull. For my class that chance is vanishingly small. I will be up for a 1 in 10 chance of being put to death. I have that hanging over me and why? Not from anything I've done. It's not my fault." She leaned in closer. "But it is yours."

Arun shook his head. "That's not fair."

"You're damned right it's not fair. Doesn't mean it isn't true. You put me in this situation, McEwan." She gripped his face, forced him to look her in the eye. "You owe me, man."

Arun's world blurred.

He'd heard that some Marines had been altered to allow messages and mood-altering hormonal packages to be passed through skin contact. *Gifting* they called it. Perhaps Xin had gifted him. Maybe the hurt, disappointment and vulnerability she'd beamed through her dark eyes had enchanted him. Or perhaps he was simply weak willed.

Whatever she'd done, or he'd allowed her to do, Arun's mind shifted someplace else for a moment, a place he recognized: a noisy world of whirring brass cogs and hot oil where the planner part of his mind was yelling at him to join her. When he blinked and found himself back in the 8-412th's mess hall he realized he'd done it. He'd agreed to join Xin.

"I'll help out," he added hastily. He paused. Gods, his head hurt. "But only because you're in my battalion. I don't want your… your *bribes*. And I don't buy your guilt trip."

"You're a cold fish," Xin sneered.

"*Me?*"

"Yeah, whatever." She flashed a smile that was undeniably beautiful but so too was the void: cold, airless, and bathed in lethal radiation, but still beautiful.

He shuddered.

"Welcome to the team, Alan," she said.

"Arun. I'm *Arun*."

"If you say so, twinkle eyes. Next team training session is tomorrow 21:55 hours in hall 5B. Don't be late and… hey, good luck telling your friends."

That was it. Xin had finished with him and walked off, quickly disappearing in the crowd, and leaving Arun lost in dark thoughts.

Darkest of all: how *was* he going to tell his friends?

—— Chapter 19 ——

No training was scheduled for Scendence Days. If you weren't competing yourself, you would be cheering on your buddies from parade halls and lecture theaters given over to Scendence and a dozen other lesser sports and shows. After laughing at your buddy up on one of the stages giving a hopeless attempt at conjuring tricks, she might get her own back by trashing you at a game of petanque. Everyone joined in the fun, because enjoying these Marine holidays was not a privilege, it was an order.

After agreeing to join Xin's team, Arun tried to lose himself in the fun going on all around him. He couldn't. He was like a ghost at his own funeral: desperate to connect with his friends in ways taken for granted in life but now impossible.

Eventually, he slipped away to the shooting range, reasoning that he'd participated enough in the Scendence events not to get into trouble.

As soon as he picked up the SA-71, he knew coming here had been the right thing to do. The feel of the carbine close to his shoulder was a comfort, the gun his most reliable friend who never judged him. He needed this. As he put round after round into the plastic targets thrown in random arcs by the range AI, every target hit made him feel better. Made him feel like he was good Marine material, despite all the drent going on. When he was inside his battlesuit, Barney did most of the aiming. Here in the range, without his suit AI, Arun was still a crack shot.

Detroit's layout was divided up by the four regiments of Marines based there. There was no rule to say you had to stick with your own regiment, but strolling into another regiment's territory wasn't something to do lightly. Arun was banking on Scendence Day being different. Humor was good, rules relaxed. Arun decided he couldn't spend the rest of the day at his range and so drifted across the border into the 420th's section of Detroit. He kept clear of the Scendence halls and visited immersion training suites, a library and even spent quiet time in one of the temples, trying to figure out what the hell was messing up his head and making him do crazy things.

Night came. The light in the tunnels and rooms changed, losing its UV content and taking on a ruddy glow. With no clear insights into why he kept inviting trouble, just a wasted afternoon, Arun wandered back to his dorm in hab-disk 6/14.

Everyone stopped and stared when he walked in. He wouldn't have felt more of an outsider if he'd walked into a random dorm in another regiment's hab-disk.

"Where have you been, man?" asked Osman.

"And why?" added Del-Marie.

Arun took a deep breath and then told them everything. He tried to explain how he had this premonition that he needed to be close to Xin and close to her Scendence team. It wasn't so much that he was leaving Moscow Express, he explained, more a merger of both teams.

The others greeted this with jeers and heads shaken with disappointment. Even to Arun his words sounded more feeble excuse than explanation.

Frakk them! I'm a Marine cadet. I don't give up.

"Hey!" he protested. "Don't give me that drent. It's not like I've joined a team from another battalion. Is it? Well, is it?" He dared them to deny the truth. But most of his comrades were already turning away.

"Xin's part of our battalion," he said. "Our scores are pooled each year. If her Scendence team scores well, it helps to keep all of us from getting Culled just as much as it does her and the G-1 companies."

"That's not the point," said Zug. "We're squad buddies. You let us down. Again. When we're in the field and get in a tight spot, we must rely on each other. Trust. Teamwork. And you've just taught us that we can't rely on you."

"But, Zug…"

With his voice of perfect calm and reason, Zug delivered his damning verdict. "No, Arun. I've nothing more to say to you." Every pair of eyes in that room was trained on Arun and Zug. Calmly, Zug picked up a softscreen, and opened it to the book he was reading. Arun recognized the title. It was an ancient work of political philosophy called *Two Treatises of Government*. Only last month, he'd discussed with Zug what kind of world its author, John Locke, had inhabited. Now that easy friendship of many years had vaporized.

Not you too, Zug! Arun had come prepared for a shouting match with Madge and Springer, perhaps Del-Marie who took a lot to anger but had a volcanic temper once roused. Arun might not have changed anyone's opinion of him, but he would have given as good as he got.

But Zug was so calm, so reasonable. So *final*. Arun had no defense against that. All the fight went out of him. Since birth he'd had drilled into him that no plan survives contact with the enemy. He hadn't expected such a practical demonstration in his dorm of all places.

Once again he felt like a ghost at his own funeral. Only one person looked at Arun as if he still lived: Springer.

"Get it over with," he said as she walked his way. "Tell me how much you hate me."

"I don't hate you, Arun."

"Really?" Arun brightened. "Sweet homecoming, Springer. For a moment there…" He shut up when saw the sour look on Springer's face.

"You're an idiot, Arun. But you're my idiot. How could I hate you for being yourself? But disappointment? The universe isn't big enough to contain all the disappointment I feel for what you did. That dirty skangat, Xin, saw what a soft dongwit you are and twisted you around her little finger as if you were one of those pretty ribbons the 420th wear. Let's face it, you have as much backbone as a scrap of ribbon. Xin hasn't one iota of respect for you. You do realize that, right?" She paused to emphasize her point and watch Arun squirm. "You were pathetic today, Arun, but I don't hate you. I hate *her*."

Her words stung. Was she right? No, Arun decided, because she didn't understand the whole picture. To be fair, neither did he. "I'm not sure how it happened. I felt…" What had he felt? He'd already tried to explain the

planner part of his brain telling him to do as Xin asked. As excuses went, it stank.

"There is a solution of sorts," said Springer.

He raised an eyebrow.

"I've checked. There's nothing to stop you continuing to play for Moscow Express and play for *her* team too. It's very rare but it's been done before. The game AIs will try to schedule the contests to avoid conflicts."

Springer was beyond wonderful. Arun almost kissed her, but stopped himself. She was still too frakked off. Then a dark thought cast a shadow over his hope. "If we did well, the two teams would eventually face each other. I can't compete against myself. What then?"

Springer rolled her beautiful eyes. "Life is strewn with choices that can't be bypassed. Haven't you learned that yet? It's through our choices that we are known."

"I get it. If I want us to stick together, I've got to make the right choice. Is that what you're telling me?"

"No." A faraway look took her. Despite the situation, Arun felt a tingle of excitement as he stared at his only remaining friend. Was he seeing a vision as it possessed her?

The violet color didn't come to her eyes. Instead she sighed and glanced up at him through old eyes that looked as if they'd seen a thousand years pass by.

"Depending on your choices," she said, "I might love you, despise you or tolerate you. But our destiny lies together. I'm certain of that. Good or bad, our futures are entwined. I've seen this many times before."

Arun groaned. Since turning cadet, he'd been threatened, manipulated, had the crap kicked out of him, and had made himself the most hated guy in the 8th battalion. All of that he could deal with, but this talk of destiny was freaking him out.

He never wanted to be a hero.

If Springer's violet visions were right, then that choice wasn't his to make.

—— Chapter 20 ——

Translation of Annotated Nest Archive
Date: 9519-244
Subject: Interrogation of Human McEwan
Key scents: Conditioning-Marines-drugs-betrayal
Filter Applied: High-value information only

CONTEXT: The human, Arun McEwan, was asked to describe small unit organization and tactics. His answers were of little value. More interesting were his attempts to steer the conversation onto the topic of his relationship with his human nest comrades. The nest scribe decided to permit this deviation, realizing it could provide valuable insights to the suspected brain-altering drug regime secretly imposed at that time on humans entering the 'cadet' phase of their lifecycle.

==INTERROGATION FRAGMENT BEGINS==
HUMAN McEWAN: Don't you think it's an overreaction? All I did was switch teams. I mean, I could understand them getting frakked off, but that was three weeks ago now. That's all! Three frakking weeks and they still act as if… Well, it's as if you'd bitten off your queen's legs and danced on her head.

SCRIBE: You mean the Great Leader.

HUMAN McEWAN: That guy, yeah.

SCRIBE: I understand. You feel your offense is minor but your human nest comrades judge you and your acts as repugnant. Are there other examples where the value that you place on things is very different from your comrades?

HUMAN McEWAN: [Pauses to think while consulting wetware memories. He nods his head. *Interpretation: (93% certainty): indicates agreement.*] No one has fun anymore. Goofing around, joking – it's an important part of human bonding but the only time I've seen my buddies loosen up recently was for Scendence Day. [*Shakes head, looking at floor (91% certainty): indicates sadness*] Even that didn't last long. I asked to keep playing for Moscow Express but Madge wouldn't let me. Last match day, they were knocked out of the competition but I won for Xin's bunch: Team Ultimate Victory. *Team Ultimate Disaster*, more like. Other than Springer, my friends hate me more than ever now.

SCRIBE: Has this been a slow and steady change or a sudden one?

HUMAN MCEWAN: It's grown, but real fast. Everything changed about the same time we made cadet. Maybe a little before.

SCRIBE: And you feel unaffected?

HUMAN McEWAN: [Rolls eyes. *Interpretation: meaning unclear*]. No, it's doing my head in too. I get wildly angry sometimes or feel so low that I whimper in my sleep. I think I'm cracking up. Oh, frakk! Frakk, frakk, frakk! I'm so flekked.

SCRIBE: Is something wrong?

HUMAN McEWAN: Wrong? I've just told you I'm cracking up. That's practically an admission that I'm not fit to be a Marine. I'll be working the mines this time tomorrow.

SCRIBE: You need not fear. The internal security systems monitor for signs of insurrection, not individual performance. We have tested this extensively. You may speak freely to me about your medical concerns.

HUMAN McEWAN: Even if you're wrong about the security stuff… [Sighs. *Interpretation: (97% certainty): indicates acceptance of an unwanted situation*]. I guess I can't make things worse.

SCRIBE: Correct. If I am wrong about the drenting security systems, then you are utterly vulleyed whatever you do.

HUMAN McEWAN: [Sets mouth into 'brittle smile'. *Interpretation: (86% certainty): acknowledgement of humor, comradeship, reasserting anxious state.*]. Good one, Pedro. A little more work on the accent and we'll be able to sneak you into the chow hall and no one will realize you aren't one of us.

SCRIBE: [spirals antennae, indicating acknowledgement of humor] Why don't you tell your medical staff or your human leaders about your concerns?

HUMAN McEWAN: [Shakes head. *Interpretation: (96% certainty) disagreement. Possibly (32% certainty) mild contempt too.*] You don't know much about humans, do you?

SCRIBE: Correct.

HUMAN McEWAN: I know. I know. It's why you want us to have these little chats. I'll try to explain. When your squad goes into danger, knowing your buddies around you are strong helps to keep you strong too. A Marine who wobbles under pressure has the opposite effect. The Corps has no use for a Marine who's going to sit down and start crying because someone is shooting at him. I can't admit my weakness. Majanita and Del-Marie already think I don't fit in anymore.

SCRIBE: If you are truly different, can you really keep this deception for three years until graduation? And beyond, as a Marine?

HUMAN McEWAN: [Shrugs. *Interpretation: (96% certainty) showing disdain for challenges faced.*]. That's something I'll have to find out the hard way. I'm not quitting. Never. That's not an option. Not me at all.

SCRIBE: Is that why you originally agreed to join your comrades' Scendence team, Moscow Express? Did you do this to regain the respect of your comrades?

HUMAN McEWAN: [Shakes head and sighs (*resignation*)] Am I that transparent? Even to an overgrown ant? [Shrugs (*resignation*)] Yes, that's why

I agreed to join in. I'm pretty good at playing Deception. Gunnery too, though Madge always wants to take that – I mean, Cadet Corporal Majanita. If I did well, then everyone sees me winning for the team. It worked too, for about ten minutes after I won my first Moscow Express match. Then the madness took me and I joined Xin's team.

SCRIBE: I am concerned for you, friend McEwan. Your wild mood swings are still unexplained. Are you worried that they will affect your Scendence performance?

HUMAN McEWAN: Not enough to stop me playing.

SCRIBE: [Pauses. Scent signal indicates exasperation that human is failing to connect the probable causes of mental state]. When I first met you, you were singing. Was that an example of your strange mental state?

HUMAN McEWAN: No, that was the… the combat drugs. [Words slowed temporarily during previous sentence. *Interpretation: (82% certainty) intense mental activity limiting speech capability. Conclusion: human has linked combat drugs with continuing mood changes.*] Combat drugs! That's it! They've been pumping combat drugs into us continuously. Low dose. They're meant to keep you focused on fighting, a robot killer. Heightens your sense of loyalty. Everything else in your head is put on standby. That would explain everything. Why I've gone wild and everyone else is a robot. And… [Makes stabbing motion with finger at scribe. *Interpretation: (81% certainty) threat display*]. You knew, didn't you? Go on, deny it!

SCRIBE: I cannot answer that.

HUMAN McEWAN: [Shakes head.] That's not good enough. If you want our talks to continue, it's got to be a two-way thing. I share. You share. We both learn from each other. The colonel will skin me alive if I don't learn anything from you.

SCRIBE: What do you wish to learn, Arun?

HUMAN McEWAN: Did you know I was being drugged?

SCRIBE: [Hesitates. Emits *deliberate falsehood* scent.] No.

HUMAN McEWAN: [Tenses jaw muscles. Narrows eyes. Adopts aggressive stance. *Interpretation: (92% certainty): dominance challenge.* Scribe shows no reaction. Human soon abandons challenge.] Answer me this, then: do you think I'm being drugged by the Corps?

SCRIBE: This topic cannot be discussed.

HUMAN McEWAN: Figures. Thanks, pal. Okay, try this. Suppose, hypothetically, the Corps was giving us combat drugs. Speculate why they might do that.

SCRIBE: This topic cannot be discussed.

HUMAN McEWAN: [Growls. *Interpretation: (99% certainty): threat display.*] Forget everything I've just said. Let's play pretend instead. Suppose traitors wanted to disable the human Marines defending the base through a non-lethal drug. As a cadet faithful to my White Knight masters and their officers, I would want to know how to protect against such an attack. How would I protect myself from being drugged without arousing the suspicions of the traitors?

SCRIBE: You humans have extremely weak natural defenses. I cannot see what you could do. A drug or toxin could be administered through the air, drink, skin contact, food, nanobots. You could be hypnotized to self-administer every night and then forget what you had done.

HUMAN McEWAN: How about you take my blood sample and use what you find to develop an antidote?

SCRIBE: [Twists antennae to indicate moral conflict.] Although I cannot discuss this topic, Arun, I make a solemn vow on the sanctity of the nest – may I be cast beyond the boundary if I break my word. I shall do whatever is in my power to aid you. Even though you might not understand nor like what I shall do, yet shall I aid you.

==INTERROGATION FRAGMENT ENDS==

[Archivist note: Subsequent events tell us that the scribe was faithful to its promise, and correct in its prediction that the human would hate the scribe for what it would do.]

—— Chapter 21 ——

"This afternoon you're going to learn a little history."

Arun groaned inwardly. With his recent frontline experience, Blue Squad had empowered their new veteran sergeant to give an insight to their future as Marines, not backward to someone else's past. Gold Squad was at the lecture too – the two squads often trained together – and looked like they felt the same. What was it to be? Famous battles of the Seventh Frontier War? Dropboat development over the centuries? Camo pants stitching patterns of the ancients?

From behind his lectern, Gupta grinned wolfishly. "I know what you're thinking. Why aren't we sweating in our battlesuits, and shooting the crap out of each other in a training environment? There will be plenty of time for that, but to win, a Marine needs more than equipment and tactics." Gupta tapped his head. "The ultimate key to victory is up here. And it's in your mental attitude that you stink the most. Until I'm satisfied with the way you think, I'm going to share examples from our forebears of what it means to be a good Marine. If any of you feels your time would be better spent capturing flags and laying ambushes for your comrades, please feel free to share your opinion with me. I hear the Aux welcomes volunteers to work the fields or clean out the head. Does anyone want to hear my history lesson?"

All the cadets rose from their desks and came to attention. "Yes, sergeant."

Gupta ignored them for several seconds before acknowledging. "Sit down, shut up, and listen good. Location: Earth. Date: Common Era 1917 through 1921. Subject: The Czech Legion."

There was a noise, a disturbance in the rigid order of the lecture. Arun followed Gupta's glare to Springer. She was writhing on her seat and screwing her face as if someone had rammed a stun rod up her backside.

Gupta ignored her. "Earth was in the grip of a major war," he said. "World War One. Total combatants approximately 70 million. Casualties: 29 million killed, wounded, and missing – and that's ignoring the civilians. Major political groupings – countries and empires – would collapse during this conflict. This was not a clash of ideology, culture or religion, but really a civil war that raged throughout the continent of Europe, although the fighting spread around the planet. Soldiers were sucked into the European battlefields from major nations on other continents, such as India and the United States.

"I've mentioned civil wars in an earlier lecture. You might think me obsessed. Well, you could be right."

Gupta smiled, which brought hesitant laughter from a few brave cadets. They were still learning the sergeant's ways. Compared to the instructors, he seemed just as strict but more informal, even outspoken.

"Brother shoots brother and bombs mother," continued Gupta. "Civil wars are just about the ugliest episodes in the human story. But that isn't what fascinates me. Civil war usually ends in the destruction of the old certainties and the emergence of something new. Even if the incumbent political authority wins on the battlefield, it is forever changed by the war."

Gupta fixed Arun with a stare. "In your orientation speech I told you Marines sometimes have to suck up the pain and survive for as long as it takes to fight back and win. That wait could last for generations. For those seeking change to the old order, civil wars *are* that chance to strike back, the one opportunity that must be seized with all six limbs."

What was this? Gupta's gaze still wouldn't release Arun.

Gupta spoke slowly and clearly. "The White Knights, for example, are an immensely powerful race, but they are no more a single unified entity than the human race. In fact the opposite is the case. Their fascination with change and mutation makes our masters particularly prone to civil wars."

The sergeant's gaze kept Arun prisoner for another few seconds before turning back to the rest of the cadets.

"Back in our Earth example, two great empires were about to disintegrate in this European civil war: the Hapsburg and the Russian Empires. Just as we humans are one of the many subservient species in the White Knight Empire, so the Hapsburg emperor ruled many distinct cultural and ethnic groupings. His empire had 27 official languages. One of these groups was called the Czechs."

Gupta looked up and stared at the cadets sitting before him. "Let's find which of you worms was paying attention in my last briefing. What often happens before a civil war battle, especially at the beginning of the war?"

Arun watched hands shoot up.

"Yes, Skull?" Gupta nodded at one of the cadets.

Skull was taken by surprise to hear the sergeant use his nickname. "Sergeant, soldiers lose the will to fight. Desertion rates are high."

"Correct. Of course, it depends on the background to the war, and how a soldier came to be recruited in the first place. In many civil wars, not only do individual soldiers desert but entire units go over to the enemy, often murdering their officers in the process."

A sense of danger snuck into the briefing hall. "Our Czech soldiers were mostly unwilling conscripts who felt a far closer cultural affinity to the enemy and only resentment to their ruler, the Hapsburg emperor. Egged on by Russian propaganda promising freedom for the Czechs and their own homeland, entire divisions deserted to the Russian side. Czech soldiers captured by the Russians were housed in prisoner of war camps. These were rich recruiting grounds for Czechs who were prepared to fight on the Russian side. These Czechs fought in their own units but under Russian orders. In their minds they fought for freedom. To the Russians, they were plasma fodder.

"Freedom is an intoxicating idea. It can drive people to extreme acts. Even I have to take care with my words. I don't want us all executed for inciting insurrection."

Arun joined in the nervous laughter, relieved that the sergeant appeared to realize the danger in his words. Gupta's near-treason hadn't gotten them killed yet.

"These turncoat units were organized into the Czech Legion. With a peak strength of about 60,000 in comparison with the Russian Army's total wartime strength of 12 million they would have been nothing more than a historical oddity if not for two things. In 1917, the Russian Empire collapsed and turned its attention to its own civil war. A year later, the Hapsburg Empire imploded and the wider war ended.

"It was as if the sea had suddenly gone out, leaving the Czech Legion stranded inside the largest country in the world. They'd suddenly transformed from a historical footnote to the only large force of disciplined troops in Russia. They were now important. By that time, all sides in the Russian Civil War distrusted the Czechs at best, and in many cases wanted them dead. What did the Czech Legion do?"

Gupta acknowledged one of the hands. It was Alice Belville, the cadet lance sergeant from Gold Squad. "The Czechs fought their way back home, sergeant."

"They did that, Belville. But their route home lay to the west, through the bulk of the forces hostile to them."

Gupta hadn't invited input from the cadets, but Arun found he had his hand up.

"McEwan?"

"They forced a passage to the east, sergeant."

Gupta nodded. "The Trans-Siberian Railway was the longest railroad in the world, running nearly 6,000 miles from the west to the east of Russia. Over the next three years, the Czech Legion forced passage along this railroad before being evacuated by sea from Russia's eastern coast."

Another disturbance made Arun glance to his left. It was Springer again. The wisp of steam over her eyes and water dripping from her nose explained what had happened. She'd never had visions so close together before. Her eyelids must be brutally scorched.

Gupta continued as if nothing was happening. "If they had simply sat in a train carriage and waited to reach their destination they would have been ambushed and wiped out before they'd gone a hundred miles. The Czech Legion became almost a nomadic state, controlling all the stations along the railroad for a hundred miles or so either direction of their force concentration, and the countryside around that stretch. They negotiated with the local people and rival factions in the Russian Civil War for supplies, security and passage. That required great skill, discipline and organization.

"Why do I mention the Czech Legion? They weren't members of the Marine Corps, but I think of them as if they were, because that is exactly how I expect Marines to think and act. So you tell me. What can the Legion teach us about some of the drent you cadets have gotten yourself into recently?"

"Sergeant," asked Majanita, "Did you pick that example because of Cadet McEwan?"

"Interesting. What makes you think I did?"

"The Czech Legion stuck together under stresses that would have crushed most units. They showed tenacity, initiative, cunning, ruthlessness, all those good things, but most of all they are a lesson in sticking together."

Gupta thought for a moment. "I would have chosen the Czech Legion's story in any case, but I did have McEwan's situation firmly in mind."

Arun almost felt he should wilt with embarrassment from the unwanted attention. He didn't. Didn't feel anything at all. For his failings to be dissected and analyzed was becoming an everyday burden.

"So tell me, cadets," said Gupta. "McEwan broke his commitment to play Deception for his squad team so he could play with… individuals from elsewhere in the battalion. How does that relate to the Czech Legion?"

Caccamo from Hecht's Alpha Section answered first. "Sergeant. Because McEwan let his team down. The Czechs didn't. By sticking together, the Legion gives us a lesson to counter McEwan's example."

Gupta frowned. "Stand up, Caccamo!" he barked. "Idiot! The White Knights consider us nothing more than cheap plasma fodder. The Jotuns hold us in higher regard. Only a few nanometers higher, but that's better than nothing. I, on the other hand, expect nothing less than for you to be Marines, the very best of the human race. We are not dumb fodder. The difference between surviving combat and being a casualty statistic is half training, half dumb luck, and half using your initiative to make your own luck."

No one dared to speak.

Gupta continued in a slightly softer tone. "Anyone who thinks I can't add up hasn't been listening properly. So, now, Caccamo. Instead of repeating what Majanita just said, use that withered lump between your ears to think. Why did I pick the example of the Czech Legion?"

"I don't know, sergeant." Arun was impressed at Laban Caccamo for keeping as cool as a cryo box under Gupta's glare.

"Don't know?" bellowed the sergeant. "You're no use to me, Caccamo. Sit down."

Caccamo obeyed.

"Anyone?"

Majanita had a reply. "The Czech unit structure was crushed. Rendered obsolete. Their army no longer existed. Even their country no longer existed. They had only themselves. Maybe…" She clammed up.

"Complete what you started, cadet. A Marine never starts anything they don't intend to see through to completion. You should know that."

"Sorry, sergeant. Maybe the parable's lesson is that the legion re-framed their world. They formed a new unit from the wreckage of the old. New buddies. New loyalties. A new team. They set themselves a new goal and set about achieving it by any means available. By teaming up with cadets outside of Blue Squad, has McEwan forged a new unit for the benefit of the battalion?"

"I don't think we know the answer to that, Majanita. Not yet. Maybe Cadet McEwan is a visionary, reacting to circumstances by creating a Marine Legion to get us out of the Cull. Or perhaps he's nothing more than a teenage boy who couldn't refuse an offer from a pretty girl. I don't care about the answer. I do care that instead of thinking through the possibilities, you all picked the lazy choice by blaming McEwan for disloyalty."

Gupta tapped at his head. "Up here! This is where you're failing me. Being able to see the same situation as everyone else, but see new possibilities within it is what makes the difference between a good Marine and the kind of half-evolved plasma fodder those other races think we are. Do you want to prove them right?"

"No sergeant!" replied both squads, Arun right up there with the rest.

The sergeant studied his cadets for a few moments. Arun wasn't sure whether the sergeant had just stood up for him. He sure felt inadequate, though.

"I can see from your faces that I've confused the hell out of you." Gupta's scowl lightened. "That's a good thing because your brains need shaking up. You're too robotic. If Blue and Gold Squads were stranded in the midst of a civil war, I would expect you to turn the situation to your advantage, same as the Czech Legion did. That's all for today. Dismissed."

As soon as Gupta had left through the door at the back of the stage, Arun made for Springer.

"What happened?" he asked her. "What was in your vision? Did you have two?"

Springer closed her eyes and shook her head. Her eyelids were brutally red, her eyes bloodshot and watering. "It isn't clear, Arun, more a vague feeling, triggered by certain words."

Majanita put a supportive arm around Springer. "Leave her alone, McEwan."

Osman stood beside her, glaring at Arun. The rest of the section waited nearby.

"No, he needs to know," said Springer. She sounded exhausted. "Arun, you and the Czech Legion are connected. I think… I think that one day you will create a—"

Majanita slapped her hand over Springer's mouth. "Shut up! Don't even think about how that sentence ends."

She doesn't need to, thought Arun. *I help to create a Human Legion. That's what she thinks. Gupta was practically spelling it out. It fits with what everyone has been hinting at all along.*

"Go away," Osman told Arun.

"No," said Arun. "Springer, can I please ask you something? I've never wanted to ask until this moment."

"I said, go away." Osman was shoving him now.

"Let him ask," sighed Springer. "What is it?"

"Your visions of the future," said Arun, grimacing uncomfortably because he didn't know how to put this without insulting Springer. "Have any come true?"

"No."

Arun relaxed. He let Osman give him a last shove and then watched his friends move away without him.

Springer paused and turned around. "But that's the thing about the future," she said to Arun. "It hasn't happened yet. But it will."

She wanted to say more but she choked back and kept silent, as if suddenly noticing the verbal minefield all around her.

The passageway crackled with tension like a G-Max cannon before an x-ray burst.

"We both know it will happen," she said, sounding as if the words were being forced out of her at gunpoint.

Arun didn't say a word. He scarcely dared to breathe. Microphones in the walls, nano-spies floating in the air. No one knew what form the surveillance systems took, but everyone agreed that they were everywhere, feeding through any signs of disloyalty to the Jotuns.

Springer spoke the three words she shouldn't, the name that meant Arun's life could never return to normal. "The Human Legion," she said.

Arun froze, expecting hidden beams of death to strike him down at any moment. There was no cover to shield him, nowhere to run. If the Jotuns decided he should die then his existence would end as surely as night extinguishes day.

But death, if it were coming, was not immediate.

By the time he unclenched, the rest of the squad had ushered Springer out of sight, on their way to the orbital elevator and dropboat training.

Arun raced after them, desperate not to be left alone.

—— Chapter 22 ——

The trips to see Pedro were worse than useless: they consumed valuable time that Arun could never get back. With graduation to qualify for, and his battalion in the Cull Zone – not to mention the Scendence commitments that were causing so much annoyance – every hour spent away from training was painful.

But Instructor Rekka had taught them that so long as your position was secure from immediate assault, if you were given a task then you should put everything else out of your mind and do that task to the best of your ability.

Sometimes that required an iron will, but Rekka was right.

Out in the field, if you were assigned to dig fox holes or latrines, then you let the perimeter guard worry about intruders and you concentrated on your digging.

And if you were tasked with a friendly afternoon chat with a seven-foot insect, then you put away thoughts of culls and graduation, you put on your most companionable smile, and you talked with the alien.

If he could, Arun would cancel his chats in an instant. Since he couldn't, he took pleasure in this excuse to roam the bustling underground labyrinth that was the Detroit base.

Pedro encouraged Arun to explore, because that way he could ask endless questions about the human levels.

Arun's hab-disk was on Level 6, near Corridor 622 that ran between Helix 62 and Helix 6, which was the main spiraling ramp in his regiment's portion of Detroit. Today, on his meandering route to Pedro, he cycled up the Helix 6 ramp to Level 3. This was a level of barracks and defensive positions. The topology of the base was the same on all levels: Corridor 622 always connected Helix 62 with Helix 6, whatever level you were on. But the route Corridor 622 took to get there was different on every level. Here on Level 3, the corridors zigzagged to prevent a single blast of firepower sweeping the entire corridor of defenders. In the hab-disks you talked of walls and ceilings, but here the tunnel structures were hardened and you had bulkheads and overheads instead. If not for the gravity keeping Arun's bike firmly on the deck, Level 3 could easily be mistaken for a warboat interior.

Level 3 was deserted. That's why Arun loved it here. There were plenty of Marines to fill the barracks and man the hardened alcoves peppering the corridor. But they were deep down in Level 10 or below, stored in cryogenic iceboxes.

Arun peddled on around Helix 64, crossed the regimental boundary and on to Helix 72. From there he took Corridor 712, which passed by the southern edge of Detroit.

He'd passed by a huddle of Hardit engineers arguing over something in their growling speech, flicking their long tails at each other aggressively. It was unusual to see them so active. When he passed the monkey-like creatures on his travels, they were more often slumped against the wall, apparently asleep.

He pushed on into a long, south-running corridor where the wall glowed red as he passed. It didn't look welcoming but there wasn't a sign or order to turn back. Up ahead should be hangars for shuttles and ground attack flyers. He doubted he'd get close enough to see them but he carried on, wanting to see how far he could get.

The answer came in the form of four Marines who came out of the distance at the double. They wore full combat armor decorated in the gold-and-black diamond pattern of the 101st Assault Marines, specialists in ground assault. They were supposed to have the thickest skulls and smallest brains, the better to survive the frantic descent from orbit to ground. Some said Neanderthal DNA had been used in their breeding program to toughen them up.

Two of these bone heads from the 101st had SA-71 carbines, one carried a plasma gun, and the other a flame thrower. They held their weapons as if they would open fire at the merest provocation. Debating their ancestry might not be a good plan.

"Beat it, kid!"

Arun hated to take that kind of drent from anyone, especially from Marines who weren't even in his regiment, and boneheads at that. Then one of them raised his carbine, and Arun hurriedly made up his mind that staying alive was the best course of action. He turned and pedaled away.

By the time he'd returned to the main ramp at Helix 6, he'd used up any spare time to go wandering, but there was still plenty to see on the ramp as he descended toward Level 9 and the tunnel that connected with the Troggie nest.

Just past Level 4, an electric truck was towing a heavy weapon strapped onto a trolley. What was that? A Fermi cannon perhaps? It was big enough. Probably something for use in the orbital defense platforms.

Between 5 and 6, Arun passed an Aux – a human manual worker – pushing a wheeled trolley down the ramp. The Aux was struggling a little. If Arun had more time, and if the Aux hadn't stank so much, he would have stopped to help.

Up ahead he could hear the sound of running. He listened closer and made out three pairs of boots thumping along the ramp. Most likely they were novices or cadets on a punishment run. He'd had plenty himself at school. If you merely looked at an instructor in a way they didn't care for then you'd be off on a thirty-klick run. The instructors didn't mind where you went so long as you did your fifty. Woe betide anyone who didn't.

The Aux…!

With a squeal of brakes, Arun came to a sudden halt. He looked back at the Aux he'd just passed.

Surely not?

He shifted gears and pedaled back up the ramp.

The Aux slunk against the wall. He seemed to know that Arun was interested in him, but instead of acknowledging the cadet politely – as Arun would expect any Aux to do – he turned to face the wall. Like many Aux, he wore a woven hat with a stiffened peak that shadowed the eyes. Arun leaned his bike against the wall and took off the Aux's hat.

Despite Arun's attempt to be gentle, the Aux flinched as if pained.

Hortez!

This was the novice Arun had admired and envied throughout school.

And it had been Arun with his escapades in the Troggie tunnels who'd taken that shining success of a cadet squad leader and turned him into … into this!

"Man, you look terrible." It was all Arun could think to say.

Hortez finally looked up, straight into Arun's face. Under his scruffy beard, the outer reaches of his face were a mix of black from deeply ingrained grime, and the angry red of flesh peeling after being burned.

Hortez stank.

The Aux who cleaned, washed, and cooked in the hab-disks were expected to be clean themselves, but Hortez didn't look as if he'd had a proper wash since that moment in Little Scar's office when Hortez's star had plummeted to these depths.

Arun looked again into his old friend's face and saw that under the grime there was another pattern, one painted in deep blues and yellows.

"Do they beat you?" he asked.

Hortez nodded.

Rage bubble up within Arun. He kept it in check, for now. "Look, pal, I know that from where you've ended up, my words are worth as much as an ice cube in the backdraft from a fusion engine, but for what it's worth … I am sorry."

"It wasn't your fault."

"I guess not but… but you're here and I'm not and that's kinda hard. I'm sorry about that."

"You're sorry? How do you think I feel?"

It took a moment before Arun realized that Hortez was trying to be funny. He'd always had a wicked sense of humor and had laid down a constant barrage of practical jokes throughout their years together at novice school. Some of that spark was still there. Not much though. Frakk! It was only a few weeks since Hortez had been his squad leader. What had they done to him?

"What are you doing here, anyway?" asked Hortez. Then he frowned and shook his head. "Forget it! You'll have to keep your mysteries, McEwan. I can't talk. Gotta go. Tell Brandt I wish him luck."

"Don't leave. Your face… This isn't right, we need to do something to fix this."

"You can't, McEwan. Don't make it worse for me."

"Why because they'll beat you? I can't stand for that. I need to let the authorities know."

After a bitter laugh that led into a hacking cough, Hortez replied: "I admire your naivety, pal. As if anyone who can make a difference would care."

The fire returned to Hortez's spirit. Arun could see it in his eyes. His spine uncurved somewhat. "They do more than beat us, McEwan. They kill us. A third of final year novices fail graduation. That's several hundred kids suddenly stuck without a role, all at the same time. There's only so much laundry work needed, man. Do you know we sleep in groups back to back because there's no space to lie down? We have to fight each other for food. It's all clean and civilized for those lucky enough to be your servants in the hab-disks, but not for us. We're excess population and the Hardits, who own and run us, take every pleasure they can in reducing our numbers. They're gonna pick one from my team tonight and kill them. Sometimes they tell us that just to enjoy our fear, but don't follow through with their threat. At other times, they killed two, just to keep the rest of us guessing. And I'm almost beginning to believe them when they say that they're only being kind. Starving to death is a tough way to go."

"What can I do to help, Hortez?"

"Stay out of it, McEwan. Don't draw attention to me and maybe I'll get lucky."

Arun took a deep breath. "Fine. I'll do as you say. Just one thing."

Hortez had already turned around and was bracing against his heavy trolley, ready to push it down the gently sloping ramp. "What?" he called over his shoulder.

"How is Alistair?"

Worse than all the horrors he'd ever seen was the deathly look in Hortez's eye when he glanced back at Arun.

"Last I heard, worse than me," said Hortez. "He's out on the surface without adequate protection against the sun's radiation. He's going to…" He shut up suddenly, his eyes widening in horror.

Arun looked behind and stared into the face of a Hardit.

If you looked past the fur and gripping tail that earned them the nickname of *monkeys*, and the three eyes set in a triangle high above the snout, the Hardits were approximately the size and shape of small humans, much more so than the massive hexaped Jotuns or the insectoid Trogs. Their attitude was what marked them apart from the other species. When they weren't snarling through their teeth-filled snouts, Hardits could often be found snoring, slumped against a corridor wall for one of their many naps. There wasn't a particular enmity between humans and Hardits, but it was a given that if a Hardit were awake, then it would be angry.

"What occurs here?" The Hardit wore a speaker on the collar of its grimy blue overalls. The synthetic voice was that of a human male, but the alien could be female for all Arun knew. If it possessed gender characteristics analogous to humans, they were completely obscured under its scruffy fur and clothing. It looked scarcely cleaner than Hortez. The difference was that it looked healthy. Arrogant too.

"Do you understand question? What occurs here? Answer!"

"It's my fault," blurted Arun. "I asked this Aux for directions. I am lost."

One of the things Arun hated most about aliens is that their faces either did not move or else their facial expressions were unintelligible. Possibly at some level – scent maybe? – the Hardit was sneering, laughing, or fuming with rage. All that Arun could tell was that three cold, yellow-flecked eyes stared at him down that long snout. It looked about to bite him.

Then the Hardit addressed Hortez. "Verify!"

"Yes, Mistress Tawfiq Woomer-Calix. I answered the request for help as swiftly as possible so that I might return my worthless attention to my duties."

This monkey-frakker, Tawfiq, snapped her attention back to Arun. "You wear a scent identifier for insect nest," she said her artificial male voice. "That

makes you even more lost than you realize. You must descend four more levels before come to nest. Insects use you for unknown purposes. You human too stupid to understand. Insects very cunning, very manipulative. They have a purpose for you that will not end well when they realize human is worthless species. Better for all of us if humans wiped from galaxy. Go away!"

Arun bowed. "Yes, ma'am. Please forgive me, Mistress Tallfat Woomer-Cat-Licks."

The Hardit growled. "It is Mistress Tawfiq Woomer-Calix. No, do not attempt to correct your speaking. Do not speak at all. Your voice irritates me. I do not forgive you. I want you go away."

Arun nodded with as much deference as he could muster. With a last glance at the pitiful figure that had been his squad leader so recently, he grabbed his bike and set off for the lower levels.

He hoped he had been sufficiently polite to deflect retribution away from Hortez, but he felt anything but deference for the foul monkey-veck.

You haven't seen the last of me, Tawfiq Woomer-Calix.

—— Chapter 23 ——

"It is a caste thing," said Pedro, after Arun had recounted his meeting with Hortez on his way over. "It is like our guardians. Our people go through many phases as they progress through their lifecycle from hatching to enriching the soil with their rotting flesh. The phases are more than just different roles, there are profound physiological and mental changes too. At the end of a long and useful life our people become a burden on the nest. We can no longer support them. They must give way so others can replace them. It is no different from your brief human lives giving way to the next generation."

"You're wrong," said Arun. He got to his feet and started pacing the hard-packed dirt floor, clenching his fists. Pedro had learned not to become alarmed by Arun's displays of anger and gave Arun time to collect his thoughts.

"We've all got to go sometime," said Arun. "I get that. But Hortez and the kids who failed school? That isn't right. It's like we toss them into a deep well of despair. Then we turn our backs and pretend to forget all about it, because if we ever peered into that well, we would be so consumed by grief that we would throw ourselves in and drown in that despair."

"You are young," said Pedro. "Mortality and youth do not sit together comfortably."

"That's what I mean. Hortez and the kids who failed school are just teenagers. They aren't spent husks like the guardians of your people. They're only just starting out in life. A caste thing? No, we humans don't have castes."

"Don't you? Tranquility is a complex multi-species planet, and part of an even more complex star system that is itself part of the White Knight empire. You humans are the lowest caste of all. And these Aux the lowest human sub-caste. You do not like this but it is the truth. You are in a caste system whether you like it or not."

Arun chewed that over. He sat down, embarrassed by his need to pace in front of the alien. "Okay – so we're bottom of the heap. How do the Hardits fit in? Are they the next layer up?"

"It is more complicated. They see themselves as equal or superior to the Jotuns but the White Knights gave the Jotuns the responsibility to run system defense and the supply of Marines. Your Marine base is a relatively recent addition to our star system. It was a mining system for millennia before that. Hardits dislike all other species, but those who share our planet reserve a special level of hatred for the Jotuns for disturbing *their* star system, as they see it, and for you humans for being the cause of the Marine base's expansion. What makes it worse for the Aux is that there are many levels in Hardit society. The Hardit you spoke to will be one of the lowest of all

Hardits, probably a criminal. From their perspective, to be tasked with overseeing human Aux workers is a humiliating punishment."

"I always thought they looked perpetually angry. The Hardits I see are failures who take out their frustration on the one group even lower than them – their human workers. Figures. But if they're such losers, why hasn't Hortez stood up to them more? He was a Marine cadet, if only for a few days. That counts for something."

Intoxicating thoughts of freedom and rebellion swirled around Arun's mind. "Tell me more about the Hardits," he asked his friend.

Pedro answered without hesitation. "The species you call Hardits originate on the planet Iradis 3. First contact with the Tans-Species Union was 0.73 million years ago. Unlike most primitive species, the Hardits initiated that contact. They are a sexual species, the sexes barely tolerating each other except during mating season. Their principal sense is smell, and the average lifespan without longevity treatment is 172 years."

The Trog gave no sign of consulting a softscreen or any other gadget. How did he know all those facts? "That's not what I'm after," Arun told Pedro. "Give me more than dull facts. Something that marks them out as different."

Pedro thought a moment. "Sometimes they are said to be able to see through solid rock. In fact they have a highly developed sensitivity to changes in gravity. In practice that means they know exactly how far they are below the surface of their planet. If two groups of Hardit miners began tunneling toward each other at opposite ends of a planet, you could be confident that the two teams would meet at precisely the same point without needing any technology more sophisticated than picks and shovels."

Arun frowned. "No, that's still not it. Tell me their weaknesses. Give me something I can exploit."

"Since we became friends, human McEwan, I have studied your planet of origin. Your Earth and the Hardit planet are unremarkable except for one aspect you both share: magnetism. Your planet has an iron-nickel core that operates as a dynamo, producing an extremely powerful planetary magnetic field. The Hardit planet's core has more sulfur than iron, and even more significantly, their planet's mantle is highly metalized. This destabilizes the dynamo effect of their core resulting in a remarkably weak magnetic field."

"So? They never grew up knowing about compasses."

"The significance is rather more than that, human. A planet's magnetic field is like a force field, shielding the surface of the planet from the high energy particle stream emitted from the local star. Stellar flares from Earth's star cause power blackouts and damage to unshielded electronics but this has not been enough to place evolutionary pressure on your species' development. With such a weak magnetic field on the Hardit planet, their star has blasted away most of their planet's atmosphere, and left the surface a sterile husk."

"Hold on a minute. If there's no life on their planet, how did the Hardits evolve there?"

"I did not say the planet was lifeless, only that the surface is."

"So they're delvers. They live underground, like you in your nests."

Pedro spiraled his antenna in amusement. "They hardly resemble us, but yes their habitat is below the planet's crust. Vast natural caverns extend for depths of many miles beneath the surface. Which is why they are used as miners. Give them a little gravity, and dirt or rock overhead, and they will be happy, whether on a planet, moon, or asteroid.

"Aliens 101 is all very well, but I asked you to give me the lowdown on their weaknesses. Do they go catatonic when you shine a bright light in their eyes? See that's something I could use. Maybe a common human cooking ingredient is a powerful narcotic? Like garlic. That's it! They go wild for garlic because it gives them such a mega-high and leaves them so blissed out they don't know what they're doing. That would work. C'mon, you gotta give me something."

Pedro flattened his feelers in disdain. "As if a human cooking ingredient would be a narcotic for an alien species. Do you realize how incredibly unlikely that would be?"

"Lay off, Pedro. It's just an example. I need to understand how to beat them, is all."

"If you had listened then you would already understand."

"Do what?"

"I have already been telling you what you asked for."

"About magnetic fields and stuff?"

"Yes."

That brought Arun up short, but he couldn't get his head around what the overgrown insect meant. "This is what our inter-species chats are all about, isn't it? Mutual incomprehension. You tell me something alien that makes no sense. Then you give me an explanation that makes even less sense. You love it. You're conducting an experiment. How much alien drent can you fill my poor human head with until my brain melts? Is that it?"

"Your words do not make sense," said Pedro through his voice box. "But I am learning your tangential ways now. I interpret what you just said as the following. One: I am angry. Two: I fear for my friend, Hortez. Three: I am too ignorant to understand your advice."

Arun shrugged. He was learning too – learning that there was no point in getting angry with aliens. "I figure that about covers it."

"Then allay your concern. It is my calling as a scribe to address the shortcomings of the ignorant. That is why I enjoy our conversations so intensely." Pedro gave a little jump. He did that sometimes when excited. "The significance of their evolution is that Hardits are agoraphobic – they do not like large open spaces in general and planetary surfaces in particular. This is not merely psychological, they are very prone to cancers caused by exposure to Tranquility's sun. Ultraviolet radiation is lethal to them. They are easily dazzled by bright lights. Tranquility's air, even the pumped and filtered air we two are breathing in this lovely chamber, is heavy and oxygen-rich to them. You humans call them lazy. They are actually an industrious species, but they find the dense atmosphere very tiring. If they exert themselves, they hyperventilate easily. You think you see them dozing but they are not asleep. They are slowing heartbeat and breathing in order to regulate blood-oxygen levels. They do not acknowledge you because you are beneath their notice."

"Yeah, I got it," interrupted Arun. "We gotta use flash-bombs." He was about to go but paused. The big insect had helped him. He hated to admit it – after all the trouble his contact with Trogs had caused – but he owed Pedro. Rewarding the big lug was child's play.

"Thanks," said Arun. The insect's antennae circled lazily, indicating his pleasure at Arun's word. "Thanks… *friend*." Pedro's antennae circles grew larger.

Arun reckoned he'd done enough alien chat for one day not to earn Colonel Little Scar's displeasure. "Gotta go now. Hortez needs me. Gonna get myself a posse."

"What does that word mean?"

"Look it up, Pedro."

"But you cannot go yet," said Pedro, his circling feelers flopping to an abrupt halt. "Our inter-species learning has not progressed enough in this session."

"You reckon? I'm gonna raise a posse and I've just explained why. That's enough to keep your feelers wriggling for a bit."

"A poss-ee…?" The voice box raised up the last syllable, indicating Pedro's confusion. Pedro must have been mulling over the word, looking it up probably, because when Arun grabbed his bike, the alien said: "You mean an affectionate term for the species *Felis catus*, especially those kept as a domesticated emotional symbiont?"

"No, I don't mean a frakking cat. P-O-S-S-E. Look it up." As he set off along the nest tunnel on the long journey back to his hab-disk, he called over his shoulder. "You wanted to learn something about humans. We have a saying: *No Marine left behind*. Watch and learn what that means, pal."

—— Chapter 24 ——

The cadet posse finally cornered Tawfiq, the Hardit bully, in a deserted passageway off Corridor 710 on Level 5, not far from their old novice school.

Only Springer and Majanita had joined Arun. As a posse it was pathetic, but at 3-1 odds they didn't fear the lone Hardit as they closed in, blocking her and forcing her to acknowledge their presence. Arun still felt dangerously exposed, and kept glancing back over his shoulder.

When he'd returned from his talk with Pedro, Arun had scoured the hab-disk and battalion chow halls, looking for allies he could trust.

Most of his squad had been in gunnery practice, but Springer and Majanita had been studying in their dorm. Cristina had been there too, and tried to convince them of the insanity of their plan. But once Madge had heard what they'd done to Hortez, nothing would stand in her way. Not reason, that was for sure.

She'd listened to Arun for about three seconds before going to the dorm armory and helping herself to three flash-bombs. Then she went back and brought out six more, which she divided between Springer and Arun.

And now, here they were in a tense standoff with the murdering alien overseer.

Arun felt the pouch on his hip that bulged with the flash-bomb within.

He undid the pouch flap.

"I saw you earlier," he told the alien. "You're Tawfiq Woomer-Calix, aren't you?"

The Hardit gave no indication that she had heard Arun speak. She was looking up at the ceiling as if inspecting a dirty patch.

"We apologize," said Springer hurriedly.

What? Arun looked wide eyed at his friend.

"We do not have experience of interacting with your people," Springer continued. "Please accept our apologies. May we beg permission to converse with you?"

Arun was all for begging permission with his fists, but maybe Springer's way would yield results faster.

The Hardit slowly lowered her head and looked at Arun. "This one thinks I should recognize him," she growled in Hardit speech, a toneless voice translating at the same time into human words through a collar-mounted speaker. Unlike the clanking gears of Pedro's box, this translator was silent and hidden. It wasn't as convincingly human, though.

"All of you look identical," said the Hardit, "and that stench humans have of rotting cheese – you stink worse than nest insects. I refuse to accept apologies. I speak with you because I want you gone and this best way to make you…" There was a pause as the alien selected the optimum translation. "Frakk off!"

"We have questions," said Arun. "About rumors we have heard concerning the human Aux. We would like to know whether they are true." He paused, but the alien gave no acknowledgment. She didn't give a refusal either, so he pressed on. "Is it true that your Aux team is given insufficient food to stay alive, their quarters so cramped that they cannot lie down to sleep, and that you sometimes kill your workers for reasons other than disobedience or treachery?"

It was hard to tell, but Tawfiq seemed to concentrate, to work through the translation. Then she reacted, bringing itself fully erect and confronting Arun.

The alien was a head shorter than the cadets but she yielded nothing to her taller accuser as she raised her head so that her snout almost rubbed on his chin. She breathed out through a wall of teeth, blowing a smell his way that was rich and meaty, and beginning to choke the back of Arun's throat.

The cadets hadn't thought this through. Arun was acutely aware of that, but he couldn't back down in front of this arrogant murderer. "Are the rumors true?" he pressed.

"I do not deny them."

Arun was trying to work out whether that meant yes or no when Madge took over. "We want assurances," she insisted. "The humans are to be well treated. Enough space to sleep properly as becomes our species. Enough food for them to be healthy. A shower once a week and an end to the killings."

Tawfiq breathed again into Arun's face. He got the feeling it was meant as the ultimate insult. The Hardit ignored Madge's words.

"We have ample food and shelter," said Springer, "and we can share what we have. Let's work something out. If your workers were healthier and happier they would be more productive. Surely that would be to your benefit."

Tawfiq stepped back. "I have indulged your foolishness." She wrinkled her nose. "And your stench. Now stand aside or face the consequences."

That was it! Arun snapped. He brought his flash-bomb out of his pouch and brandished it in front of the murdering veck. "Do you know what this is, alien?"

"We wish no confrontation," said Springer.

"What my comrade says is still just about true," added Arun. "But the prospect of confrontation is feeling better by the second."

"Our two species are allies," said Springer. "But we humans are trained to kill, Hardit. It is what we have been bred for. I think with these flash-bombs we can fight and hurt you without killing. But we might not be able to control our violent nature."

"Yeah," said Madge. "Shall we find out?" She drew out her flash bomb. "These devices stun enemy soldiers. They give out such noise, light and radiation that they can fry unhardened enemy targeting systems. Show us your human workers. Show us where they live. Let us talk with them, or we shall find out what these bombs do to you."

"You would not dare, human."

"We give you ten seconds," said Madge.

The Hardit folded her arms and looked at the ceiling.

"Nine," said Madge.

Was this an enormous mistake?

"Eight."

Madge sounded impatient to finish her countdown. But she hadn't experienced the glare of an angry Jotun. Arun was in no hurry to explain to Colonel Little Scar that he'd attacked a Hardit.

"Seven."

Arun glanced at Springer. He could see she wasn't sure either, but she was bringing out her own flash-bomb.

"Six."

He'd like to think they were a band of gallant adventurers, living up to the Marine motto.

"Five."

Never leave a Marine behind.

"Four."

But they'd been flung into this confrontation on the crest of a wave of bluster and indignation.

"Three."

Where would that wave spill them when it broke?

"Two."

Was it too late to back out now?

"One."

Madge's hand twitched but she did nothing. She must have had the same doubts all along. Springer stayed her hand too.

"You are as weak as you are stupid," sneered the Hardit. "It is your cowardice that enables us to exterminate you like the vermin you are."

Arun grabbed the flash-bombs from Springer and Majanita, and dashed all three to the ground.

—— Chapter 25 ——

The flash-bomb was so loud that the noise reached inside Arun's ears and twisted his poor brain into knots, squeezing out his awareness like sweat wrung from a sodden shirt. Arun had turned his head away from the blast just before it went off. Even so, the flash was bright enough to bore through the rear of his skull and sear a white patch onto the back of his retinas.

Unlike the Hardit veck – hopefully – the cadets had experienced flash-bombs many times before. After a few seconds, Arun's brain untwisted and the after-image of the flash began to flake away. Only a high-pitched wail continued, rising in pitch and volume to unbearable levels.

Every ounce of pain ever experienced by every sentient in the history of the galaxy was distilled into that banshee screech.

Arun opened his eyes and looked in wonder upon Tawfiq. She hadn't collapsed to the ground, hadn't even covered her ears or eyes. The alien just stood there, screeching that wail. Suddenly all three of the Hardit's eyes rolled back far enough to show the optic nerve. Then they began to dance crazily in their sockets.

Tawfiq's scream crescendoed, making Arun flinch. It was not a remotely human noise, more like a percussion drill shattering glass.

"Did we go too far?" asked Springer.

"No," replied Madge.

"Not far enough," added Arun. He spat on the alien.

"But how can we negotiate with it?" hissed Springer, the scream setting her teeth on edge. "That *is* why we're here, isn't it?"

Before Arun could reply, a change came over Tawfiq like a fever breaking. Her eyeballs snapped back into focus – glaring at Arun.

"Frakkk-kk-kkk. Frakkk-kkk-kk. Frakkkkkk. Frakk. You. Human. Filth!"

"It speaks," said Arun.

Tawfiq raised her lips, revealing the full length of her fangs. She snarled.

"Do we have your attention, darling?" asked Madge. "We have plenty more bombs…"

Arun glanced across at his cadet corporal. She was giving the pitiful creature a sultry smile. This was more like the girl who had been his friend.

"Human scum. You will learn your place. Veck. Veck."

Madge admonished with a wagging finger. "Naughty girl. And such rude words too. Don't we think that's the kind of bad attitude that got you into trouble in the first place? Hmm?"

"Give it another bomb, corporal," Arun suggested.

"Not so hasty," she said. "I've read up on animal training techniques. I reckon I can tame it." She threw a patronizing smile at the Hardit. "You are bad furry thing. If furry thing do bad things to humans, we make furry thing scream with these."

She brought out another two bombs from her pouch.

Tawfiq ceased her snarling and licked her lips nervously, her gaze never leaving the bombs.

"Not so brave when humans bite back, are you?" sneered Arun. He brought out a pair of bombs himself.

"Easy!" Springer put a hand over his arm. "Let's get our demands met. Don't push it."

Arun took a calming breath, but the heat of his anger would not cool. This skangat of an alien was reducing Hortez to a sniveling wreck, and murdering the Aux in her charge.

No, he would not take it easy.

He flourished both bombs in front of the alien's face. "I wonder what would happen if I set these off right in front of your eyes?"

"Shall we find out?" added Madge.

Arun leered at the alien, loving this. It was more than just sweet revenge. Since making cadet, he'd felt pushed ever further to the edge of the squad. Now he was in the thick of things, and Madge was backing him up for once.

He squeezed the bombs against the alien's eyes.

"No. No. Please," begged Tawfiq. She curled her tail into a circle. Was that a submission gesture? "Please let me speak first."

Arun withdrew the bombs a short distance. The alien touched a stud on her collar and then stared into space for a few moments before explaining: "I have summoned an Aux worker so that I may demonstrate the new way of things."

"I don't like this," said Springer.

"You worry too much," said Madge.

"Really? I don't think you worry *enough*, corporal. Look at her," Springer gestured at Tawfiq. "She's not cowed. She's just buying time."

"Is this one of your *visions*, cadet?" Madge sneered.

Springer seethed, but said nothing.

"You could be right, Springer." Arun tried to speak soothingly. "No matter. If the Hardit tries anything, we'll blast her with four bombs and see whether that encourages her to cooperate."

The tension between the humans was nearly as great as that between the cadets and the Hardit. Before either standoff could break into violence, an Aux worker approached, jogging along the passageway.

He was a sorry sight. Head bowed under a grease-stained cap, and face half-covered by a shapeless bush of a beard. His blue overalls were so filthy that they could probably get up and walk on their own without the human inside.

The Aux looked suspiciously at the cadets before reporting in. "I am here, mistress."

"Stay there," Tawfiq ordered the Aux. "You!" She used her tail to point at Madge. "Kiss my boots."

A chill traveled Arun's spine as he watched the youthful playfulness in Madge's face replaced by the chiseled steel of a Marine.

"I'd rather die," smiled the cadet corporal. "And if I did, I'd make sure to take you with me."

"The greater your insolence, the more severe the punishment I shall deliver."

"You can't threaten me," said Madge.

Arun readied to release his bombs.

"I think she's threatening to punish the Aux," said Springer. "Not us. Not yet."

"Correct," said Tawfiq.

"Don't you dare," shouted Arun.

The alien moved – lightning fast. Arun threw his bombs but he knew he'd hesitated too long. Tawfiq dove for the floor, her back to the bombs. As she fell, she drew a grubby black box from her overalls and seemed to activate a control, but Arun couldn't be sure because his world filled with pain and confusion as the flash-bombs drove away every other thought.

When his senses returned, the passageway was filled by the sound of screaming as before. But this time the screams were agonizingly human, coming from the Aux who was thrashing around on the floor in some kind of fit.

Springer and Madge went to aid the Aux, but Arun threw himself at Tawfiq who had risen to a crouch.

He wrestled the alien to the floor. Tawfiq was strong and managed a kick to his gut. Arun bit back the pain and landed two good punches on the alien's face.

Frakk, that hurt his fist! This creature had bones as strong as poly-ceramalloy, but the fight had gone out of Tawfiq enough for Arun to wrench away her black box.

Desperate to shut off the agonized screams from the Aux, Arun thought he'd simply thumb a control and that would be the end of it. What he saw on the box, though, was scrolling alien script that meant nothing to him. There was no icon, no red button… nothing to say *press me*. He jabbed at the face of the control box anyway.

No effect.

"You will never find it, human." Tawfiq was sitting up now, wiping blood from her snout.

"Then you turn it off, or I'll kill you," shouted Majanita.

"No."

The cadets looked at each other. The instructors had often rammed home the maxim that to win battles, you had to seize the initiative and keep it against all odds.

They'd just surrendered initiative to the alien and they all knew it.

"The pain device is still operating," said Tawfiq as if the cadets couldn't hear the Aux's screams. "It is intended to give a sharp shock. Prolonged use leads to neural pathways frying. Your fellow human will soon go from being a lowly cog in a Hardit machine to being a worn out old part that will need grinding down into components and recycled."

"What do you mean by recycled?" asked Majanita.

Tawfiq was in no hurry to reply. They listened as the Aux breached a threshold of endurance. His screams dulled and his writhing slowed.

"Tell me, humans, have you ever seen an auxiliary who was old, or injured, or otherwise functioning poorly?" Tawfiq looked at all three in turn as that Aux's screams turned to low groans. "You can't tell one Aux from another, can you? See how little you value your own kind. Well, let me inform you that you will never see an auxiliary who is unfit because such an individual has no net worth. You humans breed like vermin, which is why you need regular culling. Your human lives are cheap to spend and expensive to maintain."

Madge pointed an accusing finger at the alien. "You evil vecks. You cull the Aux?"

"Give Tawfiq the box, Arun," screamed Springer.

"And Marines too," Tawfiq told Majanita. "We cull you too, of course."

What? For a moment Arun forgot the Aux.

"No," said Springer. "You're wrong. Marines in the reserve are stored in ice."

"Stupid human. We build the ice boxes. That was my job once, in better days. We know how fast you breed and we know how many ice boxes we make. You breed faster than we can make boxes and the insect filth can build their tunnels. The older humans were even more pathetic than you slightly modified versions. Why use a valuable icebox to store an inferior model when you upgraded humans are so plentiful?"

"Wait till we tell our superiors about this," said Arun.

"No, Arun, we can't wait," shouted Springer. "Give her the box. And, corporal, you need to do as she asks."

By now the Aux worker's struggles had died away to an occasional twitch.

Tawfiq spoke to Madge as if oblivious to the life or death drama unfolding. "Do you really think your superiors don't already know?"

Arun couldn't take it anymore. He gave a last ineffectual jab at the control box before handing it over to the Hardit.

"Turn it off," he begged.

"I have machine lubricant on my footwear," she responded. "Clean it off with your tongue. Then I will consider your request."

Throbbing with humiliation, and fighting off his combat-tuned instincts that urged him to punch this veck, Arun sank to his knees, head bowed.

Tawfiq kicked him in the teeth. Not hard but enough to leave a copper tang in Arun's mouth.

He glanced across at the Aux. Froth was coming from his mouth. He was choking.

"First," said Tawfiq, "you must ask permission in the correct manner."

"Please mistress. May I lick your boots clean?"

"Good enough," said the Hardit. She tapped away at the control box, and the Aux went limp. "The Aux is free from pain."

Arun rose into a threatening crouch.

"Wait!" shouted the Hardit. "I have set the device to inflict a lethal dose of pain in eight minutes. If I am satisfied with your efforts then I shall postpone this worker's death sentence by another eight minutes while the next one of you learns your place. If you kill me, you'll kill your precious Aux. Now get licking."

Arun knelt back down, stuck out his tongue, and set to work.

—— Chapter 26 ——

Arun stood at attention, flanked by Madge and Springer. In front of them, sitting at a polished desk of real wood, was Staff Sergeant Bryant, the senior NCO for the battalion. Sergeant Gupta stood behind his superior.

Also there, to Arun's mounting horror, was Instructor Rekka. Arun had hardly seen her since that day in the colonel's office when her superior, Nhlappo, had been demoted. Rekka would be loving this chance to plant evil thoughts in the heads of the NCOs.

At least Bryant had the decency to let Arun explain what they had discovered about Hortez, about the despicable way the Hardits treated their human workers.

There was no mulling over Arun's words. No heavy sighs through steepled fingers. Bryant's reply was instant and unadorned.

"The stories of individual Aux are news to me but of no interest. The wider fact of Aux mistreatment by the Hardits is known by Detroit NCOs.

I fantasize about throttling those wretched monkey-vecks with my bare hands, but the weak cannot openly threaten the strong. And the hand we humans have to play here is even weaker than you can imagine. Therefore there will be no more talk of using even non-lethal force against the Hardits."

"But, staff sergeant—" pleaded Springer. She meant to go on, but Gupta silenced her with a curt shake of his head. Bryant chose to ignore her.

"Your actions today have brought a formal complaint from the local Hardit leader," said Bryant. "Instructor Rekka has known you for years. Sergeant Gupta has known you for only a few weeks. Even though the handover from your instructors has formally completed, I requested Instructor Rekka to advise me on suitable punishments."

I bet she did, thought Arun.

"You three are to work as auxiliaries for a week. God help you."

"This cadet begs permission to speak, staff sergeant," asked Springer.

"Granted."

"Hortez is one of our own. What about: *No Marine left behind?*"

"He is an auxiliary. A reject. He is not a Marine."

Bryant sighed and slumped a little. He wasn't enjoying this. "It's a hard galaxy," he said, "and if you survive your punishment I hope it teaches you this lesson. Do not expect justice in this life. Fight for it. Build for it over centuries. But never assume justice as your right, because if you do, you will be sorely disappointed. You, McEwan, should know that more than any here after Chief Instructor Nhlappo tried to teach you that only a few weeks ago."

Rekka started chewing them out for forgetting they were all slaves. Arun wasn't really listening. His mind was on Tawfiq and her brutal monkey friends, who would be waiting for Arun to come into their clutches. He might not survive their welcome. Since Pedro had put the idea into his head that someone was drugging the cadets, if he died, he would take that secret with him. He had to speak out about the drugs now.

"Staff sergeant?"

"Speak."

Arun looked into his superior's eyes. Could he trust the NCO? What about Gupta and Rekka?

"Well?" snapped Bryant.

He daren't trust Bryant. If the staff sergeant were a traitor, Arun would be condemning Springer and Madge to death too. No, it was too risky. "I'm meant to be playing in a Scendence match this week."

Gupta's fists clenched. Bryant's lips clenched into a tight, white line, and he glared with such intensity that Arun felt he was being sliced by a laser cutter. The senior NCO seemed to come to a decision. "You know, I must be crazy, but even though you've not listened to a word I just said, I'm going to cut you slack this one time, and pretend I didn't hear you. Despite demonstrating stupidity at every level, you did show good fighting spirit in confronting that Hardit. One day, you might make an adequate Marine. You're all to report to Auxiliary Camp Delta at 07:00 hours tomorrow for a 7-day reassignment. Short of murder, suicide, or insurrection, your orders are to obey every Hardit instruction to the letter."

"Yes, staff sergeant," they chorused.

"This cadet begs permission to speak, staff sergeant," said Arun.

Bryant frowned. He looked about to rip Arun to shreds but then stopped himself. "Granted, because I'm incredulous. What the hell could you possibly think I need to hear?"

"Thank you, staff sergeant. I am also ordered to attend a Trog liaison meeting next week. Colonel Little Scar ordered me to—"

"Yes, I know what the colonel wants of you. Very well. I shall inform the Hardits. Attend your liaison meeting but do not dally."

"Thank you, staff sergeant."

Bryant stared at the cadets, looking them up and down as if they were something foul he'd scraped off the sole of his boot. There was something wrong about the performance. When Rekka glared at you, her contempt ran solidly from her face down into the core of her soul. But not Bryant. He seemed worried.

For a moment, Arun nearly changed his mind again and confessed his suspicions about the cadet drugging. Then Bryant shook his head and hardened his face. The moment was gone.

"Learn your lesson well," ordered Bryant. "Stay alive. Dismissed!"

As Arun saluted and marched off to his fate, he felt bile rise. He nearly choked with the horror of what he was about to walk into. All his life, the truth of his slavery had been something he could push to the perimeter of his existence. This was different. Beatings, torture, malnutrition, and kissing the boots of your mistress – that's what awaited him. It wasn't the prospect of pain and injury that twisted his gut: it was the shame.

How had humans sunk so low?

Then a far better question hit him, and a lightness came to his step.

How could humans rise up again?

—— PART II ——

Operation Clubhouse

Human Legion
INFOPEDIA

Military Concepts

– Static defenses/ Defensive Warrens

If you're not familiar with star system defense strategies, then you probably think that defensive warrens, such as the infamous Detroit – constructed for our predecessors and rivals, the Human Marine Corps, on Tranquility – are designed to defend against an invader.

It's an understandable mistake. But you would still be wrong.

In fact, the primary objective of warren designers is to build a structure that will be destroyed.

Sure, the warren will have embrasures and powered hardpoints for heavy weapons, not to mention armor and force shields, and workshops buried deep beneath the surface capable of adding to the stockpiles of vehicles, weapons and ordnance.

And, yes, in addition to the broad spineways and transit corridors, wide enough for grav tanks to charge through, the narrower passageways twist and turn back on themselves so that invading troops will not only become lost, but will constantly be checking their rear for a counter attack that could come from any direction.

Then there is the key to the kind of strongly-garrisoned warren at Detroit: self-contained hab-disks that can seal themselves off for years before drilling their way to the surface and spilling out a company-sized unit of defenders bent on revenge. Hundreds of hab-disks will most likely survive the death rained from the skies by conventional munitions. They would be like weeds forever reappearing on a patch of ground you thought you'd cleared.

Warrens are built so strongly, that a better approach for an invader is to stay in orbit and play a longer game. They could douse the planet with so many dirty nukes that the planet is left a sterile, irradiated husk for millions of years to come – let's see if the hab-disks can wait that one out!

Or, if you have the tech, you could use gamma beams rather than nukes to do the same job.

But simplest by far is to nudge the orbits of comets and asteroids to slam into the besieged planet, a rain of destruction unrelenting for years.

In other words, to destroy a defensive warren, you'll probably have to destroy the planet.

Which is what the warren designers want.

Why?

Because forcing your enemy to destroy your planet denies it to him.

And if he can't use your planet for himself, why bother invading in the first place?

Unfortunately for the defenders, that logic doesn't always work: far too many wars are driven by hatred, not economic calculation.

And the story of how our galaxy's civilizations rise and clash plays out over such extended timescale that they can scarcely be conceived by humans – at least the original ones derived from *Homo sapiens*.

But the aliens who design the warrens have been around far longer than us, long enough to know one thing with statistical certainty.

If they build their warren well, then the day will surely come when it will be destroyed, along with the planet it has doomed.

Further reading

If you delve deeper into Detroit's history and design, you will soon smack up against security walls. It's no secret that Detroit held a lot of secrets. And if you need to ask what they are, you definitely don't need to know.

But whatever mysteries Detroit might have hidden in its depths, in its upper levels and hab-disks – Detroit was built as a defensive warren.

And when the invasion did finally come, it proved a tough nut to crack.

—— Chapter 27 ——

The domain of Auxiliary Team Beta lay through a restricted access side tunnel off Corridor 710 on Level 5. During their years at novice school, the cadets had used this corridor countless times, but there had never been a reason to explore the restricted passageways leading into the unknown.

Arun had expected his punishment detail would have to cross a guard post or input a security code into a locked hatch. There was none of that. The only physical barrier to prevent the curious from exploring the area was the stench. Cadets were used to showering two or three times per day. They were now entering the realm of the unwashed.

"Hello!" called Springer. "Is anybody there?"

A minute later, a dreary figure in heavily soiled overalls, that might once have been dark blue, appeared from out of the poorly lit passageway and beckoned them to follow.

"Hi," greeted Madge as they walked to meet the figure. "What's your name?"

The Aux ignored her.

It was a woman, decided Arun, a girl. Like the cadets, she was probably still in her teens, though Arun found it impossible to be sure. The overalls hung very heavily over her shoulders, more like armor than clothing. Her face was gaunt and soiled, her hair crudely cropped.

If the spark of life had dimmed in Hortez's eyes, it was guttering in the girl's, kept alive by the simmering heat of sly resentment.

None of the cadets tried again to strike up a conversation. They followed the auxiliary in silence as she led them along a long corridor, ever deeper into their banishment.

To either side were mostly closed doors, but one door had been removed allowing Arun a glimpse of a vehicle park of sorts. Instead of the hovertanks and strike flitters he's seen in other parks, here were trolleys on casters and sit-on cleaning trucks that actually looked kind of fun.

They hadn't even reported in yet but already Arun was feeling an urgent need to lighten the mood of this death march. The Hardits were humorless bullies whose language translator AIs weren't enough to stop them sounding like bumbling idiots when talking to humans. The next week was not going to be pleasant, but it would at least involve Arun mocking the hell out of the hairy monkey-vecks.

Just as he was thinking of something smart to say – anything to break the doom-filled silence – Springer beat him to it. She sprinted ahead and dodged through a door that had been left ajar.

Arun followed, hot on her heels.

A light flickered on as soon as Springer entered the room, revealing it to be a workshop. There were banks of metal boxes, neatly labeled. Tools and power sockets dangled from the ceiling over scarred workbenches.

"Hey, Arun," said Springer. "Remember the workshops on Level 9?"

He grinned back. Their class had been shown around the workshops where repairs were made for weapons mounted on the orbital defense platforms. This Aux workshop was suited more to fixing shelves, or maybe a leaky tap. But that was all right. Taps and shelves weren't as impressive as a 60 Gigajoule Fermi Cannon, but even such humble equipment had their own part to play in the life of the Corps.

Springer and Arun grinned at each other, a connection that extended for several invigorating seconds. *They were going to get through this okay.*

Wandering off for a few moments hardly counted as a great victory for oppressed humanity, but it put Arun in the mood for ripping the hell out of the Hardits.

Bring 'em on. I'll handle them.

He rejoined Madge and the Aux woman. As they pushed farther along the corridor, the air filled ever thicker with the heavy odors of unsanitized humanity.

Eventually they entered a rectangular room that had the same dimensions as the dorms in the hab-disks, though this room appeared much larger at first because there were no racks, armory cupboards or head.

There was a far more serious difference: dorms in the hab-disks housed eight cadets. In this room were fifty human auxiliaries lined up in two rows. They were hunched, faded skeletons more than people. The men, and boys old enough, wore matted beards.

"You are slightly early." The artificial voice came from the only Hardit in the room, a creature in dark blue overalls like the humans, except the Hardit's was relatively clean and, while still rough material, hung more like clothing than semi-rigid armor. The voice was male, but Arun knew that didn't prove anything.

"I am not impressed, though," said the Hardit. "Your species cowers in filth of its own fear. It is this fear that drove you here double fast, not respect for your better. By the time I have finished with you, I will teach you respect and justify your fear. Now remove clothing." The alien gestured at the Aux who had led them in. "Number 87 will provide you with new uniforms."

The cadets started stripping off their fatigues while the girl who had led them here – Number 87 – went over to a box in the back corner of the room and came back bearing three sets of soiled overalls.

"Those too, you dumb vecks," urged 87, when the cadets hesitated to remove their underwear. "As if anyone cares here."

Arun complied. But when, naked, he reached for his new overalls, his eyes popped wide. Number 87 had lied. *She* cared that they stripped off completely, but in a freak-out way. As soon as the cadets discarded their clothes, she scooped them up. Once she had the full set, she flung most them into a heap of sacking, blankets and clothing piled up in one corner of the room, but kept a few items to one side.

Was this a pile of bedding?

For the briefest of moments, the idea tickled Arun that one of these Aux would enjoy his underwear for a pillow tonight. Then he looked again at the occupants of the room. Were 53 people really going to sleep here in this one dorm? There was scarcely enough room for them all to stand.

"Hurry up or we'll all be in the drent," urged 87.

One of the Aux collapsed in a rasping sequence of coughs, attempting desperately to suppress them.

It was a reminder that Arun had new dorm-mates. He couldn't help but begin to feel responsible for them.

When he stepped into his new clothes, they felt oddly familiar – like a flak jacket, which was a crude form of armor with overlapping scales of toughened ceramo-plastics sandwiched between ablative and reflective layers.

"Which one of you threw the light-bang bomb?" asked the Hardit.

Arun raised an arm.

"Your attack caused me mild discomfort. Very little actually. I almost did not notice."

Liar!

"Nonetheless the idea that a human could attempt to harm superior sickens me to the tip of tail. Step forward!"

This was the moment Arun had dreaded. Worse! It hadn't occurred to him that it would be Tawfiq Woomer-Calix herself who would meet them. This was going to be personal.

The Hardit reached into a pouch slung on her waist.

What was it going to be? A stunner? Slow-acting poison? A whip? Maybe the creature thought humans deserved a particularly primitive form of torture, and was about to bring out a rusty knife.

The prospect of pain was something he could bear, but to stand and meekly take it… he wasn't sure he would be capable of that. The future that frightened him most was to end this punishment week alive but damaged. He would be no use as a cadet if he suffered permanent injury. They wouldn't take him back; he'd be stuck here forever.

All three cadets had made a pact. No goading the Hardits; no rising to their bait. They would suck up every bit of drent they were given and get out of here in one piece… unless he saw an opportunity to make the monkey-like aliens look like buffoons. He bet Springer would do the same.

Madge wouldn't. Even if a hidden traitor really was feeding his buddies with low-dose combat drug, it wouldn't change her. When she needed to be, Madge was as hard as a kinetic torpedo. She would stay professional throughout while Springer and he would need to goof around to cope. That was why Springer was his best buddy and Madge was his section leader.

The Hardit brought out a phial of liquid, which she dipped her thumb into and then smeared over a square fabric patch stitched into the breast of Arun's overalls.

Tawfiq replaced the phial and brought out two more – there were dozens in that pouch – mixed them together and smeared the resulting paste onto the fabric patch.

"You are designated number 106," Tawfiq told Arun. "Return to your place."

While Madge and Springer were given the same treatment, numbered 109 and 114 respectively, Arun looked at his breast. Of the alien's fluid there was no sign, but now he looked closer he could make out his new name, 106, marked in faded human numerals.

"Approach your mistress, 106."

Arun obeyed.

Tawfiq stared at him along her long snout. She appeared disappointed that he held her three-eyed gaze and glared back for all he was worth. Being a head taller than his all-powerful mistress made that a helluva lot easier.

"Keep looking into my eyes," she ordered. As Tawfiq spoke, she lifted her tail and snaked it around behind her. Strips of the rough fabric used in their overalls were wrapped around her tail from its base to a hand's width from its tip, which was left bare. The tip was flattened but curled in on itself like a rolled tongue.

Suddenly the tip whipped through the air and smacked into Arun's left cheek. He was still gasping with shock when the tail whipped back behind the Hardit and slapped him on the right.

This time, Arun was ready for it.

He hadn't broken eye contact with the alien. It was a pathetically small victory, but at this point he'd take what he could get.

After that came a steady rhythm of slaps from the Hardit's tail.

On the spectrum of torture implements he had steeled his nerve against, this slapping barely registered. In fact he suspected it hurt the creature's tail more than his cheek. It was the surprise that had made him gasp.

But that didn't mean it was easy. To stand and take a beating, however feeble it might be, filled Arun with shame. *What kind of Marine would crawl to these ugly creatures?* He bit his lower lip. His body started to shake with the effort to keep from punching that stupid alien veck between its three ugly eyes.

There was a bulbous projection on the end of the Hardit's snout that he assumed was her nose. Arun pictured grabbing that nose in his hand and pulling with every ounce of strength. Would it come off? His hands clenched with the thought. He hoped it would only come half off. Yes, that was even better.

"Return to your place."

Arun came back to himself, realizing his breathing was fast and shallow. He stepped back, still not breaking eye contact.

He was daring the alien to break eye contact with *him*.

"109, come here for whipping."

Madge stepped up and Tawfiq started to beat her the same way.

Arun was still seething with humiliation, quaking with all the anger that had pumped through his muscles but had nowhere to go.

By contrast, Madge barely seemed to register what Tawfiq was doing, which only made Arun feel more humiliated.

Standing there and taking it was bad, but to watch his friend take her slapping was far harder. They were part of a team. Even though Madge thought him no better than pond scum right now, they still looked out for each other. But Arun could only stand there and shake with impotence.

"109 is female, isn't that so, 106?"

"Right," said Arun.

"She has long and yellow hair does not she?"

"Yes." *Your translator isn't worth drent, Hardit.*

"And human males find that very attractive in human females, don't you… *114?*"

114? That was Springer!

Springer didn't answer. Arun couldn't entirely blame her. Did this monkey creature really think she was a guy? Hadn't Tawfiq just seen Springer naked? Actually, come to think of it, the alien hadn't been paying much attention. Just wait till he got back and told Osman.

"Answer," ordered Tawfiq. The voice coming through her speaker was calm, but the alien was twitching with agitation. "Are you attracted to this female's hairs?"

"Yes," said Springer. "Her yellow hairs fill me with such extreme lust that I often faint with the desire to caress them."

Steady on, Springer. Don't push it.

The alien paused, probably to translate Springer's words, before addressing Arun. "And you, 106?"

"Sure," he replied. "109 has pretty hairs and looks really hot.

"I wonder," said Tawfiq, "whether 109 will still *look really hot* by the time I have finished her whipping." The Hardit sped up her tail swipes. "Shall we see?"

The artificial voice was expressionless, but Arun couldn't help but imagine a sly quality to it. A gloating that Arun longed to smack out of the creature. He looked at the lineup of Aux, searching for support, but they glanced away, pretending not to see, or looked bored as if they'd seen it all before. Only Hortez watched from the back row, anger sketched onto his face.

"Keep watching, 106!" The Hardit's artificial voice did not change its expression, but the alien's anger registered as a louder volume. "This is only a gentle introduction to your program of torture."

Madge began to blink. Then she sneezed. The tail had whipped her cheek unerringly but with the sudden movement of the sneeze, it cut into her nose, bringing out a stream of blood. The Hardit's striking tail smeared the beads of red over Madge's cheeks.

Arun bore it for another half dozen swipes, but the sight of his friend smeared in her own blood was too much.

"Okay," he told the Hardit, "you've made your point."

The alien stopped. "The human speaks. What does it mean?"

"I said you've made your point. You're the boss. We'll do what you say. There's no point in carrying on hitting her."

"Oh, but there is. You are just too stupid to understand yet. But you shall."

Glaring at him all the time, Tawfiq's tail curled around her waist and touched a device at her hip.

Every muscle in Arun's body contracted at once. His diaphragm squeezed the air from his lungs. His knees pressed hard against his chest and he fell to the ground, unable to do anything but silently scream against the pain wracking his body.

Then the pressure released enough for him to draw a breath, and relax the clamp that his jaw had become. No wonder the overalls hung so heavily; they contained an electro-shocker system.

Before he had time to speak, the pain was back and his own muscles had been turned against him again, compressing him into a ball. He rolled over in a feeble attempt to escape the Hardit, who he thought was kicking him, but it was difficult to know what was going on since all that mattered was the need to breathe because the Hardit veck was enjoying this too much to release him from the pain. Steam blew out his mouth. Something was smoldering. It might be his skin or teeth or maybe the hairs over his body but it didn't matter anymore because…

Then he was breathing the sweet, sweet air. Gulping at it greedily, petrified that each breath would be his last.

It took some time for Arun to fully come back to his senses.

"Stand!" Tawfiq ordered.

Arun struggled to his feet.

"I assure you that I have not hit 109 while you were incapacitated." Tawfiq advanced on Arun and pressed her snout up into his face. Her breath stank of stale cabbage and fresh feces.

She growled in her throat. Then the speaker attached to her collar elaborated: "I did not wish you to miss any of 109's pain."

Tawfiq went back to slapping Madge.

After only half a dozen swipes, the beating was interrupted when another Hardit walked in. Tawfiq switched off her translator unit and the two aliens argued in their own growling speech. Their tails touched and stroked each other. Then, without any change in their conversation, their tails stretched longer and thinner and snaked through gaps in their overalls to caress each other's body.

When they began rubbing with their tails, the tone of their voices softened, taking on a crooning quality.

Arun managed to be both disgusted by the lewd alien display and grateful for the interruption to their torture.

The respite only lasted a minute or so before the two aliens broke off contact.

"I enjoyed your pain," said Tawfiq in her artificial human male voice. "But we must save the rest of the female's beating until later. Humans, you have work to do."

Tawfiq gave out the day's assignments. The newcomers were each paired with an experienced Aux, and Arun thought his luck had changed slightly when he realized he was to be paired with Hortez.

But then Madge thumped him painfully in the ribs as they walked out into the passageway.

"Thanks for nothing, you dongwit."

"What? What did I do?"

"Monkey-bitch was obviously trying to goad you. *Watch me strike this attractive female. How does that make you feel?* Well, didn't take long for us to find out, genius? Did it?"

"I got it worse than you, didn't I?"

Madge grabbed him by the shoulders and span him around, forcing Arun to look into her beautiful, blood-spattered face.

"Tawfiq wants your ass. You've just let her know that beating me is a perfect way to get to you. So guess who's going to get beaten and humiliated every chance that monkey-bitch gets."

"Lay off him," protested Springer.

At least someone doesn't hate me, thought Arun.

"Oh, I'm sorry, cadet. Did I say something horrible to your boyfriend?"

Springer stiffened at that but said nothing.

"What would you know anyway?" Madge snapped. "Monkey-bitch took one look and assumed you were a boy. If you ever wondered about your looks, then wonder no more, sister."

Arun watched in horror as his friends squared up to each other, violence in their eyes.

"Keep your mouth shut, McEwan," whispered Hortez. "Let them sort it out. I might be down and nearly out, but I still understand women better than you do. Besides, once you've finished being Tunnel-Aux scum, Madge will be your cadet NCO again. She needs to remind both of you who's in charge."

Springer and Madge broke contact and stormed off down the corridor so fast that the Aux they were supposed to be following had to run to keep up with their charges.

Hortez slowed, grabbing Arun's sleeve to encourage him to do the same. "Let them go," said Hortez "Try to make things right with them tonight. And don't be too hard on yourselves. Breaking us is about the only pleasure the Hardits have. They've gotten quite good about it."

Arun slapped his friend on the back. "I'm thinking," he hissed.

It was good to hear his friend talk when he'd pretty much given Hortez up for dead, but Arun wanted quiet to think.

Most people when they got angry just wanted to hit something, their higher order cognitive functions on temporary leave of absence. Software system architecture design, problem solving, strategic planning – these were off the menu until the fight or flight hormones had been purged from their system.

Arun was like that too – most of the time. But maybe Arun was an experimental rewiring, a test subject for the human re-engineering program. Because he could take all that anger and shunt the energy into his mind, making it whirl and dance in ways that were normally beyond him.

And that's what happened now.

The Hardits had humiliated the cadets, but had revealed many weaknesses as they did so. Inside his head, Arun pictured a mindscape of possibilities. Opportunities to exploit those Hardit weaknesses were laid out across this mindscape, scores of them. Arun knew better than to box in his thinking with conscious thought, so he unleashed his mind to roam wherever it wanted, testing the strength of those possibilities, rejecting most, promoting some. Extrapolating. Dreaming.

By the time his mind calmed, its task completed, he'd only progressed ten paces along the corridor. He couldn't point to any definite plan. Not yet. Nothing like that conviction that had told him to connect to Xin through Scendence. All the same, he was confident that seeds of revenge had been planted in his head, ready to sprout and bloom when the time was right.

He grinned, even though his mind felt bruised by its effort.

This was going to be a week the Hardits would never forget.

—— Chapter 28 ——

As far as Arun was concerned, when you pooped indoors, you did your business, flushed, and went on with your day. What happened after you flushed had never occurred to him.

Until now.

Banishment to the Aux underclass had already opened his eyes to some of the least glamorous aspects of life in Detroit.

Opened his eyes and made them water with the stench.

That first morning with Hortez, Arun learned what happened after you flushed.

Aux Team Beta was based near the regimental school on Level 5. At seven years old, the most promising kids were enrolled in the school as its new intake of novices. There the children fought, trained and competed to graduate as cadets at the age of 17.

Until a few weeks earlier, Hortez and the rest of Blue Squad had still been novices, sleeping in a 50-bed dorm not five minutes' walk from Team Beta's base. Now, for his first assignment as an Aux, Arun was back, helping Hortez to transfer novices' rotting excrement from the collection vats into wheeled storage tanks. It had been one of these slurry carts that Hortez had been pushing when Arun had first chanced across him on his bike.

Tawfiq had tasked them with clearing out one latrine block in the morning and another in the afternoon. That hadn't sounded too hard, but then Arun had assumed they would be cleaning out a single day's filth.

They weren't.

Underneath the latrines were collection vats where the output of several hundred novice backsides accumulated for 2-3 weeks before the Aux emptied them. The putrid stench hit Arun the moment he opened the door to the access passageway.

The vats were primed with an automated suffusion of bacteria, engineered to rapidly transform the dung into fertilizer, readily digestible by both the crops grown topside by human Agri-Aux, and the Troggie fungus farms in dark underground caverns.

For the first few trips, Arun and Hortez fitted hoses to drainage taps and allowed the lumpy liquid to drain into the tanks of their dung carts. The foul slurry stank and splashed but they wiped themselves off as best they could, and pushed the carts up the long looping main ramp of Helix 1, and then out past the watching Marines of Gate 5 to a topside facility. There they emptied their contents into wagons with sprayer attachments that would be towed by the Agri-Aux to their fields.

Arun had been grateful for the fresh air once they reached the surface, but Hortez had picked up pace, eager to get under cover. He'd already explained that without the protective spray of the shower block oils, Tranquility's sun burned.

Arun thought his friend was making a drama out of all this sun-worry, especially after they emerged into a topside deeply shadowed by the mountains. Even in half-light, the peeling skin and weeping sore on Hortez's cheek were now more obvious, more than enough to convince Arun to follow his friend's example by pulling his hat low and keeping to the deepest shadows. He prayed they never sent him out beyond the protective shield of the mountains.

After their third trip, the latrine slurry stopped flowing and there was no choice but to open the hatch. They got in and shoveled, the brown goop slapping around their calves and sucking at their every step. The sight of endless gallons of semi-putrefied dung churned Arun's stomach so much that he vomited the contents of his stomach into the vat. The wet slurping noise as they dug out another shovel-full was merely disgusting; far more sickening was the toxic stench. In the end, they took it in turns, one spending five minutes shoveling while the other recovered, breathing the air outside. The same putrid access passageway air that had so horrified Arun at the beginning was now sweet-smelling relief, compared with the miasma inside the vat.

A couple more trips later and Arun's sense of smell had been so violated that it finally shut down in protest.

He might not be able to smell his own stench any longer, but it became clear that other people could. They chanced across two novice boys skulking in the passageway outside at the end of a return trip back to the vats. The lads – Arun put them at about 14 – made a show of wrinkling their noses in disgust.

One of the boys placed himself in the middle of the tunnel, barring their way. "Apologize," he ordered.

His friend joined him. "Yeah, say sorry for offending decent people with your Aux stink."

Arun and Hortez halted their carts a short distance away from the roadblock.

"I'm sorry, sir," said Hortez. "Please let us pass."

Arun looked in horror at his friend. Then he turned his attention to the boys. Could he pick up these novices and shove them into the vat of dung? Probably. He started thinking through the consequences.

"You!" The first boy pointed at Arun. "You have to apologize too."

Arun scowled back.

"C'mon, man," Hortez whispered to him. "We've got more to worry about than your stupid pride."

"Sometimes it is only pride that keeps us fighting through adversity."

"You can cut that Marine Corps drent out right away," hissed Hortez. "That doesn't apply to me anymore, or had you forgotten?"

"We're waiting," said the second boy. "Do we have to report you?"

"Do it for my sake," Hortez insisted.

Arun clenched his jaw in fury. He was going to do it. He really was…

Gazing blankly into the middle distance he said vaguely: "I'm sorry."

"Not good enough," said the first boy.

"Yeah, like that would convince anyone," said his friend. "Kneel down and kiss my boots. No, you stink too much. Kneel down five paces in front of me and… and lick the floor." He laughed. So did his little veck of a friend.

That was too much! The stupid skangat was going headfirst into the collection vat and damn the consequences.

Arun had only taken one step toward the nearest boy when they were interrupted by the sound of laughter. Another two novices emerged from farther up the corridor, a boy and a girl, also about 14. When they saw what was happening, the laughter stopped. The new boy shook his head sadly and put his hands on his hips. "What do you think you're up to, Rammy?"

The two bullies looked crestfallen as they glanced at each other, trying to work out how to play the situation. They withered under the disapproving glare of the other novices.

Arun was convinced he knew what he was seeing now. These kids had arranged to meet up for a little privacy. A double date during a gap between classes.

"Well?" demanded the girl. "Why are you causing trouble, Stephan? You know you're already on a warning."

"We're punishing these Aux," replied Stephan without conviction.

"They deserve it," said the other boy, Rammy. "For olfactory offenses." He couldn't help laughing.

"It's not funny," said the unnamed boy. "Leave them alone. They can't help being Aux."

"Can't they?" said Stephan. "I reckon they can. You're not born an Aux. You become one because you're a loser." He addressed Hortez and Arun. "You are losers, aren't you?"

Hortez answered without hesitation. "Yes, sir."

"Why're you a loser?" Rammy asked him. "What didja do?"

"No, don't answer that," the girl told Hortez.

"Why shouldn't he, Ibri?" asked Rammy.

"Because I don't want to hear any of the ways in which we could end up like them. Besides, you're an utter skangat, Ramdas Tammaro. I expect Stephan put you up to this and you were too pussy to stand up to him. You're better than this."

"I don't plan on being a loser," said Ramdas. There was steel in his voice. Arun reckoned he'd already worked out that his date was a wash out. *Tough luck, you mark.*

"Yeah? Well, I don't expect those two did either," said his date, "but look where they ended up all the same."

"I still say they're frakking losers," said Ramdas.

His date glared back, daring him to retract.

Then the other boy upped the stakes. "Apologize to those poor guys," he demanded.

Arun glanced at Hortez. His friend was wearing a glazed expression as if he weren't entirely there. Arun was beginning to see how that worked. Here was an argument going on right in front of their faces. On the surface, at least, the argument was about the two Aux, but the truth was that they weren't really part of the exchange. As Aux, they were expected to wait there in silence until their betters permitted them to go about their business.

Only yesterday, if he'd come here wearing his cadet's fatigues, the novices would have stepped politely aside out of his way. Well, he decided, he was still the same person as the day before. And so he spoke up.

"There's no harm done," Arun said. "Let us go on our way."

"Stay where you are," ordered the girl. She redirected her glare at Arun, if anything, intensifying it. "You're not going anywhere until these two idiots say sorry."

Eventually, after much sighing and rolling of eyes, Stephan and Ramdas made grunting sounds that their dates decided to interpret as apologies. Hortez and Arun were allowed to get back to the collection vat.

They didn't speak for a long time, the only sound the squeak of the dung cart wheels and the slurp and plop of shoveling slurry.

"At first I didn't know what was worse," said Hortez eventually, "the novices who try to grind our face in the dirt, or the ones who pity us. Now? There's no contest. The ones who pity us sometimes throw us scraps to eat. I gulp down every morsel and thank them with every mouthful."

Arun couldn't think of a reply. He wasn't a hero. He wasn't special. It was only the hope that they would let him back into the hab-disks in a few days that separated Arun from Hortez. If he had to stay here forever, he had no doubt he would soon be begging for scraps himself.

And worst of all, it had been him who had gotten Hortez kicked out of the battalion in the first place.

He wracked his mind, trying to think of a way to help out his old friend, hoping his subconscious had worked its planning magic.

But he couldn't. Hortez's plight was hopeless.

The only question was whether Arun and the girls would be joining him.

—— Chapter 29 ——

That evening, Arun, Springer and Madge joined the roll call of 52 Aux workers, lined up in the back row. They were short one worker, Number 47 having gone off to the kitchen to fetch the evening meal.

Instead of Tawfiq, another Hardit took the roll call. From the faded blue dye in her mane, Arun identified her as Hen Beddes-Stolarz. Hortez had explained before Hen came in that she was as bored by dealing with the human workers as Tawfiq was thirsty for cruelty.

No words were spoken. The Hardit simply stood in front of the lineup, sniffing the scent markers smeared onto the breasts of the humans, and glancing from time to time at the softscreen she was holding.

All of them, Hen included, waited in silence for Number 47, who eventually returned wheeling a catering trolley bearing two metal buckets. One contained stale bread, the other held scraps left behind by the novices from their evening meal.

It wasn't much for 53 people. It wouldn't even feed 10.

Springer cleared her throat. "Mistress, I beg permission to speak."

Hen flicked her ears. Whether that meant interest or anger was something Arun had yet to learn. But when the Hardit walked over to Springer and gave her a sniff, she said in her artificial voice of a human male: "114. A new one. Yes, human, you may speak."

"Forgive my ignorance," said Springer, "but that food is insufficient nutrition for 50 humans, and by adding our mouths to your team, it is even less adequate. I can see that the workers of Auxiliary Team Beta are malnourished. May we please have more food rations so that we may work harder for you?"

Hen closed her eyes but said nothing.

What was Springer playing at? They'd agreed not to wind up the Hardits, to get out of here in one piece. Arun couldn't help admiring Springer, though, even if she was one stupid shunter.

If Tawfiq had been here, Arun had no doubt that she would have activated the pain function in Springer's suit. But Hen Beddes-Stolarz was different. She opened her eyes and waved her ears from side to side in a motion Hortez had told him indicated pleasure.

"You ask a valid question," Hen replied through her voice box, the artificial voice sounding so reasonable. "You argue that we overseers provide ineffective care for our work team. Your reasoning is not at fault, but your error is to start with the assumption that Work Team Beta consists of 53 individuals."

"Mistress, I do not understand."

"That is obvious, 114. Obvious and to be expected. It is your ignorance and stupidity that makes humans inferior. Team Beta's workforce consists of 22 humans. And yet I see 53 bodies when I include you new ones. What we have here is not an insufficient supply of food but an *over*-supply of workers. No, that is not quite right. *You* are suffering from oversupply. Team Beta has work for 22 individuals. We have accommodation and food for 22. The law of supply and demand is universal. Demand is fixed and so eventually supply must reduce to match demand."

"We don't even have food for 22, mistress," said 47 angrily. "Five thugs from Team Gamma – Cliffie's team – were waiting for me on the way back from the kitchens. They stole four of our food buckets."

"Excellent." Hen wiggled her ears. "Number 47 adds a well-timed additional dimension to this matter. We prefer our work teams to have the strongest individuals. Transferring workers between teams is simple. If you want the food back then prove you are strong enough to deserve it. Steal it back."

Springer didn't hesitate. "Team Beta!" she yelled. "Who's with me?"

To hear such fire in a human belly sent a jolt of surprise shooting through the Aux.

Arun and Madge were by Springer's side in an instant. Hortez hesitated for a moment before joining them.

A flicker of fire lit up the eyes of the other Aux.

"Don't forget, they'll be gone in a week," sneered Number 87 – the worker who'd stolen their clothes.

Her words snuffed out the Aux spirit, making them turn their heads and look away.

Hortez whispered into Springer's ear. "You're insane. And I don't mean that in a good way."

Madge ignored him and led the little team out of the room.

The Hardit made no move to stop them. Instead, she called out: "I do so love the spectacle of you humans fighting over scraps of food like flea-ridden, starving animals. Which, of course, is all you are."

The humans marched proudly away until they were out of sight. Then Madge halted.

"First question," she said. "Who the frakk is Cliffie?"

—— Chapter 30 ——

Arun took point as they stormed into Team Gamma's room. They identified Cliffie immediately. He was fat and clean shaven, the opposite of the males in Team Beta. Their room had the same discarded human clothing, except here the collection was much larger and had been neatly arranged into a crude staircase leading up to a seat. A throne, Arun realized, of tight rolls of clothing bound together by loose fabric strips.

Sitting on his throne was Cliffie.

The Gamma Aux were enjoying their meal. Arun counted eight buckets of food and 35 Aux. Team Beta outnumbered the bullies. It should be them dominating the smaller group, not the other way around!

Arun charged up the textile steps toward Cliffie. Before he reached the throne, Gamma proved their worth, dropping their meals to crowd the invaders. The four Aux who had been eating at Cliffie's feet now formed a protective wall between Arun's group and their leader.

So Cliffie had guards, and his team had discipline and full bellies. None of that was enough to stop Arun feeling this was ridiculous. The enemy was defending the crest of an artificial ridge constructed from dirty shirts and underwear. Insane! But Arun didn't doubt the look in their eyes that said they would defend this position to the death.

Madge had discussed tactics before they moved in. Success, they'd agreed, depended on speed. It was essential they overpowered Cliffie before his team could react.

This wasn't going well.

From the perspective of a full Marine, or even a cadet, the Aux were all failures for one reason or another. But as Arun felt the gaze of angry eyes pierce his body, he was well aware that everyone here was at least partially combat trained.

"We have guests," Cliffie said. He gestured at the crowd to back away. "Give them a little space to speak their piece."

Arun halted halfway up the steps, just outside of punching range of the guards. It had been Madge's idea for him to take the lead, to brutally pummel Cliffie into submission. She argued that one primal male brute ousting another would make the message clear in this primitive world. But the assumptions of macho brutishness crumbled in the face of reality. Three of Cliffie's guards were women, and Cliffie himself was clean and groomed, his voice soft and playful.

"Please," said Cliffie to Arun. "Speak."

Arun snarled his reply: "You took food that belonged to Team Beta."

"Yes." There was no malice in Cliffie's voice. He spoke as if explaining a simple truth to a child. "Did you come to inform me of this," he added while Arun was still thinking of a reply, "or did you want to ask me something?"

"Give us our food."

Cliffie tutted. "This is a grim place, to be sure, but there is no need to coarsen it with rudeness. Do I hear a please?"

"Are you mad? No, you don't get to *hear a please*. Politeness went out the door when you stole what wasn't yours."

Cliffie scratched his chin, making a play of chewing over Arun's words. "I've heard of you. Here on a forced vacation after making some ill-advised threats. Threats you did not follow up properly. But…" He stretched out his arms in a welcoming gesture. "There is no need for unpleasantness. Let me educate you. You speak of *stealing*. That is a legal term. The rule of law is very strong in the Auxiliary camps, my new friends, and our law is called *Natural Law*. Our law says that the strong must take from the weak. Team Gamma is stronger than Team Beta, and that gives us the right to take your food. There is no crime committed here. Permit me, if you will, a demonstration."

He held up one arm and clicked his fingers.

Cliffie's guards dove at Arun.

Arun picked out the one farthest from the wall and leaped at her, plucking her from the air and diving off the steps to the floor. The fall wasn't far but was enough for him to twist in midair so that when they hit the ground, the guard was beneath him and his knees pulled up into her gut, winding her.

He tried to press home his advantage by punching her in the face but one of the guards had grabbed him as he fell, and was now holding back his shoulders.

Arun's punch still thumped into the downed guard's nose, but there was no strength in his blow.

With a supreme effort he got to his feet despite the guard on his back who was throttling him, and the one on the ground grabbing at his legs.

Just as he was preparing to throw back his head to dislodge the guard on his back, the two he'd left behind on the steps fell upon him, dashing him to the ground. Pinned helplessly beneath their weight he could feel the weight of more Gamma Team Aux jump on him, kicking and punching.

Where was his backup? Then he spotted Springer and Madge, already pinned on the ground. Hortez was out of sight.

All he could do now was bring his arms up to offer a little protection for his head.

Arun was dazed. Under the crush of bodies, he was gasping for air. But even in that confused state he knew Gamma was only disabling him. They could easily have killed him but the pummeling stopped without serious damage. Instead, they hooded him, lifted him, and threw him onto one of the lower steps of the ramp of clothing. All the while, they kept enough of a crush of bodies on top that he couldn't scramble free.

He realized with a shiver of humiliation that he'd been hooded by a dirty pair of shorts. More clothing was thrown at him. The huge mound of clothing that Cliffie's throne sat atop was huge, far larger than Team Beta's collection and easily enough to suffocate someone.

Panic injected fresh energy into tired limbs. Arun tried to buck and writhe his way out, but the press was too heavy. He tried to dig out an air pocket but it was too late, the crush too strong. His desperate gasping for air had sucked in the dirty fabric of the shorts pressed into his face. But he didn't care because his head started swimming. His mind was slipping away.

He felt a brief flicker of regret for getting Springer and Madge into this mess and then… And then he was *breathing*. Through the filter of discarded underwear he was breathing air. The weight from his back was lifting. He managed to raise himself to all fours, to throw off the shorts around his head.

While Arun still knelt there with his head hung low, trying to come to terms with still being alive, he heard Cliffie crowing. "There, you see? A practical lesson in Natural Law. But your team are hungry, you say. We aren't heartless, are we Gamma?"

From around the room, all the Aux replied: "No, Cliffie."

"You, 45, give the pretty one an empty bucket. I want all of you to tear off a hunk of bread – a generous one, mind – and throw it onto the floor. If our guests want the food, they can pick it up and take it away."

The next few minutes were a nightmare that made Arun shake with shame. Every time they bent over to pick up some bread, they were kicked in the butt. So they took to scrambling around the floor on their knees, but Gamma took that as an invitation to ride on their backs, smacking their flanks and butts with cries to *giddy up!* That brought fresh waves of jeering from the crowd. The need for revenge burned ever hotter in Arun's gut.

They gave Team Gamma spectacular entertainment that night.

Gamma would pay for that!

<hr>

Once they had put a safe distance from Cliffie's team, they regrouped, the bucket of hard-won bread safely in Arun's hands. Hortez needed a rest. He was so weak he could barely walk.

Arun was fuming, unable to speak because he was too angry at having his ass kicked in every sense.

"What do we say to the others when we get back?" asked Springer.

"That's your call," replied Madge. "After all, it was your dumb idea to get Beta's food back."

"We tell the truth," Springer said through clenched teeth. "We got Beta more food. How we did it is none of their business."

—— Chapter 31 ——

"There's gotta be a Hardit weakness we can exploit." Arun scanned the slumped forms of the Beta Aux, but he couldn't detect any signs that his pleas were inspiring them. "C'mon, we've all been to the same school. We've been trained to look at a combat scenario and uncover the enemy's weak points."

"Don't you think we've tried," said a tired voice from a figure crumpled against the back wall.

"What's your name, friend?" Arun tried to pitch his words carefully: encouraging and friendly. It wasn't easy. He looked at these wretched almost-cadets. He felt pity for them, but more than that, anger. Fury that these people who were almost like him had been treated so foully, but even more rage that these pathetic specimens had allowed themselves to sink so low so quickly.

"Miller," replied the voice from the back wall. "Adrienne Miller." She sounded as if she had to search her memory for the name. Arun recognized the voice as the girl who had taken their clothes and sneered at their attempt to win back some food. Number 87.

"Well, Adrienne, I don't want to kick a girl when she's down," said Arun, "but there's one big difference between us and you. I fully intend to get out of this. That's tough on you but we all know it's true. I think my hope can spark inspiration, a fresh look at old problems. There's no harm in trying, eh?"

Adrienne simmered with resentment. Until he saw that look, Arun had recognized her voice from before but not her face. All the Aux had the same clothes, cropped hair, grimy faces and look of hopelessness. It was as if their personality had been abraded away, leaving worn stubs where once there had been people. Hortez had a little of his old flair left, and Adrienne had her resentment. Soon even those would be gone.

"How about rivalry?" suggested Madge. "Some Hardits are senior to others. That's got to mean resentment somewhere in the system."

"Never gonna work," said Hortez. "Sure they don't get along like perfect buddies. Sushantat is the number two. She resents Biljah who's in charge and so does no work. Tawfiq is treated like dirt by the others. We think she might be a lower caste. Hen thinks she's too good to be mucking out the humans. She's so deliberately lazy that she actually works hard at her laziness."

"Hold up," said Springer. "You've just given us a host of grievances. Sound like pretty much all the Hardits hate being here."

"That's right," said a new voice from the crowd. "But it won't help you. However big the divide between Hardit clans and individuals, it is nothing compared to the gulf between Hardits and humans. Most of them are arrogant, lazy, and cruel. But they aren't stupid. You'll never be able to play one off against another."

"But this *is* working," Madge insisted.

"Is it?" asked Adrienne.

"Sure it is." Madge sounded excited. "We're just getting started and already we've got a list. They're lazy. They're cruel–"

"–And we already know they struggle with the heavy air and don't like going topside," said Arun. He looked into the Aux faces. Most had turned away, already given up on the stupid newcomers. They'd taken the extra bread Springer's group had won from Cliffie, but that hadn't won the right to lead the group. Hortez was trying to look encouraging but wasn't doing a good job.

They were losing them.

"What about sex?" Arun said. That got a look of contempt and disgust, so he added quickly: "I mean between the Hardits. Are there any romances between them? A couple who would seize a chance to canoodle, thus giving us a chance to do something while they weren't looking?"

Hortez answered. "Forget it. Put Hardits together and they rub each other constantly. They don't understand privacy. I mean Sushantat will be talking to us, giving us a good yelling, and Hen or Tawfiq–"

"Or both," laughed Adrienne.

"Yeah, maybe both will be sneaking their tails inside Shushantat's overalls for a good fondle. Some of the guys think that's rubbing the team scent over each other, but I'm sure it's more than that."

"They're all females," added another voice from the crowd. "If we live long enough, we'll find out about mating season, but most of the time Hardit females and males avoid each other."

Hortez stood up. "I got something. Well, I think. I dunno…"

"C'mon, man," encouraged Arun. "Spit it out."

"It's like this. Looking after an Aux team is like mucking out the pigs."

"What are pigs?" Springer asked.

"An Earth animal," Hortez replied. "Doesn't matter. Point is, our overseers have sunk to the most demeaning job possible. They hate that. They take every opportunity to humiliate us because we're the only people even lower than them. I guess it's some kind of consolation."

"Brilliant!" Arun packed as much enthusiasm as he could as he slapped Hortez on the back. "Knew you'd come through for the team, man."

"He hasn't said anything useful yet," said Miller. "Besides. It's easy for you. *Oh, I'm so clever because I have all these fancy ideas.* You'll go back to your nice clean bunk in a week, sleeping on sheets laundered by an Aux slave, a belly filled with Aux-cooked food. How does any of this drent you've been talking actually help *me*?"

"I don't know yet, Adrienne. But I'm gonna come up with something. I promise."

Adrienne snorted. "What about you, 114?"

"Believe in him, sister," said Springer.

"I know he's annoying," added Madge. "Horden knows I'd leave him here behind with you if I could. He's unreliable, stupid, lazy…" She gave Arun a baleful stare. *"Disloyal.* Frankly, he's an imbecile whose head is ruled not by his brain but by something a few degrees south of there. But there is one thing I can't take away from him. When it comes to Scendence, he's the best Deception-Planning player I've ever seen. Some say his head is wired up like an organic battle computer. You all know that most scuttlebutt flying round the base is steaming with drent, but I am certain of one thing. If there's one person who can come up with a plan to improve your lives, it's Arun McEwan. You just need to give him a few facts to work on, and time to think."

Arun grimaced. He'd hoped to get some fresh ideas to feed into his planning brain. But he'd heard frakk all of any use and now even Madge was building him up into a messiah.

If he was going to come up with any bright ideas they'd better arrive soon, or he would be stuck in this stinking hole for the rest of his short life.

<h1 align="center">—— Chapter 32 ——</h1>

Arun leaned over and tapped Madge on the knee. "Hey, Corporal Majanita! Can I ask a question?" When she didn't immediately respond, he whispered: "Have you got a blade? I don't mean a weapon, just something that can cut."

Madge lifted the brim of her hat to give him the benefit of a foul look. "And I was having such a lovely dream."

"No you weren't. You had one eye open, watching that Adrienne. I don't blame you, either."

"Well, keep it quiet anyway," she whispered. "Springer's snoring away. I can feel her rumble through my back. She's sweet when she's asleep."

Arun tried to lean closer still to Madge without disturbing Hortez whose weight was heavy against Arun's spine. Like most of Team Beta, the newcomers slept back-to-back because with over 50 people in a room 8 meters by 4, there was no space to lie down. Even the strongest only managed to slump against the walls, using discarded clothing as a layer of insulation against the cold plastic skin of the wall and still wearing their dirty hats.

The initiation for newcomers varied depending on the mood of the Hardit overseers, but always included the order to strip naked, and don the heavy overalls through which they could send punishing shocks into their human workers. To wear any other item of clothing was punishable by death; the Hardits were very clear on that point.

At first Arun assumed the no-underclothing order was so the effect of the electric shocks wasn't diluted. That may be the case, but after the experiences of his first day, and talking with the Aux, he saw a new pattern of Hardit behavior.

The aliens had no qualms about inflicting pain, mutilation, and death, when it suited them, but they quickly tired of such things. What drove them was not sadism but the desire to lord it over the humans. The lower the Hardits could grind the humans into the dirt, the more superior they felt.

They could have destroyed the discarded human clothing, forcing them to shiver in the cold during their allotted sleep shift. Instead they were allowed to use the moldering and insect-ridden clothing as nesting material. The garments piled against the back wall during the day were now spread out over the floor and piled on top of the slumbering Aux. Forbidden to wear their own clothing, the humans were expected to be grateful for permission to burrow under these reminders of their shattered lives like feral animals.

The Hardit skangats found that very amusing.

By now, Arun had shuffled closer so he could whisper into Madge's ear, Hortez having slumped away to lean against the shoulder of another Aux.

"I know you, Madge," Arun whispered. "You're sneaky. Have you a blade, shiv, sharpened rock? Anything that would cut?"

"Get a grip of yourself, cadet." There was a hard edge to her whisper. "Out of earshot you will address me properly."

"Sorry, corporal."

She glared.

"It's those Hardit vecks, corporal. I can see how this plays out. Every day they'll make me watch you being beaten and humiliated. I can't take that forever. I'll break. I know I will. I'll punch them in their stupid snouts. And then they'll kill me."

Madge thought over his words. "Only if you let them, McEwan," she whispered back. "I know I gave you a hard time when you stood up for me this morning. That was to make you angry. I mean, sure you were dumb to do what you did, but dumb is what you are. I was trying to give you the gift of anger, though Horden knows you don't deserve any gifts after your serial frakk ups. Give in to your rage. Seethe at the injustice all around. Use that energy to fight your instincts and stay alive."

"But do you have a blade? I promise it isn't to use as a combat weapon against the monkey-vecks."

Madge sighed. "You'd better be telling the truth, McEwan." She lowered her voice to the barest whisper. "Springer and I had flexible las-blades sown into our underwear. We've got needle and thread too."

Arun nearly laughed at that but cut himself off just in time. "Good old, Rekka. She always said a well-prepared Marine always goes into battle with needle and thread. Guess she was right. "Now, don't be coy, corporal, it doesn't suit you. When you said underwear, which piece? It's not as if you're actually wearing any."

"First you tell me your plan."

"It involves you making a great sacrifice." Arun looked shamefaced: he'd not fully thought of what his idea meant for Madge. "I'm sorry. Really, but I want you to help me stay alive."

"Stop vulleying around, McEwan, and tell me what you want me to do."

373

"It involves taking off your clothes."

The flicker of disgust on Madge's face was swiftly replaced by the shock of understanding when she figured out what Arun was planning. She slid into the sexy pout she'd often worn in happier times when they'd still been novices. "For you, darling, anything," she said. "You clever boy. You'll find what you're looking for in our bras."

Springer had sensed the change of mood and woken. Hortez snored on. None of them offered to help Arun in his task of locating the undergarments in the room packed with sleeping Aux. So he set about his task, trying his best to ignore his two grinning comrades while he whispered apologies to the Aux as he jostled them awake. He rammed his hands underneath them in search of two items amongst the sea of nesting material.

His squadmates would be recording this. Of that he had no doubt. The data flow down their optic nerves would be copied into their auxiliary storage implants. If they ever made it back to hab-disk 6/14 alive, the story of Arun and his nighttime bra hunt would spread wide, and he would be a figure of fun for the rest of his life.

Couldn't the girls see that this was important? Just for once he'd prefer them to be more like robots.

Eventually Springer and Madge tired of their fun and joined the bra hunt. A confused Hortez looked on, slowly coming to his senses.

Perhaps the relative freshness of the newcomers' clothing was a highly prized luxury. Everything else placed next to their skin was greasy and stained. Their pants and shirts were in use as blankets, but the bras were more difficult to locate. They found Madge's stuffed down the front of one Aux's overalls. He said it was just insulation; they said it constituted wearing forbidden clothing. He gave up the bra without a fight.

Springer's bra was the most difficult to find. In the end it was the look on Adrienne's face that gave her away. By now, most of the Aux were awake and resentful, offering mumbled curses and scowls but not resistance. Adrienne's expression was different. Underneath the annoyance was a defensive look. She had something to hide.

When Madge and Springer searched her, they found she was actually wearing Springer's bra, even though it was so tight it must have been uncomfortable. Adrienne didn't fight back as they stripped her of the garment, but they knew they had made an enemy there, and a dangerous one. The other Aux seemed afraid of Number 87.

Once they'd gathered the underwear, the Blue Squad comrades pushed their way to one of the walls, huddled together and set to work.

Adrienne spied on them. Arun began to wonder whether she was a snitch, spying for the Hardits in return for some pathetic scraps of food or favors.

Hortez and Arun shielded the girls by standing up, arms folded and glaring at Adrienne. She pretended to lose interest but kept throwing sly glances their way.

Arun caught a whiff of burning and then Springer swapped places with Hortez who was an expert with needle and thread.

You never quite knew what would happen next with Springer, which was one reason why she was so popular. One thing was for sure: she didn't have the patience of Hortez.

The next time Adrienne spied on them, Springer gave a cry of rage and barged through the crush of people, aiming straight for her. Adrienne looked away. Then she looked back but Springer was still charging toward her. The Aux woman blanched, getting to her feet just in time for Springer to slam her down onto her butt. Springer sat down, straddling Adrienne's lap.

Springer kissed her. She embraced the Aux girl with the same furious energy that had propelled her across the room like a missile. Springer never did things by half, which is why Arun both adored her and was scared of her in equal measure. Her hands roamed down Adrienne's back, squeezing and kneading.

Arun looked on, astonished. Springer's eyes blazed with violet, a light so intense that the glow lit up Adrienne's face. He caught Springer glancing back at him. Her glowing eyes were like a laser range-finder searching for some reaction from him.

Then she was back in Adrienne's face, drawn back by Adrienne herself who had pushed Springer away at first, but was now clutching at her hungrily.

"That's quite a display," said Hortez who had finished his task. He punched Arun on the arm.

"Please, Hortez. Give our Springer some respect. She's not putting on a display for our benefit, and she's not doing that for pleasure. She's making a diversion to distract that snitch."

"Sure, man. It's that too."

Before Arun could think of an answer, Springer gave one of her own. She broke off, shoving Adrienne against the wall. Number 87 looked on helplessly as Springer hawked up a mouthful of spit. But at the last moment, Springer changed her mind and didn't unleash the gobful at the cowering girl.

From someone who a few moments earlier had shown more spirit than any of the other Aux, Adrienne now looked lost and fearful. Then she started to sob.

Springer left the weeping girl alone and rejoined her group.

Arun had no idea what that was all about but Hortez grabbed Springer's arm as she walked past. "You've still got pity in you," he said. "That's good. Don't let them drive it out of you. Don't hate us, not even Adrienne Miller. It's better that you pity us."

"You always did deep-talk nonsense, Hortez," said Springer. "I don't hate you Aux."

"Give it time," said Hortez. "You have plenty left to see."

—— Chapter 33 ——

"Step forward, 106," ordered Tawfiq.

A ragged human figure detached itself from the roll-call lineup and stood, head bowed, before Tawfiq and Hen.

"Step forward, 109."

A second figure emerged, equally cowed but distinguishable from the first by a blonde ponytail sneaking out the back of a standard Aux hat.

Tawfiq glanced across at Hen, rubbing tails as she did. "This one with long hair is an attractive female," she explained in the growling Hardit tongue but keeping her translator on automatic to give the humans the full benefit of their humiliation. "The other is male. He understands consequences of defiance. Amusing query. Can he control his protective urge toward her?"

Tawfiq appeared to expect a reply, but Hen stayed silent. "He couldn't help himself yesterday," Tawfiq continued, "so I give him level 3 pain. Today I will use level 4 if he intervenes. Do you understand, human?"

106 gave a nod.

"Stupid though these human animals are, surely even they aren't that stupid," argued Hen.

"Query? Shall we wager?"

"Agreed. Ten credits."

"Done."

The two entwined tails.

"If you understood these creatures as I do," said Tawfiq, "you would realize that the male has marked out this female as one of his harem. This means she has exchanged mating rights in return for his protection. His hormones will drive him to protect his female or die trying."

"I'd like to see one of our males claim mating rights over me!" said Hen.

"Hah! Hah! Hah!"

Both Hardits doubled over and made retching sounds. Laughter, Arun assumed, because Tawfiq's translator system accompanied the sounds with 'hah's. Hen's translator was better than Tawfiq's with normal speech. With laughter, it kept silent.

"Let us see," said Tawfiq when she'd recovered. "Stand closer, 106 and 109."

They obeyed.

"Stop staring at ground. I wish you look into each other's eyes."

They complied. There was the faintest of reactions from the crowd, but the Hardits showed no sign of noticing anything wrong.

Even Adrienne kept quiet, persuaded to keep that way by Springer and Hortez who were flicking threatening glances her way.

Tawfiq began to smack the female with her tail, while watching the male's face, daring him to react.

What the humans all saw was the results of the newcomers' activity the night before, the first part of Arun's plan – not that he'd fully worked out the rest just yet.

Arun and Madge had swapped overalls. They'd used the secreted las-blades to cut off Madge's blonde ponytail. Hortez's expert needlework reattached the hair so that it hung down from Arun's hat.

To the humans the disguise was farcically bad.

But their overseers were the products of a very different chain of evolution. Humans all looked the same to them. They suspected nothing.

Under the gaze of Madge and the Hardits, Arun endured a very mild beating that was more than made up for by knowing he was putting one over on the stupid, skangat monkey-bitch Hardits who thought they were beating Madge.

Best of all, Arun was showing them up in full view of every human there.

Eventually Hen grabbed Tawfiq's tail in hers, bringing the beating to an end. "That's enough," she told Tawfiq. "You lose upon this occasion. Time to get to work."

Tawfiq pressed some tokens into Hen's hand, and watched as Hen walked off.

After glaring at the humans for a while, Tawfiq darted into the line-up and brought out Springer and Hortez. "I have a task for new ones and–" she tapped Hortez on his head "–this one who I know is your friend. You will go up top surface. Hen Beddes-Stolarz has a delivery waiting in Bay 32 to make to the fields scum in Alabama." She paused, lips curling high about her teeth. "In fact that will be your task for rest of the week. You go to Alabama every day whether there is a delivery to make or not."

She grabbed Springer's face, squashing her cheeks together. "You do realize why, don't you?"

"Yes, mistress. We will burn."

"Correct. You will burn."

Tawfiq increased the pressure on Springer's cheeks until she winced. Satisfied, the overseer assigned the tasks to the other workers, and then stormed off.

As soon as she was out of sight, Adrienne was in Madge's face, hands on hips and a sneer across her face. "Give me one good reason why I shouldn't run after Tawfiq and tell her the stunt you just pulled?"

"Because you keep your life." Madge didn't put any aggression in to her voice, but she spoke with absolute conviction as if Adrienne's death would be as certain as night follows day.

Adrienne gave a bitter laugh. "My life isn't worth drent. Have you forgotten last night? Do I have to spell it out?"

"Yes," said Arun.

Springer sighed. "I think what Adrienne means is that she–"

"Stop calling me Adrienne!"

Arun watched in silence as a tear came to Adrienne's eye. She wiped it away.

"For a moment you reminded me of who I once was," the Aux girl snarled, beaming hatred at Springer through slitted eyes. "You veck. Your touch reminded me. Once… once there was someone special. But now he's dead and so is Adrienne. I'm Number 87 now."

"That's only what the Hardits call you," said Springer.

"No, it's what they have made me."

"Well," said Madge, "if your life has no value, how would you like more food instead?"

Adrienne pursed her lips, holding back her initial retort. "All right. How?"

"By taking it from Cliffie," said Madge.

Adrienne snorted. "That didn't work out too well last time, did it?"

"No?" Madge smiled. "Trust me. That was just reconnoitering."

"Consider this," said Hortez. "If we put Cliffie out of the picture permanently, what then?"

"Nothing," spat Adrienne. "One of his gang will take his place."

"Eventually," said Hortez, "if left to their own devices. But they will be off balance. Destabilized. Vulnerable while they fought for succession. If there was a strong man–" he looked Adrienne in the eye "–or strong woman waiting to seize the initiative, to take Cliffie's place, to stand up to them… What then? Don't forget we outnumber Gamma by 3 to 2."

Adrienne shrugged. "Perhaps. But we would need to get rid of Cliffie. I don't see how."

"Leave it to me," said Arun. "I have powerful friends and I'm only just getting started here."

Arun watched the changes come over Adrienne's face. She wasn't convinced, but just for a moment she looked away, her eyes glazing as she thought through possible futures. Better futures.

They'd given her hope.

———

Bay 32 was on Level 9 in an industrial zone of workshops and production lines where the throb and hum of motors and conveyor belts made the floor shake.

Arun's face lit up when he saw their cargo was waiting for them packed into wooden crates and already loaded onto hover-trolleys.

Hover-trolleys! Carrying their load would be easy.

Once they had swung the trolleys out of the corner of the bay on hover power, Hortez spoiled the mood by explaining that the fuel for the hover motors wouldn't be enough to get them topside, let alone all the way to Alabama, which was 17 klicks away through the Trollstigen mountain pass and out into the western plateau.

So they saved the hover capability for more difficult terrain, and had made their way up two levels of the nearest spine ramp before Madge called a rest halt.

Hortez was already tiring.

Let's crack open the crates," Madge suggested. "We'll take out some of your load, Hortez, and redistribute between the three of us."

"No," said Hortez. "We keep going as we are."

"C'mon, man," said Arun. "We're stronger than you. Don't be a dumbchuck."

"It's not pride making me say no, it's self-preservation. I don't know what's in these crates and don't want to."

"Why?" Arun asked. "What do you think we're carrying?"

"I assumed they were machine parts," said Springer.

Hortez shrugged. "They might be."

"And they might not," Arun finished for him. "Spill!"

"It's just rumors," said Hortez reluctantly. "Talk of black market smuggling."

"Smuggling? Smuggling what?" Arun said. "We get everything we need. Don't the Hardits?"

"Arun, Arun." Springer slapped him on the back. She was laughing, the sound a balm for Arun's bruised spirits. "It's not that we have everything we need so much as you lack the imagination to want for anything."

When Arun showed no sign of understanding, she added: "How did you think the corporal's hair got to be that shade of blonde? There aren't any hair salons in the hab-disks, you know."

"There's always a favor that can be done," added Madge. "A little surplus to be creamed off, help to be given. A thousand ways to make life a little more bearable. And all of that is tradable."

"The Hardits are at the heart of it all," said Hortez. "It's in their nature. They're natural traders. You gotta see it from their point of view. They were here for a very long time before the Jotuns and we humans showed up. We're like unwelcome guests to them."

"I kinda picked up on the unwelcome part already," said Arun.

"Right," said Hortez. "And guests don't go nosing around in the hidden corners of someone else's home. Not if they know what's good for them."

"All right, we'll do it your way for now," said Madge. "Now get off your butts and start moving. If we're to keep down to Hortez's pace, we can't afford to hang around."

—— Chapter 34 ——

On the far side of Trollstigen Pass, they came to a crossroads. To right and left the road hugged the foothills of the towering mountains. A simple track ran before them as straight as an energy beam, a gravel and dirt causeway leading to Agri-Facility 21, known by most of the humans as the Alabama Depot.

Although they were still in deep shadow, they could see the landscape opening up before them, the sides of the track sloping down into fields of wheat, maize and barley that waved in the gentle breeze like a golden greeting.

Indeed, it did feel as if the land were welcoming their return, even the fresh outdoor smells were inviting. All of them had been here before in happier times, as novices hiking with heavy packs or running in powered suits or unencumbered, running in nothing more than fatigues and peaked caps.

Arun knew the track carried on far beyond Alabama, as far as the timber plantations. The soil was richer there – or at least different, suitable for growing crops for Detroit's non-human residents. There was Gloigas, long-haired, twisting brown columns crowned with lush purple leaves. And the lurid green, but apparently nutritious, roots of the Tarngrip, which snaked through the undergrowth, trying to ensnare slow-moving limbs, trapping them before slowly crushing the life out of them through hydraulic pressure. The Tarngrips were far too slow to trap a human, at least while you were awake. The carnivorous plants were native to the same homeworld as the Hardits, a planet that had little oxygen in its thin atmosphere, which meant most things moved in slow motion.

Tarngrips were on the Universal Food list. Which meant everyone in the White Knight logistical supply system had their digestions adapted to consume them, human Marines included. The times when he'd seen the contorted faces of other novices forced to eat boiled Tarngrip was all Arun needed to understand why Universal Foods were more usually called *Ugly Foods*.

Arun knew all these crops well because he'd run through them, armored boots trampling great swathes through the crops to the consternation of any Agri-Aux nearby.

Instructor Rekka had once told them: "Get to know every culvert, every bank, ridge and irrigation ditch. One day you might be in them, SA-71 braced on their lip, waiting for the enemy assault to draw nearer before opening fire."

Emerging from the shadows, the bright sun swiftly warmed their spirits, despite following Hortez's advice to pull their stretchy woven hats so far over their faces that the fabric covered their eyes. As they counted down the klicks to Alabama, they peered at the world through gaps in the weave.

"In your hab-disks you go through the shower block every day," Hortez explained. "It's for decontamination and protection as much as hygiene. The spray you're given at the end is more than a dumb protective shield. Embedded into the spray oils are scavenger nanites that suck the ionizing radiation out of the air. Neutralizes it so it doesn't screw with your cells. I had no idea, but the Hardits are eager to explain that to us."

"If it works so well," said Springer, "surely it wouldn't take too much to give you Aux the spray too."

Hortez took a minute to bring himself to reply. "Sushantat told us once. You've yet to meet her. She's effectively in charge of the Aux on Level 5. She explained that the effects of the radiation take around a decade to take a hold of your body. Tumors, organ failure, deformed children. They don't want to send you lot off to war, only to have you riddled with cancer by the time you get to fight. So they give you the scavenger nanites. But the Aux? Why bother? The oldest Aux I ever heard of was 29 Terran standard years. Giving us the protective spray would not be difficult or expensive. But our lives have such little value that they're worth even less than the spray."

"Sorry, man," mumbled Arun, his sentiments echoed by Springer and Madge.

Except the girls don't feel the same as me, thought Arun. *They aren't responsible for putting Hortez here.*

It was time, he decided, to raise the matter that he dreaded most.

"Look, Hortez. I landed you in the drent because I frakked up in that exercise with the Trogs. I'm so sorry. I never knew it would be so bad here."

"Stow it, McEwan," replied Hortez. "You tried apologizing before. Don't try again."

"Fair enough. But I'm going to do more than say sorry. I'm going to ask our new company staff sergeant – Bryant – to have me swap places with you. It should be me festering in this hellhole with those sadistic monkeys."

Hortez glared at Arun who had to look away. Arun could look the Hardits in the eye, but not his friend whom he'd let down so badly.

"Do you really think this Bryant would swap us?"

"Probably not," admitted Arun. "But I don't know that for sure. I can always try."

"Make sure you do," said Hortez. He froze, as if distracted.

"Get off the road," shouted Madge. "Now!"

Arun scrambled down the bank but lost his footing, rolling down and crashing into the waist-high wheat stalks. He turned to see what had spooked Madge. In the distance, back up the way they'd come, they saw a dust cloud and heard a rhythmic pounding. They didn't need image enhancers to know what that was: an approaching squad of Marines, thundering toward them at over 30mph.

He heard a cry of frustration and noticed Springer struggling with her trolley. She'd activated hover mode and was trying to guide the trolley down the bank.

Except the load was too heavy.

Springer was pulling back on the handles, trying to slow its fall, but all she managed was to chase it down the bank.

Arun got to his feet, and rushed into the path of the trolley, hoping to push from the front, but its momentum was too great. The load knocked him flying, forcing Arun to roll away desperately, only inches from being crushed.

The trolley righted itself and came to a stop, hovering cheerfully a meter off the ground as if nothing was the matter. The wooden crate that had been on top snapped its straps and kept going, tumbling over once, twice, three times, screaming as the wood splintered and tore at its fastenings.

"Are you all right?" Arun helped Springer to her feet.

"I'm not hurt, Arun. But my crate…"

The crate had come to rest with one corner buried deeply into the soft soil, and half its sides shattered.

Arun glanced at the onrushing Marines. They looked like a wavefront of a silver sea, about to crash upon them like a tsunami. The pure gold color of their ACE-2 battlesuits was distinctive enough that Arun had no need to see insignia close up. These were veterans of the 420th, led by two Jotun officers. To deviate around the abandoned hover-trolleys would be far beneath their regimental dignity. Any second now the tsunami would break over their abandoned cargo.

The Hardits had given them a simple task, and they had already failed.

——————

The Jotun officers – a captain and a major – showed no signs of noticing the trolleys blocking their way. Cantering like centaurs on four of their six legs, massive crested heads held high, they leaped cleanly over the first obstacle without breaking stride. As their trajectory brought them down onto the second trolley, they threw their front limbs in front of them. Their hands morphed, their armored gauntlets matching every change. What had been human-like five fingers and an opposable thumb, thinned, lengthened and bifurcated repeatedly. They now looked more like waving, long-tendriled fronds held out to either side.

The rubbery fronds hit the cargo crate, pressing down against the wood like organic springs. The tension in their hands sprang back, propelling the aliens cleanly over the second trolley and the third too.

As the major and captain cantered away, a brace of senior human sergeants reached the obstruction. Running at this speed in powered armor was a skill the G-2 cadets of Arun's year had yet to master. When they had been out here as novices in their training armor, the motion had been more of a lope than a run. Not only were these Marines running, but the sergeants followed their officers' example and tried to leap over the abandoned trolleys.

Battlesuit AIs interpreted their wearer's intentions, amplifying human muscle power many-fold. The Marines soared over the first trolley like shells from a howitzer.

Out in the emptiness of space, the battlesuits could speed through a battlefield at crushing velocities. The gravity well of a planet enfeebled the propulsion units in the suits so that their flight capability was reduced to a short hop, such as over a tank.

But the officers hadn't activated their suits' flight capability and so neither could the humans who followed. They used augmented muscle power alone.

As the next rank of Marines jumped into the sky, the sergeants began to fall. The air pushed back against their bulky shapes, and the planet's gravity grabbed at the legs of their heavy armor.

Four hundred pounds of bone, muscle and poly-ceramalloy battlesuit bore down on the middle cargo crate through the armored ball of the sergeant's foot. Arun heard the crack and whine of splintering wood, but the wooden box was strong. It held.

For now.

Arun's brain had been trained and engineered to estimate troop numbers. Around five hundred Marines – three companies of veterans – were yet to clear the abandoned carts, and each one would follow their officers' example and go through rather than around.

They watched as Marines flashed past relentlessly, the smart surfaces of their battlesuits, which could make them invisible when stealthed in space, were now set to shine in regimental gold, with company markings proudly displayed on helmets and squad markings on the knee segments. Streamers tied to knees and elbows flew behind in their slipstream. These were smartfabric ribbons of pulsating color that no cadet or Marine in the 412th would be seen dead in. At least not on a planet's surface where these streamers were no more than a gaudy affectation.

Wearing ribbons in void combat was a different matter entirely; even the 412th trained for that. Inertia would spool out enormous ribbons of reflective and radar hard material behind Marines maneuvering through the vacuum. The possibility of becoming entangled with your squadmates' ribbons was a terror balanced, in theory, by the confusion they sowed in enemy targeting systems.

The Marines might only be from the 420th, but they still looked magnificent.

"Does the sight make you proud?" asked Hortez who had been watching Arun.

His companions looked at each other uneasily.

"I used to dream of being one of them," Hortez continued. "Of earning my own personal device to wear on the thigh of my suit. A bolt of lightning perhaps, or a noble hart. I wanted to belong. I used to think that was my inevitable destiny, an inalienable right. But only the best earn the right to be a Marine. Not everyone makes the grade."

"Stop it!" said Springer. "Don't you ever feel sorry for yourself. I know you're better than that. It's only bad luck that brought you here. You still deserve to be one of them." She pointed at the Marines clearing the abandoned carts.

"Sorry," replied Hortez. "You're right. But the end result is still the same. I didn't make it. There's no way back."

"I never bought into the whole Marine mythos," said Arun, wincing when a boot finally stove in the middle crate. "I'm not saying you're better off as you are, man, but life for a Marine isn't all shiny armor and the comforting heft of an SA-71. The reality is that you get stuffed into a cryo box and stored in a ship's hold. If you're lucky, then you might survive long enough to be awoken just in time to die in battle."

Arun was not a great liar. No one believed him. Even the steady thumping beat of armored feet pounding the ground sounded like the accelerated heartbeat of a super-being. The sight of the Marines, the hammering thump of their boots and faint whine of the armor muscle-amplification, even the sweaty smell vented from the exhaust outlets: everything about them filled his heart with pride.

"There's no shame buying into the dream of becoming one of them," said Hortez gently. "I did. But even if you think pride in your Marine unit is just macho dung, or Jotun brainwashing, it's still better to die young as one of them than live a lifetime as an Aux. Even if it's a short lifetime."

Arun grimaced. What could they say? Fate had dealt Hortez a hand of utter drent and they all knew it. "If I can, man, I'll get you out," he said. "I don't know how but I'll try."

Arun looked at Hortez, trying to let the sincerity show in his face, but his friend stared back with flinty disdain.

"I don't mean asking Bryant to swap us around," Arun added. "Sure, I *will* do that, but I don't hold up hope. I mean something new. Something… something I haven't thought of yet."

Hortez's stare held its scorn for a few more seconds before crumpling into laughter. "Arun McEwan, you sure are something! If anyone else had told me that, I'd have spat in their face. To give a hopeless man a false reason to hope – that's about the cruelest thing possible in an unbearably cruel universe. But you… Things happen around you, McEwan. Like you're blessed or something." Hortez stilled his laughter and regarded Arun seriously.

Arun could see a stiffening of confidence in his friend's face, in the squaring of his stance.

"I'll hook all my remaining hope onto your rising star," said Hortez. "It's like Majanita said last night. If anyone can figure out a way to help me, it's you."

Arun patted him on back. "Yeah, man! We'll do it."

For a moment, Arun thought the group was going to whoop and dance. Inwardly, though, the weight of Hortez's expectation was another burden dragging Arun to his knees. All he wanted to do was be one of the team. The half of the planet who didn't wish him dead seemed to be queuing up to label him as some kind of savior, a hero. Now he'd added Hortez to that list.

He sighed. His one great talent was for vulleying up friendships, and what was heroic about that? Those gleaming warriors, flashing by at precisely regular intervals with streamers flying in their own slipstream – the men and women who were reducing their cargo to a pile of splinters and tortured metal – they were the heroes.

Not him.

———

Tranquility's tactical Marine regiments had a nominal strength of 12 field and 8 cadet battalions, each organized into 24 companies of 6 squads plus command and heavy weapons sections. Each Marine weighed an average of 250 pounds of human meat packed into a 150 pounds of battlesuit armor, life support, motors, and powered exoskeleton.

In all, three companies stormed by, continuing on their way like a lightning bolt in slow motion, giving Team Beta no more acknowledgment than any other bolt of lightning would. What the friends had seen was probably the entirety of the 420th's veteran force that was stationed on Tranquility and awake, rather than stored in freezer pods deep in the bowels of Detroit.

It was display of strength and discipline strong enough to stir Arun's reluctant heart… and pulverize the middle cargo box and the trolley that had carried it. The other two loads on the path were damaged too: their wooden crates broken and their contents scattered.

The middle trolley was shattered far past the possibility of repair. The flat loading panel now sunken into the path was the only piece of the trolley still recognizable. Washers and bolts of metal and plastic had scattered like shrapnel, adding to the stones used by the engineers to construct the path. Amazingly, some of the boxes carried in the middle trolley were still intact.

Arun joined the rest of Team Beta in trying to salvage something from the mess, throwing cargo box shards, plastic fragments and twisted metal away from the path and onto the fields to either side. As they cleared the debris, they revealed more of the plain black boxes. None of them looked damaged.

Arun picked one up. It had a handle and indentations along its side, just like the kind of ammo case he was used to. It probably was the same design. Durable containers were humble but vital engineering patterns, so it made sense to reuse the same design for many purposes. A lock prevented him from getting inside so he gave it an exploratory shake instead. Even if the box was strong, he expected the shattered remains of its contents to rattle, but he heard nothing. Perhaps the load was okay after all.

The yellow writing stenciled onto the plain black box was written in an alien script. He had no idea what was inside. "Hey, what do you reckon these are?" he asked.

"Something illicit," replied Hortez. "Gemstones, narcotics, the colonel's art collection. Or maybe saucy Hardit lingerie."

Arun laughed. "No. I reckon it's Hardit underwear all right, but it's *clean*. Anything that didn't stink would be deviant fetish clothing to those filthy monkeys."

"Shut up!"

"What's the matter, Springer?" Arun asked.

"I know what's in them."

"What?"

"See for yourself."

Arun followed Springer's pointing finger to where Madge had taken the lid off one of the plain dark boxes. The walls of the box were undamaged but the lock hinges on the lid had shattered, allowing Madge to slide off the lid.

Inside were plasma rifles, SA-71 assault carbines, even a flenser cannon lying on a bed of matte black squares. He'd seen squares like that before: composite armor plates on a hovertank.

Cold fear overcame the warm sun and sent shivers down Arun's spine. Until that moment he had secretly believed against all realistic expectation that he would survive to shrug off the week as his *Aux Adventure*.

But now?

This changed everything.

He was part of a gun smuggling operation!

Were the Hardits the traitors? With everything else falling to drent, Arun had nearly forgotten about Pedro's hints: that someone was drugging the cadets.

He stared at one of the ammo carousels neatly stacked, ready to be slotted into an SA-71 and fired at – at what? – at Marines?

"This all fits," Arun said to himself. Then he raised his voice and announced: "There's something I need to tell you…"

"Traitors?" Madge's way of getting her head around Arun's tale of drugging and traitors was to storm up and down, looking like she wanted to smack something.

Arun looked to Hortez and Springer for support, but they were too lost in thought. "Corporal, don't you think we've all been acting strangely recently?" he called out to Madge.

She stopped and stared at Arun. He couldn't see her eyes properly through the stretched fabric of her worker's hat. But he imagined contempt there. "What has changed, McEwan, is that we're growing into Marines and you are not, and you never will do. Want to know why? Because you're a coward. You screwed up. You aren't as popular as you were. So you've invented this fantasy to justify why you're being pushed to the edge of the team."

"But it all makes sense," Arun protested.

"Does it? What evidence do you have?"

Arun bit his lip.

"There. See? You've nothing."

"If I'm right, then the drugs will wear off. The Hardits won't be keeping up our supply. We'll start to act differently any day now."

"Enough chitter-chatter!" Madge commanded. "This topic is closed. Permanently. We've a job to do. Get to it!"

In grim silence they set about salvaging what they could of the cargo, stacking it on the three surviving hover-trolleys. They ripped off the damaged lids of the wooden crates but many of the crates still had sides intact enough to layer the additional contents within.

It was heavy work and the sun blazing down punished them for their lack of drink. Hortez took it worse, wilting by the minute, until Madge told him to rest.

"No need, I'm okay," Hortez replied.

"You are not and you know it," said Madge. "Neither are you, McEwan. I think that beating took more out of you than you knew. Go keep Hortez company, out of our way."

"What? But corporal, I'm—" Arun was about to remonstrate further when Springer stomped on his foot.

He frowned a question at her.

"It's a testosterone thing, dummy," she whispered. "Hortez is weak but he won't want to admit that in front of girls. You're his cover. I told you we would be better off with single-sex units. Prove me wrong."

The situation smelled false. Madge had no formal authority over Hortez, but she could browbeat him into doing whatever she wanted. The girls were up to something but any thought of protesting was cut short by a kick from Springer.

"Hortez needs rest," she said. "Do this for him."

Arun felt sure that when the time came to go into battle as a Marine, he would charge fearlessly at an enemy defensive position, gun blazing. But against the combined forces of Springer and Madge, he knew he was beaten.

He shrugged. Hortez allowed Arun to lead him away to sit on the bank with their backs to the sun, facing away from the girls.

They sat in silence but the noises of hard work coming from behind made him feel guilty, so Arun started up the conversation no one had yet dared to broach.

"Do you think we should report the guns?"

Hortez shook his head. "Negative. Feels like we've caught them red handed, doesn't it? But we haven't. By the time we found someone to listen to us, the Hardits will have covered up any evidence. The only thing we'll be able to prove will be to the Hardits. We'll convince them that we need to be murdered to stop us talking."

"We could take some of the guns out and hide them."

"Oh, yeah. How's that gonna look?"

"Like we're planning a rebellion," Arun replied grimly.

"Exactly."

"But isn't that what the Hardits are planning? I can understand smuggling luxury items, or the means to produce them, but what use are guns other than to fight battles?"

"My friend, your thinking is too local," said Hortez. "We don't know what goes on out there in the wider star system, out amongst all those moons and asteroids, and the fuel processing plants in orbit around the gas giants. Tranquility is a small part of the system and the rest of it is dominated by the Hardits. Maybe it's one faction fighting another for the best mining sites. Perhaps it's protection against pirates."

"Pirates!"

"Why not? If something's valuable it means it's worth stealing. Stands to reason. So long as the Hardits sling their ore packets out to their destinations I doubt the White Knights care too much about how the Hardits manage their own affairs. Whatever the guns are for, it's nothing to do with us. Don't make it into our problem, Arun."

Arun said nothing. He was a Marine cadet. If anyone was taking weapons then that was something he couldn't ignore.

He decided to say no more about it for now. If he lived through today then he would be seeing Pedro tomorrow. He'd never looked forward to their meetings before, but he couldn't wait to see the insect this time. Arun had a lot of questions.

—— Chapter 35 ——

Other than the occasional dot in the distance, the party didn't see any Agri workers until the squat block of the main Alabama Depot building hove into view. Three Agri-Aux in a field of barley were sheltering in the shade of a portable canopy only a hundred paces from the path.

The Agri-Aux reminded Arun of a picture he'd seen in an Earth history book in which glamorous ladies posed in voluminous skirts, wide-brimmed hats, and long sleeves with flapping cuffs topped off with leather gloves. The ancient women seemed immensely proud of a stick-like device of unknown function called a parasol. He couldn't recall the name of the historical epoch – Victorian perhaps? – but the ornate nature of their fashion could not hide a functional design imperative: the clothing was designed to cover and shade the skin, protecting against solar radiation.

These Earth Victovians must have lived through a period of intense solar flares or ozone layer depletion.

The bombardment of high energy particles from the sun was a constant on Tranquility, which was why the Agri-Aux dressed like those ancient Earth dwellers. Multiple layers of skirts dragged along the ground, veils hung from their wide-brimmed hats, and their gloves were partially shaded under bell-shaped sleeve cuffs. Unlike the variations of lace and patterned fabrics the ancients had worn, the Agri-Aux clothing was white shot through with a fine tracery of pink. It looked as if their clothes were connected to their blood supply, feeding a network of capillaries through the cloth.

Perhaps it was.

Humans were entrusted to use the military and other technologies provided on Tranquility, but the principles that explained how they worked were forbidden knowledge.

The four Team Beta Aux took it in turns to push the three surviving hover-trolleys in single file along the path. Madge took the lead. She called over her shoulder to Hortez, who was walking behind her, without a trolley. "What are they up to?" Madge asked him.

"How should I know?" he replied.

He looked entirely uninterested but Arun hadn't lost his curiosity. Neither had Springer, who was in front of Arun.

"Carrying out some kind of tests," she said. "Soil samples or gene tests?"

"Maybe they're checking for insects or disease," Arun suggested. Then he added: "Do Tranquility's native pests and diseases attack Earth plant species?"

No one could answer. As far as Arun was concerned, food was something born fully formed on a plate. How it got there was a mystery.

"We're not meant to be here," said Madge, vaguely as if her internal thoughts had accidentally spilled out.

Arun frowned. What had that to do with pests?

"Just look at us," she continued. "Then look at them out there in their protective gear."

"We're oversupply," said Hortez. "Why waste effort on preserving our health when they prefer us dead?"

"No, she's right," said Springer, bursting with sudden enthusiasm. "Shut your sad-mouthing, Hortez, and think a moment. Tawfiq and our Hardits don't give us suits because they're smugglers and we're their expendable mules. They won't want to leave an evidence trail by requisitioning protective gear for non-existent workers to carry out tasks that don't officially exist. I don't suppose the Hardits who manage those field workers are any more big-hearted than ours, but they must treat them better if they provide protective suits."

"Let's see," said Arun. He shouted at the Agri workers. "Hey!"

They ignored him.

Under the canopy and their veils, he couldn't see their faces but Arun sensed from the way they'd momentarily frozen that they'd heard all right.

"Leave them be," hissed Hortez. "No good will come of this."

Arun ignored his former squad leader. In a hostile new environment, gather information before committing to a strategy. That's what they'd been taught and that's what he was doing now. "I know you heard," he yelled. He parked his trolley. "I just want to know whether the Hardits look after you? Do they treat you well?"

One of the Agri-Aux stopped what she was doing and answered. "We do okay."

"Do they torture you for sport?" pressed Arun.

Hortez shook his head, dismayed.

"Put it like this," replied the Agri-woman, "we'd never trade places with you sad vecks. Not from the position we've reached. Now frakk off."

Arun lifted the handles of his trolley and was about to lean into it when he stopped abruptly. Springer had let go of her handles and was racing down the bank toward the Agri-Aux.

Her legs were short but fleet. By the time Arun and Madge started to follow, Springer was already halfway to the Agri-workers.

With Hortez bringing up the rear, they chased after their comrade.

Springer was under the canopy now, remonstrating with the Agris. After a brief, heated exchange, she punched the Aux who had replied to Arun, felling her.

Arun slowed because Springer had turned around and was cutting a way through the field back to the path.

The Agris looked shocked. They didn't follow that up with action.

Springer did. She'd only made five steps before she turned back and flew again at the Agris. She punched one, shoved another to the ground, and kicked the Aux who was already down.

Once the Team Beta comrades had regrouped on the path, Springer explained: "I asked them about Alistair LaSalle. They murdered him. The vecks admitted it. He's dead."

When he'd first heard that Alistair LaSalle had been assigned the temporary role of senior cadet commander for Charlie Company, Arun hadn't been surprised in the least. Alistair was smart, strong, and enormously popular. He lacked height and bulk. The untamable waves of his light-brown hair were permanently messy, but he wouldn't shave his head like anyone else. Somehow Alistair had taken his unpromising physique and breathed such charisma into it that he seemed to have whomever he wanted in his bunk: boys and girls. And yet he never attracted envy, never needed to bully or intimidate competitors out of the way. He made success seem so easy. Arun couldn't square the Alistair he remembered with a sorry refugee who – if Springer's info was accurate – had died within weeks of his transfer.

"Murder is too harsh a word," said Hortez. "They had no choice. I often ask myself whether I would do the same in their place."

"You knew!" Arun rushed at Hortez. "You frakking knew he was dead."

Arun's hands reached for Hortez's neck but Springer tripped him as he passed.

His chin thudded into the stones and dirt of the path, filling his mouth and nose with dust. For an instant he was winded, but a Marine cadet isn't easily pushed aside. A moment later he was on his knees, ready to spring at Hortez, when Madge crashed into him, pinning him down onto the ground with her butt on his sternum. "Calm down, McEwan," she ordered.

Arun tried to wriggle free, but couldn't. Madge was lithe but strong. He'd have to attack her to get her off him.

Frakk it! He was too angry to care. Arun threw everything he had into bucking her off. He felt her lose balance, releasing her weight. As he struggled back to his feet, she came crashing down on his shoulders, splaying his legs and making him eat dirt again.

Officially they were all demoted. Madge didn't outrank him anymore. No more playing nice. Fueled by anger, he shifted his weight, trying to prepare an elbow strike at Madge's hamstring.

"Explain yourself, Hortez," said Madge. "I can't keep a leash on this attack drone for long."

Hortez hesitated before responding: "To start with, I volunteered to come up here, risking my skin to make contact with Alistair." The fight went out of Arun when he heard that. Hortez's skin was a flaming mass of burns and sores. "I saw him a few times," Hortez continued. "I waved at him. To begin with he waved back cheerfully, his old self. After a while he didn't notice me when I passed by. Not long after that, I stopped seeing him. I didn't know for sure he was dead."

"But it was a safe bet," growled Springer. "And those vecks out there confirmed it. Explain to the others how Alistair died."

"It comes down to this. To live and work out here you must have a shielded suit. There are only so many to go around. You can even out food rations so everyone gets an equal share. You can take turns at the most dangerous tasks. But you can't share a suit."

"Yes, you can," said Springer. "Take turns wearing it. A rota system, worked out hour by hour."

"Negative. The world doesn't work that way, Springer. Not out here. Alistair and another ex-cadet, a woman, were sent here. Everyone else was already established, already won the right to their suits. None of them would ever give that up. Alastair was fearless and he was fiercely determined. No one I'd rather have beside me in a fight. But he was a nice guy. Too nice to live."

Madge let Arun wriggle free from underneath her and return to his trolley, his anger drained into the dust. What would he do if he had to choose between dying or living in the knowledge that someone else had to free up his place? Probably, he decided, he'd fight the decision as long as possible before choosing to live.

What a choice!

The others seemed to be infested with the same thoughts because no one spoke until they reached Alabama.

—— Chapter 36 ——

Alabama Depot consisted of a squat building with maller extrusions around its base. A semicircle of grain silos ringed the main buildings like teeth in a jaw. On the hardened area outside the back of the main building three trucks waited, their human drivers lazing in their cabs. An ordered swarm of Agri-Aux in their pink-laced costumes loaded plump sacks onto the trucks. These sacks had the same pink tracery as the Aux suits, presumably to afford the same protection from the sun.

Without needing to say a word, Arun's group halted about fifty paces away from the Agri-Aux and assessed their options.

"They don't look riled," said Hortez. He glared at Springer. "Despite your stunt."

"I still care, Hortez," she shot back. "I'd rather die than be like you. *Faded.*"

"C'mon, focus!" barked Madge. "Are they a threat or not?"

"Negative," said Arun. "Even if they know about Springer throwing punches, they don't look like there's any fight to them. Besides, what are we going to do? Ram them with our trolleys?"

"Look in your crate, McEwan," said Madge. "Tell me what you see."

Madge made no sense at all, but Arun was too tired to defy her. Checking the brakes were on, he came around the side of his crudely patched-up crate to peer inside. "There's some plastic boxes. Can't see what's inside." He shifted the top layer of boxes aside. "Frakk! You told me they were hidden at the bottom of the load."

Poking out of the crate was an SA-71 Marine carbine, grip angled upward ready to be taken out and used. "I suppose I'd be wasting my breath to ask if it's loaded."

"You would," said Madge. "Got them ready while you boys were chatting away and we loaded the cargo. Didn't tell you because we didn't want to worry your dear little heads."

Arun was about to protest when Madge raised a hand, shutting him up instantly. Who was he trying to kid? Madge was in charge, formal rank be damned.

Madge organized them into a crude wedge formation, taking point with Arun and Springer on the flanks and Hortez – who no longer had a trolley – taking a position at the rear.

They activated hover mode and the wedge of trolleys advanced.

This is madness, thought Arun. *How have I come to this?*

From far back into his earliest childhood, Arun had taken care not to say or do anything that could be considered treasonous or disloyal. Those who didn't learn that lesson fast enough were no longer around.

Were they now so desperate that they would turn their illicit SA-71s on their fellows?

As the laden hover-trolleys breached the perimeter of the hardened loading area, Arun's fears dissipated. For starters, the idea of an attack wedge of trolleys was too ridiculous to hang on to. And far from crowding around in armed revenge for Springer's attack, the Agri-Aux shied away, as if gripped by a group delusion that if they pretended they couldn't see Arun's little unit, the newcomers would go away.

As the Agri-Aux turned to scurry away, Arun expected to see resentment of their faces. Instead, he saw shame.

Only the truck drivers high up in their cabs watched them. They must be shielded, reasoned Arun, because they wore only white vests, their heads bare.

There were three huge doors in the back of the main building, of which two were open. Madge led their wedge toward one of these open doors, a route that took them close to one of the trucks.

The driver was a fat man but powerfully built. He was in his mid-twenties or even older, which made him one of the oldest Aux Arun had seen. His face was grim set and not fearful in the slightest. He peered at their damaged wooden crates with intense interest.

Arun kept his eyes focused on the driver.

The driver stared back. When Arun drew level with his cab, the man shouted. "Hey!"

Arun let go of his trolley's handles and reached into the opening in his crate. He felt for the loaded carbine.

"I ain't seen nothing," the driver said, his voice coming from a speaker set into the cab door.

Arun's hand wrapped around the carbine's grip. The familiar shape felt comforting.

"But if I had, I might say your crates look a little busted."

Arun glanced back at the driver. He looked amused, a little contemptuous perhaps, but Arun didn't see aggression there. Reluctantly, he loosened his grip on the carbine.

"What do you mean?" Madge asked him. Arun looked her way and had no doubt what her hand was gripping.

"Me?" answered the truck driver. "I don't mean anything. I didn't see you, remember? And that goes for anything you might be carrying, because I definitely didn't see *that*. I'm just saying, in a kind of neighborly thinking out loud kinda way, that if anyone did have a busted crate, there's plenty of spare timber in the fab shop they could use to fix it."

"Thanks, man," said Hortez,

"I didn't see nothing nor hear nothing. If anyone felt thankful, they'd do well to remember that." With that, the driver folded his arms and looked out the other side of his cab.

Madge considered a moment before deciding to take the driver at face value. She picked up her trolley and pushed it the final few paces into the loading bay, the others following close behind.

Inside the main building, they pushed their loads to the far end of the bay, as far away from the main doors as possible. Hortez and Arun guarded the cargo while Madge and Springer scouted the complex.

They soon reported back that they'd encountered two humans repairing split grain sacks, and a fab shop with all the materials needed to repair the crates.

Best of all they brought back a 3 gallon water bottle, the same kind used to refresh water fountains back home.

They debated but rejected the idea of keeping some of the cargo behind. Too risky, they decided. So they set to work making good the damage to the shattered crates. By the time they had crates fit for transport onward – obviously repaired but sturdy – the grain trucks had departed and most of the Agri-Aux loaders had drifted away. A handful, though, had tasks to carry out in the depot buildings. They kept their distance from the Team Beta group.

Hortez had wheeled a few half-filled grain sacks over to where Team Beta sat with their backs to the wall, passing the water bottle between them. He arranged the sacks into a semblance of a reclining armchair. After explaining that the Hardits didn't care what you did during the day so long as you completed your task and stayed out of trouble, he spread his hands behind his head, leaned back, and relaxed.

The others followed suit, taking an unexpected breather before returning through the burning sun to the hellish dungeon that was Aux Camp Beta.

Arun was of the opinion that a Marine should grab any chance to ease off the pace, and make the most of it while he or she could. The apex of the roof about was 20 meters high which made the interior cool, airy and comfortable. There was soft ambient lighting but neither windows nor any opening in the roof, just the main loading doors. Relaxing on his nest of grain sacks, Arun felt proud of himself for being able to forget about the Hardits, who probably intended that he would not live to return to his battalion.

"You know what this could be?" said Arun suddenly.

"What?" replied Springer, without enthusiasm.

"A clubhouse."

"What's that?"

"It's an Earth concept, a place to relax. A place where you don't get bothered by your betters. You can just chill out, watch a game, chat with your friends…"

"Are you serious?" asked Springer.

"Relax."

"It'll never work," said Madge.

"Why not? The Hardits rarely come here. There's space, shielding, and plenty of seating."

"That's not what I mean," replied Madge acidly. "You can't bring your friends here to chat with them because you don't have any friends."

Arun bit back his tongue.

Madge twisted the knife further. "Oh, and I nearly forgot, we've no game to watch either. Not since our star player abandoned us and we got knocked out last round."

I would have carried on playing for you if you'd let me. As he fumed with the unfairness of his victimization, an Agri-Aux woman, approached them carrying her hat in her hand and a haunted look about her eyes. She looked a force to be reckoned with all the same, perhaps because she was older than the group from Team Beta. This woman had to be at least 25.

She introduced herself as Esther.

None of Team Beta acknowledged her, but that didn't stop Esther from standing so close that she was impossible to ignore.

"They come at night," she said.

"Who?" asked Arun. "Hardit smugglers?"

She nodded. "They use orbital shuttles."

"That's what I keep telling this lot," Hortez said to her. "I've seen the telltale scorch marks on the hardened area outside."

Madge had sat up. "Did you know Alistair LaSalle?" she asked of the Agri-woman.

Esther nodded mournfully.

"Did you try to help him?" she added.

"We sewed grain sacks together, which gave them some protection."

"But you didn't offer your suits," added Springer.

"No."

"Don't expect forgiveness from us," Madge snarled. "Is that what you thought? Come over and say sorry and then your sins would be absolved?"

Esther's face pinched with fury. Arun thought she was going to rip Madge's face off. Or try at any rate. Instead she sniffed. "I shouldn't have said anything," she pronounced, with the air of someone dealing with inferiors beneath her notice.

She started walking away.

"No, please don't go," Arun called after her.

She paused.

"What're you doing, McEwan?" Madge didn't sound pleased.

"It's…" Arun couldn't put it into words. He knew the strategy planning part of his brain was running hard because it was manifesting itself as a sense of prickly heat at the exact center of his head, and a vague sense that the Agri-Aux could prove to be invaluable allies one day.

The feeling might be vague, but he knew to trust any hunches accompanied by the prickly heat.

Springer butted in. "What he's trying to say, is that you Agris will be important allies."

Arun shot a glance at Springer. How did she know that? Behind the cute sprinkle of freckles, her eyes were focused on an ethereal sight not of this plane. They blazed with a violet intensity that made his heart race. He was in awe of Springer. He wanted to kiss her, to kneel down and worship at her feet. And at the same time, he wanted to run away from her, screaming in fear all the way back to Detroit.

What was this? Admiration or mind control?

"Horden's Bones!" Madge sounded like she felt the same. "You're a right pair of psyker mutants. Ol' Violet who can see into the future, and lover boy with a battle planner AI in his head. Not that either of your superpowers have delivered anything of the slightest value. I still can't decide whether all your mystic powers are one big load of utter drent, or whether you really are freaks. I do know that you two should never get it together in case Springer gives birth to a Night Hummer."

"Haven't they told you?" said Hortez. "Each squad has a few members whose DNA has been virally rewritten to add a few choice genes from alien species. Most of it makes no difference but every now and again something useful manifests, and they grab you for use in their eugenics program."

The cadets looked at each other, speechless.

A wicked smile planted itself on Hortez's face. "Relax," he whispered. "It's a joke."

"This is no joke!" thundered Arun as he got to his feet. "This is important! It's what Hortez said earlier – to give false hope to the hopeless is cruel. But what if we could do something for the Aux, something better than giving a gesture of hope and a finger flip at the Hardits? What if we could set an example of what humans can achieve though cooperation, an inspiration that outlasted our gesture. I want to see humans everywhere stronger and prouder. United. A force to be respected. To be granted privileges, Freedom. Isn't that a cause worth fighting for?"

Arun's speech ran out of momentum, leaving a shocked silence that Madge eventually broke. "So, all this inspirational stuff… you're still talking about a clubhouse, right?"

Arun nodded.

"And you're going to make all our lives better, and establish an interstellar human empire with you on the throne. All this by, what? Throwing a party?"

"It's more than that. Imagine if we organize a day of defiance against the Hardits. We'll light a beacon of hope that will shine for years to come into the breast of even the most wretched human slave."

"Have you ever seen him do this before?" asked Hortez rolling his eyes. "I've never heard Arun make a speech. I think the sun's gone to his head."

"No, he's right," said Springer. "Trust him."

"Trust!" Madge shot to her feet, her face reddening with fury. "I trusted him to support Moscow Express. He let us down over a frakking girl. *Twice*! We're all going to be Culled because of him. Hortez is up to his neck in drent and Alistair is dead. *Because of him*. You don't make up for that with a pretty speech, McEwan." She nodded at Esther, who was listening to all of this. "And what about your new girlfriend? How does she fit in to your party plans? Do you need her to bring a frakking salad?"

Arun spoke to Esther: "If your people could stage a diversion – I'm still working on the details – something that forces the Hardits to send us all out to the depot to deal with the crisis. A fire. Explosion. Armed revolt. Make the Hardits think they're sending their expendable Aux Team Beta into danger when actually they're sending us to the shiny new Alabama Clubhouse."

"Oh, great!" spat Madge. "I feel so much better knowing that our plan hinges on the brave Agri-Aux. Have you forgotten that they murdered Alistair LaSalle?"

"I know what I did," said Esther. "It wasn't just your friend. We're all of us alive because we forced someone else to die."

"Why tell us that?" asked Madge. "Do you want us to forgive you?"

"I'm not stupid enough to ask for that, and if I did beg forgiveness, it would be from the dead, not you."

"Let me guess how your next line goes," Madge said. "*The terrible knowledge of our betrayal eats at us every day, like a cancer.* Is that it?"

Esther shook her head and turned away. "I knew this was a mistake," she sneered.

"Wait!" called Arun. "I haven't finished with you yet. You can't ask to be forgiven because you know you don't deserve forgiveness. Not yet. What you should be seeking instead is atonement."

Esther paused. "What do you have in mind?"

"I don't know myself yet. Not exactly. But I'm working on it, and a diversion would be a good start. Think you can manage that?"

"My people will do as I say. Yes, I could arrange a diversion, if I thought the payoff worth the risk."

Arun laughed. "My people, eh? Yeah, that figures. Here," he gestured to a nearby sack, "take a seat."

Esther sat down and waited with the rest of them in an uncomfortable silence while ideas crystallized in Arun's mind.

When enough made sense to him, he explained to each of the others what he required them to do. When he later thought back to that time, it seemed to Arun that he was listening to someone else speak. Another part of him was in control. Afterward he was left behind to carry the thumping great headache that he knew was coming.

He heard himself ask Esther whether her people would help. And he remembered her agreeing that they would. "If you need to get in contact," she said, "leave a note in the cab of the dung truck. I wish you good fortune but now I must return to my duties."

As they watched Esther disappear out of the loading bay, something closer to normality returned.

"What the Aux need is hope," said Arun, feeling in control once more. A charge of excitement built within him, and why not? This could be *big*. "The Hardits expect us humans to fight each other, not cooperate. And the Agri-Aux are bent over double with guilt. Those are our two routes in. So long as we don't threaten the Agri-Aux's right to their protective suits, and don't rub their noses in their guilt, they'll do anything for a chance of atonement."

Madge groaned. "Of all your imbecile ideas, McEwan, this is the dumbest yet. I can't believe you two are humoring him."

That hurt. Just for a moment there, when Arun had been in his planning daze, Madge had listened. Now he was back to himself, she wouldn't give him the time of day.

"Leave him be," said Hortez. "He's onto something. If it sounds insane right now, that's only because the details haven't slotted into place. Just one thing, man." He slapped a hand on Arun's shoulder. "Co-opting the Agri-Aux is a good idea, but don't forget you have other allies too."

"Who?"

But even as the word came to Arun's lips, his mind had already filled with the answer: Trogs. He'd already considered the possibility of sounding out Pedro's thoughts on his plan when they met tomorrow. But what if he could persuade the Trogs to do far more than give advice?

After all, the colonel *had* ordered him to liaise with the Trogs.

Enlisting their help would only be obeying orders.

<h1 style="text-align:center">—— Chapter 37 ——</h1>

Instead of Tawfiq, roll call the following morning was conducted by Hen Beddes-Stolarz.

She paraded Springer, Madge and Arun in front of the line, scratching their faces, drawing blood from skin already red from the furious sun's exposure.

"Your skin is raw and peeling. Look–" she gouged a chunk out of Springer's cheek, making her wince but not cry out. "This one bleeds! This is good. Proof that you humans are useful. You take damage from the cruel sun to preserve the health of your mistresses."

Hen shifted position to growl in Arun's face, her breath hot, fetid and alien.

"This one is useful for other superiors than his Hardit mistresses. 106 is the most disgusting of your entire species. Today he goes to the insect nest where the hive drones keep him as a sex pet."

Hen brought her hand back as if to strike Arun.

He braced for the blow but it did not come.

"Number 106 has been immersed in insect sex fluids. He is too disgusting to touch. Tomorrow, 106, you will go to the surface without your hat. You will burn for my amusement. Perhaps the sun will sear away the stink of your depravity." The Hardit made retching noises. They sounded genuine. "I cannot bear the stink of you. Go now! Go away, human!"

Arun hid his grin as he hurried off to meet his Troggie ally.

<h1 style="text-align:center">—— Chapter 38 ——</h1>

"Yes, I can provide the equipment you have asked me for and more besides. We do not have the engineering capability to build spacecraft or nuclear weapons, but simple radio communications equipment will be an amusing diversion. We too know how to have fun, friend. And as for your abilities, human Arun, you have skills exceptional for your species. Your planning capability is similar to the way our minds work in the scribe phase of our lifecycle."

"Steady on, pal," said Arun, although he felt warm to hear his ally speak highly of him. "Nearly as clever as a scribe? I wouldn't go that far."

"No, of course not. I exaggerate."

"Hey! What do you mean, *exaggerate*?"

"I mean your mind is still inferior to a scribe's. For example, you are too fixated on your problem with the Aux. Consequently your mind can only think of solutions to that problem by ignoring your other four critical objectives. A scribe would consider all five simultaneously."

"As usual, Pedro, you're not making a shred of sense. I just want to get through the week alive."

"Yes. That is what I just said. Being a member of the hive grants me the gift of specialization. I can leave such short-term considerations as how to survive this week to others in my nest. That leaves me space to ponder your four other strategic objectives, namely: your desire to graduate as a Marine, to regain the trust of your squad, to mate with the female Lee Xin–"

"Wait! I never said that about Xin."

"Not in so many words. And the objective you have mentioned even more than this female is Scendence. Your match in 48 hours is crucial on many levels. You are the star Deception-Planning player. Yet you are banished to the Aux levels. You cannot play that game."

"You don't have to remind me. I can't be there. Done deal. I won't waste time worrying about something I can't change."

Pedro gave a slight outward tilt to both antennae, the equivalent of pointedly raising eyebrows.

"What're you hinting at? What can I do?"

"You? Nothing."

"Exactly. I need a substitute. But we're only three more wins away from immunity. At this stage, you can't just drag a player out of the spineway and expect them to perform at that standard."

"Agreed. You need a player with excellent planning ability. Preternatural by human standards."

"Right."

"An ability to think in what human opponents would regard as radically new ways. To make plays of such originality that our competitors will not anticipate them."

"I suppose."

Pedro didn't reply. He stood impassively and – to the human's eyes – without expression (or had he moved his antennae out a notch further?). Arun recognized this sudden silence. According to Pedro, this was him allowing Arun's slow human brain to catch up with the implications of their conversation. Which meant… What?

"Horden's spiny growths!"

"Indeed," said Pedro, spiraling his feelers.

"You! *You're* offering to be my substitute. And… Xin. She's already agreed to this, hasn't she?"

"There is still some slight reluctance on her part, but her xenophobia is only natural for you humans. The logic of my offer is unassailable."

Some slight reluctance. I'll bet, thought Arun, but then he remembered how to begin with he'd felt revolted by this strange alien friend. He went through all the reasons why the idea of Pedro taking his place in the Scendence match was madness. But every objection flaked away under closer inspection. He was only left with one question.

"Why? Why are you getting involved, Pedro?"

"Friends help each other in times of difficulty. And we are friends, aren't we?"

"I … yes." He thought for a moment. "Yes we are!" He knew he'd miss Pedro if he never saw the great lunk of an insect again. He also knew him well enough to suspect that Pedro wasn't telling the whole truth. Pedro persisted with this crazy alien notion that Arun was important. In protecting Arun, Pedro believed he was guarding the interests of his nest.

"And that's not all," said the Trog.

Arun's palm went to his forehead. Pedro's artificial voice lacked emotion, as always, but its volume had increased. Which meant he was excited about something. *What now?*

"I am extolling your virtues to this Lee Xin. I have learned much about you, Arun McEwan. Enough for me to embellish the truth so as to draw attention away from your many shortcomings. I am confident that on your return from your banishment to the auxiliary, this Lee Xin will be so filled with mating hormones that her skin will flush red with the need to–"

"Okay, you can stop right there!" Arun spoke from behind both his hands. Being bigged up by a seven-foot long insect. This had to be a new low. If word ever got out… "And for you information, she's Xin Lee, not Lee Xin."

"Really? Try telling her that."

Arun glared into the shiny black bulbs of the aliens expressionless eyes. Damn! He hated the creature for knowing more about Xin.

"I am serious," said Pedro. "Ask her. You and Lee Xin have a unique connection. You share a destiny. This makes the success of your courtship highly likely."

"That's enough about me and Xin! That topic is out of bonds."

Pedro dropped his antennae disapprovingly.

"I don't care what you think," snarled Arun. "That topic is forbidden."

"Very well, friend McEwan. Let us turn instead to your plan, Operation Clubhouse. I have noticed many ways in which I can improve it. My adaptations will help you to achieve the other four objectives you have temporary forgotten."

"When you say adaptations, are you talking a few slight nudges or it is more *throw everything away and start again*?"

Pedro hesitated before replying: "The second choice." It was sweet of him to act embarrassed enough to pause.

Arun shook his head. "I don't care who came up with the plan so long as it works. What I don't get is that you keep talking about me as this great being of destiny. But you think my plan's so drent you had to rebuild it. Anyone else would think you regard me as a loser, not this great hero."

"I have never described you as a hero. A person of destiny need not make all the decisions or have exceptional ideas. They might not even be a leader. Even an odious imbecile can be a great being of destiny."

"Okay, I get the picture. Maybe if I survive to have more of these discussions, I'll teach you the concept of being *too* honest."

"I haven't finished, Arun McEwan. With me you have established a friendship across species boundaries. You laugh at this but have no idea how rare that is. Perhaps that is where your destiny lies: to build a great interstellar coalition across species."

Arun sobered. A grand coalition free of the White Knights?

Was that his future? Was that the secret behind the Human Legion to come?

Arun laughed at his ridiculous hubris. "I'll leave the big picture to you," he told his friend. "Remember, my poor human brain can only cope with worrying about whether my buddies and I will still be alive this time next week. Go on, tell me your shiny new version of Operation Clubhouse."

Pedro shook his head. It looked like a negative human gesture, but indicated eagerness.

As Pedro explained his ideas, Arun's spirits lifted so high he was practically floating.

Yes, we can do this!

Arun was so excited that he decided not to puncture the triumphant mood by mentioning the other factor he was trying to ignore for now: the contents of the carts they'd helped to smuggle off planet.

The Hardits were gunrunners.

And the more he thought about that, the more Arun was convinced they were connected with the traitors drugging the cadets.

Arun wouldn't let them get away with that. But first he had to survive the week.

—— Chapter 39 ——

As Operation Clubhouse rolled out over the days that followed, radio equipment was produced in the Troggie catacombs that stretched for miles to the east and southeast of Detroit. After the comms came specialist explosives designed to give out smoke and heat but not consume oxygen. They were intended to confuse thermal and visual targeting systems in the defense of nest tunnels, where conventional explosive munitions could easily overcome ventilation, choking the defenders to death.

Amongst the Tunnel-Aux, as Arun had started calling the Detroit Aux, favors were accumulated and paid. Supplies were cached in places where the Hardits never bothered to look. Following Arun's example of exchanging his clothes with Madge, scent-marked Aux overalls were swapped freely, allowing the humans to move far out of their assigned areas.

Arun almost began to believe Pedro's fantasy that he was a man of destiny. Whenever he had these delusions of greatness, Arun reminded himself that it wasn't his genius but Hardit laziness that made the whole business possible. Rubbing those long snouts in their own drent gave Arun the greatest satisfaction of all. The Hardits had sneered about the law of supply and demand, but now the human Aux were twisting that law to their advantage. With a new sense of purpose – and a little extra food, that initially came in the form of a gray tasteless paste courtesy of the Trogs – the oversupply of human workers meant some Aux could be spared to work for their own ends.

Humans working for the benefit of others humans – for the first time in their lives. It was really happening!

After Springer managed to pass a message back to Blue Squad about the reality of life in the Aux, the word spread amongst the cadets in their hab-disks. Discrete packages of food and medicine were left in laundry bins. Cadets found reasons to wander far and wide through Detroit, making contact for the first time with their discarded brethren of the auxiliary services. But whenever the Hardits were in sight, even when lolling out of breath against walls as they often did, the Aux acted the part of broken, hungry slaves, losers far beneath the notice of any nearby cadets… until the moment the Hardits passed out of sight.

As far as the Hardits were concerned, they had work for a certain number of human workers. So long as the humans carried out those tasks adequately and didn't cause trouble, that was the limit of Hardit interest in their inferiors. They might make exceptional engineers and miners, but as bureaucrats and overseers, Hardits sucked.

Even accounting for Hardit indolence, Arun's original idea would have been a high risk gamble that might just have poked the Hardits in the eye, but would probably have paid for that shallow victory with the lives of Arun and his friends.

But Operation Clubhouse had grown far beyond Arun's initial idea, a product of cooperation between scores of individuals. Maybe more, Arun had no idea how many Trogs were involved. Thousands perhaps. Arun might have sparked the idea but it was made possible by Pedro's brains, the engineering and logistical capability of his nest-siblings, the guilt of the Agri Aux, and the bravery and tactical cunning of Springer and Madge.

And the Tunnel-Aux…

They were the greatest revelation of all.

At first the disgraced Blue Squad cadets had kept the other Aux out of the main picture, not fully trusting the others in Team Beta. Broken women and men could have sold them out for the chance of some more bread. But Adrienne was their ally here, helping to breathe some life back into Beta, enough for them to help out with simpler tasks. Perhaps she sensed that her world was changing, that this was her final chance to improve her lot, if only a little.

And it was still only pathetically little that Arun was offering his fellow Aux.

But for those with nothing, he mused one night as he listened to the ragged snoring in Beta's room, a little was a prize worth dying for.

———

Each day, Arun, Hortez, Springer and Madge would be sent off on a pointless mission to Alabama, the only purpose being to burn in the sun for the amusement of their alien mistresses. That might have been the Hardits' purpose, but the Blue Squad Aux used the time to plan, prepare and negotiate with the Agri-Aux.

Out in the fields the human workers were better organized than their equivalents servicing the tunnels. Fearful of the lethal effect of the sun's rays, the Hardits did everything they could to avoid emerging onto Tranquility's surface. That meant human taskmasters were in place, who reported daily progress toward quotas and milestones. They were very aware of the painful consequences of any slippage, but they were nonetheless free to run their own affairs.

The Hardits were so averse to the surface that it was a mystery the monkeys had fed themselves in the long millennia before human slaves were brought to the planet, the only clues being a crumbling underground ruin the Agri-Aux had discovered. Buried in the mud were plastic manacles far too big for human or Hardit limbs.

Underneath a veneer of pride and discipline a heart of darkness beat within each Agri-Aux, festering with the guilty knowledge that they were alive because they had denied others their protective suits. The outfits looked like pure white dresses patterned in pink, but they were steeped in blood.

Springer proved adept at exploiting this guilt, which she did mercilessly, although Esther put up little resistance.

Number 24 was the first to report the fruits of the Agri-Aux cooperation. She was one of the youngest in Team Beta, a girl much younger than the cadets. Despite coaxing from Springer and Madge, 24 refused to speak her real name, or anything about her former life. The only time Arun saw her smile was when she shyly came up to him one night to tell him that she had discovered protective outdoor gear, left in the topside building where she had emptied her cargo of novice excrement.

There were eight gifted outfits, crude hats and smocks sown from grain bags. Esther had spoken of them. Alistair had lived and died in one of those eight outfits. They hadn't the protective technology of the Agri workers' suits, but the outfits would ease the burn.

They were a welcome gesture.

When Esther came to see them later that afternoon in the Alabama depot, she had more help to offer. As she explained, her people weren't helping out because they were being nice. This operation was all about atonement, a gesture of contrition made for the dead, not for the benefit of the living. It would be a one off. All debts paid.

The final piece of the puzzle slotted into place when the banished Blue Squad cadets decided to let the rest of Beta in on the plan, co-opting Adrienne as their leader. The moment they saw that sly grin on her face when Springer told her what they had planned for Cliffie, they knew for sure then that Adrienne had thrown in her lot with the plot.

After three grueling days, finally everything was either in place or had to be abandoned because the countdown had hit zero.

Tomorrow was the day of the crucial Scendence matches, with the winners only two more steps away from Cull immunity.

Tomorrow was the final day of Arun's banishment to the Aux ranks. If Tawfiq's revenge was unsatisfied then she would want tomorrow to be the last day of his life.

It was time for Operation Clubhouse.

—— Chapter 40 ——

Before he faced danger, Arun was used to feeling either grim determination, utterly focused on the task at hand, or wild mania that usually led to unfortunate incidents.

But that was artificial, induced by drugs accessing the parts of his brain engineered to make him a good Marine.

There were no combat drugs in the Aux world, which he assumed was why Madge was starting to lighten up. But that meant to find courage today, Arun had to draw deep within himself. It wasn't working. Prickly heat flared along his spine, making the sweat drip down his back. The fear of letting his buddies down kept paralyzing him so that he couldn't move, could only bend over with hands on knees trying to find the courage to keep moving on his way to Team Gamma's room. The place where Cliffie had nearly suffocated him.

The opening act of Operation Clubhouse was down to Arun acting alone. When he planned this, it hadn't occurred to him that he might not have the guts to see it through.

Strangely the same fear of letting his friends down that made him pause, also drove him on, until with leaden limbs, he stumbled into Gamma's room at breakfast time. The memory of being asphyxiated under a mound of clothing made his heart flutter, and put such a wobble into his legs that he had to halt just beyond the threshold, not trusting his limbs to keep him upright if he took another step.

"Err, excuse me," said Arun, putting a quiver into his voice that didn't require much acting. "May I speak with you?"

He'd expected to find Cliffie seated on his throne, but this time he spotted the Gamma Team leader in one corner, hunched over in a secretive discussion with his lieutenants. Cliffie cast a scornful glance at Arun and then went back to his meeting. That was the extent of Arun's audience with Gamma's leader, but one of the lieutenants separated herself from the group and walked over to him.

"What do you want?" she sneered, arms folded in front of her.

She was heavy set with livid bruising around her left cheek. With a start he realized that her wound probably came from the fight the last time Arun was here.

"Please, I wish to beg for more of our food to be returned."

The lieutenant walked around Arun, inspecting him disdainfully. When she'd made a full circuit, she leaned in to his face and said: "You haven't brought any gifts to bargain with. So why should we give you food?"

"Because every day since I was last here, you've taken seven of our eight buckets. We only have one left. We're dying of starvation."

While this exchange had been going on, about a dozen members of Gamma team had formed a ring around Arun and the lieutenant. Each of them carried a handful of shorts.

"I'll give you one more chance," said the lieutenant, playing to her audience. "And think about your answer very carefully, because it will have consequences. Why should we give you our food?"

"Because Cliffie said you weren't heartless."

The lieutenant lifted her hand up high.

Arun's breath came in short gasps. He started to hunch himself over, anticipating what would come next.

"Wrong answer," said the lieutenant. She clicked her fingers and her team sprang into action.

Arun clenched his hands but didn't fight back when his assailants threw the shorts over his head and bundled him into the pile of clothing, burying him.

Events didn't play out as before. This time, Arun used the moments before the weight above him became crushing to snake his arm down into the mound of clothing and plant a gift from Pedro: a radio transmitter.

Today was a Scendence Day, when the cadets and novices would either be playing the game or watching it. The centerpiece of Operation Clubhouse was a radio show linked to the day's Scendence feeds. After all, what was the point of the clubhouse if they couldn't listen in on the game? The radio signal needed boosting from a location close to the surface. Hosting the transmitter in their room on Level 4 was to be Team Gamma's contribution to a day to remember.

As the crush began to deny him the oxygen his brain craved, and the edges of the world grew fuzzier, Arun held on to the hope that the transmitter meant Gamma would take the blame for what was to follow.

On the limits of consciousness, Arun was yanked out of the clothing pile and thrown onto his knees at Cliffie's feet.

"You have at least learned respect and politeness," said Cliffie. "I appreciate that. To show my appreciation I gift you your life. This generosity will not be repeated. If you enter this room again, my people will kill you on sight."

Arun didn't get off his knees, but did raise his gaze to look upon his master. "I understand, sir."

Cliffie raised an expectant eyebrow.

"Thank you, sir. Thank you for your mercy and generosity."

"There, that wasn't so difficult."

Arun had to keep from smiling. Cliffie was right. Playing the part of a groveling fool *wasn't so difficult*. Especially since all the while, Arun knew who the real dunkchunk was.

Natural Law finds in our favor this time, he thought. *Let's see how you enjoy it, you dirty skangat.*

—— Chapter 41 ——

"Did you do it?" asked Adrienne.

In reply, Arun could only nod. His lungs still burned. Every gasp of air was too valuable to be expended on speech.

Springer put her arm around him. "You've been a total shunter recently, but you did well today, Arun."

She gave a quick squeeze, and then the moment was gone, though the memory lingered for Arun.

Madge spoke into one of the radios the Trogs had smuggled their way. "You there, Hort?"

"Acknowledged." Now that Gamma's transmitter had boosted the signal strength, Hortez's voice came through the radio as cleanly as if he were there. He wasn't. Operation Clubhouse required someone to stay behind. Someone to take the blame too, most likely. What Pedro called the audience

chamber – where he and Arun had their chats – had been transformed into a communications hub, with Hortez at the controls.

"We're ready to roll, sir," said Madge crisply.

"Sir?" Hortez laughed. "You're a crazy one, Majanita. I declare Operation Clubhouse is a go. Good luck, everyone. And if you do make it topside, I expect you to enjoy yourselves. That's an order."

"Yes, sir." It wasn't just Madge who'd replied. Over the encrypted channel other voices respectfully acknowledged Hortez's instruction.

Before the arrival of Arun and the disgraced Blue Squad cadets, the morale of the Aux teams had been so pitifully low that none of them had tried fooling the Hardits with such tricks as swapping scent-marked overalls. Now that Arun had shown the way and Adrienne had cajoled and bullied her fellow Aux, Team Beta and their allies in other Aux teams were roaming through Detroit almost at will.

Over a hundred Detroit Aux were involved in today's operation. But the plan extended even beyond Detroit. From his Trog sanctuary, Hortez gave the signal to the Alabama Agri-Aux to initiate their diversion.

—— Chapter 42 ——

As far as Sushantat Feriek-Khull was concerned, the human animals of Aux Team Beta were lined up as normal in their two cowering rows, waiting obediently for her to complete the morning roll call and issue the day's work assignments.

Which only made her appear an utter dumbchuck to her supposed human inferiors, who couldn't help but set a charge of excitement buzzing throughout the room. Any human would instantly spot that something big was going on.

Not for the first time, the Hardit completed the roll call, satisfied that she had accounted for every human worker. The correct scent-marked clothing might be present, but not the bodies inside. Hortez's overalls were currently swamping a petite girl from Team Alpha called Kalynda. As far as the Hardits were concerned, Kalynda was supposed to be bringing food back from the kitchens for Team Alpha's breakfast, a task actually being carried out by an ally from Team Delta. The Aux had jumped into the game of swapping clothing so enthusiastically that Madge had tried and failed to rein it in. What was supposed to be their secret advantage had transformed into a game played for the simple pleasure of flipping a finger up in the Hardits' snouts.

Sushantat started issuing the assignments, giving no sign that she knew any of this.

A call came over the overseer's wrist comm, instantly clamping the room into silence. The humans had been waiting for this.

The Hardit's natural attitude was one of listlessness, as if encountering the humans was an arduous imposition that deserved a long lie down afterwards. Sushantat was the most active of the lot, officially number two, but effectively running the day-to-day Aux operations in Beta's area. That impression of laziness evaporated when the call came through. Her ears flattened against her head; her lips pulled back to reveal a jaw filled with sharp teeth through which she sucked air into suddenly purposeful muscles.

"The situation changes," she said. "All of you wait here."

Sushantat left. Striding as far as the doorway, she then dropped to all fours and cantered away, her motion making a loud skittering noise surprisingly similar to the Trogs.

"Is that it?" shouted Number 72 in disdain. There were murmurs of anger from the other Aux. She was a gaunt woman who wouldn't share her human name. "We risked our lives for what? To stay here?" She spat at Arun. "Look at him, the magnificent General 106. His plan has won us a day cooped up in this hellhole."

Adrienne confronted 72, toe-to-toe. "Shut up!" she barked.

But 72 was right, thought Arun. What had Hortez told him? To give hope to the hopeless, only to snatch it away… that was the greatest cruelty of all. And for all his big dreams, the only thing Arun had actually achieved so far was to store up a great expectation of hope.

He ran, dashing past Beta's supply store, machine room, parts room, and out in the main corridor where the smell was neutral and the floor regularly cleaned.

Sushantat was still out of sight, but Arun's hearing had been gene-optimized and augmented by amplifiers and wetware filters. Following the skittering sound of the speeding Hardit echoing off the hard corridor surfaces was simple. But the Hardit's sense of smell was acute. Could she smell him following? If she could and stopped him, then he was dead.

Too late to worry about that now, he decided.

He was committed.

He followed her in an arc around the edges of the novice area and out again to a passageway off the main corridor where the ceiling had been lowered. Nice and snug for Hardits; just the way they liked it.

As he passed more junctions, he trusted more to his instinctive sense of direction.

Finally he came to a closed door. It had been two minutes since he'd last heard Sushantat. Either she was behind that door or he'd lost her.

Nothing to lose!

He pushed the door access stud. As soon as the door slid into its housing, he was assailed by a wave of Hardit-stink.

The room had been lowered even more than the passageway outside. It was extensive, though, with banks of computer equipment winking status lights in the shadowy depths. He didn't get much of a look because rubbing together in a tail-swishing huddle were four Hardits.

"See, I told you," said Sushantat through her voice synthesizer when Arun burst into the room. "This animal has followed me all the way back from its hovel."

There were three other Hardits here: Hen Beddes-Stolarz, Tawfiq Woomer-Calix, and the boss that the humans rarely saw: Biljah Hilleskill-Khull.

They looked uninterested in Arun's arrival, as if there were more important matters. But what did he really know about Hardits and their politics? He'd have to start laying his bets or his plan would fall at the first hurdle.

"Mistress," he cried, "I beg you. Let me convey valuable information. In Ala… arghh!"

Arun's breath was squeezed from his body as he crashed to the ground, rolled up into a ball of agony. As he fell, his eyes caught sight of Tawfiq holding out the grubby little box that sent waves of intolerable pain through his overalls.

He tried to wrench his jaw open to explain, to beg… to breathe. But the pain gripped him so tightly that all he could move were his eyeballs.

He pleaded with all he had left, forcing his eyes to look up at Tawfiq. She seemed to understand, was showing him mercy, because she switched off the pain device.

Arun's muscles spasmed back into some semblance of working order. He drew in one breath. Then another. Just as he was about to tell them his lie, Tawfiq turned the pain device back on.

She hadn't shown mercy at all! She was taking care that he didn't asphyxiate too quickly. If she wanted to prolong his pain, she had to let him breathe occasionally.

Tawfiq alternated bouts of agony with the briefest of respites until Arun was too dazed and his brain too oxygen starved to feel the pain.

Amazingly, he discovered he was breathing again.

Did that mean he had died?

"… waste our time. This one is diseased. It is better to kill him quickly."

As his brain reconnected with his hearing, Arun noticed artificial human words drifting into his ears. The Hardits were speaking in their own language simultaneously with the computer translation. Each synthetic voice sounded identical, but the angry alien voices did not. Arun recognized the speaker as Sushantat, the one he had followed… the Hardit he could see bringing out her own pain controller and adjusting its setting…

Arun was engulfed in a new level of agony. Instead of his muscles locking up and feeling as if they were being skewered by a thousand viciously barbed needles, this new torture was like drowning in an ocean of hellfire. His muscles were free for him to spasm, to writhe and groan. This setting was not designed to inflict pain.

This was killing him.

He could feel his insides fry, his spirit consumed in the flames that he could feel but not see, the fire that burned inside him.

He tried again to plead but he still could not speak. His jaw muscles refused to obey because any movement was even more agony.

With a supreme effort of will, he opened a tiny gap in his mouth and tried to speak. All that emerged was a primal grunt and an acrid smell of smoldering.

He tried telling himself that this grunt had been only a start, something he could build upon. But he had expended all his reserves of courage and strength to utter it. He was spent.

The pain lessened.

He managed to glance up at Sushantat.

She was talking with the others, her hand still activating the pain device, but ignoring him now.

Sushantat hadn't reduced his punishment, Arun realized, this was his body shorting out, shutting down in readiness for oblivion. His brain numbed too. Thoughts were difficult to form. Blurring. A last thought came clearly: he was dying. This was where he ended.

No! He would not allow it!

Others had thought he had a destiny. The Aux had placed a great expectation upon him. He. Must. Not. Fail. Them.

"Al-a-bam-a," he cried. His voice heaved like a child talking through uncontrollable sobbing. "Not a… fire! Slave… revolt."

Biljah stopped speaking and looked at this writhing human.

"Guns," Arun cried.

The pain switched off.

Waves of sensation replaced the numbness.

He preferred the numbness because the alternative was worse. He screamed with the pain.

Arun sat there moaning for a long time. How long, he had no idea – his timer implants weren't functioning. Then he noticed two things. He was lying in a pool of his own vomit and Biljah was yelling at him to explain himself.

He gave himself another handful of breaths and then answered. "Mistress Sushantat said there was a fire at Alabama."

"I don't remember saying that," said Sushantat.

"You must have," said Biljah. "How else could the human have known?"

Arun tensed, praying that the Hardits wouldn't answer their own question. The humans knew about the fire because they had organized it, but the idea that humans could do such a thing was still inconceivable to the arrogant monkeys. Sushantat appeared to have conceded.

Arun continued. "I connected the news of the fire with rumors I've heard about Alabama. There are secret caches of guns and explosives. Could this be the start of a slave revolt?"

"Preposterous," said Sushantat. "He lies to save his life."

"But can we be sure what he says is not true?" asked Hen.

"If you give credence to this one's words," said Sushantat, "then we should send the Jotuns and their primitive soldiers in their shiny armor to investigate. That is their role, isn't it? To die in battle?"

Biljah considered. "I do not wish to smell their contempt if we cry panic over an incident that turns out to be innocent."

"Well, if you are so worried about them, organize the agricultural humans based at the depot to report on the situation," said Sushantat.

"I cannot," replied Biljah. "There is a crop fire fifteen miles northwest of the depot. I have already sent the local humans to extinguish it."

"What!" Sushantat looked agitated. "Why did you not inform me? I begin to believe this human's words. One or both events could be diversions. Send in the soldiers."

"No," said Biljah. "Not yet. Not until I'm sure."

"What alternative do you have?" insisted Sushantat. "Do you expect me to fight? I refuse!"

Arun looked from one Hardit to the other, trying to understand the balance of the argument. All along he'd gambled that the Hardits would be unable to ignore a major fire in the food depot, but would be so scared of accidentally revealing their gun-smuggling operation that they would be desperate to avoid bringing in outsiders, such as the Marines.

Arun hadn't considered that some Hardits were unaware of the gun smuggling, but that was the only way to explain Shushantat's attitude. She might have just tried to murder him, but she appeared to be the most honest person in the room.

Then he realized that he was best out of the argument, and cast his eyes to the ground.

"There *is* a way," said Tawfiq. "Team Beta suffers from a chronic oversupply of workers. If the situation were dangerous, then a few casualties from Beta would be to everyone's advantage, even any surviving humans."

Thank you. Tawfiq had just spoken the words Arun had been praying for.

"Too risky," said Sushantat. "We need military assistance without delay."

"Need I remind you who is in charge here?" Biljah's artificially voiced words were expressionless, but Arun was sure she was issuing some stern scents to her subordinate.

The leader of the Hardits suddenly remembered Arun was there and switched off her human translation. The argument raged on for a short while. Arun couldn't follow a word, but at the end of it, he was still alive and following Tawfiq back to Team Beta's room.

Arun had barely made it out with his life, but he'd done the necessary.

Operation Clubhouse was back on.

——— Chapter 43 ———

"Mistress, this slave begs to report our status."

Arun shook his head. Adrienne was enjoying this a little too much. Any human listening in would hear the smirk behind her words.

"Report," came Tawfiq's artificial voice through Adrienne's radio, which was turned up loud enough to fill the truck cab.

"Thank you mistress. We have caught and interrogated an Agri-Aux."

"And?"

"And they are concealing something."

"Concealing what? Explosives? Weapons?"

"We have not discovered weapons. I meant that the Agri-Aux knows something but would not reveal what she knew."

"You're playing a dangerous game," whispered Arun. He was sitting alongside Adrienne in the truck cab. Madge glowered at her from the driver's seat.

"Do not trust the crop slaves," said Tawfiq. "Stay on your guard."

"Oh, mistress. I never knew you cared."

Madge reached over and switched off the radio.

Arun could practically see the sparks fly between the two women.

"Go check the others are okay," Madge ordered him between clenched teeth.

Arun took the hint. He opened up the hatch in the cab and climbed out, leaving Adrienne and Madge to work out between them who was in charge. Arun would back his squadmate without hesitation, but he understood that Madge wanted to prove she was the commander without Arun there to outnumber Adrienne.

He heaved himself up, closed the hatch and clambered over the spine of the lurching dung truck.

The truck's powerplant was completely silent, but the heavy tread tires made enough racket to nearly drown out the angry squawks of the birds they disturbed as they drove along the same track they always used to get to Alabama.

Arun was sore all over from the Hardit's pain shocks, but his sense of balance was undamaged. He stood up and walked toward the rear, arms thrown out for balance. On the road behind them he could see Springer driving the other truck. They waved to each other.

When Tawfiq had sent Team Beta out to investigate the strange goings-on at Alabama, giving them strict instructions to never speak of what they found to anyone but her, it was Adrienne who had requested transport. The result was the trucks that ferried the broken-down human excrement from Detroit to the farmland depot: the *Alabama Dung Express*.

The poop trucks consisted of a wheeled frame to which four pods were attached by mag clamps, two pairs hanging from either side of a central spine. Instead of raw ingredients for fertilizer, today one of the pods had a different cargo.

Arun opened up the hatch on top of the pod and shouted inside. "Everything all right in there?"

He was greeted with a cheer.

"I guess that's a yes then. You want I should close the hatch?"

"No, it's a lovely day. Keep it open."

"You got it."

Arun and many of the Aux inside the pod were wearing skirts and bonnets – the full high-tech protective kit. Esther's people had donated eight crude suits earlier in the week, but today all of her Agri-Aux had decided to forego their full protective gear as part of their atonement.

Arun hoped she wasn't going to be frakked off when she learned they'd taken the dung express rather than walk.

"Hey, McEwan!" came a call from the hatch.

"What?"

"We can't get radio reception down here. Catch!"

Someone threw a speaker up through the hatch. Arun clamped his radio to the hatch, connected the speaker then settled down, sitting astride the truck's spine, looking out over the fields. Now that he was properly shielded, he could appreciate the beauty of the golden crops as they rippled in a light breeze under delicate flakes of pure white clouds. Arun could happily spend the entire day looking at clouds; they were so beautiful and he didn't often get to see them.

In the distance he could see the last few wisps of smoke dissipating in the sky from one of the fake fires the Agri-Aux had started, using the smoke bombs provided by Pedro. Hopefully they had given off enough heat to look like a genuine fire to any orbiting satellite.

Arun turned his back on the smoke. That was someone else's problem now. Having done his bit, he was looking forward to taking the rest of the day off. He'd never had a vacation before.

He settled down to enjoy the broadcast from Radio Hortez.

——— Chapter 44 ———

So there you have it, Scendence fans, The Stormers from 4th battalion, 101st Assault Regiment have knocked out Divine Inspiration from 5th battalion, 420th Tac. While we wait for the next game, stick with Radio Hortez as we return once again to Team Ultimate Victory's Deception-Planning match from earlier today, against the Fieldgrays from 1st battalion, 410th Tac.

Each match uses a randomly selected game or challenge, and for this contest the Scendence AI has selected an old favorite, Skat. It's an ancient Earth card game, folks. Skat's a popular game because it rewards bluff, risk taking, and a grasp of probability statistics. Up till this point in the game, our bug-ugly contestant from Team Ultimate Victory has lost every hand. Fieldgrays opponent, Kadian Stadeker, has kept a straight face but now I can see his expression soften, a faint smile on his lips. He's coasting to an easy victory against the surprise Troggie substitution for disgraced idiot, Arun McEwan. Or so he thinks. Let's begin our replay by hearing what our scribe friend has to say after losing yet another hand.

"You do realize, Stadeker, that I have bluffed all along. I have allowed you to win up to this point. I have just been dealt an excellent hand and I shall beat you with it. It is not that I especially wish you to lose, but I wish to win more."

"What do you mean? You want to win more than I do?"

"No. I wish to win more than I don't want you to lose."

"Eh? Your language skills are even worse than your card playing. You're talking utter drent."

"I regret to tell you, Stadeker, that you are incorrect. It is your ability to listen and comprehend that is utter drent."

Kadian shrugs that barb away, but you can see on his face that he's rattled.

"Eight of hearts."

"You what?"

"Ten of bells. Unter of acorns."

"What are you playing at, insect?"

"Unter of bells. Ten of leaves."

"Hey stop that!"

"King of leaves."

"That's frakking cheating."

"No, this is using my natural frakking advantages. I can smell your hormones the way you can see words in a book. Shall we ask the referee to adjudicate?"

Have you ever had the sense that you've snatched defeat from the jaws of victory? No? If you could only see Stadeker's face you would understand exactly what it must feel like. Only moments before he was certain of easy victory. Now he's so confused that he isn't certain of anything. If you told Stadeker that his name was Merry Madge, he'd probably believe you.

Mind you, your host on Radio Hortez can hardly believe what he's seeing either. I've watched this scene five, maybe six, times now and it still makes my eyes pop. The competitors are sitting at a small circular table covered in a black velvet cloth. Well, I say sitting, but our insect – who goes by the name of Pedro – is resting its seven-foot-long bulk on a kind of bench that leaves its back two pairs of legs free to wiggle along with its feelers. Its front pair of limbs holds a hand of cards. Its drab thorax – the middle segment of its body – is coated in fine rust-colored hairs, neatly brushed for the big occasion. Its abdomen – the lower and largest part of the Trog – is mottled in shades of brown and gray and coated in semi-transparent carapace armor that gleams like highly polished lacquer. He looks like the kind of ultimate monster. If you met our Pedro in your dreams you'd wet yourself in fright, but our insect hero is calmly lying there, holding a hand of playing cards. It's simply bizarre, my friends. Unbelievable.

Tell you what, though. Our big ant is built for these bluffing card games. It's staring at Stadeker through twin pairs of eyes like glossy black glass bowls, making absolutely no facial expressions at all. And it's speaking through a thought-to-speech device. No giveaway tells there, folks.

I'll hand you back to Pedro…

"I insist we consult the referee, because I play not only for victory but to uphold the good name of my nest."

"Your nest doesn't have a name, insect. Just a smell. A bad one too, I expect."

"On the contrary, we do have a human name. We are Nest Clubhouse."

Yeah! Let's hear it for Nest Clubhouse. Just remember who's made all this possible today. I can't name names without risking getting our benefactor into trouble. Let's just say this Scendence match had us hanging on a Cliff-edge, eh?

Back to the match. The ref confirms that trash talking to your opponent is all part of the game. As for Stadeker – get this! – now he's shielding his face, hiding it behind his hands.

"Unter of leaves. Nine of bells."

"You can cut that out. I'm not talking to you."

"Well, that's a relief. I don't want you to. I don't need to see your face either. I can smell your reaction as I name each possible card you might hold. Seven of bells. Seven of acorns."

"Damn you, skangat insect."

"You smell upset. If I were you, I'd play my first card ASAP. The longer you delay, the more of your hand I will uncover."

Stadeker makes his play. It's the ten of bells, the trump suit.

"A safe play. Very sensible under the circumstances, Stadeker. After all, I will soon know your entire hand and you have no idea what I've been dealt.

That gives me a crushing advantage, don't you think? Only a miracle of good fortune can save you from defeat.

Our bug-ugly friend, Pedro, was right. He won that hand. And the next. And every hand after that until he played the winning card and claimed a stunning victory for Team Ultimate Victory, standing in for Arun McEwan who was too busy with his vacation to make it to the match today.

They say a great Scendence player is crushing in victory and stoic in defeat. Was Kadian Stadeker calm? Was he heck! Let's fast forward to my favorite part of the match. Pedro has just won, and Stadeker is on his feet, thumping the table and hurling abuse at the big insect. Looks to me like there's going to be a fight.

"You're a skangat cheat!"

"The referee disagrees."

"The referee can go vulley herself. I'm talking about all the cadets watching this. In their eyes you're a cheat. Maybe you don't care, but the human players in your team are cheats too by association. A stench of dishonor will hang around them for the rest of their lives."

"If I were you, young human, I would sit down. It is you who risk dishonoring yourself. In your human translation of the Jotun bifurcated-noun, the game we have just played is called Deception-Planning, is it not?"

"It is. Notice the word 'cheat' doesn't appear there."

"Indeed not. To win by cheating would be vile. And since you are a much more experienced skat player than me, I planned to win by deception instead. I convinced you that I could smell your reaction when I named each card. I can't. That was a lie."

Dear, Radio Hortez fans. I'd give anything to swap places with each and every one of you right now, so you can see with your own eyes the expression on Kadian Stadeker's face.

To begin with, his face is bloated with disgust and envy. To get the idea, picture a ripe cabbage in place of his head, a vegetable bursting with greenness. Now imagine filming that cabbage being cooked for an hour in a steam bath, until it is the color of bleached bone. Finally, speed up the cabbage-cooking footage a thousand-fold.

There.

Now you know how Stadeker's expression changed as he realized how he'd been artfully played by the latest Scendence sporting sensation.

Okay, let's move on. Pedro gave an interview after the match. I warn you, do not drive, operate machinery or fire tripod-mounted weapons while listening to this interview. It is so hilarious it will have you in fits of hysteria.

Belay that! We'll come back to that laughter-fest in a moment. There's a live interview with Xin Lee just starting. I'll patch you through to the feed now.

"… whose crazy idea was it to field a Trog substitute?"

"A team effort. Everything about today has been one huge team effort. Sometimes, it seems the whole of Detroit and beyond is backing us."

"I think you're right. Team Ultimate Victory is the comeback team of this year's Scendence season. Your Trog is filling in for your previous super-sub, Arun McEwan. Was it strange to play without McEwan?"

"Not really. Arun was with us more than you realize. If you're listening, Cadet Prong, I have a hug and more waiting for you. Oh, and tell your little girlfriend, Madge, hi from me. She sent me such a sweet message telling me all about your predicament."

"Do I detect a hint of team romance, Xin?"

"I don't think so. Anyway, nice talking with you. We've won two of our four matches today, which means there are still two more to win. I'm heading over to the Gunnery arena now."

Well, what can I say? You heard it first on Radio Hortez. Arun McEwan has a little girlfriend called Madge. She sounds a sweet thing. If anyone can see Arun's girlfriend right now, please radio in a description of her face. C'mon, it's only fair. I described Stadeker for you!

While we wait for that, stick around, sports fans. Let's not forget that there are sixteen teams still in the competition and all are playing today. We've just got time to hear that interview with Pedro before the Endurance-Stoicism game between two teams from the 101st Assault Marines, Nevergation and Bluffmore Stags. Don't go away.

———

"Don't anyone say a word." Madge spoke with slow menace.

There was silence in the clubhouse for about a second before Arun couldn't help himself.

"That goes for me too," he announced. "If anyone upsets my little girlfriend, I'll be really, really cross."

Madge's punch came quicker than he'd expected, catching him a glancing blow even though he was already rolling off his lounger constructed from half-filled grain sacks. He fell onto the floor of Alabama Depot, surrounded by billows of laughter echoing from the roof high above.

—— Chapter 45 ——

"We are winning the battle, mistress. We will overcome the fire or… or…" Adrienne had to stop a moment. Otherwise she would burst out laughing and even Tawfiq might grow suspicious "Or we will die in the attempt."

"Make sure you do one or the other," commanded Tawfiq over the handheld communicator. "The food stocks are far more valuable than your lives. Are you sure you cannot simply move the food sacks out of danger? I do not understand why you say this is impossible."

Aware of her human audience, Adrienne made a show of looking around the loading bay of the depot. Most of the food stores were safely stacked on pallets to one side, but smaller sacks had been arranged into crude tables and chairs that held food, water, or lazing Tunnel-Aux gesturing for Adrienne to hurry up so they could turn the radios back on and listen to the game.

In the center of the warehouse was a stepped pyramid with a flat top. One of the two young Agri-Aux who had remained behind to greet the Tunnel-Aux had explained this this pyramid was the dance stage.

"I regret, mistress," said Adrienne with great solemnity, "the sacks are underneath immovable objects but they are not in immediate danger of burning."

"Talk with you wastes my time," said Tawfiq. Arun tried to imagine her jumping up and down in frustration. "Do not report in again until you have defeated the fire."

"If you insist mistress. I return to my endeavors. Number 87 out." Adrienne switched off her communicator to the cheers of her audience. Within moments, the commentary from Radio Hortez blared out once more from a dozen crude portable radio receivers.

"Is the monkey still buying it?" asked Springer, leaving wet footprints on the floor as she padded over from the shower.

"Yup. She's even more stupid than we thought." Arun glanced up at the roof where the young Agri-Aux had climbed the hanging rope ladders and were leaning out of a hatch to smear Pedro's fire gel onto the roof. "Reckon we've got a few hours of firefighting left."

The military-grade satellites orbiting Tranquility would spot the deception in an instant, but the Jotuns controlled those. Whatever system had told the Hardits of the fire was much cruder, possibly thousands of years older too.

For once, everything was going to plan. Arun felt invincible, or would have done if every muscle in his body wasn't still groaning under the abuse heaped on him by the Hardit torture. Even his knee was playing up again, the one he'd damaged firing grenades point blank into a Troggie horde. Setting his pains aside, he opened his arm, inviting Springer in for a cuddle.

"Oh, no," she teased. "Not with someone who hasn't washed."

Arun laughed. "How was the shower?"

Springer laughed too. "Strangely good. Here…" She threw him the sacking material she'd been using to dry her hair. "Your turn."

"I can take a hint," he said cheerfully, winking at Springer as he walked off to the fab shop.

In theory there were no showers at the depot. Why would any expense be allocated to the comfort of human slaves? But what the fab shop did have

was a small degreasing booth intended to prepare metals and other materials before powder coating them with paint and other protective outer layers.

The Agri-Aux had modified the booth for the occasion.

How bad could it be?

Arun stripped off the baggy white undergarments of his borrowed protective suit, punched the on/off button and jumped onto the conveyor belt. As the belt pushed him toward the heavy plastic strips that marked the entrance to the booth, Arun sat down, the hollow diamond pattern of the belt cutting painfully into his butt. He brought his knees up and head down; the entrance didn't look designed for comfort.

As the plastic strips parted and lukewarm water began squirting at him, he relaxed and uncurled. It wasn't as bad as he'd thought. He could almost stand up if he wanted.

Then choking clouds of de-greasing agent filled the booth, rubbed in by flailing fabric fingers. His eyes stung. So did every inch of his skin. He yelped when his brutalized muscles screamed in protest.

He was the last one through. All the Tunnel-Aux had experienced this and come out with gleaming smiles to match their grease-free hair. He'd never seen such a transformation in morale.

He squealed in protest when scalding hot water suddenly jetted up from below.

"Are you okay?" came a voice from outside the booth.

Springer's face poked through the strips on the far side of the booth. "Oh, it's you Arun. I could have sworn I heard a little girl screaming in there."

"Very funny."

"Yes, I thought so." She threw him a cheeky grin. "Don't forget to clean behind your ears, Arun. I'll be waiting for you on the outside." Her head disappeared.

Before Arun could reply, he was drenched in a sudden outpouring of cold water. The groan of a motor started up as hot air began to blast him.

He shouted into the wind: "You'd better make it worth my while, Phaedra Tremayne."

Arun smiled.

She already had.

————

Springer reached over and caressed Arun's furrowed brow. "Loosen up," she said. "Enjoy. You've earned it."

She snuggled beside him as they relaxed with a few other members of Team Beta in a nest of hay in the loading bay. "Stop worrying," she whispered.

After the stunt they'd played today, there probably wasn't going to be any future. But Arun had spent a lifetime worrying about tomorrow and the habit was too strong to break now.

"I've done something for the first time today," he said. "I've gambled with other people's lives. And…" He took a deep breath. "I think I like it."

"I know. I'm surprised at you, McEwan. You told me once that you would hate to be a leader, because you would be paralyzed by thoughts of what would happen if your plans went wrong."

"Exactly. Look around at all these happy faces. I feel so proud to see them, but then I wonder whether it was worth the risks I took on their behalf just to plant those smiles there? Even if that transmitter I planted on Cliffie puts the blame on him, we could all be executed before nightfall. At least we've a chance. Hortez hasn't. He volunteered for a suicide mission. And all that for such a gamble. It was only a guess that the Hardits would send us here because they would be scared that more official help would reveal their gun running."

"Stop it. You're beginning to sound sorry for yourself. There's nothing more pathetic than sad-mouthing, especially when you start to bend the facts to match your sob story. Coming here to the clubhouse wasn't really essential. Aux have been hiding themselves all over Detroit today, listening in on secret radios. This–" she waved around the room, at the smiling Tunnel-Aux staining their borrowed white clothes in their rush to cram food into hungry mouths – "has been brilliant, but we could still have listened in on Radio Hortez if we'd had to stay in Detroit."

Arun wasn't listening. Springer waited for him as he floundered in his thoughts, trying to turn them into words that would make sense.

"You know me better than I know myself," he told her. "The way I've used other people… have I become so cynical, or was I driven by desperation? Hortez will die, maybe others. I ought to feel guilty but I only feel stoked because I put one over on Cliffie and on the Hardits. What's happening to me, Springer?"

"Dear Arun. It's your true nature emerging. I don't think you'll like what you're becoming."

"I don't follow."

Springer kissed him. Arun noticed nearby Aux point and smile. Madge looked over from the bowl of stew she was eating and gave Arun a dirty look.

"You're fighting a losing battle against overwhelming odds," Springer told him. "Generations of selective breeding and indoctrination have brought you to this point. You can't fight such powerful forces, Arun. You're growing into a Marine."

Soon after, the main body of Agri-Aux returned, their skin hot and raw from the merciless sun.

As they made their way to the water canisters, to slake their thirst and pour cool water over hot bodies, the Tunnel-Aux smiles became guarded. The volume was turned down on Radio Hortez.

Water beaker in her hand, Esther emerged from the milling crowd of Agri-Aux. Arun rose to meet her, his own beaker raised high in salute.

"Here's to being human," he announced in a voice loud enough to carry through the crowd.

"To being human," echoed Springer, Madge and many of the Beta Aux.

Some of the Agri-Aux joined in with the toast too, but Esther waved them into silence.

Tunnel-Aux edged closer together for mutual protection.

Arun had missed something. What?

"My people will join your toast," announced Esther, "but not until we have something proper to toast with."

"Like what?" asked Arun.

Esther snapped her fingers. On the other side of the bay from the food, a cover was pulled away from a table to reveal a row of 5 gallon canisters with taps fixed at their bases.

"Like that!" said Esther.

"What is it?" asked Madge. "More water?"

"We work with the grain. We know how to extract its fruit." Esther's explanation was lost on Arun and the others.

"It's beer, man," called out one of the Aux in a peal of laughter.

"What is *beer*?" asked Arun, but that only provoked more gales of laughter. He looked to Madge and Springer for help, but they looked as puzzled as him.

Esther put an arm over Arun's shoulder. "My friend, this is a party you'll never forget."

"More likely it's a party he won't be able to remember," someone called out.

Esther ignored the heckle and steered her ally toward the beer.

"Remind me again," Arun asked Springer when the light coming through the doors to the hardened area outside was beginning to fade and redden. "What're we supposed to be doing here?"

"Partying!"

"No, I mean, like, what did we tell the Hardits we were doing?"

"Oh. Something about a fire, I think."

Arun took a moment to understand Springer's slurred speech. He remembered now. He looked up at the fake fire in the roof and frowned. He didn't remember anyone applying the smoking gel for a long while.

"Getting dark," said Springer. "D'ya think they're getting worried 'bout us?"

She and Arun looked into each other's eyes, trying to keep a straight face. They erupted into giggles.

Arun retrieved the communicator from where Adrienne had last left it. With a flourish, he activated the device.

There was the briefest of pauses before Tawfiq's voice screamed through the speaker. "Report. Report. Report!"

"Tawfiq. How're you, my fine, furry friend?"

"Who is this?"

"197 ????" Arun scratched his head. "I don't recall. I never forget a name but with numbers… I'm hopeless."

"What occurs? Report!"

"Keep yer fur on. What're we doing, eh?" He looked around at the buzzing party. The dance floor was heaving to the percussive rhythms struck from upturned metal drums. "Umm, we're busy, I guess."

"What is that noise I hear?"

"People. People doing stuff."

"Stunted imbecile. Where is 87?"

"87? Oh, you mean Adrienne? Let me see…" Arun scanned the warehouse and spied Adrienne on the dance floor, grinding out some raunchy moves in front of an eager young buck with his shirt off.

"87 is engaged in an encounter with an Agri-worker."

Springer stifled a laugh.

"I think," said Arun. "Think she's trying to go undercover to discover his secrets."

Springer exploded into laughter, bringing Arun with her in fits of giggles.

"Give it here. Silly veck-ek-eks." Arun looked up to see Madge standing over him with an open palm thrust in his face. She was bathed in sweat having just returned from an expedition to the dance floor herself, bringing back a gaggle of male admirers with her.

Arun handed over the comm.

"Corporal Majajazazaa here, ma'am." Madge's words were slurred worse than Springer's. "Firefighting party will return to home to you–"

"Do so, immediately."

"–as soon as conditions permit. Mazazeeta out."

Madge cut off the sound of Hardit protest, took aim, and threw the device 10 meters into a pan of warm stew.

Madge was so drunk she could barely stand or talk. But she could dance and – it seemed – she could throw. The communicator landed dead center in the pan and disappeared to contribute its favors to the stew.

Springer whistled in admiration. "Your targeting skills are impressive, corporal."

Arun was impressed too, but was relieved to see Madge return to the dance floor. Her hostility to him had reduced, but only by a hair's breadth.

He pulled Springer closer to him. She fitted so perfectly, snuggled under his shoulder, as if they had been engineered to complement each other.

Basking in the warmth of her embrace, he took a gulp of beer and recorded onto his implants the sights and sounds of the party, from the clumps of strangers in conversation to the pounding beat from the ever-changing lineup of drummers. He tried to memorize the scents too, though he had no means of digitally recording them: the smell of fresh perspiration, freshly-baked bread, and sticky beer spills. He nuzzled Springer's neck, drawing in her scent, the most precious of them all.

Then he settled into the simple pleasure of watching everyone else have fun.

Other than a few of the male Agri-Aux who had stripped to the waist to show off muscled torsos, everyone there was dressed alike in loose white underclothes. Arun looked from one happy human face to another, and whether they worked the tunnels and passageways of Detroit or the fields of Alabama he could not tell.

They were all of them human.

And just for a little while longer. Being human was all that mattered.

—— Chapter 46 ——

It was Adrienne who eventually rounded up Team Beta and herded them back into the dung trucks for the trip back to Detroit. She even managed to bully them back into the Aux overalls they'd left behind in the cargo pod.

After a few hours of blissful cleanliness, persuading the drunken Aux to don their stinking rags took such impressive leadership that even Arun noticed.

She's the one with the keenest eye on the future, he thought, but he kept his assessment to himself. Thoughts of what awaited them on their return pressed everyone into a somber silence as the trucks drove through the night.

Madge had driven them here but she was in no fit state now, so Adrienne took the wheel of one truck, with Springer driving the other. Arun kept Springer company in the cab while Madge slept with their passengers in their dung pod.

The drive back was bumpy and the track somehow seemed narrower because the drivers continually slipped down the bank, raising groans from their passengers.

Eventually they gave up and drove through the fields, paralleling the track.

At the topside vehicle park back at Detroit, they found a detachment of Marines waiting for them, accompanied by Sergeant Gupta, their guns leveled at the cabs of the dung trucks.

No one said a thing. There was no need. The Marines grabbed Arun, Springer and Madge and propelled them down the main ramp of Gate Three and down into the tunnels of Detroit.

"Take these," said Gupta, handing them each a capsule.

Arun swallowed his and immediately felt a blinding flash of agony followed by terrifying clarity. All the comforting fuzziness brought on by the Agri-Aux beer vanished, to be replaced by a crystal clear understanding of just how utterly flekked they all were.

As they were marched down to the battalion administrative section on Level 4, they encountered cadets, novices, Marines, Aux and Hardits. The Hardits paid them no attention, the military humans gave them wary acknowledgment, but some of the Aux recognized them. There were tears in the eyes of some Aux onlookers, despair in their hearts.

That was the hardest thing for Arun to bear, that the hope he'd encouraged in the slave workers had unraveled so rapidly. Before the day was out, the whole of Detroit would know his fate.

To give false hope to the hopeless is the cruelest deed of all.
What have I done?

———

Gupta deposited them back where their Aux escapade had begun: at attention in front of Staff Sergeant Bryant's desk.

He glowered, making them sweat for a long while before he spoke.

"I have a request from your Hardit hosts. No, not a request. It is a *demand*, barbed with the most hideous threats. Do you worms realize how dirty it makes me feel to be ordered about by those flea-bitten monkey-vecks? They demand your termination. I thought it advisable to have you escorted here directly upon your return. At least that way I'm spared the further indignity of our monkey colleagues implementing the termination of human cadets themselves."

Arun fought against the temptation to slump. He succeeded in keeping himself absolutely still, not even breathing until the shock eased. Not that he'd expected anything different, but to hear the death sentence passed… it wasn't easy.

Bryant watched with interest as Arun's dismay played out over his face.

"Staff sergeant," said Arun. "This cadet begs permission to speak."

"Go ahead." Bryant's words were filled with subtle poison, as if inviting Arun into a trap.

"I found something out there I need to report."

Madge gave a warning growl, deep in her throat, but that only steeled Arun to his purpose. He would tell about the drugs and the guns. It was a hell of a risk for everyone, but sometimes you had to take a chance. Arun didn't expect to get another one.

Then Springer gave an identical growl, and Arun's resolve melted away.

"Stop that at once," boomed Bryant. He slammed the table and then shot to his feet, his muscular bulk towering over the cadets. "It's bad enough that you stink like Hardits. To growl like them too is an insult to the Corps. Six days you've been away. Six fucking days, and you've already lost every shred of dignity." He took his seat, his face still livid with contempt. "I pity you, Gupta, to have such sniveling cowards in your squad."

Arun didn't dare to glance over at Madge, but he knew dismay would be etched into her face. Being called a coward would have hurt her more than any Hardit shock torture. To have growled like that, she must be utterly convinced that they shouldn't be talking about gun-running.

Bryant turned his stare onto Arun. "Continue."

This was Arun's big moment.

He took a deep breath… and then danced away from the truth. "I reckon my time has been up for a little while now, staff sergeant. Been dodging incoming drent so much it feels like I've cheated death a dozen times. What I mean is that it's all my fault, not the other two."

Bryant's eyebrows shot up. Arun's did too. The staff sergeant had sent them off to the Aux with a lesson about justice ringing in their ears. Arun added quickly: "I don't mean it isn't fair, staff sergeant. Justice and fairness are irrelevant. Please let me take all the blame and spare the others. That's not justice, it's efficiency because these other two have shown through their initiative that they could make good Marines one day. It would be a waste to throw them away now."

"You're wrong," said Bryant. Arun had given the most impassioned speech of his life, and Bryant had instantly crushed it with two crisp words.

But then Arun noticed a twinkle in Bryant's eye… the staff sergeant was laughing at him! "You're wrong," repeated Bryant, "because there *is* a place in the Corps for justice, even compassion. Though they are luxuries that are not often possible, we should never forget them or we will cease to be human."

Arun's heart beat faster.

"Nonetheless, request denied."

Arun couldn't keep it up any longer. He slumped, physically and mentally. This was the end.

"Unlike the Hardit request," continued Bryant. "That we cannot refuse, whether we like it or not." Why was he grinning? "They request termination and I agree. You three were sentenced to serve one week as Aux because your overactive sense of justice caused you to make grave errors of judgment. I believe you have learned your lesson. I am therefore terminating your Aux sabbatical with immediate effect. Report to the medical facility ASAP for anti-radiation treatment. You restart cadet training tomorrow."

Arun couldn't keep the smile from his face.

"We all turned a blind eye to your little adventures," said Bryant, "but no more escapades that might draw the attention of our betters. On the other hand, if I were to fish through the communal laundry shelf one morning and my fingers happened upon a packet of biscuits hidden amongst the shirts, I might put that down to one of life's little mysteries. *I might*. But don't push it too far. Understood?"

"Yes, staff sergeant," answered the cadets.

"This cadet begs permission to speak, staff sergeant," requested Madge.

"Hell no. Of all your sorry little band you are the one who should keep your mouth most firmly shut, cadet corporal. As senior cadet, your task was to keep the other two out of mischief. You failed."

It was Arun's turn to ask. He wanted to ask permission to contact the Aux, to let them know they hadn't been executed, to prevent their morale from shattering. Madge had probably been trying to ask the same thing. But as Arun's mouth moved to speak, Bryant stopped him dead with a flinty glare.

Bryant's face colored red. "You cadets have far too much to say for yourselves." He pointed an accusing finger at Arun. "You most of all."

Arun kept his eyes front as the staff sergeant's scrutiny played over him. He hated that having lifted Aux morale it would be crushed by rumors of his death. But he was too scared of Bryant to even think of crossing him.

"You're trouble, hero," said Bryant. "And you other two are only one step behind him. If you study your military history you will learn that sometimes the awkward few win finely balanced battles with their different ways of seeing things. But this is a Marine Corps unit. I do not tolerate dissent. I can maybe afford to give a few nanometers of leeway to a handful of exceptional Marines, to pander to their unconventional thinking, because one day they might make the difference between victory and death. However…" Bryant's face went as hard as poly-ceramalloy armor. "You are *not* exceptional! All I can see in front of me are three silly little teenagers. Nothing more. Do I make myself clear?"

"Yes, staff sergeant," they all replied.

"I hope so because you'd better pray to whatever gods you hold dear that you are never brought before me again. Now get the hell out of my sight!"

The cadets gave a crisp salute, turned and marched away.

Fifty paces down the passageway they stopped, looked each other in the eye and whooped with delight.

Level 4 echoed with the sounds of gleeful high fives.

—— PART III ——

The Prophecy

Human Legion
INFOPEDIA

Military Concepts

–Introduction to ships, boats & platforms

Marines will encounter a wide range of ship and boat types while on active service, as well as orbital platforms and other void-based facilities. The term 'ship' is widely use In a generic sense in the Human Legion Infopedia, but a stricter nomenclature differentiates between *ships* as vessels that have interstellar range, *boats* as vessels designed for maneuver but are not capable of interstellar travel, and *platforms* to mean space stations and other essentially static facilities.

Ship design has changed little since the development of the bacterium bomb about six thousand years ago. The ease with which this bomb — small enough to be carried by a Marine — could penetrate outer hulls made capital ships more vulnerable. This led to an emphasis on smaller vessels and on much greater numbers of Marines skirmishing in an attempt to disable enemy ships and to shield friendly vessels from the enemy's Marines. Indeed it is probable that the very existence of the Human Marine Corps, and consequently the Human Legion, owes its existence to the bacterium bomb.

Battles between warships typically occur when an invading fleet contests a defending force for control of a star system. Ships will tow warboats to strike range in the outer system, and then leave the boats to take the fight to the enemy who will defend with a mix of boats, orbital defense platforms and many hidden defenses. Some ships have high maneuver and offensive capabilities and may accompany the warboats in an attack.

Although to a Marine the distinction between ship and boat may seem arbitrary and of little interest, this is not true of navy personnel. It is vital that you learn and employ the correct terminology for any vessel to which you have been assigned. Entire Marine complements have been executed for insulting their warboat captain by suggesting she or he commanded a ship. To warboat crew, ships are flown by plodders and cowards who wait in safety while the boats do the real fighting. To ship crew, boats are minor craft, mere passengers whose crew spend most their lives in cryogenic sleep while the ship navigates the deep void between the stars.

By whatever name they are known, the vessels to which human Marines are assigned tend to be less powerful models and toward the end of their active life, many craft already having seen millennia of service.

The ship type a Marine will be assigned to depends to some degree on the regimental specialism, although Marines train for all potential roles.

Assault Marine regiments are trained for assault against a defended planet. Assault regiments can be assigned to almost any ship type. In fact, the ship or boat is unimportant, being merely to tow self-contained Marine pods, which contain habitation, cryogenic, supplies, and dropboats for an approximately company-sized unit of marines to deploy in orbit and launch an assault. The Marine pods have limited maneuver and defensive capability and will detach from the parent vessel before attack.

Void Marine regiments are specialists in vacuum and zero-g warfare. A ship's Marine complement will form a defensive screen and add offensive options against enemy ships.

Tactical Marine regiments are also trained in void combat, but are allied to a small tactical warboat to make a single combined operations unit. The most common warboat type is called a Tactical Unit (often shorted to 'TU'), a roughly spherical craft that is agile and well-armed. A TU will typically have a Marine complement of two squads and be ferried into combat by a *sleeve* ship. The sleeve consists of a command and propulsion sections attached to a hollow tube. The TU boats — and other modules such as engineering and supply pods — are stacked within the tube during interstellar travel.

Another distinction between void and tactical Marines is that the former will egress their ship through an airlock, or through a hanger opening inside a small boat. A tactical Marine will typically egress through an EVA chute which uses amniotic gel to shield the marine from physical trauma while the TU jinks at high gees to avoid enemy fire.

— Some information on this topic has been excluded as you have insufficient access privileges —

—— Chapter 47 ——

Nestled within the pattern of brilliant jewels embedded in absolute black, the precious gleam from Earth's star pulled at Arun across nearly 50 light years.

Sol was not far away, easily reached by transport ship, but no ship would ever take Arun there. Not even to one of Sol's neighbors.

Throughout novice school, the instructors had rammed home that the Human Marine Corps was a joke in the eyes of other species: plasma fodder equipped with third-rate cast-offs and so stupid that they were sent off to die actually believing they were genuine warriors.

"Look up Earth history," Instructor Rekka had once told them, "for the contempt felt by Earth peoples for Roma, Jews, lepers and dalits. That's how the others see us: unwashed, untouchable, unwanted. The word 'human' has been absorbed by alien languages, a byword throughout this region of the galaxy for the lowest of the low."

Arun wasn't so convinced. Maybe all this humans-are-useless drent was a psych trick to produce Marines who were hungry to prove their worth.

What made Sol so impossibly distant was the White Knight policy of keeping human Marine units well away from Earth. But why would they bother if humans were such a joke?

Arun would go there if he could, but he suspected that was a dream that would sour if it ever came true. He'd heard tales of Earth soldiers marching through captured cities and welcomed as liberators by beautiful girls throwing flowers at their feet. As an armed representative of Earth's oppressors, Arun guessed a more likely welcome would be a knife in the back in some dark alley.

Sol hazed and then vanished behind Tranquility's bulk as the planet swung across his field of view, but Sol was only one of myriad stars, and the circling heavens held endless fascination for those who really took the time to look.

As an underground dweller, Arun equated the starscape with clouds: both provided spectacular sights, made all the more precious because he rarely had the chance to relax and enjoy them.

"Listen up, squads. We head out in two minutes."

With a sigh, Arun reeled in the focus of his attention. Blue and Gold Squads were floating in the vacuum, like a snapshot of swarming insects. Close by was their target, a hulk of functional metal officially labeled *Assault Training Vessel 2*. The Spirit class warship was once a proudly gleaming wedge of metal, just under a klick long from bow to stern, and 300 meters from the viewing blister sprouting from the upper deck down to the main railgun slung under its belly. Now its off-white hull was scorched by beam weapon attacks and its skin riddled with holes drilled through for boarding exercises. As with most things in Detroit, the ship had been unofficially re-designated using an Earth name, *Fort Douaumont,* because — in reference to some obscure battle on Earth — the ship had been fought over countless times but never truly won.

"Ninety seconds."

A grafted-on switch in Arun's head told him that these words came over the command channel. There was no need, because Arun recognized the voice as belonging to Cadet Lance Sergeant Alice Belville, Gold Squad's leader and designated commander for both squads in this exercise.

Alice was okay. Sometimes Arun worried that she was a little too quick to press ahead without consulting with her section leaders.

"Frame-reference on my position," said Alice. "North to *Douaumont's* bow. Center on her dorsal command blister. Green layer through ship axis. Layer height 200 meters."

Zero-g combat had no natural reference for up and down, left and right, so tactical commanders defined a frame-reference for their Marines, sometimes redefining it over the course of a fast-changing battle. With *Fort Douaumont*, the framing was often the same: north corresponded to forward, right to starboard, and so on.

Arun glanced over to the two veterans observing the cadets. Their battlesuits were capable of stealthing their wearers against any means Arun had of detecting them. Today sergeants Gupta and Searl had set their suits to high visibility mode, flickering yellow and orange. They looked as if they were on fire.

Alice issued each section their orders, and reminded the cadets that the vets had given them a ten-second start before activating *Douaumont's* defensive lasers. That's when the fun would begin.

Madge would lead Arun's Blue-5 fire team in an arc over the ship at a distance of around half a klick above the ship's upper hull. Once in place, Blue-5 would watch for counter-attack, covering the backs of Alice and Brandt's teams who would lead the main assault. Del-Marie and Blue-6 would take a similar position but slightly lower and facing aft.

"All units to fire smoke at two klicks to target," finished Alice. *Frakk! That meant he would be exposed to laser fire for a klick before shielding his advance under cover of smoke. It also meant the smoke would be far denser supposing enough Marines made it that far.* "Stealth at one klick. Any questions?"

Alice had left about one minute for any debate. None of the other 54 cadets had any questions to ask, but Arun wondered whether the vets in their fiery suits were questioning why she was leaving her teams exposed for so long.

Arun concentrated his thoughts on an area of space about one half klick closer to *Fort Douaumont* until Barney acknowledged, adding a cream waypoint marker to Arun's tac-display.

"On my mark… 3… 2… 1… Mark!"

A blur of frantic motion erupted into the void from all directions, every cadet performing a crazy dance of perfect unpredictability. Arun whooped with delight in the privacy of his own suit as he corkscrewed, reversed, accelerated and stopped in a complete jinkout maneuver. All he had to do was set the waypoint and enjoy the ride as Barney plotted a constantly changing evasive course.

After about ten seconds, *Fort Douaumont's* point defense systems were activated, immediately acquiring targeting solutions. Lasers opened up, fingers of instant death reaching out to pluck the cadets from their dance.

Arun was under heavy fire, but it felt oddly unreal. It always did in space. With a ground assault you felt the crump of shellfire through your feet, and heard the whiplash crack of field railguns. Atmospheric dust would bloom beam weapons into brilliant light-shows, leaving a tang of ozone in the singed air, and an afterimage on survivors' retinas.

Not so in the serene vacuum of space. Here there were no shockwaves, the only sounds that of Arun's own breathing and the commands coming through his internal helmet speaker. With no atmosphere to scatter their light, lasers were invisible unless you looked directly down the beam.

Death was something that happened to someone else, until it happened to you. And even then, any weapon capable of slicing through battlesuit armor would kill the person inside before they knew they'd been hit.

There were no wounded in void combat.

Barney gave him a jolt whenever one of the cadets was hit. In the disorientating rush of the assault, that was the only way he could tell the lasers were finding targets. Arun hadn't time to worry about them. He set Barney a second waypoint, closer to the ship.

After another two seconds of exposing himself to point defense, Barney told him he was now two klicks from *Fort Douaumont*.

Arun fired smoke. *Yeah!* He'd made it through the most nerve-shredding part of the mission.

The defensive munitions canister flew from the launcher beneath the barrel of his SA-71. Moments later, the canister split in two, each section blasting off on different vectors. Those children split again, and then again into a total of 64 final capsules. The assault force launched around three thousand capsules, which exploded over the course of the next twenty seconds, lighting up the vacuum. Marines talked of firing *smoke*, but what really emerged was a mixed shower of decoys and material strips that unwound into streamers. The strips had a range of properties: highly reflective, thermally hot, radioactive, energy absorbent. All were designed to confuse enemy targeting systems and degrade beam strength.

It worked: Arun sensed the rate of casualties slow to a near stop.

Space seemed to have acquired a thousand new stars, a sequined shroud added to by the enemy lasers, which flashed in green or red bursts from myriad reflections.

Arun told Barney to filter out these distractions from his visor, leaving him with the target ship and his waypoints. He was about to add a third waypoint when a gut-wrenchingly abrupt change of velocity grayed and narrowed Arun's vision, robbing him of breath.

It took a few seconds for Barney to ease his acceleration enough for the blood to start flowing properly in Arun's head. As his vision returned, Barney explained that he'd made an emergency course correction to avoid colliding with another cadet. The AI was now bringing him directly to the target.

The constant jinking grew even more frantic for a few moments before slamming to a halt. Barney had matched velocity with the target ship, positioning Arun at the far left of his fire team's patrol arc. The suit was now stealthed too.

Arun tensed. If all went well, the smokescreen would have hidden his entrance so that when the cloud of defensive munitions had degraded, Arun could rely on his suit to keep him invisible. If the smoke hadn't hidden him enough… he'd already be dead.

Arun relaxed and looked around.

Springer was in position to his right and Madge farther on. If Osman had made it through then he'd be farther still, hidden by the curvature of the ship's enormous hull. Arun gave Springer a thumbs up.

She ignored him.

He had a sudden urge to talk to her, but couldn't without breaking the training protocol. The only reason Arun could see his buddy was because the stealth function on these training suits was only a simulation. If this assault were real, Springer would be as invisible to him as to the enemy. That, and the point defense lasers would have opened up earlier and at lethal strength.

Arun looked over his section of hull. There were hatches aplenty and concealed areas under the forward shield projector where an enemy counter-strike force could assemble before attacking. There was nothing to report.

He glanced down and aft to where most of the cadets in the assault force were already swarming over the boarding points, simulating breaching by holding a boarding patch to the hull and pressing down until the patch turned green. Only then could they jump through the pre-drilled holes into whatever awaited them.

There was nothing he could do for the boarding teams now except guard them from surprise attack while they were busy. Arun turned his attention back to *Fort Douaumont's* bow.

From a distance, the training ship was a sleek wedge of metal, but up close the hull was much messier. The original hull design had been infected by a boxy, urban landscape that had risen, been cleared away, and then rebuilt countless times over the centuries to leave heat exchangers, gun emplacements, storage lockers, shuttle docks, maintenance bot housing, and retro-fitted defensive munition launchers.

If the blocky hull surface betrayed that *Fort Douaumont* had never needed to cut through the thickness of a planet's atmosphere, the forward shield projector was evidence that it had to press through a far more deadly medium: interstellar dust and debris. From a human perspective, the void was a vacuum. But the gulf between the stars was not quite devoid of matter, and even a tiny dust particle would hit with the force of a fusion grenade when the ship slammed into it at its top speed of 0.7 lightspeed. The apex of the filigree crown of shield rails extended nearly two klicks forward of the bow. In flight, the shield rails charged the interstellar medium, rolling it along the ship's beams in a magnetic slipstream.

Beneath Blue-5, the shield power array was laid out like a fan-shaped forest with its narrowest point aimed directly at the boarding point. If he were a defending officer, planning to sally forth against a Marine attack on the upper hull, Arun would deploy his counter-attack through this forest, which consisted of scores of the ten-foot high spiny boxes that powered the two upper shield projectors. Then he'd wipe out the boarding teams, taking them by surprise.

Arun hung above the power array, screwing up his eyes as he tried to penetrate the crimson-tinged black shadows cast by light reflected off Antilles, the nearest of Tranquility's moons. When the cadets had launched their attack on the orbiting ship, they had kept to the cover of the Tranquility's shadow. For this simple exercise, *Fort Douaumont's* belly had been oriented toward the planet's surface, which shrouded the upper deck in that same shadow.

He switched to infra-red, but the power array was partially charged, meaning it glowed bright blue in his visor. Looking for the bots in infra-red was like looking for a flashlight on a star's surface.

It was no good. He switched back to the visual spectrum, but despite all the augmentations that uprated his sight, and Barney's best efforts to refine the image in his visor, all Arun could see were shades of black. He tried forcing his brain to concentrate harder. He was in so much drent already that he couldn't afford any mistakes. One more vulley-up and Staff Sergeant Bryant would kick him back down to the Aux levels. Alerting his section to an attack that wasn't there would be enough to earn that kicking. But the harder he made himself peer into the dark, the more it shimmered, his mind imagining fleeting patterns that weren't actually there.

What he needed were the sensors in his suit, but he was running his systems cold: active sensors could give away his position. So he left his eyes unfocused, relying on their natural motion-detection ability.

"Contact. Blue-4 going firm." The warning came from Mbizi Sesay. Arun had been good friends with Bizzy, close enough to hear the worry beneath his seemingly calm voice. "Eighteen hostiles bearing 350. Range 120 meters." Bizzy's voice cut off but that didn't mean he was dead. By broadcasting his warning, he'd also revealed his location underneath the ship. Bizzy could be moving to a new position, the g-forces unleashed squeezing off his ability to speak.

Alice's voice came over the command channel. "Gold-4 peel left. Gold-5 peel right. Enfilade hostiles in contact with Blue-4."

The temptation to turn and watch the action threatened to wrench Arun's head around, but he had his orders and they hadn't changed. Checking what was going on elsewhere in the battle was Madge's responsibility. Instead, he settled back into a watchful gaze. He'd spent countless hours in this state playing stealthsuit cat and mouse games set up between rival squads. That was good. That was routine, and routine was something he could sink into and ignore the fighting that raged behind and beneath him.

"Gold Command has boarded," said Alice. "Brandt has secured the upper two decks, and I'm forming up for attack on Target 1. Gold-3 follow. Gold-6 remain stealthed as reserve. Blue-6 maintain position. Let's show those vets what we can do, Marines!"

Not only was Alice still alive but she sounded like she was having fun. That was a good sign. 'Target 1' was the bridge. Even though the Corps' alien enemies weren't expected to understand the human language, and even though battlesuit comms had encryption beyond the ability of human crypto-experts to explain, much less decrypt, the Jotuns insisted that Marines used code words for tactical objectives.

Arun's confidence lifted still further when Bizzy reported over the command channel that the enemy counter-attack had been repulsed with minimal casualties.

Arun sensed victory, but only for a few seconds. Down there… in the shield generator array… he thought he saw movement.

He strained his eyes trying to tell whether this was an attack, but he couldn't be sure. He had to get nearer.

To remain in stealth mode, albeit simulated, his suit could only move slowly. Arun approached the suspicious area as fast as he dared, snapping a flash-bomb off the equipment patch on his hip, and slotting it into the launcher beneath his carbine.

There was something there all right.

Directly below him, hatches had opened in the hull, spilling hostiles into the cover of the shield array generators. The enemy were scurrying spider-like training bots, the size of a human child but with lasers attached to two of their limbs. A fist-sized plate was grafted onto the central 'body' of the robots. If you hit that with your laser, the robot would deactivate — a combat casualty.

Already he could see dozens. More were spilling out by the second, forming up ready to rush the boarding party. The counter-attack on Bizzy had been a feint intended to commit the cadets' reserves.

Should he warn the others? He readied his carbine to fire the flash-bomb at the bots, but he daren't reveal his presence by broadcasting a warning as Bizzy had done. Instead he asked Barney to find a tight-beam comms route. Although he could turn around and see Springer, the stealth training protocol meant Barney pretended she was invisible. The AI simulated firing tight-beam pings at the probable location of his comrades, hoping to strike it lucky before being noticed by the enemy.

"Hold fire, McEwan. Activate LBNet." Madge had found him first, bouncing her order off Springer's suit.

The instant Arun switched to Local Battle Net, Barney changed Arun's visor to tactical-display mode, adding five blue dots to indicate the positions of his section comrades. Delta Section should have seven other cadets: Brandt had been promoted out, and it looked like Zug hadn't made it through point defense.

LBNet continuously connected everyone in the team using tight-beam links. It was risky, but more secure than broadcasting on Wide Battle Net. With the suit AIs now able to share what their wearers could see, and add what the AIs suspected, scores of enemy red dots erupted like an infestation over the terrain below.

"Hey, Springer," Arun called out. "Join me at the hatch? We can drop grenades in and then take the bots from the rear."

"Negative," Madge replied. "Assigning orders."

As Barney sketched an outline of Madge's intentions, Arun scooted off to comply, while Madge used words to duplicate her orders.

The shield generator array was a funnel aimed at the boarding point, but the funnel drained between a pair of shield array projectors. The shield rails that charged the interstellar medium fed out of these 30 meter diameter tubes, which were pointed forward, angled toward the starboard and port bows. Each of the two Delta Section fire teams would take a position on top of a shield projector. When the bots passed below, the Gold fire teams at the boarding point would pin them down, and then Delta Section would rake the bots with flanking fire.

It was obvious, though he hadn't seen it.

And that was why Madge was section leader.

By the time Arun was in position, lying prone atop the starboard shield projector, and using the ridge that ran along its crest as cover, Barney was telling him the bots were already beginning to swarm on the other side of the projector.

The temptation to stick his head over the ridge to see for himself was powerful, but the fear of screwing up the operation was greater. He glanced to either side. Osman and Springer had rolled onto their sides, checking their flanks for bots. They appeared calm, but of course it was impossible to be sure in their ACE-2/T training suits. He turned back to face the enemy. Blue dots showed Madge, Del-Marie and Cristina on the reverse slope of the other projector — the two fire teams keeping in touch by means of signal repeaters slapped over the ridges.

One of the blue dots moved up the slope. It was Madge.

"Ready on 3," she said. Simultaneously, the red dots rearranged and firmed as Barney received an update on their position: Madge had sneaked a visual of the enemy surging below them.

The bots fired first. Not at Delta Section but at one of the teams at the boarding point.

"Contact!" screamed Lance Corporal Yoshioka from Gold-3. "They're coming at us from behind." She sounded surprised. Why wasn't Yoshioka in on Madge's plan?

But there was no time to worry about Yoshioka. Madge counted down. "3... 2... 1... Now!"

Arun raised his carbine over his head and fired his flash-bomb. Without waiting for its effect, he scrambled over the ridge and opened fire with his laser, Barney applying a charge to the suit that glued it to the projector on a rough approximation of standard gravity.

Barney was ready for the explosion of light from the flash-bomb, limiting its effect to be merely dazzling. The bots, though... they acted stunned.

Perfect!

Arun raked them with laser fire. From the feet of his first target, he played his aim diagonally up to the right and then down again, stitching a repeating pattern of simulated death.

They might be bots but they still acted confused, staring up, seeking for the hidden threat that was scything them down.

Yeah!

This was the therapy he needed!

He tried to imagine he was shooting Tawfiq and her skangat monkey-bitches, Instructor Nhlappo for trying to get him executed to save her butt, the traitors who were drugging his section...

"Cease fire!"

So soon? The feeling was too good for Arun to release the pressure on the trigger, but the thermal cutout on Arun's carbine obeyed Madge's order for him anyway.

He knelt as he picked a new position to switch to while his carbine cooled.

There was movement. There... from the heap of robot bodies.

He froze.

No!

But they were dead... The bots... he'd seen them fall!

The combat bots rose from death, picking themselves up on spindly limbs. One rotated its bulbous sensor node and looked straight up at Arun. It didn't pick up its weapon, just *stared*.

Arun scrambled back behind the projector ridge. "Corp—"

Too late! His warning died with his comms connection. Stiffened cords erupted over his suit, immobilizing him. Barney wasn't there any longer, and the AI had taken his tactical-display and vision enhancements with him.

That look from the bot had killed him. Arun was certain. But... but that was impossible.

The charge on his suit that had stuck him to the ship went too. As the momentum from Arun's backward scramble carried him off the shield projector, his boot snagged briefly on a cooling fin, transforming his feet-first reverse into a head-over-heels tumble away from the warship. He bumped into a laser emplacement and off into space at the speed of an arthritic worm.

The veterans would be in no hurry to resurrect the dead cadets after the exercise, which left Arun with more time than he wanted to ponder how Delta Section had messed up so badly.

His answer wasn't long in coming. Delta Section hadn't screwed up at all: the exercise had been sabotaged.

Doubts gnawed at him, growing stronger as his distance from the ship stretched ever further. Until now he'd dodged the clutches of the conspiracies swirling through Detroit. He had begun to feel as if he were acting out a daring tale of adventure, something he would look back on one day and laugh.

No longer. Although his body was tumbling helplessly through the vacuum, he knew his fate was held fast by the traitors, gripped as surely as by a powered gauntlet.

There would be no Human Legion now.

—— Chapter 48 ——

"You may turn around."

After the veterans unlocked the suit AIs of the dead cadets, they had then ordered Delta Section to stand facing the bulkhead in a passageway on Deck 14 of *Fort Douaumont* to contemplate their failure.

Now, after an hour with his visor up against a vertical sheet of metal, it was time for Arun to face the conspirators, for surely the veterans must be in on the set up.

In theory, Gold and Blue Squads had been victorious — after a fashion. Casualties had been high; tempers higher. The other cadets had taken the homeward shuttle long ago, but Arun suspected the rest of Gold and Blue had never been more than cover for what was really taking place here. Delta Section's day was far from over.

As he turned — an awkward movement without gravity but with his boots sticking to the deck like glue — all the overlays and vision enhancers in Arun's visor shut down, reducing it to a transparent bulge at the front of his helmet. Even his helmet lights failed. Gupta had taken control of his helmet.

To Arun's unaided eye, the only light in the utter black of the passageway came from the lamps mounted to either side of Gupta's helmet. They burned like fusion torches.

Arun shut his eyes. The lamps burning through his eyelids scarcely dimmed.

"McEwan!" bellowed the sergeant. "Stand at attention properly!"

Arun opened his eyes and squinted into the blazing light. Gupta held his gaze before walking down the line, halting again in front of his first victim.

"After you were in position above *Fort Douaumont*, did you hear Cadet Lance Sergeant Belville's instruction?"

In the airless passageway, there was no direction to Gupta's voice, the sound of his words coming only through Arun's helmet speaker.

"Yes, sergeant." There was a subtle note of desperation in Madge's voice. They all assumed the sergeant's words were meant to trap her with no possible means of escape.

"What were her orders?" asked Gupta.

"To guard the boarding teams against counter-attack, sergeant."

"And did you carry out that order?"

Madge hesitated.

"Answer me, Majanita! Or would you prefer me to first explain the concept of carrying out orders?"

"No, sergeant"

"Then answer, damn you. Did you carry out your orders?"

"Yes, sergeant."

"*Yes, sergeant?* Really? Then explain how your section failed to warn the boarding party of an attack coming from your sector? And why Delta's defense was such a steaming puddle of drent that you might as well have been back in Detroit, chowing down in the mess. Were there actually any cadets inside those ACE-2/T suits? Were you actually? Frakking? There?"

"Yes, sergeant."

"Then how do you explain your vulley-up?"

Arun glanced left to where Madge was pinned by Gupta's helmet lamps. Should he speak up? Shit happens, for sure, but Madge didn't deserve this. It wasn't fair.

Then he faced front, sharpish. He'd been warned before about not thinking things were fair. Besides, he bet Gupta knew what had really happened better than any of them.

"You!" bellowed the NCO.

Gupta took two bounds along the passageway to come to a position looming over Arun. He jabbed a gauntleted finger at Arun's chest.

"Do you think you're special, McEwan?"

"No, sergeant."

"Then why were your eyes on Cadet Corporal Majanita? Did you have something to say?"

"No, sergeant."

"Oh, really? Well, you do now. Tell us whether your section commander carried out her orders."

There was no hesitation. "Yes, sergeant."

"Interesting. Then explain how the enemy brushed aside your defense so easily that they wiped out Gold-3 unopposed."

"There was a fault with the bots, sergeant. We shot them but—" A red alarm sounded inside Arun's brain. A sensation he'd been trained to associate with going offline. Gupta had shut him out of the local comms net. Arun finished his explanation anyway. "We shot them, but they got back up and shot us. Frakk! They didn't shoot us. One just looked my way and I was dead. It wasn't our fault."

"Not your fault. Not *fair*? Not – *fucking* – fair? Your overactive sense of justice forced Staff Sergeant Bryant to send you down to join the Aux. Looks to me like he wasted his time. Are you hankering to reunite with your Hardit friends?"

"No, sergeant."

"Then let me remind you one final time. Life is not fair. This exercise was not fair. Wasting my breath talking to an idiot cadet is not fair. Do you still believe the bots malfunctioned?"

Did he? What was worse, lying or complaining? Lying to a superior was a capital offense, so it wasn't much of a choice. "Yes, sergeant. They malfunctioned."

"Oh, I'm sorry. Does that mean your section is off the hook? That your screw up wasn't your fault?"

"No, sergeant. Drent happens. We have to succeed despite that."

Arun pictured Gupta chewing over Arun's words behind his opaque visor. Gupta eventually responded: "I don't believe a word you've just said. But at least I detected a faint flicker of intelligence, which is as much as I can hope for. You've reported a suspected malfunction to your NCO. And now I'm telling you that I don't care. What should you do about the rogue bots now?"

"Nothing, sergeant."

"Good. You will not speak of bots that don't stay down. You will not speak of equipment malfunction. You will not talk about the events of this day at all, except to admit with the appropriate and deserved level of shame that you frakked up and let your comrades down. You will not speak of this to anyone at any time, ever. That is a direct order. Do you understand?"

"Yes, sergeant." Arun understood very clearly. If he ever talked, he would be disobeying a superior, and the penalty was death.

But there had been more meaning than that in the NCO's words. Equipment malfunction was an ever-present hazard. This was usually down to cyber-attack, not poor design or lack of maintenance. The Hardits had been mining this system for many thousands of years. Back when *Homo sapiens* and *Homo neanderthalis* were scrapping for domination of the Earth, the most valuable raw materials of Tranquility's system had already been extracted and hurled out into the interstellar trade routes by giant mass drivers.

That meant the system had long been a target for robot spies launched by rival empires. Counter-espionage bots scoured the asteroid, moons and comets forever discovering tiny automated factories pouring out nano-sized spybots to observe, challenge and test defenses.

Equipment malfunction should be investigated but Gupta was trying to snuff out any word of this. Which only confirmed what Arun already suspected: that Gupta was part of the conspiracy. And yet… Surely there were far simpler ways to silence a cadet who knew too much?

A green light clicked in Arun's head, and he knew he was back on the public comms net.

"This was your first zero-g exercise under my instruction," said Gupta. "You let me down. It is now my task to shake each of your scrawny hides until either a Marine tumbles out, or you die in the attempt. I don't much care either way. What I do care is that there should be no losers in my squad, because out there in the wider galaxy there are no losers in the Marine Corps. Why is that, Cadet Koraltan?"

"Sergeant," answered Osman briskly, "because only the best make it as Marines."

"You can cut the parade ground bullshit, Koraltan. That's for children. The reason why there are no losers in the Corps is because losers are a liability. No NCO would risk his or her entire unit in order to shield one unreliable Marine. Do you imagine the White Knight Empire provides a network of military hospitals to care for Marines who aren't fit for combat duty? Out at the front, liabilities are quietly abandoned to the void for the good of everyone else. No Marine left behind? That's a saying from long ago and far away. I don't care whether you call it murder or natural selection, but if you don't earn my trust by the time I lead your squad out to war, I'll kill you myself. Understood?"

"Yes, sergeant."

"I hope you do. And now for the good news. I've taken pity on you. Instead of going home to Tranquility, I'm going to give you a chance to start earning my trust without delay. I've booked you a place on my old boat, *Yorktown*. You're going to be doing EVA drill."

Arun kept his expression blank. Inwardly, his mind was spinning out of control. *Yorktown*? That was a Tactical Unit assault warboat, recently returned from the frontier wars for refit and upgrade. Just when he thought he was beginning to peer through the web of deceit to see what was going on here, Gupta had clouded the picture once again.

Perhaps he would find the answers on *Yorktown*.

—— Chapter 49 ——

There was a helluva lot of black in space, Arun mused, not exactly for the first time. Facing out to space from his *Yorktown* EVA chute, he saw a field of black, peppered with infinitesimally small silver dots. Sergeant Gupta would appear somewhere in the void — when he was good and ready — darting in front of Delta Section on his one-man flitter. The exercise was simple. The disgraced cadets had to keep their eyes peeled until they spotted him, and then they had five minutes to catch him. Anyone who didn't manage that would not be going home. Ever. Or, at least, so the NCO had promised them. Gupta had seemed so pissed that Arun wasn't sure whether he was exaggerating.

Arun had been entombed in his EVA chute for three hours now. The sergeant might appear in the next second, the next hour, even the next day. They had no choice but to wait, their natural sleep patterns kept at bay by their augmented Marine bodies.

Whatever changes the alien scientists had wrought on his flesh, they did nothing to stop the hunger gnawing at Arun's belly (breakfast had been 14.3 hours ago) nor did they stop imaginary lights flickering across his field of vision as his mind got its revenge for staring so hard for so long by playing tricks on him.

He issued a mental command to his faceplate to overlay astro-navigation interpretive information. Moons were ringed and named. So too were distant mining craft, as were ore shipments in their transport capsules that would shepherd them along the light years to their destinations. If he stared long enough at the tiniest dots, they would reveal themselves as stars or comets, their names appearing on his faceplate. And if he stared longer still, he would see summaries of composition, and political and economic status.

What he really wanted was to access combat mode. But his suit was not set up to show his commanding NCO as an enemy threat, no matter how Arun felt about him. Astro-navigation mode should still show up the NCO, but Arun no longer trusted his suit, and so he switched off the interpretive mode and relied upon eyeballs alone.

The ghostly blue fringe of Tranquility's outer atmosphere entered Arun's field of vision, followed inevitably by the rest of his home planet as *Yorktown* continued her spin. He had no chance of spotting Gupta against the disk of purple-tinged clouds and azure seas, so he closed his eyelids. In the cocoon of an EVA bubble, that wasn't easy, but he decided it was better to rest his eyes for a few moments.

As his eyelids shut and the dark closed in, Arun felt fear. At first, it was a curious sensation. Fear was not an emotion that came easy to a Marine's altered mind. Even in dangerous situations, such a shooting away at an advancing horde of Troggie guardians, he was always so charged with a chemically-exaggerated combat high that he hadn't time to think. But now he did. He could do nothing *but* think.

He was plastered like a squashed bug to the outside of an orbiting Tactical Unit, a spherical warboat that usually served as the assault vehicle for a squad or two of tac-Marines. In his EVA chute, he could barely move, and certainly couldn't speak or even breathe. There was a reason the chutes were nicknamed *gibberballs*.

What if his NCO never did show? What if there was some elaborate scheme to cull the oversupply of Marines? Much of what the aliens did made little sense, but Arun was absolutely certain that the value their alien masters placed on each human life was precisely zero.

Fear, boredom, hunger, and betrayal. Arun was not having a good day. He would have loved to speak with Springer, or Osman, even Madge. But

in an EVA chute, everything was stuffed with buffer gel, even his helmet and the inside of his mouth. Talking was impossible.

Tranquility slid away out of sight and Arun stared once more into the field of black.

Still nothing.

The Extra Vehicular Assault chutes were tubes set flush into the hull that terminated in an amniotic bubble filled with buffer gel. The Marine inside was supplied through nutrient and waste tubes that connected inside their bodies via their suits. The gel allowed oxygen to pass through the Marine's skin into the bloodstream, and to remove carbon dioxide through the reverse process.

In combat situations, deploying Marines to the position where they were most needed was a seriously dangerous business. The buffer gel that filled all empty spaces inside the amniotic bubble, and the suit itself, could protect a Marine against thirty second bursts of 16g acceleration while keeping at least 80% of the occupants conscious and no more than 5% fatal casualties.

Scuttlebutt had it that they were trialing a gibberball rated for 19g acceleration. The bubbles themselves were unaltered but the human occupants were upgraded by having their eyeballs replaced with artificial versions that would not pop under extreme acceleration. The brain fluid too was pumped out and replaced with buffer gel before each assault.

Arun's amniotic bubble could, in theory, keep him alive for years. Zug often insisted that this was the future intended for their distant descendants. Zug was strangely at ease with the distant prospect of cyborg Marines, but even he accepted that being encased in buffer gel – and so unable to move talk or breathe – for more than a few days would drive anyone insane.

The TU continued to spin about its center in a spiraling pattern that placed each EVA chute back to its starting position every 4.8 minutes. Thanks to the damned counters and timers he could never turn off, Arun knew for a fact that the TU was on its 38th cycle since the exercise had begun.

On cycle 39, the fear he'd experienced almost as a curiosity began to really bite. This could be the White Knights' new mode of murder: to entomb marines in their amniotic prisons until their minds were ruined. But why? It made no sense.

By cycle 41 he had it. Aliens were cruel for a reason and he knew that reason now. Disobedience was punishable by death, the sentence carried out by the assault carbines of an execution squad formed from the friends and squadmates of the guilty Marine. At least it was quick. As for death in combat, every Marine cadet accepted that was their most likely fate, one day out there in the stars, fighting for a contract signed on Earth centuries ago. Death in space combat was so quick you would never know you'd been hit. Anyone who couldn't cope with that prospect had been weeded out years ago.

But if a quick death was something they were prepared for, it would be something else entirely to be kept for a week or more in their gibberballs. Once returned to the base on Tranquility and paraded as an example, their bodies would be physically healthy but once proud young men and women would be reduced to pitiful gibbering wrecks.

Pour encourager les autres, as Zug would say.

Arun fought against the sense of entrapment. He thought of Xin, imagined kissing those vital lips… but Xin was out of his league. His fancy battleplaner brain had caused only heartache. The idea of her falling in love with him was so improbable that he only felt even more of a loser.

Alone… Abandoned… Sacrificed…

And drugged! He should be able to handle the wait but whatever they were feeding the other cadets was driving his brain wild. He'd never make it.

Desperately, he replaced Xin in his mind with Springer. It was her lips he focused on, not to kiss but to hear her speak words of comfort and reason. It helped. A little. He reinforced Springer with Zug, the calmest person he knew.

But all imaginary Zug would do was shrug and say repeatedly: "You must die to encourage the others."

That was it.

Arun broke.

He screamed!

Inside his helmet, stuffed with buffer gel, his scream sounded like distant thunder. Then the gel was pushing itself down his throat, He was drowning. He swallowed a quantity of the tasteless gloop, but when his throat released, more gel had pushed into his mouth and stuffed itself down the back of his mouth, pushing, suffocating, drowning. He knew he should shut his mouth but the need to scream and gasp for air was stronger than his sense of reason. He gagged, but the link between gagging and vomiting had long been removed, so he kept on choking and gasping and drawing in yet more gel that pushed further down into his gullet.

Arun was drowning. Every instinct screamed that he was on the cusp of death, that he must *act* now! He was drowning! Yet he couldn't die. The gel was supplying him with oxygen. He knew that, but what help was knowing because he needed to breathe and could only drown and keep on drowning?

Enough reason returned to his mind for him to order the EVA chute to launch.

It refused. Barney knew that the cadet inside him was ordering a launch for the wrong reasons. Only when the launch criteria had been met would Barney relay a launch instruction, and Barney would know when Arun was lying.

And so Arun continued to scream, continued to drown…

And drown…

Drown…

———

Arun's mind became so lost in the hinterland of death that he had no idea how long he had been drowning before Barney snapped him out of his funk with the mental equivalent of pouring an ice-cold bucket of water over his head.

Around him, he saw a glittering halo of sparkles — gloops of buffer gel flash-frozen in the cold of space. The others had launched!

He braced himself and then willed his EVA chute to launch.

Nothing happened.

He tried again. *Come on, Barney. Damn you!*

Barney explained. <Launch initiation failed. Equipment failure. Shipboard AI notified and launch override requested. Standby.>

Arun braced for launch. He calmed and relaxed his throat until the gagging eased. The idea of being deliberately driven insane seemed ridiculous now, the result of spending time in this gibberball while doped. To experience yet another equipment failure… maybe this really was a cyber-assault? That was bad, but not as bad as being murdered by your superiors.

He watched as Osman, Springer, Madge and the others converged on a jittering dot that his faceplate overlay said was Sergeant Gupta. His squadmates closed in on their target and chased it around the back of the TU and out of sight.

"Why have we not launched?" he said. Or tried to. Even Arun couldn't hear more than an incoherent grunting, and Barney made no reply.

Seconds turned to minutes.

Minutes stretched into hours.

He fought a rearguard action against the approach of insanity. He imagined resting his head on Springer's chest, his head cradled in her arms. Even in his imagination, Springer was pissed at Arun for letting down his comrades again, blaming the sabotaged training bots on him. Too angry to speak any words of comfort, her embrace offered just enough comfort for Arun to keep a fingerhold on his sanity.

—— Chapter 50 ——

His legs kicking over the pit of despair, Arun held on to his sanity by his fingertips, time stretching beyond any meaning.

And then, without warning, he was hurled back into the physical universe in a frantic blur of events.

Nutrient and waste tubes retracted. The buffer gel pulsed out of his suit, his helmet, but not his throat. He choked, panicked.

The skin of the EVA bubble blew out in a million tiny fragments and he was shot out into the vacuum, buffer gel freezing all around.

His lungs quivered, protested, screamed for the air flooding into his helmet but none could make it through the gel still clogging his gullet. Without the gel supplying air through his skin, he was choking to death.

He tried. He tried so hard but he could not breathe.

A tear came to his eye. *It mustn't end like this!*

Then a deeply embedded instinct took over. He gulped and belched simultaneously. It was confused and painful but whatever he'd done worked.

He was breathing.

He was alone.

Arun tried radioing *Yorktown*, but Barney reported the warboat was refusing comms. He decided to scan the outside for a hatch, or better still a camera that he could wave into. Then he thought better of it. The *Yorktown* crew already knew he was here. His EVA port had just opened for frakk's sake.

His answer came when a bright speck detached from the starscape and came in on a looping trajectory around *Yorktown*, decelerating to halt side-on a hundred meters away from Arun.

The distant speck had grown into a TS-32(c), a utility shuttle configured in troop carrier mode. The side of the main section facing Arun folded up, ready for boarding.

He couldn't imagine a more obvious invitation.

A whoop came from Arun's mouth, a sound as weak as he was exhausted. *That won't do*, he decided. So he flipped his suit over in a series of somersaults, the zero-g equivalent of jumping up and down while punching the air in triumph.

Someone was going to a great deal of trouble to lure Arun to a time and place of their choosing.

He laughed. This was more like it. He was living an adventure and loved it.

Too many people whose opinion he valued had called Arun an idiot recently. Well, they could go vulley themselves because he was unlucky, not stupid.

He realized that what had sapped his morale these past weeks was the fear that he would die pointlessly and unremarked, his life amounting only to a few lines in the regimental records that no one would ever read. That shuttle was as clear a sign as he'd ever get that someone powerful thought Arun was important.

Earning the contempt of his battalion had hollowed him out, leaving him a void inside a brittle shell. But if he didn't die now, he was confident he'd claw back the trust of his comrades one day, refilling that void inside with the sense of belonging that had once sustained him. He was already making good progress with Springer.

As for teetering on the brink of destruction so many times recently, that only energized him.

What was it Hortez had said on that first trip to Alabama? *Things happen around you, McEwan.* Dear Hortez. How had his friend's ending played out?

Arun instructed his suit AI to head for the shuttle.

C'mon, Barney, let's prove Hortez right.

—— Chapter 51 ——

Arun watched the external video feed to the passenger cabin as the shuttle's AI touched the craft down gently. They landed on a mid-sized lump of rock that would once have been an asteroid much farther out from the sun, but had been captured and towed to a Lagrange point between Tranquility and one of its moons. The gravitational pull between planet and moon canceled out at these Lagrange points, making them an excellent place to dump things, such as old spacecraft and tamed asteroids, because they would stay where you left them rather than clutter up the already crowded orbital paths around moons and planets.

This rock had a simple landing pad of fused and flattened rock, set a short walk away from a cavernous hole that led down into darkness.

Arun checked his suit comms. Only the shuttle's AI was registering as a node on his local ad-hoc network, and it was refusing to answer any of Arun's questions. The shuttle's cabin was airless and unpressurized, designed to disgorge a squad of armored Marines within seconds. With no one talking to him, the journey and landing had been silent, other than the sound of his own breathing.

Arun expected to be contacted by the AI controlling operations on this asteroid. But if such an intelligence existed, it was hiding from Arun. There was no sign of technology at all, other than the artificial nature of the crude landing pad.

Without a doubt, this was the most remote place Arun had ever been.

Untraceable would be another word for it.

All these thoughts floated through Arun's mind but failed to catch there. While he'd been trapped in his EVA bubble, his Marine's enhanced physiology had suppressed sleep, kept him concentrating on tiny dots in space for hour after hour, and had filled him with such a sense of threat that his muscles had powered up ready to leap and bound, but had found themselves unable to push effectively against the entombing buffer gel that had drowned him relentlessly.

The elation he'd felt when he first saw the shuttle had consumed his final reserve of strength. Now he was exhausted almost beyond the capacity to care any longer. Whoever had set this up had gone to so much trouble that it was pointless to resist. Arun thumbed the door pad, and half jumped, half floated down onto the landing pad.

He took long, bounding jumps along the path to the cavern. After fifty paces stumbling through the winding cavern entrance, Barney switched his faceplate to infrared but there was no heat source to serve as illumination: the walls were as cold as space.

He stopped and laughed. Out of habit, he'd been trying to avoid drawing attention to himself, but the idea of remaining undetected was silly, so he activated his helmet lamps.

The twin patches of illumination revealed a crudely hewn tunnel with a floor that was flattened and textured for improved grip. Arun had expected the entrance tunnels to be just large enough for him to carry out a long micro-g bound without cracking his head on the roof. It was far larger than that.

He searched his memory for zero-g mining. He knew almost nothing, but after a few seconds, facts vomited themselves out of a deep store, unpleasant to access but ready for use all the same. Whether this new knowledge came from artificial memory stores or had been implanted during Second Sleep he had no idea. But he did know that asteroids were normally assessed for mining potential by lozenge-shaped robots that would drill holes just large enough for them to drag themselves through. Larger tunnels could wait for when full-scale mining began. He saw images of asteroids being actively mined, and those fully mined out. But there were no signs of the equipment, tailings or port facilities he should be seeing in either scenario. So this wasn't a mining asteroid at all. But what was it?

It took another half hour of following twisting tunnels, and worrying whether he was circling round on himself, before he heard the hum. The tunnels were airless, but there was a faint vibration running through the floor that Barney picked up and fed in a cleaned and amplified form through his helmet speakers.

At first, Arun thought this was the electrical hum from a power source. Then, after immersing himself in the sound for a while, he changed his mind. It reminded him of listening to radio wave emissions from the sun. No, that wasn't quite it either. There was an organic quality to the hum. It was alive.

Whatever the hum's source, it gave him a beacon to aim for. Time seemed to speed up once he had a clear objective. Soon he emerged into a cavern painted with abstract symbols on its walls. Tracks ran along a ceiling, and from one of those tracks hung heavy brown drapes that ran across the room, hiding whatever lay behind from his sight. Barney was convinced that the hum's source was just behind the curtain.

"Approach the hanging barrier!"

The voice in his helmet was mechanical. Could it be a Trog? The voice was identical.

Arun walked to the curtain and then halted.

"Turn off your light and remain stationary."

Arun turned off his helmet lamps, but switched his faceplate to infrared. All he could see was a faint circular smudge right in front of him that shifted and swirled. It could easily be his mind playing tricks.

Whatever it was stayed motionless, throbbing gently in front of him. As the minutes dragged on, Arun became convinced he was making up the image, and yet something tangible was there: the hum. Under the fizz and swash, he heard – or thought he did — an echoing thump. A double pumping sound, as if twin hearts were beating.

A flash of heat came from overhead. Switching back from infra-red to visible spectrum, Arun saw that the ceiling was glowing with a diffuse blue-tinged light, and that the curtain was drawing back to reveal a… creature of some sort. But if this were a living thing, its evolutionary route was not one that had led to limbs, spine, torso, and head.

The thing was a blob, colored an impenetrable blue-black, about eight feet tall and three wide. The blob was surrounded in a rough sphere of orange liquid that fizzed and bubbled. It looked as if the orange liquid kept its shape through surface tension alone, because it wasn't inside a container. At the top of the central blob — what Arun thought of as its head — tubes connected with the orange surround, pumping out ribbons of silver fluid. A similar setup at its 'feet' sucked darkened streamers back inside its central core.

"Thank you," said the blob through Arun's helmet. At least, Arun assumed it was the blob that was speaking, but there was no sign of a translation box, no mouth parts, and no nodes registering on his suit comms.

Conversations were so much easier when you stuck to sound waves through air.

"Why am I here?" Arun asked.

"I — we — wish to see inside you."

"What? Dissection? Isn't that a bit old school?"

"It is not your body that interests us."

"You're going to read my mind?"

"We read your destiny."

"Oh."

"And your mind."

"You can…? Why?"

"Your future is — can be — important."

That's what Little Scar had told him. And the colonel had learned this from… "You're a Night Hummer!"

"You are correct."

"And all the weird stuff that's happened. Training bots that revive. Bad comms. Being left to drown for so long. That was all you?"

"I requested this event sequence. Disorientation and exhaustion is an aid to see inside your mind. To feel your path without the resistance natural to a sentient."

"Surely there must be an easier way to… to *read* me?"

"There is."

"Then why not use it?"

"You do not want the answer."

"Eh? What do you mean?"

"What I said."

Arun wanted to punch this annoying blob. Could he actually do any damage if he did? He shook his head. The Night Hummer was many levels of importance above a human Marine cadet. There would be reprisals.

"Feeding us combat meds. Running guns off planet. Was that your doing too?"

"No."

"Do you know anything about them?"

"No."

Liar. Arun was learning how deeply all the conspiracies were embedded into Detroit. Everyone knew more than they let on. And if this Hummer was in cahoots with Gupta – Arun was nearly convinced of that now – then it had to know something about the traitors on Tranquility.

The blob was probably laughing at him, those bubbles an expression of its contempt for the puny human. Nothing riled Arun more than aliens smug with the certainty of their superiority.

With difficulty, Arun sucked in his anger and snarled: "Do you realize how much trouble your little games have caused me and my squadmates?"

"No."

"Corporal Majanita will probably be demoted — that'll kill her. The battalion will be awarded demerits, which will make it even more impossible to climb out of the Cull Zone. I might be executed as a consequence of what you've done."

When the Night Hummer gave no reply, Arun prompted: "And?"

"And? Please elaborate."

"And don't you care that you've caused so much trouble?"

"I do not care."

"You're a skangat, then. You know that?"

There came a pause. Then the Hummer replied: "Yes."

"Yes? Yes, you're a skangat?"

"Correct. My translation device tells me that *skangat* is a term humans use on each other to communicate disappointment in the other's behavior, or to indicate aggression, possibly leading to physical combat. Is this correct?"

"Right on both counts, pal."

"Thank you. Then I am a skangat."

"Frakk! I can't even insult you."

"That assessment is probably accurate. Without long practice, inter-species communication is significantly less rich than between sentients of the same species. However, I estimate that if we communicate regularly over a period of no less than several weeks, and if you apply yourself to your task, then it might be possible for you to insult me."

"Is that's what's gonna happen? We're going to be stuck together for weeks?"

"No. I have completed my examination. You will leave shortly and only see me on one more occasion."

"Then why…? Oh, what's the use? Tell me this, then. What did you see inside my mind? What is my path?"

"It is best that members of your species are not given details of predestination. Your species is not evolved for that."

"And yours is?"

"Correct."

"Why?"

"Defense."

"So you — what? — see a threat coming and change the future so you avoid getting tropied?"

"The broad thrust of your speculation is correct. Our precognitive capability is an adaptation of our feeding process. It is why my kind has an understanding with the species you call White Knights. They feed and guard us. We tell them the future."

Arun thought back to the conversation with Little Scar. The Jotun had said Arun was important, another human too. Maybe two. "Luring me here," he said, "was that part of your defensive instincts?"

The Night Hummer made no reply. It rolled back a few paces before coming to a halt. Then it rolled forward again before repeating the pattern. Was it pacing?

It took three minutes before it answered: "yes."

"Then I do what? Do I shoot an invader who would otherwise have killed you?"

"Probably not."

"But I am important to your future?"

"Yes."

"Do I save you?"

"No. You are my killer."

Arun's vision reddened momentarily as combat rage took a hold of him. If the Hummer had brought his killer here, it could only be for one reason: the creature saw Arun as a threat, one to be eliminated.

Arun leaped at the blob. He had to kill the Hummer before it killed him. He sailed through the airless space aiming to bring his hands together in the place roughly corresponding to a human's neck. He penetrated the outer orange skin easily enough but then… he was gripped! The blob rolled back, absorbing his momentum, but his hands were held fast.

Arun pushed up until his feet were pointing at the ceiling. Then he swung himself back down in an arc pivoting on his hands. He never finished the maneuver. A cavity appeared in the center of the Hummer. A split second later, Arun was sailing through the vacuum to land on his back a dozen paces away. The thought just had time to run through his head that to throw him such a short distance showed restraint and skill before he hit the floor and was rolling back like a ball, and kept on rolling until he gently smacked into the wall.

The Night Hummer, meanwhile, had effortlessly kept pace with him, propelling itself by waving its surface in contact with the floor. He'd seen vids of Earth snakes move like that. It made sense if micro-g was your natural habitat.

"You misunderstand," said the Hummer when Arun had come to rest. "You are my killer, yes. But it is not your intention to kill me. You try to save me. You will fail. Probably. Hopefully."

"Hopefully? Why hopefully?"

"Because then your path is not what I foresee."

"And I'm important, right?" Arun scrambled to his feet. "Hold on! If I'm important, "

"Probably not. But the future is a forest of potential paths. You can change your future to make that more likely. This is why we stay aloof. Interference rarely works well. I have a personal interest in you because you kill me."

"What do I do that is so important?"

"You should not hear predestination."

"Who is the purple human?"

"You cannot make me tell you your destiny. Nor can you cast words and phrases in my direction, fishing for my reaction."

Okay, buddy, we'll see about that. But first, a change of tack. "Is this your natural habitat? Do you live here?"

"This facility is readied for occupation by a troop of my people. Sadly, my companions are not arriving. The White knights treat us like vegetables, to be planted in gardens such as this and tended, and weeded, left to grow information. But we are not vegetation, and I do miss company."

"So what are you telling me? That all the hell I've been through this past day… and more… it's so you have someone to talk to?"

"No!" A pressure wave coursed through the Hummer, striking the floor hard enough to lift Arun a few inches off the floor. "I am not so trivial. I must have you here to see deeper, to see the pattern of what you call past and future. Understand, human child. Your cultural history talks of the pattern of the future being a vast tapestry woven by the Fates. Each sentient life is a single thread."

"You're quoting the Loom of Thessaly, right? The Earth supremacists are always going on about the importance of Classical Greek culture."

"Perhaps they are correct to do so. The Loom of Thessaly remains the most accurate model your species has yet devised to explain the nature of reality. In this model, individual sentients are caught in the tyranny of the tapestry's pattern. They can struggle but never break free, and if you stand back a little, the struggles of individuals are invisible against the purity of the larger pattern. But sometimes special threads arise that… Your model suffers from a critical lack of dimensions at this point. Let us say that these special threads tie off the old pattern and influence the Fates to begin weaving a radically new design."

"And I'm a special thread, yeah?"

"You might be."

"Can be? What must I do to become this be this new-pattern guy?"

"You must make a choice. The pattern you make possibly saves your species from extinction and elevates the status of humans everywhere. Many other races too benefit in this future."

"Sounds nova. Where's the catch?"

"You must make an oath. It binds you to the future that saves your people. If you break your oath, the path diverges. The pattern corrupts, and you may accelerate your extinction."

"Go on."

"Do you promise to adopt my people as the client species of the humans? You must re-house, guard and cherish us. There are future times when you will choose between your friends and your promise and you must choose your promise, or the future will corrupt."

Arun laughed. After all he'd been through. Such madness! "Hummer, that's crazy talk. That's treason, for starters. The White Knights would sterilize the entire planet if they got wind of it."

"You are correct."

"I don't believe for a nanosecond that I could make this happen even if I was insane enough to try."

"I know. Yet you must promise sincerely. Saying meaningless words is not sufficient. The oath must be real."

"And in any case. The White Knights get you these hollowed-out rocks to live in. You have your understanding with them. Why change that?"

"Because the White Knights cherish randomness, mutation and the potential of creative destruction. We represent a predictable future. Our nature is utterly repugnant to them. They loath us more than any other species, and yet they cannot ignore our usefulness. Within a century from this time, we are labeled scapegoats for White Knight setbacks. They exterminate us."

"And you want me to protect you?"

"Yes."

"From the White Knights, the most powerful species I'm aware of?"

"Correct."

"You're mad."

"I can see into the future."

"You're also a liar. You refused to tell me the future because I'm not evolved enough, apparently. But you've just told me what will happen. "

"I have. I only reveal small details. They are obvious. You learn them yourself soon."

"Good for me." Arun's stomach rumbled in irritation. He hadn't eaten solid food for almost two days and his stomach wasn't one for philosophy and long-laid plans. Without food, Arun wasn't saving mad orange blobs or anyone else.

"If I refuse?"

"That is unwise. A tragedy. But you will eat and drink nonetheless, and the shuttle shall return you safely to your home."

"Food! Where?"

"Follow."

The Hummer shimmered over to the far end of the room, to the portion that had been hidden behind the curtain. If the blob had lips, Arun would have kissed them because there was a pressurized accommodation bubble. Through the clear plastic walls he could see a table and chair. There was a hotplate with steaming sauce and meat…"

"There is beer too," said the Hummer. "I am told humans enjoy beer — although you soldier-children are denied the experience. And roast meat and other palatable items. There is plenty of air, and an inflatable bedroll for you to sleep upon. When you are refreshed, tell the shuttle to return you home."

Arun knelt down to unseal the outer door of the airlock. As he started to crawl through to this one-man chow-hall, the alien spoke through Arun's helmet speaker.

"Human!"

"What?"

"Your oath. Will you swear to protect my species? To guard and cherish us?"

What was this, a marriage ceremony? He supposed it was. Perhaps this was the most important moment in human history since President Horden signed the Vancouver Accords that had bought Earth White Knight protection by selling human children into slavery. Maybe this was even more important than Vancouver.

Or maybe this was the rambling of an intelligent blob driven insane by loneliness.

He sighed. On the far side of the airlock was dinner. That was far more real than all this speculation.

"Well," said the Hummer. "Do you swear?"

"I do so swear. I shall cherish and nurture your people."

The airlock flashed a blue light and slid opened. Arun was inside, lifting off his helmet and smelling rich aromas of meat and vegetables and gravy. He shrugged. *Aliens!* If only they were all such dumbchucks.

—— Chapter 52 ——

"Since your return from the auxiliary, you have not spoken of traitors and drugging."

Pedro was lounging in the lamp heat of his basking station, his face regarding Arun with expressionless eyes as always. While the insectoid's face was physically incapable of smiling, frowning, snarling and all those other human expressions, Arun was certain he was learning to pick up on the alien's other cues, from body posture, linguistic phrasing, those tireless antennae and who knew what else?

If he was reading the signs right, Pedro was saying that this was a topic they had buried for too long.

Arun shook his head. "Not going to happen, big guy. Too dangerous."

If only they had somewhere private to talk, then Arun would dearly love to ask his friend for advice. But that first trip to the orbit could be put down to meeting on neutral ground. Meeting there regularly would look to outside observers like plotting insurrection.

"And I'll tell you another thing that's dangerous," Arun said, "continuing these little chats without you opening up. You won't tell me anything about your military capability, your population numbers, or give me a detailed map of your nest. Hell, you refuse point blank to tell me what they did with Hortez when he hung up his microphone. Colonel Little Scar hasn't yet asked me to report back on my liaison mission. But he will. So far it's been all one-way: I give you info; you confuse the hell outta me. You've helped me, for sure, but you've given me nothing that I can give to the colonel. You call yourself my friend, but on this you've let me down. Badly. Possibly fatally."

Pedro's legs were folded underneath. Each pair in sequence now pushed him up a little before dropping back down. The result looked as if Pedro were bobbing atop ocean swell.

Arun knew this meant the insect was delighted at Arun's words. Dongwit aliens! He'd been trying to tell off the Trog.

"I am not permitted to reveal certain secrets," said Pedro when he'd finished bobbing, "but I have nearly finished the compilation of a dossier containing everything else we know about ourselves, from our earliest history, through our pheromone language, and on to the best examples of our love poetry. Expressing the essence of my people using your human language proved more difficult than I thought, which is why this took far longer than my initial estimate. The greatest challenge was to transform information into understanding. *Human* understanding. The dossier will be uploaded to the base network tomorrow, and access granted to your softscreen account."

Arun didn't know what to say. The more he replayed Pedro's words, the more stunned he became. "You did all this," he said when the faculty of speech returned, "for me?"

Pedro curled his antennae in amusement. The bulky alien was laughing at Arun's expense. "No," Pedro said. "I did not do all this. A team of over five thousand assembled this for me. The majority of the nest's research capability was diverted to serve your needs. Now do you believe I have let you down? Badly. Possibly fatally."

Arun grimaced. "Sorry, Pedro. Horden's Children, big guy. Look at you. You're an overgrown ant, and yet you've made me feel ashamed. How the hell have you managed that?"

Pedro tilted his head down and folded his antennae flat against his head. He was in deadly earnest now. "It is not my people of the nest who have made you feel guilt, it is your human sense of empathy. This is important, Arun McEwan. You are important. We have offered similar information to the Jotuns on many occasions, but they lack the mindset to *understand*. You humans are far more socially elastic, enough to accept and bond with us. Jotuns are admirable in many ways but they are culturally rigid, brittle even. They can only relate to you humans as dwarf Jotuns missing a pair of arms, and with limited intelligence. And it is because they relate to you as orphaned and mutilated children that they are so protective of you — more than you realize."

"And your lot? You're tunnel-dwelling colony beings. Jotuns can't relate to you at all."

"Precisely. Which is why they wish to use you as a conduit, an intermediary to interpret the information we give you because they cannot."

Arun was about to get up to convey his thanks by rubbing the insect's head. But he held himself back because Pedro's antennae were still tight against his head.

"I'm afraid I must raise again the subject of traitors and gun-running," said the Trog.

"No. I thank you for your help, but you know as well as I do that tunnel walls hear everything."

"That is not accurate," said Pedro — still in super-serious mode. "I do not know this as well as you. I know this far *better* than you do."

Arun barely heard the words. Despite the heat from Pedro's basking lamps, the air had chilled.

"I have never spoken to you about gun-running," he said.

"Correct. Listen, please, Human McEwan. This is important. It is not only tunnels that have ears. Did you believe the surface was unmonitored? And if your words have reached my ears, then any traitors who might exist will have heard them too."

Pedro sure had a knack for springing ugly surprises. The only way the alien could top this was if Xin came walking through the chamber entrance to see for herself how the color had drained from Arun's face. Arun trembled with fear. Any one of his comrades and NCOs could be a traitor. Give him someone to shoot at and he'd fire back, no problem. But he hadn't the courage to take this.

"I perceive you understand the danger," said Pedro.

"No kidding."

Pedro acted puzzled. "I agree. This is no time for humor. I believe that very soon, events will escalate into unconstrained violence. You need a refuge, and sending you pheromone passes in the mail is inadequate."

Pedro sprang from his basking shelf, kicking a cloud of dust from the dirt floor. He jumped on Arun who was sitting in his leather sofa chair.

Arun was suddenly aware of how big his friend was. What did he weigh? Three hundred pounds? More?

Pedro ripped Arun out of the chair and flung his bulk onto the human's shoulders. Arun's vision exploded into stars when the back of his head thumped into the ground.

When the fight came back to Arun, it was too late. Pedro had him pinned down good and proper. He threw everything he had into a wild roll to the left, but he didn't move an inch.

Frakk! This Trog was strong.

A sharp claw appeared at the end of one of Pedro's upper limbs. Arun heard the claw *snikk* through his shirt and then stared in disbelief as the claw peeled open his flesh. Then the pain hit him.

"Get off me! *Get off!*"

"Hold still!" Pedro ordered calmly. "This won't hurt a bit."

Arun relaxed a tiny degree. Then Pedro cut much deeper, flicking lines of agony into Arun's chest cavity.

"Agghh!" Arun screamed continuously until Pedro paused to reach for something in his thorax belt. "I thought…" hissed Arun through gritted teeth, "thought you said it wouldn't hurt."

"I said it won't hurt a bit. It will, in fact, hurt a lot. And if you struggle it will hurt a whole lot more."

Frakk! Arun must have been around aliens too long because he actually believed Pedro. Whatever crazy thing Pedro was doing, he wasn't trying to kill him. Didn't mean it wouldn't, but it wouldn't kill him on purpose.

Arun activated his emergency meditation triggers, which transported him to a safer place in his mind, leaving the pain in his body.

No sooner had he left his body — or so it seemed — then Pedro leaped off him and the sights and sounds of the chamber colored and flavored once more.

"All done," reported Pedro.

"All of *what* done?"

"I have implanted a pheromone amplifier-emitter under your sternum."

"What the…? I mean, what makes you…" Arun sighed. Every word he spoke cost its weight in agony. "Why?

"For a start, you can throw this away." Pedro snapped off the pheromone identifier around Arun's neck. "Your new implant identifies you as a nest brother. Its scent charge should be good for about 160 years."

"For a start. You said, *for a start*." A wave of pain consumed Arun. They both waited until it ebbed sufficiently for Arun to speak. "What else have you done?"

"It is not only a dumb scent emitter. It is connected to your endocrine system."

"My what? My hormones? Are you telling me you've turned my hormones into scent signals?" The idea was hilarious. Arun vaguely noticed that the pain had gone, replaced with such giddy good cheer that the room was spinning,

"Essentially, yes. In theory you could learn to control this. You could learn the rudiments of my language."

"Look, pal. I'm seventeen. In a couple years, maybe five at most, I expect they'll ship me out on a troop ship. I don't expect to return. I'm not some kind of scribe. You're confusing me with another species. I'm a human. We shoot at people or we clean out the head. That's about the range of our career options."

"It seems that way now. Perhaps one day you could command whole legions of nest warriors with that device in your chest."

Arun stared. He waited for his friend's antennae to twist in amusement. When they didn't, he burst out in laughter that brought the pain crashing back over him.

Those visions everyone else kept having about him weren't right, after all. Arun wasn't going to become a great human freedom fighter, leader of the all-conquering Human Legion. Nope. Future annals of military history would record him as the great ant queen.

Arun the Ant Queen.

Frakk!

He was still laughing on his way back home when he was arrested on Level 7 on suspicion of taking narcotics.

He laughed all through the night in the detention cube. He laughed so much that each motion became agony, the muscles deep inside his chest bruised beyond purple and into ultra-violet.

He was still laughing as he cursed Pedro.

In the end the medics took him for an exploratory poke around in his chest to find out what the alien had done. He was still laughing as the anesthetic took him under.

He awoke with a head that felt like auto-cannons were laying down rapid fire inside. After a quick feel of his chest confirmed that Pedro's gift was still there, he groaned from something other than the pain. He was going to be a Troggie nest brother for the rest of his life.

What the hell would Xin make of that?

—— Chapter 53 ——

Arun kept his buoyant mood all the way back from this evening's Scendence team training session, until the moment he turned off Corridor 622 and into the passageway to his hab-disk. Being this close to his home soured things. He tried to wrest back his cheerfulness, but it was like grappling a cloud of smoke.

An alert in his head warned him that inspection was in only ten minutes. He stepped up his pace. Every night he practiced with Xin's Scendence team, and every time he stayed away later. Guess he was cutting it a little too fine.

He started to run.

Physical exertion usually made him feel good. So did Team Ultimate Victory. As the 8th battalion's only remaining entry in the championship, Xin and Arun's team were beginning to attract a fringe of supporters, helpers and wannabe coaches. For the first time this week, final year cadets had joined in. The next night even a few veterans had turned up to lend their support.

Despite these newcomers' seniority, no one questioned Xin's place as unofficial team leader. Arun might be the expert planner and strategist, but that was not the same thing at all as leadership. Xin took charge as naturally as breathing, and she insisted that all team members trained together, despite their different game roles.

Now that he was back in the team — Pedro having declared his appearance was a one-off — Xin had relaxed around Arun, even giving a few rare words of praise.

Arun remembered every glowing word.

And when her tight lips softened into a dimpling smile, all the threat and hardship of his life sloughed away. To catch fleeting glimpses of happiness — was that what the free people of Earth felt?

On the threshold of his dorm, with 130 seconds before inspection, Arun came to a halt. He took a deep breath. Xin might have softened, but his squadmates' coldness had solidified into ice, blaming him for all their troubles.

Only Springer backed him, although sometimes with lukewarm support from Madge.

This was an asymmetric cold war. Arun couldn't fight back because they were right to blame him.

Reluctantly, he entered his home.

"Here he is, McEwan the Maverick. Tell me, pal, is Team Ultimate Victory going to live up to its name?"

What the…? Arun took a moment to work out why his brain was buzzing in confusion. The question had come from a figure lying in Brandt's rack. But this wasn't the cadet lance sergeant. The voice was too rough, his body too slender. A novice? And why was no one ready for inspection?

The impostor sat up. His head was shaved, revealing a lateral scar burning a zigzag path across the top of his skull. He was small, but that face was too weathered to be a novice's.

"Who the hell are you?" asked Arun.

Anger lit up the newcomer's eyes momentarily, rapidly fading into a look of resignation. "Man, I'm whacked. I've been asleep for ninety years, which works out well for you, pal, 'cos I'm too tired to beat the crap out of you."

Arun looked to his comrades who were watching in silence. *Hoping I'll trip up again.*

The newcomer continued. "Name's Umarov. I'm Blue-6's replacement for the guy who got himself promoted out into Command Section."

"Arun," said Springer, "Umarov is a veteran."

Umarov snorted. "Hardly. A few days after making Marine, they shoved me into the ice store. According to my body clock's reckoning, I was iced only yesterday. You could say I've been a Marine for five days, or ninety years, depending on how you count it. Either way, you lizards are still cadets, which means I outrank all of you. For now. That's why inspection is canceled permanently. Sergeant Gupta says it's a waste of his valuable time

to schedule nursemaiding you like kids, now that I'm here. If you fall out of line, he'll kick my butt into the next star system. Simple. I like him."

None of the other cadets disputed this. Zug gave a tiny shrug. It was all true, then.

Arun saluted. "Congratulations, Marine. Days or decades makes no difference. Graduation is a proud achievement."

A frown came over Umarov. He hesitated, chewing over his next move. "You have no idea how much has changed. But this gung-ho attitude is worst of all. The others told me you don't fit in, McEwan, but you're just like the rest of them, acting as if you're proud to be in the Marines. Do you really believe it is an honor to serve in the Corps family?"

"Of course, Marine Umarov."

"No, don't call me that. And don't even think of calling me sir. That's for instructors and officers – collaborators and murderers, mostly. You call me by the rank I earned. *Carabinier*. It's the basic rank — *was* — and it's called that because our primary weapon is the SA-71 carbine. It's a title that makes sense, unlike your crap. I mean…" He glanced at Madge. "*Corporal*. And–" He gestured at Del-Marie. "–*Lance corporal*. Where the hell did those names come from? And *lance*! In the name of Horden's Hairy Hindquarters what is a fragging *lance*? Can any of you filthy skangats tell me that?"

No one answered.

"Didn't think so. Morons and lizards, the lot of you. Seems like while I was on ice they discovered the off switch for the human brain. So long as I'm still your superior, you will address me as carabinier. Understand?"

"Yes, carabinier," said Arun.

"As I was saying, we obeyed orders because my generation was too cowardly to face the consequences of disobedience. To be born in a Marine farm was to be sentenced to a hellish servitude. Are you not slaves?"

"Wait," said Madge. "You were raised on the farms? You grew wheat and barley and all that drent?"

Umarov's eyes narrowed. "It's been nine decades since I walked these passageways. I expected a few words to change. I didn't expect you to butcher the entire English language."

"With respect, carabinier," said Madge, "we speak Human, not English."

"Jeez." He grimaced. "This is a prime slice of awkwardness. You'll be my NCO sooner than you expect, but for a little while you're just a spotty little kid who doesn't know shit. Let me tell you for a fact, you're speaking English. Badly. If you don't know that, it's because of the Jotuns' eternal messing with our heads. They probably want to stamp out any sense of loyalty to the various groupings of old Earth. They didn't bother in my day. All we knew of Earth were fairy tales so corrupted in the retelling that they no longer made any sense. To us, *English* was just the name of a language. I'm guessing it means something more, now that you can read the history books."

"Carabinier," interrupted Del-Marie, but Umarov cut him dead with a cut of his hand.

"No, Sandure. Don't tell me your history lessons. I don't want to know. Not tonight."

"I wasn't. I was going to warn you. Your words could be considered… verging on disloyal."

"Good for you, kid. You might be a lizard, but at least lizards have backbone. The rest of you sorry lot are just worms."

Del-Marie brightened under the praise.

"But you score zero for intelligence." Arun nearly laughed at the look of disappointment on Del-Marie's face. "In my day the regime was so tough you had to think carefully before taking each breath. You could even be punished if you didn't go to sleep lying in your bed according to regulations; on your back, dead center, head pointing up with arms by your side palms down. For those of us who survived that crap, they loosened up a few months before graduation. They gave you back a little of your humanity to make you a better soldier, just in time for you to use it on the front line. It's obvious that hasn't changed."

"But, carabinier," said Madge. "*We* aren't nearing graduation. Your words could be dangerous for us to hear."

Umarov shrugged. "Another fair point, but still wrong. I'm not the only one to get thawed out. I just got the short straw and ended up with you freaks. There's whole companies of my class forming up. Don't you get it?

They're calling up the reserves. I don't think you gotta worry about being years off graduation.

"Anyway. Crap! Give a guy a chance to think, why don't you? I only started thawing out this morning. Brain's still running on anti-freeze. Keeps getting distracted. *Farms.* Did I plow fields of dirt or something? No, I did not! I was raised on a *Marine farm.* They tell me this place is called Detroit now. Before that it was Alpha Base. Can't have been that very long 'cos in my day this stinking hole was called Marine Farm #3 and I was crop 167. If you come from the persuasion that the simplest explanation is the one that's most likely to let you survive one more day, then you'd interpret that as meaning we'd been farmed for 166 years before my crop. Me? I'm cursed by a sprinkling of intelligence. Enough to see this world of lies for what it is, but not clever enough to do squat about it." He looked across all the cadets in the room before sniffing with disdain, "So they've prettied the words and now you love the Marine Corps. I hope there's more to this change than bullshit, because from where I'm sitting, you look a right bunch of prize chumps."

Confused looks passed between the cadets.

"Chumps! Sheesh! I mean you're idiots. *Fools.* You've all got a vacancy between your ears. They've gilded your cage and suddenly the Human Marine Corps isn't your sentence, it's your proud family! Jeez!"

"I don't think so, carabinier," said Zug, trying to put deference into his voice.

Umarov nodded at him to go on.

"I am sure you are correct that our officers have realized that fear and brutality are neither the best ways to instill fighting spirit, nor to train Marines who act intelligently. But I believe there is more to it than that. Our veterans and instructors give us such different explanations about our place in the galaxy. I guess it depends on when they were raised and where they have been stationed. But I do see a pattern. The more recently they have fought, the more likely they are to believe that we are fighting for a worthwhile cause. We fight for Earth's dignity. For humanity's right to be taken seriously by a hostile galaxy that regards us as the ultimate underclass. And it isn't just the fighting. If I were called on to carry out the Cull on my comrades, I would do so without complaint because that is just as much a part of fighting for our dignity as rushing an enemy strong point."

Umarov shook his head. "Just nine decades ago, we were farmed. I like to think we were a more specialist crop than wheat, for instance, but still a crop to be grown, harvested and shipped out to meet demand. Does a blade of wheat have dignity? Eh? Even if it did, would it make a blind bit of difference to its fate?"

Del-Marie gave his most expressive Gallic shrug. "Perhaps, carabinier, the truth does not matter. If we *act* as if we have a purpose, if we pretend that we have dignity, then our lives as soldier-slaves are more bearable. Perhaps we are living a lie, perhaps we are… *chumps*, but surely that is better than the truth if that truth is unbearably hellish?"

Umarov closed his eyes. "You're no longer human, are you? I mean, you're probably right, Sandure, but God help me, you've moved on and left humanity behind. You're all built like the back end of a destroyer, and other than you, Sandure, with your silly shrug, there's barely a hint of expression on any of you except…"

Umarov pointed at Arun. Except that one. He thinks too deeply. And she…" He pointed at Springer. "She cares too much. Thinks she's the great Earth Mother. And the rest of you? It's like they cloned the most unimaginative drones of my generation, fed them super growth hormone, and have been interbreeding them ever since. What's wrong with you? We're in our dorm! Hello? It's where you let off steam? I expect a little stupid banter, the stronger reminding the weaker ones who's in charge, and I expect grumbling. A lot of grumbling. Soldiers should always grumble. It's one of the basic laws of the universe."

"*Les grognards*, carabinier," said Zug.

"Laygronyards? That's the modern word for grumbling is it? What kind of dumbass word is that? One you never use, I'll bet, because you're all like machines on standby mode, waiting to be fully activated in the morning." He shook his head. "*Laygronyards*? Shit! You fragging scare me more than the Jotuns."

What was Zug playing at? He'd talked of these *grognards* before. It was a French word — meaning *grumblers* — that had been the nickname for a corps of elite French soldiers. Arun liked the name, though. It sounded very human.

Umarov grabbed a softscreen and started to figure out the controls. The rest of the room remained silent and motionless.

"What? Oh, for crying out loud," groaned Umarov. "You're dismissed. Go do whatever robots do in their free time. Just leave me the hell alone."

Arun considered helping the carabinier struggling with his softscreen, but decided to wait a while. He grinned. Like him, Umarov was an outsider, and one who saw immediately that there was something screwy about the attitude of the cadets.

Arun thanked Fate for bringing him a natural ally. Change was in the air, and that meant the next time he left his Spacedance training, he might have something worth coming home to.

—— Chapter 54 ——

Striding along the curved corridor of sector F7 on his way to the shower tunnel, Arun grinned when he thought back to how Umarov's arrival last night had shaken up the frigid atmosphere in his dorm.

Ever since that stupid tunnel exercise, his life had gone from drent to drenter. Zug and the guys could go vulley themselves for thinking Arun had brought it all on himself. So what if all their cold-shoulder drent was due to them being drugged? That wasn't a good enough excuse.

Arun had made his choices but he stood up for them. Why shouldn't he? He wasn't a loser. It was just the universe trying to make him look bad by conspiring to trip him up all the time.

Well, nuts to the universe too, because he was feeling good right now. It was 06:42 and he'd just finished his solo morning workout: three circuits of Ring 7 – the second-longest ring in the hab-disk – followed by a half hour pushing and pulling against resistance channels in the gym.

Even being an engineered freak, courtesy of centuries of White Knight tinkering, had its plus points. Did the humans on Earth feel such a flare of unquenchable energy first thing in the morning? From what he'd heard, they mostly fell reluctantly out of bed in a semi-torpor that would hold them for hours. Whereas, thanks to his augmented body, Arun felt not just that he could climb a mountain before breakfast, but that he needed to, or else his body would explode from all the pent up energy inside his muscles.

He walked into the F7 shower room, giving a vague wave of greeting to the other cadets stripping off on their way in, or on their way out, putting on fresh underwear and fatigues from the bins provided by the Aux.

Arun had his shirt off and was about to tug down his gym pants when he saw Zug and Osman up ahead, naked and about to enter the shower tunnel. When they spotted Arun, they glanced at each other and then grabbed gym pants from the bin and put them on.

"What's up?" asked Arun. He spoke carefully, not wishing to antagonize them.

Zug and Osman faced off against him.

Osman folded his arms. "You'll have to wait," he said. "Springer's in there."

Arun shrugged. "So?"

"So you wait till she's dressed. The tactical order chart says you're a member of our squad, but you aren't part of our team. You'll need to give our women their privacy."

"*Your* women? You're crazy, Osman. What, you think you own Springer? That she's stripping off for your pleasure? She's just getting clean, man. Stop being such a… chump."

"Yeah, I'm with Bryant's blue-eyed boy," said a voice from behind: Lance Corporal Yoshioka from Gold Squad. She threw her gym clothes in the bin.

"I don't care about your lovers' tiff. Stupid Blue Squad guffoons. I do care about whether I stink. Get out the frakking way!"

Osman stepped aside.

Yoshioka strode into the shower tunnel, giving Osman a shove for good measure on her way in. She still blamed Blue Squad for letting the combat bots shoot her from behind in that frakked-up boarding exercise on *Fort Douaumont*.

Arun dove for the gap she had opened between Zug and Osman, but they were waiting for him. Osman pushed him back so sharply that Arun slipped on the wet floor and fell onto his backside.

"It would be best for you," said Zug, "that you make an effort to be polite, whether or not you believe our request for privacy is justified."

Arun felt the anger boil over inside him. Anger directed at Zug. It was Osman who'd pushed him, but Osman had always lived life to binary extremes. You were his mortal enemy or greatest friend, sometimes both on the same day. Back before he became a cadet, any unresolved disagreements would torment Osman such that he couldn't sleep, but the next day, Osman would shrug and forget whatever had troubled him so badly the day before.

That was what made Osman such fun to be around, or used to. It also made him the exact opposite of Zug. Calm, considered, consistent, it was Zug's disapproval that had really turned the squad against Arun.

He couldn't get his revenge on Zug here. But he would. Oh, yes. Zug — *Zhoog* as he insisted it was pronounced — would get his just deserts soon enough. But for now…

"Fine," said Arun, still sitting on his butt. "I'll wait."

"Make sure you do," said Osman, his anger burning so hot that he could barely speak.

Osman and Zug threw their clothes in the bin and followed Yoshioka into the shower tunnel. Arun hovered just outside, feeling increasingly uncomfortable as a steady stream of cadets entered the shower room, or emerged naked at the other end.

The F7 shower room wasn't reserved for Blue and Gold Squads, but it was nearest to their dorm rooms, and so Arun knew most of the cadets coming into the room and giving him some hard stares.

No one said anything. They didn't have to. He was acting like some kind of deviant, lurking in the shower to steal glimpses of nude flesh.

Arun shut his eyes and clenched his fists. How had it come to this? Only moments ago he'd been buzzing.

Now Zug and Osman had ruined his morning.

Skangat lizards!

Arun stripped off and walked into the shower tunnel.

As he lifted his arms to accept the spray of foaming detergent, Arun felt eyes watching him warily. One of the girls from Gold Squad turned her back on him.

This was getting ridiculous.

Arun yelled through the spattering noise of the shower jets. "Hey! Hey, Zug!"

The big guy turned around.

"This is all your fault, man."

"No, my friend," said Zug. "It is your own doing."

"I'm not your friend."

"Yes, you are."

"You're wrong. And I'll tell you one thing, Zug the Perfect – Zug the Frakking Aloof. You'll know what it feels like one day. Maybe right now the universe is stacking the deck to deal you a frakked-up hand. Sooner or later you'll have a run of bad luck"

"I am certain you are right. One day."

"One day? Nuts to that. I don't want bad luck to happen to you one day. I want it *now*. Do you hear, Zug? I hope today is the worst frakking day of your life."

But the cadet who still called himself Arun's friend had already turned away and was lost behind the steam and spray of water.

Arun was on his own.

On his way back to the dorm room, someone leaped out of a side passageway and grabbed him by the shoulders.

Arun was about to deck his assailant when he recognized something in that touch. That scent.

He turned and stared wide-eyed into Springer's face.

Her eyes glowed violet with emotion.

Well, Arun was emotional too. He was furious at Zug and disappointed at Osman. But his anger was all jumbled up with regret and loneliness, and he'd never been angry with Springer. Everything inside churned into such a confused mess that his jaw moved up and down but he didn't know what to say.

He didn't think he needed to. Springer looked into his face and seemed to understand what he was feeling better than Arun did himself.

"Help me?" he whispered.

"I heard what happened in the shower," she said. "You need to sort this."

Arun bellowed in rage. His pulse raced, his limbs shook. "How the frakk can I do that?" Arun couldn't keep the anger out of his voice. His shoulders slumped. He hadn't wanted to bark at Springer.

Springer didn't scream back; she laughed as if this were all a game. "You're not alone, Arun." She shook her head in mock pity. Which was weird. Arun had never seen her act like that before. "It's you boys. It's your testosterone making you into idiots. I was talking this over with Majanita last night. She said she thought they give you Marine boys added testosterone to bulk you up, make you fight better. But they give you too high a dose. If not testosterone, *then they must be giving you something similar.*"

Arun nearly missed Springer's emphasis. She wasn't talking about testosterone. "I'm surprised Madge finally bought into your theory," he said, a flash of understanding connecting them as he looked into her eyes.

"I've been working on her for a while," Springer replied.

"You're amazing. I ever tell you that?"

"Not nearly enough, Arun."

"Guilty as charged." He just about managed a grin. "But I still don't see how that helps me."

Springer shook her head. "That's because you're a guy. You're no different from Zug, Osman and the others. You boys are acting as if all you understand is confrontation. Instead of a frontal assault, switch the direction of your attack. Try empathy instead."

"You mean, see it from a girl's perspective?"

"Frakk it, Arun! You've got a lot to learn. No, not at all, but if it helps you to think of it that way then, yes, try thinking like a girl."

Arun started by taking in deep breaths through his nose, holding and then blowing out a smooth stream of spent air through his mouth.

"Not now, sweetie," Springer teased. "Have you forgotten? Gupta switched schedule to put us up in orbit. *Again!* We move out in fifteen."

"I know. It's like he's deliberately keeping us off planet."

"That's not important now. Just think on something Madge said to me. It might help with Zug and the rest. She said we're all gene-modified, brainwashed, drugged-up combat kids. But deep down we're still the same species as our Earth ancestors. They evolved a set of social behaviors to cope with the challenges of life on Earth. Sometimes our minds decide they recognize the problems we face on Tranquility and reach for the bag of coping behaviors our ancestors brought with them from Earth. We act a certain way even though we don't always know why."

"So you're saying that Zug is acting like a pre-tech savage and doesn't even know it?"

Springer frowned. "Majanita sees it like this. The boys in the squad are treating me like I'm their little sister. They're closing ranks to protect me, a female, against the unwanted attention of the outsider male who wronged me, who dishonored the clan. That's you, in case your brain hasn't woken up yet. If you reason or fight them you will only make it worse. The one way to resolve this is to earn the right to rejoin the clan. Do something dramatic that proves your loyalty to our *testosterone*-addled boys. Does that make sense?"

Arun nodded. "Is that all?"

Springer rolled her eyes. "Actually, there is one more thing to think on."

"What's that?"

"This…" Springer raised herself on tiptoes, leaned in, and kissed Arun on the lips.

It was no more than a chaste peck, but Arun couldn't help but touch the spot where Springer's lips had brushed against his.

That was the most beautiful thing anyone had ever done for him.

———

Arun hurried after Springer and into a dorm filling with unhurried activity as the section prepared to spend for a stint of unknown duration practicing void combat.

Suit AIs were checked, the head visited, silent words spoken by the more spiritual. Umarov was helped through the modern drills, grumbling at all the stupid changes and venting his frustration at everyone around him in a stream of unfamiliar curses.

All that ceased dead on 07:00 when, unexpectedly, a tone sounded through the speakers recessed into the walls, followed a moment later by a woman's voice. It was not a voice Arun recognized, but it was one that was clearly used to being obeyed.

"Attention! All cadet units report to the main parade ground immediately. I say again. All cadet units report to the main parade ground immediately. That is all."

The entire force of Detroit cadets was only assembled for graduation day, the Cull, or executions too serious to be handled at battalion level. But none of those were due.

Arun's fellow cadets weren't unresponsive robots now: they looked stunned, turning to each other for explanations.

But there was one person who didn't look surprised.

"Sorry, kids," said Umarov. He was sincere too, his grouchiness replaced by hollowed-out sadness. "I guess you're gonna grow up even quicker than I feared."

—— Chapter 55 ——

Detroit nestled in a valley floor beneath the dusty red peaks of the Gjende Mountains. So deep were the shadows, it was said, that a natural-born Earth human would need a torch to pick their way around the valley floor. Arun was not a normal human. The wide avenue meandering toward the parade ground was clear for his eyes to see, as were the obelisks at either side that displayed bas-relief carvings of fantastic martial creatures. Or possibly they were portraits in sculpture of the previous residents of the base. It was not a species that Arun recognized. Although his eyes could see the path, the colors of the valley floor had been leeched out. Arun saw everything in monochrome shades of malevolent red.

If it weren't for the ominous circumstances it would be a pleasant walk. The air was thin up on the surface, but the winds were light for a change and the temperature comfortable.

At one point the avenue had been crushed under a fallen mountain top. A fresh and unadorned path detoured around the obstruction.

"What caused that?" he asked Majanita, pointing to the rock fall that blocked the path.

She shrugged. "I don't know. But it's no landslide or natural erosion."

"A meteor strike perhaps," suggested Arun.

"More likely a kinetic torpedo."

Suddenly Arun felt exposed out here on the planet's surface. That made him the opposite of the Jotuns who could not bear to be underground. At least Arun's fear was rational. A ship in orbit above the valley floor could do some serious damage. Being underground with a few hundred meters of dirt above your head was much safer.

At 07:36 they reached the parade ground, an oval cut into the side of the mountain. The gouge went back 800 meters and was 100 meters high, the roof being the smooth, flat underside of the mountain above. It was as if an impossibly large stonemason's chisel had cut a groove into the side of the mountain.

"Look!" said Brandt. He pointed to the densest concentration of cadets at the center of the oval. "Look for our battalion flag."

He must have good eyesight, thought Arun, because he couldn't see any flags himself. But as they made their way toward the center and saw that at regular intervals there were indeed square banners mounted on five-meter poles.

There it was! The gold circle on a black background of the 412th Marines with a silver number 8 in the lower left corner. It was a simple design but enough to swell Arun's heart with pride.

Sergeant Gupta was waiting for them. He marshalled them into ranks and files to his satisfaction, repositioning cadets until he was happy.

Then he marched in and out of the lines saying: "Keep your dignity at all times. Never forget. Keep your dignity!"

The cadets came to attention in perfect parade ground posture and waited. They had been bred and trained for waiting, which was just as well. The parade deck was huge, but there were around 130,000 cadets across all four regiments. Assembling them took a while.

"Welcome, cadets," came a woman's voice once all the cadets were assembled. "My name is Sergeant Bissinger."

Arun recognized Bissinger's voice as the woman who had ordered all cadets to parade. There were no obvious speakers to carry her voice, but her words reached Arun's ears with crystal clarity.

"I shall not say good morning," she added. Arun knew Sergeant Bissinger was as senior a veteran as they came. Although it was always tricky to determine the rank seniority of the human commanders due to the rule that no human could take a rank above senior squad NCO. Seniority was pretty much a word of mouth thing, but Arun's guess was that Bissinger was the de facto human base commander.

"Today," said Bissinger, "is a tragedy and a necessity."

Arun heard himself groan.

"Today you cadets face the reality of your lives. That we all of us have won freedom for our home world but that it is we who must pay the price."

If only he were in his suit. Barney would fire him the drugs to make this much easier.

"We are all of us soldiers of the White Knights, our ultimate leaders who glory in change, mutation and experimentation. They believe the elimination of failed experiments is indivisible from growth and renewal. Creative destruction is not merely an ideal that they cherish, but has been incorporated deep within their biology and planetary engineering. We humans do not mutate with the rapidity that our masters are blessed with, but the White Knights demand that all servant species perform their own emulation of our masters' ideal of creative destruction."

Arun found his eyes blinking uncontrollably. Was he crying?

"Our human way of handling this tradition – one sanctified by our masters – is called the Cull."

Frakk! He *was* crying. For years he'd dreaded this moment. It shouldn't be happening now. It was too early in the year. But off schedule or not there was a deathly inevitability about the events that would roll out over the coming minutes. All that talk of winning more points to escape the danger zone was too late now for graduation year cadets in the bottom-ranked battalions. One tenth of them were about to die, and there was nothing anyone could do to change their fate.

Eyes front, watching the officer who wasn't an officer address them from a platform almost directly in front of him, Arun was nearly surprised by Sergeant Gupta when he walked behind his rank of cadets.

"Keep your dignity. Do not disobey."

Sergeant Gupta kept repeating his litany. But what was dignified about people murdering each other? And all this pain only to ape the freakish beliefs of a bunch of faraway alien vecks?

Once Gupta had passed him, Arun's eyes drilled holes in the sergeant's back as he marched away.

Easy for you, thought Arun. *You're not up for execution duty.*

Then Arun turned his head and looked around him. Only then did he understand the layout of this grotesque exercise. The three battalions in the

Cull Zone were lined up in front of Bissinger's platform. The other 29 battalions were arranged in a semicircle around their doomed comrades. *Observers to what was about to unfold.*

There was a blur of movement and then Gupta was in Arun's face, glowering. The sergeant's breath came in short, rasping gasps. It sounded as if he was a raging bull, raring to tear Arun apart, but restraining himself from violence only by a titanic battle of will.

Snapped back to attention, Arun kept his eyes forward, which was filled by a view of his NCO's forehead. Sweat was beginning to bead in the craggy furrows of Gupta's frown.

The NCO's battle for control went on. His breath quickened even faster. Arun tensed, ready for Gupta's attack. To fight with a superior would mean immediate execution. So he readied himself to leap for the ground, where he would curl up and hope his injuries would not kill him or, worse, render him unfit for service, which would mean being dumped back into the Aux.

"You dishonor them, boy." It had taken nearly two minutes before Gupta had gained enough control to spit those words. "We are fighting a war here. A war for survival. Today is one battle. There will be casualties."

Gupta stepped back half a pace, close enough to still intimidate Arun, but far enough away that he could fix him with his glare. "Are you a coward, Cadet McEwan?"

"No, sergeant."

"Really? Only a coward would be so frightened by the thought of battle casualties that they hate their commander."

Arun's heart lurched. Had Gupta read his thoughts?

"It's good to be scared in battle," Gupta growled. "It gives you an edge. But real Marines don't stare at their commander's back, blaming them for the war. I ask you again. Are you a coward?"

"No, sergeant."

"Then what are you?"

Gupta stepped back another half pace and waited for an answer. Arun couldn't work out whether this was a drill sergeant's parade ground psycho-trick, or whether his life depended on his next sentence. Perhaps both were true.

But Arun had played this game before at school, even before then at crèche. His entire life since waking from the freezer had been lived under the hawk-like gaze of the instructors.

"I'm stupid, sergeant. Too dumb to realize I was in a battle."

Gupta rocked back on his heels, as satisfied as he was likely to get any time soon. "That's the correct answer. And stupid Marines are only one iota better than cowardly ones. Idiots get their squad killed. Today is your first real battle, McEwan. I will be watching you. If you show cowardice or stupidity, I *will* know. Understood?"

"Yes, sergeant."

Gupta considered Arun for a few moments. "Eyes front," he snapped. Then in a quieter voice he added: "Remember that no matter what you are called to do, whatever horrors you witness, you do it for the Marines. Most of all, we're fighting for Earth. Got it?"

"Yes, sergeant."

In perfect step, Gupta marched off to the front of Blue Squad, turned on his heels and faced his cadets. And waited with the rest of them.

Over the coming minutes, Arun could sense small groups of people from the condemned battalions march to the front and return a little later. He daren't get a good look after Gupta's grilling. How had Gupta seen what he was up to? Was it a veteran's sixth sense? Was he under invisible surveillance? Maybe it was just bad luck and his guilty face had given him away. Until he found out, he decided to act as if Gupta really did have eyes in the back of his head.

Then it was Blue Squad's turn. At a command barked by Gupta, they filed out in a neat column and followed him up to the platform. He thought back to that bawling out in Little Scar's office and realized he was being filmed too. He pushed back his shoulders, squared his jaw, and marched with as much dignity as he could muster.

Sergeant Bissinger stood alone on a stone platform raised about fifteen meters above the parade ground floor. It was a hexagon twenty meters across that had been carved out of the rock; or rather, left behind when the parade ground had been carved. In front of the hexagon was a polished metal drum,

and alongside, what appeared to be the same kind of armory cabinet that was scattered around the hab-disks.

Sergeant Gupta ordered the squad to halt. Then he separated off ten cadets and told them what to do. Arun wasn't in that first group. He got to watch first.

The picked cadets each put their hands into a hole cut into one end of the drum. They lined up, gripping something in their palms, but Arun couldn't see what until Gupta ordered them to open up their hands.

They were pebbles. Smooth round pebbles. Half were colored black and half white. The cadets replaced the pebbles in the drum. Those who'd picked white marched back to their place in the crowd. Those with black lined up in front of the armory cupboard.

Sergeant Gupta opened the cupboard door. Inside was a firearm rack holding five SA-71s. It was similar to what Arun was used to, except this cupboard had a feed from underneath. If these were the weapons of execution, they would need more than five. There must be scores waiting out of sight to replace those taken from the cupboard.

At Gupta's signal, the five cadets each took a carbine in turn. At his next command, they armed them ready to fire. Four of them immediately returned their carbines to the cupboard, lined up again, and then marched back to the battalion's place in the crowd.

That left one cadet holding a carbine. Laban Caccamo, his name was, from Hecht's Alpha Section. Dark hair, thick eyebrows, muscular, popular with the girls. He was an ace at flying radio-controlled drones. In happier days as a novice, Caccamo had joined in with any fun and games going around, especially if it involved playing pranks on his friends. He did what his training instructors told and he did it well, but not exceptionally.

At that moment, Caccamo couldn't help being exceptional. Every cadet in Detroit was watching him and what he would do.

Caccamo snapped to attention, saluted, and then marched around to the back of the hexagon. He was lost to sight.

Then it was Arun's turn. His group of ten included all eight cadets from Delta Section plus Lewark and Bizzy from Beta Section.

Gupta gave them instructions, but Arun wasn't listening. He was hardly going to forget what he had just seen.

By the time his turn came around to put his hand into the drum, he was convinced that it would be him joining Caccamo in the execution squad. He had to reach in deep to find it. The pebble he drew out was warm to the touch. Arun gripped it so tightly that he felt his hand bruise.

He stood in a line facing the crowd. Cristina was to his left. Zug joined him on his right, the final cadet in that group of ten.

The cadets in even the most distant battalions could clearly see Arun's plight, due to their uprated vision. If they chose to. How many of them opted to see a defocused blur instead?

"Show your hands!" ordered Sergeant Gupta.

The cadets each raised a hand in front of them, palm up, and opened their fingers.

Arun didn't feel fear as his hand opened to reveal the color of his stone; he just felt numb. Sure enough, his stone was black. He quickly glanced around him. Zug had a black pebble too. Cristina's was white.

The five cadets with white stones wheeled right in readiness to march away. Cristina whispered hurriedly to him. "If you do it now, you'll not spend the next two years fearing what it might be like."

Because I will already be damned? He did not dare to speak the words in his mind. Cristina's words were no comfort but the warmth of her sentiment was. He couldn't imagine the males in his squad offering any words of comfort.

The line-up in front of the armory cabinet consisted of Arun, Zug, Springer, Lewark from Blue-4, and Del-Marie.

Sergeant Gupta opened the armory cabinet and Arun picked out a carbine. He was so used to the heft of the SA-71 that it normally felt like an extension of his body, but this gun felt awkward. If the gun was a part of his body, then this was a part that had turned cancerous. It was sickening, alien. He wanted to throw it far away from him, but he steeled himself instead to hold it as if this were an everyday gunnery drill.

And as with a gunnery drill, Arun flicked the switch to arm the carbine and read the ammo supply from the stock display. His gun was charged and an ammo bulb was in place, but the stock display was faulty.

To his astonishment, only Del-Marie replaced his carbine in the cabinet and went back to his place in the crowd, presumably because it had no charge or no ammo. Arun and the other cadets picked for execution detail glanced at each other nervously. Then they gave smart salutes to Sergeant Gupta and marched around the back of the hexagon where the executioners were lined up, marshaled by a veteran Arun didn't recognize.

Every few minutes they were reinforced by blank-faced cadets, arriving in ones and twos, and occasionally in larger groups.

As the selection played out over the next hour, it became clear that there was a strong random element to the selection. Sometimes all the carbines in the cabinet were armed and sometimes none. But over time the numbers began to average out and Arun saw the pattern that was emerging.

There were around 175 cadets in a company, and the battalion had eight depot companies in the graduation year. That made 1,400 due to be Culled.

The G-1 and G-2 years for 8-412 had another eight companies each, which made a pool of 2,800 executioners. The G-year cadets were to be decimated: one in ten would be executed. Arun had assumed that meant there would be 140 executioners picked, but instead there was to be one executioner for every member of the G-year. Did that mean they were all to be killed?

They heard a hiss. From around the sides and top of the hexagon came clouds of lurid orange. The smell hit them. Arun swallowed hard, fought to keep control. Once he'd gotten over the shock of being gassed, it didn't smell or taste so bad. And if it was toxic, it wasn't so toxic that he could see anyone keel over. In fact it tasted of burned biscuits and almond flavoring.

Human veterans advanced toward them from out of the billowing orange. For a moment, Arun thought it was his detail behind the hexagon that were to be killed, and the veterans their executioners. But the vets led them back around the hexagon and into the heart of the unfolding spectacle.

Sergeant Bissinger cleared her throat and addressed the parade. "Every world inhabited by our masters, the White Knights, is blessed by the Sacred Mists of Renewal, more commonly called the Flek. We cannot release the Flek here on Tranquility because it would kill us all. This orange vapor we release in emulation of the Flek as we…" She paused, just briefly but Arun caught it "…reach the climax of today's ritual."

The release of the pseudo-Flek gas had been timed so that as Arun and the other executioners came around the hexagon they appeared to the waiting crowd to emerge from the mist at the moment Sergeant Bissinger finished her speech. The veterans led the execution detail to their places. They lined up facing the hexagon in 47 rows of 29 cadets. Each rank had a veteran to either side, a veteran from another battalion.

The mist cleared to reveal pale faces staring back at them. Twenty-nine cadets from the year of graduation stood with their backs to the hexagon, each a couple of paces apart. The other cadets due to be Culled awaited their fate a short distance to the left, already organized into ranks of 29.

Twenty-nine executioners would fire their carbines at twenty-nine battalion comrades. Arun understood now why his stock readout wasn't working. It was a cruel trick. All of the executioners would fire on a comrade, but only one in ten of the guns had live rounds. Arun had never fired a gun at another human being. That was just about to change. Whether he would kill his target was something no one would know until a split second after he fired.

Arun was in the third row. At least he wouldn't have to wait long to find out.

The first rank of executioners moved forward a pace and spread out a little so that each faced their victim head on.

Arun stared into the faces of the condemned, who awaited their fate with quiet dignity. In a few seconds, perhaps two or three would die. Maybe more or maybe less if this part of the Cull were as random as everything else. Most, though, would live.

That still didn't make this all right,

Gupta had called this a battle. Arun wouldn't flinch at going into battle with the possibility of ten percent casualties. But this wasn't combat whatever Gupta might say. This was humans copying their betters, a foul mockery of an utterly alien ritual. Surely it was going along with killing your comrades that was stupid and cowardly, not questioning the murder?

The front rank raised their guns.

Was Arun prepared to defy orders? Was anyone here?

The front-rank veterans faced in at their cadets, raised their arms… and then threw them downward.

A ragged volley of shots rang out. Three of the condemned slumped to the bare rock of the parade ground, bloody chunks blasted out of their bodies.

Dead before they hit the ground, thought Arun. Flenser rounds aimed at the heart. A quick death, but a messy one.

He wondered why he was analyzing the execution in such cold detail, and then realized he was distracting himself from looking into the faces of the front rank of executioners as they filed back to the rear of the execution detail.

He couldn't look upon them because in a few moments he would have become one of them. He knew he wasn't going to rebel. He didn't have the will to disobey orders.

When in doubt, obey orders. It was all he'd ever known. And if that meant he was a coward or stupid then so be it. What he did know for certain in that moment was that he was a slave.

The 26 survivors of the Cull picked up the corpses of their fallen comrades and carried them round to the rear of the hexagon. Without delay they were replaced by the next group of 29 condemned cadets, stepping carefully so as not to slip on the gore-splatter rock.

It felt dreamlike as Arun watched the front rank of executioners spread out to match their victims, raise their carbines and fire!

This time, one cadet from 8-412 fell down dead.

This time Arun did look at the executioners because something was wrong. The whole ritual was wrong, he thought, but now something had disrupted the smooth workings of the execution process.

The veteran on the right of the front rank marched in front of her detail. She halted before one particular cadet. It was Olmer, one of the original members of Xin's Scendence team.

Olmer dropped her carbine. The sound of the ceramalloy-plastic blend striking the rock floor made Arun cringe. He'd never heard the sound of a dropped gun before.

"I can't do it!" Olmer screamed. "I can't fire. You can't make me."

If Olmer was panicking, the effect of this disruption on the cadet she had failed to shoot was even more dramatic. The condemned started to cry.

The reason soon became clear.

The veteran drew her sidearm from its holster and shot Olmer in the head. Then she turned to the condemned cadet who by now had slumped down onto her haunches, her head in her hands.

The veteran shot her through the heart.

Of everything he'd seen so far that day, the sight of the cadet slumped against the hexagon waiting her fate was the cruelest by far. If Olmer had obeyed orders, then the older cadet would probably still be alive. Everyone saw that drama unfold. Everyone got the message. Arun had never attended the Cull before, but he'd attended executions. It was always the same.

Disobey orders and you will be killed.

Breathe so much as a word of dissent against the White Knights, and it won't be just you who is killed.

Arun did what he always did. Suck up the anger and humiliation and stored it for the future. Everything on this planet was designed to control the slaves who lived here. But if he survived to graduate as a Marine, one day he would get away from Detroit.

He made a vow. He swore it on the blood of his murdered cadet comrades, and on the hellish memories that their murderers would carry for the rest of their lives. Unlike Olmer, he would *wait*. Over time he would stack the chances in his favor. One day he would revenge all of humanity against the White Knights.

And then he found himself lined up opposite a tall boy with hooded eyes staring back at him with quiet dignity. Arun recognized the face but didn't know the name. Good, that made this a little easier.

Arun raised his carbine and trained his sights on the cadet, aiming for his heart. Usually when he fired, he was wearing armor and had Barney to direct his aim. Manual aim was so much more personal and if he had to go through with this then Arun preferred to do it himself. To hide behind Barney would be disrespectful to the cadet, who was calmly looking at the business end of Arun's carbine.

I will revenge you, Arun promised the condemned cadet. He took off the safety, and heard the whine as the barrel charged in preparation to fling a shell at four times the speed of sound. The gun had already been set for the required distance of an execution shot.

The Human Legion.

Desperate to think of anything other than the horror all around him, Arun clutched at a speck of hope for the future. Gupta had talked of a Czech Legion that had survived impossible odds behind enemy lines, and Springer's vision had hinted that it might be Arun's fate to lead a modern-day equivalent. He'd been too busy trying to survive to think these treasonous thoughts. Now he could think of nothing else.

One day, I swear, there will be a Human Legion. Arun made his vow in the privacy of his head and kept his mouth rigid. Even to mouth the words would be disastrous. *The Human Legion will be a beacon of hope to all humankind,* he continued silently, *and I will play my part in that story. I promise you.*

Then the veteran gave the command and Arun squeezed his trigger.

Flenser rounds consisted of an aerodynamic shell that broke apart about two meters before the target to release pairs of tiny blade-encrusted balls connected to each other by monofilament wire.

They were designed to tear great holes through unarmored targets.

Arun saw the results on human flesh. An micro-instant after he began to take in the sight, he heard the crack of the flenser casing open and the wet ripping sound as the casing's contents struck home.

The cadet's left chest disintegrated, leaving behind scored bone, gristle, and tatters of bloodied cloth from the clean fatigues she had picked up from the laundry shelf a few hours earlier.

Arun hadn't shot her. This was the cadet alongside.

An irritated whine and click came from Arun's carbine as the gun tried repeatedly to select a round from the ammo carousel, but he knew it was empty. He'd been spared.

He glanced up at the cadet that he had aimed at. He was looking back, not at Arun but at the person to Arun's right.

Arun followed his gaze and looked into Zug's face. Zug who had just shot dead a cadet from his own battalion.

Zug the Aloof, Arun had called him earlier.

He wasn't so calm now. He looked deathly pale. Then he started retching.

Arun willed his old friend to keep it in.

On the march to the rear of the execution detail Zug held it in about half way. Then he vomited, all over Arun's back.

Arun thought back to the boneheaded curse he had thrown at Zug in the shower earlier that morning.

Sergeant Gupta had been right all along. Arun's words in the shower had been those of a coward.

And a stupid one too.

Arun's shame was complete.

—— PART IV ——

You're all Marines Now

Human Legion
INFOPEDIA

Terminology

MARINE

The term, MARINE refers to both the soldiers and military organizations whose primary function is one or more of the following:
   * Close assault and boarding of space-faring vessels.
   * Defense of space-faring vessels against close assault and boarding.
   * Assault from space against the defended surface of a planet.

The term is widely used to describe the relevant military forces of most political entities within the Trans-Species Union.

The original Earthly military meaning of marine (water-borne rather than space-borne military forces) is now referred to as 'littoral marine' or 'seaborne marine'. Referring to a member of such a unit as a 'wet marine' is a sure way to start a fight.

The military term 'marine' is not capitalized in general use, although marine organizations will frequently capitalize when referring to themselves. Since the accounts you are now reading are about the Human Legion, and its predecessor/ rival, the Human Marine Corps, we capitalize as 'Marine' when referring to those organizations. We, the authors, are ourselves mostly Marines. Whatever the grammatical niceties that proper nouns might demand, it is impossible for us to think of ourselves as anything other than *Marines* with an upper case 'M'. To call us mere *marines* would be an insult.

And, we would argue, an insult to our ancestors, for we were not the first Marines by a long way.

Seaborne marines were critical in ancient Earth history. In the Battle of Salamis (-480CE) Greek Marines played a crucial role in defeating the much larger Persian forces, helping to set the cultural underpinning of what would later be called Western Civilization.

A ship-boarding technology called the *corvus* enabled Roman Marines to win naval supremacy in the Mediterranean Sea (around -250CE), ultimately meaning the Romans defeated their arch rivals the Carthaginians to become the dominant regional superpower for many centuries.

The next major innovation in seaborne Marine forces came two thousand years later with the development of a much larger self-contained, combined-arms Marine army that could fight wars almost unaided. This was the United States Marine Corps.

It is widely speculated by modern-era Marines that the military units formed from human slaves following the Vancouver Accord were inspired by the US Marine Corps. Others regard this as wishful thinking, pointing out that while the Human Marine Corps might draw inspiration from the fighting spirit of their US ancestors, the segregation and racism inherent to their command structure more closely follows the army of the British East India Company in the early 1800s CE.

Whatever the truth of that argument, we the Marines of the Human Legion acknowledge the rich heritage of our Earthly military ancestors, and indeed those from other planets. We recognize their example and transcend them, because the Human Legion is not based in the past. We have a single mission: to fight for a better *future*. A future for us all.

Freedom *can* be won.

—— Chapter 56 ——

Scorched, perforated and abused for decades — despite all that, *Fort Douaumont*'s long, lazy tumbling caught the sunlight and gleamed, an incomparable jewel for an instant… and then the moment was gone and the training hulk was space dross once more.

Fort Douaumont teased Arun. He couldn't take his eyes off her in case he missed another glint of hidden beauty.

Frakk, I must be bored!

It had been less than a day since the Cull — since Zug had shot dead an innocent cadet. After drent like that went down, the powers that be liked to split up the cadets and keep them busy.

So they'd shipped Blue and Gold squads up to Gupta's old TU, *Yorktown*, where they'd stuck the cadets into EVA gibberballs.

An orange and red flashing blob marred the serenity of the silent scene of beauty laid out before him: Sergeant Gupta with his battlesuit set for high visibility. The NCO was sitting on a flitter waiting for the exercise to begin. Hell, he must be just as bored as Arun, wishing he were wherever Gold Squad's Sergeant Searl had ended up.

They might have rushed them up here, but now the cadets were trapped in the amniotic gel bubbles, those in charge were in no hurry to launch them.

Instead of the robot defenders they normally faced, the old hulk would be defended by veteran marines, one of whom was Arun's brother, or so Gupta had said.

The exercise should be a blast. Why didn't they get it started already?

Arun had now spent hours in this gibberball trying and eventually failing to be interested in his brother. Hell, he didn't even know the guy's name. It wasn't as if he'd ever talked with his family. Instantaneous communication was possible to each Marine ship, but was far too expensive to waste on human chit-chat. Why would you care about anyone out-system anyway? You had your family right here on Tranquility.

The Corps is your family. You need no other.

It dawned on Arun why he kept thinking about family. He wasn't just bored; he was lonely too.

But talking wasn't easy when you were stuffed inside a bubble of buffer gel. After his last experience of endless drowning, he wasn't going to open his mouth no matter how much he needed to talk.

But maybe there was another way.

The TU was essentially spherical with the EVA chutes recessed into the hull. The outer surface of the amniotic bubbles pushed out from the warboat's hull like festering pustules on a victim of the red pox. But there were also vanes sticking out from the hull. He'd always assumed they were radiator fins. He should be able to bounce a tight comm beam off them. See if he could raise Springer.

Arun had plenty of experience of talking with aliens who used thought-to-speech to communicate in the human language. In theory you could do the same with a suit if its AI knew you well, and so did the AI of the person you wanted to talk with.

He tried to form the idea in his mind, to explain to Barney what he wanted. He pictured Springer. Cute freckles, a cautious smile and violet eyes.

Then he spoke the words slowly in his head.

<Springer. Can you hear me? Springer!>

<Arun. You?>

<You — what? Sorry, Springer. I can't understand you.>

<Idiot. Keep word simple.>

<OK. Understand.>

<You OK. Arun?>

<I bored.>

<Me too.>

<Zug?>

<Zug? Query?>

<Zug speak you, Springer?>

<A little.>

<Zug not speak me.>

<I know.>

<But I worry about Zug.>

<I know you do.>

<Do you?>

<Of course, Arun. Whatever explanation, we're not the same as them. You know that.>

<I suppose.> Arun had an urge to change the subject. <Your words coming through clearer, Springer.>

<Guess AIs are good at learning. Can't believe never talked like this before.>

<Usually focused on watching for an enemy. This time they've just stuck us here out the way.>

<Be loyal, Arun.>

<I am. Why do you say…? Oh, you mean loyal to Zug. I don't know what more to do.>

<Don't wimp out, McEwan. Give them time. Give them reasons to accept you again.>

<That could take years.>

<Is that a reason not to try?>

<No.>

<Don't give up, Arun.>

<I won't—>

<Good.>

<—ever give up—>

<I know.>

<—on you.>

Arun choked on a swell of adoration for Springer. Buffer gel pushed down into his mouth. Not again! He froze — not breathing — not even daring to think. When eventually he relaxed again, the gel hadn't pushed in far. He wasn't drowning. But the link to Springer was broken.

Maybe that wasn't such a bad thing. They had strayed onto the most dangerous topic, and who knew might be able to listen in? Especially with Arun unreliable due to his oversupply of emotions that ambushed him constantly. What had he meant just then with Springer? Was he in love with her? Was he reaching out for any human contact? Or was he just scared?

Arun pushed against the gel to shake his head. Man, he was such a vulleyed-up wreck, and he had no idea how much he could blame that on the mind-altering drugs he was being given. He'd sidestepped execution somehow but it could only be a question of time before he was kicked out of the Marines… probably through an airlock without a suit.

Damn these long stretches encased in the gibberball. He'd rather face an enemy battle fleet than the thoughts in his own head.

Something flew past, too quick to see properly.

Was the gibberball finally making him see things?

But when he asked Barney to replay and slow down the image — he learned it was real all right. Something was moving very fast toward Tranquility.

Barney interrupted the playback to show a real-time view of a second object flashing past. The interval between the two: 11.4 seconds.

Arun had only a limited view from inside the gibberball. Whatever had whizzed past had disappeared out of his left field of vision. He couldn't see Tranquility either, except in the planetshine brightening the side of *Fort Douaumont* that faced his home world.

What he *could* see on the extreme left of his viewpoint was a dot Barney identified as Orbital Defense Platform 74. Twelve streaks of white curled and twisted away from the platform, gyrating wildly but with only one possible target.

Horden's bones! If the defense platform had launched missiles then this was for real. Tranquility was under bombardment.

And Arun was at war!

—— Chapter 57 ——

Four objects had been launched against Tranquility, at 11.4 second intervals, followed by… nothing.

Was the attack over?

Arun tried to form another link to Springer. Perhaps she had a better view of what was going on.

Barney wasn't playing ball, though, refusing to make the comm link.

After 41 seconds, he learned that the bombardment hadn't ceased. A streak of light on a new trajectory etched a line across Arun's vision pursued by a spread of missiles from Orbital Defense Platform 74.

This time he saw the explosion as two of the defensive missiles blew up the projectile.

Yes!

His elation froze a moment later. The missiles hadn't contacted the projectile far enough away… some fragments from the explosion must have carried on. Platform 74 flared into a brilliant blue-white bloom that forced Barney to dim Arun's visor. Platform 74 was gone.

If a brace of missiles couldn't stop those projectiles, they must be moving with a staggering amount of momentum. Was this the nightmare scenario they used to scare each other with as kids? A bombardment by the mass drivers that were designed to send ore shipments across the stars? But there were failsafes. The system defense fleet could shut down mass drivers remotely. Had they turned traitor too?

Finally someone spoke. "We're all seeing this. Standby." It was Gupta, still out there somewhere on his flitter. He'd stealthed his suit but was connecting to Wide Battle Net, which enabled Barney to mark the sergeant's position with a blue dot even though he remained unseen.

The next shot slammed into *Fort Douaumont*.

The projectile passed straight through the old hulk. Arun imagined the disappointment of whoever was firing at them when the old ship didn't explode. It had no main armament, fuel or air to blow up, but the old ship was crippled all the same, just not in such a showy way. The hull twisted, sheared, broke asunder. Then another projectile hit the stricken ship, sending fragments of metal weighing thousands of tons shooting in all directions, leaving a glittering halo of shimmering shards.

The power of the projectiles was almost beyond human comprehension, but whoever was launching them didn't have much military sense. Why waste time taking out a useless abandoned hulk? Then a shock hit him when he remembered *Fort Douaumont* hadn't quite been abandoned. His brother had been on board.

Arun's concern for a brother he'd never met didn't have time to take root, because if the enemy were trying to take out the threat from nearby ships, that meant the next target was the TU!

There were mass drivers scattered on moons throughout the system, essentially the same as the railgun inside his SA-71 carbine except scaled up to the enormous degree necessary to fling packages of refined ore across the gulf of interstellar space to be received by resource-hungry star systems. Transit times between star systems were measured in centuries. But if the mass driver was on one of Tranquility's moons, its projectiles would be only seconds away from the planet.

Arun knew he was ceasing to be a bystander when, even through the buffer gel, he could feel the TU throb with a massive power build up.

Sergeant Gupta's voice came into his helmet. "Listen up, cadets. You haven't impressed me so far."

Arun's view blurred. And then settled. The TU had spun around. He was facing the dusty red ball of Antilles, the largest of Tranquility's moons.

"My advice to *Yorktown's* captain is to leave you where you are," said Gupta, "that you're a liability. She says that if we've spent all that training budget on you over the past 17 years…"

Then *Yorktown* was moving. Man, was she *moving!* Even stuffed with buffer gel, the breath was being crushed from Arun's body. Lump hammers pounded his skull tirelessly. He closed his eyes. He'd never experienced such acceleration before. It felt like he was being squeezed into a sticky dot on *Yorktown's* outer hull.

Then the lump hammers softened into wooden mallets; the vise crushing his chest mellowed into the fists of a Jotun warrior pummeling his ribs, and Gupta continued his words. "After 17 years of training you should damned well be a useful asset. *Yorktown* is moving to assault the traitors who took out *Fort Douaumont* and are bombarding our homes on the surface. We compromised and decided to offer you a choice. Are you going to take this opportunity to prove to me you're Marines? Or are you going to be spectators? Which is it to be?"

"We're Marines, sergeant."

As far as Arun could tell, every cadet in the Blue and Gold squads had answered in the same way at the same time. Himself included.

Maybe he wasn't so different from the others.

A bubble of pride put a little grin onto his face.

The TU corkscrewed sickeningly as it approached Antilles.

"Very well," Gupta growled after a few seconds. "It makes my guts crawl to call you sorry lot Marines, but here's the plan. Rebels have taken over a mass driver on Antilles. We think their main target is Detroit. Defense Command estimate a 90% chance that their defense shield can keep out a direct hit for the next hour. After that our shield effectiveness degrades rapidly, and everything that breaches the outer atmosphere is going to hit *something*. If we're lucky we might have as much as two hours to shut them down before the upper levels of Detroit are turned to slag, or buried under shattered mountain fragments."

Yorktown lurched sideways so unexpectedly that Arun's heart and lungs were left miles behind. Another bombardment shot past.

"Here's our problem," continued Gupta. "The rebels have thrown a thick cloud of rock fragments — pebbles really — above and around their base. We don't know how they've done it, but it makes for an effective barrier. *Yorktown's* weapons can't penetrate that rock cloud, but the enemy can shoot out. They've created a force tunnel through their shield that provides a launch window for their mass driver, but we can't get a firing solution through it. Friendly system defense boats are hours away. There are no other combat vessels nearby. We need boots on the ground. You!"

"But, sergeant," said Brandt, "our weapons–"

"Are training poppers only?" finished Gupta. "Did you really think they'd design and build you separate carbines just to be toy guns in training exercises? They're fully functional except we haven't given you any ammo bulbs. You've got two default modes we never told you about because you're not meant to know this yet. There's a pulse laser capability and an emergency railgun mode. Standby…"

Arun held his breath for 8.5 seconds until Gupta spoke again. "Your deployment starts in 72 seconds. Your suit AIs know how to unlock your carbines and have updated maps of the moon surface. Cadet Lance Sergeant Belville, you have command. Brandt is your deputy. Form up in the depression 4 klicks northwest of the mining base. I've marked it on your maps. We'll land a second scratch team of veterans, Force Alpha. Wait for them to attack. Then move in and—"

A familiar jolt hit Arun like a hundred Marines in full armor jumping on his spine. Then he was tossed into space with the familiar sensation of gasping for air.

By the time he was alert and had stabilized his spin, Sergeant Gupta had finished his talk and the surface of Antilles, dusty gray rocks streaked with rust, was fast rising up to claim him.

He asked Barney to fill him in on his carbine's capability. Quick as you like.

———

Arun had thought he knew all about the SA-71 carbine. Turned out he didn't. The weapon was designed to be the ultimate in robustness and flexibility with a power pack that was so long lasting that it might as well be magical. What had been hidden from them was that there were two default modes for when the standard-fit ammo carousels were exhausted. He'd always dismissed the rumors that there was secret information they only trusted Marines with once they were already on a troop ship headed out-system.

Said a lot about how humans were viewed by their betters.

One of these hidden options was a pulsed laser beam that would rapidly eat away at even the SA-71's battery charge. The strength of the laser pulses quickly degraded in an atmosphere, but in vacuum this was a credible weapon.

The second option was referred to as *shardshot*. The Marine grabbed whatever material was to hand, and packed it into a tube concealed within the weapon's stock. A combination of grinders and laser drills would chop the toughest materials into dust, which would then be compressed into ballistic pellets and shot out of the barrel in railgun mode. Barney warned him that neither the gun nor the suit could counter the recoil from shardshot rounds.

The recoil would kick like an angry Hardit.

And selecting the right material was critical to achieve a decent muzzle velocity. Something with metal content would be good.

Arun grinned when Barney told him this. The mining bases were situated on Antilles because the moon's rocky surface was rich in zinc, copper, iron, and manganese.

That should do it!

—— Chapter 58 ——

As he plummeted feet-first toward the moon, Arun could see other white smears falling like hail against the black of space. *And if he could see them…*

Gold and Blue squads looked like gunnery training targets as they descended in their gleaming white suits.

Arun couldn't help but imagine bright lines extend from the surface of Antilles, connecting a laser battery to each white blur in an obscene diagram of death.

Then Barney braked — hard enough to take Arun's breath away and make his vision blur. When his senses returned he was ten meters above the moon's cratered surface. Barney had braked early enough that he came down with only as much force as if he were stepping off a bottom stair back home.

Barney used a virtual arrow to indicate the rendezvous point.   Arun was running there from his very first step on the moon.

Turned out running wasn't easy. He kept jumping high above the ground and had to tell Barney to push him back down to the surface. It was frustratingly slow.

He was at home in zero-g where Barney could zip him around effortlessly. But in the moon's low gravity, the suit's motive power was much reduced. Barney could lob him over an obstacle, but couldn't run for him.

Arun briefly considered scampering on all fours before finding a steady loping gait that would look ridiculous if anyone were there to see it. But Arun was on his own. Alice Belville had told them to stick to Local Battle Net, which meant tight line-of-sight comms only.

A few hundred meters from the rendezvous, Arun finally encountered another cadet: Tanweer Aburto from Gold Squad. Seconds later, Barney added more dots to Arun's tac-display as the suit AIs began to ping signals off each other.

Ahead Arun saw that what the sergeant had called a depression looked like a shallow quarry pit covered by a few centuries of dust.

He couldn't see more than a few hundred meters into the depression due to the swirl of pebbles thrown up by the rebels as a defensive shield. From a distance the shield fragments looked like static. Barney speculated the pebbles were actually tailings from the ore crushers. Arun didn't care. He could already see what he wanted to know: the pebble shield didn't extend as far as the ground. There was a narrow gap underneath.

Up close, the pebble shield looked more like a miniature asteroid belt bent to the rebels' will and sped up to lethal velocities.

Arun halted. If he kept to even this low gait, he would bounce high enough to be pulped.

Aburto had the solution. The Gold Squad cadet hit the deck and rolled. Laughing, Arun copied him. It was like being a four-year-old again. Arun clung to those memories as he rolled under the rock-storm, the silent blur of death.

The ground underneath was littered with rock fragments that had fallen out of the shield. Would his training armor stand up to any rocks falling out onto him? As he spun forward, Arun grabbed some of the fallen rocks in his free hand, keeping his carbine low to the ground in the other. Maybe they would make good shardshot? He'd only collected a few small rocks before he was spinning too fast. He brought his arms beneath him as he accelerated. He was inside the depression now; rolling down the edge and picking up speed.

Then he hit the bottom and bounced — tumbling and dazed out of control and heading for the blur of swirling rocks.

Barney stabilized Arun's suit. Just at the moment that the sense of up and down began to reassert itself, the first rock hit Arun, spinning him helplessly. Then another strike.

But Barney had control now, enough to push Arun down out of the rock cloud. And once he'd touched down, Arun could run to safety because the depression was deep enough to give him plenty more headroom.

Seven other cadets were there already. He kept away from the others, keeping alert for anyone else in Delta Section to appear. Extended order drill demanded a minimum of five meters between each cadet and ten meters between sections, but that was difficult to make sense of when hardly anyone was here yet.

Some of the others appeared to be praying. Had their morale crumbled so easily?

Then he remembered about the shardshot ammo and realized they were filling their gun stocks with dirt. He joined in, using the rocks he'd grabbed out of the shield. Barney gave Arun a virtual thumbs up. Just as he'd hoped, the shield pebbles were mineral-rich tailings, not moon dust. They would make excellent shard bullets.

Arun looked up and noticed Stok Laskosk from Blue Squad's command section was nearby. He looked lost.

Arun walked over and patted Laskosk on the shoulder.

"Hey, Stopcock. Nervous?"

Heavy weapons specialist Laskosk, or Stopcock as he was universally known, looked at Arun as if trying to decide whether this was an insult. He shook his head. "It feels wrong. I always imagined I would have my missile launcher over my shoulder. Instead…" He held up his carbine. "We're firing chewed up wads of moondust. Not what I expected."

"Look on the bright side," offered Arun. "Without your launcher you're no longer a prime target for snipers."

"What's your problem, McEwan?" It was Lance Corporal Narciso, also from the command section.

"Nothing, lance corporal."

"Good. Then piss off like a good little boy. You're bad luck, McEwan. Keep away from me."

Arun retreated, almost stumbling into Springer.

"Don't mind them, Arun," she said. "Stopcock is scared, that's all."

"Are you?"

"No."

Arun laughed. "Me neither. Well, scared of letting down my buddies. Not scared of getting killed."

"Seventeen years of brainwashing and drugs and re-engineering didn't go to waste after all. Guess we're not so different from everyone else." She paused. "I'm glad you've got my back, Arun. I think that fights off the fear."

"I'm glad you're here too, Springer."

"Me too," said Osman who'd just arrived. "I mean… now the shooting's about to start. I guess I can't stay angry at you, McEwan."

"Keep minimum five meters separation," snapped Majanita to everyone in Delta Section, once they had all assembled in the depression. Privately she added for Arun's benefit: "I know it's not your fault that bad luck's followed you around, McEwan. Right now, I don't care. I think you're a liability. Since I'm stuck with you, I want you to do everything you can to prove me wrong. Can you do that?"

"Yes, corporal."

"Good. The first thing I want you to do is shut the frakk up. I don't want a peep until we contact the enemy."

Arun shut up.

Above him, the black sky was dominated by Tranquility's huge disk, its planetshine bright enough to cast shadows even though it was day on Antilles. An angry ripple spread out from a hole in the froth of cloud cover as the first enemy projectile broke through the planet's defensive shield. The fireball on the planet's surface briefly lit up the clouds in shades of orange and red.

———

As ordered, Belville made them wait until Force Alpha had launched its attack.

It wasn't difficult to see when that was.

Over the mass driver's expected location, two balls of hot violet light exploded: a pair of plasma grenades. The explosions spread fingers of jagged light in an arc over the driver but never reaching closer than about fifteen meters from the target.

"Frakk! That's some force field. Didn't even scratch it."

The words came from Force Alpha, the handful of veteran Marines deployed separately by *Yorktown*. Until this point they'd been undetectably silent, but now they were noisy. In fact, they were making as much of a clamor as possible, keeping the enemy's attention away from the hidden cadets.

"Power drain must be staggering," said another Marine. "If only we could get to the power source and shut it down."

Arun winced because that was such a clumsy hint to the cadets. But then, as he reminded himself, his time as a Hardit slave had taught him most aliens weren't interested in human languages. He had to hope there were no traitor humans listening in.

"Keep silent," Madge reminded her squad. Then: "Advance to assault positions."

The cadets scrambled up to the lip of the depression, ready to move out.

Sticking your head over a parapet was a surefire way to get your brains blown out. The designers of the ACE-2 battlesuit had solved this by providing periscope worms: an optical cable that extended out the top of the helmet. The cable was so thin that if an enemy could detect your periscope, you were as good as dead anyway.

Arun extended his periscope worm, and he saw for himself what the cadet scouts had already reported.

Gold and Blue Squads were deployed in an old quarry pit several hundred meters to the north-west of the rebel mining facility. The nearby pits had long been mined out but the buildings remained to service the mass driver. The driver was situated in a natural crater on the far side of the complex. A simple platform rested on the shallow slope of the crater. Superconducting hoops were mounted along the platform's length.

Arun watched those hoops accelerate another ore package to such speed that even if the rock shield hadn't hidden its progress from view, the projectile would have disappeared over the horizon within a handful of seconds. After a sub-orbital arc around Antilles, it would escape the moon's gravity on its brief journey toward Tranquility.

Between their position and the mine base, they could see trenches zigzagging in a ring around the buildings and extending out toward the mass driver.

Keeping to LBNet denied the cadets eyes in the sky. All they could tell was that some kind of defensive positions had been prepared for them. They might be facing an unoccupied trench, or a defensive hive protected by AI controlled GX-cannons and combat drones.

They hadn't a lot of choice either way.

From the enemy positions concentrated around the driver, dozens of streaks suddenly shot toward the Force Alpha Marines.

The missiles hit, lighting up the horizon with a series of explosions.

Force Alpha had launched two grenades. The rebels had replied with at least thirty missiles.

Arun jumped inside his suit when Barney unexpectedly lifted the worm's eye to look up into space. The silver bullet of the mass driver's previous launch had reappeared overhead. It had traveled in a slingshot around the back of Antilles and was now on its way to his home planet.

From where he waited, sinking in to the dust of Antilles surface, the projectile's silent journey looked serene. It was difficult to believe that if this glowing spark reached Tranquility's surface the impact would flatten a city.

"Look!"

It was Springer on a private channel.

Arun cut the feed from the worm and followed her finger pointing at the mass driver. He didn't understand. Not daring to break Madge's order to be silent, Arun raised a hand palm-up in a gesture of confusion.

"Look at their counter-fire."

He watched as the rebels dug in around the mass driver fired another volley of missiles at Force Alpha. This time he saw what Springer meant. The missiles didn't jink in the way that Stopcock's would if he had his shoulder-mounted launcher with him. Instead the rebels' missiles were traveling in straight lines, which meant they were crude rockets, not intelligent missiles. And rather than spread them out in a barrage pattern, the rockets were being fired straight at the firing positions the Marines had used to launch their grenades.

Didn't they realize that the Marines would have hopped and rolled away to new positions the instant they'd fired?

"The rebels don't stand a chance," said Springer. "They're strictly amateur."

Arun was beginning to agree, but then they saw movement from the enemy positions facing them. Rebels moving through the trench system to reinforce the defenses around the mass driver.

Arun laughed at his enemy. They looked so ludicrous. They'd dug these trenches but the idiots were in such a hurry that they were bouncing in the low-g, making their torsos pop into sight and then disappear as if they were on trampolines. It looked like some kind of virtual game for kids. Arun wanted to play. Doubly so because he could see the aliens were Hardits, and he had a score to settle. He itched to bring his carbine to bear and try out this new pulse laser setting on the bouncing monkeys.

But the order never came.

Arun estimated 40 rebels had moved off to tackle Force Alpha. How many remained to face the 50-odd cadets of Blue and Gold Squads?

"Go!" ordered Madge.

Time to find out.

Arun scrambled over the lip of crumbling moondust and charged the enemy trenches.

———

Miniature explosions of dust erupted all along the enemy trenches. This was the suppressive fire from the even-numbered cadet fire teams, and it was doing its job of keeping the enemy's head down because Arun didn't see any return fire.

Arun's team had to charge forward as fast as he could for two hundred meters before taking cover and providing rapid suppressive fire to shield the even-numbered fire teams as they caught up.

He wasn't scared. He hadn't time to be because all his concentration was spent on making progress without bouncing high into the sky.

One thing he did notice, though, was a missile corkscrewing from Force Alpha's position toward the mining complex.

It didn't get far.

Anti-missile defenses sprang into action from three points around the mass driver. Scores of ultra-fast missiles lifted from the ground to take out the invader. The Marine missile was nimble but not enough to evade this level of defense. It was blasted from the sky.

Arun hadn't time to regret its loss. He'd reached his first objective. He spotted a small crater and dived into it. At half a meter deep, it wasn't much, but it was better than nothing.

As he readied to fire, Arun checked his tac-display. Madge, Osman, and Springer had all taken up positions a short distance away. Barney wasn't reporting any other casualties, but he hadn't time to check beyond his comrades in Blue-5. He was zooming his visor display onto the enemy trench, about two hundred and fifty meters away, when Madge gave the order: "Shardshot. Rapid fire!"

He couldn't see any rebels, so Arun picked a segment of trench opposite him and opened up.

Frakk! The gun had given him a slap of recoil like a nuclear explosion.

He'd intended to rake the enemy position, with fire but had squeezed off one aimed shot and a handful so high they were probably heading up into orbit.

If he hadn't been in armor, the damned thing would have broken his collar bone.

He braced himself more firmly and set to work. He couldn't call it rapid fire, but it was as fast as the recoil would allow without sacrificing accuracy entirely.

"Overwatch," ordered Madge. Arun ceased firing and kept a close watch on the enemy trench, ready to shoot at any rebel brave enough to present themselves as a target.

But Madge's order confirmed what he'd already guessed. The enemy had either abandoned their trench, or were luring them into a trap.

If this were a trap, they were headed right into its jaws because the cadet fire teams made their leapfrogging advance until they reached a stopline fifteen meters from the enemy trench.

The enemy had not returned fire.

From the far side of the mining complex, Force Alpha's battle against the rebels continued its noisy progress.

The veteran Marines yelled into Wide Battle Net for backup. They fired more missiles at the mining buildings, only to see them shot down, and they gave orders to imaginary units to make flanking maneuvers. For all their efforts to pretend they were more of a threat than they actually were, Barney estimated there were only five Marines in Force Alpha. Six tops.

Then Madge gave the order to close the distance to the enemy trench and Arun forgot Force Alpha. All he could think of was what he would find waiting for him.

Blue Squad would use a boost from their suits to leap over the trench, while Gold Squad would assault inside the trench.

He sailed over, covering the trench line with his SA-71, but it really had been abandoned.

Trench warfare was the opposite of the flexibility of zero-g space combat that was the focus of Tactical Marine training. Even with his limited training on the matter, the trench looked to Arun like a hastily constructed channel. Crude cover and recently built. A far cry from the defensive warren an attacker would be faced with if they tried to assault the Detroit base from the ground.

Arun advanced, making for his next target: a cuboid segment of the mining complex that looked grafted on to the main building. This was to be their route inside.

Behind him, Gold Squad reported that they had secured the trench. There weren't any booby traps — at least no explosions — but perhaps had been motion sensors or watching cameras because moments later a volley of rockets streaked into the trench.

"Remain on LBNet," ordered Belville. "They know we're here now, but not how many of us are here. And once we're inside they will lose us. Blue Squad, hurry up and get me a breach."

Arun didn't hear Belville's orders for Gold Squad, but his tac-display showed them abandoning the trench, crawling a short distance toward the building to take up a defensive line near Blue Squad. Marines instinctively distrusted static defenses. Hiding behind a trench or rampart wall robbed you of maneuver options and surrendered initiative to the enemy. Marines

won their battles by attacking, and no one launched an attack while cowering in the bottom of a ditch.

With rocket explosions raining down rock fragments behind them, Blue Squad got to work.

———

Brandt marked out a flat section away from any bulges or exterior features, and ordered Corporal Hecht's Alpha Section to break through. Alpha tried using assault teeth, but the monofilament spikes extending from their carbine muzzles were optimized to cut through flesh and bone, the modern equivalent of the ancient bayonet. The rotating spikes skidded against the wall, scarring it, but snapping and blunting the assault teeth.

Next they tried melting their way through using their carbines on the new pulse laser setting. New to them, anyway.

Brandt assigned each section in his squad a portion of a diamond shape large enough for an armored cadet to pass through.

If Arun were in charge he would have concentrated the lasers on a single spot. Not a hole large enough to pass through but maybe after a breach the pressure escape would rip away a large chunk of wall. At least they would know how much laser power was needed to push through.

But Brandt wanted an entry point from the get go. They burned deep scores into the fabric of the building but they were burning deeper into their carbine power packs. Barney reported power had depleted by 80% already and falling rapidly.

Belville brought over a section from Gold Squad.

The mining building had shielded them somewhat from the enemy rocket volleys. But the rebels must have moved to a better position, because a fresh volley of explosions rocked the ground behind him. Their fire was increasingly accurate.

Barney marked two red crosses to show Gold Squad casualties.

It got worse. The dust thrown up was already causing laser bloom — scattering the beams aimed at the outer wall, robbing them of power.

"Move closer," ordered Brandt. "Get those lasers within ten paces of the wall."

Arun moved to obey, very conscious of what would happen if he were standing too close to the section of wall when it blew out.

"I know it's dangerous," said Brandt, "but every second we are delayed out here imperils our mission."

But they were spared that horror. Without any warning, the diamond they'd already cut through the wall flew out, landing on the moon's surface and skidding for twenty meters. Luckily no one was in its path.

Blue Squad blasted the far side of the breach with a volley of shardshot.

Arun couldn't see what was inside, because first the air, and then anything in the room that wasn't tied down, exploded out through the breach. Blue Squad was engulfed in a rain of softscreens, hats, empty plastic bottles and other detritus of what Arun guessed was a store room. The water vapor in the air flash-froze and began to fall as snow.

To anyone inside this bridgehead room, the vacuum sucking remorselessly at the air would sound like a howling gale. Outside in his suit, the violent depressurization was eerily silent.

Cutting holes into enemy warboats was fundamental to tactical Marine doctrine, so the cadets knew plenty about depressurization. Through a Marine-sized breach the air would be escaping at about 200 mph. That was plenty to incapacitate any opponents not strapped down and braced for a breach. After about 25 seconds, the wind would have died down to around 80 mph. That was when Brandt gave the order to go in.

The cadets lowered their heads and pushed against the wind. Getting through the hole was the worst part. As the cadets partially plugged the breach, the air pushed at them even harder as it tried to escape. Once they'd popped through the hole there was still enough air to hear alarm sirens above the banshee screech of the wind.

Cadet Caccamo from Alpha Section was first in. At the far side of the bridgehead room the door to an internal corridor was still open. He raced for the door but it shut before he could reach it. The wind dropped abruptly, making the cadets who'd struggled in topple flat on their faces.

Under the illumination of flashing blue lights mounted in the ceiling, Blue Squad began to form up inside the bridgehead. Even before the rest of the squad had made it inside, Hecht was by the door control with Alpha Section, ready to advance up the corridor on the far side.

"Brace for depressurization," he warned. "Opening door in 3 - 2 - 1 - now!"

Nothing happened. The door ignored him.

"Could be security lockdown," Del said, "but probably refusing to open into vacuum. Let me see if I can hack it."

"Very good, Lance Corporal Sandure," replied Brandt. Hearing his comrades refer to each other by their rank still felt freaky to Arun.

Del hadn't even reached the control panel when the door suddenly opened, and another blast of air rushed out to flash freeze as it entered the depressurized room.

Arun covered the doorway with his carbine but no one emerged. With the swirling mist it was difficult to see, difficult to even stand up against the wind. Then he saw two dark cylinders rolling his way along the floor.

"Grenades!"

Arun dove for the floor. In the low gravity, the maneuver was agonizingly slow. In fact, the wind trying to blow him out of the crude hole in the wall was stronger than gravity. He didn't even make it to the ground before the grenades exploded. The blast smacked him down and skidded him along the floor before slamming him into an equipment cupboard. Gleaming pairs of boots fell off the shelves, showering down upon him in slow motion.

The wind, he realized, had stopped.

As Arun got to his feet, Barney reported that his armor had not been compromised. Idiot monkeys! They'd used high explosive grenades — mining charges, probably. In the near-vacuum, there was hardly any medium for their shockwave to travel through. Someone standing a meter behind Arun wouldn't have felt a thing. He laughed as he got to his feet and immediately found himself in a raging firefight.

He took a moment to read his tac-display. Beta and Delta Sections had rolled, knelt or gone prone to take up firing positions that maximized fire on the door without shooting comrades in the back.

Hardit miners — about a half dozen so far — were racing into the room, spraying fire wildly. They were shooting slug-throwers: kinetic weapons that shot metal bullets powered by a chemical explosive.

A hammer blow hit Arun on his chest, which was already bruised from his drop to the moon's surface. He'd been shot by a bullet, but Barney reported his suit's integrity had been degraded but not compromised. A suit unable to cope with a few high energy impacts from small objects was little use in a real space battlefield.

Arun wanted height. Barney read his intentions, lifting his master gently off the ground and then, with a kick of brutal power, threw him to the ceiling, coming to a shuddering halt, but not so rapid that Arun blacked out. Barney had been Arun's most intimate companion for so many years that the AI knew how far he could fling Arun without breaking him. In a crowded room in the midst of a firefight, speed was vital. Gaining height was a big risk, but so too was staying in the same place when he'd already been hit once.

Arun willed Barney to reorient his visor display so that the ceiling was 'down' and the floor 'up'. Gravity might insist that it knew the correct direction of down, but it was weak enough on the moon that the motive system on Arun's suit could compensate, if it operated at maximum power. He shut his eyes, reframed in his mind, and opened them at the same time as bringing his gun to bear on… Osman. His firing solution was blocked by his friend who was attempting the same maneuver. Arun crab-walked out of Osman's way. Osman was cartwheeling through the air, firing as he went. Osman was always flashy like that. Then Osman's aerial dance missed a beat. He was jerked backward, making him fling out his hands in a primitive instinct that made no sense here, upside down on a low-g moon.

Arun watched helplessly as Osman's helmet shattered. In the low-pressure environment of the nearly airless room, the higher pressure in Osman's suit forced out a plume of blood, flesh, and faceplate splinters.

Osman was dead!

Arun braced and fired. Brandt had ordered them to conserve ammo. The pellet supply was limited without reloading, but Arun didn't give a damn as he sprayed the rebel miners. If he needed to reload, there were plenty of spare SA-71s that no one was in a state to use any longer.

Hellfire! He'd forgotten the recoil again, thumping away at his shoulder with such violence that he sprayed his fire high, which from his position on the ceiling meant firing down at his fellow cadets.

Arun lifted his finger off the trigger before he accidentally shot his friends. Shifting firing position by rolling once to the right — mentally oriented upside-down all the while — he fired again on the Hardits as rapidly as he could.

He got one, he was sure. Shot the little veck until he'd nearly decapitated it, enjoying seeing the Hardit twitch under the flail of the shardshot. Maybe it was the miner who'd killed Osman. He hoped so but in the confusion of a firefight that was more a hope than certainty.

"Cease fire!" ordered Brandt. The firing stopped. The cloud of dust and other debris began the slow process of settling to the floor, unhurried in the lazy gravity.

Madge issued an additional order. "McEwan, stay at top. Springer, stay low. Secure the corridor."

Arun, acknowledged and moved off for the corridor that led beyond the shattered door. His mind was still reframed so that everyone else appeared to him to be walking upside down. Everyone but Osman. He had to push past Osman's corpse.

Still obeying its last command, Osman's suit AI kept its master's battlesuit positioned with its boots on the ceiling, making Osman's arterial flow spray onto the floor below like a red sprinkler.

Arun snatched a glance at their dead opponents. They were in simple vacsuits — not combat hardened. He hoped to recognize Tawfiq or one of the other Hardit tormentors of the Detroit Aux, but the suit visors obscured the faces of their wearers. He imagined the faces inside stretched into shapes of agony.

Arun pushed past Springer who was hugging the door frame, using it as cover, and advanced 20 paces along the ceiling before taking a prone position behind what looked like an atmosphere scrubber mounted in the ceiling. Blue warning lights were mounted every three meters along the ceiling before it turned right after twenty meters. They flashed a decompression alert. Arun willed Barney to remove the lights from his visor display so they didn't obscure his line of sight.

There was no sign of movement ahead.

Even without air, the corridor wasn't completely silent. A hum of power transmitted itself through the material of the ceiling. Without needing to be told, Barney would be listening tirelessly for the sound of enemy footsteps.

As he waited, Arun's thoughts turned to the weapons he'd smuggled to Alabama. Had he supplied the rebels? He wanted to assume 'yes', but… Tawfiq had been smuggling SA-71s and combat armor, not these rifles with the simple kinetic rounds.

Thinking of weapons made him realize that a pressure seal somewhere ahead had closed, leaving the corridor in vacuum. *There was very little to diffuse a laser beam.*

"Setting carbine to pulse laser," Arun said to Springer.

She hesitated — probably considering the power already drained from cutting the hole through the outer wall. "Good thinking, Arun."

In his tac-display, Springer was a strong blue dot, a short distance behind him, and with a slight tail on her dot's head, meaning she was a little below him. She'd taken cover behind a trolley, her carbine barrel resting on a pile of water bottles.

"Springer…" Arun said uncertainly.

"What? Osman? Yes… I… I saw."

Never letting his attention slip from the corridor ahead, Arun spent several seconds trying to work out what he wanted to say. He couldn't talk about Osman. Not yet. But there was something else…

Eventually he said, "I'm sorry, Springer."

"Why? You couldn't have saved Osman."

"No, not that. For letting you down about Xin and Scendence. I'm sorry."

"For frakk's sake, we've been over this already. Don't get all weepy on me, McEwan. Keep focus."

"But Osman. Do you think he really forgave me?"

"I don't know, McEwan. But I do know that if you get me killed because you're too busy being sorry to keep alert, I'll never forgive you."

Barney had no difficulty keeping alert. He smeared garish orange over Arun's view of the corridor turning, meaning he'd detected something but was unsure what.

"Contact threat," said Arun.

"Confirmed," added Springer. Her suit AI would probably be giving her the same warning as Barney, but Arun had been drilled to always seek confirmation. Suits could be damaged or make mistakes. Worse, they could be compromised through electronic warfare attack.

Maybe Barney had detected the vibrations of running feet, of heat radiating from a sweating body, of unnatural light fluctuations. Whatever bothered the AI was getting stronger because the orange flash he'd superimposed had turned an angry red. Barney was sometimes wrong in his suspicions, but Arun trusted them enough to place his full concentration on the manual sights of his carbine, braced as he was, upside down behind a ceiling unit.

A Hardit head appeared around the bend, searching the corridor for threats.

Had the rebel seen them? Arun didn't think so because the monkey slunk toward them on three limbs, the fourth holding its rifle stock. The Hardit's tail grasped the weapon's pistol grip.

Barney overlaid the Hardit with a short-tailed red targeting dot, and added two more dots for the two other rebels Barney was now confident were hiding just out of sight.

"Contact three rebels," said Springer.

"Confirmed," said Arun.

"Support required?" queried Brandt. Barney zoomed the tac-display out and up from the advancing Hardits, tilting it so that Arun could see what was happening behind him. One of the Gold Squad cadets had taken up position in the doorway that fed into his corridor, his suit acting as a relay for LBNet.

"Negative," Springer answered. "We can take them out."

The lead Hardit beckoned its two hidden comrades with a wave of its rifle. If the flashing decompression lights were blinding it, then its targeting capability must be limited to three eyes staring over an ugly snout and out through a dumb transparent visor.

This would be easy!

"I'll take the leader," said Springer.

"Roger." It didn't make sense for them to both hit the same target.

As soon as Barney said he had a good firing solution, Arun opened up. The lead Hardit was just bringing its rifle to bear, its two followers not even as ready as that.

Too late, monkeys!

Using short, cutting motions, Arun fired his pulse laser at the second Hardit.

He knew he'd scored a hit. So had Springer, but then they had to face the difference between a low-power pulse laser and a full laser connected to the additional power packs they usually carried in space.

Their pulse lasers turned themselves off for a second to recharge.

They were effectively unarmed for what felt like an age. The remaining Hardit failed to make use of its advantage. All it could do was stare in horror at its fallen comrades.

Arun almost sympathized.

Their lasers had gashed open the Hardit suits but left little or no exit wounds. The pinkish spray fountaining out of their compromised suits did more than prove the Hardits had been injured, they were high pressure jets spinning the Hardits off balance. One injured Hardit got off a wild shot before both were on the floor, their weapons dropped.

Arun's carbine had recharged. He killed the remaining Hardit with a headshot, firing simultaneously with Springer.

The other Hardits were still alive, but not worth wasting battery power on.

By the time the jets out of their depressurizing suits had calmed, the Hardits would be too oxygen starved to be any threat.

"Three miners tropied," reported Springer, but no acknowledgment came from the bridgehead. They'd lost LBNet.

What were they playing at back there?

LBNet didn't reconnect for nearly two minutes. When it did, Arun's irritation vanished, because Barney updated his tac-display by planting red crosses over the blue cadet dots. Casualties. Lots of them, and they'd only captured one room so far.

Barney had added a double yellow halo to Brandt's dot, meaning he was now tactical commander.

Alice Belville was one of the red crosses.

Oh, hell!

"Listen up!" announced Brandt. His speech-making was cringeworthy at the best of times. His voice sounded doubly uncertain now. "We've suffered eight killed, two wounded. We've lost Lance Sergeant Belville, so I have command. Blue-6, reinforce Blue-5 guarding the corridor approach. Gold Alpha and Beta Sections will stay behind to guard the bridgehead and the wounded. The rest, grab ammo for yourselves and Blue Delta Section and…"

Brandt's voice faded. Arun groaned. Alice never hesitated like that. If she'd survived, they would be halfway to the base command center by now.

"Medics?" asked Brandt on the open channel. "How long to stabilize the wounded?"

"Three minutes, lance sergeant."

"The rest of us have three minutes to tear this room apart searching for anything useful. Questions?"

No one spoke.

A few seconds later, Madge took a position next to Springer, the rest of Delta Section spreading out around her.

"Good to see you, corporal," said Springer.

Arun winced. He didn't know what to say to Madge even in a simple greeting. How could he greet the remaining member of his fire team without mentioning Blue-5's missing member: Osman?

When Barney signaled another alert, Arun almost groaned with relief. He was overlaying the view of the corridor turn with a flashing orange warning.

Seconds later a Hardit head peered around the corner. Arun waited for it to move closer, to get a clearer shot. But this time the rebels weren't playing ball. The head disappeared out of sight. Barney, meanwhile, was firming his estimate. There were more rebels massing this time. Many more.

"Contact approx 20 rebels," Arun reported.

"We'll vape 'em easy," said Madge. "Two of you took out three of them with ease. Now there's six of us and they will be choked by the corridor's narrowness."

Arun thought she was talking away her fears. He didn't like the sound of that.

He readied to fire.

Any second now.

But the Hardits stayed around the corner as if waiting for something. Were they inviting the cadets to attack?

Why was no one giving orders? This wasn't a waiting game. It was a race to save his home from obliteration.

"Contact, 90 hostiles," he heard over LBNet.

Confirmation soon came from his tac-display. Out on the moon's surface, the rebels had retaken their trenches and were shooting through the breach and into the bridgehead.

The cadets were pinned down and outnumbered. Surely they had to take the fight to the enemy without delay. And who was nearest to the enemy?

Arun was.

Cold fear struck through Arun's heart. He wanted his combat meds.

Brandt's voice entered Arun's helmet. "Gold Squad will defend the bridgehead. Blue will push through the enemy in the corridor. Blue Delta Section. You're point."

Arun took a deep breath. The moment he reached the turn in the corridor a dozen rifles would fire at him.

"Blue-5, advance along the ceiling," ordered Madge. "Take the corner. Blue-6, give pulse laser covering fire. Aim low. Ready on my mark."

Arun wanted to say something — anything — to Springer. But everything he could think of sounded demoralizing. So he kept his mouth shut and tensed his legs in readiness.

"Wait!" Madge ordered.

Arun didn't understand until he glanced at his tac-display. The Hardits were advancing.

"Fire on my command!"

The last Hardit attack had been hesitant. This time the Hardits came at the cadets in a rush.

Three of them had come round the corner. Five of them. Seven. And they weren't carrying rifles. They had SA-71 carbines. Oh, frakk!

The leading rank of rebels launched grenades

"Fire!"

As he pressed the trigger to release the laser bolt, the enemy grenades exploded, filling the corridor incredibly quickly with thick smoke. Had the laser shots got off in time before the smoke grenades scattered them to harmlessness?

All he knew was that he couldn't see the end of his barrel, but Barney insisted the Hardits were still coming.

Switching to shardshot, he raked the corridor. He extended his assault teeth too.

The Hardits were firing back. Fragments of the scrubber unit he was sheltering behind flew past his face. He felt a kick in his left chest, just below the collar bone.

Then the firing stopped, all sides unwilling to fire into the fog, fearful of hitting their own side.

Barney used the brief respite to inform Arun that he had been shot. That kick he'd felt was a kinetic dart passing through Arun's body. Barney insisted he'd fixed the suit breach and anesthetized the wound. Nothing to worry about.

Good enough, thought Arun. Out of the choking mist a looming blur rapidly solidified into a Hardit rebel, carbine at the ready.

He — or she — might be better armed than the first line of Hardit defense, but not better trained. The rebel scanned ahead for targets but wasn't looking up at the ceiling.

Arun spun his assault teeth and thrust down in to the rebel's shoulder. *Let's see how you like that!*

The needle-like teeth sank in through the vacsuit, embedding into the soft tissue beyond. Then Arun set the teeth spinning at 1000 rpm, ripping a jagged hole through the suit that released a geyser of pulpy, red spray.

Before the dying Hardit had finished slumping to the floor, another attacker pushed forward through the mist and stumbled over its comrade. Arun jabbed at it with his assault teeth, but the rebel tripped before he could connect, falling headlong. The unexpected motion confused Arun. He missed. More rebels were passing beneath all the time.

The atmosphere scrubbers must be pretty powerful because the smoke was starting to clear.

When they did, they would reveal Arun to be alone in a sea of rebels.

He glanced behind him, convinced he was about to be stabbed in the back.

With a last blind jab from his carbine, he snapped his attention back to his front. No one there either, just the thinning smoke.

Stay still and die. That what the Corps had taught him.

So he moved. Forward.

The closer he got to the end of the corridor, the thinner the smoke got. LBNet was still unavailable. He should probably try WBNet but he'd been ordered not to.

He could see a heap of Hardit dead below him. Around the turn in the corridor, Barney estimated a half dozen rebels — the enemy's final attack wave.

Was he really going to take them on alone?

Arun paused, then dropped down to the floor to plug in an ammo bulb from one of the fallen Hardits. If he going to die doing something stupid, he wasn't going to do so firing pellets of chewed up ore tailings.

"You are another hero, yes?" said a scratchy voice.

Arun looked up to see a Marine on the ceiling: the replacement, Umarov. "More like another idiot, carabinier. Yes."

"Good lad."

Hearing another human voice was all he needed to restore his morale, despite the enemy waiting around the corner. And the army behind them.

Umarov shifted around so he was standing on the right hand wall of the corridor. "Stand on the wall opposite me," he ordered.

While Arun moved to comply, Umarov dropped his carbine and drew a combat blade in each hand. They were like nothing he'd ever seen: crescent moons attached to either end of a hand grip, the blades glistening with drips of what looked like fluorescent puss.

"Let's see what they make of old-fashioned poisoned carbon. Suppress them until I engage. Go!"

This was it.

Arun ran along the corridor wall, to meet his fate. At the last moment, he told Barney to select rocket rounds. He hadn't many, but they would make more of a show for the untrained rebels.

Then he was rounding the corridor and firing. His finger didn't release from the trigger until the rocket rounds were spent and he was firing kinetic darts so fast that his recoil limiter tripped out.

And still he was running at the Hardits.

Umarov was on them now, limbs extended in a whirlwind dance of cuts and kicks. Killing elegance.

Umarov had their full attention, which meant somehow Arun had survived against all odds.

He extended his assault teeth to join Umarov in the melee.

But the Hardits seemed to be getting farther away, not closer.

And gravity felt as if it were strengthening.

His legs were weakening.

What's happening Barney?

His suit AI brought up a damage summary. Arun had been shot five times. Barney had sealed his suit, but fixing the holes in his master's body was another matter entirely.

But what about the Night Hummer prophecy? I thought the future needed me?

Arun clung to that protest as everything slowed.

And went black.

—— Chapter 59 ——

A bell rang for Arun, beckoning him to his place in the afterlife.

He hadn't expected this.

To be dead: yes. But afterlife? He'd assumed that was Jotun propaganda.

"Yes, that's it. Welcome back."

The voice came through his helmet speaker. It didn't have the gravitas of a supernatural being. It sounded familiar.

He opened his eyes onto the medic tapping Arun's helmet with her gauntlet. It was Puja, or Lance Corporal Puja Narciso as she'd become. She was Command Section's medic.

He'd had a thing for her in novice school. She'd felt the same way too. Briefly.

She smiled. "I've still got it, ain't I, Arun?"

"I guess so, I… lance—"

"No!" She put a finger to his lips, or as close as his helmet would allow. "Don't 'lance' me. Not yet. You shut up and rest for a minute."

"Am I dying?" Arun croaked. He couldn't feel pain. But his body felt as if all its life-force had leeched away, leaving nothing more than dust held together by a memory of once-strong flesh and bone.

Puja paused, working out her story. She sighed. "You've taken multiple hits. A lot of trauma and blood loss. But I've patched you up and given you a transfusion. Bottom line: Stay in bed. Light duties for minimum three weeks. I'll check up on you in the morning."

"Seriously?"

"Of course not, you donker. We're heavily outnumbered and most of us are already dead. You're good to carry a carbine and that's all you need to know right now. Corporal Majanita can fill you in on the rest in a minute. Just as well you aren't human."

"What do you mean, I'm not human?"

"Well, have you ever studied a pre-Contact medical textbook?"

"No, of course not."

Puja grinned, making her visor transparent so Arun could see. "Good. Don't bother, 'cos you'd be wasting your time. Whatever the hell we are, we aren't *Homo sapiens*, that's for sure. You'd be dead if you were."

Puja's grin, flashing that cute gap between her incisors. Yes, he remembered her smile.

"McEwan?"

He tried to work out where he was but he couldn't see properly. Hey, did someone say most of them were dead?

"Frakk! Spoke too soon."

He didn't want to think of dead friends.

"Arun. Come back to me, Arun!" begged a memory of a girl who'd for an intense few weeks had meant the universe to him. Puja had been his first kiss. It seemed a lifetime ago. He closed his eyes and dreamed memories of better days, of a teenage girl back in the days when she wore too-tight fatigues, not a poly-ceramalloy battlesuit.

—— Chapter 60 ——

"You're alive then."

Arun opened his eyes. He was in a room he didn't recognize, his back propped up against something. A lot of people were rushing around. People in battlesuits. And they were glowing vision-enhancement blue because there was very little light. One battlesuit was standing over him. Inside was a woman.

"Puja?"

"Dream time's over, lover boy. I'm not Lance Corporal Narciso." She studied him for a moment. "Do you recognize me?"

The woman made her visor go clear. He squinted at her face. It seemed familiar. "Corporal… You're Corporal Majanita."

"Damn right I am."

"You don't want me."

She laughed. "What I want isn't worth squit. You're in my section and I'm giving you 60 seconds recuperation time before I need you ready to use this." She thrust something into his hands. It was an SA-71 carbine. His carbine.

"Here's the sitrep. We beat off the rebel counterattacks, but it wasn't easy. We've lost half the cadets who dropped from *Yorktown*. Cristina and Osman are both dead but, frankly, we've gotten off lightly. Gold Squad's down to about section strength."

A chill, prickling sensation marched up Arun's spine. *So many dead?*

"Where are we now?" he asked.

"Don't interrupt. We think this is the main control room. We made a mess of the doors coming in, helped by some drills the monkeys were kind enough to leave for us in the bridgehead. Del tried hacking the computer systems but doesn't think that worked. Zug had a brainwave and found power cables running through a conduit in the roof. We cut them. The main lights went out. The power hum in all the machines running here died too."

"But how do we know for certain that we've turned off power to the mass driver? Or the force shield protecting it?"

Madge hesitated. "We don't. We can't raise Force Alpha on WBNet — the monkeys are jamming us. So Brandt's ordered us to stay here. Make sure the monkeys don't sneak in and turn the power back on."

"Shouldn't we try to link up with Force Alpha? At least recon the mass driver?"

"Did God visit you in your dream and promote you to sergeant?"

"No, corporal."

"Then the lance sergeant still outranks you — thank the Fates… I think. And there's this tradition that means you kinda got to do what your superior says. Humor me. It's a Marine thing."

Madge turned away, adding: "One last thing. The base has set up pressure plugs, meaning any pressure loss is sealed automatically by a kind of gradual force field. So we can't repeat the trick of cutting a hole in a door and watch the poor vecks inside tripping over as their air rushes out. And now that we're back in an atmosphere, grenades and blast weapons — they're gonna hurt a whole lot more."

"Those pressure plugs," cut in Zug. "I've studied the theory. Playing with the laws of nature like that doesn't come cheap. Which means there must still be a lot of power running through this base. Power they could re-route to the mass driver."

"Thank you for the interruption," snapped Madge. "Makes me feel a whole lot better. I'll pass it on to the lance sergeant. You worry about keeping your eyes on the northern approach." She kicked Arun's feet. "You too. Recuperation time's over."

Arun tried standing up. There was a slight wobble, no more. There wasn't even any pain. In fact, he felt completely numb except for the tingling sensation of his gauntleted hands gripping his carbine.

Barney's medical summary explained that Arun had been stabilized just this side of death, patched up, and set running again. The reason Arun wasn't collapsing in a swoon was because, instead of using the battlesuit motors to amplify Arun's muscle movements, Barney was pretty much running the suit himself by guessing Arun's intentions. If he were outside of his battlesuit, Arun would probably be in a coma.

But at least he wasn't getting any worse. A near-coma would just have to do.

Arun was behind a huge equipment bank. He imagined it would normally be winking lights, heat and a power hum. Currently it was a cooling metal box. Even in the emergency lighting — putrid green bio-luminescence seeping out of the walls — the box looked pretty shot up by the cadet attack. With Barney's guesses helping to make up for the lack of illumination, Arun saw that he was in a 12 by 10 meter rectangular room filled with dead computers, power equipment, and consoles.

There was a door to the north which had been fused shut and then cut through and peeled back from the outside. Must be where the cadets had drilled through. A mound of spent SA-71 sabot casings on the far side of the door told the story of what had transpired.

Corpses were piled up against one wall — human and the more numerous Hardits mixed together.

To the south, a second door was propped open, leading out onto an approach corridor. The Gold Squad survivors were guarding that approach.

Arun's eyes dimmed, his breath quickened. He closed his eyes, felt like he was swaying but he knew Barney wouldn't let him fall. He didn't want to open them. Didn't want to see. Not yet; he was still too weak.

Hiding didn't help, though. He could remember what he'd seen in the tac-display clearly enough to count the Gold Squad dots. There were 8 survivors of the 31 who'd dropped from *Yorktown* just 83 minutes ago. From Blue Squad, 21 had made it this far.

He wanted his heart to feel as numb as the rest of his body, but he felt only aching loss. And Cristina… she was gone too.

A jumble of memories jostled to overwhelm him: happy times with Cristina, of arguments and impossible boasts he'd traded with Osman. He opened his eyes to escape, and tried again to take in his surroundings.

He was crouched alongside Madge and Springer behind the metal-skinned box. The alien writing and dead display screen set into the box told him nothing about its function or inner contents.

Behind a similar box next to them crouched Del, Zug and Umarov.

They were facing the northern corridor approach. They couldn't see it in visual because the boxes were in the way. They didn't need to. If anything came at them from north or south, every cadet would see it on their tac-display. Delta Section would simply leap up, fire, and then drop back down behind cover.

Arun unsnagged his mind from speculating what might be transpiring around the mass driver, and his memories of fallen comrades. He settled his concentration instead onto the dots and wire-frame schematics of Barney's tac-display.

Seconds turned to minutes.

Nothing happened.

Like the training missions where he remained floating in space, keeping watch on the void, once Arun had settled into the rhythm of observation, he could keep his concentration fixed for hours. He'd been bred for this, *engineered*.

So it came as something of a shock when his concentration was broken by someone rapping on his helmet with the barrel of an SA-71 carbine. It was Springer. Her faceplate blanked to transparency, an internal light in her helmet illuminating her features. She smiled. It was forced, but the affection warmed him.

He blanked his own visor, automatically lighting the inside of his helmet. A little glare reflected off the inside of the visor.

Arun was struck by the look of concern that shone out of her eyes like violet jewels.

Springer pursed her lips and blew him a kiss from the inside of her helmet. With faceplates touching so that the sound wave could travel directly into his helmet, he could hear the sound as if from a great depth underwater.

"That was a vac-kiss," she breathed in a voice that Arun found teasingly steamy, but he recognized was the sound of Springer speaking from her heart despite the distortion of speaking faceplate-to-faceplate. "When we get back home," she continued, "I'll give you a real one."

"Then I'd better make sure I stay alive," said Arun, grinning.

"Be sure of it. *No Marine left behind*. They used to take that seriously, you know, those old Marines on Earth. Bryant might laugh at that, but I don't. I can't leave you behind, Arun."

A burst of warmth flooded through Arun, spreading out from his heart and into an uncontrollable grin that filled his face. He fantasized entwining his suit with Springer's. There was an annoyingly rational part of his brain that Arun wished he could turn off, but maybe one day would save his life. Right now it was reminding him that human hormonal responses were dangerously amplified by combat stress, a dangerous side-effect of their re-engineered physiology that would normally be overcome by the use of combat-stim drugs.

A harsh aural assault of white noise made Arun flinch. He brought his free hand to cover his ear. Of course, that made not the slightest difference to the noise attacking him through the speakers inside his helmet.

Arun gritted his teeth and hung on tightly to his sanity until the noise ceased as suddenly as it had hit him. It had lasted six seconds.

"Cut it out, you two," bellowed Majanita inside his helmet. "You're both on a charge. Brandt's seen you. If you two loved-up shunters let yourself be distracted a moment longer, I'll be on a charge too and you will be reported for dereliction of duty. What's wrong with you, Springer? I thought you were too smart to get yourself executed."

Arun and Springer both answered at the same time. "Sorry, corporal."

Even with his attention back on the corridor approach, Arun couldn't eject from his mind the fact that Springer was standing next to him. He imagined he could feel the warmth from her body. A body that if freed from their suits would fit perfectly pressed against his own. His arms would wrap around her, gently squashing her warm flesh against his. Arun's hand would stroke through her mess of auburn curls, moving slowly so as not to pull painfully at her hair, gently untangling. Then his hand would slide down to cup the underswell of her buttock and press his fingertips into her yielding flesh…

He pushed those thoughts far enough away to realize that Majanita was right. His faulty body chemistry was going to get them both shot if he wasn't careful.

Arun let out a long breath and then ordered Barney to administer combat drugs.

He wasn't sure what they were doping the cadets with, but he couldn't shake off memories of the last time he'd been on stims. He'd ended up naked, his image plastered all over Detroit.

What would it do to him this time?

He didn't feel a thing as the meds went in, but then he felt a crust form over his heart. Fantasies of what might be were replaced with obsessively detailed observation of the here and now. Lusty romance evaporated away to leave indifference, which soured into hatred, and finally the need to kill.

"Here we go again," he mumbled.

Combat drugs were unique to each individual. Really they were a cocktail of psychostimulants and endocrine effectors blended to an individual's requirements and adjusted and tuned after each use. The exercise was made more difficult when administered into a young body still changing through the natural hormones of adolescence.

He tried to hold onto the memory of Springer's kiss, the lilac glow from her beautiful mutant eyes. He could recall the images of Springer with full fidelity, but although he could remember the fact of her love and concern for him, the emotion behind those facts had now drifted far out of reach.

Human emotion had become alien to him.

He wanted to hate that loss but couldn't. All his hatred was aimed at the enemy.

Springer had always looked out for him, ever since that time when he'd stood up for her when they were both ten years old. When the leader of the most vicious girl gang of their year had asked Springer to join, her reply had been to fill the gang leader's bed with steaming porridge, just before bedtime. Springer's other friends had thought that hilarious when the news reached them, but not Arun. He tracked down his missing friend to a disused corridor where he found her surrounded by jeering gang members. Arun stepped in to protect Springer.

His presence made no difference. Both of them were beaten senseless.

When they'd awoken in neighboring infirmary beds, she smiled as best she could through cut and swollen lips and called Arun her hero. It was the first time he'd seen her violet eyes glow, a warmth that stirred his heart. But then she said something that still chilled him: "You cared. You came because you cared. No one else did. No one else could. Thank you for caring."

Even back then, loyalty to the Corps was firmly instilled in all novices. But caring for others was a weakness, and good Marines had no weaknesses. Emotions were being eroded from the human genestock of the Corps. As a little boy, his mother had warned him never to reveal that he cared. But Springer knew his secret.

Arun shut out the memories of Springer and locked them away next to times remembered with Cristina and Osman. He had no need for such weakness.

The drugs had released him from that burden.

Now all that mattered was killing the enemy.

And killing was good.

Without warning, Arun's tac-display vanished, leaving him staring out of a dumb visor of transparent polycarbide at the big block of cold metal in front of him. In the near-dark he could barely make out the edges of the equipment block.

He jumped up, carbine ready, but before he cleared the top of the equipment box, his visor display went completely white. Words appeared on top of the white.

++ TRAINING OVERRIDE ++

++ DO NOT SHOOT! INCOMING MARINES ARE FRIENDLY ++

Was this a trick?

If the rebels could subvert the cadets' suits, then sending messages would be simple. Speaking like a human would be tricky, but any AI could write a simple sentence in any language it knew.

"Hold your fire!" The command came from Brandt, or at least that's what Barney was telling him. Brandt added: "But keep your weapons trained in case this is a deception."

That's all very well for you to say, thought Arun, *but how am I to train my weapon when I can't see out?* Barney anticipated his next thought and informed him that the air was mildly poisonous and would not be easy to breathe, but if Arun wished, the helmet lock could be released so he could take it off and see who was approaching with his naked eyes.

As he was considering whether that was wise, Brandt announced: "I have visual. It's the *Yorktown* Marines. It's Force Alpha."

Arun's faceplate lost its whiteness and his pulse calmed down. On tac-display he saw four new marines had joined LBNet. The double-halo of command had switched from Brandt to Ensign Thunderclaws, a Jotun name if ever he'd heard one. Thunderclaws was bounding toward them from the north like a swift six-legged dog, a creature Arun had seen many times in Earth recordings, though he'd never seen a dog in combat armor.

"I repeat, this is no trick," said Brandt. Frankly, thought Arun, if the rebels could fake a Jotun in a suit then they deserved to win.

"Sir, why did we lose Wide Battle Net?" asked Brandt.

The officer replied: "Our WBNet transmissions had to be bounced off *Yorktown* and boosted in tight beams to punch through Hardit jamming."

Oh, shit, thought Arun. *That meant…*

Brandt asked the question in Arun's head. "Is she lost, sir?"

"Negative," replied the Jotun. "*Yorktown* is evacuating key personnel from orbital platforms. She is merely out of range." The Jotun was speaking through a voicebox machine, sounding identical to Pedro. Arun wondered whether his friendly Trog was going to survive this rebellion, whether he would debate Arun's part in the operation with his usual alien weirdness. He was surprised to find that he looked forward to that talk.

Of course, there was the little matter of Arun surviving the day too.

Arun stood up and took a good look at the Marines coming his way.

There were three of them, in gray battlesuits, though their coloration could change in an instant. Unit insignia marked them as 9th field battalion, 412th Marines — Arun's regiment.

Two of them carried SA-71s, the third an HG-11c machine gun, which was essentially a heavy version of the SA-71 in railgun mode. Kinetic darts fired from the HG-11c reached greater muzzle velocity due to a stronger electrical charge and a much longer barrel, which was braced by a small flip-out bipod rest.

Arun counted four ammo belts slung over the machine gunner's shoulder, each holding scores of magazines, which were blocks of charged metal, pre-stressed to split along ballistic shapes, a little like perforated paper. The ammo alone must weigh well over a hundred pounds. Sometimes Marine armor was used to turn humans into beasts of burden. Unglamorous yet effective.

The machine gunner was coming directly toward Arun. Or, more likely, to take over his position.

Arun stepped back a few paces to allow the machine gunner to select his or her position, but the gunner immediately switched direction to come straight for him.

Arun froze.

"Are you Arun McEwan?" asked the Marine – a corporal according to suit markings – when they were standing toe-to-toe.

"Yes, corporal."

"Blank your visor and let me see your face."

Arun complied, standing at attention while this guy just stared at him.

Arun desperately wanted to query Barney's tac-display to ping this Marine's ID, but he couldn't do that with a blank display.

Then the Marine blanked his own faceplate. That was even worse. The Marine peered at him through bulging eyes tinted an artificial blue. The Marine's face was young — thirty perhaps? — and might have been considered handsome if not for the scar tissue that covered one cheek and cut across his nose and brow. Here was a Marine who had taken a plasma blast to the face and survived.

You didn't get to be a G-2 Marine cadet without knowing how to deal with older kids throwing their weight around. The first rule was to avoid being seen as weak. Then, if you get picked upon anyway, you took it on the chin and waited for payback until you were older.

This guy had probably picked on Arun at random. Singling him out to make an example to the other cadets to remind them who was in charge. But then, why bother? The Marine's eyes stared into space for a moment, as if recalling a precious memory. His face crumpled a little and his lips moved, preparing to say something laden with emotion.

Just before the man could speak, Springer beat him to it. She had checked her tac-display on Arun's behalf.

"Arun, he's your brother. Corporal Fraser McEwan."

But… he thought his brother had died on *Fort Douaumont*. They must have been on *Yorktown* all this time, never having set out. If Arun survived long enough for his combat meds to work their way out of his system, he expected he would feel pleased about that later on.

Fraser looked about to speak but he was interrupted by the Jotun officer. "I salute you human Marine children," said Thunderclaws speaking the human language with his own voice. He switched back to the artificial voice of the translator unit. "You have shut off power to the mass driver. The bombardment has been halted. The force shield protecting it still functions. Half of Force Alpha — three Marines — occupies the attention of the rebel positions near the driver. We have traveled here undetected, entering through the bridgehead you established."

Arun half-expected cheers to ring out. But the other cadets were, like Arun, so drugged up with the need to kill that victory didn't interest them.

"However, the engagement is not over. The rebels are sending an assault force to deal with us. Until this point, you have only encountered annoying little monkeys — not an equal foe. Now you will face their elite. They are still hardly a martial race but you should regard them with a little less than utter contempt."

Had Arun just heard a little light racial abuse directed by one alien species at another in human speech? There was a time, not long ago, when Zug would have been fascinated by that.

Ensign Thunderclaws broke off conversation, gestured at one of the Marines, and turned his attention to some other task. What that task might be, Arun was not privy to.

"I'm Sergeant Rathanjani," said the Marine the ensign had gestured to. "You've done okay for a bunch of kids but you've a shitload to learn. For starters, don't look at me! We're in a battle for frakk's sake. Keep watching the approaches to this room. That's better. Now, here's the sitrep. We estimate 10 to 20 hostiles heading our way. They will be heavily armed and armored, and their objective will be to kill us if they can, but more importantly to pin us while their engineers boot up the secondary power and control systems, and then recommence the bombardment of Tranquility."

"Sergeant," asked Brandt, "what about reinforcements?"

"Don't interrupt, cadet. Anyone else got a stupid question or maybe want a comfort break before I carry on? No? Good. System defense boats ETA two hours. Navy ships in about five. Last I heard, both were still on our side but we've traitors somewhere in the system. Tranquility orbital defense is not set up to bombard our own moon. Anything else that could help was taken out in the initial salvos. It's down to us. If these monkeys keep us pinned down here, then by the time the warboats arrive, you won't have homes to go back to."

"You're still kids," said Arun's brother. "Still believe the crap they teach you in novice school. So let me educate you. We're human Marines. We fight two wars. One is the war that the White Knights give us through their Jotun officers. The other is a longer war, a hard fought war of attrition and tiny incremental gains that will last centuries. None of us will survive to see this other war end. This is the war for respectability. Whatever bullshit you might hear in Detroit these days, the White Knights only took on we humans as a client race to piss off the Cienju. They're lizard aliens who had taken control of the Earth, and would have enslaved us all to ship them ore from the Solar System. The White Knights don't think of us as being fit enough to clean their sewers. We're only here out in the stars playing Marines as a face-saving measure, to make it look as if the Knights wanted us all along. It's down to all of us at all times to prove to our alien masters bit by tiny bit that we are worthwhile, that we are a surprisingly valuable asset. Because if we don't, then one day they will decide that the Earth and the rest of their empire will be simpler if they were no longer infested with humans. If we are to die today, make sure we die well."

His brother wasn't great with the old motivational, thought Arun. If he weren't in the grip of his combat drugs, his brother's speech would make him want to crawl into a corner, curl up, and await his doom.

The Force Alpha Marines suddenly disappeared. They must have stealthed their suits. The SA-71s attached to their invisible suits disappeared too. But Fraser's machine gun wasn't stealth-capable, hovering in mid-air as if suspended on wires.

"Cadets, keep to Cadet Lance Sergeant Brandt's deployment," said Sergeant Rathanjani. Barney used the sergeant's broadcast to place a fuzzy outline around where he thought the NCO might be. "Force Alpha will operate as mobile reserve," continued the sergeant. "Keep alert. Attack is imminent. And heed Corporal McEwan's words. I know some of you might be a little young to hear the truth, but that's hard shit. Today is the day you grow up. You're all Marines now. If you do die, then die well. That is an order. Good luck."

—— Chapter 61 ——

The door to the northern approach was still fused shut, but while the humans waited for the attack, Beta Section had used the drills to widen the opening in the door, and then post a picket guard on the far side.

"Incoming! North corridor defenses, prepare to fire."

The warning came from Sergeant Rathanjani. *He must have a better AI than me*, considered Arun because it took another few seconds before Barney picked up the threat on LBNet and threw it up onto Arun's tac-display.

Four rebels were advancing along the northern corridor, still hidden for now beyond the right turn. It almost felt like a re-run of the attacks along the corridor out of the bridgehead room, though with one difference. The rebels were plodding nearer at an astonishingly leisurely pace. Barney was getting firmer data now and was confident enough to show tight red circles to indicate the estimated position of the leading two rebels. Arun didn't get the impression they were moving slowly because they were hesitating.

They simply weren't in any hurry.

Arun decided he was frightened.

It was a weird feeling. He didn't *feel* frightened — all he felt was calm anticipation of killing the enemy – but he knew with conviction that he was scared. It was like watching someone else shaking with fear.

He glanced at Fraser's position. His brother was invisible, but his long-barreled gun was wedged securely in a slot set into an equipment console, and aimed through the opening in the north door. When his brother got to open fire on the rebels, they wouldn't stand a chance.

Then a combat fugue descended on Arun like a cool mist. His universe shrunk to his gun, his tac-display, and the enemy. An enemy he would kill.

The first rebel edged around the turn. LBNet activity flared as the suit AIs of the Marine cadets in the corridor assessed the attacker, firing packets of updated information and assessment at neighboring suits.

The AIs were MPQX-8 units: built on massive parallel quantum architecture and rated a minimum 8 peta decisions per second. That made them decidedly second rate, but plenty fast enough for Barney to start suggesting firing solutions within a tiny fraction of a second. What he wasn't offering were killshots, and that wasn't good enough. Only killing would slake Arun's bloodlust.

Arun sprung into the air, getting above the cover of the equipment bank so he could see the rebels in realsight.

As soon as Arun crested his cover, Barney zoomed his visor viewpoint onto the leading rebel, who had now advanced far enough to face Arun head on.

The rebel wore some seriously heavy armor. He looked like a column of vehicle tires stacked one upon the other, and then partially melted so the bottom was wider than the top.

Arun remembered seeing sections of this armor before — in a broken wooden cargo box on the way to Alabama.

There were no feet and no head in this armored cone, but there were two bulges at the shoulders. Two stubby little tubes ending in gauntlets showed where the hands went. One of those gauntlets held the barrel of a plasma blaster. The stock and trigger were held by a black snake that Barney whispered was the rebel's prehensile tail.

Arun aimed for the tail.

With Barney anticipating his intentions, all Arun needed to do was point his carbine roughly where it was needed and let Barney steady his suit and adjust the position of his hands and arms. As a safety precaution, Arun still had to pull the trigger.

As he did so, he felt a gentle nudge of recoil, and watched Barney register a hit.

The rebel's blaster jerked and then accelerated a ball of plasma out of its barrel — aimed at Arun. But the shot went wide, melting a section of door instead of Arun's head. Before he fell back behind cover, Arun saw the rebel's gun and tail dance under a hail of fire. The blaster was dropping to the ground now, the enemy's tail whipping back behind its body. A cloud was blooming around the rebel, debris from his disintegrating armor.

An aperture opened in one of the rebel's shoulder bulges and a stream of fire streaked down the corridor, exploding in a ball of energy.

Rocket attack!

The shockwave took hold of Arun while he was still falling back behind cover. It tossed him onto the floor.

He heard a human cry of pain and suddenly remembered that it wasn't just him and the enemy. There were other people here too.

Barney understood his new concern and showed him the cadet casualties out in the corridor. No one in the central control room had been wounded so far. The rockets must be set to low yield, the enemy unwilling as yet to obliterate the equipment in the control room.

Another rocket strike rocked the corridor.

"Aim for the skirt."

A third rocket hit.

"Aim for the skirt!"

By the time Arun had scrambled back onto his feet, Barney had marked the Marines stationed out in the corridor with a red cross. *All dead.*

"We're hurting him!"

It occurred to Arun that he was hearing Corporal Majanita's words. She was important and he was supposed to pay attention. Battle was so much easier when it was just him, Barney, and the enemy. But Barney had betrayed him, raising the volume of Majanita's words until his helmet rang like a bell.

Damn those combat drugs.

Damn reality without the drugs even more.

Arun gasped, stumbling backward. It felt like waking up suddenly from a nightmare. He shook his head. He felt normal again.

"Aim for the skirt on the lead rebel," Majanita shouted.

Standard doctrine said he should shift to a new firing position after each burst of fire to frustrate enemy counter fire. But the room was too full of Marines to offer opportunities for new cover, and the enemy fire was wild anyway.

More importantly, his urge to kill would not wait.

Arun jumped up again from behind cover and ordered Barney to hold his position, hovering a meter above the ground. He aimed through the thickening cloud of smoke, dust, and armor fragments, at the feet of the rebel, who had now advanced about another four paces toward their room.

Majanita must be right. Behind the blob of armor was a monkey with two legs on the ground and slowly walking the bulky armor their way. There must be at least some space cut away from the armor in front of the monkey's legs, or else the Hardit would trip over. Which meant the armor was thinner there. Probably.

It was the best plan Arun could think of.

Just before he put his first shot into the skirt, he heard a screaming hum of power rise to a crescendo, and unleash in a deafening whine. Barney selectively dampened the noise, which Arun recognized as a heavy duty linear accelerator powering up and then spitting out a hellfire of spinning rounds. It was his brother opening up.

Arun fired too. Rapid blasts at the enemy's skirt. He left Barney to continue firing while he looked at the other rebels. There were five in total. Two had advanced several more paces toward the room, weathering the hail of fire, uninjured so far. The three at the back were not carrying blasters. They didn't seem to be carrying anything. Other than the low-yield rockets

— which he suspected were being used as a distraction — none of the rebels were firing.

"What are they up to?" he asked.

"Don't know. Don't care," replied Majanita. "Just kill them."

And they were. The skirt armor of the first rebel gave way, splitting into a dozen fragments that spun away under the firestorm coming from the humans.

The veterans put grenades into the gap that had opened in the armor. Arun figured that was one enemy down, and shifted aim to the next rebel. His brother beat him to it, hammering the rebel with a stream of bullets aimed at his head. The rebel had no faceplate or helmet. Or if he did, it was hidden inside the mound of protective armor that offered no obvious weak spot.

No weakness, except perhaps simple physics and the concept of levers. The rebel either tripped, or the kinetic push from Fraser's fire toppled him over backward.

Arun heard a roar of shared hatred go around LBNet. He didn't join in. He was readying to aim at the three rebels who stood in a line at the rear.

But they had readied their own attack. As one, the rebels were using their dexterous tails sheltered behind their backs to throw metal objects.

Was this a grenade attack? Nerve gas?

Neither held any fear for Arun but the three round disks of metal they'd thrown hadn't been aimed at the Marines. Instead, one flew at the ceiling and two on the wall to either side.

Fraser fired on one of the rebels at the rear. Most of the humans were shooting at the rebel who had just fallen onto his back. Arun aimed at the thing on the ceiling.

An instant before his finger squeezed the trigger, a curtain of shimmering purple fell across the corridor, a force shield emitted from the devices on the walls.

Anything touching the energy barrier flashed instantly into plasma. Arun's round gave a flicker when the energy barrier disintegrated it. Fraser's machine gun rounds gave a ferocious light display but could not punch through.

The fragments of blasted armor flared. So too did the body of the second rebel who had fallen across the path of the energy field. A fist-sized swathe of the Hardit's body, running from shoulder to shoulder, had simply ceased to exist.

Arun was about to shoot through the force shield at the rebels behind, but stopped himself. He'd put such a hail of railgun darts into the armored rebels that his ammo was running low.

"Switch to laser," Brandt ordered. "Concentrate fire on the upper shield generator."

"Negative," countered Sergeant Rathanjani. "That's a 37-P tactical force shield. Save your power, we've nothing that can punch through that."

"At least there is one advantage," added Fraser. "The barrier is unidirectional. We can't fire at them. But they can't fire at us either."

"Unless they switch it off," added the sergeant cheerfully.

This was turning into a disaster.

Arun perched atop the equipment bank he had used for cover. His armored body sank into the deep pile of spent sabots. He watched the surviving rebels shuffle slowly backward and out of sight. With no shots firing into it, the energy curtain calmed. Coils of gold and crimson snaked along its surface until settling into a standing wave. Arun stared entranced at the shimmering energy field, which was framed by a corridor blackened with scorch marks and littered with the ruined corpses of his comrades. The way the rebel bodies lay amid heaps of armor dust on the ground, pointing toward the force shield, looked as if they were abasing themselves in worship of the shield's majesty. It was a horrifically beautiful sight. Arun recorded a high fidelity static image of this view, to appreciate later if he should survive this day.

What is this? he thought. *Are the drugs exciting my sense of artistic appreciation now?*

"Get a squad south," said Thunderclaws through his voicebox. "Their armor is the BA-2-G ground assault model. I know it well. Good frontal armor. Much weaker at the back. Get behind them and take them out."

"Fraser, Beder, with me," ordered Rathanjani. "Brandt, give me your best fire team."

Before Brandt could reply, Barney flashed a new threat alert. This time from the southern approach to the control room.

It was too much for Arun. Something inside him broke.

What are those disgusting three-eyed monkeys up to now? If I could just pry those frakking cowards out of their frakking armor, I'd rip their stinking fur off. And they do stink, I know them. I hate them. I wanna kill them all. Medical alert. Come here! Let me kill the frakking… frakking… Emergency cognitive sequester… Pound them! Pound 'em! How do you like that, eh? Smash the monkey bitch vecks. Every… single… last… frakking… Sequestering NOW!

Arun was alone.

He was nowhere.

He'd been angry. Yes, that was it. Run straight into the Hardit troops and beat the life-force out of them with his bare hands.

Or had he imagined that?

If he'd been running then he should have remembered seeing the room speed by. He remembered nothing like that. Couldn't remember his fists pounding alien flesh. Couldn't recall anything except anger… and argument. With Barney?

Barney, are you there?

He was a Marine — at home in the vacuum. But this was true void.

He had no existence.

Only a memory.

He clung to that memory and held on tight. He didn't want to die.

He was Arun McEwan. If he forgot that, there was no one else to remember he had ever been. There would be nothing left to rescue.

Minutes turned to months. Years stretched and thinned to become pale decades of oblivion.

Once there had been a universe and he had lived within. Time had passed there in a way he could comprehend. Night had followed day. Cause led to effect.

Now he was cast adrift in a timelike infinity. He told stories of himself, desperate to keep his memory alive because memory was all he was. For a long time he told stories about others too, but then he realized the cold truth. Those others… he'd only dreamed them.

Relentless eons of time eroded his stories, leaving weathered husks, mere rumors of a physical existence: color, heat, life. Love.

Finally, even those last nubs of memory wore away and he drifted in the nothingness. He just *was*.

Then… a change.

Still there was nothing here. No sounds. No sights. The utter void. And yet the void was bounded in a way he could not fully describe, except that boundary was *shrinking*.

Time had no measure here. A second. A century. They were the same. But time had gained one property. Time had a direction now, and it was running backward. Effect led to cause. Day preceded night.

Time was accelerating in its backward surge.

Light returned. He was moving from darkness to light. He remembered color and searched for it, but there was none.

Then taste returned.

Oblivion was hurtling at breakneck speed and tasted of bitterness and spit.

He sped through the barrier of light and out into the physical universe.

He sucked in stale air and felt it chill his teeth as he drew it in and *breathed!*

"Corporal! It's McEwan."

"What the hell's up with him now?"

"Dunno. He just, *shuddered*."

There was movement nearby.

"Arun! Arun, can you hear me?"

Arun opened his eyes and looked through Springer's blanked visor and onto her face. Her eyes gleamed with concern. He had seen this sight before. Did that mean he was still dreaming? It had been such a *long* dream.

"Arun, it's me."

"Springer?"

"Yes. Oh, yes. You've been acting weird for about ten minutes. I thought I'd lost you for good."

"I'm sorry."

"Shhh!" Springer nudged her faceplate against Arun's to speak in private. "Del thinks your suit AI shut down your consciousness and took control. We didn't want to ask the veterans if that was possible because…" She whispered. "It wouldn't look good on your record."

Arun backed away from his comrade. "I'm sorry. I'm so sorry."

"Shut up, McEwan," snapped Madge.

"Don't be sorry," added Springer, irritated but not without sympathy. "I've forgiven you."

"I know," said Arun. "I'm not saying sorry to you, violet eyes, but to all of you. To my family, the Corps. I worry too much. You know I do. I feel too much, I can't shut out my humanity and become a combat machine. Hortez should've had my place in the Corps. LaSalle. Even Adrienne Miller or the lowest Aux. I don't deserve to carry this SA-71. I'm not a Marine."

It was only when Brandt and the veterans turned to stare at him that Arun realized he'd spoken out loud. His secrets spilling out from his gut because something had torn and he couldn't hold them in. He was overwhelmed by the emotions of love and loyalty and the sense that he had betrayed himself and everyone around him. If only he'd not given into his obsession with Xin. If only he'd loved Springer back as she deserved.

Arun sobbed. Thoughts of what should and could have been grew heavier until the burden was too great for his shoulders. He shrank into a clumsy fetal ball, cowering on the floor.

People were trying to talk to him but he couldn't understand. Someone peered into his face but he shut his eyes.

A little lucidity returned. Enough to hear what Sergeant Rathanjani was saying. "I don't care whether his mind's been sequestered. I've heard enough," said the sergeant. "Shoot this cadet. I'm sorry, Fraser. I don't know whether its cowardice in the face of the enemy or combat shock. Either way, he's a liability."

"Understood."

"I don't want that cadet dead," said Thunderclaws.

Even Arun could feel the charge of surprise explode through the room. Why would a Jotun waste time with a single, unimportant cadet?

"It's his combat meds," said Fraser, "They used to do the same to me before my implants took. I know what to do. I'll make sure he's never a problem again. Come here, brother. This won't hurt."

"Quickly!" snapped Thunderclaws. "We're wasting time."

Arun stood before his brother.

"Take off your helmet," said Fraser.

Arun did as he was told. Frakk! It was cold. He took a breath. The air tasted tainted with poisons and burned his lungs with its chill.

Meanwhile Fraser had removed his gauntlet and was sneaking his hand inside Arun's clothing until he could press his palm against Arun's bare neck.

"They told you I was your brother, didn't they?" asked Fraser, using a speaker mounted in his helmet to communicate.

Arun nodded.

"Knowing the Jotuns, they never told you I am your *twin* brother."

Did that matter at this point? wondered Arun. The question seemed to consume Arun in a recursive spiral until, when his legs buckled and he slipped out of consciousness, he barely noticed.

—— Chapter 62 ——

Arun had no clear idea of what the afterlife would be like. Some Marines claimed to have preserved religious teachings from Old Earth, but he was suspicious of anything claimed to be from the home planet. The Jotuns freely provided what they said were copies of religious texts from Earth. He was doubly suspicious of that.

Soon after he'd first witnessed an execution, Arun found himself drawn to the array of temples to be found in Detroit, curious about religion for the first time.

Now he found himself floating in a sky of gold and crimson swirls. Was this purgatory? He tried to remember his religious teachings.

The memories of those visits to the temples came easily to him. He was *thinking*… his mind spinning furiously like a freewheeling supercomputer searching for a problem to solve.

That didn't sound like purgatory. Maybe this was *bardo* — the in-between state.

Then a bright light came into being in front of his eyes. It seemed to beckon him. A destiny awaited Arun, some problem that he knew only he could solve.

He opened his eyes but immediately squeezed them shut. The light was blinding.

"And he's back."

The words used his brother's voice. The light dimmed and Arun opened his eyes cautiously.

He was still in the control room of the mining base, his feet dangling helplessly in the air and held in his brother's arms. His brother was hovering near the ceiling.

Alongside, Stopcock was cradling a captured drilling machine in his arms as if he were hugging a pet quadruped. The device looked like a miniature tank with four stubby legs and a conical drill for a head.

Arun's helmet was back on, pressure seals locked.

"Welcome back, Cadet Prong," laughed Madge.

"I think he had to come back to us because he was missing his Troggie boyfriend," suggested Del-Marie. "In any case, Corporal McEwan assures me you won't keep winking out on us. No more swooning for you, boy. You're fixed"

"Not quite," said Fraser. "You may need to ask your suit AI to remind you of orders because your short-term memory is going to be shot to crap while my nanites fix you. Other than that, you'll function fine but you won't remember a thing."

"But don't expect us to forget what you said while you were delirious," added Del-Marie.

"Or what you do next," said Madge.

Springer, Arun noticed, said nothing.

"If you've quite finished…" growled Sergeant Rathanjani, though Arun sensed amusement in his voice. "All teams ready to execute on my mark… Go!"

At ground level, the sergeant led his team in a decoy attack to the south.

Fraser counted to five and then pointed to Stopcock, who activated his drill. The cutting teeth on its nose cone whirled into a blur and a pale blue lance of light erupted from its tip, the distinctive color of a Fermi beam operating in atmosphere. At the focus point of the beam, the laws of sub-atomic physics were thrown out of the airlock. The matter in the ceiling was reduced to a squirming mess, easily gouged away by the drill teeth in a shower of trailings.

Four seconds later, the roof was breached and all the air in the room was racing to escape out into vacuum outside, trying to suck Arun out with it.

That was all Arun could remember.

———

Fraser McEwan, it transpired, had experimental augmentations. Hormonal factories had been implanted subcutaneously, intended to solve the problems with combat drugs by making them self-administered and tuned by biofeedback.

There was a secondary purpose too. Human Marines and crewmembers could go for tours of decades or even centuries without leaving their ships. Troopships were not spacious. Depression, violence and other psychoses grew commonplace as lengthy tours outstripped anything evolution had prepared humans for in terms of living together in cramped conditions. The implants aimed to upgrade the very nature of human society by allowing a direct communication of moods and simple information between individuals by touching implants to the skin of another human, and using the hormonal nano-transporters to travel into the other person's system.

This *gifting*, as the Marines called it, was new and it was experimental but it worked. Fraser's biology was close enough to his twin's that he could purge the combat drugs that were messing with his head, and replace with something far better tuned to Arun's physiology than anything that Detroit's medical staff could supply.

Fraser had been right about the side effect on his memory as Fraser's nanites battled Detroit's combat drugs.

Arun remembered nothing. He had to rely on his surviving comrades to explain the events afterward. Given the number of wounds he'd taken, Arun felt lucky to be alive, his periods of unconsciousness no cause for shame. Not his surviving comrades, though, who found Arun's progress through the battle to be a constant source of amusement. They even named the engagement after him.

To the survivors, it would forever be known as the Battle of the Swoons.

———

About the time Fraser's nanites were temporarily destroying Arun's short-term memory, the assault force that contained both McEwans was scurrying away across the roof of the base. Wide Battle Net was being jammed by the rebels, but the loss of comms affected the enemy too. The thirteen heavily armored rebels were vulnerable to being cut off from each other. Fraser exploited this, making hit and run raids, drilling through walls, and surprising the enemy detachments from behind before the slow-moving rebels could turn in their bulky armor and fight back.

Arun had a brainwave. When Force McEwan sneaked back into the building via the breach they had first cut into the wall from the outside, they had found Osman still hanging upside down. Arun removed his comrade from his suit, laying him to rest in gravity's embrace, but dragging Osman's suit with him. Corporal McEwan had a more advanced form of battlesuit, one able to switch his visor to share the view anyone in his command was seeing at the time. Even dead members of his command. They'd left Osman's body behind, but his suit AI was still on active duty, buried in an armored band across the chest of his suit.

Osman's helmet and suit AI made a perfect scout, peering around corners as they played cat and mouse games with the rebels through the maze of corridors, always trying to hit the armored rebels from their lightly armored rear.

Arun remembered none of this. His first dim recollection was of their attack on the secondary control room.

The main objective of the Hardits in their heavy armor was to keep the humans pinned down while their engineers could boot up the secondary control room and re-route power to the mass driver, recommencing the bombardment before the system defense boats blew them off the face of Antilles.

The Hardits had been only a whisker away from completion when Stopcock cut through the wall, allowing Arun, Majanita and Springer to rush through while the rest of Force McEwan was pinning down the enemy fighters tasked with defending the room.

The engineers surrendered immediately, complying without hesitation when Majanita ordered them to kneel with hands on heads.

When Corporal McEwan joined them, he began shooting the prisoners and ordered the others to do the same.

Majanita complained that this was murder, and Arun could remember Fraser's reply clearly. "Murder suggests the rule of law, but in war there are no rules, there is no law. There are only winners and losers. Murder? What authority declares one action to be acceptable in wartime and another to be murder? Such a body doesn't exist."

Majanita told Arun later that Fraser had been calm throughout the rest of the battle. But when he shot the prisoners, he was impatient, as if he didn't want to give them a chance to talk. But what could the Hardits say that Arun's brother didn't want to be heard? It made no sense.

Had Arun obeyed and shot the unarmed Hardit technicians? He didn't ask and no one offered to tell him.

———

Perhaps the events with the prisoners troubled him so much that his brain commandeered all of its limited capability to record them. He had no memory of the skirmishes and raids that followed; of the victories and casualties, he knew nothing.

It wasn't until the final firefight that an image seared across his mind so vividly that it overcame all forgetfulness.

He was running, his breath hot in his helmet, his vision fogging with the exertion. Stabbing pains jolted up his legs and into his ribs, his head. Everything hurt because Arun's body was screaming its need to shut down and die, but Arun was forcing himself beyond the limit of endurance. And all because there ahead of him, on the edge of a heap of bodies blocking the blood-slicked corridor, lay Springer.

She'd been caught in a lethal rocket blast and now she was down with her lower leg blown off. Below the knee, her suit was growing an emergency seal, simultaneously fusing shut the spray of Springer's arterial blood.

"Get back, Cadet McEwan!"

The order came from Ensign Thunderclaws.

For the first time in his life, Arun disobeyed a Jotun.

Springer was down. There wasn't time to explain to the officer why that mattered so much.

Arun blacked out.

When he came to, he found he'd only been out for three seconds. Loyal, clever Barney had kept him moving forward. Arun was now coming down into a crouch over his wounded comrade. His wheezing gasps were bubbling, leaving the taste of blood on his lips.

He checked Springer's suit integrity and requested a medical update from her suit AI. She was stable, it told him, but she couldn't take any more damage. Arun had to get her away.

That was when his fogged-up brain remembered he was in a firefight.

He glanced up at the Hardit defender who'd unleashed the volley of rocket fire. He was still standing there in his huge battle armor, being blasted at by the Marines, like a titan wreathed in fire. His rocket launchers were ruined and his armor near blasted away. But behind him two more titans were turning around, ready to launch everything they had at the humans.

Where once they had set their rockets to low yield to avoid damaging their vital equipment, now they were cornered and desperate to take as much human life as they could.

Where was his carbine?

Arun tried to remember what had happened to it but the corridor was a mess of debris and blinding flashes.

The Hardit titans had nearly turned around.

Arun picked up Springer to carry her to safety.

But after he'd lifted her only a few inches, his vision swam so furiously that he had to set her back down.

How did she get to be so heavy?

The officer's voice came loud into his helmet. "Curse you, human."

Arun looked behind at the Jotun. Thunderclaws was ten meters away, in a small group of Marines in open order. He watched as the seven-foot tall hexaped dropped his weapon and closed the gap between them in an astonishing burst of speed.

A quick bunching of six limbs and Thunderclaws was tumbling up through the air, but he'd overshot — aiming for a bruising impact against the ceiling. When the officer slammed into the roof, Arun saw that this was all part of his maneuver, two limbs pushing gracefully against the ceiling and sending the bulky armored alien down to land… directly on top of Arun!

In the moment before the Jotun thumped down on top of him, Arun got on all fours over Springer, trying to shield her with his body.

A crushing weight fell over Arun, leaving him spread-eagled over his wounded buddy.

He found he was still alive, though, still breathing because the officer had extended all six limbs, using them like pillars to support the shield that was the Jotun's body.

Hardit explosions engulfed them.

Arun felt them as a white flare that seared every molecule in his body.

He should have died. He would have, a dozen times over today, if he had been a mere human. The White Knights, or their bio-engineers, had made him something far stronger than human, but Arun could push his battered body no further.

Barney could, though.

Now that the corrupting combat drugs had largely been scoured from Arun's body, Barney could implement the standing order to keep badly wounded Marines conscious. The suit AI refused to allow Arun the easy escape of slipping into blackness.

This wasn't kindness. A conscious Marine had a higher chance of staying alive long enough for a medic to reach him.

Around him, the battle raged on.

Arun's body persisted. His visor was smeared in blood. He was crushed under the bulk of Ensign Thunderclaws, unable to move his suit. The only movement from Thunderclaws was his alien blood flowing over Arun like a crimson waterfall.

Barney tried to show him a zoomed-out tactical display but Arun's mind had been beaten up even more than his body and his thoughts shied away from the fighting.

Arun was alive and conscious, but his battle was finally over.

His comrades would have to handle the rest without him.

— PART V —

A Promise Made Good

Human Legion
INFOPEDIA

Key concepts
–The regimental system

The earliest regimental system originated in the Earth continent of Europe a development of that continent's first nation states: France and England. An English regiment of the 18th century British Army, for example, would typically have three battalions. A 1st battalion of the best men and equipment would fight overseas in the continental European wars. The 2nd battalion remained in England to defend the home country. A further depot battalion billeted at the home base would train and equip new recruits, sending a stream of replacements out to the main two battalions and possibly perform garrison duties. The depot battalion would often be little more than an administrative concept, manned by a scattering of accountants, invalided veterans, and the idle rich masquerading as officers.

When the army needed to be expanded rapidly to meet the demands of a new war, all the government needed to do was raise additional battalions for the existing regiments.

The regimental system set up for the Human Marine Corps had to cope with completely different needs.

The Human Marine Corps was mostly employed in the Eighth Frontier War, a series of fluid probes and parries by the Muryani and Amilx around lightly held, minor systems situated 10-40 light years from Tranquility.

When the depot battalion in France or England sent out replacements, they would reach the front line battalion within a few weeks. But if the two depots on the planet of Tranquility sent out similar streams of replacements to frontline battalions, the journey would be not weeks but decades. European replacements could sometimes take months chasing down their battalions in a fast-moving campaign. At modern distances of light-years, and transportation cruising speed typically half the speed of light, the problem of straggling replacements looking for their unit would make the whole depot system a joke.

So instead of sending small streams of replacements to the front, fully formed companies or battalions were sent instead. As the strength of frontline units depleted due to losses, they merged and merged again. Veterans with leadership capability were sent back to leaven the green cadet battalions with a few experienced Marines.

As for the problem of how to expand the army in the face of a crisis, the Human Marine Corps solved this by constructing reservoirs of cryogenically frozen Marines to be thawed out when needed. Indeed it has often been speculated that the only purpose of sending the Tranquility battalions to the frontier was to experiment with human military units under battlefield conditions. Any military contribution to the Eighth Frontier War was coincidental. The main purpose of Tranquility was really to breed and freeze huge armies of loyal Marines who would be thawed and retrained to the latest standards when a major war sprang up.

Detroit alone was thought by some authorities to store over four million frozen Marines, each in a cryo box designed to be shielded from cosmic rays and micrometeorites and magnetized so the boxes would clamp together.

Transport ships would have towed these boxes in their millions between the stars.

It would have been an astonishing sight, like city-sized reefs of frogspawn glittering occasionally in the dark of space.

This topic entry has mentioned the Human Marine Corps, but what about the Human Legion? At this stage in the Human Legion's development, the administrative policies for battlefield replacements are something for the future, but for our human warriors, at least, no one has suggested a better approach than that used at Tranquility.

Until someone devises a better system, it looks as if the regimental system, originating from Earth's ancient history, will spread through the galaxy for millennia to come.

——— Chapter 63 ———

As soon as Staff Sergeant Bryant strapped himself into his harness he gave a thumbs up to the camera. The shuttle eased away from the orbital elevator dock without delay. Destination: the as-yet unnamed human-Trog base under construction on Antilles.

Arun and two former Gold Squad cadets were sitting on the bench set against the opposite bulkhead. The cadets had all been wounded in the attack on Antilles, and were hitching a ride back there, back to their new posting on the moon.

Bryant took his time to size up the cadets.

"You did well, Cascella," said the NCO. "You too, Abramovski. I read how you were quite the marksman, picking off enemy leaders rallying their troops to counter-attack through the bridgehead. I expect every Marine to be an expert with the SA-71, but it takes special aptitude to be a sniper. If we weren't dumping you on this frakking moon, I'd put you in for sniper assessment. I haven't the authority to get you back to Detroit, but I've made a note on your record recommending you for assessment if you do return."

"Thank you, Staff," said Abramovski coldly. Arun had liked the pale-haired girl back in novice school. She had a big heart and warm eyes, but the instant she was in the presence of a superior, her face became as unyielding as ceramalloy.

"You keep your thanks in reserve, cadet. A sniper's role is not easy." Bryant paused. "I'll say it once more. I'm proud of you two." He didn't just say the words, he glowed with so much pleasure that enemy targeting systems would mark the shuttle out as having a hot payload.

To their credit, Arun's two new cadet squadmates – even Abramovski – glanced at him with embarrassment on their faces when Bryant proceeded to ask them about their injuries and treatment. Arun didn't exist for Bryant. The senior NCO utterly blanked him, which wounded Arun deeply. After risking his life to save Springer, having put himself in the line of fire alongside his comrades, hadn't he earned enough respect to be acknowledged as existing?

Clearly not to Bryant.

Waiting for Arun on Antilles was a place in the new Indigo Squad, formed from the survivors of Blue and Gold. Would they treat him any better?

Arun turned his head away from Bryant and set his mind back to earlier that day when the medics had let him look in on Springer. She was still in an induced coma, looking scarred but peaceful, wrapped in clear sheeting like a logistics package. He'd found it difficult to believe but they'd told him she would follow in a few weeks.

Springer would never blank him. He'd done right by his buddy.

That was good enough for him.

Frakk the rest of them.

———

An hour later, Arun was on the parade deck, looking for his place in Indigo Squad's lineup. Not an easy task, because other than electric lamps directed at the front of the deck, where the officers would stand, the only illumination was a dim bio-lume red oozing up from the floor. The *parade deck* was actually a cavern literally chewed out from under Antilles' rocky crust.

How had the Trogs managed to construct all this? Just three weeks earlier, Arun had been fighting a battle about a klick from here. The dead moon of Antilles had no plant roots, water, rotting vegetation or even weather — none of the things that would produce soil on a living planet. Under a layer of powdery dust, the moon was made of cold, hard rock. But the floors and walls looked the same as the packed soil tunnels of the Troggie nest where Arun's adventures had begun. He looked again. Perhaps the walls were a slightly grayer color, and the caverns in Tranquility hadn't had those stone columns supporting the vaulted roof. It was difficult to say in the ruddy gloom that rose from the floor, transforming a parade of human cadets into something that looked more like a demonic horde assembling in the fiery depths of hell.

But his eyes soon recalibrated for the light conditions, and he found his place in the line. Madge was now leading a new Delta Section. Zug, Del and Umarov were in that section, along with two survivors from Gold Squad: a stocky girl called Azinza Sadri, and Kolenja Abramovski whom Bryant had recommended for sniper training.

There was a space left for Springer.

He thought of Cristina and Osman. There were no spaces left for them.

"Welcome back, friend," whispered Zug as Arun pushed past.

Madge ignored Zug's infraction of speaking while on parade. "Park yourself at the end of the line, McEwan," she ordered. "And for frakk's sake, try to keep out of trouble."

By the time Arun had taken his place, the two senior figures inspecting the parade were taking theirs.

Bryant was there wearing an expression like a plasma bomb two seconds from going off. He trailed half a pace behind the commanding officer. Arun didn't blame Bryant because the new ruler of all personnel on Antilles — including Hardits and humans — was a Trog!

For a moment, his heart leaped when the insect-like creature curled his antennae in faint amusement, just like Pedro used to. It couldn't be Pedro, though. Surely not. Because this was a Trog at a different stage of their weird lifecycle.

He missed Pedro's excitable nature, his playfulness. This Trog commander was very different. For a start it was much larger, almost struggling with the weight of its body. Unlike Pedro's gleaming carapace the commander's abdomen was a barrel of blisters. Dead skin — or chitin, or whatever the big aliens were made from — sloughed off as the commander walked, leaving a scabrous trail on the floor.

The alien reared up on its hind legs and surveyed the paraded humans through eyes that were milky and red-lined where Pedro's had been gleaming black jewels.

It spoke through a voicebox device that hung loosely from its neck. "Humans need ritual," it said in that familiar approximation of human speech. "I give you a ritual of welcome. And a token of our thanks."

Something made Arun snap a glance at the ceiling, noticing that half of Indigo Squad was doing the same. He started, the roof was about to collapse, crushing the life from them. But instead of death from above came… scents! Pleasant odors. Evocative ones all mixed together in a way that made no sense at all, but were astonishingly beautiful. Taking a deep breath, and closing his eyes, the smells transported Arun to ripe topside fields bathed in golden sunshine. At the same time he imagined the rich security and comfort of warm blanket on a cold night. His blanket was shared with the spicy scent of a lover impatient for his touch.

He knew the Trogs experienced the universe through smell, but Pedro had never hinted that they could do this. Arun didn't have the words to describe what the aliens were doing, and frankly he didn't want them. The experience was magic. And magic was a treasure better experienced than explained.

All too quickly, the smells dissipated. Arun opened his eyes, and once more they were an underground assembly of 34 cadets, with Sergeant Gupta lined up beside the front rank.

"I see from your facial expressions that our gift was well received," said the Trog commander. "We are pleased. In time we will grow nest warriors of our own, but that is many years away. Until then, this moon will be garrisoned by humans. You are the first human warriors to take on that responsibility. As of this moment you are re-designated soldiers of the 1st Antilles Brigade."

Bryant's face was so pinched that it looked about to turn itself inside out.

"I am not a warrior," continued the alien, ignoring the staff sergeant's disgust. "I am not a general. I was a scribe until very recently, a role that you do not have in your Marine Corps, but means I was a seeker of understanding. I understand that human warriors need the comfort of a chain of command. Whom must they obey and who must obey them? Your colonel has agreed that I shall take the rank of captain. You humans also want everyone you meet to have sex. Therefore I designate myself male, and take the human rank-role-identification as Captain Pedro, Governor of Antilles and Great Parent of the Antilles Nest."

Arun peered intently at this Captain Pedro. *Could this really be Arun's friend reborn?*

"Colonel Little Scar has also agreed to reinforce you with another squad of cadets from your battalion. They shall be a little more experienced, being one training year ahead of you."

Arun's heart skipped a beat. Pedro loved to interfere, and knew all too well of Arun's interest in one particular cadet in the year above. It *had* to be his Pedro.

But to share a distant posting on a silvered moon… It sounded like some romantic drent out of old Earth, but if that was what Pedro was angling for, Arun wasn't convinced it would end well.

"As some may know, I learned much about humans from my friend Cadet McEwan. Now that I am a great parent, I have no time for luxury. No time for friends. Soon I shall select scribes to continue my work in exploring what it is to be human, so that we may aid each other in the future. McEwan's special role is at an end, but as token of appreciation, I have decided to let him choose which squad will join you."

You conniving little veck. Pedro had set him up. *Do I choose Xin or not? She'll hate me if I do, but… but Pedro's brought her within my reach!* The lingering effect of the Troggie scent magic teased Arun's mind with the illusion that Xin was waiting for him, just out of sight… underneath that illusory blanket.

"What is your answer?" Pedro prompted, pointing a limb at Arun.

"Thank you, sir. However, I regret to say that we have a chain of command for making decisions. I defer my choice. It is Sergeant Gupta's to make."

Pedro flicked his antennae back. His body might look different, but his gesture of anger was unchanged. "With my people, to refuse a gift dishonors the one who bestows the gift. Is this so with humans too?"

"Yes, sir."

"Then do not dishonor me! The decision is yours to make alone. If you refuse then I shall decide for you. You have 20 seconds."

Skangat! Arun guessed whom Pedro would pick. Well, he wasn't going to get his way this time. "Sir. I select Baker Company, Bolt Squad."

Pedro froze. Arun felt the insect regarded him out of those watery eyes as the silence stretched on. Why had he picked the Bolters? He knew a few cadets in the squad but none of them well. He'd always liked the unusual name, and the lightning bolt emblem. The most important thing about Bolt Squad was that Xin wasn't in it.

"Very well," said Pedro eventually. "I have noted your choice. Bolt Squad it shall be." He jigged his antennae in agitation. "To my brave human warriors of the 1st Antilles Brigade, I say again: welcome, and serve well."

The humans saluted as their new commander limped out of the parade deck.

Once Captain Pedro was out of sight, Arun thought Bryant would say his piece, but all he could manage was to glower at the cadets. He appeared at a loss for words, not exactly a state Arun associated with veteran NCOs. In the end all he could say was, "What a steaming pile of crap," before shaking his head in disbelief.

"There should be an officer handling this kind of ceremonial drent," said Bryant. "The Jotuns love parades but… Well, you can tell by their absence what they think of this Antilles garrison. This 1st Brigade nonsense. We'll continue your training as best we can. I've managed to rustle you up an orbital training environment for 48 hours, but training facilities from now on are ad hoc, make do, and only if you're lucky. Sergeant Gupta has very capable hands but they can't practice magic. Isn't that right, sergeant?"

"No such word as *can't*, staff sergeant," replied Gupta, who was standing to the left of the front line.

That won a half-smile from Bryant. "Even so, I want you back in Detroit where you belong. We have plenty of trained Marines to thaw out if we need a garrison, and a regiment of engineers to build the facilities. However, Sergeant Bissinger says we should play nice with the Trogs for now. Apparently the Trog *officer*"—the way Bryant screwed his face made it plain what he thought of Pedro's place in the chain of command— "has

specifically requested that the garrison should comprise cadets because *their minds are more flexible.*" He sniffed as if assaulted by a particularly offensive odor. "Needless to say, those are not my choice of words. Nonetheless, you are here. I do not know whether you will ever graduate as Marines or re-integrate with the rest of Charlie Company. However, I am certain of two things.

"One. You are Marine cadets and represent the Corps on this moon. You will uphold the honor of your regiment and fulfill your mission to the best of your abilities. That mission is to prevent another insurrection. There are over seventeen thousand Hardit miners on this moon. The ore shipments launched from Antilles and elsewhere in this star system are the vital pulse of the regional economy. You will ensure those deliveries continue."

The staff sergeant peered at the cadets as if searching. Then Bryant's gaze found its target: Arun!

Bryant continued. "Two. Your brothers and sisters who fell here did so with honor. With one exception, you are not to blame for being posted here. I do, however, know the one individual who deserves blame. Cadet Arun McEwan, come forward!"

Arun marched with leaden legs to stand before Bryant. He felt the pressure of all those eyes staring at his back as he snapped a salute.

"Sergeant Bissinger has forbidden me to throw you out of the Corps. You can thank your alien supporters for that." He started circling around Arun, a predator seeking a weak spot. "You could, however, quit voluntarily. Will you quit, cadet?"

"No, staff sergeant."

"Due to your overactive sense of justice, I had to send two good cadets to join the Aux for a week. They were lucky to make it back. It was you, McEwan, who put your sisters in harm's way. I ask again, will you quit?"

"No, staff sergeant."

Bryant halted, and leaned in. Arun could feel the sergeant's breath on the back of his left ear.

"Hortez!" Bryant bellowed loud enough to make Arun flinch. "LaSalle! Two good young men dead. Cause of death? The colonel's punishment after you lost your mind during a training exercise, because you weren't Marine enough to handle combat stims. Will you leave the Corps and allow someone better than you to take your place?"

Arun paused. It was getting harder to say no. He hadn't thought about Hortez for days now. That was shameful. "No, staff sergeant," he said, but he knew his voice lacked conviction.

"About face!"

Arun turned around to face his comrades. Now he could see the 34 pairs of eyes all focused on him, malevolent beams of contempt in the hellish parade deck.

"No one escapes the Cull," Bryant told the assembly. "Not even on this godforsaken moon. If the battalion is in the Cull Zone in your graduation year, then you will be considered for decimation no matter where you are stationed. Some of you in Indigo Squad were forced to fire upon your battalion brothers and sisters in the recent Cull. It was you, McEwan, who ensured our battalion was chosen to endure that grief. Their blood on your hands. You brought the shame on our regiment that pushed those cadets into the Cull Zone. Do you still believe you deserve a place amongst your brothers and sisters you see before you?"

Bryant spoke cleanly and calmly, without rancor. His words, though, were barbed and tipped with the most agonizing poison of all: the truth.

The past few months had been a hellish sequence of volley-ups and bad luck. Arun hadn't deserved much of it, but he'd been the cause all the same. Back when all this crap had kicked off, the freshly minted Cadet Arun McEwan would have looked into the faces of his brothers and sisters and caved.

The staff sergeant was waiting for Arun's reply. So too were his Indigo Squad comrades.

Now that Arun's eyes were adjusting to the hell-light, he saw the Indigo Squad faces looked supportive, not contemptuous. And he'd grown up these past weeks. No longer was he just some kid trying to fit in, he had a destiny. If there was the slightest chance that his future lay with a Human Legion fighting for freedom, then that was worth the price others had paid. And more. Far more.

"Well, McEwan? What is it to be? Do you deserve your place in their ranks?"

He'd made solemn oaths. To the Night Hummer to protect its species, and to the Culled cadets to avenge their deaths. Was his word good?

Yes, it was!

"Yes, staff sergeant. My place is with them. One day I will make you proud."

"Very well, you may return to your place."

As Arun marched back to his place, Bryant addressed the squad. "The training shuttle departs Docking Bay 2 at 16:20. McEwan?"

"Yes, staff sergeant."

"Be at Docking Bay 1 at 16:10. For this exercise, you're coming with me."

—— Chapter 64 ——

With a protesting screech of its hull, the shuttle braked suddenly. The deceleration tested the harnesses of the two armored occupants of the passenger compartment, yanking them up off the bench, trying to dash their brains against the overhead.

But the shuttle was configured as a troop carrier. The harnesses were good for far more extreme stresses, and the bulkheads had already folded out of sight before Staff Sergeant Bryant had finished shouting: "Out!"

Arun slammed the harness release and pushed away. Less than two seconds later, Arun and Bryant had deployed, SA-71 carbines at the ready, and the shuttle was already blasting away.

The shuttle had braked but not to a stop. Arun had been taught long ago that there was no such thing as being at rest in space. Everything moved in relation to something else; you had to frame an inertial reference based on what was important.

Of maximum importance right now was the target of this void deployment exercise: a signal buoy orbiting Antilles. A quick check with Barney showed the shuttle had bequeathed them a textbook 3 klicks per second velocity directed at the buoy.

So far, so good. Except the point of close void assault was to concentrate your forces to overwhelm the enemy defenses. The only way to prevail was to have enough Marines to soak up the inevitable heavy casualties as you closed.

But there was no sign of the other shuttle, which carried the remainder of Indigo Squad.

It was just Bryant and Arun.

They were alone.

Just the way Bryant must have planned it.

Arun had a split second to react. Had Bryant brought him here to murder him?

There was no other possibility.

It was him or Bryant. The first to shoot would live.

Arun told Barney to initiate emergency evasive maneuvers for five seconds that would end with his carbine with safety off and aimed at the NCO.

Nothing happened!

Bryant had locked up Arun's training suit. He couldn't move.

But Bryant could. Already, the NCO was out of sight, behind Arun.

By switching to external camera, Arun got a visual on Bryant. He expected to be staring down the barrel of a gun, but Bryant had clamped his carbine to his thigh and was pressing his thumb down on a control box in his hand.

Arun flinched. But all he felt was a popping in his ears.

"EMP bomb," explained Bryant. "Nanoscale spybots are clever little skangats, but the one downside of being so small and so simple is that they aren't strongly EMP hardened. I've blasted a 50 klick privacy sphere. God help us all if I'm wrong."

Arun had learned his lesson about speaking out to his superiors. He said nothing.

"I'm proud of you, cadet. You've repeatedly shown backbone and initiative."

"But Staff—"

Bryant cut Arun's query off with a cutting gesture. "I know. I handed your ass to you in public. Now that we're in private — hopefully — consider your ass handed back, with my compliments. Best guess is that your fun and games in Alabama spooked the Hardits so bad that they thought we'd rumbled them. They launched their rebellion before they were ready. Thousands died. If it weren't for you, that figure could have been millions. The rebels could have won — at least in the short term. In the long term, even if they'd won this system, their insurrection has probably earned extinction for their entire race. Why here and now? We still don't know."

"Which makes me think the rebellion was part of a wider operation still ongoing," said Arun.

"I agree. And that kind of instant analysis combined with the initiative and planning abilities you've demonstrated leads me to think you're a natural leader. What do you say to that?"

"Thank you, staff sergeant. But I don't think I'm cut out to be an NCO. I'm not a natural leader of people."

Bryant maneuvered to take a position facing Arun. With glare reflecting off the NCO's faceplate, Arun couldn't see his face. From the jerking of Bryant's suit, Arun had the impression he was nodding in agreement.

"Right answer," said Bryant. "Good. That's what I wanted to hear you say. You're right. Maybe with a few more years on your clock you'd make a passable lance corporal. Maybe not. I'm not talking about you being a leader of men and women, I mean a commander of combat units. Armies perhaps. Commanding a unit and leading the Marines in that unit are very different things."

"You mean… like an officer, staff sergeant?"

"I do, McEwan. Last I heard there weren't any officer vacancies for our race in the Human Marine Corps."

Bryant closed the gap between them so their helmets kissed. He spoke faceplate to faceplate. "But there *will* be in the Human Legion."

Panic flared through Arun. How the frakk did he know about the Human Legion?

"NCO privilege," explained Bryant. "You're still in a training suit and I have the override. I can do more than lock your suit's motors, I can also listen in to your words. I can only hope the Hardits' human allies didn't know how to do the same."

"You think there are human traitors too?"

"How else could they have drugged you cadets? They still are, by the way. I daren't let on that I know that. They're doing it to turn you into unquestioning robots. If Charlie Company were ordered to fire on friendly units, I don't think many could shake off the drugs enough to question that order."

"But surely they can't keep this secret indefinitely," said Arun. The conspiracies were starting to make sense. "Which means… which means they will make their move soon."

"Agreed."

"But… the Human Legion? Where do you get that name? I have never uttered those words."

"Stow the chatter, McEwan. We haven't much time. You might not have said them but you did hear them spoken once, by…" He broke off to check records. "By Cadet Phaedra Tremayne."

"Springer?"

Bryant laughed. "*Springer*. Is that what you call her? I like that. Very human." He paused, keeping the faceplates in contact. "Damn. The rest of the squad is coming. Listen, trust the colonel, your Trog friend, myself, and Sergeant Gupta. And Cadet Lee. There are a few others but best you don't know who. Hopefully the traitors aren't after us specifically, but they can kill us just as surely if we get in their way. Stay alive and keep your profile low. You have a responsibility to the future. I hope one day to serve under you in the Human Legion. *Sir.*"

Arun was too stunned to reply, but amidst that explosion of surprise, he logged the mention of Cadet Lee. Did Bryant mean Xin Lee?

Bryant moved away releasing the system lock on Arun's suit, which meant Barney suddenly carried out the emergency evasive maneuver Arun had demanded when he'd tried to shoot Bryant.

Arun wasn't ready for the sudden 5g zigzags. The universe became a fuzzy blur of violent motion. When his senses came back fully, he was half a klick away at the edge of a squad of cadets deploying in open order, and his neck was screaming in protest at the whiplash. To add to his woes, Sergeant Gupta's voice screamed at him through his helmet speaker.

"McEwan. *McEwan!* Get your sorry ass into position. Did you just black out on me? Don't tell me you blacked out."

"No, sergeant. I did not black out, sergeant." Which was close enough to the truth. Arun's world had grayed, not blacked.

"Then what the hell are you doing out of position, you useless veck?"

"Sorry, sergeant."

"Umarov is worth ten of you, McEwan. Next time you screw up, you're back with the Aux permanently and I'll thaw out another Marine from Umarov's vintage. This is your last chance."

"Thank you, sergeant."

"Don't waste my time thanking me, McEwan. Just get your ass in position and we can finally get started."

Arun grinned as he maneuvered into place. It felt good to have allies.

—— Chapter 65 ——

The next two weeks were exhausting but were the most glorious Arun had ever enjoyed. Their Detroit hab-disks had housed the ultimate luxury: Aux who would cook, clean and wash. On Antilles there was no one else to plumb in the head or clean any blockage. Sergeant Gupta demanded there should be no slippage in hygiene standards, which meant the cadets not only had to cook but clean the galley afterward. Fatigues also had to be not only clean each morning, but crease free.

None of this would be possible if not for the Trogs, whose tunneling and construction ability was miraculous. They built rectangular rooms with level floors for human usage, constructed drainage and ventilation channels and hardened conduits for power and data feeds. Their arterial corridors were broad: wide enough to take ten humans abreast, plus at least one line of the monorail system which the Trogs used to transport mounds of heavy equipment, spoil, and Trog workers.

The tunnel system already stretched for several klicks around the Hardit base Arun had fought over in the Battle of the Swoons. Given a generation or two, the entire moon would be honeycombed with their tunneling.

Best of all was the pleasure of sharing honest toil with the brothers and sisters of his unit. He wasn't sure why, but he was accepted once more as part of the unit. Perhaps it was trying to save Springer's life? He also suspected that they weren't being constantly fed combat drugs any more, though he had no way to be certain of that. Sergeant Gupta had taken Arun to one side and explained that sometimes when a group of untested Marines first comes under fire, invisible bonds are forged between the survivors that are stronger than animosities built up over the preceding years.

Springer would be back soon. She'd be able to explain what had changed.

The Trogs were everywhere but it was impossible to guess their number when all scribes and all workers looked identical. The one Trog Arun considered to be an individual was nowhere to be seen… until the day before the reinforcements from Bolt Squad were due to arrive. Arun was given an order to report to a deep level where he had never been. He guessed the summons had not come from a human.

"Didn't think you were going to see me again," Arun told his old friend who had been waiting for him. Pedro seemed to be growing into his new body. The dead 'skin' had flaked away to leave a rough carapace of mottled gray, with ridges running around his body like hoops around an ancient wooden barrel. His legs had atrophied. Arun wondered whether they would eventually drop off, a body part not required in great parents.

"This is the last time I plan for us to have a conversation," Pedro replied.

"So this is for old times' sake, eh?"

"Arun McEwan, do you recall why our first planned encounter was on that orbital platform?"

"So we couldn't be overheard."

"Correct. Orbital platforms have heavy defense against infiltration by nano spies. And now too, finally, is this area of our new moonbase. We may speak freely."

"Let me guess. You're going to tell me that the Night Hummers have spoken of Xin too. That's she's part of their prophecy."

Pedro whirled his antennae in consternation. In his old body, Arun reckoned, he'd be scampering around too.

"But you are accurate," said Pedro when he'd recovered. "How can this be so?"

"I have my sources."

"This is excellent news, if surprising. Our hopes for freedom and expansion rest on both your pairs of narrow human shoulders. If you knew this already, perhaps your shoulders are a little broader than I thought."

"Nice human metaphor, pal."

"I thank you."

"What I don't know," said Arun, "is how the purple girl fits in. Little Scar talked of a purple girl."

"I know nothing of this. I do not think Lee Xin will change her color. My guess is that this purple human is an adaptation of your species bred for camouflage on worlds rich with vegetation. Foliage on most planets is purple. I enjoy speculating with you, but this is only a guess."

Arun thought that over. Little Scar had talked of someone arriving at Tranquility soon. No point guessing, though. He'd just have to keep an eye open. "You've been a great help, Pedro," he said, knowing the old Pedro would glow with pleasure at the praise. "Really. But now you're cutting me loose. I understand that, but since I'm on my own, do you have any last advice for me?"

"Only what Sergeant Gupta tells me he has been trying to tell you all along: to keep your head down and wait for your chance."

"Is that it?"

"No."

When Pedro didn't elaborate, Arun grinned and placed a hand on Pedro's rough carapace. "I know you too well for you to confuse me, my friend. Pedro, please tell me what else you have to tell me."

"You are mistaken. Anything I have not told you is self-evident."

Arun laughed. "Have you forgotten that you regard the male human brain to be blinkered and sex-obsessed? What is self-evident that we have not yet discussed?"

"That I will aid you if I can, but I have no influence outsystem. That if you need refuge in the Tranquility system I will try to provide it here on Antilles."

"Is that truly it? Nothing more to tell me?"

"There is plenty more. However, there are things it is best you do not know. Otherwise if you were interrogated…"

"Yeah. I get it." He gently caressed Pedro's feathery antennae. Under a covering of downy hairs, they were surprisingly stiff; cracked too, like perished black plastic. He'd never ditch his Cadet Prong rep if any human saw him, but Pedro was his good friend, and communicating through touch was a human thing.

"I never did get around to touching you there," Arun said. "Does it feel nice?"

"Oh, yes. Y-e-ess." The artificial voice distorted, growing fuzzier until becoming a low rumble. It had never done that before. Then Pedro's legs buckled, giving way under him,

Arun snatched his hands away, screwing face up in disgust. "You're kidding me. That's not… I mean I didn't just…?"

When Pedro recovered, he curled his antennae and answered: "Your sex obsession continues to amuse. When I was altered to morph into a new great parent, I passed by the reproductive stages, never to reclaim them. I am incapable of what you would call sexual arousal. Your touch was merely very relaxing."

"Thank frakk for that. Well, I guess if that's all you have to say, then it's farewell, you big lunk. It was good having you as a friend."

"I have not ceased being a friend, Arun, but now I must be a secret one. The action of Ensign Thunderclaws drew a great deal of attention to you. It has been noted and questioned. I gave you the choice of your reinforcements so that you could demonstrate loyalty to your nest brothers and sisters. I do not wish to further the sense that you are special. That is why this is our last meeting. Farewell, human McEwan."

With that, Pedro turned and swam through the wall.

Arun blinked, barely believing his eyes. In his morphing body, Pedro was struggling to walk, but he swam through the chewed rock as if it were his natural element.

How the frakk did he do that?

Arun inspected the wall, remembering back to that first training exercise when the Troggie guardians had emerged through the tunnel walls. Yet they had struggled to dig him out of the hole his grenades had scooped out for him. The packed earth or rock dust Pedro had disappeared into felt powdery and glistened with slime. He thrust his hands into the wall which parted until he'd nearly pushed in up to his elbows. Then the earth hardened.

Idiot! Arun yanked his arms back, but it was too late! The soil had hardened around him. He screamed for help.

He was lucky some passing Trog workers were nearby. They came racing through the passageway, milling around in confusion when they got to Arun. He waggled his upper arms, trying to communicate that he was stuck.

They looked at the wall. They looked at the human who had summoned them. They looked at each other.

Then one rubbed its antennae over Arun's shirt, over the spot where Pedro had implanted his scent communicator.

Now the big aliens understood, flinging themselves at the wall in their eagerness to free Arun.

Arun understood too. It wasn't his human screams that had summoned the Troggie workers, it was his distress interpreted by the device, and translated into pheromones, just as Pedro's box translated the scents he communicated into human speech.

When his limbs came free, the cramps he felt in his arms were excruciating, but Arun ignored that and filled his mind with a sense of gratitude.

By the way the workers scampered around, rubbing themselves against him, the Trogs were basking in his praise.

Arun grinned. Being queen of the ants could prove pretty useful. Though he started to have doubts as he dusted himself off and went to rejoin the rest of his section, who were readying to patrol the mining area where the insurrection had started, an exercise in being seen. Five Troggie workers followed in a neat column behind Arun.

He began to wonder what Madge would say if he didn't find the pheromone that told them to clear off.

—— Chapter 66 ——

On the day Bolt Squad was due to join them in the growing Antilles tunnel complex, excitement spread through Indigo Squad like a fever. By way of welcome, the cadets constructed an item that could loosely be described as a cake.

Umarov said this was madness. Having a party with Indigo would be the last thing on the newcomers' minds. If he were in their place he'd want to rip the heads off everyone in Indigo and spit down their necks.

Umarov always complained. It was just his way. But he meant what he said because he stuck close to Arun all day, explaining that the cadet needed

protection more than anyone. He even guarded Arun when they showered after the two had spent a day showing a Marine presence at a cluster of heavy element mines, about 150 klicks east of their main base.

Although they called them *showers*, water was far too scarce to be blasted at dirty cadets. Instead they stripped off and rubbed into their bodies a warmed-up ocher goop, which looked like fine moon dust mixed in with the kind of degreasing agent used to clean machine parts. Then they used plastic scrapers to lift off the cleaner. It sounded primitive but was surprisingly effective, leaving their skin cleaner and more refreshed than the Detroit showers.

"I still don't get why you're so worried about Bolt Squad," said Arun as he scooped the cleaning slime from his calves. "You've graduated, which makes you senior to them. I know Gupta asked Madge to run the section, and we could all see a few days ago that you and Madge have finally sorted between you how that works."

"You noticed our bruises, eh?"

"The limps were kinda obvious too."

"Get to the point, McEwan. Technically I outrank all the cadets in Bolt Squad. You want to know why I don't just order them to play nice."

"Well?"

Umarov shrugged. "Enlarging the group means we need to re-establish the new pecking order, same as I did with Majanita. Can't be avoided. Fighting human nature never works. I'm just here to keep you alive, pal. The rest is up to you."

Arun walked naked through the slime-coated floor and out into the passageway followed by Umarov. Clean fatigues were waiting in the dorm chamber. Back in Detroit he would've picked fresh fatigues from the bins in the shower block. Laundry was one of life's practical details they hadn't yet perfected.

"Now you've settled in, do you ever feel like taking Madge's place?" Arun asked. "Or Brandt's? *Lance sergeant Umarov.* How does that sound to you?"

"Worse than a death sentence," growled Umarov. They entered the dorm warren, making for their section's chamber. "The First Law of Soldiering still applies today. *Never volunteer for anything.* You'll learn one day."

"But Brandt, Del and Madge — none of them volunteered," protested Arun. "They were picked as NCO tryouts."

"Maybe," Umarov admitted as they entered their chamber. They waved a greeting at Brandt, Del-Marie and Sadri, who was one of the new members of the section. "But you're forgetting the Second Law of Soldiering — never stand out. Your cadet NCOs broke the Second Law and paid the price. No offense, Lancer Del."

Del-Marie looked up from the softscreen he was studying with Brandt. "None take, Grognard."

Arun laughed. Del and Umarov had understood each other from the start. The one time Arun had tried calling Umarov *Grognard*, the carabinier had given him an icy stare of warning.

Simultaneously they all fell silent when they sensed a disturbance following Arun and Umarov through the dorm chambers.

It might be Bolt Squad.

Arun climbed into his pants and hunted for his shirt. Then he caught sight of Del and Brandt getting to their feet and face the entrance. They looked seriously pissed.

Abandoning the search for his clothes, Arun turned around, just in time to duck under a flying fist. The shoulder barge that followed knocked him to the ground.

"This is your fault, McEwan."

He looked up at Xin Lee's face.

What the hell was she doing here?

"No," he said. "No, it's nothing to do with me."

"Get to your feet," she hissed, "so I can knock you down again."

Two more cadets burst in, both female.

"You kids listen up," shouted one of the invaders. "We don't want to be here." She pointed at Arun. "He is the worst of you, but I blame you all. If you know what's best for you, keep out of our way. We run this moon now. When you're off duty, you stay in your dorm. The rest of Antilles is off limits. Understand?"

Arun and the other members of the team all looked to Brandt for leadership.

"Save your threats for someone who will listen to them," said Brandt, sounding even more pissed than Xin. "You've no right to order us around. Besides, when Cadet McEwan was ordered to select a squad to join us, he didn't pick you. He picked Bolt Squad."

"But we *are* Bolt Squad." The speaker emerged from the adjoining chamber and pushed in front of the newcomers. "Cadet Lance Corporal Lee was transferred to our squad two days ago. So was I. Care to explain why?"

Xin's arrival had been a shock, but the identity of the newcomer made Arun's eyes pop so wide they threatened to explode. Standing in front of him was Chief Instructor Nhlappo. Except she was clearly in charge of the Bolt Squad expedition. Given the stripe on her shoulder, she was now Lance Corporal Nhlappo. Here, no doubt, to give him hell.

"Answer me!" she bellowed.

"Ma'am, sorry ma'am."

"Don't give me *ma'am*, McEwan!"

"Sorry, Lance Corporal."

"So now even you understand, McEwan. You *are* to blame because you are an alien-faggot. If the colonel had punished you rather than myself, Hortez and LaSalle, then you would never have been able to stick your tongue up whatever passes for Troggie butt." She frowned at Umarov, as if trying to figure out his role. Then she shrugged. "Carry on, Bolt Squad."

"Yes, lance corporal," answered Xin and the two other Bolt Squad cadets. They were panting, eyes wild and teeth bared. Eager for a fight.

"Oh, frakk!" said Del-Marie. "They're on combat stims."

Nhlappo withdrew out of sight behind a phalanx of more Bolt Squad cadets who advanced into the chamber and spread out, hugging the room's edge.

Xin nodded. It was a signal to attack. All three of the cadets who'd first arrived leaped on Brandt, pummeling him on the ground. The others in Bolt Squad — another dozen cadets — stood at the ready, daring anyone in Indigo Squad to intervene.

Arun dared. He dodged out of the clutches of a lunging Bolt Squad sentinel, and jumped onto the bundle of bodies that had formed over Brandt. He grappled, trying to reach into the writhing mass and pull attackers off his lance sergeant. Umarov was running interference behind him.

A kick to his nose threw Arun off the writhing bodies but only for a moment. He dove back in, riding the punches and kicks to get purchase. Del-Marie and Sadri were somewhere in this confusing melee too, but the mass of limbs was too confusing to make out. Finally, Arun got a good hold of a leg and levered himself backward. The legs kicked and thrashed but he pulled the attacker off Brandt.

The attacker rolled to one side before springing to her feet. She glared at Arun. It was Xin. *Figures.*

Her beautiful dark eyes flashed danger, immobilizing Arun with horror even when those eyes were coming straight at him. He snapped out of his stupor just in time, slipping under her headbutt and throwing her over his shoulder.

She grunted when her head sent a chair spinning and she landed with a thud onto her back.

Arun took in a rapid glance of the combat. Umarov and Del-Marie were on the deck, held down under a crush of attackers. It was Brandt, Arun and Sadri against Xin and the other two. Three on three. And if combat stims really were in play, this was a fight to the death!

Xin was scrambling to get up, but Arun was already over her, pinning her down with his weight through his knees. He lifted his weight momentarily, but only to get a twisting action from his hips to maximize the power behind his fist that he launched at her pretty button nose, aiming to shatter it and drive the bone fragments into her brain.

With his fist just two inches from her nose, Arun realized what he was doing and snapped out of his combat rage. He gasped, pulling his punch. It still struck home, but was a stinging slap rather than a lethal strike from a trained 17-year-old killer.

Xin seemed to snap out of her combat state too. Her eyes snapped open, staring wide-eyed at Arun. Was she shocked at her violence? Impressed with Arun?

No, neither! Xin shook spasmodically. Her stare tracked him as he twisted off her, leaving her to her fit. Something clattered to the floor beside him. It was an electro-stunner that had fallen out of Xin's fingers. She'd been about to ram it into his gut when someone had sent a shock bolt into her. Horden's frakking children! What now?

Arun got to his feet, assuming a cautious crouch as he checked for this new threat.

Trogs were swimming through the walls, bowling over the Bolt Squad perimeter from behind. Each Trog was holding two guns that looked like modified SA-71 carbines.

There were about a dozen of Trogs. The cadets of both squads were still or writhing on the ground, shocked by stun rounds.

Blowing up the enemy was simplicity itself. But to blow someone up *slightly*, without permanent damage, was anything but. Which meant these Trogs had been armed with specifically anti-human stun rounds.

Everyone in the chamber had been shot except Arun.

He put his finger to the faint bulge in his sternum. Had his pheromone implant saved him? The Trogs waved their guns at him but seemed uncertain whether to shoot.

When the shocked humans began to recover enough to sit upright, one of the big insects brought out a voicebox and brandished the speaker about its abdomen like a trophy.

"Attention, human younglings. This is a message from your great captain commander, whom we call the great parent. Your presence here is to assist in the defense of a key imperial asset. Your selection as warriors is an honor. It is mandated that you do not render each other inoperable. The great parent's authority over all sentients on this moon is paramount. Anyone guilty of… *acting naughty*… will be… *tropied*."

Arun struggled to keep a straight face as the bewildered cadets rubbed at their heads, wondering whether they had really just heard those words. Of course, this was Pedro having fun again, inserting recordings of Arun's voice toward the end of his speech. Arun's smile vaporized. Pedro had played him for a fool, giving him the choice of reinforcements and then bringing Xin anyway. Nhlappo too. Was she in the plot with the good guys?

The artificial voice came louder now. "You will all now separate and return to your respective habitation chambers to await punishment from human commander-adults."

The groggy Bolt Squad cadets picked themselves up and shuffled away, the fight shocked out of them.

As Xin passed through the door, she stopped and glanced back at Arun.

He grinned and blew her a kiss. With his chances with her well and truly blown, he might as well act as if it were all a joke.

Arun expected her to respond with the twisting hand gesture that meant she wanted to rip his heart out and devour it.

She didn't. Instead, she winked.

She *winked!*

—— Chapter 67 ——

Del-Marie set his spoon down beside his bowl of chow-hall gruel and glared at Arun across the table. "If you don't shut your mouth, McEwan, I'm going to rip out your hamstrings and use them to sew your lips shut. Permanently."

"Just making conversation, lance corporal."

"No, McEwan. You prattling on about your illusory love affair is not conversation. It's a monologue and I'm sick of it."

But she winked! Arun kept that memory to himself as he began to puff with indignation. An age ago, when Delta Section, Blue Squad were brand new cadets, Springer and Arun's prattling had lightened the section's mood. Osman's antics had also helped to entertain the unit as they made their first step along the journey toward being Marines. Osman was dead and Springer still absent. Arun was trying to keep up the morale of his exhausted comrades. Trying to turn back the clock…

A red mist enveloped Arun. He answered with venom: "Does it offend you because it is a woman that I want for a prong-buddy? Would it be better if I talked of sharing my rack with one of the men? How about Stoney from the Bolters. He's—"

"Oh, please. You're just embarrassing yourself. You never were very good at doing anger. Love is love, Arun, in all its forms. It excites us. Thrills and teases us with the promises of paradise, but we know we risk being tumbled into the lowest form of misery when love fails. Life without love would be as cold and lifeless as the void. I like to hear other people talk of love, however they experience it. Just not you."

Arun frowned. "What's the matter, Del?" When Del-Marie started up with his poetic phrases, it meant something was seriously troubling him.

Del-Marie shook his head, disappointed. "Your prattling about Xin fills the room like a gaseous emission from your backside. It's crude and stale. We all want to ignore it but it just keeps coming until we're all choking on your emanations." The chow hall — a crude cavern with a scattering of tables — was bubbling with laughter by this point. "And yet your words are ultimately nothing more than warm gas that dissipates to leave nothing behind of any consequence."

"And the rest of you?" shouted Arun at the others as he got to his feet. "Is that what you all think? That I'm a joke?"

He searched the faces for support. Madge was laughing at him, as were the cadets from Hecht's Alpha Section. Zug looked thoughtful.

"Yes, Arun," said Del-Marie. "I speak for everyone in the section. It's been nearly four weeks since this Xin creature arrived, and you still haven't stopped talking of your undying love. On the rare occasions when you do see her, you're too tongue-tied to do more than nod and grunt, and try ineffectually to reduce your drooling. She tried to gut you with an electro-stunner, for frakk's sake!"

"That's because Nhlappo gave them all stims."

Del sighed. "The girl who loves you is due back tomorrow minus her leg. You love her too, you're just too dumb to realize because you've bewitched yourself over this Xin. Snap out of it, Arun. You're not thirteen years old anymore. Act like a man. In a little over two years, you and I could be boarding a troopship to go to war. Sooner, if you believe Umarov. I don't want to fight alongside a little boy who's too scared to talk to girls. The Bolters have their own chow hall. If you're so interested in Xin, why aren't you there?"

Ungrateful shunters, the lot of them. Arun blanked Del-Marie and sat back down, contemplating his gruel.

Zug wouldn't let Arun go. "Our real problem is that we've lost Springer, just when we need her most. She isn't just the funny one with the silly ideas and spooky violet eyes. She's the one who keeps us together. Call her our emotional hub, if you like, our squad's heart. We need our heart because so many things have happened at once. First you embarrassed the colonel and then you let us down by abandoning your Scendence team mates."

"Hey, that's not fair. I thought you'd gotten over that."

"Stow it, McEwan," said Majanita. "Zug's doing the best he can to sugar coat. Would you prefer it if I told you how it really is?"

Arun kept his mouth closed.

"Rightly or not," continued Zug, "we all felt at the time that you had let us down. I've heard rumors that we have been fed low-level combat drugs for weeks or more. Maybe that's true and influenced our reaction. Then there was the Cull."

"I know," said Arun. "Sorry, man."

"I executed a fellow human being. A nineteen-year-old girl from our own battalion. Our scores were added to hers and we didn't earn enough to keep her alive. In a very small part, we are all responsible for her death, but it was me alone who killed her. It has changed me, Arun. I can't yet explain how, but I am not the same person I was when we started this training year."

"Then the frakk-up when someone rigged the training session on *Fort Douaumont* against us," said Madge. "We still don't know why. And the

rebellion. The Aux. Osman and Cristina dying. Our posting here at some whimsy of your alien friend, which has cut us off from the training system. A lot has happened in a short space of time."

"What we're saying," added Zug, "is that we've gone through a period of transition. We can no longer pretend to live in a world where innocence is permitted."

"So, what you're saying is that… what? We've all gone through drent and I should shut the frakk up because I'm too childish?"

Zug held Arun's furious gaze for a few moments before replying. "Yes, that is what I'm saying."

"Fine! You can all go vulley yourselves. Maybe Xin is a pathetic fantasy. Yes, she's out of my league. And I do see that Springer is beautiful and loving and better than I could ever deserve or hope to find in another woman, but at least I still think of love. My body is still capable of feeling passion. Is yours, Zug? Who do you dream about at night? I hear nothing from you. I don't even know whether you prefer women or men."

"Then your powers of observation are limited," said Zug.

Arun ground his jaw. "What about you, Del-Marie? There was a time when you would be forever sneaking off to spend time with Barnard. Now that he's stuck back in Detroit, you never mention his name. Weren't you in love?"

"I loved him very much." There was a catch to Del-Marie's voice. "But he loved me a little less it seems. I do not blame you for our exile to this exhausting little moon, but like it or not, it is a fact that we have been banished. It would take great sacrifice for Barnard to wait for me. Barnard is of the opinion that one must take one's pleasures where one can, while you still can, for we could all die tomorrow."

"I thought it was only Umarov who thought like that," said Arun.

Zug tapped Arun on shoulder. "Barnard was a member of the execution squad too."

"I'm sorry, I didn't know."

"Yes, well I'm not surprised," said Del-Marie. "That's kind of my point. Anyway, as Barnard says, we have to take one's pleasures where we can. I have an attachment with Jimmy Hellenstein now."

Arun knew Big Jim from Bolt Squad. Was scared of him, to be honest. "I'm glad to hear that you're happy," said Arun. "Happ-*ier*," he corrected himself when he saw misery cloud Del-Marie's face.

That was *it!* Arun was furious with his squadmates and disgusted with himself. He abandoned his chow and stormed off.

Del called it exile, but one good thing about the Antilles posting was being at liberty to wander the fast-expanding base, and having gaps in the daily schedule to take advantage of that freedom. Arun intended to check out the new lower level but only made a few hundred meters through the winding tunnels when he came across Jimmy Hellenstein coming the other way.

"Hey," said Arun in greeting. Since the violence of their arrival, the two squads had developed a rough accommodation with each other. It wasn't friendship. Not yet.

Jimmy nodded back.

"Errm." Arun felt he needed to say something but had no idea what. He wished Springer were here. "Look, ah, Hellenstein…"

Jimmy halted in front of Arun, looming over like an instructor about to chew out a novice, studying him. Judging. Jimmy was a good six inches taller than Arun and probably about the same wider at the shoulders. Arun felt like a child in comparison.

"It's Del-Marie," said Arun. "I've just left him at our chow hall. He's had a hard time and he's feeling it today. You will look after him, won't you?"

Jimmy gave a slight nod. He looked away for a moment. He seemed to be thinking over something, was about to say something to Arun but then thought better of it. Instead he rested a hand on Arun's shoulder.

"I have a message for you from Xin," he said. "She wants you to meet her in our dorm chamber."

Jimmy leaned in slightly and spoke with menace into Arun's ear. "Xin is in my section." He tightened his grip on Arun's shoulder. "I expect *you* to look after *her*."

Arun swallowed hard. Did Jimmy's message mean what he hoped it did? Jimmy was still leering down him, his expression hardening.

"Yes," said Arun hurriedly. "Xin means a lot to me. I would never do anything to hurt her." Then he remembered that he was the reason Xin was on the moon. He added quickly: "Not on purpose."

Jimmy, gave a hard stare back. After a few seconds, he relaxed a little and nodded. "Make sure you don't." Then he sighed and seemed to loosen. "Go to her now," he added, with something approaching warmth in his voice.

Then he walked off. Arun detected no joy in his gait. He hoped Del-Marie would be okay.

As soon as Jimmy had turned the corner and was out of sight, Arun forgot about Del's troubles.

He ran to Xin.

—— Chapter 68 ——

Xin was waiting on her rack, hugging her knees and deep in contemplation.

The adjoining dorm chambers were surprisingly full of Bolters, either pumped with excitement or as lost in thought as Xin. Something was up, but all Arun cared was that the rest of Xin's section had made themselves scarce. They were close enough to privacy for Arun to screw up his courage and sit beside her, stretching an arm around her shoulder.

She looked up at him with mournful eyes. He expected her to shrug him off, but she dipped her head and leaned into his embrace, shifting until her head nestled comfortably against his shoulder.

Through the thin material of her shirt, Arun's touch electrified to the feel of her muscle and bone as her shoulder gently rose and fell with her breathing.

And so they sat in silence, huddled together on a rack in a Trog-chewed underground hole under an airless moon.

This wasn't how Arun had imagined this moment at all.

Take your pleasures where you can. Umarov would laugh at him forever if he hesitated now.

Taking a deep breath, Arun slid his hand under Xin's chin and gently lifted her, gazing into those dark eyes that had been the focus of so many dreams.

He meant to kiss her but… those eyes… they were deep wells of sadness.

Suddenly he understood. *Taking your pleasures where you could* – it had never occurred to him that *he* would be the pleasure being taken, the reason why Xin had summoned him.

He drew back. "What's wrong?"

She rubbed at his lips with her thumb, as if wiping them clean of words she did not want to hear.

"Not now," she said. "Not yet."

Then the fire of her spirit ignited. The old Xin was back, pushing him back onto the rack, kissing him all the way down.

They rolled and squeezed, pressing up against each other in a frantic melee of hair, and lips, and limbs.

But as quickly as her passion had flared, it now guttered and went out, stranding Arun in Xin's stiff embrace.

He laughed. Whenever he dreamed of making love with Xin, clothing never seemed to exist. Now that he was lying on her rack in real life, not only were they both dressed, but his feet were still encased in dusty boots.

"Sorry," he said when he noticed her following his gaze down to his footwear.

"So you should be," she replied in mock anger. She scooted down the bed and removed his boots. After a salacious glance that Arun took care to commit to long-term memory, she loosened his pants and proceeded to strip him naked.

As soon as she was done, Xin darted under the covers. Arun dove in after her and started yanking off her clothes too.

She squirmed and gasped in playful protest, any resistance only part of her fun.

When they were naked together, his fingertips traced lazy circles up the softness of her inner thigh.

That didn't get the reaction Arun was after. She went rigid.

He'd pushed too far!

But then she leaned back on folded arms and released a long, long sigh — one of tension released rather than erotic passion.

"That's it, twinkle eyes," she whispered. "Keep doing that, and never stop…"

———

"I have to go," said Arun about an hour later, with as much relish as the condemned walking to their place of execution.

Xin leaned over and looked him in the eye. "Stay."

"I can't be AWOL. Not even for you."

"Stay till the end, Arun. Hellenstein was on his way to see Del-Marie Sandure. So your unit will know. They'll understand that you should be here."

"It's not my crew who bother me. Sergeant Gupta and Corporal Majanita—"

"Will understand."

Arun sighed. "It's time. You need to explain."

Xin spent several seconds searching for the right words. She looked up at the roof, ignoring Arun. "Bolt Squad will embark on the transport shuttle leaving Docking Bay 2 at 05:30. Destination: fleet transport *Themistocles*."

"What is your role on *Themistocles*?" he said carefully, dreading the answer.

"The G-year and G-1 year companies of 8th depot battalion have been detached to form the 87th field battalion. My cadet years are already over, Arun. We've all graduated. All my life I've wanted to earn my place out in the stars as a Marine. I want to go but… only when I was ready. I was having a blast back in Detroit."

He kissed her sad eyes. "Scared?" he asked.

"A little. It's whatever threat is making them rush us out when we're not ready. No one is saying what that is, but it can't be good."

Arun gave her a nod, as if he understood what she was going through. He embraced her against his chest and held her there.

Jimmy Hellenstein and the rest of Xin's section returned soon after. They made a show of ignoring Arun and Xin.

Xin tapped Arun on the head. "Don't mind them," she said. "Will you stay with me until I embark?"

Arun nearly said she ought to be spending the time with her comrades. Then he remembered she'd been transferred because of Pedro's interference. Her friends were still back on Detroit. She knew Arun better than anyone else on this little world.

From along the dorm warren, a boisterous group of newly minted Marines launched into song.

"Of course," he said. "Let's join in the fun."

—— Chapter 69 ——

Early the next morning, Arun accompanied Xin as far as the broad transit corridor that zigzagged its way to the embarkation point for Xin and the other Bolter Marines. Waving her off at the shuttle airlock, like a distraught parent, would hardly help her settle into her new role. So he hung back at the junction, applying a gentle pressure to her shoulder.

She came to a halt, turning around but not able to meet his eyes.

Xin needed him. Arun knew that. But however hard he tried to find words that would boost her morale, everything that reached the threshold of his lips sounded too trite to speak.

Eventually it fell to Xin to squeeze his hand and break the silence. "Things happen around you, McEwan. I like that about you. And you *are* kind of cute. But there's another reason why I want to stay close to you."

"Shush!" He pressed a finger hard against her full lips. "You and I are special. You know that, right? Well, so do I."

Xin's eyes went wide. He had to stifle laughter because she looked farcical with wide eyes and his finger still on her lips.

Then she gave a curt nod of understanding. How much did she really understand? Had she too talked with the Night Hummer?

"No need for us to brag about it," he said, withdrawing his finger.

"We'll be each other's little secret," she breathed, acting the part of an impassioned secret lover. "Fate is about to separate us. But we must do everything we can to let each other know where we are. One day, I believe, we *will* be reunited. Our destinies are entwined."

Then something happened that Arun would never forget but neither could he ever explain how it came about. Maybe Xin's words were too close to revealing the truth and he needed to shut her up. Perhaps he wanted to test how much of her lover's act was rooted in truth. Whatever the reason, he found he had swept his lips against hers and she was responding and kissing him greedily. She slid one hand around his neck, resting the other on the small of his back. Arun was barely conscious of his hands, and cared less about the Marines flowing around them on their way to the shuttle; his attention was limited to the brush of her lips, the warmth of her mouth.

When, eventually, they broke, it was only to take a quarter step back so that Xin could rest her gaze in Arun's.

Arun chose to believe Xin's feelings were genuine.

They stood there in silence — for how long, even Arun's time counters couldn't tell — until they were disturbed by the rattle of an ore-laden truck coming along the hover-rail out in the main corridor. With blinking eyes (was that a tear?) Xin mournfully cast down her gaze and walked away with head high, and kitbag over her shoulder.

She didn't look back.

Arun didn't look away. Not until Xin had disappeared around a turn in the tunnel.

Sighing, he made his way back to his comrades. Keeping Xin as an impossible fantasy lover would have been so much simpler.

He shrugged, managing a grin.

Simplicity was overrated.

—— Chapter 70 ——

With over an hour to go before reveille, Arun's section should have been asleep, but when Arun slunk back into his dorm chamber, he was surprised to be greeted by a ragged cheer.

Umarov had activated his nuclear-powered snore, oblivious to the universe, but the others were drifting in a place between light slumber and quiet contemplation. Not Del-Marie, though. He looked drained of blood.

Of course. Jim had been here, to say his farewells to Del.

"How was it?" Madge asked Arun.

Arun frowned unsure of the answer himself. "Not at all what I expected," he replied. "Intense. Painful."

Madge nodded back. "Tough luck, brother. I envy you. Can you believe that?"

"I'm not sure I can, corporal."

"You only had a brief time with her, Arun, but… You've come away with a powerful memory you can treasure forever. Of all of us here, only Del can claim to have experienced anything like that."

"I hope you aren't including me in your assessment!"

Arun span around. "Springer!"

There she was, framed in the doorway. Other than a walking stick, her outline looked the same as ever. A grin split her face from ear to ear. Those wild brown curls and violet eyes gleaming from her playful face were still there, despite the burns. But the dimples when she smiled had gone.

"Hello, Arun." She swung her kit bag onto the nearest rack. "Anyone miss me?"

Arun hung back while the others mobbed Springer with high-fives. Even Del planted a lingering kiss on her head.

The others gave them space, Arun and Springer facing each other an arm's length apart.

"I crept back in so as not to wake you all," Springer said. "I should have guessed you'd still be up, discussing Xin. Nothing changes, eh?"

"Just passing the time till you came back," Arun said, feeling more awkward than he believed was possible.

She gave him a look that said she didn't believe that.

Arun tried again. "She was lonely. She just wanted someone to hold her on her last night."

"Dear Arun, there's more to it than that. They brought me in early on the same shuttle that's transferring Xin's squad to the troopship. By the look on her face, when I passed by, I could tell she was leaving something precious behind. Surprise, surprise! That turns out to be you."

There was an acidic edge to her words, but the teasing glint in her eye was vintage Springer.

It was enough.

He closed the gap, trying not to look at her burn-damaged face, and kissed her.

Her lips felt as cold as stone, and her flesh didn't move quite as it should.

He hated himself for noticing these details when all that mattered was that she was alive and back with him.

He embraced her. She should fit perfectly into the snug of his shoulder as if they were built for each other, but her stance was wooden, her weight in the wrong place.

No matter. He would hold her in his arms for as long as it took until she could feel the love that permeated his embrace reach through her injuries and touch her heart.

He wanted to let her know how sexy she was too, but… but Springer could see through any lie. She was damaged and he hadn't gotten used to that yet. But he would. They had plenty of time.

Del-Marie rescued him. "Still getting used to your new leg, Springer? I noticed you limping."

Springer drew back, winking at Arun as she did.

"I'm getting there, lance corporal," she said. She walked over to the rack she'd claimed. Del was right: she limped, the soft plastic tip of her stick going *tap… tap… tap…*

"Is that permanent?" Arun asked. "I mean the new leg."

"Yeah."

"But you can't walk properly."

"So?" She shrugged. "It's powered. My new leg works well inside armor. Better than your flesh one."

Springer sounded genuine. But that was horrendous.

She must have caught Arun's look because she asked him: "Do you remember when we were novices running through the fields near Alabama? The instructors were in our face all the frakking time, telling us what pathetic weaklings we were every step of the way?"

Arun laughed. "It was easy to believe we were hopeless. We'd be gasping but they never seemed to even break sweat. The countryside was beautiful, but I used to hate those runs."

"Good, because none of that matters now. None of us will ever run through those fields again, nor anywhere else. Not in the flesh. The next time we run will be in armor."

"No," said Arun. "The Trogs can build tunnels so quickly it scares me. Even stuck here on this moon, we'll get things settled down and have miles of tunnels to run through before breakfast. Just like the old days."

Springer swung her legs over so she could lie back on her rack. "Today was Xin's turn to go to war. I expect tomorrow it will be ours. The rest of our lives will be spent either in cryo, zero-g or combat armor. No, I don't miss my leg. Now someone turn the volume down on Umarov, 'cause I want to grab some kip while I can."

Arun moved to Umarov's rack to roll him over, but stopped when he saw Springer was already asleep.

"Do you think she's right, corporal," he asked Madge. "Will we be called up tomorrow?"

Zug laughed, a sound Arun hadn't heard for a long while. "She was speaking figuratively," he said.

"True," Madge agreed with a fleeting smile, "but to answer your question, McEwan. When was the last time Springer was wrong about anything? Now, everyone, get some sleep!"

Arun tried, but he wasn't like Umarov or Springer. The room could be shaking with the retort of field artillery, the levels above collapsing under an orbital bombardment of kinetic torpedoes, but those two would sleep right through.

But when Arun closed his eyes, his mind only filled with the rhythmic *tap… tap… tap…* of Springer's walking stick.

It sounded like a countdown.

—— Chapter 71 ——

Clang… clang… clang…

A metallic beat advanced on Arun, wrenching him out of his sleepy fog.

He'd been dreaming of Springer's walking stick again — as he had done every time he'd slept in the two weeks since she'd returned — but his brain composed itself enough to insist that this noise was real. And could be a threat. He opened his eyes – muscles firing up ready for action – but the sound was only one of the ship-rats up on the walkway, here to make final sleep checks on her crop of cryo pods.

It was a surreal sight. With the pods recessed into the floor at shoulder height, the chamber did look like a field of decapitated heads, with the ship-rats their farmers.

The cryo-drugs were adding drag to every thought, making the rats walking above Arun's head look even more otherworldly than when he had boarded *Beowulf*.

It was difficult to believe the runty ship-rats had come from the same stock of Horden's children as the Marines. With their long, slender necks — and limbs to match — they could be elves of human myth, if not for the spiky hair dyed in bright primary colors. Their childlike stature brought out a protective urge in Arun, but unlike the children on Tranquility, who were bred to be Marines, the ship-rats possessed an ethereal, exotic beauty.

Arun grinned. Ship girls were hot!

He made himself think of Xin, about two light days away on *Themistocles*. Did he still feel she was a slender bundle of cuteness? Oh, yes… but compared to the graceful ship girl — who was now close enough for him to smell her perfume of machine lubricants and cryo chemicals — Xin was as bulky as… as an elephant.

He laughed, remembering his first conversation with Pedro, when the big insect had agreed that only an idiot would compare anything to an elephant.

No, this was no good. The girl had distracted him. He should be drifting away by now.

Once again he activated the calming process embedded in his mind, and felt the endorphins surge and mix with the cryo drugs in a cascade of blissful fuzziness.

A positive mental state increased the chance of surviving the revival process. The trick was to concentrate on the good things in life, to go into cryo-sleep with your head filled with all the reasons why you wanted to wake up.

He let his mind touch on memories of his unlikely friendship with Pedro, of other friends: Zug, Springer… and Fraser, who had been promoted to lead *Beowulf*'s small Marine detachment, and had been so pleasantly surprised to meet his brother on board that his handshake had carried on for ages. Then there was Xin… Umarov too… And Osman… Hortez…

Hortez.

He felt a pang of regret — he would never know how Hortez had met his end.

A new shame scoured him, guilt at how easily he'd shrugged off Cristina's death.

No! These negative thoughts were getting dangerous. If you went into cryo with worries on your mind, you'd come out a paranoid wreck.

He directed his thoughts to once again play over Xin. When he'd gone into those Troggie tunnels, she'd been nothing more than a dream. He wasn't sure what they were to each other now, but whatever it was, it was real.

As his thoughts slowed, merging into an ocean of tranquility, he felt his jaw unclench. Xin and Hortez were the kind of loose end left after every campaign. What mattered was that as a cadet he'd had just one primary objective: to become a Marine.

Arun had done that. His first campaign had ended in victory.

Now he was going to war. Two weeks after an executive order had redesignated Xin's year as Marines, the same had happened to Arun's. Calling him a Marine was an even bigger stretch of the truth than it had been for Xin, but what mattered right now was that somewhere on this ship was a full ACE-2 battlesuit allotted specifically to him — Arun McEwan — and he couldn't wait to try it on. Of course he couldn't: he'd been bred for this.

The ship-rat had reappeared over his head, checking his details on her softscreen. Her face was creamy soft, and when she glanced at him, gifting him a flirtatious smile, her brown eyes lit with character.

His drooping eyelids narrowed on the sight of her moving on to the neighboring cryo pod, fixing an image of her beautiful hair: shades of indigo and violet that ran to bright lilac at its tips.

No! He mustn't sleep. Not yet!

Suddenly Arun was fighting the drugs that were trying to still his heart before freezing him. He was swimming up from the depths of an icy sea, desperate to break the surface before everything went black.

Who are you? he asked the girl, not sure whether he'd actually spoken the words aloud. If he made any sound at all, the girl with the purple hair showed no sign of hearing him.

He closed his eyes. The icy depths claimed him, and he was sinking into darkness.

Her voice penetrated his dark tomb. "Problem?"

"Your hair," he whispered.

"My what? My hair? What about it?"

He wrenched open one eye. She was crouching down over him, her face shimmering.

He frowned. Trying to force his fading brain processes to explain why her hair was so vital.

Ship-rat fashion was to dye hair, the more vibrant and unnatural the shade the better. This girl's hair was more natural — subtle, blended shades of… Almost like…

"Your hair… it's like Springer's eyes."

She smiled but looked confused.

"I mean," he added, every word now a life-or-death struggle. "I like the way you. Color. It."

She laughed. "Thank you," she said. "Although, actually I don't color it. It's a mutation. Listen—" she paused a moment — "you really need to stop talking, Marine… Arun McEwan. But I *will* remember you. I promise. We can chat about how you like my hair when you wake. See you in six months, Arun."

The ship-rat closed the lid, sealing him inside. With his last flickers of consciousness he finally remembered what was important about her hair. This had to be the purple girl Little Scar had spoken of. The transparent lid was frosting over, but he could still see her walking to the neighboring pod, where Umarov awaited his turn. Arun wanted to shout out but the power of speech had left him.

A yearning for the purple girl was the thought that froze in his mind as his body locked solid in stasis.

———

Elsewhere on the ship, Arun's slide into unconsciousness had not gone unnoticed.

"Is he under?"

"Sleeping like a baby, ready for freezing."

"And you're set up to give him our little present before he's frozen?"

"No need. I've already delivered my package."

"Good. I don't know what makes you so special, Arun McEwan. But I *will* find out. And once I have, I'll kill you myself."

Human Legion
INFOPEDIA

Category: Equipment - personal weapons

Text copied from predecessor Organizations

— Human Marine Corps:- Detroit Base

— Category: equipment - personal weapons

— SA-71(h) carbine

— Firing options

The SA-71(h) assault carbine is designed to be the main assault weapon for space-borne humanoid troops. The (h) sub-variant has been adapted slightly to suit human physiology and responsibility level, but the ammunition and control systems are compatible with other weapons throughout the SA-70 range.

Humanoid planetary defense forces are generally equipped with the SA-72 rifle, which has a longer barrel, higher muzzle velocity, larger caliber rounds without sabots, and no energy beam or stealth capability.

The requirement to be suitable for use by space Marines gave the weapon designers a priority for robustness, endurance, and to reduce recoil, because in zero-g combat an uncanceled recoil kick will send a firer into an uncontrollable spin.

On any given day, an SA-71(h) might be shooting back at ambushers high in the jungle canopy of a hothouse world. The very next day, the same weapon might be in the vacuum of deep space, bathed in cosmic radiation and wielded by a marine encased in a battlesuit that would be his or her sole source of air, power, and ammunition for several days. The carbine has been designed to be reliable enough to cope with any environment without question.

As a result, the SA-71(h) has enormous power endurance, ammunition flexibility, and recoil absorption.

There are three main firing modes:

1. RAILGUN.

An electrical charge is applied to superconductor rails running along the gun barrel. The rails are arranged in a helical pattern to impart spin to the round as it leaves the muzzle, thus improving accuracy. The ammunition management system supplies a round of the type selected by the firer and fits it to a sabot created on the fly from the sabot resin reservoir. The sabot ensures optimum superconductance and mechanical fit to the rails. Sabots also permit the standard kinetic round to be much smaller than the railgun caliber thus allowing ammunition cartridges to hold many more rounds.

On full power, the railgun generates enormous heat and imparts a heavy recoil force at the breech of the weapon. Providing the recoil dampening system is not overcome by sustained fully automatic fire, this energy is automatically absorbed at up to 80% efficiency, being used both to heat the reservoir of sabot resin and to recharge the weapon's power pack. In limited-gravity environments the motors in an ACE-series battlesuit can cancel most of the remaining recoil automatically. [See 'Effect of combat environment on SA-71(h) carbine performance'.]

2. BEAM WEAPON.

A phased array in the gun stock can emit lasered energy beams in the x-ray and visible bands.

The x-Ray beam drains such a huge amount of energy that the maximum firing rate possible is approximately one shot per hour. The advantage and disadvantage of the x-ray beam is that it has limited interaction with physical matter. It is best employed in massed volleys against very large targets such as capital ships, space stations, and city-sized ground targets — although the usefulness is reduced for ground-based targets protected by planetary atmosphere. An x-ray beam volley can have a devastating impact, or none at all. It is the most unpredictable of all weapons available to the Human Marine Corps.

The visible laser beam is the most common firing option for use in vacuum. Beam diffraction limits effective range to around 20 klicks, though unhardened sensors can be dazzled at much greater ranges. To maximize power effectiveness, the laser beam will operate in low-power targeting mode until the battlesuit AI detects a hit, at which point it will automatically up the power rate to maximum. In the timeframe of the human operator's worldview, this shift from targeting to lethal power is instantaneous and requires no human intervention.

3. Grenade launcher.

Specialist munitions may be slotted into the launch tube situated underneath the main barrel. Grenades are low accuracy and limited range specialist munitions powered by chemical explosive. Many Marine units are now discontinuing the grenade launcher, replacing the capability by an improved supply of specialist munitions fired through the railgun.

4. Assault cutters.

For close combat situations monofilament teeth can be extended from the end of the gun barrel. They can be rotated at 1000 rpm for maximum penetration. Care should be taken if the cutters are employed in a lateral, raking motion as the blades may snap off. As well as a melee weapon, the cutters have some limited capability to act as a general purpose drill or cutting tool, although the blades will blunt rapidly. Assault cutters are optimized for cutting through flesh; they are not suitable as an entrenching tool.

— Some information on this topic has been excluded as you have insufficient access privileges —

This infopedia section was extracted from humanlegion.com

Human Legion
INFOPEDIA

Category: Strategic context:

— FTL communications

The principle behind faster-than-light (FTL) communication is *quantum entanglement* allied with bit hybridization. Channel-linked paired particles (known as *chbits*) are split into two, but retain a ghostly connection between them that is unaffected by distance (but only when measured in the three main spatial dimensions). Although 'FTL comms' is the standard term, a better practical description would be *instantaneous* communication.

Tech specialists would decry both terms because the information transferred across the channel link is neither truly faster than lightspeed, and using the term *instantaneous* obscures the potential for this method to transmit information across entangled chbits that are separated not by distance but by time.

Whatever you call it, the key is that a tiny item of information can be passed from one particle to its entangled twin, and by using many particles, data can be transmitted along the channel in the same way as, for example, electrical pulses along a copper wire. The drawback is that in passing this information to its twin, both particles lose their entanglement.

For each particle, transmission and reception is strictly single-use only, but of course the solution is to have large blocks of entangled chbits that wear away gradually with each transmission.

However, producing entangled pairs of communication blocks is a very expensive process, and transporting one half of a block of entangled material to another star system is only possible at sub-light speeds, which can take decades. As a result, although there is no theoretical limitation, these practical considerations mean that FTL bandwidth is extremely restricted. An admiral could use FTL comms to issue orders and receive reports from a fleet 60 light years away, for example, but would not expect to receive detailed telemetry, nor remotely control combat drones.

Even the local fleet commander faces the problems of sub-light communications when maneuvering the forces at her disposal. A space battle is typically fought over an area up to a light minute across. If a targeting laser reports to its weapon system that it has a firing solution for an enemy cruiser one light minute away, what it is actually reporting is that it knows where the enemy used to be located one minute earlier. If the weapon responds by sending a lethal energy pulse at the target (taking another minute), then an enemy vessel at 0.2 lightspeed would have traveled over two million miles during the intervening two minutes.

One critical difference between FTL and conventional communications is that the equipment required by the former is so compact. There is no need for the kind of concave dishes, aerials, or power sources that might reveal the location of a transmitter to an enemy. Nor is it possible to intercept or jam the signal. A node in the quantum telegraph network could be small enough to embed inside a battlesuit, or bury deep within an unremarkable asteroid. Nonetheless, even passive FTL capable comms are detectable by patient and numerous observers. And such observers exist because at a microscopic scale, war is underway in all star systems in which minuscule spy robots from enemy powers try to evade detection and report back on the location of FTL communication nodes, amongst other intelligence.

If the FTL nodes are uncovered, an enemy might launch a raid, such as in the following scenario.

A fleet of raiders descends upon a lightly defended star system, overwhelming local military forces. This could be tens of light years behind a contested 'frontier' (there are no 'front lines' in space).

One of the first acts of the attackers is to destroy FTL communications facilities, because that immediately cuts the system off from the rest of the defending empire. Almost certainly the defenders will retain hidden assets within the defeated star system, reporting back on what the attackers are doing. These may be sentient observers but will also include nano spies dispersed throughout the star system. But if the invaders are successful in eliminating the FTL comms, any further reports will be limited to the speed of light. Given the typical distance separating inhabited systems, that means a gap of 10-20 Earth standard years during which the defending empire is completely blind.

Raiders will usually take a few months or years to plunder and refit before heading off for their next target, confident in the knowledge that any relief force from the defending empire would be decades away. History also records more imaginative uses of this blind period, such as using a raid to screen the arrival of a full invasion fleet that will use this blind period to construct battle cruisers deep inside enemy territory.

***A note on the use of gender.** The Trans-Species Union recognizes four principal genders as well as a neuter state. Gender neutral literature will use all possible pronouns in such phrases as: "An admiral will use FTL comms to issue orders to his, her, sie, ser or its fleet."

Within military organizations, language needs to be fast, concise and clear. Using all five gender pronouns every time is unthinkable. The convention developed within the Human Marine Corps, and inherited by the Human Legion, is to use the female pronouns – 'her' and 'she' — to represent gender neutrality. Most senior officers of the Jotun race are female, and this convention was adopted from them.

This infopedia section was extracted from humanlegion.com

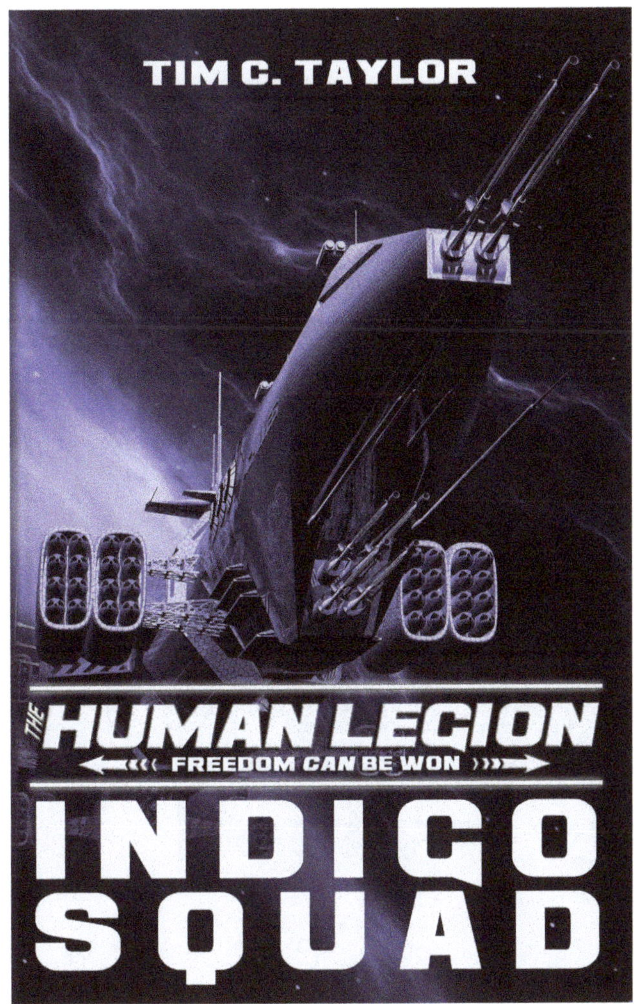

INDIGO SQUAD

…Arun grinned. The torpedoes were only a distraction, cover for the deadliest weapon in *Beowulf's* armory: its complement of human Marines. The fact that the enemy hadn't fired on the Marines meant they hadn't seen them.

Yet.

Oh, but they would do soon.

By the time they were ten minutes away, Arun was counting down the seconds before boarding, impatience adding a rasp to his breath.

He'd been bred and engineered to fight.

3,000 klicks and closing.

He couldn't wait.

Oh, but they would do soon.

By the time they were ten minutes away, Arun was counting down the seconds before boarding, impatience adding a rasp to his breath.

He'd been bred and engineered to fight.

3,000 klicks and closing.

He couldn't wait…

The story of the Human Legion continues in INDIGO SQUAD…

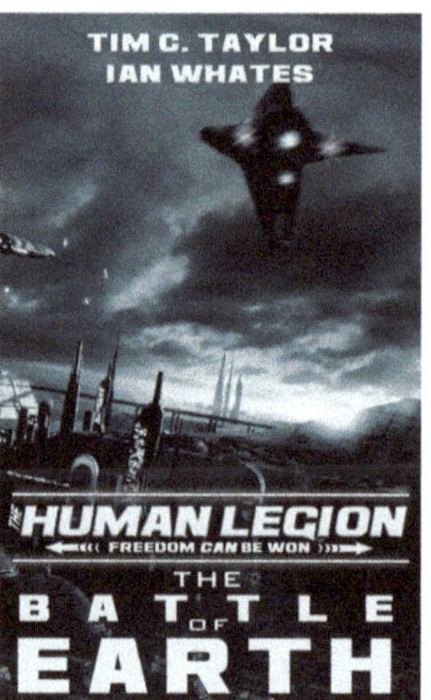

JOIN THE LEGION
HUMANLEGION.COM

THE PRESIDENT'S SON

—An exclusive Human Legion short story —

Tim C. Taylor

Alpha Depot, Tranquility-4. 2197AD

Tremmy

Oh, Simon! You're 12,000 miles up before I crash into the officers' station, and start begging the Jotun masters and mistresses to save you.

You ascend the orbital elevator another thousand miles before I stop jabbering and let my mouth drop open, because I remember that I'm in a room I'm not supposed to enter, and there are four, seven feet tall aliens baring their fangs and growling at me because they're so cross.

Cross with *me*. I'm just a girl, and not even a tall one. I almost wonder whether it was a good idea to run all the way here, but then I tell myself that I'm doing this for you, Simon.

My lips tremble and I'm so scared that I can't speak until 14,000 miles, when I blurt: "You can't let this happen. He's only an eleven-year-old boy!"

The Jotuns ignore me.

I'm glad about that. I'm only eleven myself, and that's too young to die… except it isn't. I've seen them do it – the masters I mean. I can never tell what a Jotun is going to do next. One moment they're almost caring enough to remind me of Mom and Pop on far-off Earth. Then in an instant they can turn into vicious beasts. And we humans hardly ever know why.

But, dammit, I don't want you to die, Simon. You're my best friend. Who will I talk to if you leave me?

The display the Jotuns are watching doesn't use human symbols, but I can interpret the Jotun language enough to know that the car for the orbital elevator reaches about 14,500 miles above the ground before it stops.

The hatch opens.

I can see six people inside. My heart sours when I see one of them is a Jotun. This is all official, then. The others are human children, born long ago on Earth, like me. We aren't on the same side, though. We humans need to wound each other like savage animals. Which is probably how the Jotuns like us to behave.

It takes me a while to recognize who is in the elevator because you're all wearing pressure suits. But I'm pretty sure Ling and Tomasz are there to gloat in person. Then the view zooms in to show a boy who strides to the very edge of the hatch way. I see your face, Simon Horden. Anyone else would expect you to be begging for mercy or overcome with fear, but I know you best of all. Your face looks like you've given up, just as I knew it would. For you this is almost a release.

But not for me.

"Stop it! He's just a boy!"

The mistress glances at me briefly, but the others ignore my screams, the bawling of an upset human child, of no consequence.

My cries dry up and I make myself watch the screen. You tumble through the blackness of space with such dignity. Did you jump or did you make them push you? They didn't have to attach an air tank to your suit, but I guess they want you to scream for as long as possible as you slowly descend to the ground far below. It won't be the Jotuns who gave you the air. We human children are far crueler.

How long before you burn up in the upper atmosphere? I don't know. I doubt Ling and Tomasz do either. For them it's all part of the spectacle.

We get another close up of your face. Your eyes are closed. What's going through your mind, Simon?

Are you thinking of me?

Mistress Hyndla extends one of her rubbery digits and beckons me over. I obey.

The alien finger extends and then splits and splits again, until it looks like a delicate feather. She rests her feather-hand upon my shoulder. Most kids run screaming at this point, but I know the Jotuns better than most.

Mistress is showing me kindness. She wants me to understand.

"The Cull is life's most terrible ritual," she explains in a low rumble translated into English by a box around her neck. "My child, it is also our most unavoidable. You human children are our slaves as we are slaves to the White Knights. But our masters are themselves slaves to their biology, which evolved on a planet shrouded in thick orange clouds known as flekk. Mutagens abound in this flekk, which means the clouds change everything they touch. The results are often invisible, and lead to death and disease far more than blessed improvement. The process of accelerated random mutation hasn't merely given the White Knights the strength and adaptability to dominate this region of the galaxy, it has provided the very religion that binds us. And so we too, as vassal races, must mimic the cruelness of random chance in the Cull."

"But, mistress, this Cull is false. The selection wasn't random."

The Jotun's feathery embrace hardens. Claws extend from the digit tips, ripping through my shirt and into my shoulder's flesh. "Tell me, child, on what basis was that boy selected for the Cull?"

"It's Simon Horden," I squeal. "He's President Horden's son, the most hated human on this planet."

Mistress Hyndla gives me her full attention. It's not an easy thing for me to withstand. A Jotun could crush my bones with a fraction of her strength, but I borrow some of the courage I saw on your face, Simon, and face her down.

Suddenly, her digits retract, swishing back inside her hand. I feel the blood oozing from my shoulder, but I don't care.

I can't be sure, but I think I've just saved your life.

Simon

I never expected to wake. I mean, I fell from space. You don't expect to come back from that.

Last thing I remembered, my suit had multiple integrity failures and felt hotter than the inside of an incinerator. I was about to die.

But when I tore my eyes open, even though my sight was blurry, I recognized that wide-eyed face looking down at me.

I smiled at you. For an instant, I, like, really thought I was in heaven.

"Not dead then?" you said in that cheeky little voice of yours.

I sighed. "Guess not."

You reached down to hold my hand.

And then snapped it back when I yelped in pain.

"Yeah, sorry. You're covered in burns, Simon." You suddenly went very pale and pinched in your mouth. "I wouldn't look under the sheet if I were you."

Now you mentioned it, my skin felt crusty and sticky. And I didn't look down. I'd learned to follow your advice.

We chatted for a bit, saying nothing very much of importance, but it felt nice to talk all the same.

Until *they* came and ruined it.

Ling came in first, a sneer plastered over her sly face. "Oh, look who it is!"

"Let me guess," came a hidden voice from down the passageway. Tomasz came into the infirmary with a matching sneer. "Is it an ugly bushpig with a face like a Jotun's butt? Oh! Hello, Tremmy. Didn't see you there."

I gritted my teeth and pretended to ignore our tormentors. You rolled your eyes. We all knew they only said you were ugly because you were my friend, not because you weren't pretty. I mean, has anyone ever seen a Jotun's butt beneath all that fur?

I could take a beating in silence. Hell, I was used to it by then. But when they tried to hurt you… Underneath the sheet I clenched tight fists.

Morons!

Then Ling dragged you away, and I was left alone in the infirmary with Tomasz.

He put his hands on my badly burned shoulders and pressed down hard, studying my face for any pain I might reveal. I bottled the agony inside.

"So the Cull has been postponed," he said when he finally tired of that game. "Don't think you're getting off that lightly. Your father sold us as slaves. You will *never* be allowed to forget that. At least, not as long as you live…"

Tremmy

I'm through the mountain pass, and jogging into the last prairie beyond. I'm not one of the runners in the lead pack, but I'm a safe-enough distance from the rear to get annoyed about the sticky pads for the bio–monitoring equipment. They itch but I daren't reach inside the full-bodied mesh and pull them off. That would lead to serious punishment, like pulling off a toe or something.

We're supposed to be running as fast as we can. Maximum effort. Nothing less will be acceptable. Not to the Jotuns.

I sigh and allow my feet to slow despite our instructions, because I realize what's happened. *Again.*

I take a look at the runners as they pass me. I don't see Ling, Tomasz or you.

Dirtwads!

I feel like there's gravel in my heart as I turn and run back to find you, because I know this can't possibly end well now.

I come across you in a gully, shielded from sight but not from the deadly lashing of the sun's rays.

Ling and Tomasz have enlisted the help of Serge and Randi. Jesus, but they're queuing up to take a crack at you, Simon! They've stripped you to your shorts. Your hat and protective mesh are dangled just out of reach.

You lie there and take it, not giving them the satisfaction of trying to escape the hands pinning your limbs to the hot ground.

Angry red patches bloom over your exposed skin, deepening in tone when they spread over the area still scorched from where they threw you down from space to burn up in the atmosphere.

Oh, crap. Here we go again.

I think for a moment. Do I really need to do this? Pop always used to say that bullies must be stood up to, otherwise… Then he used to mumble something about how if the American people had stood up for what was right, then Momma wouldn't have died like she had. Exactly how she died was something I knew not to ask, thinking there would be plenty of time to find out when I was older.

Wrongly, as it turned out.

They never told us how long we were frozen during the flight to this slave planet. For all I know, Pop might be long dead, dead from old age. I send him a prayer wishing good health anyway,

Can prayers cross the gap between stars? Damned if I know.

I'm close enough to you now, Simon, and the useless dumbasses still haven't seen me. I leap out of cover, swinging my pack around like a slingshot.

"Let him go!" I scream. "This isn't right!"

Ling looks up just in time for my pack to smash into her stupid face. The sound is so loud I can hear an echo coming off the rocky foothills. Boy, does that feel good!

I throw myself at Ling knowing I can't win this fight, but I can make one of the bullies regret what she's done. I punch her in the nose, and from the new angle it makes to her face, I think I've broken it.

She goes down and I know I should punch her in the same spot again and again until she stops moving, but I don't want to kill her. That's why I'm never going to win these fights. I rain down kicks and punches but it's nothing in comparison to what she deserves.

Something very hard hits the back of my head and the world goes fuzzy.

By the time I'm fully back to my senses, I'm lying next to you. My body is a mass of bruises, and they've stripped me to my shorts.

Already I can feel the sun's murderous power play over my flesh.

They're forever giving us lessons about the sun. Why you have to wear the protective gear Ling and Tomasz have stolen from us.

If you stay in the sun too long, your body doesn't work properly, you can't have babies when you're older, and you get lumps that kill you. I think

they mean cancer. My Aunt Candice died from cancer. Momma never really got over that.

This is Not Right.

I'm not like you, Simon. I can't lie here and take it. I'm seething. It's so, so, so unfair.

Then something that never ever happens except in dreams actually takes place in front of my eyes.

A Jotun screams over to us in one of those little hover platforms they use to get around outdoors. The alien orders the bullies to hand back our protective clothes.

Actually, it's even better than that. It orders them to apologize.

What does this mean?

Knowing my luck, it means I'm delirious and about to die. But I'm not so sure.

Simon

For a while I tried to atone for my father by striving for our team. I tried to win contests and impress our masters. It probably sounds hopeless – hell, it seemed hopeless at the time – but bear with me.

I'd convinced Onye and Sadri to act as flank guards in a capture-the-flag contest out in the woody, southern foothills of the Gjende Mountains. Boy, that took a lot of persuasion – but they did it. We practiced endlessly and when our time came, we made our move. Onye and Sadri's harnesses reported they had been shot dead, though really they had been no more than touched by the low-power lasers we all carried. But they had fulfilled their mission of flushing out the defenders so I could shoot them from cover. I grasped the blue-colored flag and lifted it up high. The pole was a meter long and made of hollow plastic, but its modest heft felt magnificent in my hands. Finally, I had won something!

The survivors of our Red team raised a ragged cheer that built in intensity as the realization grew that we'd actually beaten the Blues.

The teams they assigned us to were only temporary groupings, but their affiliation to our colors were not. Our colors mattered because they were based on the cities where we'd lived when we lost the lottery and had been sold as slaves.

Well, most of us had been in the lottery. The Earth authorities had taken great pains to ensure that every five-year old on Earth had an equal chance of slavery. All but one. Me. I was guaranteed a berth on the slave ships because, as the president's son, I had to be sacrificed as a token of unity. I had been Simon Horden. Now I was Slave #1, and I was different from the lottery losers.

What I hadn't reckoned with is that six waking years later, I was *still* different.

The truly horrific thing is that if I were in Dad's situation, if I were President of the International Federation and the leader of a planet caught in the devastating crossfire of alien wars, then maybe I would have done the same. I don't know for sure. It's the kind of thing where you can't be sure what you'd do unless you face it for real.

And there I was, standing with the Blue flag in my hands and wondering whether just maybe I could be accepted for who I was, not who my father had been.

Like I said, the teams were geographical, and that meant cultural and linguistic similarities too. People said things about race that they wouldn't have dared to back on Earth.

We called the Blues the Tiger Team, when we were being polite. They were mostly Japanese and Chinese as far as I could work out, which made for an awkward alliance but one that still won most contests. In Red Team we were more Trans-Atlantic, though we had a lot of Kenyans too, for some reason I couldn't figure out.

We'd never gotten our act together in Red Team. Always with the bickering and blame. But now I saw belief creep onto the faces of our team members. Could this be the start of something new – one of our teams co-operating and outthinking the Blues?

Ling strode up to me, casting a spell of silence around her that choked off the cheers.

She snatched the flag from my hand and dashed it into the dirt.

After a glare of contempt directed straight at me, she stormed away. The others followed her lead, shuffling off with heads down and avoiding eye contact.

But we had won!

Sadri moved closer. I think he was about to clap me on the shoulder or something, but he thought better of it and gave me a grimace of sympathy instead before slouching away.

I was left on my own, the symbol of my triumph lying abandoned in the mud at my feet.

It seemed no matter what I achieved, I could never escape being the president's son.

Tremmy

I'm half aware of the commotion somewhere in the girls' dorm, but if I pay attention to every beating, power play, and humiliation that goes on I'll have bags under my eyes big enough to hold a regiment of Jotuns.

I turn over in my bed, and will the disturbance away.

"Hey, Tremmy, your boyfriend's here."

I'm instantly awake.

"Weirdo."

"They're as bad as each other."

I ignore the sneering comments and the catcalls, and peer into the darkness. There's barely enough light to see Janice who's in the bed next to me trying to pretend she's asleep, but I persuade myself that I can see a figure make its way toward me.

It's you, of course.

"Simon," I snap, "you're not allowed in here."

"Kinnear snuck in last month."

"Yeah, brain box, and look what happened to him. You're taking a big risk."

"I know, I know, but I had to see you."

My heart is jumping around like a spring lamb. Are you making a dramatic gesture or are you just plain nuts? I decide I don't really care either way.

You lean in close enough for me to hear you panting. For a moment, I think you're going to kiss me. I tense, not sure if I'm ready for that. But instead you run your hand along the bed until it finds mine and squeezes my hand tightly. God, Simon, you feel so needy!

"I've been summoned to see the mistress at 05:45," you say.

"Why?"

You shrug. "Don't know. But she probably isn't inviting me for tea and biscuits. Tremmy… I came to say goodbye."

You're as tough as old boots, Simon. That's what I like about you. I've never seen you tremble but I can feel your hand shake within my grasp. I peer into your eyes, and see only infinite sadness there.

I look away. It's so dark that anything I see in your face is my imagination anyway, and I'm forever seeing things that aren't really there.

You reach over with your free hand and touch my neck. It's only for a moment, but it's the sweetest thing I've felt since they took me from my… from Earth. "Don't forget me," you say.

"I shan't. And I'm not just saying that. Don't laugh but I've got a system. I run a kind of commentary in my head, all the time."

You take your hand away and stand upright. You don't know what to say, do you? It takes an age, but you do eventually reply: "Doesn't that slow you down?"

"Since when have you ever thought of me as slow?"

You laugh. "Never!"

"Well, there's your answer. Seriously, Simon, it is a distraction at times, but that's the point. A distraction is what I need to keep me sane. My dad taught me to run a commentary after Momma died. It puts distance between me and the hell of my life." I pause, waiting for a reaction, but it's too dark for me to read you. "You think I'm nuts."

You lean in close – I can see the flash of teeth in your grin – "I do the same," you whisper. "Well, almost. I don't do the commentary thing, but I review the events of the day before I sleep."

"*Review the events of the day,*" I say in my deepest, man's voice. "Christ, Simon, you sound like your dad." I know that's a prickly subject, so I add rapidly: "And I mean that as a good thing."

"It's okay." I can hear you take a deep breath. "Good luck," you say.

"See you tomorrow," I reply. But I don't think I will.

You turn and you're quickly gobbled by the gloom.

I close my eyes and can still see you in my mind. I try to fix your image – I really do – but all I manage is a blur.

Then even that fades.

Simon, will I ever see you again?

Simon

"You are held to blame by the others," said the computer translation of Mistress Hyndla's words. "We thought your father, the President of the International Federation, insisted you were included amongst the child slave shipment to head off dissent from other humans. Were we wrong?"

"No, mistress. I believe that was my father's reasoning."

"Did you love your father?"

What kind of question was that? It was typical of the inquisitive Jotuns to extract every last drop of information from someone before discarding him as a disruptive influence. Jotuns weren't just addicted to probing for data, they had the patience of a mayfly in a hurry.

"Yes, mistress," I said just as her ear trumpets started flicking in irritation. "I loved him. And my mother. Very much."

"Excuse me one moment…"

I had to keep down a laugh and stay at respectful attention while Hyndla fiddled with some controls on her two-layered desk. I wasn't sure what was funnier, the sight of the six-limbed alien using all four arms at once, or the extreme Jotun politeness that occasionally popped out of the blue.

When she was done, she turned in her chair and asked me: "Your father, do you love him still?"

I dug inside for the answer. For four years I'd just tried to end each day as alive as I started it. The past was a hell of pain I ran from. I didn't know what to say.

"I resent him, yes…" my answer died in my throat. I still wasn't sure how I felt, but I saw mistress's ears flicker again and knew that hesitation wasn't acceptable. "I understand him. I forgive, I guess. But love? No, mistress, I cannot love my father."

I looked Mistress Hyndla in the eyes. I wasn't supposed to do that, of course, but I was starting to crack up and wasn't sure that anything I did now would change my fate.

The Jotun stared back. Her ears were still and her fangs were covered up. Her body language was saying something but I was deaf to whatever that might be. She grabbed a pair of glasses from the top tier of her desk and peered at me through them.

I couldn't stand the attention and looked away, straight in front of me with head high and shoulders back, as I had been trained.

"Mistress, may I ask a question?"

"I have asked you a difficult one," Hyndla replied. "Yes, child, of course you may ask in return."

I had to swallow an angry retort first. *Yes, of course.* This same Jotun had broken Fran's jaw for the impertinence of asking a reasonable question in the wrong manner. There was no *of course* about it.

"Why are you so interested in me?"

"Because you are significant. More than significant, you have a vital role to play."

My heart fluttered in my chest. For the first time in years I remembered what it was like to feel hope. Perhaps all the beatings and the hatred would be worth enduring after all. And, Tremmy, you'd see that I wasn't without worth, that the bruises you had earned defending me weren't wasted.

"Mistress, it is good to hear that my life is not inconsequential."

She growled, a soft yet menacing rumble in her throat. "Your life is not worthless," she said through her throat box, "but I think you misunderstand. Your language employs such weakly defined vocabulary. My Jotun dialect uses what your Earth linguists call bifurcated nouns, a superior way to capture nuance in language. What you heard as 'you' I meant as 'your likeness in the now / your pattern in time unbounded'. Your interpretation was that I meant yourself as an individual sentient. Am I correct?"

"Yes, mistress. I thought you were talking about me."

"I was not. Your life is not entirely worthless, but is nonetheless unimportant and meaningless."

The Jotun spun her ear tips around in circles. I recognized that. She was laughing at me.

"Your entire race, even your adults, seem like helpless children to us," said Hyndla. "And you, Simon Horden, are the most helpless one of all. I shall aid you. We need to test subjects to discover your physiological reaction to zero gravity. I shall reassign you tomorrow to an orbital facility where you will remain for many years. You will be largely isolated from other humans, but your beatings at their hands will cease. This is why I have summoned you. I have logged a transit plan. A shuttle leaves from Gate 4 at 07:20."

"Thank you, mistress." I opened my mouth, unable to contain my breaths that were coming so fast and strong. I'd said goodbye to you, Tremmy, but I hadn't expected to live… "Mistress, may I make a request?"

"I tire of you. Yes, but be quick."

"Please do not send me into exile. I am grateful for your mercy but if I am split from my team then I'll be separated forever. An outcast. Please let me win my place in human society in my own way."

If Hyndla had tired of me before, now I had her attention all right. Her ears pointed my way, and behind the shaggy fur-lined brow I saw her eyes narrow.

"You will fail," she said.

"Probably, mistress."

"You would rather face almost certain defeat, death most likely, than take an easier alternative?"

"Yes, mistress. It is a human weakness."

"Is it? Perhaps, but there will be times when that determination to face improbable odds will be seen as a strength. You are free to return to the contempt of your peers. Dismissed!"

I saluted and marched away, pretty convinced that I'd made the most utterly stupid call of my life.

Then an unexpected thing happened. The alien still had her translator unit on and I heard her say to herself: "They were right about these humans. Our future lies with them."

My step never faltered. Whether or not I was supposed to have overheard those words, my gut told me I must never repeat them, or it would be more than just my death on my hands.

Tremmy

Jotuns give themselves giant names. I mean, like actual giants from old Earth stories. The kind that used to battle the gods and eat villagers, that kind of thing. The aliens explained once that: *reaching into your cultural past eases your assimilation of your new role in the galaxy.*

The thing about their names comes up because Mistress Hyndla has just interrupted the report I'm giving her to tell me she thinks these Jotun names are silly.

"Hyndla is a name from an Earth story," she says. "It has no connection with who I am. I was simply assigned the next name on the list. My real name is…"

Of course, then she makes noises like someone's forced scraps of metal down her throat and now she's trying to sick them up. I don't care about her stupid name. I've got flutters in my tummy because now, after talking around in circles for ages, she's about to get to the point.

Why has she been so interested in me since that day when they pushed you out the orbital elevator? Why did they rescue us from the burning sun?

"Now you," she says.

I swallow hard. "Pardon?"

"Repeat my name."

Crap! I do my best. I growl and cough and half choke, but I wasn't really listening.

The mistress growls. It's more of a soft rumble, really, but I know to shut the hell up.

"Do not attempt to say my name again," says the Jotun through her translator box. "Your pathetic attempt was offensive. The translation of my name into English is 'Stubby Arm'. You may use that, but only when authorized"

"That's a strange name," I say. Immediately I know I've said the wrong thing because the alien growls. No mistake this time, my legs are wobbling and I want to scream.

I remember Pop taking me to Manotick Zoo when I was five. All of a sudden this huge, shaggy bear turned to us and bellowed through the bars of its cage. I was so frightened I couldn't move. I remember the shame of wetting myself in fear. I manage to hold it in this time, but it's a close run thing.

"Do not dare to toy with me." The translator box's words are calm. Mistress isn't.

"Please mistress. I don't understand. Forgive my ignorance."

Amazingly my words work. Hyndla quickly calms down. "Interesting," she says. "Your responses indicate truthfulness. I shall explain. My uppermost left limb is shorter than the other three upper limbs." Mistress stretches out all four arms. "Do you see now?"

"No, mistress. I would need to measure their length. I cannot see a difference."

"No, I believe you can't. Your eyes aren't attuned to such birth defects."

Mistress flicks her ear trumpets, which means she's really pleased. Jeez! You never know where you stand with these giants.

"You please me," says Hyndla, or dare I think of her as Stubby Arm? "I return the favor. I know you care for this boy, the Earth president's spawn, Simon Horden. Do you wish me to transfer him to another location? He could start again, anonymously."

Finally! Hyndla stops treating me like a little kid and comes out and asks for what she wants. I've been ready for her to ask something, hoping it would be this. She's already suggested to you, Simon, that you go into space, and it's not as if she can't do whatever the hell she wants whatever we say. She's not asking for our permission. I think she's experimenting on us, trying to understand how humans think.

Whatever. So long as I get my way.

"No…" I reply. "Please don't move him. And he won't ever hide behind a different name. That's not him at all. I've a better idea…"

"I'm sure you think so, but that is because you cannot bear to leave him. I was stationed in Earth orbit for more years than you have been alive. Consequently, I am an expert in the study of you humans. You love Simon Horden, don't you?"

"Love him? Like a boyfriend?" I pull a face like I've eaten sick.

I just manage to catch myself before I say something totally dumb. I can't treat her like she's my aunt or something, even if she does appear kind.

"Love?" I say again quickly before she gets impatient. I try to sound horrified. "What, you mean all that kissing and panting and stuff? No, not at all. I mean Angelique Pak does that with Kris, but she's just trying to show off and doesn't even realize she's just being like a disgusting toe louse. I don't love Simon. Don't need to for me to want to help him. I'm his friend."

"Very well." The Jotun flicked her ears as if I'd said something funny. "You may communicate your idea to me."

I do. At long last, I can tell her my plan. Well, it's not so much a plan as a hunch. A half-idea. I leave the details to mistress and concentrate on praying that it works.

It has to, Simon. It's your only chance.

Simon

Blue then amber, the emergency lights ringing the tube-shaped passageway strobed through our eyes to push our minds into breathless panic. A sub-bass rumble shook the orbital station, sending my guts into a dizzying swirl.

I retained just enough room in my head to remind myself that this crisis was fake, set up by Hardit techs on behalf of the Jotuns to test us human children. We had to run five circuits of the orbital station. Tonight's food ration credits would be distributed according to our finishing positions.

I was accepting last place, of course. If I was to eat tonight it would be through charity. What had happened to that last flicker of defiance I'd shown the Jotun mistress when I turned down her offer of exile?

Then the depressurization alert screamed into my head, expanding to occupy that last, narrow space where my thoughts had been hiding out.

I ran… panicked… Fought to get through the crush of the other children. But they were all in the same headlong stampede. The circuit ran through the bulbous chambers that formed the outer ring of the orbital station. I could see Ling and Tomasz already in the next chamber – no one would dare get in front of them – with the rest of us crammed into the curving passageway. I was still at the rear.

There was no gravity, but our boots were designed to stick to the charged walkway marked out in glowing green. I reached down to separate myself and my boots so I could float freely through the zero-gravity – sailing above the heads of the other, less imaginative, children. But we had been given strict instructions not to do that, and the awful threat of punishment overrode even my panic, bringing me to my senses enough to take stock. I looked for you, Tremmy, and found you at the front of the passageway. Instead of pushing your way in, you were looking back… at me!

What were you up to?

I heard a metallic crack loud enough to cut through all the noise. I had just enough time to wonder what on Earth this new assault on my senses could be, when the wind hit us, blowing everyone over like reeds in a howling gale.

And how it howled! Racing from behind my neck in an angry scream of protest and streaming through the hatch into the chamber beyond.

I crouched down to save my legs from snapping, praying that the force of attraction sticking my boots to the charged deck would strengthen to compensate for the emergency, and keep me attached. An unimportant nugget of information pushed to the front of my mind. That depressurization alert… It wasn't a part of the exercise.

No kidding.

Up ahead, the hatch into the next chamber sealed so quickly I never saw it move.

The wind stopped. I fell onto my face, busting my nose.

I picked myself up and glanced ahead. My pulse smoothed out a little when I saw you were still in the passageway, Tremmy. But Ling and Tomasz were on the far side of the pressure door. They'd be in hard vacuum by now, most likely. We weren't like the aliens. Our bodies hadn't been redesigned to limit the effects of decompression, but we'd all practiced the drills.

Breathe every last drop of breath out of your lungs to stop them exploding, loosen your clothing, and grab the nearest emergency pressure suit. If none were available, close your eyes and pray for rescue. You had about four minutes before you suffered permanent brain damage.

Had Ling and Tomasz followed the drill? I hadn't…

Four minutes!

That sense of a clock ticking set my legs in motion. I pulled up with my leg. My boots had adjusted to the changed circumstances and let me turn around in great clumping steps, marching back down the corridor. I counted down in my head. *Ten seconds… twenty…* Back through the chamber we'd just passed through and out into the passageway beyond. That's where the nearest airlock was located. Would it be close enough?

One minute…

I grabbed a maneuver harness and three emergency pressure suit packs from the rack, entered the airlock, and set a twenty–second delay before emergency decompression.

The suit packs are impressive bits of kit. The size of a small data pad when packed, you pull the activation strip and the suit puffs up into a bubble you step inside, arms outstretched. The smartfabric molds itself around you and seals within seconds.

By the time the airlock's outer door opened to space, my suit's pressure seal was good, my maneuver belt almost secured, and I was breathing suit air. Checking I still had a firm grip of the other two packs, I reached for the control to turn off the charge keeping my feet stuck to the airlock floor.

My hand hesitated. For the first time since the hatchway sealed Ling and Tomasz inside the depressurized chamber, I finally thought: why the hell should I save them?

I didn't have a good answer.

One minute, fifty seconds…

With them dead, my life would be a little easier. I felt a tiny sliver of guilt at that thought, but I couldn't explain why. I felt no loyalty or sense of comradeship with Ling and Tomasz. I hated them.

I don't know why but I pressed the stud, crouched down, and pushed off into space, propelled by nothing stronger than a sense of having already committed myself, of feeling foolish about backing out now.

They were probably already dead anyway.

My stomach lurched as I flew away from the bulbous orbital station – a gun platform re-commissioned as a training center. I gasped when I saw the beautiful ghost–edged planet of Tranquility hanging in silence far below my feet.

I wrenched my attention back to the station. I couldn't see Ling and Tomasz's bodies floating with me in space, but I could see that an entire panel had blown out of the chamber where they must still be.

There was no sign of the missing panel, and I began to wonder what had really happened. I had expected the jagged-edged impact hole from a meteoroid or a piece of space debris, not an entire panel removed.

Two minutes, forty-five seconds…

The panel was a mystery but it would make it easier for me to get inside.

Still floating away from the station, I directed the chest unit of my pressure suit toward the gap in the station's hull, set the maneuver belt's thruster jets to stabilize me, and fired the grappling pad.

The fluorescent rectangle of sticky material flew away, trailing strong cord behind. It stuck against the outer hull, about fifteen meters away from the missing panel. I'd missed, but was close enough.

Three minutes, ten seconds…

I reeled myself in, but realized immediately that I wasn't going to be fast enough. I set the grappling system to retract at maximum speed and was rewarded by a bruising impact when I slammed against the hull. But I held on and used the sticky pads over the suit's hands to hand-walk my way into the depressurized chamber.

Ling and Tomasz were floating like sea anemones, their boots rooted to the walkway and their bodies hanging limply. Given the angle of his lean, I guessed Tomasz's legs had snapped. I opened one of the pressure suit packs and sealed him in. He didn't stir.

Then it was Ling's turn. She was still conscious enough to glare at me. When I had sealed her and her suit was re-pressurizing she hawked up something unpleasant from her lungs. I thought she was about to say something to express her unending contempt and hatred of me, but if so she thought better of it.

No thanks came from her lips, certainly no apology. But her glare softened by degrees, and just before she passed out she gave me a curt nod.

It wasn't much, but it was much more than I was used to. I dared hope this might be the start of a new beginning.

Tremmy

"I find you interesting," says Mistress Hyndla. "Annoying but interesting. Your ability to anticipate events shows potential, and your plan to gain the spawn of Horden acceptance appears to have been successful. Yes, I think we can use you."

Use me? We've been talking across each other for ten minutes now. I still don't know why the Jotun summoned me again. Now's my chance to find out. "What do I have to do?"

"Do? Learn to keep a leash on your voice when in the presence of your betters. That would be a good start. Other than that, there is nothing you must do. It is your genetics that interest me, and your descendants who shall express your potential."

The box at the mistress's throat stops speaking. Has it broken?

The Jotun's ears fold in a little. I know what that means. *Stand to attention and keep quiet while I'm thinking.*

I wait, trembling under her gaze. I bite my lip because Jenny says it helps hold back the tears. It doesn't. Is she going to kill me? She can, you know. If they decide you've been bad… or even if you might have done something wrong, but they aren't really sure. *Bam!* There's an empty bed in the dorm for a day or two. But they soon thaw out another girl to fill the hole they've made. If Simon was standing here, he'd be head high and straight backed, but I'm not brave like Simon. Some of the ass-for-brains in the crèche think I am, but really I just rush into stuff 'cause I don't think things through.

"Remind me of your name, crechling."

"0173/921 Callista Tremayne, mistress."

"Why do you tremble so, Tremayne?"

I think on my feet. I can do that, you know. You don't get to reach eleven without quick thinking. Truth is that I'm terrified. But I've heard we're supposed to be turned into soldiers one day, to fight wars on behalf of our masters. I suppose even soldiers get scared, but I don't want to admit my terror to this Jotun, so I take a snippet of truth and build upon that.

"You said my descendants might serve you."

"I did. Explain the significance of your statement."

"Well, it's just *descendants*…. I know what that word means. It means babies, and babies mean kissing and… stuff."

Honestly? I'm not sure what making babies involves, though I'm sure it's not what Jenny Pak says, because that's too disgusting to be true. I pull a face. It's not difficult. It's the same expression I have nearly every chowtime when they feed us that stinking spew that makes our guts boil.

The Jotun jiggles her ears in circles. I think that means she either likes me or is about to kill me.

"You humans. Always in such a rush. But that, I suspect, is why you will be so important. You may go, Tremayne."

I salute, about turn, and flee.

I've only gone past the first turn in the passageway, when I have to stop. I'm bent over, hands on thighs, because I'm laughing so much. I don't know why, but I can't help it.

"You are very important," I say in my most serious Jotun impersonation. "You will have many babies."

The smile falls from my face and I swallow hard. Jenny Pak says many things. Mostly she talks out of her butt, but she says they can hear you anywhere in the base, and they're always listening. She might be right about that one.

I hurry back to the dorms, trying to forget all the weird stuff that's happened this past half hour. There's only one thing on my mind right now. I want to see you, Simon. Because for the first time since they brought us to this planet, I think you're going to be a survivor.

FALLEN WITNESS

—Vision V: England Expects—

Art: Andy Bigwood
Words: Tim C. Taylor

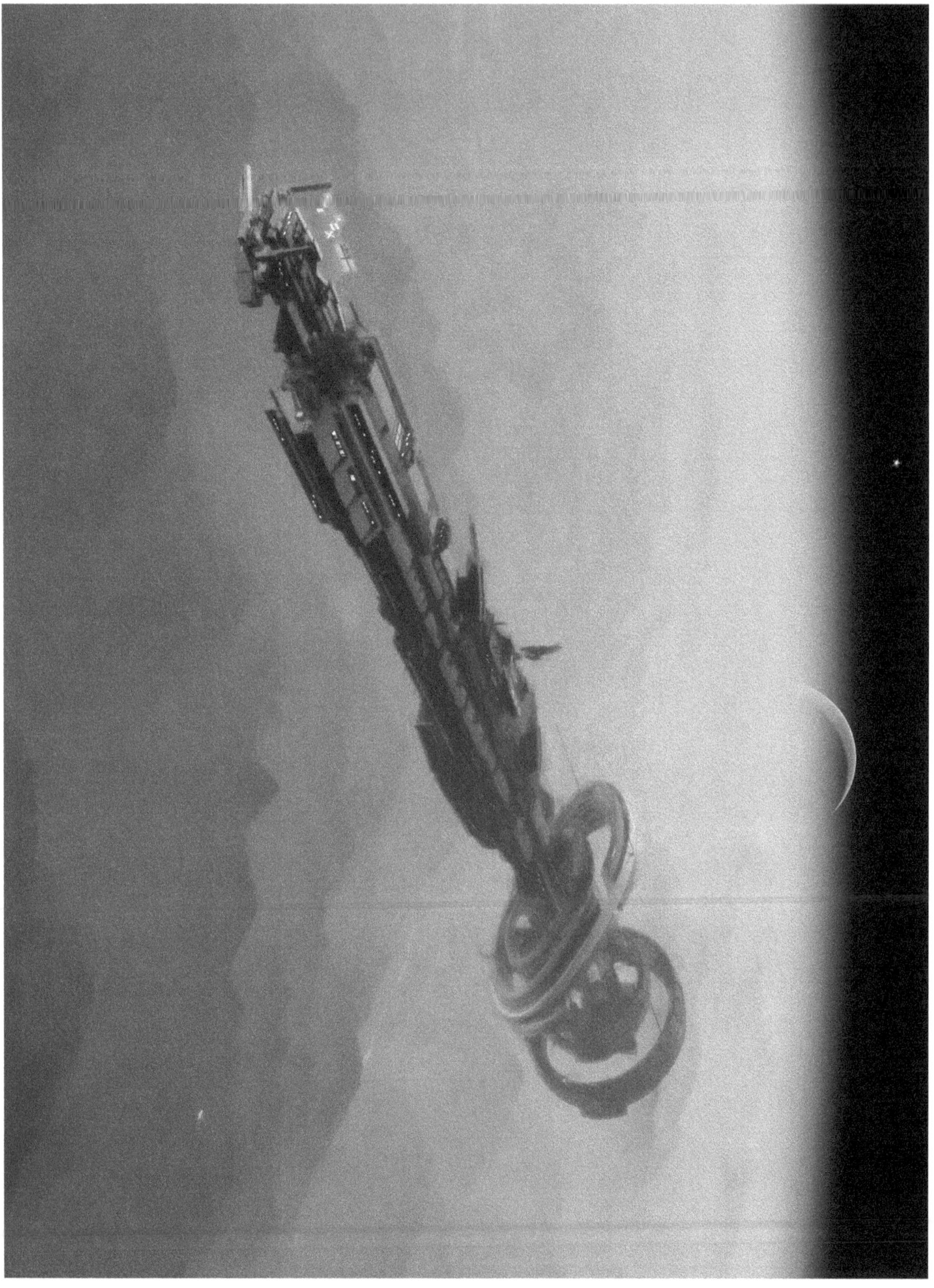

By now the children in the future lesson know what to expect. When a fifth fallen witness appears in a new cylinder of light, introducing himself as Leading Spacer Flint MacDonald, their attention is not on the android wearing military clothing, but on the image he holds above his head. It is a Warspite-class ship, but what are those markings on the prow?

"Throughout history there are examples of symbols carried by soldiers going into battle," explains MacDonald, "reminders of why they fight and symbols that help them to believe they can win. This may be a sacred gold idol, a stirring song sung by their forefathers, or a religious relic. Did you know that the English Army used to go into battle carrying the boiled bones of their great king, Edward the First? I'm serious, although not about the part of him being great. We Scots, and the Welsh too, had other words than 'great' to describe King Edward."

MacDonald let his little stab of humor relax his audience before carrying on. "In the early days of the navy, before radio and microwave beams, ships communicated with each other using flags. The glowing squares you see on the prow of the ship are these communication flags, and behind them the rectangular flag is the Royal Ensign that ships of the British Nations still use today. Sailors had stopped using the flag symbols for many centuries, but every man and woman in the British Squadron knew that particular set of flags, because it had been carried into a great battle in the time of sail. The first two trios of flag symbols cycled endlessly through codes 253 and 269: *England expects… England expects… England expects…*

"That message harked back to the greatest moment in the history of the Royal Navy until that point. Far back in time to the year by the old Common Era calendar of 1805, when Admiral Lord Nelson won a great naval battle."

The dry facts are rolling along the beams of the children's minds like the interstellar medium parted by a starship's magnetic field generator. No matter, it was all part of the setup, the choreography of the lesson.

"The name of this great historical victory?" MacDonald asks with a grin. "The Battle of Trafalgar."

The children sit open jawed and goggle eyed. MacDonald is glad he gets the best talk of the display. He doesn't want to explain the next image. The memories are too painful.

Fallen Witness Vision VI is on p469

SITREP

—The state of British Military SF —

Tim C. Taylor

The New Wave of British Military SF

At the beginning of December 2015, if you Googled for 'British Military SF' (and variants such as 'British military science fiction') you would have returned a mere handful of pages. Some referred to the authors in *The Empire at War* collection, but you would also find references to a press release announcing star British military SF author, Karen Traviss, taking on the GI Joe franchise.

And that's it.

Take out the 'British' and you would have returned nearly 20 million pages. Which only goes to prove the common wisdom about British military SF: that it doesn't really exist. Case in point: Karen Traviss is a *New York Times* bestselling author of many successful military science fiction novels. She just happens to be British, but she isn't part of a British military SF scene, because there isn't one. It isn't like space opera where commentators talked a decade ago of a New British Space Opera movement, featuring authors such as Peter F. Hamilton, Justina Robson, Alastair Reynolds and Iain M. Banks. And that's not surprising, because military SF is really an American thing, and if British writers indulge in writing such books then they are simply lured by filthy lucre to ape Americans.

Dig a little deeper and you'd come up with Warhammer 40K, the tabletop miniatures game from Games Workshop that has spawned over 350 spin-off novels. But they are just game tie-in books. Not proper novels.

Even now, this remains the conventional wisdom regarding British military science fiction.

Except it isn't true. There *is* a movement of new British military SF. It's emerging right now, and *The Empire at War* is a small sample of what this literary movement is producing.

In fact, that's why we created this collection. We wanted to mark the birth of this movement.

And the idea that the Brits didn't do military SF was never true, as we'll see shortly, but it was almost accurate to say as recently as 2010 that outside of Warhammer 40K, successful British military SF authors were either writing for American franchises (such as *Halo* or *Star Trek),* or they were space opera writers (notably Peter F. Hamilton) edging their novels with military themes, but not going as far as to bring war and the people who fight in those wars into the center stage.

That's not true now.

Things have changed because the world of science fiction books has evolved into new shapes over the last five years. It's the biggest change since at least the introduction of the paperback in the 1950s.

In short, we've just lived through the Revolution, and the New Wave of British military SF has been at the heart of this upheaval. The two are closely entwined. Consequently, some readers will be relieved to learn that this essay is about more than endless cups of tea, stiff upper lips, and beer served cool rather than cold, because in order to appreciate the state of British science fiction, we must first understand the Revolution that has swept through all of English language SF.

Freedom in the Galaxy! The Science Fiction Revolution

The Revolution erupted along two fronts.

Firstly, the Amazon Kindle eReader device transformed English language publishing. It wasn't the first eReader device, nor was its introduction the first substantial success of digital books (that honor belongs to Baen Books), but the introduction of the Kindle changed everything, and did so on an 'Internet' timescale of just a few years.

Every area of fiction publishing has changed but each has changed in different ways. The most profound changes have come to romance, erotica (without the Kindle you would never have heard of *50 Shades of Grey)* and science fiction. And here I draw a distinction between science fiction and fantasy, which was less impacted for reasons we'll soon see.

To understand why this change happened, we need to factor in self-publishing. A decade ago, self-publishing was what you resorted to when a proper publisher wouldn't publish you. Self-published paperbacks had lower production quality and higher prices than those published by mainstream presses.

Why would anyone pay more money to buy a novel from someone they had never heard of, when they could pay less to read a higher quality book from a top author in their genre?

The answer was, of course, that people didn't. The only possible route to even very modest sales was to be an excellent salesperson and go out and sell your book every weekend.

Amazon changed all that by allowing anyone to publish their books to the Kindle Store, at lower retail prices than traditional publishers, but at generous royalty rates unheard of in traditional publishing.

By 2010, a significant number of science fiction writers were self-publishing directly with Amazon (and with other retailers too). But these writers were different. Not only did the authors tend to be without traditional publishing contracts (and so 'new' to the reading public), but also they tended to write the books they wanted to read, rather than the books that they thought could be pitched successfully to a literary agent.

Science fiction readers loved it. Pioneers such as B.V. Larson were massive hits, and news that these early stars were reaching six-figure unit sales numbers encouraged more authors to follow. Choice and quality rose rapidly, and soon the idea of these new science fiction authors exceeding 100,000 sales ceased to be news. The star authors were racing for the million-selling label, and some, often aided by selling some rights to traditional publishers, have reached that milestone and are powering on to their second or even third million.

And with the huge sales numbers comes breadth and diversity of writers and topics. For example, in the LGBT category on amazon.com there are now twice as many books in Kindle format as there are in paperback. That's 22,000 books that would not have been published and probably never written if not for Amazon. In today's world, if there's a niche for a particular topic, someone will write and publish it. There are no publishers, agents or book stores with the power to create barriers to protagonists, authors or cover artwork on the basis of race, gender, or anything else. If there's an audience, anyone can write and publish to that audience, and Amazon's search tools give that audience a fighting chance of discovering any book. Take *MARINE (Agent of Time),* for example from Scottish self-publishing author Tanya Allan. As far as I know, this was the first novel to be published about a transgender space marine. It hasn't been the last, and if you read its reviews, it has clearly been discovered by an appreciative audience.

For the second cause of the Revolution, we have to step back from science fiction books and see the much larger universe of science fiction.

Back in the 1950s, fans of science fiction could enjoy occasional movies, and a few shows on radio and TV, but most of the time fans primarily enjoyed short stories and novels.

The world of 2015 is very different. As someone who earns a living writing science fiction novels, it's a little hard for me to say this, but books had become almost a forgotten backwater of science fiction, barely noticed by the vast legions of science fiction addicts who, in addition to science fiction movies and TV, enjoy tabletop games, miniatures painting, role playing games, cosplay, video games and other science fictional pursuits. You only have to look at the huge attendance figures for gaming conventions in the US and UK and compare with the far less popular flagships of the old science fiction literary world, such as Worldcon (running since 1939) and the UK's Eastercon (running since 1948), to see that the majority of people enjoying science fiction are not doing so through books.

That's not to say that the old science fiction literary establishment is irrelevant. In fact, it's the beating heart of science fiction, pumping invigorating life-force into gaming and movies and all the rest, even though most of the time this vital function is hidden away out of sight of the majority of science fiction fans.

Nonetheless, it is this huge army of science fiction fans for whom books were not hitherto a major interest, who are now being tempted by the new wave of digital books. Not only is the digital nature convenient for storage and always-to-hand availability, but in many cases the novels produced by the authors of the Revolution are closer to the kinds of science fiction stories these new SF fans immerse themselves into in their science fiction and fantasy gaming.

This talk of a Revolution is all very well, but where is the evidence that these changes are happening at a significant level?

The answer lies once again with Amazon. Like a literary voyeur's dream, for many years, Amazon has been making public its top-100 bestseller lists and overall sales ranks in the Kindle Store. Who sold the most books last year, Robert A. Heinlein or Isaac Asimov? We can't tell the answer because we don't have figures for individual author sales *outside* of Amazon, but if anyone cared to track the sales rankings, they could certainly tell who sold the most *on Amazon*. Given that amazon.com is the most important literary sales channel in the English language world, if you're not selling well on Amazon, you probably aren't selling well elsewhere. (There are exceptions, such as Baen Books and Black Library, significant publishers of military SF who both have highly successful direct sales channels).

Not only can you look at sales ranks to determine relative sales, but if you've been a bestseller yourself a few times, or pay attention to bestsellers who talk about their sales figures, then you can convert sales rank to the number of books sold.

Here's how that works.

So far, I've had three books settle in for a period ranked just outside the top 100 books in the Kindle Store on amazon.com. I've published two titles that ranked #1 in military SF. That's not enough to make me any kind of a star author, but it is plenty enough to unlock the code of Amazon's sales rank and convert to sales numbers, especially when I talk to other bestselling authors and calibrate our numbers.

For example, my title in this collection, *Marine Cadet*, spent ten days in January 2015 at #1 in military SF and space opera, and ranked at around #130 overall in the amazon.com Kindle Store. Sales were steady at around 700 per day. The book that knocked me off the #1 spot was the excellent *Warship* by Joshua Dalzelle. A few weeks later, *Warship* was still around #130 in the store. As a rough estimate, it's reasonable to assume that Joshua's book was also selling around 700 per day.

With my first two titles in the Human Legion series at the top two positions in the military SF bestseller chart, you will perhaps understand why I was looking at these charts several times a day throughout January. After having noted with pride every time my titles rose up the charts to reach the positions of my favorite authors and most beloved titles from the traditional world of publishing, I noticed something strange. The titles in the upper reaches of the space opera and military SF bestseller charts were either self-published or published by Amazon's own imprint, 47 North.

I can't talk about the first three days of January 2015 (because I wasn't yet checking the entire bestseller chart), but for the rest of that month, in the amazon.com Kindle Store only a single title by a traditional publisher managed to break into the top-40 bestseller lists in the categories of military SF or space opera. (The movie tie-in edition of *Ender's Game* by Orson Scott Card).

By mid-January I was looking at the sales ranks for the bestseller lists and estimating the total daily sales. I did this for the top-20 space opera and military SF book charts (Amazon *book chart* counts sales of paperbacks, hardbacks, eBooks and audio books). Taking care to remove duplicate titles on both charts, I estimated total sales for those top-20 charts for the whole of January, and by multiplying by twelve arrived at a crude annual figure. From that total, I stripped out sales from everyone other than self-publishers and 47 North to arrive at a figure for the bestselling books from these new publishers in science fiction who didn't exist as more than a minor rounding error five years earlier.

All sales figures to do with publishing are flawed, other than in authors' royalty reports (we hope). At least I have never pretended that my estimate for bestselling 47 North + self-published titles in military SF and space opera was more than a very rough ballpark.

Another deeply flawed sales figure is the annual estimate for US book sales by genre published in Publishers Weekly. The 2014 figure for adult science fiction books was 4.1 million.

My estimate for 47 North + self-published top-20 bestsellers in space opera and military SF was 5 million.

The overlap between both numbers was practically zero, by which I mean the sale of any given book would either be included in my estimate or the Publishers Weekly estimate, but not both.

Both figures are inaccurate, and if we could ever discover the true 2014 sales of 47 North/ self-published versus everyone else, then we would discover that both are significant underestimates of 'their' category of book. Nonetheless, I consider this to be a useful snapshot of science fiction publishing. Whether self- and 47 North-published books now represent the majority of science fiction sales is something these estimates are too crude to tell us. What they do illustrate is that the two sides of science fiction publishing, the old and the new, are broadly equivalent in terms of sales volume.

Approximate parity sounds a little weak for something I've described as the *Revolution*, but here's the kicker.

In 2014, probably the three science fiction authors contributing the most sales to traditional publishers were A.G. Riddle, Andy Weir, and Hugh Howey. If you read their comments on sales, and those from their publishers and agents, then it looks as if they made around 1½ -2 million sales in 2014. And the connection between the three is that their bestselling books originally became bestsellers through Kindle self-publishing.

There is an accelerating trend of publishers using the Amazon bestseller lists as a shopping list of authors to make offers to, often after nudges from a matchmaking literary agent. In fact, it's already happened to several of the authors in *The Empire at War*. In particular, Amazon's own science fiction and fantasy imprint, 47 North, has acquired nearly all its authors from the ranks of successful Kindle self-publishers.

I said a while ago that traditional and new science fiction publishers are in rough parity. Suppose we now stack our estimated 2014 sales figures differently. On the one hand we now have the authors who were unknown five years ago, and got their break through Kindle self-publishing, the Revolutionary authors, if you like. On the other hand, we have every other English language science fiction author. As a result, millions of sales cross the divide from old to new publishing, and tip the scales decisively.

I am convinced beyond any doubt that if you summed the 2014 sales of all the science fiction eBooks, paperbacks, hardbacks and audio books, then a sizeable majority were written by the authors of the Revolution.

Let's summarize why the Revolution has been important to lovers of military SF.

1. A whole new cadre of writers have risen to prominence, most of whom sell hundreds of thousands of books every year. The new stars of science fiction include A.G. Riddle, Andy Weir, Hugh Howey, B.V. Larson, Christopher G. Nuttall, Vaughan Heppner, Anne Charnock, Marko Kloos, Harmony Raines, and many others. Not all specialize in military SF, but a large proportion do.

2. Some sub-genres of science fiction that were not served well by traditional pre-Revolutionary publishers are now glowing with health, judging by the increase in titles and their massive popularity with readers. Notable sub-genres that have hurtled to prominence are: military SF, space opera, and science fiction romance. Incidentally, this is why I have been careful to distinguish between science fiction and fantasy. The impact of self-publishing on fantasy book publishing has also been significant, but less so than with science fiction. I believe this is because traditional fantasy book publishing was much more attuned to the tastes of the fantasy community.

3. Even though in recent years, sales of adult science fiction have dropped in traditional publishing (according to the American Association of Publishers), the total number of units sold, across all formats, has risen significantly when you include self-publishers and Amazon's own publishing imprints.

4. The total income shared by science fiction authors has rocketed even faster than the units sold (because average royalties are so much higher now).

5. I believe a key part of these trends is that the successful self-published authors have been writing novels that appeal to the broader science fiction community. After so many years when this

wider universe of SF gaming, TV & movies, comics and cosplay appeared to be largely immune to the lure of science fiction books, I find the prospect exhilarating that new audiences are now discovering or rediscovering science fiction literature. There has been a lot of talk in science fiction circles in recent years about diversity. Expanding the pool of readers and writers must surely be a good thing to broaden the range of voices in written science fiction. And while it is true that the self-published military science fiction tends to be written by men at the moment (ironically, given that women were the most prominent authors in pre-Revolutionary British military SF), and self-published science fiction romance tends to be written by women, I think the current situation is no more than a bridgehead for the future of science fiction. I love novels about space marines, and combating alien invaders, as much as the next gamer, but I don't want to read that all the time. And so, in years to come, the legions of science fiction fans flocking to space opera and military SF today will begin to look further afield for their next read.

6.   In conclusion, science fiction literature is in a healthier place than it has ever been in its history, and the future looks healthier still.

The Revolution has transformed science fiction publishing, writing, and reading. But it's not merely the backdrop to the rise of British Military Science Fiction because we have been at the heart of these changes.

But before we see how, let's rewind the clock to British SF publishing in pre-Revolutionary days.

Pre-Revolution British Military SF

If you sampled the past decade's magazines and online websites for commentaries, reviews, and essays on science fiction literature, it would be easy to mistakenly arrive at the following as the consensus view of military SF.

When played straight, military SF is fiction written by third-rate authors, and read by fourth-rate inadequates of low intelligence and dubious morals. Men, mostly. And almost certainly American men. Only Baen Books still publishes this crap, and they're such a minor aberration in the publishing world that they can be safely ignored as irrelevant. The only legitimate form of military SF is where the exhausted tropes of this embarrassing legacy of an earlier and unreconstructed decade are subverted to show how ridiculous they truly are.

As we've already seen, the consensus would go on to say about the specifically British military SF scene that (a) it doesn't exist, (b) it's a good job that Baen Books are near impossible to find in the UK and (c) yes, we know about Warhammer 40K but that's a psychotic aberration (a view I suspect would be gleefully acknowledged by Warhammer 40K fans).

The problem about paying attention to what the most prominent critics and commentators say, whether it's *Locus Magazine*, or *Interzone, Strange Horizons, BSFA Vector* (the British Science Fiction Association, or BSFA, is the premier club for British SF literature fans), or wherever the more establishment commentariat hangs out, is that these people are outliers often with little in common with regular readers.

That's not to say these self-appointed commentators don't have an interesting and vibrant sub-culture all of their own. But when you read, as I did last year, a prominent reviewer declare that the novels of Stephen Baxter and Alastair Reynolds were irrelevant, because they represented the dying embers of an old form of science fiction that no longer had anything useful to say, then I knew it was time to move on and leave the old world of critics and commentators behind, because they no longer had anything useful to say to me. And increasingly they seem cut off from the reality of what has really been going on in science fiction. *Revolution, what revolution?*

After all, if you want to find new book recommendations and explore new literary themes, Goodreads groups and reviews, and even Amazon's review system, are better for most SF fans than reading a review journal, because (barring a froth of family and friends) the reviews come from a sample of normal readers, rather than self-appointed judges of literary merit.

In a similar vein, the notion that military SF is only suited for third-rate (and American) degenerates is the kind of 'truth' that critics might believe, but only because *that's what such people tell each other.* I'm sure it doesn't feel that way from the inside, but the old commentariat has verged on a monoculture, because so many of the prominent voices have such similar tastes and interests, other viewpoints were crowded out. In real life such truths were never accepted by a very large number of British SF readers.

In fact, military backdrops feature heavily in some of the hugely successful Culture novels from Iain M. Banks. Former soldiers living in the immediate aftermath of often failed wars are the protagonists of the first series from Ken McLeod (*The Star Fraction, 1995*), Richard K. Morgan (*Altered Carbon, 2002*), and Peter F. Hamilton (*Mindstar Rising, 1993*).

Imagine a conflict where neutron stars piloted by transhumans are weapons of war to be flung at the enemy, and where the ultimate opponents are a non-baryonic lifeform so powerful that the only course of action is to flee this universe altogether. It takes an author of astonishing vision to imagine this, and Stephen Baxter is one of the few authors capable of this feat, which he delivers in the novels and short story collections of his Xeelee Sequence starting with *Raft* (1991) and continuing to the present day.

You could add Neal Asher and Alastair Reynolds to the mix of prominent British near-military SF writers of recent years, but for the most part war is a backdrop, or the off-camera cause that has made the characters who they are and explains how the worlds they inhabit came about.

One definition of military science fiction is that its main characters are active members of a realistic military organization that would be recognizable to the service men and women of today. While war, conflict, and military organization are in the background mix of British pre-Revolutionary military science fiction, most do not meet this definition of military SF.

Most, but by no means all.

Peter F. Hamilton's bewilderingly good *Fallen Dragon* (2001), and *Exultant* by Stephen Baxter (2004) are excellent novels where the lead characters are active members of a military organization, albeit a private one in the case of *Fallen Dragon*. This does not mean, of course, that the aims or even values of the protagonists match those of their commanders. Andy Remic takes a more action-oriented approach in his Combat-K series, starting with *War Machine* (2007), in which badass ex-special ops adventurers with a few loose bolts in their heads race through action and adventure.

The standard bearer of British military SF in the decade before the Revolution was Karen Traviss, whose six-novel Wess'har Wars series ran from *City of Pearl* (2004) through *Judge* (2008) and had elements of military SF, although this wasn't the main focus of the series. In the past decade, Traviss has written nine Star Wars novels, five Gears of War novels, four Halo books (all of the latter *New York Times* bestsellers), and Gears of War and GI Joe comics. Traviss worked as a defense correspondent and served in the Royal Naval Auxiliary Service, which makes her the pre-Revolutionary British writer with the most military experience, which is in sharp contrast to the many American writers of the time who had served their country in the military.

If Karen Traviss landed the plum role of writing for Star Wars, another British writer, Una McCormack, did the same for Star Trek, penning nine books in the past decade, including the *New York Times* bestseller *The Fall: The Crimson Shadow* (2013).

Outside of prose fiction, there has been a long tradition of British military SF in comics (*2000AD*), and games, such as the Mindjammer RPG, and of course Games Workshop with its extensive range of products in the Warhammer 40k range and a possessive attitude to the term 'space marine'.

In the early 1990s, the then Games Workshop supremo, Bryan Ansell, invited top British science fiction and fantasy authors to develop the concepts of the Warhammer (fantasy) and Warhammer 40K (science fiction) rulebooks into richly realized fictional universes. The initial support by many authors was lukewarm, but Ian Watson was an exception, saying that he 'had great lurid Gothic fun' writing his four Warhammer 40K novels starting with *Inquisitor* (1992) and including the much sought after *Space Marine* (1993). Ian Watson had a hand in the genesis of my Human Legion series and has recently written military SF in short form for his forthcoming collection *The 1,000 Year Reich* (2016).

As for Bryan Ansell's dream, with over 350 Warhammer 40K novels, not to mention video games and a movie, I think it's fair to say his idea came to fruition.

Which brings us to short-form fiction.

Award-winning science fiction & fantasy British small publisher NewCon Press published two collections of short fiction on the theme of conflict, *Conflicts* (2010), and *Further Conflicts* (2011), both with stunning artwork by award-winning artist Andy Bigwood, who of course is also the artist for *The Empire at War*. The leading stories from the two books were collected again in the bestselling collection, *Total Conflict* (2015). Acclaimed British military SF writers within these collections include Una McCormack, Andy Remic, Neal Asher, and Dan Abnett who is better known for his stories in both 2000AD and Warhammer 40K novels, such as the 15-novel *Gaunt's Ghosts* series that commenced in 1999. One of my early Human Legion stories is also included.

Further Conflicts was launched at the 2011 Eastercon convention, which was themed for military SF in honor of star guest, David Weber (himself a very important military SF writer most noted for his Honor Harrington series, but not a very British one).

Add in *Doctor Who* and the Doctor's often ambivalent relationship with UNIT and other forms of the military, and this then is a representative sample of pre-Revolutionary British military SF.

To summarize: other than Warhammer 40K and other franchise tie-in novels, there were very few novels of individuals serving in a military organization during wartime, but war and the military were sometimes featured as a backdrop. And that the premier literary science fiction convention in the UK could select David Weber as guest of honor and run with a military SF theme, despite a few raised eyebrows at the time, gave the lie to the idea that we Brits don't do military SF, even if it was often regarded as something of a guilty pleasure.

Year Five: Situation Report

Now that we're coming to the end of the fifth year since the Revolution began, we can step back and assess the shape of British military SF during 2015.

The pre-Revolutionary writers were mostly quiet this year, leaving the stage for the authors who have established a strong international reputation in the past few years, plus a few new names.

No new novels this year from the mainstream star of military SF, Karen Traviss, who has been busy with GI Joe comics. Una McCormack has a new Star Trek novel due after Christmas, and co-wrote a military edged space opera, *Baba Yaga*, with Eric S. Brown.

Like Karen Traviss, Dan Abnett has been largely engaged with the comic world, issuing *Insurrection*, military SF set in the world of Judge Dredd, and numerous Battlestar Galactica comics.

Christopher G. Nuttall released five new novels during 2015, including three additions to his most popular military SF series, *Empire's Corps* and *Ark Royal*, and the highly successful launch of the new *Angel in the Whirlwind* military SF series through Amazon's 47 North imprint. Audiobooks are the great growth area of science fiction publishing at the moment, and Chris launched fifteen audiobook editions during the year, many of which were top-10 bestsellers in the amazon.com military SF chart.

Michael G. Thomas added six novels to his series: *Star Legions*, *Star Crusades* and *Star Crusader*, as well as releasing many audio editions of earlier books. Peter F. Hamilton added *The Abyss Beyond Dreams*, the first of a duology that slots between his *Commonwealth Saga* and *Void Trilogy*. Phillip Richards added *Recce*, the fourth book of his *Union* series. P.P. Corcoran added two new books to his *Saiph* series. Tony Healey added eleven new books of varying lengths and mostly to his *Far from Home*, *Playlist Book*, and *Confederation Reborn* series. D.J. Holmes found some spare time when finishing his degree to write his first book, which became a hit. His novel begins a series called *Empire Rising*.

You will, no doubt, have spotted a recurring theme: Series! Series! Series!

As the British science fiction author with the most books published in the past few years (and possibly the most sold too), it's instructive to look at Christopher G. Nuttall's bibliography. You will notice that he writes nearly all his books in series, running from trilogies (*The Royal Sorceress* and *A Learning Experience*) through the eleven books so far of the *Empire's War* series. All the other authors in the collection have concentrated on their own series over the past two years: Phillip Richards with his *Union Series*, P.P. Corcoran with the *Saiph Series,* and myself with the *Human Legion*.

Another thing you will notice is we don't hang around. Other than Phillip Richards, who has to spend time looking after the soldiers in his platoon, all the British authors I've just mentioned, including Tony Healey, Michael G. Thomas and Peter F. Hamilton, are full-time professional writers of novels, which gives us plenty of time to write books. With the exception of Peter F. Hamilton (who seems to regard a book with less than 600 pages as a short story), that means we are more prolific that the old expectation of one book a year, or maybe two if you're lucky, although few authors can match Christopher Nuttall, who has published an astonishing sixty full-length novels in four years. (Yes, that's right… read that last sentence again!). The core of our audience demands the depth and breadth of immersive storytelling that is only possible with series, and they aren't willing to wait too long for the next installment.

The expectation that the wait for the next installment will be brief is hardly surprising given that we live in the world of the TV box set. Consider that most science fiction fans are not enjoying their fix through the medium of books, but through movies, TV, and gaming. Whether it's an adventure in a sci-fi role playing game, a tabletop battle in the Warhammer 40K setting, a multi-episode 'season' in a long-running 2000AD series, the latest Star Wars movie, or an episode from a TV box set, most science fiction today is a standalone 'episode' set within a much larger context.

However we may choose to rationalize *why* book series are so popular right now, the fact that they *are* what readers want is clearly signaled by our audience, thanks to the brutal Darwinism that has swept through science fiction publishing.

Anyone can publish a book these days, but the authors who can turn a dollop of luck into a thriving writing career are the ones who can repeatedly deliver a high-quality reading experience to their audience. Those who can't fall by the wayside. Sometimes bad luck or poor choices mean good writers fail anyway. Just as in nature, Natural Selection has always been about populations and not individuals. And the population of science fiction authors whom readers have selected through their book purchases tend to write books in series. (As with any 'rule' in publishing, there are exceptions to dominance of series, of course. Anne Charnock's *A Calculated Life* (2013) is a highly successful British example).

It might seem obvious that the authors who are successful are those who write what readers want, but this was not so simple before the Revolution. I think John Jarrold (an editor and literary agent responsible for launching the career of Iain M. Banks amongst many others) described this perfectly a few years ago at a convention I attended, when he explained why he wasn't taking on writers who hoped to follow the considerable commercial success of fantasy humorists such as Terry Pratchett and Tom Holt.

Jarrold explained that the Big Six publishers (as they were then) only had so many slots for new books each year, of which they would put their main marketing muscle behind a handful. All the publishers had already signed a fantasy humorist who satisfied their needs, and they didn't have space for a second; they would prefer to put all their money and time behind their proven success. Consequently, Jarrold was very reluctant to take manuscripts of that type. Even if you could out-Pratchett Sir Terry, he doubted he could sell your manuscript to a major publisher.

That was around 2010. Things are very different now. Major publishers still have their limited number of slots, but the way they fill them is changing. Many of their most successful science fiction novels of the past 18 months (from A.G. Riddle, Andy Weir, Hugh Howey) were originally self-published. And in a landmark for military SF, major imprint Harper Voyager bypassed literary agents altogether last month, and issued an open call to authors for submissions of military SF manuscripts.

The days of the limited number of publishing slots may still be with the major publishers but not for science fiction publishing in the wider sense.

Take the *Empire at War* collection, for example. As the Revolution broke out, self-publishing authors such as B.V. Larson with *Mech* 1 (2010) and *Swarm* (2010), and Randolph Lalonde with *Spinward Fringe* (2008) and *Freeground* (2008) were demonstrating that you could sell tens of thousands of copies of space opera and military SF adventure novels. In the Revolutionary world, this encouraged new writers to join the party (in fact most of these 'new writers' were already published authors, but were unknown because they didn't have a major publishing deal). Larson, Lalonde and the other early successes begat Vaughn Heppner with his breakout hit *Star Soldier* (2010), Evan Currie (now signed to 47 North) *On Silver Wings* (2011), *Michael G. Thomas *Star Crusades* (2011), Ryk Brown *The Frontiers Saga* (2011), *Christopher G. Nuttall (now signed to 47 North for some series) *The Empire's Corps* (2012), *Tony Healey *Far From Home* (2012), Doug Dandridge *Empires at War* (2012), *Mark E. Cooper *Merkiaari Wars (2012)*, Raymond L. Weil *Moonwreck: The Slaver Wars* (2012), *Phillip Richards *C.R.O.W.* (2012), Jay Allan (now signed to Harper Voyager) *Marines* (2013), Marko Kloos (now signed to 47 North) *Terms of Enlistment* (2013), Dietmar Wehr *The Synchronicity War* (2013), *Jasper T. Scott *Dark Space* (2014), Autumn Kalquist *Legacy Code* (2014), Joshua Dalzelle *Omega Rising* (2014), G.S. Jennson *Aurora Rising* (2014), *P.P. Corcoran *Discovery of the Saiph* (2014), *Tim C. Taylor *Marine Cadet* (2014), Amy DuBoff *Architects of Destiny* (2015), *Dean Crawford *Old Ironsides* (2016). (The asterisk indicates a British author.)

If you could write a manuscript, suddenly you could publish a novel. Content and covers rapidly grew more professional until today the established authors release books with production quality the equal of the major publishers. Finally, science fiction had a cadre of eager writers able to connect not only to readers who had previously bought paperbacks, but could also reach out to the untapped legions of science fiction fans who had largely ignored novels in favor of comics, gaming, or other forms of entertainment.

This was something new, something raw and feral. *This was punk science fiction.* A generation of SF fans left behind by the mainstream publishing industry reclaimed science fiction for its own. Science fiction was not merely in conversation with itself, but was now writing its own stories.

As a result, authors started reaching 100,000 sales around 2013, and today, as we reach the end of Year Five, the top authors on this list are selling hundreds of thousands every year.

Sounds easy, doesn't it?

Except it isn't.

The list above of authors and their key works includes most of the key players, though it isn't exhaustive – A.C. Hadfield and M.R. Forbes are another two very successful, authors off the top of my head – but if I listed every author who decided to try their hand at self-publishing military SF or space opera over the past five years, but who hasn't sold more than a few tens of thousands of copies, then the list would seem endless.

And notice how I'm not talking about epic fantasy, or YA dystopian futures, or superhero stories, or urban fantasy… the Revolution has definitely touched those kind of books, but not to the same extent.

All this talk about high-selling authors is not to say that only selling, say, a thousand copies of your books makes you a failure. Far from it. Writing your book makes you a *writer,* and publishing it makes you a *published author.* Even if you don't sell a single copy, the experience of writing the kind of fiction you love to read will reward you with a deeper appreciation of science fiction literature, far more so than reading an infinite number of literary review journals.

But making a success of a writing career is exceptionally hard. As writers, we need iron discipline to write fast and well, and must learn to tread a difficult path between giving readers what they've enjoyed before and pushing the boundaries to give them something new. Stray too far in either direction and we pay the price in falling book sales, blown off our feet because in the howling gale of this new competition, if we lose the interest of our readers they now have a multitude of other, talented authors to turn to.

No author is ever entitled to earn a living through their writing.

The result is a new generation of writers who have been schooled the hard way into learning how to excite readers, or have fallen by the wayside.

But there is an unexpected surprise in this list of top authors, especially the British ones. In the top flight of British military SF and military-themed space opera, the names have become more male in recent years. And that feels strange after a period when the most successful writers in the field were often female.

Given the evidence to the contrary from authors such as Karen Traviss, it's ludicrous to suggest that British military SF is an exclusively male domain. And although I've given mainly male names in the list of key military SF authors, that could be nothing more than ignorance on my part, an ignorance that results from the almost complete lack of coverage of vast areas of science fiction from the traditional voices of reviewers. When you consider that most review journals and prominent critics won't consider reading media or game tie-in novels, let alone self-published fiction, the realization hits that most science fiction book sales are from authors ignored by reviewers outside of Goodreads and Amazon. It's sad that so many science fiction fans are left in ignorance of the great explosion in popularity of science fiction, ill-served by an outdated cadre of commentators who failed to notice the greatest news story in SF since the widespread introduction of the paperback.

Take S.J. MacDonald, for example. She's a schoolteacher from Wales. I know nothing more about her except that in October 2015 she added *Dark Running* to her popular 'Fourth Fleet Irregulars' series, and entered the top-20 military SF chart on amazon.com. If I hadn't been checking the chart, I wouldn't have known that MacDonald was one of the most successful British science fiction writers of the month.

For another example, consider Jo Zebedee (the Jo is short for Joanne) who is an excellent writer from Northern Ireland. In 2015, Jo came out with a military-edged space opera trilogy (*Abendau's Heir*) and near-future drama set in Belfast (*Inish Carraig*). Both novels are now bestsellers, but I only heard of them originally via a friend's recommendation.

And that last detail is telling. How is it possible that so many new science fiction authors sell hundreds of thousands of books in a handful of years, or more in some cases, with little or no mention from the traditional SF commentariat?

I'm convinced that the explanation *isn't* a conspiracy to cut off the oxygen of publicity to the wrong class of science fiction authors, any more than there is a conspiracy of publishers to deny publishing slots to the 'wrong' kind of fiction. I know several people who are a part of the old commentariat and they aren't narrow-minded bigots at all. Far from it. They simply don't know what's been going on because they've surrounded themselves with like-minded people, and have stumbled lock-step into something of a monoculture.

So if deliberate action isn't the explanation, how is it that so many authors sell so many copies of their books, and do so in a parallel world of publishing that is invisible to large sections of the traditional science fiction literary community?

The answer, like so much else, is the internet. Why read reviews in a publication such as *Locus* or BSFA *Vector* when the internet gives you Goodreads and Amazon?

What's the best word to describe a fan of SF literature who thinks deeply about the books they read, and goes on to share their thoughts in a newspaper or magazine column, or a science fiction website? 'Critic' is the technical word, but for the purpose of this discussion, a more telling term is 'outlier'. No matter how open-minded and good-intentioned critics may be, the very fact that they establish themselves as a critic sets them apart from regular readers. They don't read books the same way as most people, and their tastes and opinions are often far removed from the mainstream.

This is true of fantasy too, but less so because the often derided 'Big Epic Fantasy' novel was too lucrative a format for publishers to move away from to the extent they allowed space opera to wither. In many ways, epic space opera and big epic fantasy are close cousins, not least in the way they can be molded by authors into many shapes, and this allowed those authors who wished to adapt epic fantasy into what some like to call 'progressive narratives'. We've seen a little of that recently in space opera, notably Ann Leckie's *Ancillary Justice* (2013), though using the space opera framework to do more than simply entertain is nothing new – witness the political visions of Ken McLeod's *The Star Fraction* (1995). Nonetheless, space opera was considered by some to be a more discredited sub-genre, too far gone to rehabilitate easily, than big epic fantasy. To summarize, the reason the rumbles of revolution have been more muted in fantasy publishing is because the major publishers didn't leave their audience behind in the way they did in science fiction.

Goodreads and Amazon reviews have their faults too, of course, but those who are Revolution-deniers are far too ready to use those weaknesses to dismiss them as irrelevant when in fact they are the engines of the science fiction Revolution. Goodreads and Amazon reviews are simply word-of-mouth recommendations for the internet age. The four authors in *The Empire at War* have barely been mentioned by mainstream media, but have amassed over 19,000 5-star reviews on Amazon and Goodreads, and have locked ourselves into Amazon's recommendation engines. That's how it is possible for three of us to earn a living writing science fiction novels.

Nineteen thousand is a respectable number, but more tellingly, consider 2014's science fiction top three stars who were or are still self-published: Hugh Howey, Andy Weir, and A.G. Riddle. As of December 2015, on Goodreads.com they have 670,000 reviews. Obviously, some of those are suggestions to stay away from their books, but that's still two-thirds of a million word-of-mouth recommendations.

Contrast that with *Locus Magazine*. Back in the days when I used to be a subscriber, *Locus* used to describe itself as the essential guide to what's happening right now in science fiction. If you look at their online index of reviews you will discover that of those three breakout authors, despite selling millions of books in the past three years, *Locus* has seen fit to write just a single book review (Hugh Howey's *Wool Omnibus* in 2013).

I don't wish to unfairly pick on *Locus*, but the magazine is an extreme case of how the old SF commentariat sometimes seems to be almost deliberately willing itself into irrelevance for most science fiction readers. And it isn't merely a bigoted attitude to self-published authors, and – let us not forget – the dismissive attitude to their legions of fans that this implies. I've mentioned the huge success of Karen Traviss and Una McCormack as the stars of pre-Revolutionary British military SF. None of their game and media tie-in novels – the ones that made frequent appearances on the *New York Times* bestseller list – none of those have been reviewed by *Locus* as a matter of review policy. That still leaves a lot of exciting titles for *Locus* to review, but it's clear the magazine has turned its back on the majority of science fiction readers and redefined itself to only address a specific niche within SF literature. That's disappointing but probably makes commercial sense.

All of which only goes to show that there may be other authors, male and female, who deserve to be on the list of military SF bestsellers that I gave above. They aren't there because I haven't noticed them yet. But unlike far too many in the old commentariat, I am at least trying to understand what is happening around me in science fiction, and am naturally disposed to celebrate success, no matter the superficial characteristics of the author or the stories they write. I urge the established commentators of science fiction to take a similarly enlightened view of this new diversity in science fiction publishing.

And that brings our reflections on the state of science fiction in Year Five to a close with the strangest observation of all.

Science fiction publishing has changed out of all recognition in the past five years. And yet many of the most prominent voices in science fiction don't seem to have noticed. It's as if a mass psychosis has gripped them, making them all turn their heads so they cannot see the immense alien mothership in the room.

But the publishers certainly have.

Consider the case of Harper Voyager who never entirely believed that military SF was dead, having published Ian Douglas for many years, the author most famous for his *Star Corpsman* series. Back in spring 2014, Harper Voyager brought in David Pomerico as editorial director from 47 North, and soon signed self-publishing stars A.G. Riddle and Jay Allan. In November 2015, they made an open call for authors to submit novel manuscripts, something that was unheard of until very recently. And Harper said they didn't want any old science fiction novel: they specifically asked for military SF.

Harper Voyager is ahead of the pack, but the rest of the old establishment will eventually throw off their group psychosis and stagger out of their bunkers, blinking under the bright skies of the new and vibrant world of post-Revolutionary science fiction.

Yes, but is it bloody British?

Now that the state of military SF has changed out of all recognition during the Revolution, is there a new style we can discern that has a distinctively British flavor?

I think there is, although it's subtle.

On the face of things, British science fiction writing has become more American. As we've seen, British military SF of the past tended to use war and conflict as a background, rather than presenting at center stage characters engaged in fighting a war. British writers were more likely to be former scientists than former soldiers.

That's all gone now. If anything the successful new British science fiction writers are even more likely to give their novels a war setting than their American counterparts. The distaste for writing action-oriented novels has also disappeared. And of the four novels in *The Empire at War*, half are written by former or serving soldiers.

Comparing British science fiction with American is like comparing James Bond to Jason Bourne, or Harry Potter to The Hunger Games. Or, for that matter, Dynasty with Downton Abbey. One is not necessarily better than the other, but they're infused with related but different cultural DNA. It's the same with British military SF and space opera (and let's not forget the Australians, Irish, and New Zealanders writing in these fields too) – we come at things from a slightly different angle to American writers, and the result is particularly successful in science fiction where it is important that the characters don't talk, act, and think the same as the everyday folk around you. If British writers drink warm beer, endless cups of tea, and say 'bloody' a lot, then we get a head start in those stakes by being peculiar from the get go.

Back in the 50s, people used to say that British science fiction was more pessimistic than American, that British novels reflected a country that had lost an empire and was coming to terms with a much reduced status in the world.

Well, we got better! Lazy commentators still use this 'lost an empire' explanation for British literary culture today, but the truth is that we had gotten over that before I was born. 'The Empire at War' it says in the collection's title. That's not us pining for the days of the British Empire, it's meant as an ironic joke.

Many examples of British military SF and space opera are not set in a future version of Britain, but those that do largely depict a future version of the diminished post-Imperial version that we grew up in. The only exception I can think of is DJ Holmes with his *Empire Rising* series, in which the political situation is largely a future projection of the Great Powers before 1914. In the future wars of most British writers, the main characters are often members of a military organization that is not strong enough to defeat the enemy alone. They need to act in concert with allies.

The complex alliances, back stabbing and confusion of Phillip Richards' *Union* series is a quintessentially British form of military SF. Alliances also feature in the Human Legion's bid to win its freedom, as they do in P.P. Corcoran's *Saiph* series, initially between human nations but then with alien powers.

Alliances show up in American writing too, of course, although not so frequently. *Babylon 5*, for example, showcases an ever-shifting series of alliances as the balance of power within the galaxy changes. The Babylon project's idealism as the 'last best hope for peace' (and later 'for victory') is reflected in P.P. Corcoran's *Saiph* series, but is an unusually idealistic form of alliance for British writers. The messiness of the alliances in Phillip Richard's *Union* series are more typical of the British attitude that says we don't want an alliance, and will probably distrust and dislike our partners, but if we aren't a first-rate power, we have little choice but to go out and seek allies because the alternative is worse. In real life, many Britons have a similar attitude to our relationship with the European Union.

In *Their Darkest Hour* by Christopher G. Nuttall, we see the famous British stiff upper lip born of weary determination to just *get the bloody job done* with the minimum of fuss. This attitude draws from a deep cultural well that would have been familiar to the British Tommies a century ago at the Somme. However, Nuttall infuses his characters with modern sensibilities. The Edwardian-era stiff upper lip can be considered a shield to insulate individuals from the hardships of the emotional and physical world around them. If so, then this shield often cracks in Nuttall's books, and the horrors of the world under alien occupation flood in.

It's also instructive to contrast Captain Smith from Nuttall's *Ark Royal* with Captain Wolfe from *Warship,* by American author Joshua Dalzelle. At a superficial level, the characters are similar, both captains of third-rate vessels, plagued with inner demons, and resenting the political interference from on high. The two authors take their characters on different journeys. Nuttall's Royal Navy captain starts as the more crumpled of the two, with a longer personal journey to progress through before he can see himself as a hero, but possessing a care-worn competence throughout, whatever his superiors may think of him. Dalzelle's Jackson Wolfe starts considerably more self-assured and readier to fight harder against political interference, with less need to prove his worth to himself. I can't say I preferred one character over the other, but that's the point I made to start this section. Harry Potter or Hunger Games? Captain Theodore Smith or Captain Jackson Wolfe? It isn't that one is necessarily better than the other. And it isn't even important to understand what makes British literature different. What matters is that British authors write a slightly different way, and the more diverse the authors the more variety for the readers. And that's got to be a good thing.

What of the successes of British science fiction as a whole during 2015?

The publishing world exists far beyond Amazon, of course, yet it remains the largest and most transparent book retailer in the world. Not only can we see who and what is selling, but if an author is not selling well on Amazon, then they aren't selling well period, unless there are special circumstances (such as the successful direct sales from Baen Books and Black Library, or popularity in non-English language markets).

According to the amazon.com bestseller charts during the year, traditional British science fiction publishing had most of its success with space opera titles, but they were outshone and outsold by the new cadre of British authors who produced most of their bestsellers in science fiction romance and military SF.

Love and war.

War stories and romance sound like polar opposites, but the success in both sub-genres comes as no surprise. Each places characters in extreme situations that test them to the limit, and that's why stories of love and war have always been popular across many cultures and many thousands of years.

The Revolution is broader than this, though, and I am sure it will broaden still further over the coming years. A notable British example is Anne Charnock, whose excellent 2013 debut, *A Calculated Life*, a subtle novel about what it is to be human, continued to sell strongly, and her second novel, *Sleeping Ember of an Ordinary Mind* reached #1 in science fiction on amazon.com in November 2015. Anne is published by Amazon's imprint, 47 North, and her deserved success is part of trends we saw during 2015 both for Amazon to promote its own imprints much more aggressively in the Kindle Store, and also to publish a wider range of fiction. For example, of the five books from various Amazon imprints due to launch on December 1st 2015, all of them were in the top-10 list of all Kindle fiction on amazon.com when they went on pre-order, including all top four positions.

I think this may have a significant impact on military science fiction. During 2013 and 2014 it often seemed that military SF and space opera utterly dominated Amazon's science fiction sales. Although sales of these sub-genres haven't noticeably reduced so far, the second half of 2015 saw a wider range of styles at the top of the SF charts.

In conclusion, British military SF ends 2015 in the healthiest position it has ever enjoyed. As a result of the Revolution in science fiction publishing, most of the major new British science fiction writers of the past few years have specialized in either military SF, or space opera adventures with a strong military theme. And no longer are British military SF authors selling only to American readers. According to Amazon's bestseller charts, military SF is, if anything, even more popular with British readers right now that with American ones.

The Future of British Military SF

As we come to the end of 2015, most of the voices eager to tell you their opinion about British science fiction are still oblivious to the idea that they have lived through the biggest revolution in SF publishing since the introduction of the paperback, and the beautiful thing about this is that *it doesn't matter.*

We veterans of the Revolution shrug our shoulders and move on. If they're happy in their ignorance then, so what? The combination of digital self-publishing with the social reviewing of Goodreads and Amazon means the old science fiction establishment has lost its power to deny readers access to books that don't fit their notions of what should be published. As we've seen, this was never about a conspiracy so much as an unconscious monoculture that stumbled away from large numbers of science fiction fans, allowing an army of self-published authors to fill the void. Perhaps those who haven't already done so will come round in a few years to accepting that science fiction is bigger than they ever imagined. Or maybe not. Either way, *it doesn't matter.*

Like a vegetarian turned born-again carnivore, it feels as if the science fiction community is cramming as much military SF into its diet as it can, guzzling on a pleasure if not denied, then certainly *rationed* for far too long. In a few years, I believe this feeding frenzy will calm, and science fiction readers – many of whom will be new readers arriving from the worlds of gaming and movies, or those returning to the fold after many years in exile – will look for science fiction literature beyond military SF and space opera.

I like to think this is science fiction's future. A new golden age of science fiction for both readers and writers that will only shine more brightly with every year.

But for now, we British writers of military SF can look upon that future and smile in anticipation… before shrugging and turning our heads back to the unfinished pages of our writing notebooks and wordprocessor files. We have hundreds of thousands of hungry fans across the world awaiting their next fix of military science fiction. Someone's got to feed them, and it might as well be us.

The Empire's still at war… and we're lovin' it!

FALLEN WITNESS

— Vision VI: The Battle of New Trafalgar —

Art: Andy Bigwood
Words: Tim C. Taylor

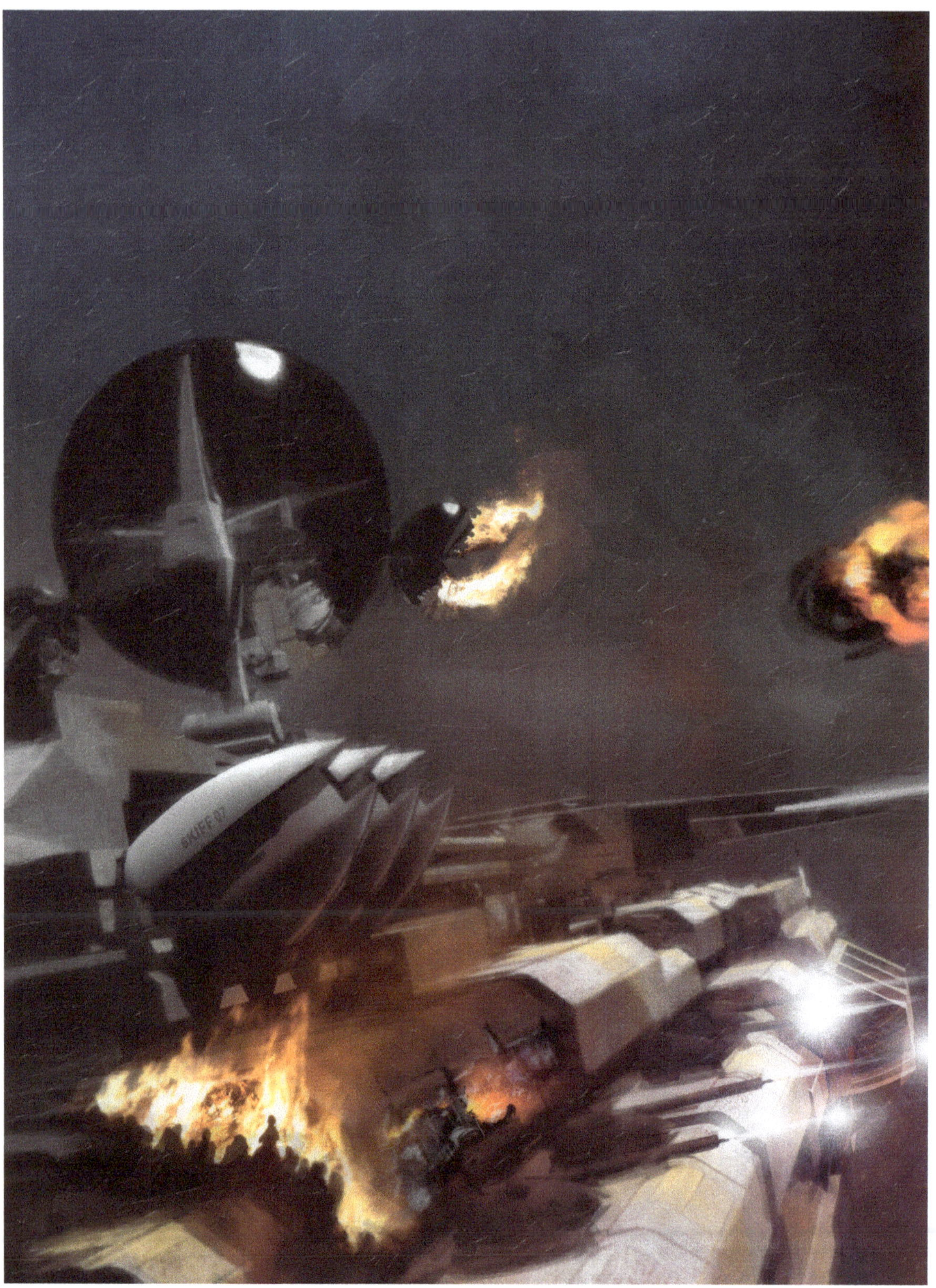

"Look at the image of the battle and imagine you are there," invites the next android, who identifies himself as Lieutenant-Commander Iain Williams. "Does it look exciting?"

Some of the boys in the audience look as if they agree that the battle was a thrill fest. Williams expects there will be a craze for playing space battles in the playground. *Let them play,* he thinks, *it is all part of the remembering.*

He waits so that those who can imagine themselves in the battle have time to do so.

"To those who were there," Williams explains, "the Battle of New Trafalgar *was* exciting. It was also terrifying. Heart rending. Desperate. And a close-run thing."

The audience hushes.

"Yes, that's right – the Battle of New Trafalgar. Most of you do not know this, but our planet is named New Trafalgar after the moment when we finally brought the enemy to battle, lured by HMS *Brilliant*. The battle was a tight affair that could have swung either way. I know because I was there. The history data will unlock to you after this lesson. Look me up! I was the XO of HMS *Warspite* until the captain was killed by an energy blast to CIC. Then I took over from my station on the bridge."

Williams winces. As the senior officer of the fallen witnesses, it is his duty to relive the most painful memories with the children. Doesn't make it easy, no matter how many times he does this.

"I was in command of the most important ship in the Royal Navy for about four minutes, and at that point the British Squadron was the most crucial formation in the entire Grand Fleet. The American energy whips had too narrow an effect, the Russian dark matter torpedoes were too easy to evade, and the Pan-African blunderbuss of nukes was devastatingly effective, but only against targets unable to maneuver. The Death Beats of the twenty Warspite-class ships of the British Squadron posed the greatest threat to the enemy… and the wraiths knew it. We ripped them apart, and they in their turn concentrated their fury upon us. Four minutes after the captain died, after my ship had destroyed the enemy's flagship, the surviving enemy ships directed their fire at HMS *Warspite*'s bridge. Even though my station was at the heart of the ship and heavily shielded, we had no effective defense."

Williams casts his gaze across the auditorium. He knows he holds the attention of every one of them in the palm of his hand.

"The result was inevitable," he says bitterly. "I was killed in action."

Fallen Witness Vision VII is on p481

ROLL CALL

—British Military SF Authors —

Tim C. Taylor

Contributors Appearing in this Anthology

Between them, the authors and artists of 'The Empire at War' have sold many hundreds of thousands of books, amassed over 19,000 5-star reviews on Goodreads and Amazon, won two BSFA Awards, been on the USA Today bestseller list, hit the #1 spot several times on the amazon.com military SF bestseller chart, and been #1 on the amazon.com bestselling science fiction authors list. Nonetheless, we are only a snapshot of the literary movement that is British military science fiction. Following the bios for the contributors is a list of other notable British military SF and space opera authors.

Andy Bigwood

Andy Bigwood is an Artist, Author, Draughtsman, Bookbinder, Cartographer, and Illustrator from Trowbridge, Wiltshire.

Trained in technical illustration, in Bath (shortly before the evolution of computer-aided art), Andy has provided artwork, cartography and cover designs for a variety of Fantasy, Horror, and Science fiction novels, twice winning the BSFA Award for best artwork in 2007 and 2008.

Andy is also a published author, with five short stories in print.

More: You can view some of Andy's artwork at his DeviantArt gallery here: http://topaz172.deviantart.com/gallery/5541499/My-Art

P.P. Corcoran

P.P. (Paul) Corcoran was born in Johnstone, Renfrewshire, Scotland in 1967. He joined the British Army in 1985 at the grand old age of seventeen and a half. After completing his initial training, he joined the British Army's elite parachute force, 5 Airborne Brigade, spending four years there until moving on to various intelligence and signals units for the remainder of his twenty-two years' service. During his career he served in many areas of operations including: Africa, the Balkans, Central America, Northern Ireland, the Middle East and South East Asia. He continued to work in the security field until recently becoming a full-time author.

He has been a fan of science fiction since his school days, his reading tastes developing to include all things military, past, future and alternate history.

Paul began writing his own stories in 2013 and self-published his first science fiction novel *Discovery of the Saiph* in 2014, and *Search for the Saiph* in 2015. *Discovery of the Saiph* reached number 1 in Amazon UK's Best Seller list in May 2015, while its sequel at reached number 1 in the same list.

In 2016 Paul will release the fourth book of the *Saiph* series and start a new military SF series, the *K'Tai War*.

Notable works: *Discovery of the Saiph* (2014).

More: Paul's website is here: http://www.ppcorcoran.com/index.html Twitter - @PPCorcoran

Christopher G. Nuttall

Born in Edinburgh, Scotland, in 1982, the same year as the Falklands War, Christopher G. Nuttall started an online alternate history magazine while studying librarianship at university, which spawned a love of writing often inspired by a love of historical speculation. His first manuscript was completed in 2005, but it was later that John Ringo gave him permission to write stories set in his Posleen Universe. Chris took on the challenges and opportunities of self-publishing through Amazon Kindle direct publishing, starting in 2011 with *Patriotic Treason*, and continuing to deliver novel after novel at his pace of 9000 words drafted per day. In the past five years, he has published an astonishing 60 novels, and these are full-length novels, not short 60,000 word affairs.

Notable successes include the eleven-book *Empire's Corps* series, the six-book *Ark Royal* series, the eight-book *Schooled in Magic* series, and entering the *USA Today* bestseller list. Chris is a 'hybrid author' being a mix of self-published, published by small presses, by Amazon's 47 North imprint, and by independent audiobook publishers. Judging by the author ranking system on Amazon.com, Christopher G. Nuttall was the most successful British science fiction author on Amazon during 2015.

Reading Nuttall at his best is to experience a masterclass in pacing and tension, because only a tiny proportion of the authors working today in the science fiction and fantasy genres have Nuttall's ability to *throw rocks at their characters*. Jim Butcher is another author with Nuttall's rock-throwing skills, and he's been known to sell a few books too. If you're not familiar with the rock-throwing metaphor, it's simply a way of describing how authors make their stories exciting. When the characters get close to solving their story problem, or realizing their goal, the author throws rocks at them.

The 'rocks' may be a form of *external* peril (enemy reinforcements, a dragon swoops down from the sky breathing fire and hate, your trusted comrade turns out to be a double agent) or an *internal* one that is in the mind, rather than in the physical world (the one you love denounces you because of your religion, you don't get the promotion because the post goes to someone with the right political connections, you have to lie to your best friend to protect them, your comrade turns out to be a double agent – which like most good 'rocks' has both an external and an internal aspect).

This is nothing specific to science fiction. Successful romance novelists are always experts in rock throwing. They have to be in a genre where the bare bones of the standard story structure is to introduce two characters at the beginning and have them fall in love at the end of the book. What makes the book interesting is the author's ability to constantly throw rocks (usually internal ones, but not always) at their romance so that it flourishes at the end of the book but only after overcoming all the obstacles the author places in their way.

Throwing rocks is a literary skill like all the others. If your rocks are too large, most authors have to rely on unbelievable explanations to extricate the characters from their peril. Throw pebbles instead of rocks, and the reader shrugs and reaches for a more interesting book. In Nuttall's *Ark Royal* (2014), every time Captain Theodore Smith thinks he has outwitted the enemy, they counter with a new tactic or a hitherto unseen threat. Survival, let alone victory, looks impossible, and yet the *Ark Royal* uses a combination of ingenuity, skill, and discipline to outwit the enemy… *just*.

There are reasons why the *Ark Royal* series has been immensely popular, and none of them are to do with luck.

But popularity hasn't yet translated into a similar level of acclaim from the prominent voices of SF fandom. That could be, in part, a consequence of Nuttall's blisteringly fast pace of releases. As these words are written in December 2015, there have been six *Ark Royal* novels since the opener was released in January 2014. The world simply hasn't had time yet to come to terms with Christopher G. Nuttall.

A complementary explanation is to do with the kind of fiction Nuttall publishes.

Writing a non-linear narrative is easy. Employing metaphors, symbolism and allegory in fiction is so easy that it's a temptation that beginning writers often succumb to before they have the skills to use these techniques well. Using a science fictional narrative to hold a mirror up to today's society and draw attention to a sociological development or injustice is a piece of cake. Anyone can write these kind of books, but *very few can write them well*. In the same way, it's easy to slap some stock art of a spaceship on your book cover and write about space battles where plucky human space-fighter pilots defend the Earth against alien battlecruisers. Very few authors can write this well.

Christopher G. Nuttall can write this exceptionally well.

Yet for some reason, some prominent voices in science fiction fandom and SF criticism place overwhelming emphasis on the importance of the literary techniques they choose to value, and are dismissive of everything else, as if one set of literary skills is objectively more worthy or easier to acquire than the other.

All of this goes some way to explain the paradox of Nuttall being one of the most successful British science fiction authors to have emerged in recent years, but being underappreciated in his home country. But then the American science fiction community has always been a broader church and it is telling that it is to America that Nuttall has been invited as guest of honor for HonorCon 2016, the prominent military science fiction convention.

Notable works: *Empire's Corps* (2012), *Ark Royal* (2014).

Trivia: If you take a look at the header on his Facebook page, you can see what it looks like to be ranked the #1 science fiction author on amazon.com

More: Chris's blog is here: http://www.chrishanger.net/ Chat with him on Facebook here: https://www.facebook.com/ChristopherGNuttall

Phillip Richards

Phillip Richards was born in Chichester, southern England. Not long after his seventeenth birthday he signed up to join the British Army, opting for service within the infantry. Since then he has served his country for fifteen years, completing a series of tours in Kosovo, Northern Ireland, Iraq, Afghanistan and instructing at an infantry training centre in northern England. He is now an infantry platoon sergeant, and spends his free time – when he gets it – pursuing his childhood passion: writing science fiction.

Phil's first novel, *C.R.O.W.*, was published in 2012, and follows the experience of Andy Moralee, a young recruit to the English Dropship Infantry. Since then further books in the Union Series have followed, telling the tale of Andy's progression: *Lancejack*, *Eden*, and *Recce*. The next book in the series, *Recce II*, is due out early in 2016. Both *C.R.O.W.* and an early view of the opening to Phil's first non-Union novel are included in *The Empire at War*.

You can follow Phil on twitter @PhilAuthor for updates on the production of future titles, as well as hearing him moan about the ups and downs of life as a Platoon Sergeant!

Feel free to email Phil at phil_richards@hotmail.com. He welcomes all ideas, comments and constructive criticism, and he always makes an effort to reply.

Notable works: *C.R.O.W.* (2012).

Trivia: Phil says that some of Andy Moralee's experiences in C.R.O.W. were inspired by his own time as a recruit in the British Army.

More: Phil's blog is here: http://militarysciencefictionblog.blogspot.co.uk/ Twitter - @PhilAuthor

Tim C. Taylor

Brought up on a diet of 2000AD, Traveller RPG, Blake's 7, Star Wars, and some particularly obscure historical and fantasy gaming activity, Tim C. Taylor started selling short science fiction in the early 2000s, set up the publishing business Greyhart Press in 2011, and self-published *Marine Cadet*, the first book of the Human Legion series over Christmas 2014. By January 2015, the first two Human Legion titles were ranked #1 and #2 on the military SF books chart at amazon.com, and so two more Human Legion titles were released that year, the most recent co-written with Ian Whates. During 2016, he will complete the six-book Human Legion series (with help from Ian Whates), publish a spin-off series written by a former US Army sergeant, and begin a new series set in the same universe as the Human Legion books, but with a very different feel.

Notable works: *Marine Cadet* (2014).

Trivia #1: *This is Free Trader Beowulf, calling anyone… Mayday, Mayday… we are under attack…* Those words are indelibly stamped on the minds of anyone who played the Traveller role playing game in the 1970s and 80s, which is where Taylor learned to worldbuild and craft science fiction stories. One of the principle starships in the Human Legion series is named *Beowulf* in acknowledgement.

Trivia #2: Taylor has been known to write short YA fantasy and science fiction under the pseudonym of Crustias Scattermush, an alien editor of the galactic anthology known as the Repository of Imagination.

More: The Human Legion website is here: http://humanlegion.com/ Twitter - @thehumanlegion

Missing in Action

Listed below are selected British writers of military science fiction, and military-themed space opera. Some are established big name writers, some have come to prominence only recently, and a few are still part-time writers; all are successful and worthy of your attention. With the sad exception of the late Iain M. Banks, and the hopefully temporary exception of Karen Traviss, all are currently active in the field.

Dan Abnett

Dan Abnett is a British comic book writer and novelist. He has been a frequent collaborator with fellow writer Andy Lanning, and is known for his work on books for both Marvel Comics, and their UK imprint, Marvel UK, since the 1990s, and also 2000 AD. He has also contributed to DC Comics titles, and his Warhammer Fantasy and Warhammer 40,000 novels and graphic novels for Games Workshop's Black Library now run to several dozen titles and have sold over 1,150,000 copies as of May 2008. In 2009 he released his first original fiction novels through Angry Robot books [*Source: Wikipedia*]

Dan is a prolific writer whose big break was the Sinister Dexter strip in 2000AD. In the grim future of the 41st millennium there is only war, courtesy of Game Workshop's Warhammer 40K game system, and the hundreds of novels that describe that future, many of which were penned by Dan. (For other Warhammer 40K authors, see also *Ian Watson* and *Graham McNeill*).

   Notable works: *Xenos* (2001), the opening to his Eisenhorn trilogy. *First and Only* (1999), the beginning of the *Gaunt's Ghosts* series.

   Trivia: Dan was featured in *Further Conflicts* (2011) an anthology of short stories that also contained a Human Legion short story by Tim C. Taylor and BSFA Award-nominated cover artwork by Andy Bigwood.

   More: Dan's blog is here: http://theprimaryclone.blogspot.co.uk/ Twitter - @VincentAbnett

Neal Asher

Neal Asher (born 4 February 1961 in Billericay, Essex, England) is an English science fiction writer. He lives near Chelmsford. [*Source: Wikipedia*]

Neal's books are mostly set in his Polity Universe and frequently feature violent action and adventure, often involving AIs, lethal drones, aliens, and something of a cyberpunk feel.

   Notable Works: *Gridlinked* (2001), Neal's breakout novel and the first set in his Polity Universe. *Dark Intelligence* (2015), Neal's latest book, set in the Polity Universe.

   Trivia: Neal had a short story in the anthology *Conflicts* which featured BSFA Award-nominated artwork from Andy Bigwood.

   More: Blog - http://freespace.virgin.net/n.asher/ Twitter - @nealasher

Iain M. Banks

Iain Banks (16 February 1954 – 9 June 2013) was a Scottish author. He wrote mainstream fiction under the name Iain Banks and science fiction as Iain M. Banks, including the initial of his adopted middle name Menzies. After the publication and success of *The Wasp Factory* (1984), Banks began to write on a full-time basis. His first science fiction book, *Consider Phlebas*, was released in 1987, marking the start of the popular *The Culture* series. His books have been adapted for theatre, radio and television. In 2008, *The Times* newspaper named Banks in their list of 'The 50 greatest British writers since 1945'. In April 2013, Banks announced that he had inoperable cancer and was unlikely to live beyond a year. He died on 9 June 2013. [*Source: Wikipedia*]

Iain Banks was a sad and sudden loss to science fiction in 2013. At their best, his post-scarcity *Culture* space opera books were exciting page-turners that employed sophisticated literary techniques. The society of the Culture had almost unlimited resources, which made for a very different setting to many other science fiction novels where fighting over limited resources is a key part of the story. Nonetheless, war between the Culture and the Idiran Empire is the backdrop for several *Culture* novels.

   Notable works: *Excession* (1996), one of the best and most accessible of the *Culture* novels.

   Trivia#1: Another great Scottish science fiction writer is Ken McLeod who was a close friend of Iain Banks ever since they went to school together.

   Trivia#2: For his novel, *Excession*, Iain coined the term 'Outside Context Problem' to describe the situation where a civilization encounters an inconceivable problem, such as a primitive civilization being 'discovered' by spacefaring aliens. Author Christopher G. Nuttall wrote a trilogy exploring this and named it *Outside Context Problem*.

   Trivia#3: Banks enjoyed stating that he set his books in the far future so he could assume technology would be so advanced as to make anything he wanted happen. That way he wouldn't have to worry about getting his science right.

   More: The official website is here: http://www.iain-banks.net/

Stephen Baxter

Stephen Baxter is a prolific British hard science fiction author. He has degrees in mathematics and engineering. [*Source: Wikipedia*]

If you want your fiction to have truly epic scale in time, space, and imagination, few authors have ever come close to the breathtaking visions of Stephen Baxter. One example who did is Olaf Stapledon with the books he called speculative philosophy, such as *Star Maker* (1937), and it's no coincidence that Baxter has cited Stapledon as an inspiration. After Stapledon, though, it's difficult to come up with a vision comparable to Baxter's. There are others who can provoke such as sense of wonder; who leave you after the final page with an elusive notion that the universe is a bigger place than hitherto thought, and yet you grasp it more fully… but Baxter does *scale* like no other.

Baxter has written many successful series and standalones and in a number of styles, including one co-written with Sir Arthur C. Clarke (*A Time Odyssey*) and another written with Terry Pratchett (*The Long Earth*). For many readers of *The Empire at War*, Baxter's most celebrated series is the Xeelee Sequence, which has so far run to nine standalone novels and dozens of shorter works that can be found in three collections of Xeelee-related short stories and novellas. The Xeelee are the most advanced form of baryonic life in the galaxy at war for megayears against dark matter entities known as photino birds. After thousands of years scrabbling to become the dominant sub-Xeelee species, humanity is able to unleash devastating weapons far beyond the imagination of the average space opera author. But when this arsenal is unleashed against the Xeelee, will they even notice?

Like many pre-Revolutionary British military SF works, the ongoing war with the Xeelee is the backdrop, and Baxter rarely drops into action/adventure mode, though he can do so to exhilarating effect. His earlier works tend to the hardest of hard-SF with works such as *Ring* (1993) sometimes interrupting the narrative to marvel at the jaw-dropping future visions. Later books are more varied in their literary approach, though usually underpinned by hard science. Perhaps the best book to follow the story of the war is the first of the short fiction collections: *Vacuum Diagrams* (1997). The novel that is most like traditional military SF, in that the war and its soldiers take center stage, is *Exultant* (2004).

Notable works: *Exultant* (2004), *Vacuum Diagrams* (1997).

Trivia#1: Baxter is something of an expert on H.G. Wells, and has presented talks on the great early-science fiction author at conventions. *The Time Ships* (1995) is the only authorized sequel the Wells' *The Time Machine* (1895). In early 2017, Baxter will release a book provisionally titled *The Massacre of Mankind*, which will be an unofficial sequel to *The War of the Worlds* (1895).

More: The official website is here: http://www.stephen-baxter.com/

Mark E. Cooper

Mark E. Cooper lives in a small town in the south of England, where he writes most mornings and evenings. His background is in mechanical engineering where he spent over thirty-two years working for Ford.

He loves reading books with strong female characters in dire situations and can often be found listening to a new book on his iPod.

Audio books are one of his passions, and he hopes to have his backlist in audio one day. His hobbies include driving his cobra–a V12 monster he built with his best friend–and reading the latest fantasy and sci-fi. His passion is writing, and he is now the author of more than ten titles in the genres he loves to read. He recently moved away from engineering to become a full time novelist, and is loving every minute of his new life. [*Source: impulsebooks.co.uk/blog*]

Mark has been publishing science fiction and fantasy novels since the mid-2000s, but of particular note to military SF fans is his *Merkiaari Wars* series, which runs to four novels so far with a fifth due out in 2016. If you like deep-space adventures with ground action, space battles and fully developed characters (both human and alien), then the *Merkiaari Wars* is for you.

Notable works: *Hard Duty: Merkiaari Wars Book1* (2012)

More: Mark's blog is here: http://www.impulsebooks.co.uk/blog/   Twitter: @mark_e_cooper

Peter F. Hamilton

Peter F. Hamilton is a British author. He is best known for writing space opera. As of the publication of his tenth novel in 2004, his works had sold over two million copies worldwide. [*Source: Wikipedia*]

If you're reading *The Empire at War*, you probably already know Peter F. Hamilton, one of the most successful British science fiction writers of recent years, and guest of honor at DragonCon 2015, no less. Hamilton often writes series of large space opera novels, such as his *Night's Dawn Trilogy* that weighs in a 1.2 million words. Armed conflict is a frequent backdrop, as are a foundation of hard

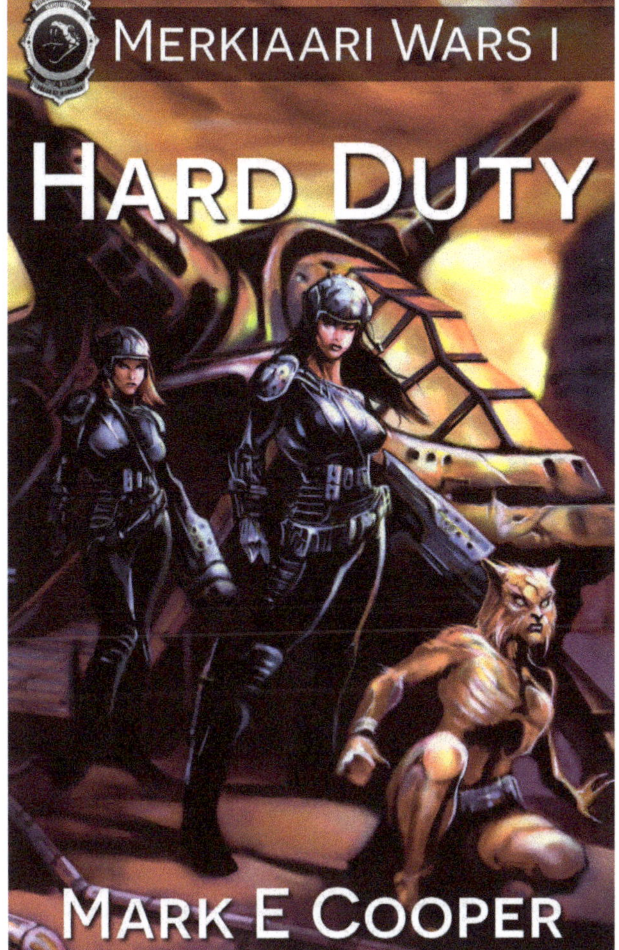

science, and taking several characters with very different experiences of the events in the novel and loosely entwining them. And then again, he sometimes takes a completely different approach as he does in his standalone novel that is the most fully in the military SF genre: *Fallen Dragon* (2009), in which a sergeant of a washed-out platoon of mercenary soldiers encounters an alien voice that speaks to his past. It's a fairly sophisticated non-linear narrative (meaning it flicks back and forward in time), but one that rewards the reader. Most of his series are now joining up into a consistent timeline, but an exception is his debut novel, *Mindstar Rising* (1993), which is the first of a superb trilogy of near future crime mysteries starring Greg Mandel, a former (very) special ops soldier. Recommended.

Trivia: Peter lives in Rutland, the smallest county in England. His *Mindstar Rising* character, Greg Mandel, lives on the shore of the reservoir called Rutland Water. In 2015, part of the Human Legion series was also written at the real-life Rutland Water.

Notable works: *Mindstar Rising* (1993), *Fallen Dragon* (2012)

More: Peter's web page has been inactive for a while, but is here: http://www.peterfhamilton.co.uk/ He is more active on Facebook: https://www.facebook.com/PeterFHamilton/

Tony Healey

Tony Healey is a Sussex-based writer and a born-and-bred Brightonian. He is the author of the best-selling *Far From Home* series.

He was a contributor to the first Kindle All-Stars short story anthology, *Resistance Front*, along with award-winning authors Alan Dean Foster, Harlan Ellison and 30 others. Tony has also contributed a piece of flash fiction to the anthology *100 Horrors*.

As well as his writing, he's interviewed numerous figures in the publishing world for his site, including Bernard Schaffer, Meg Gardiner, Alan Dean Foster, Debbi Mack, Russell Brooks and many, many more. [*Source: TonyHealey.com*]

It's Tony's *Far From Home* series we're most interested in here, the story of how a human warship is flung to the farthest reaches of the galaxy, along with the enemy vessel that attacked them. Outgunned and cut off from home, the human crew have first to survive the onslaught of attacks before they can contemplate building new alliances and strategies. Tony breathes a vividness and believability into his characters, which are flawed but competent. There's a humanity about his work, a warmness that throws the terrible situations they face into sharp relief.

Like several other top self-publishing authors (Hugh Howey's multi-million selling *Wool* series is an example), Tony has used the opportunities digital publishing provides to break free from the strictures of the novel format. The 'episodes' of the *Far From Home* series were written and released as short stories, novellas, and novels, and then collected into series, with one series released per year since 2012. This is very different from the traditional approach of a literary series being one novel per year. For modern science fiction fans used to TV box sets, Healey's approach is obviously welcome, judging by the huge popularity of the *Far From Home* series.

Notable works: *Far From Home: The Complete First Series* (2014)

More: http://tonyhealey.com/ @fringescientist

D. J. Holmes

His writing is raw, inventive, and winning a legion of appreciative fans – just read the reviews on Amazon. David Holmes is an example of how the publishing industry has transformed. *The Void War* is not just his debut novel, but his first creative writing project since he left school over a decade ago. Natural storytellers like Holmes can bypass years of creative writing courses and selling short stories to magazines, and go directly to bestselling novelist status, but note that opening qualifier well! Thousands of writers have tried to take the same route as Holmes but without his level of success (at least, not yet). Partially this is down to luck, but luck alone is not enough to reach the #1 spot in military SF – Holmes is a writer who knows how to excite his readers.

Holmes took the time to write a few words for *The Empire at War* about his success in 2015 and his hopes for 2016.

"I've been blown away with the response to *The Void War*. When I released it at the end of August I had thought that if I had sold 500 by Christmas that would be an amazing success. Needless to say, I've surpassed that and getting to number 1 spots on the military sci-fi rankings in the UK and Canada was incredible – especially as the only paid advertising I used was a £40 Facebook advert that ran for a few days.

"By far the best thing about releasing the book though has been the response from the readers. It's been really encouraging seeing people leave reviews on amazon and contacting me via Facebook and e-mail. I loved writing the story and I knew *The Void War* was the kind of story I would like to read, but when I released it, I had no idea if anyone else would like it. Overall the readers' response has been great and a real encouragement for me to get out a few more books in the series.

"Next year I hope to graduate from the university degree I'm studying and then I'm going to be writing either part time or full time for the following 12 months. I want to get another 2 or 3 books out in the Empire Rising series to see how well they do and explore the possibility of writing becoming my full time career."

Trivia: Holmes wrote *The Void War* in his spare time while studying for his degree at university in Belfast, Northern Ireland.

Notable works: *The Void War* (2015)

More: You can contact DJ Holmes through his Facebook page: https://www.facebook.com/Author.D.J.Holmes

Ceri London

Based in Sussex, UK, Ceri London is a piano tutor, following a career in IT project management, who writes science fiction / fantasy in her spare time. In 2013 she started her *Shimmer in the Dark* series with *Rogue Genesis*. Like many great examples of fantastic fiction, London doesn't allow her imagination to be limited by arbitrary sub-genre boundaries and moves freely between fantasy, science fiction, and fast-paced, military-SF conspiracy thriller. She might not have hit the big time yet, but Ceri London is an example of the talented pool of military SF writers operating below many readers' radar.

Notable works: *Rogue Genesis* (2013)

More: Blog: https://cerilondon.wordpress.com/ Facebook: https://www.facebook.com/Ceri.London.Author

S.J. MacDonald

MacDonald's fiction is an antidote to the grim dystopias that abound in current YA science fiction. Her military-themed YA space opera series is low on violence and high on the richness of her characters. She lives in Wales where she works as a teacher. Her latest entry, *Dark Running*, was a bestseller in 2015.

Notable works: *Mission Zero* (2011)

Graham McNeill

Many talented authors have worked in the Games Workshop Warhammer 40K universe, but after hundreds of novels, certain authors and their characters stand out. If Ian Watson was the father of the 40K concept of the Space Marines, McNeill led the next generation of development with his immensely popular series, *Ultramarines*. Few British authors have done more that McNeill to break down the artificial distinction between the various media in which science fiction is portrayed. McNeill took the Warhammer 40K game source material (some of which he developed himself in his then day job as a game developer), plus Ian Watson's Space Marine novels, and developed a Tolkien-like mythology around one Space Marine chapter, the Ultramarines, complete with a set of recurring characters.

These characters then fed back into later editions of the core game system before being translated into other media. If you watch the Warhammer 40K movie or video game, you are experiencing them through the eyes of characters McNeill developed on the back of Ian Watson's inspiration.

Shared universes often fade and die over time, the vision of the original contributors inevitably diluting and becoming disjoint with every new creator. Consider the number of TV, movie and comic franchises that 'reboot'. Sometimes these reboots are an attempt to reconnect with a new audience who have moved on from the people the original creators wrote for, but at least as often the reboots are a defibrillator applied to a franchise that has lost the spark of life and now lies in a coma on the edge of death.

It is a tribute to the many talented games designers and authors who have worked on the Warhammer 40K mythos that their shared vision of the grim future of the 41st millennium has become greater than the sum of its contributors. Even the earliest novels, such as Ian Watson's *Space Marine* (1993) are still on sale despite contradicting later developments of the mythos. Naturally, Games Workshop gleefully slap warning labels on *Space Marine* warning of its heretical content and promising punishment on readers not authorized to read such material, an idea completely in tune with Watson's novels of the Imperial Inquisition and their battles against heresy.

Notable works: *Nightbringer* (2002), *False Gods (2006)*

More: http://graham-mcneill.com/

Una McCormack

Based in Cambridge, England, Una McCormack teaches creative writing at Angela Rushkin University, and is a prolific writer of fanfiction and original short and long form. She is probably most notable for her tie-in novels and audio dramas in the Star Trek, Blake's 7, and Doctor Who universes, being particularly well qualified for writing the latter as she is herself a doctor with a PhD in sociology.

Although her Star Trek novels, such as *New York Times* bestseller *The Crimson Shadow,* aren't the kind of military SF that lavishes attention on military hardware and tactics, they nonetheless feature characters serving in a military organization that is fundamental to the novels. That absolutely qualifies as military SF by most people's definition. Una's novels are distinct from each other in their themes, but if there is a defining characteristic that links them, it is a fascination with how normal people experience far from normal events.

Notable works: *The Crimson Shadow* (2013)

More: Una's blog is here: http://www.unamccormack.com/

Sally Ann Melia

Melia's first trilogy, *Guy Erma and the Son of Empire,* is a YA military SF adventure that should chime well with the latest generation of Star Wars fans, with big space opera vistas, political intrigue, plenty of action, and enough grit to appeal to science fiction fans of all ages. Following swiftly on from the success of her first trilogy, the Sussex-based author plans to launch a second series in April 2016. Sally Ann Melia has been winning plenty of positive attention for her first series, and the second looks primed to add to her growing fanbase.

Notable works: *Guy Erma and the Son of Empire Book 1* (2013)

More: http://www.sallyannmelia.com

Andy Remic

Remic's work is typified by humor, violence and action. His fans love it. His breakout novel was the techno-thriller *Spiral* (2003), but it is his four-book Combat-K series, starting with *War Machine* (2007) that is a rare pre-Revolutionary example of unqualified military SF from a British author.

Notable works: *War Machine* (2007)

More: http://www.andyremic.com

Michael G. Thomas

One of the big stars of the military SF Revolution, Michael G Thomas's *Star Crusades* series has surpassed a quarter of a million sales since its launch in 2011. Beginning with the tale of the pit fighting gladiator, Spartan, who is press-ganged into the Confederation military, *Star Crusades* delivers non-stop blood-and-guts military science fiction action. Based in Monmouthshire, on the Welsh-English border, Thomas is part of the successful Swordworks publishing co-operative. As the co-founder of the Academy of Historical Fencing, the name is unlikely to be a coincidence. Although *Star Crusades* is his major work, Thomas writes other books, such as the *Zombie Dawn* trilogy.

Trivia: Michael co-wrote the *Zombie Dawn* trilogy with his brother Nick S. Thomas.

Trivia#2: Michael posted a comment to his Facebook page in December 2015 putting his total word count at 2.7 million words over the last 6 years, and 32 novels. Like Tony Healey, Christopher Nuttall, and so many of the most successful Revolutionary military SF authors, a key to Michael's success has been a ferocious work ethic.

Notable works: *Siege of Titan (Star Crusades Uprising, #1)* (2011)

More: New website: http://starcrusader.com Facebook: https://www.facebook.com/starcrusader/

Karen Traviss

The undisputed star of British military SF before the digital revolution, Karen Traviss is unusual for a British military SF writer before the Revolution in that she had some personal experience of the military, being a defense journalist and a member of the Royal Naval Auxiliary and the Territorial Army (the British Army reserve). This is in sharp contrast to many successful American writers of military SF who have military experience. Although best known for science fiction (including *Star Wars* and *Gears of War* novels) Karen's output is varied and stretches to other genres, and from prose to comics. For military SF fans, Karen is probably best known for her hugely successful *Halo* novels, all four of which were *New York Times* bestsellers. That achievement alone is enough to make Karen Traviss one of the most successful female British science fiction writers, but she has had many other successes, such as her breakout series *The Wess'har Wars*, which while not as full-on action as the *Halo* books, has strong elements of military science fiction.

Karen isn't currently working on science-fiction projects, but with her attention to detail, believability, scientific accuracy, and skill at telling a great story, she is greatly missed. Hopefully, she will return soon.

Notable works: *City of Pearl: Wess'har Wars, #1* (2004), *Halo: Glasslands* (2011)

More: http://www.karentraviss.com/

Ian Watson

Ian became a full-time writer in 1976, following the success of *The Embedding* (1973) and *The Jonah Kit* (1975), which between them won the Campbell Award, Prix Apollo, the BSFA Award, and the Orbit Award. Numerous works of acclaimed and furiously inventive SF and fantasy literature followed, as did Hugo and Nebula Award nominations. From 1990 to 1991 he worked full-time with Stanley Kubrick on story development for the movie *A.I. Artificial Intelligence*. Ian is a frequent attendee and guest of honour at science fiction conventions in many European countries, and if you get a chance to see him, make sure you do, because he is a natural performer and raconteur.

Rewind to the late 1980s when Bryan Ansell, then owner of Games Workshop, approached established British science fiction and fantasy authors to add depth and credibility to the Warhammer and Warhammer 40K game systems by writing tie-in novels. Ian wrote four of the first Warhammer 40K novels, and both set a high standard and established the psychotic sensibility for the hundreds of novels that followed. Ian's novel *Space Marine* had a particularly difficult genesis, with Games Workshop not entirely sure how and when to publish, possibly in part due to a notorious bum-branding scene. After being out of print for many years, Games Workshop now publishes *Space Marine* once again as a print-on-demand title with suitable warnings that Ian's writing must be considered heretical, and clearly written under daemonic influence.

Ian has a collection due in 2016 called *The 1000 Year Reich*, which features a new piece of military Science Fiction.

See the entries for Dan Abnett and Graham McNeill for notable authors who took Watson's psychotic visions of the far future and developed them into the mythos we see today.

Trivia: Games Workshop interviewed Ian about *Space Marine* here: http://www.blacklibrary.com/Free-Extras/A-chat-with-Ian-Watson.html

Notable works: *The Embedding* (1973), *Space Marine* (1993)

More: http://www.ianwatson.info/

Ian Whates

Ian Whates is quiet powerhouse of the British science fiction scene, running the award-winning NewCon press, organizing and appearing at conventions, editing anthologies, and writing his own fiction, notably fantasy series, *City of a Hundred Rows,* space opera series, *The Noise Within*, and new space opera series, *The Dark Angels*. Ian is currently co-writing the concluding books to military SF series *The Human Legion* with Tim C. Taylor.

Ian's writing transports the reader effortlessly across stunning vistas punctuated by intense action and often warmly reflective characters. His writing is a perfect blend between depth and readability.

Notable works: *The Noise Within* (2010), *Pelquin's Comet* (2015)

More: http://www.ianwhates.co.uk/

Jo Zebedee

Joanne Zebedee is the most recent addition to this list, hitting the #1 spot in the space opera bestseller chart on amazon.co.uk while *The Empire at War* bonus material was being written. Jo has been writing for years, but in 2015 self-published her novel, *Innis Carraig*, set in a grim future Belfast following a disastrous war against an invading alien power, and also released *Abendau's Heir*, the first of a space opera trilogy with a strong military theme (amongst many other fine attributes) published through new small publisher, Tickety Boo Press. Next year, Zebedee will conclude the trilogy started with *Abendau's Heir*.

Zebedee is a polished writer and her books are slowly winning the attention of many people. We will see a lot more of Jo Zebedee.

Trivia: Northern Ireland is the smallest region of the United Kingdom, but is a fertile ground for the new generation of bestselling science fiction writers. Bestselling authors P.P. Corcoran, Jo Zebedee, and DJ Holmes are all based there.

Notable works: *Abendau's Heir* (2015)

More: http://jozebwrites.blogspot.co.uk/

FALLEN WITNESS

—Vision VII: Listen to the Fallen —

Art: Andy Bigwood
Words: Tim C. Taylor

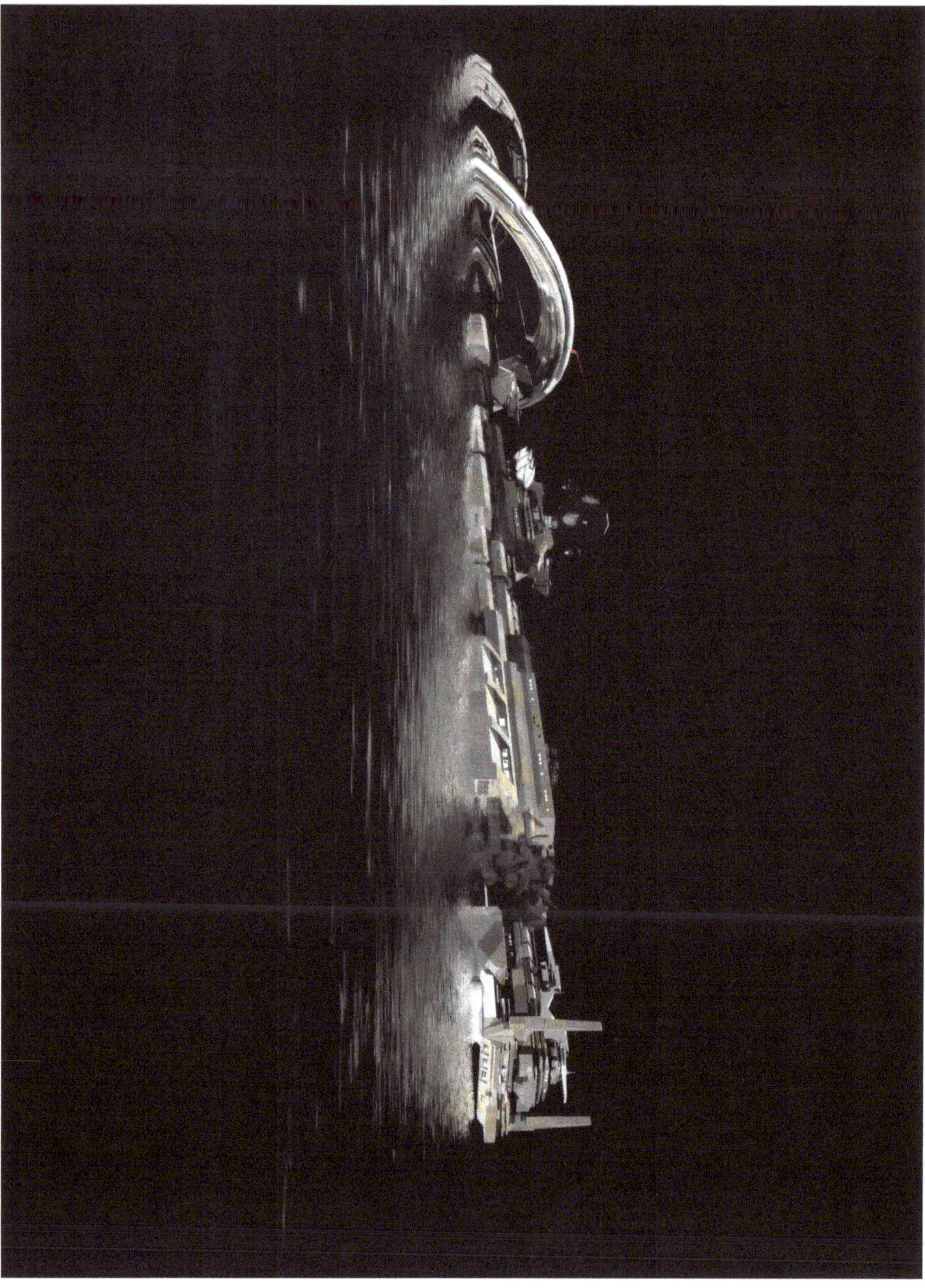

As the light snaps around the seventh and final speaker, she hides with head bowed beneath her fountain of black hair, arms crossed before her. She reveals herself theatrically until her shoulders are back and her head held high, letting the audience see that she is a flesh-and-blood human, like them.

"My name is Amelia Satrini-Khan," she announces. "I am not a fallen witness. Eight years ago I was sitting in an auditorium like you, listening to the story of the energy wraiths for the first time. Now I work for the Ministry of War, helping you to understand our history, and to shape our future."

She holds her smartscreen image up high, thankful she doesn't need to keep her arms outstretched as long as the others.

"After Lieutenant-Commander Williams died, and the ship was burning, the tertiary command team managed to crash land HMS *Warspite* in the Sea of Canaria, not two hundred miles away from where you are sitting. The survivors are our ancestors. After the victory against the energy wraiths, the remnants of the human Grand Fleet, including two other ships of the British Squadron, headed back to the core worlds. They gave us messages of support and a few supplies, but they didn't have the means to rescue the crew of *Warspite*, not now she was down in a gravity well.

"This was the genesis of the New Trafalgar colony. HMS *Warspite* was broken up. Her bones sheltered the first colonists, and the quantum foam turbines that had destroyed the bodies of the enemy, now gave us heat, light, and powered the terra-formers and the fabrication stations.

"Before the Battle of New Trafalgar, the personalities and memories of all Royal Navy personnel were stored in the ship they served upon. Petty Officer DeSouza, Flight-Lieutenant Chalmers, Spacer Cutts, Spacer Doyle, Leading Spacer MacDonald, and Lieutenant-Commander Williams were all killed in action aboard HMS *Warspite*, over four hundred years ago. Today their restored minds wear android bodies, but they are legally people with the same rights and responsibilities as you and I. They have never stopped serving the Federated Nations as Royal Navy personnel. Only, instead of serving as warship crew, and then as the first colonists braving the still-toxic air of our planet before the terra-formers rendered it safe, they now serve as fallen witnesses – as living memories of those who fell defending humanity."

Satrini-Khan spots the sparkle from a few tear-flecked eyes in the audience, and judges now is the time to strike for their hearts.

"We nearly died," she says, her voice amplified by passion. She flings her hand out to her right. "They *did* die. And that is why their duty is to go on living no matter how much they want and deserve their rest." Satrini-Khan holds her other hand out toward the audience and brings thumb and forefinger together in a pinching gesture. "We came *that* close to destruction. History teaches us that peace softens us, distracts us with lesser matters. If we forget about the possibility of a real enemy, we fight wars of rhetoric over trivial distinctions in our form of government, or launch vitriolic attacks of bitterness and contempt over arcane differences in cultural tastes. The fallen witnesses cannot be allowed their rest because their memories of humanity's darkest hour will never be diluted by peace or dulled by time. They are our direct link to that period. We must never forget, and thanks to our fallen witnesses we do not. That is why our veterans called this a *future* lesson, because *you* are our future. With our dockyards, military innovations, and armed forces, the colony of New Trafalgar has proudly served the British Nations on behalf of all humanity, ready should another invader seek to destroy us. You are schoolchildren today, but when you grow up, it will be the responsibility of your generation to keep us safe and pass on the message you are hearing today to your children."

It is easy to swell a young heart with pride. Satrini-Khan has no doubt that if she tells the children that hostile aliens lurk outside the auditorium, they will take up arms and rush the enemy. The thought is sickening, but for now she must recruit the children, not for a war of space fleets and dropships but the war of popular opinion. Their weapons will be searching questions aimed at their parents, who will be voting next year in the election. If the right party wins, then it will not be long before all in the room will bear arms.

"Even at your tender age you can help," said Satrini-Khan. "In the foyer outside you will find volunteers from British Defense League, a patriotic organization that is dedicated to a single aim – to being ready next time. If you sign up today you will receive free gifts, and a complimentary subscription to the Junior Defense League magazine. If you wish to honor our fallen witnesses, then you must become a member."

One of the children nervously raises his hand.

Satrini-Khan frowns. "Are you unsure whether to join up?"

Perhaps the sternness of her reply shocks him because he looks petrified to be singled out as the only disloyal child in the hall. "No, not at all, miss," he stutters. "I just wanted to know what we'd get as gifts."

"That's all right then. I'll let the volunteers explain what you get. All I'll say is that they were seriously fabulous when I joined up at your age. Okay, is there anyone here who doesn't intend to join? Just raise your hand now. There's nothing to be ashamed of, nothing to fear. We just want to know who you are."

No one raises their hands. They never do. The children are looking around at each other, checking they aren't sitting next to an unpatriotic maggot.

"Good," she says. "Then we have one final duty to perform." After placing her picture on the floor, she turns to the androids, who are still holding their images aloft, and snaps a perfect salute. "Fallen witnesses, we thank you for your service."

The children are well schooled. They stand to attention and salute the veterans, and the pictorial memories they hold.

Then the curtain descends and the children become someone else's problem.

Except this time the people left on the stage don't release the tension with jokes and small talk. There's a dark secret on this side of the curtain – something no one admits to knowing. But that's the thing about serving for centuries, you know so many backchannels that you sometimes learn what's what before the General Staff. And how better for ancient veterans to impress a sweet young girl than showing off how to beat the system.

Satrini-Khan wishes she hadn't listened, that she had stuck to the rules. It's too late, because now she knows it is happening again. Colonies are going off grid one-by-one, three in the past month alone. The darkness is swooping in from spinward on a direct route to Earth, a route that will pass through New Trafalgar in a few years.

The Fallen Witness program has been running throughout the Federated Nations ever since the Battle of New Trafalgar. Four centuries of preparing for the next war.

Have they done enough?

Last time the wraiths launched a surprise attack on a blissfully ignorant swathe of civilian colonies and a fleet of hastily improvised warships. This time the Royal Navy is ready. This time the beacon fires have been lit in time, and a much stronger Grand Fleet is gathering. Names swollen with glory and blood are on the move: *Temeraire, Redoutable, Enterprise, Yamato, Kirov*, and the latest HMS *Sirius*. The price will be terrible, but against a genocidal enemy, price ceases to be a factor.

England Expects… and she will not find us wanting.

Bonus Vision: Enemy Sighted!